# SEA TO SHINING SEA

# SEA TO SHINING SEA

## MICHAEL PHILLIPS

Cover by Dan Thornberg,
Bethany House Publishers staff artist.

Published by Bethany House Publishers
A Ministry of Bethany Fellowship, Inc.
6820 Auto Club Road, Minneapolis, Minnesota 55438

Printed in the United States of America

**Library of Congress Cataloging-in-Publication Data**

Phillips, Michael R., 1946–
    Sea to shining sea / Michael Phillips
        p.   cm. — (The Journals of Corrie Belle Hollister ; bk. 5)
    1. United States—History—Civil War, 1861–1865—Fiction.
    I. Title. II. Series: Phillips, Michael R., 1946–
Journals of Corrie Belle Hollister ; 5.
PS3566.H492S4    1992
813'.54—dc20                             92–15197
ISBN 1–55661–227–3                    CIP

To Judith Pella,

the greatest writing partner a fellow author
could wish for, with deep gratitude and
prayers for your best in all the future holds.
Thank you for allowing me
to be part of your life!

# Books by the Phillips/Pella Writing Team

## The Journals of Corrie Belle Hollister

*My Father's World*
*Daughter of Grace*
*On the Trail of the Truth*
*A Place in the Sun*
*Sea to Shining Sea*
*Into the Long Dark Night*

## The Stonewycke Trilogy

*The Heather Hills of Stonewycke*
*Flight from Stonewycke*
*Lady of Stonewycke*

## The Stonewycke Legacy

*Stranger at Stonewycke*
*Shadows over Stonewycke*
*Treasure of Stonewycke*

## The Highland Collection

*Jamie MacLeod: Highland Lass*
*Robbie Taggart: Highland Sailor*

## The Russians

*The Crown and the Crucible*
*A House Divided*
*Travail and Triumph*

# The Author

Michael Phillips has authored, co-authored, and edited over 50 books. He is editor of the bestselling GEORGE MACDONALD CLASSICS series and has co-written several series of historical fiction with Judith Pella, all published by Bethany House Publishers.

Nominated for fourteen ECPA Gold Medallion awards, Phillips has received much recognition for his writing and editing. Sales for his books exceed three million, and seven of his titles have appeared on the *Bookstore Journal* bestseller list.

Phillips and co-author Judith Pella began the CORRIE BELLE HOLLISTER series as a team effort, but other writing projects have resulted in the mutual agreement that Phillips continue this one on his own. Phillips owns and operates two bookstores on the West Coast. He and his wife Judy live with their three sons in Eureka, California.

# CONTENTS

# CHAPTER 1

# SAN FRANCISCO AGAIN

The setting was unbelievable!

When I first walked into the huge ballroom of the Montgomery Hotel at Pa's side, I could not take in all the magnificence of the place. Under the bright lights of chandeliers, the men sauntered around in expensive blacuits, and the women in long gowns. Waiters carried food and drinks about on silver trays, and hundreds of important people milled together in that gigantic fancy room.

All I could think was, *What are we doing here?*

But we *were* there. And as we walked in, I think Pa sensed my nervousness.

"Come on, buck up, Corrie," he whispered down to me, placing a reassuring hand on my arm. "They invited us. And you're every bit the lady any of these other women are."

He patted my hand. "So don't you go willowy on me or faint or nothin'," he added. "I'm just as nervous as you are."

When the invitation had come a month earlier for Pa and me to attend the Republican reception in June of 1860 at the Montgomery Hotel in San Francisco, at first I didn't think too much of it. But a few days later Pa said, "We oughta go to that shindig, Corrie. It's not every day a couple of country locals like us get the chance to mix with important folks. What do you think?"

"You really want to, Pa?"

"Sure, just so long as you come too."

"I don't know why they invited me," I said. "You're mayor of a town. But why me?"

"Because you're a prominent young lady writer," said Pa. "Ain't no big mystery in that."

"Maybe it was Jessie Fremont's doing," I suggested. "She and Mr. Fremont probably know every important Republican in California. Maybe they told somebody about me before they left for the East."

"Never hurts to know high-up people," said Pa with a wink. "Anyhow, what do you think—you up for a trip to San Francisco?"

And so there we were. Pa in his new suit, fresh-shaved, looked as handsome and important as ever a man could. And I wore my new dress—yellow, with ruffles and a sash, and my hair fixed up with a matching ribbon in it. We walked into the ballroom of the Montgomery Hotel to join all the men who would play a leading role in the upcoming national election of 1860.

"Hey, Hollister!" called out a voice. We both turned to see Carl Denver hurrying our way. He greeted us and shook our hands. "Come with me," he said. "There's someone I want you to meet."

Before we could say much in reply, Mr. Denver had us in tow, steering us through the crowd. Then all of a sudden we were face-to-face with one of the tallest, most handsome men I had ever seen.

"Cal," said Mr. Denver, "I want you to meet two friends of mine from up in Miracle Springs—this is Corrie Hollister and her father, Drummond Hollister, the mayor of Miracle. Corrie, Hollister . . . meet Cal Burton, an important fellow here in San Francisco these days."

Pa shook the man's hand. I just stood there watching and listening to him laugh at Mr. Denver's words.

"Come on now, Carl," he said, "you shouldn't lie to these good people. I'm no more important than the shoeshine boy on the street outside."

"Don't let his modesty fool you," said Mr. Denver, turning to me and speaking as if it were confidential. "Cal works for Leland Stanford, and from what I hear, he is moving up fast. You keep your eye on him, Corrie. He might get you a story or two that'll make you famous."

"A story—what are you talking about, Carl?" said Burton, turning away from Pa and toward us.

"Corrie here's a writer, Cal—you know, California's woman reporter."

"Why, of course!" he said. "Now I remember you telling me about her." He took my hand, but instead of giving it a manly shake, he just held it softly for a moment.

My heart started beating fast, and I could feel my face reddening all the way up the back of my neck and cheeks. My eyes had been following my hand as it was swallowed up in his. And now I found myself slowly glancing up as he released it. His eyes bored straight into mine.

I'm embarrassed to admit it, but the touch of his hand, the look in his eyes, and his smile made me feel a little light-headed for the rest of the evening. I'm sure Pa noticed, especially when he caught me staring in Mr. Burton's direction a couple of times. But he was nice enough not to say anything about it.

He was too busy anyway, meeting people and listening to speeches. I met a lot of other people too, but as I think back on the evening, I only remember a few of the names. Cal Burton did take me to meet his boss, the important railroad man and politician, Mr. Stanford. I couldn't say I actually spoke to him, because he was busy talking with some important Republicans about the election and slavery and the need for railroad development in California.

I wish I could recall more of the things I heard everyone talking about, because those were important times for California's future. The election, the railroad, and slavery were the subjects on everyone's minds and the topics of every conversation.

But I don't remember very much, because I couldn't keep my eyes off Cal Burton, and I couldn't keep down the fluttering in my chest. I thought everybody in the huge ballroom must have been able to hear the pounding of my pulse, although nobody seemed to pay much attention.

Cal was tall, with straight light-brown hair, parted in the middle and coming down over his forehead almost to his eyebrows, then falling around the sides just above his ears. He wore a fancy suit, light brown like his hair, and a ruffled shirt and polished boots. What a figure he cut, with those blue eyes that contrasted with the brown of his hair and suit and the tan of his face! He had a friendly smile and a warm tone, yet a thoughtfulness that made his brow crinkle when he was thinking about what to say.

Altogether, Cal Burton had a lively, interesting, intelligent, pleasant face. How could I help giving it a second, or even a third look?

I heard Pa's voice at my side. "He's going to get a headache if you keep looking at him like that!"

"Oh, Pa!" I said, blushing again. "I was just—"

"I know what you was doing, Corrie," Pa added. "And there's nothin' wrong with admitting you like the looks of a good-looking young man." He gave me a smile. "You just might want to not be so obvious about it."

"I didn't know I was."

Pa chuckled. "Everybody in the place is gonna know if you don't pull those eyes of yours back inside your head! Now come on, what do you say you and I go over and hear what some of those men in the fancy suits are saying about the election?"

# CHAPTER 2

## THE PRESIDENTIAL ELECTION OF 1860

As much as I had been interested in the election of 1856 because of my involvement with the Fremonts, the election of 1860 was a far more important one for the future of the whole nation. Mr. Fremont's being halfway a Californian had stirred up California quite a bit. But now even larger issues were at stake. Everything had grown more serious and heated, and even though it mostly had to do with the South and slavery, Californians were mighty interested too.

Slavery had been an issue for a long time. Pa said he remembered them talking about it back in the East when he was in his teen years. There had been preachers and politicians talking out against it and trying to get it abolished for a lot of years. But there was never anything they could do about it. Throughout the 1850s, although the debate had gotten pretty heated, the government in Washington had been almost completely controlled by the South. The southern states had kept the northern states from making any changes. And the border states were usually more sympathetic with the South, since most of them allowed slavery too.

So even though there had been growing opposition to slavery all through the 1850s, there had been nothing any of the northern politicians could do about it. I had just been growing up during those years, and hadn't known or cared much about it. But now it was 1860, and I *was* interested. So I asked people lots of questions to find out all I could. And gradually toward the end of the decade that had just passed, it began to look as if a change might be coming.

For one thing, Abraham Lincoln was becoming more and more well known, especially after the famous debates with Stephen Douglas in 1858 when they'd both been running for Congress in Illinois. Lincoln was known to be antislavery, and his abolitionist views made southern politicians angry.

Meanwhile, the country just kept growing, just like Miracle Springs and Sacramento and San Francisco and all of California had grown.

But the westward expansion meant that most new states were in areas where there was no slavery. Minnesota became a state in 1858, and then Oregon in 1859. Counting California too, there were eighteen northern and western states, while the southern and border regions had only fifteen. The southerners who had been in control for all that time started to get nervous because there weren't any new places for slavery to expand. Westward lay the Nebraska Territory and the Dakota Territory and the Colorado Territory and the Washington Territory and the Utah and Nevada and New Mexico territories. And all of those places, if they ever did become states, weren't very likely to side with the powerful slave men from the South.

All these things combined to make the year of 1860, and the election which would be held in November, one of the most important years in the whole history of our country.

Only a month before Pa and I went to San Francisco, the leaders of the Republican party had nominated Abraham Lincoln of Illinois to be their candidate for president of the United States. Against him would be running the man he already knew so well from his home state—Stephen A. Douglas.

Southerners realized the fate of slavery if Lincoln were elected, especially now that the number of slave states was in a minority. They were determined to defeat him!

That's what some of the men were discussing that evening at the Montgomery. The speeches were all about the future of the Union, they called it, and the reasons why all God-fearing and slavery-hating Californians had to do everything they could to work for Mr. Lincoln's election in California. And it wouldn't be easy—there were many more Democrats in California than Republicans.

Mr. Thomas Starr King made a speech that stirred everybody up about the need to support the northern states, even though we were so far out west. He was the pastor of the Unitarian church in San Francisco, but had only recently arrived from Boston where the man introducing him said he had been a famous preacher and lecturer. He had come from the East only a month or two earlier, and he made it sound as if debate was heated back East over which direction the nation was going to go. As for the election, however, he said he still wasn't sure how much to involve himself, being a minister.

Other men at the Montgomery were talking about issues not directly having to do with the disputes between North and South, but having to do with the future of California itself, and what the election would mean out here.

Economics and money and growth were the issues they were talking about—travel and gold and population changes and the expansion of the railroad both up and down the state and toward the East. Communication with the East was a major concern. Even though Oregon up to the north was now a state too, there had still always been the feeling that we were isolated from the rest of the country, and that the states in the West weren't as important as the other states.

Of course, nobody here believed that! To listen to them talk, California was the *most* important state! But they wanted everybody else to know it too.

The Pony Express had just started up two months earlier. At least now mail and news didn't take so long to reach back and forth across the huge continent. News used to take three weeks by the fastest stagecoaches to get across the plains and mountains and prairies from Missouri to California. Now it took only nine or ten days from St. Joseph to Sacramento! Since there were telegraph lines from there to the big cities on the East Coast, the whole country was separated from each other by less than two weeks as far as news was concerned.

Mr. Stanford was talking about this very issue. "Mail is one thing," he said, "but *people* are another. Getting *people* quickly back and forth between California and the East—*that's* what it will take before California can truly stand up and fully take its place alongside the other states of these great United States of America."

"Horses and stagecoaches," Mr. Stanford said, "are the transportation and communication methods of the past. But the future lies with machines and inventions." He went on to make a speech about how the equality and impact of full statehood could be achieved only by a railroad line stretching all the way across the country.

While I was listening to all this, I felt a touch on my arm. "Miss Hollister," a voice said, "I wonder if I might have a word with you."

# CHAPTER 3

## AN UNEXPECTED PROPOSITION

I turned, and my heart took off racing again at the sight of Cal Burton!

I glanced toward Pa, and before I knew it I was walking across the room at Mr. Burton's side. I was afraid to look at him and at the same time unable to keep my eyes off him.

"There's somebody I want you to talk to," he said as he led me through the maze of people. In another minute I was standing in the middle of a small group of four or five men. One of them began talking to me, but I forgot his name as soon as I'd been told, and I remember only about half of what he said, even though it turned out to be a conversation that changed the whole course of my life.

"I heard about you from Cal here," the man was saying, "and of course I'm on close terms with your editor, Ed Kemble. So I'm not altogether unaware of the role you played on behalf of our Republican party four years ago."

"I didn't do anything that did any good," I said, finally finding my voice.

"Perhaps not," the man went on. "You may have considered all that happened a waste of time and energy, but I would disagree with you."

"The story I wrote about Mr. Fremont was killed," I said.

"True enough. Your article was never printed. But what would you say if I told you I had read it?"

"I don't know," I replied. "I'm not sure I would believe you."

The man laughed, and all the others in the small group listening to our conversation followed his lead. It was the first time I had seen Cal Burton laugh, and I enjoyed the sound of it. His even white teeth and broad smile gave me a whole new reason to like his looks. But the man was still talking to me, so I had to do my best to pay attention.

"Well, I have," he said. "I should have known from reading your words that you would be a plain-talking young lady, even if it means calling an important man a liar to his face!"

He chuckled again, but as I started to tell him I hadn't meant anything by it, he held up his hand and spoke again.

"Don't worry, Miss Hollister," he said. "I took no offense at what you said. I admire a woman who's not afraid to speak her mind in front of men. Especially a young pretty one like you."

I blushed immediately. It was an awful embarrassment!

*I'm not pretty and you know it,* I said to him in my mind. But outwardly I just glanced down at the floor for a minute. My first reaction was that he was probably poking fun at me like Uncle Nick always did. But then I realized he hadn't been doing that at all. Neither he nor any of the other men seemed to make light of his words a bit. I recovered myself and looked up. His face was serious, and I could see that he'd meant what he'd said.

"I'm very earnest, Miss Hollister, in what I say. You see, my friends consider me a pretty straightforward man myself. So I recognize honesty and fearlessness for the virtues they are. A lot of folks who are involved in politics do so much double-talking you can't tell what they're saying. Most of them aren't saying much worth listening to. But I've always been of a mind to speak out what's on my heart, and then people can do what they want with your words. Wouldn't you agree that's the best way of going about it when you have something to say?"

"I reckon so," I answered.

"That's another thing I like about you, Miss Hollister. You don't try to put on airs. You're a country girl and you never try to hide it. You speak honestly, you speak out as the young lady you are, and as far as I can tell, you aren't much afraid of anyone or worried what they'll think." He paused and looked me straight in the eye. "Would you say that is an accurate representation of yourself?" he asked after a moment.

"I . . . I don't know," I said, stumbling a little. The man certainly was straightforward, I'll say that for him! "I wouldn't say I'm not afraid of anything. But I guess you're right about speaking my mind honestly. My minister back home, and my mother—my stepmother, I should say—"

"That would be Almeda Parrish, would it not?" he interrupted.

"Almeda Parrish *Hollister*," I corrected him.

"Yes, of course. I knew of Mrs. Parrish before I had heard of either you or your father. A woman with a fine reputation. But I don't suppose you need me to sing her praises, do you?"

I smiled and shook my head.

"And I read some of your articles about the Miracle Springs election, the whole feud between your family and that skunk of a banker Royce. You see, I do some checking to make sure of myself before I become involved with anyone. I make a habit of going into things with my eyes open."

"I can see that," I said.

"I admire your stepmother, and I have been keeping an eye on your father as well. He strikes me as a man California might hear more from one day."

"He's here," I said eagerly, "if you would like to meet him."

The man chuckled again. "Of course he's here. I'm the one who arranged for both of you to be invited! I have every intention of speaking with your father before the night is done. But right now I'm speaking with you, and we were talking about your work for the Fremont cause four years ago, and the bravery you displayed in uncovering that story. Printed or not, it was a fine piece of work, and a courageous thing to do. But a great many things have changed since 1856. Our party was just in its infancy then, and John Fremont did not have the nationwide strength to stand up against Buchanan. Even had your article made it into the *Alta*, it is doubtful it would have had much of an impact, and it would have been too late even to be picked up in the East. Therefore, what I want to talk with you about, Miss Hollister, is not your work of the past, but what you might do for the Republican party in the future."

He stopped, looking at me intently.

"I'm not sure I understand you," I said. "I don't know much about politics. I haven't paid much attention since then. Except for what my pa does as mayor, that is."

"I'm not concerned how much you know of what used to be. This is a new day, Miss Hollister. This election of 1860 is the one that's going to change the direction of this nation forever. Don't any of the rest of you tell John what I've said," he warned, glancing around at the other men in the small group before turning his eyes back to me. "But John Fremont, as much as I admire the man, represents the Republican party of the past. He was an explorer, after all. That is how he will be remembered. But the future, both of our party and of this country, lies with the man from Illinois who is heading our presidential ticket this year. I'm sure you've heard of Abraham Lincoln, Miss Hollister?"

"Of course," I answered. "There was already talk about him in 1856."

"Well, I am convinced his time has finally come, and that he is the man to take our country forward—into the new decade, into the future, and away from the Democratic control that has dominated Washington for the past thirty years."

He stopped again, still looking at me with an almost inquisitive expression.

"I'm not sure I understand," I said finally. "You're probably right about everything you say. But I don't see what it has to do with me."

"Simple, Miss Hollister. I want to enlist your support in the cause. I want you to help us with the campaign, in even a more active way than you did for John Fremont four years ago."

"Help . . . in what way? How could I possibly help?"

"Writing articles on Mr. Lincoln's behalf. Perhaps even taking to the stump once in a while. Women might not be able to vote, but men sure pay attention when a woman speaks out!"

"The stump . . . what do you mean?"

"Speaking, Miss Hollister. Giving speeches to go along with your writing, helping us raise money and votes for the Republican ticket in November."

"You're talking about speechmaking—me?" I exclaimed.

"That's exactly what I'm talking about," he replied with a broad smile. "I want you on our side."

# CHAPTER 4

## WONDERING WHAT TO DO

The rest of the evening was lost in a blur.

There was music and more discussions and a few other speeches and refreshments. I stayed close to Pa. There weren't but a handful of other women present, and I'm sure no one as young as I was. But Cal Burton seemed to be keeping an eye on me. He was very polite and not the least bit forward; he treated me as if I was the most important person there.

As Pa and I walked back to Miss Sandy Bean's Boarding House from the downtown district, the night fog had rolled in and a chill was in the air. But my face felt hot, even more so in the brisk night, and I felt so full and alive that I could hardly keep from skipping up the walk. I tried my best to keep it under control, but I know Pa couldn't help but notice.

He walked along beside me, the sound of his boots clumping along the boards of the walkways and thudding dully on the hard-packed dirt of the streets we crossed, talking and smiling and laughing lightly with me. He didn't do a thing to make me feel foolish for being . . . well, just for being the way a young woman sometimes is!

Before we parted for the night, Pa took me in his arms, gave me a tight squeeze, then said, "You're some lady, Corrie Belle. You do your pa right proud, whether it's ridin' a horse in the woods or at some fancy big-city political gathering."

Then he kissed me good-night and sent me into my room.

The next morning we left Miss Bean's and caught the steamer across the bay and up the river to Sacramento. As we moved out across the water, although it was still early, some of the fog had lifted back to reveal a portion of the city in bright sunlight. It was different than any time I'd left the city before. Instead of being anxious to get home, there was a lump in the pit of my stomach, pulling at me and making me wish I could stay. Pa seemed to know I was full of new and unaccustomed thoughts, and neither of us said much during the quiet boat ride across the bay.

About halfway across, a small cloud of lingering fog drifted by and settled down on top of the boat. With the sun gone, suddenly a chill came over me. I shivered and turned away from the railing, then sat down on a nearby bench with a sigh.

The fog seemed to fit my mood perfectly, although I didn't even know what my mood was. A cloud had settled over my spirits just as the fog had engulfed the boat in its white, quiet chill. Pa stayed at the railing, leaning over, looking down into the water as it splashed rhythmically by. I was so absorbed in my own thoughts that I was hardly aware that he had a lot on his mind, too.

It was still pretty early in the day, and as the river narrowed and we lost sight of the city, we went inside and took some seats next to a window. We floated along awhile in silence. Then all of a sudden, without hardly even thinking what I was saying, I blurted out:

"Well, Pa, do you think I ought to do it?"

"Do what?" he said, glancing over at me. He had no idea what I could be talking about.

"Get involved with the election," I answered. "You know, try to help Mr. Lincoln get elected."

"My daughter, the speechmaker!" said Pa with the first smile I'd seen on his face all day.

"Come on, Pa! You know I'll never be that kind of person. Maybe I'll just write some, like I did about the election before."

"It'd be sure to help the Republican cause," he said. "You ain't just a curiosity no more. You saw the byline Kemble put on your article last winter about the flood of California's rivers— *Corrie Belle Hollister, California's Woman Reporter.*"

"That doesn't mean much."

"Sure it does! You're not just a kid wantin' to write any more. You're just about Kemble's most famous reporter."

"But not the best paid!" I said, trying to laugh.

"You're still a woman, and you can't expect to get close to what a man does. But if Kemble knows what's good for him, he'll keep you happy. That's just what I told him too, last night."

"Pa, you didn't!"

"'Course I did. It's the truth, too. He's got all kinds of men writin' for his paper. There are hundreds of men writing for the papers in San Francisco and Sacramento. But there's only one woman. And you're it, and he's got you. So I told him he'd better treat you like the important young lady you are or else I'd tell you to take your writing someplace else."

"Pa, that's downright embarrassing."

"It's the truth."

"What did he say?"

"Aw, you know Kemble. He flustered some, but he didn't deny a word of it. That fellow Cal Burton was listening too, and he gave Kemble a few words to back up what I'd said besides."

I glanced away. I didn't want Pa to see the red in my cheeks just from the mention of Cal's name. He kept right on talking, but I'm sure he knew. Pa usually knew most things I was thinking . . . more than he liked to let on.

"I tell you, Corrie, you shouldn't underestimate yourself. You just might have the chance to influence this election. You know that folks pay attention to what you write—men as well as women. You wanted to be a writer, and you've done it. You just might be able to help elect the first Republican president this country's ever had."

"My writing's not that important. You just think so because you're my Pa."

"Well, I got a right to be proud! If you ask me, there's not a better person they could get to stand up and tell folks they oughta vote for Mr. Lincoln for president. When folks hear your name, they're all gonna know who you are. *Corrie Belle Hollister.* Why, maybe nobody thought nothing of it back in '55 when you wrote about the blizzard. But now when folks see those words above a piece of writing, they know they'd better pay attention, because *the* woman newspaper writer of California is speaking to them. And they're gonna know your name just as well if you're speaking out to a crowd of people."

"I'm not so sure," I said. "I don't know if I want to do that anyway. It sounds pretty frightening to me, getting up in front of a bunch of men. What if they yell at me or don't listen or say rude things?"

"Then you yell right back at them and tell 'em to shut their mouths and pay attention. Ain't that what Almeda'd do if a group of rowdy men got rude at her?"

I smiled at the thought. That was exactly what Almeda would do.

"Besides, if word got out that you were gonna be someplace, I got no doubt there'd be plenty of women there too, and they'd keep the men quiet."

"I don't know—"

"You got a duty to your country, Corrie. Maybe when me and Nick was fighting the Mexicans back in '47, it wasn't all that patriotic a thing. We were just a couple of men not knowing what to do with ourselves. We didn't know much about all the disputes with President Polk. But you see, now you've got a chance to do something and know it's important at the same time."

"I'd like to hear about the Mexican war, Pa."

"Ask Almeda about it."

"Almeda?" I said. "Why her? *You're* the one who fought in it."

"Nick and I may have fought in it, but we didn't know anything of what it was about. Your pa wasn't much of a literate man back in those days, I'm sorry to say, Corrie. Almeda told me what I was really fighting for."

"What was it, then, you and Uncle Nick were fighting for? Wasn't it just to keep the Mexicans from taking our territory?"

"That's the way Polk and the Democrats would like to tell it. But according to Almeda, that wasn't it at all. It was actually the other way around—we were taking *their* territory in the Southwest, just like we've been doing from the Indians in the North."

"So what *were* you fighting for?"

"You sure you want to know? It ain't too pleasant a notion."

"Of course I want to know."

"We were fighting for slavery, Corrie—nothing less than just that. Even in California like we were, that's what it was about."

"But . . . how could it have been about slavery way back then, Pa?"

"The southerners have been trying to hedge their bets for a long time. Grabbing up all that land in the Southwest, all the way from Texas to California. You see, that was the Democrats' way to get their hands on lots of new territory that would become slave states someday. Polk wasn't no fool. He was a southerner himself, and he saw the handwriting on the wall. They knew clear back then that slavery didn't have much of a chance unless they got lots of new slave states eventually."

"That's what Almeda says?"

"She gets downright hot in her breeches about slavery. Being a northerner herself, and a woman mighty full of strong ideas, she hates the very thought of it. She says that we attacked the Mexicans and forced the war ourselves, even though the government was saying they attacked us and we were only defending the cause of freedom. Hoots, that's just exactly what Nick and I was told when we joined up."

"How does she know all that?"

"She says it comes from reading what she calls between the lines, reading what nobody says but what's there if you know how to look for it."

I was quiet a while, thinking about all he'd said.

"But you see, Corrie," Pa went on, "that's all the more reason for you maybe to help Mr. Lincoln. Back then, without knowing it, I helped the South and the Democrats. Now you can do something about it on the other side."

"It still doesn't seem as if I'd make much of a difference."

"I'm telling you, Corrie, people aren't just listening to you out of curiosity. You're writing news that's important. You know as well as I do what Kemble said, that folks back East read your articles on the flooding and it was their way of finding out what was happening here. News, Corrie, not just curiosity writing. You're a genuine newspaper reporter whose words are being read from the Pacific all the way to the Atlantic. You're making a way for a lot of women who never figured they could do anything in this man's world. You're doing it, and they're proud of you—just like I am."

"You make it sound so important, Pa," I said.

"Maybe I am your pa, but I still say it *is* important. Your articles are sure more important than anything that weasel O'Flaridy's ever done!"

I laughed at the thought of Robin's condescension toward me the first time we met in Mr. Kemble's office.

"I'm glad to see you can laugh," said Pa. "You were downright furious with him over the Fremont article. Whatever became of him? I haven't heard you mention his name in more than a year."

"Mr. Kemble told me he left the *Alta* and went back East somewhere. St. Louis, I think it was at first. He always did have big ambitions, and I know it stuck in his craw that I was getting more well known than he. He couldn't abide getting outdone by a woman, and I think he wanted to get out of here and make a name for himself."

"Well, he can make his name however he pleases, but I'm proud of my own Corrie's name and what she's done with it. And I think you oughta do what the man asked you to do and help out the Republicans to get Mr. Lincoln elected."

I was quiet for a minute or so, thinking about what Pa'd said.

"But how do I know if it's the right thing?" I asked after a bit.

"You mean whether Lincoln's the right man to be president?" said Pa.

"That too, but mainly whether it's the right thing for *me* to do. I mean, just because something's there to do, and just because somebody *else* thinks I ought to do it, that doesn't necessarily make it right, does it?"

I paused. Pa didn't say anything but just kept looking over at me, and then I continued.

"I knew for a long time that I wanted to write. It was something I wanted to do inside *myself*, whether anybody else cared, or whether anybody else ever read anything I wrote. But then when something like this comes along, from the outside, so to speak, and not from inside myself, it's an altogether different thing. I just can't do something because somebody wants me to. There's got to be a rightness about it."

"I hadn't given a thought myself to the idea of running for mayor until Almeda and Avery and Nick and the rest of you all talked me into it."

"But after a bit, didn't you start thinking it was the right thing for *you* to do too, no matter what we thought?"

"Sure. I wouldn't have done it otherwise."

"That's what I mean, Pa. Even if Mr. Lincoln is the right man, I can't do it because anyone else thinks I should. It's still got to be right for *me*."

"Well, then, do you think Mr. Lincoln's the man who ought to be the country's president?"

"I don't guess there's any doubt about that. Slavery's no good, and like the man said, it's time the southern states didn't control things as they have for so long."

"So then, there's your place to start thinking about it. At least you're in agreement with the cause they're talking about. You sure couldn't do it if that weren't true. Now all you have to do is decide if it's something *you* want to do, that you feel is *right* for you to do."

"Sometimes that's not an easy thing to know."

We were both silent a while. Finally Pa reached over and took my hand, then bowed his head and closed his eyes right there on the steamer.

"God," he prayed out loud, "me and Corrie here, we've got some things to decide about our future, and about what we ought to do about some things. And we ain't altogether sure in our own minds what's best. So we ask you right now to help us, and to guide us in what we do. We need your help, God, to keep us walkin' right along the path you want us on. Neither of us want to be anywhere else but right where you'd have us. So show us where that is."

He looked up and opened his eyes. "Amen," I added.

Again we sat in silence for a while as we floated along.

"You just never know where something's going to lead you," I said at length.

Pa nodded.

"Just like starting to write and getting that first article published in the *Alta*, or walking into the *Gold Nugget*, looking for Uncle Nick that day and having you walk out instead. Things have a way of piling onto each other. Something you do today can change the whole direction of your life."

"Makes you think about being careful before you jump into something new, don't it?" said Pa. "Whether it's writing or may-oring or anything else."

"Yeah, I reckon that's what I'm thinking now. If I say that I'll write and maybe even talk to some folks about voting for Abraham Lincoln and Hannibal Hamlin, who can tell what it might mean in my life a year from now, or even five years from now? It might change things as much as writing that first article did."

"You heard what all them men in San Francisco were saying," said Pa. "This year of 1860 is just about the most important year this country's ever faced. So I reckon you're right. If this election's the most important in a long spell, then it's bound to have some effect on your life too."

"That's what I'm thinking, Pa. But how do you know what to do when you can't see up ahead what that effect might be?"

"You can't see into the future, that's for sure, Corrie."

"I know," I laughed. "Sometimes I'd like to, though."

"Well, look at it this way—if this election is gonna help decide which direction the nation's going from now on, maybe you can't see into the future, but you might have a hand in helping decide it."

"But electing either Lincoln or Douglas could change my life as much as it's sure to change the country one way or the other."

"Yep, I figure it could."

I let out a sigh. "I don't suppose there's much else to do but wait for God to show me something," I said finally.

"I reckon he will," said Pa.

"I hope so."

"If you're looking for it, he won't leave you in doubt for too long a spell about what to do."

# CHAPTER 5

# THE ROCK OF CHANGING CIRCUMSTANCES

We rode along for fifteen or twenty minutes without saying anything more. Outside, the rolling landscape passed slowly, reminding me of the time I'd first made the leisurely trip down the river with Almeda.

It seemed so long ago now!

The country was shrinking; California was shrinking. Stagecoaches ran daily to most places north from Sacramento. The Pony Express delivered mail in record time; rail lines were being laid down all over the country, and the national election seemed so much closer and important than ever before! I felt I was being stretched, so that the whole country was part of my life, my world.

Just the thought that my writing went all the way from the Pacific to the Atlantic was enough to make me stop and wonder what God was doing with me. Nobody paid any attention to what a woman did, and yet people *were* reading my words all the way back there in the East, as well as at home in Miracle Springs. It was sometimes more than I could imagine!

"You know, Corrie," Pa said after a while, "I've got a future to be thinking about too."

I looked up from the midst of my daydreaming. "You mean whether to keep being mayor?"

"There's that too," answered Pa. "But plenty more besides."

"What, Pa? You sound as if it's something serious."

Pa sighed and looked out the window thoughtfully.

"Is there something wrong?" I asked.

31

He gave a little laugh, although there wasn't anything comical in the sound of it.

"Wrong, Corrie?" he said wistfully. "No. I was just reflecting on all the changes that come even when you're not looking for them. Life has a way of bringing things to you and plopping them smack in your way so there's no way you can avoid them. You may be thinking you're heading down one road toward some-where, but then all of a sudden a giant rock falls in the middle of your path. And you figure, that's okay, you'll just walk around it. But in getting past it, without realizing it, you change directions, and then all of a sudden you're going along a different path toward someplace different. You never knew there was someplace differ-ent to go, but you're headed there, and you never set foot on the first road you was on again."

"You're going to have to try again, Pa," I said. "I don't suppose I'm used to hearing you philosophize about life quite like that."

Pa burst out laughing so hard he couldn't stop. Several of the other people in the boat turned their heads to see what the joke was.

"I must've been around you and Almeda and Avery too much," he said finally, still half laughing. "Or too long trying to make sense of being mayor to that town of miners, farmers, ranch-ers, and kids!"

"But I still want to know what you meant by the road with the big rock falling in the middle of it."

"Well, for example, Nick and I coming west, we didn't plan on all that trouble we got into. I always figured on farming my land and raising my family in what you'd call a normal way. Then all of a sudden, the rock of circumstances fell—the robbery, the shooting. Suddenly Nick and I were running from the law and heading west.

"That's what I mean, Corrie. There we were on a new path toward someplace we never figured on going. We never set foot on the first road again. I've been out West ever since, never saw your ma again. It was a long time before I could even think about Aggie without getting pretty stirred up inside. You know that, 'cause I shed my share of tears with you after finding out she was gone. You understand? A change comes out of nowhere—you don't see it coming, you don't expect it, you ain't done nothing to plan for it . . . but your life will never be the same again."

"Now I see, Pa."

"Same thing that day you and the rest of the kids showed up in Miracle. I stumbled out of the *Gold Nugget* and there the five of you was standing there, with Almeda wagging her tongue at me. And *wham*—my life took off in a new direction!

"I guess we get blindsided by circumstances every now and then. So when one of them big boulders slams down in front of you, it makes pretty good sense to look things over a spell before you start off either moving around it or in a new direction. You never know what tomorrow's gonna bring, and you just might never get back to the same place again."

"Like that man asking me if I'd help with the election?"

"Exactly like that. You see, that's a big rock in your path. It's not anything bad, like me and Nick's getting into trouble. Why, it's a real opportunity for you—might be the best thing that ever came along. But you just can't ever know ahead of time what might come next on account of it. That's why you gotta stop and take a good look at things and at the decisions you make. If you say yes to the man, it might change everything for you, Corrie. It might not . . . but then it *might*. You just can't know for sure."

As I watched Pa and listened to him, I realized that his being a father and a husband for the second time in his life, the mayor of a growing community, and a man who took his faith in God more seriously than most men did—all that had changed Pa *inside* more than even he realized. Just to hear him talk amazed me when I thought back to those first couple of years after the kids and I came to California. He might talk about the boulder and his and Uncle Nick's coming out West and being mayor, but I could see that the most important new path Drummond Hollister was walking along was deep inside his heart and mind, and maybe didn't have as much to do with all those other things as he might think.

"It's the same with the country, Corrie," Pa went on, "or with a town, a community, a family. Things come up, and then things change. Everything around here for two hundred miles is the way it is because a man named Marshall found a pretty little rock in a mountain stream up in the hills. And Miracle Springs became what it did 'cause our friend Alkali Jones found a piece of the same kind of rock in the creek up behind our place."

"According to him, at least," I said with a smile.

"You're right there, Corrie!" laughed Pa. "But *somebody* found gold there anyhow, including Tad when he was just a little runt. And then all of a sudden everything's changed.

"And this election—all those men back there were saying how important it is for the future of the country. Why, who can tell, we might look back someday and say that the election of 1860, and whoever becomes the new president next year, steered the whole country off in a new direction. You just never know what might be around the corner, and so you oughta be watching and paying attention as best you can."

Again he fell silent and gazed out the window for a while.

"I see what you are saying, Pa," I said. "And I'm sure going to take your advice and try to think carefully through what's best for me to do. If it's going to change the direction of my future, it can't be something I do without thinking and praying. But I don't think you were really talking about my decision, were you, Pa, when you first said it? There's something else on your mind, isn't there?"

He sighed, then and turned his head back and looked at me.

"Can't ever fool you, can I?"

"You said you had your future to be thinking about," I said, "more than just mayoring."

"Yeah, I guess I did say that, didn't I?"

"Yes, you did. So, what is it you've been beating around the bush to try to tell me about?"

Pa took a deep breath. "Do you know who that man was who asked you about helping out with the election?" he asked.

"I got introduced to him," I answered, "but I forgot his name."

"His name's Alexander Dalton."

"That's right, now I remember. But I'd never heard of him, Pa."

"He's not the kind of man people do hear of. Crocker and Hopkins and Stanford and Fremont—they're the public men, the famous, the names folks hear about. Lincoln and Douglas—

they're the ones running for president. But back behind men like that there are always other folks making things happen that nobody ever sees. Kingmakers, they're called. They'll never be kings themselves, but they hold power to *make* kings. You see what I mean?"

I nodded. "So, is Mr. Dalton like that—a kingmaker?"

"That's exactly what he is," replied Pa. "He's just about one of the most important men in all the West, even though he's practically unknown except by the people who need to know him. Fremont, Stanford—he's helped make them the important men they are."

"So that's why he was the one talking to me about getting involved."

"He's the top Republican in California, Corrie—the chairman of the Republican party for all of California and Oregon. It's his job to make sure Lincoln carries the state."

"Is that all he does?"

Pa chuckled. "Not by a long shot, Corrie! He's got to see to all kinds of business besides just presidential politics."

"Like what?"

"California politics, the state's future, all the kinds of things politicians think about. He's got to raise money for the party, he's got to see to the state's growth, he's got to make decisions about who does what, who's in charge of what. He's the one more than anyone else who has power to get people elected to committees and even to the Congress in Washington. Leastways, if the Republican party keeps growing like it has, he'll be doing all those things. The way I hear it, he's just about the second most influential man in Sacramento behind Governor Downey."

"You sound like you know him, Pa."

"I've met him a time or two. He's always at the mayors' conferences I got to go to. He knows everybody. He's made speeches to us about all the plans to get California split up into different states."

"So what does it all have to do with us, Pa?"

"It's got to do with you 'cause he asked you to help with the election, Corrie. He's trying to get Lincoln elected."

"But what about you?"

"Well, daughter of mine, you weren't the only Hollister that Dalton talked to last night," said Pa.

"I didn't see you with him," I said.

"It wasn't a long conversation," Pa replied. "And it was private. He took me outside for a minute."

"It sounds secretive—why, Pa?"

"Some things are best not made public until the right time, Corrie. You know how fellas like Royce can twist and turn things to their own advantage if you're not careful."

"Now you've got me dying of curiosity, Pa! What did Dalton say?"

"Well . . . he asked me to run for the state legislature in Sacramento come November."

# CHAPTER 6

# A SURPRISE IN SACRAMENTO

"Pa, that's wonderful!" I exclaimed. "Are you going to do it?"

"I don't know, Corrie. I've got lots to think about, just like you. God's bound to cause a heap of changes, like I was saying, we can't see now. It's not something you can do lightly. Naturally I gotta talk and pray with Almeda about it."

"Would you have to move to Sacramento, Pa?"

"I reckon most of the men do, but there ain't no way I'd leave Miracle. I'm not about to pack up everyone to go live in a city. And there's sure no way I'd move there myself or with just me and Almeda, and leave everyone."

"I could take care of the kids, Pa. Zack and I are adults. With Emily and Mike married and down in Auburn, that only leaves Becky and Tad. They're fifteen and seventeen. We can take care of ourselves. You and Almeda can take little Ruth with you to Sacramento and you can become a famous politician. If we have any problems, there's Uncle Nick and Aunt Katie across the stream."

"No, I'm not gonna split up my family for nobody, not for Alexander Dalton, not for my own future, not even for California. Besides, what if you decide to do what he wants *you* to do? Then you'd be gone a lot, too."

"Zack's twenty-one. He's a grown man."

"You know as well as I do that he's itching to be off wherever a horse'll carry him. He and Little Wolf are gone half the time as it is. No, Corrie, if I decide to run, and even if I win, then they'll just have to settle for a congressman who represents his people as best he can by staying with those people and going into Sacramento whenever he has to."

"I wonder how long it'll be before the train comes up that far?"

"I doubt if that'll be for years. There's lots of other places in California growing faster than us. I'm sure I'd have to travel by horse or stagecoach for a good while yet."

"Did Mr. Dalton say why he wanted you to run?" I asked.

A sheepish look came over Pa's face. I'd never seen anything quite like it in his expression before.

"Aw, he did, but you know them politicians—they're always saying things that aren't true to get things how they want them."

"What did he say, Pa?"

"Aw, he just said he and other folks in Sacramento'd been keeping their eyes on me ever since I got elected mayor, and some of them figured I was the kind of man they needed in the capitol to help set the direction for the state in the coming years."

"Of course you're the kind of man the state needs!" I said. I leaned over and gave him a hug. "Pa, I am so proud of you."

Neither of us had noticed the steamer slowing down as we approached the dock at Sacramento.

"Looks like we're to the halfway point," said Pa. "We'll have to decide on our futures later."

We got up and left the boat, walking into the bright warm sunlight of Sacramento in early afternoon. San Francisco was always much cooler, but here in Sacramento, summer was on the way.

If we had come by horseback or had left a wagon or buckboard in Sacramento, we might have made it home by late that same night. But we had taken the stage down, and the return stage north left early in the morning, so we'd have to stay over.

We got our bags and Pa hired a buckboard to drive us to Miss Baxter's Boarding House. We always stayed with her whenever we were in the city. By this time, with her keeping tabs on us and all the changes that had come in our family since we first arrived in California with Captain Dixon eight years earlier, she was as good a family friend as we had anywhere in the city.

Once we got ourselves situated at her place, we went out for a walk. Pa said he wanted to show me the statehouse where the legislature and governor had their offices, and where California's government was run from. Since we had all afternoon, we decided to go on foot. As we walked I could tell easily enough that Pa was thinking about what it would be like for him to be involved in what went on in that building. At one point Pa stopped and pointed to a construction site. "See that?" he said. "That's the big new domed capitol they're just beginning." Little did I know how much he would be involved in that building.

We walked for quite a while, back toward the downtown section of town. The day had become warmer and we were enjoying ourselves, talking about what the future might hold for us. As we crossed the street between the post office and station, in the distance I noticed a lady who caught my attention.

"Pa, doesn't that woman coming this way look like Katie?" I asked. "Or am I just imagining it?"

"There *was* something about her that struck me as familiar," Pa replied. He eyed her a little closer as we walked. "If I didn't know better, I'd swear she could pass for Katie's twin sister!"

My curiosity got the best of me. As she approached, I stopped and addressed her.

"Excuse me, but would you happen to know a lady named Katie Morgan Hollister, who lives in Miracle Springs?"

The woman's face lit up. "I sure do," she said. "Katie is my older sister."

"What!" I exclaimed. "But . . . how can—but . . . what are you—"

The woman laughed at my confusion, and the sound of her laughter left no more doubt that she was related to Katie.

"My name is Edie," she said, "Edie Simpson. Edie *Morgan* Simpson, that is. My husband died two months ago, so I decided to come out to pay Katie a surprise visit while I try to decide what's to become of my life. I take it you know Katie."

"I'm the man she came out here to marry," interjected Pa with a laugh. "Drummond Hollister's the name, ma'am, and this is my daughter Corrie."

"Corrie Belle Hollister, of course! I know your name from Katie's letters. And, Drummond, I am so pleased to meet you too. Katie speaks highly of you both." She extended her hand and gave us each a firm handshake. "How are Katie and Nick?"

"Couldn't be better, ma'am," said Pa. "Erich's gonna turn five next month, and little baby Anne—what is she, Corrie?" he said, turning to me. "A year by now?"

"Fourteen months," I said. "She was born last April, and she just started walking three weeks ago."

"I can't wait to see Katie and meet her family!" said Edie brightly.

"She doesn't know you're coming, ma'am?" asked Pa.

"No. I thought about sending her a letter by Pony Express, telling about Mr. Simpson's passing. But then I thought I might as well just come and see her in person."

"When did you get here?"

"Only this morning."

"How did you come—by ship to San Francisco?" I asked.

"I came overland by the Butterfield coach."

"The ox-bow route, huh?" said Pa.

"Yes, and I felt every bump in the whole punishing trip. I certainly got my $225 worth, and I must say I am very glad to be here at last."

She paused and laughed again. "I took the train to St. Louis. From there the coach went south through Texas, then New Mexico and to Fort Yuma. Luckily the only Indian attack was nearby and the driver outran them to the fort. Then the way led to Los Angeles and north to Sacramento. I arrived only an hour ago. I was just on my way out to locate a suitable lodging for the night."

"Well, think no more about it, ma'am," said Pa. "If you'll show me where your bags are, I'll get them for you. Then we'll get us a ride back to our boardinghouse. You can stay with us tonight, and we'll be off to Miracle bright and early in the morning."

# CHAPTER 7

## BACK HOME IN MIRACLE SPRINGS

It was late the next afternoon when the stage pulled into Miracle Springs.

We got out, and just in the time it took Pa to get our bags down off the top and walk across the street to the Mine and Freight, half a dozen people came up to greet us and ask about our trip.

"Afternoon to you, Mayor Hollister," said the man in charge of the stage office when he came out to meet the stage. He'd been in town only about a year and still acted as if Pa was about the most important man for miles. I reckon in a way he was, but Pa's old friends still just called him Drum like they always had. But even as they said it, there was a hint of a different tone to it. They knew that Pa had become something special.

As we walked across the street to the office, Edie said, "My goodness, I knew my sister's brother-in-law was the mayor, but I didn't expect *this* much attention. They act like you're a celebrity around here!"

Pa just laughed.

Above the building stood a big sign that read: *Hollister-Parrish Mine and Freight Company,* a change Almeda had insisted on even though she still ran the business pretty much herself, with my help. The *Hollister* on the sign didn't mean me, of course, but Pa.

My little half-sister, Ruth, was three years old, and she was a handful, so Almeda didn't spend nearly so much time in town as she once did. I came into the office on most days; Pa helped out

41

now and then, and Marcus Weber and Mr. Ashton took care of everything else. Almeda wouldn't have needed to come in at all, but she usually made the ride into town once or twice a week, when Pa or I would stay home with Ruth. She was too much of a businesswoman to be content always being at home.

But times had changed in Miracle Springs in the ten years Almeda had been there. There wasn't as much mining and freighting business to be done nowadays, even though Mr. Royce had closed down his competing enterprise. Mining itself had slacked off a lot; most of the men had all the equipment they needed, and Miracle Springs had become less of a gold-rush mining town, and more of a regular community made up of all kinds of people and families.

The business was still called the Mine and Freight, but Almeda and I had gradually started carrying a wider range of goods and merchandise. Now it resembled a general store for all the kinds of work men around the area did—farmers and ranchers as well as miners. We had wood tools and plows and barbed-wire and wagon parts and hand tools, even some harness and saddle equipment and seeds—lots of different things people needed. We were careful not to order goods that any of the other merchants carried; Almeda had strong feelings about such things as loyalty and competition. But if there were things folks needed they couldn't get someplace else, we found a way to get what they needed.

Pa and Uncle Nick still worked the mine several days a week, but not like they once did. They still dug gold out of it, and Alkali Jones was always talking about hitting another rich vein just a little ways farther into the side of the mountain. "Dang if there ain't a whole new lode in there, Drum," I had heard him say again and again. "I can smell it, *hee, hee, hee!*"

Whether Pa or Uncle Nick believed him, I don't know, but the persistence with which he trusted his "gold-sniffer," as he sometimes called his nose, usually brought out a wisecrack or two from Uncle Nick, and a sly wink in our direction from Pa. But he loved Mr. Jones—partly like a brother, partly like a trusted friend, even like a father. He would never do anything to hurt his feelings. Whenever the word *mayor* was used in Alkali Jones's hearing, we'd hear his high cackling *hee, hee, hee!* sooner or later.

He still couldn't get used to *dad-blamed ol' Drum being mayor to nothin' but a hill of prairie dogs! Hee, hee, hee!*

Pa and Uncle Nick didn't need to mine. The business did well enough along with the original strike to keep our whole little community of two families fed. But mining was so much in their blood that there was no way they could keep themselves from doing it. I suppose Alkali Jones's predictions of a new vein drove all the men to keep going deep down inside. Hope could be a powerful force. So Pa and Uncle Nick kept poking and picking and sometimes blasting away, and little bits of gold kept tumbling down the stream.

Pa mayored about as much as Almeda kept shop, though most of it was folks coming to him rather than him doing much of anything. He had no office in town. People knew where to find him when they wanted.

"Hey, Marcus," said Pa, sticking his head inside the livery out behind the office, "you got a wagon and a couple horses you could hitch up for us?"

"Yes sir, Mister Hollister," said a beaming Marcus Weber, coming out to greet us. "Your wife's gonna be glad to see you."

"Why's that, Marcus?"

"Little Ruth, she done took a fever."

Pa's face wrinkled in concern as he threw a couple of the bags in the back of one of the wagons. "Anything serious?" he asked.

"I dunno. Miz Almeda, she was just in here a minute yesterday, on her way to the Doc's."

"Hmm . . . then we better get out there as soon as we can," said Pa. "Corrie, why don't you and Edie go back to the stage office and get the rest of the bags. I'll give Marcus a hand with the horses and wagon."

By the time we got back, he and Mr. Weber nearly had the wagon ready to go. We climbed aboard. In two or three minutes, we were off and rumbling through the streets of Miracle and out of town toward the claim.

As much as I could with the bouncing and racket of the horses and wagon, I told Edie about the town—how it had grown and what it was like when we first came in 1852. We'd already told her all about the Gold Nugget and us five kids showing up and

Almeda going in to fetch Pa, thinking he was dead and that it was Uncle Nick inside. But now I had a chance to show her everything firsthand. In many ways the town was different than back then— bigger, less raucous, fewer saloons, more stores.

Mr. Royce still had the only bank in town. Pa and the town council had denied Finchwood another petition a year after the first, so they finally decided to open their new bank in Oroville instead. Mr. Royce had lowered the interest rate on all the loans he held to four and a half percent to match Finchwood's. Maybe he wasn't making as much profit as he once did, but folks were much more kindly disposed toward him, and you could tell from his face that he was a happier man for it, too. So nothing more had come of the "Hollister-Parrish Bank."

"It's so different than a city or town in the East," said Edie as we bounced over the bridge and out of town. "So much more primitive."

"You should have seen Miracle Springs eight years ago!" I said.

"Don't get me wrong, Corrie. It looks like a lovely town. Especially compared with some of the rough places the stagecoach went through!" She shook her head at the memory. "My, oh, my! Some of the things I saw! The territories and towns across the plains are called the frontier for good reason—every man carrying a gun! At least Miracle Springs appears to be more civilized than those places. But you really should see the East someday, Corrie."

"We came from the East," I said.

"Oh, where?"

"New York. But only the country part. I've never seen the city."

"Ah, New York is indeed the city of cities!"

"What about Washington?" I asked.

"I've never been there," replied Edie. "There's nothing there but the government. Why would you want to visit Washington?"

"I'm interested in politics," I answered. "I sometimes write about it in my articles."

"You *write* about politics! Good heavens, that kind of foolishness is for men, don't you know that, Corrie? What could a young woman like you possibly have to do with politics? We can't even vote!"

"I'm still interested in what happens to our country."

"The men will decide everything, so what difference does it make what we think about it?"

"But aren't you interested?"

"Not in men's affairs."

"What about slavery?"

"What about it?"

"Don't you think it's wrong?"

"How could it be wrong when half the country has slaves? It's not a moral issue of right and wrong, Corrie. It's just part of the economics of the country. It's how things are, that's all."

"That doesn't make it right," I insisted.

"That's what the northerners are always trying to do—make it a matter of right and wrong. But it's just different cultures. Slavery is part of the South. Northerners have no right to condemn something they know nothing about."

For someone who wasn't interested in politics, Edie seemed to have some definite ideas about slavery. And I wasn't sure I altogether liked the sound of them.

"You make it sound like northerners belong to a different country," I said. "Is there really that much difference?"

"When you live in the South, Corrie, there is. The North is a different country—and not a friendly one."

"You live in the South?"

"Of course. Virginia has always been a slave state, and always will be. My husband, the late Mr. Simpson, worked for a large landowner and had dealings with slaves all the time. It's just how things are in the South, and always have been."

"But . . . but doesn't slavery seem wrong to you?" I said again.

"I told you before, it's not a matter of right or wrong. Besides, slavery's in the Bible. Nobody in the Bible ever said it was wrong."

# CHAPTER 8

## MIXED HOMECOMING

I'd been so engrossed in the conversation with Edie that I hadn't even noticed that we were approaching the claim.

Suddenly there were Tad and Becky running toward us, followed by Almeda carrying Ruth. I expected to see Zack come out of the barn any second, but he never did.

We jumped down, and there were hugs and greetings and questions. Pa kissed Almeda and stretched his long arms around her and Ruth all at once. "How's my little daughter?" he asked, looking from one to the other. "Marcus said she wasn't feeling too well." He felt her forehead with his big rough palm.

"She was so hot yesterday," said Almeda. "I was worried and took her in to see Doc Shoemaker. "He thinks it might have been a spider bite."

"How is she?" said Pa, looking concerned. "She does feel warm."

"Better today. She's cooled off considerably and seems to be getting some of her spunk back."

All this time Edie had been standing beside the wagon. A brief silence followed, and Pa seemed to suddenly remember our passenger. He turned back toward her and motioned her forward. "But I plumb forgot our guest! Almeda, you'll never guess who we picked up in Sacramento," he said. "This here's Katie's sister! Edie, meet my wife, Almeda."

Almeda came forward and greeted her warmly. "Surely there is some logical explanation," she said, laughing. "This must be more than an accidental meeting."

Edie told about her husband's death and her decision to come for a visit, followed by her version of running into me and Pa in Sacramento. "So where do Katie and Nick live?" she said, looking around.

"Not more than a quarter mile upstream," answered Pa. "Come on everyone, into the wagon. Let's get Edie on to her reunion with her sister!"

We all scrambled back in. Pa gave Edie a lift up into the back with us kids, then took Almeda's hand and helped her up to the seat beside him, with Ruth in her lap. Then he clucked to the two horses, and off we lurched up the road alongside the creek toward the mine, where we would cross over into the woods on the other side.

What a reunion it was! I don't think I'd ever seen Aunt Katie so much at a loss for words. She was so surprised she didn't know whether to laugh or cry, so instead she just stood there with a look of silent disbelief on her face. By the time we left them half an hour later, the two sisters were talking so fast we could hardly understand them. Pa gave Uncle Nick a smile, almost as if to say, *You're gonna have your hands full now with two Virginia women.* Uncle Nick watched us go with a shrug and look that said, *What do I do now?*

When we got back to our place, Tad handed our two bags down to Pa, and we all went inside.

"Well, tell us all about San Francisco and the fancy gathering you two important Hollisters went to," said Almeda, pouring Pa a cup of coffee from the pot on the stove. "We've all been praying for you, and we're anxious to hear how God answered. So . . . did anything exciting happen while you were there?"

Pa and I glanced at each other. Pa gave me a wink, and I burst out laughing.

"What is it?" said Almeda with a curious smile. "*Something* must have happened!"

"Naw, nothing much," said Pa, "not unless you count getting asked to help Honest Abe Lincoln get elected and run for state legislature all within the same hour."

"What!" exclaimed Almeda. "Who asked . . . somebody asked *you?*"

"There was a man named Dalton," I put in. "I didn't know who he was at first, but Pa told me later that he was the most important Republican in the state. He asked me to help with the election in November."

"Help . . . how?"

"Writing . . . I don't know," I answered. "I'm not quite sure what he wanted."

"Corrie's being modest," added Pa. "I told you, Corrie, that you're an important person in this state. There was even some talk," he said, turning to Almeda, "of her making speeches on behalf of the Republican ticket."

"Corrie, that's wonderful! What do you think—are you going to do it?"

"I don't know," I shrugged. "Pa and I talked about it, and prayed together. We were both saying how you never know where something's going to lead. But Pa's news is even bigger! They asked him to run for the legislature in Sacramento!"

"Drummond!" exclaimed Almeda. "Is it true?"

"I reckon they figure there ain't no harm in asking," answered Pa noncommittally. "So ask they did."

"What did you say?"

"I didn't say anything. Just like Corrie, I said I'd think about it. I ain't about to pick up stakes and disrupt my family again. So I don't rightly see as how I could do it. But I didn't tell them anything definite."

"My husband and daughter—the politicians!" laughed Almeda. "I can hardly believe it!"

"You started it with all your notions of running for mayor!" joked Pa. "Now look what you landed me into!"

"And giving me that journal," I added in fun.

"You two aren't fooling anybody. You love every bit of it, and you both know it!"

"Corrie, tell Almeda about the new friend you met there."

"Oh, Pa, why'd you have to bring that up?" I said, blushing.

"What's this?" asked Almeda and Becky at the same time.

"Just some important young man who took a fancy to Corrie."

"Pa, he did not!" I said.

"Don't lie, Corrie," teased Pa. "You should have seen them,

Becky," he went on, "together nearly the whole evening. Why, Corrie deserted me, and I was alone for most of the reception."

"Pa! Now it's you who's lying."

"Well, maybe exaggerating just a tad."

"I want to know all about him," said Almeda.

"There's nothing to tell. He's a friend of Mr. Denver's, and he's the one who took me to meet Mr. Dalton, that's all. I'm sure he was just doing what he was supposed to do and nothing more. I'll probably never see him again."

Finally Pa figured I'd had enough of the ribbing, and he turned toward Almeda. "Where's Zack?"

Her face fell and the room suddenly got silent.

"Zack and Almeda had a big argument, Pa," said Tad finally.

"Is that true?" said Pa, his forehead crinkling as he turned toward Almeda.

She nodded. "I'm afraid so, Drummond."

"What about?"

"Something he wanted to do. I told him he'd have to wait until you got back and talk it over with you."

"What was so all-fired important that it couldn't wait a couple of days?" asked Pa.

"I don't know what got into him. He just exploded. I've never seen him like that before. He stormed away, talking nonsense about always having to go along with what everyone else wanted and nobody ever asking him what *he* thought. I don't know where it all came from, but from the sound of it, it must have been pent up a long time."

"I'll take his breeches off and tan his hide but good when he gets home!" said Pa. It was clear he was angry.

"Don't do anything rash, Drum. Zack's not a boy anymore."

"He's *my* boy!"

"He's your son. But he's grown, and whatever this storm is that's built up inside him, it's not something to be taken lightly."

"What was it he got in his head to do?"

"He said he was going to join the Pony Express, Pa," said Tad.

"That true, Almeda?"

"That's pretty much the gist of it. They were offering good money, he said, and he and Little Wolf had both decided to go.

There were some openings between Nevada and Utah."

"What about Lame Pony? What does he think?"

"I haven't seen him since. It only happened two days ago."

"And Zack hasn't come back?"

Almeda shook her head.

"He's probably up the hill at Jack's. I'll ride out there and see what's up."

# CHAPTER 9

## FATHER AND SON

None of us saw Zack for five days.

Pa went up to Jack Lame Pony's, but neither he nor Little Wolf knew where Zack had gone. Little Wolf couldn't tell him much more than Almeda had, that a fellow they had met had offered the boys jobs with the new mail delivery service and that they had talked about taking him up on his offer. Then Zack had gone home to tell Almeda about it, and that was the last anyone had seen of him.

Then as we were talking, Zack came walking through the door. We hadn't even heard the sound of a horse riding up.

I don't know where he'd been, but he looked dirty and unshaven. He gave me a little nod of greeting, but he didn't smile, and he tried to pretend Pa wasn't there. He probably knew what was coming.

"Where you been, son?" said Pa.

"Out riding," muttered Zack.

"Where?"

"Just around," said Zack, shuffling toward the kitchen area to see if there was anything to eat.

"I was a mite surprised to come home and find you gone," said Pa. "When I'm away I expect you to look after the family."

Zack said nothing. He picked up a piece of bread and bit into it.

"You don't figure you owe no responsibility to the family, is that it?"

Zack mumbled something, but I couldn't make it out.

"What's that you say?"

"I said it ain't my family no more."

"What do you mean by that?" Pa's tone was stern. It was easy to tell that he was getting riled.

"What should you care what I do? You all got your own plans. Corrie's got her writing, and you all think she's pretty great at everything she does. And you're busy being the town's important man. There ain't nothing Almeda can't do for herself. What do any of you need me for?"

"When I'm not here, I want you keeping a watch over things, that's what," said Pa, his voice icy. Zack hadn't looked at any of us straight in the face since walking in. If he was embarrassed about running off, he didn't show it. He just looked mad. I could feel the tension between him and Pa hanging in the air.

"Zack, please," said Almeda in a pleading tone, "I don't want—"

"You don't need me, Almeda. Don't try to pretend."

"Zack, that's not true," she said, turning to him with tender eyes full of anguish. "You know that I do need you—"

"Almeda," Zack said, cutting her off again, "you don't have to try to make me feel good anymore like you did when I was a boy."

"That's no way to talk to your mother, boy!" said Pa. By now he was storming mad.

"She ain't my mother!"

"She's my wife and a woman, and that means you better learn to talk to her with respect in your voice, unless you want my belt around that hind end of yours!"

"So you still think I'm a little kid too?"

"You're my son, and I'll whip you if I need to."

Becky and Tad stared at the two of them; it was all I could do to keep from bursting out crying. To suddenly have two of the people you love most in all the world arguing and yelling at each other was too horrible even to describe.

Zack turned away and laughed—a bitter, awful laugh.

"You find something funny in that?" asked Pa.

"Yeah," retorted Zack, spinning around and leveling that bitter-looking grin on Pa. "I'm twenty-one years old. I'm taller than you. I can ride a horse better than anyone for miles. But you still think of me as a little kid. You don't even know what it's like for me. I got a life of my own to live, and you don't even know the kinds of things I'm thinking about. Everything's about Corrie and Almeda or your being mayor or the Mine and Freight. You got no time for me—you never had. What do you care what I do? You just expect me to be around to take care of things so you can leave whenever you want."

"What's that supposed to mean?"

"You figure out what it means."

"None of that matters. You're not going to the Pony Express without my say-so. Whatever you may think, I'm still your pa. And I still got a right to tell you what you can and can't do."

Zack stared straight into his face, and the next words out of his mouth were so biting I could almost feel them slicing straight into Pa's heart.

"You never knew what it was like for me," said Zack. "You never knew the times I cried myself to sleep when I was a kid, hoping you'd come home. I was frightened without a father. I got teased and made fun of something awful 'cause I was little, and sometimes I came home with bruises and a black eye from trying to defend myself. I used to dream how good it would be to come home to feel the arms of a pa to hold me. I'd beg God to help us find you. But we never did, and I had to grow up alone like that. You'll never know how much you hurt Ma, and how she'd cry sometimes when she didn't know I was watching. She kept loving you and kept praying for you—always asking God to protect you and watch over you. But I finally quit praying, because I was sick of being disappointed."

Zack stopped for a second, trembling with emotion. Then he added, "So I don't reckon you got a right to call yourself my father no more. You may be my pa. But I figure I'm old enough to decide for myself what I want!"

Zack's words came so fast and were so unexpected that Pa didn't know what to do. I know Pa was hurt by what Zack had said, but his response came out as anger.

"However mixed up a job I done of it, I'm your pa whether you like it or not!"

"I'm stuck here with nothing but women and babies and little kids," Zack shot back. "You can go off and do whatever you want, and you figure I got nothing of my own that matters?"

"You got no right to talk about your mother and sisters that way. You apologize to them, or you're gonna feel that belt like I told you!"

"Ha! Your belt ain't gonna come anywhere near my rump! And I ain't apologizing to nobody! It's true, everything I said. I said to myself a long time ago I was getting out of here first chance I got. God knows I spent my muscles and blistered my hands working that mine for you all these years. You don't know how many days I sweated all day long, aching inside just for you to smile at me once and say I'd done a good day's work. But I might as well not even been there, for all you ever noticed! I don't reckon you'll figure you owe me anything for it. Well, that's fine with me. But all that's over with. I met a guy, and he's got a place arranged for me in the Pony Express. And I don't care if Little Wolf's changed his mind, I'm gonna take it. It's the chance I been waiting for to get out of this place!"

He turned and strode toward the door, still without looking at any of the rest of us. But Pa was closer, and took two giant steps and cut him off. He laid a strong hand on Zack's shoulder.

"No you're not, son," he said. "You ain't goin' nowhere without my leave. Now you get back in here, and we'll sit down and talk about it."

"I'm not talking about nothing," retorted Zack. "I've listened to all the rest of you long enough. Nobody ever seemed much interested in talking to me before. Now I'm going, whether you like it or not."

"And I'm telling you you're not."

"It's too late. I signed the papers. I start my first run next week."

"Then I'll go talk to this fella and unsign them."

Zack laughed again.

"You're not leaving home, Zack! You hear me, son? You got duties to this family."

Zack's eyes squinted ever so slightly, and his next words weren't loud but they cut deep.

"Is that how it was when *you* left Ma?" he said icily. "Duties to the family!" He laughed again. "*You* talk to *me* about duty to the family? Where were you all those years when I needed a pa? Even after we'd come all the way across the country to find you, you didn't want us. You denied you even knew us!"

Zack's back was to me as he spoke, and I could see Pa's grip on my brother's shoulder loosen. Pa unconsciously took half a step backward, as if Zack's words had been a physical blow across Pa's face. The rest of us stood in stunned silence to hear Zack accuse Pa like that.

"Well," he went on, "you talk about duty all you want, but I figure I've already about done as much as you ever did. You ran out on us, and even now you're always gone somewhere or another, but still you figure I'll do for you what you never did for me. Well, I tell you, I ain't gonna do it no more! If I go ride for the Pony Express, at least I ain't leaving a wife and five kids like you done!"

He wrested free of Pa's hand. As he did, Almeda approached, her eyes full of tears, and stretched out a hand and gently placed it on his shoulder.

"Oh, Zack," she pleaded, "if only I could make you see how much we all—"

But Zack, still backing his way free of Pa, either didn't hear her tender words of love or misunderstood her gesture. For whatever reason, as her hand touched him, thinking she intended to restrain him further, he reached up and in a swift motion threw her hand off him and took a step toward the door.

Seeing him rebuke Almeda so rudely was all Pa needed to jolt him awake from his stunned silence. Zack's reaction could not have been more ill-chosen.

Pa's eye's inflamed with rage. He leaped forward and struck Zack across the jaw. Yet even as Zack fell, Pa realized what he'd done and pulled back.

His cheek red from the blow and his body trembling, Zack slowly rose. "It's no secret where your loyalties lie," he said. "Everything for the women, but you won't lift a finger unless it's *against* your own son!"

He turned, opened the door, and stalked off, slamming it behind him. Pa half stumbled back into a chair, mortified at what he'd done. His face was white as a sheet.

The house was silent. The next sound we heard was Zack's horse galloping away.

# CHAPTER 10

## PA AND TAD

The silence, the tension, the uncertainty the rest of that day and the next was so thick and strong that we all walked around in a numbed state of sadness. Besides Pa, I think Zack's leaving was hardest on Tad. He had been a devoted son to Pa and a loving younger brother to Zack. And now suddenly the two idols of his world had nearly come to blows. He moped around in silence.

Pa managed to keep busy in the barn, going to town a lot, fixing things. He worked harder at the mine than I'd seen him work in three years, taking out his frustration on the rocks.

By the end of the second day, I sensed a gradual change come over Pa, and I was glad to see it. Zack was gone, and how long it would be before we might see him again, no one could tell. But instead of allowing it to destroy what was still left, Pa began to draw Tad closer. I suppose if good can come out of such a problem, it was good to see Pa trying to make use of what time was left him with his youngest son to build up the relationship so he didn't hurt him like he had done to Zack.

Of course Tad had been involved in the mine ever since he had found the huge nugget that had changed everything for our family. But on the second day after Zack's leaving, instead of just walking up to the mine to pound away by himself, Pa said, "Say, Tad, how about you and me seeing if we can dig any gold out of that hill today?"

Tad was still feeling pretty low, but he went with Pa. I don't know if the two of them talked much, and if they did I doubt they talked about the one person who was most on their minds. But they both came back, sweating and tired and dirty, in much better spirits than before. Hard work has a way of clearing out both the mind and the heart when they're cluttered up with feelings that are hard to understand.

The next day they cleaned out the barn together and repaired a section of the corral. Almeda and I could see that Pa was doing what he could to help ease Tad's pain and at the same time trying to give them both something—not to *take* the place of Zack, but maybe *in* the place of Zack's being there. That something was each other.

The two of them kept busy all week—busy, active, working hard, and tired. If they were going to keep thinking about Zack, they were going to have to do it in the midst of work and exercise! They got more gold out of the mountain and stream than they had in any week for three years, prompting Alkali Jones to fairly burst at the seams with his predictions of a new lode *just waitin' to spill out all over the dad-blamed valley, hee, hee, hee!*

The barn and grounds hadn't looked so tidy for a long time. They even took the wagon out into the woods and got started on next winter's firewood supply when summer hadn't even officially begun yet. At week's end, the two of them mounted up and went up into the mountains overnight—the first time Pa had ever gone hunting alone with Tad—and they came back the next afternoon with two bucks slung over the pack mules. For the first time since Zack's leaving, I saw a smile on Tad's face as he was telling us about stalking the one that he himself had shot.

"He was too far away to get a clean shot when we first spotted him," Tad said, his eyes gleaming. "So we had to work our way through the brush and trees to get closer without spooking him."

"You shoulda seen him," said Pa proudly. "He took dead aim right into the flank below his shoulder. One shot was all it needed. The big creature dropped where he stood without twitching a muscle. I've never seen such a shot!"

Tad went on excitedly telling about how they ran across the second one. I glanced over at Pa, watching him quietly. I could tell from the look in his eyes that he knew his efforts all week had paid off, that Tad felt better about Zack. Pa couldn't know it yet, but his efforts accomplished far more than just helping Tad deal with the loss of his brother. The two of them were closer than they had ever been, and were fast friends from that day on.

I knew the pain over Zack, and what Zack had said, went further inside Pa than he was letting on. Almeda knew, too, how deeply he felt it. But Pa was the kind of man who had to sort things out by himself for a spell before he was ready to talk. I was sure he would let us know what he was feeling once he was ready. In the meantime, he seemed to be putting his efforts into helping Tad figure out his frustrations.

Whatever Zack might have said, I saw a loving, unselfish man when I looked at Pa. And I wished Zack could see, as I did, how Pa had been a good father to all of us—at least once we'd arrive in California.

When we first came to California, Zack carried a chip around on his shoulder against Pa for a while, but I thought he'd gotten over all that years ago.

But I guess I was wrong. All it took for me to forgive Pa was to talk with him a few times and see how his own heart ached over the past. I had seen Pa cry and pray and grow, and I knew what kind of man he was—deep down, on the inside. But maybe he and Zack had never talked that way.

As I thought about Zack, I realized that when a person isn't able to forgive someone, a little seed of anger will eventually sprout and grow until branches and roots and leaves of bitterness come bursting out somewhere.

With Zack, apparently the forgiveness didn't get finished, and now he was gone. And Pa was feeling one of the deepest pains a man can feel on account of it.

Meanwhile, other things kept us from thinking only about Zack. The Sunday after Pa and Tad got back from their hunting trip, Aunt Katie and Uncle Nick invited all of us to their place to eat and to have a family visit with them and Edie.

That day suddenly put Zack into the background of our thoughts for a while, and got me thinking about the dilemma of my decision all over again.

# CHAPTER 11

## A HEATED DISCUSSION
## ABOUT SLAVERY

After dinner was over, Almeda and Aunt Katie put Ruth and Anne down to sleep; then the rest of us got to talking.

Pa had been telling Uncle Nick and Aunt Katie about our trip to San Francisco and about my conversation with Mr. Dalton.

"So, are you going to do it, Corrie?" Uncle Nick asked me.

"I don't know," I answered. "I'm just waiting to see what might come of it. I said to the Lord that if it was something he wanted me to pursue, then he'd have to make something happen so I'd know it."

"How could he do that?" asked Edie.

"He has lots of ways," I replied. "I just want to make sure I don't do something *myself*. If I just patiently wait, then there's no danger of making a decision all on my own. When he wants me to move a certain way, maybe in some new direction, then he'll make sure I get the message. He'll send someone or some circumstance to give me a nudge."

"That sounds like a rather passive approach to life," said Edie. "I thought all you Californians were pioneers who didn't wait for anybody but went out and did whatever you wanted to do!"

We all laughed.

"Is that what easterners think of Californians?" asked Almeda.

"That's what I thought before I became one myself!" said Katie.

"I don't mean I just sit by and don't do anything," I said to Edie. "I go on about my life as usual. But in making important

60

decisions, I want to be sure I wait for the Lord to have some say in it, too."

"So if the Lord gives you the nudge you're talking about," Uncle Nick asked again, "then do you figure you'll do it?"

"I like what they're saying about Mr. Lincoln," I said. "It seems important for the country that he get elected. I suppose I'm thinking that maybe I ought to try to help."

"If he wins in November, the whole South will rise up against it," put in Edie abruptly. "A Lincoln victory will destroy the nation."

A moment of silence followed. I think we were all a bit shocked at her strong statement, and no one had expected it of her.

"Is it really that serious?" Almeda asked after a moment.

"Before he died, my husband used to say that if the Republicans nominated Lincoln, and if the country elected him, the South would never stand for it. It's not just the slavery issue, he said, but the whole southern way of life."

"How can that way of life be justified when it is based on such a horrid thing as human beings enslaving others of their kind?" Almeda asked. "In Christ's own words, he came to set people free."

"That is an ideal not necessarily found in this life, Almeda. That's the mistake abolitionists always make—quoting the Bible and talking about God's hatred of slavery when there is nothing of the kind to be found in the Holy Scriptures."

Almeda's strong feelings surfaced. "You cannot mean you actually believe slavery to be just!" she said. "How can there be any doubt, for a serious-minded Christian, that slavery is wrong?"

"There are Christians in the South just as well as in the North."

"They cannot honestly deceive themselves into thinking slavery is *right*! It goes against every truth of the Bible."

"Abraham had slaves. The Ten Commandments mention slavery twice without disapproving of it. Jesus never uttered a word condemning slavery, although it was widespread in the world at the time he lived. Paul told slaves to obey their masters, and even returned a runaway slave to his master."

"It sounds like you met someone who knows her Bible as well as you do, Almeda," chuckled Uncle Nick.

"All of what you said may be true, Edie," said Pa, "but be honest with us. Do people in the South, God-fearing people especially—do they really believe slavery is right, deep down in their hearts?"

"I can't speak for everyone, Drummond. All I know is that church leaders and preachers all through the South are just as staunch *for* slavery as the abolitionists are against it."

"What do you think, Katie?" Pa asked.

Katie hesitated a moment, weighing, I think, how she should answer when the debate was between her own sister and her upbringing in Virginia and her new family, which had no firsthand exposure to the issue at hand.

"You have to realize," she said at length, "that slavery was common practice when I was growing up. We were all taught to accept it as the natural order of things between the races—even, some said, for the good of the Negro people. Since coming to California six years ago, I've hardly thought about it. All the disputes between the states and all the arguments over whether slavery is right or wrong—that's risen to new heights since I left. I don't even know what I think."

"Have you read *Uncle Tom's Cabin*?" I asked Edie.

"Certainly not. Harriet Beecher Stowe is hated in Virginia! That book is full of falsehoods from cover to cover!"

"I have read that its portrayal of slavery is quite accurate," said Almeda.

"Then you must be listening to a northern abolitionist. Everyone in the South knows the book for what it is—a pack of lies."

"I want to know something," I asked. "Why did you say that if Mr. Lincoln wins it will destroy the country?"

"Because he has been speaking out against slavery for two years, ever since he ran against Douglas for the Senate in '58. My husband and the men he worked with say Lincoln is sure to attempt to free the slaves. To do so would ruin the South economically. That's why the southern states would never go along with it."

"What would they do?"

"There is already talk circulating around Virginia of withdrawing from the United States and forming a new country if Lincoln wins."

A few gasps went around the room, including one from Katie herself. We all sat in stunned silence a minute. Because of my articles, we always got the *Alta*. We had read of the growing dispute over slavery between the northern and southern states, and had even seen the word *secession* more than once. But somehow it hadn't struck root exactly how serious the division was until Edie began talking about the Southern states *forming a new country*.

Uncle Nick broke the heavy silence with a laugh. He was probably the least well read of any of us, and the idea of two separate countries, a slave South and a free North, struck him as absolutely preposterous.

"That's the craziest thing I ever heard!" he said. "There's nothing in the South that could keep a country together. The South would die without the North!"

I could see Edie getting ready to give Uncle Nick a sharp reply, but Pa spoke up first.

"Don't be too sure of that, Nick," he said. "You know about the big collapse of the banks in New York two years ago and all the financial crises it caused." Pa had read more of the newspapers that came to me than I realized!

"Not much. Didn't hurt us here."

"Well, it hurt the North, and it still hasn't recovered all the way. But the South is booming. Their cotton helped save the northern banks. They can sell all they want in Europe. I tell you, Nick, there's folks saying the South is stronger financially than the North."

"There you go sounding like a politician again!" laughed Uncle Nick. "Where do you get all that stuff, Drum?"

"Well, I figure if I'm gonna have a daughter that writes for the paper, I might as well read it."

"I've read that too," said Almeda. "The North needs the South, not the other way around. If the South were to pull out, they would have plenty of resources. The cotton crop would support it."

"Exactly!" agreed Edie. "Without the South, the North would perish. If Lincoln dared to tamper with slavery, he would be cutting the throat of the very North he thinks he loves so much. The future of the United States lies south of the Mason-Dixon line."

Again there was silence for a while. At last Katie spoke. "After all this, Corrie," she said, "do you *still* think you'll support Lincoln?"

"I don't know," I said with a sigh. "I suppose there's more to the decision than I thought at first."

# CHAPTER 12

## I QUESTION MYSELF

It was a hard dilemma.

Now all of a sudden the slavery issue wasn't two thousand miles distant but right in my own backyard, even right in my own family. It had hardly occurred to me before that Katie had, indeed, come from a slave state. We had never talked about it. But now Edie's arrival, and her strong views on the subject, brought the debate closer to home.

In spite of everything she said, in my own heart and mind I couldn't see how slavery could be anything but wrong. It couldn't be right to treat other people the way slaves were treated! I was in agreement with Mr. Lincoln.

But what if it was true that his election could spell ruin to the country? What if his election caused an even more serious rift between North and South than already existed? Did I want to be part of contributing to that? What would it all mean to California?

I found myself wondering about my responsibility as a writer and a Christian in a lot of new ways. If people really were paying attention to what I said, I had to be sure of myself when I put my pen to the paper. What if I said something wrong, something that readers believed and took action on? I would be responsible for misleading them.

Always before, I'd written about things because I was interested in them. That's why I started writing—because it was something I wanted to do for myself. I wanted to express my thoughts and feelings. And there were so many things I wanted to explore! Writing seemed the natural way to express what was inside me, to communicate, even to grow as a person. That's what my journal was to begin with—just a diary of my own thoughts and feelings. It had never been meant for anybody else.

I reflected on Ma, on things she'd said to me. I had always been a reader and more quiet than outgoing. She'd made no secret of thinking I'd probably never get married. She figured I ought to read and write and keep a diary so I could be a teacher when I got older and no man would have me.

I had done what Ma said, even though I sometimes ached when I realized it took her dying to get me started. Writing in my diary back then had been a way of letting the pain out.

I was twenty-three now, and I had books and books of diaries and journals! That first beautiful book Almeda had given me, with *The Journal of Corrie Belle Hollister* stamped across the front of it, had been the first of many such volumes I had filled with memories and recollections and drawings over the years.

At first Pa and Uncle Nick had kidded me about always writing down what I was thinking. But once the articles started, and payments of two, and then four, and then even eight dollars started to come in for things I'd written, they realized maybe it was a worthwhile thing for me to be doing, after all. But even then it was just *my* writing.

Then gradually my writing started getting bigger than just *my* own personal, private thoughts. Especially as I'd written about the two elections back in 1856, I had thought a lot about truth and trying to tell the truth to people. Even from men like Derrick Gregory and Mr. Royce, I had learned a thing or two about truth and being fair. I tried to learn from everybody I met, although men like that probably had no idea they were helping to teach me and show me things, even by their deceit.

Yet I don't think it ever really struck me that anything I might say was important . . . not *really* important. I was trying to learn about truth and being a good reporter, but I figured that it was still mostly for me. Robin O'Flaridy still looked down on me, even after the '56 elections; my story had never appeared, and Mr. Fremont had lost the election. Nothing I had done or said *had* been that important, and I had gone back to writing about people and floods and how things were in California now that the gold rush was slowing down.

Mr. Kemble kept telling me that my articles were getting a wider audience in the East on account of a woman reporter being so unusual, but I didn't think much about it. I knew of plenty of women authors and it didn't seem so unusual. Julia Ward Howe wrote poems, and Harriet Beecher Stowe and Louisa May Alcott wrote, too. I didn't see what was so unusual about what I did. After all, Mrs. Alcott's poems and stories were being published in the *Atlantic Monthly*.

"None of those women are writing for newspapers, Corrie," Mr. Kemble said to me. "That's what I'm trying to tell you. Newspapers influence people. All those other women are just writing stories. They can get as famous as you please, but they're not going to be taken as seriously as a nonfiction *news* reporter."

"*Uncle Tom's Cabin* has influenced a lot of people," I said.

"It's sold a million copies," he replied. "But it's still just a story."

"You can't say Mrs. Stowe isn't an influential writer."

"She is indeed. Her book probably has started more fights and brawls and arguments than any book ever published in this country. But she's still just a novelist. You, on the other hand, Corrie Belle Hollister—*you* are more than a novelist. You are a newspaper reporter. And while it may be true that when you first came in here with little stories about leaves and blizzards and apple seeds and new schools and colorful people you had met, tricking me into thinking you were a man—"

I glanced up at him, but the little curl of his lip and twinkle in his eye told me he was just having fun with me. He never lost an opportunity to remind me of my first byline: *C.B.* Hollister.

"As I was saying," he went on, "at first I may have published some of your stories as a lark, just for the novelty of showing up some of the other papers with something by a young woman. But I've got to admit you surprised me. You kept at it. You didn't back down from me, or from the odds that were against you, not from anything. You proved yourself to be quite a tenacious, plucky young woman, Corrie. In the process, I'll be darned if you didn't start writing some pretty fair stories and getting yourself quite a following of readers—women *and* men."

He stopped and looked me over as he did from time to time,

kind of like he was thinking the whole thing through all over again, wondering how he'd gotten himself into the fix of having a woman on his staff.

"So that's why," he went on after a minute, "you're different, Corrie. Your name might not be as famous as Mrs. Stowe's. A hundred years from now nobody'll know the name Corrie Hollister, because newspapers get thrown away, while books don't. But right now, people are listening to what you say, Corrie. I tell you, you've got an influence that you don't realize."

His words kept coming back to me as I debated with myself about what I ought to do, especially after all Edie Simpson had said. It was more than just journal writing now.

What if . . . *what if* something I said or wrote really did influence the election? Even if I caused only one or two people to vote differently than they might have otherwise, it was still a sobering responsibility.

I did a lot of talking to the Lord about it in the days after Pa and I got back from San Francisco, running the pros and cons through my mind, and always remembering Pa's words on the boat. *You never know what might be around the corner, and so you ought to be watching and paying attention as best you can.* I knew Pa was doing the same thing, both about his decision and about Zack's leaving.

Ordinarily I would have talked to him or Almeda. But with slavery and the North-South dispute and the heated difference of opinion about Mr. Lincoln, I thought this was a decision I had to make alone—just between me and the Lord.

After the discussion at Uncle Nick and Aunt Katie's, I was growing more and more sure that slavery was wrong and should be abolished. But I saw more clearly now that there might be consequences—not only to my decision, but to the whole outcome of the election—that no one could predict. It might even mean disputes in our own family.

In my heart I found myself wanting to do it. I wanted my writing to *matter* for the sake of truth. If Mr. Lincoln and the antislavery people and the Republican party represented that truth, then I wanted to be part of helping people know it. But I had to be sure. So I found myself telling the Lord that I wouldn't do anything further, and that if I was supposed to get any more involved, he would have to make it clear by having somebody contact *me*, or by sending along some circumstance I couldn't ignore. I didn't want to initiate anything more all by myself.

If I never heard again from Mr. Dalton or anybody else from the Republican party, I would take that as God's way of saying no.

The dilemma of whether I should get involved with the election wasn't the only question my mind was wrestling with since hearing Katie's sister's views on slavery. But it was probably the easiest one to resolve.

In the meantime, I found myself thinking a lot about something Pa had told me about Davy Crockett. They had both fought in the Mexican War, and everyone who fought in California admired the men who died in the same cause at the Alamo.

Davy Crockett had been a congressman from Tennessee before he went to Texas, and I had read that Mr. Crockett always told folks in Washington he had based his life on the saying, *Be sure you're right, then go ahead.* I found myself reflecting on those words every day.

I kept saying to myself, "Don't go ahead until you're sure you're right."

I was pretty certain the *cause* was right. Now I just had to wait to see if involving myself in it was what God wanted me to do. Figuring that out, as well as waiting, was the hardest part of all.

# CHAPTER 13

## A VISIT WITH THE RUTLEDGES

I found myself coming away from that afternoon at Uncle Nick and Aunt Katie's with a heaviness in my heart, a confusion—not about the slavery issue alone, but rather how there could be so many different views on the same thing. I wanted to talk with someone about it, but I didn't feel that Almeda or Pa would be the right persons. I respected them as much as ever, but maybe because they'd been part of the discussion, and I knew that Almeda herself held pretty strong opinions on things, I wanted to get an outside, unbiased perspective.

Since it was a spiritual question even more than something to do with issues, I thought of Rev. Rutledge. As a pastor, he not only ought to have answers to spiritual questions, but by now I knew that he didn't usually voice outspoken views on issues people normally differed about. When it came to the Bible, he said what he had to say without fear and without backing down. But he never took sides about politics or on decisions facing the community. Pa would sometimes get riled when he wanted Rev. Rutledge's support for something the town council was getting ready to vote on.

The Rutledges had become our good friends, and we had grown to feel a great deal of respect for Rev. Rutledge since his first awkward days in Miracle Springs. He had changed nearly as much as Pa had. His teaching and his sermons and his outlook on life and Scripture and what being a Christian meant had been important in forming the person I'd grown up to be. There was a lot of Almeda in me, and a lot of Pa. But there were big chunks of Harriet and Avery Rutledge, too. They both had influenced me in different ways.

So on the Monday after the dinner and discussion, I found myself saddling up my horse and riding down into Miracle Springs for a visit with them. School had been out for a week, and I knew that Rev. Rutledge usually spent Mondays at home, so I hoped to find them both there.

Harriet opened the door. "Corrie, hello! It's nice to see you!"

"I wondered if I might talk with you," I said. "Both of you, I mean. Is the Reverend at home?"

"Yes . . . yes, he is. Come in, Corrie—Avery, we have a visitor," she called out as she led me inside and closed the door.

I followed her into their sitting room, where Rev. Rutledge was just rising from his chair, a copy of the *Alta* in his hand.

"Corrie, welcome," he said, giving me a warm handshake. "Harriet and I always enjoy your visits."

"Thank you," I said. "I've come to ask you about something that is troubling me . . . I hope you don't mind."

"Of course not. Troubled souls are in my line of work," he said with a laugh.

"It's not my soul that's troubled, only my mind."

"I was only jesting. You can feel free to share anything with me, with both of us if you like."

"I would like both your opinions," I said, glancing back at the former Miss Stansberry, whom I still sometimes had a hard time calling by her first name. "It's not what you'd call a spiritual problem, but there's something about being a Christian I don't understand as well as I'd like."

"Well, we've been through a lot of growing together, Corrie, you and I, and your whole family," said Rev. Rutledge. "You've spent lots of hours in this house talking and praying with Harriet and me, and it wouldn't surprise me if we've learned just as much from you as you might have from either of us."

"That could hardly be," I said, "when I sit and listen to your sermons on most Sundays. I've learned more from listening to you talk about the Scriptures than you can imagine."

"The best sermons aren't to be found in church, Corrie."

"How do you mean?"

"Do you remember what the apostle Peter said in his first letter? 'Ye also, as lively stones, are being built up a spiritual house.' He's saying that *we* are the building blocks and bricks of the house that God is building. Then the apostle Paul wrote to the Corinthians about our being *living* epistles or letters. 'Ye are our epistle written in our hearts, known and read by all men . . . written not with ink, but with the Spirit of the living God, written not in tables of stone, but in fleshy tables of the heart.' " He paused, then added, "Do you see the connection I'm trying to make?"

"I always like it better when you tell me instead of my trying to guess," I answered with a smile.

He laughed. "People can be stones and letters, according to the Scriptures—*living* stones and letters. In the same way, *people* can be sermons too. And living people-sermons are far more powerful than anything a preacher says in church. I suppose the point I am attempting to make is that *you* make a better sermon just by your life than any thousand sermons I may preach."

"That's nice of you to say, but I'm not sure I believe it," I said. "When you preach, people listen to what you have to say. Nobody pays that much attention to people going around just living."

"Oh, I think you're wrong about that, Corrie. As a matter of fact, I think it is exactly the reverse. People sit quietly when I'm preaching. But most of them aren't really listening, not deep down in their hearts. You might be, and a few others. But most people don't know how to *really* listen and absorb what another person is saying. There's an art to listening that most folks don't know too much about."

"I suppose you're right. But then, what about when people aren't in church?"

"People look as if they're listening in church, when they're really not. In the same way, out in the midst of life, people look as if they're not paying that much attention, but they really *are*. In other words, people listen far more to the living people-sermons around them every day than you would ever know to look at them."

"Hmm . . . I hadn't thought of that."

"Tell me, has Almeda influenced your life?"

"You know she has, in a thousand ways."

"Why is that, do you think? Is it because of the things she's *said* to you, or the person she *is*?"

"Of course it's the second, although she's taught me a lot too."

"Certainly she has. But it's the *living* sermon she *is* that's gone the deepest inside you, isn't it? Her words go only so far as she lives them out. What do you think my sermons would mean to you if you never saw my words at work in what I tried to do in the rest of my life?"

"Not much," I admitted.

"How much did you listen to me when I first came?"

I laughed.

"There, you see. And when *did* my sermons start getting into you?"

"You're right," I smiled. "When I saw the real *you*, when I saw you and Pa trying to form a real relationship."

"That's right. That's the living stone, the living epistle—the real-life sermon at work. So I stick by what I said to begin with— the best sermons aren't to be found in church, and your life is as dynamic a sermon as I'll ever preach. One that people are watching and observing and listening to all the time."

"Do you really think so?"

"You listen to me, Corrie; the Lord has placed you in many situations where you are constantly being a living epistle, a flesh-and-blood sermon to the people you rub shoulders with. You have more influence for him than you realize—and I don't mean only because you write. The person you are is the living sermon. You can believe me—people *are* listening to it!"

I didn't say anything more for a minute. That word *influence* had come up again, and I couldn't help wondering if what Rev. Rutledge had said had any bearing on the decision I was facing.

# CHAPTER 14

## TRYING TO GET TO THE BOTTOM OF TRUTH

"Would you like some tea?" asked Harriet as the room fell silent for a few moments.

"Yes, thank you," I replied, looking up again.

"What I meant to say a while ago," said Rev. Rutledge as his wife went to the stove, "is that we've been through a great deal together, and it's always a pleasure to talk and share with you about anything that is on your mind."

"I appreciate it," I replied.

"So . . . what is troubling you?"

I drew in a long breath of air, then let it out slowly. "It's hard to put into words exactly," I said finally. "We had a family talk yesterday—you knew that Aunt Katie's sister was here for a visit?"

"Yes, I met her yesterday. They were in church."

"She and Katie are from Virginia."

"Right. That's what I understand."

"Well, we all got to talking about slavery and the dispute over it between the North and the South, and I came away confused."

"About whether slavery is right or wrong?"

"Not exactly that. What I found bothering me as I went to bed last night was that all—on *both* sides—think they're right, and they've got passages out of the Bible and seemingly religious reasons for thinking what they do. How can people look at the very same thing and then think completely opposite ways about it?"

"That's been going on for centuries, Corrie. People look at things differently."

"You'd think at least Christian people would be of one mind."

"That's never been the case. Christians have had some of the world's most bitter arguments."

"It doesn't seem right."

"No doubt it isn't. But it still happens."

"Why?"

"I suppose besides looking at things differently, people also have motives of self that get mixed in with what they believe. So the stands they take on things have as much to do with what they *want* as what they believe."

"Christians ought to be able to separate the two, and take their own wants out of it."

"Perhaps they ought to be able to, but not many people can do that—even Christians."

"What about truth? Can there be something that's true down underneath everything? It seems like people ought to be trying to find it if there is."

"It always comes back to truth for you, doesn't it, Corrie?" Rev. Rutledge smiled.

"I think about it a lot. If a writer doesn't have a grasp of the truth, it doesn't seem like there's much to write about. At least that's how I've come to see it."

"Ever since that sermon I preached years ago about Jesus and Pilate."

"You sure got me started thinking with that one!"

"Yes, and apparently you haven't stopped since."

"That's another thing a writer's got to do—keep thinking."

"I'll take your word for it, not being a writer myself."

"It shouldn't be any different for a preacher."

"I suppose you're right."

Harriet came in with a tray of tea and cups. She served us, then sat down herself.

"Well, I don't care if people have always differed and argued, it seems to me that if there's such a thing as truth and right and wrong, Christians especially ought to feel the same about it. I don't understand how two people can both be Christians and believe the exact opposite. One thing can't be right and wrong at the same time. There's no sense to it!"

"Something like slavery?" asked the minister.

"Not just slavery, but that's as good an example as there is. Edie said that Abraham had slaves, and slavery is mentioned in the Ten Commandments, and then she said that according to the Bible, slavery is right. Almeda quoted the verse about being made free and then said that slavery went *against* the truths of the Bible. There they are—both Christians and yet saying the very opposite thing. Doesn't one of them have to be wrong? *Is* there a right and wrong about it?"

"Is it just slavery you're trying to understand, Corrie?" asked Harriet.

"No, I don't suppose it is," I answered. "I do have to decide if I'm going to write any articles about this election between Mr. Douglas and Mr. Lincoln. I suppose that comes down to the North-South dispute and the question of slavery in the end. But right now I'm trying to understand how two Christians can look at the same thing and see it so differently."

A silence filled the small room, and we all took a sip of our tea. I could tell Rev. Rutledge was thinking hard. That was one of the reasons I liked to talk to him, because he didn't give an answer until he had thought about it first.

"You're right about one thing, Corrie," he said at last. "There *has* to be such a thing as right and wrong. Otherwise the Bible and its whole message is meaningless. There has to be such a thing as truth, which is the opposite of falsehood."

"That's what I believe, too. Then why isn't it more clear?"

"Because people get in the way. They don't always see as clearly as they should. Their vision gets foggy and blurred, and then truth and right and wrong get muddled up in the process."

"Mixing in, like you said before, what they *want* to believe?"

"That's it exactly."

"Then if people are going by what they *want* to think instead of trying to get at what truth is, how do you ever get to the bottom of it? It seems like all you'd do is end up debating your different viewpoints."

"That's all most people do end up doing. To answer your question, if you're talking to a person who views things only through his *own* blurry vision of what he himself *wants* to be true, then you probably can't get to the bottom of a question like slavery. You just each tell the other what you think and leave it at that."

"But there we are back at the question I asked to begin with—how *do* you get at what the truth is if you don't know yourself and you want to talk to other Christians about it?"

"The first thing you have to do, I suppose, is talk and pray things over with people who also want to get down to the underneath layer, down to where truth is, even below what they themselves might want or not want. You can't get too far in a discussion unless you share that much at least."

"That's why I like to talk to the two of you," I said. "I know you want to get to things down at that level just like I do."

"I hope I do," sighed Rev. Rutledge. "But it's difficult, Corrie. Every one of us has personal biases and preferences and wants and tendencies that we can't ever escape. Laying those down, even for the sake of trying to find truth, is not an easy thing to do. I constantly try to put *myself* in the background so I can be on the lookout for something deeper."

He paused, but then went on after a moment.

"There is another way of looking at it too, Corrie," he said. "There are two different kinds of truth you can be looking for. Or perhaps I should say two different kinds of right and wrong."

"I don't quite understand that, but I'll keep listening," I said.

He laughed. "Let me see if I can explain it. I've only been thinking this through recently myself. First, there's the kind of right and wrong that's absolute, that's clear in the Bible. It's always the same, it's the same for everybody in every situation. There's no variation to it. Right is right and wrong is wrong. Lying is like that—it's always wrong. Murder, stealing, hatred—those things are always wrong. And of course, in the same way there are right things too that are *always* right, true things that are *always* true. It is true that God made the world. It is true that Jesus Christ lived and died for our sins. It is true that man cannot live meaningfully apart from God. It is true that people are supposed to treat one another with kindness and love. All those things are true no matter what anyone says. If somebody says differently—that God didn't make the world or that it's all right to be cruel—then he would be wrong. These are the kinds of things I call 'absolute' truth or 'absolute' right and wrong. There's no question about them."

"I understand all that. Then, what's the second kind?"

"Well, that's the one I've been wrestling through in my own mind lately. I haven't come up with a good name for it yet. It has to do with things that *aren't* absolute, where the Bible *doesn't* necessarily give a clear view on it, or maybe doesn't say anything at all about it. For example, is it *right* for your father to be mayor of Miracle Springs?"

"I hope so!" I said.

"So do I. And I think it is. But do you remember how the whole thing came about? It was Almeda who got involved first, and yet in the end she decided it was the wrong thing for her to do. You see, running for mayor isn't something you can say is right *or* wrong. It might be either."

"Almeda didn't think it was what God wanted for her."

"Exactly. Because of that it would have been wrong for her to do it, yet at the same time it could be *right* for your father."

"The same thing being right and wrong all at the same time. That could get a mite confusing."

"Once I started looking around, I found so many examples of this I'd never noticed before. Is rain a good or a bad thing? Both. It depends on the situation. Too much and you have a flood, too little and there's a drought. Is it right or wrong for a young lady to be a journalist? It might be either, depending on whether God wanted her to be or not."

I smiled.

"Harriet and I, of course, think that God *has* led you all along the way you've come, and we are very proud of you. That was just an example."

"I see."

"Personal decisions, like writing or being a mayor, are easy enough to see. But there are all kinds of things in the Bible that aren't black and white either. Does everybody come to God in the same way? Is there a *right* form of salvation? Those kinds of questions are very perplexing to a man in my occupation, as you can imagine. Nicodemus came to Jesus by night and the Lord told him about being born again. Paul was blinded by a great light.

God spoke to Moses in a bush. Timothy and St. Mark grew up under believing parents. So many differences! There may not be any question about murder, stealing, and lying. But what about all the deep things St. Paul wrote about in his letters? There are so many interpretations about what he meant. Does hell last forever? Will we know each other in heaven as we do now? Is the devil a real being? What does it mean to be dead to sin? Oh, Corrie, you can't imagine all the questions and issues ministers get involved talking and thinking about where there are no clear biblical answers!"

"What do you do to keep from getting confused?" I asked.

Rev. Rutledge laughed loudly. "I *don't* keep from getting confused!" he said. "I talk to my wife, and we both get more confused than ever!"

They both laughed.

"You see, Corrie," Rev. Rutledge went on in a minute, "as long as you keep a balanced perspective on such things, you can't go too far wrong. I am aware that I don't know too much about heaven and hell. But I am perfectly content not to know, because I realize we're not supposed to know such things perfectly. God didn't make them clear in the same way he made lying and stealing and murder clear. Some things are supposed to be absolute, others aren't. Where people go wrong is in adopting some personal view on one of the non-absolute things, and then saying that people who disagree with them are wrong."

"So if we were talking about heaven," I said, "I might say, 'I think we'll know each other there,' and you might say, 'I don't think we'll know each other there,' but neither of us could say the other one was wrong."

"We could say that we disagreed, but we couldn't know absolute right or wrong about it because the Bible doesn't make it clear."

"Hmm . . . that is interesting," I said. "Then it comes down to whether a certain question is absolute, like lying and stealing; or not absolute, like being mayor or what heaven will be like."

"That's what it comes down to, all right—what things fit into which category. That's where most people go wrong and start arguing with other people—they assume *their* views are more absolute than someone else's."

"But there *are* absolutes where someone *is* right and someone *is* wrong?"

"Yes. And on such issues Christians must not waver from the truth. But on all the other wide range of things, we have to give each other freedom to think without criticizing."

A long pause followed. Finally I spoke up again.

"Which kind of question do you think slavery is?" I asked. "Is it right or wrong in an absolute way, and everybody ought to feel the same about it? Or is it right for the South but maybe wrong for the North, and each side ought to respect the other's view?"

"Ah, Corrie, you've landed right in the middle of the hornet's nest with that question!"

"The whole future of the country may depend on the answer," I insisted.

"That may well be, which is why slavery is such a divisive issue. Of course, I personally find the very notion of slavery abhorrent, contrary to everything I see mirrored in the life of Jesus. Yet . . . I know there are Christians, and ministers, in the South who do not see it so. The Baptists, the Methodists, and the Presbyterians have already split over the question, their southern factions believing just as strongly *in* the validity of slavery as their northern counterparts believing it is wrong."

"How can that be?" I said in frustration, back again to the original quandary that had brought me to the Rutledges in the first place.

"People on both sides heatedly and righteously consider it an absolute issue with an absolute right and truth at the bottom of it—their *own*! Neither side will admit to anything except that the other side is absolutely in the wrong."

"What do you think? Is slavery one of the absolute issues, where there *is* a positive right and a positive wrong?"

A long silence followed. At last Rev. Rutledge exhaled a long sigh. I could tell he had already thought long and hard on the very question I had posed but without coming any nearer a conclusion than I had.

"I wish I knew, Corrie," he said almost wearily. "I truly wish I knew." Again he paused, then added, "And I fear for our country unless God somehow reveals *his* mind on the matter to large groups of people on both sides . . . and soon."

# CHAPTER 15

## A TALK WITH PA

In spite of his activity with Tad, Pa could not help but be weighed down by Zack's leaving and by the angry words he himself had spoken. Both Almeda and I knew him well enough to see that beneath the surface he was struggling hard to come to terms with what had happened.

A few days later I found him alone on the far side of the corral checking a hoof on one of the ponies. I walked up behind him.

"Made any decision about Sacramento, Pa?" I asked.

He slowly set the pony's foot back down onto the dirt, then straightened up. The weary and downcast look on his face made him seem ten years older than he was. The loose shoe was the furthest thing from his mind.

"Sacramento?" he repeated, forcing a slight chuckle. "To tell you the truth, Corrie, I hadn't hardly thought about it for a week. What about you? Got any idea what you aim to do yet?"

"No," I shrugged. "I've been thinking about it, but I don't suppose I'm any closer to knowing what God wants me to do than when we came back from San Francisco."

"I reckon getting away from all the hubbub of the city does slow the pace a mite. I suppose that's why I like it here. I couldn't abide living in no city. That's one thing I think I've decided. Whatever comes, I don't aim to leave Miracle. Zack's right about one thing. I was a fool to leave the only other home I ever had."

"He didn't say that, Pa."

"He didn't have to say those words. He may as well have said it. And even if he didn't say it, it's true anyhow, and I don't intend

81

to make the same mistake twice. I've got a home now, and I'm gonna keep it, even if it means I turn my back on everything any other man would give his eyeteeth for. No, I don't suppose I've thought about it much, but I don't reckon there's much else to do now but say no."

"Zack's just all mixed up now, Pa," I said. "You can't plan your whole future on one outburst."

"It goes a lot deeper than just the other day, Corrie. Couldn't you tell? It had been building up inside the boy for years, and I never knew it. I don't know how I could have been such a blind fool!"

He turned away and leaned over the rail fence. I knew what he was fighting against. I walked toward him and laid my hand gently on his shoulder. He didn't say anything, and after a minute I pulled away, then climbed up and sat down on the top rail of the fence, looking up toward the mine.

"Doesn't seem to me like you ought to blame yourself, Pa," I said after a minute or two.

"How can I not blame myself? Don't seem like there's anybody else I can rightly blame."

"He'll cool off and come back, Pa."

"I ain't so sure, Corrie. You saw that look in his eye. He was determined. And it's sure he's not just a kid anymore. I got a feeling we might not see him for a spell."

"Are you afraid for him?"

"No, that ain't it."

"Like you said, he's not a kid. He's old enough to take care of himself. He's been away before, just like I have. You never seemed too worried about me, and Zack's a man."

"I'm not worried about him, Corrie. Sure, I know Zack's every bit the man I was at his age. He's made of better stuff inside, too. But I can't help feeling a heap of guilt for the things he said. I haven't been the pa to him I should have been. He's right about me running out on you kids and your ma. My life isn't one to be altogether proud of. The boy's got every right to hate me. I deserve it."

He stopped and let out a long sigh.

"But even when he said what he did," Pa went on, "telling me how he'd hurt and saying nothing but what was the truth about me, like a blame fool I just got angry at him. . . ."

Finally Pa's voice broke slightly at the memory of the blow he had given his son.

"God, oh, God . . . how could I?" he said in a more forlorn tone than I'd ever heard. "Telling him I'd take the belt to him! No wonder he was mad. He had a right to be. How could I have been so blind all this time to what he was feeling and thinking?"

He stopped. It was quiet for a minute, Pa breathing in deeply, but kind of unsteadily.

"Zack was always one to keep things inside, more than me, Pa," I said. "When we first came here, he was trying to be more a man than he was. Then he took to hanging around you and Uncle Nick all the time, wanting to be grown up."

"He did grow up too," said Pa. "I don't know why I didn't let him know better how I felt about him."

"You tried, Pa."

"Not enough. But a man just gets so busy and involved with his *own* affairs that he doesn't even know what his kids are thinking. They grow up so blamed fast; suddenly they're adults and they're holding things inside them that you done. But there's no way you can go back and make it right to them."

He paused a moment, then looked up at me earnestly.

"You got anything you're holding inside about anything I've done or said, Corrie?" he asked. "It'd kill me to find out something I oughta know but not find out till it's too late."

"I don't think so, Pa," I answered with a smile. "Nothing I know of at least. You've been about the finest pa a girl could have, and I love you, Pa."

He looked away. There were tears in his eyes, both from what I'd said and from the hurt over Zack.

"Pa," I said, "I feel bad, too. I was guilty of taking Zack for granted myself. I figured Zack felt just like I did about being a Christian, but maybe he had a more independent streak in him than I did. You and I talked about your past, and you confided in me and we prayed together. I suppose I was able to put it behind me more than he did. It made me love you more, but I guess people can react to the same situation in opposite ways, and so what drew me closer to you, he resented. It's not your fault. You can't lash out at yourself for Zack's holding things against you."

"If he had a right to . . . if it was for mistakes I made."

"You said it yourself, Pa—he's grown up now, just like I have, and so he's got to be responsible himself for his reactions. That's part of growing up too, it seems to me."

"Maybe you're right. But how does a man keep from feeling guilty over not giving his own son all of him he might have?"

Neither of us had seen Almeda walking slowly toward us as we'd been talking. She came closer and heard the last of Pa's question. He glanced up, then reached out his hand and drew her toward him.

"Still wrestling with Zack, Drummond?" she said.

Pa sighed and nodded his head. I knew they'd talked a lot about it already.

The three of us were silent for a while; then Almeda began to pray softly. "Oh, Father," she said, "I ask for a special pouring down of your grace for my husband. Comfort his father's heart and ease his pain over his son."

She stopped. There was nothing else to pray. Her simple words had expressed what both of us were feeling right then toward Pa. I was praying silently myself, not knowing what I could say. Then to my surprise I heard Pa's voice.

"God," he prayed in a raspy, quiet voice, "watch over my son. Wherever he is right now, take care of him. Even if he doesn't think I care about him, Lord, show him that you care for him. And if you can, help him to see that I do too. Bring him back to us safe, Lord."

"Amen," Almeda added softly.

Again it was silent for a while. At last Pa and Almeda headed off toward the creek, Pa's arm still around her shoulder, talking softly together.

# CHAPTER 16

## SURPRISE VISITOR

The summer progressed. July was hotter than June. August was hotter than July. We heard no word from Zack.

"What are you gonna do, Corrie?" Pa asked me one day at breakfast. "That paper of yours is getting fuller and fuller of election news all the time, and I still haven't seen your name in it anywhere."

"Are you going to write for Lincoln or Douglas?" asked Tad around a mouthful of warm biscuit.

"She wouldn't support a Democrat," said Becky. "You'd never go against Mr. Fremont's party, would you, Corrie?"

All summer, Katie and Edie had kept political issues stirred up to such an extent that even Becky and Tad were aware of what was happening. We'd managed to stay clear of any arguing about it again, although Edie and Almeda kept a cool distance from each other because of their strong views on the two opposite sides of the slavery question. I'd never really thought much about Almeda being a "northerner" before. But even ten years in California couldn't take the Bostonian out of her, any more than Edie's recent trip west could take the Virginian out of her.

"I don't know, Becky," I answered. "I suppose I might be able to support a Democrat someday if he was the right man. But not this year. As far as I can see, Mr. Lincoln's the best man to be president."

"Then why don't you write an article saying so and send it in to Kemble?" asked Pa.

"I'm still a little confused over how Christians can feel so differently about the same thing."

"They do, though, so why don't you just jump into it and give 'em *your* two cents' worth?"

"What if I'm not right?"

"Do you have to be right to speak your mind?"

"It seems like if I'm going to advise people what to do, and tell them how they ought to feel and how they ought to vote, then I *have* to be right. I couldn't do it otherwise."

"Do you still have doubts about how you feel, Corrie?" asked Almeda.

I thought for a while. "No, I don't suppose I do," I answered finally. "I guess down inside I *do* think I know that slavery is wrong. It's just knowing whether I'm supposed to say that in public, and tell people they ought to vote for Mr. Lincoln—that's the thing I'm still unsure about."

"How are you going to know that?" asked Pa.

"I guess I'm waiting for some sign from the Lord, something that tells me he's urging me one way or the other. You've always said to me, Almeda," I said, turning toward her, "that when in doubt about what to do, it never hurts to wait."

"God never will discipline us for going too slowly." Almeda smiled. "I've had to learn that the hard way. We can get ourselves into plenty of trouble by going too fast, but not from holding back waiting for God's guidance."

"What kind of a sign, Corrie?" asked Tad. "Is God gonna say something to you in a dream or something?"

I laughed. "I don't know, Tad. I doubt it. Just circumstances, probably. I feel like I know what's right, and even what I'd like to do. But I also feel like I need to wait until he brings something to me, rather than me going out to do something myself."

"Well, I hope he does it pretty soon," said Pa. "If you wait much longer without making up your mind, the election's gonna come and go and leave you behind altogether."

"If that happens, then I'll just figure I wasn't supposed to do anything in the first place, and everything will be fine."

After breakfast I decided to saddle up Raspberry and go for a long ride. Somehow the day reminded me of the one more than two years earlier when I had ridden up to the top of Fall Creek

Mountain on my twenty-first birthday. It had been a while since I had a good long ride, and somehow the questions at breakfast put me in a reflective mood.

The sun was well up as I headed off east, and the earth was already warming up fast. I never got tired of the smell of sugar pines under the beating of the sun's rays. Especially if there'd been rain anytime recently, and the earth underneath a bed of fallen pine needles was moist, the fragrance of the warming dirt, the dead leaves and needles and cones, and the live breathing trees were to me the very smell of heaven itself.

It hadn't rained today, of course, because it was the first week of August, but the smell was almost as wonderful. The rugged, rough-textured bark of the trees, cracked and splitting, oozed the translucent sticky pitch that ran up and down the trunks. It was precious to me, as were all things of the forest, as indications of the fingerprints of God when he made the world.

I had been thinking for a year or more about the first chapter of Romans, and found myself almost daily awakening to its truth, that God's invisible being really was clearly visible and obvious in everything around me—that is, if I had eyes to see him.

The world tells us what God is like. But most folks don't take that truth deep enough to allow the world to really speak actively to their hearts and minds about God's character. I found myself forgetting it sometimes, too. At such times, the world around me only spoke quietly, not with the vibrant reality that the bark was speaking to me today about his creativity.

More and more I thought that God intends for the world to really *speak* to us—loudly, constantly, every day. I believed that God means for our surroundings to be a very close-up way of us getting information about him. The world God made with his own hands should speak to us just as directly and actively as the words of Jesus himself.

As I rode through the woods and meadows, I found all these thoughts running through my mind as they had many times before. I found myself thinking about the barn back at home, and how much it could tell a stranger about Pa, if that stranger took it upon himself to look past the surface appearances of things— how orderly Pa kept his tools, how he lined up the spare saddles, the stables, the feeding troughs, the wagon and buggy, the loft for hay and straw. To a casual observer, none of these things would be especially noticeable. But since I had heard Pa talk about why he had done such and such and question aloud how he should build this part or where he ought to put that, I saw evidences of Pa's personality everywhere as I looked around the barn.

I saw Almeda's personality at home and in her office at the Mine and Freight in town, too—how she kept her desk, the pictures on the walls, the books in the bookcase, how she organized the whole business. She was *there*, just as Pa was in the barn— even if neither of them happened to be there in person. The barn, the office, the house—they all reflected both characters and personalities because they had put so much of themselves *into* them, maybe even without knowing it.

In the same way, the whole world is like God's office, his barn, the room where he lives. His desk and walls and rooms are full of things that are shouting about the person he is. It's up to us to try to discover what those characteristics of his personality are. Every tiniest detail of the universe is full of energetic life.

The bear and the ant *both* reflect the God who made them— the bear, his power and magnificence; the ant, his energy and productivity and unceasing labor.

The sun and the moon *both* are pictures of God—the heat and brightness and life-sustaining force of the sun, and the reflected light that God's being is able to give, even in the darkness when the fullness of his presence is turned away for a time.

The world could no more keep quiet about the nature of God than could Pa's barn or Almeda's office about them. The world is shouting at us, so loudly that in most people's ears it sounds like silence. The thunder of his voice is so huge and so deep that it rumbles past them in awesome silence. They hear nothing.

I reined Raspberry in, slowed to a stop, then dismounted. I hadn't gone far, probably not more than an hour from home, not nearly as far up into the mountains as I had that day two years before.

Most of the ground was brown under the scorching summer's sun. Where snow had lain six months earlier, now the dirt was hard-packed, with dried mountain grasses blowing gently in the rising breeze. Among the trees all was still and quiet. The only sounds were those of the birds overhead and the buzzing of bees and flies and other tiny flying creatures.

I left Raspberry tethered to a pine branch and walked through a thicket of trees into an open meadow. I felt full, happy, overflowing with life. Thinking about God all the way up as I had ridden had filled me with a sense of how good he had been to me.

Suddenly I found myself running . . . running across the grass as fast as I could, running toward nowhere, but urged on by a feeling inside I could not keep back. I wanted to scale the heights of the hills under my feet, I wanted to run and climb to the peaks of the world, I wanted to shout and sing and laugh and cry all at once!

On I ran, my heart pounding, my legs beginning to tire. But the weariness just made me want to run all the more! I wanted to exhaust myself, to run until I dropped!

At last I could not go another step.

I lifted my hands into the air and threw my head back, gazing upward into the empty expanse of blue. Two or three white, billowing clouds hung there in the midst of it, lazily working their way across the sky. I felt great throbbing prayers inside me, yet I had no words to say. There was only a sense that God was nearby, and even that he was looking down on me right then. A closeness came over me that I had never felt before, as if his great arms of love were wrapping themselves around me, even as I stood there all alone in the middle of that meadow, hands held upward toward the sky.

Slowly I dropped my hands back to my sides and turned around and began walking down the way I had run. I was crying, although I did not know when the tears had begun to flow.

I don't think I'd ever been happier in my life than in that moment. I *knew* God my Father was with me, that he loved me, that his tender arms were about me, and that I was his.

"God," I said softly, "I want nothing more than to be your daughter . . . to be completely yours. Oh, God—take away from me any other ambitions or motives or desires than just to let you be my Father every moment. Let me be content that you care for me, as content as I am right now."

All at once the prayers that I hadn't been able to pray a few moments earlier began to bubble up out of me in an endless spring. Thoughts and prayers and feelings tumbled together from out of my heart and mind. Such a desire swept through me to be nothing more, to do nothing more, than what God himself wanted for me. Any anxieties I may have had over the future or what to do vanished. I *knew* God would direct my pathway, as one of my favorite proverbs promised.

I felt so thankful, so appreciative to God for all he had done for me—for the love of life, for the sense of his presence with me, for the peacefulness he had given me. What poured out of me was unspoken thankfulness, and a calm knowing that he *would* direct my steps, that he would keep my life in his hands, and that he would show me what I was to do and when.

I rode Raspberry back toward town and arrived at the house sometime shortly after noon. My spirit was still calm, and I could not have been more unprepared for the surprise that awaited me the moment I walked in the door of the house.

There, talking to Pa, sat Cal Burton!

# CHAPTER 17

## THE INVITATION

Inside, my knees went weak, and a lump shot up from somewhere down in my stomach up to my throat. Flushed from the exercise of the ride, I knew my face went immediately pale. A faintness swept over me, even as Pa jumped up the moment he saw me come in.

"Look who's here from San Francisco, Corrie!" he said.

I hardly needed Pa to point it out to me! Even in my state of perturbation, I knew well enough who it was!

I took his hand, feeling a slight tremble go through me at the touch, and said, "Mr. Burton . . . but I don't understand . . . what are you doing here?" Never had my voice sounded so high and squeaky! And I had never sounded so stupid in all my life.

He laughed. "I know it must come as a surprise, and I apologize for coming all this way to see you without warning."

"Don't say another word about it," Pa said boisterously. "You're welcome anytime, with or without warning. Out this far from the city we don't stand too much on ceremony."

As Pa was responding to Mr. Burton's apology, I immediately decided that he had come to see Pa. It must have something to do with them wanting him to run for the legislature in Sacramento.

"So are you going to do it, Pa?" I said, turning to him.

"Do what?"

"Run for the legislature."

"What are you talking about, Corrie Belle? What's me running for office got to do with anything?"

"Isn't that what you two were talking about?"

"I don't know where you got a notion like that," laughed Pa. "We were just sitting here passing the time till *you* got back."

The blank look of confusion on my face must have been more humorous than I intended it to be because both men laughed.

"I'm sorry," said Mr. Burton. "I was speaking to you a moment ago, not your father. It's *you* I came all this way to see."

My heart fluttered all over again! "Me?" I squeaked. "What would you want to see me for?"

Pa laughed again. He was really enjoying my discomfort! "Corrie, you just go get yourself a drink of water, then come and sit down with us. Cal here's got to talk to you."

I did as Pa said, and a minute or two later the three of us were seated.

I glanced from one to the other of them. Mr. Burton spoke first.

"What I came for, Corrie," he said, "was to ask you again, on behalf of Mr. Dalton in San Francisco, if you would consider helping us with the Lincoln campaign."

I stared back blankly at him.

"I have been thinking about it," I said finally. "But I just hadn't decided yet what I ought to do."

"Mr. Dalton thought you might not have taken his words seriously before, and felt a personal visit from me might persuade you. Let me assure you, he was quite serious. He . . . we all, that is, would very much like you to be part of the Republican campaign team."

The color began coming back into my cheeks. I didn't know what to think!

"What . . . what would I do?"

"We were sure you'd ask that. I've already spoken to your editor, Mr. Kemble, about your writing a couple articles in favor of Mr. Lincoln from a woman's point of view. Then we would like to include you among the speakers at a public assembly to be held in Sacramento four days from now. A woman has never addressed such a gathering, in this campaign at least, and Mr. Dalton feels you could have a great influence. My instructions were to convince you to say yes, and to bring you back to Sacramento with me."

I sat staring, trying to take in his words.

"Don't just sit there, Corrie," Pa said finally. "The man's talking to you."

"I . . . I don't know what to say," I stammered.

"Say the only thing you can say, Corrie," said Mr. Burton. "I was instructed not to take no for an answer. The Republican party will pay your coach fare and put you up in a nice hotel. The trip won't cost you a cent."

"Well, I have been praying about what to do."

"And do you have reservations?"

"No, not exactly."

"Then it's all settled."

"I'll have to talk to my mother and father," I said.

"Of course. I understand." He rose and shook Pa's hand. "I'm going to ride back into town. I'm supposed to see the banker Royce for Carl, and I'll be at the boardinghouse if you should need me. Otherwise, perhaps I'll drop back by later this afternoon."

"And join us for supper," suggested Pa.

"But, your wife. . . ?" hesitated Mr. Burton.

"My wife will be delighted when I tell her," insisted Pa. "Now it's my turn not to take no for an answer!"

They both laughed, and it was agreed.

# CHAPTER 18

## EMBARRASSMENT ENOUGH TO LAST A LIFETIME

I *had* been praying about it, like I'd said. But now that the moment of decision had come and I was face-to-face with it, I felt nervous and uncertain all over again. Of course, how much of that had to do with the election and how much had to do with Cal Burton himself, it was impossible for a twenty-three-year-old girl like me to know.

I couldn't help being a little taken with him. He was just about the finest-looking man a girl like me'd ever set eyes on. And so nice—how could I keep from liking him?

As much as I tried to concentrate on things like the election and what I ought to do as a writer, my mind kept filling up with Cal Burton. I wanted to say yes just because of him. All kinds of doubts would rise up, reminding me that I wasn't pretty, that a man like him would never look twice at me. I'd take to looking in a mirror and fiddling with my hair without even realizing I was doing it. When I suddenly woke up to the fact that I was day-dreaming the day away, I could hardly stand what I saw in the glass and would turn away in disgust.

One time Pa chanced by the open door of my room and saw me standing there like an idiot, turned sideways, looking at myself. I caught his reflection in the mirror as he walked by, mortified to have him see me like that. I got so flushed my skin burned, and I turned away from the mirror and ran outside. Pa never said a word, but he knew well enough what I was thinking about.

All the rest of that day I wandered about in a daze, trying to concentrate, trying to pray, trying to be rational about it. But it was useless. I'd never figured myself to be overly emotional as women were sometimes said to be. I thought my head was sitting pretty level on my shoulders.

But after this day I didn't know! As close as I'd felt to God that very morning, suddenly he might as well have been a thousand miles away. I couldn't stand it, but I couldn't help it either.

I had to talk to Almeda! But when she got back from town about an hour after Mr. Burton had left, I couldn't get up the gumption to tell her. I had always talked to her about everything, but this was different. I couldn't help being embarrassed for how I was feeling.

Cal Burton came back some time between four and five in the afternoon. I was wandering around aimlessly near the corral when I heard his rented buggy approaching. I had been working in the garden and rubbing Raspberry down, and I was positively filthy from head to foot. I quickly ran into the barn, hoping he wouldn't see me. He reined in the horses in front of the house and went inside. I watched the house for a few minutes from one of the barn windows, being careful to keep out of sight.

A little later, the door opened and Pa and Mr. Burton came out. They were talking away like old friends. Pa really seemed to like Mr. Burton. It was the happiest I'd seen him since Zack left.

Suddenly I realized they were heading straight for the barn! I jumped back from the window and hurriedly ran back into the back part of the building where it was darkest, frantically trying not to make any noises that would give me away. I was just crouching down behind two bales of hay in the far corner of the barn when I heard Pa and Mr. Burton enter by the opposite door. I held my breath and hoped the hay didn't make me sneeze!

"Corrie!" I heard Pa's voice call out. "Corrie . . . you in here?"

A brief silence followed.

"Blamed if she wasn't around just a few minutes ago," I heard Pa say. I thought I heard his footstep coming nearer. He *had* to know where I was! It would be awful if they found me like I was! What would I say? But I hadn't answered Pa's call, so now there was nothing I could do but make *sure* they didn't see me!

Silently I hunched down even more, lowering my face into my dress so if any part of me did show, at least my hair would blend in with the hay and straw around me. Why had I hidden? Now I was really in a pickle!

I heard Pa's footsteps going one way and the other, looking about. "Corrie!" he called out again. I felt like such a deceiver for not answering, but I couldn't make myself say anything now!

Pretty soon they turned and headed back out. "Can't imagine where she went," Pa said. "But come on, Cal, I'll show you the mine, and take you up to see my brother-in-law. Corrie'll be along soon enough. The two of you can talk about your business later."

These last words were faint, because by now they were outside and walking up the stream toward the mine. Slowly I crept out of my hiding place and tiptoed toward the window. I peeked carefully around the edge of it. There they were, thirty yards away, their backs to me, in animated conversation, Pa seemingly telling him all about the mining operation, which Mr. Burton seemed interested in by his questions and gestures.

I stepped back inside the barn and breathed a big sigh of relief. Then first it struck me what I must look like. I was sweating like a horse, my hair was all messed up and hanging all over everywhere, my dress was dirty and had pieces of straw and hay stuck to it all over. I was a mess! Whether I was pretty or not, I was certainly in no condition to meet a man like Cal Burton!

I sneaked back to the window and peeked around the edge. There they still were, almost at the mine now. I needed to go clean up, but I was dying to know what they were saying! What if they were talking about me?

Pa turned and led the way toward the creek. They crossed the bridge and in another minute were out of sight, walking through the trees toward Uncle Nick and Aunt Katie's. Without even thinking what I was doing, suddenly I left the barn and hurried after them, keeping out of sight behind trees and brush, just in case one of them should glance back in my direction.

I made it all the way to the bridge, then stopped. I couldn't hear their voices any longer.

Quickly I ran across the bridge, then ducked out of sight off the pathway again. From there I slowly made my way through the trees toward the clearing, moving from tree to tree, glancing around to make sure no one else was coming who could see me. I slipped around behind the house. Everything was quiet, but I knew they were inside. I crept out from my hiding place and ran to the house, kneeling down behind one of the back windows.

I was safe there. Even if someone came to the window and looked out, they couldn't see me. That side of the house faced the forest, which was close by and generally darker than the front. I strained my ears to listen.

"All this way to talk to our future Congressman, eh, Drum?" I heard Uncle Nick say.

"No, he didn't come to see me. I already told you, I'm not at all sure what I'm gonna do."

I heard a woman's voice next, either Aunt Katie's or Edie's.

"He came to see Corrie, of course," Pa answered whoever it was. "And to take her back to Sacramento with him."

Some exclamations went around, followed by some laughter. How mortifying. They *were* talking about me!

Uncle Nick must have made a joke, although I was glad I didn't hear it. Some more laughter and comments went around the room. "I'm sure Corrie will keep her head," said Katie.

Cal Burton was the next to speak. "It's all for the good of the party, I assure you," he said. "They genuinely want her involved, as they do her father, I might add. I promise to take good care of her."

"It's your chance to be a famous man, Drum," said Uncle Nick, going back to the subject of Pa's running for office.

"That's the last thing I want," said Pa. The laughter had faded from his voice, and I figured he might be thinking about all the things Zack had said. The conversation gradually subsided, and I couldn't hear everything. The next thing I did hear seemed to be Cal Burton talking to Aunt Katie and her sister. Edie had apparently said something about having recently come from the East.

"What's it been like there?" Mr. Burton asked her.

Edie laughed. Her voice had an edge to it just like Katie's, and I could hear her distinctly. "How do you mean?" she said. "Between my husband dying and political tensions, I can't say it was an altogether pleasant time for me before coming here."

"I suppose what I meant was more the weather, the scenery. It's been some time since I saw spring come out in that region, and your mentioning Virginia flooded me with memories."

"Why?" asked Katie, drawing into the conversation. "*You're* not from there, are you?"

"No, but close by. Roanoke Rapids, North Carolina, actually."

"I would never have known! What happened to your accent?"

"A casualty of coming west to California!" he laughed.

"And *you* are working for the Republicans?" put in Edie in astonishment.

"You have to take the opportunities that come your way, you know."

I had hardly paused to consider why their three voices sounded so clear. With the next words Katie uttered I suddenly knew—they had been gradually moving closer to the window I was crouched below outside.

"Is it only me, or is it rather hot in here?" said Katie.

When I heard her hand on the window latch. I panicked and ran. But it was too late!

"Why Corrie Hollister," I heard behind me. "What in heaven's name are you doing out there?"

I stopped and turned, trying to look as though nothing was wrong. "Oh . . . I was just coming around the back of the house," I said lamely. "I heard you talking and couldn't help listening."

"Eavesdropping!" said Katie with pretended annoyance. "Shame on you, Corrie!"

There stood Cal Burton right behind Katie, along with Edie, looking out the window at me where I stood like the mooncalf I was! I was so glad the trees kept the light dim. I would have died for him to see me in the state I was in!

"Well, Corrie, don't just stand there," said Katie. "You were coming in, weren't you?"

"I . . . was . . . I mean I didn't want to—"

"Come on around to the door, Corrie," she insisted. "As I understand it, this man came all the way from the big city to see you."

I hastily tried to think of some way to squirm out of the awkwardness and get out of there. But by now Pa realized what the ruckus was about. He came outside as I walked slowly around the side of the house.

"Where you been, Corrie?" he said. "I've been looking high and low for you."

"Just around and about, Pa."

"Well, come on in. Cal's back."

"No, I have to go back home and take a bath before supper, Pa."

"At least come in and say hello."

"Oh, Pa, I'd rather—"

"Come in and be sociable a minute," interrupted Pa. "You can clean yourself up later."

I knew there was no way out of it, so I sighed silently and went into the house with Pa. He may not have minded my dirty dress and mussed hair, but Uncle Nick wasn't about to miss the chance for kidding. For once I wished he'd have kept his humor to himself. Usually I didn't mind, but this time it hurt.

"Corrie Belle," he said, "you're a mess! You look like you just stepped out from wrestling with a dad-blamed hog!"

"Nick! Haven't you got any sense in your head?" Aunt Katie rebuked him sharply. "Now's not the time for saying such things."

I was grateful for Katie's standing up for me, especially since it gave me a quick second to blink back the tears.

"I think your niece looks just as nice as can be, Mr. Belle," said Cal Burton to Uncle Nick. Hearing his voice say such a thing took my breath away for an instant, and I almost forgot the mess I was in. "Hello again, Corrie," he added, turning to face me and holding out his hand.

I shook it, daring a quick glance up into his face. His eyes were looking straight at me. I glanced away almost as fast as I'd looked up.

"Honest, hard-working, robust beauty, Mr. Belle," he said, turning again to Uncle Nick. "Not the kind of thing you see too much in the city, you can take it from me. I'll take a handsome young lady from the country like this anytime!"

"Oh, Corrie," whispered Aunt Katie behind her hand, but loud enough so that she made sure everyone in the room heard her, "you better snatch up this fellow while you can! Men like that don't come along but once in a lifetime!"

Now my face *was* red! I couldn't stand it, being the center of everyone's talk. But everybody just stood there looking at me in my dirt-smeared dress. I could hardly keep the tears back now. It was awful to be stuck there like that!

"So, where have you been, Corrie," asked Pa, "to get such a mess all over you? We got a guest for dinner."

"I know, Pa," I said, trying to stay calm. "I was rubbing down Raspberry. I guess the time got going too fast for me." I wiped the back of my hand across my eyes.

Pa laughed. "You just smeared a streak of dirt across your forehead," he said. "Here," he added, reaching into his pocket for a handkerchief, "you can wipe it off with this."

Suddenly, without even realizing what I was doing, I spun around and ran for the door. I made for the woods as fast as I could, tears streaming down my cheeks.

# CHAPTER 19

## LEARNING TO LOOK FOR THE LORD'S DOORS

Somehow I managed to get through the horrid day.

After a long cry I went back home, got water for a hot bath, with Almeda's help, and was probably halfway presentable by the time Pa and Cal Burton got back down from Uncle Nick's. Almeda and I talked a little, but I think both of us realized if we talked *too* much about what had happened, I'd start bawling like a baby all over again. So she just loved me as best she could, and let me take my bath and get dressed by myself.

Pa felt bad for what he'd done, I knew that. I did my best to look at him in a way that would tell him I didn't hold anything against him, and that I knew it was my own fault. I didn't want him to have to worry about anything he'd said to me on top of his heartache over Zack.

Cal Burton kept being just as nice as he could be all evening, treating me as if nothing out of the ordinary had happened at all. But I kept my eyes away from his. Down inside I was just too mortified over having behaved like a ridiculous little schoolgirl.

"So, Miss Hollister, what about going to Sacramento to work for Mr. Lincoln?" he asked.

"I've been thinking about it," I said, "but I haven't had the chance to talk with Pa and Almeda yet."

He smiled into my eyes—a smile that almost made me forget how foolish I'd been. "I understand," he said. "I can stay for another day at the boardinghouse in town, and we can discuss it again tomorrow." Then he and Pa spent most of the rest of the

101

evening talking about politics. As interested as I'd been before, I just couldn't seem to concentrate on what they were talking about. I sat there silent the whole time, my mind muddled up with Mr. Burton's eyes, his smile, his deep resonant voice. Then I'd think about running out of Uncle Nick and Aunt Katie's that afternoon, with a dirty dress and crying, with everybody staring after me! It was a miracle I didn't cry again just thinking about it! I did shed a few more tears later, though, lying in bed trying desperately to go to sleep and put the day behind me at last.

I felt just as stupid the next morning, but at least a night's sleep put some distance between the present and my inane behavior. The sun shining into my room helped cheer my spirits somewhat. Besides, whatever I felt like, I had to make a decision about what to do.

I got dressed and walked out. Almeda was just taking the water for Pa's coffee off the stove. I walked toward her. She put the kettle down and drew me to her in a warm embrace. We stood there for a long time without saying a word. I wrapped my arms tightly about her waist and buried my face in her neck. It felt so good to know I was loved no matter what I did!

"What should I do, Almeda?" I said finally, slowly pulling away from her and sitting down.

"About yesterday, or about going to Sacramento?"

"I don't think there's *anything* I can do about yesterday!" I laughed halfheartedly. "No, I mean, should I go?"

"What are you feeling about it?"

"After yesterday it's hard to know. I thought I had things more or less worked out about the election. I was even beginning to look forward to writing something. Now I'm confused again."

"Do you feel the Lord prompting you to go?"

"Oh, I don't know!" I wailed in frustration. "I can't even concentrate enough to pray or to ask the Lord what to do! I don't know why, but it seems like a big decision. I have the feeling that whatever I decide, the results will be with me a long time, maybe for the rest of my life. But God might as well be a thousand miles away for any feeling I have of his presence."

"Do you think he really *is* a thousand miles away, Corrie?" Almeda asked.

"No, I know he hasn't gone anywhere. You've taught me better than that. I know you can't depend on your feelings. God is near, he is still with me—I know that. I just don't feel him, that's all."

Almeda smiled. "I'm so glad to hear you say that, Corrie," she said. "It doesn't concern me to hear you say the Lord seems distant as long as you know he *really* is still right beside you."

"I know it, at least in my head," I answered. "But not feeling him, not hearing his voice anywhere makes a decision that much harder. How can I *know* what his will is?"

"Could he be speaking to you in ways you're not used to?"

"How do you mean?"

"God doesn't always speak to us by giving us a strong urging or compelling to do something. The older we grow as Christians, the more he actually may *not* give us those strong inward voices telling us what he wants us to do."

"Why is that?"

"I have an idea," Almeda answered. "But it's only my own personal theory, nothing I've found in the Bible or anywhere." She gave a little laugh. "So if I answer your question, you can't hold me to it if someday the Lord shows us I'm wrong."

"Agreed," I said.

"Okay, here it is." She paused, took a breath, then launched in. "When we're young, either in age or young as a Christian, there are many things we don't know. Young people have to learn about life. And when you decide to give your heart to the Lord, there are many, many things you have to learn about what life with him is like. The Lord has to tutor us, for a while, helping us learn new habits, new attitudes, new ways of looking at things. He has to train us spiritually. He has to teach us to stand, then walk, then move forward as Christians. In the same way that a parent has to train a child in the ways of life in the world, our Father has to train us in the ways of life in his kingdom. Until we get our spiritual bearings, that training has to be very direct, very close, very personal. There is so much we don't know and that he needs to teach us."

She stopped, and a thoughtful look passed over her face. Then she laughed again.

"Oh, Corrie!" she said. "If you could have seen me that first year or two I was married to Mr. Parrish. There was so much I had to learn, not just about being a Christian, but about being a wife, about living a normal existence. Every day was a new learning experience!

"You see, that's what I am getting at. Both my heavenly Father and Mr. Parrish together contributed to that remaking process in me. But eventually I did change. Eventually I learned the new ways. And now, after all these years, I am truly an altogether new and changed person. I have matured in many ways. As a Christian, as a daughter of God, although he is still with me always—inside my heart and right beside me—I no longer require the same kind of training I did back then. I am God's daughter, but I am also a grown woman. I think God treats me in many cases like an adult rather than a child. Whereas, at first he had to show me *everything*, and had to take my hand and literally guide me through every step of life, he doesn't have to do that anymore. He has trained me, and in the same way that a parent gradually releases a child to walk on his own, I think God begins to release us—not to walk independently of him, but to walk beside him as he has shown us without his having to direct every single move we make. In obedience to him, we walk along the path he has given us to walk, without having to stop to consider every step. Does that make sense?"

"I think so," I said.

"It's very difficult to explain what I mean," Almeda went on. "I don't mean to sound as though I think I want to walk independently, or that I think God isn't there with every step I take. I do try to bring him into all aspects of my life, even more than I did at the beginning. But the more we mature as Christians, the more of our decisions he leaves in *our* hands—knowing that we are walking along the road he has placed us in, and according to the ways and habits and attitudes that he has trained into us."

"In other words," I said, "he might be leaving part of the decision of what I should do in *my* hands?"

"Exactly. If he *didn't* want you to write, I am confident he would let you know it very clearly, and I am equally confident you would obey his voice. But since he *has* led you into writing in the past, I think he will very often let *you* make the decision yourself as to what specific things you write about. He may give you a stronger sense of leading at some times than others. But there will also be times when he will trust you to go either way when you're facing a particular decision, and he will make *either* one work out for the best."

"Hmm . . . that is a new way to look at it."

"God is our Father, of course. We must look to him for *everything*. We can't breathe a single breath without him. We can't take a step without him. Yet it is one of the many paradoxes of the Christian life that he also entrusts to us a sort of partnership with him. As we walk along *with* him, keeping our hand tightly in his, it is as if he says to us, 'My son, my daughter, I have trained you and taught you and placed my life and spirit inside you. Now go . . . walk in the confidence of your sonship. I will always be at your side; if you err or misstep, my hand will be right there to help you up and guide you back into the middle of the path. But until then, walk on with the boldness that comes from having my Spirit inside you.'"

"Do you think that applies to big decisions too?" I asked. "Things like whether or not I should get involved in this election?"

"I think we always have to pray and ask the Father for his specific guidance," replied Almeda. "Then the time comes when we must make a decision."

"And if we don't seem to hear a definite answer?"

She thought a minute, then answered. "There are two ways, it seems to me, in which God can answer our prayers and direct us. He can open doors, or he can close doors. If we're standing still, facing a fork in the road, facing a decision to be made, he can either open a door going in one direction or close the door going in the other. Or, if we don't happen to see the fork, or don't see *any* possibilities clearly, it has always seemed best to me to keep moving and praying until he either opens or closes a door. I've even prayed something like this sometimes: 'Lord, I don't know for sure if this is the way you want me to go. It *seems* to be best right now, and I *think* this is what you want, so I'm going to keep moving cautiously ahead until you say otherwise. Please, Lord, if this is not what you want me to do, slam the door shut in my face.' "

"Is that what you did before the election four years ago?" I asked.

"I suppose it was something like that, although there was, as I now look back on it, an ample supply of my own wishful thinking involved in what I *thought* was God's leading. Yes, I thought I was going in the right direction, so I moved ahead. But then when God made some things clear in my thinking about my relationship with your father, I knew he was closing the door."

"And so maybe Cal Burton's coming like he has is the Lord's way of opening the door to what I've been in doubt about all this time."

"It wouldn't surprise me a bit," said Almeda.

"I've been thinking about Davy Crockett's saying, 'Be sure you're right, then go ahead.' Maybe I've been expecting the Lord to be more direct than he wants to be."

"There's wisdom in that motto," said Almeda. "Yet on the other hand, we don't always have the luxury of being absolutely sure before we *have* to go ahead. In the absence of any positive leading by God, sometimes we have to launch out according to what circumstances seem to be saying, and prayerfully trust God to open and close doors as we go along."

Both of us were quiet a minute or two, until the door opened behind us and Pa walked in. Almeda glanced up, then her face fell.

"Oh, Drummond!" she exclaimed. "I'm afraid I let your coffee get cold."

"What'd you go and do a thing like that for, woman?" barked Pa, throwing me a wink.

"Corrie and I were talking. I'm sorry."

"Cold coffee from your hand is better than a hot cup from anyone else's," said Pa, walking to Almeda and giving her a kiss.

She handed him the cup. He took a long swallow, then nodded in satisfaction. "Yep . . . not bad at all!"

"So, what do you think, Corrie?" asked Pa. "You recovered from your embarrassing little runaround yesterday?"

"Oh, Pa, don't remind me!" I said. "Mr. Burton probably thinks I'm a complete ninny!"

"Don't bet on it, Corrie. I walked him out to his buggy last night and we chatted awhile. He thinks a lot of you. Seems like all them high-up fellas in Sacramento do."

"No more than they think of you, Pa," I said.

"Naw, Corrie. A man like me ain't that unusual. If I turn down their offer, they'll just get someone else. Who knows, maybe Franklin Royce'll run instead of me! But you—that's different! If you turn them down, who else are they going to get? Ain't too many young women like my daughter Corrie Belle around!"

"Cut it out, Pa," I said. "I was a complete fool yesterday, and you know it."

"Doesn't make me love you any less, or make me any less proud of you. So . . . you decided yet?"

"I don't know, Pa."

"Seems to me that Cal's coming with a direct invitation like he brought—seems like that's just exactly the sign from the Lord you were waiting for."

I glanced over at Almeda.

"An open door?" I suggested.

"Looks like one to me," said Pa, taking another drink of his coffee. "If you ask me, I say you oughta do it!"

# CHAPTER 20

## MY DECISION

I took Pa's advice.

I may have been twenty-three, but I still figured my pa was about as dependable a man as there could be. Even if he hadn't been my pa, I would have heeded his words. His being my father made it all the more important to listen to him and obey him as fully as I could. I'd had plenty of independence at times in the past, but the older I got, the more I found myself wanting to trust his way of looking at things.

Besides, I *wanted* to do it. I was interested in politics. I knew by now that I was against slavery, and that I did want Mr. Lincoln to win the election—maybe not as much as I had Mr. Fremont four years earlier, but enough to be able to speak out and tell folks that's how I felt.

So Pa's words gave me the nudge forward I needed—a nudge, as it turned out, that would make a mighty big difference in my life.

I left the next day on the midmorning stage south to Sacramento. Pa and Almeda and Becky and Tad took me to town to see me off. I was dressed in the traveling suit Almeda had Mrs. Gianni make for me. She said it would help to save my two fancy dresses for special occasions if I had something just to travel in. It was of dark brown patterned wool on the bottom, with a loose white muslin blouse with a short wool wraparound cape if it should be chilly.

When Cal Burton took my hand to help me up into the stage, I nearly wilted, even though my heart was pounding rapidly inside my chest. I tried not to show anything on my face, but sat down, then looked out at my family while Mr. Burton took the seat next to me. They were all smiling and waving and saying their farewells to me as if I were going to be gone a month instead of just four or five days.

"Don't you worry about a thing, Mrs. Hollister," Mr. Burton said through the open window. "I'll make sure your daughter is well taken care of."

"We stopped worrying about Corrie four years ago," laughed Pa, "when she took to gallivanting off all over California by herself on horseback!"

"What's this?" he said, glancing over at me.

"A long story," I answered.

"I want to hear about it. What is your father talking about?"

"The *last* time I got mixed up in an election," I said, laughing. "I hope this one turns out better than that."

The stage jerked into motion. I leaned outside again, and they all waved. I kept looking back, waving as we picked up speed down the main street of Miracle Springs. Something about this departure was different than any other before, even though I had gone a lot farther than Sacramento in the past. Probably the difference had something to do with the man sitting next to me inside the stagecoach.

As we pulled out of town and headed south, I could not keep from thinking of the awful scene after Aunt Katie discovered me outside her window, and wondering if Cal Burton would say something about it. I didn't know *what* I was going to talk to him about the whole way!

I shouldn't have worried. He treated me with complete respect and kindness, never referred to the incident at Uncle Nick's, and was so easy to talk with I soon forgot my nervousness and began to converse more freely than I imagined possible with a relative stranger. He asked me about my involvement with the Fremont-Buchanan election, and I told him about my adventures in Sonora and Mariposa, and what had happened with my story in the end.

"I never could help feeling less important than the other people around whenever I was in the city," I said. "And everything that happened back then only made it worse."

"From what I've heard, you've stood your ground against Kemble more than once, and even made him back down a time or two."

I couldn't keep from smiling at the memory.

"That doesn't sound like a timid country girl to me."

"I suppose you're right," I said. "I did do that. But down inside, someone like me still can't help feeling kind of out of place in a big city and around important goings-on. Like that gathering in San Francisco that Pa and I went to in June."

"You seemed perfectly at ease to me."

"Oh no—I was so nervous!"

"Why?"

"I guess because I'm not used to all the big-city fancy ways. I'm more at home on the back of a horse than in a frilly dress."

"You could have fooled me. You looked as elegant that evening as any young woman I could imagine."

I blushed and glanced down at my lap. Nobody had ever used the word *elegant* about *me* before! The very thought of me being elegant would have made me laugh if I hadn't been so embarrassed at the words.

"So tell me, did you ever get to meet the Fremonts after all you tried to do on their behalf?" Mr. Burton asked.

"Yes. Ankelita Carter arranged for me to meet them when they came to California after the election."

"I imagine they were very appreciative of your efforts."

"They were very nice to me," I said. "Jessie Fremont's a writer too, and so she seemed interested in all I was doing."

"And Colonel Fremont?"

"He said he had mentioned my name to some of his friends as someone to 'get on your side when the chips are down.' I laughed at first, and didn't think anything more about it. But now I find myself wondering if it might be true, after all."

"I imagine if Colonel Fremont said he told people about Corrie Hollister, then he probably did exactly that. He and Lincoln were talked about in connection with each other for a while. You can never tell where your name might be getting around. Kemble told me that just about everything you write nowadays finds its way into print in the East. It must make you very proud to have accomplished so much as a woman, especially at such a young age."

"I guess I never really stopped to think about it," I said. "It never crossed my mind to think that I had *accomplished* anything."

"The women of this country would likely disagree. Someday they'll look back on you as a pioneer of a different kind than Daniel Boone, and John Fremont when he first explored the West."

"Me, a pioneer?" I said.

"Of course. You mark my words, the day will come when people will remember your name and be proud of you for what you did."

"Mr. Burton," I asked after a minute, "do you think it is because of something Mr. Fremont may have said that Mr. Dalton asked me to help with the election?"

"I never heard anything to that effect. It's possible, of course. But as influential as he was in helping to form the Republican party and make it a viable alternative to the southern Democrats, the party has begun to move in different directions than those of John Fremont himself. He does not have the influence he once did, as fond as you may be of him. Although you may not know it, your editor, Ed Kemble, thinks more highly of you than he probably lets on in your hearing. Word about Corrie Hollister has gotten around San Francisco and Sacramento without any help from John Fremont."

He paused, then looked over at me earnestly. "There is one other thing I have to reply to about your question," he said. "If we are going to be friends, as I hope we will, you are going to have to call me Cal. I'm only twenty-five. That can't be more than a year or two older than you. If I've taken the liberty to call you Corrie instead of Miss Hollister, the least you can do is drop the Mister."

"I'll try," I said shyly.

"If you ever meet my father, you can use Mr. Burton again. But not until then . . . agreed?"

"Agreed," I nodded with a smile.

# CHAPTER 21

## A RIDE NOT TO FORGET

We rode for some time without talking again. Cal spoke to a man and woman in the opposite seat, who were on their way from Reno to Sacramento. They, too, had spent the night in Miracle Springs.

When he turned to me again, he seemed to have returned to the subject we had been discussing earlier. "Do you really feel ill at ease in the city, Corrie?" he asked.

"Just when I have to pretend I'm something I'm not," I answered.

"Why would you want to be other than you are?"

"I don't suppose I do. But when you're in the city, around people in fancy clothes who know how the city works and are doing important things, a country person like me can't help but feel that Robin O'Flaridy had it right all along when he said I was just a bumpkin from the sticks."

"O'Flaridy?"

"Never mind," I laughed.

"He really had the nerve to call you that?"

"Robin had enough nerve to do plenty more besides that! Yet sometimes that's exactly how I do feel—especially around important people. When I'm at home and can be all by myself and write, I don't have to worry about what anyone thinks of me. I can be free with my thoughts and let them flow out onto the paper. But something like what we're going to Sacramento to do—that makes me real nervous. It makes me wish I was more used to the city and its ways so I didn't feel like a bumpkin."

"Let me tell you something, Corrie," he said seriously. "Don't ever wish to be something different than exactly the person you are. I've been in a lot of cities, and I've known many city people. But I don't know that I've ever met a family quite like yours, or a young lady quite like you, or a man quite like your father."

He stopped, then turned and looked out the window at the passing scenery. The silence lasted a long time. When he finally turned back toward me, I could see a wistfulness in his eyes, a far-off look—almost longing for something or a painful memory out of his past. I knew he'd gone somewhere far away and was now struggling to bring his mind back to the present.

Until that moment, Cal Burton had seemed so high above me, so confident and sure of himself, mingling with important people, a friend of politicians and assistant to Mr. Stanford, one of California's most influential men. All of a sudden, in the brief second when he turned back from the window and his eyes met mine, he was an ordinary person just like me, and in that instant I momentarily forgot about all of the things that made us so different. All of a sudden he did seem to be *Cal* to me rather than *Mister* Burton.

"No, Corrie," he said with a sigh, "don't ever leave Miracle Springs, or your family. It's too special a treasure. Wherever you go, whatever you do, however many people you meet, and however many big cities you visit, don't change. Don't let Miracle Springs and the country and that homestead by the creek you love so much—don't let it get away from you. You can stand tall alongside anybody, no matter how big or important they may seem to you. You've got something just as important down inside, whether anybody sees it right off or not."

I didn't know how to respond, so I kept quiet.

"So you've got nothing to be nervous about," he added after a moment. "When we get to Sacramento, you just be who you are, and that will be enough for anybody."

"I'll do my best," I replied.

"So tell me," Cal said, brightening up again with that wide smile of his, "what's it like to write? How do you do it? How'd you ever get started writing for the *Alta*, anyway?"

"I started out just keeping a journal," I said. "I wrote down things I felt, things I thought about. I just did it for myself at first."

"How'd you start writing for the newspaper, then?"

I told him about the blizzard of '55 and the story I wrote about it. "After that," I said, "I just kept doing it a little more, thinking of things to write about, getting braver about sending things to Mr. Kemble."

"And getting braver about facing him and speaking up to him, too, from what I understand."

"What do you mean—how do you know about that?"

"Dalton had me do some checking up on you," Cal answered. "Kemble was half mad, half proud of you when he told me about your facing him down and arm-twisting him into paying you eight dollars for an article he wanted to buy for a dollar."

I laughed. "How I could have been so brash back then?" I said. "At nineteen, to think I should get paid what a man did. I don't know whether it was bravery or stupidity!"

"It must have worked. You made a name for yourself. You've written a lot of articles, Kemble likes you, and you've made a little money at it, I would imagine."

"Forty-three dollars, altogether," I said.

"Is that all?" exclaimed Cal. "I would have thought it would be hundreds!"

"I got only eight dollars that once. Most of the time Mr. Kemble still pays me between two and six dollars an article, and I've written only fourteen or fifteen articles he's published. Some of them are so short I get only a dollar."

"Then you must not write for the money."

"Oh no, it's not that at all."

"What then?"

I had to stop and think a minute. "It's a lot of things," I said finally. "People, nature, thoughts, ideas, feelings . . . I don't know if I could really explain it, but what's inside me has to come out in words. When I think something or notice something or have some kind of an insight about the world, to be able to communicate that to someone else is the greatest feeling on earth."

"Are you an intellectual, Corrie Hollister?" Cal asked, with a serious and pensive look on his face. For an instant I thought he might be poking fun at me, but then I realized he honestly was trying to figure out more about me.

"An intellectual?" I repeated in surprise. "You must be joking!"

"You're certainly a thinker, almost a philosopher in a way."

"A philosopher! That's even more strange to hear you say. Didn't you hear me a few minutes ago—some people think I'm a bumpkin from nowhere."

"Ah, but they don't know you like I am beginning to," replied Cal, his eyes open wide in a knowing expression. "But you don't deny that you're a thinker, do you?"

"I don't suppose I could be a writer without being a thinker at the same time," I answered finally.

"There—you see . . . a philosopher! A philosopher is just someone who thinks and has his own way of looking at things and then writes them down for other people to think about too. Isn't that what you do, in your own personal Corrie-Belle-Hollister-from-Miracle-Springs sort of way?"

"Maybe you're right. But I don't think of it like that. I just look at things, at the world, to observe people. Then I write about what I see, describe it, and maybe try to figure out what it means."

"Tell me what *you* mean."

"Maybe it's just from living in the country. But I have this feeling that everything is supposed to *mean* something. There are two ways we can look at something—just as it is on the surface or on two levels at once—what it looks like *and* what it is saying about life and the world. Do you know what I mean? Don't you have the feeling that the whole world is talking to you all the time if you just had sharp enough hearing to listen?"

"I've never thought of it before."

"Oh, but it is!"

"Give me an example."

I thought for a minute. "There's the creek outside our house. Sometimes I lie awake in my bed at night and just listen to it singing and babbling away down the hill toward the town in the dark. Or sometimes I sit beside it on a sunny day, with my feet in the water, watching for an hour as the clear water tumbles and splashes over the rocks. I love that creek! And don't you see why? It's so much more than just water. Its splashy, wet noises are constantly bringing messages down from the mountains—telling tales of snow and winter, of secret places where it has been, under the hills where huge vaults of gold exist that no man has ever seen, telling about falls it has cascaded over and about the fish and otters that play in its deep pools. Oh, it's got so much to tell if you only stop and listen to its voice. But best of all, when you kneel down and put your lips to it in the early spring when it's icy cold, and you drink in a mouthful, then it tells about life itself and how God made it, such a simple thing to look at, as the very sustainer of everything that lives and grows. The water that comes down that creek is nothing short of a miracle."

Cal laughed. "You are indeed able to see a great deal in things that most people look right past."

"But that's not nearly all," I said enthusiastically. "If there has been a heavy snow up in the mountains and then a week of warm weather comes, the stream will grow and grow, almost hourly, until it thunders and roars and rushes down with foamy swiftness. Then the stream can tell stories about the science of water itself— how it is gathered up into the sky from the ocean, to wait and accumulate together in clouds, finally to descend back to the earth in snows and rains, hitting the earth and soaking into it and wandering to and fro in streams and springs, sometimes pausing in lakes, until it finds its way back to the ocean again. I sometimes think of all these mysteries as I sit and watch and listen to the water as I did yesterday."

"Now I know I was not mistaken!"

"About what?"

"About your being a philosopher."

"Nonsense!" I replied. "It's all there for anyone to see. That's what I love so much about the country, about life. *Everything* is just as full of marvels and secret mysteries as the stream. Just the other day I was looking at the bark on the pine trees in the woods and found myself thinking about the mysteries of how the trees grow and gather nourishment from the ground. Nothing is without a meaning, almost a personality—*if* you know how to look for it and what you are looking for."

"And what is the meaning, the mystery, the significance of it all, Corrie?"

"Why, that God made it, of course."

"I don't see what is so mysterious about that. Everybody believes that. Everything has to be *made* somehow, by someone."

"The mystery is in what it tells us about God. He put himself into every tiniest thing."

"Even an ugly old gray rock?"

"Of course. His hand can't touch anything without leaving his fingerprints behind—even on the simplest of rocks."

"Hmm . . . you do have a way of looking at things differently than most people. Is this how you write, too?"

"I don't know," I laughed.

"Have you ever written about streams and pine trees?"

"No. I just think about things when I'm watching them. Sometimes they find their way into things I write, but mostly they just get into my journal where nobody else sees them."

"You mentioned your journal before—tell me about it."

"I keep journals of things I do and think about. Sometimes I draw pictures in it or respond to books I've read. When I'm writing in my journal, I don't have to be as careful as if I'm writing an article, so I just let it be as personal as I want."

"You said journals. How many journals do you have?"

"I've filled up five—no, let's see . . . yes, five. I just started my sixth book in the almost eight years I've been keeping a journal."

He drew in a sigh, then turned to glance out the window. The pause in conversation suddenly made me realize how much I'd forgotten my nervousness and how much talking I'd been doing. A fresh wave of embarrassment swept over me.

"I can hardly believe it. I must have babbled on for ten or fifteen miles!"

"Please, don't fret about it," said Cal, turning slowly back to face me. His voice was soft and reflective. "I enjoy listening to you, Corrie. It takes me back to a simpler time in my own life when some of those things were important to me, too."

"Did you once live in the country?" I asked.

"A long time ago," he answered, and again that same wistful look filled his eyes and I heard the longing in his voice that I had detected earlier.

"I'd love to hear about it," I said.

A long silence followed. I could see a look of pain cross his face, and he turned to gaze outside for a while again. When he finally spoke, it was only to close the door into himself that he had opened just for an instant, and only a crack.

"Maybe someday, Corrie," he said slowly. "But I don't think I'm up to it right now."

# CHAPTER 22

## TRUTH OR OPPORTUNITY

We were just coming to Auburn, where the stage stopped for half an hour to pick up one more passenger, get the mail, and give the passengers time for coffee and food if anyone wanted it. Cal asked me if I'd like to join him in the restaurant for something to eat, but I said I'd rather just walk around and stretch my legs. After I'd answered him, I realized I was a little hungry, yet somehow I'd thought maybe he'd rather be alone after the way our conversation had ended. I opened my bag and pulled out the apple I'd brought along and munched on it as I walked up and down the main street of Auburn.

When we climbed back into the stage, Cal's gaiety had returned. It was more crowded now, but he was just as genial as ever, talking to the others, helping the elderly lady who had gotten on at Auburn to adjust to the bumps and noises, and speaking to me again in a way that put me completely at ease.

We talked back and forth, gradually working our way around to the reason for the ride in the first place.

"What am I supposed to say when we get there?" I asked him. "I've never made a speech before in my life."

"Are you nervous?"

"Of course. How could I not be?"

"Don't worry about a thing, Corrie. All you have to do is be yourself and people will love you."

"I've got to do a little more than that," I said. "I have to say *something*."

"Sure, but it hardly matters *what* you say. What the people

119

are coming out to see is a woman standing up there—and a pretty one!—with the men. Standing up and saying, 'Vote for Lincoln.' "

I don't know what got into me, but suddenly I lost my shyness and out of my mouth popped the words, "Come on, Cal. I'm not pretty, and you shouldn't lie like that."

The instant I said it, I wanted to retract the words! But he just laughed. "You are something, Corrie Hollister!" he said, still laughing. "Not afraid to speak your mind one bit. But you won't object if I disagree with you, will you? You're going to stand up there and folks are going to say to themselves, 'There's one beautiful young woman, and I'm going to listen to what she has to say!' So there, Corrie—like it or not. I'm not taking back a word of it!"

Now I was embarrassed again!

"But is it really true that it doesn't matter how good a speech I make?" I asked, trying to turn the discussion back toward Sacramento.

"Doesn't matter a bit. We want you there because of who you are, that's all. Dalton and the others know you're not a speechmaker."

"There's a big difference between speaking in front of people and writing down thoughts on paper when you're all alone," I said.

We bounced along for a while, then Cal asked me, "Why are you interested in politics, Corrie? How did you get involved in the first place?"

I stopped to think. "I suppose it was my mother's decision to run for mayor of Miracle Springs," I answered after a bit. "Actually, she's my stepmother—Almeda, you know. And it turned out she *didn't* run, but my pa did instead. It all happened in 1856, and we were so involved in it as a family, how could I help but be interested? So I wrote a few articles about the Miracle Springs election. Then with the presidential election going on at the same time, and Mr. Fremont being a Californian, well, I just kind of got drawn into it."

"But why did you *stay* interested? Why did you get *so* involved with the Fremont cause as to risk your life and do all you did, especially when you'd never met the man?"

"I don't know; I suppose it seemed the right thing to do."

"The *right* thing?"

"Yes. The more I found out about everything, the more I knew I had to stand up for the truth, and to write the truth so that people would know how things *really* were."

"Truth . . . hmm."

"For me there's no other reason to write at all. That's what everything's about—all of life, in fact."

"Like the Miracle Springs Creek?" suggested Cal.

"Yes," I said. "The creek, the election in '56, what kind of person I want to be. It's all about truth. The creek's got truth in it, if you know where to look for it. It seems to me that life's about learning to be a true person. That's what being a Christian is to me—not knowing a lot of religious things, but becoming a *true* person, a true daughter of God. That's what my writing's about too—learning to find life's good things, life's *right* things, life's *true* things—and then writing about them in a way folks can understand, in a way that gets down inside them. Whether I'm writing about creeks or trees or politics, I've got to make sure inside myself that it's *truth* I'm writing about."

Cal was very thoughtful for a minute. "An unusual approach to political reporting," he said at length. "And so," he added, "have you satisfied yourself that supporting Lincoln is the right and true thing to do?"

"I had to spend a lot of time thinking and praying about it," I answered. "It wasn't an easy decision. But, yes, I'm satisfied now that it's what I'm supposed to do, and so I'll give myself to stand up for the truth as I see it just as much as I did before with Mr. Fremont. What about you? Isn't that why you're in favor of Mr. Lincoln?"

Cal thought for a moment. Then a smile spread across his face. "My boss, Mr. Stanford, would not take it too kindly if I didn't," he said. "He is one of California's leading Republicans!"

"Why did you go to work for him," I asked, "if it wasn't because you believed in what he stood for?"

"Leland Stanford believes in himself," laughed Cal, "and his businesses and his railroad and making money."

"But surely you believe in *him*?"

"Of course I do. But I'm afraid it's on a more pragmatic level than because he stands for the truth. I hope you won't hate me, Corrie, but I believe in Mr. Stanford because I believe he represents the future, and therefore offers me the greatest opportunity to be in step with the future when it comes. Truth doesn't seem to me as important in this case as who holds the key to the future. Does Leland Stanford, or does former governor Latham, or does Congressman Burch with his idea of a separate California republic, or do the Breckinridge southern Democrats, or does Governor Downey, or does the state's new golden-tongued orator Thomas Starr King? Where does the future lie, Corrie? That seems to me the question. That is why I have cast my lot with Mr. Stanford and his cause. He'll be governor one day, mark my words. His railroad will span the continent. He may one day even live in the White House. And I want to be standing beside him if he does!"

"What about Mr. Lincoln? Do you believe in him in the same way?" I asked.

Cal's face turned thoughtful. "I can't say as I do, Corrie," he answered. "I think the North is very weak, both politically and economically. In a financial battle between North and South, the southern states would win hands down. With regard to the future of this nation, I do not see the North leading the way. For now it seems to me that the West is where the true future exists."

*"For now?"*

"Change that. Let me just say I came to the West because I saw the future moving in this direction."

We rode along for a while in silence. The three other passengers were occasionally making some attempts to carry on a conversation, but I think they were mostly listening to us. Whenever Cal and I stopped talking, it generally quieted down as if they were waiting for us to continue. Finally I picked the discussion up again.

"Is it all right if I ask you the same question you asked me?" I said. "Why did *you* get involved in politics?"

"A fair enough question," answered Cal. "I'll see if I can give you as straightforward an answer as you gave me."

He paused, thought for a minute, then went on. "The answer is very simple really—politics has been in my family as long as I have. Does the name Stephens mean anything to you?"

I shook my head.

"It's my mother's maiden name. My uncle, her brother, spent sixteen years in Congress in Washington, until just last year, and had served six terms in his state legislature before that. He is such a political creature that his very name raises images of the founding of the country itself—Alexander Hamilton Stephens."

"So it was in your blood?"

"In more ways than one. And I began to love it early in my life. I was only eight when my uncle packed his bags for Washington, but I remember it as distinctly as if it were yesterday. When we went up to visit him there, the sense of power the place exuded got into me and I knew I wanted to be part of it someday too. My uncle was a Whig. But he was a pragmatic man too, and he taught me to look for opportunity wherever and however it came. And so now here I am working for the new Republican party, which didn't even exist eight years ago."

He laughed at the thought.

"Don't you see, Corrie? It's all about opportunity! That's what politics represents to me. It's where the power is, where the future is. That's why my uncle said to me, 'Cal, the future's in the West. If you want a life in politics that'll take you to the top, seek it in California. That's where tomorrow's leaders are going to come from.' So I took his advice, and here I am!"

"You're involved in politics and with Mr. Stanford for where they will *take* you?"

"Do I detect a slightly negative tone?"

"I just wanted to know," I answered. "I never thought of that before, at least in relation to myself. I don't envision my writing *taking me* anywhere—at least not in the way you mean it."

"Your reputation is growing in importance. That doesn't mean anything to you?"

"I never think about it. I want to grow *inside*, as a person. But I never think about becoming important."

"Well, I do. I want to *be* somebody. I want my life to count. Don't you see, Corrie? People like you and me, young men and women with ideas and enthusiasm, we're going to be tomorrow's leaders of the country. Doesn't that excite you? Don't you want to be part of it?"

"I've never thought of it. What about what you said two hours ago about the simpler life? You told me never to leave the simple country life behind. It even sounded as if you wished you could go back to it yourself. Now you're saying that I ought to want to be important."

"I grew up in the country too," said Cal. "I suppose part of me looks back on my childhood with a kind of longing. But once the lure of politics began to get hold of me, with all the opportunities it afforded, I vowed to myself that I would use every opportunity, every situation, to the fullest."

"To the fullest . . . in what way?"

"For where it could take me, what it could do for me—for taking advantage of the opportunity in whatever ways I was able."

I fell silent, and we didn't pick up the same conversation again. Cal had certainly given me a lot to think about. We were both on our way to Sacramento to be involved in Mr. Lincoln's campaign together, and yet our reasons and motives seemed very different.

# CHAPTER 23

# SPEECHMAKING IN
# SACRAMENTO

They had offered to put me up in a big hotel in Sacramento, but I said I preferred to stay with Miss Baxter in her boarding-house.

The meeting was scheduled for the afternoon after we arrived. I must have taken an hour to get ready. Just pulling the dress over my head and trying to button the buttons with my trembling fingers was so hard I finally had to ask Miss Baxter to help me. The dress was a light brown cotton, with full sleeves, navy piping around the collar and lapels, and a matching navy ribbon around the waist. I wished Almeda had been there to help me get it all just right and brush my hair and tie it up with its ribbon. But Miss Baxter was a fine substitute. It was so nice to have a woman there to share the anxious moments with me!

Cal came to pick me up in a fancy buggy and complimented me on how I looked. But I was still dreadfully nervous.

A platform had been built downtown near the capital buildings and decorated with red, white, and blue banners. Flags were flying, and a band was playing peppy patriotic songs. Quite a crowd had already gathered, and wagons and buggies were still pulling up. It reminded me of the festive day in Miracle Springs back in '52, but one look around told me this was a much bigger and more important event. All the men were dressed in expensive suits, and just the looks on their faces told me they were probably important men in California's politics.

Most of them were, too. Cal introduced me to more than a

dozen people that day, and I can hardly remember a single one of them. I was so nervous before and so relieved after my brief time up on the platform that my mind was blank of everything else.

There were going to be speeches on behalf of all three of the candidates for president. In addition to me, Mr. Stanford and some other of his friends, Mr. Dalton and a famous orator named Edward D. Baker, all spoke for Abraham Lincoln. The Republicans were in the minority in California, as they were in the rest of the country. Up until this time, in the national elections California had always sided with the party that favored slavery. But now in 1860, when the line came to be drawn so clearly between North and South, and between slavery and antislavery, the Republicans hoped to break this record and bring California around and make it a free, pro-Union Republican state.

The split of the Democratic party, Cal told me, would help more than anything to make this possible. After the nomination of Stephen Douglas by the moderate wing of the party, the southern faction set up John Breckinridge as a candidate as well. On this day in Sacramento, many prominent Californians came out in favor of both men.

Governor Downey gave a speech in support of Douglas. I was surprised at how many famous western politicians were in favor of the southern cause and slavery. Former governor Latham supported Breckinridge, although he wasn't there that day because he was now serving in the U.S. Senate representing California. California's other senator, William Gwin, formerly from Mississippi, did happen to be present, and spoke on behalf of the southern cause and candidate Breckinridge. John Weller, also speaking for Breckinridge, actually brought up the issue of the South seceding from the Union. I couldn't believe slavery could be so important to the South that they would actually try to start a new country rather than to see the slaves set free.

I had my journal with me and I tried to write down some of what was said. But all the newspapers told about the speeches anyway, and I got copies the next day so I could read them over again. Weller said this: "I do not know whether Lincoln will be elected or not. I will personally urge every Californian to vote instead for John C. Breckinridge of the Southern Democratic party. I do know this, that if our efforts fail and if Lincoln is elected, and if he attempts to carry out his doctrines, the South will surely withdraw from the Union. And I should consider them less than men if they did not."

One speech got the biggest applause and was written up in all the newspapers of the state during the next few days—the one delivered by Edward Baker. He had been defeated a year before as candidate for Congress and then had gone up to Oregon where he had been elected to the Senate from the new state. He had come down to California and had been called upon to speak on behalf of the Republican party, freedom, and the election of Abraham Lincoln. People said afterward it was one of the greatest political speeches ever delivered in California. Baker said:

> Where the feet of my youth were planted, there, by Freedom, my feet shall stand. I will walk beneath her banner. I will glory in her strength. I have watched her, in history, struck down on a hundred chosen fields of battle. I have seen her friends fly from her. I have seen her foes gather round her. I have seen them bind her to the stake. I have seen them give her ashes to the winds, regathering them again that they might scatter them yet more widely. But when they turned to exult, I have seen her again meet them, face-to-face, resplendent in complete steel and brandishing in her strong right hand a flaming sword, red with insufferable light. I take courage. The people gather round her. The Genius of America will at last lead her sons to freedom.

After Baker's speech I wasn't any too anxious to walk up there on that platform, with four or five hundred people standing all around listening, and open my timid little mouth to try to say something. What could I say that could compare in any way with what Mr. Baker had said?

But there was no getting around it. And eventually I heard Mr. Dalton start to introduce me. I sat there listening to him, my whole body sweating and shaking, terrified at the ordeal that was about to come.

"Ladies and gentlemen, fellow Californians," he said, "you have heard from eminent statesmen today, from senators and governors and political leaders and men of industry and commerce.

But I now want to introduce to you a young lady of perhaps equal reputation in some circles, a young lady whose simple and honest words have been read in newspapers from one shining sea of this great land all the way to the other; a young lady who, I must tell you, is a bit nervous about all this. She is a country girl, yet her words ring with truth whenever she sets pen to paper. Therefore I know what she says to you today comes directly from the heart. Ladies and gentlemen, I give you Miss Cornelia Belle Hollister."

I stood up. I glanced at Cal, sitting beside me, and he gave me a smile of encouragement. I walked up the steps and to the front of the platform.

I stood there for a moment. Everyone was quiet, all eyes looking up at me, waiting.

"I've never made a speech before in my life," I began. "I don't know if this will even qualify as one now. They told me all I had to do was say what I felt and thought about things, and that would be good enough. I suppose I can do that."

My voice sounded so tiny, like a little mouse! All the other men had loud, deep voices, and I sounded like a little girl. I didn't think the people more than ten feet away would be able to hear a thing I said!

"I've been thinking a lot about this election," I said after clearing my throat and trying to speak up a little louder. "I had to think about which side I'd be on and what I ought to do about it. I can't say as I'm a Democrat or a Republican, and it hardly matters much since I can't vote anyway."

A small wave of laughter spread among the men who were listening. There were a good number of women there too, and by now most of them had come forward as close to the platform as they could. They were all watching me intently.

"I don't know Mr. Lincoln or Mr. Douglas, or Mr. Breckinridge, for that matter, who I just found out today is running too. To tell you the truth, I don't really know too much about any of the issues except for the issue of slavery and freedom. But if you want a woman's point of view, that's just about the most important issue of all. And that's the one I spent nearly all my time thinking over when it came to this election.

"The conclusion I came to is that freedom is a mighty important thing in this country of ours. The Constitution talks about it, and I guess it seems to me that if people in the United States of America can't be free, then I don't know where else in the world freedom's going to find a place to grow. Some of the Democrats might say that the freedom the Constitution talks about doesn't apply to Negroes because they aren't people in the same way as the rest of us are, so they don't have the same right to be free. But I don't agree with that. I'm a woman, and I don't have the right to vote. But that doesn't make me feel any less of a human being, and I don't figure too many Negroes feel like they're less than human, either.

"It looks to me like freedom's a thing that's got to apply to everybody, or else it doesn't mean much. It's got to apply to women and Negroes, to rich people and poor people, to folks in California just like it does to folks in Alabama or anywhere else. Some of these men we've been listening to today have said you ought to vote for Mr. Douglas or Mr. Breckinridge because it'll be better for the South, and the whole country, or because Mr. Lincoln's made so many strong remarks about being against slavery that the South will be so mad if he gets elected, there's no telling what they might do.

"All of that doesn't seem to have anything to do with freedom, if you ask me. The Democrats have been the party that supported slavery all these years. Now the Republicans are trying to change that by standing for freedom. It seems to me that's about the most important thing of all. I don't know much about money and the economy and all that. But if folks in these United States aren't free, then it doesn't seem to me that our money means much, or the word freedom or our Constitution either.

"Four years ago I tried to write some things to help Colonel Fremont get to the White House, because he was against slavery too, just like Mr. Lincoln is. He got defeated, and I figured my efforts had been wasted.

"But now I've got a chance to try to do something again, and I hope the people of this country will do better by the cause of freedom for our people than last time. That's why I decided, after thinking about it a good long while, to support Abraham Lincoln. No, I can't vote. But if I could, I'd vote for Mr. Lincoln, and it seems to me you all ought to vote for him too."

I turned and walked back down the steps and sat down. I was sweating and trembling from head to foot. I never heard any of the applause, but Cal told me they loved it, especially all the women.

The next morning, on the *front page* of the Sacramento *Union*, I was shocked to read the headline over a two-column article: *BAKER, DOWNEY, WELLER, HOLLISTER ADDRESS SACRAMENTO ELECTORATE*. And toward the end of the article, they actually quoted from *my* speech!

# CHAPTER 24

# DINNER AT LIVINGSTONE'S

By the time all the festivities of the day were finished, I was exhausted, not just from having given the speech, but from everything that had followed—talking to people, shaking hands, greeting a long line of women well-wishers who treated me like some kind of hero for "the cause," as they put it, although I had no idea what cause they were talking about.

I had tried to keep smiling and stay friendly, but by the end of the afternoon I was *so* tired. Cal stayed at my side nearly the whole time, encouraging me, telling me what to do if I got confused, picking up the conversation for me if I didn't know what to say. All day long I kept meeting people, most of whom I can't even remember. But they all looked important.

Then he took me and showed me inside some of the capital buildings, including where the legislature met. "Here's where your father will be one of these days," he said, and I thought to myself that they shouldn't count on it because Pa was an independent man who was used to making up his own mind and not having anyone else do his thinking for him. But just the thought of Pa in the midst of all these fancy, dressed-up men brought a smile to my lips. I couldn't imagine *him* making a speech in front of that great big Assembly hall! And if he did, he'd no doubt shake things up once in a while!

"What's so funny, Corrie?" Cal asked.

"Oh nothing," I replied, still smiling to myself.

"You've got something on your mind. You can't hide that."

"I was just thinking about what it would be like if Pa *was* to come here," I said.

"I hope he does," replied Cal. "This place could use more men of his caliber."

Finally, around six o'clock, Cal took me to dinner at a place called Livingstone's. We drove up to the front of Livingstone's, and Cal jumped out of the buggy, took my hand, and helped me down to the street, while someone else hopped up and drove the horses around to the back. Then Cal slipped his arm through mine and led me inside. I don't know if I'd ever felt so out of place in my life! If this was what it was like to be a *lady*, I wasn't sure I liked it.

Livingstone's turned out to be a fancier restaurant than I had ever seen—even nicer than the International House, where Almeda had taken me on our first trip to San Francisco. Mingling around the front door were several men in tuxedos and women in silk dresses. The flash of diamonds caught my eye now and then. Once we were inside, I realized all the more what a glamorous place Cal had brought me to. I heard music playing from somewhere, and the waiters were dressed up to look like preachers.

I was so nervous, I felt like I was going to stumble and fall over my dress with every step. And Cal was close to me, our arms linked together, my dress brushing up alongside him, my arm and shoulder touching his as we slowly made our way to our table behind one of the fancy-dressed waiters. As I sat down, Cal went behind me and helped scoot my chair in.

I'd never been treated like this, and I hardly knew what to do! Just the thought of Robin O'Flaridy made me laugh inside at the comparison. Cal was such a fine and gentlemanly *man*! I took stock of the white linen tablecloth, the candle in the middle of the table, the wine glasses and silver, which all made me think: What is Corrie Hollister doing *here*?

I might have been California's best-known woman reporter, but I couldn't make heads or tails of the menu. Cal helped me order. I had roast lamb with some fancy kind of potatoes with cheese mixed into them. It was tasty, but I didn't have much of an appetite. I don't know if it was because of how tired I was, but I could eat only about half of what the waiter brought me.

"You stole the show today, Corrie," said Cal across the table.

"I did not," I responded. "You heard all those other men, and the clapping after Mr. Baker's speech!"

"Those men are all politicians. Edward Baker's on his way to Washington. Speechmaking is the business of men like that. I'll wager Baker's given several hundred speeches in his life—all smooth, polished, every word just as it ought to be. But *you*—your speech was different. It was from the heart . . . it was just *you*! I saw Dalton's face as he was watching."

"What . . . what was he thinking?" I asked, wondering what he meant.

"He was sitting back in his chair with just the hint of a smile on his face. He knew well and good that he'd found the right young lady."

"He didn't say anything to me afterward."

"Alexander Dalton can be a funny man at times. But he knows politics like no one in this state. And you mark my words, you will hear from him again. I tell you, Corrie, there were some people there today paying more attention to you than anyone else who got up on that platform the whole day."

"I don't believe a word of it," I said, although I looked down at my plate in embarrassment at the same time. I couldn't help feeling pride at his words. I suppose part of me knew he was just trying to make me feel good about the day, yet another part wanted to believe he was sincere and wouldn't say anything he didn't really mean.

"Well, there's nothing I can do to convince you," said Cal sincerely, "even if I do know these men and their kind better than you do." He paused, then put his fork down and looked across the table at me. "But I will tell you this, Corrie," he added, "and even if you can't believe the other, I hope you will believe this. You were not only the prettiest speaker in all of Sacramento today, in *my* humble estimation you were also the most eloquent. If Abraham Lincoln does not carry California, it will be only because the men of this state were too deaf to heed the words of his most ardent supporter."

The rest of the evening was lost in a fuzzy blur. Even as I lay in bed hours later, I could hardly recall the specifics of it in any pattern that made sense. By the time I tried to write about it in my journal as I bounced along in the stagecoach going home, it had nearly all escaped me. The feelings inside lingered, but what we had done, where we had gone, what we had seen, and the words we had spoken—I could recall none of them.

I do know that Cal showed me nearly all of Sacramento—Sutter's fort, some of the old original houses still standing from the 1840s. We got out and walked along the river just about the time the sun was setting and the half moon was coming up. Then we rode again in the buggy, for hours it seemed, until the city was dark and night sounds faintly echoed about in the distance.

It was very quiet and still when at last Cal pulled the horse up in front of Miss Baxter's. The only sounds were the crickets in the trees lining the streets. Even the occasional shouts from the saloons down in the center of town were so faint as to be drowned out by the thunderous chirping of the tiny creatures overhead.

Cal got down, tied the reins to the fence, then came over to my side, held up his hand to take mine, and helped me down to the street. I was finally getting used to such treatment, although it still brought about a fluttering sensation all through me. But I wasn't prepared for him keeping hold of my hand as he led me up to Miss Baxter's porch!

We walked toward the house slowly, in silence. When we reached the porch, Cal stopped, still grasping my hand, and turned toward me.

"Corrie," he said, "this has been one of the most pleasurable days I have spent in all my life. You are an engaging and wonderful young woman."

He looked deeply into my eyes. The light from the moon reflected from his, seeming to draw me right into them. My heart was pounding so hard, I thought the whole boardinghouse must hear, and that windows would begin opening any moment to find out what the racket was!

Then he slowly drew my hand up, bent slightly, and kissed the top of my hand as he held it between his fingers. I just stood there, compliantly watching as his lips rested for just a second on my hand. Yet inside, my heart and brain were exploding with the sounds of a thousand waves crashing against a stormy shore.

He raised his head, released my hand, and softly uttered the words, "Good-night, Corrie."

Then he turned and was gone. I remained standing on the porch, watching him bound up into the carriage seat, and briskly urge the horse into action with a flick of the rein and a click of his tongue.

I was alone, in the silent darkness of the Sacramento night. Alone with only the sound of a million crickets in my ears and ocean waves somewhere down in my heart.

I can't remember opening the door and walking inside the house, or climbing the darkened stairs to the room I always stayed in whenever I came to Sacramento. I cannot remember taking off my bonnet, nor getting out of my long dress and tossing it across the chair. Somehow I got into my night clothes, although I don't recall that, either.

When I next came to myself I was lying on my back in the soft bed, moonlight streaming through the window into the room. Just lying there. Thinking, yet not thinking. A smile on my face, my heart full, yet my mind empty. Full of feelings, yet none that could be expressed in words.

The only words I was aware of were those three that kept repeating themselves over and over and over . . . *Good-night, Corrie.*

I don't know how long I lay there. But somehow, eventually, my eyelids closed with heaviness, the sound of the waves and the crickets gradually subsided, and sleep slowly stole over me.

# CHAPTER 25

## THE TWO LETTERS

It seemed kind of dull at home for the next couple of weeks. I couldn't find much energy to interest myself in anything. I went on long walks and rides and pretty much kept to myself. I doubt I did anybody much good when I went into town and tried to busy myself with Mine and Freight business.

Marcus Weber looked me over with his big drooping eyes of concern every day I came in, and finally, when he couldn't stand it any longer, he burst out one day, "What in tarnation be ailin' you, Miss Corrie? Blamed if I just can't stand to see you lookin' so sad!"

I smiled, but from the reaction on his beautiful, tender black face I could tell it didn't reassure him much. "Nothing, Marcus," I said. "I am just fine. Just a little tired."

I know he wasn't convinced. He looked me over for another several seconds, with an unspoken expression of concern flooding across his humble features. He gave me a nervous fatherly hug, and I almost thought I detected a tear in one of his eyes. Then he turned and went back out to the livery. In those brief moments, I felt my heart's eyes could see down into Marcus far deeper than his mere words expressed.

It was such a revelation. I could see how much he really loved me! To be loved like that, when you realize how deep it goes into somebody *else's* heart, has to be one of the most humbling things in all of life.

Pa acted the same way, looking at me with concern, asking if I was sick, telling me I ought to be eating more or I was going to waste away. Almeda didn't say much; she just smiled at me a lot, and gave me more than my share of motherly hugs whenever she had the chance. She knew what it was, and knew that I had to work through it as best I could on my own.

A couple of letters arrived early in August that helped me get back on my feet and quit thinking so much about Cal Burton. I couldn't stop thinking about him altogether, but having something to *do* at least got my brain and hands occupied with activity.

The first was a letter to Pa from Alexander Dalton. He said the time was getting very close when Pa would have to make up his mind about whether to run or not. He stressed again his assurance that Drummond Hollister was exactly the kind of man the state of California needed, and his confidence that if Pa made up his mind soon, there would be victory in November. He would handle the whole campaign and all the details, he said. It would not cost Pa a cent. All he had to do was give his consent and perhaps make two or three speeches between Miracle Springs and Sacramento—Grass Valley and Auburn, and maybe one or two other towns besides.

The second letter was addressed to me. My heart jumped for a moment, but then settled back into place when I saw the familiar handwriting of my editor at the *Alta*. Not so long ago, a note or letter from Mr. Kemble would send me into a positive tizzy. Now I found myself opening it almost with disappointment. His words, however, were sufficient to bring a tingle to my skin.

> You always continue to astound me, Corrie Hollister. I never gave you two cents' worth of a chance of succeeding in this business, but you've been writing for me for six years and are one of the most well-known reporters I have. And now you've taken up speechmaking and politics besides! Is there anything you don't do?
>
> In any case, I have heard the reports from Sacramento where, as I understand it, you were quite impressive. My Republican friends are badgering me for an article under your byline in support of the Lincoln-Hamlin ticket. Dalton says he will pay half if I will offer you enough myself to encourage you to set your pen to paper again as you did, unfortunately in vain, for the Fremont cause. He also assures me that, for the right article, he could almost guarantee publication in

most of the major eastern cities. We would like an article of some length, which men and politicians would heed as well as the women who make up your customary readership. This is the title we would like to use: "Why Abraham Lincoln Should Be President—A Woman's Point of View."

Can you do it? We will pay you a total of ten dollars. We would need the finished article by September 15 in order to get it to the east and published within the first week or two of October.

I remain, sincerely yours,

EDWARD KEMBLE

# CHAPTER 26

## A BOLD DECISION

I don't know what Pa intended to do about the letter he had received, but I needed something to occupy my mind for a while, and I liked what Mr. Kemble had suggested. I started on the article right away.

I had no sooner begun when thoughts of Zack began to intrude into my mind. Maybe it was from seeing Pa wrestling with his decision, and knowing Zack was part of what he was thinking about in it all. There still had been no word from or about Zack, and even though we didn't talk about it much, we were all worried.

I couldn't help feeling personally involved. I didn't feel responsible for his leaving, but I did feel that maybe I'd let Zack down too, that a lot of the things he'd said to Pa applied to me as well. I even felt that some of what I'd done, the opportunities I'd had and the attention I'd received, all went into making him feel less important. It wasn't true, of course, but his outburst surely made it seem like that's how he felt. I thought we were about as close as a brother and sister could be, and then I found out that he was hurting about all kinds of things no one knew about. It wasn't right for him to suffer like that, and I began to feel that it was important for me to do something about it.

At first I thought of writing Zack a letter. What better way to get in touch with him? He'd have his hands on it in just a few days!

Then I realized what a stupid idea it was. He might have his hands on it, but a letter would just be stuck inside a mail pouch in his saddlebags, and he would never see it! We had no idea where

139

he was staying, so there was no way to address a letter actually *to* him.

All the while I was working on my Lincoln article, Zack kept running through my mind. I'd see his face, first laughing, then serious. I'd see him riding on a horse like the wind. I recalled our first coming to California and how he'd tried so hard to act grown up. I remembered the pain I could see underneath the brave exterior. I remembered how he and Pa had a hard time at first, but how they had become friends—or so I'd thought. I remembered the first gun Pa gave him that Christmas and how proud Zack had been, and how much he'd loved working at the mine with the three men.

So many memories kept rising and falling into my thoughts, all now clouded over with the pain and hurt of his bitter words of anger the day he'd left.

One day a daring plan came into my mind—in its own way almost as daring, I suppose, as Zack's going off as he had. I went to talk to Pa about it.

"What would you think," I asked, "if I was to go find Zack?"

"Tarnation, girl!" he exclaimed. "How you figure on doing that?"

"I'll follow the Express route east till I get to Zack's leg."

"You're gonna ride along with the Pony Express! You're a decent rider, Corrie. But you ain't gonna keep up with *them* skinny young wild men!"

"I don't have to keep up with them, Pa," I said. "I only have to follow the route. I figure I'll go from station to station, asking as I go about Zack. Somebody's bound to know of him, and somewhere along the line I'll run into him."

Pa rubbed his chin and made like he was thinking. "It's a foolhardy enough notion for my daughter to have thought of," he said after a while, breaking into a grin.

"Is it all right, Pa?" I asked eagerly.

"'Course it ain't all right. This is crazier than any of your schemes four years ago!" Pa's tone was lighthearted, but I could tell he meant it, too.

I laughed kind of sheepishly.

"What do you want me to say?" he went on. "That I like the idea? It's dangerous out there."

"We have to find out about Zack sometime, Pa," I said.

"Yeah," Pa sighed. "And I reckon by now you *have* proved yourself, and I trust you. But I don't like the idea of you being out there alone. I don't like it for a second, and I don't see how I could do anything but try to keep you from it just like I did Zack."

"But I'd only be gone for a short time, Pa. Not like what Zack wanted to do—not to take a job."

Pa sighed. "I'm as anxious about Zack as you are. Why don't you take the stage?"

"The stage doesn't follow the same route till it gets to Wyoming."

"The wagon trail?"

"There are no wagon trains going east this late in the year. I wouldn't find anybody to hook up with that way, either. Besides, the California Trail goes north of the Express route. There's no way I can see to find him except to go straight out to Placerville and Carson City and then straight across Nevada toward Salt Lake City."

"I tell you, it's dangerous territory, Corrie. Your ma died out there from the heat. You know that better than I do. There's Indians, desert, sometimes no water."

"That was almost ten years ago, Pa. It's more civilized now. There are horse-changing stations every twenty or twenty-five miles. There are people, food, water, a place to rest. If I just told them my brother was a rider, they'd be hospitable enough, and even let me sleep the night."

Pa thought again. "Yeah, I reckon that's so," he said. "Still, I don't much like the idea of you being that far from home alone."

All of a sudden *another* wild idea struck me.

"Why don't you come with me, Pa?" I said. "Let's go find Zack together!"

Pa's face remained blank, not twitching so much as a muscle. But his eyes betrayed that somewhere deep behind them, his mind was spinning fast to take in the words I had said and to figure out what to do about them.

"You know his being gone's eating at you, Pa," I said after a minute, "just like it is me. Let's both go out there and find him and tell him we're sorry for not letting him know how we felt, and tell him we love him."

Still Pa was silent, thinking it all over. He stood there for a long time, looking out into the distance. Finally he turned to me.

"You think he'd listen to me?" he said softly, the pain and uncertainty all too clear in his voice.

"Of course he would, Pa," I said. "What son's going to turn his own pa away?"

"Seems like that's just what he wanted to do."

"Oh, Pa, no he didn't. He was just feeling pain and confusion. He didn't know what to do with it all. I think you got in the way, that's all."

"But I was the cause of it all."

"No you weren't, Pa. Kids blame their parents for all kinds of things that are really no one's fault but their *own*. They just don't want to look down inside themselves, so they blame the nearest person around."

"Did you ever do that, Corrie?" asked Pa. He and I had lots of personal talks together. But when he said those words, there was an earnestness in his voice I'd never heard before. Never in my life had I seen a man so vulnerable as Pa was at that moment, so stripped of all the barriers men usually put up to shield themselves from other people. I felt I was looking all the way to the bottom of Pa's very soul, where there was a tender human being just as capable of feelings and suffering and questions and pain and worry as any woman or any child. It's not the kind of thing most kids ever get the chance to see in their parents, but I saw it right then in my pa, and it pulled me all the deeper into him and made me love him all the more.

He was looking at me intently, almost as if he were afraid of the answer I would give him.

"When we first got here," I said, "there were a couple of times I felt hurt, Pa. But Ma had just died. I was so confused about everything, and I was only fifteen."

"Did you blame me for what happened?" Pa asked, still with the earnest, transparent, questioning probing in his eyes.

Again, I thought hard. "I can't say as there wasn't any pain, Pa," I said. "That was a hard time for all of us. But no, after we were together awhile, I never blamed you, Pa. I got to know you too well. I got to know what was inside that heart of yours. I found out how much you loved Ma, how much you loved all of us and missed us . . . and how much you loved me. How could I blame you for anything, Pa, once I really knew who you were . . . once I knew how full of love you were?"

Pa was still gazing straight at me with those manly, loving, almost pleading eyes of his. But as I was speaking they had slowly filled with tears. His lips remained unmoved, but in those sparkling eyes I could see his relief.

We just stood, holding each other's gaze for a minute. Then finally Pa did smile, and as he did he took me in his arms, drew me to him, and embraced me with a strength that almost squeezed the breath out of me.

"Thank you, Corrie," he said, his voice just the slightest bit quivery.

"Yes, Pa," I whispered.

"I'm sorry for the pain you felt."

"It's long past now."

"Not for Zack," he said.

"For me it is, Pa. And you have to remember that I know you better than he does."

"It means more to me than you can know, Corrie, that you believe in me, and don't blame me. That means more to a man than his kin can ever realize."

We stood for another minute or two in each other's arms. "I love you, Pa," I said finally.

Just a moment more we stood; then Pa withdrew his hands from around me, pulled back, and looked at me, his blinking eyes drying again. He smiled broadly.

"Then let's you and me go find Zack!" he said.

# CHAPTER 27

## THE PONY EXPRESS

The idea for the Pony Express came from a businessman by the name of William Russell, who hoped that the government would pay his company—Russell, Majors, and Waddell—to have mail delivered speedily coast to coast. He proposed that they be paid one thousand dollars a week for two trips in both directions. The government never did pay for the service, and the costs involved turned out to be as high as ten to fifteen thousand dollars a week instead.

Before the Pony Express began in April of 1860, mail took twenty-five days to go from the East Coast to California—*if* the stagecoach didn't break a wheel, run into snow, or get attacked by Indians! Compared with how isolated California had been from the rest of the country in the early 1800s, even that was mighty fast. But when the organizers of the Pony Express said they would take mail between St. Joseph, Missouri, and Sacramento in ten days or less, everyone was amazed and wondered if such speed was possible.

Naturally, with Zack's fondness for horses, we had been curious and had followed the development of the idea with interest. Like all the papers, the *Alta* carried detailed stories about the first few mail crossings. Even in the midst of all the political news of 1860, some of the Pony Express riders became nationally known heroes. I read all the news articles that had been written for over a year now about it. Zack had sent off for some pamphlets too, and I had saved all the articles I'd read from different papers. So now with Pa and me planning to go find him, I pulled out everything I'd accumulated and read through it again.

Actually, the idea wasn't really Russell's at all, because there had been something like the Pony Express during the Roman Empire. And in the 1200s, Kublai Khan, the emperor of China, had a huge system of communication with stations stretching all the way from China to Europe, and with as many as four hundred fresh horses at every station, and thousands and thousands of messengers.

But for the United States the idea was new. And with mountains and deserts and Indians and bandits and no roads and no station houses, it was all a pretty big undertaking for Mr. Russell's company to get started. We had been reading about it in the papers for months before the horses actually began carrying mail.

There were to be eighty expert light riders riding between eighty relay stations, and making use of four to five hundred fast and hardy top-quality Indian horses. Forty of the riders would be stretched out in a line going east, the other forty in a line going west—all of them going back and forth both ways from their home base. It turned out later that there were two hundred riders in all—eighty in the saddle at all times, and the others resting between rides and replacements.

The mail would be carried by a leather cover that fit right over the saddle, called a *mochila*. There were four pouches on all four corners of the *mochila*, each of which had a lock on it. The keys were kept only in St. Joseph and Sacramento—the two end points of the Express—and at Salt Lake City in the middle.

From California, the route of the Express went to Placerville, up over the Sierra Nevadas and down into Carson City, Nevada. From there it went straight across the high desert of the Great Basin and over the awful salt flats to Salt Lake. That was the only real city along the way, and was about a third of the whole distance. From Salt Lake the riders went gradually north up into the Rockies, past Fort Bridger, through South Pass, and to Casper, Wyoming. Then they started south, to Fort Laramie, and down onto the plains of Nebraska, following the same routes as the Mormon Trail and the Oregon Trail, down to Fort Kearny, into northeastern Kansas and to St. Joseph. The whole distance from Sacramento was 1,966 miles.

So many eager young boys wanted to join the Pony Express right at first that they could have probably been hired cheaply. But Russell, Majors, and Waddell decided to pay them over a hundred dollars a month—high pay for anybody! As time went on, though, even that much money wasn't enough to keep some of them riding for the Express!

I don't know how God-fearing the owners of the company were, but they must have had some religious beliefs, because every rider that signed on, besides being given a lightweight rifle and a Colt revolver, was also given a Bible to carry with him. Riders also received the clothes that became the "uniform" of the Pony Express—a bright red shirt and blue dungarees. I never did understand, given as much trouble as they had with the Indians, why they made the riders dress so brightly!

Before he was hired, every rider had to sign a pledge that read:

> I do hereby swear, before the Great and Living God, that during my engagement, and while I am an employee of Russell, Majors, & Waddell, I will, under no circumstances, use profane language; that I will drink no intoxicating liquors; that I will not quarrel or fight with any other employee of the firm, and that in every respect I will conduct myself honestly, be faithful to my duties, and so direct all my acts as to win the confidence of my employers. So help me God.

At least if Zack had to leave home, I was glad it was to work for a company with high standards of morality like that. I just hoped all those who signed that pledge kept to their word and lived by it!

# CHAPTER 28

# PA AND I TAKE TO THE TRAIL

With the history it had and the reputation the Pony Express had already gained, when Pa and I left Sacramento it was almost as if we were following in the footsteps of George Washington. It seems odd to talk about California and the West as being part of history when everything was so new out here. But if the gold rush and the Pony Express didn't make us westerners part of history, nothing ever would.

A fellow named Sam Hamilton rode the first leg between Sacramento and Sportsman's Hall. The Express left Sacramento every Tuesday and Saturday. Since we had arrived late Monday, we stayed at Miss Baxter's and decided to leave at the same time. Pa was excited, and wanted to see how long we could keep pace with him.

But Sam was a skinny little fellow, and his horse not much bigger. To give them an advantage when trying to outrun Indians, each animal's load was limited to 165 pounds—20 pounds for the mail, 25 pounds for equipment, and 120 pounds for the rider. Zack must have lied about his weight, because I knew he weighed at least 130 or 140 pounds. But little Sam Hamilton might have been only 110!

When we took off down the street out of Sacramento, Hamilton was a block ahead of me and Pa before we'd gone a mile! He glanced back, lifted his hat in final greeting, gave us a shout of *Good Luck,* and gradually disappeared in a cloud of dust. Finally Pa pulled up his horse, turned around at me laughing, and said, "We gave it a gallant effort, Corrie! But there ain't no way we're gonna keep up with him for even two miles!"

"And if we keep running our horses like this," I yelled as we reined them down to a gentle canter, "they won't make it past Placerville!"

Already the dust cloud surrounding little Sam Hamilton was fading into the distance. I could hardly imagine that the mail pouch he was carrying would be in Missouri in ten days or less!

Pa and I slowed up and walked for about ten minutes, Pa breaking out in laughter every so often at how ridiculous it was for us to think we were going to keep up with the Express rider. Then we eased our two horses on into a trot. If we didn't move at a little bit of a pace, we would never get to Nevada.

We were obviously not going to make it to a station house every night, so we would spend some nights alone out on the trail. With Pa along, I felt as safe as if we had our own private detachment of Cavalry. There would not be any danger of Indian attack until well into Nevada, and we hoped by then to have had some word about Zack.

The weather proved better for us than it had been back in April for that first "Pony" run. It was beautiful climbing up high into the Sierras, although the trail was narrow and rocky in places, with huge cliffs on the edge falling away into deep gorges and canyons. I couldn't imagine how Warren Upson had made it through here at all in the snowy blizzard of that first run!

"Listen to this, Pa," I said as we sat around our campfire on our second night out. I had been reading an account of the first runs of the Express from some papers I'd brought along, keeping track of what had happened as we followed along the same route. "It was snowing here on that very first run."

"Hard to make their time in a blizzard."

"But they did it! Want me to read it to you?"

"Sure," said Pa, sipping his coffee. "I ain't going nowhere. Maybe I'll fall asleep with you reading to me!"

I began: *"Everything had been arranged on that first day for the two riders to leave St. Joseph and Sacramento at the same time, one heading east, the other heading west. . . ."*

I stopped for a second, then said, "I wonder what it was like when the two batches of mail passed each other. It must have been somewhere in Wyoming."

"Getting a little ahead of your story, ain't you?" said Pa.

"But don't you wonder if the riders stopped and chatted or if they just blew by each other with a shout and wave?"

"To tell you the truth, I never thought of it."

"How I wish I could have been there to watch it!"

"I'm gonna be sound asleep before you have that mail pouch out of Sacramento! Now you got my curiosity up—come on, read me the story, girl."

"Yes, Pa," I said with a smile. "First let me read you a short little notice out of the *Alta*."

My paper had been involved in the Pony Express right from the beginning, and we had been watching it closely all year, especially after Zack's leaving. But only the names of the most well-known riders were ever mentioned, so we had never seen anything about Zack. The April 3 edition of that year had an article on the festivities about the first rider leaving San Francisco, and that's what I read to Pa.

*"The first Pony Express started yesterday afternoon, from the Alta Telegraph Company on Montgomery Street. The saddlebags were duly lettered 'Overland Pony Express,' and the horse (a wiry little animal) was dressed with miniature flags. He proceeded, just before four o'clock, to the Sacramento boat, and was loudly cheered by the crowd as he started. . . . The express matter amounted to 85 letters, which at $5 per letter gave a total receipt of $425."*

"Didn't you tell me that first fellow wasn't even a Pony Express rider at all?" said Pa.

I laughed again. "He was just a messenger who worked at the paper," I answered.

James Randall told me later how much he'd wished he could go farther. But he only rode three blocks to the waterfront, and then got on the steamer for Sacramento with San Francisco's part of the mail. It was in Sacramento that the route of the Pony Express *really* started, despite Mr. Kemble's attempt to make San Francisco and the *Alta* seem like the most important parts of the whole thing!

"You ever gonna get back to that story you started out of the *Bee*?"

"I'm trying, Pa." I picked up the first paper again and finally read to Pa the whole article.

*"Sam Hamilton was the first rider out of Sacramento on April 3. He rode sixty miles to the station at Sportsman's Hall, where he handed off the mochila and leather pouches to Warren 'Boston' Upson, who had to cross the treacherous Sierra Nevadas. There had just been a fresh snowfall, and a new storm was on the way. The very first day out from Sacramento proved to be one of the most dangerous. Warren found himself in the middle of a blinding blizzard crossing over the mountains, having to walk his pony on foot part of the way, and many times nearly losing the trail. At last he made it safely to his station house at Friday's Station, right on the California border.*

*"Robert Haslam took over next, riding across the perilous Great Basin to Fort Churchill, Nevada. This was one of the worst parts of the whole route, with many mountain ranges, rivers which often disappeared into 'sinks' in the ground and were hard to follow, and broken canyons, rocky terrain, wild animals, rattlesnakes, a critical lack of water in summer, snow in winter, and Indians besides. The long distance across Nevada and Utah was the most hazardous of all."*

"Not much wonder why Zack found himself an opening there," Pa interrupted. Neither of us said it right then, but it also explained why we were so worried about him. Already, in the first five months of the Express, there had been numerous attacks reported, and several killings of station people. Some whole stations had been burned to the ground.

I put down the Sacramento paper to read the account from a Salt Lake City reporter who told about the midpoint of that first run. Many of the riders in Utah were Mormon boys who knew the difficult terrain in both directions out of Salt Lake City. Although this was not an exact halfway point, it was close enough to be considered the major intersection between eastbound and westbound mail. The first riders reached Salt Lake within two days of each other. The *Alta* later ran the article that had appeared in Salt Lake in the *Deseret News* on April 11.

The first Pony Express from the West left Sacramento at 12 P.M. on the night of the third inst., and arrived on the night of the seventh, inside of prospectus time. The roads were heavy, the weather stormy. The last seventy-five miles were made in five hours and fifteen minutes in a heavy rain.

The Express from the East left St. Joseph, Mo., at 6:30

P.M. on the evening of the third and arrived in this city at 6:25 P.M. on the evening of the ninth. The difference in time between this city and St. Joseph is something near one hour and fifteen minutes, bringing us within six days' communication with the frontier, and seven days from Washington—a result which we, accustomed to receive news three months after date, can well appreciate.

The weather has been very disagreeable and stormy for the past week and in every way calculated to retard the operation of the company, and we are informed that the Express eastward was five hours in going from this place to Snyder's Mill, a distance of twenty-five miles.

The probability is that the Express will be a little behind time in reaching Sacramento this trip, but when the weather becomes settled and the roads good, we have no doubt that they will be able to make the trip in less than ten days.

After putting down the *Alta* reprint, again I read from the *Bee* as Pa listened.

*"Up through the Rockies out of Salt Lake, then through South Pass, past the famous landmark Independence Rock, and across the Platte River to Fort Laramie. This is the major stop where riders could feel a sense of civilization again. Fort Laramie is one of the major trading posts and army headquarters of the Rockies region, where trappers, Indians, emigrants, and travelers all mix with one another.*

*"From Fort Laramie down to the Cottonwood Springs station and into Nebraska, the riders regularly pass stagecoaches and wagon trains, as their route follows already well-worn paths. Through woodlands gradually descending down into the plains and across buffalo and antelope country, riders are again likely to encounter Indian lodges or tepee villages, until they arrive at Fort Kearny in Nebraska, which was originally built to protect travelers along the Oregon Trail.*

*"Across Nebraska and Kansas at this time of year, the trail is heavy with wagon trains. The Kickapoo Indians of Kansas are mostly peaceful and friendly farmers who had learned to get on very well with the white man, and thus gave the Pony Express Riders no trouble. And across the Missouri River from Kansas lay the final destination of the eastbound rider—St. Joseph!*

*"The first two runs arrived at their respective destinations at almost*

*the same time. From St. Joseph to Sacramento it had taken nine days and twenty-three hours—one hour ahead of schedule. The eastbound trip had taken one hour longer—exactly ten days!"*

I laid down the paper. If Pa wasn't asleep yet, he would be soon. It was dark and the fire was getting a little low. Everything was quiet except for the night sounds—mostly crickets. I put a couple more pieces of wood on the fire and watched them spark and flare up. Then I settled down into my bedroll, watching the flames but reflecting back on that day when the first Pony Express rider from Missouri had reached Sacramento and then gone on to San Francisco.

What a celebration there had been that April 13! I wish we could have been there, but we heard about it as if we had been. Both the Senate and the Assembly of the legislature adjourned and the whole city turned out to welcome Sam Hamilton, returning from Sportsman's Hall, where he had been waiting for Warren Upson to return with the eastbound pouches. Sam was given a hero's welcome as he hurried to the steamer to take the mail on downriver to San Francisco. He didn't arrive there until the middle of the night, but that didn't stop the torchlight celebration, band music, fire engines, cheering, booming of cannons, and speechmaking, including one from my editor, Mr. Kemble! The people of San Francisco rejoiced, for it seemed that their isolation from the rest of the world was over.

It was a significant year for the Pony Express, with so much news going on between North and South, and over the election. The news that was carried back and forth between East and West was now less than a week and a half old, instead of nearly a month old! The news people were most excited of all. An article in the *Sacramento Union* read:

> Yesterday's proceedings, impromptu though they were, will long be remembered in Sacramento. The more earnest part of the "Pony" welcome had been arranged earlier in the day. This was the cavalcade of citizens to meet the little traveler a short distance from the city and escort him into town. Accordingly, late in the day, a deputation of about eighty persons, together with a deputation of the Sacramento Hussars, assembled at the old Fort, and stretched out their lines on

either side along the road along which the Express was to come.

Meanwhile, the excitement had increased all over the city. The balconies of the stores were occupied by ladies, and the roofs and sheds were taken possession of by the more agile of the opposite sex, straining to catch a glimpse of the "Pony."

At length—5:45—all this preparation was rewarded. First a cloud of rolling dust in the direction of the Fort, then a horseman, bearing a small flag, riding furiously down J Street, and then a straggling charging band of horsemen flying after him, heralding the coming of the Express; a cannon, placed on the square at Tenth Street, sent forth its noisy welcome. Amidst the firing and shouting, and waving of hats and ladies' handkerchiefs, the pony was seen coming down J Street, surrounded by about thirty of the citizen deputation. Out of this confusion emerged the Pony Express, trotting up to the door of the agency and depositing its mail in ten days from St. Joseph to Sacramento. Hip, hip, hurrah for the Pony Carrier!

# CHAPTER 29

## TAVISH

Zack had said he would be riding somewhere between Nevada and Utah. As Pa and I rode along over the next couple of days, we hoped we would find him before we got too far. From Sacramento to Salt Lake was about six-hundred eighty miles!

The first ad I had seen for hiring Express riders was in the *Alta* earlier that year. It read: WANTED—young, skinny, wiry fellows, not over 18. Must be expert riders, willing to risk death daily. Orphans preferred. Wages $25 a week.

Zack must have lied about his age too. I heard about one Express rider named David Jay who was only thirteen, and another named William Cody who was fifteen. I don't know why they wanted them so young. A boy that age wouldn't know how to take care of himself if his horse broke a leg or if he got captured by Indians. Of course, they didn't want them to do anything but ride, and eventually they replaced the rifle with a knife. They weren't supposed to stop to fight the Indians who chased them— only outrun them! Maybe they wanted boys who had no family and who were so young that when they got killed, no one would miss them too much.

I suppose for that much pay, a lot of boys would love the adventure of the Pony Express. A hundred dollars a month *plus* board and keep was a lot of money!

They earned it, though. They rode all day and all night, changing horses every twenty or twenty-five miles over the most desolate stretches, every ten miles where it was more civilized. The places where they just changed horses were called swing stations. Each rider would ride three or four or even five horses, and then would stop at a station house where another rider would take over. Most of the time they rode seventy-five miles, usually on three horses. That took them seven or eight hours, and by that time they were ready to stop for food and sleep.

We got to Friday's Station at the Nevada border, and then down into the Carson valley of western Nevada. At the next station house, we met "Pony Bob" Haslam. Even though he was hardly more than a boy, he was already a legend from all the adventures and narrow escapes he had riding across Nevada. We spent the night there with the station keeper. Pony Bob was expected the next day in from the east, and the man kept us up half the night telling us of Bob's exploits over the last five months. When we told him we were looking for Zack Hollister, a shadow passed over his face.

"You know Zack?" Pa asked.

"Heard of him. Don't know him, though," the man replied.

"Why did you frown when I said his name?"

"On account of where I last heard he was riding."

"Where's that?" said Pa with concern.

"Nevada-Utah border. It's hot enough to be hell over there this time of year, Mister," the man said. "And the Paiutes is nasty as ever. Can't see as how I could let you and your daughter go over there and be able to live with myself later."

"I gotta see my son," said Pa.

"You stand a better chance of seeing him if you just wait for him to come home than for the two of you to head out across the Basin."

"Surely they wouldn't hurt two people just passing through," I said.

"Look, Miss," the man said, squinting his eyes at me. "Them Paiutes has been on the warpath since last May. There's over eight thousand of them. They got guns. They'll kill anybody, no matter whether they're innocent or not. They been attacking all over Nevada. We've lost half dozen stations. I tell you, the two of you'd be dead before you was two days out."

I looked over at Pa, my eyes wide. I didn't like the sound of this!

For the next half hour or so Pa and the stationman talked about the Express and the Indians. I think the man was as anxious to have somebody to talk to as he was interested in convincing us not to go any farther into Nevada. Living out there mostly alone like they did, the two or three men at the station houses got tired of each other mighty quick and were plenty happy to see visitors— especially out in the middle of nowhere like in Nevada!

Pa later said to me that this particular fellow had talked so much because I was a pretty young lady and he was trying to impress me with every tall tale he could think up to tell. I told Pa I didn't believe a word of it, but he insisted he wasn't pulling my leg. The truth of it is that the man did have tales to tell that made my blood shiver right inside me.

Pa even told him I was a newspaper writer and that he ought to be careful what he said or it might find its way into print some- day. The man looked at me kinda funny, probably not believing Pa any more than Pa said *he* believed half his wild stories. But in any case, the man grew even more talkative after that.

"I tell you, Mister," he said after pouring each of us a cup of coffee, "if I was you, I'd turn straight around and head back the way you come. Word is them blamed Paiutes is headed this di- rection again."

"Again?" said Pa.

"Yep. They was all over here three, four months back. Major Ormsby took over a hundred men from Carson City and went out after them and was beaten back so bad they had to retreat to the city. Three weeks we was without the Express at all."

"What happened?"

"Finally the army got them back up into the mountains, helped by a snowstorm—in the middle of June, if you can believe that, little lady!" he added, turning toward me with a chuckle. "Since then it ain't been too bad at this end. But they keep raiding to the east, and like I told you, word is they been heading back this way."

I took a sip of the coffee out of the tin cup the man had handed me. I couldn't keep from wincing. It was the bitterest, foulest stuff I had ever tasted! He must've crushed the beans with a hammer and then soaked them in water for a week, then boiled the water and called it coffee! I didn't care much for coffee anyway, but that thick, black syrup was awful. Pa was a regular coffee drinker, and I saw even him grimace slightly with his first drink. But he took a big gulp, swallowed it down bravely, and even had a second cup when the man offered it a little while later.

"Yeah, it's a wonder they keep any riders between Carson and Salt Lake," the man was saying. "Most of the originals have quit or been wounded or injured by this time anyway. But they keep on finding adventure-crazy young fools who'll hire on—meaning no offense to your son, Mister—but it takes a special breed of young rapscallion to put up with the dangers those boys face every day and every night out alone on the trail."

"Zack's a good rider," said Pa. "Maybe that'll keep him outta the way of—"

"They're *all* good riders, Mister!" interrupted the man. "Them that ain't—why, they'd be dead inside o' two or three days. They don't ride for the Express unless they're the best riders this side of the Ohio valley. It ain't good riding that keeps 'em alive in this foolhardy business."

"What is it?" I asked.

"It's pluck, little lady. It's determination, it's courage, it's guts, it's bravado. It's being able to look death in the face and not blink. You ever heard of Nick Wilson?" he asked, looking back toward Pa.

Pa shook his head.

"The blamed fool had a will to live beyond what any mortal oughta have to have. They left him for dead a couple of times, but he lived to tell what happened. Takes a lot of that too—a will to live."

He looked at us, almost as if baiting us to *ask* what happened before he would continue.

"We're listening," said Pa finally, taking another sip of the horrid coffee.

"Young Nick got to the relay station at Spring Valley, but there weren't nobody there. No sign of the keeper. Everything looked in order. No sign of attack. The relay horses were grazing near the cabins. So Nick, he didn't waste no time asking questions— he just jumped off his mount and started to saddle himself up a new horse.

"All of a sudden if he didn't hear a dreadful screaming whooping war cry that's the fear of every Express rider. He pulled out his Colt and started firing at the Indians that was heading toward the corral to steal the rest of the horses. The blamed fool took off chasing them to try to scare them away! But just then, from behind a tree close by, another redskin drew aim at Nick and sent a stone-tipped arrow right at him. Nick never saw him till it was too late. The arrow hit him above his left eye, and the arrowhead went right into his skull, halfway into his head. And there Nick fell and lay, right there among the trees.

"The Indians made off with all the horses, and figured they'd killed the young kid. But two men happened along a few hours later, found him, and saw that he was still alive. They tried to get the arrow out, but couldn't. All they managed to do was loosen the shaft from the stone tip, but there the arrowhead stuck, tight as ever. Weren't nothing much they could do, so they dragged him into the shade, then rode off to the next relay station to tell somebody they had a dead rider and an untended station.

"The next morning, two men came back from the station, figuring to bury the dead rider they'd been told about. Blamed if they didn't find Nick lying there, still breathing faintly! They didn't figure he'd survive the trip, but they hoisted him up across a saddle and carried him back with them to the Ruby Valley station.

"But that kid had no hankering to die just yet. He stayed alive long enough for them to get a doctor to him. He cut out the arrowhead and bandaged up the gashing wound as best he could. He hadn't woke up since the arrow slammed into his head, and no one could figure why he kept breathing! But he did, and after a few more days he woke up and looked around and asked what all the fuss was about. I ain't lying to you, Mister, when I tell you that Nick was up and riding his stretch o' the Express line in less than two months!"

"What about his wound?" I couldn't help asking.

"Yeah, well, it weren't none too pretty, and that's a fact. Ol' Nick, he don't see too good outta that eye, and he still keeps a patch over it to hide the ugly hole. But blamed if he can't still ride with the best of 'em!"

Pa took in a deep breath, no doubt thinking of Zack. But the man hardly gave us a chance to get our wits back together before he was off again.

"Pony Bob, though," he said. "He's my favorite o' the riders. Why, that young fool, he don't know the meaning of the word fear. And he don't know the meaning of tired, neither! He's saved more lives than his own, and ridden more than his share of dangerous miles. You recollect what I was telling you about pluck, little lady?" he asked, looking at me.

I nodded.

"Well, Pony Bob's made of the stuff, I can tell ya that! Why, one time he was riding along lickety-split, and rounding a bend suddenly found himself squared off face-to-face with a war party of thirty mean, blood-thirsty Paiutes! He reined in his pony, sat there a minute, this one young kid staring back at an ambush from one of the most savage tribes west of the Sioux. I tell ya, them Paiutes has killed and massacred and burned to death more settlers and workers for the Express than all the other tribes put together!

"After sitting there a spell, that young rascal just drew out his revolver, and then just ever so slowly urged his pony on. He just stared straight back into their faces, walked right up to 'em, gun held out just beside him. And without a word being said, them Indians watched him ride right through their midst and just keep going.

"Now *that's* guts!" he said, laughing and showing what teeth he had left. "Them redskins was probably so surprised that he'd challenge them right to their faces like that, they couldn't help admiring him!"

The station tender himself was almost as good a subject for an article as anything he was telling us. His name was Claude Tavish, which he only told us after Pa asked him. He had broad shoulders and big, muscular arms, which was probably a good thing for all the work he had to do around the place—building and repairing things, blacksmithing, fixing meals for the riders, and tending their horses and getting them saddled and ready. He said he had a helper who came out the four days a week when the riders came through in both directions.

Mr. Tavish had probably been a blacksmith before, and that's how he got so strong. But now he was starting to get a little fat. His hair was getting thin, too, and gray around the edges. He didn't look as if he worried too much about what he looked like. His face had four or five days' worth of beard stubble on it, and the graying whiskers stood out on the brown face. He had a pleasant enough expression, and a nice smile except for the two or three missing teeth. But he seemed tired, from more than just the work—almost as if life itself was exhausting him.

If we could have gotten him to stop talking so much about all the Express riders he knew, I would have liked to ask him about his *own* life. I had the feeling that behind all the tales he was telling us was probably a sad story of his own—maybe a family dead, or left behind. I couldn't help but wonder why he was out here like this, all by himself in a dangerous job, at his age. It was plain he liked people by the way he wanted to visit with us. But here he was miles from anybody. He reminded me a little of how Alkali Jones might have been at fifty, but without the same gleam in his eye. His eyes did sparkle some when he was talking, but behind the sparkle was a look that made me suspect there was pain somewhere back in his past.

All the time I'd been observing *him*, he had been talking about Bob Haslam. "Fortitude, that's what he's got—enough for a dozen riders! Why, during the Paiute War, he started off his ride one day with a seventy-five-mile stretch to the Reese River Station. That's all a rider's suppose to have to do in a day, but on account of the Indian trouble, there weren't nobody to hand the mail off to, and all the horses had been requisitioned by the army to fight back the Indians. So Pony Bob, he just kept on riding, hoping for better luck fifteen miles away at Buckland's. But there his replacement refused to ride from fear of all the war parties out on the loose.

"Pony Bob had already been riding some nine or ten hours, but there wasn't no one else to carry the mail. So with a fresh horse, he took off again, an' had to pass through three more stations without finding another rider to replace him. He'd ridden 190 miles almost continuously!

"An' what should be the news awaiting him? Only that the rider from the other direction had been badly hurt in a fall. Pony

Bob got himself an hour and a half of sleep before they woke him up to make the return trip. Off he rode again, only to get to the first station that he had left several hours before to find all five of the crew murdered by Indians and all the horses stolen. He kept right on, all the way to Buckland's, where he slept nine hours, waiting for nightfall when there would be less danger from Indians. Then he continued on through the night, outrunning a party of Paiutes who spotted him once, and finally arriving back here after 380 miles!

"I tell ya, I was glad to see the lad! I made him the finest meal I knew how to make, and put him to bed and told him to sleep for a week! He'd only lost four hours from the scheduled time after riding practically four days on ten hours sleep! Quite a kid! The company gave him a special hundred-dollar prize after that."

"Sounds like he's a fellow you oughta talk to and write an article about, Corrie!" said Pa.

"You'll meet him in the morning!" said Mr. Tavish. "He's due in sometime afore noon."

"How long will he be here?" I asked.

"Day or two. If there ain't no Indian trouble, he'll ride out east again day after tomorrow evening."

"Might there be Indian trouble . . . this close to California?" I asked, growing nervous again.

"There's been reports of Paiutes scouting this way. But don't you worry none about Pony Bob. He can outrun anyone. Why, there was another time when he rode into the Dry Creek Station and found the whole staff murdered. He kept going to Cold Springs, and the station was burned down and the dead body of the station keeper lying in the ashes."

As he spoke, Mr. Tavish stopped momentarily and drew in a deep breath. "Funny how fate works, ain't it?" he said reflectively. "When I first was hired by the Express, I worked the Cold Springs Station, but then I got transferred here. Otherwise, that woulda been me laying there with a Paiute arrow sticking out of my chest."

He paused again. "But ol' Bob, he kept on riding. Wasn't nothing much else he could do, I don't reckon. When he came to Sand Creek, he told the station tender all he'd seen and managed to get him to leave with him. That night the Sand Creek Station was burned down, too.

"Those were a bad couple of months back the early part of the summer! It's better now, but there ain't no one I'd rather was coming our way than Pony Bob. If there is trouble, he'll know of it and be far enough ahead of 'em to warn us."

He stopped again, and the station room was quiet for a minute or two. I looked around and began noticing all the stuff hanging up and sitting on shelves or in crates everywhere. The floor was dirt. Several bunks were built right into the far wall, and besides the bench Pa and I were sitting on, there wasn't much else in the way of furniture. Just a table, one chair, and empty crates turned up on end for people to sit on. There was a big wood stove for cooking with shelves full of supplies—flour, sugar, coffee, corn-meal, hams and bacon, containers of dried fruit and meat, tea, coffee, beans. All around the rest of the room were scattered an assortment of other things they might need—tools, brooms, candles, blankets, buckets, medicines, borax, tin dishes, turpentine, castor oil, rubbing alcohol, even sewing supplies. The alcohol was only for treating wounds or injuries. No drinking of any liquor was allowed at any of the Pony Express stations. Of course, there were lots of guns and rifles and ammunition around too.

Outside there were a couple of other buildings—a blacksmith-ing forge, a stable and barn. They had to have everything on hand that might possibly be needed for any situation—Indian attack, lame horses, broken legs, loose shoes, wounds, injury. At most of the Nevada stations, the ground was so dry that there was no grass for animals to graze on, so they had to have a large supply of oats and other feed on hand, too.

"Where'd you say your boy was at?" Mr. Tavish asked Pa.

"Not sure. Far as we know, out toward Utah."

Mr. Tavish gave a low whistle. "That ain't good, Mister. He musta come in after the Indian troubles quieted down. They brought in lots of new kids in July to replace the ones that left. When'd he join up?"

"Early July. He said he'd heard there was openings out toward eastern Nevada."

"Openings is right!" laughed Mr. Tavish. "The whole blame line from Carson to Salt Lake was open! Weren't hardly nobody left."

The look on Pa's face was not a happy one. My heart sank just to hear the stationman's words.

"Well, can't be helped now," he went on. "If your boy's alive, he's alive. If he's dead, I'd probably have heard about it. So we'll wait on Bob tomorrow and see if he knows anything. One thing's for sure, Mister, you ain't gonna take the little lady here no further east than right here. If you was fool enough to go by yourself, there wouldn't be much I could do to stop you, though I wouldn't give a plugged nickel for your chances out there alone. But with a young lady—nope, I just wouldn't let you go another mile past here."

Pa and I looked at each other. I guess this is where we'd be spending the night!

"You ever heard of Billy Cody?" Mr. Tavish asked.

"Nope," Pa answered. I nodded my head that I had.

"What'd you hear about him?" asked Mr. Tavish.

"Only that he wasn't much older than a boy," I said.

"Cody's just like Pony Bob! Guts of a man inside the body of a kid. I hope your brother's like that . . . for his sake. Otherwise, even if he is still alive, he ain't likely to stay that way for long. But let me tell you about Cody," he went on.

"They gave him an extra bit of mail one time, a box of money that had to get through. Now the Indians, they'll attack anybody or anything just to be ornery. But the bandits and thieves with white skin, they're more particular. They're after loot. Well, I tell you what happened—there'd been reports of a couple outlaws in the region where Cody was riding. And with him having to carry cash money, it was a dangerous situation. So Cody, he hid his *mochila* and mail cases under an extra leather blanket. Then he filled a couple of extra pouches with paper so that if he was held up, the robbers would think they had the real thing.

"Well, sure enough, blamed if Cody didn't get stopped as he was riding through a narrow ravine. The two bandits had guns on him and told him to get off his horse and put his hands in the air. He obeyed. One of the men rode closer, put away his gun, and reached out to grab the fake mail pouches from Cody's horse. But instead of waiting for them to take it and hope they'd leave without discovering them to be worthless, Billy suddenly flung the whole blanket up in the man's face, drawing his gun at the same instant, and shot the thief. The other man fled. Billy jumped on his horse and took off after him."

Mr. Tavish stopped in his story long enough to give a great laugh.

"That's the kind of kids out riding this part of the Express territory," he said. "Kids that can send grown men to flight! Yes sir, I hope the young fella you're looking for can take care of himself like that!"

I shuddered. Just the thought of Zack having to shoot at or possibly even kill someone was enough to turn my stomach. I could hardly stand the thought that he was mixed up in such a violent thing as the Pony Express seemed to be.

I knew Pa was thinking the same thing. He and Uncle Nick had run with a much rougher crowd, and had fought in the Mexican War. But I suppose it seemed different to Pa, thinking about his own son. Things he went through himself, he didn't want his kids to have to face. And however young Bill Cody and Pony Bob and all the rest of them were, to me and Pa, Zack still seemed too young to be part of all this.

# CHAPTER 30

## THE FRIGHT OF MY LIFE!

The rest of that night we listened to more of Claude Tavish's stories, although by the time supper was over, Pa'd managed to get him talking about something besides the Pony Express. It turned out Mr. Tavish had fought in the Mexican War too, and that kept him and Pa busy till late talking about their recollections. At least it took our minds off worrying about Zack.

I mixed up some biscuits to go with beans and a ham hock Mr. Tavish had boiling on top of the stove. He raved and raved about those biscuits, even though there wasn't anything to them that he couldn't have done himself. He didn't have any baking powder to mix in, so they were flat and hard. But he kept saying he hadn't eaten anything so good in years. "Anything tastes better if a woman's hand's gone into the making of it," he said. "A man and woman can put all the same ingredients in a bowl, and mix it up, and cook it just the same, and feed whatever it is to a passel of hungry miners or cowboys or anybody else. They'll all cuss and complain at the man for his lousy grub, but they'll rave and carry on at how wonderful the lady's food tastes. I always figured they weren't treating me none too fairly, but after tasting them biscuits of your's, little lady, I reckon I know what they been getting at all these years. There just ain't no denying that a woman's hand's got something special in it."

"They taste about the same as always to me," I said. "But thank you all the same, Mr. Tavish."

I listened with interest to the two men talk, because now every story that came out gave me new glimpses into Pa's past during those years before we were together again.

"Where was you at?" Pa had asked Mr. Tavish.

"Buena Vista, where else!" answered the stationman.

"You *were* at the center of it all," said Pa. "Me and Nick never got that close to Santa Anna."

"Lucky for you! He was a mean cuss—came at us with 15,000 men. But he hadn't counted on Zachary Taylor! No sir. Us with our 5,000 just waited in the mountains for them to attack. Dreadful night, I can tell you—wind, rain, hardly no sleep. But it must have been worse for them Mexicans, because the next day we sent 'em running!"

"Tell me," asked Pa. "What did the men think of President Polk?"

"I don't know, what's to think? He was president and we was following orders," answered Tavish.

"Did they think the war was a good one? What about slavery?"

"What about it?"

"Did you talk about how what you were really fighting for was to have more slave states in the country?"

"Tarnation, no! We were just fighting the Mexicans. We didn't know what it was about. Why, did you fellers in California talk about all that?"

"No," said Pa thoughtfully. "Back then I didn't know what it was about any more than you did. I was just curious, that's all."

When we went to bed that night, I lay in my bedroll on one of those hard wooden bunks. I couldn't get right to sleep, and as I listened to Pa and Mr. Tavish snoring, all his stories about the Indians came back into my mind. I should have been more concerned for Zack, but instead I grew more and more terrified for myself! I remembered his words about how savage the Paiutes were, and how they were headed our way, and how many people they'd killed.

Then I started to realize how far out in the middle of the desert we were—twenty or twenty-five miles past Carson City—and how we were all alone. Pretty soon every little noise I heard made me jump, and I started imagining that the place was surrounded by fifty or a hundred Indians, sneaking up on us quietly in the night, to kill us!

In the distance a wolf's cry rang out. I practically jumped out of my skin! My heart was racing, and I couldn't imagine how Pa and Mr. Tavish could just sleep so calmly through it all. All sorts of little noises I hadn't noticed before seemed to be coming out of the night—creaks and groans from the cabin, an occasional whistle of wind through a crack, now and then a bird or other animal, a sound from the stables, the bark of a wild dog, and always the howl of the wolves far off in the mountains.

I had been out on the trail alone many times, but never had I been so scared as I was tonight.

Never had the morning sunshine looked so good! The wind had died down and whatever the spooky noises had been during the night, they had gone away too. The place was calm and cheery; even Mr. Tavish looked more chipper as a result of his company and the discovery of a comrade from the days before the gold rush and California's statehood. The dull, sad look in his eyes had given way to something almost like enthusiasm.

"Well, little lady, what's you and me gonna rustle up for breakfast?" he greeted me warmly. "Flapjacks?"

"We need eggs for that," I said. "And milk."

"We got no milk, but I just may be able to lay my hands on two or three eggs," he said with a wink, "*if* my hens have been the good girls they oughta have been during the night. You just wait here, and I'll go check the coop."

He disappeared outside, and returned in about three minutes, face beaming, with two brand-new eggs in each hand.

"We'll make us up the finest batch of flapjacks this side of the gold diggin's!" he announced, and immediately began taking down pans and dumping flour into a bowl. I don't know what he needed me for!

"Here, little lady," he called out after a minute. "You take over here. We want 'em to have that female touch. I gotta go draw us some water. You get 'em cooking on the griddle there. You'll find syrup and grease up there on the shelf to the right. While we're at it, what say we fry us up some bacon to go with 'em?"

I nodded and smiled my agreement. Mr. Tavish left the cabin just as Pa came back in.

"What's Tavish so all-fired beaming about?" asked Pa with a grin.

"I don't know, Pa. Talking about the war last night seemed to perk him up."

"And the presence of a young lady on the premises might have had something to do with it!" added Pa.

Whatever it was, when the stationmaster returned ten minutes later, not a speck of gray stubble was left on his clean-shaven face. He also put on a new clean shirt for breakfast. In the meantime, his young helper, a Mexican boy named Juan who lived a few miles away, had come to help him prepare for Pony Bob's arrival. By then I had a good stack of pancakes ready, with several more on the griddle. Mr. Tavish rang his bell, and the four of us gathered around the table while he offered a simple prayer of thanks. Pa and I sat down on the bench. Juan pulled up one of the crates, and Mr. Tavish took over at the stove to watch the flapjacks and the last of the sizzling bacon. He wouldn't hear of me doing any more now. I was his guest, he said.

We had barely started eating when the sounds of galloping horses caught our attention. Mr. Tavish's smile faded. There were too many horses for it to be a Pony rider!

He threw down the metal spatula with a clang onto the stove and ran to the door. He opened it for a second, then slammed it shut with a thud and pulled the iron bolt down across it.

"Indians!" he cried. "Juan . . . get the rifles and ammo!"

Even before anyone had the chance to ask him if he was serious, one of the two windows of the cabin shattered, its glass tinkling down the wall onto the dirt floor. At almost the same instant, an arrow slammed into the opposite wall.

Mr. Tavish ran to it, yanked it out of the timber, examined it for a second, then swore under his breath. "Paiutes!" The despair in his voice filled me with a dread such as I had never felt before, and hope I never ever feel again in my life!

I looked around for Pa, but there was only time enough for our eyes to meet briefly. In that second, a multitude of unspoken thoughts passed between our hearts. But there was no time even for a word, for the next instant Juan was shoving a rifle into my hand, and Mr. Tavish was showing Pa where to crouch down behind one of the windows. I took the gun without even thinking, and before I knew it I was huddled down a little ways from Pa.

Things happened so fast there was no time for me to stop and realize, *I don't want to kill anyone . . . even an Indian!*

I don't know how much time passed. It could have been an hour. It could have been five minutes for all I know. There was a lot of gunfire, both inside and outside the cabin, and several more arrows flew through the windows, both of which were broken. After one of them, I heard Pa shout, "Corrie, you keep your head down, you hear!" His voice held such a fearful yet commanding authority, I didn't dare crane my neck up any more to try to see what was going on. I'd never heard such a sound in his voice before!

The Indians must have had guns too, because there were far too many gunshots to be coming from just the three guns inside. The rifle I still held in my hand was silent!

"Use that carbine, little lady!" Mr. Tavish called out at me, but I didn't have words to answer him. I just kept lying there on the floor, trying to stay out of the way. Pa was shooting out the window at the attackers. It all seemed completely natural at the time. Only later did I realize that he was trying to *kill* someone with that gun he was firing.

"I was praying to God the whole time," he told me later, "that I *wouldn't* have to kill no one. But when his family's in danger, a man does things he might not do otherwise. And if I had to kill to keep them Indians away from you, Corrie, I would have done it and asked God if it was right or wrong later. I'd have done just about anything to keep their savage hands off you, including getting myself killed trying."

In the meantime, it seemed as if we were all going to be killed!

*Thwaack!* An arrow flew through the window above my head, coming at a low angle, and stuck into the adjacent wall next to me only about five feet away. Pa glanced over at it. His face was white, and he was sweating.

"I got me one . . . I got one!" shouted Juan.

"Keep down, you little fool!" yelled Tavish, who was crouched down reloading his rifle. "Just because you shoot one Indian don't give you no reason to stick your head up like that and give 'em an easy target. When you've picked off fifteen or twenty, then you can shout about it!"

His rifle reloaded, Mr. Tavish turned back to the window, one knee bent to the ground, raised the gun to his shoulder, squinted his eye along the barrel, and started firing rapidly again at our attackers, his gun resting on the bottom ledge where broken glass was strewn about.

He only got off a couple more shots; then all of a sudden Mr. Tavish screamed out in pain. I looked over just in time to see him falling backward to the floor, an arrow sticking out of his shoulder.

The gunfire in the cabin ceased. Juan and Pa looked at each other as if wondering what to do now. The next instant, however, Juan was firing from his vantage point with renewed vengeance.

"Corrie, get over and see what you can do for him!" yelled Pa.

"What do I do, Pa?"

"I don't know. See how bad it is. Get a towel or something and keep it from bleeding!"

Pa turned back to the window and started shooting again. I crept over to where Mr. Tavish lay. His shirt was torn and red, and the warm blood was dripping down and soaking into the dirt. His face was white, but he managed to give me a thin smile.

"I'm sorry, little lady," he whispered. "I didn't mean to get you mixed up in nothin' like this."

"How is . . . is it bad?" I asked.

"I'll live. Them Paiutes ain't gonna get rid of Tavish so easy, but—" He winced in pain. "Blame if it don't hurt somethin' fierce, though!"

"What should I do?" I asked. Thinking back, I realize that I didn't hear any more gunfire after that. For the next two or three minutes, the whole world centered around me and Claude Tavish. "Should I try to . . . to get the arrow out?" I asked, shuddering involuntarily even as I said the words.

"I don't know if you can," he answered, closing his eyes and breathing in a slow deep breath as if preparing himself for the ordeal. "But the thing's gotta come out."

"What should I do?"

"Look in there and see how far it's stuck in. If it didn't get all twisted or lodged against a bone, you oughta be able to yank it straight out."

I bent over a little closer, trying to see.

"Get in there with your fingers, little lady! A little blood ain't gonna hurt you. Ain't no way you're gonna find how deep it's gone unless you get in there and wipe some of the blood away and see where the tip is."

I leaned closer toward him, but I couldn't see a thing. His shirt was all red and the wooden shaft of the arrow disappeared inside it. I reached out and gingerly touched the arrow right where it went into his shirt, but the same instant pulled my hand back.

"Get in there, little lady!" This time Mr. Tavish's words were a command. "You want me to bleed to death? Get in there, and if the arrowhead ain't all the way inside, then you give it a good hard pull!"

Again I probed with my fingers, tearing at the hole in his shirt to make it bigger. There was so much blood I still couldn't see. I didn't even stop to think what I was doing at the time, but later from seeing the blood all over me, I realized that I grabbed the hem of my dress as I crouched there beside him and used it to wipe away some of the blood so that I could see the wound better.

Less than a minute had gone by since he'd fallen. The blood was still warm and wet and oozing from his shoulder. I tore a bigger hole in his shirt and wiped back the blood as best I could. Then I felt all around the arrow with my fingers. The sensation of feeling his wet bloody flesh, with the arrow sticking out, was too horrible to describe. I turned away, my stomach retching. I gagged two or three times, but luckily didn't throw up. I turned back to him, took a deep breath, gritted my teeth and lips together to keep my stomach down where it belonged, and tried to examine the wound again.

I felt all about. My hands were all bloody by this time, but by now I was determined to get the arrow out. I could feel the jagged hole the rough arrowhead had made. I forced my fingers to move around it, feeling at the base of the arrow. Down low, just at the skin line, I could feel the top end of the stone arrowhead. Feeling that hard piece of stone inside his soft flesh made me gag again.

"Is the head exposed?" asked Mr. Tavish.

"It's right at the edge of your shoulder," I said.

"It ain't all covered up?"

"No, I can feel the top of it."

"Good. You pull it out."

I shuddered again, clenched my teeth, and grabbed hold of the arrow with both hands and pulled.

My hands just slid up the shaft, but it remained as tightly lodged in Mr. Tavish's shoulder as ever.

"Blood's as slippery as grease!" he said. "Wipe off your hands first."

I grabbed at the end of my dress again, wiped off my hands as best I could, then wiped off the shaft of the arrow, trying to clean if off right down to the wound.

I clutched at it again, down low right on his skin. This time I could feel my dried hands take hold against the wood. I closed my eyes, then yanked upward for all I was worth.

Mr. Tavish let out a horrible yell, rising up off the ground as I pulled, then falling back down again. The sound of his voice made me let go. When I looked back down at his face, he was breathing rapidly in obvious pain. But the arrow was still stuck in his shoulder!

"Good girl," he whispered, though his eyes were closed. "One more time and we'll have it."

I swallowed hard, then grabbed the arrow again. This time I determined I wasn't going to let go. I pulled again, but this time when I felt the resistance of the arrow sticking into him, I held on all the tighter and gave one mighty tug.

I fell backward, the arrow in my hand.

This time Mr. Tavish hadn't screamed out, although I had felt his body rise up again as I yanked. He was lying on the floor, his eyes still closed, breathing rapidly. I can't even imagine how painful it must have been for him. I don't know why he didn't just faint from the agony of it.

"Now go over to the cupboard behind the stove," he said, still in a faint, quiet voice. "Behind the black pot there's a bottle of whiskey. You go get it . . . but keep your head down."

He must have sensed me hesitate, because I saw his eyes open a crack.

"There's alcohol there on the shelf," I said.

He forced a smile. "Don't want alcohol," he said. "I want whiskey."

Still I hesitated.

"I know . . . I know, little lady," he said. "But them rules is to keep the kids in line and not for the likes of old fellers like me. You won't tell Mr. Russell, will you? Besides, I only keep it for medicinal purposes."

I got to my feet and ran over to the cupboard. The bottle of whiskey was right where he said it was. He must have had a number of wounds to treat recently, because the bottle was less than half full. I took it back to him and pulled out the cork.

Without a moment's hesitation, Mr. Tavish reached out with his uninjured hand, took the bottle from me, and took a long swig that used up half the remaining contents in one huge swallow. Then he handed it back to me.

"Pour it into the wound," he said. "You gotta get it right in the hole, or I'll die of gangrene before the month's out!"

I put the mouth of the bottle to the hole in his shoulder and poured it in. His face twisted up in an awful look of pain. He sucked in a wincing breath through his clenched teeth, his eyes shut tight. He held his breath for what seemed like a long time, then slowly let it out in a long sigh as his body relaxed.

"Once more, Corrie," he whispered. "Pour it in again."

I did, and he winced sharply just like before, though this time it didn't seem to be quite so bad.

"Now go get a towel. Soak a piece of it in whiskey and stuff it in there and try to bandage me up as best you can so's I don't keep bleeding."

I don't know when the shooting had stopped. Like I said, I hadn't noticed anything but Mr. Tavish. But suddenly it did seem awful quiet. I stood up to go find a towel. But as I turned around, my heart sank with an altogether new terror.

There stood an Indian with a rifle pointed straight at Pa!

I stood paralyzed with fear while three or four more Paiutes climbed in through the broken windows, training their guns on the rest of us.

# CHAPTER 31

## THE MOST UNUSUAL
## BREAKFAST IN THE WORLD

They must have known they'd gotten one of us when only two guns were firing at them instead of three. Then when Juan stopped to reload, the Indian had jumped through the silent window, and the next second Pa was staring down the barrel of a Paiute gun.

Pa could have tried to shoot him, of course. But then they'd both have been dead, and there would have been a dozen more Indians following right after the first. Not only would it have been pointless, Pa didn't want to shoot anyone anyway. I saw him glance over at me, all blood-stained like I was, as he set his rifle down. I knew he would have killed to save me if he needed to. But now it looked as if we were all going to die together! And the look of futility on his face said there wasn't much he could do about it.

By now one of them had opened the door, and more Indians were pouring into the cabin, some holding bows, others rifles, talking in a strange language, making gestures and signs, looking around, taking stock of the inside of the station. They didn't seem to pay any attention to my being a woman, which I know was the main thing on Pa's mind. I don't suppose I looked all that attractive to them in the condition I was in!

A few of them started taking things—some tools and supplies, what food they could carry—while two of the others talked among themselves. Then one of them gave what sounded like an order, and another ran outside and returned a minute later with several strands of buffalo rope. He threw one of them to his companion,

174

and the two of them grabbed Juan and Pa and started to tie them up. Then one of them approached me, grabbed at my arm, and pulled me over against one of the two support timbers in the middle of the cabin. He yanked my hands behind my back and tied me up too. He was none too gentle, and he smelled horrible. I tried not to cry out, but he hurt my wrists as he twisted the rope around them and yanked it tight.

I don't know what danger they thought Mr. Tavish was going to be in his condition, but one of them dragged him by the feet over next to me, then pulled him viciously to his feet and tied him up behind me. We could feel each other's hands but couldn't see each other.

"I'm sorry about this, little lady," Mr. Tavish groaned softly. "These blamed Pai—"

A blow across the side of his head and face put an end to whatever he had been going to say.

Meanwhile, the Indians who were taking things seemed to have gotten all they wanted out of the cabin and had left. Outside we could hear movement and rustling. The door was still open and I could see them dragging brush and bales of straw from the stables over toward the station. Out one of the windows I could see the same thing going on.

"What are they doing?" I whispered when the one who had been tying us up went over to check on the knots around Pa and Juan.

"Fixing to burn down the place," Mr. Tavish whispered back. "It's their favorite way—surround the place with kindling and firewood and set it ablaze."

"What about us?" I said in horror.

"It's the Paiute way of burning the white man at the stake. The good-for-nothin' savages!"

"They're going to leave us inside?" I gasped.

"Leave us inside to burn, take us outside and put arrows through our hearts—their kind ain't too particular how the white man dies."

"Pa!" I wailed.

"Be brave, Corrie," I heard Pa answer, even though I couldn't see him from the direction I was facing. "Just remember—this ain't the end of it. Our Father will take care of us, even if—"

He never finished. I heard a big *whack,* and I squirmed at my ropes, straining around to try to see Pa. I managed just to see him out of the corner of my eye. His head was hanging limp, a red gash from the butt of the Indian's rifle already swelling up from above his ear down into the upper part of his cheek. The blow had knocked him unconscious.

I found myself wishing they'd do the same to me. If I was going to get burned up, I'd rather be asleep!

There was still a lot of activity outside, but it looked as if they had just about got the cabin all surrounded with dry material that would ignite in just a few seconds. Then it got very quiet. The Indian who had seemed to be in charge walked out the door and was gone for two or three minutes. When he finally came back in, the look on his face was one of taking a last look around to make sure he hadn't missed anything. A handful of others followed him in, then stood back waiting. He walked slowly about, indicating now one thing, now another, with a grunt and a few words. The others picked up whatever he'd pointed to and took it outside. They grabbed up several blankets on a shelf that had been missed before, a shovel, an axe, an unopened bag of beans.

The leader walked slowly around the table, eyeing it carefully, then over to the stove, where he first noticed the flapjacks and bacon still frying away. By now the two large pancakes on the griddle were black on the bottom, and the thin strips of bacon burned to cinders. But the smell seemed to attract his attention. He glanced back at the table, then again eyed the stove, this time lifting the lid off the pot of coffee, which still sat there steaming hot. The smell seemed to appeal to him. He smiled, replaced the lid, took a tin cup from the shelf behind the stove, and poured out a cup of the black brew.

As he sipped at it, he must have thought more of it than I had the previous evening, because he smiled again, then called to his companions, apparently asking them if they wanted some. They all set down the things they'd been carrying outside and approached him, grabbing cups wherever they could find them, and pouring coffee for themselves.

The five or six Indians left in the cabin talked and laughed as they sipped at Mr. Tavish's strong coffee. Then before I even realized what was happening, they all sat down around the table, using *our* plates and eating up the flapjacks that *we* had cooked!

There they were, getting ready to burn the place down, and us along with it, and they were celebrating by eating *our* breakfast!

After some discussion, they finally figured out that the syrup was sweet and tasted good on top of the pancakes. They poured it on, then tore the pancakes in half with their fingers, picked them up, and ate them. It was the messiest breakfast I had ever seen in my life, and if I hadn't been about to die, I probably would have laughed myself silly. As it was, I didn't know whether to laugh or cry or look the other way and try to ignore their uncivilized antics.

But they were impossible to ignore. By now they were making quite a racket. The pancakes and bacon were gone in a few minutes, and they had syrup and grease all over their faces and hands. Then they got up and started rummaging all through the cabin to see if there was anything *else* they could find to eat! One of them grabbed up the bottle of syrup and drank down the rest of it, then set it back down on the table with a crash and a loud laugh. The rest were helping themselves to more coffee, spilling half of it in their haste. One had discovered a tin of dried venison, which all the rest now came and started to fight over.

Then suddenly, in the distance, a bugle sounded, followed by the pounding gallop of approaching horses.

All activity inside the cabin stopped immediately, and they looked around at one another. Immediately, I realized that the Paiutes had heard the sound, too, and were scared by it. They dropped everything and ran for the door. Within fifteen seconds, amid shouts and unintelligible cries, we heard their ponies galloping away in the opposite direction, followed by pursuing gunfire.

# CHAPTER 32

## PONY BOB!

It wasn't the cavalry at all who had rescued us!

Pony Bob was early in arriving on his run from the east. He'd seen signs of the Indians from far off and had ridden in shooting and firing up a storm.

He was a courageous young boy, that much we already knew, but I doubt if he really expected to scare off twenty or thirty Paiutes all by himself. But he had help that we didn't know about when we first heard him approach. All he'd been trying to do was distract the war party long enough for that help to arrive. Fortunately for everybody, he didn't have to wait for it before he got into the cabin to untie us.

We heard his horse gallop up and stop, and a few seconds later he ran inside.

"Am I glad to see you!" Mr. Tavish whispered weakly. "Get us outta these ropes, Bob!"

Pony Bob was already slicing through the cords around my hands and Mr. Tavish's with a knife. The instant I was free I ran over to Pa and threw my arms around him.

"I love you, Pa!" I said, not able to keep from crying and not the least bit embarrassed about my tears. I hardly even realized that he was still bound hand and foot and couldn't have hugged me back if he'd tried!

Pony Bob was just what I might have expected. Small, thin, six inches shorter than Zack, and with a recklessness, almost a mean streak in his young eyes. He didn't look as if he was afraid of anybody or anything. Whether it was courage that drove him,

178

or just that he didn't have anyone in this life he cared about enough to stay alive for, I couldn't tell. His face showed little trace of a beard, but his eyes had the hardness of a man of fifty. In Mr. Tavish's eyes I had seen the dull pain of loneliness; in young Bob Haslam's I saw only emptiness.

"Everyone outside!" gasped Mr. Tavish, even before Pa and Juan were free. "We gotta pull the straw away from the station. One flaming arrow and the place'll go up like a dry brushfire in a hot wind!"

He staggered outside, and with his uninjured arm began dragging back the brush and straw the Indians had piled up. In a minute all four of the rest of us had joined him.

"By now they'll know they was run off by only Bob. They'll either be back or will try to set the place off from where they're hiding!"

"In two or three minutes the army'll be here," said young Haslam.

"What?" Mr. Tavish said, breathing hard and gritting his teeth against the pain.

"Ormsby's out from Carson. He heard they'd attacked the Widow Cutt's place yesterday. I'd seen signs of the raiding party all the way in the last ten miles. I ran into his troop of men five or six miles back and told him I thought they were heading for the station. They're right behind me."

"Blamed if you ain't better'n a whole hundred cavalrymen!" said Tavish, his face flushed with fever and exertion. The next instant a shot rang out, followed by the sound of a bullet ricocheting off an iron wagon wheel next to the station house. It had come from the direction the Indians had gone.

"Them Paiutes is back!" cried Tavish. "Everyone inside!"

We rushed into the station. Pony Bob bolted the door. Pa, Juan, and Bob grabbed rifles and sent several volleys of fire out through the windows, hoping to discourage the war party from trying the same thing again. Mr. Tavish, still bleeding, made me help him get a rifle up onto the window ledge where he could rest it against his good shoulder.

But the shooting didn't last long this time.

Again we heard a bugle call, followed by thunderous hoofbeats. A minute later Major Ormsby's troop of forty men roared past after the Paiutes, who were back on their horses and making for the mountains as fast as they could. We never saw them again.

Once the cavalry had passed, Mr. Tavish sank into the one chair, and Pony Bob packed and dressed the wound.

"The army's bugle didn't sound anything like what I heard before you came," I said to Pony Bob when he had finished bandaging Mr. Tavish's shoulder.

He and Mr. Tavish laughed.

"That's because Pony Bob's weren't no army bugle, little lady. Back when the Express started, they gave every rider a horn so as to announce his coming to the station. Wasn't long before everybody knew we didn't need 'em. You can see the dust five miles away, and hear the horse's hooves a mile away, so what use was the horn? But Pony Bob, he just kept his. How come, Bob?"

"Aw, just for fun," replied Bob. "You never know when you're gonna have need of something like that."

"If the army ever heard someone trying to imitate their charge with a little tin horn like that, they'd take it from him and trample it flat!" said Mr. Tavish.

"Anyhow, the Indians believed he was a one-man cavalry charge," laughed Pa. "So I'm mighty glad you saved it, son. Say, you know a Zack Hollister?"

Pony Bob's face grew thoughtful. "Yeah, I think I heard of him," he answered after a minute. "Rides over to the east. Ain't never run into him myself, though."

"These folks come from California looking to find him," put in Mr. Tavish. "You reckon they could make it to Utah, Bob?"

"Not unless they want to go through what you've just been through every day—and that's *without* a station to hide in and no cavalry within miles."

"You reckon the Paiutes are going on the warpath again?"

"They're everywhere out there. I was lucky to make it through. You want my advice, Mister," said Pony Bob to Pa, "you'll saddle up and head for Carson and just keep right on going past the Sierras. If Zack Hollister's your kin, there ain't much you can do for him now. But if you aim to keep this pretty girl of yours alive, you'd best take my advice."

"When's the safest time to leave for Carson, you reckon?" asked Pa.

"Right now," answered Mr. Tavish. "Ormsby's driven the savages up into the hills. They won't bother nobody for some few days, and he and his men will be moving back that way, so if there was trouble, they'd be on the trail with you."

"We ought to do what they say, Pa," I said. "If we are ever going to find Zack, it doesn't seem as if this is the time to do it."

Pa thought long and hard for a few minutes. He knew we had to go back, but he was torn with wanting to find his son.

Finally he nodded. "Well then, Corrie, I reckon you and me had best saddle up our horses and get our things together."

"You could make Carson, or maybe even Friday's Station before nightfall," said Mr. Tavish.

"I'm obliged to you for everything, Tavish," said Pa, shaking the stationman's good hand. "All except for nearly getting us killed, that is!"

"You come back and visit again, Hollister," he said, smiling weakly. "And bring the little lady with you. She's a right fine nurse, along with being a cook and a newspaper writer!"

"You take care of yourself!" said Pa.

"And get a doctor to fix up your shoulder," I added, giving Mr. Tavish a one-sided hug. "I don't want to worry about anything happening to it."

Pa and I were on the trail back in the direction of Carson City in less than twenty minutes.

We rode for the rest of the morning in silence, interrupted only by Pony Bob as he passed, finishing up his run to Carson. We had probably started fifteen or twenty minutes ahead of him, but he caught up with us in no time.

We heard him coming behind us and stopped to turn around. At first all we could see was swirling dust in the middle of the desert valley floor, although the sound of the iron-clad hooves could be heard thudding loudly against the rocky trail. We squinted to watch as the cloud of dust grew steadily larger. Then a black speck began to appear in the middle of the cloud, which gradually sprouted arms and legs and came alive with movement. Across the endless level of the Carson sink, the cloud of dust grew, the now-defined horse and rider in its midst obscuring mountains and desert and sky. A show it was—magnificent to behold!

He was nearly upon us, and we watched in nothing less than awe, as if history itself resided in the four locked pouches of the *mochila* coming from the East and bound for the Pacific. Had I been able to pull out paper and pencil, to stop the motion of Pony Bob and his steed, I would have tried to capture in a drawing what I felt as he flew past. As it is, however, the scene must lodge only in my memory, for it was over in a few brief seconds.

As he thundered by, I saw the blur of four powerful black feet, Bob's arms and the reins and the bandanna around his neck all flying, and in the center of it all the huge black head of the horse, his eyes flaming, his nostrils wide to suck in all the air he could, mouth foaming, his powerful frame bulging and pulsating with muscular strength. He was by us in an instant. Only Bob's whoop of greeting, and long drawn out *Haaalllisteeeerrrrr!* lingered echoing in the wind with the suddenly retreating hoofbeats.

Like a blur, it was gone. Man and horse flew by our wide-eyed faces like a thunderstorm borne on a swift wind, then receded into the distance ahead . . . tinier, tinier, until Pony Bob disappeared in a dust cloud against the blue of the horizon. Except for the lingering whirlwind of dust, I might have believed that the whole thing had been the dreaming fancy of an overactive imagination.

But it was no dream. Pa's next words woke me out of my reverie. He had been astonished by the sight as well.

"Tarnation!" he exclaimed. "That boy does know how to ride! I reckon Tavish was right when he said they're *all* good riders!"

We rode for an hour after that without either of us saying anything. After all we'd been through, our anxiety over Zack, and even wondering where the band of Paiutes were, there was plenty to think about. I was thinking about the attack that morning, Zack, and the Indians. But Pa hadn't been thinking about those things at all I found out.

"I think I'm gonna do it, Corrie," he said after a long, long time of quiet.

"Do what, Pa?"

"Run for the legislature."

"You are? Why, Pa, that's . . . that's wonderful!" I exclaimed.

"You really think so?"

"Yes—I was hoping you would!"

"Why's that?"

"Because you're a fine man, Pa, and I want everyone to know it. What made you decide?"

"I can't rightly say," replied Pa. "Something about what happened back there just—I don't know, Corrie, it just made me think it's the right thing to do."

"Does it have anything to do with Zack?"

Pa thought for a minute. "I'm not sure. I guess I just got to figuring that everybody's gonna die sometime. We came closer than I'd like to think back there! But if I am gonna die, then I oughta have done something worth remembering before I do. Raising my kids right is probably about the most important thing a man can do, and I ain't done such a good job of that."

"Please, Pa, I don't like to hear you talk like that."

"All right, Corrie. Let's just say that *one* of my sons doesn't think much of my fathering. Maybe the rest of you still look up to me. But you're all nearly grown. Why, little Tad's gonna be a man himself in another year or two. So I figure my fathering days are nearly over—except for little Ruth, of course. Whether I've done a good or a bad job of it, maybe I oughta be looking for something else worth doing that people will remember Drummond Hollister for. You don't always get too many chances to do something important, so when one comes along, a man's gotta look at it and decide if he wants to do it, or before he knows it, the chance is gone and might never come back."

"A man *or* a woman," I added with a smile.

"Right you are there, Corrie. Which is why you've got to take your opportunities with writing and with this election, and why maybe I've got to take mine with this political thing Dalton's offering me."

"I understand, Pa."

I really did. I had been thinking along the same lines for the last couple of months—not having to do with dying or doing something important, but having to do, as Pa and Cal had both said, with taking the opportunities that came your way.

In some ways the decisions facing both Pa and me were similar too. And the choices we made were bound to have a big effect on our futures.

# CHAPTER 33

## A CONVERSATION IN SACRAMENTO

Things started to happen pretty fast after we got back from Nevada. Pa's decision to run for the California House of Representatives was like yanking up the boards to let the water from a stream into a sluice trough. Once the water started flowing, it rushed through fast! I know it didn't take our minds off Zack and the danger he was in, but it kept us busy enough that we didn't have to mope around and think about it.

We stopped in Sacramento long enough for Pa to meet with Mr. Dalton and tell him what he decided.

"I'm pleased to hear of your decision, Hollister," Mr. Dalton said.

"I still don't have much notion of what I'm supposed to do," Pa said sheepishly. I knew he felt awkward around smooth politicians like Alexander Dalton.

"You just leave everything to me. All you have to do is try to spread the word around your area that folks need to vote for you. Since you've already run for mayor a time or two, it ought not to be too difficult."

"We'll make up some more handbills, Pa," I suggested, "just like last time."

"Good girl!" said Mr. Dalton, giving me a gentle slap on the back. "I like how she thinks, Hollister," he added to Pa. "Political acumen must run in the family! Like I say, you just leave the rest of the territory north of Sacramento to me. I'll be in touch with you and let you know everything you need to do."

185

Pa nodded his head agreeably. "And as for you, young lady," he went on, turning to me, "that was some article you wrote!"

"You read it?" I asked, half embarrassed, the other half astonished.

"Did I ever! So did the rest of the state. It appeared three days ago in the *Alta*, and another half dozen papers have already picked it up. I don't suppose I should be surprised after that speech you gave here in town about freedom. Some of the people I'm in touch with are already starting to say you just might be one of the best weapons Abraham Lincoln has in this state. In fact, because of that speech of yours, the Rev. Thomas Starr King, who was in the audience that day, has decided to become even more actively involved than he had planned. He wants to work with you!"

"That's my Corrie!" exclaimed Pa proudly. I tried to hide my embarrassment. I didn't know Mr. Dalton that well, but ever since the first time we'd seen him in San Francisco I couldn't escape the feeling that he sometimes exaggerated how he said things just to make me feel good, so that I'd be more inclined to do what he might want me to do later. I suppose politicians had to do that sometimes, but I hoped what he said about Mr. King was true. I liked Mr. Dalton well enough, but I didn't like having to wonder what he *really* thought. It seemed to me a man's words ought to be exactly what they were—no more and no less. In his case, I always had the feeling they were just a little bit more than he truly meant.

Nevertheless, I was just vain enough to enjoy his compliment anyway. I hoped there was *some* truth in his words, and that my article would do some good.

"In fact," he was saying, "there are two more large rallies we've got scheduled—one right here in Sacramento and another in San Francisco. I hope you'll be able to join us both times."

I shrugged noncommittally and glanced at Pa, but the expression on his face didn't give me any help.

"I realize it's a great distance to come," he added hurriedly. "But we'll pay for all your expenses, of course, just like before. And you can know that you're having a great impact for the good of our country and its future . . . for liberty, just as you said in your speech!"

"I'll think about it," I answered him.

"I've already talked to Cal about bringing you down for them."
He paused, and when he went on I wasn't sure I liked the sly look
in his eye or the tone of his voice. "He's taking good care of you,
I understand," he said.

I nodded.

"Since you and he seemed to, ah . . . hit it off, as it were, I
took the liberty of asking Leland—that's Mr. Stanford—to allow
me to borrow young Cal now and then to help out with the election, and to make sure my favorite young newspaper writer is kept
just as happy as she can be."

Again he smiled, with a look I didn't altogether like. Now I
was sure his words said more than he meant. I knew, after all the
years he'd been involved in important things, that I *wasn't* his
favorite newspaper writer. But he'd said it just as plain as day. You
couldn't actually call something like that a lie, but it certainly
wasn't the whole truth. I didn't think Mr. Dalton was intentionally
trying to deceive me. He probably considered it a nice thing to
say. But it still wasn't the truth—the *whole* truth, anyway. I don't
suppose Alexander Dalton was the kind of man who had made
truth the same kind of priority as I had. I hoped it wasn't politics
that had made him the way he was. I didn't want Pa to get like
that if he went to Sacramento—saying one thing but always having
a slightly different meaning to it that he *didn't* say.

"You like Cal, don't you?" Mr. Dalton asked, seeing me hesitate.

"Yes," I answered, blushing a little.

"Good, good! People like to see a nice young man and woman
standing up for principles and involving themselves in the nation's
affairs. I'm very happy to hear that we'll see you again up on the
platform representing the Republican party!"

"I don't think you heard my daughter, Mr. Dalton," said Pa.
"At least, I never heard her say for sure what she was going to
do."

"Did I misunderstand?" he said, looking at me bewildered.

"I said I would think about it," I said. "And I will."

"Fine! That's all I can expect. I will have Cal get in touch with
you about the details."

# CHAPTER 34

# WARNING SIGNS

I *did* speak both times Mr. Dalton had told me about. How could I say no when Cal practically begged me? And why would I have *wanted* to say no, anyway? I wouldn't have turned down another chance to be with Cal.

The most memorable part of September, however, wasn't the two speeches I gave. They weren't much different than the first, although I wasn't quite so nervous even though there were more people listening. But after we were through in San Francisco, instead of going straight back home, Cal invited me down to Mr. Stanford's ranch south of San Francisco in a little town called Palo Alto.

"He raises horses," Cal said. "There's a big ranch house where you'll be very comfortable. I'll show you his estate. We'll saddle up two of his finest horses and I'll show you the peninsula. It's beautiful country!"

"I . . . I don't know," I hesitated. "I suppose it would be all right. It does sound fun." Inside, my heart was beating wildly. It sounded like a dream come true—a fairy tale!

"How will we get there?" I asked, not even knowing what I was saying.

"I've got one of Mr. Stanford's finest carriages here in the city. I'm heading back down to the estate bright and early in the morning. Say you'll join me!"

"But . . . how will I get back here, and then home?"

"Don't worry, Corrie. With a man of the world like me to take care of everything, you need have no concerns. I'll see to your every need!"

In the thrill of the moment, I totally believed him. Not until later, as I lay in bed that night, did I realize that something about his words had struck a tiny chord of dissonance somewhere inside my brain.

Just then, as we were still talking about it, Mr. Dalton walked up. He greeted me kindly, congratulated me on a job well done, as he put it, and then turned to Cal and began speaking more quietly and more seriously. It was clear they didn't intend for me to listen, but they made no particular attempt to keep me from hearing, either. Men have a way of ignoring women when they want to, and paying attention to them when they want to. And when they're ignoring them, they seem to think they're not there at all, or that their minds don't work because they're not being paid attention to. But women are generally smarter and more aware of things than men realize. In this case I *was* listening, and I found their conversation very interesting, even though I know they probably thought my head was off in the clouds someplace.

"One of Senator Gwin's *Breckinridge* people is making trouble for us down in the South," Dalton was saying. "There's talk of a *Breckinridge*-Douglas coalition to smear Lincoln, to insure that *one* of the two Democrats wins California. Apparently they've sent someone up this way to spread the lies into northern California, too."

"What's his name?" asked Cal.

"Jewks . . . Terrance Jewks."

"Where is he? How do I find him?"

"Their people are said to be putting him up someplace in the city."

"Don't worry about a thing," Cal said after a while. "I'll take care of it. If he's in one of the San Francisco hotels, I'll find him."

"You know what to do?"

"I've run into just this sort of thing with Mr. Stanford. I've got ways of handling his sort."

"Leland tells me you are very resourceful," said Mr. Dalton, a grin breaking over his face.

"My goal is to be useful," replied Cal, returning the smile.

"Nothing more?" queried Dalton. "Leland is a powerful man, a man whose star is on the rise."

The look on Cal's face told that he knew exactly what that meant.

"All the more reason for me to serve him faithfully," said Cal, "as well as the whole party. To answer your question—yes, I know what to do. And I've got just the people to do it. Believe me, Mr. Jewks will not prove troublesome. He'll wish he stayed in the South and left northern politics to the Republicans!"

"Good. I knew I could count on you," said Dalton. The two shook hands, and I was left alone with Cal again.

"What was that all about?" I asked.

"Nothing . . . nothing, Corrie, my dear. Just the details of politics."

"It didn't sound too pleasant."

"Politics sometimes gets a little messy, Corrie. You must know that. Your father is a politician."

"He's mayor of Miracle Springs," I replied. "I don't know that I'd call him a politician."

"Well, he soon will be, from what I understand," Cal persisted. "Once he's sitting in the statehouse in Sacramento, his hands will get dirty, too."

"Not Pa's," I insisted.

Cal laughed. "Don't worry, Corrie. I'm not talking about anything serious. But it can't be helped. Your pa will explain it to you someday. In the meantime, you and I don't have to worry about all that! How about me taking you out for a fancy first-class dinner and a night on the town to celebrate your speech today? Then I'll get you safe and sound back to Miss Bean's later, and pick you up tomorrow morning for Palo Alto!"

Cal made me feel special, more like a real woman than I'd ever imagined I'd feel. I don't suppose I really believed half the sweet things he said to me. Yet I wanted to believe them so badly that I convinced myself to ignore the uncomfortable warning signs.

Besides, Cal Burton was not the kind of man a girl says *no* to. And I didn't really *want* to say no, after all.

# CHAPTER 35

## MEMORIES ON HORSEBACK

Palo Alto was all Cal promised it would be . . . and more!

Mr. Stanford and his wife treated me as if I were the most honored guest they'd ever had on the estate. I could hardly believe that a short time ago I was out in the desolate land of Nevada nearly being burned alive by Indians, and now I was hobnobbing with one of California's wealthiest men—and, according to Cal, one of its most influential politicians too!

The Stanford estate was completely different from the primitive Fremont estate at Mariposa. Mr. Fremont was also rich, of course, but he spent so little time in California, and Mariposa was so far away from everywhere else that he never did much to fancy it up. But I could tell instantly that the Stanfords intended to live on their new estate a long time. Besides politics and railroads, Mr. Stanford loved horses, and told me it had always been a lifelong dream of his to raise them. Now that he had a place and the means to do it, he intended to make his dream come true, right there in Palo Alto.

Mr. Stanford was a good friend of John and Jessie Fremont, and once Cal explained to him my connection with the campaign of 1856, he told me many interesting things I hadn't known.

"John Fremont may have lost the election in '56," he said, "but as far as I'm concerned it was a great victory. For a man to come so close to becoming president only four years after the formation of a new party is remarkable, in my opinion, and we Republicans owe him a great debt of gratitude. We'll win this year with Lincoln, thanks to people like you throughout the country,

191

Corrie. The John Fremont campaign four years ago laid the groundwork for this year's victory."

"Was he considered as a candidate again this year?" I asked.

"By a few people. But to be honest with you, there wasn't a great deal of support for him at the convention. Lincoln represents the rising new tide of the party, Corrie, although John's name was bandied about for vice-president. I wouldn't be surprised to see him with a cabinet appointment in the new administration, however. Lincoln thinks highly of him, from what I understand."

Just then Cal walked in.

"The horses are all saddled, Corrie. Shall we head out over the hills and see what kind of adventure we can find?"

"You be sure to take her up to the top of the ridge, Cal," said Mr. Stanford. "On a clear day like this, Corrie, from up there you can see out to the Pacific to the west, down into the bay to the east, and, if it's clear as crystal like it gets after a rain, you can just make out a bit of San Francisco at the tip of the peninsula. It's the most stunning view in all of California, if you ask me. And it's right here on my estate!"

"I'll be sure she sees it," said Cal.

"I probably won't see you again, Corrie," he said. "I've got a meeting with the Crocker brothers this evening, and tomorrow I have to get up to Sacramento early to see Judah, Huntington, and Hopkins on some railroad business. But you enjoy the rest of your stay, and you let my wife or Cal here know if you need anything."

"Thank you, sir," I said. "You are very kind."

It was still fairly early in the morning when we set out. Cal led the way at a leisurely pace, westward from the house and barns, down through a grassy little valley, and then up the gradual incline at the far end. The grass was dry and brown at this time of the year, and the hills were gently rolling, with oaks scattered thinly about. The air was not hot, just pleasantly warm. There was no breeze yet.

Gradually the climb grew steeper, though still nothing like the mountains I was used to back in the foothills country around Miracle. There was no trail, but the grass was almost meadowlike. We wound around gnarled old oaks, crossed several small streams, came across little glens that interrupted the upward ascent, and if

I had let myself daydream, I could have easily thought we might crest a small rise and see the snowcapped Sierras in the distance. It was hard to believe we were actually going in the exact opposite direction.

Finally a clearing spread out before us, with a rise about four or five hundred yards farther that seemed to taper off at its crest into a flat plateau.

"There it is!" said Cal.

"What?"

"The top. That's the summit."

"The summit!" I repeated with a laugh. "That makes it sound like a mountain."

"Okay, maybe it's not a mountain peak. But it's the highest hill for thirty miles in either direction. It's the one Mr. Stanford told me to show you."

"I'll race you there!" I cried.

"You're on!" Cal yelled back, giving his horse a slap on the rump and lurching into a gallop.

I let him get about twenty yards out in front, just enough of a lead for him to look back to see me sitting at the starting point calmly. Then I dug my heels into the mare Mr. Stanford had let me pick out earlier in the morning. I had liked her looks immediately, and had tested her speed a couple times on the way up, so I was confident of what kind of mount I had under me.

By the time Cal looked back again I had closed half the distance between us, and drew alongside him before we were halfway to the top. I didn't even look over, but just leaned forward against my mare's neck and whisked by. I reached the top, reined in the mare, and was sitting calmly in the saddle regaining my breath by the time Cal galloped up alongside ten or fifteen seconds later.

"What took you so long?" I asked, grinning.

"Let me answer with a question—where did *you* learn to ride like that?" laughed Cal. "You put me to shame."

"I'm just a country girl," I answered. "I told you I've been riding for years. When you don't live in a city, you learn to ride."

"Maybe it's you who ought to be riding for the Pony Express instead of your brother!"

"I might if they let girls join," I said.

"Don't you dare! We need you too much in this campaign!"

Now that the race to the top of the hill was behind us, I had a chance to look around and see where we were.

"It's absolutely breathtaking!" I exclaimed.

Spread out, not above us as the Sierras would have been, but rather below us like a distant blue infinite carpet stretching all the way to the horizon, was the Pacific Ocean. The day was perfect. The sky was nearly as blue as the sea, with a few billows of clouds suspended lazily here and there. As we had come up over the ridge, the gentlest whisper of a breeze had met us, and now as I drew in deep breaths I could smell just the faintest hint of the ocean's fragrance.

I stretched all around in my saddle, looking down upon the long blue fingers of San Francisco's huge bay in the other direction, just as Mr. Stanford had described it. Then I turned north to see if the city itself was in view. It hadn't rained in the last several days, but it was just clear enough that I *thought* I could see fuzzy glimpses of it. If it wasn't the actual buildings of the city I saw, perhaps it was just the rounding part of the end of the peninsula, with my imagination filling in shapes where I knew the city was.

"Look over that way," said Cal, pointing northeast. "There's the mouth of the Sacramento River emptying into the bay. And Sacramento eighty miles away," he added, swinging his arm a little to the right.

As I watched Cal describing the view, I saw a subtle change come over him when he began talking about Sacramento. The capital city, it seemed, possessed a greater significance for him than all the rest.

"What is it about Sacramento that's so special to you?" I asked.

"Opportunity, Corrie," he said after a long silence. "Just like I told you before . . . opportunity."

I thought back to Pa's talk on our way to Carson City; he had said that sometimes we have to take the chances that come our way before it is too late. But I had the feeling he and Cal meant two completely different things. Pa seemed to be saying that we ought to be mindful of the opportunities God puts in our path. Cal seemed to be saying something else, although I wasn't quite sure what it was yet.

"Look around you, Corrie," Cal went on, turning in his saddle. "Look out there—what do you see?" He pointed due west.

"The ocean," I answered.

"What else do you see?"

"The sky," I said, half in question.

"What else?"

"I don't know, Cal . . . the clouds?"

"No, Corrie! Down there is the end of the land, the coast of California . . . the *end* of the country, the last piece of the United States, the edge of the whole continent!"

His face was lit up as if he had revealed the whole riddle of the universe. He kept looking at me as if expecting light to break in upon my mind at any second.

"Don't you see what that means?" he asked finally.

"Uh . . . I guess I don't," I said.

"It means the end of one kind of opportunity and the beginning of a whole new era in our country's history—a whole era of *new* opportunities!"

Again he stopped and scanned all around, at everything we could see. Slowly we began walking our horses along the plateau of the ridge.

"You see, Corrie," Cal began, "for the last century, the whole thrust of opportunity in this country was just to *get* here—to reach the Pacific. This was the frontier. It had to be explored, then tamed. Lewis and Clark, Jedediah Smith, even your own John Fremont back in his exploring days—they were men whose passion was just *getting* here, to this very place, to the Pacific coast. Then all those who came after them—trappers and traders and homesteaders and cattle ranchers, and families by wagon trains— they were coming here just to *be* here—to come west, to live, to settle, to make lives for themselves. Do you see what I mean? *Getting* west was the opportunity in itself! Then came the gold rush, and men and women poured in by the hundreds of thousands. Now California and Oregon are states, and one day Nevada and Washington will be, too. We've reached the end, the end of the frontier, Corrie. The country's come as far west as it can go. California's been tamed and settled. And here we stand, right at the very end, gazing down to where California meets the Pacific."

We rode on slowly; then he stopped and suddenly jumped down off his mount, gazing down toward the ocean below us.

"Do you know where the *next* era of opportunity lies, Corrie?" he asked.

"Where, Cal?" I said.

He hesitated just momentarily, then wheeled around, stretched his arms widely out into the air as he faced eastward, and cried, "Out there! Back where we've come from—toward the east and everywhere between this spot right here and the same spot overlooking the Atlantic coast somewhere in New York or Maryland or Georgia! It's what we *do* with this land now that we've conquered it and explored it. We've spent two hundred years just getting to this spot, Corrie. Many people shed their blood so that you and I could stand here and look out upon that expanse of blue. In the next century, fortunes are going to be made and empires are going to be built by those who lay hold of the opportunities afforded them.

"Men like Leland Stanford *came* west. That was their first opportunity. He came from Wisconsin with his four brothers and set up business in Sacramento. Getting here was his first opportunity, which he took hold of, and it made him a rich man. But he didn't stop there. Then he turned his eyes back *over* the country he had crossed, and he began to take hold of new political opportunities—the opportunity of power. He ran for governor of this state. Even though he lost, Leland Stanford is still looking for new frontiers to conquer. He came to the Pacific, but now he is seeking to *return* to the East by rail—a new opportunity. I have no doubt that he and his friends *will* one day build a railroad back to the East where they all came from, and grow even more wealthy and powerful in the process.

"Oh, Corrie, don't you see what I'm getting at? It's in the statehouses like Sacramento where these opportunities of the future originate—where the laws are made. It's there where the powerful people gather, where the money flows from. Politics, money, and influence—they are the opportunities of the *next* century! Those with vision to see such things will go far."

He turned around, his eyes glowing as he looked up at me. I sat still on the mare, listening to every word he said.

"From the Pacific to the Atlantic," I said, halfway to myself, reflecting on what he'd said a minute ago.

"Sea to sea . . . shore to shore! That's it exactly!"

"There's only one thing I don't understand, Cal," I said. "Why then do you want to have anything to do with someone like me? I'm hardly the kind of person you're talking about."

"But you are, Corrie! I knew that right from the first, when I heard about you and then when I laid eyes on you. Not only were you a beautiful young lady, all dressed up at the Montgomery Hotel in San Francisco. You also have done just what I'm talking about. You came west. The first frontier was just *getting* here and joining back up with your father and uncle. But no sooner had you done that than you turned back around and set your sights on higher goals. You started writing; you took every opportunity that you could, and now your writing is being read all the way back across the country. And the very Pony Express pouches that your brother carries across the mountains and desert have newspapers in them with *your* articles and speeches written down for folks in the East to read. You know the Fremonts and Mr. Stanford and Mr. Dalton. Don't you see, Corrie—in your own way, you're going to be an important person someday too, just like Leland Stanford!"

"That doesn't sound like me, Cal," I said.

"But it is, Corrie. You should be proud of it!"

"I never set my sights on having high goals. I never tried to *take* opportunities so I could get well known. That kind of thing never entered my mind, Cal."

"It happened all the same. And now look at you—who would deny that you're better off for all of it. For a *woman* to have done all you have, at such a young age . . . it's remarkable, Corrie! I tell you, you ought to be downright proud!"

I suppose it was idiotic of me to keep questioning him. He had been so nice to me, and a short time ago I had thought I was in love with him. Maybe I still was. I had even persuaded myself that his attentions came from feelings he perhaps shared. But I had to know.

"Is that why you want to have something to do with me?" I persisted. "Because I might be an important person someday?"

"No, of course not," he answered quickly. His voice bore a roughness, a defensiveness I had never heard before, as if such a blunt question had caught him momentarily with his guard down. It wasn't the kind of thing young women asked when men were showering them with praise.

"That is, not if you find such a motive to be offensive," he said smoothly, recovering his old composure. "I cannot deny that your accomplishments and reputation add to the charm I find so compelling about you. But even without them, I would still find you attractive above any other of the young ladies I have known. Do you believe me, Corrie?"

"I would like to."

"Then *do* believe me," he implored. His voice was so sincere; how could I possibly not believe he was in earnest? "Come, Corrie . . . get down. Walk with me." He reached up his hand and helped me down off the mare. When my feet were on the ground, however, he did not let go. My heart fluttered to feel his hand around mine, but I was too flustered to make any attempt to pull it away.

"Ah, Corrie," he said at last, "so much lies within our grasp— young persons like us, with life and opportunities and exciting new times for the country ahead of us!"

We walked on. My mind and heart were spinning in a dozen directions at once. I'd always thought of myself as rational and level-headed, but not now. Not with Cal Burton.

"Be part of it with me, Corrie," he said after a minute or two. "Let's find our opportunities together, and take advantage of them! You and I—we can be the Lewis and Clark of the next generation. You'll be a famous writer someday. And I'll—well, who knows how far we can go, Corrie, or what we can achieve! We can go back across this continent in the footsteps of Leland Stanford and men like him, and maybe even start to make our own marks in the history books of this country! What do you say, Corrie?"

I know I was being a fool, but I couldn't help asking one more time, "But . . . why me, Cal?"

"Don't you know, Corrie? Haven't you figured it out from all I've been telling you? It's because I care for you, Corrie—I care deeply. That's why, with us working together, there wouldn't be anything we couldn't do, couldn't achieve, couldn't get if we set our minds to it!"

Cal's closeness and the excitement in his tone overwhelmed me. I felt like running! I pulled my hand out of his and took off across the grass as fast as I could go.

"Hey . . . where are you off to?" called Cal behind me. I heard him start to chase after me, but I ran all the faster. I ran until I was tired, then slowed and let him catch up with me.

When he did, he threw his long arm around my shoulder and gave me a squeeze, then let go as we turned and started walking back to where the horses were nibbling at the brown grass.

We mounted back up and started slowly down the hill.

We rode down to the seashore, stopped and ran along the sandy beach, explored a watery cave, then galloped the horses miles along the sand before climbing back up inland, over the ridge of the peninsula again, and down through the woods and meadows. Even though we didn't arrive back at the Stanford estate until late in the afternoon, in spite of all the exertion and the long ride, I didn't seem to be hungry.

Dinner wasn't exactly "formal," but I did put on a different dress than the one I'd ridden in all afternoon, and Cal made his appearance in a black coat and ruffled white shirt with bow tie. He was indeed a handsome young man, and seeing him all dressed up reminded me of how taken I had been with him that night in San Francisco back in June.

When I went to bed that night, I lay awake a long time, dreaming of horses and sand and oak trees and the shining sun dancing and reflecting off the shimmering white and blue surface of the ocean. But mostly I dreamed of a tan face with brown hair flying above it in the breeze, and eyes of a blue so deep that even the sky above and the Pacific below seemed pale by comparison.

# CHAPTER 36

## HOW MANY STATES?

When I got back to Miracle Springs several days later, the two speeches I had made already seemed far in the past. But knowing nothing about my trip to Palo Alto, Pa and Almeda were full of questions about the political situation.

"You heard anything more from Mr. Dalton?" I asked him.

"Got a letter just yesterday," Pa answered. "He asked how the handbills that you had suggested were coming along—"

I had forgotten all about them—we were going to have to get busy in a hurry!

"*And,*" Pa went on, "he said he'd arranged for me to speak at a town meeting over in Marysville next week."

"What do you think, Corrie?" asked Almeda.

"What's more important is what *you* think," I answered.

"I think it's wonderful!" she said with a big smile. "I had no idea what I was starting when I got the notion of running for mayor. Now look what it's caused—Drummond Hollister running for state office!"

In California, the presidential election of 1860 in California had as much to do with the dispute between North and South as it did anywhere else in the country. The battle for supremacy of the nation, and which region was going to hold the reins of power, *was* the election of 1860. In addition to the slavery issue itself, the election would determine who was going to direct the course of the future of the United States of America.

The South had controlled the government in Washington for thirty years. But all of a sudden, a major change seemed at hand.

200

But the South did not intend to give up without a fight. The battle was to be waged on November 6, 1860.

California was one of the only states, however, where the dispute over control between North and South went on *inside* the state. California was now the second biggest state next to Texas, almost nine hundred miles from top to bottom, running north and south. The top of California next to Oregon was parallel with New York, and the bottom border ran right through the middle of Mississippi, Alabama, and Georgia. It was only natural, I suppose, that there would be debate *within* California as to which side its loyalties ought to lie on.

Even during the Mexican period in California before the gold rush, there had been a spirit of sectionalism between the northern and southern halves of the state. Especially once the gold rush came, those in the south didn't like all the activity of the north. When statehood was being discussed in 1849, many southern Californians did not want to be part of the new state and proposed dividing California in half at San Luis Obispo. They wanted to be able to go on with the slow pace of their old way of life, without being forced to be part of the frantic, growing, alien north where people were pouring in and towns were growing into great metropolitan areas overnight. Those in the south felt it unfair that they should have to pay taxes and support a state government that was located in the north, and that was expensive and heavily weighted toward the needs and concerns of the north. The south was so sparsely settled, it would even have preferred not to be a state at all, just as long as it could be separate from the north.

Statehood came to the whole state, but the desire to split the state into northern and southern halves continued as a volatile issue all the way through the 1850s. A huge movement in Los Angeles and throughout the south in 1851 tried to develop enough support to break away and form a new state. In the next two years, the southern legislators in Sacramento tried to call a constitutional convention that would divide the state. But since the north controlled the state legislature, such attempts were defeated.

Finally, in 1855 a bill was finally introduced into the California Assembly that at first called for a new state named *Columbia* to be formed. Then later the bill was changed to split California into *three* states. A new state called *Colorado* would be made of the area south of San Luis Obispo. A new state called *Shasta* would be made of the far northern part bordering Oregon. And *California* would remain as the central region of the three states.

That bill never passed, but the idea for making separate states continued, and even gradually began to be supported by some northerners. Another bill was introduced in Sacramento in 1859, again for two states, and again with the separation at San Luis Obispo, creating a new territory south of that to be called *Colorado*. This time there *was* enough support for the idea to pass both the state senate and the state assembly in Sacramento.

But the legislature couldn't split the state apart all by themselves. There were two other groups of people who had to be part of the decision, too—the federal government and the people who lived in the part of California where they wanted to create a new state.

So the legislature wrote up a bill that would create a new territory to be called *Colorado*—*if* two thirds of the people in that region south of San Luis Obispo approved of the plan, and *if* the Congress in Washington, D.C., also approved. The bill passed in the state assembly 33 to 15, and in the state senate 15 to 12. Then a special election was set up late in 1859 for the people of southern California to vote themselves on whether they wanted their part of the state to be formed into a new territory called *Colorado*.

They surely did! The people south of San Luis Obispo voted 2,457 to 828 in favor of dividing California in half, and calling their half Colorado.

Therefore, in January of 1860, Governor Milton Latham formally sent the results of the bill and both votes to President James Buchanan, asking for the U.S. Congress to approve the division of California.

No approval had yet been given, however. The rest of the nation was too taken up with other momentous events that year. The election between Lincoln and Douglas and the dispute between the southern states and northern states all made a local squabble within distant California seem a little insignificant to the politicians in Washington. Not only was California far away from the rest of the country, it was made up mostly of Spanish-speaking Mexicans in the south and gold-hungry miners in the north. At least that's what Pa said folks in the East thought about us.

"What does that have to do with splitting up the state, Pa?" Tad asked when we were all sitting talking about it a couple of weeks later.

"Nothing directly, son," answered Pa. "It's only that back in Washington I reckon they figure California's a mite different than other states, and that maybe they just oughta leave it alone to do what it wants."

"But if California wants it, all they have to do is approve it," said Becky.

"Well, there are certain kinds of things where the federal government's just not anxious to interfere. It's called *states' rights*. This country got its start as a collection of independent states that pretty much did what they pleased. The government in Washington was set up just to ride herd over the whole conglomeration, while the states went on deciding things for themselves. That's why it's called the United *States* of America instead of something else."

"You sound like a politician, Pa!" laughed Becky.

"Of course he's a politician!" said Almeda. "That's what being mayor is all about."

"I mean he sounds like a speechmaker."

"Like Corrie!" said Tad.

"I'm no speechmaker, Tad," I said.

"What about it, Drummond?" said Almeda. "Did that speech you made in Marysville last week go to your head? You *are* starting to sound a little high-falutin' for the likes of simple country folk like us."

"Now you cut that out, Almeda!" joked Pa. "You all know well and good I ain't about to start sounding like no doggone politician from Sacramento or Washington. I was only trying to answer Becky's question."

"Is states' rights why there's slavery some places and it's against the law in others?" asked Tad.

"Right you are, son. That's it exactly. It's up to the states to decide for themselves."

"What about right and wrong?" I asked. "It seems as if on an issue like slavery there ought to be more to it than everybody deciding what they want to do. That's why I decided to support

Mr. Lincoln, because of right and wrong.''

"But who's to say what's right and what's wrong? You've listened to Katie and Edie, Corrie. They *don't* see anything wrong in slavery, because they were both brought up in the South. That's why the government in Washington has always stayed out of such disputes. They don't want to get into the business of deciding right and wrong, so they let the states decide whatever *they* want to do."

"Then, why don't they let California split into two states?" asked Tad.

Pa looked at him a minute, then shook his head with a puzzled expression.

"The truth of the matter, son, is that I'm blamed if I know," he answered finally. "Maybe they just ain't got around to approving it."

"If you're elected to the Assembly, Drummond," said Almeda, "what stand are *you* going to take?"

"On what?" asked Pa.

"On the split of California. Are you going to continue to push for it next year if President Buchanan doesn't act on the measure before the election?"

Again Pa grew thoughtful. "If I do get elected to the Assembly, which I still doubt, then I'll have to figure out what I'm gonna do about a lot of things. Right now I can't say. I can't see much reason to be against dividing it up, but I got no objections to keeping it the way it is, either."

"If they won't let California do what *it* wants to do," said Becky, "then why do they let the states do whatever they want to do about slavery? It doesn't seem fair."

"Politics isn't always fair, girl, any more than the government always does what's *right*, like Corrie was saying. States' rights isn't a doctrine of governing that always makes things turn out fair. It just happens to be how this here country got put together in the first place. Besides, Buchanan's a Democrat and a southerner. Letting the states do whatever they want—that's just how the southerners want to keep it, so they can keep having their slaves and growing their cotton. No Democrat's gonna change that."

"A Republican might," I suggested.

"Yeah, you're right, daughter, a Republican just might. That's why the Democrats and southerners are so all-fired worried about this election. They figure if Lincoln's elected, it just might be the end of states' rights altogether."

"Why can't it all just keep going how it is?" asked Tad. "Some states could have slaves if they wanted, others don't have to."

"Yes, Pa," added Becky, "why can't there keep being states' rights no matter who gets elected?"

"That's what the southerners want," put in Almeda. "But Abraham Lincoln has made no secret of his revulsion toward slavery."

Pa turned to me. "Corrie," he said, "where's that paper that had your article about the election in it? Seems I recollect reading a speech of Lincoln's there."

"I'll get it, Pa," I said, jumping up.

"You see, Becky," Pa went on, "Mr. Lincoln figures we just can't keep going forever with half of the states one way, the other half the other way. He says it's tearing the country apart, making people hate each other, making it so the government can't do anything but argue and dispute and can't get on with the business of helping make the country what it ought to be. He says that we *got* to be what our name says—*united*. One way or the other— either all for slavery or all against it. We can't keep being split up like we have been. And now that there's more northern states than southern, the southerners figure that if he's elected, he's gonna try to take the *whole* country the direction he wants to go."

"Against states' rights?"

"They don't figure Mr. Lincoln cares so much for states' rights as much as he wants to do what *he* thinks is right."

Just then I returned with the paper.

"Here," said Pa, reaching out and taking it from me, "just listen to this. I'll read you part of the speech and you can see for yourselves what Mr. Lincoln says about it."

He rustled through the *Alta* till he found the speech on the second page and began to read.

In my opinion, the agitation over the issue of slavery
will not cease until a crisis shall have been reached and passed.
A house divided against itself cannot stand. I believe this
government cannot endure, permanently half slave and half
free. I do not expect the Union to be dissolved—I do not

expect the house to fall—but I DO expect it will cease to be divided. It will become all one thing, or all the other. Either the opponents of slavery will arrest the further spread of it, and place it where the public mind shall rest in the belief that it is in the course of ultimate extinction; or its advocates will push it forward, till it shall become alike lawful in all the States, old as well as new—North as well as South.

"I didn't understand that, Pa," said Tad.

"He's just saying that it's got to be all one way or all the other. Slavery's either got to be legal everywhere throughout the whole country, or else it's got to be thrown out completely, including in the South."

"What about the states that are talking of seceding, Drummond?" asked Almeda seriously. "Do you think it could actually happen?"

"No way to know, Almeda. One thing's for sure—people can be mighty stubborn and dead set against change, whether they're right *or* wrong."

"But if some states want to secede, should they have the right to?" I asked. Ever since I had decided to get involved in the election, I'd been thinking about this question because I knew it was on Abraham Lincoln's mind. I still hadn't been able to figure out even what I thought about it.

"That's the question of 1860, girl," said Pa. "It ain't so much just about slavery, but whether states' rights gives some of the states the right to pull themselves out of the United States of America altogether. If California can't split in half without the government's permission, then can some of the southern states go off and do whatever they want to do without permission either? I don't reckon anybody knows the answer to that question yet. But if Mr. Lincoln gets elected, I don't much doubt that some of 'em are gonna put it to the test and see what comes of it."

Pa surely was sounding like a politician! From a fugitive to a gold miner to a father to a mayor . . . and now he was talking about the future of the whole country as if he was personally involved in what happened.

And as a candidate for the California State Assembly, I guess he was, at that!

# CHAPTER 37

## THE ELECTION APPROACHES

In a way, the question that California politicians had been debating was just a small version of the same issue politicians in the rest of the country were wrestling with.

Should California, where the interests of the northern and southern sections were much different, be one *state* or two? And should the whole country be one *nation* or two? How far did states' rights go, anyway?

Trouble had been brewing between the North and South for a long time. There had been strong outcries against slavery for almost thirty years—going clear back to the preaching of Charles Finney in the 1830s as well as that of many others. The American Anti-Slavery Society was formed in 1833. William Lloyd Garrison had begun a radical antislavery newspaper called *The Liberator* two years before that stirred up sentiments on both sides all over the country. More societies were formed. Books were written. And dozens of preachers denounced slavery from the pulpit.

But none of that could do anything to put an end to slavery. The Congress in Washington, D.C., made the laws. And since Congress was controlled all that time by the Democratic party, which was mostly made up of men from the South, they continued to uphold the right of each individual state to have slavery if it wanted—which, of course, all the southern states did.

When the Republican party formed in the early 1850s, the Democrats and southerners weren't too worried. But it grew so rapidly—with new states and territories all being more inclined toward northern interests, and with antislavery preaching continuing to grow—that by 1856 the Democrats realized they *should* be worried. Buchanan had been elected over John Fremont only by a hairsbreadth. If two of the northern states had gone for Fremont instead, he would have become president. The governor of Virginia, Edie had told us, had been thinking of secession even back then if Fremont had been elected.

Now, in 1860, southern leaders *were* worried!

In the North, there was strong and growing opposition to the hold of the South. But the southerners had no intention of giving up their power without a fight. There were growing threats throughout the year that a number of the states of the South would simply secede, or pull out of the Union. The South was financially strong, and if it had to, it would simply form its own new nation. But it would *not* give up slavery, nor give up its right to make its own decisions.

But the election of 1860 was not as simple as Democrats against Republicans, North against South, slavery against abolition. In fact, there were *four* candidates for president. Douglas, the Democrat, was not even a southerner at all. He was from Abraham Lincoln's home state of Illinois, and was the U.S. senator from Illinois. He had defeated Lincoln for that position in 1858 after their famous series of debates.

Many southerners, in fact, didn't like Douglas. He wasn't strongly enough in favor of slavery to suit them. But most Democrats, by 1860, realized that Lincoln was absolutely sure to win if they nominated a proslavery southerner to run against him. So at the Democratic convention earlier in the year, a majority had nominated the northerner Douglas, figuring that a northern candidate was their only hope against Lincoln.

That only angered the Democrats from the deep South. Win or not, they wanted a candidate who stood *for* slavery! So they organized a convention of *their* own and nominated their Democratic candidate, Buchanan's vice-president, John Breckinridge, from the slave state of Kentucky.

Now there were two Democrats running against Lincoln!

Back in the spring, a whole new party had been formed, called the Constitutional Union party. They hoped to find some middle ground between both the Democrats and the Republicans, and stood above all else simply for loyalty to the Union itself. They hoped to attract support from Union-loving conservatives in the South. The ticket for this new party was made up of two U.S. senators, one from the North, one from the South—John Bell of Tennessee for president and Edward Everett of Massachusetts for vice president.

So those were the four candidates: Lincoln for the Republicans, Douglas for the Democrats, Breckinridge for the southern Democrats, and Bell for the Constitutional Union party.

It was a hard-fought campaign. Douglas traveled up and down New England calling on people to preserve the Union and speaking against secession—sounding almost like Lincoln himself—trying to get the northern vote while retaining southern Democratic support. Even as pro-southern as he was, Breckinridge tried to convince the voters that he, too, was opposed to secession.

In California, as in the rest of the country, the Democrats had been in control, and there was a large pro-southern sentiment throughout the state. But the split of the Democratic party also split California and its leaders. Governor Downey declared his support for Douglas. Former governors Weller and Latham and Senator Gwin declared their support for Breckinridge. And Mr. Stanford and his business and railroad associates Huntington, Cole, Hopkins, and Charles and Edwin Crocker made up the most well-known of the Republican leadership within the state.

It was remarkable to me how much pro-southern, pro-slavery support there was in *northern* California. Except for the possibility that a lot of Californians had come from the South, I couldn't understand it. I hadn't understood it back in 1856, and I still didn't understand it in 1860. If the Democratic party hadn't been split in its loyalties, I don't think Mr. Lincoln would have had a ghost of a chance in California.

# CHAPTER 38

# NOVEMBER 6, 1860

We made up the handbills for Pa. This time it was important to distribute them not just around Miracle Springs but everywhere possible in the whole section of the state north of Sacramento in the Assembly district Pa hoped to represent. Pa was running as a Republican, and though there were several other candidates—one other Republican and three Democrats all together—we hoped that he might have a chance to win. For the flyer I wrote a story that told all about Pa and who he was, adding quotes from some people in Miracle Springs saying what a good mayor he'd been.

Then I wrote an article for the handbill, like the speech I'd given in Sacramento about freedom and the future of the country. It probably didn't have much to do with Pa and whether he'd be a good legislator or not, but I hoped it would help. I didn't want to say *too* much, because if people knew that a Hollister was writing telling people to vote for a Hollister, it might not seem altogether unbiased.

Edie was still with Aunt Katie, and in spite of our differences about slavery itself, she thought it was exciting about Pa's running for office, even as a Republican. She offered to help, and the rest of us were ready to do anything we could, too. It was a lot of work, but we split up and took handbills to all the towns for thirty or forty miles around Miracle Springs—wherever we could get to on horseback and back in a day, or to the towns Pa or I passed through on our way to Sacramento. We even gave them to Marcus Weber when he had deliveries to make.

In every town we posted a copy of the handbill up on the town announcement board, or if they didn't have one, on a post somewhere near the center of town. Then the rest we'd leave at the General Store if they'd let us. Most of the folks knew something about Pa and were happy to pass out the flyers to their customers.

I didn't make any more speeches, although Pa did at a couple more towns where Mr. Dalton had made arrangements for him. He was having lots of the smaller northern newspapers print articles about Pa, too, and told us just a week before the election that Drummond Hollister was the most widely known and recognized name of the five candidates.

I got several letters from Cal in the month preceding the election, although I didn't see him again. I wrote to him several times, too, and asked him about what I'd overheard between him and Mr. Dalton concerning the anti-Lincoln move in the southern portion of the state. *It's all taken care of, Corrie,* he wrote back in his next letter. *Forget you heard a word about it.* In fact, he expressed surprise that I remembered the incident.

*It was a minor annoyance,* he went on to say, *which we took care of. I have every confidence our Mr. Lincoln will carry the day in northern California.*

The long-awaited day finally came on Tuesday, November 6. Pa and Uncle Nick went to vote, but of course it was days before the ballots were all collected and counted, and two weeks before we found out what the results were throughout the rest of the country. That Pony Express rider carrying the election news was one of the most eagerly anticipated since the Express had begun. They didn't have to ride all the way to Sacramento for the news to reach us, because by that time a telegraph had been installed between San Francisco and Churchill, Nevada. The San Francisco papers carried news of the election results on November 19.

The Democratic strategy of two candidates hadn't worked. And the Independent had done much better than predicted, carrying three states. Douglas had received the second highest number of votes behind Lincoln, but only carried Missouri and split New Jersey with Lincoln. Breckinridge got only 18 percent of the total vote. But because of his strong support in the proslavery South, he carried eleven southern states.

The final votes were: Lincoln 1,866,000, Douglas 1,383,000,

Breckinridge 848,000, and Bell 593,000.

Abraham Lincoln received 40 percent of the total, not nearly a majority. But because he carried all the northern states and seventeen states in all, his electoral vote was a huge majority. The final electoral results were: Lincoln 180, Breckinridge 79, Bell 39, and Douglas 12.

Abraham Lincoln had been elected the next president of the United States!

# CHAPTER 39

# A DREADFUL WAY TO END A YEAR

But would the United States stay *united* for much longer? Almost immediately after the election it began to look as if the answer was no!

The South was now clearly and unmistakably the minority. The once-powerful region that had controlled the nation had been defeated. Many mixed sentiments ran through the hearts of loyal southerners—pride, honor, fear of what the North might do. And stubbornness, too. They feared that their traditional and cherished ways of life would now be destroyed, their lands taken, their fortunes and businesses ruined. Their pride had been assaulted. Many southerners felt themselves superior, and that *they* were more capable of ruling the nation no matter what the election might have said. Now the mammon-worshiping materialists of the North were in power, intent on destroying the southern culture forever, and replacing it with their Yankee ways.

Their honor was at stake. They would not, they *could* not submit to such humiliation. They must save the South, even if they had to create a whole new republic to do it!

It did not take long for the southern states to act. They had prepared for this moment for more than a year should Lincoln be elected. One month after the vote, on December 6, 1860, South Carolina voted to withdraw from the Union.

Rapidly the governors of the other southern states called special sessions of their legislatures to vote on similar measures. They wanted to act hurriedly, while a sympathetic and Democratic

James Buchanan was still president. What Abraham Lincoln might do once he took office on March 3, no one knew. And the southern states didn't want to wait to find out!

I suppose that in the South during these tense months, there was a feeling of excitement, as if they were part of a historic and honorable cause, out of which a new and noble nation was about to be born. But in the rest of the country, news of what South Carolina had done caused only gloom. Why, we all wondered, would they try to tear the country apart?

We still hoped nothing might come of it. South Carolina had always been the most radical southern state. Back in 1832 when Pa hadn't been much more than a boy, South Carolina had gotten defiant and had threatened to do the same thing. But President Jackson had answered heatedly and had said he'd send in the army if he had to. South Carolina had backed down.

Many people held the opinion that they could be forced to back down again if Buchanan would act, and act promptly. But President Buchanan's party had been defeated. He had only three months more to serve, and he had never been a swift decision maker. The result was that he did nothing, and left events to take their course. He would just wait and let the new president worry about it.

In the meantime, the South became stronger and stronger in their resolve that they would *never* back down again.

As bad as all this was, it wasn't the worst news to come to Miracle Springs as 1860 came to an end. Two weeks before Christmas, a letter arrived addressed to Pa. The handwriting was a barely legible scrawl, but his name and "Miracle Springs could be made out on the envelope. The letter inside was no easier to read. It was a single sheet of paper.

HOLISTR,

I hope this here letter gits to you. I give it to Pony Bob an tol him to give hit to the next feller an to git hit to Sacremeno an that somebudy there'd no how to git it to youe. This aint no good kin of letter to have to writ to nobudy nohow, an I hate to be the one to have to do hit. But I figger youd rather hear hit from a freen than from somebudy you never heerd of. What I got to say jis this, Holistr, an Im sorry as a man kin be, but word came to us las week that yer sons horse come wanderin into the stashun without nary a trace o the kid. The mail was ther but no rider. Thats all we heerd. I sent Pony Bob back out ther an tol him to fin out sumthin mor, on account o youe bein my freen an all. I didnt want to writ you til we cud tell you jist what happen. But Bob he didnt git no more informashun, an nobudys heerd hide or hare o the boy sinse, and its been more na week now, an this time o yere nobudy kin live out in them hills past tu or thre days. Im sorry as kin be, but hit dont look good fer yer boy. Hits been snowin there tu. An the blame Piyutes. Give yer little lady my best, and tell her Im sorry tu.

Tavish

The whole rest of the week a spirit of gloom hovered all about the claim. When all the folks in town heard about it, a quiet settled over all of Miracle Springs. Pa was held in mighty high regard by everyone, and so was Almeda. The fact that Zack had been riding for the Pony Express had made people proud in a way. His disappearance affected everyone.

Rev. Rutledge prayed for Zack in church the next Sunday, and of course everybody came up to us to offer their sympathy and to say they'd be praying for all of us.

Mr. Royce was among them. "I'm sorry to hear about the boy, Hollister," he said, shaking Pa's hand. "I really mean that."

"I know you do, Franklin," replied Pa.

"The kid had spunk. Almost as much as your girl there," he added, glancing toward me with as much of a smile as Franklin Royce was ever likely to give anyone. "He was the one who saved my money and your wife's property back when the Dutch Flat gang was causing so much trouble. No, I'm not likely to forget that. If anybody can take care of himself out there, it's your Zack."

"I'm much obliged to you, Royce," said Pa.

As time went on, it was almost worse not knowing. It would have been easier to deal with and get past if we had just heard he was dead. But to not know, and to have to think of him lying somewhere with an arrow in him, or frozen in a snowdrift in some ravine—that was the worst part.

The only bright spot in the last month and a half of the year was that Pa was elected to the California State Assembly. But nobody felt much like celebrating. Least of all Pa.

# CHAPTER 40

## SECESSION!

Christmas of 1860 was certainly not a very festive day.

Almeda and Aunt Katie tried to make it as happy as they could. There were presents and we had a nice dinner with the Rutledges at our house. But Pa felt so downcast over Zack, and everyone shared his misery.

Pa now had two things to feel guilt-ridden about—driving Zack away in the first place, and then turning back when we were there instead of going on to find him—Indian danger or not!

"If only I hadn't been such a coward," Pa said a dozen times. "I might have got to him and talked him into coming back home with me. But that handful of Indians made me hightail it outta there like a scared jackrabbit!"

"There were more than a few, Pa," I reminded him. "We both almost got ourselves good and dead."

But nothing I or anyone else said could perk up Pa's spirits. And who was I to blame him? I'd have felt terrible, too. I *did* feel terrible, but not so bad as if I'd been his father. Maybe Zack was being rebellious and independent by running off as he had. But Pa didn't have the luxury of the man in the New Testament, knowing he had been a good father and yet not being able to do anything about his son's foolish youthfulness. Maybe Pa had been a decent father to Zack; maybe he hadn't. He sure had been to me. But the fact was, he didn't think so, and he believed the accusations Zack had shouted at him the day he'd left.

So it was a lot harder on him than the father in the Bible who just had to wait patiently for his prodigal son to come to his senses.

Pa had to carry guilt along with everything else, guilt for having caused all the trouble and heartbreak himself. Now thinking that Zack was probably dead, but not knowing, and knowing he might *never* know for sure—it was just an unbearable load for poor Pa. All the rest of us could do was love him and pray for him. But we couldn't make it go away.

As always, news from the East got into our papers about two weeks after it actually happened. During that first week of the new year of 1861, we began to learn of events that did not portend good news for the future. President Buchanan still hadn't done anything to block or counter South Carolina's action. Neither had he nor anyone else made any hard attempts to resolve the crisis with a compromise of some kind. These failures led to the most serious news of all: one by one, starting with Mississippi on December 20, the rest of the southern states began to secede from the Union too. Next came Florida, then Alabama, Georgia, Louisiana, and finally later in January, Texas.

Still President Buchanan did nothing. Abraham Lincoln remained powerless until he would take office on March 3. Was nothing to be done to save the *United* States of America from becoming the *Dis*united States?

As they seceded, the southern states had taken possession of federal properties inside their borders. South Carolina could not immediately seize Fort Sumter in Charleston harbor, however, because it had no navy and because the fort was held by seventy-five Union soldiers.

But South Carolina wanted the fort. Now that the new independent little country was over a month old, it was beginning to feel itself strong and important. So a committee was sent to Washington to negotiate with the United States on behalf of the nation of South Carolina to have the fort transferred to the former state.

President Buchanan refused to give up the fort. Finally he got angry and sent an unarmed steamer down the coast to Fort Sumter with more troops and supplies. South Carolina military troops fired on the ship and forced it to turn around.

It had been the first act of war. Yet even though northerners and we in the West were shocked and astonished at what the South was doing, there was still no real sense of the danger and peril yet to come.

Even if President Buchanan had *wanted* to force South Carolina and the other states back into the Union, there would probably have been little he could have done. The regular army of the nation was only 15,000 strong, and most of those men were out West protecting settlers and wagon trains and Pony Express riders from Indians. It would have taken months to get the army back to the East—and doing so would have left the West to the Indians!

Everyone loathed what the South was doing, and said it was illegal and against the Constitution to do it. Yet no one actually wanted to *fight* to stop them from doing it.

But tempers and emotions were gradually running hotter and more violent and unpredictable.

Meanwhile, the southern states were wasting no time. As northern politicians scurried around trying to set up meetings and find compromise plans, the seven states that had seceded were busy forming a new government. From the beginning, they had planned to organize a whole new nation as soon as secession had been accomplished—a new nation based on the principle of states' rights. And it was important that they do so immediately . . . *before* Lincoln's inauguration!

Therefore, delegates from the seven states met in February in Montgomery, Alabama, and founded a new nation. They called it the Confederate States of America. And they didn't waste time with an election—the delegates themselves chose Mississippi Senator and former Secretary of War Jefferson Davis as their new president.

# CHAPTER 41

# A NEW PRESIDENT COMES TO WASHINGTON

The new southern nation was confident, and in early 1861 better organized and more united than the rest of the United States. All was not lost quite yet, however, because eight more slave states of the upper and border regions of the South had remained loyal to the Union and were determined to give Lincoln a chance.

All this time, President-elect Abraham Lincoln had not revealed to the country what he intended to do about the crisis. Would he attack South Carolina? If so, with what troops? Would he try to find some new compromise nobody had thought of yet? Would he just wait and let events go as Buchanan had? Or would he accept the new nation, and go on as President of just half the former country?

No one knew. So everyone in *both* countries anxiously awaited Lincoln's inaugural speech, scheduled for March 4, to find out what his new policy was going to be.

In the meantime, out in California, there was a lot of support for the South. The South Carolina fever for secession ran all the way west to the Pacific!

But for some reason, by the time it reached California, those who felt the state ought to secede didn't necessarily want to join the Confederacy. They wanted California to pull out of the Union to start a *third* independent republic. If the North and South couldn't solve their squabbles, why should California be joined with either of them?

A year before, former California Senator Weller had proclaimed: "If the wild spirit of fanaticism, which now pervades the land, should destroy this magnificent Union, California will not go with the South or the North, but here upon the shores of the Pacific will found and establish a mighty new republic."

"It's plumb fool ridiculousness, Almeda!" exclaimed Pa, looking up from the newspaper.

"What is it, Drummond?" she'd asked.

"I'm just reading here in the *Standard* that this fellow Butts is calling for a convention to found a Pacific republic. Who is he, anyway—do you know, Corrie?"

"Judge Butts is the editor of the Sacramento *Standard*, Pa."

"Well, he's got no business interfering in politics, if you ask me."

"You better learn to get along with him when you go to Sacramento," laughed Almeda, "or you might find yourself tarred and feathered in that paper of his!

"It was just a month ago that you were laughing about that proposal by John Burch proposing the formation of a Pacific republic."

"That's because I thought it was a joke—California, Oregon, New Mexico, Washington, and Utah forming a new country! But I think Butts is serious!"

"He is serious, Pa," I said. "The *Herald*, the *Gazette*, the *Democrat*, the *Star*—they've all come out in favor of western independence."

"What about your *Alta*?"

"The *Alta*'s pro-Union all the way," I said. "You don't think I'd keep writing for a Democratic paper, do you?"

"Well, if this one Republican has anything to say about it when I get to Sacramento, California's gonna stay put right where it is— in the Union, and supporting Mr. Abraham Lincoln when he gets to be president!"

All through the elections Lincoln's opponents had made fun of his appearance—tall, thin, and gawky, with rough features and a big beak nose. He was said to sleep in the same shirt he gave speeches in, and from listening to some reports I would have thought he still lived in the backwoods log cabin where he was raised. Even after his election he was not considered "sophisticated" enough for Washington society.

But people were in for a surprise. Lincoln might not have been handsome or cultured, but he was a strong man, a shrewd politician, and an authoritative leader—just the right man to be president at such a time, and certainly better than James Buchanan. Abraham Lincoln would not do nothing. Whatever he did, it was sure to be decisive.

Lincoln left his home in Springfield, Illinois, for Washington in late February. He traveled by train and took eleven roundabout days to get there, stopping all throughout the states of the North to visit people and make speeches and let them see their new president. Everybody wanted to know what he was going to do about the Confederacy, but he wouldn't reveal his policies yet. His speeches were light—some even thought them frivolous. People began to get the idea they had elected a simpleton to the White House. He seemed almost unaware of how serious the crisis was.

At Westfield, New York, he asked the crowd if a young girl by the name of Grace Bedell was present. She was brought up to the rear of the train where he was speaking. Then he told the listening crowd that she had written him during the campaign to tell him that he would look much handsomer if he grew some whiskers. Then he stooped down with a smile. "You see, Grace," he said, "I let these whiskers grow just for you."

When he attended the opera in New York City, he did the unthinkable by wearing black gloves instead of white. High society was aghast at the thought of having such an oafish man living in the White House and in charge of the country.

In Philadelphia a private detective named Allan Pinkerton came to the President-elect with the news that he had learned of a plot to assassinate him when he changed trains in Baltimore. Lincoln would have paid no attention, except that a little while later another report came to him of the same thing.

So Lincoln let Pinkerton take charge of getting him to Washington safely. He was put up in a sleeper that had been reserved by one of Pinkerton's female detectives for her "invalid brother." They passed through Baltimore at three in the morning and reached Washington just about daybreak.

When it was discovered what had happened and that Lincoln had at one point in the journey draped a shawl over his shoulders so as not to be recognized, all kinds of mocking and cruel stories and jokes and cartoons were printed in the newspapers, especially in the South. This was the man, they said, who was going to lead the nation! People were beginning to think he was an incompetent, ignorant clown.

But Lincoln had just been beating around the bush with his lighthearted speeches. In fact, he knew exactly how serious the crisis was. He had been planning for it for four months.

The Pony Express was gearing up to speed Lincoln's inaugural address to California the moment it was delivered. I wished Zack had been able to be part of it!

It took three days for the speech to reach St. Joseph by train from Washington. Then the Express took over at an amazing pace. The speech was brought down the Main Street of Sacramento from St. Joseph in an all-time speed record: seven days and seventeen hours. Two of the riders, trying to make up for delays, actually rode their horses to death.

The speech, which Pa read to us all from the March 17 edition of the *Alta* when it arrived in Miracle Springs on the eighteenth, was certainly not the speech of a weakling or a simpleton. It was clear right away what kind of man had been elected President, and I was glad that I'd done my part to help him win California's four electoral votes. It wasn't much, out of the 180 he'd received, but I was glad they hadn't gone to anybody else.

"The Union is older than the states," he said in his speech, "and was founded to last forever. Secession is illegal, a revolutionary act." Then the new President went on to tell what he planned to do.

He did not intend to be rash, he said, or to do anything sudden or forceful. He would proceed with patience and caution for a time. And that right there, Almeda said as we listened, was the clue that showed he had no intention of putting up with the so-called new country forever—he would be patient *for a time*.

But he *would*, he went on to say, do all in his power to enforce all federal laws in *all* the states, and he would keep firm hold of federal property. Everyone knew he meant Fort Sumter.

He was not considering any forceful retribution, and there would be no threat to the constitutional rights of the states that had left the Union. If they wished to return, they could. But the government *would* act to defend itself.

Then he brought up the horrible prospect of what would happen if the southern states *didn't* come to their senses and come back to the Union. He spoke straight to the South when he said whose fault it would be.

"In *your* hands, my dissatisfied fellow countrymen," he said, "and not in *mine,* is the momentous issue of civil war. The government will not assail *you.* You can have no conflict without being yourselves the aggressors. You have no oath registered in Heaven to destroy the government, while *I* shall have the most solemn one to *preserve, protect, and defend it.*"

The closing words of his speech showed that he still wanted to believe that the people of the South deep down felt as loyal to the country as he did. Maybe their radical leaders didn't. But surely the great masses of southerners didn't really want what was happening.

"We are not enemies," he said, "but friends. We must not be enemies. Though passion may have strained, it must not break the bonds of affection. The mystic chords of memory, stretching from every battlefield and patriot grave, to every living heart and hearthstone, all over this broad land, will yet swell the chorus of the Union, when again touched, as surely they will be, by the better angels of our nature."

# CHAPTER 42

# PA IN SACRAMENTO

Those were times of peril, those first few months of 1861.

The only trouble was, no one knew how dangerous they really were. No one expected what came afterward. No one knew how bad it would be. If they had, they probably would have done things differently.

As it was, time kept passing, and everybody on both sides got more and more determined *not* to give in. They all thought *they* were right and everyone else was wrong. Sometimes that may be true, but it can still be a dangerous way to look at things. Admitting you might be a little wrong yourself is hard for most folks, but it seems like the easiest way to avoid conflicts later.

Pa had gone to Sacramento to get sworn in to the new Assembly in January of 1861. He was gone a week that first time. When he came back he was so full of stories and enthusiasm he hardly stopped talking for days. I had never seen him like that! Almeda couldn't get over him; she laughed and laughed just to listen to him. It seemed such a short time ago that he'd been just an ordinary soft-spoken man trying to make a gold strike. Suddenly he had a family and a vein of wealth right on his property, a new wife and a business. Before he knew it, he was mayor of a town, then a state legislator.

"If a simple man like Abraham Lincoln can go from a log cabin to splitting wood rails to being president," said Almeda one day, "then I don't see any reason why you can't, too!"

She made the mistake of letting Alkali Jones hear her! He'd been working at the mine with Uncle Nick, Pa, and Tad, and had just walked into the house for lunch. Whenever Pa came back from Sac-

224

ramento business, he worked at the mine for the next two or three days. "Makes me feel back to normal," he said, "to get wet and dirty and get my arms and back aching again. Too much sitting around talking like they do down there in the Capitol, it just ain't natural. A man's gotta sweat from hard work, at least three or four times a week, or things just get out of order. I gotta be working if I'm gonna think right!"

"Drum fer President!" cackled Mr. Jones, walking in on the tail end of what Almeda had said. "That's a good'n—hee, hee, hee! I can die in peace now, I've heard jist about every dad-burned tall tale a body could dream up! Drum fer President—hee, hee, hee!"

"You don't think I could do the job, Alkali?" said Pa seriously, giving the rest of us a wink.

"Oh, I ain't sayin' no such thing. Fer all I know, you'd march straight down t' them southern rascals an' look 'em straight in the eye and say, 'Now look here, you varmints! You're breakin' a passel of laws, an' worse'n that—you're all actin' like a bunch of dang fools. Now git back t' your homes; let your slaves be the free men they got a right t' be, and cut it out with all this blamed foolishness of tryin' t' start a country of your own. It ain't gonna work no how!' "

By now we were all in stitches from laughing so hard. Of course, that just spurred Mr. Jones all the more to keep going. There wasn't anything he loved better than being at the center of stories high on imagination and low on facts.

"Yep," he kept going, "you jist might make a president that'd git folks in this country t' stand up an' take notice of the kind of guts and grit it takes t' live out here. Drum for President—hee, hee! That's what them there fools back there need, all right—a Californian with the guts t' make them rascals back down and git off their dang high horses! Hee, hee, hee!"

"What would you do if you *were* president, Pa?" Tad asked.

Pa got a real serious expression on his face. The room grew quiet, and we all waited to see what he'd say.

"You mean about the Confederate states, boy?" he said finally.

"Yeah, Pa. How would you make them not do what they're trying to do to the country?"

"Well, I reckon the first thing I'd do is send my vice-president down to Montgomery to talk to 'em, to look 'em straight in the eye,

226

and to horsewhip some sense into 'em."

"Who would be your vice-president, Pa?" asked Becky.

"Why, I thought you knew, girl," answered Pa. "Alkali, of course!"

"Please, Drummond," said Almeda this time, wiping the tears of laughter out of her eyes and trying to be serious. "I really am curious what you would do."

Again Pa thought long and hard.

"I don't reckon I can answer what I *would* do if I was in Washington without saying what I *am* doing right down there in Sacramento," he answered finally.

"What do you mean by that?" asked Uncle Nick, drying his hands off with a towel and walking over toward Pa.

"Just what I said, Nick. I mean, my first business is right here and right now. I tell you, there's as much foolishness coming out of some of those southern sympathizing Democrats in Sacramento as in those renegades setting themselves up as so all-fired important down in Montgomery! It makes my blood boil just to think of it. That's why I had to get back here to Miracle and swing the sledge a few times against some good hard rock."

"How you figure it, Drum?" asked Mr. Jones. I'd never taken him as one much interested in politics, but the look on his face was serious. This dispute between North and South had *everyone's* attention!

"We sat down for our first session," said Pa. "Half of the new members, like me, had no idea what was going on or what to do or how the place even worked. Then this guy named Zack Montgomery stood up. He talked half the morning about how we needed to break away from the Union ourselves. Later I heard there was a senator named Thornton doing the same thing over in the Senate room. The Democrats are trying to get California to do the same thing as South Carolina!"

"Surely it's not a serious threat?" said Almeda, in both amazement and shock.

"You gotta realize, Almeda," said Pa, "the Democrats still outnumber us Republicans in the state. Breckinridge and Douglas together got a heap more votes than Lincoln. A lot of politicians in this state think Lincoln's a buffoon, and they're not ashamed to say so.

Lots of 'em don't have that much loyalty to the Union. They figure California's the only thing that matters, so let Lincoln and the eastern states do whatever they please. Why, there's a feller named Charles Piercy who voted for Douglas—he's not a slave man, has no particular loyalties to the South. But he stood up, just a few seats away from me, and he said he'd written up what he called a resolution condemning the Republicans as altogether and solely responsible for bringing on the secession crisis. Then he walked up to the front and handed the piece of paper he was talking about to the Speaker. Then Piercy turned around to face the rest of us—and this was after Montgomery's fiery speech—and said, 'My fellow assemblymen, for this reason, I feel most strongly that we Californians will never entirely be able to support our new president. I am urging you, therefore, to stand with me in backing the formation of a mighty Pacific Republic, as advocated by our colleague, Mr. Montgomery, earlier today. Our former governor, Mr. Latham, now in the Senate in Washington, has long been in favor of such a proposition, and would no doubt return to help us in the formation of a constitution and provisional government.' "

Pa stopped, then added, "Those are probably not his exact words, but something like 'em. Speechmaking words! And ridiculous words, if you ask me!"

"What did the rest of you do?" asked Uncle Nick.

"There were some folks saying 'Hear, hear!' and agreeing with him, but others stood up when he was done and said just what I was thinking, that it was downright foolishness. One fella got up and even brought France into it."

"France?" repeated Alkali Jones. "What do them foreigners have t' do with us?"

"Well, this fella said that if we tried to set ourselves up in a new country over here, this far away from the other states, with a thousand miles of coastline and less than a million people and no army, he said we couldn't defend ourselves against anybody—especially with the North and South at each other's throats. He said Napoleon would come right in and gobble us up and make us into a Pacific France."

"Napoleon's dead, Pa," said Becky. "Mrs. Rutledge was just teaching us about him and a place called Waterloo last month, before Christmas."

"Napoleon the Third, Becky," I said. "He's the other Napoleon's nephew. He's the emperor of France."

"Well, whoever the varmint is, let him try t' come in here an' make trouble! We'll show him what kind of stuff Californians is made of!"

"With what, Alkali?" said Pa. "We got no army, and hardly no militia to speak of. We're barely a state, much less a country that could fight off somebody like France!"

"So what happened next, Pa?" asked Becky.

A funny look came over Pa's face. Almeda recognized it immediately. "I can tell when you're holding something in, Drummond," she said. "Now tell us, what happened?"

"Well, all of a sudden I found myself on my feet," Pa answered, as if he was embarrassed to remember it.

"Good for you, Drum!" exclaimed Uncle Nick. "You gave 'em all what for, didn't you? I knew you had it in you!"

"No I didn't give 'em what for, Nick!" Pa shot back. "What do you think, that I wanted to make enemies there my first week in the capital?"

"You must have said something," said Almeda, her eyes eager to hear what had happened.

"I reckon I did," said Pa slowly. "The second I realized what I was doing, I got afraid and wanted to sit down something fierce. But I went ahead with what I'd been thinking, and I just told 'em all that I figured since we'd elected Mr. Lincoln, he deserved for us to at least give him a chance of seeing what he could do. I said we oughta let it sit a spell. Gettin' too hasty's always a way of hangin' yourself, I said. I told 'em I'd always made a practice of trying to take important decisions slow. You don't usually get in trouble from goin' too slow, I said—that is, unless you're in a gunfight. They laughed a little when I said that," said Pa, chuckling as he remembered it. "But you *can* get yourself in a heap o' trouble by rushing into something you ought not to have done. So I finished up by saying I figured we oughta wait and give the President our loyalty, and see what happened."

The room got quiet when Pa finished.

All at once Almeda started clapping, and then the rest of us joined in, just as if we'd been sitting there in the state Assembly room actually listening to Pa's speech.

"Now cut that out—all of you!" scowled Pa. I don't think I'd ever seen his face red before, but it was then. "It wasn't no big thing!"

I glanced over at Almeda. Her face was fixed intently on Pa with a look of admiration and love, and tears stood in her eyes.

"What happened next, Pa?" asked Tad eagerly.

"Well, boy, some of the folks did just what you done—they started clapping, and I sat down pronto and wished I could just sink right down into my chair and hide. I gotta tell you, I felt a mite foolish!"

"What about the resolution, Pa?" I asked. "Did you decide anything?"

"Naw. Politics is mostly talking, Corrie. There ain't much *doing*, only yammering about everything. I reckon we'll be voting on what to do one day, but I don't know when. Most likely we'll just keep talking for a long spell, and I'll keep getting my fill of it and have to spend more time up at the mine crushing rocks just to keep from going looney from all the words that don't accomplish much of anything!"

It was quiet for a long time. Finally I asked Pa the question that had been on my mind ever since he had come back home from Sacramento.

"Did you see Mr. Burton when you were there?" I said shyly.

"As a matter of fact, I did, Corrie. He congratulated me on my getting elected, and told me to give you his fond regards. Those were his words—his fond regards. *And* he told me to give you this. I was so anxious to get up and pound them rocks in the mine that I nearly forgot."

He reached inside his coat and took out a rumpled letter, then handed it to me.

My face flushed with embarrassment, but that didn't keep me from snatching the letter and getting up to go to my room to read it.

Everybody else got up too. Just as I was going into the bedroom, I heard Alkali Jones behind me, opening the door to head back outside. He was muttering and chuckling to himself.

"Drum fer President . . . hee, hee, hee!" he was saying. "Blamed if he ain't startin' t' sound like one, at that."

# CHAPTER 43

# OUTBREAK!

Shortly after the inauguration, I received another letter, this one from Mr. Kemble.

*You get to writing, Corrie!* he said. *There's foolishness and plots and subversion afoot all over this country. The Union's in trouble, Corrie, and we've got to have a strong, supportive position. Half of California's papers are advocating everything from throwing in with the Confederacy to the Pacific Republic.*

He had enclosed a clipping from one of the other San Francisco papers, which read:

> We shall secede, with the Rocky Mountains for a line, and form an Empire of the Pacific, with Washington Territory, Oregon, and California, and we shall annex all of this side of Mexico. We don't care a straw whether you dissolve the Union or not. We just wish that the Republicans and Democrats at the Capitol would get into a fight and kill each other like the Kilkenny cats. Perhaps that would settle the hash.

Mr. Kemble finished his letter: *"It's time for the Alta to take its stand, and you along with it. The Union needs us all, Corrie!"*

He hardly needed to tell me how desperate the situation was! Every day I'd been reading, not only in the *Alta* but in other papers as well, about everything that was happening in the East. With the Pony Express making news only two weeks late, everything that was going on felt so real and urgent. I saved all the papers so I'd know just what was happening, and that when I did write things, I'd have my facts straight. If I was going to help Mr. Lincoln and the Union, I had to make sure what I wrote was right and true. I didn't want anyone to be able to complain that the young lady newswoman from California wrote nothing but female emotionalism and that she didn't know what she was talking about. So I tried to understand the events that were going on and keep track of everything as it happened.

The time to have saved the country was back in November or December of 1860. If only Mr. Lincoln had been able to become president right after he was elected! But by the time he set foot in Washington, the Confederacy was already better organized than his new administration! The Republicans had never been in power before. So Mr. Lincoln had to set up an entire executive branch of government from scratch—a cabinet, and all kinds of other appointments. While he was busy having to be an executive and an administrator, the Confederacy was growing stronger and stronger every day.

Not only was the Confederacy stronger right at first, they were confident that Lincoln and the northern states could never stand against southern might. The South had economic strength, strong ties with foreign governments because of the worldwide demand for cotton, and the best politicians in the land. Now that leadership was all in the South. Washington had a group of bumbling mid-westerners and Republicans who had never governed a nation before. In addition, the South had strong financial reserves in her banks, while the North was financially strapped. Perhaps most importantly, the South had the best generals.

By the time Lincoln took office, the Confederacy had a permanent constitution, a treasury, an army, a navy, a post office, and a legal system. Its organizers had been busy. A completely functioning government had been created and was in full operation. Southern leaders had not a doubt in the world that Lincoln would be powerless to oppose them. What could he do? The Confederacy existed, and he could not undo it! If he tried to use force with the two or three thousand army troops he might muster from the northeast and midwest, the results would be laughable. The South would beat them back so fast it would make the tall, lanky rail-splitter from Illinois wish he'd never run for president!

Pa returned from his next trip into Sacramento right at the end of February with serious and disturbing news. Suddenly the dispute between North and South wasn't so far away!

A plot had been discovered, he told us, by a group of southern supporters, to take control of the government of California!

"Knights of the Golden Circle, that's what they called themselves," he said. "Once they had control of Sacramento, they were going to send an armed force down into Mexico where they would seize control of Sonora."

"They could never have gotten away with it!" exclaimed Almeda.

"They had powerful men from the South behind it," said Pa. "They had 50,000 guns on the way to California by the southern route. The knights had 16,000 supporters. They might have been able to do it if we hadn't got word from Washington. They were going to set up an independent republic of the Pacific. Their first move was to grab the Presidio to hold the entrance of the Golden Gate, then the rest of San Francisco's forts, Alcatraz, the Mint, the post office, everything of the government's. Then they were going to join the Confederacy!"

"I can't believe it—in California! Who was behind it?"

"Buchanan's secretary of war, John Floyd. He left Washington, joined the Confederacy, and from what we hear had been arranging for the shipment of guns even while he was in Washington. I tell you, Almeda, it's a dangerous situation. The South has supporters everywhere!"

If 1860 had been a dangerous year in the history of the country, as I'd heard the men discussing at the celebration at the Montgomery Hotel, then 1861 was the year when that danger climaxed and exploded. It didn't take long after Mr. Lincoln's inauguration. The day after it, in fact.

On March 5, Mr. Lincoln was told that the army men at Fort Sumter were running seriously low on supplies and food. Unless they received more soon, they would have to abandon the fort. If that happened, South Carolina would take possession of it, and their victory would make the new outlaw nation seem all the more legitimate.

Mr. Lincoln determined not to let that happen. Fort Sumter was a symbol of the authority of the United States government and its army. It *had* to remain in Union hands. Even though a ship with provisions had been fired upon and turned back in January, Lincoln decided to send several ships this time, as a relief expedition.

Early in April, therefore, he informed authorities in South Carolina that the ships were on their way.

At last the leaders of the new Confederacy showed how confident they were. They didn't want to let the ships get to Fort Sumter, or else it would reduce *their* authority in the world's sight. They wanted to prove how strong they were. In their eyes, a foreign nation controlled a Confederate harbor. So they decided not to wait for the ships to get there. They would attack Fort Sumter first and take control of it before the relief force arrived. They would show whose authority was greatest!

The Confederate commander at Charleston took an order to the Union commander at the fort demanding that he surrender Fort Sumter at once. He refused.

On the morning of April 12, therefore, the Confederate commander opened fire on the fort and blasted it with cannon balls and gunfire all that day and into the night. The small detachment of Union soldiers with scant supplies was helpless. If they didn't yield, they would all eventually be killed. On the next day they gave up and surrendered.

Suddenly the North came alive. Everyone who heard the news of the attack was outraged. It was finally clear—there was no more hope of compromise!

The President and the country had been patient long enough. The honor of the flag had been flagrantly attacked; the Rebel outlaws must be punished! As with one loud unanimous voice, the public demanded retribution against the South. There could be no two separate nations! The Union must be saved. The United States of America must be preserved . . . no matter what had to be done!

The New York *Tribune* carried the news:

> Fort Sumter is lost, but freedom is saved. There is no more thought of bribing or coaxing the traitors who have dared to aim their cannon balls at the flag of the Union, and those who gave their lives to defend it. Fort Sumter is temporarily lost, but the country is saved. Long live the Republic!

News of the firing on Fort Sumter reached San Francisco on April 24, twelve days later. The very next afternoon a great crowd assembled at Portsmouth Square. Patriotic pro-Union speeches went on for a long part of the day, amid applause and cheering. It was not a day in San Francisco to express support for the South!

Immediately President Lincoln sent out a call for 75,000 volunteers, and orders went out to the regular army troops stationed at the Presidio to be sent to the East. Lincoln's message did not actually say the word. He said that the troops and additional volunteers were needed to deal with certain "combinations too powerful to be suppressed by the ordinary course of judicial proceedings." In other words, all hope of compromise was dead.

But whether he said it or not, everyone knew that the United States was now at war.

With itself.

# CHAPTER 44

## WHICH SIDE FOR CALIFORNIA?

Everyone expected the war to be short.

The South was so sure of a quick victory they thought all that would be necessary was for them to raise an army of volunteers and march north to take Washington, Philadelphia, and New York, and that would be the end of it. There was not even a need to sign up troops for lengthy assignments. The Confederacy made the enlistment period just twelve months. That would be more than enough time. Young men and boys throughout the South volunteered in droves. They were so feverish to join the Confederate army there weren't enough guns for them all.

Four more states promptly seceded—Virginia, Arkansas, Tennessee, and North Carolina. Although they were bound to the South in many ways, the states of Missouri, Kentucky, Maryland, and Delaware all decided to stay in the Union.

In the North, the volunteer army grew just as rapidly. More practically minded as to the true depth of the conflict, the North enlisted its young soldiers for three years. Within weeks Lincoln's request for 75,000 men had been passed. By the middle of the year, the Union's army was 500,000 strong. President Lincoln ordered a naval blockade of the whole southern coastline so that ships with provisions could not get through.

Loyalties in California were more divided than ever, now that war between the states had actually come. Pa came home from a session in Sacramento in May with what he considered good news.

"Well, we finally put all that new republic and western confederacy talk to rest," he said. "Piercy and Montgomery and all their crowd oughta be silenced for a while!"

"What happened?" asked Almeda.

"We Republicans finally got our *own* resolution on the floor— a resolution strongly supporting the Union and Mr. Lincoln's government."

"Did you speak again?"

"You bet I did! And this time I wasn't embarrassed. I got up there and I said what I had to say!"

"And it passed the vote?" I asked.

"You're doggone right it did—49 to 12. California's on the Union side of this thing once and for all, and for good!"

"What did it say?"

"Just a bunch of fancy sounding words to say, 'We're behind you, Mr. President.' "

"But what were the actual words?"

"I'll see if I can quote them: 'The people of California are devoted to the Constitution and the Union now in the hour of trial and peril.' Some kind of political gibberish like that!"

But despite the vote in the California legislature, there still was more southern support in the state than was altogether comfortable. Many high office-holders had once been southerners. Not long after the war started, a group of San Francisco's city leaders wrote to Secretary of War Cameron in Washington about their concerns. Since he was editor of the *Alta*, Mr. Kemble was part of that group. He later let me read a copy of the letter.

> A majority of our present state officers are undisguised and avowed Secessionists. . . . Every appointment made by our Governor unmistakably indicates his entire sympathy and cooperation with those plotting to sever California from her allegiance to the Union, and that, too, at the hazard of civil war.
>
> About three-eighths of our citizens are from slave-holding states. . . . These men are never without arms, have wholly laid aside their business, and are devoting their time to plotting, scheming, and organizing. Our advices, obtained with great prudence and care, show us that there are upwards of sixteen thousand "Knights of the Golden Circle" in the state,

and that they are still organizing, even in our most loyal districts.

Whether blood would ever be shed in California as a result of the North-South loyalties that were so divisive, it was still too soon to tell. We all hoped not, and hoped that the pro-Union stand of the legislature, in spite of what these men had said about Governor Downey, would ultimately influence the rest of the state to support the government of Lincoln and Hamlin instead of that of Davis and Stephens.

But in the meantime, the first major exodus *out* of California since the gold rush began to occur. Young men began making their way east to volunteer for the fighting that was sure to come, some to join the Union army, others that of the Confederacy.

# CHAPTER 45

## STANFORD FOR GOVERNOR

I hadn't seen Cal for quite some time, even though I hadn't stopped thinking about him. There had been letters from time to time, but it wasn't nearly the same.

Then all of a sudden one day, there he was in Miracle Springs! I was working at the Mine and Freight when the stage rolled into town. And as I stood staring blankly and absent-mindedly through the backward letters of the word P-A-R-R-I-S-H painted on the window, suddenly there he was stepping down out of the coach.

I couldn't believe my eyes! I blinked a time or two. I must have been dreaming, I thought. But when he turned momentarily in my direction, I knew there could be no mistake.

The next second I was out the door and bolting across the dirt street—not very ladylike, but I wasn't thinking of propriety at the time!

"Cal!" I called out, clomping along in my office boots, my dress flopping about behind me, and holding on to my bonnet to keep it from flying off into the dirt. "Cal. . . !"

He turned from where he had been saying something to the driver and smiled at me in greeting. Before I knew what I was doing, I'd run right up to him and almost threw my arms around him. Luckily I caught myself in time.

"Whatever are you doing here?" I exclaimed, gulping for breath.

"What else would I be doing in Miracle Springs," he said, "but visiting my favorite writer and person, Cornelia Hollister?"

Hearing my full name from his lips sent a tingle through me, and I was glad I was already flushed from the run across the street!

"But why?"

"You don't think visiting you would be enough of a reason for a man?" he said with a grin and a wink.

"Oh, Cal, don't joke with me. You must have come for some other reason. Did you come to see Pa about some Republican business?"

He laughed. "Ah, Corrie, but you are inquisitive. Well, you're right, I *did* come on Republican business—but not to see your pa. I tell you, I came to see *you!*"

"I . . . I don't understand."

"I'll tell you everything. But don't you want to wait until the dust from the stage settles? Perhaps we could have dinner together. Is there someplace—"

"Of course! You'll come home and have supper with us tonight!" I said enthusiastically. "Everybody will be happy to see you again!"

"I had in mind someplace where we might be alone," said Cal.

I blushed in earnest.

"Am I embarrassing you, Corrie? I do apologize. It's only that I have something very important to talk over with you—something I want to discuss in private, something that concerns our future."

*What was he saying?* My head was spinning, frantically trying to think what to say, what to suggest. Before I could get another word out, Cal spoke up again.

"Now that I think about it," he said, "I suppose it would be fitting to include your father—your whole family, in fact—in the announcement I have to make."

"Announcement, Cal . . . what announcement?" I faltered.

"Oh, you'll just have to wait to hear with the rest of them!" he laughed. "I gave you a chance to hear the good news by yourself. But now you'll just have to share it with everyone else!"

He finished his statement, then just stared at me with his blue eyes and a big grin.

"So . . . do I consider that a formal invitation to supper?" he said at length.

"Uh . . . uh, yes," I stumbled out. "Yes . . . of course."

"Tonight?"

"Yes."

"Well, then . . . I know you've probably got work to do over at the office. So I'll just keep myself busy, look around the town awhile, maybe have a drink. And Carl asked me to pay a visit to Mr. Royce as long as I was coming this way. Shall I meet you out at your house this evening?"

"Uh . . . yes," I said. "I reckon that'll be just fine."

"I'll hire a buggy and be out."

He turned and began to walk away. I was still standing there in a daze. "No . . . wait, Cal," I said, finally coming to my senses. "Ride out with me. I have Almeda's buggy here. Come over to the office around five o'clock."

"I'll be there," he said cheerily.

Still I just stood there watching him walk over to the boardwalk and then toward Mr. Royce's bank.

I wasn't much good at the office the rest of the afternoon. I couldn't concentrate on anything, and it was all I could do to keep away from Marcus and Mr. Ashton. If they took one good look at me, they'd start asking all kinds of questions about whether I was sick or something. This was one time I did *not* want two old unmarried men fussing over me. So I spent most of the afternoon in Almeda's office with the door closed. But I didn't get a single thing done!

All I could think about were Cal's words, going over and over and over again in my mind.

*The announcement I have to make . . . someplace where we might be alone . . . in private . . . something that concerns our future . . . our future . . . OUR future . . .*

The ride out to the claim later that day with Cal at my side was nearly torture! He was talkative and friendly, as always, but I was about as interesting as a wet dishrag! It was the longest ride home from town I'd ever had.

I wasn't any better at supper. Pa and Almeda and the others were delighted to see Cal, of course, and he was charming and friendly, laughing and nice and hospitable. He congratulated and praised Pa, saying he always knew his star was on the rise.

They talked about politics mostly, and a lot about the problem with the Confederacy and Fort Sumter.

"Do you think there'll actually be fighting, Cal?" Pa asked.

"It seems impossible to avoid it now, with both sides so dead set against any kind of giving in."

"It's just awful," said Almeda. "The thought of Americans killing Americans is horrible! It oughtn't to be happening!"

I just sat waiting, trembling inside. How could they talk about politics and the war when was Cal going to make his *announcement*?

I didn't have too much longer to wait.

"But the hostilities between North and South isn't why I've come to Miracle Springs," he said when there was a lull in the conversation. "I have some exciting news to tell you all—news that I felt merited a personal visit."

I sat staring straight down at the table, too scared to look up. Somehow I knew, though, that Cal was looking at me.

He paused, and the others waited for him to continue.

"You both know, Mr. and Mrs. Hollister," he finally went on, "how fond I am of your daughter."

I glanced up. They both nodded.

"So fond of her, in fact," Cal said, "that I knew from the very start, right from that evening we all met back in San Francisco, you remember, Mr. Hollister, just about a year ago—I knew that here was a young lady I wanted to be part of my future. I knew too that I wanted her to meet my boss, Mr. Stanford. I just had a feeling about her—a feeling which, I am happy to say, turned out to be a positive omen of things to come."

Again he stopped briefly and drew in a breath. Then he looked over at me, reached out and placed his hand gently on top of mine, and began again.

"Just a few days ago, Mr. Stanford made public his candidacy for the governorship of California. And, Corrie, he asked me to come out here to ask you personally if you would be part of his campaign—a campaign to take control of the great state of California on behalf of the pro-Union Republican party."

He stopped. His face was bright with expectation as he gazed at me. I knew he probably thought I would be overcome with gratefulness. I was overcome, all right—but with an entirely different emotion!

"That . . . that is the announcement you told me about in

town?" I asked softly, trying to keep my voice from cracking.

"Yes. Isn't it exciting, Corrie? It's the opportunity I was telling you about . . . the future. For us to be part of together, just like I was saying when we were together in Palo Alto. An exciting future full of opportunities that we can share!"

But I only heard about half his words before I was up from the table and running to my room. I lay down on my bed and sobbed quietly. How could I possibly have been so stupid?

But even as I lay there, I remembered the other time Cal had been here, and what a fool I'd made of myself, sneaking around in the woods with dirt all over me. I could *not* let something like that happen again!

I quickly jumped up off my bed, ran to my washbasin, which still had some water in it, dashed a little on my face, dried with a towel, sucked in a deep breath, and turned around to walk back out and face the music. I would be brave, and put the best face on an awkward situation I could.

I returned to the table. "I'm sorry for leaving so abruptly," I said. "I was just overcome for a minute, and had to be alone. But I'm fine now."

I sat back down and gave Cal the biggest smile I could manage to muster. I hoped my red eyes didn't betray me.

"You can tell Mr. Stanford that I'd be honored," I said. "I would very much like to do what I could to help him."

"Good . . . wonderful!" exclaimed Cal. "I know that will please him a great deal."

With the business out of the way, the conversation again drifted toward politics. It seemed that was just about the only things folks talked about these days. With a war imminent, there was a great sense of uncertainty and tension, even in far-off California.

Then the door opened and Uncle Nick walked in with his family. Cal immediately jumped up, shook Uncle Nick's hand and greeted Aunt Katie warmly. Everyone took seats and the conversation resumed.

After about five minutes, suddenly a puzzled expression came over Cal's face. "Say, where is your sister?" he asked Aunt Katie. "Edie was her name, was it not? I had hoped to see her again too."

The room was silent a moment.

"She left for the East," Katie said. Her tone reflected the sadness she and all the rest of us had felt at Edie's parting.

"When?" asked Cal.

"Right after the Sumter incident," replied Uncle Nick.

"She said she had to go—that with the South under attack, she had to be where her home would always be."

An odd look came over Cal's face. What Aunt Katie had said seemed to strike deeply into him for some reason.

"We tried to get her to stay," said Uncle Nick. "Told her it was the South doing the attacking, and that if it did come to war, there couldn't be no safer place for her than right here."

"She hardly had any family left, anyway," said Almeda. "We told her we loved her and that we'd try to be family to her now that her husband was gone. But once news about Sumter came, she changed. She was distant after that. I knew she wasn't at home here."

"Nothing we said could change her mind," said Katie, starting to cry quietly. Almeda was sitting next to her and put her arm around her to comfort her. "I asked her what if we never saw each other again. But she just kept saying she had to be with her new country. It was almost as if we were suddenly strangers."

Katie could say no more. She broke down and wept.

Cal hadn't said another word, and the faraway look remained in his eyes for some time. He seemed very thoughtful and distracted and didn't say much the rest of the evening.

The outbreak of war between the North and South was bound, it seemed, to touch everyone in the country closely, sooner or later.

Already the pain was starting to come into people's lives.

# CHAPTER 46

## THE CAMPAIGNS OF
## THE SUMMER OF 1861

Just like Abraham Lincoln, Leland Stanford faced two Democrats in running for governor—a southern Democrat and a Union Democrat. The campaign was a short one, lasting mainly just through the months of July and August.

Stanford had lots of supporters in the state besides me. Once I began to realize just how much support he did have, in fact, I wondered why he had thought of me at all.

Thomas Starr King, now a strong ally, traveled throughout the state speaking for Mr. Stanford. And as everybody was finding out, he was one of the best orators in the whole country. A group of San Francisco businessmen who were normally Democrats backed Mr. Stanford, too. Like him, they were strong supporters of the Union even if they hadn't voted for Mr. Lincoln. A man named Levi Strauss was one of the most famous of these men, and since they were all influential, a lot of people took their advice when it came time to vote.

One person who *wasn't* so enthusiastic, though it made me mad at the time he told me, was a certain individual out of my past I'd tried hard to forget—Robin T. O'Flaridy.

I had seen his byline occasionally—he called himself *R. Thomas O'Flaridy*. When we ran into each other one day in the *Alta* building, he took me aside and spoke softly to me.

"Corrie, do me a favor and take one last bit of advice from an old friend," he said.

"An old friend?" I said, laughing. "After all you've pulled on me?"

"All in the past, Corrie," smiled Robin. "Part of the business, you know. Surely you've forgiven me by now."

"Oh, I suppose. How could I hold a grudge against a struggling fellow writer."

"Struggling?" he repeated. "Did you see my piece on the new wharf?"

"Yes, Robin," I answered, "and a great article it was, too."

"That's better."

"So," I said, "what's the advice you have for me?"

A serious expression came over his face. For a moment it almost confused me because it was so very different than the normal Robin O'Flaridy look I had grown accustomed to.

"How much do you know about Leland Stanford?" he asked.

"I don't know . . . quite a bit, I suppose," I answered.

"I mean, how well do you *really* know him? How well do you know what kind of person he is?"

"I . . . I thought I did. I've spent time with him. I like him. He's very kind to me."

"Perhaps. But I have a hunch, Corrie, that he may just be using you for his own ends."

"What! How can you possibly say such a thing?" I was annoyed.

"He's a businessman, Corrie. I've been around this city long enough to know some things. The whole deal with the railroad—I tell you, Corrie, it's not as clean and innocent as it seems. There are huge amounts of money involved. Huge, I tell you, and your friend Stanford and his cohorts are right in the thick of it."

"What are you insinuating?" I asked coolly.

"I'm not insinuating anything other than that the railroad's not primarily about politics—it's about money. I have the feeling Stanford only wants to be governor to line his own pockets and get richer than he already is. I know about these guys, Corrie—him, Hopkins, Crocker. They're businessmen, not politicians. All they are is a new breed of fourty-niner, a new kind of gold miner. Some might even call them claim jumpers."

"How dare you, Robin? I won't even listen to you. Who would say such a thing?"

"Ever heard of Theodore Dehone Judah?"

"Of course I've heard of him."

"He might agree with me."

"I don't believe a word of it. Why are you telling me this, Robin? Are you working for the Democrats in this election?" Again the same peculiar look came over Robin's face.

"Look, Corrie," he said, "I'm only concerned for you. Believe me, I just don't want you to get hurt."

"Why do I have such a difficult time believing your sincerity?" I said sarcastically. Immediately I regretted the words. The look on his face changed to one of pain.

"I'm sorry, Robin," I said. "I didn't mean it."

"Well, Corrie, I *do* mean it. Concern for you was the only reason I said anything about it at all."

"All right, Robin . . . thank you."

"Just watch your step, Corrie. That's all. And be careful about that Burton fellow too."

"Cal?" I said.

"I'm not so sure about him either. I've heard—"

"I'll watch my step, like you said, but I won't listen to you say a word against Cal," I interrupted, getting irritated again.

Robin seemed to think better of pursuing it, and he said nothing more. But the look on his face remained with me all the rest of the day. Strange as it was to say, I had the feeling he really was sincerely thinking of me. But then, I thought he was being sincere that night when we'd escaped from Sonora together, too, and he had double-crossed me!

I didn't think much more about what he'd said, and continued working for the campaign as before. Mr. Stanford himself traveled through all the northern part of the state—through all the mining regions, from Weaverville up north on the Trinity River all the way down to Sonora in the south. Naturally he came to Miracle Springs too, where I got to stand beside him and speak to my own hometown.

I didn't really do all that much for him, but Mr. Stanford took me with him to lots of the smaller places like Miracle Springs, introduced me to people as if I were more important than he was, and always let me say a few things, either about him or about Mr. Lincoln or the need to be loyal to the Union. He treated me so kindly, and told me—whether it was true or not—that I was help-ing his campaign a great deal.

The other campaign of that summer was not such a pleasant one. It was taking place twenty-five hundred miles away—and was not a political campaign, but a military one.

The attack on Fort Sumter had taken place in April. But for the next two months nothing happened. Both North and South were busy recruiting, training, and building up their armies. I later heard that the moods of the general public were very different during this time.

In the South, wealthy landowners and the leaders who had organized the Confederacy were all confident—confident that right was on their side, certain that they were doing the just and honorable thing, confident in their strength, sure of victory. Some-body I later interviewed told me it was a self-righteous kind of confidence. God and the Bible were on their side, so how could they do anything but win? The young soldiers of the southern army, though not so religious or philosophical about it, mostly felt the same way.

But hundreds of thousands of people in the South, however, neither leaders nor soldiers nor landowners, were shocked by what had happened. They believed that slavery was permissible. They believed in the ways of the South, in southern culture and their southern heritage. But whether it was worth waging a war over, such people had grave doubts. Surely, they thought, some more sensible solution or compromise could be found than to have to kill over it! Though most of these people remained loyal to the Confederacy, many of them wondered if their own leaders—Jef-ferson Davis and Alexander Stephens and General Beauregard, who had attacked and toppled Fort Sumter, and General Robert E. Lee and Thomas Jackson, and all the political leaders who had defected from Washington in favor of the Confederacy—weren't doing just as much to destroy the South as the evil Yankees and their sinister head, Abraham Lincoln. These people were scared.

As for the slaves in the South, most of the ones I talked to later didn't have the slightest notion that all the fighting was for them. They were at least the outward symbol of why the Civil War was fought, but they didn't know it. *Freedom* for them might as well have been a word in a foreign language. Even if they had freedom, they wouldn't have known what to do with it. In the meantime, their lives went on as they always had—a life of drudgery, toil, and hopelessness.

Above the Mason-Dixon Line, however, the mood was far different. People there were mad. It was time the South was put in its place, slavery put an end to, and the country made one again. The South could not be allowed to get away with attacking the very foundation of Freedom itself—the United States government. They wanted something done. They called for retribution, for punishment of the South.

Therefore, when news came that the new Confederate Congress was going to meet for the first time, and not down in Montgomery, Alabama, but up in Richmond, Virginia—only a hundred and ten miles south of Washington—the anger of the North rose to explosive heights. The call went out—the southern Congress must not be allowed to meet on July 20!

The New York *Tribune* took up the banner and repeated what it called the "Nation's War Cry" in every edition it printed: *Forward to Richmond! Forward to Richmond! The Rebel Congress must not be allowed to meet there on the twentieth of July! By that date the place must be held by the National Army!*

President Lincoln, as well as everyone on both sides, thought that the war would be short. Here was a chance, he believed, to deal a quick and decisive blow to the upstart Rebel army *and* cripple the new government of the Confederacy by taking control of its new capital—all at once!

But standing in the way, between the northern army and Richmond, were 30,000 Confederate troops. Lincoln gave the order to advance, defeat the Rebel army, and move south to take Richmond.

The battle of Bull Run near Centreville, Virginia, took place July 21.

The two armies were approximately equal in size. All kinds of maneuvering went on among the generals of both sides, trying to trick the other. But down on the fields where shots were being fired, young inexperienced boys who were hardly trained and who had never fought before were shooting guns and killing one another! Which side would panic first?

It turned out that the southern leaders were more skilled in battle tactics than those of the North. After hours of fighting on that hot summer's day, by attacks and counterattacks, they fooled the blue units of the Federal army into thinking they had more reinforcements than they really did. The boys in blue panicked and finally turned around to flee. The gray units surged forward after them.

A full retreat was on, all the way back thirty miles to Washington! The severity of the conflict was still so little understood that hundreds of northerners had ridden out toward the battle in buggies and carriages to watch. These sightseers crowded the roads, making the safe retreat of the army all the more difficult. Suddenly toward them came a streaming mass of fugitives! They turned and fled in panic too, as back to the capital rushed tens of thousands of soldiers and citizens, with the victorious and shouting Confederate army behind them!

The South had won the first major battle of the campaign. Many brave young Union soldiers had been killed.

Fortunately for the North, the southern leaders did not press the victory and keep going. Otherwise they might have taken Washington itself. For either side, Bull Run *might* have ended the contest early.

But it would not.

This was no small conflict that had any chance of being resolved politically or easily or quickly.

A full-fledged *war* had begun. The North was shocked by the southern victory. But the defeat at Bull Run only made them all the more determined. Lincoln sent out a call for more men.

Everyone was beginning to realize that this was going to be a long and difficult war.

# CHAPTER 47

# THE WAR IN CALIFORNIA

California wasn't the only state split over loyalties to the North and South. In June, after Virginia had joined the Confederacy, the western part of that state broke away and formed a new state, loyal to the Union, called West Virginia.

When news of it came, I found myself wondering if such a thing was bound to happen to California one day.

The election for governor, however, would serve to put the dispute to rest. It was a campaign fought not just along Republican-Democrat lines, but North-South as well. A famous lawyer named Edmond Randolph made fiery speeches against Mr. Stanford. He was outspoken in his calling for Confederate victories in the East, and after Bull Run, claimed that the South would put an end to the war any day. "If this be rebellion," he cried in a speech that I heard when I was in Sacramento with Cal and Mr. Stanford, "then I am a rebel. Do you want a traitor? Then I am a traitor."

There were far more Democrats in California than Republicans. But the split between them kept being the most important factor of all. The Democrats got almost 64,000 votes in September. Mr. Stanford got only 56,000.

But since he was running against *two* Democrats, he was elected governor even with a minority!

I expected Cal to be happier over the victory than he was. This was one of those "opportunities" he was always talking about. He was going to be personal assistant to the governor of the state! He had talked about it before with such a light in his eyes that I would have thought nothing could please him more. He had made it seem like getting to the nation's Capitol was his greatest goal, and that Mr. Stanford would be the one to take him there. But the southern victory at Bull Run seemed to shake him, and even after the election, he was still quieter than usual. We were all worried when we heard the army had been defeated and had to retreat. But Cal seemed more upset about it than I could understand.

Mr. Stanford was so behind the North, the Union, and Mr. Lincoln that the Republican victory ended once and for all any possibility that California would support the South or would withdraw from the Union to form a new republic of some kind. Talk of a third country, and even talk of splitting the state, diminished. The War Between the States was the most important thing on everyone's minds, and the Pony Express deliveries with papers from the East were anticipated eagerly to find out if any more battles had been fought or if anything else had happened. Nothing much did happen, though, throughout the whole rest of that summer and fall.

But just because Mr. Stanford was now governor did not mean support for the southern cause stopped altogether. It just meant the state would officially be pro-North. So all the supporters of the Confederacy—and there were lots of them!—had to go into hiding. They had lost their chance to take California into the Confederacy with the vote. So they turned instead to hidden and underground plots and schemes. There was news every week, it seemed, of some new threat that had been exposed, even threats of plots to take over California for the South.

All kinds of secret societies of southern sympathizers sprang up. Mr. Kemble told me there were as many as fifty thousand people involved, but I don't know if that was true. They caused mischief, but after the middle of 1861 there weren't any serious uprisings.

The debate over which side was "right" in the war continued. William Scott, the pastor of one of San Francisco's largest churches, the Calvary Presbyterian Church, openly preached his belief in the Confederate cause. He outraged many people in the state, including my editor, Mr. Kemble, who knew him personally.

Besides men, money was something the Union army needed more than anything. The North was not as economically strong as the South, and to feed, clothe, and pay an army was expensive.

California was too far away to help with any actual fighting. It was too small a state to be able to provide very many men. But there *was* one thing that California had more of than any other state in either the Union or the Confederacy.

That was gold. California *could* help President Lincoln finance the war, if nothing else.

The Unitarian pastor Thomas Starr King, who had become a good friend of Governor Stanford, turned his speaking skills and popularity in a new direction. He began to organize a fund-raising drive in California in order to send money to Washington.

Of course whenever money is involved in anything, there is always the chance of deception and robbery. Since the first gold miners had started pulling gold out of the rivers and streams of California in 1848, there had been claim jumpers and thieves. Now, with southern supporters carrying out their designs more secretively, and with their bitterness over losing California's support for the Confederate cause, there was worry that they would try to steal what Mr. King was able to raise.

According to Mr. Kemble, a quarter of all San Franciscans favored the Confederacy. There were even more down south in Los Angeles. After Mr. Stanford's election as governor, a lot of secessionists moved down there and kept calling, even then, for California to split in half, with southern California to become a slave state and join the Confederacy. The Los Angeles *Star* was so seditious and against the Union that Governor Stanford had it banned from the mail so that it couldn't even be delivered and read in the northern part of the state.

There weren't enough people in Los Angeles or the rest of southern California, however, to worry about actual trouble—all the mischief they could do was in writing. And because they had no gold, they couldn't do the Confederacy much good, either.

# CHAPTER 48

# A RIDER

The day was one I'll never forget. Never *could* forget!

It was late August. A hot summer's day. Hot and still. Wherever the wind from the Sierras was, it had gone to sleep that day and felt like it intended to sleep all through the afternoon. It was so still I could hear the flies buzzing about. And hot . . . so hot!

Pa had been back from Sacramento for three days. He'd been gone a week and a half, his longest stay in the capitol yet. But Tad had gone with him, and they had a wonderful time together. When he wasn't on legislative business, he showed Tad all around Sacramento, and Tad had hardly stopped talking about everything they had done together. He had gone with Pa once or twice to Assembly meetings too. When Pa first saw Alkali Jones the day after they got back, he was telling him about the trip.

"I reckon it's time you changed that motto of yours, Alkali."

"Which one's that?"

"About the presidency."

"You mean Drum fer President—hee, hee, hee!"

"That's the one. But you gotta change it now."

"How so, Drum?"

"Politics has gone and bit my son right square between the eyes. You gotta change it to *Thaddeus Hollister for President*."

Tad's face beamed at the words.

"Hee, hee . . . Tad fer President! Yep, you're right, Drum—sounds a heap more likely with his name instead of yours! Hee, hee, hee!"

But during the days since he had returned, I could see a downcast spirit coming over Pa. It had nothing to do with Tad, only that his good time with his younger son had brought back to mind the lingering doubts over the fate of his elder. We'd heard nothing about Zack all this time.

Something was different about that day besides it being so hot. There was something in the air. There was no breeze rustling the trees. But there seemed to be an invisible wind about, invisible in the way that you couldn't see it or feel it or hear it. Kind of a wind of the spirit, not a wind of the air. It was a sense, a feeling that something was coming, but you couldn't tell what.

We all felt it, I could tell. As the day wore on, I could just see a look in Almeda's and Becky's and Tad's faces that they felt it too. We found ourselves looking at one another with expressions that had no words. It was a feeling of agitation, of anticipation, as if something was at hand but nobody knew what it might be.

It was a sense of expectation, the kind of feeling people get before a big thunderstorm. Everything changes. A different kind of warmth is in the air. The breezes start kicking up, and although they don't feel too powerful, you know they are only the fingery edges of the blasts that are coming. You *feel* the storm on its way. The air smells different. Before long, the blackness begins to appear over the horizon, steadily getting larger and filling more of the sky, and you know our senses have not betrayed you.

This was a day like that. But there were no breezes, no stormy fragrances, no hints of anything in the sky other than blue going on forever in every direction.

The little breezes kicking up the leaves for a moment and then letting them settle back into place, the feeling of changes in the atmosphere . . . they were all happening inside. Every once in a while I'd catch Almeda standing at the door or window looking out, with her hand over her eyes, peering into the distance as if expecting something. Then she'd turn away with a confused expression, as if wondering herself why she'd paused to look outside, not even knowing what she was looking for.

Nobody was saying much. The day wore on, getting hotter, and everyone grew more and more quiet. Something was coming. No one knew what.

Pa tried to work at the mine some. But it was too hot. After lunch Pa went out again, walked lazily up the creek, running thin and low now in the late summer.

It was one of my times to stand at the open door looking out, with *my* hand over *my* eyes. I watched him walk up toward the mine, kicking at the rocks with his feet, one hand in his pocket. He disappeared from sight. A few minutes later I heard noises from the area of the mine. But they didn't last long.

I was still standing there, looking out aimlessly, not feeling like doing anything, when Pa came into view again, walking back down the path, this time toward the stable. Apparently he had given up on the mine again. His shirt was drenched in sweat, under his arms and down the middle of his chest. But he didn't need the work to sweat. It was plenty hot to sweat just standing doing nothing. I was sweating too, in the shade of the house and open doorway.

Closer Pa walked. It was quiet. I could hear his feet shuffling along, too tired now even to kick at the little stones along the way in front of him. Everything was so still. Only Pa's rhythmic, shuffling step broke the stillness and the silence.

I found my eyes riveted on his slow-moving feet, watching them come toward me in the distance. The soft sound of his boots along the dried dirt entered my ears in perfect cadence. *One . . . two . . . right . . . left . . .*

Over and over—right, left . . . thud, thud.

Still my eyes fixed themselves on the motion, but gradually I became aware that something was wrong with the sound. There were still Pa's feet walking along as before, but the rhythm had been interrupted. It had changed. There were too many sounds for only two feet. I heard the noise as of a footfall when Pa's two feet were on the ground and in the air not making any sound.

And . . . the sound itself was wrong.

It wasn't a thud, thud, thud anymore. Now I heard *clomp . . . clomp . . . clomp* mixed in with the shuffling thuds of Pa's boots.

It sounded like a horse.

I shook off my dreaming reverie and turned my eyes in the opposite direction. A horse was approaching from the direction of town. Of course, that was the other sound I'd heard.

Who could it be? I squinted my eyes . . .

"Somebody's coming," I heard Becky say from inside the house behind me.

"Who is it, Corrie?" Almeda asked from the kitchen.

I kept squinting, trying to see. I could tell it was a man, but all I could really make out was a hat and a light brown beard.

I stared. The horse plodded along as slow as Pa had been walking. But steadily he came closer.

Suddenly an incredible sense of recognition seized my heart! But . . . but it couldn't be!

I spun my head around and my eyes again sought Pa.

His slow step had become a rapid pounding of his boots along the path. He had seen the rider too! He was running toward him!

Unconsciously I started out the door. I looked toward the road. The rider was close now . . . there could be no mistake!

He was climbing down off his horse. I was running now too! "Zack!" I cried. "It's Zack!" I yelled back toward the house.

Out of the house the others came, following me as we ran as fast as we could toward the road.

Pa reached him first.

I stopped, ten yards away, weeping with happiness. I felt the others come up behind me, but I could not take my eyes off the scene of reunion being played out before my eyes. I felt Almeda's arm slip around me as she watched, too.

Zack had slipped off his horse, but he hadn't been able to take more than a step or two before Pa reached him. The father threw his big arms around the son and held him tight, weeping freely and without shame.

Slowly I saw Zack's hands stretch around Pa's back and return his close embrace.

The two stood silently holding each other for a long minute. The only sounds to be heard were the throbbing of six hearts in joy.

# CHAPTER 49

## WHOLE AGAIN

When the two released each other, the first words were Pa's. "Welcome home, son!" he said.

The spell of the moment was broken.

The rest of us rushed forward. For the next several minutes Zack was showered with hugs and kisses and questions and laughter. He could hardly get in a word!

"Nice beard, Zack!" said Tad.

"You little runt . . . you grew up while I was gone!" returned Zack, giving Tad a good-natured push. "And you, Becky!" he added. "When did you get to be such a beautiful, grown-up woman!"

Then Zack looked over at me. He didn't say anything at first, just gave me a long hug. Every time I tried to speak, I started crying, and all my words stuck in my throat. "Oh, Zack," I finally managed, "I'm just so glad to see you!"

"Almeda," said Zack, hugging her next.

"Oh, Zack . . . we love you so much!"

Pa had been standing back, wiping his eyes and trying to steady himself. Now he stepped up again, this time offering Zack his hand.

"How about a handshake of welcome, Zack?" he said. "A handshake between men . . . man to man!"

Zack said nothing. He just reached out and took Pa's hand. The two stood again, grasping each other firmly by the hand, gazing intently each one into the other's eyes. It was all we had hoped and prayed for! You could tell in that one moment that they understood each other, and that all was forgiven.

"Why did you grow the beard, Zack?" Becky asked after a minute.

"It's a long story," said Zack, releasing Pa's hand.

"Where you been?" This time the questioner was Tad.

"Another long story!" laughed Zack.

"How did you get back?" I asked.

"That's long too, but the why of it isn't so long," he answered. Then his face turned serious, and his eyes took on a very faraway expression. In that moment he suddenly looked older, like a true man. If I hadn't known better, I would have thought he was my older brother.

"Are you going to tell us the *why*, then?" I asked.

"I'll tell you everything," he replied, "when the time is right."

"Give the man a chance to get the dust off his feet, Corrie," said Pa. "Come on, Zack, son . . . let's get that horse of yours put up. Then what do you say me and you go up and give a *howdy* to your uncle!"

"Sure, Pa . . . yeah, I'd like to see Uncle Nick too!"

The two turned and headed toward the barn. Even though Zack was an inch or two taller than Pa, Pa threw his arm up around Zack's shoulder as they went. Zack's other hand hung down at his side, lightly holding the leather reins of his horse, which followed behind.

Almeda, Tad, Becky, and I stood there watching them go.

Just then Pa stopped and turned around. "Almeda!" he called back. "You start figuring on how to fix up the best vittles we ever had! Corrie, you make up a heap o' those biscuits o' yours. We'll invite the Reverend, and Nick and Katie—I know they'll all be anxious to see Zack. We'll have us a great time!"

He turned again, and he and Zack continued on, talking as they went.

The four of us finally walked back toward the house. "Well, Tad, your brother's home," said Almeda. "What do you think?"

When I heard Tad's answer, the tone of his voice surprised me. It wasn't just the deep baritone quality of it, but rather the maturity of what he said. It was obvious Tad was a young man at peace with his place in the family and secure in where he stood with his father.

"I'm so glad for Pa," Tad said quietly. "Something's been missing for him ever since Zack left. I did what I could to help, but I reckon a man like Pa's never gonna be quite whole when one of his kids is at odds with him. 'Course I'm glad for Zack, too. He needed Pa more than he ever could admit, probably more than I needed him, because I was younger when we came here."

He paused. "Actually," he added, "I guess I'm just about as happy as I can be . . . for *both* of them!"

# CHAPTER 50

## UNLIKELY RESCUE

A good part of the rest of that day Pa and Zack spent together. There was a lot of getting used to each other again to get done. And of course lots to talk about. But there was time for that now, and everything didn't need to be done all at once.

I could tell when I had a couple minutes alone with Pa later in the afternoon, just from the light in his eyes, that he'd been able to tell Zack the most important thing that had been on his mind all this time—that is how sorry he was. It was obvious from one look at Pa that a huge burden had been lifted from his shoulders.

We celebrated that night to make up for the last Christmas twenty times over. There was food and laughing and singing and more of Alkali Jones's crazy stories than we could have believed in ten nights of merrymaking together, much less one.

It was so strange seeing Zack with a beard! His talk, his mannerisms, his whole bearing had changed. Being out on his own had made him more confident, more independent. Zack entered into the celebration, but when I looked intently into his eyes when he wasn't watching, I could see a certain reticence too, almost a shyness at being the center of attention, and knowing that he'd caused such a fuss. I don't know that I'd call it embarrassment exactly, but it was like embarrassment in a different sort of way. Humbleness and humiliation aren't the same, though a lot of folks mistakenly think they are because their first three letters are the same. The one is always a good thing. The other isn't bad or good in itself, but can be either depending on what you do with it, and whether you let it make you humble in the end.

It had taken real humility for Zack to come home. It would probably take him a good long time to sort through the impact that act of humility would have on his manhood. Pride doesn't die easy, but humility is the only sure weapon against it. Zack had now become man enough to draw the sword against it himself. I could see the battle in his eyes . . . and I knew he was winning it!

It was well past dark before we all managed to coax Zack into telling his story. It was clearly hard for him, because of how bitter and painful his leaving home had been. But when Pa and I told him how we'd gone looking for him and what had happened, it perked him up and gave him a good place to start his tale without having to dwell on the past.

"Well, I was riding the last two stretches of Nevada and the first Utah leg," he began, "depending on the schedule, and depending on how the others were doing."

"Pony Bob told us how unpredictable it was sometimes," I said.

"It's *always* unpredictable with Bob!" laughed Zack. "That man attracts trouble like a dog draws fleas! I never rode two or three hundred miles at a time, but there were days when you'd have to keep going to another station or two."

"Were the Indians bad?" asked Becky. "Were you afraid?"

"You bet I was scared, girl!" said Zack. "The only fellas who weren't were the crazy ones, and we had a few of those, too."

"Did you ever shoot an Indian, Zack?" asked Tad.

"I shot *at* 'em, Tad, but never shot none. You don't think I'd want to hurt somebody, do you?"

"What if they came after you?"

"They did. But the Express had the best horses in the country, and no Paiute could keep with us for five minutes. So I'd just kinda stick my Colt up over my shoulder and fire back in the air and hope it'd frighten 'em away. Even if it didn't, all I had to do was stay in the saddle five minutes and I'd be out of their sight anyway."

"What if they were in front of you?"

"Then I had a problem."

"What would you do?"

"I could turn around and make a run for it. But then the mail didn't go through. Or I could head out into the desert and try to get around them. But then they'd have the angle on me, and I might ride an extra twenty miles, only to find them still there! Or I could do like Bob Haslam did a couple of times and ride right through the middle of them and hope they didn't kill me."

"What did *you* do, Zack?" asked Rev. Rutledge.

"Well, I tell you, Reverend, it only happened to me once. Funny that you should be the one asking me about it, because when it did happen I thought of you."

"Me!" said an astonished Rev. Rutledge.

"Yep. I just stopped dead in my tracks. And there they were up about a hundred yards ahead of me, right in the middle of my pathway. I just sat there in my saddle, and I started praying, and that's when I thought of you. I thought back to a sermon you preached once about problems. You were saying that sometimes you gotta face your problems head-on. Then other times, circumstances were such that you had to go around your problems to get to the other side. But there was one thing you could never do, you said, and that was ignore your problems and do nothing and hope they would just go away. They never will, you said."

Everybody in the room started laughing.

"That's just what I did," Zack went on. "I couldn't help myself. Sitting there on my jittery pony, staring at twenty hostile Paiutes, I started laughing. I couldn't stop. All I could think of was that sermon of yours, and I said to myself, just like I was talking to you, 'Shoot, Rev. Rutledge, that advice of yours doesn't do me a blame bit of good! You must not have had Indians in mind when you came up with that!' "

We were all laughing so hard by now we could hardly stop. Rev. Rutledge and Harriet had tears in their eyes—they were laughing hardest of all. Alkali Jones's *hee, hee, hee!* was nearly one continuous cackle!

"I even tried what you said you couldn't do. I stopped laughing long enough to close my eyes and count to ten. I thought that just maybe they *would* go away, that it was a dream, a winter's mirage. It was so cold last December that I thought maybe my brain was frostbit. But when I opened my eyes again, they were still there. And I still had to do what you said in your sermon—either go through them or go around them. But I gotta tell you, Rev. Rutledge, I found myself wishing I'd paid better attention that day, because I thought maybe you *had* said something else that I just couldn't remember!"

"No, that was it, Zack, my boy," said Rev. Rutledge, wiping his eyes. "Through them or around them, that's all I said." He was still chuckling even as he spoke.

"Well, I'd heard of Pony Bob riding through the band of Paiutes. But for all I knew, this might be the same band! And even if it wasn't, they were sure to have heard about the incident just as sure as I had. And they certainly weren't about to let themselves be suckered into just sitting there and letting through a lone horse-back-riding kid a *second* time! No, I figured my chances were about zero in a thousand of coming out the other side alive if I tried to tackle *this* problem head-on. This looked to me like a clear case of needing to go *around* the problem!"

"What did you do, Zack?" asked Almeda. She was sitting on the edge of her chair as if she was afraid for him all over again.

"It was in a mountainous area of some pretty nasty terrain. Spread out to my right was a huge flat plain, broken up by gulches and creek beds, and little ravines, mostly invisible from looking across the top from where we were. On the other side of the trail, it turned rocky and steep immediately, working its way up to a high plateau that ran parallel to the road below. So what I figured to do was hightail it out across the plain like I was trying to outrun my way clean around them. I figured they'd light out on an angle to cut me off as I started my swing around to outflank them. So my plan was to ride out into the plain a ways, then dip into a wash suddenly and get out of their line of view. I hoped that they would keep riding toward the plain and that I could double back, maybe staying low in a creek bed or wash, and get back to the road and head back up the other side and lose myself in the huge boulders of the hillside without them spotting me. Then I could work my way all the way up to the top of the ridge and ride along until I was out of danger, and then find my way back down to the trail.

"It worked perfectly at first. I lashed my horse off to the right.

They took out after me at an angle across toward the plain. I rode for thirty or forty seconds, then dipped into a creek bed, stopped, and waited. I got off the horse, and crouching down crept up to the edge. There went the band of Paiutes off into the plain, expecting me to appear again any minute still riding in the same direction. I crept back down, remounted my horse, and doubled back, staying in the lows and hollows and washes until I was almost back to the trail. Then I climbed up and out and galloped quickly across the trail and up into the mountainous terrain on the other side. Within another minute I was out of sight and safe. But I still had to work my way up to the top and around back on to the trail or else I'd run into the war party again.

"Up I went. It got steeper and steeper, more rocky and treacherous. The footing was bad. There was loose shale here and there, and wet because it had been trying to snow. I was still frightened and so was pushing the horse pretty hard, which was probably my mistake. By now I was so far away from the Indians I probably would have been safe, but I kept pushing. Both my horse and me were exhausted. And that's how the trouble came. I was just too tired. I'd already been riding six hours that day, and it was another three hours to the next station.

"I was three-quarters of the way up to the plateau, and I came to a little ledge that dropped off steep on one side but was flat enough for a trot along its surface. But it was narrow, only about a foot wide. I urged the horse into a trot, but it was so narrow, and with the cliff on one side I could tell she was spooked. It was stupid of me, but I lashed her on instead of paying attention to what she was trying to tell me. We got moving again pretty good, but then all of a sudden the ridge gave way right in front of us.

"It was only a jump of maybe four feet across to where it picked up again. On the flat at full gallop she'd have taken it so easily in stride I wouldn't even have felt a bump in my saddle. But she was tired. I urged her over it. She hesitated, then reared and stopped dead in her tracks. I was so tired I was barely hanging on, though I didn't realize how shaky I was in the saddle.

"Off her back I toppled, and I landed sideways on my leg. I felt the pain instantly, but I didn't have time to think about anything, because I'd fallen to the right, and I just kept falling, away down the slope off the ridge, over and over, banging against rocks, sliding down the moving shale. It was a long fall, I knew that, though I didn't know much else. I was only conscious of spinning and crunching and bouncing . . . and pain. Pretty soon, even as I was still rolling and falling, everything drifted into blackness, and my senses just faded away. I thought I was dead."

He stopped and took a deep breath, reliving the whole incident for the first time. Even just telling it had shaken him all over again. Little beads of perspiration were on his forehead. The rest of us were still. It was pretty late by now, and dark and quiet outside— all except for the crickets and an occasional owl somewhere.

"When next I knew anything it was still black. I woke up real slow, you know how you do sometimes, faint images, blurry sensations that don't mean anything. That's how it was. It was dark, and all I was aware of was an odor, faint at first, but something I recognized, and a sound that I couldn't figure out.

"I tried to make sense out of things. I tried to remember. Then the fall came back to me, and how I had faded out of consciousness while falling down . . . down . . . down.

"Suddenly I knew the smell. It was smoke! And the sound— it was the crackling of a fire. That was it—a fire and smoke!

"I was coming back into consciousness, but only slowly, and I was still half-dazed and confused. My first thought was, *That's it, I really did die . . . and I'm in hell! I'm in hell because of what I said to Pa, and how I left home!*"

I looked over toward Pa as Zack was talking. He was hanging on every word, as if he was living every moment of it with his son. I could tell these last words smote his heart. He winced slightly, but kept looking straight at Zack, waiting for him to continue.

"Then suddenly I felt the sharp pain in my leg. I don't know how I could have a rational thought in the state I was in, but I remember thinking, *I can't be in hell if my leg hurts, because if I was dead my body would still be lying in that ravine back there where I fell*. Then gradually my eyes started to focus, and I saw some light from the low flickering of the flames. Everything else was black. I couldn't see anything except the red orange of the flames.

"I struggled a little, then tried to sit up. 'Lay still, son,' a voice said out of the night.

"My eyes shot wide open in terror at the sound. I couldn't see who had spoken, but I know my eyes were big as a horse's! It wasn't a nice or a gentle voice, very deep, almost gravelly. And it had plenty of authority. It wasn't the kind of voice you disobeyed. Again the thought flitted through my brain about being in the fiery place. I didn't even want to ask myself who the voice might belong to!

"I did what the voice said and lay still for a long time, wondering what would happen next.

" 'What's your name, son?' said the voice again.

" 'Uh, Zack . . . Zack Hollister,' I answered. It was nice to find out *my* voice still worked. 'Where am I?'

" 'You're safe, that's where. You had a bad fall back there.'

"Now things were starting to come back to me. I remembered the Indians, the climb up the hill, and the fall. Now I knew why my leg hurt.

" 'But . . . my horse . . . the mail,' I said. 'I gotta get the mail through. Where's the horse?'

"The next thing I knew, the voice was laughing. If I thought it had been gravelly before, the laugh was a rockslide. If your cackle is mountain water tinkling over pebbles, Alkali," said Zack, turning to Mr. Jones with a grin, "then the laugh I heard out of the blackness was made out of boulders rumbling down the mountain after an earthquake. I never heard such a deep voice or such a throaty laugh.

" 'That horse and whatever mail was on it is long gone, boy,' the voice said. 'We're miles and miles from where you fell, and your horse was miles away before I got to you, anyway.'

" 'The Paiutes . . . did the Paiutes get her?' I said in alarm.

" 'Can't tell you, son. I wasn't looking for your horse. I had my hands full just dragging you back up out of that crevice you got yourself into. As for the Paiutes, they know better than to bother me. I saved enough of their lives to keep me in their good graces for fifty years to come.

" 'But . . . but where am I?' I asked.

" 'Like I said, miles from where you fell. You're safe, that's all you need to know.'

" 'But I gotta get back . . . back to my route. They'll be worried about me. I gotta see about the mail.'

"Again the deep laughter came out of the dark.

" 'Son,' the man said, 'You're not going anywhere. Your leg's broken in two places. You're miles from the Express line. And even if you had a horse and were healthy, we're snowed in.'

" 'Snowed in! Where are we? Why is it so warm?'

" 'It'll all make sense in the morning. You hungry? You oughta be—you been out for two days.'

" 'Two days! What have I been doing, just lying here?'

" 'That's right. I dragged you up here, splinted your leg, made you as comfortable as I could, and then just waited. I could tell you were a strong little rascal, and that you'd wake up. So—you hungry?'

" 'Yeah, I reckon I am,' I said.

"He handed me something in a bowl. I could hardly see, but it smelled good. I picked out some chunks of meat in a kind of gravy and started eating it. I didn't realize how hungry I was until the smell of that stew hit my nostrils and I tasted the meat. The bowl was empty inside of a minute.

" 'More?' said the man.

" 'Yeah,' I answered, handing him the bowl. 'What is it?'

" 'Rattlesnake.'

"I gagged and turned away.

"I heard the laugh again from the other side of the fire. 'What's the matter, son? You never eaten snake before?'

" 'No, and I got no intention of eating it again!' I said.

" 'You'll die if you don't. It's about all I eat most winters up here, so you better get used to it.'

" 'Where do you get them?' I asked. 'Ain't no snakes in winter.'

" 'Ah, you just have to know where to look. And I do. I find them hibernating in their dens. They're sleepy and cold. I kill ten, maybe twenty of them if I go out and spend a morning at it. Skin and gut them, cut up the meat, stash it in the snow to freeze it. Keeps me in meat all winter long. Just take out and cook whatever I need.'

" 'That's all you eat, and you stay alive all winter? This is the high desert,' I said. 'No man can stay alive out here, in summer or winter.'

"He laughed again. 'You must figure I'm a ghost then,' he said. 'I've been living off the hills here for eight years. There's food in the winter, water in the summer. Plenty for a man to live on—if the man knows how to find the provision the Maker put in the desert. No big secret to it.'

"Well, we talked a while longer, and gradually I drifted back to sleep. When I woke up again it wasn't black anymore. But it wasn't light either. There was just an eerie glow coming from one direction, and total blackness from the other.

"I shook myself awake, more quickly this time. My leg hurt, but I felt so much better. Despite how repulsed I had been at the thought of it, the snake meat had given me back some energy. I managed to pull myself up to a sitting position and look around. My host and rescuer, whoever he might be, was nowhere around.

"It was obvious to me now that I was inside a huge cave, and I heard footsteps coming from the inside of the mountain. The instant I heard the footsteps I was terrified. If he'd wanted to kill me or eat me or skin me alive to put in his rattlesnake stew, he'd had two or three days already to do it, but I was scared anyway.

" 'Sleep good, son?' he said, coming toward me and sitting down opposite me on the other side of the fire. The sound of his voice reassured me. It sounded friendlier in the light of day, if this dreary half light could be called day. But when I set eyes on the man, my first impression did not make me feel good about my future safety. This man *looked* like the kind who might skin a kid like me and freeze my meat to go along with his rattlesnake stew.

"His face was long and thin, with sunken cheeks and high cheekbones. His whole frame was slender, but not what I'd call skinny, and that's how his face was too. No fat, just muscle and bone and hardiness. He looked strong and tough, like he'd been in a few tangles and probably had given the other fellow the worst of it. He had lots of hair, going in all directions, but not as bad or as gray as yours, Alkali, and a full beard. His beard was black. I couldn't tell a bit how old he was. A beard always makes a man look older, but in the darkness of the cave, this fella could have been anywhere from thirty to fifty. He still had all his teeth, and every once in a while one of them would catch a shine from the flames.

"He tossed a log on the fire, and sparks danced up from the disturbance.

" 'Where do you get wood around here?' I asked.

" 'Spend my summers gathering wood for winter, spend my winters storing snow water down in the cave for summer. Everything you need's out here, son.'

"I looked in the other direction, toward the light. We were some thirty feet from the opening of the cave.

" 'Why is the light so pale?' I asked. 'Is the sun just coming up?'

"The deep laughter came again. 'Don't you know what you're looking at there, son?' he said. 'That's snow—solid snow! Only lets in a bit of light.'

" 'Snow?' I said. 'But why is it there?'

" 'We're snowed in! I told you that last night. There's twenty feet of snow over the whole mouth of the cave. You're not looking at daylight, son, you're looking at a snowbank . . . from the inside!'

"Well, he was right. I didn't see the real light of real day for two weeks, when we dug our way out after it had half melted down. But we got snowed in three more times before winter was over."

"*We?*" repeated Almeda. "How long did you stay with this man?"

"All winter and spring. Until just three weeks ago, in fact," answered Zack.

"What did you do all that time, son?" asked Pa.

"Mr. Trumbull—Hawk's what he goes by. It's a name the Paiutes gave him when he first made friends with them. Hawk Trumbull's his name.

"He never did tell me his real first name. Anyway, Hawk taught me everything he knows. He took care of me, fed me, did everything for me until I could get back on my feet, babied me like a mother hen, making sure my leg healed proper, fixing new splints for it all the time. Then when I could walk again he took me out and showed me how he lives, how to survive, where the food and water was. He taught me all about animals and the weather and the mountains, showed me where the water comes and goes above ground and below ground, showed me all his caves—"

"How many does he have?" asked Tad in astonishment.

"I don't know. I don't suppose I ever stopped to count. Eight or ten, maybe. We'd store different things in different places, use them at different times—that is, *if* a bear wasn't occupying one."

"Zack!" exclaimed Almeda.

"It only happened once," he laughed.

"What did you do, shoot it?" asked Harriet.

"No. Hawk doesn't like to kill unless he has to, unless it's life or death. No, that time we took sort of a backwards approach to your husband's advice. We stood out of the way and let the problem go past us!"

"Sounds like you owe the man your life, Zack," said Pa.

"I owe Hawk more than my life."

"How do you mean?" asked Reverend Rutledge.

"He taught me how to live, how to survive, how to see things most people never have a chance to see, and never would see even if it was stuck right in front of their noses. He's more than just a mountain man. After a while I came to realize he was almost a rough wilderness poet at heart. He was always trying to get me to look past the obvious, to look beyond what things seemed to be on the surface. That was true when we went looking for water that had disappeared into a sink somewhere. It was true when we would watch the movement of eagles up in the sky and try to detect from them what might be going on ten miles away on the ground. He was always looking *into* things, he said. Everybody had two eyes, he said, but to really live you needed *four*—two outside and two inside."

"A remarkable sounding man," said Almeda.

"Best friend I ever had," said Zack.

The house fell quiet. It had been an amazing story.

"Actually, I reckon that ain't quite true," Zack said. "He's the one who helped me see I had an even better friend than him, and had for a long time."

"Who, Zack?" asked Becky.

Zack didn't answer her directly, but just went on talking about Trumbull.

"Once he began to find out about my background, and I began to tell him about you and Miracle Springs and what my life had been before he picked me off the mountainside, he started trying to make me use my extra set of eyes to see inside myself. He helped me see a lot of things I never saw before, things about all of us, this family of ours, and—"

He stopped, hesitating. His voice had gotten quiet. It was obvious this wasn't easy for him, especially in front of so many people.

"Mostly he helped me to see," Zack went on in a minute, "a lot of things I had never seen or understood about me and Pa. Once Hawk realized how it had been when I'd left, he asked lots of questions, wanted to know how I felt about things. He probably knows you about as good as any man alive, Pa, but the two of you have never met. He told me some things about myself that weren't too pleasant to hear, even though I knew they were true. But he was a straightforward, honest man, and I knew I could trust him. So I had no choice but to believe him. And so I had to look at myself, at some of the foolish things I'd done, like running off half-cocked like I did, and blaming things on Pa that I had no right to blame on anyone.

"He made me look down inside myself, just like he made me look at things in nature. He made me look at my anger. He told me that I'd never be a man until I learned what anger was supposed to be for. And that I'd never be a man until I learned to swallow my pride and come back and say I was sorry. He said I'd never be a man till I learned to live *with* the people closest to me. 'Only takes half a man to be able to live out in nature all by yourself,' he said. 'I don't doubt that I've done a pretty fair job of teaching you that. So, Zack, my boy,' he said, 'now it's time you learned to be a whole man, a complete man. It's time you went back. Take the half of being a man you learned out here and put it to use being the other half a man. Don't make the mistake I did of never going back. I went away when I was young, and I learned a lot of things. I know how to live in the wilds. But I'm still only half a man. It's too late for me now. I've drifted for too long and too far away. And most of my people are gone now. But it's not too late for you, young Grayfox.' "

"Grayfox . . . who did he mean? Was that you, Zack?" asked Tad.

Zack smiled—a smile with worlds of unsaid words behind it.

"Yeah, Tad, it was me."

"Why'd he call you that?"

"After I'd been there a spell, that was my name up there."

"It sounds like an Indian name, Zack," said Almeda.

Again Zack smiled, the same melancholy, distant, happy, sad, full, grown-up smile he had before. "Yep," he said, slowly nodding his head. "That it was. Given to me by the Paiutes."

"Why . . . what does the name mean?"

Another long silence followed. As I watched Zack, I could tell that his memories, even for such a short time ago, went into deep regions within him that perhaps none of the rest of us would ever see. But I hoped to see into those places inside my brother—maybe even write about them someday . . . or to show him how to write about them himself.

At last he sighed deeply. "That's a long story. Maybe even longer than this one," he said. "Someday I'll tell you about it. But right now I gotta finish this one."

"You go right on ahead, son. We're all listening," said Pa, his voice full of tenderness.

"Well, Hawk and me, we talked about a lot of things," Zack continued, "and he kept on gently tugging at me, helping me to see what I needed to do. But I just couldn't bring myself to do it. I knew I needed to let somebody know I was all right. I figured that one way or another you had probably got word by then that I was missing and would be worried. But though I intended to get word to you, somehow the time passed faster than I realized, and I just never did anything about it.

"One day we decided to go down to the valley. There were a few things Hawk needed. I'd never gone down with him before. I preferred to stay up in the mountains, even after my leg had healed and after the spring thaw came. I was at peace up there, and something inside me didn't want to go back. I felt like a new person out there alone, breathing in the high mountain air, knowing that even as desolate as it was, it was a land I could call my own.

"But this time I decided to go down with him. I figured it was time I let the Express people know I was alive so they could get word to you. We rode to one of the stations, both of us on Hawk's old mule. They couldn't believe it was me, but I told them the whole story. There was even a week's back pay from months before still in an envelope with my name on it!

"They had a couple of newspapers around, extras that the guys had brought to leave off at the stations along the way to keep the stationmen up on the news. That's how I first heard about the war and everything back in the South.

"I was sitting there having something to eat. Hawk was talking to the stationman on the other side of the room. I absently picked up a copy of a Sacramento paper. I don't know what I was thinking—maybe that I'd run across something Corrie had written.

"I just was glancing through it, I think it was a paper from May sometime, and a line caught my eye that said something about a resolution passed by the legislature supporting the Union. To tell you the truth, I don't know why I starting reading it. I didn't know anything about the conflict going on. But it had been so long since I'd read anything, I was just reading the whole paper.

"Then all of a sudden my eyes shot open and stopped dead on the page. I couldn't believe the words I'd read! *According to Assemblyman Drummond Hollister, who was interviewed briefly after the vote* . . .

"*What!* I shouted to myself inside. It couldn't be!

"But I kept reading . . . *The new legislator from the mining town of Miracle Springs, where he has served as mayor for the past four years, has been an outspoken pro-Union voice in the Assembly.* . . .

"I didn't need to read another word!

"I jumped up and ran over to Hawk, shoving the paper in his face. He didn't have a notion what I was talking about. But all I could say was, 'Look! Look . . . right there. That's my pa!'

"I was so overcome that I had to be alone. Still clutching the paper in my hand, I stumbled out the door and toward the stables and the barn where all the equipment was. I wandered inside and sat down on a bale of hay. Even here, so far away from home, I couldn't escape it. Suddenly everything I saw—every leather strap, every smell, from hay to leather to manure to wood to horseflesh—reminded me of home. Everything Hawk had been saying to me over the last two months came back to me.

"In that moment, sitting there, I saw it all so clearly—what I had done, how closed off I had been to all the love Pa had always tried to give me . . . the best friend I'd ever had, and always had, just like Hawk had told me.

"I opened up the paper again and looked down there toward the bottom where the article was. Over and over I read those words about *Assemblyman Drummond Hollister*. And all I could think was what a good man that *new legislator* was, a better man and a better father than any of those people in Sacramento could possibly realize. Better than I'd realized till right then! And the one thing I knew more than anything else was that I *had* to see him again. And I didn't want to wait! I had to see him now. I wanted to go home!

"I was crying by then. I was embarrassed at the time, but I'm not ashamed to admit it now. There were tears falling all over that newspaper page, but I couldn't take my eyes off the words."

Half the room was crying by now to hear Zack tell it—at least Almeda, Becky, Harriet, and I were. I have a feeling the men were choking back tears as well.

Zack looked over toward Pa, drew in a deep breath, and then spoke again.

"I tell you, Pa," he said, "I was so proud of you when I read those words . . . so proud of who you are! I just wanted the whole world to know you were *my* pa! And I had to tell you! I had to tell you . . . how much—I had to tell you how much . . . I love you, Pa."

Both of them were on their feet by now. This time it was Zack who approached and put his arms around Pa, bending down slightly to rest his face against Pa's shoulder, weeping like the boy-turned-man that he now was. Pa's strong gentle hands reached slowly around his son and pulled him close.

Almeda rose and went to them, followed next by Rev. Rutledge. In another minute we all stood together, weeping, hugging, sniffling, and sending up lots of silent prayers of rejoicing.

As we gradually fell away two or three minutes later, Rev. Rutledge broke the silence.

"So, what happened next, Zack?"

Zack drew in a long breath to steady himself.

"I went inside, asked if I could buy a horse for the $25 in the envelope, in up-front payment, and I'd send them the rest.

"Seeing as how it was me, the stationman said, and considering what I'd been through, he didn't figure Russell, Majors, and Waddell ought to mind too much.

"I said my goodbyes, and I had to fight back the tears again when Hawk took my hand and shook it. But within the hour I was headed west . . . and here I am!"

# CHAPTER 51

# THE END OF THE EXPRESS
# AND A NEW OPPORTUNITY

Zack was home!

It was hard to get used to. Every time I stopped to realize it, a wave of joy swept over me.

It seemed as if life ought to stop, but it never did. There was still a war going on in the East, plots and counterplots in the West. Pa still had to keep going to Sacramento . . . and there was still Cal.

The very next morning, Pa came upon Zack with soap all over his face. "What in tarnation are you doing?" he exclaimed.

"Shaving off my beard, Pa."

"What in thunder for?"

"I figured if I'm going to come back to civilization, I ought to look civilized. Besides. I figured you'd want it off."

"Well, you figured wrong. I like it!"

"You do?"

"Sure I do. Makes you look like me when I was your age."

"You want me to keep it?"

"Well, it's up to you, son. But I sure think a man's beard looks good on you."

"Okay, Pa," said Zack with a smile. He couldn't have been more pleased!

In mid-October a letter came to me, in an envelope from the office of the governor of California. My heart skipped. I was sure it was from Cal, but I was mistaken. I can't imagine a letter from such an important person as the governor being a disappointment, but I have to admit that one was.

Dear Miss Hollister,

I apologize to seem to be always asking you favors. But when a man in my position discovers a person who is loyal and competent, with a handsomeness and intelligence to match, he does not find it easy to replace her. So I am coming to you cap in hand to once again ask for your help in a matter of extreme importance to the future of our nation. As you know, the soldiers of the Union have grave needs, and we of California are doing everything we can to help them. A major fund-raising effort is underway, led by my friend and yours, Mr. King, in order to raise and send to President Lincoln's forces as much cash and gold as possible. California, as I'm sure you can appreciate, stands in a unique position to be able to help in this regard.

It is my hope that you will consider allowing me to appoint you co-chairwoman of a new organization which is being formed to work alongside Mr. King's efforts, to be called California Women for the Union, and whose principal activity will be raising funds for the Federal troops. Your name is one that is recognized and respected among the women of this state, and your efforts on behalf of the Union will, I am certain, not go unnoticed.

I am, your humble servant,
LELAND STANFORD
Governor

A hastily added note was attached to the letter. It said, "*As always, my faithful Cal Burton has told me he will help you in this assignment in any way which might be beneficial to you. I look forward to hearing from you. LS.*"

I hardly knew what it would involve, but how could I not accept? I did want to help the Union. And when somebody as important as the governor asks for help, it seemed my patriotic duty to say yes. I wrote back the next day saying I would do it, but said that he would have to make sure somebody told me what was expected of me. I was willing, I said, but totally ignorant of what the appointment might entail.

In the meantime, another major event in the life of the country was taking place. It had nothing to do with the war, but, because of Zack, and because of what Pa and I had been through, it came a little closer to home.

The Pony Express was about to go out of business after just eighteen months in operation.

The Pony Express had never made a profit for Russell, Majors, and Waddell. They had from the beginning hoped for government financial help but never received it. Once the war began, the amount of mail had dwindled, since many army troops were transferred from the West back to the East, and the army had been a heavy user of the mail services. But on October 24, 1861, something else happened that made the eight to ten days to take news from coast to coast eight to ten days too long. Suddenly the Pony Express was no longer the fastest way to transmit news.

On that day, in Salt Lake City, two teams that had been working from California and Nebraska for six months met and joined the telegraph wires they had been stringing up across the country. The instant those wires were connected, Washington and San Francisco were able to communicate directly with each other over nearly three thousand miles—not in days but in minutes!

Unfortunately for him, Governor Stanford was away at the time. But in his place the Chief Justice of California sent this message to President Lincoln along the new telegraph wires:

> In the temporary absence of the Governor of the State, I am requested to send you the first message which will be transmitted over the wires of the telegraph line which connects the Pacific with the Atlantic states. The people of California desire to congratulate you upon the completion of this great work. They believe that it will be the means of strengthening the attachment which binds both the East and West to the Union, and they desire in this—my first message across the continent—to express their loyalty to the Union and their determination to stand by its Government in this, its day of trial. They regard that Government with affection and will adhere to it under all fortunes.

The riders of the Pony Express had ridden well over half a million miles. Only one rider had been killed by Indians, although a number of station attendants had lost their lives. Only one pack of mail was lost. Whatever its financial losses, in many other ways it had been a great success. But two days after the completion of the telegraph, the Pony Express officially discontinued its service.

All across the country, and especially in California, there were articles of praise and tribute for the Pony Express, now that it was gone. The *Alta* printed several, too. I had written a story about my experience with Pa at Tavish's station earlier, but now I wished I could have written one of these tributes. Mr. Kemble would have let me, but I wasn't a good enough writer to do the kind of articles that were being written. In November, in the Sacramento *Bee*, for example, one tribute read:

> Farewell, Pony: Farewell and forever, thou staunch, wilderness-overcoming, swift-footed messenger. Thou wert the pioneer of the continent in the rapid transmission of intelligence between its peoples, and have dragged in your train the lightning itself, which, in good time, will be followed by steam communication by rail. Rest upon your honors; be satisfied with them; your destiny has been fulfilled—a new and higher power has superseded you.
>
> This is no disgrace, for flesh and blood cannot always war against the elements. Rest, then, in peace; for thou hast run thy race, thou has followed thy course, thou has done the work that was given thee to do.

# CHAPTER 52

# RAISING MONEY FOR THE UNION

After the battle of Bull Run in July, there were no more battles fought in the war all the rest of that year, except for a minor skirmish here and there. Both sides now realized that the enemy was stronger than they had thought, and they spent the next six months and all winter getting their troops ready, strengthened, and trained. Both presidents and their staff of generals devised great battle plans intended to knock out the opposing forces, whatever it took.

The year 1861 had been only a beginning, the calm before the storm. It seemed that 1862 would probably be a devastating and bloody year for our country.

Therefore, fund-raising became all the more important. The Union army would need lots of money. Early in 1862, a movement was begun back in Boston to help the Union effort, and it became the focus of the nationwide effort to raise money. It was called the Sanitary Fund, although I never understood why it had such a funny name. Thomas Starr King and the other leaders in San Francisco—including me—had been raising money to send to Mr. Lincoln. We immediately organized a local branch of the Sanitary Fund.

I had a hard time thinking of myself as a leader, but I was *called* a chairwoman of the California Women For the Union. So, when the Sanitary Fund started operating in earnest, Mr. King asked me if I'd be willing to work with him as the head of the ladies' auxiliary of it. Mrs. Herndon, a woman I'd been working with on the other committee, would take that over herself. We both agreed.

As chairwoman of the Ladies' Sanitary Fund, I had to go to Sacramento and San Francisco a lot—more than Pa, in fact. He started giving me a bad time about being busier with politics than he was.

"It's you that oughta be in the legislature, Corrie," he said one day. "You spend so much time in Sacramento talking to folks about money, I oughta just turn over my seat in the Assembly to you!"

Pa sometimes had some farfetched notions, but that was about the most farfetched one I'd ever heard. The idea of a woman holding a political office like that made Almeda's running for mayor seem like nothing!

He was right, though—I was gone from Miracle Springs more than I was there, it seemed. And I hardly had any time for writing anymore—other than writing asking people to help the war effort and give whatever they could. But most of it was done in person, sitting in front of a group of people with Mr. King or one of the other men involved, listening to them give a rousing speech. They would always give me a nice introduction, saying who I was and making it sound as if I were more important than I was. And then I'd stand up and talk for three or four minutes too, urging the women especially to help out however they could.

We traveled around the northern part of the state, either by stage or in a special carriage arranged for us, or close to Sacramento by train, and spoke at lots of places. Besides being an orator who could hold people spellbound, Mr. King was a great organizer too, and he set up church meetings and town-hall gatherings and outdoor assemblies and political and patriotic festive events. Before the year was half over, San Francisco, they told me, had become the highest contributing city in the whole country to the Sanitary Fund.

We were all proud of the two hundred thousand dollars we had raised, and determined to do even better through the rest of the next year. Most of the gold was taken by ship around by Panama steamer. The stagecoach lines would have been too risky, since the Butterfield route went right through the Confederacy and was controlled by the South. Even as it was, there was always danger of the money falling into the hands of Confederate privateers.

Miss Baxter in Sacramento and Miss Bean in San Francisco each set aside a room just for me called "Corrie's room" because I stayed with them so often. Both became even better friends than before.

Cal was involved in the fund-raising too, so I saw him every time I came to the cities. We'd have dinner together most evenings when there wasn't a function to attend. More than once I turned to Miss Baxter and Miss Bean as a substitute for Almeda in trying to figure out how I felt about Cal. Neither of them had been married, but they understood about being a woman, and that was all I needed. I had never been married either, but I was finding out that I was more of a woman than I sometimes would have wished for!

Sometimes Cal would act strange, and it would worry me. I'd immediately think I had done something wrong. But if he didn't like me, why would he keep inviting me out to dinner or for a ride or walk in the evening? Often he grew quiet and distant, and his moods confused me. I would have expected him to be happy, living permanently in Sacramento, working alongside the governor, having to do with important things.

Whenever I'd ask him what was on his mind, he'd laugh and try to shrug it off lightly. But I could tell it went deeper than he was letting on. Finally I came to the conclusion that it was the war itself. The war had everybody on edge; the future was uncertain, and no matter how much money we raised, the Union might lose. Nobody liked to think it or say it out loud, but after Bull Run, we couldn't help having a gnawing worry that the South *might* win! What if Jefferson and Stephens became president and vice-president of the whole country? What if we *all* became part of the Confederacy one day? What if slavery became as common in New York and Minnesota and California and Oregon as it had been in Alabama and Mississippi?

The very thought was too horrible to dwell on!

But facts were facts. The South had won the only major battle of 1861. And as the fighting of 1862 opened, even the mighty

Union navy, which had been attempting to blockade the South, suffered a terrible defeat at the hands of the new southern ironclad warship *Merrimac*. She sank two ships her first time out, and the North's own ironclad ship, the *Monitor*, was powerless to inflict any damage upon her.

Cal had spoken about opportunity, but now that his opportunity had come and he was assistant to a governor who might run for president someday, all of a sudden it all seemed about to be destroyed. If the South won, everything would be lost for him. The Republicans—and Mr. Stanford along with them—and everything we had fought for and believed in would be destroyed. If the Union fell, so would Cal's hopes. There would be no *opportunities* left for someone like him who had so vigorously defended the Union. People like us who had worked for the Union might even be considered criminals!

As I thought about it, it became less of a mystery to me why he was downcast. I wanted him to get to have everything he'd dreamed of and hoped for. I was concerned about the outcome of the war, too, but I personally didn't have as much at stake.

I was excited when news began to reach us about Federal victories in the West along the Mississippi. It was especially exciting to hear that General Grant was leading the Union forces! I wished I could see him again.

Even after the horrible battle at Shiloh down in Tennessee in April, where neither side had been victorious, the march of Union troops toward New Orleans and Grant's control of the Mississippi River seemed to give reason for optimism. I was sure Cal's spirits would pick up.

"No, Corrie," he said, "the Mississippi's a thousand miles from the nerve center of it all. The war will be determined between Washington and Richmond, decided by who controls the two capitals. Only one president is going to emerge on top, Corrie. And right now, whatever your General Grant may be doing in the Mississippi Valley, Jackson and Robert E. Lee are threatening Washington. I tell you, Corrie, I don't expect Lincoln to last out the year!"

His voice sounded different as he spoke. Was he afraid? There was a quivering nervousness in his tone, and a light in his eye.

Through the spring of that year, as the war intensified and news continued to reach us of more battles, more bloodshed, more young lives lost, Cal grew more and more agitated. More was on his mind than just raising money for the Union, but he wouldn't say what. He didn't invite me to dinner as often either.

He seemed to be busy with other things, and often left right after our fund-raising meetings, and I wouldn't see him again for days. I didn't mind too much, but I was worried about him.

# CHAPTER 53

# A MOMENT BETWEEN PAST AND FUTURE

Late in May of that year, Mr. King asked me if I would be willing to travel to a few small communities and conduct some fund-raising meetings by myself.

He wanted me to go up into the foothill regions, the gold communities that I was familiar with, but not just near Miracle Springs—also down toward Placerville. I told him I'd be willing just so long as he told me what to do and arranged everything.

Railroads were much in the news that year. There had been all kinds of politics and debate; the companies had already been created, and a bill was before Congress in Washington to finance the building of a railroad from coast to coast. All the people of Sacramento, especially Governor Stanford, had been deeply involved in it for quite a while already. But California actually had only one railroad in operation—the Sacramento Valley Railroad, running out toward the foothills in the direction of Placerville.

I took the train out from Sacramento for the few meetings Mr. King arranged for me, where I spoke and got pledges from people for the Sanitary Fund. I didn't actually take any of the money back with me; it would be sent to the committee's headquarters in Sacramento later.

Traveling by train was exciting! I could hardly imagine being able to get into the passenger car behind a great black locomotive and ride right across the mountains and all the way to the East. But from the way everyone was talking, that day wasn't so far away. In fact, the route that had been decided on would go close to Miracle Springs. It was called the "Dutch Flat Route" and would run in the valley just on the other side of the hills from Miracle Springs. I wondered if we'd be able to ride up on the ridge and hear it chugging along someday!

During my few days of fund-raising, after I gave my short speeches about the Union and the war and the need for money, people would come up afterward and want to talk to me. And not just women; men would come up too, asking me questions and just wanting to talk in the most friendly way.

Most of these people didn't want to talk about politics or the war, but about personal things. A lot of them had read my article about the flood, or something else I'd written, even years before, and they'd want to talk about that. Then they'd tell me what *they* were thinking about, or what was on *their* minds. Everywhere I went, women would come up and invite me to supper with their family. After the first night, I didn't have to stay in another boardinghouse for the whole trip.

If it wasn't too crowded or noisy, some of them even confided things to me, problems they were having, and one or two asked my advice and what they should do. Before long I realized that my little trip out from Sacramento had more to do with individual people and what was going on inside their hearts and lives and minds than it did with raising money for the Sanitary Fund.

The most eye-opening realization of all was that the people coming up to talk to me afterward were more interested in *me* as a person, in Corrie Belle Hollister, than they were in all the things I may have been talking about. They seemed to see in me someone they could understand and who might understand them, someone they could talk to, even confide personal things in.

I came away with lots of new ideas about how my involvement in politics might have more to do with the people I ran into than it did with the bigger issues that seemed more important at first glance. Suddenly I found myself imagining people's faces, and thinking about what I could say to them and how I might be able to help them in some way. I found myself thinking more about people than politics.

I had always tended to think of myself as young and insignificant. Even with all I was doing now, I still wasn't "important" like the men were. Yet these few days changed the way I looked at myself.

It wasn't about importance . . . it was about people. It was about looking into their eyes and seeing a friend, a person who could understand and care. I found myself wondering if perhaps that wasn't the greatest "opportunity" I could ever have, the greatest "open door" of all.

I found all these things going through my mind as I stood on the last morning waiting for the train to arrive. I had completed my final fund-raising talk the night before at a church in a small foothills town. The morning train would take me back into Sacramento, and from there I would take the stagecoach back home to Miracle Springs.

The sun was well up in the sky, and it was a bright warm spring day. As I stood there on the wooden platform, holding my leather case that Almeda ordered for me out of a catalog, I thought of the changes that had come and were coming to our country, and of course the changes that had come to my own life as a result. All my past flitted by in a few moments, and I could not help but wonder about the future—if it would hold as many changes and surprises as had the past. I remembered my talk with Pa about how circumstances sometimes take us down roads we don't anticipate.

That had certainly happened to me, even just since Pa and I had talked about it! My decision to get involved in the election two years ago *had* caused things to happen in my life that wouldn't have otherwise. Here I was, raising money for the Union! Mr. Kemble and I had talked about making a book out of some of my earlier journals, about our coming to California back in 1852. That was another change on the horizon, another opportunity, as Cal would call it.

As I stood there, hearing the whistle of the train in the distance as it began to come into the station, I felt as if I were standing between my past and future—looking back, seeing the past, and waiting for a future that nobody can ever see.

I glanced toward the slowing train as it approached. Even the train itself, and these tracks right in front of me, would before long stretch all the way out of sight to the east, over the Sierras, and beyond. The very tracks themselves seemed to symbolize to me the endless stretching out of life—going in two directions. Just like the tracks, our lives stretch out behind us, reminding us of all the places we've been, all the experiences we've lived. But it also stretches out in front, and we don't know where that train track leads! We just have to get on the train and find out.

I knew where this train was going. It would take me back into Sacramento. But where was my life headed? It had been an exciting ride up till now. But I wondered where the tracks would lead me next.

# CHAPTER 54

## A DISTURBING ENCOUNTER

Late summer and fall brought more bad news from the East.

The Confederate forces had scored a stunning victory in August, matching only 55,000 men against the Union's 80,000 in a battle that was called the *Second* Battle of Bull Run.

In September, General Robert E. Lee invaded the North in force, crossed the Potomac out of Virginia and into Maryland. Not only did Lee want to get the fighting out of Virginia, his home state, so as to protect the badly needed crops for the harvest season, but he also hoped that his army might make Maryland want to secede. With Maryland in the Confederacy, the Union capital of Washington would be right next door.

He did not succeed. But neither did he fail. The standoff, and resulting battle in the valley of the Antietam Creek south of Hagerstown, was the bloodiest engagement of the war. More than 22,000 young men were killed, and neither side gained an advantage.

So much blood was being shed! There was both grief and determination throughout California—determination to help the Federal forces against an increasingly hated foe. It was all so needless! And the South was held accountable for the destruction and the dreadful loss of life.

He tried not to show it, but I know this news deeply disturbed Cal. He expected the government of the North to fall any day, and his future with it.

Not long after these two battles, an appeal came to Mr. King from the Boston headquarters:

The Sanitary Fund is desperately low. Our expenses are fifty thousand dollars per month. The sick and wounded on the battlefields need our help! We can survive for three months, but not a day longer, without large support from the Pacific. Twenty-five thousand dollars a month, paid regularly while the war lasts, from California would insure that we could continue with our efforts. We would make up the other twenty-five thousand here. We have already contributed sanitary stores, of a value of seven million dollars, to all parts of the army. California has been our main support in money, and if she fails, we are lost. We beg of you all, do what you can. The Union requires our most earnest efforts.

Immediately, Mr. King, Mrs. Herndon, Cal, and I—along with a few others—met together to plan a renewed round of meetings to gather together even more funds to help save the Union.

By the end of 1862, Mr. King's efforts had been so successful that nearly $500,000, mostly in gold, had been raised for the Sanitary Fund, more than half of it from San Francisco alone. I was proud to have been a part of it!

Usually we conducted our meeting and gave speeches. Then afterward Mr. King would pass a collection box, just like at a church service, and let people give what money they could right there on the spot. But most of the money came from pledges, and then Cal and I and some of the others would go around picking them up for the next several days. We took the money to the bank we used for the Sanitary Fund, and later sent it off to Boston by steamer. Businessmen or mining companies sometimes made their contributions in actual gold or silver bars. One time I went to a prominent San Francisco banker's office, expecting to receive a check for the pledge he'd made to Mr. King. He loaded me down with twelve pounds of gold and fifteen pounds of silver, worth almost six thousand dollars!

When Cal saw me struggling out of the bank to our carriage, he burst out laughing.

"I only got a little piece of paper," he said. "We went collecting at the wrong places."

"Next time," I panted, "I'll pick up the check, and *you* go retrieve the bullion!"

In spite of my difficulty, Mr. King was pleased.

Cal, still reading every scrap of war news he could lay his hands on, was acting disturbed and fidgety. Once he got so angry after one of our meetings that he nearly came to blows.

A man I had never seen came up to him out of the crowd and started talking rudely to him.

"Got everything going your way now, eh, Burton?" said the man derisively.

"Get out of here, Jewks!" Cal answered back in an angry tone. "What business do you have here, anyway?"

"Your business is my business now, Burton—if you get my drift."

"I don't, and I don't care to!" said Cal, trying to shove his way past the man.

"Watch yourself, Burton," he said, laying a hand on Cal's shoulder.

When Cal grabbed the hand and threw it off, I was afraid they were going to start fighting! I'd never seen such a look in Cal's eyes before, and it scared me.

"Come on, Corrie," said Cal, taking my hand and pulling me along after him, "let's get out of here."

"Who was that man?" I asked once we were away from the bustle of the crowd and walking toward our carriage.

"Nobody—just a troublemaker."

"I recognized his name when you spoke to him. What was it—I've forgotten now."

"Forget it, Corrie. He's nobody, I tell you—forget you ever saw him!"

In the expression on Cal's face, I glimpsed a flash of the look he'd leveled on the man in the crowd. He'd never looked at me like that before, and I didn't like it. Neither of us spoke again right away. We still had another meeting to attend that afternoon, but there was a chill between us all day. Later that evening, Cal said he had to go someplace. When I next saw him, everything was back to normal. He took me to dinner and was even more charming and flattering than ever.

# CHAPTER 55

# DECEITFUL SPY

The end of 1862 approached.

I was looking forward to being home for Christmas. It had been a busy and tiring year. Besides every thing else that had happened, Mr. Kemble had gotten in touch with Mr. Macpherson, an editor from Chicago, and he *did* want to publish some of my earlier journal writing into a book. That, along with the war, Zack's homecoming, and my involvement with Mr. King and Mr. Stanford and Cal, made me ready for a good long rest. After all, I had to update my journal with a whole year of keeping track of everything that had happened!

But before that, we still had one major fund-raising gathering to conduct in Sacramento—the biggest of the year, Mr. King said. We hoped to raise as much as sixty thousand dollars for one huge donation to the Sanitary Fund at the end of the year to put us over the half million dollar mark for the twelve-month period.

The meeting was scheduled for December 13, announced all the newspapers. There was a band, and Mr. King did all he could to make it festive so hundreds and hundreds of people would come. There were brightly colored banners and patriotic posters and handbills to get people to feel loyalty and enthusiasm for helping the Union. At the last minute I overheard Cal telling Mr. King he wouldn't be able to attend. He said he had some important business to take care of, but that he would be available all the following day to help gather what had been pledged. I was standing ten feet away, but I don't even think he saw me, he was so distracted. When he left Mr. King, he walked off through the crowd of gathering people without so much as a word to me. He hadn't even looked around to find me.

I have to admit, my mind wasn't on the talk I would have to give in about an hour. I couldn't help feeling hurt.

Suddenly without even thinking about what I was doing, I hurried through the crowd in the direction Cal had gone. It didn't occur to me that I was actually "following" him, I just found myself leaving the assembly under the great canvas top that had been erected for the purpose, and walking toward the business section of Sacramento. About a hundred feet ahead of me, Cal was walking briskly along the boardwalk.

I continued behind him, keeping alongside the buildings, stopping in front of a store window now and then. I would die if he turned around and spotted me!

I hated myself for spying on him like I was! But I couldn't stop. The drive inside to find out what he was doing was stronger than my good sense.

With trembling step, and even more trembling heart, I kept inching forward, ever closer—mesmerized with mingled fear and agony, yet unable to tear my eyes away from the figure in front of me.

He stopped and made motions as if to glance around.

Terrified, I ducked quickly into an open doorway.

"May I help you, Miss?" said a voice surrounded by laughter.

I looked up to discover that I hadn't walked into a store at all, but a men's barber parlor. Immediately I felt my cheeks and neck turning red.

"Uh . . . no, I'm sorry . . . I must have made a mistake," I mumbled, backing out.

I glanced up the street. Cal was just disappearing inside a building.

I ran across the street and dashed into an alley. I leaned up against the building, then sneaked a look out and over to the other side to try to see where he had gone.

I couldn't see through the window because of the glare of the sun reflecting off it. But the gold lettering painted on the glass was legible enough. WESTERN UNION it read in big letters. Underneath, in smaller script were the words "Transcontinental Telegraph Service."

I stood there waiting.

Suddenly I realized what a fix I was in! What if Cal came out and went back toward the meeting? I'd be stuck there and unable to get back without him seeing me! If the meeting started and I wasn't there, how would I explain myself?

I glanced out again. Maybe I should make a quick dash back across the street now. But it was too late—there was Cal coming out of the telegraph office!

I yanked my head back behind the building. I breathed in deeply, but couldn't get my breath. I was sure he'd know I was there and walk straight over to confront me.

*What in the world are you doing here, Corrie. Spying on me, eh! No good can come of that!* My mind played out the terrible possibilities.

Slowly I tried to look out around the edge of the building, not even thinking that my bonnet would lead my eye out into the open by at least six inches.

He was still there! I kept watching. Then he turned and continued on down the boardwalk the way he'd been going before. Several steps along he glanced down at a small scrap of paper he had in his hand, held it in front of him for five or ten seconds, still walking, then crumpled it up and tossed it into the street.

Suddenly I found my eyes following the wadded-up scrap instead of Cal, who walked on, rounded a corner, and disappeared.

My heart was pounding. *Did I dare?* What if he came back around the corner and saw me?

I waited another several seconds until I couldn't stand it any longer!

Suddenly I was out of the alley and running as fast as I could across the street in the direction of the Western Union office. I reached the other side. There it was! I ran the five or ten more yards, stooped down, grabbed up the piece of paper, clutched it in my hand, and sprinted back toward the meeting, hardly aware of the noise my boots were making along the boardwalk.

Faintly I heard some yells as I passed the men's parlor, but I just kept going. There was only one sound I dreaded hearing behind me—Cal's voice calling out my name!

There was the canvas tent, the grassy expanse where people

were standing and sitting. The meeting hadn't yet begun!

I slowed to a walk, breathing in huge gulps of air into my lungs. I skirted around the edge of the crowd, trying to calm myself down.

Just then the band started to play. I knew Mr. King would expect me up on the platform any minute. I breathed deeply again. I had to calm down! I would never be able to say a word about anything in the condition I was in.

I had to go join the others. But first I had to know what I had in my hand. I unclasped my fingers and unfolded the tiny piece of paper. I was trembling so violently I could hardly focus my vision on the few handwritten words that met my gaze.

The message was brief and made not the slightest bit of sense to me: F-BURG OURS STOP NO TIME TO LOSE.

"Corrie . . . Corrie, where have you been?" I heard a voice say behind me.

I nearly jumped out of my skin. Thinking it was Cal, I fumbled with my hands quickly, trying to make them disappear someplace in the folds of my dress.

"What are you so jumpy about?" asked Mr. King, walking up as I turned around. "It's not like you."

"Oh . . . oh, nothing," I faltered. "Just nervous, I suppose."

"Come, now—that's not my Corrie Hollister. We've got to be at our best. Shall we go? They'll be expecting us momentarily."

He led the way and I followed toward the platform where chairs were set out for us. I managed to get through it, but that day's speech was not one of my best. I kept thinking of the message written on that scrap of paper:

*F-BURG OURS . . . NO TIME TO LOSE.*

# CHAPTER 56

## IT CAN'T BE!

Cal never returned.

When the meeting was over, I was anxious to be out of there and get back to Miss Baxter's.

I was walking away from the platform when a man accosted me.

"Mind if I speak to you a minute, Miss?" he said. I looked up to see the man Cal had gotten so angry with a few months back. My first feeling was one of fear. He saw it.

"Don't worry, Miss Hollister. I mean you no harm."

I continued walking. I wasn't in much of a frame of mind for talking, especially to that man. But he fell in and started walking along beside me.

"Name's Jewks, Miss Hollister . . . Terrance Jewks."

I nodded.

"Where's your friend Burton?" he asked.

"I don't know. He wasn't at today's meeting," I answered.

"So I saw. How much do you know about him?" he asked.

"Enough, I suppose," I said, still on my guard.

"I hope he treats you better than he did me."

"What do you mean by that?" I asked.

"Just that he seems to take pleasure in ruining people."

"How so?"

"Only that a certain Democrat with a bright future ran into your friend and found himself in the hospital for three weeks, and with lies spreading about him the whole time. Lies enough to put an end to my political career."

"What does Cal have to do with it?" I asked, stopping to look at Mr. Jewks.

"He has everything to do with it. He was the one who did it to me."

"I don't believe you," I said.

"If it wasn't him personally, he was behind it. It may have taken me a while, but a few months ago I finally found out who it was that hired the thugs that pulled me out of my San Francisco hotel and left me for dead in an alley. That's when I came looking for him."

"Cal would never do such a thing," I said.

"Not even to win an election? Come now, Miss Hollister, you must know him better than that."

All of a sudden the conversation I had overheard between Cal and Alexander Dalton snapped into my mind. Of course—this must be *that* Terrance Jewks!

"Why are you telling me this?" I asked, finally more attentive to Mr. Jewks. "I'm a Republican and pro-Union. You're a Democrat, as I understand it."

"Perhaps I'm just concerned for a nice-looking young lady and I don't want her to get hurt like I was."

"Perhaps. But why do I have the feeling there is more to it?"

Jewks laughed. "You are a shrewd one, Miss Hollister! Honestly, I would like to keep you from trouble if it's possible. But along with that, I have two other motives. One is simple revenge for what your friend did to me. I'm sure you can understand that."

"I don't happen to think revenge a worthy motive," I said, "but I suppose I do understand it. What's the second?"

"Let's call it a change of heart."

"How do you mean?"

"I was a Douglas Democrat. Didn't care too much for Lincoln, but I was no southerner. Once the war broke out, I realized my loyalties were with the government, not with the South. I'm from Ohio originally. I voted for Douglas, and I'm still a Democrat. But the North has got to win this war or else the United States is all over—a dream of democracy that didn't work."

"I still don't see what any of this has to do with Cal . . . or me."

"A change of heart is what I called it," Mr. Jewks went on. "I had one, once the war started. And so did your friend, Mr. Burton. I've been following him, checking up on him, asking questions of people, using some of my old Democratic contacts. Spying on him, you might say, finding out things, without telling the folks exactly how I stood myself now, if you understand me."

"I'm not sure I do," I said slowly.

"Then let me put it to you plain, Miss Hollister, and you can use the information however you think best." He paused, took a breath, and went on. "I used to have lots of friends in the other camp. Breckinridge people. Once the war broke out, then especially after Stanford was elected, they all went underground. Had to keep out of sight. But I kept tabs on what was going on and didn't let my new loyalties be known. All the time I kept an eye out for who'd had me beaten up and what I might do about it. I found out the *who* several months ago, like I told you. And the *what* I might do to him, I just got to the bottom of this week."

He stopped.

I'm listening," I said.

"Miss Hollister . . . your Cal Burton is a member of the Knights—the Knights of the Columbian Star."

"But who . . . what. . . ?" I faltered.

"It's an offshoot of the Knights of the Golden Circle."

"No . . . it can't be!"

"It is, Miss Hollister. Believe me."

"But . . . I don't understand."

"It's really quite simple—your Cal Burton is a southern sympathizer."

"I don't believe it!" I finally burst out.

"I finally have the proof," Mr. Jewks added. Worse even than being a sympathizer—the man's a spy for the Confederacy!"

# CHAPTER 57

## CONFRONTATION, HEARTBREAK, AND BETRAYAL

The rest of that day was one of the most awful of my life.

I couldn't believe what Terrance Jewks had told me—or *wouldn't*. I was too mixed up and confused to know the difference.

I don't even know what became of the hours between my interview with Jewks and nightfall. I walked for miles, I suppose, slept in my room at Miss Baxter's, stubbornly trying to convince myself it was all a lie. Hadn't Jewks himself admitted that revenge was his motive? How better to get revenge on Cal than to turn me against him! It was a cruel hoax, an attempt to ruin Cal's reputation, and maybe even bring scandal upon Governor Stanford.

Jewks was just being a loyal Democrat. *He* was the southern spy, and his assignment had been to undermine the credibility of one of California's most loyal Unionists, the assistant to the governor himself!

It all made perfect sense! And I was Cal's weakness. They had probably been spying on me, too! I had been part of their plot all along! I had to warn Cal, and warn the governor that right here in Sacramento there were forces trying to destroy them!

But at the same time, I couldn't get rid of an uneasiness in the pit of my stomach. Cal's strange activities . . . the odd looks on his face that would come and go. I knew there must be an explanation! He would tell me everything about Jewks and set my mind at rest completely. That was the only thing to do. I had to talk to Cal tomorrow. I'd confront him with Jewks' accusations. I'd tell

299

him everything that Jewks said. He'd probably laugh the whole thing off!

Despite my attempts to reassure myself, I slept fitfully through the night. My mind told me I had nothing to be anxious about. But my stomach was quivery regardless.

The next day, the fourteenth, was a full one for all of us, contacting people, collecting money and checks and gold, confirming pledges that had been made, banking the contributions. Mr. King had called a meeting that morning to make all the arrangements and give us our assignments. It was the first time I had seen Cal since the previous afternoon. He looked and sounded like always.

We spent most of the afternoon together about the committee's work, all except for about half an hour. He knew there was something on my mind. I wasn't very good at concealing it. But we didn't have an opportunity to talk until later.

When we finally did, I just burst out and told him everything Mr. Jewks had said.

"I know it's not true, Cal," I said, nearly breaking down. "But I had to tell you so you'd know."

"Of course it's not true," he said with a lighthearted laugh. "Jewks is nothing but a two-bit politician, and a liar on top of it!" He laughed again, but the laughter sounded forced, and a little too quick on the heels of his words.

"A troublemaker, that's all he is," he added, denying the accusation too forcefully for me to feel altogether comfortable. "Probably a spy himself!" Again he laughed. But he looked straight at me as he did. I think he realized in an instant that I knew he was bluffing. I may not have been the prettiest or the smartest or the bravest person in the world, but I was able to look into someone's face and know which way the wind was blowing through their mind. I suppose up till then I hadn't made too good use of that ability with Cal. And right at that moment, I would have given anything *not* to have known what was behind his forced laughter and bravado.

Cal's laughter died away. He kept looking at me, kept watching my face for signs of what I was thinking. Then he looked away and glanced down toward the river from the little patch of grass where we were sitting. I knew him well enough to know that he was revolving things over in his mind, trying to decide what to say. Then he glanced up at me again.

Still neither of us said anything. I hadn't realized how much my face must have betrayed my doubts. But it must have, because he quit trying to deny everything. After another minute or two, a smile slowly spread across his face. A melancholy, cynical smile.

"Ah, Corrie . . . Corrie," he sighed. "You are naive."

I didn't understand his tone.

"What do you mean, Cal?" I said.

"You see the world so simply, so black and white. There's no gray for you, is there, Corrie—no in-between? Right and wrong, that's all there is."

"I . . . I don't know."

"It's a complicated, mixed-up world, Corrie. Circumstances don't always fit so neatly into black and white compartments. Sometimes there *is* gray—places where you don't know what's right and what's wrong."

"What are you trying to say, Cal?" I asked, getting alarmed by his sarcastic tone. "Mr. Jewks isn't right, is he?" I asked, still not wanting to face the truth.

"Ah, Jewks! What does he know? A low-level incompetent. If he couldn't take care of himself in this game, they should've sent somebody else!"

"Cal . . . it isn't true what he said?"

"We had to win the election. It's a rough game . . . I told you that a long time ago.

"But it's not right."

"Right? What's right? Everything has its twists and ironies. Who's to say what's right in the middle of it all?"

"What twists, Cal?" I asked. "Please . . . tell me what you mean!"

"Don't you see the irony of it? Here I am, out West, on my way up, assistant to one of California's most powerful men, when from out of nowhere my past comes back to haunt me. Suddenly the country is at war, and I am in the *wrong* place."

"What do you mean . . . what about your past?"

"I've made no secret of it, Corrie. I was born in North Carolina. You knew that. I told you about my fondness for the country, and how I admired it in you."

"Yes . . . but, what—"

"Don't you hear what I am telling you, Corrie—*North Carolina*. I'm a southerner!"

"But . . . you've been a loyal Republican. You've worked for Mr. Stanford and the Union. You left the South years ago, just like my Aunt Katie. Lots of Californians came from the South originally."

"Ah, but there's the bitter irony, Corrie. I'm not just an ordinary Californian with southern roots."

"Why?"

"Because of who I am, because of my position here. Ever since I heard about Edie leaving and returning to Virginia, I realized I had to do the same thing—not for any noble motives, but because if I didn't, everything I had worked for would be lost."

"Cal . . . what are you saying?"

"That I've got to go back too."

"Back . . . back where?"

"To the South. I have no choice."

"But . . . but *why*?" I started to cry.

"Opportunity, Corrie—remember? Suddenly all the opportunities have shifted. My golden goose, Mr. Leland Stanford, has suddenly become a millstone around my neck. My Republican affiliations, all the work I have done for the Union, even my little game with Jewks—don't you see? It will all come back to haunt me when the war's over. Men like Leland Stanford—outspoken Unionists—if they aren't in jail with Abraham Lincoln, they'll be reduced to political impotence. And unless I do something to redeem myself, something to make up for all these years when I put my money on the wrong horse—unless I do something to atone for these transgressions, as it were, I am likely to be right there with them, reduced to a life of mediocrity and meaninglessness."

"You talk as if the war is already over."

"It is . . . virtually. The North has nothing. Washington is about to fall. Lincoln could be behind bars before the year is out. Unless I make my move, and immediately, my opportunity in the new nation will be lost. Opportunity, Corrie . . . I've got to seize it while there's still time. Changing loyalties once Grant surrenders to Lee won't count for much, will it?"

"But what will you do—join the Rebel army?"

Cal laughed. "The stakes for me are just slightly higher than that, my dear naive young friend!"

"You said you always wanted to go to Washington someday."

"I wanted to get to the capital. Once the North surrenders, that will be Richmond. And I don't have to wait until someday . . . the opportunity is before me *now*!"

"I . . . I just don't see—"

"You still don't grasp it, do you, Corrie?" he said, and he sounded as though he were talking to a child. "Does the name Alexander H. Stephens mean anything to you?"

I shook my head.

"Well, he is my uncle, on my mother's side. I know I told you about him. He has been after me for some time, through discreet communications of course, to join his staff—in a very prominent position. I have simply been awaiting the most propitious time for making such a move."

I stared blankly at him.

Cal chuckled. He almost seemed to be enjoying putting me through this, seeing the confused emotions pass through me. I thought he had cared, but I had never felt so small and foolish as I did right now.

"Alexander Stephens," Cal went on, "happens to be Jefferson Davis's vice-president. When I arrive in Richmond, I won't have to wait for some distant time . . . my opportunity will have arrived! I'll be working close to the president himself!"

"There's only one President, and his name is Abraham Lincoln."

"I'm sorry, Corrie, but there is the gray again in your world of black and white. Right now there are two presidents, and before long the only one remaining in power will *not* be your friend Abraham Lincoln."

"You have made up your mind?" I said, trying desperately to be brave.

"I'm afraid I have."

"Then why did you wait until now? Why did you keep being so loyal, keep helping us raise funds for the Union, keep working for Mr. Stanford? You gave several speeches, telling people why they had to support Mr. Lincoln and the Federal troops. How could you do that, Cal, when inside you were all along planning to defect to the South?"

"Oh, I haven't been planning to defect all along. I had to keep my options alive on both sides. I have nothing intrinsically against the Union, Corrie. I told you, it's not an ethical or moral issue for me. It's opportunity, and I will go where I can climb the highest. What if I had left, and then suddenly the tide of the war turned, and Davis and my uncle were the ones being arrested for their part in the rebellion? No, Corrie—I couldn't risk that! I've had to bide my time to see how the tide of the war would go. The shifting sands of the political landscape can be treacherous if you don't watch your step. So all year I *have* been watching my step, and now that the sands are about to engulf Mr. Lincoln and General Grant and Mr. Stanford altogether, I perceive it is time for me to be off. My only difficulty will be in explaining to my good uncle, who is not a kindly disposed man, why it took me so long to come to my senses. But I'm sure I will be able to manage that."

I sat stunned. I couldn't believe all I'd heard.

"But I thought," I said at last, fighting a terrible urge to break into tears, "I thought . . . we—that is, Cal . . . you always used to talk about what *we* would do . . . about the future . . . I thought—"

I didn't know what to say. There wasn't much more to say.

"Come now, Corrie, you didn't seriously expect me to marry you, did you?"

His question was so abrupt, so stark, that I felt as if I'd been slapped in the face.

"I didn't say that."

"It's bigger than just you and me. Maybe if things had been different, who knows what might have happened? You're a great kid, Corrie. I like you. There was always something about you I admired. In fact, I always kind of figured you might be on your way up, just like me, and that we might help each other out."

"And now you don't need someone like me anymore, so that's

the end of it, is that it?" I said, my hurt turning to anger.

"Please, Corrie," said Cal, laughing slightly, "there's no need to overreact to it. It's just one of those things that happened. My uncle simply happens to have more clout than a young news writer from California, that's all. Look at it practically. But I meant every word I said—I always admired you, and I'll always wish the best for you. But this is not an opportunity I can pass up—for you, or anybody."

I sat silent again. So many thoughts and feelings were raging through me, I felt like screaming and sobbing and running and kicking something—preferably Cal Burton!

"Why don't you come with me, Corrie!" said Cal after a minute. The exuberance in his voice let me know he didn't have any idea what he'd done to me.

"Why should I?"

"Because of the opportunities there would be for you in the new government. Just think—a news writer, right at the center of power. It could put you right at the top, Corrie. You could be one of the best-known writers in the country!"

"Opportunity, is that it?" I said.

"Yes! Why not, Corrie? What's there ever going to be for you here?"

*Just my family, people I love, a good home*, I thought to myself. "I don't think so, Cal," I said. "Even if the Union falls, I'm still going to cast my lot with men like Abraham Lincoln."

"Have it your way. But don't ever say Cal Burton didn't give you the chance to hitch yourself to his star on its way up!"

Finally I got up off the grass and started to walk back toward the buggy. "Will you please take me back to the boardinghouse?" I said. "I'm getting cold, and I have to start thinking about getting ready to go home."

# CHAPTER 58

## PARTING OF THE WAYS

If I thought the last night was awful, this one was much worse. Never had I felt so isolated in my life. How desperately I wanted to feel Almeda's loving arms around me, to hear Pa's voice, to retreat to the warmth of our home!

I felt small and foolish. How could I have been so naive? Cal was exactly right—a naive kid, that's what I was, nothing more! All this time I thought I meant something to him, and now I realized it had all existed nowhere but in my own mind!

Lying on my bed at Miss Baxter's, I cried and cried, drenching the pillow with my tears.

Not until late in the evening, after my tears had temporarily dried up, did I begin to think rationally again. Should I tell somebody . . . Mr. King, Mr. Stanford?

I supposed Cal would give the governor some kind of formal resignation. We'd probably not see him again on the fund-raising platform! Now that he had decided to throw in with the South, as dreadful as it was to think it, he obviously would be hoping for the Confederacy to win as quickly as possible.

At last I concluded that it was none of my business to tell anyone. Let Cal do his own dirty work! If he was going to betray us all, let *him* tell them face-to-face. I hoped he choked on the words!

I cried some more, but managed to fall asleep around midnight. I woke up several times, suddenly remembering the ache inside my heart and longing so badly for home. Each time, however, I drifted back to sleep again, and the final time slept for several hours. When I woke up, the sunlight was streaming through the window and it was halfway into the morning.

I rose and dressed, wishing I'd gotten up early enough for the morning stage north, but it was too late now. I'd have to wait until tomorrow. The morning edition of the *Bee* had already been delivered. I greeted Miss Baxter, saw the paper lying on her table, and looked down at it. Across the top, in bold black letters, were the words: UNION SUFFERS DEVASTATING DEFEAT AT FREDERICKSBURG, MD. REBEL ARMY 40 MILES FROM CAPITAL.

I sat staring at the headlines, stunned. It was as if Cal had known yesterday.

Suddenly I ran back up the stairs, dashed into my room, and rummaged about until I found the scrap of paper Cal had thrown on the ground. I read the cryptic message again. Of course! He *had* known. The paper said the battle had taken place two days ago, on the thirteenth, the same day he had received the telegram!

But the last words of the message . . . *NO TIME TO LOSE*. What did it mean?

I stood thinking for a minute; then a terrible sense of foreboding swept over me.

*Oh no!* I thought. *What if. . . ?*

I couldn't even say it! With hardly a word of explanation to Miss Baxter, I ran back down the stairs and was out the door and heading toward the middle of town. I stopped at the first livery stable on the way and hired a horse. The instant it was saddled, I galloped off, and in six or eight minutes I was pulling up in front of the capitol building. I hardly stopped to think whether I was presentable or not. I just ran down the corridor toward the governor's office. It didn't take long to find out what I needed to know: Cal had not yet come in this morning.

I turned around and retraced my steps. How I wished Pa had some business in Sacramento right then! I could have used his help!

I got back on the horse, walked her quietly until I was away from the capitol, then urged her again to a gallop. Three or four minutes later, I arrived at the house where Cal lived. I had never been inside, but we had ridden by several times, and he'd pointed it out. Jumping off the horse, I ran to the porch and knocked on the door.

"No, Mr. Burton isn't home," his landlady said, looking me over from head to toe with a not-so-pleasant inquisitive expression. "I don't know when to expect him, either. I didn't see him come in last night, but then I don't make it a practice to be snooping into other people's affairs."

"Did he come in last night?" I asked.

"I don't know for sure. I thought I heard him, but he might have left again later. I didn't pay too much attention. I don't like to pry, you know."

I had the distinct impression that if she had known anything more than she was saying, she might have thought twice whether to tell me or not.

I ran back and jumped up on the horse's back, wheeled around, and made for downtown.

I hoped Mr. King was still at his hotel and hadn't left for his home in San Francisco! I was at the hotel in five minutes. I dismounted in front and dashed into the lobby. From all the riding, I was sure I looked a mess.

"Is Mr. King still here?" I asked the desk clerk.

The clerk gave me a look similar to the one Cal's landlady had given me. "He is."

I knew the room. We had several meetings of the committee there. I bolted for the stairs and bounded up them two at a time.

At last I knocked on the door, completely out of breath.

"Corrie!" said Mr. King, answering it, "Come in . . . you look as if you've just ridden one of those Pony Express routes you wrote about last fall!"

"Mr. King," I panted, "have you seen Cal today?"

"Why, no, Corrie, I haven't. As a matter of fact, I was going to get in touch with you to see if *you'd* seen him. I need to talk to him about what I'm sure must simply be a clerical mistake of some kind at the bank."

"What is it?" I asked.

"So, I take it you haven't seen him this morning either?" said Mr. King.

I shook my head.

"Hmmm . . . well, we're going to have to find him sooner or later to clear this up."

"What?" I asked again.

"You and he did make the collections yesterday, did you not?"

I nodded. "Nearly all of them. Several large checks, and a big amount of gold, too. I think the total was $52,000."

"Yes, it was a marvelous day—$69,000 in pledged contributions. And you say the two of you collected over forty thousand of it?"

"That's right," I said.

"Hmmm . . . that is peculiar. When I checked with the bank this morning, it seems there wasn't a deposit made to the Sanitary Fund account yesterday. But you and Cal *did* make the deposit?"

My heart began to sink beneath a dreadful weight of doom.

"Uh . . . Cal left me for thirty minutes or so after we were through," I said. "He told me he was going to the bank and asked me to run a message over to the capitol building for him. I met him afterward."

"Hmmm," mumbled Mr. King, pondering it all. "It must be a clerical oversight of some kind. I'll go check with the bank again. In the meantime, when you see Cal, tell him to come see me. Perhaps he can clear it up."

By now I was all but certain in my own mind that Cal could indeed clear it up! Whether Mr. King would ever hear about it from his own lips, however, I was beginning to seriously doubt.

I only had one more stop—the one I hoped I wouldn't have to make. I went from the hotel to the downtown district, where I pulled up in front of the Western Union office and tied up the horse. I walked along the boardwalk and around the corner I had seen Cal disappear around after receiving the telegram. It was a street I knew well from frequent use myself. But it had never occurred to me what he was doing when I'd seen him right here the other day. Three doors down was the stage office!

I walked inside and looked up at the schedule board, then went to the window.

"Morning, Miss Corrie," he said. "You ready for your ticket now?"

"Not yet, Mr. Daws, thank you," I answered. "Only some information."

"Anything I can tell you, Miss Corrie."

"Did you have a passenger on this morning's stage, a Mr. Burton?"

"Well, not exactly," replied the stationman, with whom I'd been friendly for several years. "That is, if you're meaning the same young fella I've seen you traveling with a time or two."

"That's him," I said.

"Handsome young man, eh, Miss Corrie?"

"Yes, he is . . . but was he in? Did you sell him a ticket?"

"Yes, he was in. Came in twice, as a matter of fact. But it was yesterday, not this morning."

"He was in *twice*?"

"Yes, ma'am. First time around four, five o'clock in the afternoon—"

That was the exact time when he'd sent me to his office with the message!

"He just wanted to leave his bag right then," he said, "so he wouldn't have to keep lugging it around. Once I lifted it, I knew why! Heavy as the dickens, it was! Heaviest bag I ever recollect. 'What in tarnation you got in here?' I asked him, 'solid gold?' 'That's a good one!' he laughed. 'Taking gold by stagecoach! What kind of fool do you take me for?' he said, still laughing. Nice young man, Miss Hollister."

"And then you say he came back later? But I was sure he would be on the morning stage."

"Yep, he came back later all right—around 8 o'clock. Most curious thing I ever saw. Don't know why they never told me about it."

"About what?" I asked.

"Special stage rolled up—all outfitted and ready to go. Driver said it was government business. And your man Burton, why he was the only passenger—other than the two armed guards, that is."

"What stage line was it?"

"The Butterfield."

"Which way did they go?"

"Butterfield only goes south, Miss Corrie. Driver told me they was gonna be driving all night. Said they were heading all the way to Fort Smith, Arkansas."

"That's behind the Confederate lines."

"Yes, ma'am. I . . . I thought you knew all about it, Miss Corrie." For the first time Mr. Daws' voice lost its cheerful tone, and he began to sound concerned.

"Why did you think that?" I asked.

"Well, ma'am, on account of him mentioning you, and saying you'd be along shortly. I just . . . well, I figured you'd be taking the stage out too, one of the regular Butterfield coaches, and that, well . . . that you and he'd be meeting up somewhere, or maybe that you was going all the way back East too. The way they made it sound like government business—I figured it had something to do with you."

*Cal knew that sooner or later I'd figure it out.*

"He even left a message for me to give you, Miss Corrie," the stationman added. "Makes it seem kind of odd now, him doing that, and you not even knowing he'd gone."

Cal had said it himself—the world was full of ironies.

I braced myself. I didn't want to ask, but I couldn't live without knowing. "What was the message?" I asked.

"Don't make much sense now, but he said to thank you for helping him to atone for his transgressions. He said his uncle would be very grateful, and that this would help explain things very nicely. Then he said he hoped to see you when you both got where you were going."

I took a deep breath. If Zack had to learn to be a man by facing Pa with humility, I suppose today was the day when I had to learn to stand up and be a woman by facing Thomas Starr King and Leland Stanford with honesty and humility, too.

I would have to face them both, and tell them what I knew about Cal. And I would have to tell them I had known it yesterday, in time to have stopped him. I would have to apologize. I would have to admit to the two great men of California that they had entrusted too much faith in me, and that I had not been worthy of it. And I would have to beg their forgiveness for allowing over forty thousand dollars of Union contributions to be speeding along its way south toward the government of the Confederate States of America.

"So I take it you won't be wanting a ticket, after all, Miss Corrie?" said Mr. Daws.

I sighed. "I might as well buy it now," I said. "Yes, I do want one, Mr. Daws. Give me a ticket north for Miracle Springs, on tomorrow's stage."

"Round trip, Miss Corrie?"

"No, Mr. Daws. One way will be sufficient. I don't know that I will be coming back to Sacramento anytime soon."

"Your business here all done?"

Again I sighed. "Not quite. I have some very unpleasant business to attend to this afternoon," I said. "But by tomorrow, yes, my business will be done."

# CHAPTER 59

# HOME AGAIN

It was a lonely, tearful stagecoach ride back to Miracle Springs the next day. I kept thinking I had cried all the tears it was possible to cry, and then more would come. How many tears could a girl have, anyway? There must be an end to them somewhere!

I didn't find out where the tears ended that day. By the time I reached home I had vowed never to have anything to do with politics, writing, or men again!

The minute I walked into the house I fell into Almeda's arms. I was so glad no one else was there right at that moment. She knew from one look at my face that something was dreadfully wrong, but she just let me cry and held me tight. Gradually, through my tears, I told her everything.

"Oh, Almeda," I finally tried to say, still blubbering like a five-year-old, "how could I have been such a downright fool as to think he loved me?"

She probably had seen the whole thing coming long before I had. But if she did, she didn't say so. She just kept comforting me.

"He never cared about anything but himself. He was completely self-absorbed. How could I not have seen it?"

I had done a lot of thinking all day riding on the stage. I had wanted to talk to Almeda so badly back in Sacramento. Now that I finally had her all to myself, I gushed out with everything I'd been thinking and feeling.

"Hearts can get in the way and cloud how you see nearly everything sometimes, Corrie. It's part of life, part of growing up.

313

I wouldn't feel too badly if I were you."

"How can I not? I was so blinded by everything that was going on. Cal had no real depth—it's all so clear now! All he cared about was his own ambition. We never talked about spiritual things or what really matters in life. Oh, Almeda, I just feel so foolish!"

"Time will help you understand it more clearly. I liked Cal too, Corrie. We all did. Whether he changed after the war started or was out for what you and your father could do for him from the beginning—we may never know for sure. He seemed sincere enough. I was taken in, too."

"Besides everything else, he took the Sanitary Fund money! How can I not feel responsible? I feel as if I've betrayed both the Union and God!"

"They will both forgive you."

"But it's too late about the money—he's gone."

"You said Mr. King and Mr. Stanford immediately sent some fast horsemen after the stage."

"They did, but they didn't have much hope of catching it. They had probably over a two-hundred-mile head start and would be close to the Arizona border by the time they could reach them. Even if they did catch them, it would likely have taken bloodshed to retrieve the money, and neither Mr. King nor Mr. Stanford wanted that."

"I see. I suppose in that case it wasn't worth it."

"They were a lot more worried about information Cal had to give to the South than just the money. Working so close to an important governor like Mr. Stanford, Cal knew a lot of things about the northern war effort."

A lump formed in my throat. "Almeda, how can I not blame myself? All my writing and talk about truth and being a true person, and I can't even recognize someone who isn't true when he's standing right in front of me! How could I not have seen him for what he was?"

"*Was* he untrue right from the beginning?"

"Oh, I don't know! After the way it turned out, how can I possibly know what was there inside him to begin with?"

"I don't know either, Corrie," said Almeda. "I do know we have to learn truth in stages. It doesn't come all at once. We have to learn about truth by encountering some things along the way that aren't true. Otherwise we never learn to tell the false from the real."

"Do those things that come along always have to hurt so badly, and make me feel like such a nincompoop?"

She laughed, and I halfheartedly joined in.

"A lot of times they do," replied Almeda. "Pain is one of the world's best teachers."

"The worst of it is forgetting about God all this time. I was so absorbed in Cal and what I was doing that I thought about him only once in a while, and I hardly prayed at all. I can't believe I didn't realize it!"

"It's all part of the growing and maturing process. Perhaps this will help you remember him more in the future. You've heard the expression about being older and wiser?"

I nodded.

"Well, just consider yourself an older and wiser and more truthful young woman now, after all this. If you grow and mature from it, won't it have been worth it in the end?"

I had to stop and think about that. In my present state of mind I wasn't at all sure.

"Almeda," I said at last, "when I was waiting for God to give me a sign about his will, Cal Burton was the person who finally convinced me to get involved in this election."

"Yes?" Almeda prodded when I paused.

"Well, it's just . . . maybe . . . do you think I heard wrong from the beginning? I mean, how could it have been *right* for me to be involved when Cal was so . . . so *wrong?*"

"Corrie," Almeda said gently, taking my hand, "the Lord uses many methods to open his will to us. Apart from what's happened with Cal Burton, do you think what you've done for the election—and for the Union—has been wrong?"

I thought about it for a minute. "No, I don't. I think it was the right thing to do, but—"

"Then maybe God *did* use Cal to help you make your decision, even though Cal himself wasn't aware of being an instrument in God's hands."

"I hope you're right," I said. "Right now, that doesn't seem to help me feel much better about it."

"It will in time."

"But what about my forgetting the Lord," I went on, "and not making him part of what was happening with Cal?"

"One thing about God, Corrie, that I've learned to take comfort from, is that he never forgets us—he always keeps doing his work in us, never stops working away in our hearts and minds. We may forget him, but he never forgets us. His work down inside us doesn't depend on something so unreliable as whether we happen to be thinking of him or not. His work of maturing us goes on even when we're not conscious of it. And he won't let us remain forgetful of him—not for long, anyway. He makes sure he gets our attention again eventually when he needs to, one way or another."

"Even with an incident like I've just been through?"

"The Lord will use anything or anyone. He uses all kinds of people and all kinds of situations. He will even use people who don't know him to open doors in *our* growth, like he used Cal Burton. He will use them for us, and attempt to use us in their lives at the same time."

"I doubt if I had much impact in Cal's life."

"Oh, I disagree, Corrie! I imagine God was using you to knock on some doors in Cal's heart and mind, just like he will use Cal, even in retrospect, to accomplish some older and wiser maturing things down inside you. Nothing in life ever goes to waste when we belong to the Lord—even the times when we might think we haven't been faithful to him. He takes it all and uses it for the best and deepest purposes."

"Hmm . . . If that's true, I wonder if God was knocking at Cal's heart."

"Who knows how differently it might have turned out if he'd paid attention to the small voice of God inside him speaking through you?"

"But I wasn't saying much of anything to him about the Lord."

"Your life was speaking important things to him, Corrie. I could see that the two times he was here. Your character, your bearing, your truthfulness. You may think you were nothing but a starry-eyed young lady. But your deepest self shone through like a clear-sounding bell. Cal noticed. Yes, God was knocking at his heart through you. But he chose to ignore the voice and to go his own way. So he will have to suffer the consequences, and you will have to go on with your life and learn from it all."

Suddenly the door burst open and Pa came in.

"I thought I heard the sound of someone riding up," he said, striding toward me and scooping me nearly off the ground in his arms. "Merry Christmas, Corrie!"

I'd nearly forgotten. Christmas was only nine days away!

"Merry Christmas, Pa," I said. If only I could keep from crying again!

"You show her the letter, Almeda?"

"No!" exclaimed Almeda. "I forgot, we got so involved in talking. Corrie, you have a letter!" she cried, turning and running across the room.

"What can it be that's worth all *that* commotion?"

"Wait till you see, Corrie!" said Pa, with nearly as much excitement in his voice as Almeda's.

Almeda ran back toward me, carrying an envelope, then thrust it into my hand.

"It came five days ago, Corrie! We've all been dying of curiosity waiting for you to get home!"

I took the envelope. The return address said only: THE WHITE HOUSE, WASHINGTON, D.C.

With trembling fingers I tore open one end of it and pulled out the letter. I couldn't keep my heart from pounding as I read.

MISS CORNELIA BELLE HOLLISTER,

I have been made aware of all your work for the Republican party on behalf of my election, as well as your efforts to raise money for our Union forces in this present conflict. I want to express my deepest appreciation on behalf of the nation, and to tell you that your patriotism has not gone unnoticed. It would be my pleasure to meet you here at the White House in Washington, if circumstances would permit you to make the journey. I would very much like to give you my personal hand of gratitude, as well as ask you to help me in the war effort with a new project here in Washington.

Yours sincerely,
A. LINCOLN
President

The single sheet fell from my hand and I staggered to sit down in a chair. I sat there stunned.

"What *is* it, Corrie?" asked Almeda. "Is something wrong?"

Pa picked up the paper and read it. "Nothing wrong, Almeda," he said after a moment. "It's an invitation to visit the President!"

"The President!" she exclaimed.

"Signed right here by Abraham Lincoln himself," said Pa, handing the paper to Almeda.

"Corrie . . . that's—that's wonderful!" cried Almeda.

How could it be . . . how could I possibly accept? But how could I *not* accept? Thoughts of the war and the danger and the time and expense involved—none of that entered my mind in the first seconds that I sat there. I thought only of the face of Lincoln from a picture I had seen. The President had written to *me!*

How much time passed as I sat there in a daze, I don't know. When I first became aware of voices around me again, Becky and Tad were there too, and I vaguely heard Zack and Alkali Jones outside approaching the house. Mr. Jones was laughing and cackling over something.

In the blur of my racing brain, there was Mr. Jones on the other side of the house with Zack, both of them laughing and talking. My ears weren't working right any more than my brain. They must have been playing tricks on me from the last time when I'd heard him making jokes about the Hollister clan running for office. Because of what I *thought* I heard Mr. Jones saying was, *Corrie Fer President, hee, hee, hee!*

My mind was spinning with thoughts of the war and Mr. Lincoln and stagecoaches and trains and money, and when my eyes and ears finally cleared, the room was quiet.

The whole family surrounded me, staring straight at me as if waiting for me to say something. Not a one of them said a word. They were all just gazing expectantly at me.

"Well?" said Pa finally.

"Well, what?" I asked.

"Are you gonna answer the question we've all been asking you, or are you gonna just keep sitting there staring off like you can't see or hear anything?"

"What question?"

"Are you gonna do it, Corrie?" they all shouted. "Are you gonna go?"

At last my mind seemed to start working again. I took in a deep breath.

"Of course I'm going to do it," I said. "He's the president of our country, isn't he? I can't very well turn *him* down, now can I?"

# EPILOGUE

Most of the Pony Express incidents recorded—including the breakfast incident—are true, as are all the names of the riders mentioned. Nearly all California personalities, politicians, and issues are likewise factual, and the positions, facts, and details represented, as far as can be determined, are historically accurate. Along with other sources, the following books were very helpful in researching early California history, the Pony Express, the election of 1860, and the early Civil War period:

Bartlett, Ruhl, *John C. Fremont and the Republican Party*
Hittell, Theodore, *History of California*
Lewis, Oscar, *San Francisco: Mission to Metropolis*
McAfee, Ward, *California's Railroad Era 1850–1911*
Nichols, Roy, *The Stakes of Power 1845–1977*
Reinfeld, Fred, *Pony Express*
Rolle, Andrew, *California, A History*
Roske, Ralph, *Everyman's Eden, A History of California*
Williams, Harry, *The Union Sundered*
Williams, Harry, *The Union Restored*

In addition: "The Mexican War and the Facts Behind It" by Patrick Phillips, and issue #33 of *Christian History* magazine on "The Untold Story of Christianity and the Civil War."

For all of these, as well as to Sandy Bean for the creation of Edie, the author expresses his deepest gratitude.

# A PLACE
# IN THE SUN

# A PLACE
# IN THE SUN

## MICHAEL PHILLIPS
## JUDITH PELLA

**BETHANY HOUSE PUBLISHERS**
MINNEAPOLIS, MINNESOTA 55438

Cover illustration by Dan Thornberg,
Bethany House Publishers staff artist.

Published by Bethany House Publishers
A Ministry of Bethany Fellowship, Inc.
6820 Auto Club Road, Minneapolis, Minnesota 55438

Printed in the United States of America

**Library of Congress Cataloging-in-Publication Data**

Phillips, Michael R. , 1946–
    A place in the sun / Michael Phillips and Judith Pella.
        p.   cm. — (The Journals of Corrie Belle Hollister ; 4)

    I. Pella, Judith.  II. Title.  III. Series: Phillips, Michael R. , 1946–
Journals of Corrie Belle Hollister ; 4.
PS3566.H492P5   1991
813'.54—dc20                                   91–4987
ISBN 1-55661-222-2                                    CIP

To
Michael Oliver Cochran

# Books by the Phillips/Pella Writing Team

## The Journals of Corrie Belle Hollister

*My Father's World*
*Daughter of Grace*
*On the Trail of the Truth*
*A Place in the Sun*

## The Stonewycke Trilogy

*The Heather Hills of Stonewycke*
*Flight from Stonewycke*
*Lady of Stonewycke*

## The Stonewycke Legacy

*Stranger at Stonewycke*
*Shadows over Stonewycke*
*Treasure of Stonewycke*

## The Highland Collection

*Jamie MacLeod: Highland Lass*
*Robbie Taggart: Highland Sailor*

## The Russians

*The Crown and the Crucible*

# The Authors

The PHILLIPS/PELLA writing team had its beginning in the longstanding friendship of Michael and Judy Phillips with Judith Pella. Michael Phillips, with a number of nonfiction books to his credit, had been writing for several years. During a Bible study at Pella's home he chanced upon a half-completed sheet of paper sticking out of a typewriter. His author's instincts aroused, he inspected it more closely, and asked their friend, "Do you write?" A discussion followed, common interests were explored, and it was not long before the Phillips invited Pella to their home for dinner to discuss collaboration on a proposed series of novels. Thus, the best-selling "Stonewycke" books were born, which led in turn to "The Highland Collection," and the "Journals of Corrie Belle Hollister."

Judith Pella holds a nursing degree and B.A. in Social Sciences. Her background as a writer stems from her avid reading and researching in historical, adventure, and geographical venues. Pella, with her two sons, resides in Eureka, California. Michael Phillips, who holds a degree from Humboldt State University and continues his post-graduate studies in history, owns and operates Christian bookstores on the West Coast. He is the editor of the best-selling George MacDonald Classic Reprint Series and is also MacDonald's biographer. The Phillips also live in Eureka with their three sons.

# CONTENTS

# CHAPTER 1

## ELECTION DAY

Pa walked out of the schoolhouse with a big smile on his face.

He took the stairs two at a time and ran over to where the rest of us were standing by the wagon. "Well, I reckon that's that," he said, still smiling. "Now all we gotta do is wait!"

Of course, since the rest of us were under twenty-one, we couldn't have voted, anyway—at least not Zack or Tad. But neither could Almeda, even though she was the one who got everybody for miles around interested in the political future of Miracle Springs by jumping into the mayor's race against Franklin Royce. People soon enough found out that she didn't consider being a woman to be a handicap to anything she wanted to do!

And so she stood there waiting with the rest of us while Pa went into the schoolhouse with the other men and voted. When he rejoined her, their eyes met, and they gave each other a special smile. I was well on my way past nineteen to twenty, and I'd been through a lot of growing up experiences in the last couple of years, so I was beginning to understand a little about what it felt like to be an adult. But even as the oldest of the young Hollister generation, I could have only but a bare glimpse into all that look between Pa and Almeda must have meant. If the Lord ever saw fit, maybe I would know one day what it felt to care about someone so deeply in that special way. For today, however, I was content to observe the love between the two persons I called Father and Mother.

A moment later Uncle Nick emerged from the schoolhouse, and came down the steps and across the grass to join his wife Katie and fifteen-month-old son Erich, who were both with us.

"Well, Drum," he said, giving Pa a slap on the back, "we come a ways from the New York days, I'll say that!"

Pa laughed. "Who'd have thought when we headed west we'd be standing here in California one day as family men again—and *you* with a wife and a son!"

"Or doing what we was just doing in there!" Uncle Nick added. "I reckon that's just about the craziest, most unexpected thing I ever done in my life! If only my Pa, old grandpa Belle, and Aggie could see us now!"

A brief cloud passed over Pa's face. He and I had both had to fight the same inner battle over memories of Ma. We had both come to terms with her death—not without tears—and were now at peace, both with the past and the present.

As to the future—who could tell?

A lot would depend on what Rev. Rutledge and the government man from Sacramento found out when they added up all the votes later that day. For the moment, Pa and Uncle Nick had cast their ballots in the long-anticipated election for mayor of Miracle Springs, and in the Fremont-Buchanan presidential voting. I couldn't have known it yet, but my own personal future was as bound up in the latter election as the former. I had already invested a lot in the Fremont cause, and I couldn't help but feel involved in its outcome—almost as involved as in the local election for mayor.

But for the moment, the future would have to wait a spell. As Pa had said, there was nothing else to do *but* wait.

We piled in our two wagons. Pa gave the reins a snap, and off we rumbled back to our home on the claim on Miracle Springs Creek. Pa and Almeda sat up front. In the back I sat with my lanky seventeen-year-old brother Zack, who was a good five inches taller than me, thirteen-year-old Becky, and eleven-year-old Tad. Emily, now fifteen, rode with Uncle Nick and Katie, carrying her little nephew.

That was election day, November 4, 1856. A day to remember!

But there'd been so much that had happened leading up to the voting, I reckon I ought to back up a bit and tell you about it . . .

# CHAPTER 2

## PATRICK SHAW'S PROBLEM

After I got back from my adventure in Sonora six weeks earlier, I was certainly surprised by Almeda's unexpected news.

I had just filed my story on the Fremont-Buchanan race with Mr. Kemble at the *Alta*. After that and Derrick Gregory and the double-dealings of that ne'er-do-well Robin O'Flaridy, I sometimes wonder if *anything* could surprise me! But I'll have to say I was sure excited when I got home and Almeda said, "You'll never believe it, Corrie, but your father and I are going to have a baby!" An adventure, a baby, and two elections were almost more than I could handle!

Three or four days after I returned from Sonora, we got the first inkling that Franklin Royce, the town banker, was up to his old mischief. One afternoon Patrick Shaw rode up to the house. One look at his face, and you could tell right off that he was in some kind of trouble.

Neither Pa or Almeda had to say anything to get him talking, or ask what the trouble was. It was out of his mouth the instant he lit off his horse.

"He's gonna run us off our place, Drum!" he said. "But me and Chloe and the kids, we ain't got no place else to go. What am I gonna do, Drum? I don't know nothing but ranching, and with a family and the gold drying up everywhere, I can't pack up and try to find some new claim!"

"Hold on, Pat," said Pa. "What in tarnation are you talking about?"

"He's fixing to run us out, just like I told ya!"

"Who?"

"Who else—Royce! There it is—look for yerself!"

He thrust a piece of paper he'd been holding in Pa's direction. Pa took it and scanned it over quickly. He then handed it to Almeda.

"He says we got thirty days to get out!" Mr. Shaw's face went red, then white. If he hadn't been a man, he probably would have started crying.

Almeda read the paper over, taking longer than Pa, her forehead crinkling in a frown.

"It might as well be an eviction notice," she said finally, looking up at the two men. "And if I know Franklin, it's no doubt iron-clad and completely legal."

"What happened, Pat?" Pa asked. "How'd you get into this fix?"

"Well, it ain't no secret my claim's just about played out. I wasn't lucky enough to have any of your vein run across to my side of the hill. Though I suspect Royce thought it did, the way he's been after my place."

"What do you mean?" asked Almeda.

"Why, he's come out offering to buy the place three or four times the last couple of years."

"And so now he figures he'll get your place without paying a cent for it!" said Pa, the heat rising in his voice.

"A few of my cattle got that blamed infection last spring when my pond had the dead skunk in it. It spread around the herd, and I wound up losing thirty or forty head. I missed a good sale I was gonna make, and so couldn't make a few payments to the bank."

"How many?"

"Four."

"So how much you do owe him—how far behind are you now?"

"I pay him a hundred sixty-seven a month."

"So you're—let's see . . . what, about six, seven hundred behind," said Pa, scratching his head. "I'll help you with it,

Pat. I can loan you that much."

"No good, Drum! I already thought of that. I knew you'd help if you could, so when Royce delivered me that there paper, I said to him, 'I'll get you the six sixty-eight—that's how much he said I was in arrears, is what he called it. I told him I'd get it to him in a few days, because I knew you'd help me if you could. But he said it wouldn't help. He said now that I defaulted, the whole loan was due immediately, and that if I didn't come up with the whole thing in thirty days, the claim and the house and the whole two hundred-fifty acres and what cattle I got left—he said it'd all be his."

"How much is your loan, Mr. Shaw?" Almeda asked. "What do you still owe the bank?"

"Seventeen thousand something."

Pa let out a sigh and a low whistle. "Well, that's a bundle all right, Pat," he said. "I'm afraid there ain't much I can do to help with *that*. Nick and I couldn't scrape together more than three or four thousand between us."

"What about me, Drummond Hollister?" said Almeda, pretending to get in a huff. "I'm part of this family now too, you know! Or had you forgotten?"

"I ain't likely to do that anytime soon," replied Pa smiling.

"Well then, I insist on being part of this. Parrish Mine and Freight could add, perhaps, two or three thousand."

"I appreciate what you're trying to do," said Mr. Shaw, his voice forlorn. "But I could never let you loan me that kind of money, everything you got in the bank. It don't matter anyhow. Between all of us, we ain't even got half of what it'd take!"

"Yes, you're right," sighed Almeda. "And it wouldn't surprise me one bit if your loan had a thirty-day call on it even if you weren't behind in your payments. Franklin as much as told me that's how he structured all the loans around here. Of course, I couldn't say for certain without seeing the loan document, but my hunch is that your getting behind is only an excuse for the foreclosure, that legally he is perfectly justified in calling your note due at any time and giving you no more than thirty days notice."

A little more talk followed. But there wasn't much more to be said. Mr. Royce had the Shaws in a pickle, and nobody could see anything they could do about it.

# CHAPTER 3

## ALMEDA'S DECISION

The next surprise came a couple of days later.

Almeda had been rather quiet ever since Mr. Shaw's visit. The terrible news of what Mr. Royce had done seemed to weigh on her, and I knew she felt almost desperate to find some way to help him. Yet there just wasn't enough money to get him out from under the call on his loan.

It was getting on toward late in the evening, Pa was sitting with Tad and Becky in his lap reading them a story. I was trying to draw a picture of Zack from memory. Zack had taken Rayo Rojo for a ride that afternoon, and for one moment, just after he'd mounted, she reared up on her hind legs. Zack leaned forward, his feet tight into her flanks, one hand flying in the air, and his eyes flashing with the closest thing to pure delight I'd ever seen. The sketch wasn't turning out too well, but I didn't want to let myself forget the mental picture of that wonderful moment.

Suddenly Almeda's voice broke out loudly, as if she had been struggling all day to keep the words in and couldn't hold back the dam a second longer.

"It's just not right for a man like that to be mayor!" she exclaimed. "Drummond, I'm sorry for acting rashly, and I hope you'll forgive me, but I just don't know what else to do. We've just got to stop him, that's all there is to it! Pregnant or not, and despite his threats, and even if I am a woman—I don't know what I can do but go ahead with it! It *must* be done for

18

the good of this community—I am going to run for mayor after all!"

For a few seconds there was silence. Everyone stopped and looked at her. Pa was still holding the book steady on his lap, but his and Tad's and Becky's eyes all focused intently on Almeda where she stood over by the stove.

"If that don't beat all!" Pa said finally, shaking off the two kids from his lap, climbing to his feet, and walking over to her. "Sometimes I wonder whether I married me a wife or a hurricane! Well, if I'm gonna have me a new son or daughter, he might as well have a ma for a mayor to make up for the fact that his pa's such an old man!" He smiled and gave Almeda a big hug. I knew he was proud of her decision, even though maybe it wasn't the same one he would have made if he had to decide.

So many things immediately began to run through my heart!

What about all those threats Mr. Royce had made about what he would do to Almeda if she didn't keep out of the race? He said he'd cause trouble for Pa and Uncle Nick with the law, that he'd investigate the ownership of the land and their claim! All along we'd worried about what Royce might do to all the miners and ranchers and people around Miracle Springs who owed money to his bank if he didn't win. The incident with Patrick Shaw showed that he wasn't fooling, and I didn't see how Almeda's running would help, even if she won.

Worst of all, he had threatened *me* too! He had told me to stop interviewing and talking to people about the election, and as good as said that if I didn't, he would let it be known to powerful slavery people that I was a pro-Fremont reporter, and that I would be in danger. And after what had happened in Sonora I knew it was no empty threat! The powers behind the scenes in the national election were real . . . and *were* dangerous! For all I knew Royce might be somehow connected to senator Goldwin and his people! After my story appeared in the *Alta* exposing the falsehood of Mr. Gregory's claims against Fremont, they might try to track me down and do something to punish me. I was still so new to this whole world of politics and news reporting, I had no idea what to expect. And I certainly didn't want Mr. Royce getting me in more trouble than I was already in!

With all this worrying about Mr. Royce and his threats against *me*, I hardly even remembered at first what he'd said about opening a supplies outlet and freight service of his own, and putting Parrish Mine and Freight out of business.

But Almeda hadn't forgotten. She weighed everything, and over the next few days talked to Pa a lot. They prayed, and in the end they both concluded that her decision to run was the right one after all, and that they had to go ahead and see the election out to its conclusion on November 4.

I think Almeda felt a little like I had with the Fremont story, that there was more at stake than just the outcome of the election itself. She felt that it was her duty to fight against what Franklin Royce stood for, to fight against his underhanded and deceitful methods. She felt she was standing up for what was *right*. Even if she lost, she felt she needed to take a stand in the community for what was right and honest and true.

It was not an easy decision. Everything Royce had said was true. He *could* hurt her and her family if he chose to. He *could* put Parrish Freight out of business. He *could* challenge Pa and Uncle Nick's ownership of their land. He could hurt a lot of other people in the community, just like he was doing to Patrick Shaw, if he decided to start calling loans due. Franklin Royce was a powerful man!

But in the end Almeda and Pa decided to take the risk— because it was the right thing to do. Maybe it wouldn't help the Shaws keep their claim and their ranch and their home. But they had to do something to show that Royce couldn't just do whatever he wanted without any opposition. A man like that simply shouldn't be allowed to work his will in a town and come to power without anyone standing up to him. Sometimes you just have to do what's right, no matter what the consequences.

Realizing all the risks involved for Pa and Almeda in their

decision, within a day or two of Almeda's surprise announcement to the family, I made a decision of my own.

I decided to start up again with my article on the Miracle Springs mayor's election. And whether Franklin Royce liked it or not, I was going to pick up where I'd left off interviewing people. I *would* write at least one article, maybe two, on the election. There wasn't much time left before November, but what there was I would use. And I wouldn't settle for $1 an article either! If Mr. Kemble wasn't willing to pay me at least $3 or $4, I'd submit it to another editor—even the *Globe*, if I had to! But I was sure the *Daily and Weekly Times* in Sacramento would print it. Sacramento was closer, and both Mr. Royce and Almeda were a little bit known there.

So I dusted off my writing satchel, read over the notes from interviews I'd done earlier, and tried to figure out how I could go about telling people in the rest of the state about this election in what Mr. Kemble would call an "unbiased" way. Then I started going to visit folks again to find out their thoughts, now that the election was getting close and Almeda was back in it.

# CHAPTER 4

## MY FIRST INTERVIEW

One thing I was learning about being truthful was the importance of being out in the open with folks—not only being honest in what you said, but coming right out with things so that nothing was ever said or done behind another person's back. I don't think there's anything more destructive among people than thinking and saying things about someone that you're not willing to tell them to their face. And I knew that if I was going to be a writer—especially if I was going to write about people—I had to show integrity in this straightforward way.

So I figured there was only one place to begin my article about the election, especially if I was going to be fair and unbiased.

Therefore, that very afternoon, I rode into town, left Raspberry with Marcus Weber at the stable, and crossed the street to the bank. I went straight to Mr. Royce's office, knocked on the door, and walked in.

If he was surprised to see me, he certainly didn't show it. But neither did he smile.

"Mr. Royce," I said, "I would like to talk with you, if you don't mind. Either now, or some other time."

"Now will be fine, Miss Hollister," he replied, still sitting behind his desk, still not smiling or showing any sign of emotion. He motioned me to a chair with his hand.

"I imagine you know," I said, "that my stepmother has

decided to remain a candidate for mayor after all."

"So I understand," he replied. "It is of course her decision to make, but it is an unfortunate one that will, I fear, have most unpleasant consequences."

The squint of his eyes as he looked steadily into my face confirmed his meaning. I took a deep breath to steady myself.

"Well I have decided to go ahead with what I was doing too," I went on. "I am going to write the article or two I was planning about the mayor's election. And to do a good job I am going to have to continue talking to people around town and interviewing them."

"I am very sorry to hear that," said Mr. Royce. But his tone held a threat. "It would deeply grieve me to see a promising young writer such as you find herself on the wrong side, shall we say, of powerful interest groups and individuals who—"

"Look, Mr. Royce," I said, "I know you're trying to scare me by making it sound like I'm going to be in danger if I don't do what you say. But if Almeda can do what she's doing in spite of all the trouble you could cause her and our family, then I figure I can too. I'm going to do it whether you like it or not, and you might as well just stop trying to frighten me off by talking like that."

He stopped, his mouth half open, shocked that I would cut him off and dare to speak so brazenly.

I probably shouldn't have interrupted him, or spoken quite so boldly. But he was starting to make me angry with all his cool words and hidden threats, sitting there behind his big fancy desk as if he owned the world and could tell everyone else what to do! And I knew he was especially annoyed that Almeda and I were causing him so much trouble. He wanted us to stop interfering with his plans and the powerful grasp he used to hold on to everything around him. I'm sure he figured he could scare us into submission. Well I didn't like it! My face got red and my voice sounded a little edgy, but I couldn't help it.

For a second or two he just stared, probably wondering

whether he should threaten me further, or stand up and throw me out of his office! But before he had a chance to do either, I spoke again. And this time I went on and said everything I'd come in to say. I didn't want to give him a chance to cut *me* off.

"Now, doggone it, Mr. Royce," I went on, "I'm gonna try to be fair in this article I'm writing. It's not going to be something that's supposed to make people favor Almeda. I want to present both sides and talk to folks who are gonna vote for you *and* for her. My editor Mr. Kemble said he didn't think I could write a fair and unbiased article, being so closely involved like I am. He said I couldn't be objective—he called it a conflict of interests."

I paused to take a breath, but only for a second.

"But I'm going to prove him wrong, Mr. Royce," I said. "I'll show him that I *can* write an unbiased article about the election that will interest the people who read his newspaper. I intend to be fair, but you're not making it very easy for me to think unbiased thoughts when you're telling me and my Pa and my mother the things you're going to do to us if we don't just quit and let you run for mayor all by yourself. What would folks think if I wrote about what you said to us?"

"I would deny every word," replied the banker coolly. "It would be my word against that of a teenage girl desperately trying to sway people in favor of her father's wife. No one would believe a word you said."

"You might be right, for all I know," I said. "I don't want to write those things, and I'm not going to write them. What I came here for was to interview *you* and to ask you to give your side on some things. Whether you believe me or not, I want to write what's fair and truthful about you as well as Almeda. And it would be a lot easier to be fair to you if you'd give me a little help instead of talking mean like you're doing."

I stopped. Judging from the expression on his face, people didn't normally speak quite that plainly to Franklin Royce. And if I'd stopped to think about it, I probably wouldn't have either. But I'd done it, and it was too late to take my words back now!

He sat just staring back across his desk at me. The office was completely silent. His face didn't give away a hint of what he was thinking. I'd heard Pa and Uncle Nick talk about poker faces, and if this was one of those, then I understood what they meant!

Finally Mr. Royce's voice broke the quiet.

"What do you want to know?" he said. The red was gone from his cheeks and the meanness from his tone, although he was obviously not pleased with the whole affair.

"Why do you want to be Miracle Springs' mayor?" I asked, getting out a sheet of paper from my satchel and inking my pen. "What made you decide to run?"

He cleared his throat, but kept looking at me almost warily. The question *sounded* like what a newspaper reporter would ask, and yet he didn't quite believe it was coming from the mouth of a girl he wasn't sure he trusted.

"I, uh . . . feel that the town, growing as it is, must look to its future, and who could be better qualified to lead such a diverse community forward than one like myself, who has been such an intrinsic part of helping in its growth up till now?"

I wrote quickly to get down all his words.

"So you feel you are the most qualified person to be mayor?"

"I do."

"Because you are the town's banker?"

"That of course is a large part of it. In that role I have, as I said, helped this community grow. I have helped to finance much of the building, most of the homes. I have a stake in the community because of who I am and what I have done. As mayor I will always be looking out for the best interests of its people."

Again there was silence for a while as I wrote. Mr. Royce was getting used to the idea of an interview. He was starting to sound like he was delivering a campaign speech.

"Your opponent, Mrs. Hollister, could no doubt say the same thing about her history in the community and all the ways *she* has helped the miners," I said. "What real difference is there between you and her?"

His eyes narrowed for an instant, and I knew he thought my question meant more than I intended.

"Of course she could *say* it," he answered with just an edge of derision. "But there is a clear difference between a $13,000 loan to build a house or buy a spread of acreage, and a store where you buy a fifty-cent gold pan or a five-dollar sluice box or pay a few dollars so that a free black man can freight your supplies somewhere for you. A little supply store and a bank are hardly equal in their impact upon the community, and I am sure the voters in this area will have the good sense to acknowledge that difference on November 4."

"Do you think your position as banker might be a drawback in any way?"

"What do you mean? How could it possibly be a drawback?"

"There are some people who have said they might have trouble trusting you as mayor."

"What people?" he said, his voice rising and his eyes flashing.

"I cannot say *who*," I replied. "But I have talked with some folks who aren't sure they'd altogether like a banker in charge of their town."

"Look, Miss Hollister," he said angrily, "if you want to ask me some questions, that's one thing. But if you're going to come into my office and tell me to my face that I'm not to be trusted, and then put the lies people say about me in your article, I'll have no part of it!" He rose from his chair. "I believe it is time for this interview to come to an end. You can't say I didn't warn you what might happen if you persist in this folly. You tell that fool father and stepmother of yours that for their own good they'd better stop fighting me. I won't be denied what is rightfully mine, and I will not be responsible for people who stand in my way! Good day, Miss Hollister."

I remained seated and returned his stare. That man made it real hard to keep a Christian attitude! But I kept sitting there and didn't get up and leave like he wanted me to. Finally I spoke again, as calmly as I could.

"Please, Mr. Royce," I said, "I was only saying what some people have told me they're thinking."

"During your so-called interviews about the election!"

"That's right," I answered. "And if I'm going to write a fair article, then I ought to know how you would answer those people. Otherwise, if you just make me leave and I have to write the article with only their side of it to go on, then your perspective never gets to be told. I'm trying to give you a decent shake here, Mr. Royce, but you're making it downright hard! Do you want me to tell what *you* think or not? If you want me to leave, I will. But then I have no choice but to write just from the other interviews I get. And I am going to write this article, Mr. Royce, with or without your cooperation!"

He stood looking down at me just a second or two longer, then slowly sat down, like an eagle smoothing his ruffled feathers.

"Go on, Miss Hollister," he said calmly, "what is your next question?"

"Perhaps I should go about this differently," I said. "Why don't you tell me, Mr. Royce, how and why you first came to Miracle Springs, and how you became involved in banking in this community."

On this safe ground, Mr. Royce started up and was soon talking comfortably. I kept taking notes, and asked him more questions about himself, and the rest of my time in his office, while not "pleasant," was calmer than the beginning. When I left fifteen minutes later I had plenty of information to offer a fair look at Royce the candidate—if "fair" is the right word, considering what I knew about Royce that I couldn't say.

I never asked him about the business of calling Mr. Shaw's note due. I knew I could never mention it in the article. And for the time being I'd rather he didn't know I knew about it.

# CHAPTER 5

## TALK HEATS UP

I didn't need worry about trying to keep it a secret that I knew of the Shaws' problem.

Within a few days *everyone* knew. And most everyone was plenty riled. If the election had been held right then, Franklin Royce wouldn't have gotten a single vote!

Word had just begun to circulate back through the community that Almeda was going to run after all . . . *and* that she was in a family way. Those two things alone had people talking, and the "Hollister For Mayor" sign back up in the Freight Company window kept it all fresh in people's minds. But when the news got around about Mr. Shaw getting evicted by the bank, Franklin Royce wasn't exactly the most popular man in Miracle Springs that week!

Pa kept saying he couldn't figure out why Mr. Royce did it. "Gotta be the stupidest thing I can think of doing," he said, "just before the election. Why, Tad could run against him now! Anybody in the whole town could beat him hands down."

Almeda was both furious and delighted. This foolish move by the banker suddenly made it seem as if she had a good chance of winning the election. But on the other hand, what good would that do Patrick and Chloe Shaw? Even her being the town's mayor wouldn't get them their house and land back.

Finally Almeda decided to make the Shaws an issue in her campaign, to try to use it to make people think twice about voting for Mr. Royce, and at the same time to coerce the banker into giving the Shaws another chance if they could get caught up and current again with their payments to the bank. "I would gladly sacrifice the election," she said one night at the supper table, "if Royce would negotiate some equitable terms with Patrick."

"Might be that you can do both, Almeda," said Pa, "win *and* make him back down."

"I'm going to do everything I can to try," she replied. "But the first order of business has to be somehow getting the Shaws out of their dilemma."

Almeda planned to give her first campaign speech the very next Sunday after church, right on the main street of town in front of Parrish Mine and Freight. Pa and Marcus Weber got busy building a three-foot-high platform for her to stand on, and the rest of us fanned out all over the community telling everybody to come, that we needed their support. She had some important things to say.

"And, Corrie, Zack, all of you," she said, "make sure the women know how important it is for them to come, even if they can't vote. If they're there on Sunday, and they hear what I say, their husbands will hear every word eventually! Women, children, dogs, horses . . . we just need a good crowd! We've got to show people that we are serious and that the opposition to Royce is real. That's the only way they'll give earnest consideration to voting for me."

By Friday, the whole community was buzzing! One of the town's most well-liked men was on the verge of getting run off his place. A pregnant woman who couldn't even vote herself was running for mayor against the town's powerful banker, and a campaign speech was scheduled in two days. Folks were talking of nothing else!

What a "human interest" item all *this* would make! I began to wonder if the article I was writing would be any good at all, leaving out all the things people were talking about. But I was almost done with it, so it was too late to start over. I thought maybe I should write a second one to come about a week after the first. I'd have to see what Mr. Kemble said.

Before I had a chance to worry about that, it began to come clear to Pa why Mr. Royce had taken the action against Mr. Shaw about his loan.

"He's a schemer all right," Pa grumbled. "He's making an example of Pat, showing folks what he'll do if things aren't to his liking."

"And demonstrating that he isn't afraid, even of what people think of him," added Almeda with a frustrated sigh. "I really don't know how to stop him, Drummond. Right now everyone's mad at him and saying they'll never accept him as mayor. But when it comes down to their decision, and their *own* homes and land that he holds the mortgages on, I'm afraid they'll worry less about how much they like Franklin Royce and more about their own security. And I can't say that I blame them. I don't want people voting for me if they're going to be hurt by it."

"He can't foreclose on everybody," said Pa. "He'd be a fool. He'd be cutting his own throat. His bank would be out of business."

"But don't you see, he doesn't have to follow through with his threats. Just the fear that he *might* will be enough. People won't run the risk. They'll give in to him. That's why he called Patrick's note due when he did. At first it looked like a foolish campaign move. But in reality it conveyed just the message to this community Franklin wanted it to—*I hold the power and the purse strings in this town, and I am not afraid to use them. I don't care if you like me. I don't even care if you all hate me. But just don't cross me or you'll end up in the same dilemma as Patrick Shaw.*"

"In other words," growled Pa angrily, "vote for me . . . or else!"

"I think that's the basic message he hopes the men of this community will glean from the Shaws' trouble. He doesn't care a bit about all this anger circulating around right now, as long as once it dies down he's succeeded in getting that message across."

Almeda sighed. She knew she had taken on a tough opponent who apparently held all the cards. Her initial enthusiasm was fading some, I could tell, and I knew from her washed-out complexion that she didn't feel well either.

"Well you just give 'em your best in that speech on Sunday," said Pa, trying to bolster up her spirits. "Maybe we can beat that rascal yet!"

Almeda smiled back at him, but it was a pale, wan smile. She rose slowly to her feet and walked to the door and outside. She needed to be alone a lot during those days. Pa knew it and let her go without any more talk between them.

# CHAPTER 6

# CAMPAIGN SPEECHMAKING

On Sunday morning church was packed, and folks were waiting for what was going to happen that afternoon.

A little after one o'clock, we all rode up to the front of Parrish Mine and Freight in the wagon. A few people were milling around already, and soon others began to arrive for the speech, which was scheduled for 1:30.

More people turned out than we had imagined possible! Not only were there dogs and horses and every woman for miles around and all their children, but a lot of men turned out too. Almeda was noticeably excited. By the time she was ready to stand up, the whole street was filled in front of the freight company office, all the way across to the stores on the other side, and stretching down the street almost to the Royce Miners' Bank. There must have been four or five hundred people, maybe more! The one person I *didn't* see was Franklin Royce, although I was certain he knew of the event.

At about twenty minutes before two, Pa jumped up on the platform and held up both of his hands. Gradually the crowd quieted down.

"I know it ain't necessary for me to make introductions," he said in a loud voice. "If any of you don't know who this is standing here with me by now, then I don't figure you got any business here anyway!"

Laughter rippled through the crowd.

"But this being our first campaign, well I figured we ought

to do things proper. So here I am making the speech to introduce our candidate who's gonna speak to you all today. And
that's just about all I reckon I'm gonna say! So here she is,
Miracle Springs' next mayor, and a mighty fine-looking woman
if I do say so myself, Mrs. Almeda Parrish Hollister!''

All the women clapped as loud as they could, and most of
the men joined in. Pa gave Almeda his hand and helped her
up the steps to the platform. Then he jumped down onto the
ground. Almeda turned to face the crowd.

"I can't tell you how much it means to me that you've all
come here today,'' she began. "As my husband said, campaigning for public office is not something we are experienced at,
and to tell the truth, I'm more than a little nervous standing
up here facing so many of you. I don't really know what a
political speech is suppose to be like, so I am simply going to
tell you what I think of this town, why I love Miracle Springs,
and why I want to be its new mayor.''

She paused, looked out over the faces, and took a deep
breath before continuing. As she did, some of the people sat
down on the ground.

"When I came here, as a few of you know who were here
at the time, the town of Miracle Springs was a far different
place. My late husband and I had just arrived from Boston,
and I have to tell you, all of California seemed pretty wild and
rambunctious to me—Miracle Springs included. There were
more saloons than stores, more gold than bread, more mules
than women, and it was every man for himself. They said California was a state back then in 1850, but it wasn't like any
state I'd ever seen!''

The listeners laughed and some joking comments could be
heard from long-time residents who knew first-hand what she
was talking about.

"That's right, Mr. Jones,'' Almeda called out with a smile.
"I heard that. And you are absolutely correct—it was a fun
place to be back then! But it was a hard life too, for those who
didn't make a strike. And I don't know about the rest of you,
but for myself, I will take the Miracle Springs of today to the

Miracle Springs of 1850. Yes, times have changed—here as well as in the rest of the state—and throughout the country. It's a new era. Our fellow Californian John Fremont is campaigning through this great land for the abolition of slavery. And we've all been hearing recently about some of this state's leading men, like Leland Stanford and Mark Hopkins, who are earnestly pursuing the railroad linkage of east and west across this great country. California is becoming a state with a future.

"My point, ladies and gentlemen, is that as the country is changing and growing, we citizens of Miracle Springs must change and grow with it. Gold brought many of us here, and it first put California and Miracle Springs on the map, but gold will not insure our future. When the nuggets turn to dust, and when even the dust begins to dry up, gold will no longer sustain businesses. Gold will not feed hungry stomachs. Gold will not educate. Gold will not keep the bonds of friendship and love deep. Gold will not raise a church. Gold will not attract the kind of families a community needs to put down roots and sustain itself and grow strong that it might endure.

"You are all familiar with towns, once booming and alive with activity, which have now become silent and empty because the gold is gone. Ghost towns—dead today because they failed to look to the future, they failed to establish a community fabric where roots went down deeper than the gold they feverishly sought."

Almeda stopped, thought for a moment or two, then took in a deep breath and started up again.

"Now, in a few weeks you men have to decide how to vote in Miracle Springs' first election for mayor. And I suppose I'm telling you why I think you ought to vote for me—even though I'm a woman!"

A little laughter went around, but mostly some cheers and clapping could be heard from the women present.

"So I'm going to tell you why you should vote for me," Almeda continued. "I love this town. After my first husband died, I was miserable for a time. I seriously considered returning to the east, but in the end decided to stay here. And I cannot say it was an easy time. Some of you men made it very difficult for a woman, alone as I was, to keep a business going."

The smile she threw out as she said it showed that her words were meant in fun, not bitterness.

"Yet, on the other hand, most of you were good to me. You were considerate, you brought me your business. You treated me with courtesy and respect. And we managed to forge a pretty good partnership, you miners and Parrish Mine and Freight. This town became my home. And as the town grew, I loved it more and more. The church and school were built. A minister and schoolteacher joined our community—"

She smiled and pointed to where Rev. Rutledge and Miss Stansberry were seated together in the minister's carriage.

"Families came in growing numbers. Wives joined the miners—some from as far away as Virginia!"

She turned and threw Katie a smile behind her where she stood with Uncle Nick.

"And now I feel it is time for me to give this community back a little of what I feel it has given to me. I love Miracle Springs, and with everything that is in my heart, I desire to see it grow into a community whose strength lies in its people, and in their bonds with one another. I love it too much to see it become a ghost town, abandoned because the gold is gone from its hills and streams. My friends, even if the gold were to disappear tomorrow, you and I are what make this community vital! And that is the future to which I want to dedicate myself, as your next mayor.

"Now . . . why do I think you men ought to vote for Almeda Hollister? The chief reason is this: a Hollister vote is a vote for the future of Miracle Springs. It is a vote for the whole fabric of this community, not just one aspect of it. Money and gold may make men rich. But when they are gone, money and gold also make ghost towns.

"I am committed to the whole of Miracle Springs' future, not just its financial future." She paused, thought for a moment, and when she spoke again her voice had grown softer and more serious.

"What I say next is not easy for me," she went on. "But I suppose perhaps it is necessary in light of the purpose for which we are gathered. From the beginning, I have been instrumental in helping Miracle Springs become a real town, not just a gold camp. I helped organize the church and the school, and brought Reverend Rutledge and Miss Stansberry here. I truly believe I am qualified, both by experience and by commitment, to be your mayor. I suppose my greatest drawback as a candidate is that I am a woman, and that may be the reason many of you feel you should not vote for me. But on the other hand, perhaps that is the greatest asset I have to offer Miracle Springs, too. The fact that I am a woman makes me, I feel, sensitive to some of the deeper and longer-lasting interests of this community, important things that I fear a one-dimensional focus on gold and mining profits cannot adequately see."

I don't know whether she saw him at first, because she kept right on with the conclusion of her speech. But as I looked up I detected some movement at the back of the crowd, and then realized that a figure had emerged from somewhere near the bank and was now walking slowly forward.

"In closing then, my friends of Miracle Springs and surrounding communities," Almeda was saying, "I simply want to ask for your votes on election day. In return, I pledge to you my commitment to do all that lies in my power to insure a happy and prosperous future for all of us. Thank you very much for your attention and support."

She turned to step down off the platform, amid a lot of clapping—mostly from the women and children and *our* family, and a few enthusiastic men, like Pa and Uncle Nick and Rev. Rutledge. But suddenly the noise died down abruptly. Almeda turned around to see the cause, just as the crowd split down the middle to make way for Franklin Royce, who was striding purposefully toward the platform.

# CHAPTER 7

## ROYCE'S REBUTTAL

Silence fell over the street as everyone waited to see what would happen. Almeda remained where she was, watching him approach.

"Well, Mrs. Hollister," said Royce in a loud but friendly voice, "that was a very moving speech. You wouldn't deny your opponent equal time in front of the voters, would you?"

"Certainly not," replied Almeda, obviously cooled by his appearance, but trying not to show it.

The banker climbed the steps to the small platform, where he joined Almeda. He flashed her a broad grin, and then, as if he was just going on with the conversation said, "But surely you do not mean to suggest that gold and the financial interests which accompany it are of lesser importance to this community than these other things you mention?"

"I did not use such a term, Mr. Royce," said Almeda. "But now that you put it like that, I suppose I *do* believe that money is less important than people, than friendship, than churches and schools and families."

"Come now, Mrs. Hollister," said Royce with a patronizing smile. "You know as well as everyone here that gold drives this community. Without the gold Miracle Springs would not exist."

"Perhaps not. But I believe it *will* exist in the years to come, with or without gold."

"You are a businesswoman, Mrs. Hollister. You know that

37

money is what makes everything work. Without money, you are out of business. Without money none of these people would have homes or clothes or wagons or horses. I'm all for friendship and schools and children and churches. But a community needs a solid financial base or all the rest will wither away. Money is what makes it go, money is what it is all based on."

"Money . . . such as that represented by the Royce Miners' Bank?"

Royce smiled, although he did not answer her question directly. "And all that is why I'm not sure I can agree with your statement that a Hollister vote is a vote for the best future of Miracle Springs. In my opinion, the future must rest upon a solid financial base."

"In other words, with a vote for Royce," she said.

The banker smiled broadly. "You said it, Almeda . . . not I." Some of the men chuckled to see him getting the better of her. "Let's be practical, Almeda," he went on. "Everyone here may have done business with you at some time in the past. But I am the one who has financed their homes, their land, their businesses. Why, Almeda, I have even lent money to you to help *your* business through some difficult times! None of these people would even be here today if it weren't for my bank and what I have done for them. And the future will be no different. If Miracle Springs is to have a future, even the kind of future you so glowingly speak of, it will be because of what *I* am able to give it, both as its banker *and* its mayor."

Everyone was quiet, waiting to see what Almeda would do. Clearly, Mr. Royce meant his words as a direct challenge to everything she had said and hoped to accomplish with her speech.

When she spoke again, her voice contained a challenging tone of its own.

"Is the kind of future you have in mind for Miracle Springs the same kind as you're imposing on Patrick Shaw and his family?" she asked in a cool tone. "That is hardly the kind of future I would judge to be in the best interest of this community, no matter how much your bank may have done for it in the past."

A low murmur of agreement spread through the crowd. Her words had touched off the anger at Royce that had been circulating all week. A couple of men shouted out at him.

"The lady's right, Royce," cried one voice.

"Shaw's a good man," called out another. "You got no call to do what you done!"

Mr. Royce did not seem angered by her question. It almost seemed as though he had been expecting it, and was ready with a reply.

"Surely you must realize, Almeda," he said, "that politics and business don't necessarily mix."

"Well maybe they *should*!" she shot back. "Perhaps the incident with the Shaws tells us what kind of mayor you would be. Is this how you envision looking out for the best interests of the people of Miracle Springs—making them leave the homes they have worked so hard for?"

By now Almeda had the support of the crowd. Although not a single one of the men present would have dared go to Mr. Royce in person and tell him what he thought, in a group, and stirred by Almeda's words, all the anger that had been brewing in the community through the week spilled over into mumblings and shouts of complaint against what Royce had done.

"Listen to them, Franklin," she said. "Every man and woman here is upset by what you have done. They want to know why. They want to know if this is what you mean when you say you have *helped* the community grow! Is this the future you offer Miracle Springs—a future whose road is strewn with failed loans and eviction notices? If so, I do not think it is the kind of future the people of Miracle Springs have in mind!"

By now everyone was getting into the argument, calling out questions and comments to the banker. From the look and sound of it, it didn't seem that Royce could have any possible chance in the election! But as Pa had said earlier, Mr. Royce wasn't the kind of man who should be underestimated.

He held up his hands to restore quiet. When he could be heard again, he turned to Almeda. "What I said, Mrs. Hollister," he replied, still in a calm tone, "was that the future of

Miracle Springs must rest upon a solid financial base. Without a financial base, there can be no future."

He paused, looked into her face for a moment, then continued. "Let me ask you a question," he said. "As a businesswoman, have you ever extended credit to a bad account?"

He waited, but she did not answer.

"I'm sure you have," he said. "And what did you do when a customer did not pay you? Did you continue to let him take merchandise from you, knowing in all probability he would never pay you?"

"There are plenty of people here today who know well enough that I have given them credit during some pretty tough times," she answered at last. "When I trust someone, I do what I can to help them."

"As do I," countered Royce. "I have made loans and extended credit and helped nearly every man here. But in the face of consistent non-payment, I doubt very much if you would blithely let a man go on running up a bill at your expense. If you operated that way, you would not have survived in business so long. Well, in the case of the Shaws, I have been extremely lenient. I have done all that is in my power to keep it from coming to what has transpired this past week. You ask Patrick Shaw himself—he's standing right back there."

Royce pointed to the back of the crowd, and heads turned in that direction. "Ask him. What did I do when he missed his first payment . . . his second . . . his third? I did nothing. I continued to be patient, hoping somehow that he would be able to pull himself together and catch up and fulfill his obligations."

Royce paused a moment, seemingly to allow Mr. Shaw to say something if he wanted. But Shaw only kept looking at the ground, kicking the dirt around with his boot.

"I would say that I have been extremely patient," Mr. Royce went on. "I have done nothing that any honest businessman wouldn't have done. If you were in my position, Almeda, you would have been forced into the same action."

By now the crowd had begun to quiet down. They may not

have liked it, but most knew Royce's words were true. They didn't know he was only telling them half the truth—that he had refused to rescind the note-call even if Mr. Shaw made up the four months.

Royce turned and squarely faced the crowd. He spoke as if Almeda were not even present beside him, and gave her no opportunity to get in another word.

"Let me tell you, my friends, a little about how banking works. Banking is like any other business. When my esteemed opponent here—" he indicated Almeda with a wave of his hand, without turning to look at her, "—offers you a gold pan or a saddle for sale, she has had to buy that pan or saddle from someone else. Now as a banker, the only commodity I have to offer is money. She sells mining equipment. I sell money. Now, I have to get that money from somewhere in order to have it to lend. And do you know where I get it?" He paused, but only for a second.

"I get it from the rest of you," he went on. "The money I loaned Patrick Shaw for his house and land came from money that others of you put in my bank. I lend out *your* money to Mr. Shaw, he pays me interest, and then I pay *you* interest, keeping out a small portion as the bank's share. Mr. Shaw didn't borrow money from *me*. In a manner of speaking, he borrowed money from the rest of you! All of you who have borrowed money from the Royce Miners' Bank have really borrowed it from one another. You who receive interest from the bank are in actuality getting that interest from your friends and neighbors."

Everyone was quiet again and was listening carefully.

"If someone doesn't pay the bank what he has agreed to pay, then how can the bank pay the rest of you the interest due you? What I have done is the most painful thing a banker ever has to face. The agonizing inner turmoil it causes a man like me to have to find himself in the odious position of calling a note due, it is so painful as to be beyond words. And yet I have a responsibility to the rest of you. How can I be faithful to the whole community and its needs if I ignore such problems? My bank would soon be out of business, and then where would this community be?"

He waited just a moment to let his question sink in, then answered it himself.

"I will tell you where it would be. When a loan gets behind and goes bad, the real injury is to *you*. As much as I don't like to say it, Patrick Shaw really is indebted to the rest of you, his friends. His failure to make his payments hurts *you* as much as it hurts the bank. He has not paid *you* what he owes. And if that sort of thing is allowed to go unchecked, it puts the bank in a very serious position. Before long, I might have to call another loan due from another one of you, in order to raise the funds to make up for the note which has been defaulted upon. Do you see, my friends? Do you understand the problem? Do you see the dilemma I'm in?

"All the loans I have made are subject to a thirty-day call, just like Mr. Shaw's. In other words, the bank can legally call *any* note due at any time. Now a banker hates to call a loan due, because it is a very painful experience, as painful for a sensitive man like me as it is to a family who must pack up and leave a home where they have invested years. But if a loan is allowed to go bad, then another loan must be called from someone else, to keep the bank healthy. And so it goes. One can never tell when circumstances may force a banker to begin calling many loans due, in order to carry out his wider obligations to the entire community.

"This is why I said earlier that *if* Miracle Springs is to have a future, it must rest upon the solid financial base that I and the Royce Miners' Bank can give it. Without that solid base, I fear many loans may have to be called due, and Miracle Springs could become one of those ghost towns Mrs. Hollister spoke about. As your mayor, I hope and pray I will be able to keep that from happening."

He stepped back and began to descend from the platform, then turned back for one final statement, as if wanting to avoid any possible confusion.

"I want it to be very clear that if I am elected mayor, I will work strenuously toward a strong financial base, to make sure that what has befallen our friend Mr. Shaw, with whom I deeply sympathize, does not happen to any of the rest of you. In other words, I do not see a string of foreclosures in any way as inevitable, so long as the bank, and I personally, are able to remain in a strong position in the community. I clarify this because I did not want any of you to misunderstand my words."

No one did. Franklin Royce had made himself perfectly clear to everyone!

# CHAPTER 8

## POWER

The banker stepped down, passing close to Pa.

"If you know what's good for that wife of yours, Hollister," he said quietly but with a look of menace in his eye, "You'll get her out of this race before election day. If she's going to continue her attacks against me, she'll find two can play that game! And I warn you, the consequences will prove none too pleasant for either of you!"

He walked on. Pa did not say a word.

Mr. Royce strode straight back toward the bank. The crowd of people quietly began to disperse toward their homes. Hardly a man or woman anywhere liked the banker, but everyone was afraid of him. As sorry as they were for the Shaws, no one wanted to find himself in the same position. And as much as they'd have liked to help, no one had the kind of money it would take to do any good.

Almeda followed Royce down off the platform. She looked at Pa with kind of a discouraged sigh.

"Best speech I ever heard!" said Pa.

She tried to laugh, but the look on her face was anything but happy.

"I may as well have been talking into the wind for all the good it will do," she said.

"Everyone loved it," I told her. "You should have seen their faces! And they clapped about everything you said."

"Both of you are determined to cheer me up," she said,

laughing now in earnest. "But you saw what happened—Royce has let it be known that if he doesn't win, more foreclosures will follow. Nobody's going to take that chance, no matter what I say, even if they might actually prefer to vote for me."

That evening it was pretty quiet. I could tell Almeda was thinking hard on her decision to go back into the race and wondering if she had done the right thing.

"Why don't I just go to Franklin," she said at last, "and meet with him privately, and tell him that if he will reconsider the terms of the Shaws' note, I will withdraw from the race? Maybe I was wrong to think we could take him on and actually stop him. But at least maybe we could save the Shaw's place."

"Won't work, Almeda," Pa said.

"Why not? He wants to be mayor, and I'll give him the election. He will have won. He'll have beaten me."

Pa gave a little chuckle, although it wasn't really a humorous one. "As much as you like to complain about us men not understanding women, and about how your kind are the only ones who *really* know how things work, I must say, Almeda, you don't understand men near as much as you might think."

"What do you mean, Drummond?"

"This election isn't about being mayor. It might have been at first, but not anymore."

"What's it about, then?"

"It's about manhood, about strength . . . about power."

She cocked her eyebrow at him.

"Don't you see, Almeda? You challenged Royce for the whole town to see. You've had the audacity not just to run against him, but to pass out flyers, to make speeches, and to ignore two or three warnings from him to stop. You're challenging his right to be the most powerful person in these parts. And your being a woman makes it all the more galling to him. He was there this afternoon. He could see as well as everyone else that folks like you better than him. And he hates you for it. It's gone past just winning for him now. Down inside he wants to crush you, punish you for making people doubt him. Winning isn't enough. He's got to make you pay for what you've done. It wouldn't surprise me if he did what he's done to Pat to get back at us, besides telling the rest of the town not to fool with him."

"Then that's all the more reason we've got to find some way to help!"

"I don't see what we can do," said Pa.

"But why wouldn't he be satisfied with me withdrawing? How does it help him to foreclose and take the Shaws' place?"

"Well, for one thing," Pa replied, "something tells me he wants Pat's place. I don't know why, because according to Pat the gold's about played out. But if I know Royce, it's no accident that he set his sights on Pat's note. And that's just the other reason it ain't gonna do no good. He's gonna find some way to get back at you, and he's also gonna make an example of Pat that folks around here aren't likely to forget anytime soon."

"What harm would it do him to simply let it be known, 'If you elect me mayor, I'll let the Shaws keep their place. But let this be a lesson to you not to cross me, or you might find yourself in the same position'?"

"Power, Almeda—I told you already. If he did that, it would be like backing down. You would have arm-twisted him to letting Pat off, and the whole town would know it. Royce would think you made him look weak. Everyone would know that he was capable of backing down, and so they wouldn't take his threats as seriously. No, I tell you, he's not gonna back down about the Shaws, no matter what you or I or anyone else does. The memory of Pat and Chloe and them kids of theirs having to pack up and leave—that'll keep folks in line as far as Royce is concerned for a long time. Everyone'll know he means to follow through with what he says. He may hate it that folks like you better and would vote for you if they could. But he wants them to fear his power even more than he wants them to like him. And now that you've challenged that, he'll be all the more determined to run Pat off his land, *and* hurt you any way he can in the process."

Almeda sighed. "I just can hardly believe any man would

be so vindictive as you say—even Franklin Royce."

"Believe it, Almeda. I saw the look in his eye when he got down off that platform this afternoon. I've met men like him before, and I know the kind of stuff they're made of. And it ain't good."

"Do you really think he'll try to hurt me?"

"He won't go out and find a man like Buck Krebbs to send after you, if that's what you mean. He might have done that to me in the past, but he'll use different ways on you. I have the feeling we've only seen the beginning of his campaign tactics. If I know Royce, and I think I do, it's already a lot bigger in his mind than just the election. I think we may have made an enemy, Almeda, and the town might not be big enough to hold both of us."

Pa was right. It didn't take long to see that Mr. Royce did not intend to stop with mere speechmaking.

Three days later, on Wednesday morning, when Almeda and I arrived in town for the day, a man high up on a ladder was painting a sign across the front of the vacant store-building two doors down from the bank. In the window was a poster that said "Coming Soon."

By noon the words the man was painting in bright red had become plain. The sign read: *Royce Supplies and Shipping.*

# CHAPTER 9

## THE ARTICLE

Meanwhile, I had finished the article I'd been writing.

Going around telling folks about Sunday's speech gave me the chance to get some last interviews. Folks were really ready to talk to me now! I had a long conversation with Almeda on Friday, and then spent the rest of that day and most of Saturday writing and rewriting the final copy. By this time there was a stage running on Saturday too, and I sent off the article to Mr. Kemble by the afternoon mail, along with a letter.

Mr. Kemble had said earlier that he'd pay me $1 for an election article, but things had changed now on account of the Fremont article. I told him that since he'd paid Robin O'Flaridy $4 for his small article about Miracle Springs, I figured what I'd written here was worth at least $7. But I would be willing to settle for $4 because I knew he couldn't pay a woman more than a man. But I would not take one penny less than $4. If he didn't want to pay me that much, he could send the pages back and I would print it somewhere else.

At the end of the letter, I asked Mr. Kemble when the article about Mr. Fremont would be appearing. I thought it important that the *Alta* run my version before the *Globe* had a chance to do a story based on the false information and quotes and interviews of Derrick Gregory. Had it already run and somehow I had missed seeing it? I knew that really couldn't be possible since we got the *Alta* in Miracle Springs (though still two days late), and I had been watching for it every day. I couldn't for the life of me figure out why it hadn't run yet. Nearly two weeks had passed, and the election was getting closer and closer, and I wanted the people of California to know the truth about Mr. Fremont.

Six days later, the following Friday, in the same mail pouch that brought the copies of the *Alta* to Miracle Springs, was a packet addressed to me from Mr. Kemble. In it was a check for $4, and a copy of Wednesday's edition containing my story in full. There was no letter, and no answers to any of my questions. But I hardly cared about that right then! There in the middle of the fifth page, running across two columns, were the words in bold black type: "Mayor's Race Matches Business-woman Against Town Banker."

I found a quiet place, then sat down to read over the words I had written.

> *Among the many mining towns of northern California, most of the big news in recent years always had to do with gold. But in the growing community of Miracle Springs, no one is talking about gold these days. Instead, people are talking about the town's first election for mayor, which will be held on November 4, concurrent with the national election between John Fremont and James Buchanan.*
>
> *This election is big news because of the two individuals who are running against each other. As reported in this paper last month, the election matches longtime Miracle Springs banker Franklin Royce against equally longtime businesswoman Almeda Parrish Hollister.*
>
> *That's right! Businesswoman. Mrs. Hollister, one of the first women in the west to seek office, will not even be able to vote herself. Yet she hopes to sway enough men in the community to upset rival Royce, who must be considered the favorite.*
>
> *The campaign between the two town leaders is a hot one, with emotions and reaction among the voters running high.*
>
> *Franklin Royce first arrived in Sacramento from Chicago in early 1850. He was sent west by the banking firm Jackson, Royce, Briggs, and Royce—a company begun by his father and uncle—to explore possibilities for branch offices in the new gold rush state. He opened an office in Sacramento, but later that year took out*

a $40,000 loan and moved north to the foothills community of Miracle Springs, where he opened the doors of Royce Miners' Bank. When asked why he chose Miracle Springs, Royce replied, "I wanted to become involved in banking closer to the source, where men were actually digging gold out of the streams. That seemed to me to provide the greatest opportunity for me as a banker, as well as open up the greatest potential for helping a young community grow and prosper."

Within two years, Royce had made Miracle Springs his permanent home and had completely withdrawn from his position with Jackson, Royce, Briggs, and Royce of Sacramento and Chicago. Since that time Mr. Royce has played an active role in helping the young community to grow. According to Royce, his bank has financed the building of 80% of the community's homes and has been an active supporter of the miners and their interests. "Who could be better qualified to lead such a diverse community forward than one like myself, who has been such an intrinsic part of helping in its growth up till now?" said Royce.

Mrs. Hollister came to Miracle Springs a few months before her opponent. She was Almeda Parrish then, and she and her husband had come to California from Boston. After a brief stint attempting to find gold himself, Mr. Parrish started the Parrish Mine and Freight Company. Upon his death from tuberculosis in the early winter months of 1851, his wife decided to keep the business going and to remain in Miracle Springs.

She has been there ever since. During those years, Parrish Mine and Freight has been involved with the miners of the region in nearly every phase of supply and delivery, from small gold pans to the ordering and installation of large equipment for some of the major quartz operations in the surrounding foothills.

Two years ago, the businesswoman and widow married Miracle Springs miner Drummond Hollister.

When asked why she felt qualified to become Miracle Springs' mayor, Mrs. Hollister replied, "I realize the new state of California has never had a woman mayor before. However, I feel that changing times are coming, and that women will play a vital role in the future of this state and this great country of ours. As mayor of Miracle Springs I would bring an integrity and forthrightness to the office, and the families of this town would be able to trust that their future was being watched out for by one of their own."

*All the women, of course, although unable to vote, expressed strong support for Mrs. Hollister. "I think the idea of a woman mayor shows what a wonderful thing democracy is," commented the local schoolteacher, Miss Harriet Stansberry.*

*Among the men, opinions were strong on both sides. Several miners and ranchers expressed reservations about a banker as mayor. "I ain't never yet met a banker I had much a hankering to trust further'n I could throw him!" commented one old miner who said he had been in Miracle Springs longer than both candidates put together. The same prospector added, "Why, if anybody oughta be mayor of this here place, blamed if it don't seem like it oughta be me. I'm the first one in these parts to find gold anyway!"*

*Others, who did not want to be identified, also said from their dealings with the two candidates, they felt more trusting toward Mrs. Hollister. "She ain't one to short a feller so much as a penny," said one man. "Don't matter what kind of dealings you have with her, she always gives you the best price and a little more than you asked for. But you're never gonna get something for nothing at no bank, that's for sure!"*

*Many of the men said they had nothing but the highest regard for Mrs. Hollister, but some expressed concern. "She's a nice enough woman, but that don't mean she ought to be mayor. It's a man's job. I just can't see that I want no woman being leader of my town. Somehow it just ain't right. Mayoring's gotta be something a man does."*

*Among such men, the comment of one local saloon owner seemed to sum up what many thought, "It don't really matter what I think of Mr. Royce or Mrs. Hollister, there's only one man running. And since only men can vote, I figure they'll stick by their kind."*

*Whether that proves to be true, and the men of Miracle Springs elect as their mayor the only man on the ballot, Franklin Royce, or whether they go against the odds and elect California's first female mayor, Mrs. Almeda Hollister, the fact is that this election is one to watch. It is surely one of the most unusual elections in all California this year. Whether she wins or loses, Mrs. Hollister is a pioneer in a state full of pioneers. And if she should win, not only the rest of the state, but the whole country will be watching.*

# CHAPTER 10

## THE RUMOR

We all thought Mr. Royce's decision to open Royce's Supplies and Shipping was a pretty underhanded thing to do. By the time his sign was finished, word had gotten around town about it, and a lot of people were upset that he'd try such a deceitful, lowdown tactic as attempting to run Almeda out of business.

But we didn't know the half of it yet. Within a week of Almeda's speech, we began to get wind of a rumor circulating about town. Almeda, according to the gossip, had presented herself falsely to the people of Miracle Springs. She had left Boston and come to California to escape the worst tarnish a woman's reputation could have. Some even said she had met and married Mr. Parrish on the ship north from Panama.

But the worst rumors had to do not with Almeda's past, but with her present. They said that the baby she was carrying was not a Hollister at all.

Franklin Royce, of course, never appeared as the author of the rumors surrounding Almeda. He remained too skillfully concealed behind the scenes for anyone to suspect that he was doing anything other than expressing mild curiosity at the tale as it had been told to him by others.

When the whisper first awoke it was merely the hint that the former Mrs. Parrish had not been a Parrish at all in Boston. In its later stages was added the idea that her former name—however well hidden she had kept her past—was one that all

Boston knew. Furthermore, it was said that whatever she had done, although no one could say of a certainty what exactly it was, it was enough to have barred her from the society of respected people. She had escaped the East on a steamer, leaving more than one broken heart behind her—some even said a child. On the boat she fell in with the late Mr. Parrish. The evil gossip reached its culmination with the final suggestion having to do with Pa and her present predicament—something about the chickens of her past coming back to roost. Or, more aptly, the roosters.

We went about our business as usual. Not many people came in to the freight office, and neither Almeda nor I thought much about the occasional peculiar looks on the faces of those people we saw. Whether Marcus or Mr. Ashton had heard anything, I don't know. They acted normal. It did seem activity in town was quieter than usual toward the end of that week. But still we remained in the dark about the talk that was spreading from mouth to mouth.

Sunday came, and we all went to church. The service was quiet and somber. Afterward nobody came up and greeted Pa or Almeda, but just walked off silently in the direction of their horses and wagons. It was eerie and uncomfortable, but still we suspected nothing. We all figured it was a result of the scare Mr. Royce had put into everyone the week before. But the fact that some of his best friends had seemed to avoid him and hadn't come over at least to shake his hand got Pa pretty agitated during the ride home.

All that day none of the whispers and lies and gossip reached the ears of the Hollister and Parrish and Belle clan out where we lived on the edge of Miracle Springs Creek.

Early Monday morning, a buggy drove up carrying Rev. Rutledge and Miss Stansberry. They came to the door while we were eating breakfast. Both wore serious expressions.

"We just heard," said the minister.

"Heard what?" said Pa, rising to invite them in with a smile.

"One of the children who came early to school was talking,"

he went on. "That's how Harriet heard. She put one of the older children in charge, then came right to me. We drove out here immediately. Believe me, Drummond, Almeda . . ." he glanced at them both as he spoke, still very seriously. "Believe me, I don't believe a word of it. What can we do to help?"

Pa glanced around dumbfounded, then let out a good-natured laugh. "Avery," he said. "I don't have the slightest notion what you're talking about!"

"Almeda?" said Rev. Rutledge.

"It's the truth, Avery. What is it that's got the two of you so worked up and so glum?"

"You really don't know," said Miss Stansberry, almost in amazement. "Oh, you poor dear!"

"Drummond, we have to have a serious talk," said Rev. Rutledge. "What we have to discuss has to be talked about alone."

Pa gave me and Zack a nod. "You heard the Reverend," he said. "Go on . . . git." We silently obeyed, but curious beyond belief.

We heard nothing from inside for probably ten minutes. Then the door of the house was thrown open and out exploded Pa, his face red, his eyes flaming. I'd never seen any man, much less Pa, so filled with anger!

"Drummond, please!" called out Almeda, coming through the door after him. "Please . . . wait!"

"There ain't nothing to discuss, nothing to wait for!" Pa shot back as he strode to the barn. "It's clear enough what I gotta do!"

"We don't know it was him."

" 'Course we do, woman! You told me yourself what he said. No one but him knows anything about Boston. It was him, and you know it!"

Pa was inside the barn, already throwing a saddle over his favorite and fastest horse. Almeda followed him inside.

"At least let me go talk to him first," she pleaded.

"Time for talking's over, Almeda. A man's gotta protect his own, and now I reckon it's my turn to do just that."

"Drummond, please . . . don't do something you'll regret!"

"I won't take my gun with me, if that's what you mean." He was cinching up the straps already.

"Drummond," said Almeda, more softly now, putting her hand on his arm and trying to calm him down. "I can live through this. You don't have to defend me to that evil man. The Lord has healed and restored and remade me. And I am at peace in his love, and yours. I don't care what people say, or even what they think. Drummond, don't you see? I know that God loves me just for who I am—past, present, and future. And I know that you love me in just the same way. That's all I need."

Pa seemed to flinch for just a moment in his determination. Then he said, "I understand that, Almeda. And I'm thankful for what God's done. But sometimes a man's got to stand up for truth, and stand up and defend maybe his own reputation, or maybe his wife's. And even if it don't matter to you, it matters to me what the people of this town think. That man's got no right to say dishonoring things about my wife, or about any woman! And I aim to show this town that he can't get away with it without answering to me! I'm sorry, but I just ain't gonna be talked out of this. I gotta do what's right!"

Pa pulled himself up in the saddle, then paused again and glanced around where all the rest of us were watching and listening, in fear and worry, having no idea what was happening.

"Zack, Corrie," Pa said after a couple of seconds, "you two come with me. At least having my own kids around might keep me from killing the scum!"

In an instant Zack and I were throwing saddles on our horses, and in less than two minutes we galloped out of the barn, chasing Pa down the road toward town.

# CHAPTER 11

# FIGHTING MAD

Zack and I never did catch up with Pa. By the time we rode into the middle of town, we were just in time to see him dismounting in front of the bank.

We galloped up, jumped off our horses, and ran inside after him. The bank had only been open a few minutes, so there were several early-morning customers inside. By the time we got through the door, Pa was already in Mr. Royce's office. His voice was loud enough that you could hear it through the whole building. Everyone else's business had ceased, and they stood stock-still with wide open eyes, listening to the argument going on in the next room.

"Look, Royce," Pa was saying, "I never had much liking for you. But I figured maybe that's just the way bankers were. So I kept my distance and held my peace. But now you've gone too far!"

"I don't have any idea what you're talking about," replied the banker, keeping his calm.

"I ain't ashamed to tell you to your face, I think you're a liar!"

"Careful, Mr. Hollister. Those are strong words."

"Not too strong for the likes of a man who's so afraid of losing an election to a woman that he'd drag her reputation through the mud and spread lies about her. Only the lowest kind of man with no sense of shame would do a thing as vile as that!"

"I tell you, Mr. Hollister, I don't know what you're referring to. I confess I have heard some rumors lately that—"

"Heard them?" exploded Pa. "You started them!"

Slowly Zack and I inched our way toward the open door of the office. I was terrified! I think Pa forgot us after telling us to come with him.

"Accusations, especially false ones, can cost a candidate an election, Mr. Hollister. You would do well to guard your tongue, or your wife will suffer even worse consequences on election day than she has already suffered because of her past reputation."

He still sat calmly behind his big desk, almost with a look of humor in his expression. Pa was standing, leaning over the desk at him. If Mr. Royce was afraid, he didn't show it. He looked as if he had expected the confrontation, and was glad other townspeople were hearing it.

"I ain't said a false word yet!" exclaimed Pa. "Do you deny to my face that you've been talking about Almeda and making up this gossip about her life before she got here?"

"I do."

"Then I tell you again, you're a blamed liar!" Pa's voice was loud and his face was still red.

"Look, Mr. Hollister," said the banker. His eyes squinted and his voice lost whatever humor it might have had. "I've taken about all of your ranting accusations I'm going to take. Now unless you want me to send for Sheriff Rafferty and have you locked up for harassment, you had better leave."

"Simon, lock me up?" roared Pa.

"You and I both know there are worse charges that could be brought against you. When I am mayor, I may find myself compelled to have the sheriff look into *your* past more carefully."

"Simon knows all about my past! And you ain't gonna be mayor of *this* town, Royce, you scoundrel. Not while I have anything to say about it! Any low-life who'd try to hurt a woman to make himself look good ain't the kind of man who's good enough for anything but—"

"Your wife doesn't have a reputation worth protecting, Hollister!" interrupted the banker, finally getting angry himself. He half rose out of his chair. "You know as well as I do that everything that's being said about her is true. If you don't, and you married her thinking she's the unspoiled preacher-woman she pretends to be, then you're a bigger fool than I took you for!"

"Do you dare to tell me to my face that my wife—"

"Your wife is nothing but a harlot, Hollister! Anybody in Boston could tell you—"

But his words were unwisely spoken. Before another sound was out of his mouth, Pa had shoved the banker's desk aside. He took two steps around it, and the next instant his fist went crashing into the white face of Franklin Royce.

Stunned, Royce staggered backward. Losing his balance, he fell over his own chair and toppled backward onto the floor.

Quickly he started to scramble up. But seeing Pa standing over him, fist still clenched, trembling with righteous anger in defense of the woman he loved, apparently made Royce think better of it.

Then Royce noticed the blood flowing from his nose and around the side of his mouth.

"You'll pay for this, Hollister," he seethed through clenched teeth while his hand sought a handkerchief to stop the blood.

"Your threats don't mean nothing to me," said Pa. "You do what you think you can to me, Royce. Do it like a man, face to face—if you got guts enough! But if I hear of you speaking another word against my wife, I tell you, you'll answer to me! And next time I don't aim to be so gentle!"

He turned and strode with huge quick steps out of the office, hardly looking at us, but saying as he passed, "Come on, kids, let's get out of this scoundrel's hole!"

We followed Pa to the door, while the customers and two clerks watched in shocked silence.

Mr. Royce came running to his office door, a handkerchief to his nose and mouth, and shrieked after us, "You're through,

Hollister—you hear me? You're through! You'll regret this day as long as you live!"

But Pa didn't even slow down, only slammed the door behind us with a crash.

# CHAPTER 12

# REPERCUSSIONS

All Pa said on the way home was, "I'm sorry you kids had to see that . . . but maybe your being there kept me from doing worse."

About halfway back, we met Rev. Rutledge and Miss Stansberry. Pa stopped, and the minister drew in his reins.

"I'm obliged to the two of you for coming and telling us," Pa said. "I'm afraid you wouldn't approve of what I done, Reverend."

"I understand, Drummond," he replied.

"Well, I'm thankful we got you two for friends," Pa added, tipping his hat, and then moving on.

When we got home, Almeda's eyes were red. I knew she'd been crying. Pa kissed her, then put his arms around her and the two of them just stood in each other's embrace for a long time. Nothing more about the incident was said that day.

Almeda considered whether to go into town at all, now that we all understood why folks had been behaving so strangely.

"We gotta face this thing head on," said Pa. "You go into the office—I'll go with you if you like. We gotta go on with our business and show folks we ain't concerned about Royce and his rumors. We'll go around to people one at a time and tell 'em to pay no attention to what they hear, that it's all a pack of lies drummed up to make you look bad before the election."

"You know I couldn't do that," Almeda replied softly, looking Pa directly in the eyes. "But you're right—it's best we go

60

on with our lives as usual. Corrie and I will go into the office."

"You want me to go into town with you for the day?"

"No, I'll be all right. I'll do my best to put on a brave face."

In the four years I'd known Almeda, I'd never seen her quite like this. Her voice was soft and tired, without its usual enthusiasm and confidence. It was easy to see this was really a blow to her, and that she might not get over it so quickly. All day long her eyes remained red, though I never saw her cry again. I guess the tears stayed inside.

By the time we walked into the Parrish Mine and Freight office two hours later the whole town was stirred up all over again by news of what Pa had done to Mr. Royce. Old widow Robinson had been in the bank at the time and had heard every word. And that was enough to insure that within an hour, every man, woman, and child for ten miles around knew about it! The widow's reputation for spreading information certainly proved itself true. Franklin Royce himself never appeared for two days after that, so the news had to have come through someone else who was present, and most bets were on Mrs. Robinson. In all likelihood, she was the one Royce had used to plant the rumors about Almeda. He probably told her in hushed tones, making her promise to keep it to herself, no doubt saying that he'd assured the person *he'd* heard it from that he would say nothing to anybody.

Suddenly the first rumor was old news, and began to take a back seat to steadily exaggerating tales of what Pa had done. At first it was just that he had given the banker a good sound thrashing. Then mention was made of sounds of violence, angry threats yelled back and forth, sounds of scuffling and furniture being broken, and even blood, along with vows to get even. All in all, the story as Marcus Weber said he'd heard it was a considerably wilder affair than what Zack and I actually witnessed with our own eyes.

But it did manage to lessen the impact of what had been circulating about Almeda. Even though they feared him, not too many people liked Franklin Royce much. I think the incident was talked about so much because everybody was secretly pleased to see Royce get his due for once.

Yet they were afraid too, for Pa and Almeda. If Franklin Royce promised to get even, they said with serious expressions, he was not one to make empty threats. As for the election, who could tell now? Royce was a dangerous opponent, and *they* sure wouldn't want to have crossed him! They wished someone else could be mayor, but they had to admit, with Royce as an enemy, the prospects didn't look too good for the Hollisters.

With Almeda, the distance and silence and curious looks turned into sympathy. Pa silenced the gossip once and for all, and nobody was inclined to spread the rumors any further and run the risk of Pa finding out. Whether folks believed what they'd heard—and after what Pa did, I think most figured Royce had made it all up—they didn't show it, and talk now centered around Pa.

When Mr. Royce began to be seen around town again, he kept his distance. However, he continued his subtle tactics both to make sure people voted for him, and to pressure Almeda into capitulating. By the end of the week, the sign across the street was done, and there was activity inside the place, as well as some merchandise displayed in the shop windows. Almeda muttered a time or two, "Where can he have gotten that stuff so quickly?" But there seemed to be no question about it—he *had* it, and *was* going to open a business to compete with Parrish Mine and Freight. And obviously his intent was not merely to compete, but to drive her out of business. A second paper soon appeared in the window: "Mining, ranching, farming tools, supplies, and equipment at the least expensive prices north of Sacramento. Shipping and freight services also available."

That same week, whispers of a new kind arose. If Franklin Royce did not become Miracle Springs' next mayor, it was said that he would be forced to review all outstanding loans, and would more than likely be compelled to call a good many of them due. As much as they respected Pa for standing up for his wife's honor, and as little as they cared for Royce, most of the men were agreed that they just couldn't take the chance of having what had happened to Pat Shaw happening to them. They *had* to vote for Royce. They just didn't have any other choice.

To make matters worse, Pa got an official-looking letter from some government office in Sacramento saying that the title to his land was being challenged in court by an anonymous plaintiff, and that investigators would be contacting him shortly for additional information.

"Well, if that don't just about do it!" said Pa, throwing the letter down and storming about the room. "The man's not gonna stop till he's ground us into the dirt and got our land and our business and everything!"

He walked angrily out of the house. Almeda picked up the letter and read it, then showed it to the rest of us.

"I think we'd better pray for your father," she said softly. We all sat down and took hands, while Almeda prayed out loud for Pa, for the claim, for Mr. Royce, and for God's purpose to be accomplished through all these things that were happening to us. "And show us what you want us to do, Lord," she concluded. "Make it plain, and give us the strength and courage to do it—whether we're to give in, or whether we're to stand up and fight for what we think is right. Help us not to act in our own wisdom, but to depend on you to show us what you want."

When Pa walked in a few minutes later, he was calm and quiet. He sat down, rested his chin between his hands, and let out a big sigh. Anger had obviously given way to defeat and frustration.

"We gotta quit, Almeda," he said at length. His voice was soft and discouraged. "I wish I'd never got you into this."

"You didn't get me into a thing, Drummond. I made the decision to run for mayor on my own. I brought this trouble on the rest of you."

"Well I sure didn't make it no better, flying off against Royce like I done. Though the rascal deserved it!"

"Now we've got to decide what's to be done. With Franklin threatening two claims, ours and Shaws', there's no telling where it'll end. Not to mention the business in town."

"We gotta give in," said Pa, in as depressed a voice as I'd ever heard from him. "He's got us licked. If we let him have the election, maybe he'll lay off from all this other harm he's trying to bring us."

# CHAPTER 13

# FIGHTING FIRE WITH FIRE

I don't know if all marriages work this way, but I'd noticed that Pa and Almeda were both quicker to defend each other than they were themselves. When Franklin Royce started spreading gossip about Almeda around town, Pa got so filled with anger that he went right into Royce's office and knocked the banker down and bloodied his nose. Pa knew it was *his* duty to defend Almeda's honor, not hers.

And in the same way, Almeda would fight for Pa. When folks were talking about her, Almeda couldn't help the discouragement it caused. But now that Mr. Royce was threatening Pa and was threatening to take away all Pa had worked for and held dear, it was *her* turn to get fighting mad, like a mother bear protecting her family. The banker could threaten her reputation and her business all he wanted, but once he dared threaten the husband she loved—look out! She wasn't about to take that lying down!

"He's not going to lay off, Drummond," she said to Pa's last statement after a few moments thought. "There are times when to lay down your arms and surrender is the best course of action. Jesus said we must deny ourselves, and do it every day. But there are also times when wrong must be fought with aggressiveness. Jesus did that too. He laid down his life without a word of self-defense, but he also drove the moneychangers out with a whip and strong words. How to know when to do which is the challenge for a Christian. And I can't help thinking that this is a time for the whip and strong words."

"We've already tried it," said Pa, "you with your handbills and your speech, and me with my ranting and raving like an idiot in Royce's bank. All we've done is made him madder and made it worse for everyone around here."

"The Lord will show us what to do. The children and I were just praying while you were outside. We asked him to make it plain what we're to do and to give us the courage to—"

She stopped and her face got serious a moment, then lit up.

"You know, I just had a thought," she said. "A wild, crazy, impossible idea!" She pressed her hands against her forehead and thought hard again. "It's too unbelievable an idea ever to work, but . . . if God is behind it . . . you just never know what can happen!"

"What in tarnation is it?" exclaimed Pa. "Your face looks like you swallowed a lantern. It must be *some* notion that's rattling through that brain of yours!"

She laughed. "It is, believe me. It just might be the highest-stakes poker game you ever played, Drummond Hollister, with the mines and homes of every man in Miracle Springs in the middle of the table—winner take all. And if Franklin Royce doesn't blink first and back down, and if he decides to call our bluff, then it just might cost more people than the Shaws their places."

"Sounds like a mighty dangerous game."

"I'm afraid it is. That's why we have to pray hard for God to show us if this is *his* idea, or just something my own mind cooked up."

"Then let's pray that right now," said Pa, "before it goes any further." He got down on his knees. "Come on, kids," he said to all the rest of us. "We got some serious praying to do, and it's gonna take all seven of us. We've gotta do what the Book says and ask the Lord above for wisdom, cause if we do wrong a lot of folks are gonna be hurt. We gotta be sure we're doing what the Lord wants."

We obeyed, and Pa started to pray. We'd all heard him pray before, but somehow this time there was a new power in his voice that seemed to come from deep down in his heart. When we all got up a few minutes later, I think every one in the room had the sense that God had spoken both *to* Pa, and maybe *through* him to the rest of us. I know what *I* felt inside, and judging from the looks on Pa's and Almeda's faces I think they too thought the answer was to go ahead.

"Well, don't keep us in suspense, woman," said Pa with a smile. "What's this dangerous new plan you're thinking of?"

"Before we could even know if it had a chance to succeed," she said, "it would take a trip to Sacramento. And with the election coming up so fast, there might not be time. But here's what I'm thinking."

She paused and took a breath.

"Back when we started, and Franklin was doing everything he could to threaten us, he made a comment that I haven't forgotten. He said, 'Two can play this game as well as one.' He was, of course, referring to my flyer and Corrie's interviewing and what he considered our going on the attack against him. But the moment we started praying about what to do his words came back to me, and I suddenly found myself wondering what is to prevent us from applying the same principle. If he's going to try to undercut us by taking away business from Parrish Mine and Freight, and if he's going to start hurting our friends and neighbors by calling up their loans, then why don't we use the exact same tactic, but in the opposite way? We will take business from *him*, and will try to *help* people at exactly the point where he's trying to hurt them and pressure them into supporting him!"

"Fight fire with fire, eh?" said Pa grinning.

"Exactly! There are times to back down and admit defeat. But I don't think this is one of them. Not yet at least."

"But you shouldn't travel, not in your condition," said Pa. "Whatever's to be done in Sacramento, I can do."

"No, I have to be the one to go," insisted Almeda. "I'll need to see my friend Carl Denver and get his advice. I don't know whether there's anything his company can do, but he might know someone else in the city who can help."

"I'll at least go with you, to make sure you're all right."

"I'll be fine. Besides, you ought to stay here," said Almeda, pointing to the letter that still lay on the table where she had laid it.

The look on Pa's face said he wasn't convinced.

"I'll be fine," she repeated. "I'm a strong woman. Corrie," she said turning to me, "can you handle things at the office?"

I nodded.

"You shouldn't go alone. That I *won't* let you do," said Pa. "Zack," he said, turning his head, "you want to ride to Sacramento with your stepmother, keep her company and protect her at the same time?"

"You bet, Pa!" Zack replied brightly.

"I'm going to let you take my rifle," Pa added. "But unless there's trouble, you keep it packed in the saddle case. No foolin' around with it."

"Yes, sir."

"Do you really think that's necessary, Drummond?" asked Almeda.

"Maybe not. But I don't want to take no chances with the two of you out there alone. I don't trust Royce. It ain't been that many years ago he was hiring no-goods like Buck Krebbs to sneak around and set fire to houses. I'd feel safer if I knew Zack had the gun."

"Can I go too, Pa?" asked Tad.

"You couldn't keep up, you pipsqueak!" laughed Zack.

"I could so!" insisted Tad. "I can ride just as fast as you or Little Wolf!"

"That'll be the day! I could ride from here to Little Wolf's and back twice before you'd have your horse out of the barn."

"That ain't so! Why I could—"

"Hey, the two of you—cut it out!" interrupted Pa. "Time's a wastin', you gotta hit the road. Tad," he said, "I gotta have you here with me. If Zack's gonna be protecting your Ma, then I'll need your help here watching over the claim. You'll be my number one man, and I can't have the both of you gone."

Almeda rose, Zack ran outside to the barn, and the rest of

us did what we could to help them get ready. In less than an hour we were watching the dust settle from Almeda's buggy and Zack's horse after they'd rounded the bend in the road and disappeared from sight.

# CHAPTER 14

## PATRICK SHAW'S SOLUTION

Those next days waiting for Zack and Almeda to get back were dreadful, wondering all the time what was going to come of it.

How wonderful it would be if there was a railroad to Sacramento! They were laying down track for new train lines between the big cities, and the talk of a train connecting the two oceans was enough to make your head swim. I could hardly imagine it! Wagon trains took months to cross the country. Overland stagecoaches, along the southern route where there wasn't as much snow, usually took between thirty and forty days. And stories were told of madcap horsemen who rode their horses to their deaths to make it from St. Louis to San Francisco in fifteen to twenty days. I'd thought about trying to find such a man to interview for an article sometime, to find out if the stories were true about dashing across the plains at a hundred miles a day. But I could barely imagine going across the country in a comfortable train car in only eight or ten days.

Well, they didn't have a train to ride on. But they had good horses, and Zack and Almeda returned faster than Pa had expected. They left on Saturday, and about midday of the following Wednesday Zack and Almeda rode in.

It was obvious from the lather on the horses that they'd been riding hard. Their clothes and faces were covered with dust, and they both looked exhausted. But the instant Almeda saw Pa, she flashed a big smile.

"I got it!" she said excitedly, patting the saddlebags next to her on the buggy seat. "Go get Pat and we'll tell him the news!"

Pa helped her down from the buggy, then gave her a big hug and kiss. "You're a mess, woman!" he laughed, standing back to look over her dirty face.

"Don't push your luck, Drummond Hollister," she replied. "You know how a woman can get riled when she's tired!"

"Well, you heard your ma," said Pa, turning around to the rest of us. "Who wants to ride over the hill and fetch Mr. Shaw here?"

"I will, Pa," I said. "Come on, Tad. Wanna go with me?"

But he was already scampering toward the barn to start saddling his pony. One thing about Tad—he never had to be asked twice!

We took the quickest way to Shaws, the back trail around the mountain. All the way back Mr. Shaw kept quizzing us about what was up, and I said I didn't know all the details, which I didn't, but that Pa and Almeda had some exciting news for him and they'd tell him everything as soon as we got back to our place.

By the time we arrived back at the house, Almeda had gotten herself cleaned up and had changed clothes. Her eyes looked tired, but the smile still shone from her face.

"Come in . . . come in, Pat," said Pa, shaking Mr. Shaw's hand. "Sit down. Want a cup of coffee?"

"Yeah, thanks, Drum," he replied. "But what's this about anyway?"

"We'll tell you everything, Pat. Just have a seat, and I'll get you that coffee."

Bewildered, Mr. Shaw obeyed.

Pa returned in a minute, handed Mr. Shaw a steaming blue tin cup, then sat down himself. Almeda joined him.

"This has been Almeda's idea from the start," Pa said, "so I reckon I'll let her tell you about the scheme she hatched to try to foil ol' Royce." He cast her a glance, then sat back and took a sip from his own cup.

"It all began last week," Almeda began, "when we were

praying about what to do about the election. We were asking the Lord whether to quit and give in, or whether to fight on somehow, even though it seemed, as you men would say, that Franklin held all the right cards. Your note had been called due, we'd just received word that the title to our land was being questioned, and word was going around town that a vote against Franklin Royce would result in the same kinds of things happening to others. We just didn't see what could be done. But then I had an idea! And I think it was God speaking providentially to us. I certainly pray it was, but I suppose time will tell. I have no idea if it will work. And if it goes against us, it could mean doom for everybody."

"I don't understand a word of what you're talking about," said Mr. Shaw. "From where I sit, it don't appear there's nobody in any danger except you folks and us."

"Just hear her out, Pat," said Pa. "Go on, Almeda, quit beating around the bush. Pat's dying of curiosity!"

Almeda smiled. "I just returned from Sacramento," she said. "I rode down there with Zack, and on Monday morning I went to see a man I've known for several years, Carl Denver. He is one of three vice-presidents of the banking and investment firm Finchwood Ltd. I think they're connected somehow to a bank in London, but I don't know for sure. My late husband knew Carl, and when we first came west, Carl helped my husband secure a small loan to open our business in Miracle Springs. That loan was paid off long ago, but Carl and I have kept in touch through the years and I've borrowed from them a time or two, and have done some freight business with his firm as well. And now Carl's risen to a fairly prominent position.

"Well, I explained our situation to him. He said he'd read about the mayor's race in the *Alta*, and I told him the article was written by my stepdaughter."

She looked over in my direction. I couldn't help but be pleased that somebody Almeda knew had seen it!

"When I told him some of the things that have happened, he became positively livid. 'Anything I can do to help,' he said.

'Anything!' But when I mentioned the sum of eighteen thousand dollars, his enthusiasm cooled. 'That's a great deal of money, Almeda,' he said. I knew that only too well! I'd never borrowed more than five or six thousand from him before. I told him I'd secure it with my house and the business and what stock-in-trade I have, although that wouldn't amount to more than ten or twelve thousand. I knew it would be going out on a limb for him, but I assured him that the other property involved—that's yours, Mr. Shaw—was solid, and that we could add to the collateral amount later to more than cover the full amount of the loan. He said he'd have to discuss the matter with the higher-ups of Finchwood, but that he'd do everything he could on my behalf, and to come back about noon."

"So Zack and I left and I showed him around some of Sacramento. We had a good time together, didn't we, Zack?"

Zack nodded.

"We returned to Carl's office just before twelve. From the big smile across his face, I could tell he had good news!

" 'You'll never believe this!' he exclaimed. 'I don't believe it myself. But we hit Mr. Finch on just the right day!'

" 'What do you mean?' I asked.

" 'He knows Royce,' Carl answered. 'And in plain English, Almeda—he hates him! Seems several years ago, when different companies were new to California and were trying to get firmly established, Jackson, Royce, Briggs, and Royce pulled some underhanded things against Finchwood. Nearly put them out of business, the way I understand it. And ever since, the rivalry between the two has been fierce . . . and bitter. Just last week, Mr. Finch told me, the old man of the outfit, Briggs, stole one of Finchwood's largest clients away from them. And that's why Finch is roaring mad. I told him that this Royce you're dealing with isn't with his father's firm any longer, but Finch said he didn't care. "A Royce is a Royce!" he said. "And besides, I still owe that young weasel of a Royce a thing or two from '51!" Anyway, I went on to explain your whole predicament to him, and almost before I was done, he said, "Look, Carl, you bring that lady-friend of yours in to meet me. I want to shake hands with the woman with guts enough to square off in an election against that snake. And then you tell her we'll back her up. We don't need her collateral either. I trust her from what I know of her, and your word vouching for her is good enough for me. I'd love to see her put that pretentious imposter out of business, though I don't suppose we could be *that* fortunate!" ' "

Almeda took a breath and smiled.

"I still ain't sure if I see how my property has anything to do with your banking friends," said Mr. Shaw.

"I'm just about to get to that," said Almeda. "Well, Carl took me right into Mr. Finch's office. The president of the company treated me like royalty—got a chair for me, offered me something to drink, and then shook my hand and said what an honor it was for him to meet me! Can you imagine that! An honor for *him* to meet *me*!

"We talked for quite a while. He said he'd investigated the northlands up around here a time or two, and had even thought of expanding and investing in this direction but nothing had ever come of it. The more we talked, the more interested he became, he even scratched his head once and said he thought he'd heard of the new strike at Miracle Springs. 'Had something to do with a kid getting caught in a mine and being pulled out by his brother, didn't it?' I said that indeed it did, and that those two boys were now fine young men and that I was privileged to call them my sons."

Tad was beaming as she spoke.

"He said that if worse came to worst, and he wound up holding mortgages on half a dozen pieces of property, he'd consider it a good investment, and worth every penny to put a corrupt man like Royce out of business."

Finally Almeda looked straight into Mr. Shaw's face. "The long and short of it, Patrick," she said, "is that I brought the solution to your problems with the Royce Miners' Bank home with me from Sacramento right in these saddlebags!"

She picked up the leather pouches that had been sitting beside her, stood up, and turned them upside down. Bundles of paper money poured out onto Mr. Shaw's lap.

All of us gasped. Almeda laughed at everyone's reaction as the fortune in greenbacks spilled onto the chair and floor.

"Thunderation, woman!" roared Pa. "You came all the way from the city with *that* in your bags? What if you'd been stuck up? *Tarnation*, that's a pile of money!"

"I had your son to protect me," Almeda replied. "How could I be afraid? And Zack and I prayed for the Lord's presence to go beside us. We read Psalm 91 together, and we took our Father at his word."

All this time poor Patrick Shaw just sat where he was, in speechless silence, gazing down at more money than he'd ever seen in his life.

"It's to pay off your loan, Pat," said Pa at length. "How many days you got left on the call?"

" 'Bout nine. Chloe's already started to pack up our things."

"Well you tell her to *un*pack them," said Almeda firmly, "and you ride straight into town and march into Royce's bank and put this money down on his desk, and you say to him, 'Mr. Royce, here's your money, just like your notice-of-call said. Now if you don't mind, I'd like a receipt and the clear title to my property.' "

Still dumfounded and bewildered, Mr. Shaw managed to stammer out the words, "But I can't take this . . . this ain't my money."

"Don't worry, Mr. Shaw," said Almeda. "We'll make everything legal and tidy and you don't have to be concerned about us. We're not *giving* you this money, we're *loaning* it to you. I borrowed it from Mr. Finch at four-and-a-half percent interest. We will make you the loan at the same rate. You pay off the Royce bank, and next month begin making payments to us instead. We will then pay back Finchwood Ltd. as you pay us. And since the interest rate is less, your payments every month will be less than Franklin was charging you. You'll be out from under his yoke, you'll have your land back, and as long as you keep the payments up from now on, everything will be fine."

"I—I don't know how to thank you," said Mr. Shaw.

"No thanks is needed, Pat," said Pa. "You'd have done the same thing to help us if you were in a position to."

"It's an investment for all of us," added Almeda. "For us and for Mr. Finch, for the future of Miracle Springs and its people, and against the scare tactics of Franklin Royce."

"Well, I reckon I can understand that. But I can't see how it'll help anyone else around. They're still gonna be too afraid to vote against him for mayor. And Royce is liable to be so mad he'll start calling other folks' loans due, and then we'll just be making it worse for everybody."

"You've put your finger right on the risky part of our plan," said Almeda. "Before I left for the south I told Drummond it was going to be like a giant poker game. And here's where we have to hope our bluff works."

"How's paying off my note gonna bluff him?"

"Because you're gonna tell the other men around just what you've done," said Pa. "You're gonna tell them you paid Royce off with money you borrowed, and that there's more where that came from."

"But you can't tell them where we came by it," added Almeda. "Just say that you borrowed it. And then you tell them that we'll back anybody else up whose loan gets called too."

"You mean it?" exclaimed Mr. Shaw in disbelief.

"We mean to try," answered Pa. "You just spread the word around town that nobody's got to be afraid of voting for Almeda on account of what Royce might do with their loans. You tell 'em that *you're* gonna vote for her—that is, you *are* gonna vote for Almeda, ain't you, Pat?"

"You're dang sure I am! After what you've done, how could I not? It's not every man who's got friends like you! You two are just the kind of mayoring this town needs, and I aim to tell everyone I can too!"

"Well, you tell 'em to vote for Almeda and that Royce's not likely to do a thing to 'em. If he tries and starts threatening other folks like he did you, then you tell 'em to come see us."

"I still don't see how you can do such a thing."

"What my husband has been trying to say is that we'll back

up our promise as far as we can," said Almeda, "and we're praying it's far enough. Mr. Finch said he would support us up to fifty thousand dollars. That should enable us to protect three or four others from being evicted by Royce. If he persists beyond that, then we could be in trouble. That's when we have to hope he won't call our bluff."

"Well, I'll do what you say."

"Just remember—you keep quiet about all this we talked about," said Pa. "Pay off your loan and start talking up *Hollister For Mayor*. Then we'll leave our friend Royce to stew over it."

# CHAPTER 15

## INTO THE HORNET'S NEST

If we thought Almeda's handbill caused a commotion, or Pa's marching in and smacking Mr. Royce in the face while the widow Robinson got an earful in the other room, that was *nothing* compared to the uproar caused when Mr. Shaw walked into the Royce Miners' Bank that same afternoon, calmly asked to see Mr. Royce, and then dumped eighteen thousand dollars in green United States bills on the desk in front of him, asking for his change, a receipt, and the cancelled mortgage note and clear deed of trust for his property.

The exclamations from the bystanders, and the look on Mr. Royce's face, according to Mr. Shaw telling us about it later, was a sight to behold.

"His greedy eyes got so big seeing all that money in front of him," he said, "for an instant I thought he was gonna dive right on top of the desk after it! But then the next second he suddenly seemed to remember this money meant he wouldn't be able to get his hands on my land *and* wouldn't be getting that six-and-a-quarter percent interest no more.

" 'What kind of a trick is this, Shaw?' he said.

" 'Ain't no trick,' I answered him. 'You called my note due, and there's the payment, just like you asked—nine days early.'

" 'Where'd you get it, Shaw?' he asked.

'Nothing in your notice of call said I had to tell you everything I do. You said I had to pay you, and I done it.'

" 'I know you don't have a dime to your name,' he growled.

And watching him when I put that money in front of him made me realize that he wasn't after the money at all, but that he wanted my place. 'What did you do, hold up a stage? Or is it counterfeit?'

"By now I was enjoying myself, and I decided to pull a little bluff of my own. 'Mr. Royce,' I said, 'that is good U.S. legal currency. I come by it perfectly legal, I'm paying you off in full with it. Now, if you don't write me a receipt and give my note back showing it's paid in full, with the extra from the eighteen thousand I got coming back, then I'll just be on my way over to the Sheriff's office!'

"Well, he blustered a while more, but finally he took the cash and put it in his safe, and got out the papers and signed everything over to me. But he didn't like it, I could tell. There he was with eighteen thousand dollars, and a look on his face like I'd gotten the best of him. And he gave me back the extra—there's $735 back from your $18,000!"

He plunked the money down on the table.

"Keep it, Pat," said Pa. "You use that to clear up your other bills, and if you still got extra, then it'll help make the first few payments."

"Then you come by the office tomorrow," added Almeda, "and we'll draw up a note and some terms. At four-and-a-half percent, it shouldn't be more than $135 or $140 a month."

"I can't tell you how obliged I am to you!"

"You just get folks over being afraid of voting for us!" said Almeda.

"Oh, I've already been doing that! Once that money fell out onto the desk in Royce's bank, it was like I'd stirred up a hornet's nest! I no more'n walked out the door of the bank and it seemed the whole town knew already. All the men came pouring out from the stores and their houses, cheering me and shaking my hand and hitting me on the back. Why, you'd have thought I struck a new vein under the mountain! And of course the question they was all asking was, 'Where'd the loot come from, Pat . . . where'd you get that kind o' cash!' But I just kinda kept to myself, smiling like I knew a big secret, and said,

'Let's just put it this way, boys. Wherever I got it from, there's more where that came from. And so you don't need to be one bit afraid of what's gonna happen if you vote for Mrs. Hollister for mayor. Matter of fact, boys,' I added, and I let my voice get real soft like I was letting them in on a big secret, 'matter of fact, it's come to my attention that our old friend Royce is charging us all close to two percent *more* interest than the going rate down in Sacramento. Unless he's a dang sight dumber than I think, he ain't gonna call your loans due. He's been making a killing on us all these years, and he ain't about to upset his money-cart now.' "

"What did they say to that?" asked Almeda. Pa was laughing so hard from listening to Mr. Shaw that he couldn't say anything!

"They were plenty riled, I can tell you that. And once I told them that I had it on the word of a man I trusted that they'd be protected in the same way if Royce called their loans due, they all walked off saying they weren't gonna vote for no cheat like him for mayor!"

"You done good, Pat," Pa said finally.

"Did you tell anyone that it was us who was behind it?" asked Almeda.

"Rolf Douglas came up to me afterward, kinda quiet. Said he was two months behind with Royce and was afraid he was gonna be next. I told him to go see you, in your office, Mrs. Hollister. I think you can likely expect a call from him real soon."

"Rolf ain't no Widow Robinson," said Pa. "But I don't doubt that word'll manage to spread around."

"Maybe I shouldn't have told him," said Mr. Shaw, worried.

"No, no, Patrick, it's just fine," said Almeda. "Word had to get around. Just so long as folks don't know *how* we were able to do what we have done—at least not for a while. We want to keep Franklin off guard and guessing."

# CHAPTER 16

## PA PLAYS POKER—EYEBALL TO EYEBALL

Word got around, all right—in a hurry!

Two days later we got a call from Franklin Royce that was anything but friendly. Pa must have sensed there was fire coming out of the banker's eyes while he was still a long way off. The minute he saw the familiar black buggy, he said to Almeda, "I'll handle this," and walked a little way down the road away from the house.

"I'm here to talk to you and your wife, Hollister," said Mr. Royce, hotly reining his horse up in front of Pa but remaining seated in his carriage. As he spoke he glanced over to where Almeda and I were standing near the door. His eyes threw daggers at us.

"What you got to say, Royce," replied Pa, "you can say to me. I'm not about to put up with any more of your abuse or threats to my wife or daughter. If you haven't learned your lesson from what happened in your bank last week, then maybe I'll have to knock some more sense into that head of yours."

"You dare lay a hand on me, Hollister, and I'll have you up on charges before the day's out!"

"I don't want to hurt you," said Pa. "But if you dare to threaten anyone in my family again, I won't stop with bloodying your nose. Now go on . . . say your piece."

"I'd like to know what the two of you think you're trying to do, paying off Patrick Shaw's note like that?"

"We made him a loan. I don't see anything so unusual in that."

"You're mixing in my affairs, that's what's unusual about it!"

"Ain't no law against loaning money to a friend."

"You don't have that kind of cash!"

Pa shrugged.

"I want to know where you got it!"

"There also ain't no law that gives a banker the right to meddle in someone else's private affairs," Pa shot back. "Where Pat Shaw got the money to pay you off is no more your concern than where we might have gotten it to loan him— that is *if* we had anything to do with all this you're talking about."

"You know good and well you have everything to do with it, you dirty—"

"You watch your tongue!" shouted Pa, taking two steps toward Royce's buggy. "There are ladies present. And if I hear one more filthy word from your mouth, I'll slam it shut so hard you won't speak *any* words for a week!"

Cowed but not humbled, Royce moderated his tone.

"Look, Hollister," he said, "I know well enough that you are behind that money of Shaw's. It's all over town. You know it and I know it and everybody knows it! Now I'm here to ask you—the two of you—" he added, looking over at Almeda, "businessman to businessman, having nothing to do with the election, I'm asking you what are you trying to do by meddling in *my* affairs! Banking and making loans is my business, and you have no call to step into the middle of my dealings with *my* customers! I want to know what your intentions are."

"I figure our intentions are our own business," replied Pa coolly.

"Not when they interfere with *my* business!" Royce shot back. "And word around town is that you intend to continue sticking your nose into my negotiations with people who owe my bank money. So I ask you again, Hollister, what are your intentions?"

"Our intentions are to do what's right," answered Pa.

"Paying off other mens' loans, even when they are in legal default?"

"I ain't admitted to doing any such thing."

"Cut the hog swill, Hollister!"

"You want to know my intentions," Pa said. "Then I'll tell you straight—it's my feeling that a man's duty-bound to stand by his neighbors, whatever that means. And that's what I intend to do. I'll tell you, Royce, I'm not really all that concerned about you or your banking business, because from where I stand it seems to me you're looking out for nobody but yourself. Now you can do what you want to me. You can say what you want, you can spread what lies you want. You can sic some investigator on me to try to run me off my land. You can beat my wife in this election. And maybe in the end you *will* run me out of Miracle Springs and will some day own every stitch of land from here to Sacramento. But nothing you do will make me stop standing up for what's right, and for trying to help my friends and neighbors so long as there's anything I can do for them. Now—is that plain-spoken enough for you?"

"So you intend to continue backing up the loans of others around here even if they should be called due, as people are saying?" repeated Royce.

"I said I aim to do what's right."

"What are you trying to do, Hollister, open a bank of your own?"

Pa shrugged. "I got nothing more to say to you."

"You can't do it, Hollister. You'll never pull it off. You can't possibly have enough cash to stand up to me."

Almeda began walking toward the two men.

"Franklin," she said approaching them, "do you remember just after I entered the mayor's race, you said to me, 'Two can play this game?' You were, of course, insinuating that you could be just as underhanded toward me as you thought I was being to you by the publication of my flyer. I think anyone with much sense would say that this last month demonstrates that you have few equals when it comes to underhanded tactics."

"How dare you suggest—" the banker began, but Almeda cut him off immediately.

"Let me finish, Franklin!" she said. "You have spread rumors about me throughout the community. You threatened my daughter and my husband in different ways. And now you are opening a store just down from mine intended, I presume, to drive me out of business. All we have done is help a friend. That hardly compares with your ruthless and self-serving behavior. And if it takes our going into the lending business to keep you from hurting any more of the families in this town, then so be it. Your own words condemn you, Franklin. Two *can* play this game! And if you feel compelled to enter the supplies and freight business, perhaps we will feel compelled to open a second bank in Miracle Springs, so that people can have a choice in where they go for financial help."

"That is utterly ridiculous!" laughed Royce with disdain. "The two of you—a miner and his shopkeeper of a wife— financing a bank! I've never heard of anything so absurd! It takes thousands, more capital than you'll ever have in your lives! The very notion makes me laugh!"

"You are very cocky, Franklin," she said. "It may well prove your undoing."

"Ha, ha, ha!" laughed Royce loudly.

"It isn't only capital a business needs. Besides money, it takes integrity and a reputation that people can trust. I would say that you may be in short supply of those latter assets, Franklin, however large may be the fortune behind your enterprises."

"A bank takes money, and nothing else. I don't believe a word of all this! You may have stashed away a nest egg to help that no-good Shaw, but you won't be so lucky next time."

"We were hoping there wouldn't have to be a next time, that you would see it will do you no good to call the notes you hold due."

"Don't be naive, Almeda. I'm a banker, and money is my business. And it's not *yours*! So stay out of it!"

"If you call Rolf Douglas's note, or anyone else's, Royce, you're going to find yourself straight up against us again," said

Pa, speaking once more. His voice rang with authority.

"I don't believe you, Hollister. I've checked your finances, and I know your bank account. You don't have that kind of money."

"Then go ahead and do your worst, Royce," said Pa.

"You're bluffing, Hollister. I can call any of a dozen notes due, and there's no possible way you can back them up."

Pa stared straight into Mr. Royce's face, and for a moment they stood eye to eye, as if each were daring the other to call the bluff. When Pa spoke, his words were cold and hard as steel.

"Try me, Royce," he said, still staring into the banker's eyes. "You just try me, if you want to take the chance. But you may find I'm not as easy an adversary as you think. People in these parts know I'm a man of my word, and they can trust me. I don't think you'd be wise to go up against me."

"What my husband is trying to tell you, Franklin," said Almeda, "is that you can call notes due and try to foreclose all you want. We've let it be known that if people find themselves in trouble with you, they can come see us. You may call those dozen loans due, but once they are paid off, what are you left with? A vault full of cash. Without loans, a bank cannot make a profit. You'll wind up with no loans, no land, no property, and before long the Royce Miners' Bank will be out of business, Franklin."

"That's too ridiculous to deserve a reply!"

"Do you think the people of this town will think it ridiculous when they learn that the six-and-a-quarter percent interest you have been charging them is almost two full percentage points *higher* than the current rate in San Francisco and Sacramento?"

"Rates are higher further away from financial centers."

"Your rates are two points higher than what *we* intend to charge people on *our* loans."

"You would dare undercut me?"

"No, we merely intend to charge our borrowers the fair and current rate."

"I don't believe you!"

"If you don't have better manners toward women yet, Royce," interrupted Pa angrily, "than to call them liars to their face, I suggest you go see Pat Shaw and take a look at the note we drew up for him. Four-and-a-half percent, just like my wife said! You can squawk all you want about it, but when folks find out you've been taking advantage of them, they won't take too kindly to it. They're gonna be lining up at your door begging you to call their notes due so they can borrow from us instead!"

He paused just long enough to take a breath. Then his eyes bore into Franklin Royce one final time.

"So like I said, Royce," he added, "you go ahead and do your worst. You think I'm bluffing, then you try me! You'd be doing this community a favor by calling every loan you hold due, and letting the good folks of Miracle Springs pay you off and start borrowing from somebody else at a fair rate. Then you can see what it's like trying to make a living competing with my wife in the freight and supplies business!"

Mr. Royce returned Pa's stare as long as he dared, which wasn't long, then without another word, flicked his whip, turned his horse around, and flew off down the road back toward town.

Pa and Almeda watched him go. Then she slipped her hand through his arm, and they turned and walked slowly back to the house. They seemed at peace with what they had done, because they knew it was right, but they couldn't help being anxious about the results. If Royce *did* start calling notes due, there wasn't much they could do to stop him beyond helping a handful of other men, and that would only make it worse for everybody else. If they did bail out Rolf Douglas and whoever followed him, once they reached the $50,000 limit that Mr. Finch had promised, they would have no more help to give. And then, once word got out that the Hollister-Parrish "bank" had run dry, Mr. Royce would get his chance to foreclose on everybody in sight, run Parrish Mine and Freight out of business, gobble up all the land for miles around, get elected mayor, and gain control of the whole area.

Everything Pa and Almeda had said was true, and they meant every bit of it. But there was a lot of bluff in their words too. Now there was nothing left to do but wait and see how Mr. Royce decided to play his cards.

"Well, Corrie," said Pa with a half-smile as they came toward me, "I reckon we've done it now. Your next article may be about the end of Miracle Springs and the beginning of Royceville!"

Almeda and I laughed. But all three of us knew Pa's joke was a real possibility, too real to be very funny.

# CHAPTER 17

## THE DOC'S VISIT AND PA'S SCARE

The election was less than two weeks away.

The moment Franklin Royce disappeared down the road in his black buggy and we went back inside the house, a last-minute let-down seemed to come over Almeda.

There was nothing more to be done. She wasn't going to give any more speeches or write any more flyers. And as far as visiting and talking with folks was concerned, she said everything had already been stirred up plenty. The people had more than enough to talk about for one year, she said, and Franklin Royce had enough fuel to keep his hatred burning for a long time. It was best just to wait for events to unfold.

Almost immediately, her whole system seemed to collapse. Even as they walked away from the conversation with Mr. Royce, her face was pale and her smile forced.

The minute they were inside, she sat down heavily and breathed out a long and weary sigh. Tiny beads of perspiration dotted her white forehead. Pa saw instantly that she wasn't feeling well at all. She didn't even argue when he took her hand, helped her back to her feet, and led her into the other room to their bed. She lay down, and Pa brought her a drink of water. He wiped her face for a minute with a cool, damp cloth, and before long she was sound asleep.

Almeda remained in bed the rest of that Friday and all day Saturday, only getting up to go to the outhouse. Pa tended her like a mother with a baby. When Katie or Emily or I would try to take Ma something or sit beside her or help her on one of her many walks outside, Pa would say, "No, she's my wife. Nobody loves her as much as me, and nobody is gonna take care of her but me. Besides," he added with a wink, "I got her into this here fix, so I oughta be the one who helps her through it!"

The rest of us fixed the meals and cleaned up the house, but Pa took care of Almeda. He even sat beside her while she was sleeping, held her hand when she got sick, and read to her now and then, either from a book or from the Bible. If the rest of the town could only have seen him, some of the men might have made fun of him for doting on her. But no woman would have thought it was anything short of wonderful to have a husband love and care for her so tenderly as Pa did Almeda.

In the midst of all the turmoil over the election and loans and money and rumors and legal questions about Pa's claim and the future of Parrish Freight, it had been easy to forget that Almeda was in the family way. Except when she'd get sick for half an hour or hour every few days, she didn't seem any different, and she wasn't showing any plumpness around her middle.

But Pa started to get concerned about her condition on Saturday afternoon when she still lay in bed, looking pale and feeling terrible. He sent Zack and Tad off on their horses to fetch Doc Shoemaker.

When the Doc came an hour or so later, he went immediately into the sick room with Pa. After examining Almeda he shook his head, puzzled.

"Everything seems fine," he said, "but she's weak, and mighty sick. I don't quite know how to account for it. Came on her sudden, you say?"

"Yep," answered Pa. "She was fine and full of pep for a day or so after she got back, and then she started to tire out pretty bad."

"Back from where?"

"Sacramento."

"Sacramento? How'd she get there?"

"In her buggy, how else?"

"She bounced around on a buggy seat for that whole trip and back?"

"I reckon so," said Pa reluctantly. By now he realized Doc Shoemaker was mighty upset.

"Drummond Hollister, you idiot! What in blazes did you let her do that for!"

"She didn't exactly ask," said Pa. "She just said she was going. I asked if she wanted me to go with her, and she said no, that I oughta stay here, and I didn't think any more about it. She just went, that's all."

"This lady's between three and four months pregnant! She can't be doing things like that. I'm surprised she hasn't already lost the child from the exertion of a journey like that. She still may."

All the color drained from Pa's face. I had never seen him so scared. "I—I didn't think of all that," he stammered. "She's the kind of woman who's used to doing what she likes, and I don't usually stand in her way."

"Well, you're her husband and the father of the baby she's carrying. So you'd just better start telling her to take it easy. If she doesn't like it, then you put your foot down, do you hear me? Otherwise you might lose both a baby *and* a wife!"

"Is she really in danger, Doc?" Pa's voice shook.

"I don't know. I hope not. But she needs rest—and you make sure she gets it!"

# CHAPTER 18

## A FEW MORE CARDS GET PLAYED

Almeda was up and out of bed some by Monday. Most of the color had come back into her cheeks and she was smiling again.

Pa made her stay in bed most of the day, and the minute she even had a fleeting thought about going into town or doing any last-minute campaigning, he wouldn't hear of it for a second!

"Corrie can manage the office fine without you," he said. "And whatever campaigning's to be done—which I don't figure is much—I'll do myself. There's not much we can do anyway, and the best thing for you is more rest. I don't aim to take any more chances!"

"Why, Drummond Hollister," she said, "I declare, if I didn't know better I'd take you for one of those slave-driving husbands who thinks his every word is supposed to be absolute law!" Her voice was still a little weak, but it was good to hear her joking again.

"Well, maybe it's time I started exerting my authority a mite more over an unruly wife who sometimes doesn't know what's for her own good," Pa jibed back. But joking or not, he still was determined to make her stay home and stay in bed as much as he could.

I went into town to the office, but I quickly discovered that while Almeda had been sick and we had been thinking only about her, the rest of the town had been talking about something else. And although the election was only eight days away, the elections to vote for mayor or United States President were not on people's minds.

I came back home on Raspberry about half an hour before noon. "Pa," I said, "I don't know what to do. The office has been full of people all morning."

"Don't ask me," he answered, "you and Almeda know the business, not me."

"It's not the business they're coming in about, Pa. It's about money and the worries about Royce."

"Who's been coming in?" he asked.

"Several of the men—asking to see Almeda . . . or you, when I told them she was sick. Mr. Douglas was one of the first."

"Rolf?"

"Yes, and he didn't look too happy."

A worried look crossed Pa's face. "Royce musta called his note due," he muttered. There was no anger in his voice, only a deep concern. Mr. Royce had apparently decided to play another card and call Pa's bluff.

Pa let out a deep sigh. "Reckon I'd best head into the office and see what's up," he said, "though I'm not sure I want to. What's going on now?" he added, turning to me. "What's Ashton doing?"

"I told him I was coming home to talk to you and to tell anyone who asked that I'd be back after a spell."

"Okay . . . I'll go saddle up the horse in a minute, and we'll ride back in."

He went into the bedroom to talk to Almeda a minute, then said to Emily and Becky, "You girls take care of your mother if she needs anything. And if she tries to get up and about too much, you tell her I told you to make her lie down again."

"Yes, Pa," said Emily. "Don't worry about her at all. We'll see that she keeps resting."

"Good. Corrie, we'd best be off." He went out to the barn while I went in to visit with Almeda for a few minutes. She was feeling a lot better, but she seemed quiet and thoughtful and a little sad. I suppose she was anxious about the men in town, and maybe about the election.

When Pa and I rode into town, we saw a small group of men standing around the door of Parrish Mine and Freight. A few were leaning against the building, and a couple sat on the edge of the wooden walkway, chatting aimlessly and waiting for Pa. When we rode up, they stood and turned in our direction. Worry filled all their faces. Rolf Douglas was at the head of the line right next to the door.

"He done it, Drum," said Mr. Douglas as we rode up, holding the paper he held in his hand up toward us.

"Thirty days?" said Pa, dismounting.

"Yep. I already been to see him to ask whether he would reconsider if I got back up with the two months I'm behind. But he said nope, got to have the cash or be out in thirty days."

"Well, come on in," said Pa, opening the door and leading the way into the office. "We'll see if we can't work something to help you out."

"What about the rest of us, Drum?" someone else called out. "We've got loans with Royce too."

"Any one of us could be next," called out another.

"Hold your horses, all of you," said Pa. "Right now Rolf here's the one with immediate problems with Royce. Let me get him taken care of first. Then we'll talk about what's to be done next."

He and Mr. Douglas went into Almeda's office. Ten minutes later they emerged and walked back outside. Mr. Douglas's expression was completely changed, and even Pa had the beginnings of a smile on his face. In that short time, the assembly of men outside had grown to ten or twelve.

Pa gave Mr. Douglas a slap on the back, then the two men shook hands. "You come back and see me in three weeks, Rolf," Pa said. "That'll give you eight or ten days before the money's due to Royce. We'll finish up our arrangement then."

Mr. Douglas thanked him, and by then all the other men were clamoring around, asking questions, wanting to know how things stood with them if they suddenly found themselves in the same predicament.

I don't know whether Pa was aware of it or not, but I thought I could see the outline of a familiar face in the bank window down the street. Word of the goings-on outside the Parrish Freight office would get back to Royce's ears soon enough.

"Listen to me, all the rest of you," Pa said. "We can't help you out until Royce tries to foreclose on you. Even the Hollister-Parrish bank's got limits, you know!"

He laughed, and all the men joined in.

"But we'll help you out when your time of need comes, you can depend on that. So long as we're able, whatever we got is yours. The minute Royce sends you a paper, you come see me and we'll sit down and talk. Until then, all of you just hang tight and go on with your business."

"Thanks, Drum . . . we're obliged to ya. We all owe you an' your missus, and we won't forget it!" called out several of the men as they began to disperse down the street."

"Just remember," Pa called out, "you men vote according to your consciences a week from tomorrow. I ain't gonna mention no names, but you just remember that as long as you got friends you can trust, no one is gonna be able to hurt you no matter what they may threaten to do."

He didn't have to mention any names. Every one of the men understood perfectly what Pa meant.

And as the week progressed and the days wound down toward the election, this statement of Pa's spread around town and became a final campaign pledge that stuck clearly in people's minds.

Judging from his action, it was obvious that Franklin Royce had heard Pa's statement about friends you could trust too.

# CHAPTER 19

## WOMAN TO WOMAN

By the middle of the week Almeda was back to a normal schedule and was going into town for at least a good part of the day. But she was unusually quiet, and it seemed as if something weighed on her mind. I didn't know if it had to do with the election or the Royce trouble or anxiety about the baby.

After all that had gone on with the build-up to the election, the last week was completely quiet—no speeches, no rumors, no new banners. No one saw Mr. Royce. Almeda kept to herself. There were no more threats of foreclosure. Business went on as usual, and Tuesday, November 4 steadily approached. The most exciting thing that happened had nothing whatever to do with the election. That was the news that Aunt Katie was expecting again. The two new cousins were both scheduled to arrive sometime in the early spring of 1857.

Time had slipped by so fast that I didn't have the opportunity to get a second article written about the election. But almost before I had a chance to think through the possibility of a post-election story, which I wasn't sure I wanted to do if Mr. Royce won, all of a sudden a realization struck me. I still hadn't seen my Fremont article in the *Alta*!

What could have happened? Did I miss it? I'd been so preoccupied with everything that was going on, I hadn't read through every single issue. Had it come and I hadn't seen it?

I couldn't believe that was the case. Mr. Kemble always sent me a copy of my articles separately. He had done so with

every one he had ever printed. Then why hadn't *this* article
been printed? It was the most important thing I had ever written, and it was almost too late!

I rushed home that day and frantically searched through
the stack of *Alta*s from the last three weeks. It was not there.
My article had still not been printed!

All that evening I stewed about it, wondering what I ought
to do. By the next morning nothing had been resolved in my
mind. So when we got ready to go into town, I asked Almeda
if I could ride with her in the buggy instead of taking Raspberry
like I usually did.

I began by telling her about the article's not appearing, and
about Mr. Kemble.

"After a while," I said, "I started to get so tired of him
looking down on me because I was young, and because I was
a girl, that I became determined to show him that I could write
as well as anyone else. But sometimes I must have sounded
mighty headstrong, like I wouldn't accept anything but my own
way. Do you know what I mean?" I asked.

Almeda nodded.

"I know there are times you've got to fight for something
you believe in. You've taught me that. But then again, Mr.
Kemble *is* the editor, and he *does* have years more experience
than I do, and I *am* young. Sometimes I wonder if I'm pre-
suming too much to think I'm so smart and such a great writer
that I can just tell him what I want."

I glanced at Almeda. She was obviously thinking a lot about
what I was saying, but still she let me keep talking.

"And not only am I young and inexperienced, I *am* a
girl—"

"Not anymore, Corrie," Almeda interrupted. "You're a
woman now."

I smiled. "What I mean," I said, "is that I'm not a man
. . . I'm a girl, a lady, a woman—a female. I wish Mr. Kemble
could look at something I write and *not* think of it as written
by a woman. But there's a division between men and women
that affects everything—it affects how people look at you and

what they expect from you and how they treat you. And as much as I find myself wishing it *wasn't* that way, there's no getting around that it *is*. There *is* a difference between men and women, and maybe it *is* a man's world, especially here in the west. I don't know any other women newspaper writers. There aren't any other women in business around here but you."

I stopped, struggling to find words to express things I was feeling. "Maybe Mr. Kemble is right when he says that it's a man's world, and that a woman like me can't expect to get the same pay or have it as easy as I might like it. Maybe it *is* a man's world, and I've been wrong to think things are unfair because Robin O'Flaridy can get paid more than I do for the same article. Maybe that's just the way it is, and it's something I have to accept."

"How did your article's not being in the paper lead you to think about all that?" asked Almeda.

"I don't know. It's just hard to know how to fit being a woman into a man's world."

"Very hard!" agreed Almeda. "Believe me, Corrie, I have struggled with that exact question almost from the moment I arrived in California."

"My first reaction was anger," I continued. "I wanted to march right into Mr. Kemble's office and say, 'Why haven't you published my article?' A time or two I've been really headstrong and determined with him. Part of me still says that's the right approach. That's how a man would probably do it." I paused for a moment.

"But another side of me started thinking in this whole new way," I went on, "wondering if the way I've handled it in the past wasn't right."

"It's the Spirit of God putting these thoughts in your heart, Corrie," said Almeda. "You're maturing as a daughter of God. He's never going to let you remain just where you are. He's always going to be pulling and stretching you and encouraging you to grow into new regions of wisdom and dedication to him. And so he'll continually be putting within you new thoughts like this, so that you'll think and pray in new directions. He wants you to know both him and yourself more and more intimately."

"If it's God's Spirit speaking to me inside, then what's he trying to tell me?" I asked.

She laughed. "Ah, Corrie, *that* is always the difficult question! It's often very hard to know. Separating the voice of God's Spirit from our own thoughts is one of the Christian's greatest challenges."

The look on her face changed to one of reflection. "It's funny you should bring this up," she said after a minute. "I've been facing a real quandary myself. Different from yours, I suppose, but very similar at the same time."

"You mean about knowing if it's God saying something to you?"

"Partly. But more specifically, the issue of being a woman, and how to balance the two sides that sometimes struggle against one another inside."

"That's just it!" I said. "I feel that there's two parts of me, and I'm not sure which part I'm supposed to listen to and be like. One part wants to do things and be bold and not be looked down on for being a woman. That part of me resents hearing that it's a 'man's world' and that a woman's *place* is supposed to be somewhere different, somewhere less important, doing and thinking things that men wouldn't do. That part of me wants to think that I'm just as important as a man—not because women are *more* important, but just because I'm a human being too. Do you know what I mean?"

"Oh, I know exactly what you mean, Corrie!" answered Almeda. "Don't you think I've wrestled with that same question five hundred times since my first husband died? I've spent years trying to run a business in this 'man's world!' I always had to prove myself, to show them that I could run Parrish Mine and Freight as well as any man. Oh, yes, Corrie, I've struggled and prayed and cried over these questions you're asking!"

"Then you must feel the other half of what I've been feeling too," I went on.

"Which is?"

"Well, maybe it's not altogether right to expect to be treated the same as a man. Maybe it *is* a man's world, and I've got to accept my place in it. Even if Mr. Kemble says or does something I don't like, or even something I don't think is fair, maybe I have to learn to accept it. After all, he *is* the man, he *is* the editor, and maybe he has the right to do what he thinks best, whether I like it or not. After all, it isn't *my* newspaper. So who do I think I am to think that I have a right to expect Mr. Kemble to do what I want?"

Almeda drew up on the reins and looked at me intently. "Corrie," she said, "it seems there are two principles at work here. Maybe you're feeling the need to accept Mr. Kemble's judgment about the paper and your articles. But it's not just because he's a *man*—it's also because he's in a position of authority, and deserves your respect even when you disagree with him."

I nodded. "I guess so."

"But there's more to it than just the question of who makes the final decisions about your stories, isn't there?"

"Yes. I guess the last couple of years, since I started trying to write more seriously, I've been wanting the people I meet—first Mr. Singleton, then Mr. Kemble, and then even Robin O'Flaridy or Derrick Gregory—to treat me like an equal and not look down on me just because I'm not a man. But maybe I'm not supposed to be an equal. Maybe that isn't the way God wanted it to be. I don't like the thought that I'm not as important in the world as a man. But I've been wondering if that's the way it is."

"Corrie . . . Corrie," sighed Almeda, "you've really hit on the hardest thing of all about being a woman, especially out here in the west where we sometimes have to fend for ourselves and be tough."

"You mean accepting the fact that we're not equal to men, and that what we do and think isn't as important?"

"Oh no—not that. We *are* just as important. The question isn't about equality, Corrie, because in God's eyes, men, women, children—*all* human beings—are equal and precious. The soul of the poorest black woman is just as important to God as the soul of the richest white man. The President of the United States, in God's eyes, is no more important than a child dying of starvation somewhere in deepest India or Africa. No—men are all equal, and by *men* I mean all of mankind—men *and* women. You are just as important as Mr. Kemble or anyone else, and your thoughts are just as valid. Never think that you're not as *good* as someone else—as a man. On the other hand, never think that someone else isn't as good as you! Equality works in all directions."

"Then what's that hardest thing about being a woman?" I asked.

"I said you were wrong about us not being *equal*. But you were right when you said we were *different*! And that's what is so hard about being a woman—trying to find how we're supposed to be equal and different at the same time. That is the struggle, Corrie."

"It's a struggle, all right. Half of me wants to tell Mr. Kemble off, and the other half wonders if I've got any right to."

"That's where women make a big mistake, Corrie. We want to be treated equally, but we forget that we really *are* different. We're supposed to be. God didn't make men and women to be the same. He made us equal but different. And so we're supposed to fulfill different roles. And the minute we try to start turning our equality with men into *sameness* with men, we lose sight of what it truly means to be a *woman*. I think we become less of a woman, in the way God intended womanhood when he created it, when we try to compete with men and do everything men do."

"Do you mean maybe I *shouldn't* be trying to be a reporter, because it is something mostly men do?"

"No, it's not that at all, Corrie. I think it's all right to *do* many of the same things men do. There aren't certain limits or restrictions God places around women. But even though we may be involved in many of the same pursuits, we're still women, not men. There's still a difference. There is still a leadership role which God has given to men, and a follower's role God has given to women. That's part of the difference I spoke of. Equal but different. Man is to be the head, the spokesman, the leader. A woman is to fit into that arrangement, not try to compete with it."

"You mean, like Mr. Kemble being the editor of the paper, and so I have to realize the importance of his position?"

"Something like that."

"And even if it weren't for his being editor and me just being a raw young writer, him being a man and me being a young woman makes it that way, too."

"I suppose in a way, although I wouldn't want to assume that any man, just because he *is* a man, has the right to control your life and your decisions. I believe that God has set certain men—a husband, for example, or an employer—into positions of leadership. As women, we need to acknowledge that God-given leadership. But I have to admit that I don't always know how it works out in practice. Lately I've been struggling with it a lot myself."

"Is that how it is in a marriage too?" I asked. "Like between you and Pa?"

She didn't answer immediately, but looked down and sighed deeply. I glanced away for a moment. When I looked back toward her, to my astonishment I saw that Almeda was crying.

# CHAPTER 20

## ALMEDA CONFIDES

"What's the matter, Almeda?" I asked. My first thought was that something I'd said had hurt her feelings.

"I'm sorry, Corrie," she said, looking over at me. I'd never seen such an expression on her face. To me, Almeda had always been so strong, so in control, so much older and more mature than I. For three or four years she had been the one I had looked to for help and advice. I guess before that moment it had never crossed my mind that *she* had inner struggles too. But that look on her face, with tears silently running down her cheeks, was a look of confusion and uncertainty and pain—a look I had never expected to see from Almeda!

I reached over and took her hand.

The gesture made her cry even more for a minute, but I kept my hand on hers, and she held on to mine tightly. Finally she reached inside her pocket for a handkerchief, then blew her nose and tried to take a deep breath.

"I've been struggling with this for several days," she finally said, "ever since coming back from Sacramento and getting sick. I suppose I've needed someone to talk to. But I haven't even been able to bring it up to your father yet, because I haven't known how to put into words all that I was feeling."

"What is it?" I said. "Is there something wrong between you and Pa?"

"Oh, no. Nothing like that. Although it certainly has to do with your father." She paused, took another breath, then took my hand in both of hers again.

"I've always been a pretty independent sort of woman, Corrie," she said. "Just the other day, when I was sick, I heard your father saying to the doctor that I was the kind of woman who was used to doing what I liked. When the thought of going to Sacramento came to my head, just like your father said, I didn't ask him, I just said I was going and that was that—I went. Perhaps getting sick, and hearing those words of Drummond's, and realizing that my impetuousness could have cost our baby's life—all that set me to thinking about some things I hadn't ever thought of in quite the same light before. And last week, as I lay in bed recovering, I spent a lot of time in prayer. And I must tell you, I'm having to take a new look at some things in myself. It's not an altogether pleasant experience!"

She paused for a moment, dabbed at her eyes, then went on.

"Ever since I was a child I've had a determined streak. And that's not necessarily a bad thing. My past was anything but a spiritual one. I did not begin walking with God until I was in my mid-twenties, and before that I was a much different person than the one you have known. I did much that I am not proud of. And when I discovered who my heavenly Father was, and realized that he loved me and desired something more for me than what I was, I set my heart and mind to give myself to him completely. As a Christian, my inner determination has been a good thing. I have wanted to settle for nothing less than God's fullest and best for me. I have determined to give my all to him, in every aspect of my being, to let him re-make me into what *he* wants me to be, rather than just settling for what I have always been. And thus, I really am a different person than I was fifteen years ago. He *has* created in me a new heart, a new mind. And I am thankful that he gave me the determination to seek him with my whole being. Some people do not have that hunger, that earnest desire to give their all to God. But he gave me that hunger, and I am glad.

"After Mr. Parrish died, I'd have never made it in business in Miracle Springs without being what your Pa calls 'a mighty determined lady.' I had to fight for what I wanted to do, and prove myself to people, mostly to the men of this community. It's just like what we have talked about before, Corrie—fighting for what you believe in. God puts that fight, that determination into women's hearts too, not just men's. He fills women with dreams and desires and ambitions and things they want to do and achieve, and I really believe that God wants determined daughters as well as determined sons, willing to believe in things strongly enough to go after them. Like your writing. I think God is filling you not only with the desire to write, but the determination to fight for it, even when it might mean occasionally standing up to Mr. Kemble and speaking your mind.

"But on the other hand, there's a danger women face that men don't. Sometimes a single woman, who has only herself to depend on, can get too independent and lose sight of what it means to live in partnership with someone else. After I lost my first husband, I got accustomed to doing things for myself, in my own way, without asking anyone's permission or what anyone thought. I had to, I suppose.

"But when your father and I were married, I continued thinking pretty much the same way, even though I was a wife again. I didn't really stop to consider that maybe now I had to alter my outlook. I still thought of my life as *mine* to live as I saw fit. Once when we were talking about your future, I told you that I was the kind of woman who believed in exploring all the possibilities for yourself that you could. When your father suggested shutting down Parrish Freight for a while, so that I could be a more traditional wife and mother, I nearly hit the roof. I wasn't about to have any of that, and I told him so!

"The trip to Sacramento and getting sick last week suddenly made it clear to me that I have carried that independence into my marriage with your father. I haven't stopped to consider things, or to ask him about what I do, or to defer to him in any way as my husband, I've just gone on ahead and done what I wanted to do. And the instant I realized it—I have to tell you, Corrie, it was very painful. I love your father so much. Realizing that I haven't been to him what God would have me be fills me with such remorse and sadness and—"

She stopped and looked away. I could feel her hand trembling in mine. I knew she was weeping again. After two or three minutes of silence, she continued.

"Your father has been so good to me," she said. "He has never pressured me, never said a word. He has let me be myself, and even be independent. Yet now I see that I have done some things that perhaps he wouldn't have wanted me to.

"Why, this whole thing of running for mayor—I never *asked* him about it, Corrie. We prayed about it when I decided to get back in the race, but I never really sought your father's counsel as a man of wisdom. The initial decision for me to run was a decision I made. I never even sought his advice as my husband and as the leader of this family. I genuinely thought I was being led of God, and perhaps to a degree I was. But the point is, I never consulted your father in any way or allowed him to help me arrive at a decision. You were there that evening last July—I simply walked in and announced that I had decided to run against Royce."

Again she stopped, tears standing in her red eyes. "Don't you see, Corrie—I haven't been fair to your father at all! My determined nature just lost sight of the fact that we're not supposed to act independent of men, but *with* them, and following them, and allowing them to help guide us. God made women to live *with* men, not to act independently of them—especially in a marriage. And I haven't done that with your father, the man I love more than anyone else in the world!

"Probably God was trying to get my attention even before last week. From the very start of the election, all the mischief and deceit Franklin has been up to—maybe that has been the Lord's way of telling me some of my priorities haven't been as he would have them. When he started spreading those rumors about me, even then God was stirring me up, though I didn't know what he was trying to say."

"But what could all those lies about you have to do with what God wanted to say to you?" I asked.

A faraway look passed across Almeda's face. "Yes, a good portion of what people were saying was false, Corrie," she said softly. "But not everything. I lived for many years outside God's plan for me, and I had much to repent of. He had many things in my character to change. Perhaps I will have the opportunity to tell you about it one day. I would like that. Your father knows everything. I have held no secrets from him. And it is to his great credit that he married me knowing what he knew. I love him all the more for it.

"And so when Franklin began stirring up the waters of my past, God began to probe the deep recesses of my heart as well. And now I find myself wondering if this whole election came up, not so that I could become mayor of Miracle Springs, but so that I would finally face some things in my own heart that I had never let go of, so that I would put them on God's altar once and for all."

"But surely you can't want Mr. Royce to be mayor!" I said in astonishment.

"Wouldn't it be better for me to withdraw from the election, even if it means giving the mayor's post to him, than to go ahead with something that is outside of God's will for me?"

"I suppose so," I answered hesitantly. "But I just can't stand the thought of Mr. Royce getting his own way and gaining control of this town."

"I can't either," she replied. "But he is not a Christian, and I am. Therefore I am under orders to a higher power. To *two* higher powers—the Lord God our Father, and to my husband Drummond Hollister. And maybe it's time I started to ask the two of them what I am supposed to do, instead of deciding for myself."

"I just can't abide the thought of Mr. Royce being mayor."

"Look at me, Corrie," she said tenderly, placing her hand gently on her stomach. "The baby that is your father's and mine is beginning to grow. Before long I will be getting fat with your own new little brother or sister. Do I look like a politician . . . a mayor?"

"I see what you mean," I said.

"Do you remember what you said when we first started talking, about the two parts struggling inside you?"

I nodded.

"It's the same thing I've been wrestling with. It's hard. It's painful. That's why I've been praying, and crying. I *want* to be mayor. But at the same time, my first calling is to be a woman—to be your father's wife, to be a mother to his children, and this new child I am carrying. Balancing the two is very difficult! That's why I don't know what to tell you to do about your article and Mr. Kemble. Because I don't even know what I'm supposed to do in my *own* dilemma."

We both were silent for several minutes. "What will you do?" I asked finally.

"I don't know," Almeda answered. "But the one thing I *do* have to do is talk with your father—and pray with him. This is one decision I am not going to make without him!"

She looked at me and smiled, wiping off the last of the tears on her face with her handkerchief.

"Thank you for listening, Corrie," she said. "You are a dear friend, besides being the best daughter a woman could have. Pray for me, will you?"

"I always do," I replied. I leaned toward her and gave her a tight hug. We held one another for several moments.

"Oh, Lord," I prayed aloud, "help the two of us to be the women you want us to be. I pray that you'll show Almeda and Pa just what you want them to do. And help me to know what you want me to do, too."

"Amen!" Almeda whispered softly.

When we released each other, both of us had tears in our eyes. They were not tears of sadness, but of joy.

# CHAPTER 21

# FRANKLIN ROYCE SURPRISES
# EVERYBODY

All day Thursday after Almeda and I had our long talk, neither of us could concentrate on work. About three in the afternoon, Almeda suggested we go on home.

We hadn't been back more than forty or fifty minutes when Alkali Jones rode up as fast as his stubborn mule Corrie's Beast could carry him—which wasn't very fast!

Pa was just walking down from the mine to wash up and have a cup of coffee. We'd been inside the house, but hadn't yet seen Pa since getting home. Mr. Jones spoke to all of us at once as he climbed down off the Beast.

"Ye left Miracle too blamed early!" he said to me and Almeda. "Weren't five minutes after ye was gone, ol' Royce come out o' his bank, an' starts talkin' to a few men who was hangin' around the Gold Nugget. Told 'em he was gonna be givin' kinda like a speech tomorrow mornin', though not exactly campaignin'. But he said whatever men owed his bank money oughta be sure an' be there. He said he'd like to notify 'em all by letter, but there weren't enough time, so would the men spread the word around town."

"And what else?" asked Pa.

"That's it," said Mr. Jones. "He's gonna be sayin' something he says is mighty important an' folks oughta be there."

Pa looked at Almeda. "Well, I reckon this could be it," he

108

said. "Looks like he's gonna call our bluff and foreclose on the whole town at once."

"He wouldn't dare," said Almeda.

"As long as you've known Franklin Royce," said Pa, "you still think he'd be afraid to do anything? Nope, that's what he's gonna to do all right. One last threat to finalize his election on Tuesday."

"I just can't believe he'd have the gall."

"He'll do anything to win."

Everybody was silent a minute.

"Well, I can't be there," said Almeda finally. "I wouldn't be able to tolerate that conniving voice of his addressing the men of this town. I'm afraid I would scream!"

"I'm not gonna be there, that's for sure!" added Pa. "I'd be afraid I'd clobber him, and then Simon'd have to throw me in the pokey. Alkali, you want to go and hear what the snake has to say? You'd be doing us a favor."

"You bet. Maybe I'll clobber the varmint fer ye! Hee, hee, hee! I don't owe him nuthin'. He cain't do a thing to me!"

"No, you just stand there and listen. Won't be doing our cause no good for *anybody* to clobber him, as much as I'd like to!"

They went into the house and had some coffee and talked a while longer, and then went back to the mine where Pa worked for another couple of hours.

That evening was pretty quiet. It felt as if a cloud had blown over the house and stopped, a big black thundercloud. I think Pa and Almeda were afraid that whatever Royce did in the morning would send a dozen or more men running to them for help with their loans, and then the cat would be out of the bag that they didn't have enough money to help them all. They didn't actually have any money at all! Once they were forced to admit that fact, like Pa said, the jig was up. Royce would then have everyone over a barrel and could do whatever he liked.

The next morning we all tried to keep busy around the house, but it was no use. We were on pins and needles waiting for some news from town. I think Pa was halfway afraid that he'd suddenly see ten or twenty men riding up, all clamoring for help with their loans, and when he had to level with them and say there was no way they could back them all up, that they'd turn on him and lynch him from the nearest tree!

The morning dragged on. Two or three times I could tell from Pa's fidgeting that he was thinking of riding into town himself to see what was up. But he stuck with his resolve, and attempted to busy himself in the barn or around the outside of the house.

The first indication we had that word was on the way wasn't the sight of dust approaching or the sound of galloping hoof-beats rounding the bend. Instead it was the high-pitched voice of Mr. Jones shouting at his mule as he whipped it along. Long before he came into view, his voice echoed his coming.

"Git up, ye dad-blamed ornery varmint!" he yelled. "Ye're nuthin' but a good-fer-nuthin' heap o' worn-out bones! If ye don't git movin' any faster, I'm gonna drive ye up the peak o' Bald Mountain an' leave ye there fer the bears an' wolves—ye dad-burned cuss! Why, I shoulda left ye in that drift o' snow last winter! Ye're slower than a rattlesnake in a freeze!"

By the time he rounded the bend and came in sight, Pa was already running toward him, and the rest of us were waiting outside the house for news.

Seeing Pa and the rest of us, Alkali's jabbering changed and his face brightened immediately.

"Ya done it!" he shouted out. "Ya done it, ye wily rogue!"

"Done what?" said Pa. "Who's done what?"

"*You* done it!" repeated Mr. Jones. "Ya made the rascal blink, that's what! Hee, hee, hee!"

"Alkali, I don't have a notion what you're babbling on about!"

"He backed down, I tell ye! Your bluff worked!"

"What did he say, Mr. Jones?" said Almeda, "Are you telling us he *didn't* call all the mens' notes due like we feared?"

"He didn't do nuthin' o' the sort, ma'am. Why, he plumb was trippin' over his own tongue tryin' to be nice, 'cause he ain't used enough to it."

"What did he say, Alkali? Come on—out with it!" said Pa.

"Well, the varmint got up on top of a table so everybody could hear him. There was likely thirty, forty men gathered around, all of 'em that owes the rascal money. An' they was all worried an' frettin', and your name came up amongst 'em afore Royce even got started, and they was sayin' as how they'd have to be over t' see you next.

"But then Royce climbed up there, all full of smiles, and said he'd been thinkin' a heap 'bout the town an' its people and about his obligation as the banker an' the future mayor. An' he said he had come t' the realization that ye gotta have friends ye can trust when times get rough—"

"He stole that from you, Pa," I interrupted.

Pa just nodded, and Mr. Jones kept going.

"An' he said that as Miracle Springs' banker, he was proud of bein' a man folks could trust. An' then came the part that jist surprised the socks clean off everybody listenin'. He said that he'd been thinkin' an' was realizin' maybe he'd been a mite too hard on folks hearabouts. An' so he said he was gonna do some re-figurin' of his bank's finances and had decided fer the time bein' t' call no more loans due. An' he wanted t' git folks together 'cause he knew there'd been some worry around town and he wanted t' put folks' minds at ease.

"An' then blamed if he didn't hold up a piece a paper, an' he said that it was the call notice on Rolf Douglas's note. An' he said he'd reconsidered it too, an' then all of a sudden he ripped that paper in half right afore our eyes! An' then he said he wanted them all to remember that he was their friend, an' a man they could trust."

"That was all?" asked Pa, stunned by the incredible news.

"The men was jist standin' there with their mouths hangin' open, an' no one knew whether t' clap fer him or what t' do, they was all so shocked. An' then he said he hoped they'd remember him on election day. But if ye ask me, gatherin' from the gist of what I heard as the men was leavin', I figure the only person they's gonna be rememberin' next Tuesday is this here missus of yours, Drum, now that they don't figure they need to be afeared of Royce!"

He stopped and looked around at all our silent amazed faces.

"Hee, hee, hee!" he cackled. "Ye all look like a parcel of blamed ghosts! Don't ye hear what I'm tellin' ye? Mrs. Hollister, ma'am, I think you jist about got this here election in the dad-burned bag!"

Pa finally broke out in a big grin, then shook Alkali Jones' hand, and threw his arm around Almeda.

"Well, maybe we have done it after all, Mrs. Hollister!" he exclaimed. "I just don't believe it."

But Almeda wasn't smiling. One glance over in my direction told me this latest news was like a knife piercing her heart. Knowing that suddenly she had a chance after all was going to make what she had to do all the more difficult.

# CHAPTER 22

## TWO OPPOSITE MOODS

All the rest of that Friday Almeda was quiet and kept to herself, while everyone else was happy. Around the house Pa was all smiles, laughing and joking. I'd hardly ever seen him like that! To know they had gone up against a skunk like Royce and won was more than he'd expected. We still didn't know what effect it would have on the trouble he was trying to cause about *our* claim. But at least the men with overdue loan payments appeared out of danger.

Uncle Nick and Katie came down to the house, and the minute they walked in, Pa took Katie's hand, even in her condition, and did a little jig, and then said to her and Uncle Nick, "The two of you watch how you talk around here from now on—this is the home of the soon-to-be mayor of Miracle Springs!" And that set off the celebrating all over again!

Even more than being glad about Royce's backing down about the loans, Pa was jovial because he figured Almeda was a cinch to win the election on Tuesday! Pa was so excited he could hardly stand it. They were going to beat Royce in two ways!

Despite Royce's last-minute ploy with his speech, tearing up Mr. Douglas's call notice and trying to convince folks he was their friend, the word around town was that most of the men were going to go with the person their gut had told them all along they could trust. The words *Mayor Hollister* went down a lot smoother than *Mayor Royce*.

Uncle Nick was in town a couple of hours after the banker's speech, and when he came back he confirmed exactly what Mr. Jones had said. People were relieved at what Royce had done. But a lot of them said they hadn't been that worried anyway because they knew Drum would help them out. And now more than ever they knew who they were going to vote for, and it wasn't the man with all the money in the fine suit of clothes from New York.

"Everybody's sayin' the same thing, Drum," said Uncle Nick, "and what Alkali said is right—she's just about got the election in the bag!"

When Almeda and I went into the office for a couple of hours, people on the street shouted out greetings. Mr. Ashton was all smiles, and when we saw Marcus Weber a bit later, his white teeth just about filled his dark face in the hugest grin I'd ever seen him wear. The two men did everything but address her as Mrs. Mayor.

Poor Mr. Royce! He had tried being mean, and now he was trying to be nice. But neither tactic made people like him nor trust him.

Almeda was silent, unsmiling, even moody. Pa, and I think most other folks, just figured she wasn't feeling well on account of the baby.

But I knew that wasn't it. I knew what she was thinking— she was going to withdraw from the election! After all that had gone on, she had victory in her grasp . . . and now she was going to have to let go of it and hand the election to a man she despised.

It took her the rest of the day to get up the nerve to talk to Pa, because she knew how disappointed he would be. Finally, after supper, she asked him if he'd go outside with her for a walk. He was still smiling when they left. But when they came back an hour or so later, his face was as downcast as hers had been all day, and Almeda's eyes were red from crying. I knew I'd been right. She'd told him, and the election was off.

The instant they walked in the door, a gloomy silence came over the five of us kids. All the rest of them knew something was up, just from Pa's face, although neither Pa nor Almeda said anything about what they were thinking.

Before long we got ourselves ready and off to bed, leaving Pa and Almeda sitting in front of the fire. The last thing I remembered before falling asleep was the soft sounds of their voices in the other room. I couldn't tell if they were talking to each other or praying.

Probably both.

# CHAPTER 23

# THE COMMITTEE GETS TOGETHER AGAIN

On Saturday, three days before the election, when I got up Pa was already gone. Almeda was still in bed. Pa finally returned a little before noon. His first words were to Almeda, who was up and about but who hadn't said much to any of the rest of us yet that morning.

"You still want to tell everyone all at once?" he asked her.

"I think it's the best way, don't you?"

"Yeah, I reckon. They gotta know sometime, and it's probably easiest that way."

Then Pa turned to the rest of us. "Listen, kids—we're going to have another meeting of our election committee. So you all be here right after lunch. Don't go running off if you want to hear what your mother and I have been discussing, you hear? Plans have changed some, and we're gonna tell you all about it."

He spoke again to Almeda. "I already told Nick and Katie to come down. What do you think—anyone else we ought to tell personally, so they don't just hear from Widow Robinson and the rest of the town gossips?"

"Maybe it would be good to tell some of our friends," suggested Almeda, "now that you mention it. I'd like Elmer and Marcus to hear it from us."

"And Pat," said Pa. "And maybe the minister—"

"And Harriet," added Almeda.

116

They both thought another minute.

"Guess that's about it, huh?" said Pa. Almeda nodded.

"Zack, son," said Pa, "You want to ride over to the Shaws' and ask Pat if he could come over around half past one?"

"Sure, Pa."

"Come to think of it," Pa added, "ask him if he's seen Alkali today. Alkali's gotta be here too."

"He was by Uncle Nick's earlier," said Zack. "I heard him say he was going into town."

"Well, we'll round him up somewhere. Between him and his mule, it shouldn't be too hard to find him."

"Corrie, would you ride into town and deliver the same message to Mr. Ashton and Mr. Weber?" said Almeda.

"Can I go see Miss Stansberry?" asked Emily. "I'll tell her."

"Sure, said Pa. "What about Rev. Rutledge? Who wants to ride over—"

"I'll ask him to come too," said Emily. "He'll be at Miss Stansberry's—he's always with her."

"You noticed, eh?" said Pa with a smile.

"Everyone knows about them, Pa," said Becky. "They're *always* together!"

"Okay, all of you get going with your messages. Tell everyone we'll meet here at half past one."

Two hours later, we were all back, and the house was full of the election committee and our closest friends—sixteen in all, probably the most people we'd ever had in the house at one time.

"We're obliged to you all for coming," Pa began. "What we've got to tell you isn't exactly the best news we could have. But we talked and prayed the whole thing through and this is the way we figure things have to be. You all are family, and the best friends we've got, and we want you to hear how things stand from our own lips instead of just hearing it around town.

"Now in a minute Almeda's got some things she wants you to know about how she's been thinking. When she first unburdened all this to me, I didn't see what the problem was with her being mayor. But I gotta tell you, we done some praying on this dilemma last night, and I went out myself for a couple hours this morning and was asking the Lord some mighty hard questions. And I'm coming to see that maybe what she's doing is the right thing after all.

"You see, we've been thinking mighty hard about this here marriage of ours, and we've been asking God to show us how things are supposed to work between a man and a woman who say they want to live together and try to be one like the Book says they're supposed to be. Almeda figures maybe she hasn't been deferring to me like she ought to have been. At first when she said it, I didn't see how that should prevent her from running for mayor. But I have to respect what she thinks is the right thing to do. And then something began to speak inside me too. I have to hope it was God's voice, just the same as I have to think it's him that's speaking to Almeda's heart.

"I began to see that maybe I had some changing to do too. Maybe I haven't been quite the leader of this marriage that I'm supposed to be. I mean, I don't have any complaint with what Almeda does or wants to do. And I don't want her asking my permission to do things. She's a grown woman, and she's a heap sight more experienced than I am about trying to live the way a Christian should and listening for how to obey what God wants us to do. When it comes to that sort of thing, why she's the one who ought to be leading me! If she comes and says, 'I don't know what to do about such-and-such, and you're my husband and I want to do what you think is best,' I'm more'n likely to answer her, 'You're a grown woman, and I trust you, so do what you think's best.' In other words, I don't figure she needs me telling her what do all the time.

"Yet I can see that maybe I need to take more responsibility in the way of thinking of myself as head of this family and this marriage. I'm not really sure what that will mean because all this is mighty new to both of us. But I reckon that if you don't start someplace, you're likely never to get the thing done. So we're aiming to start here and now, even though it means having to turn back from something we worked so hard get. If we got started with this election on the wrong foot, then it's not gonna do nobody any good to keep pushing forward. The only way to make things come out right in the end is go back and start over, even if it means having to let go of something in the process."

He stopped and let out a big sigh. The whole house was silent as Pa looked around the room. His eyes fell on Almeda last of all. "Well," he said, "I reckon I had *my* say . . . now it's your turn."

"Drummond has really put his finger on what has been bothering me for the last week," Almeda began. "This whole election thing, as he said, got off on the wrong foot. I am coming to see that perhaps I'm a more independent woman than I realized—more independent than I should be. I have been in the habit of doing and thinking for myself, of making up my *own* mind about things, of running my *own* life and never really asking how what I do affects anybody else. And I see that in certain ways I have been headstrong when things stand in my way.

"I suppose it all boils down to the simple question: Is this the way for a woman, a wife, to behave in a marriage? I can't say as I even have the answer. As Drummond told you, neither does he. I don't intend to suddenly start asking him about everything I do. And I know the last thing he would ever do is to start lording it over me like a king. He is the most tender, most thoughtful man I have ever known.

"Yet somehow, we need to make some changes about my being less independent, and maybe him being a little more forceful. Neither of us understands very much about what we're trying to explain, because it's new to both of us."

Almeda then went on to tell how she had made the decision to run for mayor on her own. She shared some of what she and I had talked about, how she realized she had brought her independent streak into the marriage with Pa. And now, she said, she felt that the only way to make right what she had done was to go back and undo it, and then start anew.

"Drummond explained how I feel," she said. "I should have paid more attention to his initial hesitations, but I was determined it was the right thing. You can't make something come out right in the end if you got started with it in the wrong way. You have to go back and start over. The foundation has to be built right, or else everything that comes along and gets put on top of it will be shaky. It's like the old parable of building a house on either rock or sand. And I fear my running for mayor of Miracle Springs was a decision built on sand. Nothing I can do now will change that, or change the sand into rock. I don't know anything to do but go back and rethink the original decision in a new light."

She stopped, drew in a deep breath, and then went on with the hardest part of what she had to say.

"This new light cast on my decision to run for mayor, shows me that it was an ill-advised decision—one made independently, maybe even with some pride mixed in, a determination not necessarily to do what was right or what God wanted, but rather to do something that pleased my ego—that is, prevent Franklin Royce from becoming mayor. I never stopped to ask whether running for mayor was right for my husband, for this wonderful family of mine—"

Her hand swept around the room as she spoke, and she glanced around at all of us.

"I just said to myself, 'I can do this. I *will* do it!' And so I did. I made the decision without consulting a soul. Of course I prayed about it. But even my prayers were so full of self that God's voice could only speak to me through a heart that was still thinking independently.

"Well, the long and the short of it, as I'm sure all of you have guessed, is that we feel we must go back and undo that original decision I made.

"Now, no doubt you will all find yourselves full of reasons to try to convince us to reconsider. I know Franklin Royce is a dangerous man to let become mayor. I know every possible thing you could say to try to convince me to remain in the race. I've said them to myself. At first Drummond would not hear of my withdrawing, and he gave me every reason he could think of too. But as we talked and prayed, and as time settled our thoughts, we both became convinced that this is the right and proper course of action. Neither of us can give you every reason why—but we feel it is the right thing to do. So please, don't try to change our minds, unless you truly feel we've missed something God might have wanted to say to us.

"So," she concluded, in a quiet tone full of resolve, "I have decided—that is, *we* have decided . . . together, both of us— that it is best for the name Almeda Hollister to be withdrawn from consideration in the election for mayor of Miracle Springs. Since it is obviously too late for my name to be taken off the ballot, I would like to make a public announcement tomorrow at church, if that would meet with your approval, Avery, and simply tell people that I am no longer a candidate. If despite this, people still check my name on the ballot on Tuesday, I will not accept the position. In any case, Franklin Royce will become the next mayor of Miracle Springs."

# CHAPTER 24

## WHAT AN IDEA!

The room was silent.

Pa and Almeda both felt relieved, I think. I could tell a burden had been lifted from Almeda's shoulders. The peace on her face was visible. And since I had been expecting it, the shock wasn't as great for me.

But for everybody else, the news was awful!

I knew every single person wanted to start shouting out reasons to make them reconsider. But because Almeda had said not to, no one spoke.

The silence went on and on for a minute or two. Finally Rev. Rutledge broke it.

"Does this represent your decision too, Drummond?" he asked. "Is this what you want?"

"I reckon," Pa answered. "At first I didn't like it any better than the rest of you. And she's right—I spent an hour trying to convince her that I *did* want her to be mayor. But then after a while I saw what she'd been driving at. And so I reckon I do agree that maybe a woman—at least a wife, who's carrying my baby!—ought not be mayor. I'm not saying that *no* woman should do something like that. But we got ourselves a family here, and it's gonna be an even bigger family in a few months. We got our hands full without her trying to manage a town's business besides. So yeah, Reverend, I'm in agreement with this decision, even though I can't abide the thought of Royce being mayor any more than the rest of you can."

The silence fell again, and Rev. Rutledge seemed satisfied. A long time passed before anyone said anything.

"Well, I reckon there ain't but one solution t' this here fix," cackled Mr. Jones at length.

Pa looked over at him with a blank expression. I know he was expecting one of his old friend's wisecracks.

"And what's that, Alkali?" he asked.

"Fer you t' take the lady's place. Hee, hee, hee!"

As his high-pitched laughter died down, silence again filled the house. We could all *feel* an unexpected energy of hope rising out of the disappointment of only seconds earlier.

Faces gradually started glancing around the room at each other. Eyes grew wider and wider.

Mr. Jones' words were like a stick of dynamite exploding right in the middle of the room! For the first few seconds everyone wondered if they'd heard him right.

Then light began to dawn on face after face!

Uncle Nick was the first to say what everyone else had felt instantly. "If that ain't the dad-blamedest best idea I've ever heard!" he exclaimed, jumping out of his seat. He walked over to Pa and stuck out his hand.

Dazed, Pa shook it, still hardly believing what he'd heard. The moment he took Uncle Nick's hand, everyone in the room began letting out cheers and shouts of approval. The next instant we were all out of our seats and crowding around Pa, who still sat bewildered.

"Drummond," said Rev. Rutledge somberly, "I think Mr. Jones has hit upon an absolutely wonderful idea."

"The perfect answer!" chimed in Katie and Miss Stansberry almost in unison.

"Will you do it, Drummond?" asked the minister. "We're all behind you one hundred percent."

Almost in a stupor in the midst of the sudden excitement, Pa still didn't seem to grasp what all the fuss was about.

"Do what?" he said.

"Take Almeda's place, you old goat!" said Uncle Nick. "Just like Alkali said."

Still Pa's face looked confounded. The idea was just too unbelievable for him to fathom.

Finally Almeda turned from where she was sitting beside him. She took one of his hands in hers and looked him full in the face with a broad smile. "Drummond, what these friends of yours are saying is that they want *you* to run for mayor . . . *yourself!*"

"*Me* . . . run for mayor?" he exclaimed in disbelief. "The notion's crazier than Alkali shaving his beard and taking a bath!"

"No crazier than me being hitched and having a family, Drum," rejoined Uncle Nick.

"This here's Californeee, don't ya know! Things is done a mite looney out here. Hee, hee, hee!"

"Times are changing. You might as well change with them," added Mr. Shaw.

"But I'm no politician," objected Pa. "I don't know anything about that kind of stuff."

"Nobody else does either, Drummond," said Almeda, growing in enthusiasm over the idea herself. "I'm no politician either, and Franklin is only running so that he can gain more power for himself and his bank. Surely you don't want *him* to be elected?"

Her words sobered Pa and quieted everybody down.

For the first time the look on Pa's face indicated that he was giving serious thought to the reality of the possibility—as outlandish as the whole thing still seemed to him.

"My name's not even on the ballot," he said at length.

"If enough people voted for me and I should happen to win," suggested Almeda, "I could then step down and appoint you mayor."

"Is that legal?" asked Miss Stansberry.

"Royce would probably challenge it and call for a new election," said Katie. "Something similar happened in Virginia a few years back."

"And then once that happened, he'd think we'd deceived him and would no doubt start in again with his shenanigans and financial pressure on everyone," said Almeda, thinking aloud.

"There's got to be some way to get Drum elected mayor," said Mr. Shaw, "even if the election's only three days off."

The room got quiet for a minute. When Almeda spoke next, her voice was soft and earnest. It was almost as if the two of them were alone, continuing a conversation they'd been having in private.

"Drummond," she said, "it seems to me that this could be exactly what the Lord has had in mind all along. Perhaps this is the reason things have worked out as they have, and why he unsettled my heart about my being out in public view trying to make something of myself. Maybe all along God wanted me, and perhaps the whole community, to be looking to my husband for leadership. I see God's hand in the way events have unfolded. And I can't think of a better way for me to defer to you, and for you to move up a step in taking hold of the firm hand God might want you to exert, than for me to step aside so that you can take the lead in this election."

She paused, and her eyes were filling with tears of love as she went on. "I can't tell you how pleased it would make me," she said softly. "It would make me feel as though these past two months had not been in vain, that maybe God was even able to use my independence to accomplish his purposes. But of course," she added, "it has to be your decision, and I will understand and stand by you whatever you think is best."

She stopped, and now all eyes rested on Pa as he considered everything that had been said. A long time—probably two or three minutes—passed before he said a word.

"Well, you're all mighty convincing," he said finally. "And I have to say it's flattering that you'd think I could even do the thing—that is, if I had a chance in the first place."

He paused and took a breath.

"But it occurs to me," he went on, "that one of the first things a mayor probably has to do is make decisions of one kind or another. And it occurs to me, too, that if I'm gonna start taking more of a lead in this marriage partnership Almeda and I are trying to figure out, then I have to get more practiced in finding out what the Almighty wants me do, instead of just taking things as they come, or figuring that Almeda's supposed to handle most of the spiritual side of things, while I just go on without paying much attention.

"All that is my way of saying that I guess I *do* have to make the decision myself. I appreciate all your thoughts and advice. And I'd appreciate all of you praying for me, because I'm gonna need it. But first I have to get alone and ask God what decision he wants me to make, and then hope that he'll put the thoughts into my heart and head plain enough that I can figure out what he's saying."

He let out a deep sigh, then hitched himself to his feet.

"So that's what I'm going to do before I say anything else, and before you all try to do any more convincing."

He went to the door, opened it, and walked outside.

Gradually those of us left in the house started talking a little. Katie had to entertain little Erich, and Becky and Tad had had enough sitting for one stretch and had to get themselves moving again. Almeda went into her and Pa's bedroom and closed the door, to pray for Pa and the decision he was wrestling with.

About twenty minutes later Mr. Shaw was about to leave, and Rev. Rutledge was helping Miss Stansberry with her coat, when the door opened and Pa walked in.

From the look on his face, every one of us knew instantly that he'd made his decision.

Almeda had heard him return and emerged from the bedroom just as he spoke. "It'd be a shame to waste all those good 'Hollister For Mayor' signs and flyers," he said with a big grin. "So if it's not gonna be one Hollister, it might as well be the other! Move over, Royce—I'm in it now too!"

"Now the varmint'll find himself in a *real* scrape!" cackled Alkali Jones. "Hee, hee, hee!"

More hollering and hand-shaking went around the room, while Mr. Shaw and the others took off their coats again. Over to one side of the room I could see the person more involved in this turn of events than anyone but Pa, and she wasn't yelling or whooping it up.

Almeda closed her eyes briefly and softly whispered the words, "Thank you!" Then she opened them, and walked forward with a smile to join her husband in the midst of the commotion.

# CHAPTER 25

## DEVISING A STRATEGY

"Well, I suppose you'll still be wanting to make an announcement at church tomorrow," said Rev. Rutledge at length. "Although it looks like it will be quite different than what you first had in mind, Almeda!" he added with a big smile.

"I don't know, Reverend," replied Pa hesitantly. "I don't know if it strikes me as quite right to use your pulpit to further my own plans. Seems like it might have been okay to make a public announcement like Almeda was fixing to do. But without Royce having the same advantage, it hardly seems like it'd be fair for me to do it."

All this time Pa had been so angry at Mr. Royce for everything he'd done, and now all of a sudden he was worrying about being fair—even to him. It didn't take long for him to start thinking like a politician—and a good one at that, not like the kind who are always trying to twist things for their own advantage. Maybe Pa was gonna be cut out for this kind of thing after all!

"Aw, come on, Drum," said Alkali Jones. "How considerate has that snake been t' you an' yer missus here?"

"All's fair in love and war—and politics—that's what they say, Drum," added Mr. Shaw.

"Now let's have no more of this, the rest of you," said Almeda. "My husband has made his first decision as a candidate for mayor, and I think we should support him to the fullest in it. And besides that, I think he's absolutely right. Ethically speaking, it would give him an unfair advantage to speak in church."

"Not to mention mixing religion and politics," added Miss Stansberry.

"Even if there weren't anything wrong with it," Pa said, "Royce'd squawk and complain of an unfair advantage and might get so angry he'd start causing who knows what kind of mischief all over again. Just because I have to be fair to the man doesn't mean I trust him any more than I ever did—which isn't much. No, there's not gonna be no speaking out about this change of plans in church. If I'm going to win this election, I'll do it fair and square, so that Royce hasn't got a straw of complaint to stand on."

The room got quiet and people sat back down again. Only Pa remained on his feet, slowly pacing about, as if he had to keep moving while he was trying to think. But when he spoke, since he was standing and all the rest of us were sitting, it was almost like a speech, although I knew speechmaking never crossed Pa's mind. I couldn't help being intrigued by the changes I saw coming over him already! He was taking command of the situation, just as Almeda had said she had hoped he would.

"And that brings us straight back to the question I asked a little while ago," Pa went on, "which seems to be the crux of the whole matter. My name isn't even on the ballot. I don't see how I *can* run against Royce for mayor, even if I want to. There just isn't enough time."

Silence fell again. He was right. Time was short. What could be done? The ballot obviously couldn't be changed.

"What about a write-in vote?" suggested Katie after a long pause.

"What's that?" asked Pa.

"A write-in vote. People write in someone's name who isn't officially running. You hear about it all the time in the east—although nobody ever wins that way because they just get a few votes."

"That's it! That's the perfect way!" exclaimed Almeda excitedly. "What do you think, Drummond?" she asked, turning toward Pa. "We'll get word out that everyone who was going to vote for me should write in your name on the ballot instead."

"That's a lot of folks to get word to," replied Pa, "because I still don't want an announcement made in church."

"We could do it, Pa," said Zack, getting into the spirit of it. "Look how many of us there are right here. We'll just go out and tell everybody!"

"He's right—we could!" said Almeda. "With eight or ten of us, each calling on five or six families, telling them to let it be known—why, the whole community would know in no time."

"What are we waitin' for?" cried Uncle Nick. "Let's get the horses saddled and the buggies hitched and be off!"

"Hold your horses!" said Pa loudly. "I figure if all this is going on because of me, I ought have some say in it too!"

Everybody quieted down and waited. Pa thought for a moment. He was still standing up and slowly walking back and forth.

"All right," he said finally, "like I said a bit ago, I'm in this thing, so maybe Zack's got himself a good idea. If you're all of a mind to help, then you've got my permission to tell anybody you want—"

A fresh round of whooping and cheering went around the room. Even Rev. Rutledge dropped his normal reserve and got into the act with some noise.

"Wait a second . . . hold on!" shouted Pa. "Don't you go chasing off before the wagon's hitched! I was about to say you could tell anybody you want . . . *but* ye gotta keep word of this quiet—just one person to the next. I don't want this being talked about on the streets of Miracle Springs. I don't want Royce getting wind of it. You just tell people to spread the word around quietly and not to make a big ruckus about it, but just to walk into that schoolhouse on Tuesday and do what they feel they oughta do. The less Royce knows the better. I don't want to give him any more fuel to try anything else that's gonna hurt somebody. After the election's done, he can come and see me if he's got a complaint."

"That sounds easy enough," said Uncle Nick. "Now can we git going, Drum?"

"Nobody goes anywhere till after church tomorrow," answered Pa. "I don't want it talked about, you hear? Tomorrow afternoon, once folks are back home, then we'll see what can be done. But we're all going to go to church as usual, and we're not going to say anything. You all promise?"

Everyone nodded, although Uncle Nick and Alkali Jones didn't like the idea much. I think they would have liked to go and shout the news in the middle of the Gold Nugget so the whole town would know everything in five minutes!

Rev. Rutledge rose from his chair and walked over to Pa. "May I be the first to offer you my congratulations, Drummond?" he said, extending his hand. "I think you have chosen a reasonable and a wise course of action, and I want to wish you the best."

"Well, I reckon we'll see what'll come of it in a few days!" replied Pa, shaking his hand. The two men looked at each other for a couple seconds as their eyes met. I can't say it was a look of love so much as a look of mutual respect, and even friendship. They had sure come a long way together.

We went to church the next day, like Pa had said, but we all sat there with half-smiles on our faces, as if we all knew a secret we were keeping from the rest of the town.

Which, of course, we did!

But we didn't keep it from them for long. That afternoon, everyone who had been at our place the day before—everyone except Pa, that is. He didn't feel he ought to go to people and ask them to vote for him—rode on horseback or by buggy all throughout the community to pay short visits to everyone we could. Almeda and Miss Stansberry and Rev. Rutledge had planned out where we would all go. Even Tad and Becky had their calls to make.

The visits continued on Monday, although Almeda and I went into the office and tried to conduct a normal day's work in spite of the distraction of knowing the election was the next day. Smiles and nods and whispered words of hope and encouragement as the day progressed told that the word of Pa's write-in candidacy had spread through the town as quickly and successfully as anyone could have imagined.

Late in the day, Franklin Royce paid another call. He came into the office, asked for Almeda, then extended his hand and shook hers in one last election formality.

"Well, Almeda," he said, "by tomorrow evening this will all be over. So may the best man win, as it were."

Almeda smiled, thinking to herself—as was I—that he could not possibly have realized the significance of his own words. He obviously knew nothing about Pa, or Almeda's decision to remove herself from the race.

We all went to bed tingling with anticipation and excitement . . . and a little fear besides!

The next morning, the fateful day of November 4, 1856, we all got up and rode into town in the wagon with Pa, so he could cast his vote.

# CHAPTER 26

## ELECTION RESULTS

The voting stopped at six o'clock that night.

The government man from Sacramento, Rev. Rutledge, and a few people they'd gotten to help locked the door right then and started to count the ballots. They figured to be done and announce the results by eight-thirty or nine o'clock.

By eight a pretty big crowd was beginning to gather around the schoolhouse. Lots of people had come back to town, whole families in wagons, carrying lanterns and torches. At eight-fifteen, Mr. Royce drove up in his fancy black buggy. We were all bundled up warm in the back of our wagon. People came over now and then to speak briefly to Pa and Almeda, but mostly we just waited nervously. We tried to figure out how many voters there were. Pa and Almeda thought there would be somewhere between three and five hundred men who lived in and close enough to Miracle to vote for its mayor. There were probably another hundred or two hundred men who lived farther away who would have come to town to vote in the presidential election.

At about eight-forty the door to the schoolhouse opened. Some men came out, and everybody who was waiting came and clustered around the stairs to hear the news. The government man held a paper in one hand and a lantern in the other.

"I have some results to report to you," he said, and silence fell immediately over the crowd. "First of all, in the election you're most interested in, that for mayor of Miracle Springs,

133

we have tallied the unofficial vote as follows. These will have to be re-confirmed, but this is the first count. For Mrs. Almeda Parrish Hollister, the first name on the ballot, there were 67 votes cast."

A small ripple of applause scattered about. Already I could see a smile starting to spread across Mr. Royce's face where he stood not too far away.

"For the final name to appear on the ballot, Mr. Franklin Royce, we have a total of 149 votes."

Again there was some applause, though it was not as loud as Royce had expected. His smile grew wide. The turnout was not very high, but he was willing to take the victory any way it came. He began making his way through the crowd and toward the steps where he was apparently planning to address the people of Miracle Springs with a short victory speech. He had just taken the first two steps when he was stopped by the sound of the man at the top of the landing again.

"And in what is a most unusual and unexpected occurrence, we have a third unregistered candidate. . . ."

Everybody could almost feel the chill sweep through Mr. Royce's body. The smile began to fade from his lips.

"This candidate has received a sizeable number of write-in votes. In fact, by our unofficial tabulation, a certain Mr. Drummond Hollister, with 243 write-in votes, would appear to be the winner. . . ."

Before these last words were out of his mouth, a huge cheer went up from the crowd gathered there in the darkness. Instantly scores of people clamored around Pa and Almeda, shouting and shaking hands and clapping and whooping and hollering. In the middle of it, suddenly Mr. Royce appeared. His smile was gone, and even in the darkness I could see the rage in his eyes.

"I don't know what kind of trick this is, Hollister," he said. "But believe me, you won't get away with it!"

Without waiting for a reply, he spun around and walked back to his buggy. No one took any notice as he turned his horse and cracked his whip and flew back toward town. Nothing ever came of this last threat. There was not a thing he could do. Pa had won the election fair and square!

# CHAPTER 27

## LOOKING PAST THE ELECTION

After the headlong rush of events for the four or five months leading up to the election, the months of November and December of that year seemed like a sudden calm. Like a river tumbling over rocks and through white, foamy rapids, our lives suddenly opened out into a calm pool.

Everyone, myself included, felt like just sitting back and breathing out a sigh of relief. It was good to know there were no more stories I had to write immediately, no more dangers facing anyone, no more elections, no more trips, no more handbills to pass out. The next morning I lay in bed for a long time, just enjoying the quiet. I didn't want to get up, I didn't want to write, I didn't want to think about anything!

The whole town seemed to feel that way. People seemed relaxed, but they were talking plenty about the election results! The men spent a lot of time hanging around the street in front of the Mine and Freight, although we hardly had a customer for three days. They weren't interested in seeing any of *us*, or in doing business. They were waiting to catch sight of their new mayor!

When Pa rode into town that Wednesday afternoon, I knew by the look on his face that he had no idea what was waiting for him. He was such a down-to-earth and humble man that he still didn't realize that he was suddenly a local hero. He had hardly gotten past the first buildings of Miracle Springs when

word began to spread, faster than the time it took him to ride
the rest of the way in. By the time he got off his horse and was
tying the reins to the rail in front of the store, fifty men and
women had gathered around him—shouting, cheering, throwing out questions—with kids running through the streets like
miniature town-criers, telling everybody that the new mayor
was in town!

Pa just looked sheepishly at everybody, confused and not
sure what all the fuss was about. After a minute or so they all
quieted down, as if they were waiting for Pa to make a speech
or something. But when he finally spoke, all he said was, "Tarnation, what are you all raising a ruckus about? I just came to
fetch my wife, and I can't even get through the door!"

———

Almeda wasn't due until April or May, but Katie, who was
due earlier, was starting to show a lot. And once the election
was over, the anticipation of two new babies on their way into
the Hollister-Belle-Parrish clan started to take more of everybody's attention. I could see both Pa and Uncle Nick treating
Katie and Almeda with more tenderness, pampering them
more than usual. Katie still could be reserved and distant, and
every once in a while she would say or do something that made
me wonder whether she liked Almeda at all. Sometimes I saw
a look on Uncle Nick's face as if he might be thinking, "What's
going on inside this lady I married?" Nick tried to be gentle
with her, helping her across the bridge with his hand, or fixing
her some soup when she didn't feel well. Sometimes she'd be
appreciative and smiling, but at other times she seemed to resent it, and would snap, "Let me alone. I can take care of
myself!" Uncle Nick would stomp around muttering, or go off
for a ride or a walk alone in the woods if Katie got after him.
It was obvious he didn't know what to do. Being a husband
was still pretty new to him. But Almeda never seemed to take
it personally or be hurt by it. Once she said to me quietly after
Katie and Uncle Nick had left and we were alone for a minute,
"I know what she's going through, Corrie, and I know how
hard it is."

"What is it?" I asked. "You mean with the baby and feeling sick and all?"

She smiled. "Oh, that upsets our system a bit," she answered, "but there's more to it than that. The Lord is at work in your Aunt Katie's heart, Corrie, and she doesn't like it. We must continue to pray. Her time is coming."

That was all she ever said. But ever after that, when I'd look into Almeda's face when Uncle Nick and Katie were around, or when we'd go up to visit them or to help Katie, I saw an even more tender look in Almeda's eyes. Maybe she was praying at those times too. After what she'd said to me, I noticed Almeda paying all the more attention to Katie, looking for every opportunity possible to help her or do something for her. I wondered if she would say something to Katie about God as she had with me several years before. But as far as I know, nothing was ever said.

In the meantime, more visitors began to show up around our place, men coming to ask Pa's advice about things. They came both to the claim and to the office in town. Sometimes it was about a little thing that didn't have anything to do with Pa, but maybe they figured that since he was mayor and was a man they could trust, he was the one to ask. And once he realized this was going on, something in Pa's bearing began to change. There seemed to be a confidence growing inside him. Around town, people would greet him with, "Hey, Drum!" and he'd wave and answer back. Gradually he seemed to get used to the attention folks paid him and quit minding it so much, as if he realized it was his duty now to be something more to them than he had been before.

# CHAPTER 28

# DIRTY POLITICS

It took some time before we found out the results of the national election. We knew the following week that Mr. Fremont had lost his home state of California, but it was weeks before we found out that he had lost the rest of the country too. James Buchanan had been elected the 15th President of the United States.

By that time I was sure my story had never run in the *Alta*. I was disappointed for the Fremonts, and I didn't know what to think about my story. I was sure it would have helped counteract all the rumors and lies being told about Mr. Fremont during the campaign. And Mr. Kemble had seemed to want the information so badly. I couldn't imagine what had happened. I wrote to Mr. Kemble to find out, but it was well toward the end of November before I got a reply from him.

*Dear Miss Hollister,*

*I understand your concern over your Fremont article, especially after the hard work and dangers you undertook on the* Alta's *behalf. It was a fine bit of legwork you did, and now that I have been able to extract more of the full scope of what happened from your colleague, Mr. O'Flaridy, I realize just what a powerful article it was and how fortunate I am indeed to count you as one of my reporters. I commend you once again for a fine piece of journalism!*

*Unfortunately, as it turned out, I was unable to run the story in the* Alta *prior to the election. Apparently your man Gregory got back to the* Globe *and immediately began trying to cover his tracks with accusations against you and our paper. I received a not-so-friendly visit from the editor of the* Globe, *and he told me that if we tried to run a pro-Fremont piece there was sure to be trouble, for the paper as well as for you. I told him I didn't believe a word of it and that I fully intended to stand by my reporter and run the story. The world needed to hear, I said, that what was being said about John Fremont was nothing but a pack of lies. He left in a huff and I made plans to print your story just as you gave it to me.*

*However, the next day my publisher ordered me to kill the story. "What?" I said. "They didn't get to you, did they?" He didn't say anything except to repeat his order. "Listen," I told him, "the country's got to know the rumors and charges against Fremont are unfounded. It could turn the election!"*

*"It doesn't matter now," he said. "You just kill that story. John Fremont will have to take care of himself without any help from us. If we run that story they could ruin us—both you and me and the paper, do you understand, Kemble? And they could hurt your young reporter friend too. We have no choice. They've made that clear, and I don't intend to see how far they're prepared to back it up."*

*"Goldwin?" I asked.*

*"Goldwin . . . and others," he answered. Then he left the room.*

*So I'm sorry, Miss Hollister, but he left me no choice. My publisher's a strong man, and a major influence in this city. I don't know how they got to him, but whatever they were holding over his head, it must have been powerful. I've never seen him so beaten down and defeated. But it was for your good as well as the paper's that we didn't run it, as much as it galled me to see the* Globe *get away with printing Derrick Gregory's phony interviews. I truly believe your story could have influenced the election, if it had run in time to be picked up by the Ohio and Pennsylvania papers. But sadly, we will never know.*

*Perhaps John Fremont will be able to make another run at the White House in 1860, and we can try to help his cause again. In the meantime, I hope you will be working on some articles for me. You have shown a flair for politics as well as human interest. I would be happy to see you pursue more along that line in the future.*

*O' Flaridy sends his regards. I remain*
*Yours Sincerely,*
*Edward Kemble, Editor*
*San Francisco* Alta

I almost expected my reaction to be one of anger. Most of Mr. Kemble's letters aroused all kinds of hidden emotions in me and put me through all kinds of ups and downs and doubts and questions. But this time I just put down the letter with a deep sense of sadness and regret. It almost confirmed everything Derrick Gregory had told me about politics being a dirty business where everything depended on money and what people wanted out of you rather than truth. Was that really what political reporting boiled down to? If so, then I for one didn't want to have any more to do with it. However flattering Mr. Kemble's words might have been, I would stick to human interest from now on. And as for Robin O'Flaridy's regards— those I could do without!

During the next several days I alternated between being upset, then depressed and disillusioned all over again. I had spent so much time and had invested such effort in that story, not to mention risking my life! And for what? The bad guys had won anyway. The powerful senator had used his influence to get his way and to keep the truth from being printed. A slave supporter would be in the White House for another four years. And all I *thought* I had accomplished seemed wasted. It really made me stop and question why I wanted to be a newspaper writer in the first place.

But then I got to thinking about the *other* election I had been part of. Who could deny that good *had* come through in the Miracle Springs mayor's race? It wasn't that I had much to do with the outcome—I probably hadn't at all. But the truth did come out in the end. The most truthful person, Pa, had won the election. And so in this case at least, politics wasn't a dirty business at all. The good guy had defeated the underhanded banker!

I never did come to much of a conclusion about myself and whether I would do any more writing about politics. But I finally realized that politics itself wasn't necessarily a bad thing. If you're going to run a country or a state or a town you've got to have elections and officials and Presidents. And I was glad that Pa was mayor now rather than Franklin Royce. Maybe what was needed was for good men like him to be in politics, not men like Mr. Royce and Senator Goldwin. I just hoped Mr. Buchanan would be a good man too, and a good President, and that some day someone would get elected who would free the slaves like Mr. Fremont had wanted to do.

I wrote to Ankelita Carter about returning Rayo Rojo to Mariposa. I had wanted to do so before the election but there hadn't been time. I told her about the article being scuttled and how sorry I was for the way the election had turned out. When I heard back from her, shortly before Christmas, she was furious. She said she was sure the election would have turned out different, especially in California, if people had known what she told me. She'd written to the Fremonts before the election and told them about what I was trying to do. She hadn't heard back from them since news of the loss, but she knew what Jessie and Mr. Fremont must be going through, and she said she intended to write them that very day with news of what had happened with the *Alta* story. There was nothing Mr. Fremont could do about it now, but he ought to know what Senator Goldwin had been able to do, even in far off California. She wanted to see me again, whenever it might be possible, and if I wanted to do *another* article on the Fremonts, she would be more than happy to oblige. There was no hurry about getting Rayo Rojo back, but when I was able to come, I should plan to spend at least two or three days with her.

She wrote as if I were her friend, and it set the wheels of my mind in motion again. Why couldn't I do an article on Mr. Fremont about the lies that had been told? It might not win him the election now, but at least it would vindicate his reputation and might help him in the future.

Time would tell. In the meantime, I wanted to think of some less controversial subjects to write about.

# CHAPTER 29

## PREPARATIONS FOR THE HOLIDAYS

Our Christmases always seemed to be times of exciting announcements, high-running emotions, family, friends, guests, food, and the unexpected. The Christmas of 1856 was no exception.

We had been looking forward to Christmas all the month of December. Almeda had such a way of making the holiday a happy time, and of course my sisters and I couldn't have enjoyed anything better than being part of all the preparations. We made decorations out of ribbons and popped corn, colored paper, and greenery cut from the woods, bells and dried berries.

And what Christmas celebration would be complete without a feast, and people to share that feast with? So along with everything else, we were thinking of who to invite to our place for the day. Pa and Almeda always included all five of us kids in most of the talking and discussion that had to do with our family. Sometimes they'd talk alone, walking together, or whispering in low tones in their room late at night, but they included us in everything they could. It really made us all feel that we were a *whole* family. And both of them would include *me* in even a more personal way in their decisions too. To say I had a *friendship* with my own Pa sounds a little funny, but in a way, that's what it was. He *was* my friend! And so was Almeda— friend and mother and an older sister all rolled up into one.

142

And so we talked and planned the Christmas as a family. Of course we intended to invite our friends like Alkali Jones and Rev. Rutledge and the Stansberrys, and of course Uncle Nick and Katie and little Erich. Zack said he'd like to invite Little Wolf and his father, and after a brief glance at Almeda, Pa looked back at Zack and replied, "I think that's a mighty good idea, son. You go right ahead and ask them if they'd join us for the day!"

Pa fell silent for a few moments. I hadn't noticed the look that had come over his face, but when he next spoke I could see in his eyes that he'd gone through an intense struggle just in those brief moments. The tone in his voice spoke much more than the words that came out of his mouth.

"You know, Almeda," he said quietly, "there is someone else we might pray about asking to join us."

"Who's that, Drummond?"

Pa paused again, and when he answered her, though his voice was soft, the words went like an explosion through the room.

"Franklin Royce," he said.

Becky and Zack immediately let out groans, but Almeda's eyes were fixed on Pa with a look of disbelief and happiness at the same time.

"You're right," she said after a moment. "He is a lonely man, with probably no place to go on Christmas."

"It just seems like the right thing to do," Pa added. "I'm not all that anxious to strike up a friendship with him after what he's done. But we have to put the past behind us, and I believe it's got to start with us. One thing's for sure—he's not going to be inviting us to his place anytime soon!"

Almeda laughed. "I think it's a wonderful idea, Drummond!"

The rest of that week before Christmas we did lots of baking—wild huckleberry pies, an *olia podrida* (a stew with a lot of meats and vegetables mixed together), and honeyed ham. Then Christmas morning we baked biscuits, potatoes, carrots, yams, and two pumpkin pies.

There was also a lot of sewing and stitching and trying-on to be done too, everyone pretending they didn't know what it was all for. Almeda made Pa close his eyes to try on the new vest she was making him, telling him to pay no attention to anything that was going on. I did the same for a shirt I was making for Zack. We kept poor Mr. Bosely so busy that week—buying extra bits of linen or cotton fabric, lace, buttons, and thread.

It was so funny to watch Pa going about Christmas business of his own, and with Zack and Tad. Men have such a hard time knowing how to do and make things, especially for wives and sisters and daughters. Most of the preparations at holiday time came from the women. But Pa entered into the spirit of it, and kept his little secrets too, and would sometimes shoot a wink at one of the boys about the things that *they* were planning that none of us knew about. I could tell it made Almeda love him all the more to watch him try to do his part to make it special.

# CHAPTER 30

# A CHRISTMAS DAY TO REMEMBER!

Christmas morning everyone was up at the crack of dawn.

It was one of those crisp, sunny winter days that made me love California so much. And as the day wore on, though it would never get hot, I knew it would warm up enough to draw the fragrances up out of the earth and from the trees and out of the grasses and pinecones and dew. Days like that always made me want to go find a quiet place in the sun where I could just sit down and lean my back up against a tree trunk and read a book or draw or just think.

While Pa stoked up the fire with a new supply of wood and Almeda put the ham in the oven to bake, Tad scurried around making sure the rest of us were up and ready. Then he was off across the creek to fetch Uncle Nick and Aunt Katie to make sure they got down to our place the minute they were dressed. He didn't want to have to wait one second longer than he had to before Pa turned him loose in the pile of packages and presents next to our Christmas tree.

If the giving of gifts at Christmas is an expression of a family's love, then there couldn't have been a greater outpouring than there was that year. Pa gave Zack a beautiful new hand-tooled saddle with a matching whip. If Zack could have carried the saddle around with him all day, he would have. He *did* carry the whip, feeling its tightly wound leather handle, smelling it, examining every inch with his fingers and fine eye. He was truly a horseman, and nothing could have pleased him more.

Almeda gave me a beautifully-bound copy of *The Pilgrim's Progress*, and a new journal. Like Zack, I carried around my two new books most of the day, just looking at them and feeling them.

She and I had made dresses for Emily and Becky. We three girls, with Katie's help, had nearly completed a new quilt for Pa and Almeda's bed, with a big "H" in the middle of it. But we had to give it to them not quite finished, saying we'd get the stitching done later.

There was a new doll for Becky, scarves for all three of us girls, a harmonica for Tad, Pa's new leather vest, and other smaller things—candies, fruits, nuts—as well as what we gave Uncle Nick and Aunt Katie.

Two of the most memorable gifts of the day were given to the two mothers. Almeda had bought a small New Testament. She had been praying a lot for Katie, and trying to find ways to talk to her about her life with the Lord. And so I knew how deeply from the heart the gift of the small book was. But when Katie opened it and saw what was inside the package, she was very quiet for a moment. "Thank you," she finally said, her words stiff and forced. When I glanced over at Almeda, I saw clearly the disappointment on her face from Katie's lack of enthusiasm.

Pa had made Almeda a nice wood shelf for the wall in her kitchen. It had three levels, with a decorative top-piece he'd carved out with a design. Almeda raved excitedly about what fine workmanship it was and all the things she would put in it. But then Pa pulled out one last wrapped package, one he'd kept hidden somewhere.

"Well, you've gotta keep a place on one of the shelves for this," he said as he handed it to her. "This is what gave me the idea of making the shelf in the first place, so you'd have somewhere to put it so you could see it."

She took it from him and opened it. Out came a beautifully painted little china replica of a two-story house, like I'd seen drawn in books and magazines of city buildings in the east.

"I ordered it from one of Bosely's catalogs," Pa said, and I could tell he was excited. "It's called 'Boston Home.' The minute I saw it, I wanted you to have it."

Almeda fought back tears. "Thank you, Drummond," she said finally in a soft voice. "It is beautiful."

"And look there behind," said Pa, taking it from her hand and turning it around, "here's a place for a candle, so it lights up and looks like there's lights in the windows. I hope you like it," he added. "I thought it would remind you of your home back East."

She looked up at Pa, then reached forward and kissed him.

"Whenever I look at it," she said, "it will remind me of how grateful I am to be here with *you* in California!"

Then she stood up and left the house for a few minutes. There *were* tears in her eyes by now. The room was silent for a short spell, then Pa tried to liven things up again.

"Play us a tune on your new mouth organ, Tad, my boy!" he said.

That was all the invitation Tad needed! He started blowing furiously with puckered lips, which was enough to send the rest of us scattering. Pretty soon we were all occupied with looking over our new things, and I didn't even notice when Almeda came back in. I happened to glance up from my book about ten minutes later and there she and Pa were over against one wall trying to find the best place for Pa to nail up her new shelves.

The rest of the morning we spent cooking—Almeda checking on the ham from time to time, the rest of us cutting up vegetables and peeling potatoes. Becky and I mixed up the biscuit dough. Katie and Uncle Nick went back to their place for the morning, until all the others came for dinner in the afternoon.

Alkali Jones was the first to arrive, and as always he kept things pretty lively the rest of the day. Then Rev. Rutledge and Harriet and Hermon Stansberry came, all together, Hermon riding his horse behind the carriage. When the minister helped

Miss Stansberry down, I'd never seen him so gentle with anyone. Of course with her crippled leg, she needed assistance
getting in and out of carriages and climbing steps. But he took
hold of her arm so firmly, yet with such a kind look in his eye,
I could tell she felt really safe. It was easy to see that he cared
a great deal for her.

About half an hour later Little Wolf rode up with Mr. Lame
Pony, each of them on beautiful horses. Little Wolf always
seemed to be riding a different animal, always spirited but well
behaved, always groomed and shining. It was obvious the Indian father and son took great pride in their animals, and loved
them as if they were part of their family.

Pa and Lame Pony shook hands, and Pa made every effort
to make him feel welcome and at home with us. After tying up
his horse, Little Wolf walked over to see me and Zack. We
chatted a while, then he said, "This is a hard thing for my
father. But the more he knows your father, the more he will
trust him."

"Look," I said, "it won't take long." I pointed to Pa, already leading Lame Pony toward the stables to show him our
horses. Pa had his arm slung around the Indian's shoulder and
was talking good-naturedly. I knew he would win Lame Pony
over and make him a friend in no time. Pa was like that with
people nowadays.

When Katie and Uncle Nick came back down from their
place not too long after that, however, I wondered if the spirit
of Christmas was going to be spoiled. Little Wolf had been
around enough that Katie had gotten used to him, although
she never spoke to him or was very friendly. But now when Pa
introduced her to Little Wolf's father, she was noticeably hostile.

"Nick, you know our neighbor from over the ridge," said
Pa as he and Lame Pony walked toward them as they approached from the bridge over the creek.

"Best horses in California," replied Uncle Nick, giving him
a shake of his hand. "Nice to see you here, Jack."

"Katie," Pa went on, turning to her, "this is Jack Lame

Pony, Little Wolf's father. Jack, this is—"

Lame Pony nodded his head in acknowledgment toward Katie as Pa spoke, but before Pa could complete the introduction, Katie turned toward Uncle Nick and abruptly said, loud enough for everyone to hear, "What's *he* doing here?"

"He's our friend and neighbor, that's what," answered Uncle Nick hastily, obviously embarrassed by her rude comment, and a little riled at her at the same time.

"Well, neither of them are *my* friends," shot back Katie, and then marched off toward the house, leaving the three men standing there, Pa and Uncle Nick mortified at her behavior. And poor Lame Pony! What was *he* supposed to think after such an outburst?

But Pa didn't wait for the dust to settle around Katie's words. He said something about wanting to show Lame Pony something at the mine, and then I heard Uncle Nick trying to apologize for Katie, and adding something about women doing funny things when they're carrying young'uns. By dinnertime everything seemed to be smoothed over, although Katie was pretty sullen all day.

None of the rest of us could understand why she was so prejudiced against Indians, especially with what a good friend Little Wolf had been to our whole family. But we had learned to accept that Katie didn't think like the rest of us. She'd never been very friendly toward Rev. Rutledge either, as much as she knew he meant to the rest of us all. And although she was usually pretty tolerant, every once in a while she'd make some comment that let everyone know how ridiculous she thought trying to live like a Christian was.

"Going to church is one thing," she said once. "And though I don't have much use for it myself, I don't mind folks going themselves. But all this talking about God in between times, and praying, and trying to act religious about everything else you do—that's just taking it too far. Church is one thing, but you've got to live life without trying to bring God into every little thing. I've got no use for that kind of thinking. It's just not natural."

Almeda had been praying for her and hoping to find opportunities to share with her how she felt. I didn't know what Uncle Nick thought of it all. He never said much.

Mr. Royce was the last one to arrive, all alone in his expensive black buggy. Pa and Almeda greeted him as if he were an old family friend, and the look on his face made it clear he didn't know *what* to make of it. What he thought of getting the invitation in the first place I don't know, but being greeted and welcomed as a friend was altogether too much! Maybe he was so used to folks being suspicious of him that courtesy and friendliness made him uncomfortable. He was pretty reserved the whole day, yet entered into the spirit of the occasion as much as he was able to.

Once everybody had arrived, we went inside the house. The whole place was filled with delicious smells! The table was set as fancy as we had been able to make it, but Pa asked everyone to sit around in the big room where the chairs were rather than at the table.

"Almeda says the ham still has about half an hour," he said, "so that's why I arranged the chairs out here. There's some things I want us to talk about before we get down to the business of the dinner."

Everyone took a seat and it got quiet. Pa stood up in front and everybody waited for him to continue.

"Ever since me and the kids got together four years back," Pa began when everyone was situated, "we've kept up the tradition of reading the Christmas story together, kind of in memory of our Aggie, the kids' ma, and in memory of what this day's supposed to be all about."

Pa turned behind him and took down Ma's white Bible and flipped through the pages.

"This is our fifth Christmas together in California," he went on. "And, Avery, with all respect to you being our preacher, I think I'm going to keep this privilege all to myself today."

"Wonderful, Drummond!" said Rev. Rutledge with a smile. "It is a great blessing for me to be able to listen to you."

"So I'd like to invite all the rest of you to listen, though I guess I'm mostly reading this to the five of you kids. And you be sure to remember your Ma when I read, 'cause she got us going with this tradition, and I don't doubt for a minute that it's on account of her prayers that we're all together like this, doing our best to walk with the Lord like she did."

He drew in a sigh. I looked at Almeda out of the corner of my eye as he spoke. The radiant smile on her face was full of such love! I knew there was no confusion in her mind—or in any one else's—over the love Pa had for both her *and* Ma, and the special place both the women God had given him held in different corners of his heart.

"*And it came to pass in those days,*" began Pa with the familiar words out of Luke, "*That there went out a decree from Ceasar Augustus, that all the world should be taxed. And this taxing was first made when Cyrenius was governor of Syria. And all went to be taxed, every one into his own city. And Joseph also went up from Galilee, out of the city of Nazareth, into Judaea, unto the city of David, which is called Bethlehem; (because he was of the house and lineage of David:) To be taxed with Mary his espoused wife, being great with child. And so it was, that, while they were there, the days were accomplished that she should be delivered. And she brought forth her firstborn son, and wrapped him in swaddling clothes, and laid him in a manger; because there was no room for them in the inn. And there were in the same country shepherds abiding in the field, keeping watch over their flock by night. And, lo, an angel of the Lord came upon them . . .*"

As he read the story, Pa's voice filled the room. Everyone sat quiet, not just listening, but *absorbing* his words. It was a different voice than the one who had read the Christmas story four years earlier, just after we had arrived in California. This was the voice of a man of confidence, afraid of nothing—not even afraid to stand up and talk to other people about his God and the birth of His Son. Just listening to him read—well, it was no wonder that the people around here had come to respect and admire him. Now it was *Pa* reading from the Scriptures, and Rev. Rutledge sitting and listening with a smile on his face, as if he was proud of Pa and what he was becoming. Pa's voice seemed to have a *power* in it, even though he was reading softly.

As we sat there listening, I looked at the faces around me. What did Mr. Lame Pony and Little Wolf think of our Christmas religious practices? Franklin Royce's eyes were fixed on Pa as if he was trying to make sense of this man who was extending forgiveness toward someone who had done his best to destroy him. I saw something in that lonely banker's face, and a little spark of love for the man stirred in my heart.

Alkali Jones sat there more still than I'd ever seen him. He was staring down at the floor, so deep in thought he looked like he was a thousand miles and forty years away. I wondered what memories he was re-living as Pa read. Had *his* mother read him this passage as a child? What *was* going through that old mind? And Katie—she sat there, still looking solemn. I couldn't read a thing in her eyes. But I knew she was thinking.

Pa's voice pervaded the room, and the very sound was weaving a mood upon us. I don't think I've ever been so aware of what it might be like for God to be speaking through a man as I was that day. I felt as if God himself was telling us the story of Jesus' birth, and using Pa's voice to do it. It was hard to imagine that Katie had a hard time believing, or that Mr. Royce had ever been Pa and Almeda's enemy, or that there could possibly be enmity between Indians and white people. There was such a good feeling in the room, a sense of oneness. The story of Jesus' birth was so alive that we were all sitting on the edge of our seats to hear how it would all turn out.

"*. . . And when eight days were accomplished for the circumcising of the child, his name was called JESUS, which was so named of the angel before he was conceived in the womb.*"

Pa stopped, and the room remained silent. Pa closed the Bible, and then after a short pause started talking again.

"I don't aim to start infringing on our good Reverend's territory. That'd be just a different kind of claim jumping, wouldn't you say, Avery? But it strikes me that a few more words might be in order on a day like this. Since this is my house and you all are our guests, then I reckon nobody'll mind if I take the liberty of delivering them myself."

A few people chuckled, and everybody relaxed in their seats. "You go right ahead, Drummond," said Rev. Rutledge. "I'm sure these good folks are sick of my preaching and will welcome the change!"

"Well, I thank you," replied Pa, "but I ain't gonna preach, and I don't aim to keep them as long as *you* do on Sundays!"

More laughter followed.

"I guess I just figured this was a good time for me to say a thing or two about what Christmas means to me," said Pa. "And what my family means. Somehow you need to say these kinds of things to other people once in a while for it to get all the way down to where it's supposed to go. So I'm going to tell you who're here with us today."

He paused, took a breath, then continued.

"Christmas is a time for giving and good food and friends," Pa said. "And for the youngsters there's always some toys and gifts and candy. So now and then we can get our eyes off what's the *true* meaning of this day. On this day God's Son, the little baby Jesus, was born. We need to remember that, because without his coming to the earth when he did, and living his life and then giving it up for us, there wouldn't be any life for the rest of us.

"But then I've been thinking, there really *is* something special about families at Christmas. So I just want to say how thankful I am that God gave me this family of mine—every one of these kids that Aggie gave me, God bless her. And for Almeda and the one that she's bearing right now, and for Nick and Katie and their family. I just feel about as full and blessed as any man ought to have a right to feel. And I'm thankful for the rest of you too, because you're what you might call a part of our bigger family.

"So, God bless you all—thank you for sharing Christmas with us. Let's not forget that Jesus was born on this day a long time ago. And let's never forget that good friends and family are what makes this world a pretty special place."

Pa stopped and sat down. In earlier years he might have shown a little embarrassment at making a speech like that. But not this time.

"Amen to every word, Drummond!" said Rev. Rutledge. "We are blessed to be part of your family, and that you are part of all of us too."

Pa nodded while a few other comments filtered around.

"And now, might I be permitted a word or two also?" the minister added, glancing first at Pa and then at Almeda.

"Of course, Avery," said Almeda.

"This won't take long," said Rev. Rutledge, standing up and then clearing his throat. He sent a glance and smile in Miss Stansberry's direction.

"I have a little announcement to make," he went on, "and I—that is, we—thought it would be nice to wait and tell you all about it all at once. And what more fitting time and place than here on Christmas day?"

He took in a big gulp of air, then plunged ahead. "And what I've got to tell you is this: Harriet and I are engaged to be married. . . ."

I think he was going to say something more, but before he could get another word out of his mouth, Almeda was on her feet nearly shrieking with delight.

"Oh, that's wonderful!" she exclaimed, hurrying over to Miss Stansberry and taking both her hands in a tight clasp.

In the meantime Pa and Uncle Nick had joined the minister and were shaking his hand and slapping him on the shoulder. In another minute everyone else was on their feet joining the hubbub and well-wishing.

"Couldn't keep from stealing the show, eh, Reverend?" laughed Uncle Nick.

Rev. Rutledge knew he was being kidded only because of how happy everyone was for him, and joined in another loud round of laughter with the men. His boisterous laugh could even be heard above Alkali Jones' *hee, hee, hee*! The fact that Pa and Uncle Nick and Avery Rutledge were laughing and joking and talking together like they were showed how much things had changed in those four years since our first Christmas together. Who could have foreseen it all?

I glanced over at Almeda. She'd been talking with Miss

Stansberry, but then looked over across the room at the men. For once she wasn't looking at Pa, but at Rev. Rutledge. She had tears in her eyes. She had cared for him, in a different way from Pa. And I knew his happiness meant a lot to her.

But she only watched the celebrating men a moment, then clapped her hands a few times and raised her voice above the din.

"Enough everyone!" she cried. "You can do the rest of your visiting and carrying on at the table. It's time to eat, and the food's hot! Come now, find your places!"

# CHAPTER 31

## THE FEAST

What a group that was!

Pa stood up by his chair at the head of the table and raised his hands to quiet everyone down for the prayer.

"Before you take your seats," said Pa, "let's all bow our heads and give thanks to God."

Everyone calmed down. A quiet settled over the room.

"God, we thank you for this day," said Pa solemnly. "Help us all never to forget what it means. And help us every day of the year to remember how much you loved us, and the whole world, to give us your Son. And thank you for family and friends, and the good food and fellowship you give us together. Amen."

"Okay, everyone," said Almeda, walking toward the stove while everyone got into their seats, "we've got ham and sweet potatoes, biscuits, stew, vegetables, and a special treat that Lame Pony and Little Wolf fixed for us—what did you call them, Jack?"

"*Pozoles*," answered Little Wolf's father. "That is Mexican word. Little Wolf and me, we just say pig's feet."

"So all of you try one of Jack's *pozoles*," added Almeda—handing two large pewter platters, one to Pa, one to Mr. Royce—"while we start this food around the table. But save room for the pies!"

It didn't take long for everyone's plate to be piled high, and within five minutes the sounds of eating and conversation and laughter echoed around the table. There was a harmony in it, almost like music. I sat with Becky on one side and Little Wolf on the other, trying to listen to Mr. Jones on the other side of Becky and Rev. Rutledge a little further away. I was especially curious about what Pa and the banker were talking about. So the whole meal for me was a mixed-together jumble of half-conversations, laugher that I didn't know the cause of, words, smiles, and always passing food and exhortations from Almeda to eat up on the one hand but to save place for dessert on the other.

Alkali Jones was in good form, as always, and must have told two or three of his famous "totally" unbelievable stories. But as interesting as they always were, on this day I found myself most eager to hear what was going on across the table, and I strained to listen whenever I could.

"Glad you could be with us today, Franklin," Almeda had said.

"I must say your invitation came as a surprise."

"Why's that?" said Pa. But when the banker turned toward him to answer, I couldn't hear what he said.

". . . put it in the past," I heard Pa say next. "Learn to live like neighbors and brothers. . . ."

"What my husband is talking about, Franklin, is forgiveness," put in Almeda. "Don't you think it's time to let bygones be bygones?"

Mr. Royce said something, but I couldn't hear it. He didn't seem altogether comfortable with the direction of the conversation. It was as if he didn't know how to react to it being so personal.

"That's exactly what I was trying to say," added Pa. "I figure if I'm gonna be mayor, even though you wanted to be when this whole thing started, then I've got to be your mayor too. And that means doing the best I can for you just like everyone else. And so we figured the best place to start was to invite you to our home and shake your hand like a friend and neighbor, and say, 'Merry Christmas, let's put the past behind us.' "

". . . kind of you—kind of you both," Mr. Royce said, "certainly more hospitality than anyone else in this town has ever shown me."

"We want to be your friend, Franklin," said Almeda, and although I was too far away to see into her eyes, I knew from her tone what kind of look was on her face.

"Even though I tried to put you out of business and have opened a store to compete against you? A Christmas meal may be one thing, but do you seriously think I can believe you want to be my friend?"

"Believe what you want, Royce," answered Pa, and now it was quieting down a bit around the table as more of us were listening to this most interesting conversation. "Whether you can understand it or not, we're supposed to be your neighbor and to try to do good to you and to love you. That's what the Lord God tells his folks to do, and it don't matter what they do back to you in return. So Almeda and I've been praying for you, and we want to do good for you however we can. I don't reckon I've been too neighborly to you in the past, and I hope you will find it in your heart to forgive me for that. In the mean time, I aim to change. I aim to forgive you for what you've done, to keep praying for you, and to do my best for you however I can."

He stopped, and the table was silent for just a moment. Mr. Royce just shook his head and muttered something at the same time as Alkali Jones let out with a cackle, "Hee, hee, hee! If that don't beat all! Mayor and preacher all rolled up into one!"

Then Tad asked for another biscuit and Almeda started passing food again, and pretty soon the conversation was once more at a loud pitch, although I never heard any more serious goings-on between Pa and Mr. Royce.

The only person who didn't enter much into the lively talk was Katie. She hardly said a word, and didn't seem to be enjoying the Christmas celebration at all. She was either feeling mighty poorly, or else had something brewing in her mind.

When the meal was done, the men went outside to light pipes and talk about horses and weather and whatever else men talk about. We girls and Miss Stansberry and Almeda got busy cleaning everything up, talking and chatting away, mostly about Rev. Rutledge's and Miss Stansberry's surprise news, and when they were planning the wedding and what kind of dress she would wear. Katie still didn't participate much. Claiming to be tired, she left and went back up to their place.

An hour or so later, when we had the place looking tidy again, the men came back in and we cut into the huckleberry and pumpkin pies. Uncle Nick had a piece of pie, then took little Erich and went to check on Katie.

By this time even Jack Lame Pony seemed to be feeling real comfortable and he and Pa and Rev. Rutledge were talking freely. Hermon was asking lots of questions about the horse-breaking work they did and was even planning to go up to their place in a day or two to look for a new horse. Zack and Little Wolf and Tad were off shooting their guns. Franklin Royce was even entering in a little to the conversation, though I still don't think I'd seen him smile the whole day. But at least the scowl that I'd always associated with him was gone from his face, and every once in a while I'd hear him say something to one of the other men. He seemed a little out of his element, however, with the others talking about such man-things as working and mining and shooting and horse-taming, and him there with his suit and white hands that hardly looked like they'd seen a day of work. But you almost had to admire him for entering in as much as he did.

Mr. Royce was the first to leave, late in the afternoon, but the others stayed a while longer, drinking coffee and nibbling now and then at the ham or one of the pies.

Around dusk, Uncle Nick and Katie and little Erich came back down the path, holding a lantern. The most memorable part of that Christmas was about to begin.

# CHAPTER 32

## KATIE'S OUTBURST

Katie was still quiet and sober. Everyone greeted her kindly, but she didn't say much. Uncle Nick looked a little nervous, and would glance at her now and then, although he entered into the spirit of the evening with everyone. I wondered if they had an argument, because they didn't say much to each other.

Everyone but Mr. Royce was still there. The day cooled off quickly. Pa stoked up the fire, and we sat around the hearth talking and chatting. I don't think I'd ever seen Rev. Rutledge so jovial and in such high spirits. Even he and Alkali Jones laughed together more than once about something one or the other said. Mr. Lame Pony was a little more reserved when Katie got back, and every once in a while I'd catch a glimpse of him glancing over at her, probably wondering what she thought. But he stuck around, visiting with the men, and I was glad of that. I hoped he and Pa might become friends!

As the evening progressed, the talk got more subdued and quiet, even serious at times. How different Pa was! He talked with Rev. Rutledge about spiritual things on equal footing, not as a miner talking to a preacher.

"What do you think, Avery," Pa was saying, "about how God lets folks know what he wants them to do?"

"Do you mean how he speaks, how he guides in our lives?"

"Yeah. How can you tell if God's telling you something or if it's just your own thoughts? Like me being mayor. I figure something ought to be different about my mayoring if I say I'm

160

trying to follow God in what I do. It ought to be different than me just following my own nose like most folks do, and like I spent most of my life doing."

"That's exactly what being a Christian is, Drummond, bringing God into all you do."

"It's easier for you, because religion's your business, ain't it, Reverend?" piped in Uncle Nick.

"Just the opposite, Nick," replied Rev. Rutledge, turning toward him. "Maybe you're right in one way," he added slowly. "It is easier for me to *talk* about things of God because people expect it of me. But it's no easier for me to have God's attitudes inside than anyone else. And, you know, I sometimes think being a preacher is a handicap."

"How's that?"

"Because my very presence gets it into people's minds that there is a difference between religious and non-religious people. Like I said, they expect me to be religious. After all, I'm a preacher, I get paid to talk about God. I can never go into any situation, any discussion, any group of people and just be my-self—Avery Rutledge, a man with feelings and thoughts like everyone else."

The others were silent for a minute. Even the quiet showed that what Rev. Rutledge said was true, and that they *hadn't* thought of him as anything but a preacher. I knew that was true about me. The only ones among us who had really seen him as a *person* beneath the minister were probably Almeda and Miss Stansberry.

"I reckon you're right, Avery," said Pa after a minute. "That is how folks see you, and that's me too. I reckon maybe I owe you an apology."

"Think nothing of it, Drum," laughed Rev. Rutledge. "I wasn't looking for sympathy, only telling you how it is with me."

"Still, I aim to take your words to heart. So if I ever forget and start talking to you like you're only a preacher, and you need me to be a friend just as one man to another, then you stop me and say something. I want you to do that, you hear, Avery?"

"Agreed," smiled Rev. Rutledge, and I could tell Pa's words meant more to him that he was letting on.

"That goes for me too, Reverend," added Uncle Nick. "You can count on the two of us as your friends, whether it's preacher-business or not."

"I thank you too, Nick."

Alkali Jones and Mr. Lame Pony and all the rest of us were watching and listening to this exchange with a sense of wonder. Men rarely talk honestly and about their feelings with one another, and we'd never heard these three men talk like that. I knew what Almeda was feeling. I didn't even have to look at her. And I suppose something of the same mood was upon all of us. Christmas had brought a gift nobody had been looking for, the realization that these men weren't just "acquaintances" who got together for dinner, but *friends*.

"Okay then, well *I* got a question fer ye," piped in Mr. Jones, to everyone's surprise. I'd never heard a single word even hinting at religion from his mouth. Heads turned toward him. "How *do* you figure to bring God into yer mayoring, Drum? Sounds like a kinda crazy notion if ye ask me."

"I don't know, Alkali," Pa answered. "That's why I was asking the Reverend here. But there *oughta* be a way to do things different if you're trying to walk with God."

"So whatcha got in mind, Drum?" Mr. Jones asked again. Still he hadn't let out one of his cackling laughs. He seemed genuinely interested in the answer.

"I don't know. I figured maybe if there was something I had to do, or some decision to make that affected the town, I ought to pray about it, or maybe get together with some of the rest of you and Avery here, and try to find out what the Lord wants to happen. It seems like that'd be a better way to go about things than just barging ahead and doing whatever I think of to do. Nick and I did that for a lot of years, and I can't say as it always turned out so good. Maybe it's time I tried to learn a new way of going about things. The idea's just a little new to me. It'll take some getting used to. I don't know my way around too well yet with thinking like this."

"None of us do," said Almeda, speaking now for the first time. "Look at how long I've been trying to live as a Christian, and yet only a few months ago there I was out chasing my dream of being mayor without ever stopping to ask what God or my husband might have to say in the matter."

"It is easy to hitch our own horse to the wagon instead of letting God be the horse and us being the wagon."

"That's a good one, Reverend," laughed Mr. Jones. "Hee, hee, hee!"

"You could put that in your next sermon, Avery," added Pa.

Now it was Zack's turn to get into the discussion. "I'm not sure I see what you mean about the horses and wagon, Rev. Rutledge," he said. The serious expression on his face showed he was really trying to grasp the deeper meaning.

"I was only saying that sometimes we've got to stop and take a look at who's doing the leading and who's doing the following," replied the minister.

The puzzled look on Zack's face didn't disappear.

"Come on, Avery," said Pa good-naturedly. "If the boy takes after his Pa, he's likely a little thick-headed." As Pa said it he shot a wink in Zack's direction to show he meant only fun. "He's gonna need more explanation than that."

"You don't want me to preach a sermon, do you, Drum? You've got to be careful what kind of openings you give a preacher, you know."

Pa and the rest of us laughed.

"Don't try to fool us, Reverend," laughed Uncle Nick. "You'll take any chance you can get to convert us sinners! Remember that first Christmas in town at Almeda's?"

A huge roar of laughter followed. Now that they *were* friends, they all remembered that awkward discussion around the dinner table with affection for each other.

"I *did* do some preaching at you that day, didn't I!"

"I never wanted to see your face again," said Pa, still laughing.

"I figured it'd be up to me to save the new minister's life,

164

hee, hee, hee!" said Mr. Jones. "I'd never seen ol' Drum so riled up!"

"Well, those times are all over now," said Pa, "and I for one am thankful for that. I was a plumb fool about a lot of things back then, and I don't want to remember it any more than I have to. So on with your sermon, Avery. Tell us about horses and wagons. We're all waiting."

"Are you sure? You know what I'm like on Sundays. Once you get me going, I can't stop!"

"Course we're sure. You still wondering about your question, son?"

"Yeah," answered Zack. "I'd like to know what you have to say, Rev. Rutledge."

"You listen to these men, Avery," said Almeda almost sternly. "They are all your friends, and they *want* the benefit of your experience and insights."

Rev. Rutledge took in a long breath. "All right," he said. "I suppose you asked for it. But I'll try to make it a *short* sermon."

"Agreed," said Pa. He looked at me with a quick smile and wink, as if to say, *Bet me, eh, Corrie! He'll never keep it short!*

"I've always thought the horse and wagon picture perfectly illustrated our relationship with God," Rev. Rutledge began. "It's easy to talk about what we call 'following the Lord,' but how we actually go about living through the day is much different. In practice, we try to be the horse, and we drag God along behind us as if he were the wagon. When it comes to deciding where to go and how fast to go and which forks in the road to take, *we* lead the way, just like a horse pulling a wagon.

"What God wants, of course, is that we allow him to take the lead and let *him* be the horse. He can do a better job of leading than we can. He knows how fast to go, which roads to take. Our responsibility as Christians is to follow."

"How do you follow horse you not see?" said Mr. Lame Pony, speaking up for the first time in a long while. He had been listening to everything intently.

"That is both the difficulty and challenge of life as a Christian," replied Rev. Rutledge. "It is no easy task. We have to unlearn a lot of habits because our natural inclination is to just gallop off, like Drummond said a while ago, following our *own* nose. That's the way we're made—independent. When Drummond says to himself, 'I want to find out what *God* wants me to do about this instead of what *I* might have thought to do,' he changes the whole order of his life around. He says, 'I'm going to become a wagon now, and stop being the horse.' And it takes a great deal of practice because we're not used to thinking that way. At least most adults aren't. I suppose children follow their parents when they are young. But then once they get out on their own, they take charge of their own lives. The way God really intended it, however, is for adulthood just to mean that we change horses—from letting our parents do the leading in our lives to letting God lead. It's a hard thing to do—especially because, as Jack says, we often cannot see the horse. We don't know what God might be saying to us about which path to take here or there. It takes a lot of practice, many new habits. It's a challenge that lasts a lifetime."

He fell silent and nobody spoke for a few seconds.

"Do you see what I mean, Zack?" Rev. Rutledge added. "I don't suppose I was real specific about *how* it all works. That's something God has to show every person individually, because he leads all of us on different paths and in different ways. But do you see what I mean about the principle of the horse leading the wagon?"

"Yes, sir," replied Zack.

"So in answer to my original question," said Pa, "about how God lets us know what we're to do, you're telling me that you don't exactly know what he's gonna be saying to me, but that I have to keep listening anyway so I don't accidentally get out in front of the horse, is that it?"

"Like I did before the election," added Almeda.

"I suppose that's about it," answered Rev. Rutledge with a smile. "An answer that maybe isn't an answer you can do much with until the time comes when you have to ask God for yourself what he's saying to you."

I found myself thinking back to the words of his sermon about how God speaks to us through our thoughts, and about pointing our thoughts and prayers toward God so that he could point his toward us. But before I had a chance to think too much about it, Tad's voice broke the silence.

"Who's driving the wagon?" he said.

Everyone laughed.

"That's the trouble with any illustration," said Rev. Rutledge. "There's always someplace where the parallel doesn't work. Maybe God is driving the wagon, and the horses are Jesus or the Holy Spirit. They're who we're supposed to be following, while our heavenly Father directs everything. It's difficult for it to make exact sense. But I think we all see the principle involved in trying to apply Proverbs 3:6: 'In all thy ways acknowledge him'—that's the part of letting him be the horse, the driver, the guide of our lives—'and he shall direct thy paths.' But thank you for your question, Tad. We need young fellows like you to keep us on our toes."

The whole conversation had been lively and warm. Just from the looks on their faces, I could tell everyone felt involved and felt the same thing I did, that it was all the more special this time since the men were open and talking freely with each other. Everyone except Katie, that is. She had been sitting the whole time a little ways off from the rest. I didn't want to look at her, but out of the corner of my eye I could see that she wasn't enjoying it. I couldn't tell if she was sick or angry. She'd had a sour look on her face all day. I felt bad for her not feeling well on Christmas.

Pretty soon Almeda got up and made some fresh coffee, and the conversation picked up again in other directions.

Little Erich was waddling around talking to himself. I listened more closely and heard the words, "God drive wagon . . . God make horse go." Just then Uncle Nick walked by and scooped his son up and tossed him up into the air.

"What's that you're saying, boy?" he said, catching him and burying his face in the plump little belly.

Erich just giggled.

"He was talking about God driving the wagon," I said. "He must have heard what Rev. Rutledge said."

"A little preacher in the making, that's what you've got, Nick," said Almeda with a smile as she held out a cup of coffee for him.

"That'd be a mighty hard one for my father to imagine!" laughed Nick. "Why the very thought of it—"

He never finished his sentence. Katie had had enough, and was suddenly on her feet.

"The thought of it's enough to make me completely sick!" she yelled. "You stay away from my son with any more of your talk of making him a preacher, do you hear, Almeda! And as for you," she added, spinning around and glaring at me, "you mind your own business, Corrie!"

In an instant there was silence in the whole house.

"Now wait a minute, Katie," said Uncle Nick, trying to calm her down. "They didn't mean no harm. There's no call to go yelling at—"

"You stay out of it, you big lout!" she snapped back at him. "You're the worst of the lot, talking about horses and wagons and God and the Bible like there was anything to any of it. It's all such ridiculous trash, you talking away with that minister and that Indian like you're some saint! You big hypocrite! I know you better than anyone here, and I daresay *you're* not holy!"

"Just you quiet down a minute! Just because you're not feeling so good doesn't give you the right—"

"I'm feeling fine!" Katie retorted, shouting louder now. All the rest of us were shocked silent. It was terrible to be in the middle of such an argument, especially with her having just yelled at me and Almeda, and now pouring out all her anger on Uncle Nick. "I'm not going to quiet down. I've been quiet too long! All this talk about God and religion—I hate it! I can't stand it one second more! Hypocrites, that's what you all are, and you're the biggest fool of them all, Nick, if you believe one word of all that! I'm getting out of here!"

She grabbed little Erich out of Uncle Nick's arms, and

turned around for the door before anyone could say a word.

"Katie, you just wait," said Uncle Nick, going after her. "You may be able to say what you want to me. But you ain't got no right to go shouting at Corrie and Almeda, or calling the minister or anyone else names. If you're bound and determined to go, then you owe them an apology."

"An apology! The only thing I'll apologize for is coming back down here at all. I should have stayed home! You and this family of yours are nothing but a pack of religious do-gooders, and I hate every bit of it!"

She was out the door with the final words trailing behind her. The door slammed in Uncle Nick's face with a loud crash. He opened it and went after her, leaving the rest of us in stunned silence. The only sounds in the whole room were the faint noise of the fire and the boiling water on the stove.

# CHAPTER 33

# A TALK ABOUT GOD'S TIMING

Almeda was still standing there holding the cup of coffee she had meant for Uncle Nick. Her face was deathly white. I suppose mine was too, after what Katie had said to both of us. But neither of us felt anger, only hurt and sadness to find out what Katie had been keeping inside all this time.

Slowly Pa got up, walked over, took the cup from Almeda's hand, and led her to a chair. "Don't think anything of it," he said. "It wasn't you she was upset at."

Almeda nodded and sat down. "I know," she said. She took in a breath and let out a long sigh. "Poor Katie," she said softly. "She's got so much turmoil inside, and so many mixed up ideas. She thinks God is her enemy, when really he's the only source of life she's ever going to find."

"Why don't you tell her that?" I suggested.

"Now?" replied Almeda, looking over at me. "Oh no, Corrie. She's in no frame of mind to hear it now—especially from me. Right now she needs some time to cool off and settle her mind down. And I'm sure she and Nick will have to work some things through after this, and he needs to be the one standing beside her."

"But she needs to know God's not at all like what she thinks."

"All in good time, Corrie," said Pa. "God can't be rushed in what he's about with people. Look at me. Sometimes it takes a good long while for him to break through the outer layers

169

people have got up all around them. And from what I know about Katie, I reckon she's got a few for him to break."

"That doesn't sound too pleasant," I said.

Rev. Rutledge went to stand next to Pa. A look of deep concern filled his face.

"Pleasantness isn't always what the Lord is after, Corrie," he said. "His purposes are beyond what someone feels— whether they're happy or sad on a given day. He's after hearts and lives he can get inside of and possess more than he's after making a person happy."

Almeda let out a sigh. "I think we need to pray for our dear Katie," she said softly, then looked up at Pa.

He nodded, then sat down and immediately started to pray. I'd never heard Pa pray for another person like that. He seemed totally unconcerned about everybody else in the room listening. And everybody joined in silently, I could tell, even though only Pa and Almeda and Rev. Rutledge actually prayed out loud.

"Lord, we ask you to take care of Nick and Katie, and to calm Katie down so she can see how it really is with all of us."

"Oh, yes, God," Almeda went on. "And let her see how it is with our Father. Let her see that you love her, and that our lives are deeper and richer because we live them with you."

A short silence followed, then the minister prayed.

"Heavenly Father, we join together in asking for your touch to be upon Nick and Katie and their small family—right now, even as we pray. Give Nick the words to say to soothe and comfort his dear wife. And we pray that in your own way and time, you would draw Katie and open her heart to the influences of your life and love."

"Give us opportunities to show her that love, Lord," added Almeda. "Let your Spirit flow out from us to her. Help Katie to know that we do love her."

"Amen," said Rev. Rutledge.

As the room fell silent, gradually some of the others began getting ready to go. The mood of the wonderful Christmas we'd spent together was broken, and no one seemed inclined to try to be jovial any longer.

Hermon Stansberry got up and slowly put on his coat. Little Wolf and Lame Pony got up also and gathered their hats and coats.

"I suppose we ought to be heading back to town as well," said Rev. Rutledge, smiling toward Miss Stansberry. "But we will be in prayer for the situation here."

"Thank you, Avery," said Pa, shaking his hand. "And thanks for being part of our Christmas."

"*Thank you,* Drummond," rejoined Miss Stansberry.

"Oh, and we are so happy for the two of you!" added Almeda.

The minister and schoolteacher smiled. Almeda gave them each a big hug, and Pa led them to the door. In another few moments only our family was left inside, and everything was quiet. It had been a wonderful Christmas, but suddenly none of us felt very much of the Christmas spirit. Nobody said anything as we slowly gathered around the fire. Katie was weighing heavily on our hearts.

A few minutes later, Uncle Nick came back through the door.

"Well, I apologize to you all for what happened," he said with a sigh, taking off his hat and plopping down in a chair.

"Think nothing of it, Nick," said Pa. "It wasn't your fault. Just one of those things."

"I didn't make it any better by trying to shush her up. I shoulda just kept my mouth shut. But it's done now. I just wish I coulda said something to the others, though I did see the minister and Harriet outside."

"I'll go talk to Little Wolf and his father tomorrow if you'd like," said Zack.

"Would you, boy?" said Uncle Nick. "I'd be obliged to you if you did. You give them my apologies. That'd mean a lot to me."

"Sure, Uncle Nick."

Uncle Nick sighed again. He was really looking sad and downcast, more than I'd ever seen him.

"It's going to work itself right in the end, Nick," said Almeda after a bit, reaching out and laying a hand on his arm. "This is often the way God works. The storm has to come to clear the sky, and the rain falls to bring life. God is at work in your wife, Nick."

"I don't know how you can figure that, Almeda. She hates any mention of God. Didn't you hear what she said—she was sitting here stewing and fretting and getting more and more annoyed at all our talk."

"Those are only surface reactions, Nick. Down inside, God's Spirit is moving, making her think, and—I believe with all my heart—drawing her. The more people resist and argue against God, and the more they dislike hearing Christians talk about the way their lives are *with* God, the more they are actually being drawn by God. The resistance is a natural human tendency when we feel change in the wind blowing toward us."

"Hmm, I reckon I see what you mean," replied Uncle Nick slowly. "Though I can't say as I could picture Katie *ever* having anything good to say about religion. She can't stand any mention of it. I sure ain't no religious kind of guy, but I got my beliefs like anyone else, though my father'd probably be surprised to hear me say so! But alongside Katie you'd think I was a preacher. Why, just last week she got mad 'cause I tried to teach little Erich to pray before we ate. It was just a harmless little prayer, but she wouldn't have a bit of it."

"Her time will come, Nick. Everyone's time comes eventually. We all have to face God personally and decide what we're going to do with him. I don't think that time's come yet for your wife. She sounds so much like I was before I gave my life to the Lord."

"You?" said Uncle Nick, glancing over at Almeda with a surprised look on his face.

Almeda laughed. "You should have heard me back then! You wouldn't have even known me. I was pretty bitter about God myself."

"Bitter?" I said. I couldn't imagine Almeda being bitter about anything.

"I had plenty to be bitter about—in my thinking, at least.

My life hadn't been easy, and I took it out on God. So I know what Katie's going through."

"That's what I asked before," I said. "Don't you think it would help Katie if she knew that?"

"And your father's answer shows what a wise man he is, Corrie," replied Almeda with an affectionate smile. "It's all about time, Corrie—*God's* time. God wants *every* single person to know about him. But he's got to get a person ready so that he can hear the good news properly when that time does come. Some people's ears are so plugged up with wrong and distorted notions about God that even if Jesus himself were to appear to them and tell them about his Father, they *still* wouldn't hear, wouldn't be able to receive it. They would hear the words, but their minds and hearts would be so mixed up they might turn and walk away from the very Giver of Life himself."

"I know that's right," said Uncle Nick, " 'cause I was like that when I was young. Such a fool hothead I was! And now things are making more sense to me than they ever did, things I recollect my father telling me, and my Ma, things I learned in church. But I don't understand why it's gotta be that way. Is it just growing older?"

Almeda glanced in Pa's direction, seeing if he wanted to reply.

"Don't look at me, woman," he said laughing. "I'm still too new at this myself to know what to tell him. You're the philosopher here. You've been at this Christian life longer than any of the rest of us. So since Avery's on his way back to town with his wife-to-be, I reckon you're the most qualified. You just speak on!"

Almeda laughed.

"You married a long-winded woman, is that what you're trying to say, Drummond Hollister? Who, if she can't be a politician, will keep on being a woman-preacher!"

"You said it, not me!"

We all laughed, and it felt good after the tension and uneasiness following Katie's outburst.

After the laughter settled down, Almeda became serious again.

"Growing older's part of it, Nick," she said after a moment. "But not the most important part. Circumstances have a great deal to do with it. Through circumstances God gets us to a place where we're ready to listen and really *hear* his voice. You see, we hear with our hearts, not our ears. And our hearts have to be ready. It's exactly what Drummond said when you were gone with Katie. It takes a long time for God to break through the outer layers so he can get inside us. He uses the events of our lives to break down the layers of our resistance. Then, when the time is right, he comes and shows himself. If we have been listening and paying attention, and if our heart is open at that time, then we are able to receive his love, and say yes to him."

"Like you and me chasing around the country, getting into trouble, making fools of ourselves," said Pa. "Who knows but that God was using all that to get us ready for this time now when we're listening to him a mite better than back then."

"Sometimes it takes a crisis, a real moment of heartbreak, before our inner ears—our hearts I should say—are unplugged enough to hear God's voice. For you, Drummond, I suppose it was that moment when you learned your wife was dead and you were standing staring at your five children. Suddenly all you'd run away from came back upon you in an instant."

"You're right there," said Pa. He had a faraway, thoughtful gaze in his eyes. "All the layers of toughness I had tried to surround myself with all those years just started to break and crumble away in that moment."

"So that God's life could begin to come in," added Almeda. "Do you see what I mean, Nick? Circumstances. For Corrie," she went on, glancing at me with a smile, "there was her mother dying in the desert and her feeling of aloneness. Out of that pain, God was able to enter into her life in a greater way."

"What about me? There ain't been no great big thing like that for me. You saying I've still gotta face some awful thing before God's gonna be able to do anything with me?"

"Not at all. It doesn't work that way for everyone. God can also come into lives slowly, a little at a time. The more a person listens to him, the more he or she becomes open to God's influences. It's different with everyone. But *sometimes* it takes a crisis, some major change in outward circumstances, to open a person's heart to be able to listen. And judging from Katie's agitation and hostility right now toward spiritual things, I have the feeling God is speaking more and more loudly to her. I hope she will listen. I hope and pray she doesn't have to be broken by circumstances any more than she already has been. But I do have the sense that God is speaking to her and that she is trying to resist."

"Well I hope it don't take too long for him to get through," sighed Uncle Nick. "I don't know how much more I can take of her being so irritable."

"Have patience. Besides, she's carrying your child."

"I know, and I do all I can for her. But sometimes she can be the most ornery woman!"

Almeda laughed softly, then became very thoughtful. "I will talk to her, Nick. I've been praying for an opportunity. Perhaps this is it."

"I'd be mighty obliged, Almeda," said Nick.

"All in God's time. You just join me in prayer for the right opportunity."

# CHAPTER 34

## PRAYING FOR KATIE

We didn't see Katie or Uncle Nick much the whole week after Christmas. Katie kept to herself in their house up across the creek. No more was said by anyone about what had happened, but it was obvious she was avoiding us. From Uncle Nick's behavior it was clear he still felt mighty bad about what had happened. And from the look on his face it didn't seem that things were so well between him and Katie either. He'd walk down to our place most evenings, and although he didn't say much, his face said plenty. He loved Katie, I could tell that, but when she got in one of her moods, he didn't know how to help. Eventually it started to bother him that she wouldn't pay any attention to what he tried to say or do. And of course none of the rest of us were too anxious to get involved. Katie had made it plenty clear what she thought.

After a week and a half, one afternoon Almeda finally said, "Well, it's been long enough. I'm going up to see Katie. If she's not ready to see me yet, she ought to be. This isn't doing anybody any good."

She packed up some food, asked Becky to carry it up for her, and took a small pot of soup she'd made. The two of them headed for the bridge. We'd been sending things up with Nick, but this was the first visit any of us had paid in person. They were back about in about fifteen minutes. Almeda's face wore a smile.

"How is she?" I asked.

"The same," she answered. "Sullen, quiet. I didn't get a single smile and hardly two words out of her. But it's an open door, Corrie. Before long, when the time is right, I'm going to sit her down and have a long talk with her. And by then I think she'll be ready to listen."

"With the heart?" I said with a smile, recalling our conversation of the other evening.

"Yes," she smiled back in return. "Katie's heart is nearer the surface than she lets on. I saw something in her today, Corrie, for the first time since I've known her—hunger. Something in her eyes tells me she knows she isn't as self-sufficient as she wants everybody to think. She *is* being broken and made ready. I can see it! It's exciting. The Lord is tilling her soil, making her ready for the moment when he comes to her and says, 'Katie, it's time to let me in.' "

"But what about everything she said about God?" asked Becky, who was still standing beside Almeda. "She said she hates it when anybody even mentions him."

"Oh, but Becky, that's the best part of all!" replied Almeda. "The closer the Lord gets to a person's heart, sometimes the more that person resists and shouts and complains. That can take many forms, like Katie's outburst the other night. It's just a sign that God is getting ready to take hold of her heart. It's a sign that circumstances are pressing in closer and closer around her, that thoughts and ideas about God are on her mind, that she is watching and observing all the rest of us, seeing the part God plays in our lives. You see, Katie is aware of all that, aware that we are trying to live in a certain way. She says she hates it because way down deep inside she actually *wants* God living with her too. She wants him but she doesn't want him at the same time."

"How can that be?" said Emily, joining the discussion. The two boys were off with Pa at the mine, and it was special, just the three of us girls talking with Almeda.

"The human heart is a complicated thing, Emily," said Almeda with a smile. "It finds no difficulty at all in wanting and not wanting the same thing at once. That is especially true of a woman!

She chuckled, obviously thinking something to herself, then laughed outright. "If you doubt that, girls, just ask your Pa!" she said, still laughing. Gradually she got serious again, and then went on.

"It's also especially true in spiritual things, because just like love, our spiritual beings live in our hearts, not our heads. We both want God and don't want him. He created us to need him, to hunger for him. Life can never be complete unless we are living in a relationship with God. That's the only way we can be fulfilled as human beings. The *only* way. But at the same time, we've all got a stubborn streak. And that part of us wants to keep hold of our independence. We want to *think* we don't need anyone—God included. We want to think we're self-sufficient and strong.

"That's the great conflict down inside all of us—every man or woman, every boy or girl—until the time comes in our lives when we realize we need to walk *with* God, not independently from him. It's just like the minister was saying about horses and wagons. And I think Katie's time is coming, and so the independent part of her is fighting and resisting and complaining and yelling inside."

"Inside *and* outside," added Becky.

We all laughed.

"Yes, Becky," said Almeda. "But it's not any of us she's angry at. She's not really even angry at God. It's just her independence fighting to keep control, while all the time her Father in heaven is drawing her heart closer and closer to his, so that he can pour out his love to her and give her his life."

"But what if she doesn't want his life, doesn't want to be a Christian?" asked Emily.

"Then God may keep bringing circumstances to her that are harder and more painful, until one day she finally comes to the point of realizing happiness and freedom and contentment are not qualities she can have without him."

"So it's just a matter of time?" I asked.

Almeda shook her head. "Maybe. But God never forces people to accept him. Katie still has a choice—we must pray that she chooses to accept God instead of rejecting him."

We were all silent again, thinking about Almeda's words.

"Can we pray for her now?" said Becky.

"I think that's a wonderful idea."

We all bowed our heads and closed our eyes, and softly we prayed for Uncle Nick's wife. Almeda prayed for an opportunity to speak with her, the rest of us prayed that she would be open to God's voice and that we'd have chances to do things for her and show her how much we cared about her.

Praying with other people you love always makes you feel closer to them—especially when you are joining together to pray for someone else you love just as much. The rest of the day I found myself thinking about people praying together. I wondered if that was one of the reasons Jesus told us to pray in groups of two or three. In addition to the answers to the prayers, maybe praying itself brings those two or three people closer together.

Our prayers did get answered, although we sure couldn't have seen ahead of time how it was going to happen. It's a good thing Almeda told us about God sometimes using painful circumstances. That way, when the time came, at least we were a little more prepared for it.

# CHAPTER 35

## DEEP PAIN SURFACES

Several days later, out of the blue, Almeda said to me, "Come on, Corrie, we're going to see Katie."

She began gathering up some things in the kitchen, then to my questioning look added, "It's time, Corrie. From the moment I woke up this morning, I had the strong sense that today was the day."

"The day for what?" I asked.

"For doors to open."

The puzzled look on my face didn't go away with her answer.

"I can't even say that I'm sure myself what that means. But sometimes God puts within you a sense of purpose, a sense of urgency, a sense that it's time to *do* something, say something, take some action that will move things in his kingdom."

"Are you saying you think Katie will be open to God today?"

"I don't know. That's something I have no way of knowing. God holds the keys to our hearts, and nothing we do can open or close *those* doors without there first being nudgings and promptings and openings from his Spirit. I don't know what's going on in the deepest regions of Katie's heart. That's God's domain, not mine. Our responsibility is to obey his promptings *in us*, not concern ourselves with what he is saying to others."

"So what is it you think will happen today?"

"I have no way of knowing that. I wouldn't even want to.

God is in control of Katie's destiny, and her heart, not me. Yet sometimes God will place inside us an urge to do or say something that fits in with the groundwork he is doing inside someone else. The result is that a door opens. It's impossible to say what exactly that means, how it will come about, or what will be the eventual outcome."

"What will you say?"

"I won't try to plan that. To speak of holy things at the wrong time, before someone is truly ready to receive them, can do more harm than good. We must rely on God's guidance to provide the fit opportunity, and we must move slowly. I don't know what Katie needs to hear. God knows that. So I just want to be available."

We packed up some food, and two knitting projects we had been working on, and then set out for Uncle Nick and Aunt Katie's—just the two of us. All the way there Almeda said nothing. From the intense look on her face, I knew she was praying.

When we arrived, Katie was alone with Erich. Uncle Nick was at the mine with Pa and Zack. All the other kids were in town at school. It was the middle of the morning, and the men would be working for another two or three hours before lunchtime.

Katie did not seem particularly overjoyed to see us, but she went through the motions of being hospitable.

"How are you feeling?" Almeda asked.

"Well enough, I suppose," Katie answered.

"We brought you some fresh bread. I know sometimes it's difficult to keep up with baking when you're not feeling so well."

"I tell you, I'm feeling fine," replied Katie, a little crossly. "I don't need your help, Almeda. I'll get through this fine on my own. Just quit worrying about me so much."

Almeda looked away for a moment. "I'm sorry," she said after a bit. "I'm only trying to be a good sister-in-law to you, and a good neighbor, and I know how it feels to be alone and far away from—"

"Look Almeda," Katie interrupted. She turned and faced Almeda. Her face did not seem to be angry, but there was no trace of a smile to be found anywhere on it. She was cool, distant, reserved, and obviously not interested in returning Almeda's friendliness. "I know what you're trying to do. I know you feel sorry for me. But just don't bother. I can get along fine without you or anybody else's sympathy. Keep your bread and all your religious notions about neighborliness to yourself, and just leave me alone!"

The words stung Almeda; and the slight wince that flitted across her face showed that they had stabbed her right in the heart. I would have done anything to disappear right then and not be in the room with them.

How thankful I was for Erich. Little children are so innocent, and sometimes they can stumble right into the middle of a hornet's nest without realizing it. On this particular morning he toddled in and rescued us from any further embarrassment.

"Look, Aunt Corrie," he said, holding something up to me, "Papa make me wood bear."

I stooped down to look at the piece of wood he was holding, so relieved for *something* to do. After I'd seen it, he marched over to show it to Almeda. She had looked away after Katie's rebuke, but now she stooped down, put an arm around his shoulder. Though her face was still a little pale she flashed him a bright smile and asked two or three questions about his toy "bear," which looked like a stick that had been whittled on. Katie went about something on her stove without another word, and Almeda and I talked for a few more minutes with Erich.

When he finally waddled off to another part of the house, Almeda threw me a glance which was followed by a deep sigh. This did not seem to be turning out to be much of a visit.

Slowly we rose, still holding the things we brought. Almeda walked over toward Katie, whose back was still turned toward us.

"I brought the stockings I've been making for Erich," Almeda said quietly, "and the sweater for your husband. I thought you might like to see them."

Katie did not reply for a moment. Then, still not facing us, she said, "You can leave them on the table if you wish."

"They're not finished. I thought you might like to see how I'm planning to—"

"Then take them with you and finish them any way you like. Leave them if you like, or take them. I don't care."

Almeda winced again, as if she had been struck across the cheek.

Almeda stood still, facing Katie's back, looking helpless. She wanted so badly to be Katie's friend.

Finally she drew in a breath and said, "I suppose we'll be going now. I'm so sorry, Katie. I didn't mean to cause you any pain, or to intrude where I don't belong. Please, if you can find it in your heart to forgive me, I would appreciate—"

"Forgive you!" repeated Katie, spinning around. Her face was red and her eyes flashing. "Forgive you for what?"

"I don't know," stammered Almeda. "For upsetting you, for intruding when you wanted to be alone." I'd never seen Almeda so flustered and unsettled. "I'm just sorry to have caused you any more grief."

"The only grief you cause me is by trying to be so good and self-righteous all the time!"

"Oh, Katie, I'm so sorry," said Almeda in a quavering voice.

"Sorry . . . forgive . . . don't you ever get sick of being so *good*? Do you ever stop, Almeda? Don't you ever want just to be normal and let people live their own lives, without always being nice, always smiling, always doing things for them, always preaching to them with all your holier-than-thou notions of God? Sometimes you make me sick with all your talk of God and forgiveness, and that happy smile on your face—always with a kind word, always doing somebody a good turn, never getting upset, never getting angry!"

I sat shocked at what I was hearing, my eyes glued to Katie as she poured out her fury. Poor Almeda just stood standing in front of her, defenseless, tears pouring down her cheeks.

"Do you know what it feels like to be around someone like you who's always so good?" Katie went on. "It makes me resent every word I ever hear about God! What about the rest of us, Almeda, who can't be as good as you? What does God have for people like us? I'm sick of it, do you hear? I hate God, I hate you, I hate California, I hate this stinking house, I hate the whole rotten business, and I never want to hear another word about God as long as I live!"

I don't know if she was going to say anything else. Before her outburst was finished, Almeda ran out the door, one hand held over her face. The bread and knitting lay on the floor where she had dropped them.

The sound of her footsteps and sobs woke me from my trance. I looked hard at Katie and saw tears in her eyes too. The next instant I ran out the door after Almeda.

She was hurrying away from the house, but not down the path to our place. She stopped on the edge of the woods, and I caught up with her leaning against a tree.

She was sobbing harder than I'd ever seen before, from the depths of her heart. I walked up to her slowly and laid my hand on the back of her shoulder. It was hot and wet. She kept crying but reached up and grasped my hand with one of hers, clutching it tightly.

We stood there, alone and quiet next to that tree, for several minutes. Gradually her weeping calmed down, then finally stopped.

Slowly she turned around, looked deeply into my eyes, and attempted a smile.

"I am so thankful for you, Corrie," she said softly. "I don't know what I'd do right now if I didn't have you here to share this with me."

I had no words to say. I just put my arms around her and held her.

"Do you know what's the hardest thing of all, Corrie?" she said at last.

"What?"

"Being so misunderstood . . . having your motives—which

you thought were good—questioned as if you had some selfish end you were trying to gain."

"She didn't mean to hurt you," I said.

"Oh, I know. She has no idea what she's done. But to have love turned back on you as if you were trying to injure rather than help and minister . . . that's such a painful thing."

We were silent another minute.

"But of course she didn't mean it," Almeda went on. "I have no doubt she's hurting more right now than I am. And it must be especially bitter for her in that she has no place to turn, no source of help. I do. But she is alone with her anger and her frustrations. So of course I don't blame her for lashing out at me." Her voice was soft and clean, as if the tears had washed it.

"It's not you anyway, is it?"

"No. Katie's not angry with me. She just doesn't know where to turn for help."

By this time we had stepped back, and Almeda was leaning against the tree again. I could tell she was thinking about the last words she had said.

It was quiet a long time. Then Almeda took a deep breath, looked at me, and smiled.

"We do know where to turn for help, don't we?" she said. "Maybe this is the door I had the feeling the Lord was going to open. It just might be time I told Katie some things. As painful as it will be, I think the time has finally come. Let's go back to the house, Corrie."

She turned and led the way back toward the cabin.

I followed Almeda through the door. She didn't knock or wait to be invited in. Katie was sitting in a chair staring straight ahead, her face white.

"Katie, I know you and I haven't always seen eye to eye on some things," Almeda said. "And I know our views on religion are very different. I'm sorry if I've hurt you or done things to bother you. I've honestly tried to be a good neighbor and friend to you. I'm sorry if it's seemed otherwise to you."

Katie just sat there saying nothing. She looked spent, like

the storm of her anger had left her weak and with no more words to say.

"But there's one thing you've got wrong, Katie," Almeda continued. "And that's about me being good. When you said 'someone like me who's always so good,' your words felt like a knife piercing right through my heart. And so whether you like it or not, Katie, unless you actually demand that I leave your house, I want to tell you what I used to be. You've got to know some things about God that you have all mixed up in your mind. After you've heard what I have to say, then if you still think faith is ridiculous and want to hate it, that will be your choice. But I intend to tell you what I have to say."

She paused for a breath. She was still standing, looking straight down at Katie. Katie sat with her eyes focused on the floor. But she said nothing.

Almeda sat down in front of her, took another deep breath, and began to speak.

# CHAPTER 36

## ALMEDA'S STORY

"The person I was many years ago in Boston," she began, "was a different person than you have ever known me to be. Completely different, Katie. Do you understand what I mean—black and white, night and day different?"

Almeda paused momentarily, but apparently she wasn't waiting for any answer, because she went right on.

"My father was a wealthy Boston merchant. I was one of three daughters—I hesitate to say it, but three *beautiful* daughters. I was the eldest. My father was a conniving man who would do anything—including sacrifice his own daughters— to turn a profit or to make a deal that would pad his bank account."

A painful look passed across Almeda's face as she said the words. Then she took in a deep breath, as if she was trying to gather courage to continue.

"I have to tell you that even after all the years I have been a Christian and have been trying to forgive him deep in my heart, the very thought of what he did to us still causes resentments to rise up within me. He was not a good man. For many years I despised him. At least now I can say that is no longer true. I have learned to accept what happened, and his part in it, and to know that through it I discovered what I might not have discovered otherwise. To say that I am thankful for my past would not really be truthful. But I do accept it, and have come to terms with it.

"What my father did was to flaunt us before his important clients. From the time I was fourteen or fifteen he would make me put on scanty dresses and alluring silk stockings, then he would pour perfume on me and take me out in the evening with him. There he would meet men I always assumed he was doing business with. I was too young at first to have any idea what was happening to me. I just went along obediently. There I would sit or stand beside my father while he would talk or drink. Sometimes it would be for dinner, other times we would go to saloons or taverns. Soon enough I realized that he was talking to the men about *me*. They would look me over, and there would be laughing and winking and whispered comments, then more laughing, all with a lewd, suggestive tone to it. My own father was hinting to his various associates that he would let me be available to them in exchange for their business.

"At first it wasn't so awful. The men would try to joke with me or take me alone over to the bar to buy me a sparkling water to drink while they had their whiskey. But it got worse the older I grew. They wanted to touch me and put their arms around me and feel my hair, always leering at me through toothy grins and evil eyes.

"I hated it. I hated the men, and I hated my father. But there was nothing I could do except go along with it. If my father thought that I wasn't being 'friendly' enough, or wasn't doing enough to please his associates, he would yell at me and hit me when we got home, and say horrible and abusive things to me. Sometimes he beat me even when I had done my best to be agreeable, just because a certain client decided to take his business elsewhere. One time—"

Even as Almeda spoke, the memory made her shut her eyes and a momentary shudder passed through her. She took a deep breath and continued.

"One time, he stopped the wagon on the way home, shoved me down from my seat, jumped down after me, and struck me over and over, knocking me to the ground until my nose was bleeding and my dress was torn and I was covered with dirt and mud, then threw me in a heap in the back of the wagon. I had learned years before not to cry aloud in his presence. He hated it when I cried, and he would beat me all the more. So I had to learn to stifle my whimpered sobs, and bury the agony of pain from his beatings.

"That night riding home in the back of the wagon, blood and dirt on my face, my ear and shoulder splitting with pain from his blows, I realized, perhaps for the first time, that my father was not a good man, and that I hated him. And from that moment, something began to rise up from inside me, a determination to escape from his clutches whenever and however I could.

"But it wasn't as if I could just leave home. I was only sixteen, and I was still completely dependent upon my parents. They never gave any of us any money. What could I do, where could I go? We had no relatives, no friends I could turn to. My mother knew what he was doing to us, but she was just as afraid of him as we were. I could never understand why she didn't stand up for us and protect us from him. But as I grew older I saw that she felt just as helpless as we. I tried to confide in her about what he did when he took us out in the evenings, but she would only suffer with us in silence. I don't doubt that she had more than her share of beatings from his hand as well. Probably if she had tried to say or do anything, he would have punished us all ruthlessly—all of us. So she just must have figured it best to keep silent and hope we could endure it.

"Once I even tried to talk to my father. It was late in the afternoon, around dusk. He was out in the barn working on a new saddle he'd bought. How naive I must have been to think he would listen, that he would care. But something had come over me that day with more clarity than ever before that what he was doing was just *wrong*. It was so plain to me all of a sudden, with my little girl's trusting heart, that if I could just say it to him he would see it too. I was wrong.

"I walked up to him slowly. He had his back turned. I don't even know if he heard me approaching. I stopped a few feet from him, terrified. I mustered all my courage and blurted out, 'Daddy, I want you to stop doing what you're doing to me. It's wrong. I don't want to go out with you again to see any more men.'

"That was all I said. I stood there trembling, just looking at his back in the quiet of the barn. He said nothing, and what seemed like a long time passed, though it was probably only a minute. Then he slowly turned around and bore his eyes into me. His face was blank. It was not even a look of anger, just a total lack of feeling, an emptiness, a void. Then slowly a cruel smile spread over his lips. He just looked at me with that horrid half-smile. It was the same kind of expression I'd seen in the men he made me be friendly to. Then slowly he turned back to his saddle, never uttering a word.

"I don't even remember when or how I left the barn, or how I spent the rest of the afternoon. But I remember the night distinctly enough. He took me into town again, and it was an absolutely horrible evening. My father joined with the men in saying things about me—half of them I didn't even understand, but I felt ugly and small and dirty just from the looks and laughs and winks that went along with their words. And that night he made me go to a man's room alone. Nothing much happened; I suppose once he got me alone the man felt sorry for me because of how young I was, and he was almost nice to me when he saw how terrified I was.

"So he took me back downstairs to my father a little later. And then on our way home, out somewhere desolate where even if I did scream no one would hear me, my father gave me the worst beating of my life. He never said a word. He didn't have to. The message was clear enough: I must never speak boldly to him again like I had that afternoon in the barn. I had to stay in bed for two days. My mother hardly even came into my room except to give me something to eat. I knew she felt guilty, but powerless at the same time. So she did the worst thing of all—she did nothing. She didn't even offer me so much as a look or a smile of consolation, not even a glance to say, 'I understand . . . I'm sorry.' "

Almeda stopped. Her voice had grown quiet, and now she

looked down, took a handkerchief from her pocket and dabbed her eyes.

"You know," she went on in a moment, her voice soft and husky, "during all the years I was growing up, I never once remember hearing the words *I love you*. Not even from my mother. Love was nonexistent in our family. I don't know what my two sisters felt. But all my life I felt unwanted, that my parents would have gotten rid of me the moment I was born if they could have."

She paused again, crying now.

"Do you have any idea what it's like," she said through her tears, "never once all your life to be told that you are loved—by *anybody*? Not once. Never to be touched except in anger. Never to be held . . . never to feel arms wrapping themselves around your shoulders in tenderness . . . never to—"

She couldn't continue, but finally broke down and sobbed, her face in her hands.

I don't know what Katie was thinking. Part of me didn't want to look at her. Besides, I was far too occupied with my *own* thoughts and feelings. I was shocked, of course, but that was only part of my response. I could feel the hurt, the ache, in her voice. And because I *did* love her—oh, so much!—it made what she'd gone through so much harder to hear. I just wanted to go back and take that girl she had once been in my arms and wrap her up and protect her from any more hurt and any more unkindness.

On another level, as I listened I could hardly believe what I was hearing. From the very day I had first seen her, Almeda had been to me the absolute picture of strength, and Christian virtue, and maturity. I had never seen her "weak." There was never a time when I didn't know she could be depended on, no matter if everyone around her fell or faltered or even ran away. To hear her describe her past was like looking into a window inside of someone else. And I couldn't manage to make the two images come together into the single person I had always known. Suddenly there were two pictures of Almeda—the stately, solid lady, full of grace, capable and mature, and the young girl, frightened, alone, and unloved.

How could the two be the same person? Yet there sat Almeda, the same loving woman I had always known, my stepmother now, opening up this window into her soul.

Slowly I got up from where I was sitting and walked over to Almeda. I knelt down in front of her, took one of her hands in mine, and looked into her face, red with tears and the anguish of reliving the ugly memories of the past.

"Almeda," I said softly, "*I* love you . . . I love you more than I can ever tell you!"

At the words a fresh torrent of weeping burst out from Almeda. I put my hand around her waist and tried to comfort her, but she had to go on crying for another minute or two.

"Oh, Corrie," she whispered at length, "you'll never know how precious those words are to me! Your love is such a priceless treasure to me . . . words cannot express the joy you give me."

She blew her nose, then looked down at me with a radiant smile. I guess it's true that pain makes a person more capable of love. Almeda's face at that moment was more filled with love than any face I'd ever seen. Our eyes met and held. I felt I was looking right through her, not into her heart or into her past life, but into the deepest parts of *her*—the whole person she was, the person she had always been, the person she was still becoming. Maybe in those few seconds I had a tiny glimpse of what God sees when *he* looks deep into us—a glimpse into the *real* person, the *whole* person—apart from age or appearance or past or upbringing.

All these feelings passed through me in just a second or two. Then Almeda gave me a squeeze and took a deep breath.

"I want to finish," she went on, "or I might never get this far with it again. And I want both of you to hear what I have to say. I care about the two of you, and I want you to know me—to know *all* about me."

I stood up and went back to where I had been sitting.

"It's difficult for me to describe what I was feeling back then," she continued, "because I suppose I didn't even know myself. I was terrified, and yet at the same time I was growing more and more determined to escape from that awful life. I suppose there was a part of me that was a fighter. I've been called headstrong more than once, as you know, Corrie, from the very first day when we saw each other."

She looked over at me with a smile.

"You weren't afraid of anybody when you went into the saloon looking for Uncle Nick, that's for sure," I said.

"No, I don't suppose I was," she replied. "And as afraid as I was of my father, by the time I was sixteen a part of me inside was biding my time until I saw an opportunity. And after he'd done it once, my father started trying to make me go upstairs alone with men again. The next time it happened, knowing what I was in for, I refused to go. 'I just won't do it,' I said, which silenced the joviality around the table where we were sitting. And the look of daggers my father threw at me told me there was a beating waiting for me, the likes of which I'd never felt.

"And of course after that, nothing my father could say would make the man he'd been talking to take me away anyway, even if I'd given in. So I just sat there in silence, trembling about the ride home.

"Luckily my father had an appointment the next night with another man, a whiskey distributor I'd met before. I had never liked him one bit. The smiles he would give me, and the pinches and little jabs, were so horrible. It never took long in that man's company to know what kind of man he was. My next younger sister still had a black eye from the hand of my father, and he wanted to make sure I was presentable because whiskey was one of my father's main sources of income. So he didn't beat me that night, although he made sure I knew full well that as soon as the *next* night was over, I was going to be so black and blue I would be in bed for a week and would never refuse to do anything he asked of me again.

"All the next day I plotted my escape. I stole what money I could find in the house, packed a few clothes in a bag, and hid it in a field nearby. Then I waited for evening to come, filled with fear and anticipation all at once.

"This time I was as nice as I could be, and I just smiled when the men called me 'Honey,' as if I enjoyed it, and I went right upstairs with that awful man. But on the landing I managed to get ahead of him, and since I knew what room we were going to, I ran in and locked the door behind me, then climbed out the window onto the landing and scrambled down to the alley.

"I ran away from there as fast as I could, hardly even knowing what direction I was going. I ran and ran, through alleys and streets, but always with the vague intent of moving in the direction of our home, which was on the edge of the city.

"After that it all becomes a blur. I can't even say how I spent the rest of that night or the next few days and nights. I managed to retrieve my bag of things, but where I went and what I did after that I honestly can't even recall. There are just images that sometimes flash into my mind—a face, a place, or a set of surroundings.

"Actually that's all I remember for the whole next year. How I survived I don't know. Now I can say that the hand of God was upon me, but then I knew nothing of God, and certainly cared even less. If I thought it had been bad at home with my father, now my life turned black indeed. I don't even want to remember all the things I did, or what I got myself mixed up in. I lived on the streets, sometimes in the countryside, in saloons and cheap hotels, getting what jobs I could find. I stole, I drank, I used people if I thought it might get me a free meal.

"I knew my father probably hated me all the more for making him look foolish, and that he was no doubt looking for me. But I didn't care. I told people who I was and exactly what I thought of him. Over the next several years, as I got older and more capable, I was able to hold jobs for longer, and even to do a man's work when I had to. Living like I did made me tough and independent. I could take care of myself, and I wasn't afraid of my father finding me. I knew he'd never be able to get a hold on me again. I suppose I even had something of a reputation as a pretty hard, tough young lady—which no doubt is how Franklin found out about my past last year.

"To make a long story short, when I was about nineteen or twenty I fell in with a man who more or less took me under his wing. He was a confidence man, a card shark, a high-stakes swindler, but he lived a fast life, and I found that appealing. I didn't love him, and I know he didn't love me either. I was just a pretty girl for him to have around. I had no idea what love was and at that point in my life never stopped to even ask if such a thing as love existed. Life was survival. To survive you had to be tough, you had to take advantage of what opportunities came along, and you had to put yourself first. If other people got hurt in the process, that wasn't my concern. Life had dealt me a pretty bad hand, and I wasn't about to start getting pangs of conscience over anyone else.

"So I lived with him for a while, stole for him, set people up for him, and in the process lived better than I had for several years. At least I knew I was going to have a roof over my head, a warm bed, and a good meal. It was the closest thing to stability I had known in a long time. How much longer it might have gone on like this, or what might have become of us in the end I don't know. Because then something happened which changed everything."

Again Almeda stopped, and again I knew from her face and the tone of her voice that she was struggling within herself for the courage to say something that was painful.

The room was silent for a minute or two. I chanced a quick glance in Katie's direction. She was looking intently at Almeda, listening to every word. Every trace of anger was gone from her face.

"There was a child," Almeda said at last. She stopped again and hid her face in her hands.

I saw Katie gasp slightly, and I felt myself take in a quick breath. I couldn't believe what I'd just heard!

"I'm so ashamed to tell you what I have to say next," she went on, crying a little again. "The minute he learned I was pregnant, I was nothing to him but baggage. I woke up one morning in the hotel we'd been staying in to find myself alone with nothing but my carpetbag and a few clothes left in the room. I never saw him again. He left me ten dollars, and I was back on the street.

"I was too angry even to cry. It just drove my bitterness toward men—toward the whole world, and I suppose toward God too—deeper. The old hard determination rose up in me again, and I struck out after that day all the more mistrusting, all the more independent. I was a different person, I tell you—selfish, hateful, caring for no one but myself.

"When the baby was born—God forgive me!—I took it to an orphanage. I didn't want to—"

Almeda broke down and wept. I wanted to comfort her, but I was so stunned by what she'd said that I couldn't move.

"Oh, how many times I've relived it in my memory, wondering where I might have changed this course I was on, wondering if I did right or wrong. I was so unprepared to be a mother. Yet something in me has often wished—"

Again she stopped to collect herself, then continued.

"The birth of my baby sent me lower still. By now I was in my early twenties and something in that hard independent spirit slowly began to break. Guilt over what I had done began to set in. Gradually it ate away at me, burrowing deeper and deeper into my heart. I didn't realize it at the time, but now I see that all the hard, determined independence was only my young way of covering up my desperate hunger to be loved. The more I tried to assert my strength, the more my soul was being torn apart. I didn't have any idea who I was. My whole identity had come from my father. To him I was just an object to be used. No one had ever loved me. How could I do anything but despise myself? And even the most precious thing a woman has—that purity which is the only thing she has to offer her husband—I let slip away. And I gave away the child that should have been the wonderful outcome of love between a man and a woman. I was no better than my father! I didn't even want my own baby! Oh God . . . how could I have been so shameful . . . how could—"

Again she broke down and sobbed quietly.

"There is no way I can tell you what that time was like for me," she finally said after a while. "I felt so guilty, yet I tried to hide it. Inside I was slowly dying to all that life should be, sinking into a pit of despair, yet making it worse by the obstinate hard-bitten image I tried to keep up.

"I started drifting, caught trains to New York and Philadelphia. I worked here and there, stealing what I needed, living among some really rough men and women. I even got to be pretty handy with my fists when I had to be. It was a dreadful life! It wasn't life at all, it was a living death."

She paused once more. By now her tears had stopped. She breathed in deeply, and looked out the window off into the distance. As if she had suddenly become unaware that Katie and I were in the room with her, she seemed miles and years away. I'd seen that look before, a look of mingled pain and remembrance. Now at last I knew why those clouds had passed across her face.

She continued staring out the window for a long time, then suddenly came back to the present and turned and focused her gaze onto Katie.

"So you see, Katie," she said, "when you spoke of me as someone who's always so good, as if God was somebody I could understand but you couldn't, do you see why your words bit so deep? I *wasn't* good, Katie! I was about as despicable a person as they come. For the first twenty-five years of my life, I did everything wrong! I did not know love. I was miserable. I was mean and bitter and vengeful. I hurt people, I did more horrible things than I could count.

"If you're going to think of Christianity as something that's only for a certain kind of person, then you'd better leave me out altogether. If you think God reserves his life for churchy 'good' people, where does that leave me? All those things you said about me—nice, always smiling, holier-than-thou, forgiving, doing good turns, never getting upset, never getting angry . . . don't you understand, Katie—none of that was me at all! The person you think you see, the person you have known these last couple of years, wasn't me at all not so very long ago. I don't say that to be critical, Katie. But if you're going to criticize me for how I am now, then I think you should know the whole story. And that's why I wanted to tell you."

Still Katie just sat numbly, not saying anything.

"So what happened?" I asked finally. "How did you . . . I mean, how could everything have changed so much?"

Almeda turned toward me and smiled. Her eyes were a little red still, but the radiance that was normally on her countenance had returned. Having told us everything, reliving it as she did, she was ready for the sun to come back out.

"That," she sighed, "is almost an equally long story."

# CHAPTER 37

## ENCOUNTER WITH A SHOPKEEPER

"One day," Almeda began again, "when I was back in Boston, I was walking in one of the better sections of town. I don't even remember why I happened to be on that particular street because it really wasn't a part of town I went to very often. Fate, I suppose I would have called it back then. I would call it something else now.

"In any case, I walked into a shop that sold a mixture of many things—dry goods, some fine linens, with one glass case of some very expensive jewelry. I wandered in, probably looking every bit the street-tramp that I was. I must have stood out like a sore thumb, but I didn't really think of that myself.

"As you might imagine, my eyes immediately focused on the case of jewelry. I sauntered toward it, saw that it was filled with expensive gold and silver rings and necklaces and pendants. The proprietor of the shop was occupied along one of the far walls with a lady who was picking out some fabric, and the jewelry cabinet was out of the man's direct line of vision. All I would need would be a second or two. If I could get my hand inside the case and snatch three or four pieces, I'd be able to dash out the door and all he'd see was the back of my heels. I'd done the same sort of thing a hundred times and had the utmost confidence in my cunning and my speed once I lit out. The only question was whether the case was locked.

"I moved up to the case and searched quickly for a lock but

didn't see one. The back seemed to be open. I eyed the pieces I thought I could nab. Then with one motion I stretched over the top of the case and reached into the back. My fingers grabbed two or three rings. I hurriedly put them in my other hand, then stretched out again and reached for two pearl necklaces that were close by. Just as I'd laid hold of them and pulled my arm back, ready to make a dash for the door, I felt the grip of a strong hand seize my shoulder.

"The store owner had sneaked up behind me and now he had me redhanded. I winced from the pain because he'd grabbed me tight. His only words were, 'Drop them on the counter, Miss.' There was no anger in his voice, only a calm tone of command. I instantly did what he said. I had no choice.

"He relaxed his grip slightly, but still held on. The other lady had left the store and now we were alone. Still holding on to me, he walked me over toward the door and locked it. I was too feisty and stubborn to be scared. I squirmed a little, but he was strong and it did no good. I couldn't have escaped if I'd tried, and now with the door locked I settled down and decided just to wait and see what would happen next.

"The man was younger than I'd first realized, only a few years older than I was—in his mid-thirties. He led me, still with a strong hand, back behind the counter of the shop and into another room, which was his home, attached to the store. He sat me down in a chair, then finally let go of my arm and shoulder. He took a chair himself and sat down opposite me. He must have seen my eyes darting about already plotting my escape.

" 'There's no way out, young lady,' he said. 'All the doors are locked, and even if you did manage to find a key to one of them and get out, I'm quite a fast runner and I'd catch you before you were halfway down the street. And the sheriff's office is only two blocks away. So if I were you I'd just sit still for a moment or two.'

"His voice still had that calm, deep tone of authority. I couldn't help but find myself arrested by it. And though I slouched back in my chair with a look of angry resignation on my face, already I found myself wondering why he hadn't yelled at me or wasn't already on his way to the sheriff's with me.

"The longer I sat there, the more confused I became, although I wouldn't have shown the man a bit of what I was thinking. He just sat there for the longest time and stared into my eyes. I found his gaze annoying and looked away. I kept looking all over the room, but still he kept focusing in on my eyes and my face. It was very disconcerting. Yet at the same time I couldn't help thinking that there was something in his expression that I had never seen before, though I had no idea what it was.

"Finally he spoke again.

" 'Why did you try to steal from me?' he asked.

"I shrugged.

" 'If you were hungry, why didn't you just ask me for some food? I would have given it to you.'

"I still had nothing to say.

" 'If you needed money, why didn't you come in and tell me about it? Perhaps I could have helped.'

"*What is this?* I wondered to myself. *If you're going to have me thrown in jail, then get it over with.*

"Yet inside curiosity was already starting to well up in me about this strange man who didn't seem bent on condemning me but instead sounded as if he was interested in me.

"Well, I sat there for the next hour while he continued to question me and talk to me, always in the same calm voice, with his eyes probing into me in a way no one ever had before, and gradually he began to coax some words and then some whole sentences out of me. By the end of the hour, we were actually carrying on a conversation. Over and over he kept saying, 'I don't think you really want to be a thief. I think you want to be a lady, but you just don't know how.'

"I hardly knew what he meant. But the compassion and caring in his voice was real enough, and the commanding tone and the purposefulness of his eyes, slowly began to speak to me. I found myself listening with more than just my ears. I found myself *wanting* to listen, wanting to hear more of this strange man's words . . . wanting to *believe* that he was right, wanting to believe that perhaps he really did see something of worth and value as he looked into my face, saw something that maybe I didn't see, and had never seen myself."

Almeda paused and took a breath, but quickly kept right on going.

"After a while he offered me something to eat. I took it eagerly. I hadn't had much to eat all day and was famished. He heated me some soup on his stove, and poured me a cup of coffee.

" 'How about a slice of bread to go with it?' he asked. 'I made it just yesterday.'

"I nodded between spoonfuls of soup, half glancing up now and then with one of my eyebrows raised in puzzlement over this strange man who was treating me so nicely.

"I must have looked like a ravaged animal sitting there!"

She chuckled and the faraway gaze came into her eyes again.

"When I said earlier that my father had three beautiful daughters, I meant no boast in any way. Our faces were a curse, if anything, because they made men look upon us differently than they would have otherwise. A plain face is a young girl's greatest gift and greatest protection against many of the cruelties of this world, though most never discover that fact for forty or fifty years. But as I sat there in that man's kitchen, I can tell you I was anything but beautiful. My face had grown bitter, hard, calculating. There was a perpetual scowl on my brow. My cheeks were sunken, my hair ratted and messy, my clothes dirty, even torn in places. It was not an attractive sight. That man had absolutely nothing to gain by befriending me. I hadn't bathed in two weeks, and the plain fact of the matter is that I was foul. I looked and smelled ugly, inside and out.

"But he—"

Almeda paused and looked away, suddenly overcome again with emotion. I saw her handkerchief go to her eyes once more.

"But he saw something in me. Why . . . how . . . I hadn't any idea. I know now it was because God's love resided in him, but I didn't know it then. He *saw* something in me! Something that he considered of *value*. And you just can't understand what that did to my starved, confused, lonely, encrusted heart. It was as though he took hold of my eyes, looked deeply into them, and then said, 'Look, young lady. Look here—into my eyes. Gaze deeply into them, and you will find someone who has compassion on you, someone who cares about you as a person.'

"As I ate his food, he just kept watching me, quietly talking, and I'm sure praying too, though I was oblivious to that. And that same message kept coming through, even in his silence: *Here is someone who cares about you.*

"And then another strange and unexpected thing happened. As I was finishing up my second bowl of soup and starting to think about being on my way—that is, if he was going to let me go instead of having me thrown in jail—the man got up, pulled a book from a shelf nearby, sat back down, and said, 'Did you know there's a description of you in the Bible?'

"No," I answered.

" 'Well there is,' he replied, 'and I want to read it to you.'

"*No harm in that*, I thought as I kept eating.

"He flipped through the pages, stopped, and then began to read: *Who can find a virtuous woman? for her price is far above rubies. The heart of her husband doth safely trust in her, so that he shall have no need of spoil. She will do him good and not evil all the days of her life. . . .*

"I found myself listening more than I let on. Was this the man's idea of a cruel joke, calling me *virtuous*? *Me!* Couldn't he see that I was anything but good? I didn't even have a husband, but if I did I'd be the last person on earth anyone would say such things about! I had just tried to rob this storekeeper, and now he was reading words like, *She will do him good and not evil*, and saying it was a description of *me!*

"But when he got to the end, he paused a moment, then looked intently into my eyes with a piercing gaze and said: *Many daughters have done virtuously, but thou excellest them all. Favor is deceitful, and beauty is vain: but a woman that feareth the Lord, she shall be praised*. That's when I suddenly knew beyond any doubt that I'd landed in the house of a man whose wits had left him. There was that word *virtue* again! I knew how black I was inside! That hidden part of me that I tried so hard to keep anyone from seeing—I knew that part was selfish and horrid through and through!

"But even if he was a madman, he had been nice to me, after all. So I simply finished up my soup, then stood and asked if I was free to go.

" 'If you want to,' he replied. " 'But the day's almost over. It's going to be cold tonight. Do you need a place to stay?'

"*So that's it*, I thought to myself. *All this just to lure me into his lair! He's no different from everyone else!*

"Then he added, 'I have a guest room. I'd be happy to put you up for the night. You could take a hot bath, have breakfast with me in the morning, and then be on your way.'

"I eyed him carefully, squinting to see if I could detect some motive. But try as I might, I could see nothing. I don't think the man would have been capable of taking advantage of another. And even if he did try something, I thought, I could take care of myself.

"So I shrugged, and said, 'Sure, I suppose a bath and clean bed would feel good for a change.'

"That night changed everything, and altered the whole course of my life. The man could not have been a more perfect gentleman. He treated me like a queen, heated water for my bath, gave me clean clothes to sleep in, fixed me tea and brought it with some crackers to my room before I went to bed. I didn't know it at the time, but when I was bathing he took my clothes out to be cleaned by a lady around the corner.

"You can imagine the changes I was going through in my mind as I lay there that night. One part of me was laughing inside that anyone could be such a sap. I would sneak down in the middle of the night, find my way into the store again, and make off not with just three or four pieces of jewelry, but with everything in the case. My head was resting on a nice clean pillow cover that would hold everything.

"But somehow another part of me was feeling things I had never felt in my life. This storekeeper—madman or sap or religious nut, whatever he was!—had treated me with courtesy and respect and kindness and graciousness like no other human being in the world ever had. So the deeper part of me was hardly anxious to leave! It felt good to have someone care and treat me kindly. I was not consciously aware of these feelings at the time. Inside I was still pretending it was all ridiculous.

"But he had shown me my first real glimpse of love. He had reached out, looked into my face, and said, 'I see a person of value and worth inside there.' He'd even used that silly word *virtue* and said the passage he read was a description of me. No matter how I might rave and bluster on the outside about it all being syrupy and stupid, I couldn't help feeling cared about and loved.

"So even though I lay there plotting and scheming my escape and all the loot I would make off with, the deeper part of me gradually went contentedly to sleep. And I slept like a baby and didn't wake until I heard the man's familiar voice. I opened my eyes. Sunlight was streaming in through the window, and there he stood with a tray in his hands and a cup of steaming coffee on it, and saying with a bright expression, 'Good morning, young lady. I hope you slept well!'

"In just a few short hours, this place—a place I had walked into to rob, run by this man standing there whose name I didn't even know yet—had become more like a true home to me than any I had ever known. And as I lay there, suddenly the most unexpected thing happened. I felt tears in my eyes. I looked up at him, blinking them back as best I could, and then another unexpected thing happened. A smile came across my lips, and I said, 'Yes, I did. Thank you.'

"He left the coffee, and I lay back in the bed and cried. But they were like no tears that had ever come from my eyes before."

Almeda glanced over at me and smiled. Her eyes were glistening.

"Needless to say," she went on, "I didn't leave immediately, or rob him, or anything like that. I stayed for breakfast and for all that day, then for another night, and before I knew it I had been there a week. He gave me new clothes from his shop, he fed me, I had a bath every day and a room completely to myself. Within a couple of weeks he moved me into a boarding house just down the street and offered me a job in his store.

"The long and the short of it is—I became a new person. Life such as I had never known began to come up out of me. I began to notice things that had been dead to me before. People took on a whole new meaning, and I found within myself a desire to reach into them and find out about them.

"Well . . . if you haven't guessed it by now, the man who took me under his wing and helped me to believe in my own worth was none other than Mr. Parrish. The year after I first wandered into his shop I became his wife.

"What a transformation took place within me during that year! That wonderful man simply reclaimed me from Boston's gutters, pulled me up, gave me a place to stand, loved me, believed in me, spoke encouragement and worth into me, and showed me how to *live*. He was God's provision for me. I was dead to all that life was, and he rescued me. I became a new person, thanks to him—completely new, the person the two of you know today.

"Do you know what he did?" Almeda smiled tenderly at the memory.

"After that first day, he read that passage from Proverbs 31 to me every day until we were married. He kept reading it to me, over and over, and kept saying to me, 'You *are* that woman of virtue, Almeda. You are virtuous and pure and capable.' He kept telling me that, and kept reading those words to me, until they began to sink into my soul. God began to wash me clean with those words, and with many other passages from the Bible. Washed me clean from my past, at the same time as he was implanting within me a new picture of the person I could become. It was really quite a wonderful process, nothing short of a full transformation. The old fell away under the influences of this man's love and God's love, leaving the new free to emerge and then eventually to spill out onto others. All my life I had lived under a dark cloud—first from feeling unwanted, then from the awful things my father did, and then finally the cloud of my own blackness of heart that I had been carrying for many years. The clouds were swept away. Someone *did* want me and *did* love me. The horrible memories of my father were replaced by the present reality of a man who was caring and compassionate, a man who loved me and would never hurt me. And the blackness in my heart was cleansed and healed by his belief in me, and by his gentle and tender and encouraging words. The sun came out for the first time in my life. He gave me a place to stand in life, a place of warmth and smiles, and a contented feeling when I went to sleep at night.

"Of course, on a deeper level what was really happening was that he was giving me my first glimpse of God's nature and character. For what he did was exactly what Jesus did when he encountered people—he looked into their eyes and reached down inside them to touch the *real* person down at the core. That is what God is always trying to do in people's lives, in a million ways, sometimes using other people, sometimes on his own. He has a million ways to love us, a million ways to try to get through to us, if we're only able to hear that voice that is sometimes so hard to hear. We are locked away in the cocoons that life surrounds us with. Yet all the while the freedom of the butterfly lies hidden deep inside, and God is constantly trying to find ways to loose our wings and let us soar and be happy in the flight of his life.

"That's what Mr. Parrish did. He looked inside me and said, 'You are someone special. You are a gem that can shine—all we have to do is polish it a bit.' And he went to work polishing.

"At first it was just his words, his kindness, his caring, his love. He made me believe in myself, and believe that he loved me. I listened to him read the Scriptures, and I listened to everything he said about God, but the Lord was still distant. God was not someone who had yet touched my life in a real way. I listened and I probably absorbed more than I realized.

But it was still some time later when I awoke to the immediacy of God's relation to *me*—me personally! It took some time for God to steal closer and closer, until that moment when I was ready to surrender my heart to Him, as well as to Mr. Parrish."

# CHAPTER 38

## ENCOUNTER WITH THE FATHER

"How influences from our Father in heaven begin to penetrate our consciousness," Almeda continued, "is one of life's great mysteries. I know ever since the moment I met Mr. Parrish, God began speaking more directly to me. But for a long while, as I said, I was not aware of it.

"We worked together in the store, then expanded the business a little, and by and by built a pretty good life there in Boston. I was obviously not what you would call a 'society lady,' yet in a way my husband did succeed in making a lady of me. He would take me to the theater and sometimes to social gatherings, without the least shame in the kind of person I had once been. He knew everything about my past—about my father, about the men who had been in my life, about the baby. Yet nothing could stop him from continually saying to me, 'You, Almeda, are a woman of virtue and uprightness and righteousness. God made you in *his* image. He loves you, and I love you. Yesterday's gone. Your past has been washed clean.'

"All that couldn't help but make all of life new to me. The sun was brighter. The raindrops sparkled with a new radiance. Flowers took on such a wonderful new meaning. One day a little bee flew against our window and stunned himself and fell to the ground. I scooped him carefully into my palm, and just gazed upon him with a tenderness I didn't even know was in my heart. When he began to come to, I lifted him into the wind and blew him off my palm. And as I watched him fly away, tears came to my eyes, althought I didn't even know why.

"Life was happening all around me, but it wasn't an *impersonal* life. Somehow everything was very personal. It all seemed to touch my heart so. To breath in deeply of the fragrance of an orange or yellow rose touched chords in my being I can't even describe. The smell itself was holy, as if it went back to the very foundation of the world itself, and then had come into being just for me, that I might smell that rose on that particular day. There are no words to convey what I felt. The smell was almost sad in a way, calling forth a yearning for something more than just the aroma of the rose's perfume, but a longing for something that could never be had, never be found. I think that's what it was with the bee too, a longing after something, a hunger—oh, I don't know!—to somehow be a sister, a friend, to that bee in the shared life of the creation we were both in. Yet the bee was just a bee, without the capacity to let me share his life, without even the capacity to know that such a thing as people existed. And somehow as a result I found tears in my eyes.

"Birds in flight held my gaze, something about their seeming freedom called out to me to join them. Sunrises, sunsets . . . even tiny green blades of grass—*everything* began to speak to me. Not speak in words, but speak in feelings. Just to see the intricacies of creation was to find feelings of love rising up in me for those things—for the rose, the bee, the bird, the blade of grass—each unique and so beautiful in its own way.

"Yet there always were tears to go along with the love. For a long time I didn't know why. But then a day came when at last I did.

"The moment came when we were on our way here to California. My husband got a business scheme in his head, and we sold everything and booked passage to join the rush to California.

"One night I was standing along the rail, gazing out across the expanse of the Pacific. It was late, and I was alone. There was a bright moon out, and its light spread glistening out across the water as far as I could see. A few clouds now and then slowly went across it, dulling the reflection for a few moments, and then it would return.

"All these things I have been telling you were filtering through my mind, images out of my past, the changes that had come, how alive and full I felt, such a great thankfulness that the downward path of my former existence had been stopped and that I'd been turned around. And I was thinking of the bee too, and wondering why it had caused me to weep. All the time I was gazing out upon the glow of the moon on the water. The ocean . . . the moon . . . the water . . . the clouds . . . the mystery of the silence . . . it all began to have a saddening, yearning effect on me and as I stood there, I found tears welling up in my eyes.

"But it only lasted a moment. The next instant a voice spoke to me. I don't mean out loud, but it was so clear in my heart it might as well have been an audible voice. It said: 'It's *me* your tears are meant for. *I'm* the one who put my life into the things I have made, and it's that life which calls out to you. All along I have been calling out to you through the fragrance of the pine tree and the buzz of the honey bee and the winged freedom of the butterfly . . . and this very moment I am calling out to you through the moon's light on the sea.'

"And I knew it was the voice of God speaking to me. And suddenly I knew that he had been there all along, all my life, speaking, calling out to me, trying to love me and touch me and heal me—and care for me. I knew that he knew all about my father and everything that had happened to me. And I knew that he had sent my husband to help pull me up and make a woman of me.

"Yet somehow, even in knowing these things, I continued to weep. I was filled with a sense of remorse because I hadn't seen God before this moment, even though he had been beside me, so close beside me since the day I was born. I had smelled the roses and picked the blades of grass, but I had never seen the *life* that was in them, the life that was God, so close as to be in my very hand, yet unseen.

"In that moment, in a sense, my whole life swept through my memory, and I saw for the first time my own responsibility in what I had allowed myself to become. Even as awful as my father had been, I saw that if I had seen that God *was* with me even then, and had listened to his voice, I could have shared that time with him, and that he could have protected me and kept me from what followed in my life. But my independence kept my eyes on myself, and until Mr. Parrish came along I just looked at nothing else but *me*.

"Right there on the ship, I dropped down onto my knees. And still clinging with one hand to the railing, I began to pray to God from the depths of my heart.

" 'Oh God,' I prayed, 'I want to live! And I want to live with you. I want you to be my Father. I said I'd never let anybody near me . . . I didn't think I could trust anyone, not even you! All those painful years growing up, people were so cruel . . . they only wanted me for what they could get out of me. I learned to be tough, and when anyone tried to come close, I'd just push them away . . . but inside I was truly afraid . . . I only wanted someone to love me. But there's been no one . . . until this dear man you sent me to . . . and *you* Lord! Please forgive me . . . it just hurt *so* bad. But now I see how much I've always needed you. Be the Father to me I never had. Oh Lord, forgive me for my stubbornness and independence when I was younger. I'm so sorry I didn't know you were there, didn't pay attention. Help me now to live, and to live for you! Help me to get my eyes off myself and onto others. Let me be a help to those who may not know love, just as I didn't. Oh God, please help me. I want to be your daughter. I want to be your woman. Do whatever you want with me, Lord, whatever it takes to transform me into the person you want me to be.'

"When I was through praying I got up and went back to our cabin. I knew there had been a change. And from the moment we got to California I was a new woman. Mr. Parrish had begun the process by picking me up off the ground. Now the Lord continued the transformation deep in my being, all the way through every part of me.

"And it goes on every day. I still have to struggle with my independence, as you both know from the events of the election campaign. But as I said when I began, even though the work God has to do in me goes on every moment, the difference between fifteen years ago and now is like night and day. You, Corrie, are very fortunate to have begun so early in your life to make the Lord part of your life. I hope and pray that you will one day give your heart to him too, Katie. Because there is no abiding contentment in life apart from him. I can tell you that, not because I am a good Christian lady, but because I've known life without him too, and I know how empty it is."

Almeda stopped. We had been sitting for nearly an hour and a half. It was the most moving story I had ever heard anyone tell, and I still could hardly believe Almeda was telling about her *own* life! She was visibly drained.

"What about all those rumors Mr. Royce was spreading around town last fall?" I asked finally.

Almeda smiled—a sad smile, yet without bitterness.

"There were elements of truth in everything that was said, Corrie, as you can now see for yourself. But like all rumors, it was half fact, half fiction, with usually the fiction parts being those aspects of it people are most eager to believe. All that ridiculous talk about meeting Mr. Parrish on the ship and marrying him practically the next day—I don't know where some of that was dredged up from."

"Does Pa know all this?"

"Everything," she answered. "I wouldn't have let him marry me without making sure he knew what he was getting. I told him every detail. And do you know what he said? He said, 'Everything you tell me just makes me love you more, not less.' He's quite a man, Corrie, that father of yours!"

I nodded and smiled.

"I suppose there's no disrespect in saying this," she went on. "But I'm just now seeing just how much I really do love your father. Mr. Parrish taught me that I could *be* loved. He showed me love. He gave me love. He opened up so much of himself to me. But once I came to know your father, Corrie, I found hundreds of new things opening in *me* that weren't there before. Or at least if they were there, I hadn't noticed. In knowing him, suddenly love began to pour out of me in a new way. Of course I loved Mr. Parrish, but—well, I suppose I just wanted you to know that your Pa is special to me in a completely unique way. There is a part of my heart that is only for him and no one else."

Again she was quiet. Still Katie sat without moving.

Almeda rose. "I suppose it's time we were going home," she said.

Then Katie rose and finally spoke. "Almeda," she said, "I am sorry for the things I said. I had no right."

Almeda smiled. "Think nothing of it, Katie. I just wanted you to understand." She gave Katie a hug, which Katie only half-heartedly returned, and then we left.

"What do you think she thought?" I asked as we walked home.

"That's something only God can know," Almeda answered. "He does everything in his own time, especially in the matter of the human heart. Katie's time will come just as surely as mine did on the ship. But what did you think, Corrie?" she added.

"I guess I'd agree with Pa," I said.

"How so?"

"That your story makes me love you more, not less."

She slipped her hand through my arm and we walked the rest of the way in silence.

# CHAPTER 39

## THE TOWN COUNCIL

Almost the moment we got back to our place, exhaustion came over Almeda from all the energy it had taken to pour herself out like she had. She slept for two or three hours that afternoon, and I went into the office in town. When I came back that evening and our eyes first met, she smiled at me, and there was something new in her look. I suppose I saw for the first time how much depth there had always been in that smile. And I could tell she was glad that I knew everything. It was like a smile exchanged between sisters who know each other completely.

Nothing much changed otherwise. Things returned to normal with Katie. No more sullenness, no more outbursts, but neither was there any exuberance or special friendliness. I was sure Katie had been touched by Almeda's story, but you could see nothing of it on her face or in her actions. I hoped something was going on inside her.

Meanwhile, business at the Mine and Freight hardly seemed to suffer at all on account of Mr. Royce's competition up the street. Now and then we'd hear of some sale he made to someone, or of something he was doing. But most of our customers remained loyal to Almeda. And of course the way the election turned out and what Pa and Almeda had done for Shaw and Douglas and had promised to do for the others—all that just deepened people's allegiance to them.

I thought that after Christmas dinner Mr. Royce might

eventually close down his store. But he kept it open, although he was pretty subdued about promoting it. He probably knew it wouldn't do much good anyway, and I think he was starting to realize that maybe Pa and Almeda weren't the adversaries he had always imagined them to be. He also stopped making so much noise about making trouble for Pa and his claim. Maybe getting beat in the election sobered him into recognizing that he wasn't quite as all-powerful in the community as he had thought. He made good on his promise to call no more notes due. In fact, just shortly after the first of the year he lowered the interest rate on a few of the larger ones, not wanting folks to be mad at him for what they'd heard about Pa and Almeda's arrangements with Mr. Shaw.

Mr. Shaw kept paying them, and they kept paying the fellow in Sacramento, and so in the long run it actually worked out better for the Shaws than it had been before.

As it turned out, I didn't get the chance to visit again soon with Ankelita Carter. She wrote saying that she was sending some men to Sacramento for supplies, so Zack and Little Wolf and I arranged to go to the capital and meet them and return Rayo Rojo without having to ride all the way down to Mariposa. But I still hoped to meet the Fremonts some day!

Even with Christmas and the beginning of the new year behind us, I still couldn't get myself in a frame of mind to do much writing. Somehow the motivation was missing after the events leading up to the election and disappointments about my article and Mr. Fremont's loss. I tried to write a few articles throughout the first months of the year, but they were nothing I wanted to send in to Mr. Kemble. I found myself wondering if I'd ever write much again. I drew lots of pictures and kept writing in my journal, and otherwise spent most of the daytime in town at the Mine and Freight. Almeda kept working too, although by the beginning of March her pregnancy was far enough along that she had to slow down and take most afternoons off.

Several interesting things happened in town during those early months of 1857. Some meetings were held in Sacramento about town planning. Now that the gold rush was gradually giving way to the growth of California and the concerns of statehood and settlement, the state's leaders in the capital seemed to think communities like Miracle Springs needed some help figuring out what to do with themselves. Because of my articles, someone there had actually heard about the election and knew of the outcome. And so Pa received a personal invitation to come to the meetings. They asked if he'd be willing to make a short talk about the problems and difficulties he felt *he* had in being a leader in a former gold-boom town that was now growing into a more diverse community.

When the letter first came, everyone was excited about it, and Alkali Jones was laughing and cackling about Pa running for president himself next. Everyone was excited, except Pa. His response was just what you might have expected—casual and disinterested.

"I can't see what you're all making such a fuss about," he said. "They most likely sent this same letter to a hundred other men just hoping that *one* of them would show up with something to say."

But inside I could tell Pa was mighty proud, and a time or two I caught sight of him alone re-reading the letter, so I know he was thinking about it more than he was willing to let on.

He did go to Sacramento, and he did speak a little to the meeting of town leaders who were there, although he downplayed that when he got back, too. But it was obvious that he was different after that—more serious about being mayor, talking more about problems that needed solving in the community, thinking about the impact of things on the people he served as well as his own life and family.

One of the results of Pa's going to Sacramento was a town council.

"It's the way a town ought to be run," Pa told us, "so no one man can tell everybody else what to do. They can vote on things, and that way it doesn't all just rest on the mayor's shoulders. And besides that, the council gives the mayor someplace to go for advice, other men to talk to—"

"Other *men?*" repeated Almeda with a sly smile. "Are only men allowed on the council?" The rest of us laughed.

"You're dang right, woman!" said Pa with a grin. "You don't think after what you put this community through last year that anyone's going to stand for a woman on the town council!"

"They just might! And I suppose you're going to tell me that only men can vote for the council too?"

Pa smiled, drawing it out a long time, waiting until everyone quieted down and was watching for what he would say next.

"Well, actually what they recommended," he answered finally, "is that the mayor himself pick the people to be on the first council, instead of trying to call an election."

"And so no women will get selected?" persisted Almeda.

"I think you've just about got the gist of how California politics works at last," said Pa.

We all laughed again, Almeda louder than anyone.

"Seriously, Drummond," she went on, "are you really going to pick the council yourself? How will you choose?"

"I don't know yet. But I gotta have some folks I can talk to besides just you and Nick and Corrie and Alkali and the rest of you. That was all right for trying to decide about the election last year, when we all just got together and discussed everything. But what would folks think if that's how I did my mayoring, just getting my advice from my family? One thing's for sure, I'd never get re-elected! No, folks want to know their voice is being heard somehow. That's what they called 'representative government' in Sacramento. We all know that everybody votes for president, but they said the same thing's important in a town too, that the mayor and council represent all the people, not just their own interests."

Pa was starting to sound like a politician!

"They said those towns without a council yet ought to get one appointed so they can get it working and get the bugs worked out of how town government's supposed to function. Then in two years—that'd be in fifty-eight, when the next state elections are held—they can have people run for town council and mayor, and make it all more official."

"How many are on a council?" asked Zack.

"Oh, depends, son. In big cities, maybe ten or twelve. But for a little place like Miracle Springs, four or five, maybe six, is plenty."

"What does a town council do, Pa?" asked Becky.

"I reckon they just help the mayor decide things."

"But who says what the mayor decides and what the council decides?" I asked.

"Well, another thing they talked about in Sacramento is a town drawing up a set of what they call bylaws. That's like a set of instructions of who does what and how rules and laws are made. So that's something we got to do too, after we get a council. They've got some from other places we'll be able to look at and work from."

"What if the council votes and it's a tie?" said Zack.

"That's why you have to have a wise mayor who knows what he's about," replied Pa with a smile. "In cases where they can't make a decision, the mayor casts the deciding vote and they do what he says."

As it turned out, Pa wasted no time in getting together the first Miracle Springs town council. He went around and talked to folks, got lots of opinions and suggestions of who people'd trust to sort of be their community spokesmen and leaders. The first man he selected was Mr. Bosely, the owner of the General Store, and then Simon Rafferty, the sheriff. Those two surprised no one because they were men most folks knew and respected. Next there was Matthew Hooper, a rancher who lived about five miles from town. Pa said he wasn't sure if him being on the council was exactly legal, since he didn't actually live in town. But that could all be straightened out later, he said, and if it wasn't, then a change could be made at the next election. For now he and most folks around thought Mr. Hooper would be a real good help for speaking up for ranching interests. And to represent the miners, there was Hollings Shannahan, who had been in Miracle since 1850. But the last two—Pa had decided on six for the council—shocked everybody. The first was Almeda, and she was the most surprised of all!

"What will people say, Drummond?" she said. "Picking a woman's bad enough . . . but your own wife!"

"I don't care what they say, woman. You're one of the most qualified people around here, and everyone knows it. You ran for mayor. And what anyone thinks is their own business—I want you on my town council."

But his final selection made everyone for miles throw their hands up in the air wondering if Drummond Hollister had finally gone loco once and for all. He wouldn't say anything to any of us ahead of time, and on the day when he made the announcement of the council members to a gathering of people in town, he saved the surprise name for last.

"As the sixth and final person to help look over this town," Pa said, "I name a fellow I've had a difference or two with, but who I reckon has just about as much a say in the things that go on around here as anyone—Franklin Royce."

So that was Miracle Springs' first town council—Bosely, Rafferty, Hooper, Shannahan, Parrish-Hollister, and Royce— with Drummond Hollister mayor over them. As time went on, everyone saw Pa's wisdom in picking the people he did. Everyone came to have a real confidence in the council to make decisions that were for the whole community's good. Even Mr. Royce began to be seen in a new light. I think it meant a lot to him that Pa had picked him, although he wouldn't do much to show it.

The first meeting of the town council was a celebrated affair that was held, of all places, in a back room of the Gold Nugget, which they cleaned up for the occasion. Lots of people were there, curious to see what was going to happen. But for the meeting itself, Pa wouldn't let any spectators in.

"There may be time enough one day for all you gawkers to see us do some of our town counciling. But for this first time together, we aim to just talk among ourselves, and get a few matters of business settled."

Then he shut the door and disappeared inside, leaving all

the onlookers in the saloon to drink and talk and wonder out loud what there could possibly be for a Miracle Springs town council to talk about, anyway.

When Uncle Nick was telling us about it afterwards, he said, "There was more than one of the men that said, 'What in tarnation's got into Drum, anyhow? He's done got hisself so blamed official about everything since the election! He ain't no fun no more!'"

But mostly Uncle Nick said the men had a lot of respect for how Pa was handling the whole thing.

When Pa and Almeda got back later that evening it was already pretty late, but we were dying of curiosity. Pa didn't say much, but Almeda went on and on about it.

"You should have seen him!" she exclaimed. "Your father ran that meeting like he was the Governor himself! Why, he even had to shut me up once or twice."

"You told me to treat you like all the others and not to give you preferential treatment on account of us being married," said Pa in defense.

"I didn't mean you had to silence me in mid-sentence."

"You were carrying on, Almeda," said Pa, "and I didn't see anything else to do but shut you down before you made a fool of yourself by what you were saying."

"A fool of myself!"

"You were talking like a woman, not like a town councilman. And maybe you are a council*woman*, not a council*man*, but you still gotta act like a councilman. I'm just trying to protect you from getting criticized by any of the others."

Almeda didn't say anything for a minute, then added, "Well, even if I am still vexed with you for what you did, I still think you ran that meeting like the best mayor in the world, and I'm proud of you."

"What did you talk about, Pa?" asked Emily.

"Oh, not too much, I reckon. A town this size hasn't got all that much that anyone needs to decide. We just looked at a copy of some bylaws I brought from Sacramento and talked about some of the stuff, trying to decide how *we* ought to do things here in Miracle."

One of the things they decided over the course of the next few meetings had to do with growth and new businesses that might come to Miracle Springs in the future. With the way the state was growing so fast—and this was something Pa said they talked a lot about at the meetings in Sacramento—communities like ours had to make some decisions early about how much they wanted to grow and in what ways. Pa and the council members decided that the council would vote on any new businesses that wanted to come and start up in Miracle, so that they'd have the chance to determine if they thought it was a good idea or not.

As it turned out, this decision was one of the first ones to be tested, and the results were different than anyone had expected.

# CHAPTER 40

## PA'S FIRST BIG DECISION

As a result of all the ruckus the previous autumn about money and foreclosures and all the threats Mr. Royce had made about calling notes due, an unexpected turn of events landed Pa and the rest of the council in the middle of a controversy. Pa and Almeda were even more in the middle of it than anyone else.

When Almeda's friend from Sacramento, Mr. Denver, had helped to arrange with his boss, Mr. Finch, for them to borrow the money to help Patrick Shaw, the incident had apparently stirred up Mr. Finch's old antagonism toward Franklin Royce. Mr. Denver told Almeda that there was a time when his boss had thought about expanding their financial holdings into the northlands, and now it seemed that uncovering his old grievances had brought that desire to life again.

One day out of nowhere Carl Denver rode into town to see Almeda. Almeda's first thought was that something had gone sour on their arrangement with Mr. Finch and that he was about to call Pa and Almeda's money with *him* due. But that wasn't it at all, Mr. Denver assured her.

"Finch couldn't be more pleased to be involved with you people up here," he went on with a smile. "In fact, he's hoping this is but the beginning. Which brings me to the reason for my trip."

He reached into his coat pocket and pulled out several papers. From where I was standing in another part of the office, they looked like legal documents of some kind.

"Mr. Finch wants to open a branch of Finchwood Ltd. right here in Miracle Springs!" he announced. "He's already had all the documents drawn up, and he sent me up to find a site and begin making specific preparations."

"That's wonderful," replied Almeda. "But I can't imagine . . . why Miracle Springs? Finchwood is a sizeable investment firm. What can there possibly be here to interest you?"

"All of California is growing at an explosive rate. Mr. Finch is a shrewd businessman, and loses no opportunity to get in on the ground floor, as he calls it. He's convinced that Miracle Springs will one day become a sort of hub for this region north of Sacramento. And I have to tell you, Almeda," he went on, "no small part of that has to do with your impact upon him. He was quite taken with you—with your resolve, your determination. He's watched what went on here, followed the election, and then saw your husband at the recent town-leader meetings down in Sacramento."

"Mr. Finch met Drummond?"

"No, they didn't actually meet. But Mr. Finch has been considering a move of this kind for some time, so he went to the meetings to explore possibilities. He heard your husband address the meeting, and was duly impressed with him as well. Out of all the growing communities represented at those meetings, he came away thinking more strongly than ever that Miracle Springs was the town he wanted to invest in—with a new bank, with investment opportunities for the miners who happen to be doing well and need a place for their funds, and perhaps with other businesses as well."

"I must say, Carl, I'm . . . I'm rather speechless. It's so unexpected—to think that Miracle Springs could one day grow into an actual city."

"There's no *could* to it, Almeda. If Mr. Finch has his way— and he usually does—there will be no way to stop Miracle Springs from growing by leaps and bounds. A population of 10,000 or more within three to five years would not be out of the question. And you know what that means?"

"I imagine it would mean a great number of things," replied Almeda slowly, her expression turning very serious. "But what do you think it means, Carl?"

"It means money, Almeda, opportunity, jobs. Your business, even if no changes were made, would positively explode. But as I said, Mr. Finch is very taken with you and your husband. He would lose no chance to make some very attractive and lucrative opportunities available to you. He would like to help you expand your business. He told me to convey that to you personally. He would invest money in your husband's re-election campaign when the time comes. He even hopes to persuade one of you to join him in Finchwood in some capacity or other—perhaps with a stock option—in order that you and your husband might be influential in securing Finchwood access into the community, so that we would be able to gain people's trust, as it were."

"I see," responded Almeda, thinking heavily.

"It's a once-in-a-lifetime opportunity, Almeda. If the growth happens as Mr. Finch is convinced it can with his money pouring into the area, in five years you and your husband could wind up in a very secure position—even wealthy, by the standards of most people. Your husband would be mayor of one of California's leading small and growing cities. And who knows what opportunities can open up politically, with your being so close to Sacramento. Not to mention the vast influence you would both have right here in your own community. You would become its first man and first woman, with the prestige and wealth to accompany it!"

Almeda was silent a moment. It was clear Mr. Denver didn't understand her hesitancy.

"There is one thing you have perhaps not considered in all this," said Almeda at length.

"What is that?"

"The town council."

"Oh, not to worry. A mere formality," said Mr. Denver buoyantly. "It's money that runs politics, not politics that runs money, Almeda. Once the people of this community realize all

the good to come of the kinds of investments and growth Finchwood will bring, they'll be begging us to come."

"A recent town ordinance was passed which says the town
council must authorize any new business within Miracle
Springs."

"Yes—and aren't both you and your husband on the council?"

"I am. Not Drummond."

"But he's the mayor. Why, with the two of you behind this
thing, it can't lose!"

"There is one person who *will* lose from it, that much is
certain," said Almeda."

"Who's that?" asked Denver.

"Franklin Royce," she answered. "His bank won't survive
six months once a new one opens its doors."

"Mr. Finch *did* think of that," Mr. Denver observed with
a sly smile. "He's been waiting for a chance to put him out of
business for years. And ever since you came to us for help last
year, he's been slowly hatching this scheme in that clever brain
of his."

"Seems a little too bad."

"Too bad! Royce is a no-good crook! You as much as said
so yourself. I thought the two of you hated him as much as Mr.
Finch does. Hasn't he tried to put *you* out of business?"

"Yes, there's no denying he has . . . several times."

"Then here's your chance to get even and rid Miracle
Springs of him forever."

Again, Almeda was silent.

"And from what I understand, he's opened a supplies outlet
in direct competition with you," Mr. Denver added.

She nodded.

"Well, now do you see how well this will work out for
everybody? Kill two birds with one stone, as the saying goes—
drive Royce out of business, and his bank and store with him!
And all the while Miracle Springs will be growing and you and
your husband will be making money and gaining power. What
more could anyone hope for!"

"What more, indeed," repeated Almeda, her voice filled with reservation in spite of Mr. Denver's enthusiasm. "But you do know that Franklin is on the council too?"

"Of course. I've done my background work before coming here. One vote won't hurt us. Five to one is just as good as six to zero. Besides, everyone in the whole community hates Royce too. We'll be performing a service to the whole area by getting rid of him! And just to make sure, I'll be contacting the other council members to outline the advantages to them personally for voting with Finchwood."

Almeda did not reply, and then the conversation moved off in other directions. Finally Mr. Denver left to go to the boarding house where he would be staying.

Miracle always seemed to be in the middle of *something* or another that had people stirred up and talking and taking sides. And no sooner had all the election hullabaloo settled down than we were smack in the midst of another upheaval. Carl Denver saw to that! He started right off talking to the members of the town council—all except one. Within a few days it was all over town about Finchwood's plans and all the growth and prosperity that would come to Miracle Springs and how good it would be for all its people.

Folks talked about it a lot, and almost everyone seemed to think it was a good thing. You can't stop progress, Mr. Denver had been telling them, and no one seemed inclined to try. Besides, they said, new businesses and new money and new investments in the community couldn't help but be good for everybody. And if California was going to grow, why shouldn't Miracle Springs get right in and grow as fast as anyplace else?

Undoubtedly the change would do damage to the Royce Miners' Bank, especially because Mr. Denver let it be known that Finchwood would probably lend money for land and homes at lower interest than Mr. Royce. I don't think most people wanted to hurt Mr. Royce, but at the same time they weren't all that worried about him, either. "If he can't keep up with the times, that's his own fault," Mr. Shaw commented to Almeda when he was over visiting. "Wouldn't bother me none at all to see him run out of here for good!"

Of course, Mr. Shaw had good reason to dislike Franklin Royce, but a lot of other people would probably have agreed with Alkali Jones assessment of the situation: "Serves the dang varmint right, hee, hee, hee!" he cackled. "He ain't been out fer nobody but his blame self for years, an' now it'll just be givin' him a dose o' his own medicine!"

Pa and Almeda were surprisingly quiet through the whole thing. I knew they were talking and praying together, but they didn't tell anyone what they were thinking. Almeda had remained somber ever since the day when Mr. Denver had come into the Freight office. I didn't understand her hesitation, if that's what was making her quiet about it. It seemed to me that it couldn't help but be good for her and Pa and the business. And in a way they'd already thrown in with Finchwood months before with their dealings over the Shaw and Douglas notes. I'd heard them talk once or twice about the possibility of getting even more money to lend to people if Mr. Royce got troublesome again. Pa had even jokingly said something about the new Hollister-Parrish "bank," and then laughed. So it seemed that what Mr. Finch was proposing fit right in with what they'd been thinking of themselves.

A special town council meeting was planned to vote on it, so that Mr. Denver could get the papers signed and finalize everything before he went back to report to Mr. Finch. During the week he was here, he had a sign painted, and the day before the meeting it went up in the window of an empty building two doors down from Mr. Bosely's. It read, *Future Home of Finchwood Ltd.*, with the words, *Investments, Banking, Securities* underneath in smaller letters. No one saw much of Mr. Royce all week.

On the morning of the meeting, I said to Pa at breakfast, "How are you going to vote, Pa?"

"Don't you know, girl, it's the council's decision to make, not mine."

"Then how's Almeda going to vote?"

"You're asking me? She doesn't tell me ahead of time.

When it comes to the council, she's not my wife. She's representing the town, not me. And I don't want to know what she's thinking, because then one of us might try to do some convincing for our own side, and that wouldn't be right for the town, now would it?"

"I guess not," I answered.

Just then Almeda walked in from the other room.

"Corrie asked me how you're going to vote," Pa told her.

"And what did you tell her?"

"That I didn't know, which I don't."

"When we're representing Miracle Springs, Corrie," Almeda went on, "we've got to do our best to lay our personal feelings aside. If we're going to be faithful to the town and its people, we've got to vote our conscience, even if it sometimes means being on the opposite side of a certain issue. Both of us have spoken to a lot of people, and we've prayed together for wisdom, but that's as far as our communication on the subject goes."

The meeting of the council was scheduled for six o'clock that evening. Because so many people were interested, Pa had arranged for the tables and chairs in the Gold Nugget to be moved aside and organized so that the meeting could take place in the main part of the saloon—the biggest single room in all of Miracle Springs.

When the time came, the place was full, with another twenty or thirty people milling around in the street outside. The council members sat up in front at a long rectangular table with Pa in the middle. Mr. Denver was full of smiles and greetings for everyone, and sat down in the front row of chairs. It was the first time our whole family had been in the Gold Nugget together since that first church service when Rev. Rutledge was new in town. There were chairs for us and for all the women who came, but most of the men had to stand.

Pa called the meeting to order by banging his fist down on the table two or three times.

"Quiet down!" he called out. "Hey, quiet . . . we have to get this meeting called to order!"

Everybody gradually stopped talking and buzzing. "This is a meeting of the Miracle Springs town council for the purpose of deciding whether to grant this petition—" Pa held up Mr. Denver's papers which had been sitting on the table in front of him. "This petition is from Finchwood Limited in Sacramento to set up a bank here in Miracle Springs."

You could still hear quite a bit of noise coming from the men standing around outside, but Pa ignored it and kept right on going.

"So before we decide, I need to ask if anybody's got anything to say. You've all got a right to speak to the council before we vote if you think there's anything we need to hear before making the decision."

Pa waited. The room was silent for a moment. Then Mr. Denver rose to his feet. He talked for about ten minutes, half toward Pa and the others up in front, but turning around into the saloon a lot too, saying mostly the same kinds of things he'd been saying all week about all the good Mr. Finch wanted to do for the people of Miracle Springs.

When he sat down, Pa said. "Any of the rest of you got anything to say?"

Mr. Shaw came forward.

"All right, Pat. What do you have to tell us?"

"Only this—that I think it's an opportunity we might not get again. And as for the folks of Finchwood, it seems to me we can trust them just as far, if not even further, than some of the people we've been having our financial dealings with up till now."

A small buzz went around at his pointed words. Mr. Royce sat in front not moving a muscle, but everyone knew what Mr. Shaw was talking about. Since Patrick Shaw had almost been thrown off his land by Mr. Royce, if anyone had a right to be saying what he was, it seemed that Mr. Shaw did.

"So I say we give them all the approval they want," he added, then went back to where he'd been standing.

From the nods and expressions of agreement, it was clear that most of the men present felt the same way.

"Anyone else?" said Pa over the hubbub.

"Get on with the votin', Drum!" called out someone. "We all know well enough what's gonna happen without no one talkin' 'bout it no more."

"Do yer mayorin', Drum!" cackled Alkali Jones. "Hee, hee, hee!"

"Okay, that's enough from you ol' coots," said Pa. "But I reckon you're right. It's time to get this thing decided and over with. So if there's nothing more to be said, I'm going to call the vote."

Immediately there was silence, and Pa called on the council members one at a time.

"Hooper,'" said Pa. "How do you vote—yea or nay about Finchwood's petition?"

"Yea," said Mr. Hooper. Another round of chatter spread through the room.

"Bosely?" said Pa.

"Yea."

"Rafferty?"

"I vote against it," said the sheriff. At his words the noise got immediately louder.

"What you got against 'em, Simon?" called out someone.

"Quiet down," said Pa. "You can't interrupt the voting like that. You all will just have to keep your opinions to yourself till we're done."

"I just got a feeling about it, that's all," said the sheriff, not paying any attention to Pa but answering the man anyway. "I just can't see all the good it'll do for Miracle to grow so big as they're saying. It'll make my job all the harder, that's for sure. And that's why I'm voting no."

"Royce?" said Pa.

"Nay," replied the banker. Everyone had expected that.

"Shannahan?"

"Yea."

Now it *did* get quiet. Everybody had figured the vote to be five-to-one, with Mr. Royce being the only person to be against it. Now suddenly it was three-to-two, with one vote left. No one had expected it to be close. And they sure hadn't expected what came next.

"Almeda," said Pa. "Looks like you're the one who's going to decide this thing."

"I wish you'd have remembered to let ladies go first, Drummond," said Almeda with a smile. "Then all this pressure would have fallen on one of the other men."

"Couldn't be helped," replied Pa. "It's just the way you were all sitting around the table. Besides, on a town council everyone's equal."

"Well, I'd still feel more comfortable not being last because I'm afraid I'm not going to clarify matters much. I vote no."

The silence instantly erupted into gasps and oohs and ahs and comments all filling up the room. The certain outcome was suddenly three-to-three—a tie vote on the first major decision the town council of Miracle Springs had to make!

"What you gonna do now, Drum?" someone called out.

"He's gonna vote himself," said Uncle Nick loudly. "That's what we got a mayor for!"

"Well, I reckon now we're about t' see what kind o' stuff our mayor's made of, ain't we?" said someone else.

"What's it gonna be, Drum—yea or nay?"

"Yeah, Drum, don't keep us in suspense! How you gonna vote?"

"Well, maybe I'd tell you if you baboons'd shut up long enough to let a mayor get a word in edgeways!" shouted Pa into the middle of all their hollering and talking.

Gradually the noise subsided, and within another minute the place was dead silent, with every eye in the room fixed on Pa, who was standing up behind the table where the other council members were sitting. He waited a moment longer. I don't know what he was thinking about, but everyone was listening for him to say just a single word—yea or nay. When he finally spoke, he said neither.

"I aim to say a few words before I cast my vote," he said. "You all know I'm no speechmaker. But I reckon a mayor's gotta get used to making a speech now and then, and so maybe now's as good a time as any for me to have a start at it. I didn't plan this out, because I didn't figure I'd have to do any voting today. But since it looks like I have to cast the deciding vote, I suppose I ought to tell you what I've been thinking about this week."

He stopped and took a breath, as if he was getting ready to jump into an icy river and wasn't too pleased at the prospect. Then he plunged ahead. And if I didn't know it was my own Pa, I would have taken him for a downright politician! It was just about one of the finest speeches I'd ever heard!

"We've got a lot of things to consider," Pa finally went on, "if it's gonna fall on our shoulders to say what should be the future of this town of ours. Now I've been talking to a bunch of you this past week, and doing a lot of thinking. Most of you say you figure change and new business and more money would be good for everybody, and so we ought to just let it go ahead and happen. And I guess we all figured that's how the vote would go, too. Probably most of you are a mite surprised that we've got a tie on our hands. And I'm as surprised as anyone. But even as little as I know about it, because I take my mayoring seriously, I did a bit of thinking these last days about what I thought too, and what I'd do just in case I did have to vote. And a couple of things stuck in my mind."

He stopped for a couple of seconds, just sort of looking around the room at all the eyes on him, then went ahead.

"The first thing I found myself wondering is this—if all this change and growth that Mr. Denver's predicting *does* happen, what kind of place is Miracle Springs going to be five or ten years from now? I'm sure he's right, because he knows more than a man like me about bringing in lots of money and new people. And maybe we'd all get rich. But that's what they said about the gold too, and not too many of us in *this* room are getting fat from having so much money stashed in Mr. Royce's bank."

A ripple of laughter spread through the room.

"Maybe we would get rich," Pa went on. "But it still strikes me that we'd have to ask what kind of place Miracle would be with five or ten thousand people here. Speaking just for myself, I'm not at all sure I'd want to be mayor of a place like that, or would even want to live here. Can you imagine Miracle with ten thousand people? Why, tarnation, the place'd spread so far in every direction, the Hollister place would be in the middle of town! We'd have no woods, no creek, no mine! Even half of Hooper's spread would have streets running through it!"

He paused for a minute while everyone laughed.

"Why Miracle would be a dad-blamed city! There'd be no room for mines anymore. Every inch for miles would be taken up with buildings and people! And I guess I'm just not at all sure I like the idea of that. I don't know about you, but I kind of like Miracle Springs the way it is."

Suddenly everyone quieted down as Pa's words sank in. It was obvious nobody had thought about the question quite like that, and Pa's questions got everyone sobered up in a hurry.

"The second thing that bothered me is gonna surprise a few of you. It surprises me to find myself thinking like this too! But you all know that besides my mayoring, I've been trying to take living as a Christian seriously too, so I'm not afraid to tell you that I pray about things a lot more than I used to. And I've been praying about this vote too. When you pray, every once in a while you find an answer from God coming your way that you didn't expect. And this is one of those times.

"What I got to thinking about was loyalty, and what it means. Loyalty to other folks—not just to friends and family, but to all sorts of others we owe something to. Seems to me loyalty's in short supply these days. Everyone's out to get all he can, and we don't stop too much to consider what we should be doing about those people Jesus calls our neighbors. But he tells us in the Good Book that we're supposed to do as we'd like to be done by. And that means standing by our neighbor whether he stands by us or not. It means being loyal whether someone's been loyal to us or not. It means trying to do good wherever you can, no matter what anyone else has done to you.

"So I found myself thinking a lot about a certain individual in this town of ours by the name of Franklin Royce—"

Another buzz of whispers and movement went around, then quickly settled down. Everyone was anxious to hear what Pa was gonna say.

"Now, you all know that Royce hasn't been a particular friend of mine, or anyone else's around here. He's pulled some pretty lowdown stuff, and he's hurt more than one upstanding man with his greed."

I glanced over at Mr. Royce. His face had a scowl on it, but he didn't dare move a muscle. I could almost feel the anger rising up from his reddening neck into his cheeks!

"He's tried to take my place a time or two, and would've taken Shaw's and Douglas's if Almeda and I hadn't stopped him. So I'd have to say that Mr. Royce has been a mean man, and maybe some of you'd just as soon be rid of him and his bank altogether.

"But you know, if it hadn't been for his bank, half of you in this room wouldn't have your houses and farms and ranches. Almeda's store used money from Royce's bank a time or two, and so did I. Much as we don't want to admit it, Franklin Royce has done a lot for this community. Even if we don't always see eye to eye, he's just as much a part of Miracle Springs as I am or as you are. Why, he was almost your mayor! And it was money from Royce's bank that saved the life of my Becky.

"Maybe Mr. Royce, for all his faults of the past, deserves a little of our loyalty too. He's put five or six years of his life into this place, and I'm not so sure I can be party to watching his business get ruined because he hasn't treated me so kindly. Seems like when times get rough, folks have to stick together and show their loyalty to one another. Maybe this is the time when we need to show Mr. Royce that the folks of Miracle Springs can be loyal too."

There was another pause, this time a long one, while people shifted around in their chairs or shuffled their feet.

"So here's what I figure to do," Pa continued finally. "I think we ought to think a little more about what kind of future we want for this place we call our home. Do we want it to stay the nice little town it is, or do we want it to become a city that's growing faster than we can keep up with? Then I want to go have a talk with Mr. Royce. And I want to tell him I'm willing to give him my hand and be a friend to him, and show my loyalty to him, even if he does try to put my wife's store out of business!"

More laughter erupted, and people shifted about nervously.

"What I aim to say to him is this: 'Now look, Franklin, it's no secret that you're charging more interest than some of the big banks in Sacramento. Why don't you be neighborly, and show *your* loyalty to the folks of Miracle Springs, by lowering the rates on everybody's loans to match what Finchwood would give them? They'll like you all the more for it, and then there won't be any reason for a new bank to open up. What do you say, Franklin?'

"That's what I'm going to say to our friend and banker, Mr. Royce, first chance I get," said Pa, glancing around the table where the council sat. Everyone chuckled when he looked straight at Mr. Royce.

"And in the meantime, since we've got town business to conduct right now, I'm going to cast my vote. I vote no."

He was immediately interrupted by sounds throughout the room. I had been looking at Mr. Royce, and my eyes drifted to Almeda, who was sitting right next to him. She was crying. She was so proud of Pa—we all were!

"So, Mr. Denver," Pa was trying to say, "I'm afraid you're going to have to tell your Mr. Finch that the petition's denied for right now. But you tell him how much we appreciate his interest in Miracle Springs. And you can tell him for me, that if he is still interested in Finchwood coming up this way, try us again a year from now. That'll give us a chance to think about all this a little more slowly. And it'll also give us a year to decide whether we think Miracle Springs is in need of some more competition in the banking business, or if the bank we've got seems to be operating to everyone's satisfaction."

Again Pa glanced in Mr. Royce's direction. The banker's face had a look of stunned joy on it, realizing that the man he styled his arch enemy had just saved his bank from another enemy.

I think Pa's final words were lost on Mr. Royce for the moment. But there would be plenty of people to remind the banker of their significance in the coming months!

People began moving around the room, and lots of men were already walking up to the bar to start ordering drinks. The women and children who had been there made haste to leave. The members of the council stood up, and some talking and hand-shaking followed.

Then almost as an afterthought, Pa shouted out: "This meeting of the town council is adjourned!"

# CHAPTER 41

# UNCLE NICK LEARNS TO PRAY

Pa's speech and vote sure did show what the new mayor was made of! Pa had shown his mettle in front of the whole town, and there couldn't have been a prouder, happier bunch of kids and a wife than we were riding home in the wagon that night after the meeting! It didn't even matter about the vote—it was what Pa'd done. He'd been a leader, a mayor. And it felt good to see him strong like that, and courageous to speak out.

Things seemed to change after that. The mayor and town council were more than just formalities now. They had made a real decision that changed something that would have happened without them. And if Mr. Royce did lower interest rates like Pa hoped he would, then as mayor Pa would have done everybody a lot of good. Miracle Springs might not grow as fast as some of California's new towns and cities. But at least from now on, folks around here knew they had people they could trust looking out for them.

One of the other events that happened early that spring before the babies were born was a big town picnic. But first I want to tell you about a conversation Pa and Uncle Nick had. I didn't actually hear it. Pa came in late one evening, got me and Almeda and Zack together by ourselves after the others were in bed, and told us about it.

"Nick's worried about Katie," he said quietly. We all waited for him to explain further.

"She's still quiet and moody. Of course, that's no surprise

to any of us," he went on, "because we can see it well enough. But he thinks it's his fault in some way, that he must have done something, or that he isn't being all to her he ought to be."

"Bless his dear heart," said Almeda tenderly.

"I told him it's not his doing—"

"Of course not," added Almeda. "He's a fine husband and father."

"That's exactly what I said," Pa went on. "Why, nobody from the old days would even recognize Nick! He's that different."

"So what did he say?"

"Aw, he just kept going on about how Katie wouldn't talk to him and was sullen and quiet and how he didn't know what to do. He was frustrated, I could tell that much. Seemed like he was ready to get angry with her one minute, but then the next remembered her condition and felt bad for not having more patience. He just doesn't know what to do, that's all."

"What did he say?"

"He said, 'She's been downright impossible lately. When I married her I didn't bargain for no wife that's moody all the time. What kind of marriage is it when you can't even talk together? But she ain't saying nothing no more, and I wind up talking just about the weather and the mine.' He'd go on like that, but then suddenly stop himself and feel bad just for saying it."

"It could be the pregnancy, you know, Drummond. It's harder on some women than others, and she's a good seven months along."

"So are you," said Pa.

"Are you saying I'm fat?"

"Just good and plump," replied Pa with a smile. "And you aren't moping around like you're mad at the world."

"But then I have you for a husband," said Almeda with a loving smile.

"Yeah, I guess you do at that!"

"But it's not really the pregnancy," Almeda mused. "That probably is wearing her out some, especially with little Erich to keep up with. But there's more than that—it's down deep. She's a troubled woman, Drummond. It's her spirit that's in turmoil, not her body."

Pa sighed. "Yeah, I know you're right. That much is plain from one look in her face. She's just not at peace with life."

"Does Nick know that?" she asked.

"I think so. I asked him when it all started. He said that it had been growing gradually for a long time, but it seemed to start getting worse a while back after he'd gotten her to go to church with us one Sunday. Avery preached a sermon about how we've all got to make God a regular part of our life every day, not just here and there."

"I remember the day very well. And now that you mention it, she was particularly quiet that afternoon."

"Nick said he had a feeling she was thinking about it. 'You remember when she first came' I asked him, 'when she said her aunt used to go to church every Sunday and prayed and did all kinds of religious stuff, but then didn't really live by it much the rest of the week?' Then I told him that she was more than likely watching all the rest of us mighty close, and especially him, to see if our religion was something we lived by. 'I don't mean no offense to you, Nick,' I said, 'but you gotta make sure you live by what you believe.'

" 'What do you mean?' he asked. 'I'm doing the best I can. But it ain't easy, Drum, tryin' to be helpful with her grumpy all the time and ignorin' me.'

" 'Calm down,' I said, 'I know what kind of man you are. I'm just saying you can't go on with your business like maybe you done in the past. You gotta go out of your way to help her.'

"I kept reminding him that she most likely had lots of things brewing down deep inside that had nothing to do with him, but with what she thought about God, and other memories out of her past like her aunt. I told him that all those things and attitudes were probably coming back at her now.

" 'Why won't she tell me about it then?' he asked me.

" 'Can't tell you that, Nick,' I said. 'It's not easy to talk about the past sometimes, especially for a woman like Katie who's used to being independent and in control of things. She probably doesn't want to admit to having any kind of trouble inside herself. That's just the way some folks are.' "

"Sounds to me like you gave him pretty good advice," said Almeda.

Pa shrugged, then continued his story. " 'Well what am I supposed to do?' Nick asked me.

" 'You just be as nice and as gentle to her as you can be,' I said. 'And keep remembering that she's carrying your little son or daughter inside her.'

" 'I'll do it, Drum,' he said.

" 'Then you pray for her, Nick,' I told him. 'You pray for her real hard, and you pray for her all the time.'

" 'What am I supposed to pray? I ain't no praying sort like you and Almeda.'

" 'Well then it's high time you became a praying man,' I told him. 'You look here, Nick—that wife of yours needs you now more than she's ever needed anyone in her life. And she needs more than just you being nice—even though she needs that too. She's got something going on down inside her, and she needs God to be her friend. And that probably isn't going to happen without lots of prayer, because Katie's mighty headstrong when it comes to God. And you being her husband, your prayers mean more than anybody else's because you know what her needs are. We'll all be praying too, but you being the man of that house, and Katie being your wife, you're the one who can take charge of the situation with your prayers. So you gotta do it, you hear me? You gotta pray for her.'

"Well, he shrugged and didn't say much for a long time. He wasn't used to thinking of himself like that. He's like most folks with that fool notion that praying's something you hire the preacher to do, and that living like a Christian's something you do on Sunday and forget the rest of the time. But I told him he's got to get to the business of being God's man in that family of his if he wants to pull his wife through this.

" 'But I don't know how to pray, Drum,' he said again.

" 'You can't have forgotten all your ma and pa taught you,'

I said. 'Even I knew them well enough to know they taught you and Aggie better than that. You know how to pray well enough. You just got out of practice because you haven't done it all these years. And now it's time you got at it again!'

" 'But what do I *say*?'

" 'There's nothing special you have to say. Just talk to God, that's all.'

" 'Out loud?'

" 'God doesn't care if it's out loud or not, Nick. Just talk to him, like he was right there in the room with you. You don't have to say a lot of words to get his attention. He's there. He's waiting for you to make him part of what you're about. He's not like us, Nick, who can only talk to a few folks at a time. He can be with all his children at once. So just tell him what you're thinking and feeling. And pray for Katie. Pray that he would open up Katie's heart.'

"He was quiet again. He was thinking pretty hard on what I was saying. I think it was like lots of things coming back to him from when he was just a kid, things he hadn't stopped to think about for a long time.

" 'But I don't know what's supposed to happen, Drum.' he said.

" 'Well, if you're praying for God to open up Katie's heart, then that's what's gonna happen,' I told him. 'That's the way it works. That's the kind of prayer God wants real bad to answer.' "

Pa looked around at the rest of us with a smile. " 'Look at me,' I said. 'That wife of mine—before she was even my wife, I don't doubt—and my daughter, and maybe even my son, for all I know—they were all praying for *me*. And lo and behold if some places down inside me didn't eventually open up and I begin to remember things and think about how I ought to be living and how I ought to be listening to God more. And pretty soon, Drum Hollister's praying out loud and trying to live his life as a Christian, and even some of his old friends are calling him *Reverend*.'

" 'So you see, Nick,' I said, 'that's just the way it works. If you pray for somebody, one way or another there's gonna be a change in their life. You remember what kind of man I used to be! It ain't gonna be all that tough for God to get through to a woman like Katie, just so long as you keep praying.'

" 'She can be a mighty headstrong woman,' said Nick. When he said it he sighed, and I could tell he wasn't being critical. It was just that frustration coming out again.

" 'Well, maybe that's so. But we'll all be praying with you, Nick,' I told him. 'And some time or another, something down inside her is going to tell her she's not as in control of life as she's always figured. That time comes sooner or later to everyone. For me it was Aggie's dying and the kids showing up. All of a sudden, my whole world changed and a little door somewhere inside me opened a crack. And that's when God started poking his head through, and for the first time in my life, I was ready to listen.

" 'Well, that time will come for Katie too. So when I say you have to wait, that's what you're waiting for—that time when the little door inside of her heart opens up a crack and she looks out and says, "Maybe I do need to know God more than I've always thought." Then you can pray with her.'

" 'I'm not sure how,' Nick said.

" 'You're the man,' I told him. 'You gotta take the lead and show her that you can pray. Just ask for God to be in both of you and to show himself to you, and pray that you'll be open to let him do what he wants to do in your hearts. And then if she's willing,' I said, 'then you encourage her to pray that same thing, that God would show himself to her and that he'd live in her heart and help her to understand things better and be a friend to him like she hadn't been up until then. If she'd pray that, I think you'd have yourself a new woman, Nick—one with a smile on her face.'

"He was real quiet again. This was all pretty new to him. I'm not sure he even liked it much. But I could tell he knew it was true, and knew what he had to do."

The cabin got real quiet. From the look in Almeda's eyes I could tell she was far away. But this time it wasn't the look of pain that came from memories of Boston. It was a contented, peaceful look. I knew she was reflecting on the changes that had come to us all, to her, and especially to Pa. Even though no one said anything right then, we all *felt* so complete—a genuine *family*, talking and praying together about the deep and important things in life.

The late-night silence was broken by footsteps as Emily walked out from her room.

"I'm sorry, Pa," she said. "I wasn't asleep, and I couldn't help listening. I was concerned about Katie."

"Come over here, girl," said Pa. Emily walked over to him, and he stretched out his arm around her waist and pulled her close to him. "I'm glad you came out to join us. We're gonna pray for Katie, and I want you to pray with us."

"Thank you, Pa," she said, then sat down on the floor at his feet. Pa kept one of his great strong hands resting on her shoulder.

"After Nick and I were done talking," Pa went on in a moment, "I asked him if he wanted to pray right then with me. I think it took him by surprise, the thought of two grown men praying together like that. But he just nodded. Then he waited to see what I was gonna do. So I bowed my head and reached across and put my hand on his arm, and then I closed my eyes and started praying for him and Katie. Afterward he told me he was surprised to hear me pray in just normal words, without trying to use a bunch of church-words like the Reverend does on Sundays. But I told him, 'Nick, the Lord's not much concerned with a batch of big words that sound like they come out of the Bible. He only wants us to talk to him, that's all, like the people we *really* are, not like someone we're pretending to be. That's what I told him afterwards. But right then I just closed my eyes and prayed for him and Katie, and especially that Katie would come to see that God wasn't her enemy and that he wanted to be her friend. Then I prayed that Nick would find the courage to pray for her and to be the man he was supposed to be. He hardly moved a muscle, and when I finished it was quiet a long time.

"I kept waiting with my eyes closed, 'cause I wanted him to pray, so he could see it wasn't such a fearsome thing after all. It seemed to take him forever to get up the gumption, but finally he said, 'God, I ain't much practiced in this kind of thing. But if you'd give me a hand now and then, I'll try to pray more. So I ask you to help me do what Drum says and pray for Katie. Help me to know what to say to her. And I ask you to make her be able to listen when people talk about you without getting her dander up. Help me to know what to say and do. And help me to be able to listen to you too.'

"Anyhow, that's something like what he prayed," Pa added.

"Good for him," said Almeda softly. "What a wonderful beginning! I know many doors will begin to open for the two of them very soon."

"And now let's us pray for them both," said Pa. "Five of us praying, especially five of us who love Nick and Katie—why, that's a powerful lot of prayer for God to be able to use!"

He took his hand off Emily's shoulder and placed it around her little white hand. Then he reached out with his other and took hold of Zack's. Almeda and I joined hands to complete the circle. We all bowed our heads and one at a time prayed for Uncle Nick and Aunt Katie.

# CHAPTER 42

## SPRING PICNIC

One of the next decisions Pa made as mayor was to announce that there was going to be another town picnic on the first day of spring that year. He told us that he'd been thinking about the gathering we'd had three-and-a-half years earlier at the church's dedication, and thinking it had been too long since we'd done something like that as a community together. So he figured that if he was mayor, he ought to be able to do something about it.

He announced it in church one Sunday early in March.

"On the twenty-first of March," he said, "that's on the Saturday two weeks from today, we're gonna bring in spring with a picnic right out here in the meadow between the church and the town. I want you all to come, and we'll celebrate the day together. That's on orders from your mayor!"

Everyone chuckled, and Pa moved to sit down. For the next two weeks, the whole town looked forward to the chance to get together again. Most of the women—and there were a lot more of them now than there had been in 1853!—spent the time cooking and baking. It was almost like getting ready for a fair!

When the day came, it couldn't have been prettier. There had been rain through the week, and Pa was wondering what to do if it rained on Saturday. But the storm passed on into the mountains and the sun came out Friday afternoon. It was a bit chilly on Saturday, and still a little wet, but *so* fresh and clean!

As I walked into the meadow that afternoon, there was still

moisture and dew all about in the shady places, and where the sun shone the grass sparkled. It looked as if the whole area was covered with thousands of tiny glass prisms, all reflecting the sunlight like diamonds.

We were the first to arrive, and as I walked through the meadow, in the distance by the edge of the woods I saw a deer calmly nibbling on the fresh wet grass. She lifted her head and looked around, her tan coat gleaming when the sun hit it as she moved through the shadows. With each movement her velvet-like body shone with the essence of freedom I had always dreamed about.

I looked up and breathed the crisp air with pleasure. The sky was blue with clouds billowing gently across the sky. A whisper of cool wind blew by me, and I smelled again the fragrance of clean, fresh, springtime air.

Gradually more people began to arrive. The women were dressed brightly in colorful spring apparel, the men wearing dark trousers and flannel shirts. A few of the women were carrying parasols and twirling them around—some red, some pink. As the people slowly came and the meadow filled, all the colors and sounds and sights reflected the joy that was felt by everyone.

The men got tables set up and then we arranged food as it arrived and got everything ready. As the crowd enlarged, most of the younger kids went running off, some playing tag and other games.

"What can I do?" asked Becky, as Almeda was preparing one table.

"Hmm . . . let's see," replied Almeda, "why don't you go see if you can pick me some nice wildflowers to use here on the table."

Becky was off in a second, glad to be of some help. "But don't get near those woods again!" yelled Emily after her. Almeda and I both laughed.

After a while we were ready to begin eating. As the men were gathering around the table and the women were spreading out the last of the food, Rev. Rutledge asked if he could say a few words before we began.

"Ye mean we's gonna have t' listen to another one o' yer sermons?" said Alkali Jones, loud enough that everybody could hear.

A great laugh went up from those nearby.

"I will try to make this one as short as possible," said Rev. Rutledge, laughing himself and joining in the fun.

"You know preachers, Alkali," said Pa. "Whenever they see a crowd of people, they immediately start thinking of something to say!"

"And if they don't think of something right off, then they pass the collection plate!" added Rev. Rutledge. His joke got another good laugh out of everybody.

"When I was a child," the minister began as the laughter died away, "my parents always had a celebration like this to start off the season of spring. Most of our friends remembered the coming of spring on Easter, and in the church we went to, Easter was always a busy day. But my parents wanted to preserve Easter as a day spent thinking only of the resurrection and the true meaning of the day. Thus our family celebrated the first day of spring separately, as we are doing now."

The minister paused a moment to look around at the townspeople gathered in the meadow.

"Spring is the season of new life," he went on, "when new things begin to grow and new life bursts forth out of the earth. During springtime we witness the cycles of life and nature emerging in their newness, and all about us we see God's creation alive in the earth. But spring is also the time of year when Jesus Christ rose from the grave. And so the resurrection is the true basis for what spring means. We can let ourselves be reminded of the life that Jesus gave us when we see the new life that nature gives us during this wonderful green, growing, fragrant time of the year.

"So I would like to give a special thank you to our mayor, Drummond Hollister, for arranging this picnic today. As you can see, it is especially meaningful for me. And I would like to thank you all for being here."

Then Rev. Rutledge prayed, and immediately everyone began to eat. I don't know if I'd ever seen so much food before. There was every kind of meat and salad and fruit and bread imaginable. Afterward, people gradually began getting up and going about, visiting, the children playing, men smoking their pipes or chatting and playing horseshoes or discussing their claims and the latest gold prices, while the women worked on clearing up the tables and leftover food.

When no one else was around him for a minute, Mr. Royce walked up to Pa.

"Hollister," the banker said, "I think the time has come for me to acknowledge what you did for me at the town council meeting."

"I meant what I said," replied Pa.

"Nevertheless, I want you to know that I'm extremely appreciative."

"It was for the good of the town."

"*And* for me," said Mr. Royce. "Your vote more than likely saved my bank, and my whole future. And I want to say thank you."

He extended his hand. Pa took it and gave it a firm shake. Then the eyes of the two men met. Pa still held on to Mr. Royce's hand.

"I meant what I said about loyalty, Royce," said Pa. "And about being a friend and neighbor to you."

"I know you meant it, Hollister. You've proved yourself a man of your word. I didn't think I could admit this several months ago, but I have to say now that the best man won last November. Miracle Springs is better off with you as its mayor than it would have been with me."

"Well, I'm just glad you're on the council," said Pa, "and that we can start working together on the same side from now on." He relaxed his grip and let the banker's hand go.

"Well, thank you again, Hollister. And as for the question

on interest rates, I'm looking into all that. I want to be fair to the people. If you'll just give me some time to get the details worked out—"

"Certainly, Royce," answered Pa, then added with a smile, "just don't wait too long. The people are all anxious to know what you're going to do."

"I'll move along as quickly as I can, believe me. Just tell the people they can count on me."

"Done!" said Pa. "They will appreciate it, Franklin."

The picnic that day gave us our first sight of someone who would be part of the Hollister future, though we had no idea of it at the time. There were quite a few people at the picnic that I didn't know. New families were coming to Miracle Springs regularly.

After we were through eating, I saw Zack over on the other side of the field throwing a ball back and forth with someone I didn't know, a boy who looked about Zack's own age. Then a while later, when I looked at them again, there were four or five others who had joined them scattered about. The stranger was hitting the little ball with a stick and the others were chasing after it. A few minutes later Zack brought the new boy over to where Pa and Almeda and Emily and I were seated on the grass. He was every bit as tall as Zack, and wearing a straw hat with a white shirt and blue knickers (which I found out later to be of some significance). He had light brown eyes and curly red hair with lots of freckles on his face.

"This here's Mike, Pa," said Zack. "His family just got here from the east."

Pa stood up and shook his hand. "Mike what?" he said in a friendly voice.

"McGee's the name, and baseball's the game," the boy replied. The instant he let go of Pa's hand, he reached into his pocket and pulled out a little white ball, the same one they had been playing with earlier.

"Baseball . . . what's that?" asked Emily.

"What's baseball!" exclaimed Mike McGee. "Why it's just

the newest, most exciting game there is. They call me 'Lefty.' "

"Well none of us have ever heard of it," said Pa. "Why don't you tell us about it? Is that stick you got there something to do with it?"

"This stick," said McGee, holding up the rounded piece of wood, "has *everything* to do with it! This is called a bat, and you've gotta hit the ball with the bat."

He took a few steps away from us, then tossed the ball up into the air, slung the bat up over his shoulder as he grabbed it with both hands down near one end. As the ball came back down, he swung the wood around fast. It hit the ball with a loud cracking sound, and the ball went sailing out across the meadow in a big arch, landing over next to the woods.

"Just like that!" he said. Tad, who had just walked up to join us, was off like a flash to retrieve the ball and bring it back to Mike. By now a few more people were gathering around, but something told me young McGee was paying more attention to my sister Emily than all the other people put together.

"You hit it a long ways!" exclaimed Tad, running up puffing with the ball.

"That's nothing. You should see how far they hit it in a real game. My older brother Doug took me to see the first baseball game played between two regular teams. He played for the New Jersey Knickerbockers himself. That was back in '46. I was just eight then. They played against a team from New York."

"How'd it turn out?" asked Zack.

"I was nine before the game ended," replied Mike. "That first game took almost a year because they'd stop and then start again later. Nobody really knew how to play, so there were arguments and disputes through the whole game. My brother was so sick of the arguing, on top of losing the game 23 to 1—"

"Tarnation, boy!" exclaimed Uncle Nick, "that ain't no game, however you play it. That's more like a slaughter!"

"That was the score, all right. And my brother said he'd never play baseball again. So he gave me this here bat and ball and uniform. Now, do any of you want to get up a game?"

"But how do you play?" asked Zack.

"I plumb forgot—none of you know how to play!" he said. "Well, one team hits the ball and tries to run around the diamond and score an ace."

"What's an ace?" asked Emily, looking up into Mike's face.

"That's what it's called when you score a point by running in from third and touching home plate."

"Home plate . . . diamond . . . third? You're not makin' sense!" said Zack.

"And in the meantime," Mike went on without paying any attention to Zack, "the other team tries to catch the ball and throw it ahead of the runner so one of his teammates can tag him out before he gets to the base."

"It sounds mighty confusing," said Pa laughing. "I doubt if you're gonna get many around here to play. We can't understand a word you're saying! How many does it take to play?"

"Eighteen—nine on each team."

"Eighteen! You'll *never* get eighteen people in all of California to make heads or tails of what you're talking about!"

"If nobody knew how to play for that first game, how did anybody know what to do?" asked Emily.

"It sure sounds like one side knew how to play, judging from the score," Uncle Nick said.

"To answer your question, Miss," said McGee, "all the fellers who were there knew how to play, but everybody had their own brand of the game, coming from different places. You see, it was already played a bit before that, but not in an organized way or anything. That's why the game took so long. The arguments got so fierce they had to keep stopping it and figure out a way to agree on the rules before continuing on. The one game had three different sessions to it, like I said, stretching for almost a year."

"Well that's about the dad-blamdest kind o' game I ever heard of!" piped up Alkali Jones. "Weren't no *game* at all, from the sound of it, but more like a war. Hee, hee, hee!"

Everybody had a good laugh, and after a little more talk,

Mike managed to get half a dozen or so of the boys to join him. They walked over to the far end of the field where he began explaining the game to them. Emily followed to watch.

I got up and walked toward the hillside overlooking the meadow, where over three years ago I had looked down on the gathering we'd had to celebrate the completion of the building of the church. That other day seemed so long ago and much had happened since. Yet up there on the sloping hillside, everything still looked the same. It reminded me of how God had watched over us during the years since then.

Wild lilies were in bloom, and the birch trees were just beginning to get their fresh growths of new bark and tiny green leaves. The wildflowers brought back to my mind Rev. Rutledge's words, *"We can let ourselves be reminded of the life that Jesus gave us when we see the new life that nature gives . . ."*

I walked up the hill, turned around, and looked down on the meadow just at the same spot I had that day three years before. When I was alone, questions about my future always seemed to nag at me. I wanted God to have complete control over my life in whatever I did, but I couldn't keep the fears and anxieties from bothering me from time to time.

Down on the field I watched the group of boys playing with "Lefty" Mike McGee. Every once in a while I heard his voice yelling out some kind of instruction to them, or pointing to get them to go stand someplace else. He didn't seem to be having much success explaining the game of baseball to them. I couldn't help laughing a time or two as I watched.

Zack and Tad were in the middle of it. My eyes followed Zack around. I knew that occasionally he struggled with the same kinds of questions that I did, although being a boy I don't suppose his anxieties went as deep. Boys have a way of being able to take things more as they come, while girls have to think everything out on a dozen levels.

"What are you going to do, Zack?" I asked him once.

"What do you mean?"

"Well, we can't just stay at home and live with Pa and Almeda forever, you know."

"There's the mine," he said. "I figured I'd work the mine with Pa and Uncle Nick."

"No mine lasts forever. Then what?"

"I don't know."

"Don't you find yourself wondering about things, about other places you might go, things to see, people to meet?"

"Not much. I like it here in Miracle. But I reckon you're right, we can't just live with Pa when we get to be adults."

"Hey, I've got an idea, Zack!" I said. "We could go live in Almeda's house in town. It's been empty all this time. Then we could stay in Miracle and do whatever we'd be doing, but it'd sorta be like being on our own."

"You think she'd let us?"

"Sure. She's said once or twice what a shame it is for the house not to be used."

"But what if one of us gets married?" suggested Zack.

"Well *I'm* not worried," I answered. "There's no fear of that about me! *You're* the one some girl will come along and want to grab."

"Nah, not me! I ain't gonna get married."

"Then what are you gonna do if the mine plays out?"

"I don't know. Maybe Little Wolf and I will raise horses like his Pa. And we've talked about going riding together, but I don't know where. I reckon you're right—there is a heap of world to see.

"What about you, Corrie?" Zack asked. "You got plans? What're you gonna do?"

"I don't know. I want to keep writing. But it's hard to say if something is always going to be what God wants for you. I'd like to travel."

This conversation was the most I'd ever gotten Zack to talk personally about himself, and I hoped we'd have the chance to talk like that again.

I didn't stay up on the hillside for too long, just long enough to quiet myself down. I got up from the base of my favorite old oak tree, gave its gnarled trunk an affectionate pat with my hand, and then started back down the slope to rejoin the picnic.

In fact, I thought to myself, maybe I'd go join in whatever Lefty McGee was trying to teach the others about his new game. I'd like to see if I could hit that little ball with that stick!

# CHAPTER 43

## UNEXPECTED LABOR

Doc Shoemaker figured Katie would be due to give birth around the last of April or first of May. He said Almeda would probably follow about two weeks later. So both of them were mighty big around the middle by now and were moving slow, with Pa and Uncle Nick worrying and fussing over them every minute. At the picnic it seemed the women talked about nothing else to Almeda. Katie stayed home. Almeda was still spry enough and went into town every other day or so, but she also stayed in bed longer and took lots of rests. Pa saw to that.

Tuesday night in the second week of April, the doctor had been out that afternoon, had seen both Almeda and Katie, and had left with a smile on his face. "Won't be long now, Drummond," he'd said from his buggy. "Everything looks good. Both your wife and sister-in-law are healthy and coming along just fine."

In the middle of the night I was awakened by a loud banging on the door and shouts outside. I bolted awake and knew in an instant it was Uncle Nick. And from the sound of his voice I knew something was wrong.

I jumped out of bed and put on my robe, but by the time I got out of my bedroom Pa and Almeda were already at the door and talking to Uncle Nick.

"It's Katie!" he said frantically. "Something's wrong, Drum—she's yelling and carrying on—"

"I'll go right up there," Almeda said as she started to throw

256

a coat around her robe, then sat down to put on her boots.

"You ain't in no condition to—" Pa began.

"Don't even say it, Drummond," she interrupted. "This is a woman's finest hour, and the hour of greatest need."

"But you gotta take care of—"

"I will take complete care of myself," she said. "Katie needs me now, and I am not going to sit here and do nothing. Are you ready, Nick?" she added, standing up and pulling her coat tightly around her. The door was still open and a cold wind was blowing right into the cabin.

Uncle Nick just turned around and hurried back outside into the night. "She's in terrible pain, Almeda!" he said.

"Then you go on ahead, Nick! Tell her I'm coming. And put water on the stove!" Uncle Nick had already disappeared toward the bridge across the creek.

"I'll need the good lantern, Drummond," Almeda said, "so the wind won't blow it out."

"I'll get it lit," replied Pa as he went toward the fireplace. "Then I'll take you up there."

"You must go for Doctor Shoemaker," objected Almeda.

"I ain't gonna let you walk up there at night alone. You fall, and we'd have two women in trouble in their beds! Corrie," Pa said turning to me. "Go see if Zack's awake, and get him in here pronto."

By the time I got back into the room with Zack, who was still half asleep, Pa had the lantern burning bright.

"Zack, you gotta ride over and get the Doc, you hear me, boy!"

"Yes, Pa."

"We need him fast!"

"I'll bring him, Pa."

"Corrie, you get out there and saddle up—let's see, who's fastest in the dark, Raspberry or Dandy?"

"At night, probably Dandy, Pa," said Zack.

"Then Corrie, you get to saddling Dandy. Zack, you get dressed and get going!"

Then he turned to the open door, holding the lantern in his

left hand while Almeda took hold of his right, and the two of them walked out as quickly as they could to follow Uncle Nick.

In another five minutes, Zack was off, and the sound of Dandy's hoofbeats died in a moment. Suddenly I was left alone. I stoked up the fire with a couple of fresh logs, and lit another lantern. Then I went into the girls' room and woke up Emily, who was already stirring from the noise.

"Emily," I said, "Katie's in trouble. Pa and Almeda are up there already, and Zack's gone for the doctor. I'm going too."

"Should I come, Corrie?" she asked.

"I don't know, Emily," I said. "There probably isn't anything we can do to help, but I've gotta know if Katie's all right. You stay here with the others, and if they need us, I'll come and get you."

I was glad Pa had gone with Almeda! A storm had blown in while we'd been sleeping, and the wind was howling fiercely. I had trouble keeping my lantern from blowing out.

By the time I arrived at Uncle Nick's cabin, it seemed like an hour had already passed! Things were happening fast and I could feel the tension the minute I walked in. Pa stood at the pot-bellied stove watching a kettle of water that was nearly boiling. Alongside, a pot of coffee was brewing. Uncle Nick paced around with a horrified look on his face. I'd never seen him like that before—so helpless, so concerned, wanting to help yet looking like a lost little boy who didn't know what to do. Even though it was his house and his baby being born, it looked like he felt out of place.

Both of them glanced at me as I came in but hardly took any other notice. Just as I closed the door I heard a scream from the other room. Uncle Nick spun around. "Oh God!" he cried. He took a couple of quick steps toward the bedroom, then stopped. Pa went over and put an arm around Uncle Nick's shoulder, and from the slight movement of his lips, I knew he was praying hard.

*Oh God,* I breathed silently, *whatever's going on, I ask you to be close to Katie and take care of her. And Uncle Nick too.*

"Anything I can do, Pa?" I said.

He gave me a wan smile that showed he appreciated my being there. "Could you check on Erich? He's sleeping in the other room," he answered. "And pray that the Doc'll get here in a hurry."

Almeda came in from the bedroom. She was so obviously pregnant, walking with a bit of a waddle, and her face was a little pale. But otherwise you'd have thought *she* was the doctor! Still wearing her robe, she had her sleeves rolled up. Her hair was loose and hanging all out of place. And you could see the perspiration on her forehead. She looked like she'd been on the job working with Katie for an hour already.

She came up to Uncle Nick and attempted a smile. "You have nothing to worry about, Nick," she said. "The baby's just a few weeks early, that's all."

"Why's she crying out and screaming then?" said Uncle Nick, still looking frantic.

"That's what labor is like, Nick," she answered. "You weren't here when Erich was born, were you?"

"No, you and the Doc made me and Drum get outta here."

"And this is exactly why," said Almeda, smiling again. "It can be harder on the husband, who's fretting and stewing in the other room, than for the woman herself."

"But is Katie . . . is she all right?"

"Of course. She is fine. Labor is a long and painful process, Nick. It hurts, and sometimes we can't help crying out. It might not be a bad idea again for you and Drum to go down—"

Before she could finish another shriek came from the other room. A horrified look filled Uncle Nick's eyes. You could tell the sound pierced right through to his heart.

"It's another contraction!" said Almeda, turning to return to Katie. "Drummond, why don't you take Nick down to our place. And take little Erich with you."

"We oughta at least wait till the Doc's here."

"We'll be fine. Corrie, come with me."

Nick bundled up little Erich, still half-asleep despite all the commotion, and he and Pa took the lantern and started down the hill to our house.

I followed Almeda into the bedroom. Katie lay there with only a sheet over her. She yelled out again just as we came in. I was frightened, but Almeda walked straight over to the bed and took Katie's hand.

"Go around the bed, Corrie," she said to me. "Take her other hand so she has something to squeeze. It helps with the pain."

I did as she said.

Katie was breathing hard, her face wet and white. Her eyes were closed and a look of excruciating agony filled her face. Just as I took hold of her, she cried out again and lurched up in the bed. She grabbed on to my hand like a vise and held it hard as she pulled herself forward. The pain lasted ten or fifteen seconds, then she began to relax and lay back down, her face calming, her lungs breathing deeply. Still she held my hand, but not as hard. Slowly she opened her eyes a crack, glanced feebly at the two of us, managed a thin smile, then closed her eyes again. It was the first smile either of us had had from her in a long time.

Almeda left the bedside and wrung out a towel that had been soaking in a bowl of hot water. She pulled back the sheet and laid it over Katie's stomach just below where the baby was.

"Corrie," she said, "we need some more hot water. Go in the other room and fill this bowl from the kettle on the stove."

"That feels good," I heard Katie murmur as I left the room. "Thank you, Almeda," she added, and then all was quiet.

I got the hot water and went back into the bedroom. Katie was resting peacefully for the moment. Almeda sat by the bedside holding her hand. The look on my face must have been one of anxiety, because Almeda spoke to me as if she were answering a question I hadn't voiced.

"Don't worry, Corrie. This is just going to take some time, and Katie's not done hurting and crying out. She needs us to be strong for her."

Just then another contraction came. Katie winced and held her breath for a minute, then suddenly let it out in a long wail of pain. She lurched forward, holding her breath. I hurried over to the other side of the bed and took her hand. She grabbed on to it for dear life until the pain began to subside a minute or two later.

It went on like this for a while. In between contractions Almeda changed the hot towel while I wiped off Katie's face with a cool cloth, went to get water, or did whatever else Almeda said. It must have been a half an hour or forty minutes before we heard the outside door open.

"It's Doc Shoemaker," a voice called out. Doc walked into the room, carrying his black leather case. "How is she?" he asked.

"The contractions are coming about every two or three minutes now, Doctor," Almeda replied.

"She's getting close then," he said with a sigh that didn't sound too enthusiastic. "Three weeks early," he mumbled to himself as he approached the bed. "Hmm . . . don't suppose that's too worrisome in itself."

I stood aside and the Doc spoke softly to Katie, then put his hand on her stomach where the baby was. He held it there a long time with a real serious expression on his face. He didn't say anything.

Another contraction came. Katie winced and cried out. The doctor kept one hand on the baby and with the other took hers. I stood on the other side of the room watching. The Doc's face was expressionless.

When the contraction finished and Katie fell back on her pillow, the Doc let go of her hand and again felt the baby, this time with both hands. Still I couldn't tell a thing from his face. Almeda, too had her eyes fixed on him, looking for any sign that might betray what he was thinking.

He looked over at Almeda, then back down at Katie, then glanced up in my direction.

"Corrie, do you mind if I have a few words with Almeda," he said, "alone?"

"Sure," I said. "I'll go put some more water on the stove."

I left the bedroom, wondering what the matter was. I scooped out some water from the big bucket Uncle Nick had pumped up from the stream and added it to the kettle sitting steaming on the stove. Just as I was putting another log or two on the fire, I heard Katie cry out again. It wasn't quite as loud as before, but the tone sounded so painful, more like a wail than a scream. It shot straight into my heart and a shiver went through me. I heard the Doc's voice too, though I couldn't make out anything being said. I hurried and shoved the wood into the stove. Then I tried to find something else to keep me busy, but there wasn't anything to do but pace around the floor.

Another scream came from the bedroom. It had been less than a minute since the last one! I was getting worried, and I wished they'd call me back in instead of making me wait outside.

Almost the instant the cries and sounds stopped, the bedroom door opened. It was Almeda. Her face was pale.

"Corrie, go get your uncle."

"Is everything—"

"Just get Nick, Corrie," she said. "Get him now!"

I didn't wait for any more explanations. I turned around and ran from the house, hearing another mournful cry from Katie just as I shut the door. I was halfway back to our place and stumbling along the path beside the stream before I realized I'd forgotten both a lantern and my coat. I would have known the way blindfolded—and I might as well have been because of the dark! The wind was still howling. Finally I saw the faint glimmer of light from one of our windows. I crossed the bridge, still running, and ran straight up to the house, tore the door open, and ran inside.

"They want you, Uncle Nick!" I said, all out of breath.

"Is the baby born?" he asked, jumping up and throwing on his coat.

"I don't know. They just said to get you quick."

He was already out the door at a run.

"What is it, Corrie?" Pa asked.

"I don't know, Pa. They made me leave the bedroom, then Almeda told me to go fetch Uncle Nick."

He had his coat on now too, then grabbed the lantern and

headed out the door after Uncle Nick. I followed, running after him, although the bobbing light ahead of me got farther and farther away as we made our way up the trail along the creek.

By the time I reached Uncle Nick and Aunt Katie's place, I was breathing hard. The door to the cabin was open, and Doc Shoemaker was standing in the doorway. Nick was trying to get by into the house but the Doc was holding on to him trying to talk to him.

"Not yet, Nick!" he said. "Give her a few minutes."

I didn't see Almeda. Pa was standing beside Uncle Nick. He saw me coming and stretched out his arm to put around me. I came up close and he drew me to him tight, but just kept looking at Uncle Nick.

"I gotta go to her!" said Uncle Nick frantically. "I gotta know if she's—"

"She's fine, I tell you, Nick. But she's just been through something awful, and you must let her—"

"Get outta my way, Doc!"

"Please, Nick, just wait for two or three minutes until you calm—"

"I ain't waiting for nothing!" said Uncle Nick. He pushed the doctor aside and ran inside.

"Nick, please!" Doc Shoemaker called after him. But it was too late. Uncle Nick was through the door and the tromping of his heavy boots thudded across the floor toward the bedroom.

The doctor sighed, looked at Pa with a helpless expression, then followed slowly after Uncle Nick.

"What is it, Pa?" I said finally, feeling a great fear rising up inside me.

"The baby's dead, Corrie," he answered. I'd never heard such a sound of grief in his voice in my life. He squeezed me tight with his arm again. I felt the sobs tugging at my breast even before the tears came to my eyes. Pa knew what I was feeling. I knew he had tears in his eyes too, even in the darkness, even without looking up into his face. I just knew.

Slowly we walked inside. Pa closed the door. The next moment Almeda emerged from the bedroom. Before she got the door shut behind her, I heard the sound of the doctor's voice again, and Nick's. Uncle Nick was crying.

Almeda walked toward us. She was very pale, her face covered with sweat, with splotches of blood on her robe. Her eyes met Pa's and they looked at each other for a few seconds, almost as if they were wondering in the silence whether something like this was in store for them in the near future.

Then Almeda glanced at me, and gave me a thin smile. Pa put his arm around her and Almeda embraced us both. The three of us held on to each other for a long time. I knew Almeda was crying, too.

"God, oh God!" Pa said after about a minute. "They need your help now more than they ever have. Be a strength to them."

"Yes, Lord!" Almeda breathed in barely more than a whisper.

Again they were silent. Slowly Pa released me and led Almeda to a chair and made her sit down. He turned toward the kitchen and found a towel, dipped it in the bucket of cold water, then gently began wiping Almeda's face and forehead with it.

She sat back, closed her eyes, and breathed in deeply.

In another minute Doc Shoemaker came back from the bedroom. He walked over to Pa.

"Drum," he said softly. "You've got yourself a mighty brave woman there. But she's in no condition for all this. This has taxed her more than I like. You get her home and into some fresh things and to bed."

"Yes, Doc."

"Then you send one of your kids—Zack or Corrie, or if you want you can go yourself—but one of you go into town and get Mrs. Gianini. You'll have to rouse her, but she'll come right out when you tell her I need her. She'll spend the night with Katie and help me clean up and get the baby ready for burying."

"You need any more help, Doc?" Pa asked.

"She'll know what we need, Drummond. Don't you worry

about anything but that wife of yours. She's put in a hard night's work. If we need anything, I'll get one of your girls. As soon as things are in order here, I'll come down and check on Almeda."

"I'll be fine, Doc Shoemaker," said Almeda softly.

"I will check on you anyway. And, Drummond," he added, again to Pa, "fix me some place to spend the night. The barn will be fine. I want to stay close."

"You can have my bed," I said.

"Doesn't matter to me," replied the Doc. "I appreciate it, Corrie. But I'm sure I'll be able to catch a little sleep anywhere!"

Pa helped Almeda get slowly to her feet. Then we began our way home, both of us helping her so she wouldn't stumble in the dark. It was a slow walk, but within half an hour Almeda was in her own bed and sleeping peacefully.

# CHAPTER 44

## BITTER WORDS

Almeda was tired the next day, but otherwise fine. She stayed in bed the whole day except for about an hour when we had the funeral for Uncle Nick and Aunt Katie's little stillborn daughter.

Mrs. Gianini helped get everything cleaned up and tended to Katie through the night. Then in the morning she got the baby ready. Once the new day came Uncle Nick showed what a strong man he had become. His tears were now past and he did everything he could for Katie, being tender and serving her when he could, being brave and in charge when that was necessary too.

Doc had spent the night getting what sleep he could, but checking on both Katie and Almeda every hour or two to make sure they were all right. Katie was weak and stayed in bed all the next day, although Doc Shoemaker said she would recover and be fine in a week or two. She didn't even get out of bed for the burial.

A few people came out to pay their respects to Nick and to stand with him at the graveside—the Shaws and Miss Stansberry and a few others. Rev. Rutledge, of course, took care of things, read from the Bible, and prayed before the tiny box was lowered into the ground. Pa had dug a grave not far from the apple trees Katie had planted from Virginia. The little cross marker on the grave, so near the trees that were a symbol of hope and new life, became a poignant reminder that things don't always go the way we expect or want them to, and that frontier life in this new state sometimes brought hardship along with it.

I cried. So did the other women—Becky, Emily, Almeda, and the others. Pa and Uncle Nick were pretty straight-faced and serious. Afterward people shook Uncle Nick's hand and tried to say encouraging things to him. They wanted to go in and pay their respects to Katie too, but she wouldn't see anybody.

Doctor Shoemaker went home after the funeral, got some fresh clothes, and came right back out. He wanted to spend the rest of the day near both ladies. They were all right, so he managed to get a good bit of sleep during the afternoon. After checking on them early in the evening, he went home. He kept coming out every day for a while.

Almeda stayed in bed for another day or so. She said she felt fine, but the doctor had told her to rest, and she complied with his wishes. Katie hardly got out of bed except when she had to for two weeks. We all admired the way Uncle Nick tended her. But through it all Katie was sullen and cross, hardly speaking, even to him. She just lay there in her bed, either sleeping or staring straight ahead across the room, not even noticing when people came and went.

Pa and I tried to help Uncle Nick, and after a few days Almeda went up to visit Katie. I went with her. We took a pot of soup and some bread we'd made. Little Erich was glad to see us, but the look on Uncle Nick's face made it clear he was feeling awkward about Katie's moodiness. We went in to see her. Almeda tried to be as cheerful as she could, but sensitive too.

"I'm so sorry, Katie," she said, sitting down beside the bed and taking Katie's hand. Katie continued to stare straight ahead. Her hand just lay limp in Almeda's. She didn't act as if she was even aware that anyone was in the room. She didn't move a muscle to acknowledge us.

"Is there anything I can do for you?" Almeda asked. "Anything you need or would like to eat or drink?"

Katie said nothing. There was a long silence.

"Would you mind if I prayed for you?" Almeda asked at length. Suddenly Katie's eyes shot wide open and her nostril's flared. She yanked her hand from Almeda's and turned on her with red face.

"How dare you talk to me about prayer!" she shouted angrily, as loud as her condition would allow. "After God's just taken my baby, and you want to pray to him?"

"It's impossible for us to understand his ways," said Almeda softly, smiling sadly down on Katie.

"I suppose you're going to tell me next that I ought to thank him for what he's done!"

"We just can't know what's in God's heart, Katie. All we can know is that he loves us more than we can imagine, and that everything he does can work for *good* if we allow it."

"Good! Ha!" she shot back, seething now. "I suppose if he takes *your* baby, you will smile and give him thanks—is that what you're telling me?"

"I would try to have a heart of gratitude, in spite of the pain I'm sure I would feel."

"Well, you're a foolish woman, Almeda!" said Katie bitingly. "You're more of a dimwit than I took you for! Don't you even know what it's like to feel a woman's worst grief? I don't think you have any feelings at all, Almeda!"

Almeda turned away. The words stung her to the heart. Her cheeks reddened, and hot tears rose to her eyes.

"Katie," she said, looking back toward the bed, "I'm so sorry. I didn't mean to sound unfeeling. I understand the pain you must feel, and I want you to know—"

"*Understand*! What could you understand about what I feel? Spare me your sympathy, Almeda. I don't need you feeling sorry for me any more than I need your idiotic prayers! Just leave me alone!"

"Oh, Katie, please let us—"

"Get out, Almeda! You and Corrie just go. I don't want to see you . . . or anybody!"

Again Almeda turned quickly away, fighting back emotion.

Slowly she rose and without any further words the two of us left the room.

We closed the door behind us. I think Uncle Nick had heard everything because he was standing close by. The look that passed between him and Almeda was enough. They both seemed to understand what the other was thinking and feeling.

"You come get us if there's *anything* any of us can do, Nick," said Almeda. "Fixing something to eat, cleaning up, taking Erich for a while . . . anything."

Uncle Nick nodded, then went into the bedroom. We left and started the walk home in silence, going slowly on account of Almeda's condition. I kept hold of her arm. We were barely out of the clearing toward the creek when we heard Uncle Nick running up from behind. We stopped.

"She's crying," he said. "She won't say a word, she's just sobbing."

"Did she ask for us?" said Almeda.

"Not exactly," replied Uncle Nick. "But I can tell she's sorry for how she treated you. Won't you come back and try to talk to her?"

"It's got to be in her time, Nick."

"But she's hurtin' something terrible, Almeda."

"I know. Anybody can see that, Nick. But she's so angry and bitter toward God that she can't hear anything we try to say, and she can't receive any love we try to offer her."

"But won't you just try?" His voice sounded almost desperate.

"Of course we'll try. We'll be back every day. We'll do all we can. And yes, I'll come back and try to talk to her. But right now, Nick, I just don't think she's open to anything I have to give or to say. Come down this evening and let us know how she is. If you think she would like to see me, you know I'll be on my way that very minute. Corrie too—any of us. We'll stand with you through this, Nick, whatever comes."

"But what do I do for her in the meantime?"

"Pray for her, Nick. She is fighting against some things that have been with her for a long time. God is moving closer and closer to her heart, but she is resisting him. She needs your prayers now more than ever."

"I'll try," sighed Uncle Nick, turning back toward his cabin.

"You pray, and then you serve her and love her every minute," added Almeda. "When she finally breaks, it will be your love that will see her across that unknown gulf she's so afraid of."

"I'll try," repeated Uncle Nick. He walked back to the cabin, frustration showing in the slump of his shoulders. We turned and continued our way back down the slope toward the creek.

# CHAPTER 45

## REMORSE AND CONFUSION

Almeda was quiet the rest of the day. It was hard to hear the kinds of things Katie had said to her. She had done so much for Katie, only to be spoken to so rudely because of it. I have to admit, as sorry as I was about the baby and for the grief Katie was feeling, her angry words toward Almeda got me more than a little riled. But Almeda kept saying, "It's not me she's angry at, Corrie. She needs our patience and our love now more than ever. The Lord is pushing aside her outer shell, and she needs us to stand with her until he breaks through to her."

She asked me to go back up that evening to ask about Katie. Emily and I went. Uncle Nick came outside with us.

"She's calmed down and is feeling better," he said. "She slept most of the afternoon."

"That's good," I said. "Almeda said to tell you that if you think she wants to talk again, to come get her."

"I wish she would," he replied. "I don't ever know what to say when she's feeling down and upset like she gets."

We took Erich back down to our place with us for the night so Uncle Nick would be free to look after Katie and get some sleep. He looked tired.

Nothing much happened for another day or two. Uncle Nick was still downcast from worrying about Katie. Doc Shoemaker came out again. He pronounced Katie fit and said she could get up and about for a few hours a day if she wanted. But she remained glum, and stayed in bed.

He told Almeda to take care of herself. "Only three or four weeks for you now, Almeda," he said. "Don't you go getting any ideas about going back into town or doing anything around this house. You've got three daughters for all that. You just keep yourself rested, you hear?"

"Of course, Doctor," she laughed.

The next day, early in the afternoon, Uncle Nick came running down to our place. His face looked more full of life as he came through the door than I'd seen it in weeks. Pa was outside, but he came straight to me.

"She asked to see you!" he said out of breath.

"Katie?" I said.

He nodded.

"Me?"

"You and Almeda."

In an instant I was off to tell Almeda in her room. She was dressed but lying in bed. She got right up and came out to where Uncle Nick was still standing. The look on his face was bright and excited.

"Did she really ask to see us, Nick?" Almeda asked.

A sheepish expression crossed his face. "Well, we were talking," he said, "and I happened to say as how I thought she'd been a mite hard on the two of you last time. She was pretty quiet, you know how she's been of late. Then she just kinda nodded and said, 'I suppose I was at that.'

"So after a minute I said, 'What'll you do if Almeda or Corrie comes calling again? You gonna send 'em away like you never want to see them again?' I reckon it was a hard thing to ask her, but doggone if she wasn't beginnin' to try my patience with all her surly scowls and irritable talk."

"She can't help it, Nick," said Almeda softly.

"I figured that," replied Uncle Nick. "Well, anyhow I said it, and she didn't say nothin' for a while, then she said, 'No I wouldn't send them away.' I figured that was about as good an invitation as you was gonna get, so I came down when she fell asleep to tell you."

Almeda looked at him for a moment with a blank expression. Then her face broke into a laugh. "You are something, Nicholas Belle! You really love that wife of yours, don't you?"

"I reckon so. I just can't cotton to you and her being apart and for her to be angry with my own kin. Will you come?"

"Of course we'll come," she replied with a smile. "You go on home. We'll come up for a visit sometime this afternoon."

A couple of hours later we walked up. I had made some shortbread to take, which I knew was one of Katie's favorites.

Uncle Nick met us at the door and took us straight into the bedroom. Katie was awake. I told her I'd made her some shortbread. She tried to smile, but it was one of those smiles that showed there was something on her mind behind it. I think she was embarrassed about what had happened before.

"How are you feeling, Katie?" Almeda asked.

"Oh, better, I suppose. You?"

"Very well."

"How much longer?"

"The doctor said probably three weeks."

"I hope . . . I hope it goes well for you," said Katie. It was hard for her to say.

"Is there anything you need?" Almeda asked after a minute. Her voice was so full of tenderness and compassion, and her eyes so full of love as she stood beside Katie's bed. Katie looked up at her and her eyes filled with tears.

"Almeda, I'm sorry for the things I said before," she said.

"Oh, Katie, dear, think nothing of it." Almeda sat down on the chair at the bedside and took Katie's hand.

"It's just that I was so afraid of dying," Katie went on, trying to maintain her composure. "When I was lying here having the baby, it hurt so bad! I was more worried about myself than . . . than my little daughter! Every time I screamed out, I was sure it was going to be the last breath I breathed. It was so much worse than with Erich!"

"There, there," said Almeda, running her hand gently along Katie's head and smoothing down her hair. "It's all right, dear."

"And then when she came out, and the doctor told me she

was dead," Katie said, sobbing now, "I felt . . . I just felt so guilty! All I had been thinking about was myself! And all the time, even while she was inside me . . . my poor little daughter was—"

She couldn't even finish the sentence, but let out a mournful wail of such bitter remorse that it went straight into my heart and my eyes filled with tears. Poor Katie!

"She was dead!" sobbed Katie. "Dead, and the whole time I was worried about *myself!* I can hardly bear the thought of how selfish I was! Oh God, why couldn't you have taken me instead of her?"

I could hardly keep from crying. I wondered if I should leave and let Katie and Almeda be alone. But when I looked at Almeda as she stared down into Katie's forlorn face, I could tell she was praying even though her eyes were open. I had seen her pray for others like that and I always knew when she was talking to the Lord. Then I thought maybe it would be best for me to keep sitting right where I was.

I closed my eyes and began praying for Katie myself.

"He wanted you to live," said Almeda softly.

"But why? Why should he want me to live, instead of my baby?"

"I don't know, Katie. He loves you, Katie. I know that. He loves you, and your baby."

"Oh God!" Katie wailed again as if she hadn't even heard. "How could I think of myself at a time like that!"

Almeda didn't reply. Katie was sobbing.

"I've always thought more of myself than anyone else," she said. "Nick's so considerate to me, but I don't show him half the love he does me! I've acted dreadfully to you . . . to both of you! I'm so selfish! I hate the person I've become! I'd rather it *had* been me that had died! You'd all be better off without me!"

"Don't say such things, Katie. Don't you know that we love you?"

"Love me! How could you love me? Look at me! There's nothing to love!"

"God wouldn't have made you if you weren't special to him."

"That's ridiculous! Why should God care about me? I've never given him a thought! Why should he love me?"

"He loves us all."

"You, maybe. But I've always told him to keep away from me."

"Don't you remember all I told you, Katie? I used to be further from him than you could ever be."

"I don't know if I believe half what you told me, Almeda." I opened my eyes. One look into Katie's face told me the old anger was coming back. Her voice had changed, too.

"Oh, Katie, I would *never* tell you something that wasn't true."

"Well, I don't care anyway. I never had any use for God, and I certainly don't mean to start now."

"Oh, but Katie . . . dear! You need him now more than ever."

"I won't need him! I refuse to need him," she snapped back. "If he's going to take my baby, then he's not going to have me! He took my parents from me! He's taken everything I ever cared about. I've had to make my own way. It's little enough he's ever done for me! And now he's taken my daughter! I won't need him, I tell you!"

"Perhaps he took your little girl because he loved her so much he wanted to have her near him," said Almeda after a moment, still speaking calmly.

"That's absurd, Almeda!" said Katie angrily. "If there's a God at all, which I doubt, then what right has he got to toy with our lives like that?"

"He doesn't toy with us, Katie. We just can't see how much he loves us. But everything works for good if we will only let—"

"There you go again, saying it's good that my baby died!" interrupted Katie. "I suppose you'll tell me next that it's good I'm such a hateful and selfish person! If that's your God, Almeda, then curse him! I hate him, too . . . I hate you all . . .

I hate myself . . . God . . . just go . . . leave me alone . . . just
let me die!"

She turned over in her bed, sobbing bitterly.

Almeda looked over at me, sick at heart. She closed her
eyes again. Then after a moment she sighed deeply, rose from
the chair, and together we left the room. Katie was still weeping.

"Your dear wife really needs you, Nick," Almeda said to
Uncle Nick. "Love her, Nick. Give her all the love you can.
She's more alone right now than she's ever felt in her life. God
is right at the threshold, but she doesn't know it. That tough
self-sufficient outer layer is nearly broken. And when it does
break, she's going to need you there to help her."

Uncle Nick nodded. We left the cabin and started home.

We had nearly reached the bridge over the creek when Uncle Nick overtook us. This time he had a message directly from
Katie's lips.

"She told me to get you," he said. Almeda looked him
intently in the eyes. "She *wants* to see you," he said.

We turned around at once and walked back up the trail.
Almeda took Uncle Nick's arm, and I followed behind them.

# CHAPTER 46

## THE ANGELS SINGING

Once again we walked into the bedroom. This time Uncle Nick went in with us.

Katie was sitting upright, propped up by several pillows. Her face was red and her eyes puffy, but she wasn't crying any more, and there was a look of determination on her face.

"Please forgive me, Almeda . . . Corrie," she said. "Please have patience with me for my rudeness."

"You are forgiven," said Almeda softly, smiling at Katie. I walked over to the bedside, leaned down, and gave Katie a hug. She put her arms around me and squeezed me in return. The feel of her arms around my shoulders filled me with such happiness I started to cry again. I pulled back and sat down across the room. Almeda again sat down next to the bed.

There was a long silence. Finally Katie spoke again.

"Do you *really* believe that God intends everything for our good?" she asked. For the first time her voice sounded as if she genuinely wanted to know.

"Oh yes, Katie," smiled Almeda. "He is more wonderfully good, and his ways are more wonderfully good than we have the faintest notion of."

"Then why did my parents die . . . why did he take my baby?" said Katie, starting to cry.

Almeda took her hand. "I don't know, Katie," she replied with tenderness. "There's so much we *can't* understand about life. Corrie lost her mother also. I have had to struggle with all

277

of the *whys* my past life. There are hurts every man and woman has to face and wonder about. There are disappointments. We can be lonely. We lose things and people who are precious to us. But there is one thing I've learned in the years since I gave my heart to the Lord, and I think it's just about the most important lesson our life in this world has to teach us. Do you know what that lesson is?"

Almeda stopped and waited. Finally Katie spoke up. "I don't suppose I do," she said.

"It's just this, Katie," Almeda continued, "that when life's heartaches and hurts and disappointments come, running *to* God, not *away* from him, is our only hope, our only refuge."

"Is that what I've been doing—running away?"

"I'm not sure, Katie. I don't know that it's my business to say. Only you would know for certain. But you haven't been running *to* him." There could be no mistaking the love in Almeda's voice, in spite of the directness of her words. I knew that at last Katie realized Almeda loved her and wanted to help her. She began to weep softly.

"I know you've suffered hurts and losses, Katie," Almeda went on. "But they've made you bitter and resentful toward God, when actually he was the one you should have gone to for help. He would have borne the pain *for* you. But by keeping him away, you had to bear it all alone.

"Katie, I'm so sorry about your daughter! I grieve with you! But don't you see, the only place for the pain to go is into the hands of Jesus. Otherwise it will tear you apart inside. Instead of turning *from* him, and blaming him, and crying out *against* him, he is the one you must go *to*. He did not take your daughter to inflict hurt. He loves that precious little girl, who is now radiantly alive in his presence, more than any of us ever could! And he loves you, Katie! His arms are wide open, waiting for you to run into his embrace. He is waiting to enfold you in his arms and draw you into himself, waiting to pour out his love in your heart, waiting to fill you with his peace."

Still Katie wept softly.

"I'm ready to listen to what you want to tell me," she said

finally, her voice barely above a whisper. "But I don't know what to do, how to do what you say, even if I want to."

"There's nothing to do, Katie, except to receive the love he offers, the love his arms are waiting to wrap around you."

"How do you receive his love?"

"Just by telling him you want to be his."

"You mean . . . praying?"

"It doesn't matter what you call it, Katie," said Almeda. "God is a friend we can talk to. He is also our Father. We can crawl into his lap and let his arms wrap us up tight, and we can tell him we're tired of being wayward children and we want to stay close to him from now on. Whatever you say, however you say it, he understands. And once you open up your heart to him like that, he will be with you from that moment on, for the rest of your life. With you, and *inside* you! The Bible says that he actually takes up residence inside our hearts and lives with us forever. It's what Jesus calls being born again. That's what it means to give your heart to God. It's what Mr. Parrish helped me to do, and it changed the whole course of my life forever."

A long silence followed.

Without another word, very softly Almeda rose from her chair. With the slightest gesture of one hand she motioned for Uncle Nick to take her place beside Katie's bed. Uncle Nick got up, a momentary look of confusion on his face, not exactly sure what she meant. As he approached Katie and sat down in the seat where Almeda had been, Almeda and I quietly left the bedroom and closed the door. Then we left the cabin and started toward home.

"I'm glad Erich is down at our place," Almeda said after we were a ways along the path. "The two of them need to be alone for a while."

"Why did you get up so abruptly to leave?" I asked.

"Was it abrupt? I didn't mean it to be. I just knew there was nothing else for me to say right then. The next step was Katie's to make, and I felt it was best she have some time to reflect on everything I'd said. God's timing cannot be rushed."

"I know," I said with a smile. "You've taught me that."

"Katie has finally stopped fighting against God. That is a good beginning. How far she goes now, and at what pace— that will be up to her. But I would never want to push someone too fast. We do great harm when we impose our own timetable on the work of the Spirit."

We walked on to the creek and alongside it in silence.

"What do you think will become of Katie and Uncle Nick?" I asked finally.

"Oh, Corrie," said Almeda excitedly, "life is just beginning for them! Everything that's happened up till now has just been preparing them for this time, getting them ready to walk with God in a new way. I truly believe that!"

"And the baby?"

"Sometimes I don't understand God's ways anymore than Katie does. But he turns all for good—when we let him. The two of them losing their daughter is no exception. If they allow him to use it in their lives, it will draw them both closer to him . . . and to each other."

We walked the rest of the way without talking again. When we got home, Almeda lay down.

About an hour later I saw Uncle Nick coming toward the house. Pa was out in the barn. I'd been talking to him and was just coming out when Uncle Nick came up. He had a great big grin on his face and his step was lighter than I'd seen it for several days.

"Where's Almeda?" he said.

"In bed."

"And your Pa?"

"In the barn."

"Well, get Almeda up and I'll go fetch Drum. We'll be inside in a minute."

"What for?" I asked, dying of curiosity.

"Never you mind! I'll tell you all at once," said Uncle Nick, heading off in the direction of the barn. "I got news, that's all I'll say." He was still smiling.

A few minutes later Pa and Uncle Nick walked into the

house, Pa's arm around Uncle Nick's shoulder.

Uncle Nick scooped his son up in his arms. "Well son, your ma did it!"

"Did what, Nick?" asked Pa. "Come on, out with it!"

Uncle Nick was beaming, both from embarrassment and pride all at once. "She prayed, just like you said she ought to, Almeda," he said. "Dad blame if she didn't grab my hand the minute you two left and say, 'Nick, will you pray for me? I want the life that Almeda and Corrie and Drum and the others have. I don't want to be like this any more!' Then she started crying, and I didn't know what to do. 'Please, Nick,' she said, 'you've got to help me! I don't know what to do, but I want to live with God. I don't want to live alone in my heart any more.'

"So I just got up what courage I could muster. Except for that one time with you, Drum, I've never prayed out loud before, but I just said, 'God, you gotta help us, 'cause I don't know what to do. So I ask you to just help Katie, like she said, and show her how to let your arms go around her.' "

"Well, at that, she starting bawling as if she couldn't stop, and I just sat there wondering if I'd said something wrong, getting kinda worried. She just kept crying. But then all of a sudden she burst out praying herself, and she prayed on and on, asking God to forgive her for being so ornery all this time, and for being angry and resentful and for treating people rude and for being selfish. She was crying out how she had hurt so deep inside, saying things I never thought I'd ever hear her say. It was like she was a different person once the shell around her broke apart. There was a look of pain on her face worse than when she was having the baby. She seemed far away in a place all alone—it was a place even I couldn't reach her, though I was sitting beside her holding on to her hand. She was talking to God like I'd never imagined anyone doing, as if he was sitting on the other side of the bed from me—saying . . . all kinds of things."

He stopped and took a deep breath.

"And. . . ?" said Almeda expectantly.

"I guess you could say she and God were having their own

private time together. She said, 'God, I've been so lonely, my heart has felt so cold . . . but now I feel like a little girl again . . . Oh God, why did you take my mother and father from me . . . why did you leave me all alone? I felt so unloved, God . . . no one needed me or wanted me. And now my baby's gone! Was it because of me that you didn't let me keep her . . . wasn't I good enough? Oh, God!' And then she really started to wail—stammering out stuff about being mad at him and getting angry when people would talk about him, and resenting people who went to church. She cried, 'Nobody ever really understood me, Lord . . . no one wanted to be near me, and I took it out on you . . . oh, forgive me—please, Lord! I don't hate you . . . I'm not angry at you any more . . . I *need* you . . . I want so much to trust you . . . so much to feel your love, to know that your arms are wrapped around me like Almeda said. Oh God, I want you to hold me like my daddy never could!' "

Again, Uncle Nick stopped. All the rest of us were silent, hanging on his every word. It was such a moving story, there was nothing to say!

"That was about it," he said, but then a sheepish expression came over his face. "After she was done praying," he continued, "she opened her eyes and looked over at me with a smile, just about the happiest look I'd ever seen on her face. Then she said, 'Oh, Nick, you've been standing with me a long time, and putting up with a lot from me. How can I possibly thank you?' "

"Well . . . what did you say?" asked Pa when Uncle Nick stopped.

"Aw, not much. I just told her I loved her and that it weren't no big thing I done. Then she opened up her arms to me, still smiling, and I sat over on the edge of her bed and leaned over and gave her a hug. And, tarnation if she didn't nearly squeeze the insides out of me! That's when I knew she'd got back most of her strength!"

"Hallelujah!" said Almeda quietly. "God *is* good!" She closed her eyes, and I knew that inwardly she was giving praise to God.

We were all awestruck at what we'd heard.

"God bless her!" said Pa. "I told you if you prayed for her, everything would come out right in the end, Nick."

"What happened to Aunt Katie?" asked Tad, not quite understanding all that was being said.

"The angels in heaven are singing, boy," said Pa, "that's what."

"Your Aunt Katie just gave her life to Jesus, Tad," said Almeda.

"What did you two say to each other after that, Uncle Nick?" I asked. Another sheepish look came over his face.

"Well, if you wanna know," he said, "I prayed again. You see, I'd been sitting there listening to everything you said, Almeda, and it was going down mighty deep into me too. Now you all know I went to church when I was a kid, and that was fine as far as it went. But then I went my own way for a lot of years, as you know better than anyone, Drum. And now I been trying to live my life a mite different, now that I'm married and got myself a family. And I been praying like you said, and trying to remember what I used to know about being a Christian.

"But while you was talking, Almeda, it just sorta dawned on me all of a sudden that I didn't know if I'd ever actually done what you was talking about—prayed, you know, and told God all that about wanting to be different and have him live in my heart. I reckon what I'm saying is that I didn't know if I'd been what you called born again *myself*. I just couldn't say for sure. So I figured it couldn't do no harm to pray all that again, even if I was already on my way to heaven.

"So I did. I prayed it just like Katie'd done. I was still holding her hand, and I closed my eyes and told God I wanted him to live with me too, just like Katie, and I asked him to help me, and to help us both do what he wanted us to, and to be the kind of people he wanted us to be for a change. And when I was all done I stopped, and then I heard Katie whisper a real soft *Amen*. I looked down at her and her eyes were closed again, and the most peaceful look was on her face. I just sat there a long time, her hand in mine. And pretty soon she was asleep, with just a faint smile still on her lips. So I slipped my hand out from hers and came straight down here to tell you what we done."

Our house was so quiet! The only dry eyes in the place were Tad's and little Erich's.

Pa's hand was on Uncle Nick's shoulder again. "You done good, Nick," he said. "You done what you needed to do. It takes a real man to do what you did, to stand up in prayer for himself and his wife. Aggie and your ma and pa'd all be proud of you." He paused just a second or two, then added, "And I'm right proud of you too!"

"Amen!" said Almeda.

I was so happy! We all were. And even though nobody said anything for another spell, all I could think of were Pa's words. And I knew he was right—there was rejoicing going on right then in heaven!

# CHAPTER 47

## GOD'S LITTLE COMMUNITY

The next few days were a joyous time. Uncle Nick's and Almeda's faces showed that a weight of concern had been lifted from them. And among all of us there was a sense of calm and peace, a good feeling, that would erupt every so often in laughter. Pa played with Tad like I hadn't seen him do in a long time, and Emily asked if she could invite Mike McGee to the house for dinner the next Sunday afternoon. Uncle Nick could be seen bounding all over the property and up and down between the two houses with Erich on his shoulders, laughing and carrying on like they were two little kids. There was really a change in him. How much had to do with Katie, and how much had to do with what he'd done himself, I didn't know.

It didn't matter. A new spirit was suddenly alive among us all because Katie had opened up her heart—and it was wonderful!

Almeda remained quiet. I knew she had to take it slow on account of the pregnancy, and every time Doc Shoemaker came to the house he would say, "Now you just don't let yourself get excited about anything, you hear me, Almeda?" But I think her joy went deeper than it did for anyone else. She probably knew in a more personal way how hard it had been for Katie, and knew more of what Katie was feeling because she had felt the exact same things herself. She had shared her own life with Katie, painful as all the recollections were, and endured the emotional pain over what Katie had said. After all that, and the loss of Katie's child, to have Katie finally say that she wanted to know God's love for herself meant more to Almeda than she could have expressed.

She went up to see Katie the next morning. I asked her if she wanted me to go with her.

"Walk me up to the creek, Corrie," she answered. "But then you can come back down here. I want to talk to Katie alone."

She was there a long time. When she got back home she was clearly tired but there was a peaceful smile on her face. Pa asked her what had happened.

"We had a long talk," Almeda said. "A more personal time than we've ever had. She opened up whole new areas of her life to me. She's really a changed woman! I think we're at last ready to be sisters. And then we prayed together, for the first time, and when I left *she* hugged *me*."

There were tears in Almeda's eyes even before she was through telling about it. She turned and went inside and straight to her bed. Pa just put his arm around my shoulder and gave me a squeeze, and said nothing for a minute.

"The Lord's really up to some unexpected things around here, ain't he, Corrie?" he said finally.

"You can say that again!" I said.

"Nick's just as changed inside as Katie," he said. "And I aim to sit him down like Almeda's done with Katie, and talk about some things and get him to praying too. It's time all ten of us—well, at least the nine of us except for little Erich—it's time we all started praying together and bringing God into *everything* we do around this little community of ours."

"Community, Pa?"

"Yeah, Corrie. Don't you see—we got two houses, two families, nine or ten people, however you count them—"

"Soon to be eleven," I put in.

"Yeah, well I reckon you're right—eleven. But you see, here we are a little community within the bigger community. And if all of us—this nine or ten or eleven of us dedicate ourselves to live in what we do by what God tells his folks to do, then it just seems to me that other folks around might sooner or later stand up and take notice, and say, 'Hey, I want to be part of living that kind of life too.' You see, Corrie, it's gotta start someplace, people joining themselves to live together like God's people. I've been thinking a lot about this, and now with Katie and Nick doing what they've done, I figure God might be about to do some new things among us that we haven't seen before."

"That sounds exciting, Pa," I said. My mind flashed back to my talk with Zack at the picnic, and I wondered if I *wanted* to leave this little "community," as Pa called it, of the Hollister-Belle families. Pa made it sound like there couldn't be a better place to be than right here in the middle of where God was at work. "What do you think he's going to do now?"

"How could I know that?" he answered. "I'm not about to start trying to figure God's ways out ahead of time. I'd have never figured a bunch of people like us would be all together like this. Almeda's from Boston, and Katie's from Virginia! But God's got a way of bringing folks together from places about as far apart as we can imagine, and then, *boom*—there they are together and he starts working among them. So how could I try to figure what he's gonna do *next*?"

"I see what you mean, Pa."

"But I'm sure of one thing."

"What's that?"

"When God sets about knittin' folks together—just like weaving threads to make a piece of cloth—when God starts doing that, then good things happen. Just like all of us here—good things are gonna happen, Corrie, I can just feel it. Other folks besides Katie and Nick are gonna find out what it really means to live like God's people."

"How will they find out?"

"Who can tell? They just will. I don't doubt my being mayor's got something to do with what the Lord's up to. It's no accident I got elected when nothing could have been further from my mind. And your writing, Corrie. People read the things you write."

"But I don't write anything about God or what's happened here in our family."

"You might someday. And when you do, people are gonna pay attention to what you say. They're gonna listen, and they're gonna say, 'Hey, I want to live the kind of life Corrie Belle Hollister talks about . . . I want to be a Christian like that . . . I want to pray and know God's love.' You see, Corrie, there's all kinds of stuff God's gonna do with all of us, and with lots of other people too. We've only just seen the beginning!"

# CHAPTER 48

## NEW LIFE

Katie was up and out of bed within two days. Everything about her was changed. You'd have never known she just lost a baby. It was as if she had made a decision to be different from now on—which she had!—and was determined to act accordingly. And of course, God living inside her made the biggest difference of all!

All of a sudden, she was down at our place all the time. It reminded me of the time before Pa and Almeda had been married. There was Katie again in our house, bustling about the kitchen, helping with everything. Now Almeda was being pampered and cared for—with Katie and the three of us girls all taking care of her. I usually went into town to handle the business at the freight office. Doc Shoemaker came out every day. Pa wandered about, not able to get much work done for nervousness, but hardly able to get near Almeda—as much as he wanted to help—for all the women tending to her!

After all that had happened, the birth of Pa and Almeda's baby came almost as a routine event in our lives. It was, of course, one of the greatest things that had ever happened, but there was no huge crisis like there'd been with Katie. One morning about two and a half weeks later, Almeda calmly said to Katie, "I think my labor's begun. You'd better send Drummond for the doctor."

The birthing wasn't routine for Pa! He scurried around like a nervous old lady! He sent Zack for Doc Shoemaker. He didn't

289

leave Almeda's side for a second until the Doc came and shooed everyone out of the bedroom.

Almeda's labor lasted about five hours. I don't know whether it was as painful as Katie's, but she didn't cry out like Katie had. About the middle of the afternoon, all of us except Doc and Katie were gathered in the big room. Suddenly we heard some shouts and exclamations, followed by the cry of a baby.

Pa jumped out of his chair and was off to the bedroom like a shot! The doctor tried to keep him out for a few more minutes, but it was no use.

For the next hour the whole house was like a beehive—nobody could sit or stand still for a second. There were kids and men and women, the doctor and Katie and Uncle Nick—everyone moving to and fro, cleaning and congratulating and laughing and talking. Mrs. Gianini was there too—there was hardly a birthing for miles around Miracle Springs that she didn't attend.

Late in the afternoon, after things were more or less back to normal, Doc Shoemaker let us go into the bedroom one at a time and have a visit with Almeda and to see her and Pa's little daughter. Almeda gave me such a smile when I walked in! For the first time in my life, I found myself wondering what it would be like to become a mother.

"What do you think of your new baby sister, Corrie?" she said.

"She's wonderful." What else could I say? She truly was!

They named her Ruth. "Ruth has long been one of my favorite Bible women," said Almeda. "God took a foreigner from a strange land and grafted her into the royal line of his people. That's just how I feel to be married to your father," she told me. "So blessed of God beyond what I deserve. Our daughter's name will always remind me of God's goodness in bringing me, like Ruth, from a distant place to give me a new life here."

There was a bit of a dispute over little Ruth's middle name, with both Pa and Almeda showing that they wanted to honor the *other* above themselves.

"*Parrish* has gotta be her middle name," said Pa.

"But I was only a Parrish for a few years," objected Almeda. "How can we name *our* daughter after my first husband?"

"Ain't no different than naming her after my first wife." Almeda wanted to use the name *Agatha* in honor of Ma.

"That's completely different," said Almeda. "Your Aggie is the mother of *my* children now. I love her because of them."

"That may be," said Pa. "But I'm still mighty grateful for what Mr. Parrish did for you. If it hadn't been for him, you wouldn't be walking with God now, and wouldn't be my wife. I owe the man plenty, and some day I'm gonna shake his hand and tell him so. Besides, I first knew you as a Parrish, and I kinda like the name!"

In the end they compromised and used both names. She became Ruth Agatha Parrish Hollister.

# CHAPTER 49

## TWENTY-ONE

The rest of the spring and then the summer passed quickly. What a difference a little baby made to life in our little community! There was new life all around—on Katie's face, in little Ruth's crib, in Uncle Nick's walk, and in Pa's stature as a leader in town and among his acquaintances. I could see what Pa had said to me happening—that people would be taking notice of the life that was flowing out on the Hollister-Belle claims.

I had done a lot of thinking about what he'd said about my writing too. And so later that summer I started devoting myself to it again. I didn't write any major articles, but I started spending more time thinking about stories I could write, and dusting off some of my old ideas. I sent some stories to Mr. Kemble and he printed them all in the paper, and was always encouraging me to write more. As I did, I found myself thinking more and more about how I could work God into what I wrote in a way that Mr. Kemble would still find newsworthy. I wanted people who read my articles to know that I was living my life as a daughter of God, not as a person who never thought about him.

I also kept writing in my journal. I wrote about Rev. Rutledge's and Miss Stansberry's wedding. Rev. Rutledge asked Pa to perform the ceremony, and then the men in town *really* started teasing Pa about being a preacher! But he didn't mind. And pretty soon Harriet was expecting a baby too!

I also filled several pages of my journal with the story about Emily and Mike McGee. He didn't just come for dinner that Sunday. He started coming out to the cabin nearly every day. And just before Christmas later that year, he came to see Pa and asked if he could marry Emily. Pa was shocked! Everybody liked Mike, even though he always talked about that new game he liked to play. But *marry* him! "The girl's only just seventeen!" Pa must've exclaimed three dozen times.

But the most important entry in my journal came in March of 1858. It was my twenty-first birthday, and in a lot of ways it was a day when something inside me said, "Well, I suppose I'm getting close to being grown up now."

I wanted to do something special, something I would always remember. For several weeks I'd been considering the idea of taking a ride up into the high hills east of Miracle Springs, maybe even as far as the lake region by Grouse Ridge or Fall Creek Mountain. I didn't really have any definite plans—I just wanted to get high up so I could see the sunrise over the Sierras further east.

It was still dark when I got up, and for the first hour of riding I had to make my way slowly until the faint gray light of dawn gradually began sending the darkness away. In the distance, as I climbed higher and higher over the rugged terrain, gnarled weathered oak trees sat on the horizon, silhouetted against the clear early morning sky that was gradually brightening in the east. Everything was so still and quiet—just a horse and rider moving as one through a smooth grassy meadow of the foothills, dotted sparsely with massive trees, then suddenly encountering the steep rockiness of the mountain region.

Of all the horses I had known and ridden, Raspberry remained my special friend. He was a golden brown color, except for his white stockings and the blaze of white running from between his ears forward to his nostrils. His bulging muscles glistened with sweat. *What a magnificent beast he is*, I thought as he glided with liquid ease, responsive to my every change of the reins, alert to everything around him. I think he enjoyed the morning's ride as much as I did! We galloped across the gently sloping meadows, then slowed to ascend steeper paths upward, and I almost felt Raspberry knew what I was thinking ahead of time!

For an hour we rode, many thoughts passing through my mind, the beauty of the surroundings giving way to reflections on what this day symbolized. What was it that made this, my twenty-first birthday, different from all the ones that had come before? I didn't *feel* any different . . . or did I?

Perhaps it was a deeper sense of accountability—accountability toward others . . . toward God . . . an accountability for my *own* life, my own self.

Even though there were still areas of my life where I felt like a little girl—tentative, unsure of certain things—people would look at me from now on as a "grown up" adult. I was no longer a young girl, but a woman. On this day I was stepping over a threshold into being totally responsible for my own actions, my own thoughts, my own attitudes—accountable for my own decisions, and responsible for making good and right decisions.

God had brought me so far!

Such a short time ago, it seemed, I hadn't known much of anything about what life truly was. I didn't know about God and how he was involved in people's lives, how he wanted to be intimate with us. I hadn't known much about who I was or where I was going, or even who I wanted to be and where I wanted to go.

Yet God had given me such a sense of purpose, so many desires of who and what I wanted to be and become as a person, as his daughter. I wanted to be pure before him. I wanted to love God with my whole being. I wanted to be able to love others with his love. I wanted to be able to tell people about him, about my life with him, about the thoughts and feelings that were in my heart toward him. I wanted to meet and know people who shared that same commitment, those same desires—people who were also on that same road of life.

When I found my thoughts drifting toward marriage, I surprised myself. I didn't think such things very often, and usually figured I'd never marry. But on the occasions when it did cross my mind, I wondered what kind of man God might have for me to share my life with. I'd even fall to imagining about it sometimes. And then I'd realize that in spite of what I'd said to Zack, I did have certain feelings and ideas about the man I would marry, *if* I did. He would be strong and sensitive and loving. But strong in an inward way, not strong the way boys and men talked about strength. *Strong* to me was the quality of character that made someone willing to stand up for what they believed, even to make sacrifices to do it. Almeda was strong in that way. So was Pa. And *sensitive* to me meant the kind of man who could tell what another person, especially a woman, was thinking. Sensitivity meant respecting the thoughts and feelings of others, a gentleness, and especially the ability to talk and share and be open with feelings. Women didn't have much trouble doing that kind of thing, but men usually did. I wanted to marry a man who knew how to talk and share and feel—a man who knew how to cry and wasn't ashamed to be an emotional, open, tender man. That was sensitivity to me. I wondered if such men even existed! As hard as it had been for him at first, Pa was learning to be that kind of man, and I loved him so much for it!

And of course *first* of all, such a man would have to be a Christian, sharing with me the desire to follow God with all his heart in *everything*. How could a man and woman be friends for a lifetime if they didn't share that most important thing of all? And if marriage was something God had for me, I didn't want to just be a wife, and have a husband. I wanted to have a best friend to live the rest of my life with!

Raspberry stumbled momentarily on a rock in our path, and suddenly my thoughts were jolted back from marriage to the present. We were climbing pretty steeply now. It was completely light, and over the mountains ahead of us hues of pink were starting to spread upward from the horizon. The summit up ahead looked like a good place to stop. From there I'd be able to see the sun rise over the peaks in the distance. I urged Raspberry on.

But in spite of the difficult climb, I couldn't keep my thoughts on the ride itself. I found myself thinking about myself and what kind of person I was—the kind of thoughts you usually keep to yourself and don't tell anyone, even your parents or closest friends.

God had given me certain talents and strengths, although sometimes it was hard to admit good things, even to myself. But I knew I had done a lot of growing up in the five-and-a-half years since we had come to California. I'd been fifteen-and-a-half then, and so young. Now here I was looking at life as an adult would. And I wanted so badly to put to good use all that God had given me. I wanted to use the gifts and abilities and strengths he had put inside me to help other people, to grow still closer to him, and to glorify him.

"Oh Lord," I found myself praying, "help me to cultivate what you've given me. Don't let me waste anything. Help me to grow to the fullest, so that I can be the person you want me to be!"

Even as I prayed I realized how much he had already done within me. The growth hadn't all been easy. I'd cried a lot of tears since Ma's death out on the desert. I'd cried with Almeda. I'd cried with Pa. And I'd cried alone. Yet I had grown and matured so much through it all!

And I wasn't the only one who had changed. I'd seen so many other relationships develop and deepen, from Pa and Mr. Royce to Uncle Nick and Katie, Little Wolf and Zack. Mr. Lame Pony was having more to do with people in the community. Rev. Rutledge had changed and become a friend to our family. I saw so much growth in so many people.

I thought about what it was like to toss a pebble into a pond. The rock starts a motion of ripples that spread outward in concentric circles, which eventually goes the entire length of the water in every direction. I was reminded of Almeda, one woman, left alone at her husband's death, yet with faith alive and growing inside her heart, like a rock thrown into the middle of this community.

Then we had come. And through Almeda's walk and life with God I saw something I desired to share, something I wanted and knew I needed. As I searched for the truth, with Almeda helping and guiding and teaching me, our friendship developed and deepened, as did my faith. I became a daughter to her in many ways.

Then Pa was gradually drawn by the same thing I had felt. His faith in God began to grow deeper too, not just from Almeda, but maybe even from me and seeing Rev. Rutledge reach out to him. God was already spreading his life out into the community through more than just one or two.

After Pa and Almeda were married, the circles of deeper faith continued to widen. As Zack and Emily and Becky grew, we all started praying more together as a family. Then things began changing for Uncle Nick. And then God, in his mysterious ways, worked through tragedy to bring Katie into the ever-widening circle.

*God, O God,* I thought, *you have transformed me and the people around me in so many extraordinary ways! Where will it go from here? What are you going to do next? Whose life will you change . . . whose heart will you get inside of next?*

As we crested the peak, Raspberry struggled up the final bit of the steep climb. Then the path leveled out and continued along for some distance over the high ridge.

I reined him in and sat still in the saddle for another moment or two, glancing around in all directions. What a beautiful view! The long ride, the climb . . . it had all been worth it for this one moment!

Slowly I dismounted, taking the reins in my hand, and walked to a lone tree, growing by itself on the high plateau. I tethered Raspberry to its trunk and patted the red splotch in the middle of his white forehead, the reason for his name.

I walked on farther, climbed onto a big boulder, and sat down on top of it. The sky in the east was now full of vivid colors, all melting into each other as the brightening flame on the horizon gathered in intensity.

Suddenly, from behind a snow-capped peak in the distance, a sliver of the sun shot into view. The intense ray pierced my eyes like a blinding arrow. In a second the whole eastern horizon was changed as brilliant, flashing rays spread out in all directions. All other colors instantly vanished in the core of blinding orange fire.

I turned around and looked in the direction from which I had come. Down in the distance the early morning haze still clung to the trees and ridges and hollows, some of which wouldn't see the sun for several more hours. And then, still farther off, I could just glimpse the big valley into which all the rivers of these mountains poured.

*I am twenty-one*, I thought to myself. *Twenty-one*! It hardly seemed possible! What would my future hold? I wanted so much to do what God wanted me to. I wanted always to be growing in my knowledge of him, growing in what the Bible called righteousness. I never wanted to let myself relax in my faith and take the easy way. I wanted to hold on to the standards that God had established, the way he wanted his people to walk.

"God," I prayed as I sat there, "I want my whole self to belong to you. I give my all to you. Show me how to do it. I know I can only do it with you beside me and in me."

I could feel the warmth of the sun's rays on my back. I sat still for a long time. Everything was still and quiet. The only sounds to meet my ears were the songs of birds celebrating the sun and the springtime.

Seized by a great surge of joy, I wished I could soar like those birds. I had grown in the years since coming to California from a timid and uncertain young girl into a confident, though occasionally still struggling—could I actually *say* the word?—into an—*adult*.

As I sat there basking in the sunrise, the dawn reminded

me of the day Almeda shared her story and her feelings with Katie. Almeda had said that Mr. Parrish gave her a place to stand. I remembered her words, and I could almost hear her voice when she said, *"Not only was he giving me a place to stand, it was a place of warmth and smiles."*

I got down off the boulder and walked back to the tree where Raspberry was waiting patiently for me. I mounted and we moved on for a short distance in the other direction, gazing toward the mountains, then back westward toward the valley below, where the sun's rays were now probing the hollows and caressing the ridges above them.

Suddenly the overpowering radiance of the sun became a revelation to me. *I have been given a place to stand, too,* I thought. *A place right here, a place in this new state, "the sunshine state." God has given me a place in the sun!*

A sense of calm and peace and assurance flooded over my being. Even as I felt the sun's warmth on my arms and back, I felt God's presence wrapping around me.

I sank to my knees on a patch of nearby grass. Lifting my face toward heaven, I was filled with a heart of gratefulness.

"Thank you, God, for being so near to me, so present with me. Thank you that I am here. Thank you for bringing me to California. Thank you for the place you have given me to stand . . . and to walk. And thank you for everything my future holds . . . whatever it may be."

I lingered a while longer on the grass, soaking in everything I was feeling. Then I slowly stood.

The sun was already climbing into the sky, its fiery beams waking up every inch of the sleepy earth. I walked back toward Raspberry, gave his nose a pat, untied him, and remounted.

"It's time we headed back, my old friend," I said.

Down the way we had come, we made our way toward home. I knew my family would all be up by now and wondering where I was. I smiled at the thought. I probably should have told someone where I was going. But I had wanted to be completely alone, even in the knowledge of where I was!

My heart was still welling up within me, full of God's peace and love. My thoughts and prayers seemed to take up where they had left off on the ride up.

"God," I prayed again, "help me take care of the good things you are doing inside me. Never let me take for granted all you've given, and the life you've put within me. I give my life to you, Lord, and place into your hands whatever my future holds."

# ON THE TRAIL OF THE TRUTH

# ON THE TRAIL OF THE TRUTH

## MICHAEL PHILLIPS
## JUDITH PELLA

**BETHANY HOUSE PUBLISHERS**
MINNEAPOLIS, MINNESOTA 55438

Cover illustration by Dan Thornberg,
Bethany House Publishers staff artist.

Copyright © 1991
Michael Phillips/Judith Pella
All Rights Reserved

Published by Bethany House Publishers
A Ministry of Bethany Fellowship, Inc.
6820 Auto Club Road, Minneapolis, Minnesota 55438

Printed in the United States of America

**Library of Congress Cataloging-in-Publication Data**

Phillips, Michael R. , 1946–
    On the trail of the truth / Michael Phillips and Judith Pella.
      p.   cm.   (The Journals of Corrie Belle Hollister ; bk. 3)

    I. Pella, Judith.  II. Title.  III. Series: Phillips, Michael R. , 1946–
Journals of Corrie Belle Hollister ; 3.
PS3566.H49205   1991
813'.54—dc20                         91–6660
ISBN 1–55661–106–4                CIP

To
Gregory Erich Phillips

# Books by the Phillips/Pella Writing Team

**The Journals of Corrie Belle Hollister**

*My Father's World*
*Daughter of Grace*
*On the Trail of the Truth*
*A Place in the Sun*
*Sea to Shining Sea*

**The Stonewycke Trilogy**

*The Heather Hills of Stonewycke*
*Flight from Stonewycke*
*Lady of Stonewycke*

**The Stonewycke Legacy**

*Stranger at Stonewycke*
*Shadows over Stonewycke*
*Treasure of Stonewycke*

**The Highland Collection**

*Jamie MacLeod: Highland Lass*
*Robbie Taggart: Highland Sailor*

**The Russians**

*The Crown and the Crucible*
*A House Divided*

# The Authors

The PHILLIPS/PELLA writing team had its beginning in the longstanding friendship of Michael and Judy Phillips with Judith Pella. Michael Phillips, with a number of nonfiction books to his credit, had been writing for several years. During a Bible study at Pella's home he chanced upon a half-completed sheet of paper sticking out of a typewriter. His author's instincts aroused, he inspected it more closely, and asked their friend, "Do you write?" A discussion followed, common interests were explored, and it was not long before the Phillips invited Pella to their home for dinner to discuss collaboration on a proposed series of novels. Thus, the best-selling "Stonewycke" books were born, which led in turn to "The Highland Collection."

Judith Pella holds a nursing degree and B.A. in Social Sciences. Her background as a writer stems from her avid reading and researching in historical, adventure, and geographical venues. Pella, with her two sons, resides in Eureka, California. Michael Phillips, who holds a degree from Humboldt State University and continues his post-graduate studies in history, owns and operates Christian bookstores on the West Coast. He is the editor of the best-selling George MacDonald Classic Reprint Series and is also MacDonald's biographer. The Phillips also live in Eureka with their three sons.

# CALIFORNIA.

Golden Regions.

# EMIGRATION TO
# CALIFORNIA !

Do you want to go to California ! If so, go and join the Company who intend going out the middle of March, or 1st of April next, under the charge of the California Emigration Society, in a first-rate Clipper Ship. The Society agreeing to find places for all those who wish it upon their arrival in San Francisco. The voyage will probably be made in a few months.— Price of passage will be in the vicinity of

## ONE HUNDRED DOLLARS !
### CHILDREN IN PROPORTION.

A number of families have already engaged passage. A suitable Female Nurse has been provided, who will take charge of Young Ladies and Children. Good Physicians, both male and female go in the Ship. It is hoped a large number of females will go, as Females are getting almost as good wages as males.

FEMALE NURSES get 25 dollars per week and board. SCHOOL TEACHERS 100 dollars per month. GARDNERS 60 dollars per month and board. LABORERS 4 to 5 dollars per day. BRICKLAYERS 6 dollars per day. HOUSEKEEPERS 40 dollars per month. FARMERS 5 dollars per day. SHOEMAKERS 4 dollars per day. Men and Women COOKS 40 to 60 dollars per month and board. MINERS are making from 3 to 12 dollars per day. FEMALE SERVANTS 30 to 50 dollars per month and board. Washing 3 dollars per dozen. MASONS 6 dollars per day. CARPENTERS 5 dollars per day. ENGINEERS 100 dollars per month, and as the quartz Crushing Mills are getting into operation all through the country, Engineers are very scarce. BLACKSMITHS 90 and 100 dollars per month and board.

The above prices are copied from late papers printed in San Francisco, which can be seen at my office. Having views of some 30 Cities throughout the State of California, I shall be happy to see all who will call at the office of the Society, 28 JOY'S BUILDING, WASH- INGTON ST., BOSTON, and examine them. Parties residing out of the City, by enclosing a stamp and sending to the office, will receive a circular giving all the particulars of the voyage.

An Agents are wanted in every town and city of the New England States, Postmasters or Merchants acting as such will be allowed a certain commission on every person they get to join the Company. Good reference required. For further particulars correspond or call at the

## SOCIETY'S OFFICE,
# 28 Joy's Building, Washington St., Boston, Mass.

Propeller Job Press, 142 Washington Street, Boston.

# CONTENTS

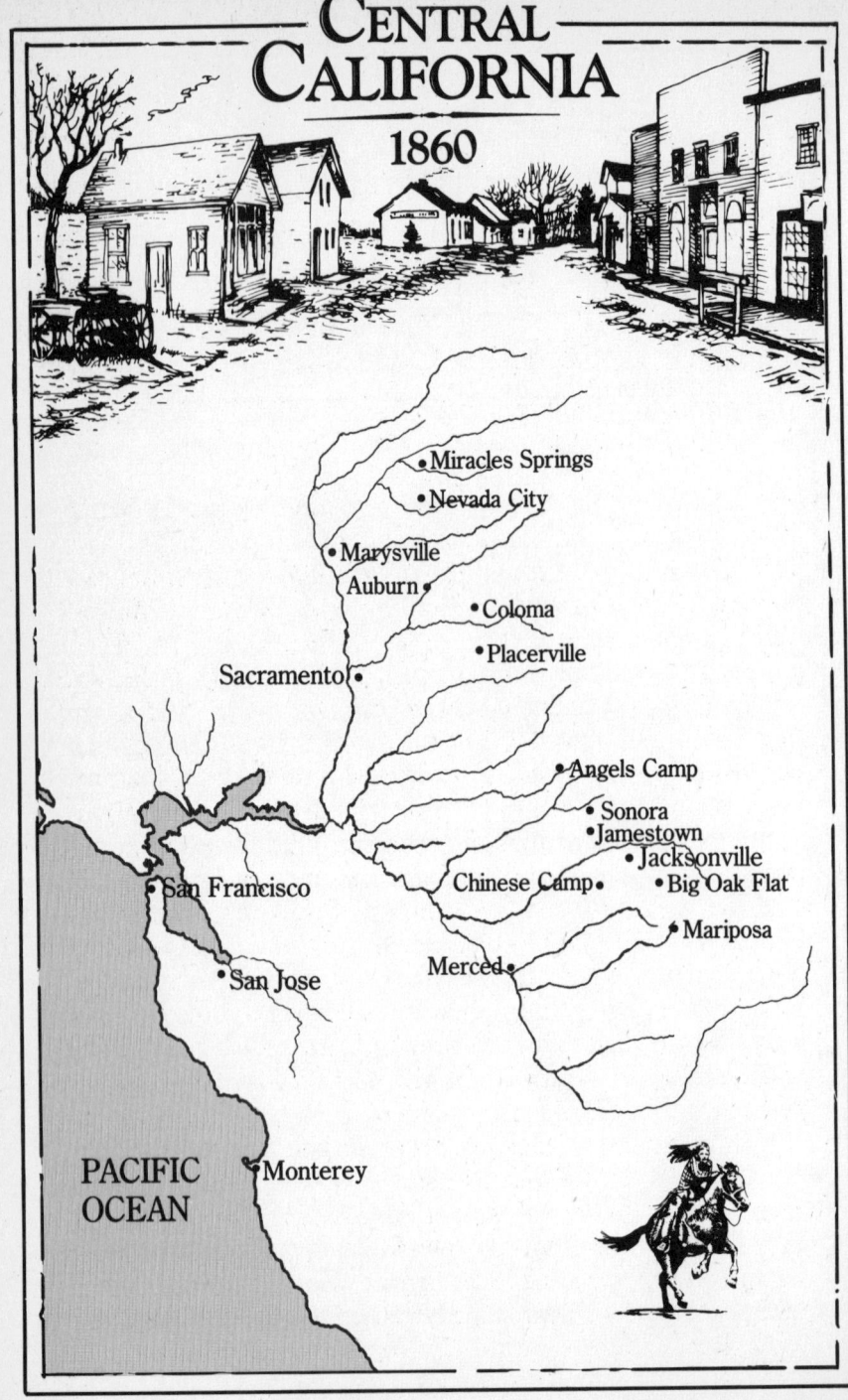

# CENTRAL CALIFORNIA

## 1860

• Miracles Springs

• Nevada City

• Marysville

Auburn •

• Coloma

• Placerville

Sacramento •

• Angels Camp

• Sonora

• Jamestown

• Jacksonville

Chinese Camp • • Big Oak Flat

• San Francisco

• Mariposa

Merced •

• San Jose

PACIFIC
OCEAN

• Monterey

# CHAPTER 1

## REFLECTIONS

I remember the last time I was here listening to Miss Stansberry play the wedding march on the church piano. Two months ago, back in June, I was sitting down in the front row waiting for what I thought was going to be my pa's wedding to Katie Morgan.

But that wedding never happened. Uncle Nick crashed in, shouting that Katie should marry *him*, not my pa, and to my amazement, Pa agreed. I was filled with a lot of feelings that seemed to be fighting inside my head. I wanted Pa to be happy, but down inside I just didn't feel right about him and Katie. Right from the beginning they somehow didn't seem like the kind of man and woman that were meant to be together. Not married, at least. Not when I thought of Ma. An hour later, I was there again—only this time sitting *next* to Pa, watching Katie becoming Mrs. Nicholas Belle. Instead of marrying Pa, Katie had ended up married to Uncle Nick.

So this day in the second week of August 1854, I felt a heap different than I had the last time I heard the wedding march. No seventeen-year-old girl could have been happier than I was standing up there in front of the church alongside Mrs. Parrish. Uncle Nick stood on the other side next to Pa, with Rev. Rutledge in between. It was the perfect ending to the last eight or nine months, since that day toward the end of last year when Pa announced to us kids that he was planning to get married again. For weeks—ever since Nick and Katie's wedding, ever

13

since I saw Pa and Mrs. Parrish walking quietly away from the church after Uncle Nick had busted in—I'd been so happy and distracted, I hadn't been able to think straight. And on the big day, even standing there in front of the church, I couldn't keep my mind focused on what was going on. All of a sudden I realized the music had stopped and Rev. Rutledge was talking and telling folks about what the wedding vows were supposed to mean. By the time I started listening in earnest, he was already getting on with the business of what we were all doing here! As he said the words, my brain was racing, remembering so many things. I had to stand there, straight and quiet next to Mrs. Parrish, smiling and acting calm. But inside I was anything but calm.

*"Do you, Drummond . . ."*

When I thought back to the first day I heard that name, and how Pa and Mrs. Parrish squared off on the street in front of the Gold Nugget, I just wanted to laugh. He was *Mr.* Drum then. None of us knew who he was or what was to come from that day. He and Mrs. Parrish sure didn't like each other much at first!

"So, Mr. Drum, what might be your intentions now?" I could still hear her stern voice, her glaring eyes bearing down on Pa's bewildered face.

And he roared back, "I reckon it ain't none of your dad-blamed business!"

Mrs. Parrish said she aimed to *make* us kids her business and told him he ought to be ashamed of himself. Pa said he had no intention of having a woman tell him what to do, and then he rode off through the middle of town.

What a beginning that had been! Who'd have ever figured it would come to this?

*"Take this woman to be your wedded wife . . ."*

Wife . . . his *wife*! My first thought was of Ma. But instead of showing sadness or regret or sorrow when her face came into my memory, she was smiling. I knew she understood and was watching with pleasure, glad that the Lord had sent such a good woman to this man and his kids.

At first Pa was looking mostly at Rev. Rutledge, but now he glanced over toward me and Mrs. Parrish. He wasn't looking at me but her, and he looked right into her eyes. I couldn't see her face looking back at him, but from the look of love in Pa's eyes, I didn't see how he could possibly concentrate on what the minister was saying. Pa's eyes were so full it must have taken all his concentration just to fill them with that look. I don't think I'd ever seen such a look in his eyes before.

I couldn't help remembering the meeting of their eyes on that day he and Katie were supposed to be married, after Uncle Nick had run in and the uproar had started. Pa had a sheepish, embarrassed look on his face as he stood next to where Mrs. Parrish was sitting, and she looked back at him sort of half-crying.

That memory sent me back further, to a day when Pa and I were talking in the barn. He told me that when he looked into Katie's eyes, it just wasn't the same as it used to be with Ma.

Now as I saw Pa and Mrs. Parrish looking at each other, everything seemed to be coming right after a long time of wondering how it would all turn out. No one would ever replace Ma, but you could sure tell there was something pretty special for both Pa and Mrs. Parrish.

"*. . . to have and to hold from this day forward, for better, for worse, for richer, for poorer, in sickness and in health . . .*"

During the last few weeks, getting ready for the wedding, I often found myself wondering when Pa actually started thinking differently about Mrs. Parrish. I thought back to that day of the first church service in Miracle Springs, when there wasn't even a church yet, when he stuck up for the minister. I wondered if he had done that for her, maybe without even knowing it himself. Or that first Christmas dinner at Mrs. Parrish's house, when Pa got mad and we all left early. I wondered if they really liked each other back then, if some of their arguments were just to cover up feelings that might have been sneaking up on them from behind. I guess that's something I'll *never* know!

"*. . . to love and to cherish, till death do you part, according to God's holy ordinance?*"

I asked Pa about three weeks before the wedding, "When did you first notice Mrs. Parrish?" He looked at me as if to say *What are you talking about, girl?* But he knew well enough what I was driving at. "When did you look at her different than just another woman, Pa? You know what I mean."

He kept eyeing me, serious as could be, then a little grin broke out on his lips. Once he got to talking about it, I think he enjoyed the memories. We talked about the meetings for the school committee, and he sheepishly admitted that we had gone early a couple of times so he'd be able to see Mrs. Parrish before the minister got there, just like I figured. "And you got all cleaned up and shaved and smelling good too, didn't you, Pa?" I asked. "And that was on account of her, wasn't it?"

"I reckon," he answered. "But don't tell no one."

"Everyone knows by now, Pa," I laughed. "There ain't nothing more to hide!"

He blustered a bit after I said that, but in a little while he started talking again, and this time it was about Katie. He said almost the minute she got to California, he realized he'd made a mistake, but he didn't know what to do about fixing it.

"Why didn't you just call the whole thing off?" I asked.

He said he could see it all perfectly clear now and couldn't imagine he could have been such a fool, thinking it might work if he just went ahead and didn't say anything. "But by then, Corrie," he said, "my head was so blamed full of that Parrish woman I couldn't even think straight. I was so muddled I pretty near got myself hitched to the wrong woman, just like Nick said. I was just a downright nincompoop 'bout the whole thing!"

"It's a good thing Uncle Nick came when he did," I said.

"Tarnation, you're right there, girl! Yes, sir, Nick saved my hide but good! And that more'n made up for all the times I hauled him outta his share of the scrapes we got ourselves into. Yep, I figure we're about even now."

It was quiet for a minute, then I asked Pa, "How come you wrote off for Katie in the first place, Pa?"

Pa thought a minute, scratched his head, and finally said, "I don't know, Corrie . . . I just don't know. I been wonderin' that same thing myself for quite a spell."

"Maybe for Uncle Nick," I suggested with a grin.

"Yeah, probably," said Pa. "But you know, Corrie, folks sometimes say there's times a man's just gotta do what he's gotta do—which is just another way of saying that a man is sometimes determined to go his own fool-headed way no matter how stupid it might be. And I reckon that's how it was with me back then. I was already startin' to feel something inside for the Parrish lady, and I reckon it scared me a little. At the same time, I wasn't sure if I even liked her, 'cause she could sure be ornery sometimes. So maybe I figured gettin' me a bride like Katie would put a stop to the crazy thoughts I was havin'. But it didn't work at all! The minute Katie got here I found myself thinkin' of Almeda all the more."

I smiled, and that was the end of my conversation with Pa.

Whatever his mistakes and uncertainties back then, he sure wasn't making one now. And he wasn't having any more second thoughts. For when the words *I do* came out of his mouth, the whole church heard them, and I couldn't keep from crying.

Then the minister and all the eyes of the people turned toward Mrs. Parrish.

*Do you, Almeda . . .*

Poor Rev. Rutledge! It must have been hard for him to utter those words. Mrs. Parrish had brought him here, and they had been together so much the whole first year. It was hardly any secret that he was sweet on her. Everybody in town figured they were going to get married one day. And now he was having to marry her to somebody *else*! But ever since Rev. Rutledge came to Miracle Springs, folks have been surprised at what a fine man he turned out to be—building the church, pitching in with all the rest of the men when anything needed to be done, helping folks, going to visit anybody who was sick. I think he'd earned the respect of just about everybody in the whole community. And now he was marrying Mrs. Parrish to Drummond Hollister with his head high and being a real man about how things had turned out.

*" . . . take this man to be your wedded husband . . ."*

Only about a week before the wedding, one Sunday afternoon Mrs. Parrish came out to our house for dinner. Of course she'd been spending a lot of time with us, but she wouldn't come there to live till after the wedding. She was there, along with Katie and Nick and everybody else, and the talk was getting lively and everybody was laughing. Katie asked the question, but I'd wondered about it too, just like I had with Pa.

"Now tell us, Almeda," she said, "when did you first fall in love with this cantankerous gold miner?"

Mrs. Parrish laughed, and Uncle Nick chimed in, "Yeah, that's somethin' I'd like to know! How any woman in her right mind could think o' marryin' a coot like him, I can't figure it!"

"Aw, keep your no-good opinions to yourself, Nick!" Pa shot back, but neither of them were serious.

When it quieted down a bit, Mrs. Parrish told about how much she'd admired him when he stood up in church, and even when he'd stomped out after Christmas dinner that time. She said part of her was angry with him for ruining her nice dinner, but at the same time she couldn't help respecting him for wanting to stand up for what he thought was right, and for not wanting things said about him that he didn't think were true. "But I suppose the very first time my heart thought about fluttering must have been that day, not long after the children and I had gone on a picnic out in the country, when I was getting ready to leave on a business trip. Drum rode up in a great flurry of dust and noise, jumped off his horse, and came striding up to me so determined-looking I didn't know what he was about to do! But when he took me aside and told me he was the children's father, and then apologized for not coming forward sooner—well, right then I think something began telling me this was an unusual man."

"No, you were already after me sooner'n that!" said Pa seriously, but with a twinkle in his eye.

"What do you mean, I was *after* you?"

"You know perfectly well what I mean. You always were a mighty headstrong woman, and you—"

"Headstrong! Drummond Hollister, I ought to—"

"You know well and good you're headstrong. And you know you were out to get me right from the start."

"There is no truth in that whatsoever."

"Come on, Almeda, don't lie in front o' the children." Pa threw a wink at us. "Do you deny you went out on that picnic intentionally to get near to my place here?"

"I simply said that—"

"There! You can't deny it! Right from the start you were trying to weasel in closer toward me."

"It was only for the sake of the children. I've told you that before."

Pa laughed. "I don't believe that for a minute. You had your sights set long ago. Once you took a look at me, you couldn't help yourself. Go on, tell Katie the truth."

By now everybody was laughing at their good-natured argument. Mrs. Parrish didn't say anything for a minute. I was beginning to wonder if Pa'd hurt her feelings. But I guess she was just trying to think up some good way to get the best of him. Finally she burst out:

"Well, it worked, didn't it? I got you in the end!"

" . . . *to have and to hold from this day forward, for better, for worse, for richer, for poorer, in sickness and in health.* . . ."

I suppose after the incident with Becky's kidnapping by Buck Krebbs and the thing with Royce and the ransom money, there could hardly be any doubt that Mrs. Parrish was prepared and willing to give everything she had for Pa and us kids, even if it meant she *would* be poor from then on. After what she did that day, the minister hardly needed to ask if she was pledged to Pa for better or worse and richer or poorer. She'd proved that already!

Pa didn't realize what she'd done right at first. He didn't know how she'd twisted Royce's arm to give her the money. If I hadn't seen her go into the bank with that parcel of papers, and then seen that horrible look on Mr. Royce's face later when she left, none of us might have ever known, because Pa and Uncle Nick had already gone to the sheriff's.

But later that night when I told Pa what I'd seen, he jumped up and, hurt as he was, rode into town right then to get the money back to her. And almost as quickly, she lit off out of town for Royce's home, even though it was past banking hours.

Pa told us later that she'd signed over the deeds to all her property, her business, her home and office, and all her supplies and equipment as collateral against the $50,000. If she hadn't gotten the full amount of money back to Royce within twenty-four hours, everything she owned would have become his! That was how much she cared about Becky's safety, and how much she trusted Pa!

The minute Pa learned what she'd done, he must have known that their lives were made to be intertwined together somehow. After that, his future could have no one in it besides her—not after all they'd already been through together, and how close it had brought them toward each other.

That's when, he told me later, he suddenly realized he loved Mrs. Parrish *himself*, and not just because she was nice to us kids.

So when Mrs. Parrish answered the minister's question, every single person in that church knew the depth of love behind the vows.

*". . . to love, to cherish, and to obey till death do you part according to God's holy ordinance?"*

And with eyes brimming full of tears, and a radiant smile

of love and thanksgiving spread all across her face, Mrs. Parrish answered: *"I do."*

Ten minutes later, as I walked back down the aisle in time to Miss Stansberry's playing, my hand on Uncle Nick's arm, I was following my pa and my brand-new mother!

# CHAPTER 2

# RICE, BOUQUETS, AND GARTERS

As Pa and Mrs. Parrish walked through the front door of the church and outside, I heard shouts and yells, followed by Pa's loud voice and then Mrs. Parrish's laughing.

Uncle Nick and I were right behind. As the sunlight hit our faces, there were six or eight of the saloon girls gathered around, tossing handfuls of rice in the air at them. The whole rest of the church was right on our heels, and within a minute or two they were all getting into the act. Katie had made sure everyone in Miracle Springs under the age of fifteen—and a lot of those older, too!—had a good supply of rice. And before you knew it the whole town was after them, whooping and hollering.

Mrs. Parrish could hardly move fast enough to get away in her beautiful white wedding dress, the same one as she'd worn in Boston and which she had packed away all this time. Most of the folks weren't after her at all. Pa had by far the worst time of it with the rice! But I knew he loved every second, yelling and running and pretending to be trying to get away, while at the same time letting Tad and Becky and the other kids get him good a few times. When it was all done, and people were laughing and panting and hand shaking and back slapping, Pa's hair and black broadcloth suit looked as if he'd walked out in the middle of a hailstorm.

There'd been a big afternoon of festivities planned. Pa had

fussed about it ahead of time. "Let's just get the thing done, and then slip outta town, Almeda," he'd said. "There don't need to be a big to-do on our account."

Pa still didn't understand. Mrs. Parrish took me aside and said, "Your father, bless him, is so humble he has no idea how folks around here look up to him!"

She was right! If people around Miracle Springs were interested in Pa's getting married before, *now* with him marrying Mrs. Parrish—and almost two months after Nick and Katie's wedding for word to spread about it—why, folks had hardly been talking of anything else! The little church was packed, with people standing up all around the outside walls. Lots of folks from the hills and neighboring towns knew there'd be no room inside, so they just came and waited around outside for the festivities afterward. Rev. Rutledge had made sure the doors and all the windows were open, and so folks peered in however they could. Then afterwards the tables were set up and filled with food, with the big wedding cake in the middle. When everyone started gathering around, I reckon there were more people than would have filled the church three or four times over, and a lot of faces I'd never seen. Mrs. Parrish herself was a pretty well-known woman, so no doubt lots of people were there on account of her.

It's not often a man gets married with his kids right there with him. Pa had the five of us—me and Zack and Emily and Becky and Tad—come stand beside him and Mrs. Parrish. It was such a proud, happy moment! We were a *whole* family again! Uncle Nick stood right there in front of us with his arm around Katie. Zack's best friend, Little Wolf, was there, as well as Miss Stansberry and her brother and Rev. Rutledge and all the other folks that we'd come to know. I hardly know how to describe what I was feeling—complete, I reckon. None of the pieces were out of place or missing anymore.

Then Mrs. Parrish took Pa's hand and together they began to cut the cake. Uncle Nick and Alkali Jones kept the men stirred up with their catcalls and poking fun at Pa, and there was plenty of laughter to go around, with Pa getting in his share of jibes back at his two friends. Then they handed out slices of the cake, first to the kids and then to everybody else, and there was more handshaking and well-wishing and congratulations offered to the bride and groom. A few of the women cried again, but most of the tears, mine included, had come and gone in the church. By now everybody's spirits were pretty high.

"Time to throw the bouquet!" someone called out.

I glanced up, but couldn't see who it was. It had been a woman's voice—probably someone wanting to get it herself! Mrs. Parrish had told us earlier about the custom of the bride throwing the bouquet over her shoulder to the women of her wedding party and family and whoever else wanted to join in. "And whoever catches it," she said, and eleven-year-old Becky's eyes were big and wide listening to every word, "that woman's going to be the *next* one to get married."

"Really?" said Becky slowly, full of wonder.

"That's what they say," answered Mrs. Parrish.

"Then *I'm* going to catch it!" said Becky, more as if she was speaking fact than hope.

Emily didn't say anything. She was thirteen, and turning into a pretty young lady. It wouldn't be long before fellas would be turning their heads to look at her twice. And I couldn't help wondering what *she* was thinking about the bouquet. Flowers or not, I had no doubts she'd have half a dozen handsome young men courting and sweet-talking her before *anybody* threw a second look toward me. Maybe that's why I had the feeling that Mrs. Parrish would try to toss her bouquet in my direction.

"All right . . . all right," she answered to the call, coming out from behind the cake table. "Ladies, girls—all of you gather round right over here in front of me!"

A scurry and bustle followed. All the little girls came running, some of the saloon girls, laughing to themselves but wanting to join in the fun and maybe hoping for a chance to grab at the bouquet, the three of us Hollister girls, and the few unmarried women that were there.

"Are you all ready?" she said, and as she did her eyes caught mine. I wasn't sure I *wanted* to catch it.

A chorus of high-pitched shouts went up.

Mrs. Parrish turned around, her back to us, picked up her bouquet from the table, and gave it a mighty heave up in the air back over her head.

I was right; it did come in my direction—but not nearly close enough that I could even have jumped up and touched it. The bouquet went sailing over my head!

Becky cried out in disappointment. Sounds of *oohs* and *aahs* and various cheers went up. I spun around to see a red-faced Miss Stansberry, standing far toward the rear, holding Mrs. Parrish's flowers with a look of shock and surprise in her eyes.

We all clamored around her, while the men clapped and cheered, and a few winked and kidded each other with knowing expressions of significance on their faces.

"And now, Drummond, it's time for you to throw my garter," said Mrs. Parrish.

"Yeah, Drum!" several called out. "The garter . . . throw it to me!"

Now the men *really* erupted with shouts and yells and laughter. Above it all I could hear Mr. Jones's *hee, hee, hee!* and Uncle Nick's whooping. All the men were having a good time trying to make Pa feel as uncomfortable as they could!

Mrs. Parrish pulled up the corner of her dress to the knee, and now all the yelling changed to whistling, while the women tried to shush up their husbands. But nobody was going to be denied making sport of anything they could on this day. Mrs. Parrish took her time, throwing Pa a smile as she slowly slipped the garter down over her calf and ankle.

"Here, Drum, will you help me a moment?" she said coyly. Pa stepped up and lent a steadying hand to her free arm to keep her balanced.

"No, Drum," she said. "I want *you* to slip the garter over my shoe."

A red flush crept over his face. Pa stooped down to one

knee and began the process, while the whistling and calling out doubled in volume.

When he finally stood up, the garter in hand, he shouted, "Cut out all your hollerin', you pack of baboons! Can't you see there's ladies present!"

But the men just fired off more teasing and jesting at Pa all the louder.

"All right, then, you loco varmints!" shouted Pa back. "Any of you characters who's fool enough to want to get yourself hitched come up here and get yourselves ready, 'cause I'm about to give this little thing the heave-ho."

All the boys hustled forward, nine-year-old Tad right in the front.

"Throw it to me, Pa!" he cried.

"You gotta fight for it with everyone else, boy," Pa answered. "Get in there, Zack . . . Little Wolf . . . come on, all of you get ready."

Not nearly so many men gathered around as women, even though there were twenty times more men available for marrying than women.

Pa turned his back to them and threw the garter in the air behind him. Zack made a halfhearted reach for it, Tad leaped up in the air, but neither was even close. Like the bouquet, the garter flew over the top of them, and I saw it hit Rev. Rutledge on the back of the head. He'd been talking to Patrick Shaw and wasn't even paying attention to what was going on behind him.

The minute it hit his head, the minister's hand unconsciously shot up to investigate the disturbance he'd felt. He then turned around to see every face upon him, the garter hanging from two of his fingers, a bewildered expression on his face.

When the truth of what happened dawned on him, a broad grin spread over his face, followed by an embarrassed laugh.

"Well, Reverend," called out Uncle Nick, "I reckon you're next!"

"No, no, not me," insisted the minister. "Here, this souvenir ought to be your pa's," he said, leaning down and handing the garter to Tad, who had scampered through legs and bodies and now stood next to Rev. Rutledge.

"Yes, sir!" exclaimed Tad, taking it from him, a happy smile on his face. He ran back to Pa and held it out to him.

"No, boy, you keep it," said Pa. "Who knows? Maybe you *will* be next—with the Reverend there performing the ceremony!"

Everyone laughed again, and then settled down to the serious business of consuming the cake and other food people had brought.

# CHAPTER 3

## A GLIMPSE AHEAD

Pa's marriage to Mrs. Parrish was just about the happiest day of my life.

By the time we all got to bed that night, I was exhausted, and I think everyone else was too. Being too happy for too long at one stretch can wear a body out just as much as hard work.

But as I lay in my bed on that warm August evening, even though I was so tired I didn't think I could have kept on my feet another minute, sleep didn't come for a long time. Once my feet and hands quit being so active, my brain figured it had to get some exercise. The instant my head rested against the pillow, my mind raced off and I had no choice but to follow.

This day wasn't just the first day of Pa's and Mrs. Parrish's life together as husband and wife, I thought. It was also *my* first day, I guess you'd say, as a grown-up.

I *wasn't* grown up yet, of course. And it's ridiculous to say that all of a sudden, on a *certain* day, you just up and become an adult. I was only seventeen, and plenty of seventeen-year-olds *did* have to fend for themselves and were a lot closer to full grown and independent than I was. But I knew on the day of the wedding that a lot of things were going to be changing for me real soon.

I'd been so busy the last two years since Ma died, acting like a mother to the other kids, helping Pa with the chores and the cooking and cleaning. Suddenly I realized time was passing quickly and I was getting older in a hurry. Ma had been right about the prospects of my marrying. And even if I did have any prospects—which I didn't—I don't think I'd have relished the idea anyhow. If I ever did get married one day, it'd have to be the Lord who saw to that part of my life, because there was a heap of living I wanted to do, things I wanted to see, places I dreamed of going.

It began to dawn on me that maybe now I *could* do some of those things, go to some of those places. Now that Pa was married, Mrs. Parrish would be taking care of everything that I'd been doing—all those housekeeping and wife and mothering things I'd sorta done because there was nobody else to do them.

Pretty soon I'd *have* to figure out something to do besides just being underfoot around the house. I was pretty close to being past schooling age, and I suppose I could study to be a teacher someplace else, like Miss Stansberry. Pa and Mrs. Parrish would have kept me at home till I was fifty—that's just how wonderful they both were. But somehow I wasn't sure that'd be exactly right—or if it was what I wanted.

Something inside me started stirring that night. Ma and Uncle Nick and Pa—they all used to talk about the "Belle blood," as if when your name was Belle, you had no choice but to get ornery and stubborn and independent every so often. I didn't think I ever got too much that way, but once in a while when I'd get riled or headstrong over something, Pa'd mutter about the Belle blood.

Maybe it was my Belle blood stirring. I started thinking about going off alone to some strange new place just to see what it was like, thinking about meeting new people, about being a grown-up who had to take care of herself because she didn't have to tend to her Pa and brothers and sisters anymore. I found myself wondering what Los Angeles was like, and thinking about the Oregon territory folks were talking about. I wanted to know more about the mountains and the miners and Indians and trappers who lived in them and what kind of people they were.

Even a month earlier I would have been afraid at the prospect of going someplace by myself, of being away from Pa and the others, of having a job of my own somewhere besides Miracle Springs. But it didn't frighten me now. It was kind of exciting, adventurous.

Maybe that was what the Belle blood did to folks. Maybe that's why Uncle Nick was always in trouble and then came out here—that adventurous spirit in his blood.

So when I say it was my first day as a grown-up, I don't mean that anything really *changed* all at once. But my thoughts and my outlook toward things began to change—no longer a little girl way of viewing. I began to think, *This is my life, and I'm getting older. Pretty soon I'm going to be out doing things and going places because I decide to, not because my ma and pa decide for me.*

Maybe that's what growing up is more than anything else—being on your own, relying on *yourself* to decide what's going to become of you instead of looking to somebody else like you've always done. And as I lay there that night, that was the question that kept coming to me: *What AM I going to do with myself now?*

It wasn't as if I needed to decide anything before I got up the next morning. With Uncle Nick and Aunt Katie still there in the cabin with us, and with Pa and Mrs. Parrish off to Sacramento and San Francisco for a week, for a while it'd be just like the last six months. School would be starting up again in a few weeks, and I had already agreed to help Miss Stansberry again this year.

But Uncle Nick was already building a new cabin for him and Katie up past the mine in a little clearing in the woods, about five or six hundred yards from ours. Zack was now fifteen and had been growing like a weed. He was still quiet, but his voice had deepened and he was apt to be as tall as Pa in another six months. He'd be thinking man-thoughts before long.

Mrs. Parrish and I'd already laughed several times over what I should call her. She told me, "I would be honored, Corrie, to have you call me *Mother*, but only when you feel comfortable doing so. And you must never call me what you called your real mother."

"I called her *Ma*," I said.

"Then you call me whatever you like." She smiled and put her arm around me. "I will always call you just Corrie. But I want you to know that I do think of you as a very special daughter—a spiritual daughter, a daughter whom the Lord gave me first as a friend . . . a daughter of grace."

"Thank you," I replied. "But I'm afraid you will keep being *Mrs. Parrish* for a while yet."

She laughed, that laugh that always seemed to have music at the back of it. "Oh, I do love you, Corrie Belle! I will be as happy as can be to keep being *Mrs. Parrish* to you forever!"

I gave her a tight squeeze. I loved her too—differently, but I think by now probably just as much as I loved Ma and Pa. I couldn't believe how good it was of God to bring together the two people I loved most in the world.

Just then some of Ma's last words came back to me. It had been two years, but I could almost hear her voice saying them like it had been yesterday.

*You turned out to be a right decent-looking girl,* she said. *You're gonna get along just fine, Corrie. I know you'll make me and your pa proud.*

I cried thinking about her. It was still the happiest day of my life, but sometimes happiness and sadness get all mixed up in a girl's heart, and then tears come out and you don't quite know why.

Then Ma's words about women getting on in the world came to my mind, her telling me—as she did more than once—to be strong and have courage and to try things.

"Don't be afraid to go out and do things, Corrie. And never worry what folks'll say or think. How else is a woman gonna get on in the world if she don't try?" That wasn't the kind of thing you heard most women talking about. But I guess Ma had plenty of the Belle blood in her too!

When I finally began to get drowsy, the last thought I can remember was praying that God would make me strong and would give me the courage to go out and do whatever it was he might want me to.

But I don't think my prayers were completely finished when I fell asleep.

# CHAPTER 4

# POSSIBILITIES

That next week I found myself wondering even more about what my future held. Katie and I took care of things, the kids played, Uncle Nick worked on his new cabin, but most of the time I kept thinking about Pa and Mrs. Parrish getting back home. Now that they were married, it didn't seem *right* with them not here.

But their being gone did give me and Katie a good chance to get to know each other better. I reckon with it all settled between Pa and Mrs. Parrish, I found myself able to see a lot in Aunt Katie that I hadn't seen before when my feelings were getting in the way placing her up alongside Mrs. Parrish and comparing the two. Now, Katie was . . . just Katie! And I discovered I really liked her a lot more than I ever thought I would. We talked about many things, and she told me about growing up in the East, and even some about her and Uncle Nick. She treated me like a friend, and I found myself thinking about her as mine too.

But she also had an annoying side. Now that she and Uncle Nick and Pa and Mrs. Parrish were married, she seemed to figure it was *my* turn. That whole week whenever we'd get to talking, she'd make little comments how I needed to be practical and look ahead to the time when I'd be starting my *own* family, and how I oughtn't wait as long as either of them. According to Katie, it was high time I either got a job or got married.

"There's that new young fellow up the pass, Corrie," she reminded me more than once, "not much older than you, and a nice young man. He's going to be looking to settle down with a wife before long."

She just didn't understand that I wasn't interested in marriage yet. Maybe I would be later, maybe I wouldn't. I didn't know. But right now there were other things I wanted to think about. Still, Katie kept whispering these kinds of things in my ear. She was determined to be practical, a realist, while Mrs. Parrish had always encouraged me to think about my dreams.

As much as I missed Pa and Mrs. Parrish, the time without them helped me to see this difference between Katie and Mrs. Parrish, and to think more about myself too. Mrs. Parrish was always telling me that *everything* has a good side, if you know how to look for it and find it, and I reckon this was one of those times.

Mrs. Parrish had asked me to go into town once or twice while they were gone to check in at the Freight Company, just to make sure everything was in order. I thought it a mite strange—she'd gone on lots of trips before without anyone having to check up on the business. But I wouldn't find out why she'd asked me to do that until a few days after they got back.

In the meantime, I did ride into Miracle Springs one afternoon. When I walked into the Parrish Mine and Freight Company office, Mr. Ashton immediately stood up from the desk where he was sitting and gave me a very pleasant, though awfully formal, greeting.

"Good morning, Miss Hollister," he said.

*Miss Hollister!* I thought. *It's only me, Mr. Ashton—Corrie Belle!*

But instead of saying what came into my mind, I just answered, "Howdy, Mr. Ashton. Mrs. Parrish said I should come in to see you while they were gone and see how you were doing."

"Everything is smooth as can be, Miss Hollister," he replied, still in a stiff but friendly voice. "Marcus loaded up the

Jefferson order this morning and is off to Nevada City with it. And the invoices for the shipment of tools and that sample for the new kind of sluice box came—" He picked up some papers off his desk as he spoke and held them up to show me. "So I have no doubt the merchandise will be arriving in the next day or two. Several of the men are anxious to see the new box."

I hardly had a notion what he was talking about, but when he was done he kept looking at me like he was expecting me to say something.

I gave a halfway sort of nod. "Uh . . . so Marcus Weber's not here today?" I said. I had intended to say hi to him too.

"That's right, Miss. On his way to Nevada City. When do you expect Mrs. Parr—"

Mr. Ashton caught himself and smiled with an embarrassed grin.

"When do you expect Mrs. *Hollister* back, I should say, shouldn't I, Miss Hollister!"

"Takes a heap of getting used to the idea, doesn't it, Mr. Ashton?" I said. "I don't know what to call her either."

"Yes, indeed! Many changes, indeed."

"I don't know exactly, Mr. Ashton," I said, finally answering his question. "I figured it'd be about a week, like maybe we'd see them back on Sunday or Monday."

"Yes, yes, that's what I thought, too. I only wondered if you, now that you and Mrs.—Mrs.—*Hollister*—now that you are family, you know—I thought perhaps you might have heard something differently. But yes, Sunday or Monday . . . I'm sure that's about right."

As I left the office I couldn't ever recollect seeing Mr. Ashton act so strangely. He was talking to me like a perfect stranger! And I was at a loss to figure how Mrs. Parrish marrying Pa would make him behave so downright peculiar to me.

But it started to come a little more clear after she and Pa got back from their honeymoon trip.

On Thursday, after they got back to Miracle on Tuesday, Mrs. Parrish said, "Corrie, it's time you and I had a talk."

"Woman to woman?" I said, smiling. I loved the chances

we had to be alone and talk for a long time, especially about
living as a Christian and thinking more about God in the things
that went on every day. I wanted to be a woman like Mrs.
Parrish, a godly woman who was different than other folks. I
had already learned so much from her, but there was still a lot
I didn't understand. She was teaching me to find out answers
for myself by praying and searching in the Bible. So I was
expecting another talk like that when she took me aside.

"Yes, woman to woman," she replied. "But perhaps even
more . . . mother to daughter," she added.

"I like the sound of that," I said.

"So do I." But from the look on her face and the serious
tone of her voice I could tell something different was coming
than the kind of things we'd talked about before.

There was a long pause. A knot twisted in my stomach, as
if something bad was about to come, although Mrs. Parrish
had never said or done anything to make me afraid. Finally she
spoke up.

"This is very difficult for me, Corrie," she said, then paused
again. "You know how much I love you—both your father and
I?"

"Yes, ma'am—of course," I said.

"Well then, Corrie, you must take what I'm about to say
as coming from a heart that loves you very much."

I nodded.

"Well, Corrie," she went on, "I have to be honest with you
and say that I've been thinking a great deal about you—about
your future. Both your father and I have. And we have discussed what some of the possibilities might be for you—alternatives, things you might do."

I didn't like the sound of her words. Was she going to start
getting like Katie and try to marry me off? Had she and Pa
spent their week away planning out my whole future?

But I kept my first feelings to myself and decided to hear
her out. And I realized after a while that nothing had changed
at all, and that she still wanted me to be able to dream, yet to
be practical at the same time.

"You see, Corrie, most women don't spend a great deal of time thinking about what they might like to do. They just live a day at a time and life comes along, and they just do what they do without ever stopping to wonder if they might do something *else*. Or if they might *have to* do something else. I have thought about this because of losing Mr. Parrish. Women are more vulnerable. They need to be prepared in case they are suddenly on their own. But most women never think of that until it is too late. I certainly never did. Do you see what I mean?"

"I think so."

"Men don't do that, at least not most of the men I've known. Men plan and dream and work to see their dreams fulfilled. Most of the men around in these parts have dreamed of getting rich in the gold fields. Now, most of them won't, and their dreams will never come true. But at least they think and plan and *try* to do what they dream of doing. Other men want to get a spread of land they can call their own, maybe have a farm or a ranch and raise horses or cows or grow wheat. I've known other men who dream of going to sea. Some of the things they want to do happen, others don't. But most men are thinking and planning about how they want their lives to go.

"But most women, Corrie, they just take life as it comes. They're so dependent on men that they figure what happens to them will depend on what the men in their lives do—brothers, fathers, husbands. They think the men have to make the plans and do the figuring and try the new things and explore the new places and make the money and stake the claims . . . and all the while the women just have to follow along."

She stopped, this time for longer. She took a couple of deep breaths, and I could tell she was still thinking.

"I'm not saying that's wrong. In one sense, God made men to be the leaders and the doers and he made women to be the followers. God made the woman to be man's helper, that's exactly how the Bible says it, Corrie. The men are supposed to be the ones that are in charge of how the world goes, and the women are supposed to help them, not run off trying to do their own kinds of things independent of men.

"But not every woman gets married. And, married or single, a woman's still got to know how to think and how to make decisions. How else can she be a good *helpmeet*, as the Bible calls it, if she doesn't use the mind God has given her?

"And some women—and this is what I wanted to get to, Corrie—some women don't have men to depend on. Women like me, when my husband died—and like your mother, after your father left. Some women find themselves in circumstances where they *have* to be able to make their own decisions, to fend for themselves. If they take life just as it happens to come to them, well, they never know what is going to become of them.

"When my first husband died, Corrie, I had to do a lot of thinking and praying. I began to realize that a woman's got to be able to think and plan and have alternatives too. Some women more than others. When I suddenly found myself all alone, I realized that *I* had to make the decisions about what was going to become of me. I had no man to depend on. My life was *mine*. That's when I started thinking that a woman needs dreams and plans and thoughts of her own. You can never tell when *you're* going to be making the decisions that will determine what becomes of you. Do you see what I mean?"

"Alternatives?" I asked.

"Yes. Possibilities—different things you can do, choices you can make. Most women don't *have* many alternatives because they never give life or their future enough thought, and never think about the different possibilities. But some women have to. If there's no man to do it for them, they have to take hold of the reins of their own lives. And they do so because they *want* to—they *want* to make the choices that will decide what they do. Most men nowadays aren't too comfortable with women doing that. But more women than ever are getting an education and even getting jobs everyone figured were just for men."

"Like Miss Stansberry?"

"Yes. Harriet said she had wanted to be a schoolteacher ever since she was young. And though she has her brother with her, I have the feeling she probably would have come out here anyway, even if she was by herself."

"She is an adventurous lady," I said.

"But women are doing things other than just what folks figure are women-things, like teaching."

"Running a business like you do sure isn't what too many women are doing."

Mrs. Parrish laughed. "I'll say! And it was hard for many of the men around here to accept at first. But like I said, after Mr. Parrish died, I *had* to think of my options—should I go back East, take over my husband's business, try to get married again? I decided to become a businesswoman, and I've never regretted it. I love what I have done, and I am so thankful that such a possibility was available to me, even though my first husband had been the one to open the door to it for me.

"Your mother too, Corrie—it was much the same for her. She was left without a man, with a family, with decisions to make."

"Ma didn't have many things she could have done," I said. "We just stayed on the land like always. Of course, she had kin there to help us."

"What if there hadn't been kin, or what if you hadn't had the farm? Then she would have had to consider other possibilities."

"But we did decide to come west in the end."

"Exactly! You see your mother *was* a strong, thinking, deciding, trying-to-figure-what-was-best kind of woman. She did more than just take life as it happened to come. She made decisions about what she thought was best for her and her family. And, Corrie, I suspect there are a lot more women like that than some of the men realize. That's why men always seem so surprised when women like your ma or Miss Stansberry—"

"Or you!"

She laughed. "*And* me—why they seem so surprised when a women stands up and does something different than 'the weaker sex' does."

She laughed again, a humorous laugh, as though she and I were in on a secret no one else knew about. "But we have to be patient with them," she said, still chuckling. "It may take them a while, but in the end men usually come around to seeing things reasonably, as long as women aren't too pushy to begin with. Why, nearly all of my customers are men, and by now they are used to doing business with a woman, used to the fact that I have men working for me who consider me their boss. And I think most of my customers have learned to respect me as a fair and honest and intelligent businesswoman, though most of them laughed at the very notion when I first announced my plans to continue the company after my husband's death. Men just sometimes need a little time to get used to things, that's all."

A silence fell between us. I was thinking about everything she had said. I guess Mrs. Parrish was considering what to say next, because she started in from a whole new angle, talking about me this time.

"Do you see what all this has to do with you, Corrie?" she asked at length, very serious sounding again.

She stopped and waited a long time for me to answer.

"I think maybe," I replied slowly. "You figure maybe I ought to be thinking about my possibilities, too, because I'm not—"

"No, Corrie," she interrupted, "not for any reason other than because I love you very much, and I think you are an extremely gifted young woman. I want only the absolute best for you, and so I think we—your father and I *and* you—all ought to be thinking and praying about what that might be. We need to consider choices, alternatives, that are before you."

I laughed sheepishly. "I've told you what Ma said, haven't I?"

"About you not being of a marrying sort? Yes, Corrie. But if your mother could see you now—and I believe she *can*!—she would know you are the most beautiful, wonderful daughter she could ever have hoped for! That's not at all what I had in mind, Corrie."

"I'm not sure I want to get married, Mrs. Parrish," I said.

"I know. But whether you do or don't, I think a young

woman still owes it to herself to think about things *she* might want to do in life—even if she does get married."

"Is it because of you and Pa getting married," I asked, "that you figure now it's maybe time for me—you know, with me getting older and getting past school age, that I move—?"

"Oh no, Corrie!" She put her arm around me and squeezed me tight. "I love you so much! I would keep you here with us forever if I could. I never want you to go someplace away from us. Never, Corrie! And I know your pa feels the same way, too. He's real proud of you, Corrie."

You can't imagine how happy it made me to hear that! "So it isn't that you think I ought to be finding myself a man, or looking for job someplace, since I'm not a kid anymore?"

"No, Corrie. It's just that we want the best for you. We want you to be happy. And more than anything, I want to see you become the woman I think God had in his mind when he made you—a woman doing some exciting things."

"What kinds of things?" I asked.

"That's just it—I don't know, Corrie. I simply think there's a life full of opportunities out there waiting for you. And as much as I would like to always have you by my side, you're right about one thing—you aren't a child anymore. And that's why your pa and I have been talking about some of the ways you might begin preparing for whatever the future holds."

"I have wondered about teaching school," I said. "Seems that's about the only thing a young woman like me could do— like Miss Stansberry."

"Teaching is one possibility."

"I'd have to go to college."

"I thought of that," she replied. "Your father and I would have enough money to send you away to a normal school to get your certificate. Though I would hate to see you have to go away."

"There's always the newspaper writing," I added.

"That's what you *really* want to do, isn't it?"

"Oh yes!"

"But how to get you started. . . ?" Again her finger found her lips, pursed together now.

"That's another one of those areas where men don't figure a woman has much place, isn't it?"

Mrs. Parrish laughed. "Men figure that about *everything*! I'll let you in on a secret. I think they are uncomfortable because they don't like the competition. They're afraid a woman might do something just as well as they! But I fear you are right—it could be very difficult for a newspaperman to take articles by a woman seriously."

"Like Singleton," I sighed.

"There is something else I've been thinking about, Corrie," said Mrs. Parrish.

I looked at her, just waiting.

"You've had some experience teaching, helping Harriet. So that's one alternative you might explore. You've helped your pa with your brothers and sisters for two years, so we already know you could make a good wife and mother. You want to write for a newspaper, but maybe the time hasn't come quite yet for that. What would you think of learning a little about my business?"

"The Freight Company?" I asked, surprised.

"Yes. How would you like to work with me?"

"I'd never thought of that before," I said. Then I couldn't help smiling. "Did you talk to Mr. Ashton about this?" I asked.

"I think I may have mentioned it to him," she answered. "Why?"

"Well, I went in to your office last week, like you asked me to— Say, is *this* why you wanted me to do that?"

Mrs. Parrish nodded.

"I wondered what you could possibly want me to check up on. I don't know anything about the business."

"I just wanted to see what you'd think about being my family representative while I was out of town. But go on, tell me about Mr. Ashton."

"He talked to me real peculiar, all formal and stiff, calling me *Miss* Hollister! No one ever calls me that!"

Mrs. Parrish laughed loudly. "He probably thinks I'm going to make all sorts of changes now that I'm married again. He probably figures I'll turn it into a family business and he'll be out of a job."

"That's why he was being so polite."

"I'll have to talk to him and put his mind at ease," she said. "But I did speak to him about the possibility of your working in the office a little—when you're not helping Miss Stansberry, of course. What do you think, Corrie?"

"I—I don't know . . . it's such a new idea."

"I'd pay you, of course."

"You wouldn't have to do that, ma'am," I told her.

"But I *would* do it, Corrie. You're old enough now to have a money-earning job. It would be good experience. There's nothing like being in business to gain valuable knowledge. You meet people, you learn how things are run, you sometimes travel to new places. Whatever other things the Lord may in time lead you into—and we must be faithful to pray for *his* guidance—helping in the Mine and Freight Company will give you experiences you'll be able to use anywhere. And perhaps one day you'll be running the business in my place, who can tell? I've suddenly got a family to manage. I might find myself with more than I can handle."

"I'm willing to try, I reckon," I said finally, "if you think I can do it."

"I know you can, Corrie."

# CHAPTER 5

## ADJUSTMENTS

For the whole next year I worked with Mrs. Parrish at the Freight Company. I kept going to school every day, both to learn and to help Miss Stansberry. But most days after school I worked a couple of hours, and I even got to make some deliveries with Mrs. Parrish and Marcus Weber to some of the outlying areas in the hills.

Mrs. Parrish had been right. I learned things and met a lot of new people. I still didn't figure I was cut out to be a businesswoman like her, but it never hurt to have a few more possibilities of things I might be able to do if I needed to.

That fall after the wedding, Pa and us kids all moved into Miracle Springs to Mrs. Parrish's house so that Uncle Nick and Katie could have the cabin to themselves while they finished building their own place. Mrs. Parrish's house had seemed so huge before, but all of a sudden it was a pretty tiny place with seven of us living there!

Pa went out to the claim every morning, the kids and I went to school, and Mrs. Parrish went to the freight office. Pa and Uncle Nick would work mornings at the mine, and then afternoons on the two cabins—finishing Uncle Nick's and adding on to Pa's to make more room. Alkali Jones was there most days, and on weekends several of the other men would come out and help too. Usually Rev. Rutledge was there pounding nails or carrying lumber just about every Saturday.

Katie stayed at the claim nearly all the time, helping too,

feeding the men. The grass and trees she'd brought us from the east were all growing, and she'd started clearing a garden spot up by their new place for next year. She had plenty to keep her busy, though she started feeling poorly later in the fall and had to keep to her bed a lot. Pa said it was probably just the weather starting to turn cold.

Mr. Alkali Jones, who always seemed to know everything about everything, was now ranting every day about what a miserable winter we were fixing to have. "Them squirrels got twice the winter fur I seen on 'em in fifteen years," he'd go on. "An' they're hidin' acorns in places I ain't seen afore. I tell ya, we're in fer a heap o' snow an' cold!"

They finished the adding on to our place about the middle of October, and then with the work concentrating all at Uncle Nick's, they got his and Katie's new home closed in and the roof and the doors and windows on by about the second week of November, just before any of the big rains Mr. Jones predicted began to fall.

Two days after they moved and got Katie comfortably settled—though she was feeling better by this time—a huge storm came through. It rained for two days and the streets around Miracle turned to mud. Up in the hills to the east a lot of snow had fallen. Alkali Jones said that with a start like this—as early as it was—it was "unmistakably gonna be the dad-blamest, coldest, most ornery winter ya ever done seen!" He finished off his words with that high-pitched cackle and gave his beard a scratch with his dirty fingers. But what he said sure turned out to be right!

Once the storm had passed and the sun came back out to start drying up the mud and grass and fields, leaving big ruts in the roads with muddy water standing in brown pools in the low spots, I figured we'd all be moving back out to the cabin, especially since now it was bigger and they'd added on a couple of rooms. That's what Pa'd been thinking too.

But Mrs. Parrish was having some second thoughts about it. It was so hard not to keep calling her Mrs. Parrish! I knew someday I'd probably have to start calling her either *Mother* or

*Almeda*. But right then I wasn't ready for the first or old enough for the second, and I just couldn't keep from calling her Mrs. Parrish like I'd always thought of her.

Anyway, one morning I heard Pa and my new mother, Almeda Parrish Hollister—that ought to take care of just about anything I might think of calling her!—talking. The conversation was getting louder than usual. I'd never heard them argue before, and I didn't figure they ever *would* argue! But I suppose even married people who love each other have differences of opinion now and then, though never having been married I can't say for certain.

They began talking about the two houses, but pretty soon they were talking about lots of other things.

"It only seems, Drummond," Mrs. Parrish was saying, "that since we are all here now, and since the children and I all have to be in town every day, perhaps it would make more sense just to stay here in my house—at least through the winter, as long as the children are in school."

Pa was quiet for a minute. I had to admit what she said made sense, even though I hadn't thought of it before. I'd never stopped to consider what would happen to Mrs. Parrish's house when we all went back out to the claim.

Finally Pa spoke.

"I reckon you got a good point there," he said, "but I got the place all fixed up so there's more space. You and I can have a room off to ourselves, and the boys got a room, Emily and Becky can share a room, and the little one Corrie can have by herself. It's a dang sight more space than we got here, Almeda."

"But the trips back and forth into town every day, and in the cold and wet of winter . . ." She didn't finish the sentence.

"Yep, I know. But it just don't seem right somehow, livin' at a woman's house when a man's got a place of his own."

"The woman's house is not as good as the man's?"

"I didn't say that. I just said it don't seem altogether right. It's kinda like it'd be if you kept on with your Freight Company and I quit working the mine. I know we talked this out a while back. But I been doing a lot o' thinkin' on it since."

"As I told you when we discussed this before, I intend to keep my Freight Company, Drummond."

"I know, for a while. But you know as well as I do that it ain't right for a woman to support a man, and that's kinda like it'd be if we kept on living in—"

"What do you mean *for a while?*" she interrupted, her voice sounding a little agitated.

"I mean I know you can't just shut down an operation that size right away. It'll take you some time."

"Shut down? Drummond, I have no intention of shutting down my operation at all. You didn't think my marrying you meant I would give up my business? There was never any talk of that when we discussed it before the wedding."

"I guess I figured that was sort of understood." Pa's voice was quiet. I couldn't tell if he was embarrassed or was slowly getting riled. He got the same kind of quiet in both moods.

"It was not understood by me," said Mrs. Parrish. "I thought it was understood that we both had been married before, we both were involved in livelihoods of our own—your claim and my company—and I had no idea you were thinking that any of that would change. Why, I would never think of asking you to give up *your* claim or *your* cabin because of marrying me."

"That's different. I'm a man."

"What's different about it?"

"A man's work—well, it's more important than a woman's. Maybe you had to run your company so as to provide for yourself. But you got me now. You got a husband to take care of you, so you don't have to anymore."

"And if I want to?"

"Women ain't supposed to be out doin' what men do, not unless they have to, and you don't have to no more."

"Maybe I *want* to. Did you ever consider that I enjoy what I do, that maybe I'm a good businesswoman, and that I don't *want* to just be at home sweeping the floor and fixing a supper for you to eat when you're through with *your* work? Did you ever consider that?"

"I reckon I never did. Women are supposed to be at home, men are supposed to be out working. What you're saying just ain't natural. I know I never said this to you before, but it just ain't done that way."

A long pause followed. When Mrs. Parrish spoke again, her voice was calm but determined.

"Look, Drummond," she said. "I know most men, and even most women, might agree with what you say. But I'm not most women. I'm *me*! And after my first husband died, I found out some things about myself. I found out that I had a strength down inside that I could depend on. I found out that I was a good businesswoman, that I could fend for myself in this rough California world, a man's world. I found out a lot about the person I am down inside by having to stand up for myself and make it on my own when my husband was suddenly gone. I liked what I found, Drummond. The things God built into me during that time—I'm just not willing to let go of. I love you, Drummond Hollister. You are the best thing that has happened to me since my first husband died. I will love and obey and cherish you all my life. But that doesn't mean I will stop being myself—a woman, a person with my *own* dreams and goals and things I want to do in life. Please don't ask me to give up my business for you, Drummond. I would do it if you asked, because I will obey you. But I don't know what would become of me if I did. A piece of me would die. Please, don't ask me to do that."

It got quiet for a long time. The next thing I heard was the sound of Pa's boots on the wood floor, and then the back door opening and then shutting again. I guess he had to think about it all. And usually when Pa was thinking he went someplace alone, outside or in the barn or on the back of one of his favorite horses.

I never heard the two of them discussing the business or the houses again for a long time. I think they did, though, because every so often I could tell from the quiet between them that they'd been talking and had seen things differently.

But however they decided to work it out, nothing much

changed. Most of the time they were as loving and pleasant as could be to each other. Mrs. Parrish went to her office every day and the Mine and Freight Company kept doing business just as before. I went on working there after school. And Pa seemed pleased with me learning different aspects of the business. Pa kept mining with Uncle Nick and Mr. Jones, and they continued to bring gold out of the stream and out of the mountain the deeper into it they dug.

I guess Pa saw that Mrs. Parrish's idea about the houses was pretty smart. Most of the time that winter we stayed at the house in town—Mrs. Parrish's house—during the week, and then on Friday night Pa'd come in to fetch us all with the big wagon and take us out to the claim. Since there was no school, Mrs. Parrish didn't go into her office on Saturday, and so we'd stay there all weekend, and ride back in on Monday morning for the week. During the week, Pa'd come into town every evening for the night.

It was a bit of a cumbersome arrangement. But we were kind of an unusual family, and it was gonna take some time for things to get figured out.

# CHAPTER 6

# WINTER 1854–55

Without even thinking about it, Christmas dinner was becoming a kind of tradition. Maybe our Christmases stand out in my mind because each of the three was so different, and every time I remembered them it reminded me of how fast things had changed since we'd been in California, and how much the Lord had done for us.

This Christmas was no exception. It was the best ever!

Now we were two happy families, and Mrs. Parrish was there with us. I hadn't been happier since her and Pa's wedding day. All morning she and us three girls worked and sang away in the kitchen, baking pies and sweet potatoes and a big ham, while Pa was outside with Zack and Tad. Pa'd got Zack a new rifle for his very own, and Zack could hardly stand it, he was so excited. So as we were working, we heard the shots firing in the woods where Pa was giving him a lot of instructions about aiming, which Zack really didn't need.

We loaded the food and some extra chairs into the wagon about noon, and took it up to Nick and Katie's new place where we were going to eat. It was their first chance to show off the new cabin, and they'd invited a couple of other families, and of course the Stansberrys and the minister. Katie had been excited for days, planning and telling us she had a surprise for everyone.

We got there first, and soon the others began to gather. When Rev. Rutledge's buggy drove up, Miss Stansberry was with him, alone, with the news about her brother. Hermon Stansberry had taken sick and wasn't going to come. We all prayed for his health before sitting down to dinner, and Miss Stansberry took a nice basket of food back with her for him when the day was over.

But Katie's announcement was the highlight of the whole day!

"I have some big news to tell you all," she said, with a wider smile than I'd ever seen on her already wide mouth. "Some time along about the middle of next summer"—she looked at the five of us kids—"your Uncle Nick is going to stop being *just* an uncle and start being a pa himself!"

Mrs. Parrish was on her feet, exclaiming excitedly almost before the words had left Katie's lips. She gave Katie a great hug, which was followed by the other women doing the same, while Becky tugged at my arm asking me what all the yelling was about. I whispered to her that Katie was going to have a little baby. "And it'll be *your* cousin," I said.

The men were slapping Uncle Nick on the shoulder and shaking hands. Then Uncle Nick went to the fireplace where he picked up a small box from on top of one of the stones, and started passing out cigars that he'd bought. The minister didn't take one, but Uncle Nick shoved one into Zack's hand with a laugh.

"It's high time you tried it, Zack, my boy!" he said.

"Can I, Pa?" said Zack, expecting the usual answer.

Pa shrugged. "Maybe your Uncle Nick's right, son. I guess if he's finally old enough to be a pa, I reckon you're old enough to try one of those things."

Uncle Nick wasted no time. With a grin on his face, he struck a match and held it up to the end of the cigar that was now sticking six inches out of Zack's mouth. Zack sucked in a couple times, got a few puffs going as the tobacco caught fire, and Uncle Nick cheered him on. Pa seemed to know what was going to come of it and just stood back watching, with a half grin on his face.

It didn't take long. After only about an inch had burned

off the end, Zack's face began to turn pale. All of a sudden, amid what must have been an embarrassing roar of laughter for poor Zack, he handed the cigar back to Uncle Nick and bolted for the door and outside to get fresh air. In a minute or two Pa followed with a look on his face that seemed to say that he knew what Zack was going through, while Katie and Mrs. Parrish were talking about "these ridiculous rites of passage that men insist on putting each other through," both with disgusted looks on their faces.

But even Zack's getting sick from the cigar couldn't spoil the impact of Katie's announcement about the baby coming, and the other memories of the happy Christmas Day.

Alkali Jones was right. It was a rough winter—cold, wet, with lots of snow and frost. The stream got bigger than I'd ever seen it, and the men were saying that if the rains kept up, maybe they'd wash down lots of new gold from up in the mountains. It was so wet a time or two that we stayed at the house in town for two weeks each time. The stream was so full of water rushing by that Pa and Uncle Nick had to pull all their equipment out and couldn't do much work. They worked some inside the mine, but with the cold and wet it was a miserable job. They gave that up, too, after a while, waiting for a break in the weather. But everybody was talking about the rain being good. It had been uncommonly dry, they said, for the last couple of winters, so the crops and pastures needed the rain, and the miners were glad for it, hoping it'd shake some new gold loose. Probably the only people who weren't thankful for the rain were the children, who had to stay cooped up inside the schoolhouse all day long on the worst of the wet days.

Throughout the winter, I learned a lot about the freight and mining business and took several wagon rides with either Mr. Weber or Mrs. Parrish to deliver things that people had ordered. Mrs. Parrish always introduced me real proper-like to the people we were doing business with, saying, "Mr. So-and-So, I would like you to meet my daughter Corrie, who is helping me now in the business." She had such a way of making me feel grown-up, like she respected and appreciated me! Soon

I knew most of the roads for twenty or thirty miles around Miracle, and had been to nearly every little town or hamlet or gold camp around those parts. I'd never realized how many customers Mrs. Parrish had all over. Some of the places we went and people I met were pretty rough-looking. But she always marched right into wherever we had to go with her head high and without showing a bit of fear. That's probably why the men came to respect her, because she could be as tough as they were if she had to. And that was something I would have to learn, too—if I planned on making my way alone in California.

That winter some of the town leaders got together and decided Miracle Springs ought to have a mayor. The town had grown a lot in the last two years, and was still growing some, with new families coming in. There was no election, it was just announced one day that a retired banker, recently come from the East, had agreed to act as mayor. He'd had experience in that sort of thing before. So Jason Vaissade became the first mayor of Miracle Springs.

# CHAPTER 7

# LEARNING TO LET GO
# AND TRUST GOD

The weather had been nice for a couple of weeks. It was warming up and folks were saying the winter had finally broken and spring was on the way. We were more than a week into March, so any other year they would probably have been right.

One morning, when we were staying at Mrs. Parrish's house in town, I woke up before dawn. I usually got up pretty early, and liked to lie in bed and read or go for walks before the rest of the family got up.

This particular morning I got up while it was still dark. I put my clothes on and sneaked out of the house as quietly as I could. The morning was beautiful. I felt as if I were the only one alive. I took in the cold morning air in long breaths. A few stars still twinkled in the sky, with just the faintest hint of the gray dawn starting to mix in with the blackness.

I walked out into the street. It was cold and I had several layers of clothes on, but I could tell the sun was going to come up and it would be a nice bright day. Everything was completely quiet. Marcus Weber wasn't out in the stable with the horses yet, and he was usually the first person to be up and at it most mornings in Miracle Springs. The roosters weren't even about their business yet either, although they likely would be before long.

I love early mornings! After I've been up a little while, my mind gets awake and active and has its best thinking times.

Maybe it's the quiet, maybe being alone. As much as I like people, I never get tired of being alone either, and my brain always seems to take alone times to turn about some of its best thoughts. Morning is always the best for praying too.

I suppose the two go hand in hand—praying and thinking. When you're praying you *are* thinking, kind of thinking in God's direction, pointing your brain toward God and then letting your thoughts go *out* of you and *into* him. At least that's how I like to imagine what it's like when I'm praying. And the other side of praying, listening to God, works just the reverse— I try to pay attention to the thoughts that are coming *into* my brain. And if I've been talking to God about something, then I figure those thoughts coming toward me are the thoughts coming out of God toward *me*—his thoughts that he's sending in *my* direction.

Well, on that particular morning I was thinking and praying, and opening my thoughts toward God and trying to listen to his thoughts toward me. And I found myself remembering the talk Mrs. Parrish and I had about alternatives, and choices, things I might some day find myself doing, and how a young lady like me ought to be preparing herself for the future and thinking about what she wants to do. And pretty soon I was walking along not even paying attention to where I was going, talking back and forth with God—talking in my thoughts I mean, not out loud—and asking him what it was that *he* wanted me to do and prepare for.

My favorite passage in the Bible is in the third chapter of Proverbs, verses five and six: "Trust in the Lord with all thine heart; and lean not unto thine own understanding. In all thy ways acknowledge him, and he shall direct thy paths." That morning I felt as if God was directing my footsteps, because without even thinking where I was going, I found myself walking about the town praying and talking to God as I went.

I walked for five or ten minutes, and found myself standing in front of the Gold Nugget saloon, where we'd first met Pa and where we'd had our first church service in Miracle Springs.

Then I walked farther on down the street past Mr. Bosely's

General store. My heart was full as I recalled everything that had happened, all that God had done since those first days here.

As I passed the bank, I thought about Mr. Royce and all the evil that had come because of him. But seeing his bank also reminded me of what Mrs. Parrish had done to save Pa's mine. Maybe that incident was the beginning of her and Pa loving each other like they did now.

God had brought me so far, would he bring me safely the rest of the way? Yet even seeing how everything had worked out in the past, it was still easy to slip into worrying about what was going to become of me.

"I'm growing up, and sometimes it's hard to know what I'm supposed to do!" I had told Mrs. Parrish in one of our talks.

"God will let you know in his time," she said. "You can trust him. If you let him, he will work in every bit of your life—you can depend on it."

Even as I was thinking these words of Mrs. Parrish's, I found myself coming back around to the Freight Company and to Mrs. Parrish's house—our house.

*Oh, God,* I found myself thinking, *you have been so good to me! We were so alone back then . . . and now you've given us so much! Thank you for Pa, for what a fine man he is. Thank you for Uncle Nick, for Katie, for the claim and the cabin, and for the life you've given us here, and all the new friends we have.*

I stopped and looked around me. I was standing right in front of Mrs. Parrish's office. The light was creeping up in the east, and it wasn't dark anymore, though it was still only a gray light. Inside through the window, the office was empty and black. On the glass was painted in small gold letters: *Parrish Mine and Freight Company.*

"How can I thank you enough, Lord, for . . . for my new mother?" I whispered. There was nothing else to say—that one prayer was enough. My heart was full of gratitude for her—for all she'd been to us, for the friendship she and I had, for how she had helped me love Pa better, for all she had explained to me about living with God, for how she had helped me understand myself and my own feelings more deeply, for the talks we'd had, for our trip to San Francisco, for how I'd learned to pray and bring God into the little things of my life because of her. I wouldn't have been half the person I was if it hadn't been for Mrs. Parrish—and I sure wouldn't have been standing there praying, and thinking about verses from the Bible, if she hadn't taught me how important it was to live my life with God as part of it.

I didn't even realize it at first, but suddenly I was crying— quietly, just a few tears. And a great sadness was coming up out of my heart, although I didn't know why right at first.

*I don't want to leave this place, God,* I thought. *I love these people and Pa and Almeda and Zack and Tad and Becky and Emily . . . and Mr. Weber, and everybody, Lord! I don't want to leave . . . I don't want to, Lord!*

All at once I knew why I was so sad. I'd been filled with such happiness only a few moments before, in the memories of this town and people. But retracing steps along the sidewalks where I'd walked dozens of times in the last couple of years was a little like saying goodbye to Miracle Springs.

"Is that why you woke me up so early, Lord," I asked, "and drew me out of bed—to say my farewell to this place?"

My future and what was to become of me *had* been on my heart a lot—ever since the day of Pa's and Almeda's wedding. Even when my mind wasn't actively thinking about it, down deeper the question was still running around inside me. Every once in a while the doubts would surface and I'd get to thinking again about that conversation we'd had about a girl preparing herself for her future, or I'd remember what Ma had said about me needing to think about growing up. I suppose I was growing up slower than a lot of girls might—especially being a reading, thinking person always trying to figure things out in my head. But maybe now it was time that I *did* get on with the business of growing up, and I couldn't help thinking about it a lot.

The town still surrounded me, still quiet just like a moment before, but now I felt a pang of pain at the sight, as if I would not be able to hold on to it forever.

"What are you fixing to do with me, Lord?" I asked.
"Where are you leading me? What do you want me to do?
Where do you want me to go?"

*Go!* Out of my own prayer the word slammed against me.
"Oh, God, you're not gonna make me go away, are you? But
I don't want to go! I've only had my pa back two years, and
now I've only had a mother again less than a year, and I don't
know if I can stand to be torn away from them! Please, God,
don't make me go away! I don't want to be *Miss Hollister,* God.
I want to be just who I've been all these years! I want to keep
being a daughter for a while longer. I'm not ready to be a
woman, a grown-up all on my own yet!"

I was crying hard now. The praying words dried up, but
not the tears.

Two or three minutes later the tears began to stop. And as
they did another set of words from the Bible crept into the back
of my mind. I hadn't thought about them for a long time—I
couldn't even remember when I'd heard or read them, but all
at once there they were, as if God had sent them to quiet down
my spirit and remind me of something I needed to remember
right then. The words were: *Delight thyself also in the Lord; and
he shall give thee the desires of thine heart.*

"Do you really mean that, God?" I asked. "Will you give
me what *I* want? You won't make me leave Miracle Springs?"

I started walking again. By now the first colors of pink were
showing in the sky to the east. Folks would be stirring before
long. The roosters were hollering their heads off all over town.

As I walked I knew God was talking to me. I didn't hear
an actual *voice* speaking out of the sky. But I had been thinking—and even crying—in God's direction. And after I'd "had
*my* say," maybe it was God's turn to do the talking. Walking
along I felt my mind and heart filling up with words, ideas,
feelings, verses from the Bible, reminders of things Mrs. Parrish had told me or things I'd heard Rev. Rutledge say in
church, about feeding on God's truth. When I look back on
the experience of that morning, I think God was using everything going through my mind to speak to me. *His* thoughts

were now coming in *my* direction.

I felt God speaking to me that morning. The thoughts and feelings came too fast and in such a jumble, and of course I didn't understand everything all at once. But as I wrote it down and thought about that morning after it happened, more and more of it made sense to me. It was as if God was *saying* something like this to me:

"Yes, Corrie, I *will* give you the desires of your heart. I do that with all my children who delight in me. But I cannot do it unless a man or a woman, a boy or girl . . . unless *you*, Corrie, do indeed *delight* yourself in me. That's what the psalm means. *If* you delight in me, *then* I will give you the desires of your heart."

*I want to delight in you, God,* I said to myself, *but I don't think I know what that means.*

Again I felt God's thoughts coming into my mind.

"Just this, Corrie—to delight in me means that you want to do what I want, not what *you* want. Your desire is to do *my* will rather than your own, because you trust me to take care of you, you trust me about everything. I created you, I created all things, and I love you so much more than you can possibly realize. You can trust me to do the very *best* for you in every way imaginable—the very best!"

*I don't understand. I thought that verse said you would give me the desires of MY heart?*

"When you trust me completely, as your Creator and Father and friend, when you trust me so much that you know I will do the best for you, when you trust me enough to want *my* will in your life, that becomes the desire of your heart. The desire of *your* heart is to do *my* will. And when you want *my* will for your life, and you want that more than anything else, then I will give you that—I will certainly work out my will in your life. And it will be the best possible life you could ever have! You will have the desire of your heart, and everything you could possibly hope for shall be yours—because your life is in my hands, not your own. Do you remember how that whole passage from Psalm 37 goes, Corrie?"

Suddenly I *did* remember! Rev. Rutledge had preached from Psalm 37 about two months ago and I had loved the words so much I'd memorized them:

*Trust in the Lord, and do good; so shalt thou dwell in the land, and verily thou shalt be fed. Delight thyself also in the Lord; and he shall give thee the desires of thine heart. Commit thy way unto the Lord; trust also in him; and he shall bring it to pass.*

"I do not always fulfill the worldly desires of my children. I do not give them everything they selfishly might *want*. But for those of my sons and daughters who want *me*, who want to know me, I will fulfill that heart's desire. And everything else in life will be given in abundance along with it. I cannot give myself without giving my blessings and my love and my abundant provision."

The flow of thoughts stopped. I was outside town now, unconsciously walking in the direction of the church and school. I looked up. There was the building off in the distance. I thought of the laughing, yelling voices of the children that'd be echoing from inside it in a few hours. I thought of Miss Stansberry and wondered if I would someday be a schoolteacher too. Then I thought of the church, about that summer when it'd been built, and about Pa and Rev. Rutledge, about the dedication of the building and the picnic and seeing Mr. Grant and the soldiers. I thought about all the many church meetings and services we'd had in that building since then, and all the growing I'd done—sometimes having to do with the church services, sometimes not.

Had the Lord directed my path here, like the proverb said, so that I could say goodbye to this church and school building like the rest of the town? Something down inside was telling me a change was coming in my life, and I was afraid. I wasn't sure I liked the idea at all.

"Trust me, Corrie . . . you *can* trust me!"

This time the words came into my mind so clearly that I *knew* exactly what God was saying.

I drew in a deep sigh from the cold morning air. Even though I was all alone, I felt suddenly embarrassed, because I knew my worrying about my future was silly. Of course I could trust God to take care of me! Even if I didn't want to leave Miracle Springs, God wouldn't lead me to leave unless it was best. I *did* want my life, my future, everything I was as a person—I wanted it to be what *God* wanted, not what I wanted. I *did* want God's will. I wanted to be able to trust him, even for my future and all its unknowns.

Then I started to realize that maybe God hadn't gotten me up early like this and had me walk around town, filling me with these thoughts about my future and what I might be doing a year, two years, three years from now, because I was going to *leave* Miracle Springs. I might leave someday, or I might not, but maybe the *goodbyes* weren't to the buildings and the things I had looked at that morning, or to the people. Maybe God was trying to get me to think about my life in a new way, wanting me to say goodbye to the old way of looking at things, goodbye to worrying about what was to become of me. Maybe the future God was wanting me to move into wasn't necessarily in a new *place,* but in a new way of trusting him, of delighting in what *he* wanted for me.

Sunrise had filled the sky with brilliant reds and oranges. I could hear the sounds of the morning in the distance—dogs barking, a few wagons moving. Marcus Weber's hammer slammed down on the anvil, ringing in the distance. He was likely fixing a wheel or shoeing one of the horses.

I walked a little way off the dirt road, behind the trunk of a huge old twisted scrub-oak tree, and knelt down. I immediately felt the cold on my knees, because the grass was still wet from last week's rain and the morning dew. But I didn't mind. I bowed my head and prayed again, this time out loud, though just barely above a whisper.

"Oh, Lord, I *do* want to delight in you! I want your will for my life, whatever you want me to do. If you want me to teach children in a school, or if you want me to keep working in the Freight Company, I'll do either of those if you want me to, God. Or whatever else. I want to trust you, and so, Lord, I want to give my life to you, like Rev. Rutledge was talking

62

about that Sunday, to make the kind of lady you have in mind for me to be. I do give you my future and whatever you want to do with it, even if it means someday having to leave Miracle Springs, though I don't want to. Please help me to trust you more completely. I'll do what you want and go where you say, 'cause I know you know what's best for me."

That was all. No more words were there. I slowly got up and began walking back toward town, breathing in deeply of the morning air.

I felt good! In church you sometimes hear people talking about "burdens being lifted" off their shoulders, and maybe that's a little what it felt like. The worry was gone. It felt as if I had given it to God, and he had taken it, just as if I'd handed him a heavy sack and now I wasn't carrying it anymore.

I'd been crying earlier, thinking about having to say good-bye to familiar sights and faces. But now I felt like smiling. The future was going to be exciting, not fearful! Because I had given all of it to God, even though I didn't know what *it* was, and he was going to make it the very best for me—because it would be what *he* wanted for me. Maybe I felt lighter and happier because for the first time I really was trusting God to make things turn out, instead of worrying about them.

As I walked into town, more thoughts from God started coming into my mind. They were different, yet still part of that psalm which said we would be fed by truth. I hadn't thought of that part of the verse before, but now I found myself considering what it might mean. Maybe I had to get to the point of saying to God "I trust you" before he could make sense out of the rest of it to me. In my mind, God seemed to say:

"Wherever you go, and whatever you do—here in Miracle Springs or far away to wherever I might send you someday— I want you to love and follow the truth, and live by it, and let it feed you. *The truth*, Corrie Belle Hollister, my daughter that I love. I am making you into a woman, and I have plans for you—whether people call you Corrie Belle or Miss Hollister. Whatever they call you, wherever you go, whatever you do— follow the truth, Corrie . . . follow *my* truth. Find out what my truth is. Then follow it, live by it, and never let it go. For in *truth* shall you be fed, and so shall you dwell in the land, and by following the truth will I be able to give you the desires of your heart."

Like so much of what happened to me and what passed through my mind that morning, I didn't fully understand those words at the time. But now, years later, I can see how the Lord was giving me those words as a way of pointing me ahead toward a certain desire that was in my heart, getting me ready for it. That morning was the beginning of where the Lord was going to take me, the beginning of the part of my life when I began learning to trust him more completely.

At the time I realized none of this. But in going down on my knees and giving myself and my future to God in a way I never had before, I see now that when I got up and walked back into town, I had left the things of my childhood behind.

# CHAPTER 8

## THE BLIZZARD

The Lord shoved me right into something that was going to play a big part in my future almost immediately. But I didn't realize the significance in my life until I looked back on it years later.

That same day when I'd gotten up early to walk and pray and talk with God, about the middle of the afternoon huge clouds started to roll in from the North, coming toward the Sierras. By evening the cold, icy, blustery winds had begun to blow.

The next morning, just after dawn—which seemed later than usual on account of the dark clouds—it started to snow, very lightly to begin with. Even at noon there was no more than a fine layer of dust on things and it still wasn't collecting on the roads or where people walked.

But it kept falling, and by the middle of the afternoon the flakes were bigger and whiter, and an inch had collected. People were bundling up and starting to pack in extra firewood and oats and corn for their livestock.

Pa built a huge fire in the house that night, and it was warm and cozy. Every now and then he'd get up and go and peer out the window into the blackness. Sometimes he wouldn't say anything. Sometimes he'd come back into the room muttering. Once he just said, "I don't know, Almeda," and then he shook his head. "It looks like it could be a bad one!"

When I woke up the next morning, Pa was already down-

64

stairs in the parlor, standing still, staring out the same window into the morning gray. I walked to his side, he put his arm around me, and we both just looked and looked, neither of us saying a word. Everywhere was white—nothing but white. You could hardly tell there was supposed to be a town out there. It was just hills and mounds and bumps of white. It had to be over a foot deep, and still the sky was filled with the down-fluttering flakes.

"Ain't never seen it like this," Pa finally said. "Never this much so low down. Must be taller than a man's head up in the foothills! I hope Alkali got back to the cabin."

"Where is he, Pa?" I asked.

"He set out yesterday morning for Dolan's place, up to the high flat on Relief Hill above Missouri Canyon. He was aiming to get himself a mule. Dolan was in town last week and had several he wanted to get rid of. But Dolan's ranch'll be plumb snowed in for weeks now." He stopped and sighed deeply. "Alkali, Alkali . . . I hope you made it back in time, you old buzzard!"

The day wore on slowly. School was cancelled. Most of the places in town didn't open. If they had, nobody would have come anyway. Almeda went to her office, but only for part of the day. I could tell she was worried about Pa, he was acting real fidgety. Somehow he just had a sense that things were going wrong out there in that snow. He just kept staring out the window.

It stopped snowing about noon. A few footprints and horse tracks cut through the thick white blanket, but not too many. After lunch Pa put on his heavy winter coat and started to climb into his boots.

"You're not going out?" Almeda said.

"Can't stand sitting around here any longer, Almeda. I'm going over to Rafferty's, maybe the Gold Nugget. I gotta find out if anybody's heard anything." He made for the door.

"Can I come, Pa?" asked Tad.

"I need you to stay and protect the womenfolk, son," said Pa. The gleam in his eye said he hadn't forgotten about Marcus

Weber, who was pounding and working away out in the stable, but that he wasn't going to mention him.

"Zack, you come with me. Might be that I'll need you," he added.

Zack was in his boots and after him in a flash, leaving the rest of us sitting there wondering what Pa figured doing out in the middle of the blizzard.

Eventually we found out.

A couple of hours later Zack burst through the door.

"Pa said to get a couple of horses saddled up right away," he panted. "He'll be back in a minute."

"I'll get Marcus to help you," said Almeda, starting toward the back door. "What is it, Zack?"

"There's been an avalanche down on the west side of Washington Ridge. I guess the snow gathered so fast up on a ledge overlooking the little ravine that the powder couldn't hold together. Two or three cabins down in the wash was plumb buried. All the men are heading out there to try to dig the folks out."

"Who is it—any women or children?" asked Mrs. Parrish.

"No, ma'am. Just some old miners that camp out up there."

"What about Mr. Jones?" I asked. "Is *he* in danger too?"

"Don't know," said Zack. "Nobody's seen him."

"Let's go see to the horses," said Almeda.

"Come to think of it, we'll need three, cause Pa said to tell Mr. Weber to come too." The two of them closed the door behind them.

About ten or fifteen minutes later, Pa came in the front door almost exactly as Zack and Almeda returned from the stable.

"Horses ready, Zack?" he said.

"Yes, sir."

"I don't know when we'll be back, Almeda. Marcus coming?"

"He's in the stable."

"Good. Pray we'll find those fellas! There's a lot of snow up there—must be a good thousand feet higher'n we are here in Miracle. Come on, Zack."

They made for the back door where their horses waited.

"Oh, Almeda," Pa said, turning back at the door. "Hitch up a wagon—one with the highest axle to get through the snow—with two of whatever horses are left. The workhorses would be best in this weather. I ain't sure what we'll find, but if we need a wagon for hauling some gear up there, I want it ready."

"It will be," she replied. "Drum . . . be careful!" she added, gripping his hand.

Pa nodded seriously, then he and Zack were gone. Almost the minute they left it started snowing again.

# CHAPTER 9

# A RASH DECISION

About an hour and a half after Pa and Zack and Mr. Weber left—the whole time it had been still as death, hardly a sound either in the house or outside—we heard the door of the livery crash open.

Mrs. Parrish jumped up and ran out back to the stable, and I followed.

"Hey!" a man's voice was calling. "Hey . . . ain't nobody in there? Marcus, where are you, man?"

Just then Mrs. Parrish opened the stable door and looked inside. "Mr. Ward!" she exclaimed. "What are you doing here?"

"No time to explain, ma'am! Where's Weber, Hollister? I can't find any of the men around. I gotta have me some help an' I ain't got time to go tryin' to track 'em down!"

"I'm afraid all the men are gone. There was an avalanche down across the Yuba on Washington Ridge."

The man swore, slapping his hand to his forehead. But I could tell it was fear he was feeling, not anger. His face turned pale and he started to collapse.

Mrs. Parrish rushed forward and caught him in her arms before he hit the floor. "What *is* it, Mr. Ward?" she said in alarm. But the moment she felt his body and saw his face close up, she knew. "The man's nearly frozen to death!" she exclaimed back in my direction. "Corrie, come help me—we have to get him into the house!"

Together we half dragged the poor man, whose legs could hardly support him another step, back into the warm parlor of Mrs. Parrish's house. By the time we got him slouched in a chair he was nearly unconscious.

"The boots, Corrie!" she said. "We've got to get his boots off!" She grabbed at one as I pulled on the other. The leather was soaking wet, and when we got his boots and his stockings off, we could feel that his feet were just like ice.

"He might already have frostbite—it's a wonder he didn't die from the exposure," she said, pulling his limp legs in the direction of the fire. "We've got to get some dry cloths around his feet."

In a few minutes Mr. Ward began to come to, and almost immediately started to ramble in a panicky, exhausted voice. "My wife and three girls," he said, ". . . trapped up on Buck Mountain . . . snow caught us last night . . . blizzard up there—had to get 'em to town . . . wind blew the storm right down on top of us . . . snowing so hard I couldn't see a thing . . . too far to turn back . . . got off the trail, and the wagon went in a ditch . . . wheel broke—"

He stopped, then looked around at the two of us. His eyes were wide, as if he suddenly had become aware he was sitting in a warm room in front of a fire. His expression showed no recognition of who we were.

He struggled to rise. "Gotta get out of here," he mumbled. "Got to get back . . . gotta find help . . ."

"Mr. Ward, you can't go anywhere," Mrs. Parrish said firmly but gently. "Your feet and hands are frozen, and all your clothes are soaked."

"I've got to get back . . . they'll die if I don't . . . got to get help!"

"Where are they?" she asked.

"Snow was everywhere . . . wagon was broke down—wheel shattered . . . couldn't get us all out on the one horse . . . sheltered them best I could under the wagon . . . unhitched the horse, took off for town. But I pushed the beast too hard in the snow . . . stumbled . . . broke a leg . . . walked rest of the way here . . . got to find some men . . . got to get back out there . . . they'll freeze to death in the blizzard!"

"Where are they—*where*, Mr. Ward?" asked Mrs. Parrish, urgency in her voice.

"Halfway down the Buck . . . off the road from our place . . . got to get back there!"

Again he struggled to rise, but fell back, unable to stand.

"There's no way this man's going out again any time soon," said Mrs. Parrish, half to me, halfway thinking aloud to herself. She paced toward the fire and back again.

Without really stopping to think, I suddenly found myself running to grab my thickest coat, putting on my gloves and hat, and then running back out to the stable and throwing the big double doors wide open. I climbed up on the seat of the wagon Marcus had hitched for Pa, and took the reins in my hands.

"Corrie, what do you think you're doing?" exclaimed Mrs. Parrish, rushing out of the house behind me.

"I gotta go after them," I said. "Mrs. Ward and the young'uns!"

"The horses can never make it! The snow's too deep, and it's still falling!"

"I can do it—I know the way."

"It'll be dark soon. Please, Corrie . . . don't. Come back inside with me." Her voice had a pleading sound in it. I could tell she was worried.

"I'm sorry, Almeda, I've *got* to. I can make it—I know I can!"

She stood there for a moment, just looking at me as if seeing me for the first time. "All right, Corrie," she said at last. "But wait a minute."

Faster than I would have thought possible, Mrs. Parrish ran into the house and came back with a package wrapped in a dish towel, with several blankets thrown over one arm.

"Some food and water," she explained. "And blankets." She threw the blankets in at my feet and stepped back. "Be careful, Corrie," she said briefly. "And God go with you."

I flipped the reins and called out to the horses, and in a few seconds I was plowing my way through the blizzard. I didn't look back. But inside I knew Mrs. Parrish was crying, and would immediately go back into the house and get on her knees to start praying. I knew God was with me, but I was glad to have two of us praying at the same time! If Pa'd been there, I might not have done what I did, but *if* I had, he'd have probably been muttering something about "that blame fool Belle blood" as he watched me disappear up the street. He probably thought the same thing when he heard about it later.

I didn't realize it then, but that was the first time I ever called Mrs. Parrish *Almeda*. I suppose I was moving toward being a grown-up faster than I realized.

I headed out of town northward, where I could still see Mr. Ward's footsteps in the snow. But I wouldn't follow them all the way. I had made a delivery up to the Wards' place last month with Mr. Weber. He had showed me a ravine along the foot of Buck Mountain where he said the snow didn't fall. He was laughing about it then, but now it just might save those peoples' lives! I'd take the wagon to the foot of the mountain, then along the length of the ravine and up the cutoff road that joined the main ridge-road about halfway to the Wards' place. Marcus had shown me where it turned off when we'd been on our way back down the mountain.

About halfway through the canyon, I heard the bray of a donkey, a strange sound through the quiet of falling snow. I stopped, and heard it again. Then I heard a familiar voice yelling and cursing. Suddenly the sounds coming from the animal made sense!

I urged my horses toward the sounds, and as I got closer I heard the voice again, this time calling out to me. "Hey! Who's there? Hold up . . . whoever ya may be!"

I called my horses to stop. Then I heard the voice again, from part way up the hillside on the slope of Buck Mountain. But it wasn't from the trapped members of the Ward family at all. I wasn't anywhere close to them yet. Instead, the voice was coming from the mouth of a small cave.

Presently a figure appeared in the black opening, looking out into the white blizzard. It was Alkali Jones!

"Mr. Jones!" I called out in astonishment. "What are you doing here? We were all worried about you!"

"I was halfway down from Dolan's when I figured I'd better git me an' my mules hurryin' a mite faster or we'd be buried by this dang blizzard. Then one o' 'em stumbled an' went lame on me an' I figured this here cave'd be 'bout the best I could do till the blame snow quit—hee, hee, hee! But am I glad to see you!"

"But you're only six or eight miles from home. Couldn't you have made it?"

"You ever tried t' pull a mule through a foot o' snow—an a lame one at that? Hee, hee! I might as well o' got on my hands an' crawled home on my knees. This blasted beast won't budge! An' I jest gave Dolan six-fifty fer the blame critter, an' I weren't about to part with my investment, ya might say, hee, hee."

"Well, come on down from there and get in! We got folks trapped up the mountain!"

Alkali left the injured mule tied at the cave and tethered the healthy one behind us. The old miner jumped into the wagon with me, and we continued on to the end of the ravine, which ended abruptly about six hundred yards farther up the canyon.

"You'll never git this pile o' lumber even halfway up the hill," said Mr. Jones. "Ain't no way a wagon like this is gonna make it up that steep path. I don't know what ya was aimin' t' do fer them folks."

"I thought there was a road from the canyon up to the ridge on top. When Mr. Weber and I were up there, he pointed down this way, and it looked like a fine road leading off down toward here."

"Fine road fer maybe two hundred yards, till it's outta sight! Then it turns into a steep trail switchin' back an' forth up the side o' the mountain. Ain't hardly wide enough fer a man, much less a beast. Jest look at it! Ain't no wagon can climb up that!"

We looked up toward Buck Mountain, one side looming against the canyon on our left. Tiny flakes of snow were falling, but above us, the mountain was lost in a dense fog of thick snow.

"'Sides that—look at it!" said Mr. Jones, still pointing upward in the direction I had been hoping to go. "Why, the snow up there's comin' down in a white blanket. There's likely a foot or two foot o' powder, maybe three, up t' the top where the other road is. That trail comin' down off the mountain t' this here ravine—why, it drops a thousand feet! Ain't no way, even if there was a road this wagon'd fit on—which there ain't! No way ya'd git it through that blizzard, not with them horses ya got."

"They're Mrs. Parrish's best," I said.

"They ain't snow animals."

"What are we going to do, Mr. Jones? Those people are trapped up there, and night's coming, and the snow's still falling!"

"That's what I was askin' you—what ya was aimin' to do."

"I thought I'd be able to get there with the wagon."

I hesitated. "What about the mule?" I exclaimed. "Could your mule make it up the steep trail?"

"'Course he could. He could make it up a mountain with no trail."

"In the snow?"

"That critter's been with me in worse snows than this! He ain't no blame tenderfoot like that beast o' Dolan's!"

"Then we'll take the mule up to the top!" I said.

"Jest how ya figure that'll help? How many of 'em ya say there was?"

"Four—Mrs. Ward and three young'uns."

"Hmm . . . lemme see, we might oughta—"

"We could bring them out one at a time, with the mule, and get them to the wagon!"

"Take too long! I tell ya, it's a three-quarter mile o' steep, rugged trail. Time ya went back an' forth, whoever was sittin' down in the wagon waitin', why they'd be plumb froze to death!

If we're gonna git 'em outta there, we gotta git 'em all at once, git back down here, an' high-tail it back to town to git them young'uns someplace warm afore nightfall brings another three foot o' snow an' they're buried till next spring!"

We were at the end of the canyon, and the trail up the mountain wound up and out of sight. I now saw the impossibility of what I had hoped to do. The wagon could go no farther. A light wet snow was falling where we were, and up higher the snow was falling in huge, thick flakes.

We stopped and I tried desperately to think.

"We'll have to try it with these horses," I said at last. "They're the best workhorses Parrish Freight has, and it's our only chance."

I jumped out of the wagon and began unhitching the straps from the two animals.

"What'n tarnation ya thinkin'?" said Mr. Jones.

"We'll both ride up there!" I answered, working my fingers as fast as I could in the biting cold. "We'll take the horses and your mule . . . leave the wagon here, then bring them all four down at once!"

"Ya got spunk, I'll say that! Let's git goin'—we still gotta find where they's broke down," said Mr. Jones, already out of the wagon and untying his mule from the back. "An' that ain't gonna be easy, neither!"

In another three or four minutes we were making our way up the narrow trail. It seemed to take forever, but we made it safely to the top. When we reached the main road that ran along the ridge, we stopped.

"Which way's the Ward place?" said Mr. Jones, half asking, half trying to remember himself.

I glanced all around. In the eerie quietness of the snowy wooded area, everything looked different.

"I . . . I'm not sure," I replied, glancing about for something I might recognize.

Suddenly Mr. Jones jumped off his mule and tromped forward in the snow several paces.

"Look . . . there's wagon tracks!" he shouted back at me

as he pointed ahead. "They been along here all right!"

He glanced hurriedly to the right and left.

"The slope's climbin' this way," he said, jumping back onto his mule. "That means they was headed down."

"Let's go!" I cried, urging the horses toward the faint wheel tracks.

Alkali Jones nodded. "I jest hope we ain't too late."

# CHAPTER 10

## THE ARTICLE

What happened next . . . well, I've kinda got to jump way ahead to tell you about it. You know I'd always wanted to write, and had even hoped to write newspaper articles someday— more than the one or two little things I'd done for Mr. Single- ton. As it turned out, what happened to me and Mr. Jones in the blizzard was the thing that my first really big article was about. Of course, it wasn't printed in the paper till a couple months later—that's the jumping-ahead part.

But as I was writing about the blizzard, it just seemed that perhaps the best way to tell what happened would be just to let you read the article I wrote afterward. And I'm kind of proud of the article too, even after all these years, since it was the first one I got published in a big city paper. So here it is:

Sometimes danger brings with it adventures that would never have happened without it. That's how it was during the blizzard that struck the foothills northwest of Sacramento last March. Folks had already been calling the winter of '55 a bad one, and the sudden fall of snow that dropped on all the gold- mining communities of the region sure made it seem like they were right.

The blizzard brought danger, all right, because most of the citizens weren't expecting it, since it struck so suddenly and all, before anyone was prepared.

The first sign of trouble came when word got to the men gathered in Miracle Springs' Gold Nugget—one of the town's only establishments open at the time—that an avalanche had just occurred on Washington Ridge east of Nevada City, burying three cabins in the ravine below, and endangering the lives of six or eight miners trapped inside. Immediately all the town's available men set out through the snow to try to dig the men out.

No sooner had the men left Miracle Springs when another emergency came. Mr. Jeriah Ward staggered into town, nearly dead of exposure in the bitter cold and in danger of frostbite, frantically in search of help. Finding no one at the saloon or the sheriff's office, Ward made his way to the Parrish Mine and Freight Company. In a state of collapse, he desperately told Mrs. Almeda Parrish Hollister that his wife and three young girls were trapped underneath their broken-down wagon halfway up Buck Mountain.

The words had barely passed his lips when one of Parrish Freight's young employees set out through the snow with a high-axle flatbed wagon pulled by two sturdy workhorses. The Parrish Freight wagon first headed north through the snow-blanketed white countryside on the main road toward North Bloomfield and Alleghany. Following Humbug Creek, swollen full from the winter's rains, the wagon left the main road at the base of Buck Mountain, dropping down into Pan Ravine, a narrow gulch running along the south flank of the mountain. There the snow, which had been between six inches and a foot and a half deep on the main road, was only an inch or two thick. According to Mr. Marcus Weber of the Parrish Mine and Freight Company, who was interviewed afterward, this unusual phenomenon, which keeps most snowfall off the floor of Pan Ravine, is known only to the oldest natives of the region, but has been responsible for saving the lives of more than one person in winter snowstorms like this one.

Up through the ravine the young freight driver urged the two workhorses, who found the footing easier. But as the elevation steadily rose, so did the snow on the ground.

About halfway through the canyon the familiar voice of longtime Miracle Springs miner Alkali Jones was heard. Jones had left the previous day, prior to the beginning of the blizzard, for the Dolan ranch on the higher ground beyond Buck Mountain, and had been feared trapped or even lost in the snow. Like a ghost peering out from the darkness of the cave where he had been trying to wait out the worst of the storm, Jones appeared and joined the rescue effort.

The two made their way to the end of the ravine where they left their wagon. Then up the narrow trail into the blizzard they went, Jones leading on the back of his sure-footed mule, followed by his young friend on the bare back of one of the horses, pulling the other.

Steadily they climbed up the side of Buck Mountain, the snow falling heavier and heavier, but the trail under the thick foliage of the trees remaining visible. The way was slow, but all three animals proved true to their sure-footed reputations. Up the steep way they went, switching back often, always climbing, until at last they reached the main road that ran along the ridge. Snow over a foot thick covered the way.

"I hope they're still alive!" cried out the young freight driver as they began their search for the broken-down wagon.

"Ain't likely they can last long in this cold!" said Alkali Jones. "We gotta find 'em quick!"

As rapidly as they could in the thick snow, they trudged along the road, following the barely visible indentations of wagon tracks, which were growing fainter and fainter by the minute.

"I think I see it!" shouted the young driver at last. "There . . . off the road, all covered with snow!"

"Could be a wagon," replied Jones, giving his mule a hard kick in the side.

"Mrs. Ward . . . Mrs. Ward!" the two shouted as they approached, jumping down and staggering through the deep snow. "Mrs. Ward—you there?"

"Thank God!" said a faint voice from underneath the half-buried wagon. "Who is it?"

"I'm from the Parrish Mine and Freight Company. Your husband came looking for help. His horse broke a leg and he couldn't get back to you."

The two bent down. Under the wagon, protected from the snow, sat the freezing woman, the chill of death in her eyes, huddling her three children close to her under two or three blankets. The bed of the wagon, partially sloped against the wind, had kept them dry, and the blankets had preserved at least some of their body heat as the woman clutched the three children close to one another. Otherwise, all four would have been dead.

"Why, Alkali Jones!" exclaimed the woman, recognizing one of her rescuers for the first time.

"In the flesh, ma'am," replied Jones. "I haven't seen ya since last spring."

"You two can visit later! Let's wrap up the girls in these blankets. We've got to get back down to the canyon before this snow gets any deeper!"

Helping her to her feet, Jones assisted Mrs. Ward onto the back of his mule—the most sure-footed of the three animals—then handed her the smallest of the girls, tightly wrapped in a blanket. Then the other two remounted, each cradling one of the children securely.

Ten minutes later, the three animals were retracing their hoofprints toward the steep trail they had recently ascended. Downward they went this time, in tracks they had carved through the powder on the way up—still visible, though snow continued to fall. Jones, on one of the horses, with seven-year-old Julie bundled on his lap, led the way, followed by Mrs. Ward with the baby on the mule, and then the last Parrish workhorse with four-year-old Tracey in the rider's lap. In a rainstorm the footing on the steep trail would have been muddy and treacherous, but in the frozen snow the hoofs of the animals found solid footing; and though the way was slow, they made the descent into the ravine below without stumbling once.

The waiting wagon was loaded with the four Wards while the two-horse team was once again hitched to the wagon. Then the intrepid group turned for Miracle Springs.

"What about your other mule?"

"Leave it!" replied Alkali Jones, referring to the second of his two mules that he had tied back at the cave. "He couldn't make it afore ya came, an' he ain't likely t' feel none different now. I'll come back fer him when the storm breaks. You jest whip them two horses o' yers along an' git us back t' town! I'm as blamed anxious t' git outta this cold as the Missus an' her young'uns. My fingers is likely already froze clean off!"

And so the rescue of Mrs. Jeriah Ward and her three daughters off Buck Mountain took place. When her husband next saw her, Mrs. Ward was sitting trying to get warm, drinking a cup of tea, while her two older girls sipped hot milk and vanilla in front of the fireplace at Mrs. Hollister's. Waking up in a chair he could not remember being dragged to, with his family warm and safe and recovering, Ward took a cup of coffee from the hand of Alkali Jones, full of more questions than he could ask at once. Then, with many interruptions of "hee, hee, hee!" from the old miner, the relieved father and husband heard the entire story.

In conclusion, it should be mentioned that the rescue of the miners trapped on Washington Ridge was also successful, though it was after nightfall before most of the men returned to Miracle Springs.

# CHAPTER 11

## HOW IT GOT PUBLISHED

Well, that's the article I wrote about what happened, though you can probably tell I had a little help with it here and there. Mrs. Parrish and the man from the newspaper office added a few words and made it sound a little better, but mostly it's mine.

The Wards all turned out to be fine, and stayed in town at Mrs. Gianini's boardinghouse for five days. It snowed on and off for another two days, then it took a while before Jeriah Ward could get a wagon back up the mountain with his wife and girls. He never let the fire go out in that cabin all winter and spring, and kept his wagon in good repair. I went up to visit them several times, and they treated me like a hero, telling me that if it hadn't been for me they might have died in the cold. I hadn't really thought about the danger, but the men around had such a respect for the mountain and for the fierceness of the weather in winter that they insisted there *was* more danger to all of our lives than I realized. Although I never felt much like a hero, it was nice to have them appreciate what I did. And from that time on, the Ward place became kind of like a second home to me, and I got quite attached to Lynn— Mrs. Ward—and her three girls.

Alkali Jones went back to the cave off Pan Ravine the next day during a lull in the storm. I half think he was hoping the mule he'd left there would have frozen to death or run off so he'd have an excuse to go back to Mr. Dolan and try to get his

81

$6.50 back. But no such luck. The mule was still there and still lame. Mr. Jones managed to get him back to town, and got him healthy again, although he still curses at him, calling him "the blamed orneriest dang mule I ever stuck rawhide t' the rump of!" Maybe because he figured my coming along sort of saved his and his mules' lives too—or at least saved his new mule's life by keeping him from killing it himself!—he named it *Corrie's Beast*. That's what he's been calling it ever since, though most of the time he's swearing at it so loud he never has a chance to say the critter's name at all!

I wrote in my journal all about what happened during the blizzard with the Wards—even longer than I did in the article. I wasn't in the habit of showing Mrs. Parrish everything I wrote. My journal was still a private thing I did just for myself. But she asked me what I'd said about the blizzard, and if she might see it, and I agreed.

"Corrie, this is just great!" she exclaimed after she'd read only about half of it. Then she kept on reading, with a bright look in her eye. When she finally set the book down, she looked up. She was still smiling, but she tried to sound serious so I'd know she really meant what she was saying.

"Corrie," she said, "we could get this published, I'm sure of it!"

"How?" I said.

"In a newspaper. This is real news, Corrie. Papers want this kind of thing, especially personal accounts."

We talked about it some more and I asked her what I should do.

"Write it again, Corrie. Write it on separate paper, and as good as you can make it. Think of it as a newspaper story. Pretend telling folks in San Francisco or up in Oregon or back in Kansas City what it was like during that blizzard. Pretend that you're telling *real* people about what happened, and then just write it like a story."

"Should I mention my name?" I asked.

"Hmm, that is hard to know," mused Mrs. Parrish. "Why don't you see if you can write it without letting on who you are," she said after a minute. "That way it will seem more like real news reporting rather than that you're just telling something that happened to you."

Later I learned ways to do "reporting" and tell about things I was involved in without including myself. But this first time it was difficult. After I wrote everything down again as a story, Mrs. Parrish helped me make some corrections. She suggested I add a few words here and there, like *foliage* and *phenomenon*. Actually she suggested quite a few things to change, but all the time she made me think it was all my own doing.

When we were done she helped me send it to Mr. Singleton in Marysville. When he wrote back two weeks later, saying that the *California Gazette* regrettably would have to decline interest in the blizzard account, she was so upset she stormed and fumed around the house with a red face.

"That old rattlepate Singleton wouldn't know a good story if he was hit over the head with it! How he ever got into the newspaper business I can't imagine!"

All at once she had an idea. That's when she thought of her friend. "I know what we'll do, Corrie," she said. "I have a friend on the staff of the *Alta* in San Francisco. He's in advertising, but I've done quite a bit of work with him for the business. I'll send him the story, tell him it's authentic and that a friend of mine here in Miracle Springs wrote it. I'll twist his arm a bit and ask him to show it to the news editor—Kemble's his name, I believe."

"Do you really think they might print it?"

"You never know unless you try, Corrie. I've given the *Alta* a lot of my business, not just in advertising, but for various printing jobs I've needed. I think upon my recommendation, they just might consider it."

When Mrs. Parrish's friend first wrote back to us, he said, "The article's fine. Matter of fact, it's better than fine for a new reporter. But doesn't he know how important it is to identify who the hero of the story is?" He thought I was a *he* because Mrs. Parrish had suggested I send him the story as written by *C.B. Hollister*, so his editor wouldn't say no to the idea of publishing it just because I was a girl.

Mrs. Parrish answered the letter and explained why the freight driver's name shouldn't be used in the article. He responded immediately. "Kemble liked the blizzard piece. Not too well written, he said, but exciting and realistic, which is what our readers want. He complained like I did about the heroic wagon driver not being mentioned, but I told him that was a condition you'd put on publication. Anyway, he thought the piece was fine enough regardless, especially for a new reporter. Enclosed is $2.00. Whoever your friend C.B. Hollister is, Kemble says for him to get in touch. Might be that we can use something else of his in the future. Kemble likes firsthand accounts and has been looking for this kind of thing from the foothills country. We'll send you a copy of the issue when it appears."

She threw her hands in the air and let out a whoop and holler.

"Corrie, Corrie! Do you see this?" she exclaimed, shaking the check in my direction. "A check for two dollars! Corrie . . . you are going to be a published, professional newspaper writer!"

I'd been sitting beside her as we read the letter. My heart was pounding and my hands were sweating, but not because of the $2.00. In fact, I hardly even noticed that. Over and over the words from the letter spun through my brain: *Whoever C.B. Hollister is . . . get in touch . . . something else of his in the future.*

I could hardly believe it! Not just that *this* story was going to get into a newspaper—they might even want another story later, if I could write another one!

It was too good to be true!

By this time winter was over, and the story didn't appear until toward the end of April. I'll never forget what it was like sitting around the house that night after the copy of the *Alta* came, the whole family huddled near the fire, everybody looking over shoulders and around heads and through arms. Tad and Becky sat on the floor, Emily and Zack and I squatted Indian-style, Alkali Jones, Katie, Uncle Nick, Pa, and Almeda

all crowded together to read the article in the *Alta* with BLIZ-
ZARD RESCUE ON BUCK MOUNTAIN in big bold black
print across the top, and underneath the words: *by C.B. Hollister, Miracle Springs, California.*

Between the storm and the article, I'd turned eighteen. And
there couldn't have been a better birthday present than this.

When everybody was finally done reading it, Katie congratulated me, and Uncle Nick threw his arm around my shoulder and pretended to pinch my cheek. Mrs. Parrish, bubbly
and happy that it had all turned out so well, was saying things
about all the articles I was going to write in the future.

But Pa was the quietest of all. He didn't say a word until
the hubbub from everyone else had died down. Then he just
stuck out his hand toward me. I took his hand and he gave
mine a big firm shake and looked me straight in the eye.

"Corrie Belle," he said, "I reckon you're a woman now.
You done this on your own, without me or your ma, though I
guess you had your share of help from Almeda here. But no
matter—*you* went out there after them kids. And that was a
right brave thing to do—though maybe a mite foolhardy—"

Everyone laughed.

"You went after 'em. Then you thought how to write it
down. You done that too. And with whatever help you had, I
figure it's you that newspaper guy and them girls got to thank."

He paused, then added, "Anyhow, Corrie Belle, what I'm
trying to say is that you're a mighty fine young woman—and
you done your pa proud."

I held on to his hand an extra moment or two, my eyes
glistening with tears as I took in the face I loved so much. God
had been so good to me!

In that moment I was more full and more thankful and
more proud than I had ever been in my life.

# CHAPTER 12

## SUMMER OF '55

The snowstorm, the article, and what Pa said to me that night, all seemed to be part of the Lord pointing me toward my future. Hindsight makes it easier to see those kinds of things when your life takes new directions. And as I've looked back, I've felt that God may have brought about the events of the blizzard and then the article getting published right after the prayers I'd prayed about my future.

Even as I was still down on my knees praying in the wet grass behind that oak tree near the school, somewhere up in the clouds way up high in the sky those snowflakes were getting ready to fall. God was telling me, "You see, Corrie, even before you're through praying, I'm already sending the answers down to you. You may not realize it, but these little snowflakes are going to come down onto you, and I will use them to show you that I am answering your prayers, and will send you out into your future. I will use these snowflakes to show you that I am giving you the desire of your heart too, Corrie, which is to write."

That time of prayer and trying to give my whole self more completely to God, and then the article that came later, set me on a path I would never turn back from. I said to God, "Here is my life, my future . . . here are my worries . . . You know what I want to do . . . I am willing to do and be anything you want me to be." And then God seemed to say back to me, "I will take your life, Corrie, and I will work my will in it, and at the same time I will give you more than you could ever hope for, even more than you prayed for."

Ever since, whenever I see snowflakes falling to the ground, I think of them as beautiful tiny little remembrances of God's answers to prayer. For every prayer we pray, even before we're through praying it, God is *already* sending millions of answers down to us, answers we may not see or recognize, but they are from him nevertheless. Falling snow always helps me remember that God is so completely above us that we can never escape his quietly falling blessings and answers to prayers and his love and care.

Thus, I always look back on that time as the end of my childhood and the beginning of my being an adult. Not just because I'd turned eighteen, but because I'd let go of my worries (which kind of represented my past), and God had sent me out toward my future with a glimpse (that first newspaper article) of what it was I would be doing in the years to come. Just as Pa's and Almeda's life together was just beginning, so too was mine as a grown-up.

For the rest of that school year I kept helping Miss Stansberry at the school, and then after I was done, working at the Freight Company two or three days a week. But even before school broke off for the summer in June, I think I'd decided not to be Miss Stansberry's assistant the following fall when it started back up again. Whether it was the thinking and praying about my future, I don't know. And I still considered teaching school one of my "options" that perhaps I'd think about someday. Maybe I figured it was time to take a break from school, even though I liked being part of it. It might be that God was, like the verse said, "directing my path" by getting me to think about different things. It's hard to say. I was still too new at trying to figure out about what Almeda called "God's guidance." But I felt I ought to do something else for a spell. So my plan was to work more at the Freight Company that next year, and of course Almeda thought it was a terrific idea.

The summer of '55 was one of the happiest times I can remember. The weather was nice, and everything went perfectly. The mine didn't cave in and nobody got hurt and everybody got along real fine. We all moved permanently from the house in town out to the claim. That made Pa happy, because he'd fixed up the house so nice, and it was plenty big—big enough for all seven of us.

Tad and Becky weren't just little runts anymore, but were ten and twelve. No one worried about them getting lost as we had when we'd first come, and they were all over the place. Emily was fourteen, still quiet and beautiful. Zack was well past sixteen and was a strapping tall young man with the beginnings of a beard showing on his face and muscles gradually starting to bulge out on his arms. He helped Pa at the mine on most days, although he was over at Little Wolf's most days too, riding and breaking horses. Pa'd mutter about the two of them being "plumb loco" on account of what they did with the horses. But it was plain to see that Pa was proud of Zack's being such a tough and hardworking kid. Alkali Jones was around a lot too. His hair was gradually getting more gray in it, and he seemed to do a lot more cackling and talking and directing up at the mine than working.

Uncle Nick and Katie's son Erich, named after Katie's grandfather who immigrated from Europe, was born on the next to last day of July. Uncle Nick said he had been thinking about naming the baby after his father, Grandpa Belle, if it was a boy, or if it was a girl calling her Agatha after Ma. But in the end it was Katie's name that prevailed. So we had a new cousin in the family and were mighty pleased to have him.

As you can imagine, having Katie *and* Almeda around sure did liven up the place! When I think back to that first winter when it was just us kids and Pa and Uncle Nick in that one little cabin, all I can do is laugh. The two women sure made it different, more homey, more lively. There was more laughter in the air, more flowers on the tables, better smells coming out of the pots hanging over the fires, and everything was a lot cleaner than back then!

But I think it was a good thing there were two houses separated by six hundred yards, a stream, and some woods. Those two strong women under one roof would have been like Pa putting too much dynamite in the mine! As it was, they were able to be good friends and visit and talk and invite each other over and borrow things and help each other, while they both kept track of their own houses. Just like with the naming of Erich, Katie usually got what she wanted, and anybody who knows Katie knows she was more likely to stay Katie Morgan Belle than to become *Mrs.* Anybody! She may have been Uncle Nick's wife, but she was still "Katie" to everybody around!

I suppose you could say the same of Almeda too. She had been on her own for a long time and was used to thinking independently, unlike most women with a husband and five kids. Yet she was different than Katie in how she went about things. If Katie and Uncle Nick had a dispute about something, they'd say their mind—sometimes loudly!—and somehow or another figure out what to do. They laughed and kidded and sometimes hollered at each other—you could hear them clear down across the creek at our place! They argued, and then worked out their differences, kissed, and went on. Sometimes Uncle Nick got his way, but mostly Katie got hers.

It was different with Pa and Almeda, although they laughed and had fun together too. Maybe it was because they were older, and both had been married before. Maybe it was because there were hurts in both of their past lives. They'd each had to face the death of someone they loved very much and were now married again, but with memories still lingering from before.

Both Pa and Almeda were quieter when there'd be something to decide, more thoughtful, I guess. And if they had a difference of opinion—like earlier about the houses and where to live—it would get real quiet for a spell. In some ways yelling and arguing about things like Uncle Nick and Katie did was better for the other folks around. At least you didn't have to wonder what people were thinking! When Pa and Almeda got quiet and quit talking to each other much for a day or two, it was eerie and unpleasant in the house and all us kids would tiptoe around, not knowing what to say.

But I came to realize at such times that being quiet was

their way of thinking about things. It may have been awkward for a while, but I came to see that maybe they were both quiet, not because they were angry or upset, but because they loved each other and didn't want to say something that would hurt. They needed to think and maybe pray too. And then when they did talk, you could tell they were trying hard to think of each other, not just themselves.

Both marriages were a year old that summer, and watching them develop was interesting for me. I'd never thought much about what it might be like to be married, and I wasn't thinking about it in connection with *myself*. But being older, and being Almeda's friend and getting to know Pa so much better *before* they had married made me look at them through different eyes than I could have when I was just a little kid. I did find myself wondering *if* I ever got married, way off in the future sometime, what it would be like. What kind of wife did I want to be, like Katie or like Almeda?

I didn't come to any conclusions, only that it was interesting to me, especially seeing how Almeda would try to yield to Pa as her husband. I knew that was hard for her, since she'd had to think for herself since Mr. Parrish died. And in matters like the house and how to run her business, she'd been accustomed not only to making all the decisions herself but also to thinking like a man, because she was trying to run a man's business in a man's world.

Now she was married, but she *still* had her house and business along with a husband and a family. She had to live two different lives. She'd never had children of her own before, and here she suddenly had five! Yet she still walked into her office or met with customers who looked to her as the businesswoman she was.

On most days she and I would go into town together in the morning. I was learning more about how the office itself operated and would process orders that came in through the mail or write up invoices. Mr. Ashton still called me *Miss* Hollister! With me to help in the office, Almeda had more time to go out and call on miners and see potential customers, and the incoming orders picked up as a result.

"Your being here makes a big difference, Corrie," she said. "If the business keeps growing, we'll have to change the name to *Parrish & Hollister,* or *Parrish & Daughter!*"

"How about just changing it to *Hollister* Mine and Freight Company?" suggested Pa that same evening when Almeda was recounting the conversation she'd had with me earlier. "You ain't a *Parrish* no more, you know, Almeda."

I don't think Pa meant anything by it other than just a passing comment, but afterward it was quiet for a while, and I know Almeda was thinking about how all the pieces fit. I know now that she was thinking about praying about *her* future and *her* options too, just as she was helping me do in my life. Eventually she did share with me that she went through a time of real doubt and wondering about what she and Pa ought to do. She found herself wishing Pa would give up the mine and join her in the business. Then she realized maybe she wanted it because that's the decision Mr. Parrish had come to, and that it would be hard for Pa to want to be a part of *her* business if it meant sacrificing something which was *his* own, *his* dream— like the mine was. And she had to battle within herself whether she was going to be *Mrs. Drummond Hollister,* or if she was going to keep being *Almeda Parrish* with a new last name added on. Was she going to keep everything as it had been and add Pa's family, or was she going to *become* part of the family, even if it meant sacrificing some of what she had been before?

Later, when I was quite a bit older and she told me about some of these things, she said, "Every woman doesn't have to face it the same way, Corrie. Most women just get married and their husband's home and livelihood is about all they have to consider. And they're perfectly content to just be part of their husband's world. But when I married your father, it was different. And I'm so thankful that he understood. He respected me, respected that other part of my life too that had been going on before I knew him and wanted to keep going afterward as well. I think he knew I'd never want to sell the Freight Company, or would want to change the name. As proud as I was to be Mrs. Drummond Hollister, to become a 'mother' and join your family, I couldn't help wanting, I suppose, to keep a part of myself—not 'separate' exactly, but keep it as my *own,* to keep being the *me* I have always been. As much as a man and a woman become 'one' when they are married, there is still that part of you that needs to know you are your *own* person even though you are married and have given that personhood to your husband too. I don't know if other women think about it quite like that, but I have. Anyway, I *wanted* to keep the business, and to keep calling it by the *Parrish* name . . . because of something in me that didn't go away when I married your father."

And she did keep both halves of her life going just great from what I could tell—the Almeda Parrish part and the Mrs. Drummond Hollister part. I only hoped I could do as well if there ever came a time in my life when I had to.

Some days she'd go home early, in the middle of the afternoon, and get working on supper—we were a pretty big household to feed!—and I'd ride out later by myself. On other days we'd get a big pot of beans or stew prepared in the morning to sit all day on the fire, and Emily and Becky would make corn bread or biscuits to go with it. On those kinds of days we might both come home together after the office closed. It was always different. Maybe one or the other of us would be on a delivery and would be late, and the other would tend to the supper. Almeda was gracious about making me feel like I was still needed. And I suppose I *was,* even though it took some getting used to at first, not having the others depending on me for everything. Pa was a big help. He didn't mind giving the stew a stir or adding some extra water to the pot of beans or tending lunch for the rest of the kids when neither Almeda nor I was there. We were an unusual family, but Pa didn't seem to mind that.

We had Katie to think about that summer too, and most evenings one of us would go up and help her with the washing of clothes or whatever else she had to do. Emily spent half of most days helping Katie with her new little baby cousin. Becky went over there a lot too, and tried to pitch in. But Becky always thought she was a bigger help than she really was! I could tell when Emily held little Erich that she wouldn't mind being a mother herself someday!

Even with all that was going on around home, and with the work at the Freight Company to keep me busy, I kept thinking of those words in the letter to Mrs. Parrish: *Whoever your friend C.B. Hollister is, Kemble says for him to get in touch. Might be that we could use something else of his in the future. Kemble likes firsthand accounts and has been looking for this kind of thing from the foothills country.*

All summer I kept racking my brain trying to think up some other "firsthand account" I might write about to send to the *Alta.* A little dose of success was enough to make me think I was ready to be a real-live reporter!

All of a sudden, about the middle of August, the idea hit me. Of course! I had the greatest possible story right in front of my nose! If it'd been any closer it would have bit me!

The minute it came to me I was filing the July invoices in the file drawer in the oak desk. I jumped up.

"Almeda," I said, trying to stay calm, "would it be all right if I went home early today?"

"Certainly, Corrie. Is something the matter? Don't you feel well?"

"I feel great. It's just that I think I've thought of the next story I might write and send to the *Alta.*"

"Wonderful! What is it?"

"I'd rather not say till it's done, ma'am. But I'll let you read it first."

"Go, then, Corrie!" she exclaimed, breaking into a laugh. "Go and write it. Your reading public is waiting!"

I charged out the door and onto my horse and galloped all the way back to the claim. I hardly stopped at the cabin, but ran right up to the mine where, just like I'd figured, Alkali Jones was sitting on a rock and giving out advice to Pa and Uncle Nick and Zack.

"Mr. Jones . . . Mr. Jones!" I said, all out of breath as I

ran up to him. "I gotta talk to you."

"Hee, hee, hee!" he laughed, looking me over from head to foot. "Can't be that one o' my mules has got me in a fix. I got one right there." He pointed to a tree where his trusty favorite was tied. "An' Corrie Beast's tied up where she can't git loose nohow! Hee, hee, hee!"

"No, it ain't that, Mr. Jones," I said, trying to catch my breath. "Please, would you just come down to the cabin with me for a few minutes?"

"Okay by me, Corrie Belle," he answered, "but I don't know if yer pa an' uncle can find any gold in that there stream without me. Hee, hee! I know this creek better'n I know that blame mule yonder. An' it ain't just nobody what gits the gold outta it. That's why I'm here, to show 'em where t' put their sluices an' pans an' where t' aim their shovels."

"We'll manage for five minutes, Alkali!" shouted Pa from where he stood knee-deep in the water. He threw me a quick wink as he spoke. "But don't you keep him long, Corrie! I don't want me and Nick and Zack wasting *too* much time when we don't know where the gold might be!"

"Okay, Pa," I answered him seriously. "I'll take care of my business with Mr. Jones as fast as I can."

The old prospector got up from his rock, grinning and cackling his high-pitched *hee, hee, hee* to himself, and followed me down to the cabin. I can't imagine what he thought it was all about, but once inside, as soon as I had grabbed a pencil and fresh sheet of paper, I started asking about his first days in California and about his discovery of gold in the creek, about how he first yelled "It's a Miracle," and how the stream was named, and then how the town started to grow. All it took was my first question and he was off retelling it all faster than I could write!

Well, that was my first "interview." And I never had a more willing talker! I could have written a whole book just about the adventures and exploits of Alkali Jones—founder of everything in California that was of any importance, friend of everybody, who had been everywhere and seen everything and done things nobody else in the world could hope to do! I probably would have had to call the book *Alkali Jones, the Most Important Person Ever in California's History.*

As it was, I wrote a two-page story that I called "How Gold Was Discovered on Miracle Springs Creek."

I finished it four days later. That's when I showed it to Almeda.

"It sounds just like an experienced writer, Corrie!" she said. "I am excited! Do you want me to send it?"

"If you don't mind, I'd like to send it in from myself," I answered. "I've gotta try sometime."

"You're right. And they did say to have 'my friend' get in touch with them," she laughed. "Are you going to use your whole name?"

"I don't know," I answered. "Do you really think they'd mind it being from a girl?"

"If I know men, Corrie—and I do, because I do business with them all day long!—yes, I do think they'd mind. They might not say so. No man will *admit* to looking down on those of us of 'the weaker sex.' They will always talk about 'respecting' and 'admiring' us, and they'll be more than happy to be courteous and gentlemanly if it suits them. But let a woman try to *do* something on her own, especially something they think ought to be done by a man, and they don't like it. They want to keep women what they like to call 'in their place.' And they *especially* don't like a woman doing something *well* that they think is a man's thing to be doing. Don't ask me why, Corrie— but they just don't like a woman to be successful at anything except *woman* things—you know, feeding babies and sweeping floors and washing clothes and boiling water and setting dinner on the table. Not that there's anything wrong with doing those things, but a *few* of us women, like you and me, want to do some other things besides. So to answer your question again, Corrie, I would say this—I think that if you sent in your story exactly like it is, and the editor, that Mr. Kemble, figured it was from a woman—especially just an eighteen-year-old one!—I doubt he'd even read it. But if he thought it was from a man, even though the words were just the same, I think he'd read it and like it. That's just the way the world is, Corrie, if you're a woman and you want to do something that maybe is a bit out of the ordinary for a woman to do."

"Then I reckon I ought to keep being just *C.B.* Hollister for a spell longer."

She laughed. "You boil my long-winded lecture on the frustrations of being a businesswoman right down to the basics, don't you, Corrie?"

So I sent my story to the *Alta*. I addressed it to Mr. Kemble, Editor, and included a letter. I introduced myself as the C.B. Hollister who had written the story about the blizzard, and thanked him very much for the two dollars. I had written another article, I said, which I hoped they might be able to use, and it was enclosed. The letter was in my best handwriting, and I tried not to make it look like it was written by a girl.

Two and a half weeks later, an envelope came to the freight office addressed to me, with a return address from the *Alta* in San Francisco.

The instant I saw it I started trembling with anticipation. I grabbed it out of Mr. Ashton's hands, and my sweaty fingers fumbled frantically to tear it open.

"Dear Mr. Hollister," the letter began—and I was so nervous that I didn't even notice the *Mr.* at first.

> We won't be able to use your article. Stories about gold being discovered in creeks around the foothills are what we call yesterday's news. Nobody cares about that anymore. We're looking for stories about people—*real* people. Your Alkali Jones sounds more like fiction than fact, and if he does exist, I don't believe a word of what he told you.
>
> I remain, Mr. Hollister,
> Sincerely yours,
> Edward Kemble
> Editor, California *Alta*.

I was too disappointed to think about being angry about what he'd said. As much as I wanted to be grown-up about it,

I immediately felt my eyes starting to fill up with tears. I had been so sure this story about Mr. Jones was even better than the blizzard one! At that moment, I never wanted to write another word!

I dropped the letter down on the desk and quickly went out the back door before Mr. Ashton saw me start crying and blubbering right there in the office. I was glad Almeda happened to be out on the street with Marcus Weber, checking the load for an order he was taking up to French Corral.

I went out into the back of the livery, and by then I was crying. But at least I was alone, with the smells of hay and horses and leather to calm me down instead of having to face any people.

I guess I left the door open behind me, because I never heard Almeda enter. The first I knew she was there with me was when I heard her voice close behind me and felt her hand on my shoulder.

"I guess I was wrong," she said softly. "Even from a man, he didn't like the article!"

I laughed and turned around. She was holding the letter from Kemble in her hand, and a tender smile of compassion was on her face. She knew the hurt I was feeling.

But I couldn't help it—the tears kept coming!

"No matter how old a girl—or a woman—gets, Corrie," she said, "there are times when you just have to cry. Right now, won't you just let me be—if I can say it—won't you let me be a *mother* to you?"

She opened her arms and drew me to her breast.

I laid my head against her, wrapped my arms around her waist, and melted into her tender embrace, quietly weeping. My emotions were so full, but I didn't know if it was from the letter, or from the happiness I felt at having Almeda love me as much as I knew she did in that moment. Sometimes you can't tell whether you're happy or sad, but you just keep crying anyway.

We stood there for two or three minutes, neither saying a word, holding each other tight. It was such a wonderful moment of closeness, I didn't want it to end.

Finally I felt her arms about me relax.

"You really wanted that story about Mr. Jones to be published, didn't you?" she said, looking down into my eyes, still red but at least dry now.

I nodded.

"And you thought it was . . . maybe not the best—but as good as the article you wrote about the Wards?"

Again I nodded. "I can't see that it was as much worse as Mr. Kemble said."

"But you're afraid he's right, and that you'll never amount to anything as a writer if something you liked is really as bad as he says. Is that how you feel?"

"I reckon that's about it. And he didn't say a thing about sending them anything else. I thought he said he wanted first-hand accounts. Now I'm just back to where I was before the blizzard—which is nowhere!"

"Not quite, Corrie. There's one big thing that's changed."

"What's that?"

"You *did* write that article, and it *did* appear in the *Alta*, and you *did* get paid for it. Don't you realize what that means, Corrie—you *are* a professional writer! You have done it. Maybe only once—but that's a start!"

"But what about this?" I said, pointing to the letter from Kemble.

"It's nothing! If Singleton, and now Kemble, aren't smart enough to see a future-budding reporter right under their noses, then you can send what you write to someone else. Somebody *will* be interested!"

"In my story about Alkali Jones, do you think?"

"Perhaps. But maybe not. Kemble *may* be right about it being yesterday's news. But you can't let that stop you. You'll write another article, and then another. Some of them will be published, and some won't. But that can't stop you from writing them, not if you believe in what you want to do, and believe in yourself to do it."

She paused. "*Do* you believe in yourself, Corrie—as a writer, I mean?"

"You mean, do I think I'm a *good* writer? I wouldn't say that."

"Maybe not a 'good' writer. But do you believe in yourself as someone who's *going to* be a decent writer someday—even if some day way in the future? Can you believe that about yourself? Can you believe that God can do that with you . . . and maybe even that he *wants* to?"

I thought a minute. "I reckon I can believe that," I replied.

"And you *want* it to happen, am I right? That is, if God opens the way for it to happen, then you want it?"

"Yes."

"Well, that's how I felt about this business, Corrie, after Mr. Parrish died. I desperately *wanted* to make the business work. I *wanted* to succeed, maybe because I figured most of the men around thought I'd pack right up and be on the next ship back to Boston. But no I *wanted* to stick it out, even during the hard times, and *make* it work. And it seems to me maybe that's what you might have to do too—stick it out, even through the hard times, and not give up, because you're *determined* to make it work . . . and to do it."

"That's what you mean by believing in yourself?"

"That's right. There are times, Corrie, when you've got to go after something you want, even when you think you're all alone and when nobody else believes in you or thinks you have a chance to do it. There are times when you've got to plow ahead with your own determination to succeed. That can be especially true for a woman trying to do something on her own. You can do it, Corrie. You *can* write . . . and you *will*! The day will come when you can march right into Mr. Kemble's office and lay your papers down on his desk and say, 'I'm *Corrie Belle* Hollister, if you please, and not *Mister* C.B. Hollister, and my story is as good as you're gonna get from any man-reporter!' "

"I could never do that!" I said, laughing.

She laughed too. "Maybe not in those words. But if that kind of determination is inside you, and you believe in yourself that much, then I can promise you, *Corrie Belle Hollister*, yours is a name people are going to see in print someday."

"So what do I do now," I asked, "if I'm going to try to keep believing in myself like that?"

"You keep looking for ideas, and you keep writing in your journal, and you keep thinking up stories and articles to write . . . and you keep writing them and sending them to Mr. Singleton and Mr. Kemble. And with everything you write you're going to learn a little something more, and one of these days those editors will start paying attention when they see your name on a story. Believe me, Corrie, Mr. Kemble has not seen the last of you!"

I laughed again. It was nice to hear her say it, though I couldn't be quite that confident myself.

The article about Alkali Jones never did get into a newspaper, though every once in a while I still think about writing a whole book about his life. Almeda's other words, however, about determination and believing in yourself—I never forgot them. Her encouragement came back to me more than once later, because that was not the last rejection I got for something I wrote. There were a lot more to come!

And her joking about what I might someday say to the editor of the *Alta* was something I remembered too. When that day came, it didn't happen just as she'd predicted, but I couldn't help thinking back on her words nevertheless.

# CHAPTER 13

## LEARNING TO BELIEVE IN MYSELF . . . AND WRITE

The following school year was very different for me. For the first time in my life I *wasn't* going to school, either as a student or a teacher's helper. It made me realize in a whole new way how much things were changing.

For everybody! Zack wasn't in school anymore either. He spent his time about equally between helping Pa and Uncle Nick at the mine and helping Little Wolf and his pa with the riding and training and selling of horses. Now that Central California had been being settled for five or six years, there were a lot more than just gold prospectors coming into the state, including farmers and ranchers. Little Wolf's pa had developed a fair business in horse selling. There seemed to be a continually increasing need for good riding and cattle horses, and they brought even more money if they were already broke and trained—which was where Zack and Little Wolf came in. The two of them loved it! Anything to do with horses made them as happy as could be.

Anyhow, with Zack and Little Wolf and I gone, and Elizabeth Darien married and moved to Oregon, Miss Stansberry chose a new helper—Emily! During that year she turned fifteen, the same age as I was when we came to Miracle Springs.

Without older boys like Zack and Little Wolf and Artie Syfer in the school anymore—and there weren't any fourteen-or-fifteen-year old boys coming up in the class—Rev. Rutledge

101

came to check up on Miss Stansberry usually once a day, to see if she needed any help moving a desk or lifting something. She was such a capable lady it was easy to forget about her being lame, but the minister didn't forget. He was always trying to find ways to make it easier for her. Sometimes when I was on my way home from town late in the afternoon just before suppertime, I'd see Rev. Rutledge's buggy out in front of the school where he was still helping Miss Stansberry. I suppose, though, with the two of them sharing the building like that, using it both as a school and as a church, they probably had plenty to keep them both occupied.

We continued living in the cabin out at the claim. Almeda and I would take a buggy into town with Emily and Becky and Tad every morning and return in the afternoon. Sometimes only one of us might go into town. Occasionally I'd want to stay home and work on something I might be writing, and other days Almeda would want to spend part of the day with Pa. By that time, whenever she did want to stay at home, I knew most of what needed to be done at the freight office. When she wasn't there, I wasn't Mr. Ashton's or Mr. Weber's boss. They knew what to do too, and we all did our jobs together and talked about any decisions to be made before Almeda got back. Yet they would ask me questions, almost as if I *were* their boss, just because of me and Almeda being in the same family now. Although it was a mite peculiar, I got used to it—but I'm glad she was there most of the time.

I didn't forget Almeda's words about having to work for something you believed in. I figured if I had the Belle blood in me, like Pa sometimes said, then I ought to put it to work for me.

So I didn't let myself get discouraged because of that letter Mr. Kemble wrote, saying he didn't believe what I wrote about Mr. Jones was true. I just said to myself: "Well, we'll see, Mr. Editor! I'll show *you* who can write around here! You're not just talking to anybody, Mister—you're talking to a Hollister, half of whose blood is *Belle blood*! Yeah, Mr. Editor, we'll see about what's true and what's not! And what's true is that I'm gonna be a reporter for your paper someday!"

That's what I said to Mr. Kemble in my thoughts. But I was nice as could be whenever I sent a story to him. And I kept signing my name *C.B. Hollister*. Almeda had talked to me about believing in myself, but I wasn't ready to believe in myself quite enough yet to start using my real name! I figured what he didn't know about who *C.B.* was wouldn't hurt him for the time being.

So I wrote stories on anything that I thought might be interesting to the folks either in San Francisco or in Sacramento. If it seemed more to do with Sacramento, I sent it to Mr. Singleton in Marysville. If it seemed more appropriate for San Francisco, I sent it to the *Alta*. Since I didn't know exactly what kinds of things a newspaper editor would be likely to publish, I tried all kinds of different approaches. Here's one I tried.

> This fall the school in Miracle Springs begins its third year. Teacher Miss Harriet Stansberry reports an enrollment of twenty-four students, up eight from the previous year, though she says the average age of her children is younger than before.
>
> When asked about the future of the school, Miss Stansberry answered: "There are still new families coming to the area, even though the rapid growth has slowed somewhat. From the age of my students, it seems as if the enrollment will probably stay about where it is for some years to come."

I then went on to tell a little about the school and what kinds of subjects the children studied, and even had a quote or two from some of the students, including one from Emily.

I sent this to Mr. Singleton, reminding him that he had printed the very first thing I had written about the opening of the school back in December of '53. I don't know whether it was that, or whether maybe he was afraid of losing the Parrish Freight advertising, but he did print this new article about the school, though he cut most of it out, including all the quotes from Emily and the others. When it appeared it was only two paragraphs long and didn't have my name anywhere on it. And

Mr. Singleton never paid even fifty cents for anything I sent him. I began to wonder if that $2.00 was the last money I'd ever see for anything I wrote. But even if it was, I still wanted to write newspaper stories. I'd just have to keep doing other work besides.

I can't say that anything I wrote was any good compared to *real* authors like Thoreau or Hawthorne or Cooper or Irving or Walter Scott. But I wasn't trying to be a real author, only to write for a newspaper, and it didn't seem to me that you'd have to be as good to do that. Besides, I figured maybe writing was one of those things you had to learn how to do just by doing it a lot. So that's what I did—I wrote about a lot of different things, and practiced trying to make my writing more interesting. Like this one:

> Mr. Jack Lame Pony, a full-blooded Nisenan Indian, has turned his skill in training horses into a livelihood. "When white men come to California in search of gold," says Lame Pony, "many of my people went farther north, and to mountains and hills. But I had son, cabin, land. I not want to leave."
>
> After two or three years trying to scrape food out of the soil and sell furs trapped in the high Sierras, Lame Pony began to acquire a stock of riding horses. He was very bitter against the intrusion of gold-seekers into what he considered the land of his people. But when men began coming to him one by one in search of sturdy and dependable horses, he found that most were reasonable and not as different from himself as he imagined.
>
> Slowly, word about his horses spread throughout the region north of Sacramento, and he had more requests than he had horses. He also found that doing business with ranchers and farmers, and even some gold miners, was not as difficult as he had thought.
>
> "As my anger left my heart," he says, "I sold more horses. Soon had no time to trap. Had to find more horses—always more horses, then break them, train them, teach them white man's ways."
>
> Perhaps even Lame Pony's name might have helped his

reputation as the best horse trainer in the region. Wherever one goes in the foothills north and east of Sacramento, the mention of the name Lame Pony always brings a chuckle and the words, "Whatever his name says, his horses are the best." A rancher from Yuba City, who has purchased eight different horses from Lame Pony for his hands, was quoted as saying, "None of my men ever been throwed by one of his horses yet!"

Recently Lame Pony and his son Little Wolf, with the help of neighbors, enlarged their corrals and added another stable. With the continued growth of California, they foresee an even greater need for well-trained horses in the future and want to be prepared for it.

Of course I asked Little Wolf's father if I could write about him first, and Little Wolf talked him into agreeing. Mr. Singleton printed this article just as I'd written it—*after* he had signed up a small advertisement for the Lame Pony Stables to appear on the same page. The neighbors I mentioned were Pa and Uncle Nick and Zack. I didn't really talk to the man from Yuba City, but Marcus Weber knew him and heard him say those words.

I wrote a short article about Patrick Shaw, our neighbor from over the ridge, who in his spare time was getting to be a pretty well-known banjo-picker and was often invited to hoe-downs from as far away as Coloma and Placerville. I drew a picture of him playing, too, to go along with the written part. But that was one of my articles that never actually made it to a paper. Mr. Shaw did ask me, though, to do a drawing of him and his banjo for him to use on a sign if he was going to be playing somewhere.

Another article I wrote was about a new church that was getting started down at Colfax. They didn't have a building yet and were meeting in a great big house. Rev. Rutledge went down there every two weeks and was more or less in charge of it, though he had people in Colfax helping a lot too, like Almeda had done when he first came to Miracle Springs.

Both the minister and Almeda were excited about the opportunity for new churches starting throughout this part of California, something I know they'd been wanting to see happen from the very first. Of course, as interested as we all were—and he would tell us what was happening in other areas on Sunday—Almeda didn't actually participate in his plans as she did at first. But at least he didn't have to make that long ride back and forth to Colfax alone every time 'cause every once in a while Miss Stansberry would go along with him to keep him company.

Religious news didn't seem to be something most folks were interested in, because that was another one of my articles that never got into a paper.

One that did, however—and I admit it surprised me, because I wrote it just for fun—was an article I called "Virginian Finds New Home After Unusual Beginning."

> When Miss Kathryn Hubbard Morgan stepped off the steamer in Sacramento in May of 1854 as a mail-order bride, she could little have foretold the strange turn of events that would make her future so different from what she had planned.
>
> Miss Morgan carried with her that day a handful of apple seeds, a seashell, a rock, a tuft of grass, some Virginia moss, and a piece of dried bark—all as remembrances of her past in Virginia and as symbols of the new life she was starting in California the moment she set foot upon the bank of the Sacramento River.
>
> As it turned out, Miss Morgan, now Mrs. Nick Belle of Miracle Springs, did not marry the man who had paid half her passage to the west, but his brother-in-law instead.
>
> "You cannot imagine the thoughts that were racing through my mind as I stood there in my wedding dress," Mrs. Belle said, "only to have the ceremony so suddenly interrupted and thrown upside-down."

I then went on to tell a little about the wedding and what Uncle Nick had done and the story leading up to that day, including quotes from Pa and Uncle Nick, and another one or two from Katie. When I was asking them questions, Uncle

Nick got to laughing and talking and said this, which people who read the article liked best of all: "When I lit outta here on the Thursday before the wedding, I figured I might never come back. I was so mad at Drum I coulda knocked his head off. But I didn't know whether to be mad at Katie and just say good riddance to the both of them, or if I oughta come back and just grab her away from him and tell her she was gonna marry me. I tell ya, I didn't know what to do. I was just all mixed up inside! And so when I rode up and saw that the wedding was going on, I don't even remember *what* I said or did!"

Then I finished the article like this:

> So now Mrs. Belle, still known to all her friends simply as "Katie," has found a new life as a full-fledged Californian. Like all Californians, she came from someplace else, but now calls this her home. Her seven-month-old son will be a Californian born and bred, one of the first in a new generation of Californians who will carry the hardy breed of pioneers— from Virginia and every other state of the union—into the future of this western region of these United States.
>
> When Katie looks out her window, if she lets her eyes go to the edge of the pine wood, she will see a thin apple tree, still too young to bear fruit, but a growing reminder of where she has come from. At its base, a different variety of grass and moss than can be seen anywhere in the surrounding woods is growing—also a reminder that this is a big land, and that its people have roots that stretch far away.
>
> One day Katie's young son will eat apples from that very tree, Virginia apples, and Katie will be able to tell him the story of how its seeds ventured to a new and strange place called California, and put down roots and began to grow, in the same way that his own mother did.

The "hardy breed of pioneers" and the "venturing to a new and strange place called California" and "roots that stretch far away" were all Mr. Kemble's words. But the ideas, even at the end were my ideas, and he just helped me to say it better.

Having this article published surprised me, especially since most of the things I'd written had been sent right back to me. But Mr. Kemble was real interested in this one. He sent me

$3.00 for it—the first time since the blizzard article that I'd gotten any money. And afterward, about a week after the story had come out in the paper (we sent for ten copies! Katie had lots of folks back east she wanted to send them to), a letter came to me from the *Alta*. I hadn't sent anything else to them and couldn't imagine what it was. But when I read the letter, the tears that came to my eyes were not tears of disappointment like the last time the editor had written to me.

Mr. C.B. Hollister
Miracle Springs, California
Dear Mr. Hollister,

Your recent article "Virginian Finds New Home," etc., has been very well received, both by the staff and the readership of the *Alta*. I must say, your writing has improved very much since your first story with us, "Blizzard Rescue on Buck Mountain."

As I read those words I couldn't help thinking of what he'd said when he sent back the Alkali Jones story about finding gold in the creek. I wondered if he remembered. I read on—

I would be interested in seeing other such pieces in the future. There have already been two inquiries as to when the next piece by C.B. Hollister is going to appear. I hope to hear from you soon.

Sincerely,
Edward Kemble,
Editor, California *Alta*

I sat down and handed the letter to Almeda. She read it.

"There, you see," she said. "You never know what can happen if you believe in yourself and just keep moving in the direction you think God wants you to go."

*And if you practice your writing a lot,* I thought, *and don't mind getting most of your things sent back to you!*

But in an instant this one brief letter seemed to make the earlier disappointments all forgotten.

# CHAPTER 14

## I WRITE TO MR. KEMBLE

I took the letter from Mr. Kemble not just as an encouragement but also as an opportunity.

There was that determination in my Belle blood coming out again! But I figured I ought to make the most of the fact that he'd written and seemed interested.

So I decided to write back and ask him some questions so I'd be able to know what to do differently in the future. I had thought the story about Alkali Jones was good, and hadn't expected anybody to pay much attention to what I'd written about Katie. As it turned out, my figuring was exactly opposite from Mr. Kemble's. Not only that, two months after his letter, *another* letter came, telling me that a paper from Raleigh, Virginia, had written to ask permission from the *Alta* to reprint the Katie story! The name C.B. Hollister was going to be read clear back on the East Coast!

I wrote to Mr. Kemble and asked him just what it was about the "Virginian" article that his paper liked and wanted more of.

About three weeks later I got a reply.

"There're two kinds of stories," he told me. "First, there's straight news reporting. That's when you've got to tell your *who, what, where, when, and why.* Those are your *w's,* and no reporter better forget them for a second.

"But then you've got your human interest kind of stories. They're more personal. The *who* and the *why* are still important, but you're telling about people instead of just facts, so the other things aren't quite so important.

"Now, you take your 'Virginian' story. That was human interest if ever I saw such a thing. Once you got folks interested in your Katie Morgan, they kept reading. They weren't trying to find out news or facts; they were reading because you were telling a story about a *person*.

"I've got lots of reporters who can give me the five *w*'s. One rambunctious kid on my staff chases around this city night and day and is the first person on the scene of anything that happens. Now *he's* a newshound!

"I'm not saying that if you brought me some noteworthy news like that I wouldn't print it. Maybe I would. But from the two stories of yours we've run so far, something tells me your talent tends more toward the human interest side. You seem to see interesting things in people. And if you can keep doing that, keep finding interesting people and keep finding interesting ways to tell folks about them, then I don't doubt you might just have a future in this business. Leave the five *w*'s to the newshounds like that Irish kid on my staff I was telling you about. Stick to the personal angles, Hollister, and let me see anything you come up with."

He didn't say it in that same letter, but much later when he and I were talking about similar things, he said some other things along this line.

"Women and men are different in how they read a paper," he told me. "Now we've got more men than women in California, but we still have thousands of women readers, and we've got to please them, too.

"Men want to know news and not much else. They're your five *w*'s readers. Give them what happened, where, when, and why and they'll put the paper down and get on with what they got to do. Men want to know whether it's likely to rain, what kind of damage the flood caused, what price gold is fetching, whether there've been any new strikes, and how much a new pick or a fifty-pound sack of beans is going to cost.

"But a woman'll look through the paper while she's drinking her tea, and she'll want to read about Polly Pinswiggle's garden that the rain washed out. That woman reading about Polly doesn't care a hoot about how many inches it rained or about what the seed is going to cost to plant a new garden. All she's thinking about is poor Polly!

"The women are your people readers. And that's why we've got people like you writing human interest stuff. You've got to go out and find interesting people who are involved in interesting things and then write about them, mixing in a little news too, and getting three or four of the *w's* in there to please your traditional men-editors like me.

"In other words, you've got to sort of *pretend* to be a reporter, a newsperson. But really you're not. What you are is a journalist, a writer about people, not facts. And as long as you keep writing about people, you can count on having readers, whether you ever dig up any hard news or not."

All this he didn't tell me, as I said, until later. But even now, without realizing it, I think this was the way my interest in writing was heading. I'd been keeping a journal all this time, not just to record the facts of my life, like where I went and what I did and what the weather was like—what Mr. Kemble would have called the five *w's*. I kept a journal to write about a person—a person who happened to be *me*—and what she was thinking and feeling inside.

In a way, the other writing that I was starting to do now— about Mr. Jones and Katie and the Wards and Jack Lame Pony—was kind of like the writing I did in my journal, but about other people instead of me.

Having Mr. Kemble tell me about the two different kinds of writing helped me understand it a lot better. But besides the five *w's* and the human interest kind of story, there was one other ingredient that I came to see was an important part of *any* writing that anybody did. Maybe it was the most important ingredient of all.

And I have Rev. Rutledge to thank for putting this other factor in focus for me.

# CHAPTER 15

# A SERMON ABOUT TRUTH

One Sunday morning Rev. Rutledge preached about *truth*. Nothing he said had that much to do with writing, I suppose, but I found myself listening carefully, trying to understand everything and applying it to my own life.

"Truth means different things to different people," he was saying. "To some people truth means a set of *ideas*. Therefore, if we were talking about five statements, we might ask which of them were true:

"The sky is blue and the sun is shining today.

"California is smaller in size than New York.

"It is raining outside.

"There is no gold in Miracle Springs Creek.

"This building is used for a church and a school."

He paused a minute and let the words sink in, and then repeated the five statements.

"Now then," he went on, "which of those are *true* and which are false? We can look outside and see the sunshine and the blue above, so we know that it is *not* raining. How about New York and California—which is larger? Any of you youngsters of Miss Stansberry's school know the answer?"

Someone piped up that California was the second biggest state behind Texas.

"Right," said the minister. "So saying California is smaller than New York is a *false* statement. How about the gold? *Is* there gold in the creek?"

112

Some laughter spread through the room.

"Depends on who you ask, Reverend!" called out one of the miners whose claim was known not to be doing so well.

More laughter followed.

Rev. Rutledge joined in the laughter. "However, I think we would all agree that there is *some* gold still around," he said, then added, "even though it might be unevenly distributed!"

He let the chuckling gradually die away before he went on. "Then, finally, is this building used for both a church and a school?"

"Yes!" went up a chorus of young voices, enjoying being able to participate during the sermon time for a change.

"Right you are again!" said Rev. Rutledge. "Now, think back to the five statements. How many were true, and how many were false? Let me repeat them for you."

He did so. Then he waited a minute.

"All right, now—how many statements were true?"

"Two," answered someone.

"Are you all agreed? Two true, three false?" said Rev. Rutledge.

A nodding of heads and general murmur went around.

Again he waited until everyone had quieted down. When he finally started speaking again his tone was different and he was more serious.

"I must confess that I tried to trick you," he said finally. "I hope you will forgive me, but I wanted to get across a point that many people misunderstand. Now—let me answer my own question. How many *true* statements were there? My answer is . . . *none*."

He waited to let the word sink in. I don't think anyone in the whole church understood what he meant, but we were all listening for what would come next.

"Two statements were *correct*—two statements of fact; three statements were *incorrect*—three statements of *error*. But my point this morning is that *truth* is a very different thing from correct 'facts.' That's why I said in the beginning that to most people truth has to do with the factual correctness of a set of ideas. But in reality, as the word *truth* is used in the Bible, it means something very different."

He stopped, opened up his Bible, then went on. "Let me read to you what the Bible calls truth. In John, Jesus says, 'I am the truth.' He doesn't say that such-and-such an idea, or a certain set of statements or facts are the truth, he says that *he* is the truth.

"Do you remember when I said that truth means different things to different people? Let me show you two people in the Bible to whom truth meant completely different things. In the eighteenth chapter of John, after Jesus had told his disciples that *he* was the truth, Jesus stands trial before Pilate, and he again brings up the subject of truth. Jesus says to him, 'Every one that is of the truth hears my voice.' And then Pilate asks one of the most profound questions in all of the Bible. He says to Jesus, 'What is truth?'—the very question we're examining this morning.

"Can you get a picture of these two people in your minds— Pilate and Jesus—both talking about truth?

"But they mean very different things by the word. When Pilate asks 'What is truth?' he is asking for a set of ideas, facts, opinions—just like the list of statements we talked about. Pilate wants Jesus to tell him what facts and ideas comprise what he calls 'truth.' But Jesus gives him no answer. Jesus says nothing. Why doesn't Jesus answer him?"

Rev. Rutledge paused a moment.

"Jesus doesn't answer him because truth is not at all what Pilate thinks it is. There are no *ideas* that would make up what Pilate calls truth. Not even any religious ones.

"What is the truth, Pilate wants to know. Jesus *himself* is the truth, and he is standing right in front of Pilate. Pilate *has* the truth but doesn't know it!

"In other words, the truth is a *person*, but Pilate wants mere *ideas*. And even true ideas, even correct facts, are not the truth. 'The sky is blue today' is a correct statement of fact. But it is not a truth. Only a *person* can be true."

Rev. Rutledge stopped again, and took in a deep breath. I

was concentrating hard to understand what he was saying.

"I hope I've made myself clear," he said, "about the difference between truths and facts, and about the contrast between Jesus and Pilate. I know I've gone on a long time, but there's one more very important point I must make. If I don't say this one last thing, then my whole sermon may mean nothing to you. My whole sermon could amount to nothing more than just a nice set of 'ideas' that I have given you, without there being any *truth* in it.

"So, here is my final point: Jesus is not the only person who can be of the truth. So can you and I!"

Again he stopped to let his words sink in.

"Jesus said that everyone who is *of* the truth hears his voice. In other words, Jesus is *the* truth, but others—people like you and me, people who hear his voice and obey him—we can be *of* the truth. Jesus is the first truth, but we can be *of* the truth if we follow him and do as he did."

As I pondered Rev. Rutledge's words afterward, what he said next was the thing that stood out most in my mind. "Truth is people and how they live. If we want to *be* of the truth, like Jesus said, it's in how we live and what we do, not in what we think about ideas and facts. Someone sitting right here this morning—one of you in this church building—may have been mistaken in all five of those statements I gave. You might have missed every one. Yet you might be more an of-the-truth person than another one sitting here who got every answer correct— if that person with all the wrong answers went out and *lived* the truth by what kind of person he was—lived following Jesus' example.

"Was Pilate a true man?

"After asking 'What is truth?' what did he do? Knowing Jesus was innocent, knowing the charges against him were lies, and even admitting that he could find nothing wrong in him— knowing all this, Pilate still gave Jesus over to the Jews to be crucified. Pilate may have wondered what truth was, but he was not a 'true' man. He did not stand up for what he knew to be right. He was weak. He was not *of* the truth."

The minister paused again, took a breath as he closed his Bible, and went on.

"Truth is not ideas, not even religious ideas, not even Christian ideas, not even correct ideas. Truth is *life*, not thoughts. Truth is a person. That person is Jesus. And he wants us to be *of* the same truth as he is—by how we live.

"As Christians we are to be *true people*. Jesus was of the truth. Pilate was not. Jesus *is* the truth. Pilate wanted ideas, but was not a strong enough person to *live* truthfully.

"Each of us has to make the choice which of these two men we are going to be like. How are we going to live? By the truth or not? Who is going to be our example? Are we going to *live* truth, or only think and talk about it?"

# CHAPTER 16

## A TALK ABOUT GROWTH

It probably seems like I was forever taking walks and thinking and writing in my journal about what was going on in my mind.

But I did also try to write down things I was doing—however, the most important thing about life to me was what was going on inside me. Maybe it isn't this way for everyone, but I liked to try to figure out the meanings behind things. When I read a book, I think about what the author said, and I like to read for the ideas as much as the story. I reckon that's why I liked Mr. Thoreau so much. There was hardly *any* story in *Walden* but it was full of ideas that made me think.

Maybe that's why I wanted to be a writer, so I could think on paper, and so I could get to know other people and find out what they were thinking and write down their ideas for others to get to know too.

Ever since I began keeping my journal and started learning more about what it really meant to live as a Christian, something inside me wanted to grow, to learn, to stretch and think and explore and be more than I was. I wanted the inside part of me to get bigger so it could hold more. Thinking and talking to God and reading and writing down my thoughts and feelings in my journal were all ways to stretch and enlarge that deep-down part of me and make it grow.

Almeda and I talked once about growth. I told her this feeling I had inside about wanting to stretch that inside part of

117

me, and to be more than I was.

She thought for a long time, and then said that she felt the process of growth inside each person's heart and mind was one of the greatest gifts God has given to us.

"There is nothing in all the world," she said, "quite so wonderful as an individual soul expanding, reaching out, coming awake to itself, to its Maker, to other souls around it. The awakening of the soul, then its growth and development, then its reaching out to touch other souls that are similarly growing along the same journey—there is hardly anything in all of life so wonderful."

Her voice became quiet and her eyes misted over.

"Like you and me?" I suggested.

"I think so, Corrie," she replied in a soft tone. "I truly think so."

"What makes some people want to grow like that, and others content just to stay where they are?" I asked.

"That's a huge question, Corrie! Who could possibly know the answer to that?" she laughed.

"Is it because some people are made to be thinkers?"

"People like you, I take it you mean?"

Now it was my turn to laugh. "You know what I mean," I said. "Not everybody keeps journals and thinks about everything like I do."

"Maybe people should think more."

"But I figured God made some folks to be thinkers and others not to be. Isn't everyone different?"

"That's true. But I have the feeling God wants *everybody* to think, though maybe in different ways and to different degrees. It has nothing to do with being smart, but with using the brain you do have. The book of Proverbs, the whole of Scripture really, is full of urgings and promptings to learn and understand. One of my favorites is 'Apply your heart to understand, incline your ear to wisdom.' That sounds to me as if God meant for every person in the world to try diligently to understand things, and to get wisdom. It also says to *seek* for wisdom like silver, and to *search* for it like hidden treasures. That sounds to me like we're supposed to think!"

"It sure doesn't seem as if everybody thinks like that. Or at least they don't talk about it so you'd know."

"Most people don't think, Corrie, not like God wants them to. They aren't searching for wisdom and applying themselves to understand, and that's why not even very many people who call themselves Christians are growing as they could be."

"You mean you can't grow if you're not thinking about everything?"

"No, that's not it exactly." She paused and thought for a little bit. "Let me try to explain it another way," she said finally. "To grow, I would say—yes, you *do* have to apply yourself to understand, and you have to search and pray for wisdom, just like the Bible says. Both those things imply not only prayer but also a lot of thought. And if you're *not* doing those things, your thinking and growth and wisdom muscles, so to speak, are going to lose their power to think and grow. If you don't use a muscle, it gets weak. In the same way, if you don't think and make an effort to grow and, as Proverbs says, *apply* yourself to understand, then pretty soon you won't be able to, and you will stop growing. You become capable of thinking by thinking. You become capable of growing by growing. And thus you grow as a Christian . . . by growing. And certainly thinking and praying and searching for wisdom are all part of that process.

"But growth isn't *only* a matter of thinking—most important of all is the *doing* that goes along with the thinking. Thinking all by itself won't stretch that inside part of you. It won't make you bigger inside, won't draw you closer to God, won't make you *more* than you are now, as you said. The real growth comes *after* the thinking, when you *live* what you've been thinking about. The growth comes when we *do* what God wants us to.

"In other words, Corrie, it's a process that has two parts. First we have to try to understand, we have to search and pray for wisdom. But then after that, as the second part, we have to *live* out what our understanding has shown us. We have to *do* what Jesus says. We have to put others first, we have to be kind and do good, speak pleasantly and behave with courtesy and trust God and pray, and do all those things Jesus told us to do. That's the active part of getting understanding and wisdom.

"There's the thinking part and the doing part. And growth only happens when *both* are at work in your life together. That's how the inside part of you, the *real* you down in your heart, will stretch and grow, and will always be becoming more than it was the day before."

# CHAPTER 17

## A WALK IN THE WOODS

After the church service, I needed time alone to try to understand Rev. Rutledge's sermon more clearly. I had a feeling God might have more meaning for me in his words than I could know just from sitting in the church. I had to think about it some more.

So I told Pa and the others to go on ahead home without me. I'd walk back in a while. Then I went out into the woods behind the church, the same woods where Becky'd gotten lost. On the way as I walked, the conversation I'd had with Almeda about growth came back to me, and I found both her words and those of the minister mingling in my mind, trying to sort themselves out.

As all of it was tumbling through my mind—living truth instead of just thinking about it, growth, understanding, wisdom, the thinking kind of person I was, everything Almeda had said about growth and doing and Proverbs—it came to me how important all of it was if I was going to be a writer.

You couldn't even write the five *w's* without being able to think and understand things, I thought to myself, because one of them was *why*. So if you were going to write, you'd *have* to think and understand!

Then I found myself thinking, not just about the kinds of writing that Mr. Kemble had talked about, but about *why* I wanted to write in the first place. At first it had just started with journal writing. I had only needed to express myself, to think out loud.

But now I realized there was more to it. I still liked to think on paper—whether in my journal or in something I was trying to write. But now that I thought about it in light of Rev. Rutledge's and Almeda's words, I found myself realizing that I wanted my writing to amount to something more than *just* writing. I wanted it to *mean* something, even though I'd never really stopped to think about it before.

Then I found myself reflecting back on that early morning walk I had taken just before the blizzard began, when God had shown me so many things and when I had prayed about my future. I recalled how on that day I had thought about the *truth* too, and had felt God telling me to find the truth and to follow it and live by it and be fed by it. The scripture I had thought about that morning came vividly back to me: *In truth shall you be fed, and so shall you dwell in the land.*

Suddenly it all made so much more sense!

The truth was so much bigger than just giving a factual account of the five *w's*. Anybody could do that. That was the Pontius Pilate side, the facts, the statements, the lists of ideas that might be half correct and half wrong. That might be "reporting," but that wasn't what I wanted to spend *my* life doing.

I wanted to *grow*—in understanding, in wisdom . . . in truth.

And I wanted my writing to be true. Not just with correct facts, with the five *w's*—though that might be part of it too. But true like Rev. Rutledge talked about truth—true to the kind of person I was, true to the Bible, true to the man who *was* truth—Jesus, God's Son. I wanted my writing to point to the truth, to be *of* the truth. I wanted it to make people think and help them to grow. Even if I was writing a story about something other than Jesus, who was the truth, I wanted how I said it to make people think in a true way, not a Pontius Pilate sort of way. I wanted people like Katie, who didn't believe in spiritual things, to read my writing and think in a little more of a true way. Katie herself had said, after my article about her, that she could never think about the apple tree in quite the same way after reading what I wrote. Well, maybe if I could get her thinking about apple trees and people and roots in a true way, someday that might lead her to think about God in a more true way too.

That's what I wanted my writing to be able to do, even when I was writing about something that didn't have anything to do with God on the surface.

I remembered the verse Rev. Rutledge had quoted in church just a little while ago, the words Jesus had said: "Everyone that is of the truth hears my voice."

"Help me, God, to hear your voice," I prayed. "I want to hear your voice so that I can grow and understand. I want to hear your voice so I will know your wisdom, and so that what I write will be true."

I was deep in the woods now, the church and all the buildings of the town long out of sight.

I stopped and dropped to my knees among the decaying leaves and dead pine needles of the forest floor. I clasped my hands and closed my eyes.

"Oh, Lord," I prayed aloud, "make *me* a true person! When I hear your voice, give me strength to do what you say. Give me your wisdom and your understanding. Be the guide to my thoughts, God, and then help me to *do* what you want me to. Make my life be a true life, so that my writing will be *of* the truth."

I drew in a deep sigh, and my nostrils filled with the fragrance of the forest. It was such a lovely smell, and I couldn't help thinking right in that moment that God had made it only for me. It reminded me all over again how much he loved me.

*Me*—just me! The God of the universe loved little me, Corrie Belle Hollister!

Almeda had been telling me that simple truth for three years, and now I really grasped it on my own. Now maybe it was my turn to find ways to begin telling *other* people the same thing, as she had told me.

I stood and turned around and began retracing my steps out of the woods. Everywhere I looked were the signs of growth, from the fresh buds on the tips of the pine branches to the shrubs and undergrowth of the forest. Overhead the early afternoon sun poured through in tiny rays split into millions of arrows by the infinite, green needles on the trees.

I had always loved the woods, the mountains, the streams, the sky, the clouds. Yet the older I grew the more alive it all became to me. Every time I went out alone something new revealed itself to my consciousness. This was not the first time I had walked in this pine wood. But I think it was dearer to me on this day than it had ever been before. The mystery of its loveliness was somehow almost sacred. From the church building that the men of Miracle Springs had built, I had stepped into God's presence itself—into his greater, living church. All about me were signs and reflections of God himself, things he had made.

And as I left the wood that afternoon I found myself wondering about the *truth* contained in the trees and the bushes and the grass, even the truth of the blue sky and the sunshine and the smells I so enjoyed. Were all these things "true," as a man or woman might also be "true," because they came out of God, and reflected part of his nature?

That was far too big a question for my mind! I thought about it all the way home, and was no nearer to figuring it out than when I left town.

# CHAPTER 18

## NEW TIMES COME TO MIRACLE SPRINGS

By the time I got back to the claim, the afternoon was half gone and it was snowing again. Not real snow—it was toward the end of May, and though snow that late wouldn't have been out of the question higher up in the mountains, down in the foothills where we lived it would have been close to impossible.

A storyteller might call it snowing "figuratively." Sometimes a writer says something that has more than one meaning, like the apple tree when I was telling about Katie. So when I say it was snowing, I mean that God had already begun to answer my prayers again, my prayers about wanting to be true and to write in a true way. Like the last time, when it was *really* snowing, I didn't recognize the things that happened as God's little answering snowflakes coming down into my life.

The invisible snowflakes of answered prayer are falling down all around, millions of them. But it takes a special kind of sight to see them, and most folks never know that kind of snow's falling. You have to learn to hunt for them, learn to see them, train your eyes—your *inner* eyes, the eyes that look out of your heart and your mind. Just about everything having to do with God and the spiritual side of life is like that—they're things you have to train yourself to see.

And so I've been trying to train myself to look for buried, hidden, *invisible* things the more I grow as a Christian—the hidden meanings that are all around us, the invisible little glimpses of God that most folks don't notice.

When I got back to the house, there sat Rev. Rutledge's buggy out in front. I didn't think anything much about it until I went inside. Everyone was sitting there all quiet and talking in low tones. The reason the minister'd come was to tell us that our mayor, Mr. Vaissade, had just died, and the pastor was making the rounds to tell as many people as he knew would be interested.

Mr. Vaissade was an older man, and I don't suppose his death was all that much of a shock. But he had been in church with us just three or four hours earlier, and now suddenly was dead. He'd collapsed right on his own front porch after walking back to town from church, and was found lying there by a neighbor an hour later.

Although we all liked Mr. Vaissade, we weren't close friends, so his passing away like he did wasn't in itself an event that changed everything for me or for our family. But it turned out to have a huge effect on the future of the town, and an even bigger effect on our family.

Mr. Vaissade had been mayor of Miracle Springs for a year and a half. I don't think during all that time I heard of one thing in particular that his mayoring had done or changed. He just *was* the mayor, and everybody went on about their business as usual. Maybe he had to sign papers or something, but I never heard anything about it, and didn't really see what difference having a mayor made to Miracle Springs.

But folks had gotten kind of used to the idea of having a mayor, and almost immediately talk began to stir up about who was going to replace him. Miracle was a respectable town now. Including all the folks round about in the foothills and farms and ranches for several miles around town, there were fifteen hundred or two thousand people, and the area was growing back into the kind of size it'd boasted right after the first gold strikes. No town of the importance of Miracle Springs, they said, could be without a mayor. And in addition, political fever was in the air that summer of 1856 after Mr. Vaissade's death.

California had changed so much, even in the four years we

had been there. *We* were by now among the old-timers, the early settlers in the West. For the first several years, just about everybody coming to California from out East was coming because of the gold. Right at first it was the gold miners themselves, then later the people like the Parrishes and others—businessmen and suppliers and merchants and others who hoped to make a living *because of* the gold rush, though they may not have been directly involved themselves.

But by now, people were pouring into the West to settle it and live here, just because there was space and freedom and adventure, and because they heard the land was good. Schools and churches were being built all over the state, and thousands of families were putting down roots. Farmers were turning the valleys into land that produced food. Cities and towns were growing. Railroads joined the different parts of California, and there was even talk of a railroad someday to hook up California with the rest of the states back East.

California wasn't the only place that was growing. People were coming west—the *whole* west. California'd been made a state in 1850, and by this time there was lots of talk that Oregon would be the next new state. Settlers were coming across the Oregon Trail by the thousands.

It wasn't only because of all the new people coming west that folks were more interested in politics that year. In the only other election since California'd been in the union, statehood had been so fresh and the gold rush so much on people's minds that folks just didn't pay that much attention. After all, Washington, D.C. was thousands of miles away, and Californians didn't figure it made much difference whether they voted for Franklin Pierce from New Hampshire or General Winfield Scott.

But now in 1856, everything was different!

A new political party, the Republicans, had been formed only a couple of years earlier. The issue of slavery, though not really involving California too much, was still talked about, because the new party was more or less based on anti-slavery. I suppose Californians were interested in the Republican party too because one of the state's most well-known men, John Charles Fremont, was one of the leaders in getting it established. Fremont was rich from the gold that had been discovered on his huge estate. He had been one of the first explorers to California, had fought the Mexicans, and was one of the first new senators in 1850 right after California became a state. All in all, John Fremont was the most famous Californian there was.

And now, for the presidential election of 1856, the new Republican party had chosen John Fremont as their nominee.

That made all of California stand up and take notice of national politics. Now it made a big difference who people voted for—James Buchanan from far-away Pennsylvania, or John Fremont *from California*! We may have been the newest of the Union's thirty-one states, but all of a sudden we were one of the most important.

"Why, just think of it," everyone was saying, "a Californian in the White House!" That election of 1856 was just about the biggest thing to hit California since the discovery of gold!

John Fremont was one of those kinds of men that not everyone liked. When people talked about the election, lots of folks like Alkali Jones didn't have that much nice to say about him. But one thing was for sure—he was *our* John Fremont . . . from *our* own state! And folks figured that made him worth voting for no matter what else they thought.

So politics and John Fremont and Washington, D.C., and slavery and Republicans and Democrats were all topics in the air and on people's minds and lips that summer.

And as part of all that, and maybe because of it, almost immediately after Mr. Vaissade's death, folks started saying Miracle Springs needed to have an election for mayor.

# CHAPTER 19

# THE CANDIDATE

An election for mayor in a little town like Miracle Springs may not sound like a big event, especially with an important presidential election going on at the same time. But around the Hollister-Belle claims, the minute Franklin Royce announced that he intended to run for mayor, all discussion about Buchanan and Fremont faded completely into the background. The Miracle Springs mayor's election was all at once the only election anyone cared about!

"I told ya afore, an' I ain't changed my mind none since," said Alkali Jones. "The man's a polecat!"

"A snake!" put in Uncle Nick.

They were sitting around the table in our house talking about Royce and the election. Alkali Jones' high laughter had ceased. The men didn't seem to know whether to be angry or miserable over the turn of events. So they wound up being a little of both.

"You talked t' Rafferty again, Drum?" asked Mr. Jones.

"I've talked to him half a dozen times," Pa answered, "and so has every other man in town. But he says he's got all he can do as sheriff, and he don't want to be mayor too. None of us can convince him."

"Ol' Vaissade didn't do nuthin'. What makes Rafferty think he can't jest combine the mayorin' an' the sheriffin'?"

"He says the town's growing, and needs both a mayor and a sheriff."

"Well, one thing's for sure," added Uncle Nick. "The mayor's job won't be a do-nothing job no more with Royce in it."

"Simon says he can keep him from doing any mischief," said Pa. "That's another reason he doesn't seem too worried."

"What harm *could* he do?" asked Katie, who had been listening from the other side of the room, where she and Almeda were sitting. "After all, he's still got his bank to manage."

Pa turned his head, then gave a shrug in answer. "Who knows? But if you give a man like Royce a chance, he'll find *some* way to turn it to his advantage, and I reckon that's what has the rest of us worried. Especially if we just let him have the job for the taking."

"I'll tell you what he could do," said Almeda. "Once a man like that's in power, he can do all kinds of things. I've seen it happen in other towns. There's been corruption in the governments of Sacramento and San Francisco, and any time you have money involved in political decisions it can be dangerous. As mayor *and* the town's only banker, Franklin Royce could control this town. He could bring in his own people and set up a town council. He could control decisions that were made. He could levy taxes, commission building projects, change laws. He already dictates how the money in this community flows. He could put Parrish Mine and Freight Company out of business if he wanted to. What if, as mayor, he wanted to get rid of Simon Rafferty as sheriff and appoint one of his own men? I'm sure he could find a way to manage it. Before we knew it, warrants on Drum and Nick would start to appear from the East. I tell you, the possibilities are frightening. I don't trust Royce, even though I'm forced to do business with him."

"But the mayor's never had that kind of power. Vaissade couldn't have gotten rid of Simon if he'd wanted to."

"Power has a way of sneaking up on you if you put it into the wrong hands. Once you start something, it's sometimes impossible to undo it. I for one would feel a lot more comfortable if the door were not opened in the first place."

Uncle Nick now spoke up again. "He's always wanted this land of ours," he said.

"An' every other piece he could git his slimy white hands on," Jones added.

"Then, why doesn't one of the other men in town run against him?" asked Katie.

"No one wants to," replied Pa. "Bosely, Simon, Lewis, Miller, Griffin—me and Nick and Rutledge, we talked to all of them. I even tried to get Avery to consider it, but he keeps saying religion and politics don't mix."

"Wouldn't do no good anyway," said Uncle Nick. "Royce would win, whatever anybody else tried to do. He holds mortgages and notes on eighty percent of the property in the whole area. Nobody's gonna cross him up when it could mean he'd call due what they owe him."

"But they could still vote against him," I suggested. "I can't see why everyone can't simply choose not to vote for him, or vote for nobody. "He'd never know."

"Economics, Corrie," said Almeda, looking over toward me. "Sad to say, money dictates power. If Royce doesn't win, he could call *everyone's* mortgages due. When they can't pay, he forecloses on whatever properties he wants, and winds up owning all the land for miles. Such a prospect might even be worse than calling him our mayor. Nobody *knows* whether he'd do that, but just the threat can be enough to frighten people into doing what a man like that wants. He wouldn't even have to say anything—a mere rumor circulating that foreclosures would result if he wasn't elected would probably be enough to insure his victory. That is *if* someone was running against him. As it is, he probably won't even have to go that far."

# CHAPTER 20

## THE TWO CAMPAIGNS

Mr. Royce continued to be unopposed in the election for Miracle Springs mayor, which was scheduled for November 4, the same day as the presidential voting between Fremont and Buchanan. He gave a couple of speeches in town in June, but nobody paid much attention since he was the only one running. And after that, he didn't do much else. About the only sign that would let a stranger know there was even an election going on was a banner in the window of the bank that said, "Royce for Mayor."

Nobody liked the idea of Franklin Royce being mayor of Miracle Springs, but gradually they got used to it and the hubbub and complaining slowly died out. Out in the open, no one really said much. I guess what Almeda said was true—they didn't want to get on Royce's bad side for fear of what would happen. Royce didn't have any "paper" against our claim (that's what Pa called it), but Parrish Mine and Freight still had business dealings with the bank, so we had to be careful like everyone else.

One other thing quieted down all the initial worries, something that was a surprise to everybody. Mr. Royce started making himself agreeable. He didn't give any more speeches, but he walked around town, smiling, shaking people's hands, visiting in the stores. He even came into the freight office a time or two for a minute, saying he was checking up on his customers, seeing how they were doing, wondering if there was any way the bank could be of service to them. He was so polite and friendly you almost couldn't help liking him!

The words "election" or "mayor" were never mentioned once. He never said a thing about asking people to vote for him. Of course, he didn't need to—there was no one else they *could* vote for!

Mr. Royce knew, I suppose, that folks were suspicious, not only of him but of bankers in general. And he probably knew that he wasn't the best liked man in Miracle Springs, and that people were nice to him only because they had to be since he was the banker.

That could hardly make a man feel too good about himself, knowing people had more fear than liking for him. I can't imagine anyone finding it pleasant inside to know that people were afraid of him. But I figured that Mr. Royce decided he'd rather have people liking him as mayor than being afraid of him, so he had vowed to himself to change his ways and be nice from now on. Rev. Rutledge talked sometimes about giving people what he called "the benefit of the doubt"—thinking the best of them. Maybe that's what I was trying to do with Mr. Royce.

When he'd come around, I'd watch his face real careful and look into his eyes to see if I could see the change. I like to watch people and try to imagine what they're thinking. But I couldn't see anything in Mr. Royce's face. His mouth had a nice smile on it when he talked, but there was just no way to tell what he was thinking. His eyes didn't seem to look exactly at you when he spoke. It was like he was looking just a little bit off to one side, and so the conversation back and forth was just a tiny bit crooked, though such a little bit that I doubt anyone else even noticed. I didn't talk to him much myself, only to answer when he'd come into the office and say "How are you today, Corrie?" before going on to talk a minute with Almeda or Mr. Ashton. So maybe that crookedness was just something I noticed that he didn't do with everyone else. But his eyes didn't sparkle, they just kind of looked past me.

I watched other people, too, as they talked to him. I was

real curious about this changed friendly Mr. Royce. Mr. Ashton seemed to be drawn into the banker's friendly smile, and their words back and forth were jovial and lighthearted. Almeda, however, always seemed to be looking into those dark gray eyes of Mr. Royce's as if she was trying to figure out the thoughts behind them too. She smiled and was very gracious, and their talk was polite. Her eyes didn't sparkle at such times either. Despite the smile on her lips, her eyes remained serious and seemed to be turning over more thoughts inside than her words let on.

Even Pa and Uncle Nick gradually started speaking more kindly about their future mayor.

"We may as well get used to him," said Pa one evening. "I never liked the man, an' I'd rather see someone else run. But we're stuck with him. He's gonna be the mayor and he's gonna be the banker, and it's for sure we don't want to be on the wrong side of *his* fence once he's *that* important."

"I reckon you're right," said Uncle Nick, "though I'll still feel a sight better once I get the $450 I owe him for lumber paid back. I don't like to be indebted to no man, least of all him. Politicians *and* bankers are both a mite too full of smiles to suit me!"

"I don't trust the varmint nohow!" put in Alkali Jones. "Jest like I don't trust ol' Fremont neither. Anyone what's been in California as long as me knows too much 'bout what Cap'n John's *really* like! I ain't gonna vote fer neither o' the skunks!"

"And a big difference *that's* gonna make, Alkali!" said Pa, laughing. "Fremont's gonna carry California so big they might as well take Buchanan off the ballot, and Royce don't need nobody's but his own vote to win."

"It's the preenciple o' the thing, I tell ya, an' I ain't gonna vote fer neither o' 'em!"

Pa chuckled to himself, but said nothing more.

"Well if *I* could vote," said Katie, who had been following the conversation with interest, "I would vote for anybody, just to have my say in what happens. You men are lucky, Alkali, to be able to vote. You shouldn't throw the chance away just because you don't like the candidates."

"Aw, but Drum's right. What blame difference is it gonna make anyhow who we votes fer, or even iffen we votes at all?"

"It's the American way, Alkali," said Pa, smiling, and giving his friend a poke in the ribs. "When you came out West it was just a wilderness. Now we're a state and our man's running for the White House, and we got our duty as citizens to do. Come on, Alkali, you got to get into the right spirit for this election!"

I couldn't tell at first how serious Pa was, but when I saw him throw Uncle Nick a quick wink, I knew. I think he meant the words but was using them to make Mr. Jones squirm a little.

When they'd get to talking about Mr. Royce, Pa was pretty kindly disposed toward him and seemed willing to forget about the past. Uncle Nick was more cautious, but not as critical as they had both once been, though he did say one time, "It's easy for you to forgive him, Drum. You don't owe him a dime. Why, you got four thousand dollars *in* his bank! But me, I gotta still worry some, till I get that house all paid for."

Pa only laughed. He'd worked hard in the mine these last two years, getting enough to add on to the house, and save money besides. Since they'd both got married, Pa and Uncle Nick had kept their earnings separate, and as much as Uncle Nick had settled down, he still wasn't half the worker Pa was. And Zack had by now begun to make a pretty big difference in the Hollister share of the output of the mine. I didn't know how Pa's and Almeda's money was being handled now that they were married—the Mine and Freight Company, that is. That's something they never talked about to me.

All through the conversation about Royce and Fremont and the elections, Almeda remained silent, although I don't think it had anything to do with the money. I could tell she was listening to every word and was *very* interested in what was being said—that much was plain from one look at her face. Just as clear was that she was thinking real hard. But what she was thinking about, she didn't let on so much as one little peep.

The weeks of summer went by. Royce kept up his pleasantness campaign. The leaves on a few of the birch trees started thinking about turning yellow. Both Mr. Singleton's *Gazette* and Mr. Kemble's *Alta* were full of the Fremont-Buchanan election, and there wasn't much room left for an aspiring girl-writer from a little foothills gold town. I hadn't seen anything of mine in either paper since May, though I kept writing. Mr. Kemble was still looking at two more articles I'd sent him— one called "Summer in the Foothills of Gold Country," and the other one of what he called his "human interest" stories about Miss Stansberry and the school, and especially about how she had learned to use her lameness as a strength instead of a weakness.

The Summer-in-the-Foothills one was mostly about the beauty of the countryside and how summer was such a special season. I had the idea out walking one day, watching Pa and Uncle Nick and Zack and Mr. Jones all working away in the stream and mine from where I was standing up on a hill behind the house. I had been thinking how much I loved the countryside God had made, and when I saw them laboring away after little pieces of gold, the realization came to me that the land itself was really the treasure, not the gold. The "real gold"— that's what I called it in the article—was the land and its people, not just the nuggets that they were digging out of the streams and rivers. Someday, I said, there might not be any gold left, but there would still be this wonderful land, and there would still be people to love and cherish the land, and that was more lasting than any riches any miner could ever dig out of even the wealthiest mine. So the article had one of those "double meanings," because I meant the word "gold" in the title to stand for the wealth of the land itself.

Anyway, I figured Mr. Kemble would be sending it back to me some time real soon. But I hoped the article on Miss Stansberry might get published. And in the meantime, the papers were full of editorials about the election and reprints from papers out East and articles about the slavery question and where the two presidential candidates stood on that and all kinds of issues. There were also other elections going on for California's senators and representatives in Washington. So much was happening so fast. Everything was growing. Sacramento had just been made the capital of all of California two years before in 1854. Now that we were so close to the center of politics, the elections for state offices had gotten everybody's attention too, and even a time or two men came through making speeches and telling everybody to vote for them, though half the time no one had ever heard of them.

# CHAPTER 21

## ALMEDA SURPRISES
## EVERYBODY!

One evening toward the latter part of July, Almeda was late coming home from town. I'd been home for some time. Supper was all ready, Pa had quit working and was cleaned up, but still she didn't come. Finally Pa said we should just go ahead and eat, though it wasn't like her to be so late. At first I think he might have been a trifle annoyed, but by eight o'clock, when she still wasn't home, he started to worry.

Finally Pa got to his feet. "I'm going into town," he said, "to find out where she is and if she's okay."

He walked out the door and toward the barn to saddle his horse. But not two or three minutes later, Almeda's little buggy came around the bend and up the road toward the house.

A moment or two passed before she and Pa came through the door together. From the look on Pa's face, she still hadn't told him what had caused her delay.

Without sitting down, she waited until everyone was quiet. We all had our eyes fixed on her, wondering what she was going to say. Her face was serious but bright, and it was obvious something was brewing inside her head that she was dying to tell us all about.

"I'm sorry to be so late," she said. "I didn't expect this, but as I got ready to come home, suddenly a great . . . a great sense . . . of God speaking to me began to come over me and I knew I had to be alone for a while. As it turns out, I've been thinking, praying, and crying for over two hours! But now . . . I believe I know at last what he's been trying to tell me."

She stopped and took a deep breath. Then she got a big smile on her face, and was clearly excited about what she had to say.

"I've reached a decision," she said. "Hopefully with God's help—"

She paused again, then announced:

"I've decided to run against Royce . . . for mayor!"

Silence fell like a heavy cloud throughout the house. No one said anything. Everyone was too shocked.

Becky was the first to break the silence by bolting past Almeda and through the door.

"Where ya going?" called Pa after her.

"To tell Uncle Nick and Aunt Katie!" shouted Becky back at him, already halfway to the bridge over the stream.

That was all Pa said for a while. He was real quiet, and from the look of expectation on Almeda's face I could tell she was waiting for him to say something.

"Well, if that don't beat all," he finally said. "You are a lady full of surprises, I'll say that for you."

Almeda laughed, and finally sat down, showing some relief. I brought a plate and set it down in front of her at the table.

Pa didn't say anything more, just sat there thinking about this turn of events. From looking at him, I couldn't tell whether he approved or not. I guess it was quite a thing for a man to get used to, his wife saying she was going to run for politics. It wasn't the kind of thing women did, or that men usually approved of!

I decided to break the silence myself. "What makes you think you can do it?" I asked. "If a woman can't vote, I wouldn't think they'd let you *run* for an office."

"Well, women *ought* to be able to vote," she replied, "and I intend to run whatever anyone thinks."

"Anyone . . . including me?" said Pa finally, looking over at her.

"Well, I . . ." Almeda hesitated. "I just thought, Drummond, that you'd be all for it. I've heard you say yourself you didn't like the thought of Royce as mayor."

"You're right, I don't. I reckon I just wish you'd said somethin' to me first, that's all."

"I'm sorry, Drummond," she said, genuinely surprised, as if she'd never thought about talking to Pa ahead of time. "If you'd rather—"

"No, no," interrupted Pa. "I ain't gonna stand in your way."

Then he tried to lighten the tension some by letting out a laugh. "Who knows, maybe I'll like the notion of bein' known as the mayor's husband! But what about Royce?" he asked, serious again. "He ain't gonna like this one bit!"

"Franklin Royce can think what he will. If he calls my notes due, I'll borrow the money from *you*! I don't owe him more than a couple thousand dollars."

Pa laughed again. "Well, you're determined enough," he said, sounding as if he was getting gradually used to the idea. "I reckon I'll give you my vote. But since women can't vote, and men being what they are, I can't see how you'll get many more."

"What about everything you and Nick have been saying about none of the men around caring for Royce?"

"That was before. Now that he's changed, I ain't so sure most of the men wouldn't still prefer him to voting for a woman."

"Are *you* prejudiced against the idea?" asked Almeda, still wondering what Pa thought.

"I'm just tellin' you how folks'll see it, and you know as well as I do how men are about women doing 'men's work.' "

Almeda sent a glance in my direction, as if to remind me of the conversations we had about that very same thing.

"We'll see," she said. "I'm not so sure Royce has changed as much as everyone thinks. I have a feeling he's just as conniving as ever, and if folks have a choice in the election . . . well, we'll have to wait and see. I just think they ought to have a choice."

In a few minutes Katie and Uncle Nick, led by Becky, came in. Uncle Nick was carrying fourteen-month-old Erich, but set him down as soon as they were inside. He'd been walking about three or four weeks, and now he went toddling about while Becky and Tad tried to keep up with him. Still sitting at the table, Almeda did her best to eat some supper and answer everyone's questions. Her surprise announcement caused an uproar in the house. No one knew what to think, but everybody had plenty to say in response!

"I think it's exciting!" said Katie over and over. "If I'd thought of it myself, why *I'd* have run!"

"Being the wife of this character," said Pa, tossing his head sideways toward Uncle Nick, "I wouldn't exactly have recommended you as qualified for the position."

"Why, Drummond, how dare you!" she said.

"I'm only saying," laughed Pa, "that Almeda here's got a reputation as a businesswoman that goes further back in Miracle Springs even than Royce's—when *did* he come to town, Almeda?"

"I think it was late '51 . . . maybe early '52."

"There, you see," continued Pa. "Parrish Mine and Freight has been doing business in town since '50." He stopped. "Hmm, now that I think about it, maybe you *can* put up a campaign against Royce."

"Sounds like a campaign slogan to me," said Katie. " 'Hollister for Mayor—Part of Miracle Springs from the Beginning!' "

"How about being my assistant, Katie?" said Almeda.

"No, no, no!" interjected Uncle Nick. "If a woman's gonna try to go up against a man, at least you gotta have a man runnin' it for ya."

"Are you suggesting, *Mister* Belle," said Katie, "that two women would not be able to do it?"

"*Three* women!" I added.

Katie and Almeda cheered and clapped to have me joining their debate. "Now we three outnumber you two!" said Katie. "Perhaps we should *vote* on who should be the campaign manager, right here and now!"

"Make it three against three!" chimed in Zack. "I'm sixteen. My say oughta count as much as Corrie's!"

"Now you're talking, son!" said Pa. "You just stand aside, Katie, and let us men figure out the best way to go about this thing!"

By now we were all laughing, including the kids, who had never seen a family squabble line up quite so definitely with the women against the men. It was sure good to see Pa entering into the spirit of it now, after his initial hesitation.

A lot more lively discussion followed throughout the evening. Despite all the suggestions the rest of us were free to give, the wisdom of the candidate prevailed when she said, "Perhaps the best idea is that we let this whole *committee* manage my campaign. What do you say—we six, three men, three women? That way we'll be able to give even voice to the concerns of the men *and* the women, the young *and* the old, the married *and* the unmarried, the business persons *and* the miners. We'll have our whole Miracle Springs constituency represented right on our 'Hollister for Mayor' committee—do you all agree?"

Everyone looked around at each other. What she said made sense.

"Maybe you *are* cut out to be a politician, Almeda," said Pa. "That sounds just like the kind of solution a mayor oughta be able to figure out—with a little speechmaking thrown in!"

We laughed.

"And the first thing for the committee to get busy on," she said, "is publicity. That, I think, would be your department, Corrie," she added, turning toward me.

The result could be seen the next afternoon in the window of the Parrish Mine and Freight Company, with a hand-lettered poster where the words *Vote Almeda Hollister for Mayor of Miracle Springs* suddenly declared to the whole town that the poster in the bank's window wasn't the only political message to be heard anymore.

This election had now become a two man—that is, a two-*person*—race!

It took only the rest of that day and half of the next morning for the poster to be seen and for word to begin to get around. But when it did, the news spread like a brushfire in a hot wind. Before the week was out there wasn't *anything* in the mouths of people for miles around other than what they thought of Almeda going up against Franklin Royce. Some folks thought it was ridiculous. Others said privately they would vote for her if they could, but they just couldn't afford to rile Royce. A lot of the men said women ought to stay where they belonged and keep out of politics. Of course, all the women admired Almeda and loved the idea, but none of them could vote. And most of the men, whether they liked the idea or not, said she had guts to try it, although some added it would probably ruin her business in the end. Royce wasn't the kind of man you got on the wrong side of, they said.

All of a sudden, the Fremont-Buchanan election seemed far away and uninteresting!

# CHAPTER 22

# THE CAMPAIGN
# GETS STARTED

With the town all a buzz, there was still not much active
support for Almeda against banker Franklin Royce.

People were talking *about* the election, but nobody was
coming out and saying they actually supported Almeda. If anything, business around the office was quieter than usual. Almeda was right in the middle of a hurricane of talk and interest
and discussion, but the Parrish Mine and Freight office was
quieter than a tomb. And even the people who did come in
seemed reluctant to mention the election. They just took care
of their business and left without more words than were necessary.

"You know what it is," said Almeda one day in frustration
to me and Mr. Ashton. "They're all afraid Franklin is standing
behind his window over there watching!"

The bank and freight office, two of Miracle's busiest places
and biggest buildings, sat looking right at each other across the
intersection of the two main streets. There they sat, with the
General Store and the sheriff's office and jail on opposite corners and lots of other little stores and buildings in between,
making up the central square block of Miracle Springs.

And there stood the posters in the windows of each, saying
nothing out loud, but silently saying so much about what really
made Miracle Springs work and operate and "function" every
day as a town. *Royce for Mayor*, said the one, promoting the

144

man who owned the bank and who as a result co-owned or part-owned three-quarters of all the farms and ranches and businesses and homes for miles around. And in the other window folks read the sign I had made that said *Vote Almeda Hollister for Mayor of Miracle Springs.* Everyone knew that it was Almeda who had gotten them their gold pans and sluice boxes and their bags, shovels, wagons, spare parts, picks, saddles, ropes, and nails. At her livery half their horses and mules were tended, and at her blacksmith's forge Marcus Weber repaired their tools, re-shod their horses, and fixed their broken wagon wheels.

I don't suppose any two people had done more to make Miracle Springs what it was in 1856 than Franklin Royce and Almeda Parrish Hollister. Yet it seemed more than likely that most folks would end up on Royce's side. Even though through the years Almeda had given credit to most of the men of Miracle Springs one time or another, she didn't hold mortgages on their property. And if she went out of business, as sorry as they might be, they could always get what they needed someplace else. If she was gone, probably Royce himself would set up a new business to replace hers!

"What we need is a flyer, a pamphlet!" Almeda exclaimed, after a few moments pause, still staring out the window, looking toward the bank. "Folks are just too nervous to be seen talking to me. But if we distributed something they could take home and read when they're alone, then they wouldn't have to worry about being seen by you know who."

She spun around and faced me. "What do you say, Corrie? A flyer—you can help me write it, and I'll take it down to Sacramento to have it printed up. We'll get five hundred, even a thousand printed up. We'll scatter so many of them around that everybody will see it eventually!"

We got started on it that very afternoon.

Almeda told me what she wanted to say. I wrote it down in the best way I could, she made some changes, and then I wrote it over again. I started to work on a couple of pictures for it, too, so that it would look interesting—a sketch of Almeda's face, and another one of the front of the Freight Company office, as a reminder of what Parrish Mine and Freight had meant to the community.

During the evening we all sat around and talked—what Almeda still called her campaign "committee"—trying to figure out what we ought to say. Katie kept talking about needing a campaign slogan, and Almeda finally settled on: Almeda Hollister—A Hard-Working Part of Miracle Springs' Past Who Will Be Faithful to Its Future. She Will Put *Your* Interests First."

That slogan would go on top of the handbill. Under it would be my sketch of Almeda. At the bottom would be words like: Integrity, Experience in Business, Familiar with Needs of Miners, Dependable, Friend of Miner and Rancher and Farmer, Working Hard for Your Prosperity.

All that would comprise the front page. Inside the fold, people would open it up and read the written part about how Almeda had come to Miracle Springs, how the business had been started, and how much she had done for the miners through the years—helping get what they needed, giving them extra time to pay if needed, delivering things at odd hours or even in rain or snow if something was needed right away, opening up her livery or blacksmith's shop in an emergency even if it meant getting Marcus up in the middle of the night—and finally saying that as mayor she would continue to do all those things for the community, always looking out for the interests and well-being of the people she represented.

During those first couple of weeks, Mr. Royce continued to be his same smiling, friendly self. In fact, three days after the poster went up in our window, we were astonished by another personal visit by the opposing candidate himself. Mr. Ashton had spotted him out the window walking in our direction from the bank.

"Here comes Royce!" he said, and he hurried back to his chair and tried to busy himself with the papers in front of him. Almeda and I braced ourselves for—well, we didn't know what, but I don't think either of us expected it to be pleasant.

But Mr. Royce walked in the door, a big smile on his face, and went straight up to Almeda.

"Well, Almeda, I must say this is a surprise! Welcome to the race!" he said.

"Thank you, Franklin," she replied, shaking his hand. "You are being most gracious about it."

"Whatever our differences in the past may have been, I congratulate your intrepid decision. California needs more women like you!"

Almeda smiled, the two wished each other well, and then the banker departed, leaving Almeda with a question on her face. "Have I completely misjudged that man?" she said after a moment, speaking more to herself than to either of us. Her eyes remained fixed on the door Mr. Royce had just left for another few seconds. Then she shook her head and went on with her work. Was she doubting whether she had done the right thing?

Thereafter, Mr. Royce kept being nice about the whole thing. Whenever anyone asked him about the election, or mentioned Almeda's running against him, his response was something nice and friendly.

"It's a free country," he might say. "Anyone is able to do as his conscience leads him, and I salute Mrs. Hollister's courage to stand up for what she believes in."

Or: "She is a strong woman, and Miracle Springs should be proud to have her as one of its leading citizens."

Or: "It is remarkable, is it not, what women are able to achieve when they persevere? She has done a great deal for this town, and I for one have the greatest respect for her as a businesswoman in what is predominantly a man's occupation."

Whether he was truly being nice, or just didn't think he had to worry about Almeda's hurting his election, I didn't know. One thing was for sure, folks were starting to change their opinion of him, and his nice comments about Almeda only made them like him all the more.

But some people didn't believe a word of it. Like Katie. When she heard that last remark he'd made to Patrick Shaw—

which his wife had told Katie—she got downright riled.

"I tell you, Almeda, he's talking out of both sides of his mouth!" she said. "All those nice words don't fool me a bit."

Almeda laughed. "Why do you say that?" she asked.

"He may be saying nice things about you, but he makes sure he always mentions that you are a woman, and that this is a man's world. He doesn't *have* to say anything—it's obvious he wants people to think for themselves that being a mayor's no job for a woman."

"He's never said a word to that effect, Katie."

"He doesn't need to. He's relying on the men around here to draw that conclusion for themselves. Patronizing, that's what it is. He's being nice to you so that folks won't take you seriously. It's almost as if he treats your running against him as a joke that doesn't *really* mean anything as far as the election's concerned."

"I don't know, Katie," Almeda replied with a thoughtful look on her face. "It just may be that Franklin Royce has changed his ways after all."

# CHAPTER 23

## I SURPRISE MYSELF!

Right in the middle of all the excitement of getting the handbill ready and everything else to do with the election, a letter came from San Francisco that caught me by surprise.

"Dear Mr. Hollister," it read. "I would like to run your article about Summer in the Gold Country in the *Alta* next week. Enclosed is $4 for it. I have to admit your pieces continue to surprise me. Some of the people on our staff tell me your writing is among the most favorably received of anything we print among our women readers. I don't know how you do it, but you seem to have a good feel for the kinds of things that women enjoy reading about. Keep it up! I am confident we will be able to sell this article to several eastern papers as well." It was signed, "Edward Kemble." Then underneath had been added: "It may be that we will also run your story about the lame schoolteacher. It will depend on whether we have space to spare. You're getting the picture about 'human interest.' But of course, right now we're swamped with election news."

I was elated. This was the most positive thing he'd ever written me! He actually said there were people who *liked* reading what I wrote!

Over the next two or three days, I read his letter several times. My conscious mind couldn't help feeling good at the words "favorably received," "good feel for what women enjoy reading," "keep it up" and "you're getting the picture." But down deep something was bothering me.

149

At first I didn't know what it was.

Then gradually thoughts began coming back to me about that Sunday when Rev. Rutledge had preached on truth. He had talked about *people* being true rather than *ideas*. I found myself wondering about it further, questioning how to make my writing "true." It seemed like I was getting to do what I had always wanted to do. Writing for a newspaper had been my dream, and now here I was actually doing it! And if I was going to keep on doing it, I wanted to write truthfully.

I thought about the two articles and about what I had written, and about what Mr. Kemble had said about them. The more I thought about them, the more I did feel like I could be proud of those articles as truthful. I honestly *did* feel there was something more special about the gold country than just the gold itself—and that was the land. And I hoped what I'd written about Miss Stansberry overcoming her lame leg would show folks something about her down inside that was a good thing for them to see, a part of her true character.

Yet something kept eating at me inside. I'd written about ideas and thoughts and feelings and people in a good and honest way, even in a way that people might like reading about. But something was still wrong.

I remembered Rev. Rutledge's words: *Truth is not ideas . . . only a person can be true.*

All at once I knew what was wrong with the two articles. It wasn't anything I said about Miss Stansberry or the gold country. It was in Mr. Kemble's letter. All the nice things he'd said were pleasant to hear. But the words that now suddenly jumped off the paper as I looked at his letter again were the very first ones: "Dear Mr. Hollister . . ."

*Mister* Hollister . . . Dear *Mister* Hollister . . . *Mister* . . . *Mister*. . . !

That's what was wrong! Truth wasn't the ideas, it was the person, and I was the wrong person! Mr. Kemble didn't even know who I was! He thought I was a man. How could I possibly be a writer who was trying to write about true things when I *myself* wasn't being true?

Then the words that had come out of my own mouth that same day came back to me, the words I had prayed to God in the woods after the church service: *Lord, make me a true person!*

If my writing was going to mean anything, no matter what it was I happened to be talking about, then I had to be true *myself*! And maybe this letter from Mr. Kemble was my opportunity to start. After all, being a true person isn't something you put off and figure you'll get around to some other time. You either are or you aren't. And if I had let this little lie slip in about who I really was—even though neither Almeda nor I had a thought of deceiving Mr. Kemble at first—I couldn't wait for some other time to set it right.

Setting something right is a thing you have to do now, not later. So I figured I'd better do something about this situation . . . and soon.

I'd gotten the letter at the office in the morning. All day long I thought about it. And by the middle of the afternoon I'd made a decision that surprised even me.

So that night, in as calm but determined a voice as I could, I said to Pa and Almeda:

"I'm going to San Francisco."

Almeda's eyes opened up wide as Pa exclaimed, "What in tarnation for, girl?"

"If I'm gonna keep writing for his paper," I said, "there are a few things I need to talk to Mr. Kemble about. And I just don't figure there's any way to do it but in person."

I reckon they both sensed from the resolution of my tone that there was no way I was going to let them talk me out of it.

But that didn't stop them from trying. In fact, at first Pa said if I was determined, one of them would have to go with me. But in the end, after endless instructions and warnings, they sent me off with the boys keeping me company for at least half the way.

# CHAPTER 24

# FACE TO FACE
# WITH MR. KEMBLE

Zack and Little Wolf went with me on horseback as far as Sacramento. We camped out for one night somewhere between Auburn and Folsom. We lay around the fire and talked until after midnight before I finally drifted off to sleep.

I left my horse at a livery in Sacramento and went on to San Francisco alone. Zack and Little Wolf said they'd keep busy and see the city and would meet me back at Miss Baxter's Boarding House in three days. Miss Baxter could hardly believe it was us, and said she'd never have known Zack if he bumped into her on the sidewalk. What a feeling it was, the three of us—still kids inside, I reckon, but alone in the city and knowing we could handle ourselves. Well, Zack and Little Wolf could handle *them*selves, and I felt safe enough as long as I was with them!

Not until I was alone on the steamer floating down the Sacramento River did it begin to dawn on me what I was doing. I was on my way to the biggest city in the West—alone!

I'd climbed tall trees when I was little—terrified that I was going to fall, too frightened to look down, yet tingling with excitement as I kept climbing higher and higher . . . afraid, but glad to be afraid! And not so afraid that I didn't want to get as high up as I could.

That's how it felt as I looked out over the river and watched the shore glide past and felt the warm breeze on my face and in my hair. I was nervous, and thought that anyone who saw me would have noticed my knees shaking under my calico skirt. But I wouldn't have wanted to be anyplace else.

I thought of traveling to San Francisco with Almeda exactly three years earlier. I was so dependent on her back then. It had been *her* trip about *her* business. *She'd* made the arrangements. *She* knew what to do and where to go. I had been just a little girl.

And now here I was, not only going to San Francisco alone, but going there on my *own* business, about something that concerned *my* life. It had been *my* decision to come, and I was on my own to figure out what to do. I had the name and address of a boardinghouse run by a friend of Mrs. Gianini's, but that was all.

I still felt young, but I knew I was starting to grow up. I was going to San Francisco by myself and, as fearsome as it might be, I knew I could figure out what I should do. And if I couldn't, then maybe it was time I learned. I had to grow up sometime. And maybe the best way to learn how to stand on your own two feet without your pa or ma helping you is to just go out and start walking on them without anyone's help.

I thought too about how dependent I had been on Almeda spiritually. She had been the one who had first told me how God felt about us, and about how he wanted us to think and live and behave. I hadn't known anything about God and his ways back then. When I think back to some of the questions I used to ask her, I can't help but be embarrassed at how naive I was. But on the other hand, that's how you grow and learn— by wondering, by asking, and by having someone you can look up to who can help you as you're trying to figure things out. So I'm glad I wrote in my journal about some of those lengthy conversations Almeda and I had. I still go back and reread them now and then—the talk we'd had about what sin meant when Mrs. Gianini was working on the dresses, the talk we'd had right on that same Sacramento River steamer about faith, the Easter Sunday afternoon just after I turned seventeen when I'd prayed that God would make me into the person he wanted me to be, and the long talk on the way home about obeying. Every one of those talks remains so special in my memory, and makes me love Almeda all the more as a mother.

Now those truths she had given me were part of *me*. She had taught me, helped me, encouraged me, and loved me. But the most important thing she had done for me was to help me stand on my *own* spiritual feet. She had helped me to think for myself, helped me as I learned how to pray, and encouraged me gently as I grew.

I had been grappling with the whole prospect of what growing up meant, and about my future. But the fact that I was thinking about options, about writing, about what truth was, and about growing to be a woman. The fact that I was asking God about them, showed that maybe I *was* growing up after all—or at least starting to.

And now here I was on my way to San Francisco! I would never have imagined it just a few months ago. But now . . . who could tell what the future might hold.

If being so far away from home wasn't enough to make my knees quake, the thought of facing the editor of one of California's biggest newspapers sure was! The more I thought about it, the more foolish this whole thing seemed. Yet I still knew I had to go through with it, even if it meant I never saw another word of mine in Mr. Kemble's newspaper . . . or any other newspaper! If growing as a Christian and being a "true" person had anything to do with becoming an adult, then I had to do this thing I had come to do, no matter how hard it might be. I'd never *keep* growing if I didn't do the thing that was set before me.

Another idea had been running around in my mind since just before we got to Sacramento. The closer we got to the big city, the more I found myself thinking about it—and it had to do with the election back home between Almeda and Mr. Royce. By the time I walked into Mr. Kemble's office the next day, I had figured out exactly what I wanted to say to him.

Of course, the conversation didn't quite go the way I had planned it!

The lady in the *Alta* office seemed a little surprised when I asked to see Mr. Kemble. I don't know why. I tried to look as professional as I knew how, and I had brought along my best clothes to wear. But I couldn't hide my age.

She asked if he was expecting me. I said no. Then she asked my name, and I said he didn't know me and that I wanted to wait to tell him my name in person.

That kind of annoyed her, and she told me to sit down and wait, which I did. It was a *long* wait, and I think maybe she hoped I'd get tired and go away. But I kept sitting there, and finally she got up and went somewhere out of my sight. When she came back a minute or two later, she said, "Mr. Kemble will see you now, young lady," and she led me down a hall to the editor's office.

The instant I walked in the door, a panic seized me, and I forgot everything I'd intended to say!

There sat the man I took to be Mr. Kemble behind a big desk, looking up at me with a half gruff expression that said, *I don't know who you are or why you're here, but I'm busy. So get on with your business and say what you have to say before I throw you out!* Before he had a chance to say anything, all of a sudden I was talking, hardly knowing what was coming out of my mouth.

"Mr. Kemble," I said.

"That's right," answered the man.

I walked forward and stood in front of his desk.

"My name is—"

My throat went dry suddenly and I couldn't get out the words.

"I'm not going to hurt you, Miss . . . Miss whoever-you-are. You don't need to be afraid to tell me your name."

"That's just it, sir. When I tell you my name, you may say you never want to see me again."

"I doubt that. But come on—out with it. I haven't got all day."

I tried again. "My name is—*C.B. Hollister*. Corrie Belle Hollister.

"What? You're C.B. Hollister? I don't believe it!"

"I'm sorry, Mr. Kemble. I never meant to not be truthful . . . it was just something that happened at first, and then I never had the courage to say anything once you started calling me *mister* in your letters."

I was shaking from nervousness and fear and from wondering what he would do. But at least I had said it.

"You're just a kid," he said at length. "And a girl, besides!"

"But I want to be a newspaper writer," I said, though my voice was trembling. "I *am* sorry," I apologized again, "and that's why I came here to see you, to tell you the truth about who I was, and so that the rest of any articles I write can have my full name on them, so that everybody else will know too."

Mr. Kemble leaned back in his chair, thinking for a moment.

"You came all the way to San Francisco for that?" he asked. "Just to see me and set the record straight on this *C.B.* business?"

"Yes, sir."

"Hmm," he mumbled. "That shows some spunk—I like that." He paused again. "But as to your doing any more writing for the *Alta* . . . most of my reporters are older, and—"

"I'm nineteen," I said. "Halfway to being twenty."

He chuckled. "That's hardly old in this business!"

"You said folks liked reading what I wrote," I ventured cautiously. "They didn't care how old I was . . . or that I was a young lady instead of an old man."

He leaned forward and eyed me hard for a minute. Now I *was* afraid I'd said too much!

All of a sudden he threw his head back and laughed. "You *do* have spunk, young Miss Hollister! And you're not afraid to say what's on your mind," he added more seriously, "or to come a hundred and fifty miles to make something right, even if it's for something you shouldn't have done in the first place. I like that. Those are good qualities for a writer—spunk and courage. So tell me, what's on your mind to write about now—

same kind of human interest stuff our former friend C.B. Hollister's been sending me?"

He smiled at his own humor, but I had my answer ready. I'd been thinking about it all the way from Sacramento.

"I want to write about the election in Miracle Springs," I said. "I'd like to write three articles on it."

He laughed again. "The election's being covered by more experienced reporters than there are gold miners in the Mother Lode. If Fremont ever so much as sets foot in the state, there will be a hundred writers waiting. You'd never get near him!"

"I don't mean that election," I said. "I mean the Miracle Springs election—for mayor."

"What could my readers possibly care about that?"

"They'd be interested because a woman is running against the town's banker. You've heard of Parrish Mine and Freight Company."

"That's right," he said. "Run by Almeda Parrish—fine woman, from what I hear. And you say *she's* running against the town banker?"

I nodded.

"What's his name?"

"Franklin Royce."

He let out a low whistle. "I've heard of him too. A slick operator, and with plenty of dough. And you think you can write something my readers will be interested in?"

"You mentioned your women readers liking my articles—don't you think they'll want to read about a businesswoman in politics?"

"Yeah, you're probably right," he said thoughtfully, nodding his head slowly. "The thing is unheard of—though everything's new in California these days."

After a minute of silence he went on. "Now you understand, Miss Hollister, that if I agree to print something of yours about this election—well, for that matter, anything of yours in the future—"

"Three stories on the election," I reminded him.

"Whatever—whether it's the Royce-Parrish story or something else—you understand that I can't pay you near what I did before. Women only fetch a third or a half a man's wages, and a girl who isn't even twenty yet . . . let me see—I doubt I'll be able to give you over a dollar an article."

*A dollar!* I shouted inside. Whether it was my mother Agatha Belle Hollister or my stepmother Almeda Parrish Hollister rising up inside me—or some of both of them!—what Pa called my Belle blood started to get riled. Why should the exact words that might have been worth three or four dollars a week ago be worth only *one* dollar now? Because he had found out that I was a lady instead of a man, and a young lady besides? It didn't seem at all fair!

But before either of us said another word, the door of Mr. Kemble's office opened behind me.

# CHAPTER 25

# A FAMILIAR FACE

Into the editor's office walked a tall young man, carrying a stack of papers. He wore a cap tilted to the right down over his forehead, which kept me from being able to see his eyes at first, though there was immediately something familiar about the way he walked and the few blond curls coming out from beneath his cap.

The instant he spoke I remembered the voice as if I had just heard it yesterday!

"Mr. Kemble," he said, "I've got those files you asked me to dig up on—"

He stopped, apparently just as surprised to see me as I was him.

"If I didn't know better . . ." he said, pausing to look me over from head to foot. I couldn't think of a single word to utter as I stood there, probably with my mouth hanging open.

"It *is* the girl from off in the backwoods gold country!" he finally exclaimed. "Are you still trying to get into the reporting game?"

"You two know each other, O'Flaridy?" asked a bewildered Mr. Kemble.

"We ran into each other a couple years back, though I can't remember your name," he added, looking again at me.

"Robin O'Flaridy, meet Corrie Belle Hollister," said Mr. Kemble.

"Hollister, that's it!" he said. "Miracle Springs, right?"

I smiled and nodded. "It looks as though you've moved up a few notches from delivering papers yourself," I said. "Are you really a reporter now?"

He shifted his weight onto his other foot, as if he was embarrassed for the editor to hear me ask the question, and the pause gave me a quick chance to assess the changes that had come over the first acquaintance I had ever made in San Francisco.

In the last three years, Robin O'Flaridy had shot up, and stood a good head taller than me. But he was still lean, with a smooth face and blond hair, though a bit darker than before. And his voice, though not boyish, was still high-pitched for a man. All that made it just as hard to tell his age as the first time I had seen him as a scrappy kid delivering papers and hanging around hotels. I figured him for twenty or twenty-one, and he certainly looked as at home and comfortable in the offices of the *Alta* as he had in the lobby of the Oriental Hotel. Maybe he hadn't been exaggerating as much as I thought back then about his association with the paper. He seemed every bit the newsman now.

"Of course I'm a reporter," he answered, a little defensively I thought. "I told you that back then."

"Don't listen to a word he tells you, Miss Hollister," laughed Mr. Kemble. "To hear him talk, you'd think the *Alta* couldn't possibly put out a single edition without him. But he does occasionally bring me something I can use."

Robin's neck reddened slightly. He tried to get the conversation off himself. "So I take it you're here because you still hope to write for a newspaper someday, eh? But I can tell you from experience, just being a pretty face won't get you anywhere with this editor!" He grinned and threw Mr. Kemble a wink.

"Now don't get too cocky, O'Flaridy!" said the editor. "Miss Hollister has already written several articles for us—a couple of them have appeared back East. You may have seen the name *C.B. Hollister.*"

If Robin was surprised, even halfway impressed, he wasn't about to let it show.

"What do you know about that!" he said. "So you've moved up from that other rag from the sticks! Good going, Hollister!" He gave me a slap on the back.

Now I remembered what had so irritated me about Robin O'Flaridy before. I smiled, but my heart wasn't in it. My Belle blood was flowing again!

"Careful, O'Flaridy, she may be taking your job someday! I was just about to offer her three articles on an election they're having up her way," said Mr. Kemble. "That's besides the two I've already got in the files. Can't recall *you* ever bringing me good writing quite so fast as that." He was kidding Robin O'Flaridy, that much I could tell from his tone, but whether he was being serious about my writing or making fun of me— that I *couldn't* tell.

"Three articles, huh!" he said. "That *is* something! I guess I better get my pencil busy. I can't let some girl cub reporter from out in the hills of the Mother Lode show me up!"

He set the files on Mr. Kemble's desk and then turned to leave. "See you around, Hollister!"

"Well, I think that about concludes our business too," the editor said to me before O'Flaridy was even out the door. "A dollar an article, as agreed. When will I see the first piece?"

"Uh . . . in a week or two," I said, trying to get my mind back on what I had come for and off the surprise interruption by Robin O'Flaridy.

"That sounds fine."

Mr. Kemble stood up behind his desk and offered his hand. I shook it.

"Good day, Miss Hollister," he said.

I turned and left his office, my mind half numb from all that had gone on inside, part of me thinking of the things I had intended to say to Mr. Kemble but hadn't. The whole interview now seemed awkward, even though I had accomplished what I'd wanted—he now knew who I really was, and he had agreed to let me write about the election. But somehow I still felt unsettled inside.

"Hey, Hollister, where you staying?" said the familiar voice of Robin O'Flaridy from where he was leaning against the wall of the hallway, apparently waiting for me.

I told him, then began walking toward the door where I had entered the building. He pushed himself off the wall, skipped a couple of steps to catch up with me, then continued to walk alongside me.

"That older lady with you again?" he asked.

"No."

"You came to the big city alone, eh?"

"That's right."

"And how long you planning to be around?"

I said I didn't know. To be honest, I had thought about remaining for another day or two. It was such an adventure being there on my own, I wanted to see a little of the city. However, I wasn't so sure I wanted Robin O'Flaridy escorting me around—even with his blue eyes, blond curls, and air of confidence, as if he considered the whole city and everything in it his own personal domain. I suppose most nineteen-year-old girls would have been dazzled and flattered. But something about his attentions caused me to squirm.

He started in telling me all about his latest escapades as he moved closer to my side. I felt his hand slip through my arm. Immediately I knew my cheeks were turning red.

"Say, how about I come over to Miss Sandy Loyd Bean's Boarding House tonight," he said; "and you and me, we'll go out to dinner someplace, and then I'll show you San Francisco by night?"

We were just about to the door. He opened it for me with his free hand, then continued on outside with me.

"What do you say, Corrie?"

"I . . . I don't know—I'd made plans to eat with Miss Bean. I told her I'd be back for dinner. Besides, I couldn't possibly go out with you—alone!"

"Aw, forget Miss Bean. You can eat a home-cooked meal anytime! And who needs a chaperon? Who'd ever know about it, anyway?" He laughed. "When else are you going to have an invitation to go out to a San Francisco restaurant with one of the city's well-known journalists? You're a good-looking girl and I'm not too bad-looking a fella, and it just seems right that we ought to spend some time together, you being here alone like you are. Especially with us both in the same profession now. What harm could there be in one evening of fun?"

"I really don't think I ought—"

"Listen," he said, cutting me off as I hailed a horse-drawn cab for myself from the corner of the block, "you talk to your Sandy Bean and put your mind at ease. I know she won't mind your not being there once you explain that you ran into an old friend who invited you out for the evening. I'll be by at seven o'clock."

Without giving me an opportunity to say anything further, he took my hand, helped me up onto the cab seat, gave the cab driver fifty cents and told him where to take me, then turned back toward me, smiled, tipped his cap, and as the horse's hoofs clopped off, said, "See you tonight!" He turned and pranced off down the street, obviously pleased with himself.

# CHAPTER 26

# WHAT TO DO?

I tried to see some of the city during the afternoon, and even took a cab out to Point Lobos where Miss Bean told me the Pacific Mail steamship was due to reach the Bay with letters and newspapers from the East. But all day I was distracted by thoughts of Robin T. O'Flaridy! There was such a battle going on inside my head that I could hardly enjoy myself.

One side of me kept thinking that I ought to throw caution to the wind and go with him. I imagined putting on my nice cream dress with the pink lace around it. He was a decent-looking young man—he'd been right about that. And we were both interested in newspapers and writing. And how many opportunities was I going to have like this? He had talked about showing me the town and it was bound to be fun.

I could hardly believe that the thought of marriage would cross my mind at a time like this! I'd never in my life thought *seriously* of getting married! But now all at once I couldn't keep the idea from entering my brain. I always figured Ma was right about me not being the kind of girl that fellas would stand in line to marry. Maybe I ought to take the few opportunities that come along and not let them pass by.

Why shouldn't I go with Robin? I might have a good time, and he probably wasn't such a bad fellow. It might be years before another young man took an interest in me. And even if he wasn't a Christian, maybe I could do him some good, or even talk to him about some of the things Mrs. Parrish and I talked about.

But the other side of me said something entirely different. I couldn't help thinking of the people who mattered to me, and what they might think. What if I did go out to dinner with him? Would I be proud to tell Almeda or would I be embarrassed? I couldn't help wondering if Robin T. O'Flaridy was the kind of person I *wanted* her to know I had been with. Was he a good person, the kind of young man she would respect and admire? And what would Jesus think to see me alone with someone I hardly knew?

The more I thought on it, the more doubts I had about what they might think. If Mrs. Parrish walked in on us together at some fancy restaurant, I *would* be embarrassed. He wasn't her kind of person—unselfish, kind, and thoughtful of others. In fact, he'd always struck me as a little egotistical and conniving. That certainly wasn't the sort of person I wanted to marry, if I ever *did* get married. If I didn't think enough of him to figure he was worth marrying, and if I would have been embarrassed to have Almeda see me with him, then what possible reason could I have for accepting his invitation? To accept would not be true to what I was thinking and feeling inside. Something about him made me very uneasy.

When Mrs. Parrish and I had first come to San Francisco, the desk clerk had said, "Nobody even knows where the boy lives. He's always on the street looking for some likely target to fleece." Robin just delivered papers, but he had told me he was a reporter. He wasn't a very honest person.

Robin T. O'Flaridy and I were different sorts of people. I couldn't believe he was a very godly young man. What would he say if I told him about how I prayed every day to obey God more and to be true?

He'd probably laugh. Or if he didn't laugh, at least he'd probably make some comment like, "Well, all that religious stuff is okay for girls and women. But I'm a man and I can make it just fine on my own without all that stuff about God."

Was that someone I wanted to spend time with, see San Francisco with? We'd be talking together and smiling and trying to have a good time, but our *real* selves would be miles apart. That didn't seem right, didn't seem honest or truthful, didn't seem any way to have a friendship between a young man and a young woman—pretending on the surface to be people we really weren't. There was really no decision to make. I couldn't even say I actually wanted to be with him. To go with him would be compromising my convictions.

By the time evening came, I had made up my mind.

He came to the door promptly at seven. I heard the knock, and my stomach lurched with a queasy feeling. I said a quick prayer as I went to answer it.

"You ready?" he asked. He stood there dressed up in a coat and tie, flowers in his hand. "These are for you," he said, holding them out toward me.

A giant knot suddenly tightened in my stomach. This was awful! A hundred doubts shot through my mind about the decision I had come to earlier. Maybe I had completely misjudged him. He probably wasn't such a bad young man after all! Yet in spite of my last-minute misgivings, I found coming out of my mouth the words I had been practicing to myself for the last hour:

"I . . . I've decided . . ." I stammered.

"Decided? Decided what?"

"I've decided that I really shouldn't go," I finally blurted out. "I'm . . . I'm very sorry."

He stood staring at me blankly, as if he hadn't heard.

"I don't believe it," he said at last. "You can't be serious?" I could see him getting angry.

"I'm really sorry. I—I—just feel I shouldn't . . . And I never really said I would go with you."

"But I had so much planned for us. I've dressed up and brought you flowers," he said, glancing at the bouquet still in his hand. "I just can't believe you'd do this to me!"

I didn't know what to say. I felt dreadful.

He just stood there staring at me, his face gradually filling with color—not the red of embarrassment, but of anger.

"Well then, enjoy your ridiculous meal in this dull boardinghouse, and your evening alone! You'll probably sit in your room reading some boring book when you could have been having the time of your life out in the city!''

With a last spiteful, glaring look, he spun around and started to leave. Then he noticed the flowers in his hand. With an angry motion, he threw them into the dirt in the street. Then he looked back at the door.

"But just don't you come crawling to me when you're a lonely old spinster!" he said vengefully. "Or when you realize you can't make it as a reporter without the help of people like me. Robin T. O'Flaridy doesn't get made a fool of twice!"

He strode off down the street with long steps, and never looked back.

I shut the door slowly and turned back into the boarding-house. Then I ran back up to my room and lay down on the bed and started to cry. All I could think was how hard it had been to refuse him when I saw his face so alive with expectation. I had almost given in and walked out the door with him. Yet even as I lay there crying, I knew that something inside me had been strengthened, and that I would look back on this moment as one more marker on the road of my spiritual life.

Robin was right. I did spend the rest of the evening alone in my room, mostly reading. I'd brought along a book of Mr. Fremont's about his exploration of Oregon and Northern California in 1843–44. Since he was running for President, I was interested in his early years in the West.

My adventure in San Francisco had lost its excitement. I had never in my life felt so lonely and far away from everybody I loved. But still I knew I'd done the right thing.

# CHAPTER 27

## THE CAMPAIGN HEATS UP

I tried hard to enjoy the city the next day. Miss Bean told me some things I ought to see, and I walked around a little, and took one cab. But I was afraid I'd run into Robin O'Flaridy around every corner. So it was with a great sigh of relief that I boarded the steamer the next morning back to Sacramento. And I was so glad to see Zack and Little Wolf later that afternoon that I gave them bigger hugs than I ever had before.

"What's that for?" asked an embarrassed Zack as he half returned my embrace.

"Just to remind me how much I love you," I answered. He was satisfied, in the boyish sort of way that avoids talking about such things, and I wasn't inclined to explain any further.

Little Wolf hugged me back, smiled, and pretended to give my face a little slap. Even though we were two days from Miracle Springs, I already felt like I was home! Without people to love, you can get awfully lonely in a big hurry!

Back in Miracle, the mayor's campaign had started to heat up. While I had been gone, Almeda had gotten the box of completed handbills back from the printer in Sacramento—one thousand copies printed on bright colored paper. Already Tad and Becky and Emily had been putting them around town, and Almeda had begun to call on some of the leading townsfolk, both to take them a handbill and to explain what she was doing and why. With the excitement over seeing the handbill, and then telling Pa and Almeda about my trip and the incident with

Robin O'Flaridy, it was late in the evening before I remembered my most important news of all.

"But guess what?" I said. "Mr. Kemble said he'd print three articles on the election if I'd write them!"

"The state election?"

"No—Miracle Springs . . . you and Mr. Royce."

"That is something—and *three*! My goodness, you *are* turning into a genuine newswoman, Corrie!"

"For pay?" asked Pa.

"More or less," I answered. "A dollar each."

"Three dollars!" exclaimed Almeda. "They paid you four times that just two weeks ago for that countryside article."

"That was before he found out I was a girl."

"Why—why, that is the most despicable, low—"

"Now hold on to your breeches, Almeda," said Pa. "Don't get all riled. You know how the world is. If Corrie's gonna try to do a man's job, she's gonna have to expect this kind—"

"A man's job! Drummond Hollister, not you too! Corrie can write just as well as any man her age, and better than some a lot older, and there's no reason she shouldn't be paid according to her ability."

"Maybe you're right, but then I figure that's Corrie's decision, not yours or mine. And if she doesn't want to write an article for a measly eight bits, she don't have to. And if she does, then it ain't nothing for you or I to stick our noses into."

Pa's practicality silenced Almeda for a minute, then she smiled broadly. "Well it's a start, Corrie." She paused. "I'm really proud of you. Proud of your courage in standing up to a powerful man like Mr. Kemble, but even more proud of your honesty, your integrity." She reached over and squeezed my hand. "Proud to have a young woman like you as my daughter."

I thanked her, inside thinking how much I would like to have known what Robin O'Flaridy made for each of *his* articles.

With the handbill circulating and Almeda making visits to people, the whole feeling of the mayor's campaign changed. People had been talking earlier, but I think it was mostly from

interest's sake, almost curiosity. Just the fact that Miracle
Springs was going to have an election was an event in itself.
Having two of the town's most well-known people in it against
each other made it all the more a topic of interest and conversation.

But now the initial novelty had worn off, and people were
starting to ask more serious questions about the election.
Which one of the two, Royce or Hollister, would actually make
the best mayor? Who would do the most for Miracle Springs?

Almeda's visits and the handbill got people to thinking
about more than they had at first, and wondering if maybe she
just *might* be a better person to vote for than the banker. But
she *was* a woman, and having a woman for mayor just wasn't
done. And Royce was not only a man—he was the banker, and
he still had financial power in one way or another over just
about everybody around Miracle.

After several days Mr. Royce made another call at the
freight office. This time none of us had seen him coming down
the street, so when he walked in it took us by surprise.

"Almeda," he said, "I'd like to talk with you for a minute."

His voice was more serious than the last time he'd come
into the office. He was trying to smile as he said the words, but
you could tell he had more than just lighthearted conversation
in his thoughts.

"Certainly. What is on your mind, Franklin?"

"In private?" he suggested.

Almeda nodded, then led him around the counter and into
her small office. But when they went inside she made no attempt to close the door, and he did not particularly keep his
voice down.

There was a pause while they both sat down. Mr. Ashton
and I looked at each other sort of apprehensively and kept about
our work as quietly as we could.

"Are you really sure you want to do this, Almeda?" asked
Royce.

"Do what—you mean the election?"

"Yes, of course that's what I mean. What's the purpose?

You're doing nothing but getting people stirred up and confused. And what good can it possibly do in the end?"

"The last time you were in, Franklin, you welcomed me to the race and said you congratulated my intrepid decision, as I believe you so eloquently phrased it." I could almost see Almeda smiling faintly as she said the words.

"That was then," he replied, a little quickly. "I had no idea you were going to take the thing so seriously. I thought perhaps it was a ploy to help your sagging business."

"My business is not sagging. We are managing just fine."

"Nevertheless, you have taken it beyond the casual point, Almeda, and I simply suggest that it is time you paused to consider the implications. People are talking and, quite frankly, some of the talk has negative features to it that are not going to help *my* reputation and business if they persist."

"And therefore you want me to withdraw?" asked Almeda. She wasn't smiling now, that much I knew.

"Be reasonable, Almeda," Mr. Royce said. "You've had the excitement of the campaign. You've thrust yourself into the center of attention. People respect you. It cannot help but heighten your image as a businesswoman. But now it's time for you to face the realistic facts. No town is going to elect a woman mayor, and the longer you continue, the more the potential damage to *my* reputation and *my* business. And if I'm going to be the next mayor of Miracle Springs, both the bank and my image in the people's thoughts need to be solid. And all this is not to mention the lasting impression your loss will leave. Right now you are riding high in the public mind. But after the election, your image, and perhaps even the reputation of your business itself, will be tarnished and you will be seen as a loser. All I'm attempting to convey to you in the most reasonable manner I can—from one business person to another, from one *friend* to another—is that it is time you stand aside and let Miracle Springs move forward without all this dissention and strife your being part of the election is causing— for your own good, Almeda."

A long silence followed.

"So then, Franklin, you consider the outcome of the election a foregone conclusion?" said Almeda at length.

"I didn't think there was ever any doubt about that," said Mr. Royce, with the hint of a laugh.

"Maybe not as far as you're concerned," replied Almeda. "But I didn't join this race to help my business or my reputation, as you call it, or anything else. I joined it to make every effort to win."

"Surely you can't be serious?" Royce sounded genuinely surprised.

"Of course I'm serious. I wouldn't do something of this magnitude for frivolous or self-seeking motives. If you think I care about what people think of me, Franklin, then you do not know me very well."

There was another pause.

"Well, if you're determined to see it out to the bitter end," Mr. Royce finally said, "I wish you'd at least discontinue the distribution of this brochure of yours, and visiting people—a good many of them my friends, Almeda—and stirring everybody up and spreading talk about me that isn't true."

"Franklin, I have not said a single word about you to a soul! I'm surprised you would think I would stoop to such measures."

"People *are* talking, Almeda. How can it be from anything other than your stirring them up against me?"

"I tell you, I am doing no such thing. I have never even hinted anything about you. I have only been talking to people about what I feel I would be able to offer Miracle Springs as its mayor."

After the pause which followed, Mr. Royce's tone cooled. He apparently realized he was not going to dissuade Almeda from anything she had her mind made up on.

"You can't win, Almeda," he said. "The thing's simply impossible."

"We'll see," she replied.

"You're wasting time and money."

"You may be right."

"You're determined to go ahead with it?"

"I am."

"Will you stop making calls on my friends and customers?"

"They are my friends, too, Franklin. You are free to call on them yourself."

"In other words, you will not stop?"

"No."

"Will you withdraw the brochure?"

"I will not. Again, Franklin, you are free to circulate one of your own."

The next sound was that of Mr. Royce's chair scooting back on the wood floor as he rose to his feet. "At least it appears we understand each other," he said.

"So it would appear," repeated Almeda.

"Good day, Mrs. Hollister," said the banker, and the next moment he reappeared from the office and walked briskly to the street door and out, not acknowledging me or Mr. Ashton in any way as he passed. We both pretended to be busy with the papers and files in front of us.

Two or three minutes later Almeda came out of the office. Her face was red with anger.

"That pompous, egotistical man!" was all she could say before she started sputtering and pacing around the office like a caged animal. "The nerve . . . to say that I stood no chance whatsoever! To ask me to withdraw from the race, because—because of his reputation! *His* reputation—ha! Calls on his *friends*! I doubt he even has that many friends around town—everyone is too afraid of him! What harm could *I* do *his* reputation!"

She walked around the office another time or two, then burst out again:

"I've got to get out of here!" She looked at the two of us. "I'm going for a ride. I'll be back in about an hour."

With that she left the room with as much grace as she could manage. When Mr. Ashton and I heard a yell and hoofbeats galloping away down the street a couple minutes later, we looked at each other and laughed. It was plain her horse was in for a time of it!

Almeda didn't pull out of the mayor's race, which continued to get livelier and livelier as we got into the month of August.

Mr. Royce paid no more visits to the Parrish Mine and Freight Company office.

# CHAPTER 28

## I TRY MY HAND AT SOMETHING NEW

I wanted to get right to work on my first article about the election. It was early August, and there were only about thirteen weeks to go.

I began by just trying to tell the five *w's* of the situation. I figured the first article needed to be a straight "news" kind of story that told folks about the election and what was unusual about it. Then for the next two I'd maybe try to write what Mr. Kemble called "human interest" things about the election and the two candidates, and maybe even about Miracle Springs itself.

I started off writing down the facts like I had for the poster about Ulysses S. Grant that Almeda had put up.

> The mining town of Miracle Springs, sixty-five miles northeast of Sacramento, will hold its first mayor's election in November of this year. The local election will be held at the same time as the general election for President and other offices. But what has the people of Miracle Springs all roused up isn't just that they're having their first election, but *who's* running in it!

Then I talked about Mr. Royce and Almeda being two of the town's leading citizens, about the bank and the Freight Company and how everyone for miles around depended on both of them for different parts of their livelihoods. But of course the fact of Almeda being a woman couldn't help but be

175

the main thing that would make folks interested in the election—and in my articles.

>The Miracle Springs mayor's election is one of the most unusual elections in all of California this year because a woman, who herself cannot even vote, is running against one of the wealthiest and most powerful men in the community. It is not known whether a woman has ever before run for such a high position as mayor in the United States, but Mrs. Hollister must certainly be considered one of the first. One might say she is a pioneer in a state full of pioneers. And if she wins, the rest of the state—if not the entire country—will be watching her, just as it is now watching the most famous Californian of all, John Charles Fremont.

I was planning to write a little bit about both of their businesses and how they both came to Miracle Springs, and then finish off the article with the last of the *w's*—a quote from both Mr. Royce and Almeda about "why" each had decided to run for mayor.

But before I got quite finished with the first article, an idea came to me that I just couldn't wait to get started on. I started putting together what I'd need for the second article, and so I got delayed a while getting the first one finished and in the mail to Mr. Kemble.

My idea was this: I'd go around to people around Miracle Springs, in private without either Mr. Royce or Almeda knowing what I was doing, and I'd ask them questions about what they thought of the election. I'd ask them their reaction to the two candidates, about what things would probably decide who they voted for, about whether they had business dealings with either candidate, and what difference that made. I would ask what they thought a mayor of Miracle Springs ought to do, what they thought was going to be the future of the community, what they themselves were most concerned about. I might even ask them who they planned to vote for.

It was such an exciting idea, I could hardly wait to get started!

If I could, I would get quotes, but if people wanted me not

to use their names, I would promise not to. I'd just tell everyone I wanted to get an idea how the whole town and its people were feeling about the election but without giving away any secrets or making it awkward for anyone.

Mostly, since they were the ones who could vote, I figured I'd talk to all the men I knew, and then to those I didn't know. And then another idea came to me! I could interview women too. Even though they couldn't vote, it would be interesting to get their opinions—especially since, according to Mr. Kemble's letter, it was the women readers of the paper who liked the kinds of things I had been writing. And I could ask the men (the married ones, at least!) if they might vote any different on account of what their wives thought.

What a great "human interest" article I could write if the women all put enough pressure on their husbands that they actually voted for Almeda! Even though the women couldn't vote, might it be possible that they could still influence the outcome? Or were there even enough women around Miracle Springs to make a difference? If the women started putting that kind of pressure on their husbands, what might the unmarried men do? There were still more unmarried men around than families. And what might Mr. Royce do?

I didn't know the answers to all my own questions. In fact, I kept thinking up new questions. And I figured the only way to find out some of these things was to get out and start talking to people and getting their ideas.

This would make a great article! It'd show Mr. Kemble I could write an article of news *and* human interest. And one worth more than $1!

The first people I talked to weren't the kind you could get a fair opinion from—they were all people who were friends of Almeda's—Pa, Uncle Nick, Katie, Mr. Ashton, Marcus Weber. But I had to begin someplace, so those were the folks I started with. I hadn't ever done anything quite like this before, so I had to learn how to ask questions and write down what people told me.

Gradually I started to talk to other people—the Shaws and

Hermon Stansberry gave me some interesting ideas, so did Mrs. DeWater, though her husband didn't say much. Rev. Rutledge was visiting Mr. and Miss Stansberry when I called on them, and so I got to talk to all three of them at once. The minister tried to be gracious toward both sides. Though obviously he had always felt fondly toward Almeda, he said some nice things about Mr. Royce too. Miss Stansberry took the woman's point of view completely, just like Katie had.

So far most of the people I'd talked to favored Almeda. But I knew to be fair I had to get the opinions of Mr. Royce's friends too. It would probably be harder than I thought to write an article that fairly represented both sides and all the people in the town!

But even as I interviewed people, I knew I had to get my first article finished up and in the mail. I went back to it, added the few parts that had been missing, rewrote it all, and then put it in the mail to Mr. Kemble. Then I got right back to visiting people, asking them questions, and writing down as much as I could about what they thought.

# CHAPTER 29

# I GET ANGRY

By this time there were daily stage runs from Sacramento up the valley and into the foothills. Mail usually took two or three days from Miracle Springs to San Francisco. And we'd get San Francisco newspapers most of time just two days late. They'd get the issue right off to Sacramento on the morning steamer up the river, or across the Bay and onto the train line that was now running between the two cities. Then the next day the papers would be taken by stage up the main routes to the north, which usually took a day and a half by the time it reached Miracle.

Almeda had always gotten the newspapers from Sacramento and San Francisco, besides Mr. Singleton's *Gazette*. But now that I was writing for them, I was more interested than I used to be, and the minute the stagecoach arrived in town at between two and four every afternoon, I'd be out of the office and on my way over to the depot to get whatever mail there was for Parrish Freight *and* our newspapers. On most days I spent the next ten or fifteen minutes looking over the paper, seeing what other reporters were writing about, getting ideas, reading some of the news. Then usually at night Pa and Almeda and I would pass the paper around until we all three had read every word.

The day of August 8 is a day I will always remember. At about four-thirty in the afternoon, I was sitting down in the freight office, scanning through the copy of the *Alta* that had arrived about an hour before on the stage. Mostly it was full of election news. There were quotes from a speech Mr. Buchanan had made in Philadelphia, and a lot about Mr. Fremont, including two long editorials. He had been campaigning all through the East, but news of his travels and the issues surrounding the election continued to make daily news in California. The slavery situation, events in Kansas, the question of Fremont's religion had all contributed to heated debate and discussion, as well as legal battles involving title to Fremont's Mariposa estate down in the foothills east of Merced. There was a short article entitled "Fremont Estate Embroiled in Campaign Controversy," though I didn't stop to take time to read it.

A few moments later my eyes fell on a small article on the bottom of page four. When I read the caption, my pulse quickened. There was no way they could have gotten my article into print this soon, yet there were the words in bold black type: "Woman Pioneer Seeks Office in State of Pioneers."

Hastily my eyes found the small print of the article and began to read:

> The place is Miracle Springs, foothills mining town some seventy miles north of Sacramento on a tributary of the Yuba River. The occasion: an election for mayor between two of the area's most prominent citizens and members of the business community—one, the town's only banker; the other, the owner of one of the largest mining supply and freight companies in the northern foothills.
>
> What makes this an election that many observers will be watching with interest, however, is that it pits a woman—who cannot even vote in the election—against a man of great influence in the community.

I couldn't believe it! This wasn't my article, but it might as well have been—all the information was the same!

With my heart pounding, I read on:

> According to research done by this reporter, the Miracle Springs mayor's race marks one of the very few times a woman has sought higher public office in these United States, and

never has a woman held office west of the plains. It should prove a groundbreaking election insofar as the future of this great state of California is concerned.

Almeda Parrish Hollister, owner of Parrish Mine and Freight Company and recently married to one of the town's miners, has thrown her hat into the ring against Franklin Royce, Miracle Springs' only banker and financier.

There were three more paragraphs telling a little about Miracle Springs itself, and then a brief background of Mr. Royce and Almeda and their businesses and how they had come to California, with the final sentences: "Experts interviewed for the purpose of this article give Mrs. Hollister no chance to win the election. They say that besides the disadvantage of being a woman, she has taken on a man owed too many favors by too many people. But just the fact that she is in the race is of interest in its own right."

If those words weren't enough to make me downright furious, those immediately below them were:

*Reported by Robin T. O'Flaridy, staff reporter for the California Alta.*

I threw the paper down and jumped to my feet. How could he do this to me? The rat!

And what about Mr. Kemble? He had no right! Why, they'd stolen my ideas, my words! And if Mr. Kemble wasn't in on it, how did Robin ever get his hands on my article in the first place? They must have done it together! It wasn't so much losing the dollar. They'd taken *my* idea—and even used some of my exact words. And then, most of all, they put Robin's name under them!

I was so angry I would have clobbered Robin if he had been there! I knew why he'd done it. He wanted to get even with me for the incident over the dinner and the flowers. He was paying me back for making him feel foolish.

*Well, Mr. O'Flaridy,* I thought to myself, thinking up all kinds of things I could do to *him* in return to get revenge, *we'll just see who gets the last laugh!*

I fumed around the streets of town, my brain reeling back

and forth, not even stopping to think about whether my anger was right or wrong, not once thinking about God or what he might think. All I could think about was Robin O'Flaridy and how I could fix him!

And what made it even worse was that his article was *better* than mine. I couldn't stand to admit it, but he was a better writer!

I don't know how I spent the rest of the day. I think I walked around town a while longer—but for sure *this* walk wasn't one I spent in prayer! I must have gone back to the office, but whether I did any more work, I can't remember. I was just so mad!

By evening I had cooled down. In fact, I was embarrassed at myself and had to go outside for a while alone to talk to God a little about it. I told him I was sorry for getting so angry, because I knew it wasn't right. I'd been thinking so much recently on being true and everything that *truth* involved. I suppose that's what vexed me so much about what they had done—that they weren't being truthful at all, not to the people reading their paper or to me. But after a while I realized I had no business thinking about whether *other* people were truthful or not. There was only one person I had the right to criticize for not being truthful, and that was me. It was none of my affair what Robin O'Flaridy did about living honestly and doing things right. But what I did—that *was* my affair!

I walked around a while and thought and prayed. But when I went back inside I still didn't have everything figured out.

We talked about it, and Pa said something that helped me see a little more inside the situation. I had just told him and Almeda about realizing that I had to take care of myself and whether I did the right thing, rather than criticizing others for what they did.

"That's right, Corrie," Pa said. "One of the biggest things about growing up is to take responsibility for yourself without forever blaming other folks for everything that you don't like. That's something me and your Uncle Nick's had to learn—and sometimes the hard way. It still ain't easy for Nick, who gets to blaming your grandpa for things he done. And I used to blame Nick for things that I later had to face up to myself. Blame's a terrible thing, Corrie. A mind that's set to blame other folks all the time is eventually gonna destroy any chance of setting things right, 'cause all it's doing is looking at everything that's wrong.''

He stopped for a minute and gave the log in the fireplace a poke with a stick.

"But on the other hand, Corrie, if you're gonna write for this man Kemble, and you're gonna work for his newspaper, then you gotta be able to trust him, and you gotta know where you stand. It's a sight different than blaming a fella when you try to get your business dealings straight so you know what's up and what's down. If I'm gonna have some kind of a deal going with your uncle or Alkali or if I walk into Royce's bank and say I want to borrow some money, then there ain't nothing wrong with saying, 'Now, Nick, here's what you gotta do, and here's what I gotta do, and since we're both men of our word, then we'll do what we say. Then we shake hands and agree on it, and that's that. Or I might say, 'Now, Mr. Royce, I don't exactly like you, but I want to borrow some money. How much'll it cost?' And then he might say, 'I don't like you either, Hollister, and I don't like your wife running for mayor against me, but if you want to borrow money, it'll cost you 6 percent.' Then if it's agreeable, we shake hands and that's the deal. We don't have to like each other, but everybody's got to know where everybody else stands, otherwise you can't do business together.''

He stopped, and I waited for more. But he was finished.

"Is that all, Pa?" I asked. "What is it you think I ought to do now?"

Almeda, who had been listening to everything, laughed.

"In his wonderful roundabout way," she said, "I think your father's been trying to tell you that even though you may have to get over your anger and blaming, you still have to find out where you stand and why they did what they did. Otherwise, how can you go on writing for the *Alta*?"

"Maybe it ain't as bad as it looks, Corrie," added Pa. "Are you sure it's your article?"

"Some of the exact words, Pa. I told you about the pioneer in a state full of pioneers."

"And you and Kemble had a deal for the article."

"Well, we didn't shake hands that I can remember," I said, "but he told me he'd pay me a dollar each for three articles on the election."

Pa shrugged, and nodded his head thoughtfully.

"It sounds to me, Corrie Belle, reporter of the Mother Lode, that you need to get some things straight with your editor," said Almeda.

I gazed into her earnest face, and realized she was right. I let out a deep sigh, then got up and went into my room, where I sat down and immediately began a letter to San Francisco.

"Dear Mr. Kemble," I began. "I have to admit I was given a considerable surprise when I opened the copy of the *Alta* that arrived in Miracle Springs this afternoon. . . ."

I then went on to ask all the questions that were on my mind, as nicely as I could, though I did ask him right out if he'd let Robin put his name on my article—and if not, then how was it that I found some of my very words appearing in the paper?

It was a long letter, but I finally got everything said I wanted to say. Once I'd done it I felt a lot better. For a writer, getting your thoughts said to *somebody*—even if it's just on paper—is always a great feeling of relief. I wondered if I ought to send it at all—this might be the last I'd ever hear from Mr. Kemble. But like Pa said, I had to know how things stood if I wanted to keep having dealings with him.

The letter went south on the next morning's stage.

# CHAPTER 30

## MR. KEMBLE'S REPLY

The next five days were torture!

I knew I couldn't possibly hear anything back from Mr. Kemble for at least six days, yet even on the fifth day I couldn't help being there to meet the stage and frantically looking through the mail.

During that time I must have wished I had the letter back a thousand times. *What an idiot I was!* I kept saying to myself. *He's never going to print another thing I write! He's never going to even answer my letter!*

But that didn't keep me from meeting the stage every day.

I tried to do my work and to keep up with my interviews about the election just in case I got another chance with the series. But I was so distracted I finally just gave up.

On the eighth day, the seventeenth of August, there among the rest of the mail was an envelope with the return address: The California *Alta*, Montgomery Street, San Francisco, California.

I grabbed it and ran off down the street. I had to be alone. I was so afraid of what might be inside that envelope!

Finally I wound up inside the livery of the Freight Company, up in the loft. No one was around, and the silence and smells calmed me down like they always did. At home the barn was still one of my favorite places.

I took several deep breaths, then looked down at the envelope in my hands. My fingers were shaking. My whole future as a writer might be at stake. It might even be over already.

Finally I scratched off an edge of the stuck-down part, then jammed a finger through and tore the top off the envelope. Then I reached inside with two fingers and pulled out the letter, unfolded it, and began to read:

Dear Miss Hollister,

Your letter raises some interesting questions.

First, you said you thought we had a deal about you writing on the Miracle Springs election. But we had no such "deal." I said I'd pay you a buck a piece *if* you sent me something acceptable. But at the time in question I hadn't seen a word from you yet. And time was wasting! We are a *news*paper. People buy the *Alta* to read news.

In the meantime, O'Flaridy came to me with a legitimate news article. He'd researched it in our files and the limited library we have here at the *Alta* and it was a decently done bit of writing. What am I to do, turn it down? I'm an editor, he's a reporter; he brought me news, I printed the story. It's as simple as that.

Face it, Miss Hollister, he scooped you on this one. You may not like it. Maybe it doesn't seem fair. But then nobody ever accused the newspaper business of being fair in the first place. And maybe that's why you don't see too many female reporters. It's a tough business, and the reporter who gets the goods gets published. There's no place in this business for feminine emotions and for getting your feelings hurt. Talk is cheap. If you don't deliver, you get left holding the paper and reading it, while somebody else does the writing and reporting.

Now as to your chief complaint, the O'Flaridy article was set to go before I received yours in the mail. He did not take a word of yours. You can trust me on that. I would never condone such a thing. If I'm tough, you'll also find me a fair man. The title for his piece was taken from your words. That was my doing. It was a clever phrase that caught my eye and I would have written you acknowledging the fact except that your letter beat me to it. I apologize if I overstepped my bounds. I will make it up to you in the future.

As to your question about pay, I gave O'Flaridy $4 for the

article. It was solid news, and before you think of complaining, remember that he's a young man with plenty of experience that you don't have. That's why he's on our staff and why I offer him a bonus incentive like this one for bringing me something in addition to his regular assignments. If you think it's unfair, remember, this is a man's business. If you don't like the offers I make to you, then take your writing elsewhere.

Now to something more serious on my side. Given the false impression you gave initially over the whole business about the *C.B.* name, I do not feel that the payment I offered you is unfair, since you are a woman. But it does not seem you have learned your lesson about false impressions! Robin tells me this woman running for mayor is no longer Mrs. *Parrish* as you told me, but rather Mrs. *Hollister,* and none other than your own stepmother. I must tell you, Miss Hollister, I was highly annoyed when I learned that fact. You should have been clear on that point up front. It could look like you were attempting to further the campaign of your stepmother rather than to carry out objective news writing. That fact did, I must confess, contribute to my decision to run Robin's story.

We have a term in this business called "conflict of interest," and it looks to me as if you have landed yourself squarely in the middle of it. How do you possibly expect to remain objective and unbiased in writing about an election of which you are such an intrinsic part?

My first inclination was to withdraw any and all commitments and cancel all plans to publish anything else of yours, including the two prior ones I am still holding. But upon further thought I realized you may not have intentionally tried to deceive me. Thus, I have decided to keep an open mind, and if you present me with anything publishable on the election, I will run it as per our one dollar per article arrangement. Given the circumstances, I do not feel obliged to hold to our two-dollar "deal." I originally offered you one dollar, and one dollar it will be. But it will have to be well-done and objective, or I will have no choice but to send it back to you.

The two previous articles will also be run at payment of $1 each rather than the $4 stated originally. Under the circumstances, I think that is more than generous. The article received last week concerning the Royce-Hollister election, I will obviously not be able to use.

I remain, Miss Hollister, sincerely yours,

Edward Kemble

By the time I was finished reading, I was crying. Part of me couldn't help but be outraged at Robin for "scooping" me, as Mr. Kemble had called it. He'd done it on purpose, just to spite me—I knew that. And I was angry at Mr. Kemble for talking down at me about my "feminine emotions" and my "hurt feelings." No, it didn't seem fair that Robin would get $4 and I only $1! The whole thing wasn't fair!

But then my logical mind reminded me that Robin's article *was* better than mine had been. That made me mad all over again—but mad at myself, mad for being so stupid as to think I could be a writer.

I was no writer! My writing was nothing compared to everything else in the *Alta*! A dollar was too much to pay for my writing.

I thought about all the rest Mr. Kemble had said. I hadn't meant to hold back the truth about Almeda. It just never came up about our being related. I'd never even thought about what he called a "conflict of interest." That made me mad all over again. Mad at myself.

I *had* made a mistake! I hadn't told him the complete truth. Maybe it hadn't been on purpose, but what difference did that make? Why should he trust me after twice giving him the wrong impression?

I sat and cried for a long time—sad, angry, disappointed, hurt, and irritated at myself. I couldn't help but feel like a complete fool. I had wanted to be a writer, and now I realized I wasn't fooling anyone.

For years I have kept Mr. Kemble's letter. Every once in a while I get it out and read it again, because in a lot of ways— though I don't think he intended it necessarily—Mr. Kemble's words helped me in the growing-up process. Writing the letter to him had forced me to face a situation squarely. And his reply helped me to see for the first time what was involved in being part of the newspaper business. Although I didn't want to admit it, Mr. Kemble was right—it *was* a tough business.

It was time I gave it up and tried to get on to doing something else with the rest of my life.

# CHAPTER 31

# "HOW BAD DO YOU WANT IT?"

I moped around for a few days, keeping mostly to myself. I didn't even talk to Almeda or Pa. I was too dejected and defeated to want to talk about it.

They gave me room to wallow around in my self-pity for a while. But then eventually they both began to try to encourage me out of my despondency. When you're in one of those holes where you feel everything in your life has failed, part of you doesn't even want to get out of the hole you've dug for yourself. Strange as it seems, you almost enjoy feeling sorry for yourself.

But Pa and Almeda wouldn't let me do that.

"Ain't it about time you got back to your article writing?" Pa asked me the second evening after I'd got the letter.

I shrugged and said I didn't know if I'd do any more articles.

"What?" he exclaimed. "This from my daughter who wants to be a newspaper reporter more than anything? What're you talking about, girl?"

Finally I showed them the letter.

They both read it quietly and seriously, and neither of them said much else that night. But over the next couple of days both Pa and Almeda found a time to be alone with me.

"There's times when a body's just gotta force himself to keep going," Pa told me, "even though maybe inside everything's screaming at him to do something else. If something's the right thing to do, then you just gotta do it."

He looked at me carefully. "You want to keep writing, don't you?" he said.

"Of course I do, Pa. But everything Mr. Kemble said is true. And besides, my writing is terrible, and he doesn't think I was honest with him."

"But it's something you still want to do?"

"Yes."

"Then how else you figure on gettin' any better at it if you don't do it? And how you figure on gettin' Kemble to trust you if you don't keep going to him and writing for him and showing him he *can* trust you? Ain't no other way but to keep at it."

"I just don't know how I can, Pa, after that letter of his."

"I reckon it's a setback for you, all right. And I can understand how it'd hurt a mite, those things he said. But don't you want to prove him wrong, prove to him that you *can* do it, prove that a woman *can* write as well as that O'Flaridy kid?"

"Yeah."

"Then you gotta toughen up, Corrie! Get that Belle blood working for you. Toughen up, fight back, keep writing and don't let either Kemble or O'Flaridy take your dream away. Maybe they stole your idea, and even your words. But don't let them steal your dream. Fight for it, Corrie. And if Kemble doesn't like what you write, then do like he said and take it someplace else. But don't let him rob you of what God gave you just 'cause he don't have the good sense to see what a fine writer you're gonna be someday."

He gave me a hug and a kiss, and I cried a little again. It made me feel better just knowing that *he* still believed in me.

Almeda told me what it was like for her after Mr. Parrish died.

"After my husband died, Corrie, I was absolutely despondent. I felt so alone and out of place in this world. We hadn't been in California much longer than a year and our business was just getting going. I was the only woman in Miracle Springs besides the saloon girls. Mr. Parrish and I had dreamed of the life we would build in the new west, and all of a sudden it was shattered."

"But you probably didn't fall apart like me," I said.

"Oh, I did," she answered.

"I cried thousands of tears, so I think I know a little of what you are feeling right now. I wanted to just sit down and die at times. Then at other times I would decide to pack everything up and go back East. I had my reasons for not wanting to go back to Boston. Someday, when the time is right, perhaps I'll tell you about that period of my life. In light of what I've seen and been through, Corrie, God has been so wonderfully good to me. But it wasn't because of being afraid of my past that I decided not to go back. No, Corrie, it was because I finally realized I couldn't give up. That wouldn't have been fair to my husband and to the dream we'd had of a new and happy life in California. And it wouldn't have been fair to me!"

She stopped, and it was real quiet. I hadn't seen that distant look in her eyes since she and Pa had been married, but there it was again. I knew she was thinking about another time and another place, and I didn't want to disturb her.

But as usual, the silence only lasted a few moments. Then her face suddenly brightened and she spoke again.

"In every person's life, Corrie, there come times like you're going through right now. Usually everyone has several such moments, when everything you think you wanted seems suddenly gone, destroyed, unattainable. At those times a woman's got to stop and take stock of herself. Just like in business. We have to do periodic stock-checks, inventories of supplies—just like you and Marcus did out in the supply room last week. We had to know what we had on hand so we'd know what to do in the future.

"A person has to do that too—take inventory, check the supply room. Especially when you come to what you might call 'crisis' times, or times of evaluation and question, when you have to ask yourself where you're going as a person, where your life is headed. You have to take stock. You have to find out if where you've been going is still where you *want* to go, or if you need to *change* directions."

"And you think maybe that's where I'm at now?"

"Quite possibly.

"Sometimes God allows difficulties and hardships and questions and heartbreaks to come our way because he wants us to change directions. And so whenever they come we have to stop and try to listen to his voice and ask him what he's trying to get through to us. But there are other times when the disappointments come not to get us to change directions at all, but to strengthen and toughen us, so that we will be all the more dedicated to accomplishing what we felt God was leading us toward in the first place. Do you see the difference, Corrie?" she asked.

I nodded. "Like how hard it was when us kids and Pa got together," I said. "I think we all wanted to find some way out of that situation—especially Pa!"

Almeda laughed.

"But we knew we had to stick it out because it was the right thing."

"Exactly! And that's why I decided to stay here rather than go back East. After taking stock of myself, I realized that I *wanted* to make it work. I had to ask myself how willing I was to fight for what I wanted to do. And I decided I was willing to fight for it, even though I knew it would be hard and that men would probably be against me at first. But I was determined to fight for what I believed in, to fight for my dream.

"Now you're facing almost exactly the same thing. You've had a bad letdown. You're a woman up against stiff odds. The man you're up against—in my case it was the men of the community whose support and business I had to have to survive. In your case it is an editor you have to prove yourself to—such men don't necessarily make it easy for us. Now you have to take inventory of the direction you've been going and ask yourself if it's *still* the direction you want to *keep* going.

"What it boils down to, Corrie, is this—how bad do you want it?"

"I *do* want to be able to write," I said.

"I had to ask myself the same question. How bad did I want to see my business succeed? What sacrifices was I willing to make? Was I willing to fight for what I believed in? In the same way—how bad do *you* still want to be a writer? Are you willing to fight for it? What sacrifices are you willing to make? If you don't think you're a good writer now, how hard are you willing to work to improve? Are you willing to work twice as hard as a man would have to, and get only half the pay?"

She paused and looked into my eyes. "How much do you want it, Corrie?"

"I think I want it," I answered lamely.

"Well, if after taking stock of yourself, you decide you *do* still want to be a writer, then don't let Kemble or O'Flaridy or anyone else stop you. Go after it! It's your dream—so fight for it, and don't let go of it."

# CHAPTER 32

## MY DECISION AND
## WHAT CAME OF IT

Even before Almeda was through talking, I knew what my decision was!

This was one time when I didn't need to go out in the woods for a long time to think and try to figure things out. I knew what I wanted—and that was to keep writing! And if it meant working even harder than before and trying to make my writing better than it had been, I'd do it! If it meant getting only $1 an article, maybe I'd do that too. But then maybe I'd tell Mr. Kemble I wanted more. And if he said my articles weren't good enough to pay more, then I'd *make* them good enough! I'd improve my writing. I'd practice. I'd learn.

How bad did I want to do what I'd dreamed of doing? I figured I wanted it bad enough to fight for it, just like Almeda had.

Within ten or fifteen minutes I was in the saddle and on my way back toward town. It was Saturday afternoon, a good time to interview some more people about the election. If my first article wasn't good enough for Mr. Kemble, then I'd make my second one all the better—with facts and the five *w's* and human interest all put together! I'd make it so interesting even *he* would enjoy reading it! And since I'd gotten behind during this last week, I couldn't afford to waste another minute. Most of the people in town had seen Almeda's flyer. Mr. Royce had put up a great big new banner on the side of his bank building

just three days ago, which said in big letters and bright paint:
ROYCE FOR MAYOR. MIRACLE SPRINGS' FUTURE
PROSPERITY DEPENDS ON YOUR VOTE. Folks were
really interested and were talking a lot about everything. Now
was the time to see everybody to get their thoughts and reactions while interest was high and they were willing to talk.

But about halfway into town a huge new idea suddenly hit
me! It was such a great idea I completely forgot about Mr.
Royce and Almeda and Miracle Springs in an instant. If I could
write an article about someone *really* important, about news
that was significant to the whole country, not just a little town
like Miracle Springs, then Mr. Kemble would *have* to print it!
And he'd see that I could be a reporter who could write about
more than just pretty leaves and sunsets and interesting people
nobody'd ever heard of.

I yanked back on the reins, swung my horse around on the
trail, dug in my heels to her flanks, and galloped back to the
house.

I ran straight inside and began searching through the pile
of old newspapers Pa kept by the fireplace to start fires with. I
hoped it was still there!

Then I remembered. I'd saved the August 8 issue with my
own articles. I ran into my room. There it was, right with the
others! Hurriedly I scanned through the paper until I found it.
I read the brief article again, then went back into the big room
where Pa and Almeda were sitting with puzzled expressions
watching me scurry around.

"Look!" I exclaimed, pointing to the paper still in my hand.
"It says right here that there is a controversy about Mr. Fremont's estate, but it doesn't say what it is. What if I could find
out? That would sure be a story Mr. Kemble couldn't refuse!"

"There ain't no mystery there," laughed Pa. "Everyone
knows they been trying to claim jump and get his gold mines
away from him ever since he found gold on his land."

"Who, Pa? Who's *they*?"

"His enemies, people who want his gold—neighbors, claim
jumpers, drifters, Mexicans. Anybody who's rich and powerful

always has a pack of people trying to do him in, and John Fremont's both. All this time he's been back in Washington senatoring and now running for President, folks back here's trying to get their hands on his gold."

"But *who*, Pa?"

"I don't know. I suppose there's lots of 'em."

"Well, I'm gonna go find out," I said determinedly.

Pa laughed again. "What you figure on doin', girl?" he said. "The man's running for President of the United States! And *you* figure on uncovering some mystery about him that no one else knows?"

"I don't know, Pa. It's probably downright foolish—but I *know* there's a story there. I can *feel* it! A story for me . . . if I can just find it!"

"And how you figure to find this story that's waitin' just for you?" I know the smile on Pa's face wasn't meant to be making fun of me, but at the same time he just couldn't keep from chuckling. I was serious.

"I don't know. Maybe I'll just go out there and start looking around. I guess maybe that's what a reporter's got to do sometimes, and maybe it's time I learned how."

"Go where—Mariposa? That's a hundred and twenty, maybe a hundred and thirty miles."

"Through the mountains," added Almeda. "Through Sacramento and the valley roads, more like a hundred seventy-five."

"If that's what I gotta do for a story, then maybe that's just what I gotta do."

I reckon I'd been swept along in this conversation by the emotion of the moment. But the minute those words were out of my mouth, suddenly the reality of what I'd said seemed to strike us all. There was silence for a moment, and I guess somehow in the very saying of the words a determination rose up within me to *do* what I'd said, even if the words had been spoken lightly. I think Pa and Almeda realized, too, that a change had come in that instant. And maybe inside, both of them had to face how they were going to react to my growing up.

Almeda's next words were not what you'd expect from a mother who was worried about what her son or daughter was about to do, and who wanted to talk them out of it.

"I think it's a sensational idea, Corrie!" said Almeda. "If you are going to go after something and follow a dream you have, you might as well go straight to the top."

Pa had been serious for a minute, but now he chuckled again. "You're a determined one," he said. "Once you make your mind up about something, I wouldn't want to be the one standin' in your way. But how do you figure on going all that way . . . how do you figure on findin' something out that other folks don't know?"

"I don't know," I answered again with all my innocent youthful enthusiasm. "I'll find a way."

"You want me to take you down there, maybe go with you?" he asked.

I hesitated a minute before answering. "I don't know, Pa," I said finally. "Something inside me wants to do this alone, though I'm afraid at the same time. Maybe one of you should go with me . . . if you could." I was already starting to get cold feet about my idea.

A little frown passed over Almeda's forehead and I could tell she was thinking. But the reply she gave startled me.

"I don't think we ought to, Corrie," she said after a minute. "This is your idea, and you're the one who wants to go down there and uncover a story you think is waiting for you. I think it's time you figured out the best way to go about it yourself. I can give you the names of good boarding houses all the way, people I know and that we can trust. But I think perhaps it's time you saw what you were capable of. You can do it—I know you can."

"It is a fearsome thing, to go so far alone, not even knowing what I am looking for, not even knowing who to talk to, not knowing if anybody will listen to me." My earlier resolve was fading fast.

"They will listen to you, young lady. You can be very determined . . . and very persuasive! Besides, part of the process

I was telling you about of fighting for your dream—part of it is learning to stand alone if you have to, facing the dangers and uncertainties, and learning to go where maybe no one else has gone in just the same way, or asking questions no one has voiced before. That's part of growing up—finding your own inner strength with God. Something inside tells me this might be one of those times. If there's a story there meant for you, then you have to be the one to find it."

"I don't know, Almeda," said Pa. "I ain't so sure I agree with you. There's bears and varmints and who knows what kind of hoodlums all the way up an' down that way. I don't like it. I'll go with her, just to keep an eye on things."

Neither of us said anything more. From the sound of it, Pa had made up his mind, and I knew what he said was the logical way to look at it. So I was surprised the next morning when he announced that he'd changed his mind, and that if I wanted to make the trip alone, he wouldn't forbid me. He'd still rather he or Zack went with me, but he'd trust me to make the decision.

Naturally I was fearful at first as I anticipated such a trip, such a quest for the unknown. Later I looked back at this as another one of those growing experiences. And I came to thank Pa and Almeda afterward for not doing it for me, for giving me encouragement but not actually helping me, and for forcing me not just to believe in what I wanted to do—but for forcing me to believe in myself too. Whatever I felt at the time, Pa and Almeda didn't try to make it easy for me. They pushed me out from under their wings to go after this story—whatever it was!—by myself, showed me that they really did believe in me, and were ready to treat me like an adult. There's just no other way to get your legs strong unless you stand on them without holding on to someone else. And that's what I was about to do.

I would have to finish my interviews and articles about the Miracle Springs election for mayor later. Whatever was waiting for me at the Fremont estate, I figured it had more potential for being something that Mr. Kemble would take notice of.

Two days later, my decision had been made!

With saddlebags full of a week's supply of food, and with blankets in case I couldn't put up at a boardinghouse for any reason, I set off on my faithful horse Raspberry alone, headed for Sacramento.

# CHAPTER 33

## TO MARIPOSA

The two-day ride to Sacramento was by now a familiar one. I had traveled the road three or four times in each direction. It was almost like coming to another one of my "homes" to stay at Miss Baxter's boardinghouse again. When I told her where I was going, she gave me several names of people she knew along the way where I could lodge.

"If you go down the valley," she said, "there are nice women who will put you up in Lodi, Modesto, Turlock, Merced. I'll write their names down for you, dearie."

I thanked her.

"But if you take the short route through the foothills, it's rougher, and mostly men. I don't know of a single reputable place from Angels Camp down through Chinese Camp and Moccasin Flat. No, you'd best stick to the valley and then cut east from Merced."

She wrote the names down for me, and having them in my pocket gave me a feeling of security. Then we talked a little about our old trail boss, Captain Dixon. She said he was just about due, and I told her to give him a hug for me.

"He'll be so proud when I tell him how you've grown and how you're a real reporter for a San Francisco newspaper!" she said.

"Not a reporter," I corrected her. "Just barely a writer, and only sometimes at that!" I laughed.

"Perhaps that will change when you find what you are seeking in Mariposa," she said.

I hoped so, too, although inside I was getting more and more fearful that I was on what Pa would call a fool's errand. But I wasn't about to turn back now, even if I did come back empty-handed.

I left the comfort and security of Miss Baxter's and Sacramento early the next morning, and went straight south on the road leading through Lodi, Stockton, and Modesto. It was hot and dry and dusty, and I was glad I had plenty of water with me. There weren't too many people on the road—now and then a rider on horseback, and two stagecoaches headed to Sacramento.

At first I rode pretty hard, but before the morning was half gone, I knew I had to slow down or poor Raspberry would drop from exhaustion in the heat. Stockton was fifty miles, and I'd thought of spending my first night south of Sacramento there. But I passed through Lodi well before noon, so I decided I'd try to make it all the way to Modesto, where I had the name of a boardinghouse. That extra thirty miles in the afternoon sun nearly wore me out, and when I got to Modesto that night I didn't think I could ever get in a saddle again in my life!

I didn't start nearly so early the next morning. I only had to go thirty miles that day, though on my sore rump it was far enough! I got to Merced in the middle of the afternoon, found Harcourt's Boarding House, took a bath, and then fell fast asleep until dinnertime.

The next morning I prepared to go to the Fremont estate, only fifteen miles from Merced. I told Mrs. Harcourt that I might be back that night, but that I couldn't be sure.

When I set off east from Merced toward the foothills, the rising sun was in my eyes. As it rose in the sky, the hills came closer and closer, with the mountains in the distance behind them. It was probably ten-thirty or eleven in the morning when I approached the Rancho de las Mariposas, estate of presidential candidate John Charles Fremont. In my heart, I must confess, I felt about as uncertain, scared, and intimidated as I had ever felt in my life. If this was "following my dream," as Almeda had put it, I began to wonder if it wasn't time to just give the whole thing up and turn around! I had no idea who I'd run into or what they'd say to me . . . or what I'd say to them!

*Lord*, I prayed silently, remembering my prayers before the blizzard and the article I'd written about the Wards, *I don't know what I'm supposed to do next, but please guide my steps . . . and show me what you want me to do.*

And then, taking in a deep breath of the warm dry air, I rode forward toward the gate of the estate, about half a mile outside the little village of Mariposa.

I learned later some things about the estate I didn't know at the time. In 1847, the explorer John Fremont gave a friend $3,000 to buy some land for him near San Jose, just south of San Francisco where he hoped to settle with his family. By mistake, however, the man bought a huge estate eighty miles too far inland, across the flat, dry San Joaquin Valley. At first they were disappointed, but as soon as the Fremonts saw their new land, they realized perhaps the mistake had been a blessing in disguise.

And as I entered the estate, I understood why! The Fremont ranch covered over 44,000 acres, with mountains and streams, waterfalls, trees, forest, pools, meadows, areas of rich soil, and even two small towns. I had already been through the first, for which the ranch was named, and I would later get to know the town of Bear Valley, and spend several nights in Oso House, the small hotel owned by Fremont himself. Fremont named his estate *Mariposa* after the millions of beautiful, tiny winged creatures that flew and fluttered all about it—Ranch of the Butterflies.

Even before Fremont had set foot on the land himself, farther to the north James Marshall and John Sutter discovered gold at Sutter's Mill along the American River, and the California gold rush was on. Only a year later, in 1849, huge amounts of gold were also discovered at Mariposa. Overnight John Fremont was a rich man. He had been well known already because of all the exploring he had done throughout the West for years; he became even more famous for the stories of the gold found on his land. When California became a state in

1850, John Fremont was immediately elected one of its first senators. Fremont's wife Jessie was the daughter of the well-known United States senator from Virginia, Thomas Hart Benton. Fremont was therefore a nationally known politician throughout the whole country. So when the new Republican party was formed in 1854, they nominated John Fremont to run as their candidate for President.

Fremont had not even been back to California during the whole campaign, so I didn't know what kind of story I figured to get by coming here. And as I rode up to the gate I desperately wanted to turn around and go home. But I was here, and it was too late to turn back, so I might as well see what happened.

A man was sitting in a little shed by the gate, which stood open. A painted sign on the fence read *Rancho de las Mariposas*. The man looked like a Mexican, and he stood up as I approached and glanced over me and my horse. He wasn't carrying a rifle, though he had a pistol in his holster at his waist, and he didn't seem too friendly. I suppose he was standing guard on account of the trouble Pa talked about with the Fremont mines.

"I . . . I'm a newspaper writer," I said hesitantly. "I've come to—"

But he didn't wait for me to finish and didn't seem to care what I was doing there. With a wave of his head, he motioned me to come through the gate, then pointed along the road toward some buildings in the distance, which I assumed was the ranch itself. I urged my horse along slowly, and the man sauntered back to his shed and sat down, never speaking a word.

*Well,* I thought to myself with relief, *at least I made it past the outside gate!*

As I approached the house, which wasn't big and fancy at all like I had expected, I could hear the sound of machinery and voices and wagons and workers in the distance. I knew that must be the gold mining going on. And as I got closer I saw more and more people about—all men, lots of Mexicans—but none of them paid any attention to me. There were several buildings, mostly adobe, a barn with corrals and stables attached with both horses and cattle in the enclosed areas. Several log buildings were scattered about, with a few men going in and out of them, and I figured maybe that's where the mine and ranch workers lived. The main house was made of wood planks, but it didn't look impressive like the house of a U.S. President. The Fremonts had never actually lived here, however. They spent most of their time back in Washington, D.C.

I stopped, got off my horse, tied her to the hitching rail in front of the house, and took in a deep breath. I looked around again. Still no one had taken any notice of me. I walked up onto the porch, then knocked on the door, my knees shaking.

The door opened and another Mexican appeared. He could not have been much older than I was.

"Hello," I said, trying to sound confident, "I am a newspaper writer and I have come to write an article—"

I paused just for a second, wondering from the fellow's blank stare whether he understood English. But even before I opened my mouth to continue, he spoke quickly.

"Sí, you come see Mrs. Carter!" He motioned me inside. "Venga aquí, you seet down . . . you seet here," he said, pointing to a chair. "I get Mrs. Carter—she veesit you!" And before I realized it, the young man had left the room and I was alone again.

A minute or two passed. Then I heard footsteps coming down the hall in my direction. A woman appeared and came toward me.

"I am Ankelita Carter," she said. "Felipe says you want to see me about something for a newspaper."

I liked Mrs. Carter immediately. From her dark brown skin it was plain at once that she was Mexican, and her broad smile of white teeth put me instantly at ease. Despite the color of her skin and her overall appearance that seemed to me at first glance that of a servant or maid, she spoke flawless English without even the hint of an accent. There was even a cultured sound to her tone, which made me immediately curious.

She was a stocky woman, not fat, but strongly built, and looked well accustomed to work. She might have reminded me of Katie, though she was taller and her broad shoulders had almost a manly quality. She was not "pretty," although her brown complexion was clear, her eyes bright, and her smile so infectious that you couldn't help but consider her attractive to gaze at and converse with. Her hair was pure black without a trace of gray, but from the rest of her appearance I would have guessed her to be somewhere in her mid-forties.

"I write sometimes for the *Alta*," I said, "and I was hoping to be able to write something about the estate or the Fremonts. My name is Corrie Belle Hollister."

"Well, Miss Hollister," replied Mrs. Carter, "I am very pleased to make your acquaintance." She held out her hand, and as I shook it I was further reassured by this woman with the friendly smile. "You must have come a long distance." She sat down in a chair opposite me.

"I have ridden four and a half days," I said.

"My, you *are* dedicated! But I must admit to some surprise. You are a woman, and a very young one at that. How do you come to be a reporter? I've never heard of such a thing."

"I don't suppose I'm *really* what you'd call an official reporter," I replied. "I try to write things I'm interested in, and then I hope the editor will want to print them."

"And he is willing to print something written by a woman?"

"Actually, the first few things he's printed appeared under the name C.B. Hollister. To tell you the truth, he hasn't printed anything of mine since he found out I was a girl not even twenty years old yet."

"How old are you, Corrie?" Mrs. Carter asked.

"Nineteen."

"Well, you are brave to try what you're doing." She paused. "Hmm . . . C.B. Hollister, you say?" She seemed to be thinking. "Did you write something about, let's see . . . it's coming to me—something about a lady from Virginia who went out to California as a mail-order bride and planted an apple tree?"

"Yes, yes!" I answered excitedly. "Did you actually read it?"

"I did indeed," she said. "It was very well done."

She smiled at me again, and gave a little nod, as if she was looking me over again for the first time.

"My, but isn't this something! For us to meet like this—a year later and all the way across the continent."

"What do you mean?" I asked. "I've only just come from north of Sacramento."

She laughed broadly. "That's not what I meant," she said. "I read your article in Virginia, when I was there with Mrs. Fremont."

"It really did get printed back there?" I said. "Mr. Kemble said it was going to be, but I never knew if it really did."

"Oh, yes, we all read it. Mrs. Fremont, the Senator."

"You were there with the Fremonts?" I asked, my surprise showing through.

"I've been with Mrs. Fremont since they were in Monterey in 1850. Her father, you know, is Senator Benton, and we were at their Virginia estate of Cherry Grove often, until the house burned down two years ago. After that and the death of Mrs. Fremont's mother, we went south less frequently. Though that is still where we encountered your article. Jessie herself is a writer, or at least she helped her husband a great deal with the memoirs of his travels. She hopes to write again one day. Just wait until I tell her I've met you! She will be thrilled. I know she will recall the article and your name because it made an impression on her at the time."

"I can hardly believe it," I said, in wonder. "To think that someone that far away actually read something I wrote out here!"

We continued to visit, and Mrs. Carter turned out to be as interesting herself as the Fremonts or the election or the estate. From a wealthy Mexican family, she had been well-educated in eastern United States, had returned to Mexico where she had married a California businessman. Her husband had been killed and most of her family's wealth lost during the Mexican war, and in Monterey, Jessie Fremont had taken her into her household, at first as a domestic. But soon realizing Ankelita's training and education, Mrs. Fremont put her in charge of most of the household, including the Fremont children. The two women fast became friends, and Ankelita had been part of the Fremont home ever since—in Washington, D.C. , during Mr. Fremont's term as senator, back in California, accompanying them to Europe. Only two months earlier had she left the Fremonts to return to California.

"But this recent trip," she concluded, "was *so* much more pleasant, now that there is a railroad across the Isthmus instead of having to walk or ride a donkey or be carried and pulled in carts by Indians." She laughed at the memory.

"Why did you return to California?" I asked.

"I felt it would be best for the campaign," Ankelita replied. She stopped as a look of sadness crossed her eyes. "I love Mr. Fremont," she went on, "and Jessie is like a sister to me. But politics is a field that attracts many enemies, where cruel things are said and done in order that men might gain their selfish ends. And many things have been said about Mr. and Mrs. Fremont that are untrue, things that others would use to defeat Mr. Fremont in the election. Some newspapers began to report that he was a Catholic. Though it is not true, the mere report has damaged him greatly. His own father-in-law, Jessie's father Mr. Benton, has spoken out harshly against Mr. Fremont, even against his own daughter."

"But why?" I asked.

"Because Senator Benton is a Democrat and his son-in-law is a Republican. The Republicans are against slavery, and most of the Democrats are in favor of slavery. And though Senator Benton himself is from the slave state of Virginia, he is personally against slavery. Yet he cannot make himself cross the party line to support his own son-in-law, though he shares his views. I find it appalling that his party has more influence than his own conscience."

"Is that why you left?" I asked.

Mrs. Carter drew in a deep sigh, and I saw a look of something like sadness on her face, even pain.

"I came to feel that my presence would ultimately do him more harm than good in the election," she said at length.

"Being raised as a Mexican, I am Catholic. It was only a matter of time before Buchanan's press writers would have discovered about my religion, and they would have used it against the Colonel. And there were those who were beginning to talk against Jessie because of me, implying that I was Mrs. Fremont's 'Mexican slave,' as they called it. Not a word of it was true. But just the darkness of my skin was enough to feed prejudices, and the hint of such a thing would have been enough to hurt the Colonel because of his strong anti-slavery position. All through the campaign people have been trying to link Mr. and Mrs. Fremont to slavery, digging up Jessie's Virginian upbringing, and asking pointed questions about their black servants, all of whom were perfectly free just like me."

"It doesn't seem fair," I said.

"Politics is never fair, Corrie. Politics is politics, and it's a matter of winning however you can and by whatever you have to say about your opponent. But *fair*—no, politics is rarely fair."

"It just doesn't seem right!"

"No, I don't suppose it's right any more than it is fair. But if you're going to be in politics, that's just the way it is."

"Did the Fremonts ask you to leave?"

"No, Jessie would never have done that. But when I told her of my decision, she knew it was best. She gave me money for passage and asked me to come back here to watch over their household affairs. Not that I could really be of much help with the business of the mine, but they want to know there is someone here they can trust completely who can tell them what is happening. So I returned, and I have been here a little over a month. After her husband is elected President, Jessie wants me to come back and live with them in the White House."

"Oh, wouldn't that be wonderful!"

"And then *you* could come visit us, Corrie, and write a story about President and Mrs. Fremont. *That* would surely make that editor of yours stand up and take notice of you—even if you are a young woman!"

I laughed. But just the thought of me ever visiting the White

House was too unbelievable to fathom.

"But you cannot have come all this way just to listen to me," Ankelita said. "You must have known the Fremonts have not been in California for five years. What did you want to write an article about, Corrie?"

I shrugged sheepishly. We'd been talking for almost an hour and the subject of my writing had hardly yet come up. If Mr. Kemble wanted "human interest," Ankelita Carter was the perfect subject. She was as "interesting" a person as I'd ever met! I could write several stories about her, without having to worry about the Fremonts or the election or the mine or anything!

"Actually, I didn't have anything to write about," I admitted. "I saw the article a few days ago in the *Alta* about the mine here having some controversy, and I just decided to come here and hope that I might find out about it. The editor of the paper has been pretty hard on me after the C.B. Hollister business, and I just have to find something to write about that'll make him see that I can be a reporter even if he doesn't like the fact that I'm a young woman."

"So you didn't knock on the door asking to see me as Felipe said?"

"No, ma'am," I said. "I just knocked on the door and was praying that somebody would be here who would take the time to talk to me and wouldn't mind that I had come."

"Well, I don't mind a bit!" she said. "And I have enjoyed talking to you."

"What is the controversy about the estate?" I asked.

"Oh, nothing new. The Colonel's mine has been in legal battles from the very beginning. Most of the miners in California believe in 'free mines'—whoever first stakes out a claim has right to the area. Colonel Fremont bought all this land before anyone knew there was an ounce of gold anywhere around here. But after 1849, miners invaded his property, and he has been having to fight them off ever since. The miners feel entitled to stake claims even though the land belongs to Mr. Fremont. And just a few months ago the Supreme Court back in Washington confirmed his title to the whole estate and Mr.

Fremont had all the independent miners driven out by force. That all happened earlier this year. But it hasn't been the end of the trouble. That's why you saw Hector out at the gate wearing a gun, and there are guards posted all around the main mining areas. Some of the anti-Fremont newspapers are stirring up the Mariposa title issue again, trying to make sure the miners of the state stay mad at Fremont until the election."

"Won't Mr. Fremont win easily here in California?" I asked. "That's what my pa says."

"I don't know, Corrie. Money and greed and power do strange things to men. Many powerful Californians are jealous of Mr. Fremont because of his fame and good fortune. They want him to fail. And they will stop at nothing. There are bad men involved, ruthless men. I have even heard Mr. Fremont say there are politicians willing to have people killed to further their own causes. It is hard to believe such people run our government. And such men are fanning the fires of contention about the title to the estate, and spreading many other false rumors about the Fremonts."

"That's terrible!" I exclaimed.

"I agree. But gold is not the only issue involved. Here in California the issue over mine ownership is big in the minds of the miners. But on a national scale, slavery is the overriding issue. And there are millions of dollars at stake over the future of slavery in the South, just as there are millions of dollars at stake over where a man is entitled to mine here in California. The pro-slavery forces of Buchanan are equally ruthless at times. They are determined to keep John Fremont out of the White House. If Fremont is elected, he will probably abolish slavery, and then their whole southern way of life will be ruined. They feel they *have* to stop him."

"Are *all* politicians like that?" I asked. "Greedy and mean?"

"No, there are many good men. Yet when otherwise seemingly good men support something intrinsically evil like slavery, it does something to them. They become different, and in a bad way. But during my years with the Fremonts, I have met many good men too. I've never forgotten the time I met a young Illinois lawyer by the name of Lincoln. The look in his eye told me that *he* was a different breed than these kinds of men I've spoken of. In fact, this Lincoln was almost Mr. Fremont's running mate for Vice-President this year, but lost out to Mr. Dayton. Lincoln is staunchly anti-slavery, just as is Mr. Fremont, and I overheard the Colonel say to his wife shortly after the nominating convention in Philadelphia last June, 'That fellow Lincoln is one to watch. I doubt the country's heard the last of him.' "

She stopped and the room grew quiet for a minute or two.

"But all this can't be that interesting," Mrs. Carter said finally.

"It's interesting to me," I replied.

"But nothing so interesting you could make an article out of. The papers have been full of this kind of thing for a year."

"But not from a woman's perspective," I said with a smile. "Maybe I could write something about Mr. Fremont in a different way that women readers would enjoy more."

"You want something women would like to read?"

"Mr. Kemble says that's one of the reasons he printed some of my articles, because women enjoyed them."

"Well, if you want a woman's story, I'll give one to you!" said Ankelita excitedly.

"What is it?" I asked eagerly.

"The best story of all in this election isn't the candidate or the election at all. It's the candidate's wife. If Mr. Fremont wins and gets to the White House, he's going to have Mrs. Jessie Benton Fremont to thank for it. *She's* the real story!"

"Should I get out my paper and pen?" I asked.

"You get them! And then you sit right here and I'll tell you all about Jessie. And when we're through, Corrie Belle Hollister, young woman reporter, we're going to have an article that editor of yours won't be able to refuse, an article that will make your name read in newspapers all over the country! Jessie's story is one that only another woman could write, and you're the first woman writer I've ever met. Oh, how I wish Jessie herself were here! She would so love to talk with you!"

I started to get my things out of my satchel, but before I got seated again, Ankelita was out of her chair.

"Let's eat some lunch together first, Corrie," she said. "Felipe!" she called down the hallway, then turned to me again. "Then afterward we'll sit down and I'll tell you everything."

Felipe appeared and she spoke a couple of hasty sentences to him that I didn't understand, then indicated for me to follow her.

# CHAPTER 34

# HEARING ABOUT JESSIE

An hour later we were seated in the same chairs again, each with a cup of tea in our hands.

Lunchtime had been an interesting assortment of people coming and going as we sat around a wooden table eating beans and tortillas. There were several children, an older woman, Felipe and two or three other young men about his age, and Ankelita and I. Most of the conversation among the others had been in Spanish. The ranch and mine workers must have had their midday meal someplace else, and I never did quite figure out how Ankelita was involved with everything that was going on. She could not have been in charge of the whole household, because she had only recently arrived, yet I saw no one else who seemed to be higher in authority. At least she spoke to those in this particular house in a confident manner. Maybe this wasn't the main house, even though it had been the first I had come to. There were a few other buildings about with people coming and going from them.

Once we were alone again and had seated ourselves, Ankelita began telling me about Jessie Benton Fremont, from their first days together in Monterey, right up to the present.

"It was just before I had become part of their home," she said, "that gold was found here. I've heard Jessie tell the story so many times I feel as if I'd been there: how Colonel Fremont rode up on his horse and ran into the room they were renting in Monterey and plopped down two big heavy sacks in front of her. 'Gold, Jessie!' was all he said. 'Gold! The Mariposa is full of it in every stream!' "

She told me about the Fremonts' life in Monterey before that.

"Monterey was then the capital of California, but it was a hard life for Jessie. They had no money, and Jessie had little fresh food. They had no milk, no fresh eggs. Jessie talks about eating rice and sardines and crackers during those days."

She paused and chuckled.

"A couple of months ago during the campaign, a woman started criticizing Jessie for being rich and pampered, for having tea and cake between meals.

" 'I find it a comforting break in my often wearying day,' Jessie answered her.

" 'But you allow yourself to be served by a maid?' the lady asked, thinking to make Jessie look foolish. But Jessie turned the tables on her.

" 'Yes, I confess it,' she whispered. 'But just between us, I think I make better tea myself. I had no maid in Monterey. I heated the water in a long-handled iron saucepan over a smoky fire. And instead of French cakes to eat, I lifted a sardine from his crowded can and gave him a decent burial between two soda crackers.'

"The lady and all the people around laughed, and in the next day's paper it was reported that Jessie Fremont was a good down-to-earth woman who could cook over a campfire."

We both laughed at that, and I found myself wondering if the story had made its way to the California newspapers. If not, it would be the perfect thing for me to use!

Then we talked about the Fremonts' trip to San Francisco following the discovery of gold on their estate. At San Jose, which later replaced Monterey as the capital of California, they hired some Indian women to wash their clothes by pounding them with stones in a brook. They were met there by a workman from the Mariposa, bringing buckskin bags filled with gold dust and nuggets—wealth from their foothills mines.

After Colonel Fremont's election to the Senate to represent

the newest state in the Union, the Fremonts set sail for New York. For the next year, Jessie, who had long been a senator's daughter, now found herself a senator's *wife*.

"The years came so rapidly and were so full," Ankelita said. "Colonel Fremont was in the Senate only a year, and then we returned to San Francisco in 1851 to a beautiful big home. But within months there were two terrible fires and the house was gone. Then we spent a year in Europe before returning to the East. Jessie's mother died, her father lost his Senate seat, and the house at Cherry Grove also burned, all within a few months. And now they are running for the White House! The Fremonts' lives, especially with three young children, have been so busy and eventful."

We talked most of the afternoon. I must have asked a hundred questions. It was all so fascinating! Ankelita told me what Jessie looked like and what she felt about some of Mr. Fremont's political decisions, about the heartbreak of their decision to become Republicans, knowing that it meant driving a wedge between them and Jessie's southern relatives. She told me about the children, about what it was like for Jessie to try to be a good mother in the midst of Washington politics. She told me how Fremont would consult Jessie about political decisions, not something very many politicians did. That, too, would be perfect for an article women would really enjoy. Even though they couldn't vote, women were more interested in current events than men sometimes thought. And Jessie Fremont was the shining example of what impact a woman could have standing beside her husband in American politics.

"During the early part of the campaign, Corrie," Ankelita said, "Jessie was sometimes as popular as her husband. Crowds would call out her name after the Colonel's speeches, wanting to see her too. One campaign song went like this:

*And whom shall we toast for the Queen of the*
   *White House?*
*We'll give them "Our Jessie" again and again.*

"I only wish I could be there to see the election through,

although I know it's best that I am here."

By the end of the day, I truly felt as if I knew Jessie Benton Fremont myself. If I could just figure out how to best put it down on paper, Mr. Kemble was sure to print it! And if he didn't, I would take it to another newspaper. The Fremonts hadn't been in California since 1851 and things had been much different back then. Now Jessie Benton Fremont was only a month or two away from being the most important woman in the whole nation, and I had personal stories about her that Mr. Kemble could not possibly have heard before.

I was so excited, and hoped I'd be able to somehow write about Jessie Fremont in as interesting a way as Ankelita Carter told about her!

By the time our conversation was over, the shadows were starting to lengthen outside. The day had gone by so quickly, and had been better than my wildest dreams.

"Well, young lady," said Ankelita, "we'd best get Felipe to see about getting your horse put up for the night, and then getting you settled in your room."

From my puzzled expression she could tell I didn't understand.

"You weren't thinking of riding back down the mountain to Merced, were you?" she asked in a voice of astonishment.

"I figured I would," I answered. "To tell you the truth, I hadn't really thought about it since this morning."

"Well, you're not going anywhere, Corrie. You're staying here with us tonight. I have an extra bed in my room. Besides, you have to get started on that article of yours. And what better place than right here?"

I had supper with them around the same table, with most of the same people. Then later, at a little table with a candle, I pulled out several sheets of blank paper, got out my pen and ink, spread out my notes, and began to write the article I had come to Mariposa to find.

At the top of the page I wrote for a title: "The *Real* Jessie Benton Fremont: The Woman Behind the Candidate."

# CHAPTER 35

## MR. KEMBLE ONCE MORE

Five days after I'd first set foot on the Mariposa estate, I once again walked through the doors of the offices of the California *Alta* on Montgomery Street in San Francisco.

I'd arrived in the city late the evening before. I spent the night at Miss Bean's Boarding House. After a bath and a change into fresh clothes, I felt much more confident than the first time I had been there. In my hand I held eight sheets of writing, an article I was genuinely proud of as being different and publishable, and something that no other reporter could have, especially no San Francisco reporter. If Robin O'Flaridy had scooped me last time, now it was my turn!

I didn't feel like a little girl begging a powerful editor to publish my little article. For the first time I guess I felt like a real "reporter" who had uncovered a story. As I walked down the hallway—and was I ever glad there was no O'Flaridy in sight!—I felt tall and good inside.

I went straight to Mr. Kemble's office, without even asking anybody if he was in or if I could see him, and knocked on the door.

I heard a muffled sound from inside, so I opened the door and walked right up to his desk, where the editor sat just like last time. His head was down and he didn't even look up right at first.

"Mr. Kemble," I said, trying not to let my voice quiver, "I have a story for you."

At the sound of my voice he glanced up.

His eyes surveyed me up and down for a second, then it seemed to gradually come to him who was standing there in front of him in his office.

"Ah, Miss Hollister," he said, leaning back in his chair. "Come to deliver your next article in person, eh? So you can be sure no one steals any of your precious words? Long ways to come, isn't it, just to deliver a short piece?"

I think he was trying to be humorous, but I didn't smile.

"This isn't on the Miracle Springs mayor's election," I said. "It's got to do with the national election."

"Oh, national news! My, oh my!" he said, still with a little grin on his lips. "You've broken some major new story that all the other hundred newsmen in this city have never heard?"

"No, it's not a major new story," I said. It's 'human interest,' I believe you call it. However, I think you will find it of interest to your readers. And to answer your question, no, I don't think any of your other newsmen do have access to this information."

I stood straight and confident before his desk, the papers still in my hand. Gradually the smile disappeared from his face, and he eyed me carefully. I think he was starting to realize I was serious.

"All right, Hollister," he said at last. "Let me see it."

He held out his right hand. I handed him the top page.

He took the sheet, glanced over it quickly. His eyes darted up to mine again, as if looking for some clue. Then he looked down at the sheet again and read it start to finish. As he completed the last line he again held up his hand.

"I'll give you more when you agree to publish it," I said.

"Don't toy with me, Hollister!" he snapped, dropping the page. "I don't play games with my reporters, especially nineteen-year-old women!"

I reached forward and took the page from his desk, then turned around and made a step toward the door.

"Okay, okay," he said, still brusquely but apologetically. "I'm sorry. That was rude of me."

I turned back and faced him again.

"It looks good, Hollister," he went on. "I'm sure I can use it. May I please see more?"

I shuffled through the sheets and handed him page five.

He took it, and the moment he saw what I had done, he glanced up at me again, bordering on another outburst, I think. But he controlled himself, and read the page through. He set it down on his desk, leaned back in his chair, put his hands behind his head, and looked at me for a long moment.

"What is this little game you're playing with me?" he finally said.

"I just want to protect my article," I said. "What happened before was very upsetting to me. I felt we had an agreement, even if we didn't shake hands on it, and I don't think what you did was right. Now, I'm very sorry I didn't get the chance to tell you all about Mrs. Parrish being my stepmother. That was wrong of me. But it was an honest oversight. When Robin O'Flaridy walked in, I forgot a lot of what I had intended to say. But all that's past, Mr. Kemble. You explained yourself very clearly in your letter, and you were very plain about how things are if I intend to write for your paper. Therefore, it seems best to me that I make sure we come to an agreement beforehand. And after we've reached an agreement, then you can see the entire article."

While I spoke his face changed first to red then to white. I don't know if he'd ever been spoken to by any of his reporters that way, but he certainly wasn't used to it from a nineteen-year-old woman!

When I finished, I stopped and stood still. I half expected him to yell at me, or throw me out of his office and say he never wanted to see me again.

There was a long silence. I don't think he knew what to do with me either. He probably *wanted* to throw me out! But then again, I knew he wanted the article on Jessie Fremont!

Finally he spoke again.

"Where did you get this stuff?" he asked.

"My sources are confidential," I answered. I'd been practicing that line all the way from Mariposa! Ankelita told me that's what I ought to say if asked where I'd got my information.

"Nobody could know some of the things you say unless they knew the lady personally. *You* don't know Jessie Fremont . . . do you, Hollister?" His voice was incredulous at the very thought, even though he *knew* I couldn't possibly know her.

"Confidential," I repeated. "I can tell you nothing about where any of this came from."

He squirmed in his chair. I could tell he hated not being in control.

There was another long silence.

"All right . . . all right, Hollister, you win! I'll print it. I don't know how you got it, but it's good, it's original, and I want it."

"And the matter of pay?" I said, still holding the rest of the pages.

"I told you before I would pay you a dollar an article . . . until you've proven yourself."

"I think this is worth more than what I've sent you before."

"So now it's you who's welching on a deal, eh, Hollister?" He chuckled.

"I never agreed to a dollar," I said.

"Okay, you're right, this is worth more. You've done some good work here. I'll pay you two dollars for it."

"I want eight dollars."

"Eight dollars!"

I didn't say anything.

"That's highway robbery! I can't pay that kind of money for a single article. If word got out that I'd paid a woman eight dollars, the men would be wanting sixteen for every little thing they brought me."

"This has nothing to do with whether a man or woman wrote it. Somebody had to do the work to uncover this story, and whether it was a man or a woman, it seems to me the words would be worth the same. And I figure the words of *this* story are worth eight dollars. She might be our next first lady, and nobody else has some of this stuff I've written here."

"You are a huckster, Hollister, a downright rogue! All right, I'll give you four. I can't pay a penny more!"

"I'm sure the Sacramento *Union* or maybe the *Courier* would like to take a look at it."

"You can't do that. You're under contract to me—don't forget, we have a three-article deal on the other election."

"A deal you did not feel you needed to honor a couple weeks ago," I said. "I'm under no obligation to the *Alta*; I simply wanted to offer the story to you first."

I reached for the page five still lying on his desk.

"Good day, Mr. Kemble," I said, and again turned to go. This time I made it almost to the door before I again heard his voice. Even as he said it I could tell from the grating tone that it killed him to give in to the demands of a woman.

"Six" came his voice behind me.

I stopped, and slowly turned around. He was standing behind his desk, both hands resting upon it, sort of leaning toward me, his face glaring.

I stood where I was and returned his stare. Two seconds went by, then five. It seemed like an eternity that we stood there, looking deeply into each other's eyes. Whether it was a struggle of wills, or a contest of stubbornness, I don't know. But in that moment, I was thankful for Ma and her Belle blood!

Finally I spoke. My voice was very soft, but very determined. I had made up my mind even before I'd entered his office, and I wasn't about to back down now.

"Mr. Kemble, I said I wanted eight dollars. I believe the article is worth eight dollars. And if you want it for the *Alta*, you are going to have to pay eight dollars. Otherwise I am going to walk out this door and take what I have to one of your competitors."

Several more seconds went by.

Finally Mr. Kemble sat down and exhaled a long sigh.

"All right, you win. Eight dollars." His voice sounded tired. I could hardly believe it—I had beaten him.

"I'd like the money today," I said.

"Do you never stop, Hollister?" he asked in disbelief.

"Don't you trust me for payment?"

"You told me yourself, Mr. Kemble, that the newspaper business was a tough business. I'm just following your advice. You also told me that if I thought it was unfair I could take my articles elsewhere. It seems that your own advice would apply to you too. If you do not like my terms, you do not have to accept them. I'm simply saying, my terms for this article are eight dollars in advance, and then you may have my article on Jessie Benton Fremont."

He sighed again.

"Go see the cashier," he said. "Tell him I'm authorizing payment for an article. He'll check with me, and then you'll have your payment."

I turned and left his office and did as he said. An hour later I was walking back up the street to Miss Bean's. I felt like shouting at the top of my lungs.

*I had done it!*

# CHAPTER 36

## LAST NIGHT ALONE
## ON THE TRAIL

Two nights later I was camping between Auburn and Colfax beside a blazing fire. I'd be home the next day.

I'd spent the previous night with Miss Baxter in Sacramento, and I could have slept this night in Auburn. But somehow I felt that I wanted to finish off this adventure alone, by myself, beside a campfire I had built, sleeping under the stars. I suppose it was a dangerous thing for a young woman to do. After all, even if Buck Krebbs was gone, there were a thousand more just like him, and California was still no tame land.

But I wanted to do it. By the time I rode back into Miracle Springs tomorrow, I would have spent eleven days alone. It was like nothing I'd ever done before. I'd gone off chasing a dream—in search of a story I didn't even know existed. I had found it, written it, and sold it for eight dollars! I'd met some interesting people. I'd taken care of myself. I'd faced some scary situations and come through them. I was eleven days older, but I felt about eleven years older! Something inside me had changed. I had learned some things about myself, about what I was capable of. And this seemed the fitting way for me to spend my last night.

I had also learned to pray in some new ways, and to depend on God more than I'd ever had to before. And now I knew a little more about what that verse in the Bible really meant about God guiding our steps. He had really guided mine!

I guess I felt I had grown up a little bit. Well . . . grown up a lot. Especially standing there staring back at Mr. Kemble and saying if he didn't pay me the eight dollars, I was leaving. I had met a lady who knew the man who might be the country's next President. The next first lady had read one of my articles, and now I'd written an article about her. Why, I practically had an invitation to the White House! I felt like I'd gone halfway around the world in those eleven days. I'd talked about and thought about some big and important things. And now here I was going back to little Miracle Springs in the foothills of the California gold country. Yet another part of me had been opened to a bigger and wider world, and I knew I'd never be the same again.

I *could* be a writer now; I already was a writer. Maybe I'd do other things. Maybe I would teach or keep working for the Freight Company. But at least I knew I *could* do it. I could go into the office of an editor of a California newspaper and put my pages down on the desk and say, "There's a story that Corrie Belle Hollister wrote, Mister. I wrote it, and folks are going to want to read it!"

So I sat there staring into my little fire, eating dried venison and hardtack and some apples Miss Baxter gave me. I felt peaceful inside. Peaceful and thoughtful and even a little melancholy. This had been an adventure, but now it was over. I knew I'd face disappointments in the future, and probably write a lot more articles that wouldn't get printed. And there would probably be times Mr. Kemble would win and would stare *me* back into a corner and make *me* give in and do it his way.

But I would always have the memory of this journey, of feeling a story calling out to me though I didn't even know what it was, of going out and uncovering it. Next time I'd have more courage to ask questions and to knock on doors and to search and try to uncover something. I was lucky this time, meeting Ankelita Carter. But I had met her because I struck out and tried something scary. Maybe next time, though it would be different, God would lead me to someone else, to a different set of circumstances that would take me in the direction of the story I was after.

There were no sounds around me but the crackling of the fire and the crickets in the woods. I hoped no wild animals came. I was especially afraid of bears and snakes, and I didn't even have a gun—only a small knife.

But God would protect me and take care of me. He had so far. Why would this night be any different?

Maybe that's one reason I wanted to spend the last night alone like this on the trail. I had been nervous and anxious plenty of times in the last ten days. Yet I hadn't been in any situation that was downright "dangerous." I wasn't really in any danger now. But I wanted to prove to myself that if I had to, if I was out tracking a story again sometime, and I did have to fend for myself—up in the mountains, or down in the valley where there was no town—I could do it. Maybe someday I'd even travel farther from home, or back East—or maybe I *would* go to the White House someday. Wherever I went, I wanted to know that even if I was all alone, I could stand on my own two feet and say to God, "Well, it's just the two of us, Lord. And that's plenty to handle just about anything that comes along!"

My eyes were fixed on the bright orange coals of the fire, and I found myself praying quietly as I sat there.

"Lord, I am grateful to you for doing like you promised, and for guiding my footsteps on this trip. I don't know whether I trusted you very well or not. I tried to, but then sometimes it's hard to remember. Yet you just kept taking care of me, anyway. And, Lord, I thank you, too, for the article, and for all the ways you have been helping my writing this last year. You showed me a while back that trusting you is the way you give us the desires of our hearts. But you've let me be a writer too! You've given me that dream, Lord, and I am so thankful to you! Help me to write just like you want me to. And teach me to trust you more! I really do want to, God. I want to do just what you want me to do, and I want to be just exactly the person you want Corrie Hollister to be."

I drew in a deep breath. I felt so peaceful. God had been good to me!

The night air was getting chilly. I lay down and pulled my blankets tight around me. And still staring into the fire, the sounds of the crickets in my ears, I gradually fell asleep.

# CHAPTER 37

## HOME AGAIN

I'd left Miracle on a Monday. It was now Friday afternoon, a week and a half later, the 29th of August. I wondered if Almeda would be at the office, but I was actually relieved when she wasn't. I wanted to see everyone at once.

I can hardly describe the feelings I had inside as I went around the last turn in the road and the house came into view. I felt as if I'd gone to a foreign country and was now returning after many years. Yet it had only been eleven days!

Almost immediately Becky saw me. But instead of coming to meet me, she turned around and ran inside, then out again, then up the creek, screaming at the top of her twelve-year-old lungs, "Corrie's here! Corrie's home . . . it's Corrie . . . Corrie's back!"

Within seconds people were pouring through the door of the house, and out of the corner of my eye I saw Pa and Uncle Nick and Mr. Jones running down from the mine. By then my eyes were full of tears; everybody was hugging and laughing and shouting and asking questions, and I could hardly tell who was who. I was so happy, yet I couldn't stop crying even at the same time as I was laughing and smiling and trying to talk. And I don't even remember getting off my horse, but there I was surrounded by the people I loved so much, arms and hands and voices all coming at me at once. Every once in a while I'd hear a voice I knew—Katie's one minute, then Alkali Jones's high *hee, hee, hee,* and of course all my sisters and brothers shouting at once. The only two voices I don't remember hearing were the two whose sound I loved more than all the others. But Pa and Almeda and I got a chance to visit quietly alone later. The three of us stayed up and talked around the fire way past midnight, and I told them everything.

"I've got to tell you, Corrie," said Almeda when I was through, "we were mighty concerned about you."

"I know," I said. "I'm sorry."

"You're starting to remind me of myself, girl!" said Pa with a smile. "Maybe it ain't just the Belle blood, but some of the Hollister too. Tarnation, but I'd like to see you in ten years! You're gonna be some woman, that's all I got to say."

I could tell that in spite of Almeda's concern, Pa was proud of me. I suppose he'd figured I was a mite timid—which I was!—for a daughter of his. So I think he liked what I'd done. He'd been acting a little different toward me all evening—not just treating me like I was older and wasn't a little girl anymore, but also more like a son who had done something brave. Being gone a few days wasn't all *that* courageous a thing. But because it was *me*, timid little Corrie Belle, I think it gave Pa kind of a special feeling to see his daughter do it. Zack acted different, too, as if I'd proved my right to be the oldest Hollister.

Once the article on Jessie Fremont appeared in the August 30 issue of the *Daily Alta*—on the *second* page with a big bold caption over three columns, with my name right under the title!—my life would never be the same again. Whether I liked it or not, ever after that I *was* a reporter, a writer, and much would change as a result. How many times I must have read those words over: "The Real Jessie Benton Fremont . . . *by Corrie Belle Hollister*." I was so thankful inside, so thankful to God. More and more, as I reflected back on those eleven days, I realized that none of it would have happened had he not been guiding my steps just as he promised. Even though I wasn't aware of it at the time, and even though I hadn't even been thinking of him through some of it, he had been there all the time, going along the path just in front of me.

As I read over the article and the caption and my name

underneath, I couldn't help wondering if I shouldn't have used my full given name, *Cornelia*. But when I later suggested it to Mr. Kemble, he said, "Too late, Corrie. Folks know you now. And once you're writing with one name, you can't change it any more than you can change horses in mid-river, as the saying goes. No, you stick with Corrie. It's a good name, and folks are starting to recognize it."

The excitement of my trip and the article died down, especially after church on Sunday when everybody asked me all about it, and then the following Monday I went into the office with Almeda and spent a regular day working in town.

I'd almost forgotten about the Miracle Springs election. Almeda hadn't said much about it since my return, but all of a sudden the church service on Sunday seemed to stir it up again, even more than before. People came up to me afterward, welcoming me home, asking me about the trip and what I'd done, and most everybody said something about my interviewing them earlier about the mayor's election. Sometimes it was just a little comment, like, "I been thinking about that conversation we had," or they might say, "I might like t' talk t' you again, Corrie, if yer still gonna do interviewin' about it."

Most of the folks were quiet about it, as if they didn't want anyone to hear them talking to me. And Mr. Royce acted pretty friendly at the service too, like I reckon a fellow ought to be if he's trying to make people vote for him. He was greeting the men and their wives and shaking hands. And he even came up to me and gave me a light slap on the shoulder and said "Good to have you back, Corrie!" before he went on to visit someone else.

But in the background amid all the hubbub of the after-church visiting, lots of people seemed as if they wanted to talk to me again about the election. My getting back to town seemed to stir up people's thinking in a new way.

All day Monday my mind was on the interview article, going over what I'd done and things people had told me and thinking of how to go about starting to write the article. There were only two months left before the election, so I couldn't delay too long. On Tuesday, the *Alta* came with my article in it, which set my mind running in a hundred directions at once! So it wasn't until Wednesday that I really settled myself down enough to think about the interviews and article again. That morning I gathered my papers together and put them in my satchel to take with me into town to work. I hoped to see some of the people who'd talked to me at church. There were still a few people in town I hadn't interviewed yet. As I went through my notes and quotes from what people had told me before and started to consider actually beginning to write the article in a way that Mr. Kemble'd like, I found myself getting enthusiastic about it again.

But that very evening something happened that suddenly changed my thoughts not only about the article I wanted to write but about the whole mayor's election.

# CHAPTER 38

## THREATS

Not long after Almeda and I got back home from town, we heard a single-horse carriage approach outside and then slow to a stop. Pa went to the window, and when he turned back inside, his face wore a look of question and significance.

"Franklin Royce" was all he said, half in statement, half in question.

We all looked at one another, but the knock on the door came before we had the chance to wonder fully what the visit could possibly be about.

Pa opened the door.

"Good evening, Mr. Hollister," I heard the familiar voice say, "might I have a word with your wife?"

Pa nodded, stepped aside, and gestured Royce into the room. Almeda stood and offered her hand. Royce shook it, though without conviction.

"Mrs. Hollister," he said rather stiffly, "I would appreciate a few moments of your time."

"Of course, Franklin," she said deliberately. It was clear from his tone this was no social call. "Please . . . sit down." She pointed to an empty chair.

"In private, if you don't mind," he added.

"Anything you have to say to me can just as well be said in front of my husband," she replied, her voice betraying a slight edge to it. I think she was perturbed by his unsmiling seriousness. She continued to look right at him, but neither said another word.

Pa had a hesitant look on his face, not seeming to know what he ought to do. But finally spoke up.

"It's no never-mind to me, Almeda," he said. "Come on, kids, let's go outside. But I'm warning you, Royce," he added to the banker. "I'm going to be right outside this door, and if you say something my wife don't like, I'll be right back in here and throw you out on your ear!"

Every one of us was curious what Mr. Royce's visit was about, but we all got up and started trooping silently toward the door that Pa held open for us. I was the next to last one, but before I reached the door, I heard Royce's voice again.

"Perhaps *Miss* Hollister could join us," he said, speaking to Almeda but gesturing his head in my direction. "What I have to say concerns her as well as you."

I glanced up at Pa. He shrugged. "If he wants to talk to you, it's okay by me." But as he said it he was staring daggers at Mr. Royce.

I turned around and went back to where I was sitting, while Pa and Zack filed outside with the others and closed the door. Once we were alone, Mr. Royce still did not take the seat Almeda offered him, but began speaking immediately.

"Almeda, when you first announced that you were going to run against me for mayor, like everyone else I was surprised, interested, even curious. And for a while I was willing to play along with your little charade of pretending to be a politician. But when matters grew more serious and when people began to talk and I began to fear for the business of my bank, then I grew concerned. You were visiting people and rousing them up against me. I came to you in your office, and I tried to be reasonable. I asked you as cooperatively as I was able to cease and desist, and to withdraw before more harm was done. But you refused. You have persisted in your efforts to undermine my reputation. Your flyers continue to circulate. And now you have set your stepdaughter to do your dirty work, talking with everyone in town, asking their opinions."

He stopped, but just long enough to take a breath of air.

"Now," he continued, "I'm here to tell you—both of you—

that I want this to stop. It's futile, it's useless. You cannot win the election, Almeda, and I will not have you stirring up the community against me any longer. I've been patient for as long as I can, but it's time I put my foot down. I want it to stop. And as for you, young lady," he said, turning and looking me straight in the face, "I do not want you talking to anyone else about the election."

"You leave Corrie out of this, Franklin," said Almeda heatedly. "This election campaign is between you and me."

"Then *you* tell her to stop with these ridiculous interviews."

"I will do no such thing. She is a newspaper reporter in her own right and I will not tell her what she can or cannot pursue."

"Newspaper reporter! That's a good one," he laughed. "That's almost as humorous as a woman mayor!"

By now we were *both* more than a little annoyed!

"My editor in San Francisco is paying me for two stories about the Miracle Springs election," I said. "I have done nothing to hurt you in any way."

"Except get people talking."

"It's hardly *our* fault if people talk," I said. "And you can't blame *us* for what they think of you."

I shouldn't have said it, but the words were out of my mouth before I realized it. Now Royce was angry too, and he made no more attempt to mask his true intentions.

"Look," he said, "Hollister may pamper the two of you in your little schemes! But he never did have much backbone. It's a rough world out there, and no two interfering women are going to spoil my plans, no matter what their fool of a husband and a father lets them get away with. Two can play this little game of yours, and you don't want to play it against me. Stop now, or I'll make life miserable for all of you!"

"How dare you talk that way of the finest man in Miracle Springs!" cried Almeda, rising from her chair.

I expected to see Pa burst through the door any minute and slam his fist into Royce's face.

"You are meddling in what is not your business, and he is a weakling if he cannot prevent you."

"You are the fool, Franklin Royce, for not knowing a real man when you see him! And as for the election, my campaign is *not* a charade. I have not roused a soul against you, and have never once even mentioned your name in a single discussion with anyone. Corrie is absolutely right—you can hardly hold *us* responsible for what people may think of you! I have done *nothing* to undermine your reputation. And I would never think of resorting to dirty work, as you call it, still less of asking Corrie or anyone else to do it for me. I resent your charges against me, Franklin, and I will *not* withdraw from this election!"

"It will not go well with you, Almeda, if you do not reconsider."

"What's more," she added, "not only will I see it through to November, after today, Franklin, you have shown me more clearly than ever that for Miracle Springs to elect you its mayor would be a grievous mistake. You have made me more determined than ever to *win* that election!"

"If you do win, Almeda," and his voice was deadly serious, "you will live to regret it! I will make life so miserable for you and your family that you will have no choice but to resign, and I will be made mayor eventually anyway."

"What can you possibly do to us?" she shot back. "You hold no mortgages on either my property or Drummond's. The little my business owes you is unsecured."

"The people of this community who *are* indebted to me will find themselves compelled to reconsider where they purchase their supplies. In fact, I have been thinking of opening a supplies outlet and freight service myself, as an adjunct to the bank."

"Dare to go into business against me, Franklin, and you will find I am a strong businesswoman, with more contacts and experience than your money alone will buy you."

I had never seen Almeda like this. She was seething.

"Perhaps that is true," replied Royce, with a sly smile. "But you will not be able to survive long without customers. And the men of this community will know they had better deal with me or else find themselves foreclosed upon. Most of the mortgages I hold have a thirty-day call."

"You are an unscrupulous man, Franklin!"

"It's called 'the fine print,' Almeda. Every standard banking contract has its share, and I simply use it to my own advantage, as does any wise businessman when it comes to matters of finances."

"When the people find out you are trying to blackmail this town into electing you its mayor, they will never stand for it!"

"They will have little choice. If they do not vote for me, I will simply call their loans due. Within a year I'll own the whole town. In the meantime, you'll be out of business for lack of customers."

"Well, you don't own *us*, Franklin! You may blackmail the rest of this town, and you may put Parrish Mine and Freight out of business. But you will never control me, or my husband, or our family! If it comes to that, I will leave the business and move out to the claim. We will manage with or without the Parrish Freight."

"Ah yes . . . the *claim*," said Royce, drawing out the words with a significant expression. "That brings up an interesting point which I have been looking into. You are correct, Almeda, in that I hold no mortgage on the property your husband and his brother-in-law claim as their own. However, according to my investigations there may be some question as to the validity of their ownership of the land."

"That is preposterous, Franklin!" Almeda nearly exploded. "You know the doctrine of *free mines* as well as anyone else in California. Whoever first stakes out a claim has exclusive right to the land. Drummond and Nick have been on that property since 1849, long before you ever got to California!"

"Granted, they have right to *use* the land, but that does not make the land itself theirs. I have been looking into the deeds to actual land ownership in and around Miracle Springs, and let us simply say the results may surprise many people."

"You wouldn't dare try to run the miners around here off their land! You wouldn't survive a month as mayor!"

"There are laws, Almeda," Royce said, trying to sound calm. "California is a state now. There are legalities to be observed. Surely you know of the recent Supreme Court decision in the Fremont case *against* free mines. I tell you, Almeda, your husband's position may be very tenuous indeed, and he may find it more pleasant to have me as his friend rather than his enemy. Especially when the authorities who might be compelled to look into the matter discover his criminal record, and learn that he is still wanted by the law in the East. I very seriously doubt that they'll uphold his claim to the property, especially given the Mariposa ruling."

"You are full of threats, Franklin," replied Almeda, and she had now grown calm as well—calm and cold. "But Sheriff Rafferty put the matter of my husband's past to rest long ago."

"Rafferty is a weakling, too!" Royce spat back. "There are others who might find his failure to uphold his duty cause for his removal as well. As mayor of Miracle Springs, I may well find that I must—"

"You will never be mayor, Franklin! Not if I can help it. You will not get away with all this!"

Suddenly the room grew silent. Royce stared back at Almeda with piercing eyes. When he next spoke, all anger, all passion, all intensity from his voice was gone. His words were icy, measured, and the look in his eyes hateful.

"I have tried to be as reasonable as a man can be, Almeda. But you have left me no choice. As a gentleman I am loathe to stoop to such measures, but you force my hand."

He paused, and his eyes squinted in a glare of evil determination.

"If the hurt to come to the rest of the town, if the loss of your business, if danger to your husband, and if the loss of all this property here on your so-called claim—if all these things do not convince you that it is in everyone's best interest for you to withdraw from the race, then perhaps what I have to tell you now *will* convince you.

"There are men in this state, even now, who will stop at nothing to see Fremont defeated in the general election, men whose interests will be more preserved under a Buchanan presidency than one led by an anti-slavery westerner."

He looked over in my direction.

"Our budding reporter here is taking a decidedly pro-Fremont stand in the *Alta*. Should these men I speak of learn that she is perhaps, as the daughter of a miner herself, planning to come out with an appeal for the miners of California to vote for Fremont, they would take such news very badly, and I would hate to see anything happen to Corrie as a result."

"I am planning no such pro-Fremont story," I said quickly. "I only wrote a story about his wife."

"Ah, but don't you see, Corrie," replied Royce, "these men do not take kindly to *any* such favorable articles. And word could begin to spread that you intended to take a more affirmative stand, and—well, you can see how a man in my position would . . . be powerless to stop such a rumor."

"Franklin, you are despicable!" said Almeda, practically shouting. "Are you now threatening Corrie with what is purely a false and—"

"Enough, Almeda!" Royce interrupted angrily. "I will do whatever I have to do! I have had people investigating you too, Almeda, as well as your husband and his daughter. If danger to your stepdaughter from the slavery people does not pound some sense into that stubborn brain of yours, then perhaps the people of Miracle Springs would like to read a little flyer that I might circulate just prior to the election concerning what I have recently discovered from my contact in Boston. You have an interesting past, Almeda!"

At the word *Boston*, Almeda's face grew white. She spoke not another word, and sank into a chair as if she had been suddenly struck a devastating blow.

"Forgive me, Almeda," said Royce. "I do not want to use the information I possess, either against you or your stepdaughter. I admit it is not the gentleman's way. But you are a stubborn woman, and I will do what I have to!"

He spun around and quickly left the house.

# CHAPTER 39

## MEETING OF THE COMMITTEE

The rest of that night and all the next two days Almeda was practically silent. Not a word was said about Royce's visit. Pa asked no questions. I guess he knew Almeda would tell him about it when the time was right. I didn't say anything either. I figured it was her business to share, not mine.

On the evening of the second day, Almeda got the six of us together—Zack and I, Katie and Uncle Nick, and she and Pa—for what she called a campaign committee meeting. Then she told everyone else about Mr. Royce's visit and that he'd promised to do some pretty bad things to a lot of people if she kept on with the election.

"I believe you men have an expression," she said, trying to force a smile, "when you are playing poker and realize you can't possibly win the pot. Well, I finally realize there is no way I am holding a winning hand, and it's simply time for me to throw in my cards, as you say. So I've decided to pull out of the mayor's race."

A few groans went around, but then it got quiet again.

"I am very disappointed too," she went on. "And I am convinced that Franklin Royce is more of a louse than when I began. But it just is not fair for me to continue. Too many people could be hurt. And it isn't worth it just for my pride to try to defeat him."

"But you *can* defeat him, Almeda," insisted Katie.

"The price would be too high. Many of the miners and families around Miracle Springs could be hurt."

"How?" asked Uncle Nick. "What can he do if you win?"

"He's a banker, Nick," she replied with a thin smile. "He can do whatever he wants. Specifically, he can make it very hard for folks whose mortgages he's holding. He as much as threatened to begin foreclosures if I didn't withdraw." She told them what Royce had said.

"The man is a ruthless skunk!" muttered Pa.

"But it isn't only the townspeople I'm concerned about," Almeda went on. "He threatened all of you too." She told about the questions he'd raised about ownership of the land, and about his threats to reopen Pa and Uncle Nick's problems with the law.

By now Uncle Nick was pacing about the floor angrily.

"We can fight him!" he said, waving his hands in the air. "Me and Drum ain't afraid of him. We been up against worse odds dozens of times!"

"He's a powerful man, Nick," said Almeda. "I'm not willing to run the risk of us losing our land here, or the mine. We've got a good life and I just can't take that chance. And besides all that, he threatened Corrie as well."

"He what?" Pa roared, his eyes flashing. "If he dares lay a hand on any of my—"

"Only on account of my writing, Pa," I said quickly. "He's not about to hurt me himself."

"What can your writing have to do with it? What did he say?"

"I didn't really understand it all myself, Pa," I answered, "but he said there were rich and powerful slave-state men who were determined to see Mr. Fremont lose in California, and who would do anything they could to stop him."

"His implication was that something could happen to Corrie if she got in their way," said Almeda seriously.

"What could Corrie possibly have to do with the outcome of the election?" asked Pa.

"After her article in the *Alta* about Mrs. Fremont, she could be seen as a Fremont supporter, especially if she wrote more such articles."

"Then she doesn't need to write any more."

"That's what I told him too, Pa," I said.

"Franklin implied that he knew some of these men, and that if I didn't do as he said, he would start a rumor to the effect that Corrie Hollister, a miner's daughter, was planning a major story to try to persuade California's miners to vote for Fremont. Even if it wasn't true, if he did what he said, it could endanger Corrie . . . and every one of us. The man has no scruples, and I have no doubt that he would do it just to spite me."

The room was quiet. I think any of us would have been willing to go up against Mr. Royce if the only danger was to himself. But when harm could come to so many others, no one was quite willing to take that chance.

"So you see," Almeda said at last with a sigh, "why I just cannot continue on with the election. The risk to all of you whom I love, and to others in the community, is simply too great. I'm afraid I'm just going to have to go into town and face Franklin again. And as much as it galls me to have to give in, I'm going to have to tell him he's won."

She took a deep breath, looked around at the rest of us, then got up out of her chair and slowly walked outside and away from the house. No one followed. We all understood that she needed some time alone.

During the whole discussion she had not once mentioned Royce's threats to her business, or what he said he had discovered about Boston. And after seeing the look on Almeda's face just before Royce had left, I certainly wasn't going to bring up the subject. Whatever it meant, it was clear there was a great deal of pain involved for her. Still, I couldn't help wondering how much these words of Royce's influenced her decision.

After about five or ten minutes Pa followed Almeda outside. It was an hour before the two of them came back inside. Almeda's face was red, and I knew she'd been crying. Pa was serious, but the rest of that evening whenever he'd look at her, his face was more full of love than I'd ever seen it.

Both of them were quiet, and neither said a word about their time alone together outside.

# CHAPTER 40

## A SURPRISE LETTER

The rest of that week things were pretty sullen and quiet around the office and at home. We were all disappointed and angry, yet there was nothing we could do. Mr. Royce had us over a barrel.

I didn't write a word or interview anyone. As much as I hated to quit on something I'd started, a dollar or two wasn't worth getting Almeda or Pa in trouble with a man like the banker of Miracle Springs. As for what he'd said about me, I have to say I didn't think of it that much. I didn't see how anything I wrote could possibly put *me* in any danger. Almeda didn't say anything to Mr. Royce, though she took the banner down from our office window.

The thought did occur to me that perhaps I could still write an article or two about the election, even maybe with some of the quotes from talking to people, if I showed it to Mr. Royce first and he didn't see anything wrong with what I'd said. I would hate to do that! But it did seem like a possible way to be able to do the article. Maybe this was the other side of the question Almeda had put to me before I went to Mariposa: How bad did I want to write? Did I want it bad enough to crawl to Mr. Royce for approval? I didn't know if I wanted it *that* bad.

Fortunately I didn't have to decide. All of a sudden I was thrown into the middle of a new story, one that made the Miracle Springs election—or what was left of it, anyway—seem small and far away.

The following Monday a letter arrived for me in the mail. I immediately recognized the *Alta* envelope. I opened it and read:

Miss Hollister,

A major story is about to break which will doom Colonel Fremont's chance for election. We can still stop it, but time is short and I need your help. After your article on Mrs. Fremont—which I must confess turned out to be worth the $8 from all the favorable response it has received—it could well be that you have the necessary contacts to get to the bottom of this scheme to ruin the Colonel's reputation.

I must warn you, however, there could be danger. Powerful men with great resources behind them are involved. If you want to help, the *Alta* version of the story will be yours to write. I hope this reaches you in time. If interested, I will be at the offices of the *Daily and Weekly Sacramento Times* at two o'clock on the afternoon of Wednesday the 12th. Meet me there.

Edward Kemble
September 8, 1856

I could hardly believe my eyes! Mr. Kemble was asking *me* for help!

I ran across the street and burst through the door of the office. "Look at this!" I cried, waving the letter in my hand.

Almeda took it and scanned it quickly. Then she just looked up at me with raised inquiring eyebrows.

"I've got to ride home and pack my things," I said. "I've only got forty-eight hours to get there!" I reached for the letter and was ready to head back out the door.

"Are you sure you know what you're doing, Corrie?" asked Almeda.

"This could be my big chance!" I answered.

"And the danger?"

"How bad could it be? No one would try to hurt me."

"People do awful things sometimes when you try to thwart their plans. You remember what Royce said."

"This doesn't have anything to do with that."

"Just be sure, Corrie, that's all."

I paused, my hand on the knob of the half-opened door, and looked back at Almeda. Her eyes were filled with concern.

"I'm not sure," I said. "But maybe the only way I'm going to be sure is to go ahead, and see what God does. But I'll talk to Pa . . . and I'll pray. I'll try hard not to do anything foolish."

"Then God go with you, my daughter. I love you . . . and I too will pray!"

For one moment our eyes met, and in that moment worlds were spoken between us. The next instant I was out the door, onto my horse, and dashing toward home as fast as Raspberry could gallop, my hair streaming out behind me, the early autumn wind chilling my nose and ears.

I was at home in less than an hour. I threw together what food I could find, rolled up three blankets, and repacked my little tin fire box. It wasn't cold yet, but the nights would be chilly so I dressed up as warm as I could, and put extra clothes, a warm coat, an extra pair of boots, a rain slicker, and several old newspapers in a bag. Then I got together my writing satchel.

Once Pa read the letter, he figured it was too late to try to stop me. He probably wouldn't have tried, anyway. The look in his eyes said to me that he thought I was ready to face whatever the world might throw at me. And if I wasn't, then maybe it was high time I learned to be.

"You go and do your name proud, Corrie Hollister," he said. "You're a Belle *and* a Hollister. And when anyone tries to give you a hard time, you just remember that, and remember you're tougher'n any of 'em. And you're God's daughter and Drummond Hollister's little girl too—and I figure that gives you a winning hand against just about anybody. Now you go and show that fella Kemble what kind of stuff you're made of!"

"Thanks, Pa," I said.

"I love you, Corrie Belle," he added. His voice was soft and shaky.

I wheeled Raspberry around. I couldn't say anything back because of the big lump in my throat and the tears in my eyes.

I dug my heels into my mare's sides and took off down the road. Before I was out of sight, I glanced back and waved. There was Pa still standing in the same place, his hand in the air.

# CHAPTER 41

## SACRAMENTO

I walked into the office of the Sacramento *Times* at ten minutes after two on Wednesday.

I had ridden my mare as hard as I dared, spent both nights on the trail, and arrived in Sacramento just in time to go to Miss Baxter's to take a bath, change into presentable clothes for seeing an editor, and get directions where to go. I didn't know Sacramento very well, and it was growing so fast that it seemed to have changed every time I came.

A man sat at a desk inside an open office just inside the main door. He walked out and looked me over.

"I'm here to see Mr. Edward Kemble of the *Alta*," I said.

"Yes, I was told to expect you," he replied. "Right this way, Miss Hollister."

He led me down a hall and opened a door for me. I walked inside. He stayed outside, closing the door behind me.

Mr. Kemble sat at a table in the center of the small office. There was no one else in the room.

"I'm sorry I'm late," I said. "I came as quick as I could. I left the minute I got your letter."

"Good . . . good, Hollister," he said. "Sit down." He pointed toward the chair opposite him.

I sat down and took off my coat. He started right in.

"I don't know how much you know about California politics," he said, "but it's a real mess this year. You would think that with Fremont's ties to the state, he'd be a shoo-in to win California."

"That's what my pa says," I added. From the look on Mr. Kemble's face, I gathered this was a time he wanted to listen to himself talk, and wasn't particularly interested in my responses. I settled back in my chair and listened.

"Well, it isn't necessarily so. Fremont's in a bunch of trouble here, and California's one of the critical states that's going to decide this election. It's all split right down the middle of the Mason-Dixon line—Fremont and the Republicans above it, Buchanan and the Democrats below it. But even with all Fremont's exploring and connections to the West, and the anti-slavery sentiment of the North, his chances are still shaky in some places—like California and Pennsylvania. The Republican party is too new. The Democrats are just plain a stronger party. They've got the South all sewed up, while at the same time there are bad fractures in the northeast and west.

"The trouble is, there's a lot of folks who don't like the idea of slavery, but they have always been Democrats. And there's some of us who are afraid that in this election we're going to find out they're more *for* being Democrats than they are *against* slavery.

"Now, you take the Germans. There's likely a hundred, maybe a hundred and fifty thousand Germans who are going to vote next month; most of them are Democrats and always have been. They don't like slavery, but they're Democrats and nobody knows how they're going to go. And so both parties are trying to win them over and are giving them money, and there are editorials aimed at the immigrant vote in the New York *Tribune* and the Cleveland *Herald* and the *Ohio State Journal* and the Detroit *Free Press* and the Cincinnati *Enquirer* and every other paper in the country. And the Democrats are stirring up fear of a Southern secession from the Union if Fremont wins. The Philadelphia *Daily News* and the *Pittsburgh Post* and the Washington *Daily Globe* are full of that stuff. The fear is worst in Pennsylvania. Listen to this."

He stopped a minute and rifled through several papers on the table in front of him. I didn't understand everything he was saying, but it was interesting, and I didn't want to interrupt again. He found the paper he was looking for.

"Listen—this is from the *Daily Pennsylvania* just a couple months ago: 'There is no disguising the fact that the great question of union or disunion has been precipitated upon us by the mad fanatics of the North, and that it is a direct and inevitable issue in the presidential contest.'"

He put the paper down and glanced across the desk at me. I think he was almost surprised to see that he'd been delivering his political speech to no one but me, who barely understood half of it.

"Do you get what I'm driving at, Hollister?" he asked.

"Some of it," I answered.

"I'm talking about this country splitting apart—that's the kind of fear the southern Democrats are putting into the people of the North. They're blackmailing the voters, threatening to pull the South out of the Union if Fremont is elected. But if Buchanan is elected, then the South wins . . . and slavery wins. The Democrats are saying, 'Give us the victory, put our man in the White House, let slavery remain, and we won't destroy this nation.' Now I ask you, can we allow this country to submit to that kind of blackmail? Of course we can't. Slavery is wrong, Hollister, and that's what John Fremont stands for, and that's why he must be elected in November. The Southern states will never secede from the Union, even over slavery. The secession issue is a bluff."

He stopped, took a breath, but then went right on.

"It's the Southerners, the Democrats, these blackmailers holding the threat of secession over the rest of the country, who are trying to ruin Fremont. They're spreading all kinds of lies and rumors about him—saying that his parents weren't married until after he was born, ridiculing him for his beard, claiming that he had once been a French actor, saying that he is secretly a Catholic, that he hates Germans because of his French blood, and hinting at improprieties, even illegalities, in how he came by his wealth. And the rumors involve his wife too—that's where you come in, Hollister. There are reports circulating that Jessie Fremont has never forsaken her Virginia upbringing, that she still keeps slaves and even watches while they are beaten at her orders, and that she herself was suckled by a slave mammy on her father's plantation.

"They're all lies. Vicious lies. But they are damaging Fremont's chances. And I don't have to tell you what that means to California. Buchanan stands for the interests of the South. His election will mean that the West will be forgotten.

"Many people feel that the future of California depends on a rail line between Chicago and Kansas City and the Pacific. Mark Hopkins, Charles Crocker, Leland Stanford, C.P. Huntington, and others like them are backing Fremont for that reason. They know that the only hope for a transcontinental railroad lies with the Republican party. And that's why our paper, the *Alta*, and the *Daily* and *Weekly Times* here in Sacramento are doing our best for him. But our competitors are working just as hard to discredit him. The Sacramento *Union*, the *Courier*, the *Democratic State Journal* are all backing Buchanan. And the worst is the *Morning Globe* in my own city, where some of my own former colleagues have defected.

"Fortunately, I have a spy at the *Globe* who keeps me informed, and only last week I learned that they are planning a major story to run just a week before the election, a story they hope will utterly ruin Fremont and insure his defeat. Their timing is intended to sway last-minute voters, and I fear they may have similar stories they will break in some of the eastern papers as well."

He paused and gave me a long, serious look.

"You understand what it's all about, don't you, Hollister?" he said after a minute. "It's slavery . . . and power . . . and greed. You've got to understand all this so you'll know the kind of men we're up against. We may be fifteen hundred miles from the nearest slave plantation, and California may be a free state. But there are men here who work for some of the most powerful and wealthy men in the South. And they're doing whatever it takes to put Buchanan in the White House and keep their power from eroding. The South controls the country right now, and they don't want to lose their hold on Washington. Men like Fremont, and that young lawyer from Illinois, Lincoln, who aren't afraid to speak up, are in danger. And *we* may be in danger too. But we've got to do what we can, and we've got to try to scoop them on their story before they print it. We've got to discredit everything they say before they say it, and print our own major new pro-Fremont piece. We may not be able to change what they do in Pennsylvania. It's too late for that. But if we can swing the vote in California, it may be enough to put your friend Jessie Fremont in the White House."

"I didn't say she was actually my friend," I corrected him.

He looked at me crooked for a second. "I thought you did," he said finally. "Well, that makes no difference. You obviously have *some* connection."

"What do you want me to do?" I asked. "I don't know anything about politics. I don't see how I can be of much help."

"One of Senator Goldwin's men is supposed to be up in the Mother Lode somewhere, digging up the last of the dirt they're planning to use against Fremont."

"Who's Senator Goldwin?"

"Herbert Goldwin—just about the most powerful man in the U.S. Senate, an entrenched slave owner, and filthy rich from his huge cotton plantations in South Carolina. Also one of the most unscrupulous men in Washington. He'd lie or cheat, steal, maybe even kill to keep his little empire secure. Fremont's spoken out against him, and Goldwin hates the Colonel. Of course he'd never soil his lily-white hands with his own dirty work. But he has plenty of people to do it for him. And one of them's up Sonora way rousing up all kinds of mischief—getting falsified documents against Fremont, getting interviews from miners Fremont supposedly ran off the Mariposa at gunpoint. Then there's the Catholic angle, and the rumors against Mrs. Fremont. My contact at the *Globe* says this guy's due back in San Francisco in a week and a half with the last pieces of the article which will, his editor claims, 'nail down the coffin on the presidential bid of John Charles Fremont.' We've got to locate that guy and find out what he's got so we can see if there's any substance to it. If they're making claims, we need to find out whether they're true or false."

"What's the man's name?" I asked. This was getting mighty interesting!

"We think Gregory, or something like that. Only heard the name once, so we can't be sure."

"And you don't know exactly where he is?"

"I had someone else on it, but they lost his trail. Sonora's the last scent we had, which makes sense—there's a lot of anti-Fremont talk among the miners that close to Mariposa. Lot of 'em think they ought to be entitled to the gold on Fremont's estate, and they don't like him getting rich while they're scratching away for tiny little nuggets. And just between you and me, I wouldn't doubt if what Goldwin *really* wants is the Mariposa for himself! Rich guys like him can't stand when a man like John Fremont comes into a lot of dough overnight. They want all the wealth and power for themselves, and it makes them crawl to have to share it."

"What do you want *me* to do?" I asked. "Why do you think *I* can help?"

"Maybe you can't, but it's worth a try. So here's what I want you to do. Find this Gregory, or whoever he is, and find out what he's got. If he has something on Fremont or his wife that's not true, then use your contact to write an article discrediting Goldwin's charges."

"How could I possibly find him? I'm just . . . a girl!"

Mr. Kemble laughed. "Here all this time you've been wanting me to overlook that fact. And now when I drop something really important in your lap, you tell me you're not old enough to do it!"

"I didn't say I wasn't old enough. I just don't know what you expect me to do when your other man couldn't do it. I don't have experience tracking someone like that."

"Don't you see—you're the perfect one, Corrie. No one will suspect you of a thing. I doubt if anyone who's involved with Goldwin will even recognize your name. I could send one of my experienced men. But they'd spot him right off. No, I think you might be able to find out things someone else couldn't. You shouldn't even have to lie."

"I couldn't do that."

"I don't think you'll have to. But you won't be able to tell them what you're after."

"I still don't see why you want *me* to follow somebody."

"I'm not just sending you to track this fellow. I'm sending you after a story. You've got to get on the trail of this thing, find out what's at the bottom of it, and then write a story that tells the truth and shows up their lies for what they are. Once their story runs, it's too late. You've got to find the guy and uncover what he's trying to do. I don't know how, but that's what you've got to try to do. I can't do it, and none of my regular guys can do it because they know them all. But you can, Corrie—at least I hope you can, 'cause the outcome of the election in California may depend on it. You get to the bottom of it, find out the truth behind the things they're planning to say, and I'll make you a reporter, Corrie Hollister. You find this guy and uncover what Goldwin's up to, and get me the story I want *before* their charges can appear in the *Globe*, and I'll give you a monthly article of your very own, as an *Alta* regular."

I was stunned. It was the very thing I'd dreamed of. Yet how could I *possibly* do all he asked? I must have said something, or asked what I should do first, though I don't remember. But I do remember his answer.

Mr. Kemble's expression changed from concern to relief. "The first thing you do is get yourself out to Sonora and start asking questions and nosing around. Real quick you'll start to find out if you're *really* a reporter, or just a kid who wants to be one. And whatever you find out, it's got to be on my desk by noon on the 22nd or else we're done for. That's ten days, Hollister. By then we'll know what kind of stuff you're made of."

# CHAPTER 42

## SONORA

Everyone in California had heard about Sonora. Except for the area around Sutter's Mill farther north, it was one of the heaviest populated, roughest, and richest regions of the Mother Lode. There were stories told—and we'd heard them all the way up in Miracle Springs, thanks to Alkali Jones—of single nuggets worth thousands of dollars. One was found that was supposed to have weighed twenty-eight pounds!

The whole place had been fabulously rich in the few years after the rush. There were twenty or thirty separate little towns all within ten miles of Sonora. Every one had seen thousands of hopeful miners pass through, all with a hundred stories to tell. In Shaw's Flat, only a mile away, eighty-seven million dollars had been taken from its streams. Columbia, four miles away, supposedly had a population of 30,000 with over a hundred gambling houses, thirty saloons, twenty-seven food stores, a stadium, and a theater. Farther north, Mexican Flat and Roaring Camp and Columbia and Angels Camp and Sawmill Flat—they all could have laid claim to equal riches and equal notoriety. I'd heard stories of fights and jumped claims and even murder. Most of what I'd heard, coming from the mouth of Alkali Jones, was probably considerably bigger in the tale than in the reality, but that only made it all the more fearful for me as I rode into the heart of the Mother Lode—alone, and not even knowing what exactly I was looking for. I had been praying harder than ever before in my life since leaving Sacramento! And I hadn't been about to spend the night alone in this country—at least not my first night. I'd stayed at the National Hotel in Jackson, although it wasn't much better than sleeping outside. I'd heard yelling and singing and piano playing all night, and a couple of gunshots. But at least I'd been able to lock the door to my room!

Late the next morning I rode into Sonora, still praying, still thinking every other minute of just forgetting the whole thing and galloping back to Miracle Springs as fast as I could! But I knew I couldn't. Even though Pa didn't really approve of me riding down here alone, Mr. Kemble was counting on me. And maybe Mr. Fremont too, and Jessie Fremont, and even Ankelita Carter. So I had to do what I could. Even if I failed, I had to try.

I walked my mare slowly through the main street. I hoped I could find a boardinghouse in town instead of a hotel, because most of the hotels were connected with saloons, and stayed pretty loud and raucous all night long. But I didn't see anything that looked even halfway civilized. Every other building seemed to be a saloon, and from the sounds coming from them they all seemed full of men drinking and yelling. The people on the streets were all men, and I didn't see a friendly face anywhere. The ones who noticed me looked me over as I passed, and a few yelled and whistled at me. But I just kept going and tried to keep my face from turning red. I was beginning to think I was the only female in the whole place when two or three saloon girls came out of a place called the Lucky Sluice. They started calling out worse things than the men. I didn't like their looks at all!

Finally a little ways farther on, I spotted a building with just the word "Hotel" printed across the door. I rode toward it, stopped, got down and tied my horse to the hitching rail, and walked inside.

I was glad there was hardly anyone inside, though a few tables in the lobby indicated that probably card playing went on at night. A man stood behind a counter, and I walked toward him. But before I even got across the floor, a whistle behind me let me know that the man at the counter wasn't alone after all. "If it ain't a real live female woman!" someone said.

"Hey, Fence," a voice called out, "check her into my room!"

I ignored the noises behind me and went up to the counter. Before I'd said a word the man they called Fence pushed the register in my direction.

"Excuse me," I said, putting on my bravest-sounding voice, although I probably didn't convince anyone, "do you know if there's a boardinghouse in town?"

"I got a boardinghouse, Missy!" called out a voice, followed by footsteps slowly coming across the floor.

"Shut up, Jack!" said the hotel man. "Can't you see she's just a kid?"

"So much the better!"

"Get outta here, Jack. I don't want no trouble." Then looking down at me, the man said, "There's Miz Nason's place, little lady. Down the next street to the right, 'bout a quarter mile down."

Just as I was about to turn to leave, a thought occurred to me.

"You don't have a man by the name of Gregory registered here, do you?" I asked. I glanced down at the register and tried to scan the names on the page without being too conspicuous.

"Nope. But half the fellas what come to the diggin's ain't usin' their real names anyway."

"Thank you very much," I said, turning around to go. As I did I almost bumped into the man the hotel manager had called Jack. He had been standing right behind me. I didn't know how I couldn't have known it, because he smelled terrible. He must have been working for a month without a bath! He looked even worse, and I walked on past him toward the door without even looking into his face, though he muttered a few words as I went by. Just as I was going through the door, the hotel man's voice called out after me, "If you don't find no room, Missy," he said, "I got one you can have fer four dollar a day. The lock works, an' I personally keep Jack an' his kind off the second floor."

Four dollars! When Almeda and I went to San Francisco, she'd only paid six dollars a night at the fancy Oriental, and that was for *two* of us! And he wanted four, just for me, in this ramshackle place that looked like it hadn't been cleaned since the day it was built! I kept walking back out to the street, ignoring the voices and laughter coming from behind me.

I mounted my horse again and set off again in the direction that I hoped would lead me to Nason's boardinghouse. In five minutes I found myself approaching a decent-looking two-story wood house. At least the paint wasn't peeling and some grass was growing in front. A small hand-painted sign on the fence simply said "Nason."

I stopped, got off my horse, and walked up and knocked on the door. In a minute or two a stout, broad-shouldered black-haired woman opened it. She looked me over up and down, without the slightest change in her expression, then just stared at me, waiting.

"I'm interested in a room," I said, "if you have any available."

"Rooms? 'Course I got rooms!" she said back, a little too gruffly to make me feel altogether comfortable. "How many you got with ya?"

"It's just me, ma'am."

"Just you!" she exclaimed. "You expect me to believe a young thing like you's travelin' in *this* country alone?"

"I'm sorry, ma'am, but I really am by myself."

"Well, then, guess I can't hardly send you away. Yeah, I got a room, if you got two-fifty a night."

"Two-fifty!" I said in astonishment before I could keep it from slipping out.

"Two-fifty, and a bargain at that! Only two other houses in town—one of 'em's full of dance-hall girls, and the other's full of drunken miners. An' both charge the same. If you want to stay in one of the hotels, you'll take your life in your hands—someone's gettin' shot over some gold fracas every week. An' you'll pay more besides. So it's two-fifty a day—in advance! Breakfast's included, but if you want supper, it's another two-bits."

Every other boardinghouse I'd stayed at was a dollar a night, including supper—except for Miss Bean's in San Francisco, which was a dollar-fifty. It was a good thing I'd brought money along!

Finally I nodded my head and said that would be fine. Mrs. Nason opened the door and led me inside.

I followed her through a large parlor and toward a flight of stairs. "Might you have a man by the name of Gregory lodging with you?" I asked.

"Never heard of him," she answered without turning around.

We continued up the stairs in silence, and she opened the third door we came to. "This here's the room," she said. "How many nights?"

"I—I'm not altogether sure just yet, ma'am. I guess I'll pay you for two to begin with."

"With supper?"

"Yes . . . thank you."

"That will be five dollars, four bits. And I believe I did say in advance?"

"Yes, ma'am. I'll go down and fetch my things from my horse."

"Ain't a good idea to keep nothing of value unattended in this town. They'll steal you blind. You better go down and make sure your horse is still there."

"Yes, ma'am," I said, turning back the way we'd come.

"If you want to put your horse up, there's a barn out back, with stalls an' fresh oats."

"Thank you, that will be fine."

"It's another two-bits for the horse," added Mrs. Nason. I sighed, and walked back outside to where my mare was waiting patiently.

An hour later I sat down on the edge of the bed in the bare little room. I'd fed and groomed Raspberry and put her up in the barn for a well-deserved rest. Now I had to think about what I was doing here.

I supposed if I was being a newspaper reporter investigating something, then about the only place to begin was by asking questions. No doubt Mr. Kemble might have other ideas. He'd probably have all kinds of sneaking-about-kind-of notions how to find this fellow who was working for the *Globe* and for that Senator Goldwin. But I didn't know anything but just ask around and try to find him. And if I did, then try to find out what he was up to, even if it meant just going up to him and asking him. I didn't have to blab right out that I was working for the *Alta* and that my editor told me to sabotage him.

I wasn't sure how to do what Mr. Kemble sent me to do and still be honest at the same time. This was a part of being a reporter I'd never thought about. I had always wanted to write just to express myself and tell interesting stories to people. Now all of a sudden here I was in the middle of trying to investigate a situation where wrong was being done. But even if wrong *was* being done, I couldn't do wrong myself to try to uncover it. I just hoped I'd be able to keep straight what was right myself, no matter what anyone else was doing!

I got down on my knees beside the bed.

"God," I prayed, "I'm not sure what's going to happen here. But I ask that you'd show me what to do and where to go, and guide my thoughts as well as my steps. Help me to be true, like I prayed before, and help me to find out the truth behind this article they're trying to hurt Mr. Fremont with. Help me to be a good reporter, and to be a good daughter of yours."

# CHAPTER 43

## THE LUCKY SLUICE

All that afternoon I walked around the town of Sonora.

After a while I got used to the rowdiness and the yelling and the horses running through the streets, and even the men talking to me and calling after me. I saw a few other women about who didn't look like they belonged in a saloon, and that helped. And luckily there hadn't been rain for a while, so the streets were dry instead of muddy.

I went into several stores, peeked over the swinging doors into a saloon or two, and got up my courage to go into two or three more of the town's hotels to ask about the fellow named Gregory. I felt rather foolish just wandering about, and it didn't seem like I was having much luck. Later on I saddled my horse and rode out of town.

I took a ride clear around through Jamestown, Rawhide, Shaw's Flat, Springfield, and Columbia. I saw signs pointing off to Brown's Flat, Squabbletown, Sawmill Flat, and Yankee Hill. I had no idea there were so many little towns and mining camps—though most of them were just a few buildings sur-rounded by claims up and down the streams. Once I got out of Sonora no one bothered me much. The men I passed would stare or watch to see where I was headed, but most of them were too intent on their work to mind me. All around were the sights and sounds of gold mining—men panning in the streams, mules laden down with equipment heading off the roads up toward the high country, the sounds of heavy equipment and dynamite and quartz machinery. It seemed that every square inch of this country was being dug up or mined by somebody!

Riding back to town, I decided that the only way to go about this search was to start at the beginning of Sonora and go to every hotel and boardinghouse and ask about Mr. Gregory. Then I'd go ask the sheriff. After that, I'd have to do the same things in whatever places there were in the little surrounding towns where he might be staying. I'd never find him just wandering about. There were thousands of people around here! I'd have to go to every lodging place one by one until I found where he was staying. At least by then I'd know for sure if he was in Sonora or not. If he wasn't, then I'd be able to tell Mr. Kemble I'd done everything I knew to do.

I arrived back at Mrs. Nason's just in time to unsaddle and put up my mare before supper. When I went in, Mrs. Nason introduced me to the others around the table, including her own husband who'd been out working their claim all day. Besides Mrs. Nason I was the only woman, but the men were all nice enough, although they spent most of their energy gulping down the biscuits, potatoes, roast beef, and cooked cabbage.

"She's lookin' fer a feller named Gregory," said the landlady to her husband. "You ever heard o' him, Jed?"

"Can't say as I have," the man answered. "What you want him for, Miss?"

It was the first time I'd been asked that, but I'd already planned out the answer to give.

"We're in the same line of work," I said. "And I need to ask him a few questions."

" 'Bout what? You look kinda young to be in *any* line o' work in these parts. What do you do?"

"We're in the newspaper business."

This seemed to satisfy Mr. Nason. His wife's expression didn't look like she approved, but she hadn't smiled once since I'd arrived, anyway.

Just then one of the other men at the table spoke up.

"There's a Gregory over at the saloon, least he was a couple nights back. But he weren't no newspaper man, I can tell ya. A shyster's more like it! The guy took me for my whole two days' worth of dust in an hour of five-card stud."

"Where was that?" asked one of the other men.

"The Lucky Sluice."

"The Lucky Deuce, you mean!" said the other. "They play a game of faro there with deuces countin' triple and always goin' to the player, *if* you lay down a double bet ahead of time. So if you hit it wrong, the house gets rich and you lose everything in a hurry. But they keep bringin' the suckers in! I gave it up after losin' my whole wad to 'em twice."

"When was the last time you saw this man?" I asked.

"Couple nights ago, don't remember exactly. I ain't been back since."

"Maybe I'll go over there and see if he's back," I said.

"It gets mighty wild there, Miss," said Mr. Nason. "You don't want to be mixing with drinkin' men, especially if they happen to be losin' their gold at the same time."

"Well, if it's the man I'm looking for, he's not a miner, so I won't have to worry about that. And as for the drinking, I reckon I'll just get my business done and get out before anything rough gets started."

Nobody said anything else. None of them seemed to think I was too smart to think of walking into a saloon alone. But on the other hand, they didn't seem to care that much either way. Sonora was the kind of place, I guess, where folks were in the habit of doing whatever they pleased, and where everyone else minded their own business.

After supper I went out to the barn. I was about to saddle up my horse when I remembered Mrs. Nason's words about the stealing that went on around here. Maybe it wasn't such a good idea to tie the horse on the main street of Sonora at night. I decided to walk up to the middle of town instead.

Even while I was still a block away, I heard the laughing and yelling and music coming out of the Lucky Sluice. There weren't many people out. I'm sure all the respectable people were in their homes—if there were very many of those in this town!—and the rest were already inside the brightly lit saloons.

When I got to the double swinging doors of the Lucky Sluice, I took in a deep breath, breathed a silent prayer, and, trying to hide my shaking knees, pushed through the doors and walked inside.

I was dressed in denim breeches and a man's flannel shirt, and most of the men were absorbed at the dozen or so card tables, so I didn't attract too much attention at first. If I had, I probably would have turned back around and run right out! Against the right wall a man was playing lively music on a piano, and a few women in short, bright-colored dresses were lounging about and talking with some of the men.

I walked straight to the bar, ignoring the few heads that turned and watched me. The big burly man behind it walked toward me, still finishing something he was saying to somebody else. When he looked down at me, surprise showed on his face, and I think he might have been about ready to throw me out because of how young I looked. But I didn't give him the chance.

"I'm looking for a man named Gregory," I said quickly. "I was told he might be here."

The bartender stared at me like he might *still* be thinking of throwing me out. Nobody in this town did much smiling, but they sure stared a lot! Maybe I was funnier looking or more out-of-place looking than I realized.

But finally he turned his head and shouted off toward a table near the piano, "Hey, Hap, that friend o' yers from Frisco here tonight?"

"Naw . . . who wants t' know?"

"Little lady here's askin' fer him."

The man named Hap sat up in his chair and looked in our direction. If I'd hoped to be inconspicuous, there was no chance of that now! The rest of the men he was playing cards with glanced up too, and a round of whistles and catcalls followed. But I tried not to pay any attention to them.

"I'm afraid yer luck's done run out, Miss," said Hap. "Derrick lit off fer Chinese Camp yesterday. But maybe I can help ya out, Miss," he added with a smile, and a wink at his friends. "I'm better lookin' than him by a dang sight!"

"Can you tell me where I might find him?" I asked.

"Try Shanghai Slim's at Chinese Camp, or else he might be stayin' at old lady Buford's place in Jacksonville."

"Is that a boardinghouse?"

"You can call it what ya want, Miss. Derrick's called it worse things than that! But if ya mean a place where a body can get a bed an' a meal, then that's what it is."

"Thank you kindly," I said, nodding toward him and the bartender. Then I turned and walked out as fast as I could!

I went back to Mrs. Nason's. I'd paid for the night, and it was nearly dark and much too late to think of doing anything else. I'd head south to Jacksonville in the morning. I had no way of knowing if Hap was talking about the same man as I was trying to track down. But the bartender did say Gregory was from San Francisco, and that's where the *Globe* was. So I figured I ought to follow the lead and see what came of it.

# CHAPTER 44

# DERRICK GREGORY

Chinese Camp was about ten or twelve miles south of Sonora. I figured I'd ride there first.

There probably wasn't much chance of finding anybody in the morning, but I could look around, ask, and then I could go on to Jacksonville three or four miles farther on and see about getting a room for the night at that boardinghouse. I didn't much relish walking into strange hotels and saloons and asking about a man I didn't know. I still couldn't figure out why Mr. Kemble had sent *me* after this Gregory when, like he said, he had other more experienced men. I couldn't believe it was only that he wouldn't recognize me. Especially when I didn't have any idea what I was supposed to be doing, or how I'd find out the information Mr. Kemble needed. But I noticed that every time I walked into a strange or uncomfortable situation, it got easier the next time.

So when I saw the sign above the door advertising "Shanghai Slim's" as I rode into Chinese Camp, I didn't feel nearly so queasy in the stomach at the thought of walking inside. I wasn't looking forward to it, but at least I knew I could do it.

I got off my horse, tied her to the rail outside, and went in.

It was obvious in a minute where the place got its name—both the town and the saloon. Inside, the decorations looked more Chinese than anything I'd seen before in California. And although there weren't very many people there, more than half of them were Chinese. A man wearing a green apron was sweeping the floor in front of the bar. From his appearance I thought he must be the owner.

"Pardon me," I said, "are you Mr. Slim?"

He stopped his broom, glanced up at me, and answered in a thick Chinese accent, "You bet. I Shanghai Slim." The look he gave me seemed about the friendliest I'd seen in a long time, and he almost hinted at a smile. But I couldn't be sure.

"I'm looking for a man by the name of Gregory," I said.

The short little man pointed behind me, then without another word returned to his sweeping.

I turned around and saw, among the half dozen empty tables in the room, a group of men involved in a poker game at one of the tables. From the looks on their faces, I wondered if it had gone on all night, or if it was just getting started on a bad note. The only one apparently having a good time was one jovial Chinese man with a pile of money and some little bags of gold sitting in front of him. Several others who had apparently dropped out of the game stood by watching.

Slowly I approached them. No one even saw me. A pile of coins, some paper, and a couple of small nuggets of gold lay in the middle of the table, and all six of the men had their fingers curled tightly around their cards. Most of them had creases on their foreheads and were examining their hands intently. Finally a Chinese man broke the silence.

"Not me. I fold," he said throwing his cards face down in front if him. "I out this hand."

"I'll stay," said the man next to him. "That is, if you'll all take this nugget as good for the fifteen-dollar call." He held up a piece of gold between his thumb and first finger that looked to be about a half an inch thick all the way around.

"Okay by me," said a player across the table, and his words were followed by various nods and mutterings of approval.

The first man tossed the nugget into the middle of the table, where it sounded against the other coins there and rolled to a stop.

"I'm in," said a third man, laying two paper bills into the pot.

The next man eyed his cards carefully, then sent his thin Oriental eyes squinting one at a time around the table of his companions as if trying to penetrate either their thoughts or see through the backs of their cards. Finally he spoke. "I only once see man draw two cards to inside straight, and his face not look like yours. So I think you bruffing."

The look of satisfaction I had noticed on this man's face at first from his obvious winnings had now disappeared.

"I call your fifteen," he said. "And another fifty."

He reached into the pile in front of him and first tossed in two coins for the fifteen. Then with great deliberation he dropped five more ten-dollar gold pieces one at a time into the pot.

Sighs and exclamations went around the table. A couple of the men threw their cards down immediately.

To the left of the rich Chinese, a grubby looking miner laid his cards down and leaned back in his chair. "Well at least I'm glad you did that before I called with the fifteen. It's all yours, Ling. I'm out."

To his left, however, a well-dressed man, who looked somewhat out of place among both Chinese and dirty unkempt miners, cracked a tiny smile as he glanced again at his cards, then looked over into the eyes of the Chinese man who had just raised the bet to fifty. When he spoke, in spite of a deep serious look in his eyes, there was humor in his tone.

"Now, Ling," he said, "you asked for two, I took one. You figure me to be going for the inside straight. And I figure since you're so confident, then you must have three of a kind. My gut tells me you didn't pick up either the four or the full house, and that you're still standing with the same three you were dealt."

He paused, and now smiled broadly at the man called Ling.

"So if you want to see if I *did* hit on my inside straight, I'm going to make you pay for the privilege."

Still with his eyes on the other man, his hand went down in front of him and found five coins, which he tossed into the pot. It left him with only five dollars in his own pile.

One by one, all those who had previously called threw in their cards until it came again to Mr. Ling.

He laid his cards down in front of him, face up. "Three kings," he said.

"Well, Ling," said the man who had raised, "it appears at last your string of luck has come to an end. For you see, I picked up the straight . . . jack high!"

He laid down the five cards with a triumphant look of satisfaction and let out a great laugh, while various reactions and exclamations went round the table on the part of the others.

While he was scooping up the pot he had just won, I walked timidly the rest of the way to the table. He didn't see me until I was almost beside him.

"Uh . . . excuse me," I said shyly, "would you by any chance be Mr. Gregory?"

"That's me," he answered, still raking in his money. "Who wants to know?"

At last he glanced up to where I stood, and before giving me a chance to say anything more, let out an exclamation.

"Well, well! It looks like you came just in time to change my luck, honey! Derrick Gregory, at your service!" he said, flashing a grin.

He stood, took off his hat, and gave an exaggerated bow. As he rose from the table I saw that he was taller than I had realized, with curly black hair and eyes of the same color. He appeared to be in his early thirties. The smile revealed his teeth, though his voice and look didn't appear altogether genuine.

"I would like to talk with you," I said.

"Oh, I'd be right pleasured t' speak with ya, Miss," interrupted one of the other card players, a dirty man with a leering face I didn't like at all. "Now you jest come right over here t' me, an'—"

"Snap your big trap shut, Frank, or I'll stuff my fist into it!" said Mr. Gregory in my defense.

"Tarnation, Greg, I didn't mean nothin' by it."

"Well, just stay out of it!"

And though Frank didn't say another word, I still wasn't

sure what to think of Derrick Gregory either.

"Now, girl," he said, towering in front of me, "who are you, and what are you hankering to tell me?"

"I'm Cornelia Hollister," I said, "and I understand you're a newspaper writer."

The smile faded from his face. He started to lead me toward the other side of the room, saying as he did, "You fellas go on without me. I figure I owe this little lady a few minutes, the way she won that pot for me!"

As we moved away, a few whistles and jeers followed us.

"Don't pay any attention to them," he said to me. "And don't one of you think of touching my pot!" he called out over his shoulder. "I'll count every penny when I get back!"

He led me out the door and into the bright sunlight.

"You see, none of those men in there—they don't know *exactly* that I'm a reporter. They know I've been around a while asking some questions, but as long as they can keep winning some of my money at poker, they don't care too much about what I'm up to. And that's the way I'd like to keep it. So what is it *you* heard about me—what'd you say your name was?"

"Cornelia."

"So what makes you think I'm a writer?"

"I just heard about you, that's all."

"And what did you hear?"

"That you're writing about the election," I answered.

He sat down on the edge of the wood sidewalk, his long legs stretching out into the dirt street. Then he looked up and scanned me up and down as if taking stock of me for the first time.

"So you're interested in the election, eh, Cornelia?"

I nodded.

"That all?"

"I've always wanted to be a newspaper writer too," I said.

He smiled again. "A girl wanting to be a writer!" he exclaimed. "And so you figured I could give you a few pointers, eh, is that it?"

I didn't answer right off, but he didn't seem to mind.

"Cornelia what?" he asked.

"Hollister."

"Hmm . . . Hollister . . ." He rubbed his chin thoughtfully, then after a few seconds went on. "Well, Miss Hollister," he said, "I'm not saying anything one way or another about what I may or may not be. But I figure I owe you one. Ol' Ling in there'd been beating me all day and all night and had just about cleaned me dry till you walked up. So just maybe this is your lucky day as well as mine."

He didn't seem to take me seriously. But on the other hand, he didn't mind talking to me either, which was all I could have hoped for.

"Where do you come from, Cornelia?"

"I rode down from Sonora."

"Well, I'll tell you what," he said, getting back to his feet. "I've been staying at a place down in Jacksonville, and I got some folks I gotta see down at Big Oak Flat. If you want to ride along with me, I'll tell you a thing or two about this election, and maybe let you watch me conduct a real live interview in person. You game?"

"Oh yes, thank you very much!" I said enthusiastically. "I would like that."

After just a few minutes with him, I wasn't worried about riding off alone with Derrick Gregory. There was nothing about him that frightened me, although I couldn't help being on my guard. He talked to me as if he were sharing his great experience and wisdom with a little kid, which in this case I didn't mind.

"Let me go back in there and get my loot and tell those old coots that we're leaving. And then we'll hit the trail, *Miss* Hollister."

# CHAPTER 45

# I FIND OUT MORE
# THAN I OUGHT TO

For the rest of the morning we rode south and chatted easily. Mr. Gregory seemed perfectly willing to talk to me about his work, and didn't appear to mind my questions. Gradually I learned a lot about him and what he was doing. Apparently he thought of me as nothing but a raw novice who knew absolutely nothing.

In a way I guess I *was* just a raw novice. But I knew more than he thought I knew, and I wasn't so innocent of motive as he thought. I wondered if I was doing wrong to deceive him. But I hadn't actually said anything that was untrue, he had drawn his own conclusions. I wasn't trying to hurt anyone but was just trying to get at the truth, and I thought that what I was doing was justified. If it wasn't, and if I was doing wrong, I'd have to deal with my conscience when it started to nag at me. It was a hard question, and wouldn't be the first time as a reporter when I'd wonder about the line between honesty and not saying enough. Maybe it's a problem a reporter never completely gets a handle on.

One thing was for sure, Derrick Gregory wasn't in the least concerned about truthfulness in what *he* wrote. He treated me nice enough. But he didn't care if he was fair to Mr. Fremont. Before we'd gone very far at all, he'd confided in me that his job was to get whatever he could in order to destroy John Fremont's reputation.

"But what if you write something that's not true?" I asked.

"Nobody pays you for truth, Cornelia. They pay you to watch out for their interests."

I reached into my saddlebag and pulled out a notepad and a pencil. "A *real* reporter's supposed to take notes, isn't she?" I asked innocently. "Do you mind if I write down some of what you say? I want to learn as much as possible."

Derrick looked flattered. "Atta girl, Cornelia! You wanta be a writer, you gotta *act* like a writer!" He paused, and an expression of importance crept over his face. "Now, Miss Hollister, listen close, and you might learn something about being a real newsman."

Writing notes on horseback is not an easy thing to do. My pencil went all over the page, but at least I got down the important parts. Mr. Kemble wouldn't print anything unless I was sure I had the facts straight, so I wanted to make sure I could back up what I wrote.

"If you're writing about election news," I asked Mr. Gregory, "don't you have to report the facts?"

"Facts are slippery things. One fella might look at a fact one way, and somebody else in another way. The people who hired me pay me to dig up facts that they can use against Fremont. They don't care how I get them, or even whether they're true. If they can make people *believe* they're true, then they'll have what they want, and I'll get paid handsomely for my efforts. You see how nice it works out!"

"But that's not being honest to the people who read what you write, Mr. Gregory," I said.

"What is honesty? Like I said, I don't get paid to be honest, but to do a job. And the senator who sent me out here always gets what he wants. So why shouldn't I profit from his greed?" He patted his saddlebag. "So I've got a whole lot of things here that are just what the senator wants, sworn statements, quotes from guys who saw Fremont do such and so. Why, by the time I get through writing it up, the election's as good as decided in this state. And by the way, Cornelia, no more of this Mister Gregory stuff. If you and I are going to ride together and I'm going to teach you the business of being a reporter, then you at least ought to call me by my name. Fair enough?"

I nodded. "But then why—uh, Derrick—why did you come clear out here, all the way from the South, to write stuff about Mr. Fremont?"

"That's the beauty of the senator's scheme! Right here's where Fremont kicked around before he got famous. Why, his estate runs clear up to just a few miles from here. Anything we can uncover here, people'll believe it just like it's gospel, because it's from the man's *real* past, what he was like before he got into politics."

He stopped, with a serious expression on his face, and looked around behind us.

"You hear a horse back there?" he asked, pulling his own mount to a stop. I reined in alongside him and listened. I didn't hear anything.

"Maybe I'm just too jumpy," he said, urging his horse along again. "But I've had a feeling like I'm being followed for more than a week now. Maybe I'm just nervous till I get this article written and these papers back to Frisco. But I still don't like not knowing who's watching me."

"Who would be watching you?" I asked.

"Fremont's people—maybe even Senator Goldwin's people, for all I know. Politics is a dirty business. Those guys play for keeps. To tell you the truth, it wouldn't surprise me if the senator had eyes on me, to make sure Fremont's people don't buy me off. If I will do *his* dirty work for a price, then he's got to figure I'd pull turncoat for a higher offer. You always gotta be figuring how these powerful guys think. Those slavery people are the worst. Right and wrong means nothing to them— it's strictly dollars and power."

"*Would* you turn your information over to Fremont's side— for a higher price?" I asked.

"Nah, they couldn't pay me enough to make me cross Goldwin. He'd have me killed inside a month."

"What do you have that's so valuable to him?" I asked.

"I've got the election in my saddlebag—the end of Fremont's political career forever, that's what. Once this stuff hits the press, Buchanan's election is secure. Goldwin's happy; he and his slavery boys stay in power in Washington. The anti-slavery forces go down in defeat with their champion, John Charles Fremont, caught with mud on his face and skeletons in his closet. Just think, the Union may owe its preservation to none other than an investigative reporter and man of the hour, Derrick Gregory! And you, Cornelia Hollister, had the good fortune to take it into your head to ask his advice about becoming a reporter right when he was about to finish the story that would sway the election of 1856! You are witnessing history in the making, Miss Hollister!"

"But I still don't see what you could have discovered way out here in the middle of nowhere that could be so damaging to Colonel Fremont," I said.

"All right, just for an example, take that little place where you found me, Chinese Camp," he replied. "My time there was spent doing more than playing cards. You might have seen it on your way in—little Catholic Church, St. Xavier's. I've got a quote from a Chinese man back there as an eyewitness that he saw John Fremont going into the church with a priest last time he was out here, for a private Mass."

"That can't be true," I said in disbelief. "John Fremont isn't a Catholic . . . is he?" I added, suddenly unsure of myself.

"Who knows? But haven't you been listening to anything I been telling you about this game of political reporting? Doesn't matter if it's true. Doesn't matter that I had to slip the guy ten bucks to encourage his memory along after I hinted at what I was looking for. If folks think it's true, it's good enough and you've done your job. No one's gonna come checking up on it. They couldn't check it anyway. The source's name will never be mentioned. My name won't appear on the story, won't have anything to do with it as far as the public's concerned. The story's untraceable. But the charge will persist, and even if it is only a rumor, it will do its job."

"It hardly seems right."

"Right, wrong—who cares? A reporter has a job to do, and

he gets paid by people in power with money to pay him. A writer doesn't decide right and wrong, he has to do his job. Facts are just what you make of them, no more, no less. There was another reason I was at Chinese Camp. You know about the Tong war a few months back at Crimea Flat? Well, I've got it on good authority that Fremont's men rode up from Mariposa and instigated the whole thing because Fremont hates the Chinese and doesn't like so many of them so near his estate."

"What kind of authority—same as about the church?"

Derrick laughed. "Now you're catching on, Cornelia! No, it's a little more reliable than that. Miners in these parts hate Fremont. They're jealous of his gold, they think some of it's theirs. A few of them who got run off the Mariposa at gunpoint for poaching are willing to say just about anything to bring down Fremont. I've got sworn statements that Fremont used Chinese slave labor along with the Mexicans when he first started mining the Mariposa, that he falsified surveying reports to change his boundaries to include the richest claims. I got quotes saying they saw Negroes in chains on the Mariposa, and even that Fremont used to get away at night with barmaids, leaving his wife alone at home. I got all kinds of stuff from interviewing people around here. Fremont's dead when it all gets out."

"What are you after today? Some other quote from someone who doesn't like Mr. Fremont?"

He laughed again. "In a manner of speaking. We're almost to Big Oak Flat. I'm gonna see Jack Savage, Jim Savage's brother—they founded the place and got rich from it. The Savage brothers and Fremont go back a ways. Savage and his brother led the Mariposa Battalion. Jim got himself killed by the Indians. They were the first white men into the Yosemite valley, and he has a thing or two to say about how Fremont got his clutches on all that land when he wasn't even here in person. From what I've gathered, the senator's promised Savage a big chunk of the Mariposa if he can give him enough information to contest Fremont's title. If I can get what I need, it not only makes Fremont out a crook, it might put the Mariposa right in Senator Goldwin's lap. Half of the old fat judges on the Supreme Court owe their appointments to him, and they would back him up if it came down to a law suit between Fremont and Goldwin."

"Do you think this man Savage will go against Fremont?"

"Sure. Disputes over money makes men more unforgiving than anything. Gold men and slavery men—there aren't any two groups in this country to hold a grudge longer. It would gall Savage to the core to see his old arch-rival over these gold fields be made President of the United States. I have no doubt he'll say anything and everything I want him to. And to make matters even better, Savage was involved with the Palmer & Cook Company back then at the same time Fremont was. He'll be able to confirm Fremont's role in that as well—and that one *does* happen to be in the area of true facts."

"What's that all about?"

"Just a couple months back, Palmer & Cook got into trouble for an illegal breach of faith in handling some securities belonging to the state of California. Fremont was closely involved with them when he was last here. It's the perfect smear."

We'd been talking a long time, and within another ten minutes we rode into the little village of Big Oak Flat. Derrick seemed to know where he was going. We rode straight through town, made two or three turns, and eventually arrived at the ranch called the Savage Diggings, the original name of the town in 1848. Mr. Savage must have been expecting him, because we went right in and sat down and the two men started talking. I just watched and listened, and they paid me no heed. But as I glanced around the room I noticed some old copies of the *Alta* lying around, and a momentary panic seized me.

As I sat there listening, I was astonished at what I heard. Mr. Gregory didn't just ask questions and write down Mr. Savage's answers. The two of them talked back and forth and discussed what would make it look the worst for Mr. Fremont—sometimes laughing, even making up situations and other people. By the time Mr. Gregory got to writing down some of the things they'd talked about, it might as well have been fiction. He wasn't trying to find out what *really* happened at all, but to make up what he called "facts" and quotations that he and Mr. Savage could agree on that would put Mr. Fremont in a bad light. They said things about Jessie, too, that I was sure were untrue, and I got angrier and angrier. Everything Derrick had told me on the way there was bad enough, but now I saw the deception and lies going on right in front of me, and it made me mad. How could he call himself a reporter, a newsman? He was telling lies to the whole country for that rich Senator Goldwin.

"But you say Fremont got out of the Palmer & Cook Company several years back?" asked Derrick.

"Oh yeah," answered Savage. "He's got nothing to do with this current mess of theirs. But it doesn't matter. His financial involvement in the company can be documented, and by the time he has a chance to refute it, the election will be over. Use it, Gregory. It'll bring him down in the business circles in Frisco."

Derrick was busy with his pen. He had written several pages since we'd got here, full of accusations, quotes, names, dates, places, illegalities, rumors—all slanderous against Colonel Fremont.

"But don't forget what I told you about the purchase of the Mariposa," Savage went on after Derrick's pen stopped. "It all hinges on Thomas Larkin, the guy Fremont used to buy the estate. Larkin was U.S. Consul at the time, but he had dealings back to the mid-forties with Alvarado and Michelorena, who owned the property first. I've never been able to get to the bottom of it, but if the senator could get to Larkin and, shall we say, win him over with a few hundred dollars on the side, I have the feeling Larkin might be able to provide all the ammunition the senator needs to mount a challenge to Fremont's title and get the Supreme Court to overturn their ruling."

Derrick was writing as fast as his fingers could move. Finally he glanced up.

"You are a devious one, Savage," he said. "I'm sure the senator will be deeply indebted for all your help in putting the final pieces of this article together."

"I am counting on it," smiled Savage.

"I will pass along your sentiments when I next see the senator after the election."

A pause followed. Derrick looked over his several pages of notes, then put them in a leather case along with his pen and ink. He snapped the buckle shut, patted the case with his hand, and let out a long sigh.

"Well, it's all here," he said. "I'll be writing up the article in the next few days, and within a week you should be reading the political obituary of one John Charles Fremont in the San Francisco *Morning Globe*. I'm sure future President Buchanan will be grateful for your part in effecting the demise of his opponent."

Derrick rose and extended his hand. Mr. Savage shook it, then offered me his hand also as I got up.

"Nice to see you too, Miss—"

"Hollister," I reminded him.

"Ah, yes—hmm . . . Hollister . . . seems as if I know that name. You from these parts?"

"My father's a miner," I said, evading the question. I hoped his mind didn't wander to the *Alta* right then!

"Hmm . . . well, I don't know . . . your name just seems familiar, that's all."

Derrick and I left the house, got on our horses, and started back north the way we had come.

"Looks like I've got everything I need, Cornelia!" Derrick said with a smile. "All I have to do now is write it up and take it to the city and my job's done!"

"Why do you bother with interviews," I asked, "if you're just making everything up, anyway?"

"You've got to at least give the appearance of credibility, you know! Besides, if anyone does question my sources, I want to have a credible list to give them."

We rode on a while in silence.

"Why so glum?" Derrick asked. "You've just seen political reporting at its best, firsthand. Why, you're watching how Presidents get elected!"

"It just doesn't seem right, somehow," I said.

"Still worried about honesty, Cornelia?"

"I reckon."

"Forget it. If you want to be a news reporter, this is how it works—who you know, and what kind of deal you can make with them. And watch out for your own best interests! It's the only way to get ahead in this game—just like in politics."

We were quiet again for a while.

"Are you going to Jacksonville now?" I asked.

"Nah, we still got plenty of daylight left. I think I'll get on back to Sonora and bunk there for another day or two while I'm writing this all up. I got a nice room above the Lucky Sluice where I can work."

"Maybe I could come and see what a finished article looks like," I suggested.

"Sure. Come on around, that is if your folks'll let you into a place like that." He hesitated. "But I guess if you're old enough to be tracking me down to learn how to be a reporter, you're old enough to go where you like without your pa's permission." He laughed, then sobered and asked, "Your pa's a miner, huh?"

I nodded, and immediately felt a pang of guilt for not telling him that I didn't actually live in Sonora.

All the rest of the way back that afternoon, Derrick seemed to be watching and listening, as if he still thought someone was following him. But we never saw anybody and nothing ever came of it.

# CHAPTER 46

## AN UNEXPECTED REUNION

We didn't get back to Sonora till pretty late in the evening.

We parted at the edge of town. "See you around, Cornelia," Derrick Gregory said, then took off toward the middle of town and the Lucky Sluice. I rode back to Nason's boardinghouse, hoping I wasn't too late to get my room back—payment in advance!—for the night.

Mrs. Nason almost seemed glad to see me, in her grumpy sort of way. She even heated up some of the supper things for me to eat and said that because they had already gotten cold she wouldn't charge me for the meal.

As I lay in my room that night, I couldn't get to sleep. All I could think of was the day I'd spent and Mr. Kemble, and the election, and what I ought to do with everything I'd learned. Finally I got up, lit a lamp, and for the next couple of hours went over my notes and tried to remember everything I'd seen and heard that day. I wrote it down in as much detail as I could. Whatever came of it all, at least I had to be sure of the truth of *my* facts. I had to be accurate about Derrick's falsehoods if I was going to tell them to Mr. Kemble in a way that would help Mr. Fremont. My notes weren't very neat, but I managed to get down most of the names of people Derrick said he'd talked to and quoted from, as well as what he'd told me about making things up and bribing people to say things. And I tried to reconstruct as much of his conversation with Jack Savage as I could so that I'd be positively accurate in my *own* quotes when it came to disproving the lies that were being told against Mr. Fremont.

When I finally got to sleep, it was after midnight and I slept late the next morning. But when I woke up my thoughts were less confused and my head was gradually coming clear about what I ought to do. I didn't really stop to consider that the plan was probably foolhardy and dangerous.

First, I'd have to find out what room Derrick was in. After that I'd have to watch him and try to figure out his writing habits. If they were anything like mine, every once in a while his hand would cramp up and his brain would get dizzy and he'd have to take a break and go for a walk or something. And after that . . . well, then I'd just have to hope for the best!

A little after noon I decided to walk up to the saloon just to see if I could run into Mr. Gregory. I didn't really know what I'd do or say, but whatever happened I had to keep him in my sights. If he left town without my knowing it and got back to San Francisco ahead of me, everything was lost.

There weren't many men in the Lucky Sluice at that hour, but a couple of tables were occupied. Almost before I was fully inside I heard Derrick Gregory's voice raised in laughter and talk. He had just won a hand and was celebrating at the expense of his companions. As I walked toward him, I noticed something awfully familiar about the tall thin form sitting beside him with his back to me. Across the table facing me as I approached sat two mean-looking men—one with a beard who looked like a miner, the other clean and well dressed in an expensive suit. If they were together, they sure made an odd-looking pair!

Derrick half turned and spotted me out of the corner of his eye.

"I should have known you were somewhere close by, Cornelia!" he exclaimed. "Gentlemen," he said to the rest of the men sitting at the table, "this is my good luck companion, Cornelia Hollister. Whenever she's around, I win!" Then glancing back at me, he added, "Cornelia, these two fellas are the men I was telling you about that work for the senator and are supposed to keep me in line." He threw me a quick wink, as much as to say that in spite of their rough appearance, *he* wasn't worried about them. "And this young buck just got in from the big city," he said, indicating the young man sitting next to him.

"Meet Rob Flaridy."

It was all I could manage to keep from stumbling over my feet and gasping in amazement! I'm sure the shock must have shown on my face. I must say, if he was as surprised to see me as I was him, Robin hid his reaction better than I did mine.

"Charmed," he said, half rising from his chair and tipping his familiar cap with a smile. I knew he enjoyed my discomfort.

"Sit down . . . sit down, Cornelia!" said Derrick. "Bring me some more good luck!"

"I . . . I really can't stay," I fumbled. "I was just . . . I thought I'd find out how your article was going. I didn't mean to interrupt."

"No interruption at all!" he said boisterously. Now that I was close to him I could tell he'd been drinking, although he wasn't really drunk. "I'm half done, Hollister . . . the election's practically in the bag! I'm just having a little break with my friends here! By tomorrow at this time I'll be on my way to San Francisco, and the boys here will be on their way overland with a copy of everything I've found for the senator's use in the East."

"You have a loose tongue," growled the man with the beard.

"Relax. Miss Hollister's on our side!"

In spite of his expensive suit, the expression on the other man's face was anything but friendly. "You just keep your mouth shut and your hand busy, and get those papers copied out for us! We're a day behind schedule as it is."

I couldn't help but notice that both the strangers had rifles leaning against their chairs. The man with the beard also wore a gun belt. The other eyed me with a questioning look.

I turned to leave.

"You come back around tonight, Cornelia," said Derrick. "I'll be right here at this table, and I'll be ready for another dose of your good luck."

I nodded sort of noncommittally.

"And maybe by then I'll be rid of these two brutes," he added, gesturing across the table, "and we can have some fun!"

I left the saloon without looking at Robin again.

I walked straight across the street into the dry goods store and pretended to look around. I kept close to the window with one eye on the swinging doors of the Lucky Sluice. In about twenty minutes the two men came out and walked up the sidewalk toward the north end of town. Five minutes later Robin emerged. He stopped, looked up and down, then started in the opposite direction, crossed the dirt street to the side I was on, and continued on toward the first hotel I had gone into when I'd got into Sonora.

I watched for another minute or two to make sure Derrick wasn't coming out. I didn't want him to see me chasing down the street after Robin. But finally I figured he'd gone back upstairs to his room. I left the store and walked southward as quickly as I could without attracting attention. I saw Robin up ahead of me, sauntering along slowly. I went out into the street so my boots wouldn't make a pounding noise on the wood walkway, and started running after him. I caught up with him just as he was passing a narrow alleyway that ran along the near side of the hotel.

Before he saw me coming, I ran alongside him and gave him a hard shove sideways into the alley and behind the building. He lost his balance and let out an exclamation, while he struggled to get back his footing. I jumped behind the edge of the wall after him, and grabbed him before he could yell.

"What are you doing here?" I exclaimed as loudly as I dared without attracting attention.

"I could ask you the same thing," he retorted. "And get your hands off me!" I hardly realized that I had hold of his coat and had pushed him up against the building.

I relaxed and took a step back.

"I am here because Mr. Kemble sent me," I said.

"As am I."

"He sent *you*?"

"How can I put this delicately, Corrie?" he said, finally cracking a meaningful grin. "He wasn't sure a girl of your tender years could—shall we say—*handle* such an important assignment. So he sent me along to make sure you didn't foul it up."

"Foul it up?" I cried, getting angry. "*You're* the one who's going to foul it up. I've practically got Gregory's whole story!"

"Ah, but I know that he's in room fourteen, and I know where those other two men are staying, and I know their whole scheme."

"How long have you been tracking him?" I asked.

"Couple weeks."

"Kemble told me he had someone on this but that it dried up and they lost Gregory's trail."

"Well, that was unfortunate. He eluded me for a while, but then Kemble told me to follow you up here and see what you turned up, and to move back in if I could. Experience, you know," he said with a superior smile. "He felt even if you did track down Gregory, I'd be better able to get what we need in the end."

"Why, that conniving rascal!" I said. "He gave me all that runaround about me being the perfect one for the story and about the election and truth all hanging in the balance, and all the time he was just using me! And you're trying to tell me that I was just a decoy so that *you* could get the story in the end?"

"The truth is sometimes painful, Corrie," said Robin, still smiling with that look of superiority.

I turned away and strode off a few steps deeper into the alley. I felt like crying and screaming all at once!

But if I was going to prove that I could compete with men like Mr. Kemble and *Mister* Robin T. O'Flaridy, I couldn't do either. I couldn't give in to all the female emotionalism flooding through me right then. I couldn't cry. I couldn't scream. I couldn't go over and punch Robin in the nose. Somehow I had to see this thing through, and prove that I was made of stronger stuff than either of them might think.

I took a deep breath, then turned back around.

"So it *has* been you following Derrick recently," I said calmly. "And you were on our trail down to Big Oak Flat yesterday."

"And you've got to admit I did a pretty good job too," said Robin. "Neither of you saw me, did you?"

I shook my head. "But Derrick knew somebody was back there."

"Nah, he knew nothing. He was guessing."

"Don't be too cocky, Robin," I said. "If you're not careful you could put your foot right in the middle of it and get us both killed."

"What could go wrong?"

"Plenty. You just watch your step. We're too close. I don't even want to think what those two men might do if they catch us or if they find out we know each other."

"They'll never find out a thing!"

"Just watch your step. Both of our names have been in print recently. It wouldn't take much and we'd be in way over our heads."

"I tell you, you worry too much, Hollister."

"And maybe it'll be my worrying that'll get you through this," I replied. "Where you staying?"

"Right here," he said, indicating the hotel.

"Well, I'm in the boardinghouse down the street. Which is where I'm going now—I've got to do some thinking. You stay out of trouble!"

In reply, he only flashed another smile of unconcerned indifference.

As I left the alley and walked off alone down the street, it hardly occurred to me how much everything had changed. I wasn't afraid of Robin anymore, as I had been in San Francisco. In fact, I'd acted as if *I* were the older and more experienced one of the team.

And for better or worse, I suppose that's what we were now, at least for a couple more days—a team. Something inside me told me it was up to me if we were going to get out of this in one piece. Robin was too cocky for his own good.

# CHAPTER 47

# DISCOVERY AND BETRAYAL

I didn't see either Robin O'Flaridy or Derrick Gregory for the rest of the afternoon. I spent three hours finishing writing down what I'd learned.

I didn't really know what to do next. But I had to get my hands on Derrick's batch of papers before those other two men headed east with them. If I waited too long to figure out some plan, Robin might louse it up and get us both into a heap of trouble.

Finally, late in the afternoon, I went outside. I had to do *something*. I'd been praying and thinking all afternoon, but without any ideas coming to me.

I wandered up the street toward Robin's hotel. I went inside and walked up to the counter.

"Do you know if Rob Flaridy's in?" I asked the man called Fence.

"Left an hour or two back, Miss."

"Alone?"

"Couple of men with him. They'd been lookin' fer him earlier."

"Friends of his?" I said.

"Didn't look too friendly to me," said Fence. "Looked to me they was takin' Flaridy against his will. But I don't ask no questions. You get too curious in this town, Miss, an' it's a good way t' git yerself a plot o' ground out in the cemetery."

I went back out into the street and walked back in the direction of the Lucky Sluice.

I approached the saloon on the wood walkway, but the instant I reached it and started to push one of the swinging doors open, I froze. Over the top of it I saw Robin seated at a table, his hands tied behind his back, with the three other men standing facing him, asking questions and talking among themselves. It was obvious in a second they'd discovered he was trying to foil their scheme. But how much they knew, I couldn't tell.

I backed up quickly so they wouldn't see me in the doorway, leaned against the wall, and strained my ears to hear through the door just to my right.

They were speaking softly to avoid attracting attention, but because they were so close to the door I could hear them clearly. It was still early. The saloon was nearly empty, and the piano player hadn't started.

"I say we take him out and put a slug through his head right now," said the man with the beard.

"No, no, Jake—too messy," said the other friend of Derrick's. "There are certain rules to be observed, even in our business. No, we'll wait till we're set to leave town, then there'll be no tracing us."

"I don't like it," I heard Derrick mutter. "I knew there was somebody trailing me!" He swore a couple of times, giving Robin a cuff on the side of the head. "But I never thought they'd send someone the likes of you after me!"

"Who's in it with ya, kid?" asked the bearded man, grabbing Robin's shirt around his neck and giving it a yank. "Tell us, an' maybe we'll go easy on ya!"

"Please . . . please! I don't know anything about what you're doing. They just told me to follow you, that's all, but I didn't find out anything. Please . . . let me go . . . I'll never say a word to anybody."

While he was whining, the nicely dressed man was apparently rummaging through his clothes.

"Well, look at this!" he said. "We shoulda searched him when we first found him snooping around your room, Gregory. It would have saved us the trouble of trying to beat the information out of him. His name's not Flaridy at all, but *O'Flar-*

idy—Robin O'Flaridy . . . and he works for the *Alta*."

"I should have known!" said Derrick. "Kemble's rag. They sent him here to kibosh the story! They've been backing Fremont from the beginning!"

"Look," pleaded Robin in a forlorn tone, "you caught me red-handed, and you know I've got nothing that can hurt you. Let me go, and you go your way and do whatever you want about the election, and I'll never say a word. You can trust me to—"

"Shut up, ya whimpering brat!" shouted the bearded man. I heard the back of his hand slap across Robin's face, and he cried out in pain.

"Wait a minute!" said the man in the suit, snapping his fingers as if he was thinking. "Wait . . . it's coming to me . . . Derrick, that girl you were so friendly with—the one you said brought you good luck."

"Yeah, what about her?"

"What'd you say her name was?"

"Hollister."

"Her first name, you idiot!"

"Cornelia . . . Cornelia Hollister. But what has she—"

"You are a bigger fool than I thought!" the man said spitefully. "I knew there was something familiar about her name the minute you said it! Blast, why didn't I think harder—don't you know who she is?"

"Yeah, she's just some miner's kid from around here who wants to be a writer."

"And you thought you'd give her a few pointers, eh?"

"I didn't see any harm in—"

"You lunkhead, she *is* a writer. And she doesn't need any pointers from you! She writes for the *Alta*, too! The name Corrie Hollister mean anything to you?"

Derrick shrugged.

"You dolt! She wrote a big pro-Fremont piece just a couple of weeks back. She's a friend of Fremont's wife! She's in it with this snivelling little creature here!"

"That's impossible—she's just a kid!" cried Derrick in disbelief.

"Impossible, huh? I saw that look in her eyes. She was watching and listening to a lot more than you thought."

"I can't believe it."

"The senator will love to hear this. What did you tell her, Gregory?"

I could hear Derrick sitting down and letting out a bitter sigh. "She was with me all day yesterday. I told her everything. She was there for the Savage interview."

"Well, you know what you got to do, Gregory," said the bearded man viciously. "The senator don't like mistakes like this. You make a mess, then you clean it up—that's what he always says."

"Yeah . . . yeah, I know," sighed Derrick. "I kinda liked the kid too, and she did seem to bring me luck at cards."

"Yeah, she brought you luck all right. *Bad* luck! She's got to be eliminated, along with this trash here!" snarled the man in the suit. "Jake'll do the boy, but *you've* got to pull the trigger on the Hollister girl, Gregory! Otherwise the senator won't know if he can trust you in the future."

"I know," sighed Derrick. "You don't have to tell me. I know the senator as well as you do. If we let these two survive, he'd be after me next."

"Where's the girl?" the suited man asked Robin.

I'll have to say this much for him, he didn't give me away immediately.

The next sound I heard was a blow to the side of the head. I was terrified! My first thought was to flee. But something held me back. I *had* to find out all I could. I looked around the corner, just in time to see Robin crashing to the floor. The terrible-looking man grabbed roughly at him and raised his fist to smack him again. "The man asked you a question!" he yelled. "Where is she?"

"You'll . . . you'll let me go if I tell you?" whimpered Robin. His mouth and forehead were bleeding. "I don't know anything . . . it's her you want, not me."

"Yeah, okay—you win, kid," said the suit-man. "Take it easy, Jake—let him loose." They set him back down in the chair.

"Okay, you got a deal, O'Flaridy. You tell us where she is, and we'll let you go."

"She's . . . she's staying at a boardinghouse—down the side street from my hotel."

I leaned back against the wall in disbelief. He had *betrayed* me!

But I didn't have time to stop to consider the implications. Immediately I heard the sounds of chairs being pushed aside and boots on the wood floor walking my way.

I turned and ran, darting into the alleyway, running alongside the edge of the saloon. I hurried into the darkened passage, and ducked quickly down behind some big oak beer kegs sitting by the back door. A few seconds later I heard the three men pass by along the sidewalk, dragging Robin along with them.

"We'll take O'Flaridy out back of the livery and tie and gag him," the suited man was saying. "You finish what you got to do, Gregory, and later you go down to that boardinghouse and sweet-talk that Hollister kid into coming out for a walk with you. We'll grab her and stash her with the kid."

"Hey, you promised to let me go!" cried Robin. "I told you what you wanted to know."

I couldn't hear what they said back to him, because by now they were too far down the street. But the man with the beard let out a huge laugh that sounded full of glee and evil intent at the same time.

I waited a few minutes after they had passed, inched out to the edge of the alley, looked both ways to be sure it was clear, then I darted across the street and made my way back to Mrs. Nason's through the back streets and alleys and over a few fences. I knew it was dangerous to go back there after what had been said. But I had to risk it.

# CHAPTER 48

## A RISKY PLAN

I gathered my things quickly and stuffed them into my bag. I'd already paid for the night's lodging, but I thought it best to slip out and not tell anyone at the house. The less they knew, the less chance Derrick would have of finding me.

Dusk was just settling as I sneaked out my window and down the back stairs outside the house. I could still hear workmen's voices inside the Nasons' barn, so I crept out behind it, sat down in the grass and waited. It gave me time to collect myself, catch my breath, and rest. I was hungry, but food would have to wait! I had to spend my time thinking of a plan, not my stomach.

When time came for supper, I heard the men in the barn leave for the house. A few minutes later I heard Mrs. Nason call my name a couple of times. But eventually she gave up, and I knew everyone was at the table eating. I crept into the barn, saddled my horse as quickly as I could in the dark, then led her out and around back.

I didn't know Sonora very well, but I thought I could make a big circle around to the other side without going through any of the main streets where I might be seen. It took me twenty or so minutes to get where I was headed. I rode out past the edge of town, but stopped where most of the buildings were still visible. I got off my horse, tied her securely to a tree. I had my bag tied down behind the saddle too so I would be able to make a quick getaway when the time came.

The only thing I took back toward town with me was a handful of blank writing pages from my satchel.

Now I retraced my steps back to Nason's boardinghouse. I found a place across the street, behind some bushes, where I could see both the front door and up the street toward the hotel and the main street of town. I was sure Derrick would come that way when he came looking for me. I just hoped I wasn't too late!

I waited for a long time. I started to shiver from the cold, and I could tell the dew was beginning to creep up out of the ground. But eventually my patience was rewarded. Sure enough, in the distance down the street from the main part of town came Derrick Gregory walking toward Nason's boardinghouse.

The thought that he was coming to lure me away was incomprehensible! But I didn't have time to reflect on that now. I had to get to the Lucky Sluice and safely away before he found out I wasn't there and had time to get back to his room.

I jumped up and ran in the direction I had planned, through a couple of gardens, over a fence or two, through an alley, across a back street, into somebody's yard, through another alley, until I arrived at the main street just next to the dry goods store across from the saloon. Looking right and left I darted across, behind the saloon, and had arrived at the back stairway just about the same time, I hoped, as Derrick was knocking on the door and asking Mrs. Nason to see me.

Now came the risky part! If he got suspicious from my not being there and ran back, or if I had trouble getting in, he could catch me right in the act of breaking into his room—then I'd be a goner for sure! I only had five minutes at the most to get in, grab what I wanted, and get out!

I took the saloon's back steps two at a time as quietly as I could on the toes of my boots. I tried the door. It was open! I crept inside. The hallway had a narrow strip of carpet down the middle, which kept my footsteps quiet. I walked slowly forward.

There it was! Room 14, the second room on the right.

I tried the latch. It was locked!

The next minute I heard voices coming up the stairway from the saloon below at the other end of the hall.

I turned and bolted back for the back door, and had just closed it behind me when I saw a man and a woman come into view. I watched through the window from the landing where I stood. Luckily they didn't come much farther, but stopped and went into a room at the far end of the hall.

Now what should I do? The door to Derrick's room was locked, and he was probably already on his way back here from the boardinghouse!

I glanced around where I stood on the landing of the back stairs.

A thin ledge ran around the building at the height of the second floor, a board about six inches wide. I stuffed my batch of papers inside my pocket, then I climbed over the railing and began slowly easing myself away from the landing. If I could just keep my balance and find enough for my fingers to grasp on to!

Slipping along sideways across the ledge, my fingers barely keeping me upright by holding on to window moldings, gutters, and other projections from the building, I came even with the window of the first room. Luckily it was empty!

I continued on, my heart pounding so hard that I was afraid its beating would knock me off backward. I didn't know which would be worse—to die from a gunshot through the head, or to die of a broken neck from falling twenty feet onto hard-packed dirt!

I came to the second window. This should be Derrick's room!

As I had hoped, the window was open a crack. I got my fingers under it and jerked upward. With a great scraping sound, it gave way and opened about nine inches. I got both my hands underneath and yanked again, but only managed to open it another two or three inches.

It would have to be enough.

I leaned down, stretched one leg through, then my left arm,

then squeezed the rest of my body through.

In a few seconds I was standing alongside Derrick's bed, with visions of him already walking into the Lucky Sluice below and hurrying up the stairs three at a time to catch me red-handed!

There was enough light from the moon showing through the window for me to see his writing table. I walked toward it. There was his satchel, full of papers, as well as a stack of the papers he had just been working on. A half completed sheet lay on top of them, his dried-out pen lying across it.

Quickly I opened his satchel and grabbed out all his papers. There must have been twenty or thirty pages—interviews, quotes, names, dates, lots of notes of his own. I picked up the fresh pages off the table, apparently his completed article about Fremont and the copy he was making for Senator Goldwin. I put them all in a stack together, folded them once, and stuffed them into my coat pocket.

Then I took the blank pages I had brought with me and replaced about the same number into his satchel, and on the tabletop. I hoped that at a quick glance, seeing papers still there and still in his case, he wouldn't stop immediately to think they weren't his papers.

I hurried back to the window and started to squeeze my way back through to the outside.

Suddenly a thought struck me. One look at the table and he would instantly know his writing had been tampered with!

I reached into my pocket and grabbed the papers. I removed the half-completed top sheet. Quickly I read it over in the light of the moon. Still I heard no voices. I read it again so that it would stick in my memory.

Then I went back to the table, replaced the half-written sheet of Derrick's on the stack of blank pages I had put there, and smoothed out the fold. I laid the pen down exactly as it was before, then stuffed the rest of the pages back in my pocket, and left through the window.

It closed easier than it had opened. I crept back across the ledge, over onto the landing, and back down the stairs onto the street.

Just as I started down I heard the heated voices of Derrick and the other two men entering the hallway from the saloon. They sounded like they were in a hurry. "We'll ride out of here early tomorrow and dump the kid and the girl in a ravine up in the mountains someplace," one of the men was saying. "Then you can put a bullet into both of them. You got it, Gregory?"

I didn't want to stick around to hear any more. I leaped down the stairs three at a time, and dashed off into the night.

# CHAPTER 49

## ESCAPE

Taking back streets and finding my way as best I could by the light from the night sky, I hurried toward where I thought the livery stable was.

The smells and the sounds of the horses and mules inside told me I had reached the right place. I approached from out in the back of the livery. There wasn't a door into it from where I was, but I could hear two men talking on the other side of the wall. They weren't voices I recognized, probably only stable hands cleaning up and tending to the animals.

I glanced around. Where could they have stashed Robin? Inside one of the stalls? Not likely, or those two workers might have spotted him.

What had they said? I tried to remember their words. *Out back of the livery*—that's what they'd said.

He must be here someplace. There were several shacks nearby. I ran to the first and opened the door.

It was pitch black and cold inside—must have been the ice house. "Robin . . . Robin, you in here?" I said just a little above a whisper. There was no reply.

I shut the door and ran to the next little outbuilding. From the smells of leather and dirt and the shovel and pitchfork I nearly stumbled over, I figured this to be where they kept tools for repairing harnesses and wagons. "Robin . . . Robin!" I whispered. Again, I heard nothing.

I looked around yet once more. The last possible spot was

a shed for storing bales of hay and straw, made of three walls and a roof, with the one open end facing southwest, probably to protect it from the wind and rain.

I ran to the shed and inside. All I could make out in the dim light were piles of baled hay.

"Robin . . . Robin?" I called out, a little too loud, I'm afraid. But I was getting desperate. I knew those men were going to be after me any minute!

"Robin O'Flaridy, you low-down rat . . . where are you?"

I stopped and looked all around, wondering where else I could search.

Then I heard a muffled groan!

"Robin, is that you?" I cried.

The sound came again, from the back of the shed. I ran toward it, struggling to throw aside bales, and climbing over them to get to the back of the shed.

There he was, tied up in the corner—wrists and ankles bound tight, a rag stuffed in his mouth, lying on his stomach, his face buried in loose straw, and a couple of heavy bales leaning sideways on top of him. He'd probably been trying to free himself, and they'd toppled over on him, knocking him into the ridiculous position where I found him. Luckily there was no one guarding him.

As fast as I could I went to work at the ropes around his legs. But they were too tight!

I fumbled in the darkness for the knife I'd tucked at my waist, found it, and quickly slit the cords.

"Get on your feet!" I said. "Let's get out of here!"

I pulled at him to get him up. He moaned and motioned at his hands and mouth.

"After what you did to me," I said, "you want me to set your mouth free to start yapping again? You betrayed me once tonight already, Robin O'Flaridy, and I'm not likely to forget it anytime soon. And if I'm going to save your life, I don't want to have to listen to your explanations or excuses! I'll just leave your hands tied behind you and your mouth gagged until we're safe. Now come on, before those ruffians get here!"

I yanked at his arm and half-dragged him back over the bales the way I'd come. If I had seen the dried blood on his face and the welts above his eye and the bruises on his shoulders, I probably would have been a little kinder. As it was, I was both angry at him and terrified that we'd be caught any second. And by the time we got out of the shed and back out into the moonlight and I did see his condition, we were in too big a hurry. My compassion for loose-tongued and cowardly Robin O'Flaridy would just have to wait until later!

"This way!" I said, still holding on to his arm, pulling him to follow.

I ran toward the woods behind the livery, toward where I'd tied my mare earlier.

Robin was stiff and sore from being tied up, and he could barely keep to his feet. I knew I'd have to untie his hands or he'd keep stumbling along and falling every other step. I stopped and got out my knife again. But just as I was slitting through the last of the cords, I saw a figure come running out from the front of the livery to the back. He made straight for the hay shed, then stopped the instant he saw us standing about thirty yards from it toward the woods. There was no chance to hide. We were exposed in the pale glow of the moonlight.

It was Derrick Gregory!

Robin and I froze. Derrick walked slowly toward us. I hadn't noticed him wearing a gun before, but he had one now, and he pulled it from his holster.

I could feel Robin trembling and he began pulling away. I went with him and we inched backward.

"You're a clever one, Cornelia Hollister," he said, still advancing. "You had me completely fooled."

"I'm sorry, Derrick," I said, "but I had to know if you were going to write the truth about Mr. Fremont."

He gave a laugh, though this time it rang with bitterness. "I told you before, a reporter can't worry about that. You've got to do your job, that's all. And right now *my* job's to get those papers back from you."

"What papers?" I stammered nervously.

"Come on, Cornelia," he said with a sneer. "You know as well as I do you took them from my room. Now, hand them over!" He waved his pistol at us, but still we kept inching back.

"How did you know?" I asked.

He chuckled again. This time there was a little of the old humor in his tone.

"Every writer has his own little secrets, his own way of doing things. You must know what I mean, Cornelia. One of mine is that I never fold my pages. I can't stand papers with folds in them! You tried to smooth it out, but it didn't work. Very clever of you to leave the top sheet. If you hadn't folded it first, I'd never have noticed it till hours later. But then I saw all those blank papers substituted for my own, and I knew it had to be you. You're a smart girl, but I've got to have those papers back!"

"Where are the other two men?" I said.

"I sent them on a wild goose chase to the boardinghouse to look for you. I figured you'd be here, trying to save that coward who turned you in to save his own skin."

"And if I don't give you the papers?"

"Look, I don't want to hurt you, Cornelia. But I've got to have those papers! The other men'll be here any second. Now just give me the papers and get going. I'll tell them you got away. But if they get here first, they'll kill you both! Now come on, Cornelia, don't make me do something I don't want to have to do!"

He quickened his pace toward us. Robin and I began moving backward toward the woods. Derrick was still twenty or twenty-five yards from us.

"Robin," I whispered. "Make for the woods. My horse is straight up that little rise about fifty yards away. Untie her. I'll be right behind you! And you wait for me, you scoundrel!"

He hesitated.

"Get going!" I yelled, shoving him up the hill. He needed no more encouragement. He'd broken the last strand of rope on his wrists and took off for the woods as fast his spindly legs would carry him.

"Stop, Flaridy!" cried Derrick. "Stop, or I'll shoot!"

Robin kept going and in a couple of seconds was out of sight.

"Derrick," I implored, still walking backward after Robin, "you don't want to shoot anybody. I don't think you're willing to kill either of us for the sake of your rich senator."

"You'll never get away from them," he said.

"I'll just have to get back to San Francisco before you or your friends."

Behind him I heard the sounds of running footsteps and shouts.

I turned and sprinted into the woods!

My heart nearly stopped when I heard the explosive fire of Derrick's gun behind me. But he couldn't have missed! I was sure he intentionally shot wide and over my head! I heard shouts again and I knew whose voices they were. Derrick's pistol echoed in the blackness with two more deafening shots.

"They got away!" I heard Derrick yell. "After them . . . this way!"

More shots sounded, but they were not close. I reached the horse only seconds after Robin. He was fumbling with the rope.

"I'll get it!" I cried.

I loosened the rope from the tree, then jumped into the saddle and helped him up behind me. "Hang on!" I called. "If you fall off, I'm not stopping for you!"

I dug in my heels and off we galloped.

Hearing us, more gunfire rang out. It was the sound of rifles this time! Bullets smashed into trees and clipped off branches around us. But we kept on. Finally the gunshots stopped.

"Get to the horses!" I heard the man with the beard cry out. "We'll chase 'em down . . . they can't get far!"

I lashed poor Raspberry on as fast as she could go, circling the town and working our way down onto the main road west toward Chinese Camp and Modesto. Reaching the road, we pushed on as fast as we could go. But I knew the other three riders were only a minute or two behind us.

We rode hard for a couple of miles. When we came to the

junction of the southern road, I eased up on the reins, then found a place to pull off the road and hide behind several boulders and large pine trees.

A couple of minutes later, the thundering hoofs of our pursuers' three horses approached and passed us, continuing on the westward route. Once the sound had died away, I led my horse back out into the clearing, and onto the road leading south.

The stop had given Robin his first opportunity to pull the rag from his mouth.

"Hey, this isn't the road to San Francisco," he said as I urged the mare to a gallop again.

"Is that all you have to say after I just saved your skin?" I shot back at him over my shoulder.

"Of course, I'm grateful, but I only wondered where we're going."

"Well, for the moment at least, we're *not* going toward San Francisco. That is the direction they think we're going, and I don't want to make it too easy for them to find us. I happen to value my life, Robin, even if *you* don't!"

"They would never have hurt you, Corrie. I knew that. I would never have said a word if there'd been any *real* danger to you!"

"Ha!" I said. "I don't believe that for a second!"

"Where are we going?"

"Don't worry, I'll get you back to San Francisco. But first I've got a little unfinished business with regard to Mr. Gregory's article."

"Where?"

"At the Fremont estate."

The moon was practically full and I could see well enough to ride with tolerable speed. I couldn't see my map too well, but I had studied it back at Sonora. There were enough markers along the way so that I knew we were on the right road to Mariposa.

We rode pretty hard for half an hour, then eased back. The horse wouldn't be able to keep it up all night at this pace, and all I wanted to do was get far enough from Sonora so that I'd know we were safe.

We stopped about midnight. We hadn't gone very fast, but we had ridden for several hours and had covered a good distance. By my reckoning we were only eight or ten miles from Mariposa and could make it there easily in the morning. I pulled off the main road, and found a clearing two or three hundred yards away where we could spend the night.

We got down off the horse. I built a small fire, making sure to use dry wood so as not to give off any visible smoke, then got out some dried food and my canteen. I tried to wash Robin's wounds as best I could, then gave him something to eat and tried to make him comfortable with two of my blankets.

"You get to sleep, Robin," I said. "You're going to need it. I'll keep watch for a couple of hours, just till I'm sure no one's tracking us."

He was real quiet, not like his usual self. When I'd look over at him, he was just staring into the fire like he was thinking.

"How'd you learn to do all this stuff, Corrie?" he said finally.

"All what?"

"Ride a horse, escape from guys with guns, build a fire, take care of yourself out in the wilderness."

"I don't know," I said. "I never thought about it. I just did it. I guess I've been taking care of myself for a lot of years."

"Yeah," he said after another minute of staring into the fire. "I suppose it's the same for me in the city. I can take care of myself there, just like you do out here."

"The city scares me," I said, laughing. "But out here, I don't know, for me it's more like home."

"Give me buildings and lights and people and city-sounds any time!" said Robin, and for a minute I thought he might be going to laugh too.

"Not me," I said. "I love the crickets and the far-off howl of some animal and the wind in the trees and the sound of a stream."

It got quiet again.

"How's your face?" I asked. "They roughed you up pretty bad, didn't they?"

"It hurts some, but I'll be okay." He paused, but then added, and I could tell from his voice that the words were hard for him to say, "Thanks, Corrie, for what you did back there. I didn't deserve it."

"Aw, think nothing of it."

"Why did you do it? Why'd you risk everything to save me?"

"Anybody'd have done the same," I said.

"I doubt that. I'm not sure I'd have had the guts to do what you did, especially after what I did."

"Well, look at it this way," I said. "I couldn't very well go back to Kemble with the lowdown on Gregory's article and with all the papers of his, and then at the same time tell him I left his star reporter for dead. How could I tell him *that*? Don't you see, Robin, I had no choice. I *had* to save you to keep on Kemble's good side!"

Now he did let out a little chuckle, but quickly put his hand to his mouth from the pain.

"Well, whatever your reasons, thanks anyway."

"Any time," I said. "And I'm sorry I was so hard on you back there, Robin," I added. "I didn't mean to yell and call you names. I was just upset, that's all."

He nodded, then turned over and pulled the blankets around his shoulders. In two or three minutes I could tell from his breathing that he was sound asleep.

I took off my coat, wrapped my blanket around me and lay down, staring into the fire, thinking of the terrifying, unbelievable day I'd just had. At least it felt good that Robin O'Flaridy was no longer my adversary. That was one positive thing to emerge from the dangerous escapade of this night.

Still I stared into the fire, growing sleepier and sleepier, until at last I knew no more.

# CHAPTER 50

## MARIPOSA AGAIN

When I awoke, the gray light of dawn was just giving way to the reds and oranges of the coming sunrise.

The fire was out cold.

I glanced around. Robin wasn't where I'd left him. He must have gone down to find a stream to wash and get water.

I got up, stretched, and wandered in the direction where I figured he had probably gone. But before I had gone far, I stopped and turned back.

It was too quiet. Something wasn't right!

I ran back to the clearing where we had slept. There was no sign of Robin anywhere. And my horse was gone!

Frantically I looked around. There was the blanket I'd slept in and my coat—that was all. He'd taken both my two other blankets, my canteen of water, and all the food. I checked my coat. My notes! Every single sheet of Derrick's notes and the article he had written for the *Globe* were gone!

"Why, you underhanded rascal!" I cried.

At least he'd left me my carpetbag! There it lay on the ground right where he'd thrown it off the horse. I walked toward the bag, and then spotted a scrap of paper on the ground alongside it, torn from the bottom of one of Derrick's pages. I picked it up.

I'm sorry, Corrie. It's an awful thing to do to a colleague.
But I just couldn't afford to miss a shot at a really big story.
I always wanted to write politics, and this is my chance! I'll

make it up to you someday.

Fond regards,
R.T. O'Flaridy

*Fond regards!*

I crumpled up the paper and threw it to the ground. "And *I'll* make it up to *you* someday too, Mister O'Flaridy—just you wait and see!"

I grabbed my blanket, stuffed it inside my carpetbag, put on my coat, and headed back to the road, so angry I could have walked for a week! The only trouble was, time was short and I was stuck out in the middle of nowhere!

I soon found out that even anger in the absence of food won't keep your energy up forever. After two hours, I was beat. My feet hurt, my legs ached, and I was hungry!

But still I trudged on, my carpetbag getting heavier and heavier. I don't know how far I walked. It had to be at least ten miles, although it felt like thirty! Somewhere in the middle of the morning, when the sun was getting high in the sky and the day was beginning to get uncomfortably warm, I finally reached the little village of Mariposa.

Half an hour later I was sitting with Ankelita Carter, telling her my story. Watching the various expressions on her face change from shock to grief to anger to sympathy to outrage was nearly enough to take my mind off my own trouble. As irritated as I was at Robin, Ankelita's chief concern was for her mistress and her husband.

"You must stop them, Corrie!" she exclaimed when I was through telling her everything that had happened. "You must not let them print such lies! The Colonel and Jessie are good people—these are nothing but lies!"

"I'm will do my best," I said. "But I will need your help."

"Anything!" she replied.

"First, I need to borrow a horse," I said. "A fast horse. Robin will have at least a twelve-hour lead on me. Though I doubt he will be able to ride straight through to San Francisco," I said with a smile. "He does not exactly have the adventurous pioneering spirit! Still, I have to catch up with him before he does any mischief with Gregory's parcel of papers. For all I know, he might try to sell the pack of lies back to the *Globe* rather than take it to Kemble."

"We have horses. I will have Felipe saddle for you the fastest in the stable."

"Then I need to ask you some questions, Ankelita," I said. "I need whatever proof I can get that will disprove the claims Gregory was going to make in his article. You probably know the Fremonts better than anyone in California."

"You get out your paper and pen and ask, Corrie!" she said enthusiastically. "You've got to get back to San Francisco and write the truth about Colonel Fremont! He's *got* to win that election, for the sake of the Union. We just can't let a slave man into the White House!"

"Before we start," I said with a sheepish expression, "would you mind if I had something to eat?"

She laughed, jumped out of her chair, and was on her way to the kitchen before all the words were out of my mouth.

A couple hours later, we had gone through just about everything I could remember of Derrick Gregory's charges against Colonel Fremont. I don't suppose the words of a Fremont friend and maid would constitute proof in a court of law. But perhaps they would shed sufficient doubt on the credibility of the *Globe* story to keep them from running it. I hoped so, at least.

"You can't trust anything Jim Savage might say," Ankelita said. "Why, he's been mad at the Colonel for years because he didn't get his hands on this land! And as for all that foolishness about Negroes in chains and Chinese slave labor and false surveys—why, they're just lying to make Mr. Fremont look bad. Felipe!" she called out into the other end of the house.

The young Mexican appeared after a minute. She spoke to him in Spanish, and he ran outside.

"I told him to get Bernardo. You couldn't ask for a more honest and upright man than Bernardo Garcia. He has been the Colonel's foreman here since the Colonel purchased the property. He will tell you himself that these things are not true."

"Thank you," I said. I was writing down everything as rapidly as I was able, though my fingers were already getting cramped. I would have to rely on the old newspaper gimmick of quoting "reliable sources at the Mariposa estate," and my words could be persuasive enough to convince people that what I was writing was the truth.

"As for the Colonel and barmaids in the village," Ankelita went on, incensed at the very thought. "I can tell you that Jessie never believed such things. She once told me that neither of them had ever been unfaithful to the other. She said—"

"Wait," I said, "just let me get that written down."

She paused until I caught up, then finished her sentence as I kept writing.

"What about his stirring up the Chinese in that Tong war?" I asked.

"I don't know what to say about that, except that the Colonel had nothing against the Chinese any more than he did the Negroes. But you should ask Bernardo about that. If anything like that did go on among the men here, Bernardo will know of it."

"And the rumor that Mr. Fremont is secretly a Catholic?" I asked.

"Ridiculous!" exclaimed Ankelita. "The Colonel and I had more than one discussion about matters of faith, and I know he always took the Protestant view and I the Catholic one."

"How did the rumor get started?"

"Mr. Fremont's father came from France, you know, and so I presume he was a Catholic. When he was young Mr. Fremont was educated for a time at a Catholic school, and he and Jessie were married by a priest. From all this, people merely assumed he was personally a Catholic, and his enemies stuck the label on him. He is such a private man in religious matters that he never went out of his way to refute it. His enemies knew that if it could be proven, he could never be elected President. That is undoubtedly why they are trying to dig up this old story about St. Xavier's. But don't you believe a word of it, Corrie!

John Fremont may have attended some services when he was at school as a youth, but the grown man John Fremont never attended a Catholic Mass in his life!"

"How can you be so sure?"

"Because when we were in Charleston two years ago, he showed us the church where he was baptized at the age of eight—a Protestant church!"

"Then why doesn't he make a public statement?"

"I don't know, Corrie. But just before I left the East he and Jessie had given all three of the children's baptismal records to the *Daily News* to be made public, with their admission into Protestant churches."

"Then that refutes Derrick's story completely," I said.

Just then Felipe returned, followed by a man Ankelita introduced me to as Bernardo Garcia. His English was not as flawless as hers, but I was able to understand him well enough to get along. I questioned him on all the points that were still fuzzy, especially the charges about the boundary surveys, the Chinese and Negro labor, and the treatment of local miners over squabbles about the ownership of the land. He confirmed what Ankelita had told me about Jim Savage, and was definite about everything else as well. We spoke for an hour, and when we were through I knew I had all I needed.

Bernardo went back out to the mines. Ankelita and I stood. It was already midafternoon.

"Now I must get your bed ready for you again, Corrie," she said.

"Oh no, Ankelita, I mustn't stay!"

"The article cannot get into print in less than a day," she replied. "You should stay with me again, get some rest, eat well, and sleep. Then leave early in the morning."

I stopped to think. If I took the rest of today and this evening to write my article, then I would be prepared the moment I saw Mr. Kemble. Whatever Robin might tell him, I had to have my own facts straight. And if I could have an article completed, so much the better.

I nodded. "You're right, of course. I'll stay tonight and

leave with the first light of the morning."

She led me into the room where I had slept before. I immediately began spreading my notes and previous papers over the table. I had to make sense of everything I had learned, and try to put it together into an article that was factual and true.

I worked long into the night. And when at last I laid my head down to sleep, it was with a satisfied feeling. Despite the fact that I had a journey of a hundred and fifty miles awaiting me, and even then I didn't know what might be the outcome of my efforts, at least I knew in my heart that I had uncovered the truth of what I'd been sent here to find, and I had done what I'd set out five days earlier to do.

Tomorrow was the 18th. If I gave it everything I had, just maybe I could make it to San Francisco before the offices closed on the 19th.

I might even make up the ground I'd lost and beat Robin O'Flaridy at his own game!

# CHAPTER 51

## SHOWDOWN

Ankelita awoke me the next morning before dawn.

She had packed food, a canteen, and an extra blanket, and Felipe already had the horse saddled and waiting for me.

"Her name Rayo Rojo," he said. "She . . . este caballo corre como el viento!"

"She's the filly of Jessie's favorite mare," added Ankelita. "She's of good stock, and Felipe's been training her to race one day."

"She run like no horse miles 'round," said Felipe excitedly. "Rapido . . . like tornado!"

"If any horse in California will get you to San Francisco ahead of that O'Flaridy scamp, Rayo Rojo will!" said Ankelita.

"What does her name mean?" I asked.

"Do you see the reddish star on her white forehead?"

I looked and did indeed see the reddish-brown star. The rest of the top of her head was white, though her predominant color was a tan or light brown.

"That red star was there from the moment of her birth. Jessie had always called the horse's mother Big Lady Red because of her color. So when the foal was born, they called her *Little* Red—until they saw how fast she could run! Then she became Rayo Rojo, or *Fast Red*. I had never seen her until I arrived back here at Mariposa recently, and Jessie has still not seen her. But we both have felt we knew her from the reports Bernardo sent. She is a favorite with all the men on the ranch."

Felipe handed me the reins, then offered his hand to help me up into the saddle.

The moment I was on her back I felt a surge of the animal's life and energy. The look in her eyes did not fully reveal the power contained within her frame and her thoroughbred legs and muscles.

"Now go!" said Ankelita, giving Rayo's rump a little swat. "Go . . . and may God be with you, our friend Corrie."

"I will get Rayo Rojo back to you as soon as I can," I shouted over my shoulder. But already I was halfway to the gate. At my slightest urging, the young filly accelerated with an ease that was astonishing. The breeze flew through my hair and I leaned forward to be sure of my seat. With my right hand I grasped the saddle horn and reins, while my left sought to make sure my hat was tied securely around my chin.

This was going to be like no ride I had ever experienced. Truly this was a faster animal than I had been on top of in all my life. I had never known such speed. Perhaps I would overtake Robin after all!

We flew through the village and eastward along the Carson Creek road, past the quarry at Negro Hill and around Cathey's Mountain, and were already in Cathey's Valley before the sun had risen over the last of the mountains in the east. I was to the central valley and Bear Creek by midmorning, and Merced by noon. I stopped and looked up Mrs. Harcourt and asked her if I could feed and water and rest my horse in her stable and refill my water canteens. The hottest and driest part of the journey still lay ahead.

It was midafternoon the following day before I reached San Jose. Poor Rayo Rojo! She was indeed fast, but I had pushed her hard, and her stamina was not equal to such a sustained effort. Now we had to walk and take many rests between gallops. She was a brave one, though, and whenever I would urge her forward, she would obey faithfully.

I rode up to the office of the San Francisco *Alta* at about half past five that afternoon. I tied Rayo outside and ran to the door. I turned the handle and it yielded. I raced down the hallway to Mr. Kemble's office.

The door was closed. I tried the handle. It was locked. I rapped on the marbled glass. There was no reply.

I turned and walked slowly back. I stuck my head in at one of the other offices where I heard someone busily at work.

"Is Mr. Kemble here?" I said.

"Gone home for the night, Miss," was the answer.

Dejectedly I left the building. Well, at least it would give me time to clean up and take a bath, I thought—and to put the finishing touches on the article I planned to present to the editor in the morning. I just hoped Miss Sandy Loyd Bean had a room left! Rayo Rojo would no doubt welcome the rest much more than I did!

Miss Bean did have a room, and I slept very soundly that night after two days of bouncing along on Rayo Rojo's back.

At seven-thirty the following morning I was standing on the walk outside the lobby of the *Alta* building, my writing satchel in my hand, awaiting the arrival of head editor, Mr. Edward Kemble.

A little while later Mr. Kemble approached along the sidewalk, with none other at his side than Robin T. O'Flaridy, walking along laughing and talking amiably together. No lady would say the things that came into my mind at that moment. Fortunately, I swallowed them and managed to keep my mouth closed. Robin wore a bandage over one corner of his mouth and chin, and one eye was pretty badly swollen and discolored, but otherwise he didn't look too much the worse for wear.

"Ah, Miss Hollister!" exclaimed Mr. Kemble the moment he saw me. "Robin told me to expect you sometime soon."

Robin gave me a nod and a smile, and I gave *him* back a look that shot daggers. I wasn't feeling much like a loving and forgiving Christian at the time!

Mr. Kemble led the way inside and down the hall to his office, and I followed in silence.

"Quite a business you and Robin got into up there, eh, Hollister?" Mr Kemble said the moment the three of us were alone. "And it looks like he scooped you again! Tough break too. I thought this was the one where you might really prove yourself."

"Scooped *me*!" I exclaimed, at last finding my tongue. "What are you talking about?"

"Right here," he replied, slapping his hand a couple times on a stack of papers that sat on his desk. "When Robin arrived yesterday afternoon—looking a mess, I have to tell you!—and put this in my hands, I knew everything had paid off in the end. Not only had he unearthed the whole of that bum Gregory's story, he had actually made off with the thing—notes, interviews, quotes and all! Can you believe it, Hollister? He scooped the whole *Globe* story—stole it out from under their noses! With this in our hands, they can't run it against Fremont!"

"What?" I stammered.

"How was I to know that he'd go back out there on his own after I pulled him off the story and sent you? Mighty determined reporter he's turning out to be! It really is too bad, Hollister, for O'Flaridy to scoop you twice in a row. Lucky for you he was there, though—to save you from those ruffians!"

The whole time Robin was standing by with a smug smile on his face, not saying a word.

"He—he told you all that, did he?" I said. I'm afraid my voice did not sound too calm.

Mr. Kemble chuckled. "He *also* told me you'd be furious and would try to tell me *you* had done it all. Look, Hollister, you're young . . . you're a bright kid. But another thing you've got to learn in this business is not to be a sore loser. When you're up against someone more experienced than yourself, like Robin, you've got to expect to be beat out for a story now and then. But you're learning."

I sat down finally, took some deep breaths, and tried to calm down. It would do no good to argue or yell or complain or call Robin a liar. That would only confirm what Mr. Kemble already thought, that I was a young and emotional female not able to think rationally. And I suppose the first two *were* true, but this was one time I had to *force* myself to think rationally!

Finally I looked up at the editor and spoke again, softly and without anger.

"And just what sort of article did Mr. O'Flaridy provide you to run in opposition to this information of Gregory's that *he* brought you?" I asked.

"We hadn't exactly settled on our response. Perhaps Robin will write a pro-Fremont piece. Perhaps you could even join that effort. Perhaps nothing need be done with regard to this aborted *Globe* information." He patted the stack of Derrick's papers again.

"I see," I said, then paused thoughtfully. "And has it occurred to you that Derrick Gregory is also an experienced writer with perhaps more at stake than either of you, and that he would be well able to reconstruct from memory much of what he was planning to divulge? Do you think that just because you have his notes and perhaps a rough draft of his article, you have stopped him entirely? I wouldn't doubt that he is already back in Sacramento or right here in San Francisco, in a hotel someplace, writing furiously to redo the very article that you think you have stopped." I pointed to Mr. Kemble's desk and the papers that I had taken from Derrick's room.

Mr. Kemble and Robin were both silent, thinking over what I had said.

"If that is true, your possessing his notes and original material will do you no good whatsoever. He'll still run his story in the *Globe*, and Colonel Fremont will suffer just as much damage as ever."

I paused and looked straight at Mr. Kemble. "What you need," I said, "is a story that refutes Gregory's charges and strengthens Mr. Fremont's position."

"And where can I get such a story?"

"I happen to have one—right here!" I patted the writing satchel on my lap. "Completed, ready to print, and refuting nearly all of Gregory's charges."

"May I see it?" asked Mr. Kemble. I think he was beginning to wonder if he'd misread the whole situation.

"Not until we have worked a few things out," I replied. "For now, I will just hold on to it myself."

"If it's what you say, Corrie, I'll pay you well. I'll give you your eight dollars without an argument this time."

"You can't buy my submission quite so easily now, Mr. Kemble. You sent me up to Sonora, as you said, to find the truth. Well, I found it. I found Mr. Gregory when Robin couldn't. I found what he was going to print. I found what I am satisfied is proof against his charges. I risked my life to steal that for you—" I pointed to the papers on his desk.

Suddenly I stopped, and the impact of what I had done hit me square in the face. I had determined not to lie to get my story, and yet I had done something just as wrong—I had broken into Derrick Gregory's room and stolen his papers, and at the same time I hadn't given it a second thought.

"Mr. Kemble," I said at last. "When I took Mr. Gregory's article, I didn't even stop to consider if it was right or wrong— I just knew I had to get my hands on that information. I had to stop his article from being published, to save the Fremonts from his deception." I paused, then went on.

"Maybe that makes me just like Derrick—willing to do anything for a story. But maybe it's different because my reasons for doing it were better. I don't really know, and I haven't had time to sort it all out yet. Maybe it doesn't matter at all to you, but it matters to *me*, and it may take me a while to get over what I've done. But your willingness to believe falsehoods about *me* is just as bad as the *Globe* being willing to print lies about John Fremont!"

I stopped, trembling with both anger and apprehension as I thought about my actions.

"I am deeply sorry, Corrie, if there has been some misunderstanding," Mr. Kemble said.

"There has been no misunderstanding. It seems simple enough to me. What Robin brought you is nothing." I turned to Robin. "That was your one mistake, Robin, leaving me my carpetbag," I said. "That's where *my* notes were. I had been with Derrick the whole previous day, and had written down everything he'd told me. He even admitted to bribing half the people he quoted! He as good as told me himself which of the charges against Mr. Fremont were false. And all *that* was in my carpetbag, which I still have. And at the Mariposa I got the rest of what I needed to destroy the credibility of Derrick's story. But you had none of that, which is why stealing Derrick's papers from me didn't do you a bit of good!"

I was angry again, and even the pale look on Robin's bruised face wasn't enough to renew the kinship I'd briefly felt with him four nights ago around the campfire.

"And you know what else you don't have?" I continued. "You don't have the last page that Derrick was in the middle of writing when everything exploded back there in Sonora. I left it behind. But I know what that page contained, and it would be dynamite if used against the Colonel. I know what that page said, and I am able to refute it. But neither of you have any idea as to either."

I looked around again at Mr. Kemble as I said these last words. I stopped and the room was silent. I had the best of the argument, and both men knew it.

"Now, Mr. Kemble," I said. "When I left, you told me to get to the bottom of the story and to find out the truth, and to have it on your desk by the 22nd. Today's the 20th. I've done everything you said with two days to spare. I reckon it's time for you to decide what you want to do about this matter, and it's time for me to decide what I want to do with what I've found and with the article I've written. I'll be staying at Miss Sandy Bean's Boarding House if you want to contact me. Otherwise, I'll be back to see you, perhaps tomorrow. That is, *if* I don't decide to take what I have to another paper!"

I got up from the chair and approached his desk, where I reached over and took hold of the stack of papers. "And if you don't mind, I think I will take these with *me*. I'm sure Robin will be glad to tell you how things *really* happened in Sonora."

I took Derrick's papers, put them under my arm with the satchel full of my own, and walked out of the office.

# CHAPTER 52

## COUNTDOWN TO NOVEMBER

The trip back to Miracle Springs from San Francisco was peaceful and thoughtful for me. I'd gotten my Raspberry back from Robin, and would return Rayo Rojo to Mariposa later. With both horses it was a much slower ride, and it gave me a chance to reflect on all that had happened.

After my conversation with Mr. Kemble, I went through all sorts of doubts about what I had done. Even though I was trying to stop others from doing wrong, the thought kept coming back to me that I had taken what didn't belong to me. And as I sat at Miss Bean's wondering what to do, I couldn't help finding myself confused. Finally I just had to say to myself, "Well, right or wrong, I *do* have Gregory's papers, so now I have to decide what to do with them." Maybe I'd never find any hard and fast rules that would help me know the answer to every situation I was in. I had to trust somehow that God would lead me through the dilemmas I might face as a writer.

In the end I left my entire Fremont article—explaining the charges that were being brought against him, and then showing how many of them were fabricated just so that he would not be elected—with Mr. Kemble. He said that its appearance would be a major boost to the Fremont campaign and should insure that the Colonel carried California in the election.

I took Derrick Gregory's papers to the *Globe* for them to return to him. He couldn't do much damage with them any longer, and I didn't feel right about keeping them. Without my even having to dicker for it, Mr. Kemble said he'd pay me $10 for the work I had done. He called it a "major effort" in the Fremont cause. He also said the *Alta* would pay the expenses of my trip to Sonora. He would have a check sent to me for $29. We didn't get around to discussing the pledge he'd made earlier to give me a regular article in the *Alta*. But I hadn't forgotten, and I planned to remind him of it before long!

On the afternoon of September 26 I finally rode into Miracle Springs. I was so glad to be home—I'd had enough adventures for one month!

I rode up to Parrish Mine and Freight Company, stopped, dismounted, and walked inside. Almeda wasn't there, but Mr. Ashton and Marcus gave me greetings and hugs enough for all three of them.

"Miz Hollister, she left for the claim," said Mr. Weber. "She got big news for ya all, Miss Corrie! You best git on yer horse an' follow her as quick as you can."

"Can you take care of Raspberry for me, Marcus?" I asked. "As you can see, I came back with an extra horse."

"No trouble, Miss Corrie."

"Then I'll see you both again tomorrow," I said, and hurried back outside. Now I was ready to give Rayo Rojo a run, and she was ready! We flew out of Miracle Springs so fast I'm sure a few heads turned as we passed the Gold Nugget. We clattered across the first bridge over the creek and headed up the incline in less than two minutes. Never had I covered the distance so fast. *Just wait until Zack and Little Wolf see this magnificent animal!* I thought.

I galloped all the way home. As I was dismounting, all the family poured out of the house, and just like after my other trip, there were hugs and tears and shouting in plentiful measure.

I was anxious to find out the "big news" Marcus Weber was talking about. A flood of questions came out. I had all but forgotten that nobody else knew a thing of what *I'd* been through for this last two weeks. The only responses I heard were the clamoring questions of six other people shouting out and wondering what had happened to me!

Finally Pa managed to make his voice heard above all the rest. "*Everybody* inside!" he shouted. "The only way we're gonna get to the bottom of all this is to take it one question at a time!"

We trooped inside, still loud and laughing and talking. It was a happy moment. Every one of the others had big smiles on their faces and I knew they had something to tell me.

Pa got us all sat down and got my brothers and sisters to quiet down. Then he said, "Now, Corrie, tell us all about your trip."

"Oh, Pa," I groaned, "there's too much! It'll take *days* to tell you everything that happened! I want to hear *your* news! Something's up—it's written all over every one of your faces!"

The laughter erupted all over again. I had never seen Almeda so gleeful. She was laughing like a little girl.

"Come on . . . out with it!" I exclaimed, looking around at everybody. "What is going on here?"

"Well, Almeda," said Pa, looking down on her with a smile, "I reckon it's more your news than anyone else's. Go on . . . tell her!"

Almeda, who was sitting beside me on the couch, took one of my hands in hers and looked me tenderly in the eye.

"You'll never believe it, Corrie, but your father and I are going to have a baby!"

"That's . . . that's wonderful!" I exclaimed.

Without even realizing it, I discovered that I was crying. All the emotions and fears I'd had to keep to myself for the past two weeks broke loose into a well of tears that spilled over to everyone in the room. Even Pa was half laughing and crying at the same time!

When I finally dried my tears, I found that I still could not find any words to express all that was in my heart. Every word I tried to speak only started up the tears all over again.

Almeda finally came to my rescue with a long, tight hug that only a mother can give and only a daughter can receive.

At length we did manage to take some deep breaths and get

back to some normal conversation. I had so many questions, especially with the election now getting so close, and wondering what had been going on in Miracle Springs. But they were nothing compared to all *I* had to tell about my adventures!

So much had happened in two weeks, and so many stories remained to be told! In the *next* few weeks the Hollister-Parrish-Belle clan would witness a whole new series of events that would turn our lives topsy-turvy again—permanently.

All of our lives were changing. In a period of two weeks, I had found myself facing more adventure and danger, struggle and doubt, than I would have ever thought possible. I had grown so much! I'd gone out on the trail of the truth, and in finding it, I had found a little more about myself as well.

And yet in some ways the adventures were still only beginning!

———

The story that followed, and what happened in the two elections . . . you can read about in *A Place in the Sun*, The Journals of Corrie Belle Hollister, Book 4.

# DAUGHTER
# OF GRACE

Published by Bethany House Publishers
A Ministry of Bethany Fellowship, Inc.
6820 Auto Club Road, Minneapolis, Minnesota 55438

Printed in the United States of America

**Library of Congress Cataloging-in-Publication Data**

Phillips, Michael R. , 1946–
    Daughter of Grace / Michael Phillips, Judith Pella.
        p. cm. — (The Journals of Corrie Belle Hollister ; bk. 2)

    I. Pella, Judith.  II. Title.
III. Series: Phillips, Michael R. , 1946–    Journals of Corrie Belle
Hollister ; v. 2.
PS3566.H492D38   1990
813'.54—dc20                                    90–42092
ISBN 1–55661–105–6                                 CIP

# DAUGHTER OF GRACE

## MICHAEL PHILLIPS
## JUDITH PELLA

**BETHANY HOUSE PUBLISHERS**
MINNEAPOLIS, MINNESOTA 55438

To
Robin Mark Phillips

# Books by the Phillips/Pella Writing Team

## The Journals of Corrie Belle Hollister

*My Father's World*
*Daughter of Grace*
*On the Trail of the Truth*
*A Place in the Sun*
*Sea to Shining Sea*
*Into the Long Dark Night*

## The Stonewycke Trilogy

*The Heather Hills of Stonewycke*
*Flight from Stonewycke*
*Lady of Stonewycke*

## The Stonewycke Legacy

*Stranger at Stonewycke*
*Shadows over Stonewycke*
*Treasure of Stonewycke*

## The Highland Collection

*Jamie MacLeod: Highland Lass*
*Robbie Taggart: Highland Sailor*

## The Russians

*The Crown and the Crucible*
*A House Divided*
*Travail and Triumph*

# The Authors

The PHILLIPS/PELLA writing team had its beginning in the longstanding friendship of Michael and Judy Phillips with Judith Pella. Michael Phillips, with a number of nonfiction books to his credit, had been writing for several years. During a Bible study at Pella's home he chanced upon a half-completed sheet of paper sticking out of a typewriter. His author's instincts aroused, he inspected it more closely, and asked their friend, "Do you write?" A discussion followed, common interests were explored, and it was not long before the Phillips invited Pella to their home for dinner to discuss collaboration on a proposed series of novels. Thus, the best-selling "Stonewycke" books were born, which led in turn to "The Highland Collection."

Judith Pella holds a nursing degree and B.A. in Social Sciences. Her background as a writer stems from her avid reading and researching in historical, adventure, and geographical venues. Pella, with her two sons, resides in Eureka, California. Michael Phillips, who holds a degree from Humboldt State University and continues his post-graduate studies in history, owns and operates Christian bookstores on the West Coast. He is the editor of the best-selling George MacDonald Classic Reprint Series and is also MacDonald's biographer. The Phillips also live in Eureka with their three sons.

# CONTENTS

# Prologue

Well, I suppose Uncle Nick was right.

When we let Mr. MacPherson, the publisher from the East, make a book based on my diary of our life in Miracle Springs, I didn't know what would happen with it. But Uncle Nick said folks would like reading it, and I guess he knew what he was saying, judging from all the mail I've received.

Pa's kind of proud, too—not just of being in a book, but seeing that folks admire him and his family. He walks around town with his head up high, knowing he doesn't have anything to be ashamed of anymore. And I think too, though he's never said it, that he hopes some of the folks back in New York might get hold of the book and read it, and will find out he wasn't as bad a man as some of them might have thought.

Of course Mr. Kemble still blusters around like the whole notion of a book's a crazy idea. And he still tries to talk to me in the same gruff way. But things are different now, and he knows it. Sometimes I can see a little light in his eye when he's looking me over that says he's almost proud of me, though he would *never* say it! I think he's a little proud of himself too, because he's the one who's pretty much responsible for getting it made into a book. But he won't admit that, either!

11

12

All of them have been hinting at me to tell more about what happened after we found the gold, and about how Miracle started to grow, and about Uncle Nick and Mrs. Parrish and Pa. And I did have to agree with them. When we were first talking about the idea of a book, it seemed like a mighty farfetched notion. But now that I've done it, there's an incomplete feeling about it all. The story is only partway told. So *much* happened after my birthday when Pa shaved off his beard, and that spring day early in 1853 when we watched the wagons heading East. It hardly seems right that I should tell only part of it, and not what came afterwards.

So that's what I'm going to do now. I'm going to try my hand at a second book, picking up where I left off with the first.

I hope you like it!

Corrie Belle Hollister
Miracle Springs, California
1863

# CHAPTER 1

## THE DEDICATION . . .
## LOOKING BACKWARD

In September of 1853, the first service was held in the brand-new Miracle Springs church, and the dedication was followed by a big town picnic and celebration.

It was a warm, beautiful, fragrant day. As I sat there in the freshly painted new building, with Pa on one side of me, and Zack, Emily, Becky, and Tad on the other, my sixteen-year-old heart was full of happiness as Rev. Rutledge led us in the singing of the morning's hymns.

Then he said he had a special addition to the morning service. He asked Mr. Peters, a German man who had settled in the area recently, to come to the front with him. "Hans asked me if he could read an old German hymn for us today," said Rev. Rutledge. "And I told him we'd be delighted."

"This is my favorite hymn," said Mr. Peters in his thick German accent. "It maybe is because I like animals. This song vas written by St. Francis of Assisi, who loved all God's creatures. I loved in ta old country to sing it, but I think no one knows it here. So I make ta vords into English so gut as I can, and I read them to you for ta church dedication today."

He stopped to adjust his spectacles and take a breath, then began to read from the piece of paper he was holding. As he went along, my mind started filling with all kinds of memories of everything that had happened. All the words of the song, and Mr. Peter's explanation of how he'd turned it into English, reminded me of little parts of last year.

*All creatures of our God and King, lift your voices up*
*and sing with us, Allelulia . . .*
*You, the sun that burns bright and gold, and you silver*
*moon with soft gleam . . . praise Him! O praise Him!*

All the memories weren't happy. That sun in the desert had been *so* hot. There'd been times I'd cursed God for that sun, burning down day after day, infecting Ma with its heat, till she couldn't cool off—even at night.

Heat . . . heat. Every day her hands and forehead got hotter, her voice weaker, till there was no voice left but Captain Dixon's, trying to comfort us kids, trying to help us in the only way he knew.

I remember walking a little ways away from the wagon camp the night Ma died. Walking, stumbling aimlessly, I hardly had strength to put one foot in front of the other. Ma had been my whole world, and now she was gone. I couldn't even stop to think what we were going to do now. There was nothing but emptiness inside, not even sadness at first . . . just an awful empty feeling.

I looked up and there was the moon—about half a moon, staring silently down at me. Everything around me was quiet. The desert sounds were way off in the distance, and I didn't even hear them. Back where the wagons were, everyone knew about Ma and they were being real subdued. I guess death always makes people quiet. All I could hear was some of the horses shuffling around, and Becky and Emily still crying once in a while back where I'd left them. Tad hadn't cried yet. But he'd understand later, and then the hurt would catch up with him. Zack wanted to cry, I know, but something in him couldn't let it out.

I looked up at that moon, quiet and cold, with the cool

of the summer night closing in all around us. I wanted to yell up and curse that moon for not bringing its coolness sooner! The cool had come to the desert, and Ma's face was cool now, too. But the cool had come too late!

How could I praise Him, how could I sing? Ma was dead! Didn't God know what He'd done? I was angry and hurt. The last thing I could do was praise Him!

Tears filled my eyes out on that lonely, quiet desert. *Why, God . . . why! Was it my fault, for not praying enough? Was Ma a sinner that You had to take her away? Why, God? Were You angry with us . . . with Ma . . . with me? Was it on account of Pa that You took Ma away out here in this hot, horrible, empty, lonely desert?*

And still that silent, silver moon looked down, mocking me in my misery. It was blurred now, and my eyes were all wet. "Go away!" I shouted. But then quickly I stopped, shocked to hear my own voice in the middle of all the stillness.

Hearing my outburst sobered me for a minute. I took in a deep breath, trembling like I always do when I've been crying. But I got the air all the way in, and then I looked up at the moon again.

It was still there, still the same, quiet and bright and cool. But now there seemed to be a softness in its gleam. A peaceful feeling gradually came over me, a feeling that maybe God was like the moon, looking quietly down on us, that He hadn't forgotten after all, and that maybe His coolness, His peace, His tenderness would be there even through all the pain we were feeling. I didn't actually think all that right at the time, out there in the desert as I stared up at the moon. But there must have been a feeling in my heart that maybe God hadn't forgotten us, and I wrote it down later.

*You fast-blowing wind so strong, and you clouds blowing along through the heavens, O praise him, Allelulia. . . .*

*Rejoice in praise, you morning rising up . . . You flowing
water, clear, pure, make music for our Lord to hear, Allelulia, Allelulia. . . .*

I looked up at Mr. Peters reading, with Rev. Rutledge
standing beside him smiling, and I quickly wiped the sleeve
of my dress across my eyes. Thinking about that day the
year before had brought tears back to my eyes without my
even realizing it!

God *had* watched over us. I know that now, although I
didn't at the time. He had blown the past away with his
strong wind. We couldn't realize it then, but as my sisters
and brothers and I continued our journey over that desert,
and then over the Sierras and down into California, not
knowing what was to come, the clouds above us and the
winds blowing about us were God's way of brushing away
our past life and getting us ready for everything He had for
us there.

A new morning had come to us in Miracle Springs. Suddenly there were new people, like Mrs. Parrish and Alkali
Jones and some of the neighbors and townsfolk. Best of all,
there was Pa, and of course Uncle Nick. It was like God's
way of letting the sunlight that had died with Ma rise again—
as the sun does every new morning—on Pa's face. I don't
know if it makes sense. Sometimes when people try to use
words to say something they're feeling down inside, it
doesn't always come out quite right. But I felt like in Pa and
in the other folks in Miracle, and in everything that happened, a new morning came to our lives, and maybe I could
learn to rejoice in it.

And the water—the wonderful, bubbling, sparkling water! How many walks alone had I taken this year up that
stream by the cabin, where the deer came down to drink?
Beside that stream I first talked to Little Wolf. Pa and Uncle
Nick worked there every day, and we all carried that water
up to the cabin in buckets to do the cooking and washing.

Most folks from around here, and from all over the country, praised the water only because it carried the gold from inside the hills and mountains out into the light of day where they could see it and mine it and sell it and make their fortunes with it.

If it weren't for the water, pure and clear, and the shiny gold it brought with it down to Sutter's Mill, Mr. Marshall would never have found what he did and no one would ever have found out about all the riches filling the veins that criscrossed these hills and mountains of California. It would all have sat there for years and years, maybe forever, and no one would have ever known it. But the water changed history, and made California a state, and Miracle began to grow so fast there were new folks coming to town every day on account of the strike. And lots of the other men hereabouts dug deeper into the hills than before, following Pa and Uncle Nick's example, and some of them found new veins too. Folks said ours was one of the most famous new strikes around, because so many of the original places had started to run out of gold.

But even if it weren't for the gold, even if little Tad hadn't found anything in the mine after the cave-in, and even if we were poor as could be, the water flowing in that stream outside the cabin would be just as musical to me, and I would be just as content. It isn't the gold that makes folks happy. The Lord knows how many around here *aren't* happy for all the bags of gold they've taken to the bank!

If a person's going to be happy, it's got to come from somewhere else. That's one thing I've learned this year! It comes from having a family, and friends, and probably more than anything from learning to be thankful for whatever comes your way.

But the next words Mr. Peters read both filled me with joy and made me have to fight back the tears. They showed me all over again how much had changed, and how thankful

I was to God for making us kids part of our father's world, and for making him part of ours, too.

Mr. Peters' words set me to thinking so deep that I didn't come back to myself till he was sitting back down and Rev. Rutledge was talking again.

# CHAPTER 2

# A MAN OF TENDER HEART

These were the words Mr. Peters was reading:

*Allelulia, O praise Him, all you men with tender
hearts. . . .*
*Allelulia, forgive others, you who must bear sorrow and
pain, Allelulia. . . .*

When it came to changes in our lives, I doubt anything
could match the change in Pa! These last months with him
had been wonderful.

Nothing could make up for Ma being gone, and I still
missed her, but not as much as at first. In my head, I still
missed Ma just as much as ever; I doubt I'll ever get over
loving her till it hurts. But my heart was getting used to the
idea of going on in life without her. I knew it was hard for
the three younger kids not having a ma around the place. Pa
wasn't a woman, and never could be. And though I did what
I could, I was only their sister after all.

But Pa was real kind, even more so to the younger ones,
I think, because he knew they needed mothering. I know he
loved Ma, but now I think he missed her more for the kids'
sake than his own, because he felt so helpless to give them
all they needed. Mrs. Parrish would come out once a week
or so, and I think she might have liked to help more with
the younger kids, but Pa seemed kind of reluctant—as

though it was his duty to take care of his family and he didn't want help. He felt that he had to do more for us now on account of his being gone from us and leaving Ma alone for so long.

So Pa'd tuck Emily and Tad and Becky under their covers every night. And though he never said much about religious things, he took us into Miracle nearly every Sunday for Rev. Rutledge's church services, because like the rest, he thought getting some religious teaching was important for us kids. He wouldn't have gone if it hadn't been for us—it was simply one more way he was trying to be a good Pa.

Pa and I never had another talk like that one outside the cabin after last Christmas. Since that day, we'd had a silent understanding between us. And because of it, Pa treated me more like one of the grown-ups around the place.

The change I noticed most about Pa had to do with Uncle Nick. They still worked and laughed and talked together like the friends and partners they were. But there was another side of Pa that I started to see, a little part of him that seemed to think of himself as Uncle Nick's pa, too. In so many ways Uncle Nick was still a kid at heart. He'd do silly things and chase off after ideas Pa called "just a blame fool ridiculous notion!"

Now it was like the partnership and older-brother was only half of Pa's relation to Uncle Nick. The rest of the time he was his pa, just like he was Pa to all the rest of us—a pa who had to tend his family, work his mine, be careful with his money, see to our training, fix up the cabin, and sometimes read us stories. He never gambled or drank any more, and he took his fathering duties as seriously as any man ever could.

More than once or twice those last months Uncle Nick would come home after squandering some of his gold in a poker game or on something he didn't need, and Pa would get after him like he was an irresponsible little kid.

"Don't you know no better'n that!" he'd say. "Those fellas in town see you coming and say to theirselves, 'How can we fleece ol' Nick today?' Sometimes you're just a downright fool, Nick! That mine could dry up any day, and then where'll you be?"

"But, Drum," Uncle Nick would whine like a whipped puppy dog feeling ashamed of itself, "I figured maybe you'd ride into town with me and help me win the money back."

"You figured wrong!" Pa would answer, and that would be the end of it. Uncle Nick wouldn't say much for a day or two, and would try to work harder at the mine. But then he'd just go out and do something foolish again a little while later, and they'd have the same argument, but over something different.

I can remember two conversations I heard, one the previous May and the other more recently, that really showed me how much Pa'd changed. The first was a conversation with Mrs. Parrish and Rev. Rutledge one Sunday after Pa'd taken us in for the little service in Mrs. Parrish's house.

As we were getting into the wagon to head back home, while Pa was tightening a strap on one of the horses' necks, Mrs. Parrish and Rev. Rutledge came up to him.

"Could we have a few words with you, Mr. Hollister?" said the minister.

Pa turned to face them, gave a nod, and continued fiddling with the strap.

"Mrs. Parrish and I have been thinking a great deal about your children and their future," Rev. Rutledge began. Pa shot him a quick glance, and I think the minister figured Pa was going to light into him like he had that day of the Christmas dinner. But before anything else was said, Mrs. Parrish jumped in.

"It isn't what you may think, Mr. Hollister," she said quickly. "Actually, Rev. Rutledge and I've been commenting on what an admirable job we think you are doing with your family. We think it's a fine thing you're doing, and both of us are proud of you. We consider you a real example to some of the other men of the community."

Pa didn't exactly seem comfortable with the compliment, but it did settle down the irritation that seemed ready to rise up. He just nodded and said, "I'm obliged to you for thinking so."

"We really mean it, Mr. Hollister," added the minister. "And with more men like you, and women too—you know, family folks—coming to the area, we've been thinking that we should be giving more attention to the future of our young people. The church is going to be up before you know it, with facilities for a school during the week, and we think it's high time something was done in the way of preparing ourselves for the changing times that are coming. We'll need books and desks and paper and supplies. It'll take a fair sum of money to outfit a new school."

He paused, and Pa, thinking they were finally getting around to the point of what was on their minds—that is, asking him for money—started to reply.

"Well, I'm as much in favor of educating my young'uns as the next man. You can count on me to give my share. As long as our mine's producing, I don't mind contributing what I can. Tad's the one that found the gold, and if he's gonna be schooled, then I figure—"

Mrs. Parrish interrupted him with a laugh.

"You misunderstand us, Mr. Hollister! We didn't come asking for your money, although the time for that may come later."

Pa stared back at her with a confused expression.

"We think you're doing such a fine job with your children, and being one that the men of this community look up to, we wanted to ask if you'd be on the committee to help get the Miracle Springs school organized, and to help us locate a teacher."

"Me? A committee? Why, I don't know nothing about such things, and I ain't—"

"You don't have to *know* anything special, Mr. Hollister," she went on. "You're a man of character, and whether you like to admit it or not, you're one of this community's leaders. You have children who will be directly involved in the outcome of whatever decisions the committee makes, and we think you are a logical choice and would do a fine job."

Everything was silent for a moment.

Sitting in the wagon, we were hanging on every word, as still as a robin listening for a worm under his feet. Rev. Rutledge and Mrs. Parrish had said what they had to say, and Pa just stood there, his right hand hanging over the horse's neck, staring off in the distance as if he was still shocked by their request but was thinking it over real seriously at the same time. The silence only lasted a minute.

Then all of a sudden he turned his head back toward them. He had a look on his face I can't even start to describe. I'd never seen quite the same expression from him before, though as I thought about it later I realized it was that look on his face that showed me Pa was changing. It was such a different expression than what I'd seen that first day we got to Miracle Springs and he came walking out of the saloon.

"I'm right honored that you'd ask me," Pa said. "And I figure I owe it to the kids . . . so I'll do it."

He turned toward the wagon, jumped up onto the seat, flicked the reins and gave a click with his tongue, and with nothing more than a "Good day to you both," we were suddenly on our way back home. I turned around to wave to Mrs. Parrish. She had a smile on her face, but she wasn't looking in my direction. She was smiling at Rev. Rutledge.

After that a committee was formed, and besides Pa and Mrs. Parrish and the minister, there was Mrs. Shaw who lived nearby, and Mr. and Mrs. Dewater from over on the other side of the valley. They met a few times and started sending out notices advertising the need for a teacher in Miracle Springs. And Mrs. Parrish, from her business contacts in some of the nearby cities, got information about desks and blackboards and schoolbooks.

The kids were all excited because there was even talk of the school starting up this year, as soon as the church was finished, and getting to go to school again and see other kids every day was just about all the younger three could think about. I was getting a mite old for school, though I still thought some about being a teacher when I grew up. And Zack didn't say much.

But being on the committee wasn't the only change. The way Pa helped with the building of the church and school showed me, too, that he was determined to be different than he had been for so long, that he wanted to be the family man Ma had known him to be. I'm sure he remembered that argument he and Rev. Rutledge had had last Christmas when they'd got to talking about the building of a church. Pa'd gotten mad when the minister started saying Pa was a fine Christian man who he was sure would help support a new church. But in spite of their differences, all through the summer Pa *did* help, probably more than any other man besides the minister.

The second conversation that showed how much Pa was changing happened about two weeks before the dedication of the new church and school building. Pa and Uncle Nick were just cleaning up from a day's work at the mine, and I was fixing to put supper on the table for them. All the rest of the kids were still outside. It had been a beautiful fall day and none of them were anxious to stop their playing and come inside. Maybe the sounds of them laughing and yelling outside, and me keeping quiet toward the kitchen end of the cabin made Pa and Uncle Nick forget I was there. I'd never heard them talk quite like this before, though from their words I gathered it wasn't their first time.

"Ya wanna come into town with me tonight, Drum?" Uncle Nick said while he washed his hands in the big porcelain bowl.

"Don't think so, Nick."

"Why not? We'll quit plenty early."

"No, it's not the time. I just don't want to go, that's all."

"Why not?" insisted Uncle Nick. "You got other plans?"

"Nope."

"Then what's so blamed important to keep you here? There's a big game tonight. What're you gonna do at home?"

"I don't know. Read, fix that loose hinge on the door."

"Read? Tarnation—"

"Maybe read to the kids some."

"What in blazes has got into you, Drum?" exclaimed Uncle Nick.

"How many times I gotta tell you, Nick?" said Pa, his voice finally starting to rise a little. "Things are different now."

"Aw, come on! You ain't no fun no more! Why, back in the old days, you—"

"This ain't the old days, Nick!" interrupted Pa, and he almost shouted the words. I wished I could slip out of the room, but I couldn't help wanting to hear the rest of it too. "I rode with you, and we did lots of things. I tried to do some good, and I reckon I did a heap of things that wasn't so good. But the whole time I was ashamed of leaving Aggie, and so now maybe I got the chance to make a little of it up to her by being a better Pa to her kids than I was when I was trying to take care of you! I ain't your riding partner no more, Nick! What do I gotta do to get that through your thick head? I may be your partner in running this mine. But other'n that I'm the husband of your sister, and these are my kids, and I aim to do the best for 'em I can, though Lord knows there ain't much a man like me can do all by himself."

He stopped and took a breath, and Uncle Nick, like he

always did when Pa got after him, got quiet and looked down at the floor.

"So I ain't going to town with ya! You can throw away your hard-earned gold, but not me! I gotta think of these kids' future. And if I wanna read to my own kids, then you can keep your thoughts on the matter to yourself!"

Uncle Nick sort of slunk toward the door and went outside. About five minutes later I heard his horse coming out of the barn. Pa ran outside.

"Where you goin'?" he called out.

"I don't know, maybe down to Barton's."

"No you ain't, Nick! You stay away from Dutch Flat! Them's a bad bunch down there and I half suspect Jed o' knowin' more about us than I like. You keep away from 'em, you hear!"

"You think ye're my ma now too?" Uncle Nick shot back.

"You just keep clear o' those varmits, that's all," said Pa, and came back into the house. A minute or two later we heard Uncle Nick's horse gallop away toward town, and none of us saw him again for five days. Supper that night was quieter than usual, and Tad asking Pa every three minutes where Uncle Nick was didn't help Pa feel any better about yelling at him. Whenever Uncle Nick went and did something foolish like that I think Pa blamed himself.

But however Pa felt, it made me warm inside to think of Pa's words, and how much he cared about us as a family. And as I thought about it over the next two weeks I began to think that maybe all the change wasn't in Pa after all. I recalled Ma's words when she said he was a good husband and father, and that she couldn't have asked for any better. What I got to thinking was that maybe I was just starting to see some of what Ma had seen all along. Maybe this was how Pa had always been deep inside, or at least had wanted to be.

Whatever it was, it sure pleased me to think that he'd rather stay home and be with us than go into town for a night of poker with Uncle Nick. So when I heard those words, "You men with tender hearts," I immediately thought of Pa. More and more I was seeing how good a description of him that was.

The next words Mr. Peters read made me think of Pa too, but in a different way. "Forgive others, you who must bear sorrow and pain." There was hurt in Pa's life. He had allowed me to share a little of it with him, though now that I'm older I understand more than I was able to then. A lot of wrong had been done, and he'd suffered and had to bear pain and sorrow for long years. And there were a lot of people Pa knew he had to try to forgive before the hurts from the past would go away—the bad men of that gang, probably Uncle Nick, and old Grandpa Belle, who never thought of him as anything but a low influence on his daughter.

Most of all, I reckon, Pa had to learn to forgive himself. That was the hardest thing, especially with Ma dead and Pa feeling like he had done her such wrong never to come back to us. That's why he wanted to be a good pa, so maybe it all had a way of coming together for good. I'm not sure I understand all of what he was going through because fathers are harder to really know than mothers. But I did know that Pa was trying hard to get rid of his past, and I loved him for it.

More than that, I just loved him for the man he was. He really was a man of tender heart! Whatever the men in town might have thought, and however much Mrs. Parrish might have preferred a religious man like Rev. Rutledge to an uneducated, hard-working man like Pa; however much Grandpa Belle may have thought he shouldn't have married Ma, as we sat there that day in September hearing those

28

words in the new Miracle Springs church building, I couldn't think of anything I was more thankful for than my Pa sitting beside me. *He's* the one I would thank God and say *Alleluia* for!

# CHAPTER 3

## THE DEDICATION . . .
## LOOKING FORWARD

"My friends of Miracle Springs . . ." Rev. Rutledge was saying, and I glanced up in surprise to see that Mr. Peters had finished and was just settling back into his seat. "My friends, this is indeed a great day for all of us! This is far more than the dedication of a new building. Of course, I would not downplay the importance of what a new church can mean to a community, nor what having a school building right here in our town will mean to the future of our young people. But this is more than the dedication of a building to these noble and worthy ends, for we stand embarking on a new era. . . ."

I know I was distracting Pa, and I hoped Rev. Rutledge didn't see me, but I had brought paper and a pencil with me, and I was trying to write down some of what the minister said. I knew this was a big day for Miracle, and I wanted to be able to put as much in my journal about it as I could. Pa didn't cotton to the idea of my writing so much, though by then he was starting to get used to it.

Rev. Rutledge was still talking ". . . it's a time, my friends and neighbors, when many communities around this expanding nation, communities like our own, are growing, a time when families are putting down roots. The pioneering days of uncertainty and lawlessness are drawing to a close. The statehood of our great California symbolizes the westward reach from shore to shore of a destiny that surely can be seen as in the Almighty's plan to tame this land and make it fruitful and prosperous among the nations of the world.

"And part of that destiny is surely the establishment of churches throughout the land, and the education of our young people with schooling. Therefore, I count it a privilege and a blessing to stand here today, as one of God's representatives, in this building erected with the toil and sweat and the hard-earned money of a good number of you men, and to take my share along with you in dedicating it to God's purposes, and to the future generations of Miracle Springs. . . ."

As he spoke, I thought about how much Rev. Rutledge also had changed in the months since he came. That first day he spoke to the townsfolk in the saloon, he seemed none too sure of himself. After yelling out his first sermon, even us kids could tell he was more than just a little nervous when the men started to rile him. And afterward he left the building like a dog with his tail between his legs.

But he'd gradually improved since then, and tried to say things so folks could understand them better. He still sometimes talked with a lot of religious words, and Mrs. Parrish had a way of saying things I could grab onto better, but I was getting so I could follow him easier than before. As I watched him today, speaking out with confidence and all the folks listening to him, I realized that he'd become a part of the community too. Men like Pa might not have thought of him as a friend exactly, and everybody wasn't in favor of a church building coming to town, but I guess they were used to the minister enough to tolerate his staying around. Most of the grumbling about "too much civilization" had nearly ended by the day of the picnic. Even the men who were set against it at first managed to have a happy time too.

I glanced up and realized I'd been daydreaming again.

"So I thank you personally for your support of this building project," Rev. Rutledge was saying. "Men of stout heart and vigor have given a great deal to this school and church, and you can all be proud of them—men like Mr. Hollister there—" Pa squirmed a little as he said it—"And Mr. Shaw and Mr. Timmons, and so many others of you. And not just the men, but you women too, with food and drink and encouragement—and some of you even drove a few nails!

"But in addition to the construction of this church, I owe you thanks for the support you have given me as your minister. When I came to Miracle Springs last November there were a good many of you unsure whether you wanted a parson in your midst! And I must admit to being disheartened at times along the way. But owing to the encouragement of the faithful among you, I think we have managed to become accustomed to one another, and can now begin to move forward, growing together spiritually."

I knew he meant Mrs. Parrish. She had been his only friend for the first several months, and even now was the only person in Miracle Springs who was with him very often. Some of the other folks would have him over to their place for a Sunday dinner, but you'd see Mrs. Parrish and him together during the week, and it seemed like every time I went to visit her, he was either coming or going or staying for supper. Folks more-or-less figured that someday they'd get married. I guess I figured that too, because Mrs. Parrish had wanted him to come to Miracle so bad and had seemed more than just a little partial to him since then.

And Rev. Rutledge was softer-spoken now on account of being around Mrs. Parrish so much. He didn't preach about hell hardly ever anymore, and he seemed glad to have some of the rowdy men come to meetings on Sunday even if he knew they'd be drinking and fighting again later in the week. So it seemed Mrs. Parrish was taming Rev. Rutledge, and I suppose that's part of what a woman's supposed to do when she marries a man.

I could see why he'd admire her, for Mrs. Parrish was a fine lady. She was always thinking of others and trying to do what she could to help them. I knew how much she'd done for me in just a year. Even as I scribbled down what I could of what the minister was saying, my mind went back to that day a few months earlier when she'd come back from Sacramento. She rode all the way out to the cabin to see us, and when she got me alone for a moment she handed me a little package, wrapped up in pretty blue paper.

"Open it," she'd said as I stared back at her, not exactly knowing what to think.

I untied the ribbon, then slipped my finger through the edge of the paper and unfolded it. Inside was a gorgeous little book with green and orange flowers designed on a cloth cover, bound together by a tan leather spine.

"What *is* it?" I asked. "It's beautiful!"

"Open the pages," she said, smiling so big she could hardly contain it. I opened the book right in the middle and found nothing but blank pages staring back at me. I flipped all through it and there wasn't a single word anywhere.

I must have looked puzzled because she started laughing.

"It's for your journal, Corrie," she said. "I had it specially bound for you in Sacramento."

"But it's . . . it's—it's just like a book!" I exclaimed in disbelief.

"It *is* a book. Real book pages, bound in calf-leather. I had it made at a bindery."

"Oh, Mrs. Parrish!" I said. "I don't know what to say! How can I ever thank you?"

"I thought it was high time you graduated from that tablet I got for you last Christmas. But look inside the front cover!"

I did so. There, embossed in gold, just like it was the

title of a book, were the words—*The Journal of Corrie Belle Hollister.*

I treasured that volume, carrying it with me wherever I went for the next two weeks, being extra careful over everything I wrote in it, trying to make it as neat as I could so the inside would look as good as the outside. Pa was probably right about me being a mite fanatical, and when Mrs. Parrish gave me the book, it only made me think about writing things down all the more.

So I could see easily enough why Rev. Rutledge would be taken with Mrs. Parrish, and would want to say his thanks to her, even though he didn't do it in so many words. For the way I figured it, that church building was as much *her* doing as it was Pa's or the minister's or anybody else's. If it hadn't been for her, there wouldn't have been a Rev. Rutledge in Miracle, and no church built either.

As I'd been thinking about him and Mrs. Parrish, the minister had gone right on talking.

"So let us be hopeful as we move into the future together—hopeful that blessings will come as a result of this building we have built. Let us now join our hearts together in prayer to the God who has given us strength to accomplish this task in His name."

He paused, and throughout the small building everyone bowed their heads.

"Almighty God, we thank thee for blessings thou abundantly bestowest on us thy servants and children. And now, our Lord and our God, we dedicate this building to thy service and thy glory. May we be ever mindful of thee when we enter herein, and may this church be a light to the lost and weary of the world. We pray, too, that the school which will also utilize this building will be a beacon for the light of truth for every child who comes here to learn. Let those of this community support both this church and this school with our time and our resources and our energies for the ongoing work. May both the church and the school of Miracle Springs grow to influence this town and this community for good and for thy glory. In the name of the Father, and the Son, and the Holy Ghost we pray. Amen."

# CHAPTER 4

# THE TOWN PICNIC

As we rose from our seats and walked outside, everyone had a smile on his face. It was such a good feeling to see the whole town friendly and together. For once there were no bickerings or disputes or differences. Even the saloons had agreed to close down for the whole day. Of course, not everyone was in church, but many were, and I figured there'd be a lot more at the picnic.

As we made our way to the door in the slowly moving crowd, folks were talking and laughing and visiting. Pa came behind us, chatting a bit with Doc Wiley. Up by the door Rev. Rutledge was shaking people's hands as they left the church, and I could see that Mrs. Parrish had joined him and was on the other side of the door doing the same. I found myself wondering if she hadn't wanted to be a minister's wife instead of a business woman—she looked like she enjoyed it. I steered the kids in her direction.

"Well hello, Tad!" she said as we reached her. "Becky, how are you today? And Emily—how bright you look in that pretty dress! Zack, it's nice to see you," she said, giving Zack a firm handshake. Then she turned to me. "Oh, Corrie," she said, giving me a hug, "isn't this a great day? We've waited for it so long!"

I can't even recollect what I said—it must not have been

anything too important. There was a lot of noise and folks were pressing all around us. And the other four kids were already out the door and running off yelling like dogs that had been cooped up in a shed for two days.

"I have something I must talk with you about later," Mrs. Parrish said softly into my ear, ". . . maybe during the picnic." Then louder to Pa as he came up behind me, she added, "Perhaps your family can join Avery and me this afternoon."

I glanced back hopefully at Pa, but he just gave her one of his in-between sort of looks and answered, "We'll see, ma'am." Before anything else could be said, we were out the door and Mrs. Parrish was greeting the people behind us.

The town picnic! The images of that day stood out in my mind so clearly I could hardly go to sleep that night. It wasn't so much that any single thing happened. It was more the *picture* of the whole day—the sounds, the faces, the food, the kids all running about, the fiddle music and dancing, and most of all the togetherness of the townsfolk. It was one of those rare moments when people put aside their differences and came together in friendship, as a community instead of a bunch of separate parts squabbling about things that didn't even matter.

I couldn't get out of my mind the picture of Pa and Mr. Royce, the banker, shaking hands, or Rev. Rutledge helping one of the saloon ladies to her seat. The looks on the faces—most of all, the smiles and laughter—were so vivid! I didn't want to ever forget that people *could* be this way to each other. I wanted to remember every detail of the day—every face, every sound, every bit of laughter, every smell, every taste.

Sometime around two o'clock in the afternoon, I went off by myself for a spell. I walked up the sloping hillside east of the grassy meadow next to the church building. I must have walked five or ten minutes, while the shouts and sounds behind me were gradually growing fainter in the distance. Finally I sat down next to the big trunk of a gnarled old oak tree and turned around to look back.

It was just like I'd hoped it would be! There was the church, white and shining in the sunlight, off to the left. Then all over the meadow below me were the townsfolk, in big clusters and little clusters, men talking, kids running about playing games or chasing a dog or each other. Two long rows of tables had been put up with boards where the ladies were spreading out enough food to feed an army. We were supposed to start eating in about an hour, which was just enough time for what I wanted to do.

I opened up my satchel and pulled out a big sheet of drawing paper and my drawing pencil. Once Mrs. Parrish found out I liked to draw as well as write, she got me some sheets of extra big paper, and now I spread one out in front of me, trying to capture the picture of the picnic. I'd be able to write about the day in my journal later. But to make a memory I could see—that was something I had to do right then!

I started with the church building. I guess that was the natural place to start, because that's what the picnic was about in the first place. Then I drew in some trees, a few of the town buildings in the distance, the tables with the food on them. And then it was time to start trying to fill in the people.

I couldn't help noticing Mr. Alkali Jones first of all. Even way up where I was sitting I could hear the high cackle of his voice, although I couldn't make out what he was saying to Patrick Shaw. He was probably giving him some kind of advice on how Mr. Shaw could get more gold out of his mine. The Shaw claim ran over the hill right next to ours, but up till now Mr. Shaw hadn't found nearly the rich vein folks thought he should have from the way Pa and Uncle Nick's vein ran. Mrs. Shaw was over by one of the tables cutting up a turkey she'd roasted, and her two children, Sarah and Josiah, were nearby with Tad and Becky, throwing a stick out for Marcus Weber's dog Mutt to fetch. I didn't see Zack right then. Emily was sitting down in the grass a ways off with Amanda Jenson, who was a couple of years older than Emily. Marcus Weber was just driving up with one of Mrs. Parrish's wagons. I guess his dog had jumped down off the back early and had come running and barking to join the fun. The wagon Mr. Weber was pulling was empty, and he drew it to a stop at the far end of the meadow, away from the tables, and proceeded to unhitch the horses.

Pa was with a group of men talking. I could see Mr. Dewater, Doc, Mr. MacDougall, and Mr. Larsen. They were probably talking about mining. Just then Uncle Nick walked up. He hadn't been at church and was just now arriving. Mr. Larson gave him a big slap on the shoulder, and whatever Uncle Nick said in reply must have been funny, because I could hear the laughter that burst out from the men all the way up where I was.

Mrs. Parrish was carrying a ham over to the table from her basket. I couldn't see the honey dripping from it or the pieces of clove stuck into the sides, but she'd told me how she baked hams. I could practically smell it.

A little ways off to one side three or four men carried a big chest of ice they'd brought from the icehouse, then set it down with a heavy thud. A little dog cart sat nearby with four big milk cans standing in it. I knew they'd been brought by Mr. Peters, who didn't care about gold nearly as much as he did about his dairy cows. In the short time since he'd immigrated from Germany, his farm had come to supply folks thereabouts with nearly all their milk and cheese, and he'd brought thick cream today for the ice-cream freezers later in the day.

All around the meadow were other folks. There must have been two hundred altogether, maybe three hundred.

Most of them were standing around, a few sitting on the grass or leaning against trees. There weren't many chairs, not even enough for the ladies with dresses, though I saw Mr. Bosely and Sheriff Rafferty carrying a few chairs Mr. Bosely'd brought from the back room of his store. Some other men were setting long planks of wood on chair-height wood chunks for benches.

Even Mr. Singleton showed up for the day. His *California Gazette* paper had started up as sure as he promised, although he never got around to doing all the stories he talked about at first. He was mighty interested in the new strike at Pa and Uncle Nick's mine, and when I went to talk to him about writing something for his paper, at first his eyes lit up as though he liked the idea. But when I told him Pa wouldn't let anything get printed that used any of our names, his interest fell mighty fast. I tried to write something for him too, but when I showed it to him, he just handed it back to me and said, "Well, we'll just have to see." He was nice enough, but I could tell he didn't like it much and I was too embarrassed to try again anytime soon.

Mr. Singleton went out to talk to Pa a time or two about letting him write the story, but Pa was firm with him that he wouldn't let a word be said about *us*. And that pretty much doused Mr. Singleton's enthusiasm for it, because by then there were other men finding gold all around and he had plenty to keep him busy.

By summertime (the summer of 1853), Mr. Singleton was printing his paper every week. But he was printing it in Sacramento, so it didn't really turn out to be a Miracle Springs newspaper after all. It was the *California Gazette* of Marysville, Oroville, and Miracle Springs. Most of the news seemed to have to do with the other towns, and the paper didn't get to Miracle until two days after it was printed. Besides that, Mr. Singleton set up the office for the paper down in Marysville.

So by the time the paper was established, folks in Miracle Springs figured they'd had a big celebration for Mr. Singleton the year before for nothing, and some of them were downright perturbed at him. Most of the articles and advertisements were for the other towns too, though Mrs. Parrish would put in a notice about her freight service every month or so.

I kept secretly hoping someday I'd get a chance to see my name in the *Gazette* no matter where it was printed and no matter what anyone around Miracle may have thought of its owner!

My sketch was about as full as I had time to make it. The hour had gone by quickly, and I could hear the bell down below signalling dinnertime.

# CHAPTER 5

# MIRACLE'S SURPRISE GUEST

About an hour later—after most folks were done with their fried chicken and baked ham and turkey and rolls and all the other stuff that had been brought, and the kids were off yelling and romping again, and most of the men were standing around with tins of coffee in their hands—we heard horses coming through town.

At first the sound was just in the background. As it came closer and closer, folks started turning their heads to look. The horses and riders were coming right toward us, and everybody got up and started making their way in the direction of town.

I didn't recognize the name *Grant* at first, though after I thought about it, I did seem to remember hearing it someplace before that day. But at the time it was just a name, nothing more. My first reaction to the man leading the small procession of soldiers wasn't on account of recognizing his name, but because of the look and bearing of the man himself.

He sat up tall and straight on his horse, a rugged, almost stern man with a short sandy beard. Wide-eyed sixteen-year-old girl that I was, I was impressed. I didn't exactly fall in love, but I sure stared a lot. Then he got down off his horse and began shaking hands with the men, and there was lots of talking and laughing. The women hung back and the kids just gawked.

Most of us had never seen men in uniform before. The bright blue shirts and trousers, with yellow stripes down the side, and their yellow scarves and big wide hats—it was a sight to remember! I was already starting to think I should make another sketch of that picnic day to include the army riders and their horses!

Then the handbell started ringing again. I looked around and saw Sheriff Rafferty swinging it, trying to quiet everyone down. When he finally had folks' attention, he shouted out so he could be heard.

"This here's our special guest!" he called out loudly. "My friend, Captain Ulysses Grant! I'm sure most of you men heard of him from the fracas with Mexico a few years back, where he and I served together."

A few cheers went up, followed by everyone clapping their hands in welcome.

"Well, Captain Grant wanted to see some of the gold fields in California, and I invited him up here to see ours."

More applause and shouts.

". . . so after a bit we'll all gather round and listen to what Captain Grant might have to say to us!"

The noise and hubbub broke out again. The captain and the eight or ten soldiers with him got down and tied up their horses. Several of the women went over and invited them to sit down and eat, and that didn't take much persuasion! For the next thirty minutes the whole sound of the picnic changed. The high-pitched shouts of small children running and playing were gone. Now the kids were standing around just watching the men talk. I was real curious, but I didn't dare get too close. I could see Pa in the center of the crowd, and once or twice I saw him talking to Mr. Grant himself.

A while later everyone started moving toward the edge of the meadow. The sheriff jumped up onto the back of the wagon Mr. Weber had brought, then Captain Grant joined him, and all the folks gathered around in front of the wagon and sat down on the grass.

"Well, folks," the sheriff said, "the captain's just been promoted from being a lieutenant in the Mexican campaign, and he's now on his way to a new duty up north of here."

He turned and spoke to Grant for a minute, then faced us again.

"He's going with the 4th United States Infantry to be stationed up overlooking Humboldt Bay. That's where he's headed. But now I'm going to let him tell you what it's like being a genuine army hero!"

Some cheers went up while Sheriff Rafferty stood back and Captain Grant took his place.

"I ain't much at speechmaking," he said, "and I ain't going to get up here and pretend to be a politician! And if Simon here hadn't saved my life once down in Mexico, I wouldn't have agreed to do this at all. But I would like to visit some of your mines and like I said, I owe your sheriff my life, so here I am!"

He was a shorter man than I'd figured from seeing him on his horse, three or four inches shorter than Pa, who was six feet. But he was so stout and rugged that he seemed big. His nose was large and straight, his eyes firm and steady.

"What's up north that they need an important man like you?" shouted out Uncle Nick. "I ain't heard of no gold up there."

"No gold," he answered, "just Indians. There's a lot of trees up there as good as gold, some folks think. So they built a fort to protect this little lumber port town, and I guess they figure I'll be able to keep the Indians from burning it down."

The talk and the questions went on for a while, mostly settling around the captain reminiscing about the Mexican War during '46 and '47. After a while I wasn't paying much attention to the words anymore. I heard them off in the background but wasn't focusing on what they were saying. Instead, I was trying to sketch the scene on my paper.

On one side of it I tried to draw the captain and his men as they had ridden up on horseback. I'd practiced a lot on horses, and could draw a decent one. But a group of eight or ten, with men on them, with people gathering around as they came, was harder. It wasn't much good as a drawing, but at least it would remind me what the scene had looked like when I wanted to remember it. Then on the other side of my paper, I drew Mrs. Parrish's wagon with the sheriff and the captain on it, talking to everyone sitting around on the grass.

Well, the day went on, the speeches, music and ice cream ended, and we didn't get back to the cabin until nearly dark. The three younger ones were sound asleep in the back of the wagon even before we got there, because it had been a long, long day. I was wide awake though, and lay in my bed later for two more hours with my eyes open, thinking about lots of things, none of which was going to sleep! Mrs. Parrish had had her talk with me later in the day, as she'd promised at church, and I was so excited I could think of nothing else.

But before I say what she asked me, I want to tell what happened to the sketch I'd made. I showed it to Mrs. Parrish a few days after the picnic.

I knew it wasn't a great picture. But when she saw it she got all in a dither over it. I figured she was just trying to make me feel good. But then she asked if she could put it up on the board outside her office, for the men to see who hadn't been to the picnic or those from out in the hills who hadn't heard about Captain Grant's visit.

"And, Corrie," she said, "why don't you write something brief on the bottom of it. Just explaining the picture, you know. You have such pretty writing. It'll make it all the nicer."

Well, if Mrs. Parrish was trying to make me feel good, she sure was doing a good job of it! Who can turn away a nice compliment like that? I tried to act nonchalant about it, but inside I was happy that she liked my picture.

I asked her if I could borrow Mr. Ashton's desk for a minute, seeing as he wasn't there, and a pencil. She cleared a place for me, and then I sat down.

I wrote on the bottom of my drawing:

On September 17, at approximately 3:30 in the afternoon, the mining town of Miracle Springs, California, was honored by a visit from United States Army Captain Ulysses Grant, shown here on his horse with his men. The visit took place during the town picnic in honor of the newly completed church and school building. Captain Grant spoke for a while to the people in attendance, also shown in this picture. The Captain was on his way to his new duty at Fort Humboldt, at the northern California lumber town of Eureka.

I couldn't help adding at the bottom of that, but in smaller letters: *Picture by Cornelia Belle Hollister.*

It was sure no photograph. But we didn't have photograph machines in Miracle like they did in Sacramento. Mrs. Parrish liked it all the same, and she marched outside with my picture and tacked it up with a hammer right then for the whole town to see.

Mr. Singleton saw it the next time he was in town and asked Mrs. Parrish who wrote the brief article on the Grant visit. I laughed when she told me about it—him calling it an "article"! And I do have to admit that he treated me a little more like a grown-up next time we talked about my working on something for his paper.

For the time being, about all that came of it was that every once in a while Mrs. Parrish'd ask me to draw something for her board—sometimes just for fun, sometimes showing the men some new mining contraption she had for them to buy. And always she'd ask me to write something to go along with the picture.

Pretty soon the writing part of it got to be more than the drawing part. She'd ask me to just write up a notice about such and such a thing for the board, with no picture. And by the time she thought about printing up a little flyer about her company, well I guess I was the natural one she thought about to do most of the writing for it, even though she told me what to say.

So as it turned out, my first chance to see my words in a real newspaper was in an advertisement for the Parrish Mining and Freight Company. And by the time Mr. Singleton and I talked again about real article-writing, he'd gotten used to my being someone who could write a little, even if up until then it had just been little advertisements.

Captain Grant, I read later in one of the San Francisco papers, hated the cold and wind and rain and fog at Fort Humboldt so much that he got despondent, and some folks said he started drinking real bad. The *Alta* article in 1854 ended by saying, "Captain Ulysses Grant resigned at thirty-two years of age. He has now left the army, apparently for good, and returned to his family in Ohio."

Ever since his first visit to Miracle, whenever I saw news about Mr. Grant, I copied it down. And, of course, he didn't stay out of the army forever, but came back to become one of President Lincoln's generals in the Union army. But I didn't know that would happen when I read of his resignation in the *Alta* in 1854, and the news made me sad.

# CHAPTER 6

# THE ADVENTURE

Even though I'd lain awake in bed long after everyone else was asleep the night after the picnic, I was the first one up the next morning.

Pa was still snoring in the other room, all the kids were quiet and still, and it was just beginning to get light. I got out of bed quietly, dressed, and went outside. I was too keyed up even to think about staying inside! Mrs. Parrish's words of the previous afternoon had been ringing through my head all night.

The minute Pa came out of the cabin half an hour later, I ran toward him. I guess I didn't exactly use a subtle approach to get him to agree to what I was about to ask. I'm afraid I didn't even give him the chance to get to the outhouse!

"Pa, Pa, can I go to San Francisco with Mrs. Parrish?" I shouted, running up to him.

Poor Pa! I don't think he even knew I was out of bed!

He glanced up, bewildered. "What're you talking about, girl?" he said as he fiddled to straighten one of his suspenders.

"San Francisco, Pa! Mrs. Parrish asked me to go with her!"

"If that woman ain't always—" Pa muttered to himself.

47

But then he stopped and said to me, "I don't know, Corrie. I ain't heard nothing about it till just this minute, and—"

"She asked me yesterday at the picnic, Pa, and—"

"Tarnation, girl! Hold on to your britches! Just gimme a minute to take care of myself!" As he was talking he hurried off toward the outhouse at the edge of the woods.

When he came back a few minutes later, he looked considerably more relaxed and ready to listen to me.

"Now, what's this all about, Corrie?"

"Mrs. Parrish has to go to San Francisco for some meeting or something, Pa. Some place where they show off new stuff for folks like her to buy to sell the miners."

"Something like a fair or exhibition?"

"I don't know, Pa. I reckon. But she asked *me* if I could go with her! Can I, please, Pa!"

I was trembling inside. I could hardly stand the thought of getting to see the great city and the Pacific Ocean! But Pa just stood there still for a minute thinking. He was such a kind man, and I loved him. But sometimes I couldn't help being just a little afraid too. This was one of those times, and I was so afraid I'd start crying or something if he said no.

"Well . . ." he finally said, although his tone showed he was still in the thinking stage and hadn't really made his mind up yet. "Well, I reckon I don't see no reason why not, just so long as—"

"Oh, thank you, Pa!" I shouted, and gave him a big hug. "Thank you! I'll be real good, Pa, and you won't have to worry on account of me!"

And without realizing I hadn't even given him the chance to finish his sentence, I turned and ran off up toward the mine. I wasn't going anyplace in particular—I just had to run to get out all the excitement that was built up inside me.

Pa never did get a chance to tell me what he was going to say. I guess he figured he'd said enough to get the idea across that he wasn't going to oppose the idea. And he always stuck by his word.

———

I could hardly wait for the next two weeks to pass! Every moment, every hour was a torture. I couldn't think of anything but getting to go to San Francisco. For a girl who'd come all the way across the country, it might seem that the thought of visiting one more city wouldn't be so exciting. But San Francisco was different. Sitting right there on the Pacific Ocean, it was growing just about faster than any city in the country because of the gold rush.

And to get to stay in a hotel with Mrs. Parrish! Why, I'd never dreamed of such a thing! The other four kids were full of envy, but I reminded them that I was the oldest and that maybe when they were my age *I'd* take *them* to the city for a visit. That seemed to satisfy them, and no one really begrudged me in my enthusiasm.

Pa couldn't see what the fuss was about. He'd been to San Francisco, he said, and it wasn't so all-fired special. I asked him if he'd stayed in a fancy hotel, and he just laughed and said, "Not exactly." But he was glad I could go, and when we left gave me a kiss and a wink, and said, "Have fun, Corrie!" Then he said to Mrs. Parrish, "You keep her away from the docks!" with a serious voice, but as I looked at him I think he might have been joking.

Mrs. Parrish laughed real loud. "Don't you worry about a thing, Mr. Hollister," she said. "Corrie'll be with me the whole time!"

"Maybe *that's* what I'm worried about!" Pa answered back.

Mrs. Parrish laughed again, then flipped the reins, gave a "H'yaah!" to her two horses, and we were off!

Mrs. Parrish said Sacramento was about sixty miles— one day for a man on a horse, three or four days by mule or wagon train. She said we'd make it in two with the new surrey she'd just bought pulled by her two best horses. It was early in the day when we left, and we first returned to Miracle Springs to fetch Rev. Rutledge, who was riding with us as far as Grass Valley. Then we'd go on to Auburn where we'd spend the first night.

I sat in the back seat, but my hindquarters didn't get sore like on the wagon coming out west last year; Mrs. Parrish's new surrey had padded black leather seats. The minister and Mrs. Parrish talked most of the morning about wanting to get churches started in Grass Valley and some of the other communities around the gold-mining region. I suppose I should have been interested, but my mind was filled instead with the week ahead of us.

Mrs. Parrish was quiet for the hour or so after he left us, but by mid-afternoon she was back to her old self and we were laughing and talking about all sorts of things. I imagined we'd have some serious talks too. We always did when I was with Mrs. Parrish, and I liked that. But that first day of my big adventure was mostly just fun, and when we got to Auburn I hardly even felt tired.

The next day wasn't quite so long, and we arrived in Sacramento before suppertime. We stayed at a boarding-house where Mrs. Parrish knew the landlady. I was hoping I'd get to see Miss Baxter, who had been so kind to us all a year ago, so after supper Mrs. Parrish took me to see her.

"Why, Corrie Hollister!" exclaimed Miss Baxter after I reminded her who I was. "I'd have never known you! You done a heap of filling out in the year since you was here!"

"Have you seen Captain Dixon?" I asked. "Has he been back again?"

"He's due just next month—maybe even in two weeks. Land sakes, wouldn't *he* enjoy seeing you!"

"Oh, I wish I could see him again!" I said. "There's so much I'd like to tell him about how we're getting on."

"Well, you'll just have to come back . . . and bring that parcel of sisters and brothers with you!"

"I'm afraid it might be a little farther out to Miracle Springs than you realize, Miss Baxter," put in Mrs. Parrish. "Nevertheless, perhaps you could have word sent to me when Captain Dixon does arrive. It might be that I can schedule a freight pick-up for that time." She wrote down something on a piece of paper and gave it to the landlady, and after a few minutes' conversation we left and went back to our boardinghouse.

The next day was the most exciting day I'd ever had in my life!

Bright and early we took a horse-cab down to the river landing. There, waiting to take us down the Sacramento River was the most beautiful white steamer I could have imagined! Walking on board, I felt as if I were stepping into a fairy tale adventure! The deck was full of people waving and shouting and jostling about, but by the time the captain shouted "Cast off!" and his men below unhooked the big ropes, I was in a world of my own. Slowly we inched away from the dock, and gradually I could feel the swaying motion beneath my feet as the captain guided us out into the middle where the current began to take hold.

Beside me Mrs. Parrish was saying something about never getting over the thrill of being on the water and feeling the motion underneath her, but I hardly heard the words.

# CHAPTER 7

## THANKFULNESS FROM
## BEHIND THE CLOUDS

Floating down the Sacramento River, I got to thinking about the new church in Miracle Springs. I thought about the building of the church, and how much Pa had helped with it.

After Rev. Rutledge came to Miracle Springs, he held services of some kind every Sunday, usually at Mrs. Parrish's. When summer came, work got started on the new building that was going to be used both for a school and the church. By then there were enough new folks in town that it was crowded in her house. But that just made Rev. Rutledge and Mrs. Parrish all the more enthusiastic for the work that was going on at the building site.

And I think it gave them both a quiet kind of good feeling to see Pa and Uncle Nick helping with the new building more than all the other men, even though Uncle Nick might not have done it on his own, without Pa making him.

They provided lots of the lumber too. Pa said the Lord gave us that gold in the ground, and he figured he should give some of it back. So whenever they needed more boards, he'd hitch up the horses and go into Sacramento to buy a wagonload. And some of the big beams and timbers he cut right from trees on our own claim.

Pa still never said much out loud, but he was thinking about a lot of things, I could tell. I knew Rev. Rutledge was downright thankful for Pa's support with the church building, though the two of them still were formal to each other. I doubted they'd ever be friends, but at least they were able to work side by side without arguing. And probably it helped Pa in his impression of the Reverend to see him with his shirt off in the hot summer sun, sweating with the rest of the men, helping to hoist a beam into place or driving in the nails of the wall supports or climbing up on top of the roof to help steady one of the joists. I think he was a little surprised that Rev. Rutledge was such a hard worker, and it gave him more respect for him than he'd had when we first went to Mrs. Parrish's for dinner.

All through the summer months, the men of Miracle would get together two evenings a week and most of Saturdays to help with the church. By the middle of the summer it was looking like a real building.

Rev. Rutledge was excited about a place to hold church services, of course, but some of the other folks in the community—mothers of young children, mostly—were thinking of the uses for the place during the week. Mrs. Parrish organized a committee of seven people in Miracle to start looking for a teacher to come, and they wrote to papers in Sacramento and some of the other cities and towns around to advertise their need.

Mrs. Parrish was excited about helping civilize this rough and wild place, and gave more and more of her business affairs to Mr. Ashton to run while she spent as much of her time as possible on "community affairs," as she called them. Pa wasn't about to pack up and go someplace else, because the mine was doing well, but I couldn't help thinking he wasn't altogether in favor of the changes. At the same time, I know he was trying his best to put his past behind him and to be a good family man to us kids. So he helped with the church and was civil to Rev. Rutledge and down-right friendly at times to Mrs. Parrish. Some of the folks around Miracle were beginning to look to Pa as one of the town's leaders—though Pa himself would have hated to hear me say such a thing!

"What does 'Alleluia' mean?" I asked Mrs. Parrish all at once.

"What makes you think of that as we're floating down the river Corrie?" she said, turning to me.

"Oh, I don't know," I answered. "I was thinking about the church getting built. That made me think of Easter day and that hymn we sang, you remember, *He Is Risen! Alleluia!* I've been wanting to ask you ever since. Then that song Mr. Peters read said *Alleluia* a lot too."

"Hmm," she said, "what would be a good way to explain it?" She thought for a minute, placing one of her slender fingers across her lips, between her chin and her nose like she always did when she was thinking real hard.

"You know how it is, Corrie," she finally went on, "when something is just so wonderful you want to tell everybody? Like a beautiful sunset, or some idea you've had, or maybe a precious possession—a favorite doll or a piece of fine jewelry?"

"Like Pa and Uncle Nick always talking about mining every chance they get?"

"Yes. That's the idea. And when you talk about something you treasure like that, when you can't say enough good about it, then you're *praising* it. That's what 'praise' is. And *Alleluia* is a word of praise—it's a way of saying that you think God is wonderful and loving and kind. The word means *Praise ye the Lord*."

"I think I see."

"There is another side of it, Corrie," said Mrs. Parrish. "It's easy to give praise to God when you are *feeling* it inside. There are times when the sun is bright and you're happy

inside, and you know God is out there making the world
beautiful and keeping you safe in His hand. But there's even
a better time to thank Him for being such a good and loving
God. And that's when it's gloomy and cold and cloudy, and
maybe you're sad, and you're *not* feeling like God's anywhere
around at all."

"Why's that a *better* time?"

"Because that's when it takes *faith* to praise God, to thank
Him for being good, to tell Him 'Thank you,' for taking care
of you and watching over you and loving you. It doesn't take
any faith to do it when you're feeling it inside. But when
your mind and heart try to tell you it's dreary and that life
is sad and that maybe God doesn't care about you after all,
that's when it takes faith to believe that He still *is* there just
the same."

She paused, and then her face lit up. "Think about your
father's and uncle's mine," she said. "It was the same mine
two years ago, wasn't it? The same hillside, the same dirt.
The gold was even there back then, wasn't it?"

I nodded.

"But your father and uncle didn't know it! To them it
*looked* like a worthless, played-out mine, when really it was
a wonderful mine full of gold."

"I see," I said, but I didn't really see what meaning she
was intending. I guess she saw the confusion on my face
despite my words.

"You see, Corrie, it doesn't take any *faith* now for folks
to believe your father's mine has gold in it. Anyone can go
up there and look and see it with his own two eyes. There
doesn't need to be any faith, because you can *see* it! But two
years ago, if someone had said, 'This mine has a rich vein
of gold in it,' back *then* it would have taken faith to believe
such a statement, because no one could *see* it."

"I understand that."

"It's the same with God! If the sun hides behind the

clouds for a few days, we still know it's there. But sometimes when God hides himself behind a cloud, we let ourselves start thinking He's gone, instead of using our *faith* to remind us He still *is* there, and is just as good and loving as always. That's why it's best to give God thanks when we don't feel especially thankful. That's how we learn not to trust our thoughts or feelings *about* God, but to trust in God himself. We can even trust Him when we can't see Him!"

"That seems hard," I said.

"I don't know why it should be harder than believing the sun is still in the sky even when we can't see it," she answered. Then a look of thoughtful sadness came over her face briefly. "But it *is* hard sometimes, Corrie, you're right. And it can be a very painful lesson, learning to say *Alleluia* to God in trying circumstances."

She said nothing more, and I looked out the window at the passing landscape again. One thing I was sure thankful for was Mrs. Parrish. She treated me like a grown-up and never seemed to mind my questions. I was learning so much about life and God from her.

"It won't be much longer now, Corrie," said Mrs. Parrish after a bit. "We'll be to Richmond in two or three hours. We'll stop there to take on some more passengers, and then it's across the bay to the great city!"

San Francisco! I could still hardly believe it! It's more than I would have dreamed or hoped for a year earlier, to see the big ocean that went all the way to China!

Mrs. Parrish then tried to explain to me about San Francisco Bay—she said it was shaped like a huge, tall, skinny ear—with towns and harbors all around it where ships came in, and with San Francisco itself sitting on a little piece of land on the other side. "It's the bay that makes it possible for the ships to come in to the city from the Pacific," she said, "but it also makes getting to and from the city kind of difficult if you're not coming by boat."

I couldn't really get a picture of it in my mind, but she said I'd understand when we reached the pier in Richmond and could look out across the bay to see the opening into the Pacific where the ships go through, and see San Francisco on the peninsula, she called it, just to the left.

We finally did get to Richmond in the early afternoon, where we docked for about an hour. But we couldn't see San Francisco at all. There was fog so thick we could hardly see the water in front of us, although I could hear it slapping up against the wood of the pier and the rocks on shore. And when we started moving out across the bay, going slowly through the fog, it was an eerie feeling.

The chilly fog was full of the smell of water and fish, and I could imagine we were sailing out to sea to unknown places. Even though Mrs. Parrish pointed to me through the fog to show me where San Francisco was on the other side, something in me wanted to make the adventure all the bigger by thinking that the captain of the boat might miss the city and go sailing out through "the gate," as they called the opening, right out into the Pacific!

It was cold standing out there on the deck in the fog, and after a while Mrs. Parrish said she wanted to go inside. But I didn't want to miss a thing, so I stayed outside by myself, leaning over the railing looking down into the water as the boat plowed a furrow through it, then glancing up again at the mists blowing about. Every once in a while a portion of something in the distance would appear, whether the shore or another boat I couldn't tell, and then would fade back into the depths of the white-gray cloud we were going through.

I was gazing again down into the water, deep green with white from the boat splashing through it, when suddenly off to our left the mist broke apart, and through the middle of it, as if I was looking through a tunnel of light, I saw the shore and the buildings of the city scattered about the hills of San Francisco.

I stared in wonder. It was like a vision from God, and as far as I could tell I was the only one who could see it, for all about the boat and the water the misty fog still swirled to and fro. But right at the place where I stood, a bright window through it looked in upon the city. It was there all the time, just where Mrs. Parrish had pointed. I thought immediately of the conversation we'd had earlier about the sun being behind the clouds even when you couldn't see it.

Then just as suddenly, as if God swept a giant curtain over the window He had opened briefly for me, the fog filled up the space again, and I couldn't see past the end of the boat's front. But still I stared, wondering if I had dreamed the whole sight.

I never forgot that moment. And sometimes when I can't see what's ahead, I remind myself of Mrs. Parrish pointing through the fog telling me where the city was, and think that maybe sometimes God's telling me the same thing, that He knows what's up ahead even though I can't see it, that He's steering the ship and knows where it's going. And I think that if I'm paying attention, maybe He'll give me a little sight through the fog to help me trust Him even when I can't see where He's taking me.

# CHAPTER 8

# SAN FRANCISCO!

There is no way to describe our three days in the great city of San Francisco! I wish I knew more of what Uncle Nick calls "them fifty-cent words." Maybe then I could give a better idea.

The fog seemed attracted to the water, because as soon as we got away from where our steamer landed, the sun started peeking through hole after hole. Before long, everything was shining in the bright afternoon sunlight.

We took a horsedrawn cab from the pier to the hotel, and on the way Mrs. Parrish pointed out many of the sights. She even had the cabman take a short detour up a steep hill so I could look down on the city from the top. She showed me where some of San Francisco's newspapers were, where the *Star* began on Clay Street, and down by the waterfront where the *California's* offices were located.

She pointed out a bookshop—"That's where I go whenever I'm here to see if I can find something for you," she said. "We'll visit it later"—and a dressmaker's shop, which she also said we'd visit.

Everywhere there was building going on. Mrs. Parrish said San Francisco was growing faster than any city in the country. Although our hotel must have been half a mile or more up the hill, we could see and hear the workers all day long and half into the night working on the huge Montgomery Block. Mrs. Parrish said there had never been anything so big or so elegant built anywhere in California. It was four stories tall and the walls were three feet thick. It was so huge there were going to be offices in it, a big hotel, restaurants, saloons, and all sorts of places. Mrs. Parrish said when it was done it was sure to be the center of San Francisco's business and social life.

I had never seen so many Chinese people as I saw in San Francisco, come to help with the construction. The cab driver told us that hundreds of these Chinese men worked eighteen-hour days hauling big numbered blocks of granite for the new Parrott's bank building. I can hardly believe it myself, but he said every piece of granite came from China— along with the men to put them up—and they all had to go in a certain place. It was a four-story building too, but there were so many workmen it was done in just a few months.

Usually when she came to San Francisco, Mrs. Parrish said she stayed at a boardinghouse. But this was a special occasion, she said, and she intended to treat me first class. I wasn't prepared for all the sights that met my eyes when we pulled up in front and then went inside the Oriental Hotel, a fine new building on Hyde Street.

The foyer was carpeted in a rich red and black carpet. There was a chandelier overhead and velvet chairs and couches all around in the lobby. It was the kind of place I'd only imagined in cities like Paris, France!

A man in a red coat took our luggage right away. Mrs. Parrish spoke with the clerk at the front desk, while I just stood on that thick carpet and kept staring all about me, probably with my mouth hanging open and my eyes full of country-girl wonder!

"Must be your first time in the city," came a voice into the middle of my musing.

"What?" I said, looking around.

"First-timer, eh?" he said again. "I figured—I can always tell."

I saw a boy, around my own age, maybe a little older, standing looking at me. He wasn't much bigger than I was, and since he was slender, I couldn't really tell his age. He looked young, but he sounded so sure of himself and confident that he must have been seventeen or eighteen, though he only looked fifteen. His voice was high-pitched. His eyes were as blue as the night, and looked somewhat mischievous. He wore a dirty, gray hat that was tilted to the right. Out from under it stiff blond curls fell onto his forehead.

"Yes, it is," I answered, finally getting hold of my wits.

"Yeah, I knew it. Being in the newspaper business, you see, I got a nose for people." Now he was starting to sound cocky, and I had the feeling he was looking down on me. But then I noticed the bundle of newspapers he was carrying under his arm and thought maybe he deserved another chance.

"You work for a newspaper?" I said, probably a little too eagerly.

"That's right."

"What do you do? You're not a reporter . . . a writer?" I asked.

"I do whatever they tell me," he answered. "I'm what they call in the business a jack of all trades. So, yeah, I've done a little reporting in my time—" The superior slant of his mouth crept back. "You see, my editor, he knows that a fella like me, out on the streets, is likely to pick up better stories than them desk reporters."

"I'd like to write for a newspaper some day," I said.

"Where you from?"

"Miracle Springs."

His first response was a great laugh. "Boy, are you from the sticks! You ain't gonna do no newspaper writing there! Ha, ha, ha!"

"What do you mean?" I said back, my face getting red. "We have a newspaper there."

"You mean ol' Singleton's rag! Ha, ha! It ain't nothing but an advertising sheet—mining tools, mail-order brides, spent claims, and worn out jackasses! We cover *real* news stories here in the city. You must have just lit fresh from the overland trail! So, what are you doing in San Francisco?"

Even as he asked the question he was still smiling that patronizing smile of his, and I didn't know whether to be hurt or mad.

"We're just—that is, I came with that lady over there," I glanced to where Mrs. Parrish was just finishing up with the clerk.

"Well, sounds to me like the two of you could do with a guide while you're here, and I know this city like the back of my hand. Robert T. O'Flaridy is the name! And besides newspapering, I offer my services to out-of-town young damsels such as yourself to keep them out of distress! My rates are most reasonable, and I—"

He was interrupted, just as Mrs. Parrish walked up, by the desk clerk's irritated-sounding voice calling out from behind the desk.

"Robin O'Flaridy, what are you doing accosting my guests again!"

Robin—that fit him better than his fancy "Robert T."—flashed a big grin, sheepish, but with a dash of cunning in it too.

"Just trying to make a living, Mr. Barnes," he answered, throwing a wink in our direction.

"Well, your job is not to bother our people, as I've told you fifty times, but to deliver those newspapers. If you can't do that properly, you may well lose that job, too!"

"Okay, okay!" He tipped his cap toward us. "It was a pleasure meeting you ladies. Remember, I'm the best guide in this city."

He deposited the bundle of papers on the desk and made a hasty exit.

"I apologize for the annoyance, ma'am," the clerk said.

"No trouble at all, Mr. Barnes," replied Mrs. Parrish. "Perhaps if he is as good a guide as he says, we might consider engaging his services."

"Believe me, ma'am, the boy is all wind. All he does is deliver papers to a few of the large hotels in town, and he tells everyone he's a reporter."

"He *doesn't* write for the paper?" I said.

"*Write!* Did he tell you that? Ha, that's a good one! He's nothing but a confidence man in the making. No, ma'am, if you employed him as a guide, you'd have to chain your pocketbook to your arm. Nobody even knows where the boy lives. He's always on the streets looking for some likely target to fleece, and an hour or two a day he delivers papers and pretends to be the senior editor's right hand man! No, I've seen him mixing with some bad customers, and wouldn't want you associating with him."

"Well, I appreciate your candid advice, Mr. Barnes," said Mrs. Parrish. "But surely, the boy could be trusted. If you hire him—"

"I don't hire him, ma'am. If I had my way, I'd never see him setting foot in my lobby again. No, he's the newspaper's doing, and I'm stuck with him. But the paper isn't the only outfit he runs errands for, if you get my meaning," he added with a look of significance. "And like I say, some of the other types he hangs around aren't the sort a lady like you wants to have anything to do with."

With plenty to think about, we followed the man with the red jacket up to our room. I didn't realize it, but I must have been so tuckered out that I fell asleep in my clothes almost the minute I lay down on the beautiful soft bed.

Mrs. Parrish had a short nap, too, but when I woke she was sitting at the dressing table fixing her hair. She suggested that if I felt rested enough, we get a little something to eat and then see more of the city. We still had most of the afternoon ahead of us, and her meetings didn't start until the next day. She didn't have to ask me twice! I jumped up and washed my face and was ready in a twinkling.

Mrs. Parrish hired us a carriage, but she didn't need a guide. She knew the city as well as any native, or any guide like that O'Flaridy boy said he was. First she took us up onto Telegraph Hill to see the windmill, and then clear across town to the point overlooking the "Gate," where we could see the Pacific and the opening of the bay on the other side. It was beautiful when the fog still clinging to the water would lift or part. It was pretty windy, though the sun was shining warm. What you could see of the water was so blue, just like the sky, and when the sun was just right, even the patches of fog swirling around here and there could be pretty. I thought San Francisco was about as grand a place for a city to sit as anywhere in the world!

Wherever we went in the city we saw different sights— fancy business men, Chinese workmen, fishing boats of all sizes, and big ships from all over the world. On the waterfront I heard many strange languages being spoken. And of course, there were lots of saloons with rough-looking men coming in and out of them.

I guess it was what you would call "colorful," but Mrs. Parrish said that lots of terrible things happened around there. They even called one stretch of the waterfront the "Barbary Coast," after the pirate coast of North Africa. She said that there were bad men and women in those saloons and boardinghouses, and I have to admit I didn't like the looks of the ladies who came out of them, dressed in bright colors with painted faces and red lips, sometimes hanging on to men in fine clothes with ruffled lace shirts. Those men had a different look than the businessmen you saw around the Montgomery Building. And after our day's outing when she took me to see the city, I was glad when we got away from there.

Just as we were climbing into our cab, while Mrs. Parrish was telling the driver where to go, I glanced back for one last look at the waterfront, with its saloons and people and the fishing boats and bay behind it. My mind was on the whole panorama of blue sky, clouds, the pretty expanse of water, but my eyes fell instead on a figure just at that moment stumbling out of one of the buildings nearest to where we sat.

My mouth fell open in disbelief. It couldn't be! And just as quickly as I saw him, I turned my head away. Even if it was, I didn't want to see that face a second time. I *never* wanted to see it again!

I stared down at the floor of the cab, afraid to say anything to Mrs. Parrish. Yet, somehow I sensed that, drunk as he was, the man had seen my face too, and was even now walking uncertainly toward us.

What a relief when at last the cabman shouted to his horse and I felt the cab lurch into motion. I didn't look back. I never wanted to see the Barbary Coast again!

I kept quiet most of the way back to the hotel. I wanted to tell Mrs. Parrish, but something inside me couldn't. I was afraid, flooded by so many unpleasant memories so unexpectedly, and I just wanted to try to forget. By the time we got back to the hotel, we were talking again and I tried to put the incident behind me and out of my mind.

I'll never forget that evening as long as I live!

When we got back to the middle of the city, it was late in the afternoon and the wind coming in off the ocean was pretty chilly, but some shops were still open. Before we returned to the hotel, the carriage stopped in front of the dressmaker's shop Mrs. Parrish had pointed out earlier.

She told the cabman to wait, then took me inside and said she was going to buy me a new dress. After all she'd already done for me, I could hardly bear thinking of her doing even more!

But she insisted, and said, "Corrie, you have to let me do this for myself, for the pleasure it will give *me*! I doubt I'm ever going to know the joy of having a daughter of my own, and you're just about the closest to one I'm likely to get."

As she spoke her eyes started to get big and shiny from the tears filling them, as she sometimes does when a conversation gets real personal, and I knew I couldn't argue with her. I couldn't help thinking about Rev. Rutledge, and I was about to say something about maybe her getting to have a daughter of her own after they were married. Whether she had an inkling of what I was thinking, I don't know, but before a word got out of my mouth, she put a finger softly to my lips to silence me.

"You're like a daughter to me in many ways, Corrie. I'm so thankful to God for you! Sometimes I think maybe it's even more special to have a friend like you I can think of as a daughter in the Lord, than to have a daughter of my own flesh. Because in you I'm always reminded of God's love and goodness and grace. Now, let's have some fun, and find you a bright, pretty new dress—and maybe even a bonnet to go with it!"

And it was fun! We stayed in that shop for an hour, Mrs. Parrish and the woman from the shop holding up dress after dress to me, draping them over my shoulders, having me look in the mirror and asking me what I thought. They made me feel so special that I might have cried if we hadn't been laughing and talking and enjoying ourselves so much. I must have tried on six or seven different dresses in all colors. I forgot all about the cab driver waiting outside and the time passing.

The dress we finally picked was the prettiest of all, mostly a light green. I wouldn't have chosen pink as a color to go with green. A couple of the other ones I tried on mixed yellow with green. But this particular dress had such light colors that the two blended in a way I just loved. It was made mostly out of polished cotton, with a full skirt in green. The skirt was loose and soft, but not so full that I had to wear hoops and petticoats underneath. It felt comfortable, like I could walk around free and easy. Above the waist, the bodice was pink, and a wide collar folded down over the pink all the way around, with a green piping around its edge. They called the sleeves leg of mutton sleeves, the full part from my shoulders down to just below my elbows made of the green, with the tight forearms in plain white. Only the top in front and in back was pink, and little pink fabric-covered buttons stretched all the way down the back, matching those on the sleeves.

Best of all was the satin and lace—dark green, with rows of satin stretching down from the shoulders over the pink and down to the waist where the green began. The wide waistband was dark green satin, with a bow tied in back. In between the satin stripes, which were three inches apart down the bodice, were sewn little delicate strips of lace, a lighter green than the satin, but darker than the dress. The same lace went down the wide part of the sleeves too, all the way to where the narrow white began.

The bonnet must have been made at the same time, because the wide floppy brim was of the exact same light green as the dress. The crown was of the same pink, and around the base of the pink was a wide strip of the dark green satin that exactly matched the waistband of the dress. It was all so pretty, and made me feel so fine and grown-up!

Walking out of that shop carrying that parcel, the smile on my face must've been six inches wide.

When we went back to the hotel, Mrs. Parrish dismissed the cabman. We walked up to the second floor to our room and got ready for the evening. We put our dresses on—Mrs.

Parrish had bought a new one for the occasion too. Then
Mrs. Parrish fixed her hair up all nice and then helped me
with mine, so it would look nice flowing out from under the
pink and green bonnet. At last we left the room and walked
back downstairs.

As we walked through the hotel lobby, I saw several
men's heads turn in our direction. I could feel the red coming
up my neck and into my cheeks, but Mrs. Parrish just kept
straight for the door without even flinching at some of the
calls at her.

I guess that's one of the things I always liked about her,
that she could be such a lady, so tender and nice, and could
cry with you and talk about girl things. But she could be
strong in a man's world like San Francisco too. I'd never yet
seen her cowed by anyone, man or woman. And walking
through that hotel lobby beside her, I felt as safe as if I'd
been with Pa and Uncle Nick and Captain Grant—all three
of them!

Mrs. Parrish took me to dinner that night at a fancy
restaurant. It was close enough that we could have walked,
but she said this was our "night out in San Francisco," and
that we were going to "go first class all the way." So she
ordered another cab—a covered one, this time, with fringe
hanging down all the way around—and we rode down Montgomery Street, lit up with the brand-new gas street lights,
to the International House restaurant.

On the way I asked her why we didn't eat at the dining
room of the hotel. "The Oriental is one of the city's nicest
hotels," she answered, "but there is an element present there
which I would rather avoid. Sam Brannan and other of the
city's leaders may have suites there, but I do not choose to
dine with them, and I do not think most respectable women
would care to do so either."

I felt like such a lady that night, sitting there in my new
dress in that expensive restaurant, with well-dressed people

all about—businessmen, Mrs. Parrish said, from all around the world. I didn't even know what half the food was that Mrs. Parrish ordered, but she explained it all to me, and everything was delicious! There was music playing as we ate too—real music—and a lady who sang. It was like being part of a world I never even dreamed of seeing but had only read about once or twice in books.

By the time we got back to the hotel I was tired—but happy, too! What a wonderful day it had been! As I lay down in my bed, all the things that I'd seen and heard that evening ran back and forth through my mind.

But not for long, because I was asleep before I knew it.

# CHAPTER 9

## BRUSH WITH THE PAST

The next day Mrs. Parrish had to go to her meetings. She asked me if I wanted to go with her, but I said I'd rather stay at the hotel and either try to read in the book I'd brought or else write in my journal. There was already *so* much to tell, and I wanted to remember every minute of my visit to San Francisco! She said she had to meet some people in the morning, would be back for lunch, and then would be gone for three or four hours in the afternoon.

The morning passed quietly. I read some, but mostly wrote in my journal. Mrs. Parrish was back almost before I realized she had left. We talked a while and had lunch, and then she left again for her afternoon meetings.

About an hour later, I started to get restless. I'd been in that room most of the day, and I wanted to get a little bit of fresh air. Mrs. Parrish said everything would be fine, but that I ought to stay in the room or maybe go into the hall or down to the lobby to stretch my legs.

But I had too much of the outdoors and the country in me for my own good. I just had to get outside where I could feel the sun and wind on my face and breathe air that had been mixed with the clouds and the trees and the wind, instead of just sitting in a stale room for hours on end.

Finally, I got up and walked downstairs and into the lobby.

I had hardly set foot off the stairs when I heard a familiar voice: "Well, if it isn't the country girl who wants to be a newspaper reporter."

I glanced up and there was young O'Flaridy, again with a bundle of the day's papers.

"Having a pleasant visit in the city?" he added.

"Real nice," I answered, smiling but feeling a little cautious after what Mr. Barnes had said the day before.

"Even without my services as a guide, eh?" he said, with kind of a sly smile as he approached me.

Unconsciously I backed up a step, while I answered, "We saw all kinds of things. Mrs. Parrish knows the city pretty well."

"And where is your lady friend this fine day?"

"She had some meetings to go to."

"What kind of business she in?"

"Freighting and the like."

"Mighty peculiar field for a lady to be in. Say, who is she, anyway? She can't be your mother. She your aunt—your older sister?"

"She's a friend."

"Sort of took you under her wing, did she?"

I wasn't sure I liked his being so nosy about our affairs, but luckily he spotted Mr. Barnes eyeing him, so he made a beeline for the counter to dump off his papers. Then he sauntered back in my direction.

"Say," he said, "maybe with the lady gone to her meetings and you all alone like you are, you'd like me to show you around some."

"No, thank you." I tried to sound confident. "I've got plans of my own."

"Aw, what could—"

"Hey, O'Flaridy!" interrupted a man's deep voice from the other side of the hotel lobby. We both looked around, and the instant he saw who the speaker was, Robin left me and hurried over to him.

"I thought you was gonna run them papers down to McCready's for me," said the man, his voice quieter now, but still so I could hear. I didn't like the sound of the man, and he looked like a rough sort, though he was dressed in a black suit. They spoke a minute in quieter tones and I decided it was time for me to make my exit. I didn't want to have any more to do with Robin O'Flaridy or anyone he knew. I turned and walked through the lobby, past the desk, and toward the exit doors.

"Hey, you're not going out alone, are you?" came the persistent O'Flaridy voice yet again from behind me, just as my hand touched the door.

I hesitated. I still didn't know whether to be frightened or flattered by the attentions of this seemingly worldly-wise San Francisco lad. He hurried up to me again.

"I've got to make a delivery down by the waterfront," he said. "How about joining me?"

"I don't think so," I said. "I really have to be going."

"This is a big city, you know. No place for young girls to be roaming the streets without someone to watch out for them. Why—" His voice got real low and he came up close, like he was letting me in on a secret. "Why, I could tell you stories of that fella there I was just talking to, stories that you'd never believe! It's rough out there, and I wouldn't want anything to happen to you."

"I can take care of myself," I retorted before I knew what I was saying, with more courage than good sense. I wanted to get away from him. He was too pushy! I shoved the door open and walked out onto the street. He'd likely keep after me, so I turned and walked quickly away, without looking back.

It was a little chilly. The fog was just starting to blow away, and there were patches of bright showing through all around, but there was still enough fog to give me one of the best memories I had of San Francisco: breathing in that fresh-feeling fog that made my lungs feel so full and alive. I breathed in a few times when I got outside, then I started to walk down the street.

I went down the sloping hill of California Street toward the center of town. I figured if I walked straight down and then straight back up to Hyde I'd be able to remember where I was, and I'd been that way in the cab a couple of times already. I had walked for maybe ten minutes, then all of a sudden I felt a strong hand close around my arm just above the elbow.

"I thought it was you, missy," growled a deep, raspy voice. "I knew if I followed you an' that lady an' watched this fancy place, I'd find my chance t' git even!"

I didn't even need to turn around. His was a voice I could never forget! And besides the voice, I could smell him too. In an instant I knew I'd been right in what I thought I'd seen the day before.

It was Buck Krebbs!

"Come with me, missy," he was saying, shoving me forward and toward the side of the walkway where there weren't so many people. "You an' me's got some talkin' to do!" Only later, when my arm got a big purple bruise, did I realize how hard he was pinching me. But at the moment I was much too scared to feel anything. "I wanna know where yer pa hid my loot! An' ye're gonna tell me!"

Not more than five or ten seconds had passed since he first grabbed me, but when you're scared, time seems to freeze as if it's happening to somebody else in slow motion. I've had dreams like that where I couldn't move even though something bad was about to happen if I didn't run away or jump to safety. Those first few seconds I was that way. Like a frog that a snake had just grabbed, I was so paralyzed I couldn't move or scream or even think.

But the second Buck said the word *pa*, something unfroze inside me, and all of a sudden woke up.

I don't exactly know what happened next. I read some-where that fear makes you stronger than you really are. I guess I must've twisted my arm hard. Maybe that's when I got the bruise, or maybe I was stronger than Buck thought I'd be. I started screaming too. I remember being shocked at the loudness of my own voice! Everything all at once took Buck by surprise. I could feel the pain in my arm stop, and then I was running as fast as my legs would move. I didn't even know where I was going, I just ran as fast as I could, and I could feel my hair flying all about my face. Behind me I could hear the pounding of Buck's boots on the wood walk, and him yelling after me, "I'll git 'im, ya hear me, missy! I'll git that pa o' yours! I'll git the loot! I'll git ya all! I'll git it if I have t' kill ya all first!"

I kept running along the street, then turning, still hearing Buck chasing behind me. I ran past the Armory Hall and turned up Sacramento. I didn't know what I was doing at the time or where I was, or I'd have stopped right there and got one of the Guard men to help me.

A couple of blocks later I was in front of the *Eldorado*. People were staring at me, and some of the men hanging around called out rude things to me. I must have looked like a mess, a young kid of a girl running along the street, all alone in front of San Francisco's most famous gambling house.

I turned again, down the hill this time. I found out later it was Washington Street.

I stopped for a spell, caught my breath, and looked back for the first time.

I couldn't see or hear anything of Buck, and I didn't figure with his heavy boots and the whiskey I could smell on him that he'd be able to run too far. But all I could think of was getting back to the hotel before he did, and safely into my room again. I'd never leave that room alone now, because

I was sure he'd be waiting for me if I ever came out of the lobby again!

A few minutes later I found myself back on Montgomery Street, which I recognized. I ran toward where the work was going on for the big new Montgomery Block building.

I went up to a man, dressed real fancy, who was just walking inside. I figured he was probably on his way to one of the lawyers' or mine owners' offices that was already open up on the second floor, and was a safe enough man to talk to. He didn't look too pleased at being accosted on the street by what must have looked like a tramp. But when, all out of breath, I asked him where the Oriental Hotel was, he didn't give me more than a *hmmp* or two as he looked me over, then pointed out the way with a half-scowl on his face. Somehow I got back onto California Street, and then ran all the rest of the way back, not even slowing down as I went through the lobby and up to the desk to ask for the key to our room, panting and sweating like a runout horse all lathered up.

When I'd been running through the streets trying to get away from Buck Krebbs, I'd have probably welcomed the sight of his face, but at the moment I was grateful Robin O'Flaridy wasn't anywhere around to see the fix I'd gotten myself in by not taking his advice! I took the stairs two at a time up to our room, hurriedly locked the door behind me with my fingers shaking, and then threw myself down on the bed and tried to catch my breath.

I didn't get much more reading or writing done that afternoon!

But I didn't start crying till Mrs. Parrish got back and I told her all about it. Having her take me in her arms and say comforting things to me made me feel safe again, and that's what made the tears start to come. She said her meetings were all done and that she wouldn't leave me alone for another minute of our time in San Francisco, and she said that

Buck Krebbs would never dare come into the hotel and try to harm us, so we were safe enough.

We were to start home the next morning. The man in the red jacket brought our luggage down to the lobby and Mrs. Parrish took care of her last business at the desk.

I could hardly believe it when I heard a familiar voice once again, "Leaving town so soon?"

I turned around and found myself again staring straight at none other than Robin O'Flaridy! This time he had no newspapers. If I didn't know better I'd think he was waiting for us.

"Yes, we are," I said, silently thinking to myself, *Not him again!*

"Well, I wish you safe travels all the way back to—what's that town out there in the sticks you say you're from?"

"Miracle Springs."

"Oh yeah, that place. Well, I wish you and your lady friend safe travels back to Miracle Springs. Say, how're you getting back there?"

His voice actually was starting to sound nice for a change.

"We'll take the boat up to Sacramento," I said.

"Hmm," he said with a serious expression, "I hear the bay's been pretty rough these days."

Outside I could see that the sky was blue and it didn't look any more windy than usual, so I decided to pay no attention to his remark. And the more I looked at him the more I realized that he took nothing he said very seriously himself!

"You still hankering to be a newspaper reporter?" he asked.

"Some day perhaps."

"Well, the next time you come to the city, you stay right here and be sure to look me up. I'll give you a few tips that helped me get started in the business. What do you say?"

To my relief, Mrs. Parrish had just finished at the desk and came up to us.

"Our cab is waiting outside," she said. "Good bye, Mr. O'Flaridy."

He quickly hastened to the front door and opened it for us with a flourish, annoying the man in the red jacket.

When we were finally on the steamer heading back across the bay toward Richmond and Sacramento—on perfectly calm waters!—Robin O'Flaridy quickly left my mind. Once again my thoughts filled with what had happened the previous afternoon. I couldn't wait to get back home to tell Pa what Buck Krebbs had yelled after me as I ran away from him. His words were mighty frightening to think about!

Probably because I was so worried about him and talking about it, on the way home Mrs. Parrish asked me lots of questions about Pa. I was glad for the chance to tell her what a fine man he was, though something in her tone made me think she didn't need to be told.

We laughed together about those first few weeks after we'd gotten to Miracle last year and how awkward it had been for everybody right at first. A faraway look came into her eye after I told her why he had left New York years ago, and I think she felt truly sorry for how she had misjudged Pa.

"There appears to be a lot more to your father than just what shows on the surface, Corrie," she said.

"Oh yes, ma'am," I answered. "Why, I'd hardly know him now from that man who first walked out of the saloon when Captain Dixon brought us into Miracle!"

———

When we got back to Sacramento, we dropped in to see Miss Baxter again at her boardinghouse, and who should be sitting there in her parlor but Captain Dixon himself!

Before I knew what I was doing, I ran toward him, and

he stood up and I threw my arms around him and gave him a big squeeze. He seemed almost as pleased to see me too, and hugged me in return. He said his wagon train had arrived early, and then he asked about Becky and Emily and Zack and Tad.

When I told him how well we were doing with Pa and about the gold in the mine, he seemed genuinely relieved. He said he'd thought about us almost every day and was glad to hear everything was working out so well.

Miss Baxter fixed us some tea and we had a pleasant visit. Next to Pa and Mrs. Parrish, I reckon Captain Dixon was more responsible for helping us kids through Ma's death and coming to California than anyone else.

When we left to go, he and Mrs. Parrish shook hands. "I hope you might one day be able to come out to Miracle for a visit, Mr. Dixon," she said. "I know the other children would love to see you."

"I may just do that, ma'am," he answered.

We spent the night in Sacramento, then got Mrs. Parrish's horses and surrey from the livery stable where she'd left them, and early the next morning began the ride to Miracle.

We talked about so many things on the way home! Since that very first day on the street outside the Gold Nugget, I had always felt that Mrs. Parrish was my friend, but she had seemed a mite distant all the same. She never really kept herself aloof from me, but she was just so tall and confident, older, and a successful businesswoman, that it made me feel small by comparison.

But after this trip together, and her asking about Ma and Pa and our family, and with us talking about so many things, I felt that I was her friend too. She never seemed quite so distant after that.

We met Rev. Rutledge again, this time in Auburn, and he rode all the rest of the way back with us. He was in high spirits and talked practically the whole way about people he'd spoken with and the great opportunities he said existed for "the field of harvest." I didn't know what he meant by that, and I must admit I didn't pay much attention to him. It just wasn't the same after he joined us, and I was disappointed that my time alone with Mrs. Parrish had to come to an end. Mrs. Parrish was unusually quiet that day too. She didn't seem quite as enthusiastic about the minister's plans as she had been several days earlier.

# CHAPTER 10

# TROUBLE AT DUTCH FLAT

As we approached the cabin, I hardly waited for the surrey to come to a stop before I was out and running toward it yelling.

"Pa! Pa!" I called out. "Pa . . . I saw that man Krebbs and he said he's gonna—"

But when I threw open the door I was stopped short by the sight of Zack standing there staring me in the face. The other three were behind him, and I guess the worry in my voice frightened them, cause they were all silent. Even though I'd been gone most of a week, none of us thought to hug or greet each other.

"Where's Pa?" I asked, out of breath.

"He's gone to fetch Uncle Nick outta trouble," piped up Tad.

I glanced at Zack.

"He rode off on Jester this morning," Zack said, but before he had the chance to explain, Emily was adding her version of what happened.

"He was real mad," she said, "and his face was all red. I hope he doesn't hurt Jester."

By now Mrs. Parrish had come up behind me and was listening. I was still waiting for Zack to fill in the details.

"He rode out to Dutch Flat in the middle of the mornin'.

He didn't take time to tell me nothin'. He just heard about Uncle Nick, and the next thing I knew he was saddlin' up Jester and ridin' off, tellin' me to keep everyone inside and to go over to Mr. Shaw's if we had any trouble."

I glanced back at Mrs. Parrish. Inside I couldn't help feeling that some terrible danger was approaching. I didn't know what had happened with Uncle Nick, but I was worried something awful about what Buck Krebbs had said. I was afraid seeing me had put it into his evil mind again to come back to Miracle and try to hurt us.

"I've got to warn Pa!" I said, turning and running back out to the surrey to grab up my few things and bring them into the cabin. Then, almost before anyone knew what I was doing, even before *I* knew what I was doing, I ran to the barn and started saddling Snowball.

A couple of minutes later I heard the door open behind me. It was Mrs. Parrish, her voice calm.

"Corrie, please," she began, "let's go inside and talk about this. It might be best if—"

"Don't try to stop me, ma'am," I interrupted, not realizing how rude I sounded, especially with her having done so much for me and just getting back from taking me to San Francisco.

"I won't try to stop you, Corrie," she went on, still calm. "You're practically a grown woman now, and I know it's not my place to tell you what to do. But it's late in the day and it's a long way to Dutch Flat—"

"Only fifteen miles. I can ride that in a little over an hour!"

"But you don't know where your father has gone."

"I'll find him! I know I can!" I said, tightening the saddle straps.

"Besides, Corrie, dear, you don't know what the trouble is. There may be danger."

"It can't be worse than Buck Krebbs trying to kill him!

It was only about a month ago that Pa was sayin' the men down at Dutch Flat might know something about the men who were after him and Uncle Nick. I didn't think anything of it at the time, but now I see it could have to do with Buck Krebbs. Don't you see, Mrs. Parrish, I gotta go! I gotta warn him! What if Buck Krebbs is back around here already!"

"I understand," she replied. "But I think it would be best if you waited until tomorrow morning. You and the children can spend the night with me, and tomorrow we'll talk to the sheriff and—"

I don't know why all of a sudden I was acting so ornery and stubborn. But deep inside I just knew I had to find Pa and not wait a second longer. Zack was always telling me I was mule-headed. I figured it was because he was my kid brother. But maybe he was right. Pa had said a time or two that as I grew older I reminded him more and more of Ma. And I knew she could be mighty determined once she set herself to do something.

Anyhow, by the time the next words came out of my mouth, I was getting ready to swing up onto Snowball's back. "I'm sorry, ma'am," I said, "but I just gotta try to find him, and I just can't wait till tomorrow!"

I turned Snowball's head toward the door, but before I was even outside Zack called out, "I'm goin' with you, Corrie!" I hadn't even noticed him follow Mrs. Parrish into the barn, where he went straight to Blue Flame to start saddling him.

"You know the way, then," I called back. "You can catch up!" I knew Blue Flame would be able to catch Snowball in a quarter of a mile once he was on the open road. But even though I was in a hurry, I wouldn't have trusted myself to him. Zack had learned to handle him pretty well, but he was too spirited for me. I dug my heels into Snowball's flanks and was off.

"Corrie, at least take something to eat!" called out Mrs. Parrish's voice behind me.

The words brought me to my senses in the middle of all the emotions that were flying through me. I reined in Snowball, stopped, then turned and trotted back to where she was standing beside the barn. "Let me at least put some things in the saddle bag for you," she said. I nodded, got down off Snowball, and followed her back to the cabin.

By this time Zack was out of the barn with Blue Flame. He tied him to a post and ran inside.

I saw at once that he was thinking more straight than I was, cause when he came back out he was carrying a couple of blankets and his overcoat, in case we didn't make it back by nightfall. He was growing up, maybe in some ways faster than I was!

Five minutes later we were back on our horses again, this time with food to last us a day or two, blankets, and coats. Mrs. Parrish hadn't said anything more about trying to talk me out of going. She looked up at me, straight into my eyes.

"I'm sorry, Mrs. Parrish," I said, "to go running off like this the minute we get back—"

"Don't you worry about a thing, Corrie. I understand! And I trust you to do the right thing. I know the Lord is with you."

"Thank you," I answered. "And thank you for taking me to San Francisco! This isn't exactly how I figured it would end, but I *am* grateful to you for everything!"

She reached up and gave my hand a squeeze, still gazing straight into my eyes. "It was a wonderful time for me, Corrie! But we'll talk about San Francisco more later! Now, you go and find your father! I'll have Tad and Becky and Emily at my place in town when you get back!"

"Come on, Zack!" I said, and we galloped off. But before we were out of sight, I glanced back for a last look at the three young'uns and Mrs. Parrish. I couldn't help thinking how nice it looked with her standing with them in front of our place. I found myself wishing she'd still be there when we got back, instead of in town in that big house of hers.

# CHAPTER 11

# GRIZZLY HATCH

Zack and I rode hard most of the way, at least where we could.

We went over the hill first, crossing the Allegheny road north of Miracle, then along the trail leading from French Corral to Soda Springs till we were across the South Fork of the Yuba. After that we headed south, up and across Chalk Bluff Ridge, down through Deadman's Flat, then across the Bear.

I was proud of Zack. He knew the way exactly and didn't need my help at all. Not that I'd have been much help. I'd only been this way once with Pa, and then not all the way to Dutch Flat. But I guess Zack had come two or three times with Uncle Nick.

We made good time. I think we were there in less than two hours. But even so, it was late and the sun was starting to think about bedding down for the night. Zack told me there'd be a half moon tonight, though, so if the clouds stayed away we'd be able to make it back home after dark if we wanted to.

There wasn't much to Dutch Flat, that's for sure. All it amounted to was a little valley between the Bear River and Canyon Creek where they'd discovered gold. There were claims here and there on the streams, and a shack or two, one of them a saloon. I don't think there was one respectable family in the whole place.

We hadn't really talked about what we would do when we actually got there, or how we thought we would find Pa. I'd been praying all the way that God would help us. I'd remembered a verse in the Bible that Mrs. Parrish had told me about God guiding someone's footsteps if you give yourself to Him.

Now I remember—if you *acknowledge* Him was the word she used. If you *acknowledge* Him, He will lead you. I asked her what "acknowledge" meant.

"If you say that God is in charge of your life," she answered, "if you agree to go along with His leading instead of you trying to lead yourself, then you're recognizing that He is your Lord. That's what *acknowledge* means—just saying that He is holding the reins of your life instead of you yourself. And when you do that, it's like He tells the horse where to go and all you have to do is follow. If you acknowedge Him, He will direct your path. That's what He tells us in Proverbs."

Now her words came back to me, and I'd been praying that God would help us know where to go and what to do. But riding into that little place was a fearsome moment. All of a sudden we were there and we didn't know what we were going to do. I think we figured we'd see Pa's horse right off and there he'd be. But it didn't turn out that easy!

There were some horses tied up in front of a rundown building, but none I recognized. Voices came from inside. Zack and I looked at each other, sort of half-shrugged, then as if by unspoken agreement went slowly toward it, dismounted, and walked timidly inside.

It wasn't well-lit, but I could make out a table with men sitting around it. It looked like they were playing cards and a bottle of whiskey sat in the middle of the table. Most of them had glasses in front of them half filled with the amber liquid.

A couple of them glanced up when they saw us in the doorway, one leaned back in his chair and tilted his hat back on his head as if taking in the sight thoughtfully. One by one the rest of the card-playing company noticed us, and slowly the game came to a halt. There were some muttered comments and some snickering. "Well, what do we have here, boys?" said a voice, followed by a low laugh I didn't like the sound of.

I stepped farther into the room. "We're looking for our Pa," I said. "We wondered if any of you could help us. His name's Drum. Sometimes he goes by just that. Sometimes by Drum Hollister."

"Ya don't say? Yer Pa, eh?" mumbled another.

"You all the way out here alone, girl?" said another of the men, drawing out the word *alone* with a sinister tone.

"No, she ain't alone," piped up Zack, walking forward to join me. I know he was trying to sound brave, but it didn't work.

"Well, if that don't change everything now!" said one of the men. "You hear that, boys? She ain't alone! She's got this tough gunslinger here to protect her! Ha, ha, ha!"

"Please," I said, starting to get a little scared, "have you seen him?"

"Nobody sees nuthin' in these parts, girl! It ain't healthy to be stickin' yer nose into other folks' business."

"I ain't seen yer pa, girl, but I can't say I'd mind seein' you a mite closer!" said the man with the low laugh, rising up out of his chair and moving slowly toward us.

"You leave my sister be," said Zack, stepping forward and pulling me behind him. It was so brave of him. If we hadn't been in such a fix I'd have hugged him right there! I didn't know what he would do, because the man who was walking toward us was twice his size. But still Zack just stood there waiting for him, keeping me behind him.

I was about ready to bolt for the door and make a run for our horses when another voice interrupted the slowly approaching steps of the man's boots on the wood floor.

"Now just hold on, Barton," the new voice said. "Those kids don't mean no harm. Leave 'em be."

"You leave *me* be, Duke! Keep to yer own affairs an' let me have a little fun!"

"I've seen what your kind of fun leads to, Jed," said the other voice. "Especially when you've got whiskey in your belly. Now back off, I tell you, or you'll have to go up against me. And you don't want to do that. Just remember what happened last time you tried it!"

The man called Jed Barton stopped, threw several bitter curses over his shoulder toward the voice coming from the dark end of the room, then slunk back to his seat. I heard the sound of a man hoisting himself up from a table and walking toward us. Once I could see him halfway plain he didn't look much better than Jed Barton, but everything I'd heard from him up till now told me this fellow called Duke was our friend.

"Your pa was here, kids," he said. "Leastways I reckon it was your pa. Two, maybe three hours back. But not for long. He was trailing someone else—"

"Our Uncle Nick!" I said eagerly.

"Musta been. He just walked in, called out, 'Name's Drum. I'm lookin' for Nick Matthews. Any of you seen 'im?' and he was outta Dutch Flat in five minutes."

"What did you tell him?" Zack asked.

"That some of the boys there were playing a friendly game of cards with Matthews when ol' man Hatch wandered in and wanted to join in. Your uncle thought he saw an easy mark, and before it was over he near got his head blown clean off. That Hatch is a looney ol' cuss, and he lit outta here after your uncle, sending every one of us for cover. I don't know how your pa got wind of it so fast. I told him the last I seen of Matthews he was high-tailing it outta here in the direction of Blue Devil Diggings. Course, he mighta been heading for Gold Run. And Hatch was after him with pistol and rifle, both shooting at once!"

"So where do you think they are now?"

"Who can tell? But I know Hatch spends a lot of time in these here parts, and if he gets your uncle—or your Pa, for that matter—boxed into one of them canyons down that way, they'll never be able to outfox him. If he chases Matthews into Squires Canyon, your uncle might already be dead."

"Which way is it?" said Zack, already moving toward the door.

"Southeast of here, off the road to Gold Run," he answered. "You kids be careful, you hear?"

"Don't worry," I said. It was a stupid thing to say, cause I was terrified myself from what the man said. But I wasn't about to show it.

He followed us outside and watched us get back on Snowball and Blue Flame, still not believing, I think, that we were really going to chase off in the direction Pa and Uncle Nick had gone.

"Thanks, mister," I called out as we galloped out of Dutch Flat, and as I glanced back he was still standing there staring after us, his hat in his hand, scratching his head.

We ran our horses for only about three or four minutes when Zack, who was up ahead, signalled me to stop. I came up even with him and could tell he was listening for something.

"What is it?" I whispered.

"I thought I heard shots."

We listened again.

"There! Did you hear it?" he said. "There it is again!"

It sounded like a single shot from a rifle, followed by

some yelling I couldn't make out.

Slowly we started up again, then left the road off to the right and made our way up a grassy ridge, hoping we could get to a point where we could see further. Every once in a while we'd hear a voice call out and we moved toward the sounds. About a quarter mile off the road I spotted a horse up ahead of us, tied to a tree.

"Zack!" I said, speaking softly. "Look! Isn't that Jester?" I hadn't forgotten what that man Duke had said about Hatch killing Uncle Nick, and I was afraid if he found us sneaking up on him, he'd kill us too.

We got down off our horses and led them the rest of the way. It was Jester, so we knew Pa must be close by. We tied Snowball and Blue Flame, then kept going on foot. We were on the top of the ridge now, but still hadn't seen anyone.

The next time a voice shouted out it was so close it made me jump nearly out of my skin. I didn't know the voice, so it must have been the one Duke called Hatch.

"Ya might as well come on out, Matthews!" he shouted. "Ya got nowhere to hide!"

There was no reply.

"I know ya's in there, Matthews, ya cheatin' scum, an' I mean to fill ya full o' lead!"

I looked at Zack and he looked at me. Both pairs of our eyes were wide open, but we didn't dare utter a sound!

We crept forward on tiptoes, inch by inch, trying not to let the dry leaves and twigs crack under our feet.

All of a sudden I tripped, but halfway through my fall I felt a huge pair of arms grab around me. I started to scream, but just as suddenly a great hand clamped itself over my mouth and held it fast.

My heart was beating like a frightened rabbit's, but I looked up to see myself safe in the loveliest arms I could imagine.

"Pa!" I whispered as he released his hand, motioning

for silence with his finger over his mouth.

He looked us over, from one to the other, bewildered, then whispered, "What in tarnation are the two of you doing here?"

"Oh, Pa," I answered back, "it's my fault. I had something to tell you that I didn't think could wait even another day. But now with that man down there trying to shoot Uncle Nick, it doesn't seem so important now!"

"Yeah, you're right," he replied softly, glancing around again down the hill. "That Grizzly Hatch is just crazy enough to kill us all! Now listen to me, the two of you. I want you to go back the way you came. I don't know what horses you have or how you ever managed to find me out here in the middle of nowhere looking down on Squires Canyon. But I want you to go back and get on them horses and get out of here! If Hatch finds out there's four of us, he's likely to get crazier'n ever!"

"Maybe we could help, Pa," suggested Zack.

"There's nothing to do, boy! I been here two hours already myself. But he's got Nick down there trapped in that little cave at the end of the canyon. He may be crazy, but he ain't stupid. He's got Nick's horse, he's got a full view of the mouth of the cave. Nick can't make a move Hatch won't see, but I can't get a clean sight of Hatch. Now get outta here, I tell you!"

"But, Pa, maybe with four of us . . ." Zack said, letting his voice kinda trail off.

Pa turned toward him, slanting his eyebrows like he does when he's thinking. Then a slow smile spread over his mouth.

"You may just have something there, Son," he said after a minute. "You're right—now there's four of us! Only Hatch doesn't know it! If we can make him think it's still just me and Nick, we might be able to lure him away from that cave opening."

He stopped, thinking some more, glancing down toward where Hatch was watching the mine, then along the canyon, then back up along the ridge where the three of us sat. "Yeah," he muttered to himself, "it just might be crazy enough to work! Zack, my boy," he said, turning to Zack, "we'll try it! Now—do you think you can shoot my gun?"

"Yes, sir!" said Zack eagerly. "At Grizzly Hatch?"

"No, no! For heaven's sake, we don't want to kill anybody! We just want to give him something to think about. Okay, here's what we're going to do."

Five minutes later, after Pa was done explaining his plan, he stood up. "Now you wait till you hear me throw a rock over in your direction. That'll be the signal I'm in position up behind the cave. The minute you hear that rock, Zack, you start shooting. But aim right where I showed you! I don't want you accidently hitting him. We just want him to *think* we're firing at him! Then I'll yell at Hatch and try to get him to leave his position and come after me. At first he won't believe I'm Nick. But then you gotta call out something from up here. Doesn't matter what, just make your voice sound low enough to be mine. Say something like, 'Hey, Nick, how'd you get outta the cave?' If Nick'll just keep his fool trap shut till Hatch comes after me, this oughta work! Now, Corrie, when you see him climbing up the other side there—"

He pointed with his finger and I followed with my eyes.

"—when you see him coming after me, you know what to do."

I nodded.

"But remember, he's got to only think there's me and Nick!"

We both nodded our heads, then Pa went back up toward the horses to start making his way around and down the other side of the ridge to the back side of the cave, while we sat and waited. He said it could take him more than half an hour to get in place.

Silently we crouched where we were and waited. It seemed forever, and we never saw or heard anything more from Pa. Hatch yelled and shot at the cave a couple of times, but that was all. Finally we heard a small stone land not far away from us.

I looked at Zack. He looked at me, then he fired Pa's gun in the direction Pa told him to. Immediately when the echo had died away, we heard Pa's voice shouting from across the canyon, off to the right and behind the cave.

"Hey, Hatch, ya ol' buzzard!" he called out. "Thought you could keep me down, did ya? But ya didn't know that cave had another way out! Nice shootin' Drum! Give him another one so I can get outta here!"

Zack fired two more shots, then called out, trying to make his voice as deep as he could, "Come on, Nick, let's get outta here!"

Then for the first time I saw the man Pa had called Grizzly Hatch. He stood up from behind the rock where he'd been crouched. He looked toward the cave, then up in our direction, then back toward where Pa's voice was still badgering him.

I lay real low so he wouldn't see me, but I could see him looking back and forth and could tell Pa's plan had worked. He was getting confused and really thought Pa was Uncle Nick. He was stocky and squat, not particularly tall, though he looked strong. He wore a beard but not a long one like Alkali Jones'—it looked more like he just forgot to shave for a couple of weeks. His hair was dark black and so long it came down over his ears, and he wasn't wearing a hat. I was too far away to make out much about his features. But even from where I was watching, I was glad I couldn't see them. He looked mean.

"I'll join ye directly, Drum!" Pa was shouting. "Just as

soon as I work my way 'round the mouth of this canyon. You just keep that ol' coot Hatch where he is! The old weasel will never catch me!"

Zack fired again.

By this time Grizzly Hatch was downright in a boil, which is just how I figured Pa wanted him so he'd quit thinking about the cave. He didn't seem too worried about Zack's shooting in his direction—or maybe he was crazy like everyone said.

All at once he lit out from where he was, ran down the hill shouting out curses in the direction of the cave. It had been so quiet from inside it I began to wonder if something had gone wrong and Uncle Nick *had* disappeared somehow!

Zack fired again and shouted, "Hey, Hatch, come back here, ya varmint! Look out, Nick, he's comin' in your direction!"

Hatch was now scrambling up the other side of the canyon in Pa's direction, shooting and yelling wildly.

I stood up. Now it was my turn.

"If he comes back, you yell out a warning," I said to Zack. Then I began making my way down the hill toward the cave from the left, where Hatch couldn't see me even if he looked back. When I got to the floor of the canyon I looked around. By now I couldn't even hear anybody else, just an occasional shout in the distance. I ran across the flat ground and up the short incline to the cave on the other side.

"Uncle Nick . . . Uncle Nick!" I said into the black opening as loud as I dared. "You in there?"

All was quiet a moment. Then I heard, "Corrie . . . that you?"

"Yes! Come quick! Pa got the man away from the cave!"

I heard Uncle Nick's shuffling steps from inside, then he stepped into the light, holding his hand up to his squinting eyes. The sun was just setting behind the ridge and shining right toward us.

"How'd he manage that?" he asked.

"Come on, come on!" I said, grabbing his hand and pulling him along. "I'll tell you later. We gotta get outta here before he comes back!"

I ran back down the way I'd come, still trying to keep as quiet as I could, half pulling Uncle Nick behind me. Finally, he broke into a run himself and we made our way back up the hillside to where Zack still sat with Pa's gun.

"Why, dad-blamed if that don't beat all!" exclaimed Uncle Nick. "I been busted outta my prison by two kids! You know how to use that thing, Zack, my man?"

"Who do you think was doing all that shooting you heard a minute ago?" I said. "Zack used that gun just fine. But now we gotta get back to the horses to meet Pa!"

Zack and I quickly retraced our steps to where we'd left our horses with Jester. Still bewildered by the events of his sudden rescue, Nick shuffled along behind us, asking where Pa was. But we didn't stop to answer. I was still afraid of Hatch sneaking up behind us!

In a couple of minutes we reached the horses. We stopped, breathing hard. My panting was only half from running down to the cave and back up the hill. The other half was from still being afraid for Pa. Now *he* was out there with Grizzly Hatch after him!

It was a terrible wait. Every so often we'd hear an explosion of gunfire or some shouts. Once or twice I heard Pa yell out something too. Then everything was dead quiet for about five minutes.

Suddenly through the brush came a trampling sound making right for us. Without thinking, I grabbed at Uncle Nick and jumped behind him. But almost the next second Pa broke through the trees running toward us as fast as he could.

"Mount up!" he yelled the instant he saw us. "Let's get outta here!"

"But my horse, Drum! He ran my horse off!" said Uncle Nick, hesitating.

"Dad-blame ya, Nick! It's your own durn fault! Now get up there on Snowball! Having your skin in one piece is better'n a horse!"

"But that was a new saddle, Drum!"

"Get up there, Nick! Hatch is right behind me! I don't wanna tell ya again!"

"Snowball? Why, that's just a kid's horse!"

"After this little escapade, I ain't so sure you can handle anything more!" said Pa, clearly irritated. "Zack, you take Blue Flame, Corrie, you get up on Jester with me, and Nick, *you get on Snowball!*"

We all mounted up, though I could feel Uncle Nick almost pouting as he did, hardly noticing that Pa'd just saved his life by risking his own. Pa jumped up on Jester's back, then reached down and hauled me up in one quick motion. I held on to the saddlehorn as tight as I could, Pa reached around me with his arms, took the reins in one hand and squeezed me tight with the other, dug his heels in, and off we went. Zack on Blue Flame was right behind us, followed by Snowball and Uncle Nick.

As we sped along the ridge, I thought I heard shouts behind us. A couple of gunshots rang out. Pa'd been right. Hatch was right behind us. But dusk was settling in and Hatch was nowhere near his horse. In another minute or two I knew we were safe.

# CHAPTER 12

## AROUND THE CAMPFIRE

Pa lashed Jester's rump with the reins and the poor horse galloped for all he was worth.

I was bouncing up and down in front of Pa, and if his arms hadn't held me in on each side, I'd have wound up off in a ditch. Zack didn't have any trouble keeping up, but Uncle Nick fell a little ways behind, though Pa still kept pushing as hard as he could go.

Before I knew it we were speeding through a clearing, then we were on a wider road like before, and a small cluster of buildings came into sight. Pa later told me it was Gold Run, but at the time I was hanging on too hard to ask. A few men were standing outside the saloon watching us as we tore past. A couple of them yelled at us, but Pa just kept on going without even slowing down.

Just past the saloon he turned left onto another road, and in less than a minute we were past the little collection of shacks and racing again through the brush and trees and woods.

After about ten more minutes, Pa finally slowed the pace, though he still couldn't let Jester stop and walk. At last, after another five minutes, he did stop.

By now it was night. The moon was shining on the water as it passed in front of us, but even without the light, I'd have known we had reached a river from the rushing sound.

"This here's the ford across the North Fork of the American," Pa said.

Over the sounds of the river, I could hear the heaving of all three horses. "Once Hatch tracks us to Gold Run and them fellas at the saloon tell him which way we was goin', this is right where he'll figure we're headin'."

"We gonna cross that river, Pa?" asked Zack.

"Naw, but we're gonna make Hatch think we did. Come on, follow me."

Pa urged Jester forward toward the water, then stopped. "No, wait. We've gotta leave him a clue to find—somethin' he'll recognize as ours, somethin' that'll make him know we came by here and went on—"

He stopped, thinking, looking around at all of us. Then he said, "Nick, gimme that hat o' yours."

"Not my hat, Drum!"

"You got us into this mess! Now do I hafta take it from you, or are you gonna give it to me?"

Silently Uncle Nick took his hat off his head and handed it to Pa. "He'll know this, all right," said Pa. "He came near shootin' a hole clean through it!" He tossed the hat down a couple of feet from the water's edge, then continued out into the river.

"It's shallow all the way across," he said to me. "Even in the dark, these horses won't have a problem. But we ain't goin' all the way across."

"Why not, Pa?" I asked.

"Cause we're headin' south, Corrie. Can't you tell? Home's back behind us. But I don't want that ol' cuss Hatch findin' out where our claim is. I heard o' him for years, and I heard he's a bad 'un. I don't think he knows who we are or where we're from, and I wanna keep it that way! So we'll make him think we're headin' down to Indian Hill, then we'll double back up by Grass Valley and head home that way."

We walked the horses twenty feet out into the river, then he pulled Jester's head around and began leading him downstream to the right. Zack and Uncle Nick followed. Slowly we made our way, following the shoreline, till we were well out of sight of the place where Pa'd thrown Uncle Nick's hat. Still he kept leading the way down the river for ten more minutes. I could hear louder sounds from the river up ahead when Pa finally turned again toward the bank. "Hear them rapids up ahead, Corrie?" he said. "Time for us to get back on dry land and head back north. I don't think Hatch can track us now!"

"You really think he'd try to follow us, Pa?"

"Fellas like him don't forget when they've been made a fool of! I still gotta find out from Nick what went on back in Dutch Flat, but yeah, I think Hatch'll do his blamedest to find us. I don't doubt he'll be askin' around in Dutch Flat an' Gold Run tonight, an' it won't be long before he's standin' at that ford back there, cursin' to himself as he's holdin' Nick's hat, an' vowin' revenge. Let's just hope he's mad enough to ride across the river an' just keep on goin'!"

"We gonna ride all the way home tonight, Pa?" I asked.

"From where we are now, Corrie," he answered, "with no trail to follow for the next three or four miles, in the dark with only half a moon, we're likely three hours from Miracle."

"Zack and me brought some food, Pa. And blankets."

"And the young' uns?"

"They're with Mrs. Parrish."

"Then maybe it'd be best for us to find some place to bed down for the night. But we better get up past Grass Valley . . . maybe near Nevada City somewhere. Then we'll be outta Hatch's territory."

We rode on in silence for a while, and I leaned back

against Pa's chest. I felt so safe and protected with him behind me and his arms around me. Even if he had decided to go straight back to Miracle, I could have ridden with him like that forever! By now nothing could have been further from my mind than what had sent me and Zack after Pa in the first place.

———

A couple of hours later the four of us were sitting around a small fire, munching on the biscuits, dried venison, and apples Zack and I had brought along.

"Wish we had some coffee," said Uncle Nick.

I half expected Pa to make some sour reply. He hadn't been any too nice to Nick the whole time, though I suppose he was right about Uncle Nick getting us into the tight spot we'd been in. But once he had the fire going and I pulled out the food we'd brought, Pa seemed to relax a little.

"Yeah, coffee and some o' them beans ol' Grimly used to make," replied Pa. "That'd be 'bout as good as it gets. How that ol' coot could get so much from a pot o' beans and an old worn out ham-hock, I could never figure."

"Them wasn't all bad times, ya gotta admit—eh Drum?"

Pa half smiled as he stared into the flickering fire. Maybe it was just the dance of the light over his forehead and eyebrows, but a look came over his face that I had never seen before. It was a faraway look. All at once he seemed to be someplace else.

"Yeah, they had some good moments," said Pa after a spell. His voice sounded the way his eyes looked.

"An' you recollect his flapjacks?" Uncle Nick went on. "Can't ya just smell 'em? After a hard afternoon's riding—"

"Likely runnin' from a posse!" added Pa with a little laugh, but not taking his eyes off the fire.

Uncle Nick laughed, too. "Yeah, an' then beddin' down for the night someplace in the hills and sleepin' so hard nothin' could wake ya, till that smell o' his cakes on the griddle worked its way into yer nose, and suddenly you was awake an' the sun was halfway up the sky, an' it was time to eat and get in the saddle again!"

Pa smiled, but said nothing. Zack and I didn't want to say anything. We were both listening to them reminisce about the old days. But after a while I found myself as fascinated with watching Pa's face as listening to his voice.

The light from the flames of the fire seemed to bring different things to my mind as I watched. One moment I saw the hard, stern man I'd been afraid of when I first laid eyes on him that day outside the Gold Nugget in Miracle Springs. The slight squint of his eyes and just the hint of an indentation below his cheekbones made him look cold, as if he didn't care much about feelings. But then when the light hit more full, and I could see *into* his eyes, then all at once I saw that maybe he had felt things *too* much.

Maybe the severe look was really a soberness that had come from years of feeling things so deeply that he tried to keep his face from showing what was going on inside. I thought I could see a tiredness in the eyes, too—a weariness from the unsettled life of being on the run for so long. And now here he was again having to hide from someone who was after them, and because of Uncle Nick, just like before.

It was probably silly of me to sit staring at my own Pa, trying to figure out things like that. But ever since I'd started keeping a journal, I found myself thinking more and more about the inside of people and experiences instead of just the outside. And so I couldn't help doing that when I looked at Pa's face and heard him talk about when he and Nick rode together.

It was a good face, I thought—even with two or three days' whiskers. Rugged, I suppose, but I wouldn't call it craggy or sharp. The cheekbones, the chin, the nose were all hard-edged. Pa didn't have any extra fat on him, although his shoulders were big and he wasn't lean. And his dark brown hair coming down just over his ears and spilling down his sideburns onto his cheeks, with just a little bit of gray showing here and there—all put together, I liked Pa's looks. He showed himself as a man that could take care of things. Yet the few times we'd talked seriously, and the time when he'd first told me about leaving the East, there was an earnest tone in his voice that showed he was sensitive, too. Pa looked like the kind of man who wouldn't be out of place in either a gunfight or a quiet talk with a woman.

I found my thoughts drifting to Mrs. Parrish. I wished she could see the deep look in Pa's eyes that I was seeing right then. I wanted her to know what a fine man Pa was, even though he'd had a past life that was different from her Rev. Rutledge. I wanted her to be able to see the feelings that were beneath the hard shell that Pa showed to the rest of the world. They were certainly getting along better now than at first, but I wanted them to become friends. Well, maybe someday . . .

"What are you thinking about, Pa?" I said finally, not planning to say it and almost surprised at the words when I heard them.

For a long moment Pa just kept looking into the fire. Then he took a deep sigh, pulled his gaze off the orange and red coals, and looked over at me. "I was thinkin' about your ma, Corrie," he said, then gave me a little smile. Even in the firelight, his eyes were bright with tears. I smiled back.

Then all at once he turned to Uncle Nick and said, "Now, Nick, I wanna know just what the devil happened back there in Dutch Flat to get Hatch so all-fired hot to put a slug through you!"

Uncle Nick laughed. "It was a card game," he answered.

"Somehow I ain't surprised," said Pa.

"But ya shoulda seen it, Drum! It was the perfect set-up! I couldn't lose!"

"Except that you were settin' up to fleece Grizzly Hatch! Ain't you heard of him?"

"Yeah, but I never believe half the things I hear."

"Well you shoulda believed it in his case! So tell me what happened."

"Well, Barton was dealin', and he called five card stud. I had the seven of clubs underneath, an' my first up card was the seven of hearts. Well, nobody else had much of anythin', and when the seven of diamonds fell down on my pile for my fourth card, showin' just a measly pair o' sevens, I was high man. Now Hatch, meanwhile, had all spades but nothing else. But he was startin' to put some good-sized money in the pot, an' when the fifth card came his eyes flashed, an' he threw in all he had. That's when I knew he didn't know nothin' 'bout that declarin' rule—you heard of it, ain't ya?"

"Yeah, I heard somethin' about it," answered Pa, "but I ain't never seen no game run that way. I heard there's talk of takin' it outta the rulebook."

"Well, they ain't taken it out yet," said Uncle Nick. "An' so ya see, Hatch had to figure he had me cold. The second his last spade came up, he knew he had his flush and he had to figure me for three sevens at most. He had me an' he bet the pot. But *I* knew I had *him*! My only risk was whether they had a Hoyle around. So I called him, an' the pot musta been two or three hundred. His eyes lit up an' he turned over his last spade, and reached out to scoop in the dough.

" 'Just a minute, Hatch,' I said. 'Far as I can tell, you got nothin' that can go up against my three sevens. That pot's mine.'

" 'What're ya tryin' to pull, Matthews?' says Hatch. 'Open yer fool eyes! I got me a flush.'

" 'I can see that,' I said, 'but in this game, three of a kind beats a flush.'

"By this time Hatch was gettin' plenty riled.

" 'Anybody got a book o' Hoyle around here?' I asked. The feller that runs the place said he did. He went behind the counter, got the book, gave it to me, and I found the spot where the special poker rules was discussed. I read it real slow an' deliberate-like: 'In five or seven card stud poker, the flush and the straight are not played unless it is declared in advance by the dealer.'

"Everybody's mouths fell open, an' Barton grabbed the book outta my hand mutterin' that he hadn't never heard o' that rule. But then when Hatch asked him what it said— that fool Hatch can't read a word himself—after a couple seconds Barton just said, 'I'm afraid he's got you dead to rights, Grizzly. That's what the book says.'

" 'An' I didn't hear no one declare it,' I said. 'So I reckon my three sevens is high after all.' "

"And what happened to the pot?" asked Pa.

"Well, it was no secret now that the game was over. I put the money in my saddlebag an' left."

"So now Hatch has his money back, your money, *and* your horse! When are you gonna learn, Nick, that it never pays? And now you got him tryin' to put a bullet in yer hide besides! You don't need that kind of trouble! You're just gonna land us back into the same kind of fix we were in back in New York if you don't cut out that kind of nonsense!"

Uncle Nick fell into one of his quiet, sulking moods.

"It's just a good thing these kids showed up when they did! If it hadn't been for them, Nick, you'd be a dead man by now! There was nothing I coulda done to get to Hatch the way he was positioned, and if he'd kept firin' into that cave, he'd have got you sooner or later."

Pa paused, then looked over at me.

"By the way, you ain't told me why you two *did* come,

Corrie. And how in tarnation'd ya find us, anyway?"

Suddenly I remembered!

"Oh, Pa, I forgot!" I exclaimed. "Everything started happening so fast after we got to Dutch Flat and those men said you were in trouble. I plumb forgot what I had to tell you!"

"Well, what is it, girl, that's so all-fired important you had to track me all over the country to tell me?"

"It's him, Pa! Buck Krebbs! I saw him in San Francisco!"

A cloud instantly spread over Pa's face that neither the darkness nor the flickering of the dying fire could hide.

"You *saw* him. Is that all?" he asked solemnly.

"No, Pa. He saw me too, and he followed me and Mrs. Parrish to our hotel, and then when I was alone he sneaked up and grabbed me again, like up by the mine, and I think he was going to hurt me, but I got away and ran from him!"

By this time Pa was real serious and staring intently at me.

"Go on, Corrie," he said. "Tell me everything."

"I got away from him. I ran all around through the streets and got back to the hotel."

"Where was the Parrish woman?"

"She was at her meeting, Pa. It wasn't her fault. Please don't be angry with her! She took real good care of me, and she told me to stay in the room till she got back. It was my own doing, going out alone like that."

Pa nodded.

"But, Pa, after I got away from him, he ran down the street after me and was yelling all sorts of awful things, saying he was going to get you and the money, even if he had to kill us all to do it! I was so scared, Pa. I thought he might be fixing to come to Miracle right then! He sounded so evil, and I thought that seeing me again must have put it into his mind to come back here. And I just had to warn you, Pa!"

I stopped, thinking I was going to start crying. But I forced myself to hold it in.

Pa looked over at me. He knew what I was feeling. He reached out, placed his big hand on mine and gave it a squeeze.

"Everything's gonna be fine, Corrie Belle," he said. "Don't you worry none. Buck Krebbs ain't gonna kill nobody."

"But the money, Pa! He's not gonna stop till he gets the money."

"There ain't no money, Corrie."

"But how we gonna convince that loco fool Krebbs o' that?" said Uncle Nick.

Pa sighed again. "All the more reason, Nick," he said finally, "for you to keep outta trouble with characters like Hatch. We ain't out from behind the trouble from the East that keeps on houndin' us, an' it's gonna take all we can do to get rid of it once an' for all."

Again everyone got quiet. Pa stood and grabbed up some more of the wood we'd gathered and threw it on the fire. Then he came back and sat down, staring into the flames again. But this time I didn't see a faraway look. Instead it was a look of worry, concern, like he was thinking about what he ought to do.

The next words out of his mouth caused *me* concern.

"Nope, this ain't no proper place to raise no kids." He said it quietly, as if he were thinking out loud. "Nope, it sure ain't," he repeated. "Not for a man like me, alone, the law after me from the East, crazy men trailin' me lookin' to put a piece o' lead in me. No place at all! My kids in danger . . ."

His voice trailed away. I knew he was blaming himself.

"Pa," I said, "as long as we're together, everything'll be fine in the end, won't it?"

"I don't know, Corrie," he said. "It just seems I ain't no

fit pa to take care o' five kids by myself. Buck Krebbs tryin'
to hurt you, bullets flyin' outta Hatch's gun. You an' Zack
in danger there today! That ain't no way to run a family!
And me ridin' off this mornin', leavin' Zack an' the
young'uns alone. What if Krebbs'd shown up then? No, I
tell ya, things ain't right the way they are! I can't let it keep
bein' this way. You kids need a proper bringin' up! And I
gotta do something to get you one!''

"We're happy being with you, Pa!" I said, but I don't
think he was listening. He stood up again and walked away.
If I had learned anything about Pa, I knew he was thinking
real hard.

Pretty soon Zack and I lay down on the softest piece of
ground we could find near the fire and pulled the blankets
over us. If it hadn't been for the last bit of the talking, this
would have been one of the most pleasant nights to remember since we came to California. It was so peaceful lying
there, looking up into the black sky, the faint crackling of
the fire in our ears, and the sounds of the crickets and other
creatures of the woods.

After a while Uncle Nick pulled his harmonica out of his
pocket and started playing softly. I was glad he hadn't put
*it* in his saddlebag! What a perfect way it was to go to sleep.
I could hardly believe this day had started with Mrs. Parrish
and Rev. Rutledge in Auburn!

Before long I heard Zack's breathing change, and I knew
he was asleep. The last thing I remember was wondering
what Pa could mean to do to get us what he called a proper
upbringing. I said a prayer for him, wherever he was right
then, out alone walking, and asked God to help him do the
right thing.

# CHAPTER 13

## PA'S SURPRISE DECISION

When we got home the next morning, the trouble with Grizzly Hatch died down, and things pretty much went back to normal.

Uncle Nick was upset about losing his horse, and every once in a while he would start muttering about going to get it away from Hatch. But then Pa would remind him what got him into trouble in the first place, ending by saying that if he tried to find Hatch, he'd shoot Uncle Nick himself first.

Everything got back to normal, that is, except Pa. I knew he was thinking about something serious. He'd been different ever since the night around the campfire when he'd gotten up and walked off. Riding home the next day he was quiet, and he'd been like that ever since.

Every so often he'd say something—more to himself than to any of us—like what he'd said that night, about this being no way to bring up a family. But we were all afraid to ask him what he meant or what he was fixing to do. I know I couldn't help wondering if he was thinking again about sending us kids back East someplace. In my heart I knew Pa would never do it, but I couldn't help fearing some terrible change. Sometimes he'd go off alone in the woods and just sit, and once I came upon him alone in the barn. He was sitting there on a bale of straw, holding my picture of Ma in his hand, like he was asking *her* what to do.

When he glanced up at me, I saw one tear roll down his cheek. In that moment, suddenly I wasn't worried about myself any more, but I hurt for Pa. All at once I realized how hard this decision must be for him—whatever it was about. Maybe he was thinking about packing us all up— him and us together—and leaving Miracle Springs!

That would sure be hard enough on him to make him shed a few tears, because I know he loved this place and the mine. He'd built a new life here, and now he had his family again, and a good claim. Yet there was Hatch and Buck Krebbs and always the danger of something out of his past catching up with him. And Uncle Nick was still wild enough to get Pa and the rest of us into a scrape now and then.

Maybe Pa was right that this wasn't a proper place to bring up five kids. What if he was thinking about taking us kids and going someplace else, and leaving Uncle Nick behind? Most of the trouble had Uncle Nick's name on it, one way or the other. Even the trouble with Buck Krebbs and whatever else might follow them from the East had all started from Pa's trying to help his wife's younger brother.

But I knew that even though he sometimes treated him like a kid, Pa really loved Uncle Nick. They'd been through all kinds of hardship together, and had been partners together, and sometimes when working at the mine they'd have a good laugh over something. They were friends too.

That would be a hard decision, if he was considering splitting up and leaving. And it was something he might be thinking he had to talk to Ma about, even if all he had left was that picture. After all, Uncle Nick was her brother, and she had loved him too.

All this was just nothing more than speculation in my own mind. I didn't talk to anyone about it. We were all walking around softly, not wanting to do anything to get Pa upset. But many things ran through my mind—like Pa sending us away, or him going away someplace else with us, or making Uncle Nick leave, or changing all our names from Hollister to something else so nobody could find us. I even feared that one day we'd wake up and find Pa himself gone and never hear from him again. I suppose I knew Pa would never do that again. But sometimes fears and hurts come back out of the past to grab at me and make me think things I don't want to think.

Then one day all the fears seemed to come true. I woke up one morning, and Pa was gone.

I was always the first of us five kids awake. I'd get up and go outside for a walk, or I'd read in one of the books Mrs. Parrish had brought me from her trips to Sacramento, or I'd write in my journal. About half the time Pa was up before me, sometimes sitting in front of the fire in the other room in the cabin, sometimes out in the barn or up at the mine.

But on this particular morning, the instant I opened my eyes, I had a feeling that something was different. I got up quickly. Pa wasn't anywhere in the cabin and there was no fire started. With a growing feeling of dread I jammed my bare feet into my boots and ran outside and to the barn. Jester was gone, along with Pa's best saddle.

Panic began to seize me, and as I ran out of the barn and up toward the mine I was starting to cry, but I didn't want to stop and give in to it. I didn't expect to find Pa at the mine, but I had to look everywhere. He hadn't said a word about needing to go anywhere, and now he was gone.

If I had stopped to think about it all reasonably, I'd have trusted Pa, but Mrs. Parrish says that people sometimes think with their hearts instead of their heads. And this was one of those times. As I walked slowly back to the barn I was crying, probably more because of the things *I'd* been wondering than any real fear that Pa had left us. But I wanted to get my crying done and my tears used up before I saw the other kids or Uncle Nick. I didn't want to try to explain to them how worried I was about what Pa might be fixing to do.

Pa came back about the middle of the afternoon. He didn't act different or tell us where he'd been right off. But the second he rode up and got down off his horse, I could tell from his eyes that something had happened. His smile and hug were enough to make all my fears vanish—for right then, at least. It was a smile that seemed to still have some of the same anguish in it that I'd seen in his eyes when he was gazing at the picture of Ma. But at least it was a smile, and I was grateful.

It seemed to say that he'd come to some decision. I didn't know what it might be, but he was more like himself after that and he started talking again to us. I think everybody, even Uncle Nick, was relieved. I hoped by and by he'd tell us what had brought on the change.

But he didn't, and things settled back into their old routine. The other four kids seemed to forget all about Pa's temporary moodiness, and sometimes I wondered if Uncle Nick ever paid much attention to those kinds of things.

But I kept watching Pa, hoping maybe he'd tell me, even if he didn't want to tell everybody. And he kept behaving strangely every now and then, going to town and not telling what for, and once riding all the way to Marysville.

"Where've you been, Pa?" I asked him when he got back. It was late in the day and he'd been gone since morning, and his horse was bushed from hard riding.

"Marysville."

"What for? I never heard you talk of knowing anybody there," I said.

"I had to see your newspaper feller, Singleton."

"Why him, Pa?"

"I had some business with him, that's all."

And no matter what I did, I couldn't pry out of him what he was up to.

But he was up to something, I was sure of it. He went into Miracle more often too, and started paying more attention to the *Gazette* every week than he ever had before, though why the sudden interest in Mr. Singleton and his paper I didn't have a clue.

Most curious of all was my suspicion that he went to see Mrs. Parrish some of the times he rode into Miracle. I found out he'd been by her office by accident once when I was talking to her.

I mentioned it to Pa casually. "Mrs. Parrish said you paid a call on her," I said, to see if he'd say something. But he replied gruffly, "Weren't no *call* on the lady. We just had some things to talk over 'bout the school committee, that's all."

And then a few days later, Pa was sitting by the fire in the evening looking through a Sacramento paper. I couldn't figure any way he'd have gotten his hands on it except from Mrs. Parrish. More and more I just kept noticing things about his behavior I couldn't account for.

Then all of a sudden his interest in newspapers stopped, and so did his rides into town. I would have forgotten about everything, except that about a month later, as the weather was turning cold, all at once his peculiar habits returned. Now all of a sudden he took an unlikely interest in the mail delivery. Every two weeks, regular as clockwork, he'd ride in to the new General Store where the mail came every other Friday, and he'd wait for it.

We'd never had any mail that I could recall. Who'd send us anything? Yet there was Pa waiting for that stage every Friday when it was due!

Finally, in the later fall, as we were thinking about looking forward to our second Christmas in California, whatever Pa'd been waiting for must've come on the stage. That particular Friday he came home from Miracle with a different look on his face—not exactly a smile, and not even a "happy" look, but just a different look, with a light in his eyes, like something good was about to happen.

That evening, I finally got answers to all my questions about the peculiar goings-on for the last two months. Pa sat us all down, Uncle Nick too, took a big deep breath, then told us he had some real important news to tell us. Suddenly, I found myself thinking about all those same fears I'd had after the Grizzly Hatch affair. But I kept still and Pa started talking.

"Well, I reckon you all think I been actin' mighty ornery these last coupla months. An' I'm sorry if I ain't been too cheerful, but I had a heap o' things on my mind." He stopped, took in another breath, then started up again.

"I been thinkin' a lot about this life o' ours here. An' I guess we got a parcel o' things to be thankful for. But I still can't help thinkin' it ain't no way for a family to live. Why, with varmints like Grizzly Hatch wantin' to take their piece outta our hides, and with Buck Krebbs sneakin' around wantin' to put a slug into me an' Nick and tryin' to hurt Corrie, and with us still havin' to wonder every day 'bout the law catchin' up with us from the East an' runnin' us to the pokey—why, it ain't no life for kids! Things are still too rough out here in the West, an' I ain't no sort o' man who can make a good life for the five o' you like things are now."

It sounded like he was getting ready to say something awful, like that we shouldn't be together, and I couldn't keep from interrupting him.

"We don't mind it, Pa!" I said. "As long as we're with you, everything's gonna—"

"Let me finish, Corrie," said Pa, almost sternly. I sat back in my chair and waited for what would come next.

"I tell ya, there's still too much goin' on here, and I can't tell what might happen. What'd you all do if Krebbs *did* kill me? Then what?"

It was terrible to hear Pa talk like this! I looked at all the others and they were staring at him with their eyes wide open.

"I can't take the chance of you bein' left alone again," Pa went on. "I gotta do somethin' to protect you young'uns. I just can't take the chance no longer of trying to do what I can't do myself."

I couldn't help breaking into his talk again. "Mrs. Parrish'd take care of us, Pa," I said, "if something happened to you or Uncle Nick. There's nothing to worry so much about, Pa! And Zack and me, we're practically old enough to take care of the young'uns!"

"Hush, Corrie, let me have my say! This ain't easy for me neither. Now whatever you say may be true, but it ain't enough. Mrs. Parrish ain't kin, an' out here in the West, kin is what matters most. An' you an' Zack are a mighty fine young woman an' young man, I gotta admit that. But this here's the West, and things are different. If I was gone, you'd need help to get by—family kind o' help."

He stopped again and took a deep breath. He seemed getting ready for what he'd been trying to tell us all along.

"Well, ever since that Hatch deal, and Corrie tellin' me about Buck Krebbs tryin' to get her and threatenin' us, I realized I needed help with you kids. I ain't no good as a ma to you. Lord knows Corrie's a fine cook and all, but by the time school starts up in Miracle, she ain't gonna have so much time, and you younger ones is gonna need more tendin' especially when Corrie gets older. Besides that, I can't help worryin' about what might happen some day if our past catches up with me an' Nick.

"So a while back I made myself what folks call a resolution, that I was gonna do my best to fix it so you wouldn't ever be alone, no matter what might happen, and so you'd have someone to fix your meals an' help you better'n a man like me is able to.

"It wasn't an easy decision to make, and I spent a lot o' time talkin' to your Ma about it, though I don't reckon folks like Rev. Rutledge'd take much stock in prayers prayed like that to someone else! But I can't help what he might think, my Aggie's the one this here decision concerns more'n anybody else, and somehow I had to know what she'd think of what I'm doin'. An' so in the end what I decided was that you kids need a woman around here. I gotta see about gettin' me a new wife. And so that's what I'm fixin' to do."

# CHAPTER 14

# THE LETTER

The moment the words "a new wife" were out of Pa's mouth, I felt a rush of warmth race into me. I'd never actually thought such a thing could be possible, knowing how Pa had felt about Mrs. Parrish. But they had been getting friendlier, and . . . well, it just seemed too good to be true!

The very idea of her as . . . as . . . the idea was just too wonderful to think about! Both my hands went to my cheeks in shocked reaction. My face was flamed, and in my brain already little bells were going off—wedding bells! I hardly stopped in that passing moment of bliss to remember Rev. Rutledge, and the look I had seen on his face when he looked at Mrs. Parrish. And I didn't hear too well what Pa said next, I was too busy thinking about Mrs. Parrish.

Finally I became aware of Pa's voice again. ". . . so you see, that's why all the fuss with the newspapers, I had to investigate, you know, and find just the right woman. It's always a gamble, because you can't see no picture and you don't know if they're tellin' you the whole truth about themselves. But you gotta do the best you can and hope things'll turn out okay.

"Well, I looked in them papers and sent some letters out to an agency in the East that said they'd advertise for me what I was lookin' for in a woman, and I read about some women whose names were in that Sacramento paper Mrs. Parrish was kind enough to get for me, but none of them seemed quite right. I told 'em not to put my name in any paper within five hundred miles of New York. And, well, this here's finally my answer. I already wrote her back and I told her about the trouble with the law, but that I was a decent man. I don't reckon we'll hear back from her for a couple of months, but after that, if she's still of a mind to come, I figure it'll be the best thing fer all of us."

Pa pulled a white envelope out of his pocket and held it up for us to see. It was rumpled. I could tell he'd read it two or three times already.

Then Pa started to read the letter out loud to us:

Dear Mr. Drummond Hollister,

My name is Katie Morgan. I am from southern Virginia, as you will see from the address on my letter. I saw your advertisement in the newspaper from Raleigh south of here. I have never been married. I am thirty years old and now live with my younger sister. But she is to be married in two months. She and I have lived with an elderly aunt and uncle for twenty years, since our parents were killed in the Black Hawk War in 1832. Our uncle has not been well recently and died three months ago. Our aunt is returning to New York to live the rest of her days with another aunt, her sister. With my sister marrying, I feel it is time for me to seek a new life for myself.

I have not had many adventures in my life, though eight years ago a young entrepreneur (that's what he called himself) from New York asked me to marry him and come to live in the big city. That would have been an adventure, but I felt it my duty to remain with my aunt and uncle. Now, however, I feel perhaps the time for my life's adventure has come. My parents dreamed of settling in the West, but after they were killed by Chief Black Hawk's followers, my sister and I were sent back to Virginia. Now perhaps it is time to realize their hope, and mine. I have dreamed of travelling to California ever since 1849.

I am not beautiful, but neither am I altogether plain. I am quite short, with brown hair, a good complexion, and rather stocky build. I am not accustomed to niceties, for we have never had money to spare. I like children, and animals. I know hard work and do not mind it. I am anxious enough to come to California that I will spend the little I have saved to get me there. I have saved only about half the $450, however, required to make the sea voyage by way of Panama. If you would like to see me, and would send the rest of what I need to complete the trip to Sacramento, I will stay for a month. You do not need to marry me if you do not care to. I am determined not to be a spinster, and in California I do not doubt I will be able to find a suitable man. I am not overbearing, but neither am I timid—or so my aunt has always told me.

I would like to know about your children. Your advertisement said you also live with your wife's brother? And of course, I am most interested in you. I hope to hear from you soon.

Very truly yours,
Kathryn Hubbard Morgan.

The room was silent a minute.

I had my own thoughts and emotions swimming around inside my brain trying to get over the shock of Pa getting married again—and to a stranger.

Uncle Nick had got over his initial whooping and hollering and was now sitting quietly, staring down at the floor. I reckon he was thinking about Ma, because he finally said, "It don't hardly seem like the right way of treatin' the memory of my sister, Drum, writin' off for some mail-order bride you never seen!"

Pa took in a deep breath, as if the words stung him a bit. A quick flash of pain went across his face, but it was lost as he answered Uncle Nick.

"I know what you're thinkin', Nick. I been strugglin' with the same thing for weeks an' weeks. But I gotta think this is what Aggie'd want."

He stopped, took another lungful of air, then added, "It's for her kids too, Nick—mine *and* Aggie's—that I'm doin' it. I gotta see to the raisin' of *her* kids—and I gotta do somethin' better'n what you and me can give 'em!"

Again it was quiet and nobody said anything for a long time.

"Will we have to call her Ma, Pa?" asked Becky after a spell.

There was such an innocent worry in her voice. But Pa didn't chuckle or even crack a smile. He just got up, went over and picked Becky up in his great big arms and looked into her face. Then he smiled, trying to put her mind at ease.

"You'll always have just one Ma, Becky, and nobody's gonna ever take her place. You'll call her Miss Morgan at first, and then later maybe Mrs. Hollister, or Miss Kathryn. I don't rightly know, Becky. Maybe you'll even find you like havin' another woman about the place, kinda like an aunt or somethin'. But I doubt any of you'll ever call her Ma."

"What'll she be like, Pa?"

"That I don't know, Becky! That's somethin' we're all gonna just have to wait to find out."

# CHAPTER 15

## SCHOOL

One of the most important things about to happen in Miracle Springs during this time, at least as far as the kids were concerned, was the opening of the Miracle Springs school.

Pa and Mrs. Parrish and the school committee had met quite a few times, and I'd been hopeful about Pa and Mrs. Parrish as a result of working like that together and seeing each other more regularly.

Pa did go to her house pretty often, and sometimes he'd take me, and it got so they were downright friendly to each other. Mrs. Parrish'd greet Pa with a smile and say, "How are you today, Mr. Hollister?" and Pa'd tell her something about the mine or what we kids had been up to while he handed her his coat and hat.

Of course most of the time Mrs. Shaw and the Dewaters were there. Rev. Rutledge was *always* there, and looking so at home and comfortable you'd think he lived there. He was always the first to come and last to go.

Nobody said anything about it, but I got the notion that people noticed his being with her so much and wondered when the new church was gonna have a pastor's wife to go with the new hymnbooks and freshly painted walls. I wouldn't've *dared* ask her something like that, but I had the idea Mrs. Parrish might be wondering the same thing.

That wasn't the kind of thing that Pa and I talked about, but I know it crossed his mind now and then too. Once, coming home from town, he was quiet most of the way, and then finally, like he'd been thinking about them all the way since the meeting, he all of a sudden said, "Yep . . . she's a fine woman, that Parrish lady! I may have been wrong about her, Corrie. Ol' Rutledge's a lucky fella—the two o' them's gonna be a mighty fine thing for this town, though I never thought I'd be sayin' such a thing."

I was dying inside to ask him more of what he meant, but by then we were just coming around the bend and the cabin came into sight, and it was too late. Another meeting was scheduled the following week. Pa was taking me almost every time.

I don't know if his agitation had anything to do with what he'd said to me in the wagon, but when time for that next meeting came round he seemed nervous the whole day and quit work at the mine early so he could wash and spruce up.

When he and I got into the wagon later in the afternoon to go to town, he looked cleaner than I'd remembered seeing him in months—his hair washed and combed back, with a clean shirt and pair of trousers. I looked at him, smiled, and said, "You look real fine, Pa."

"Well, a man's gotta scrape the dirt off hisself some-time," he mumbled. "I just didn't figure I oughta be trackin' it into Mrs. Parrish's place, that's all."

Pa'd gotten ready so soon that we left earlier than we needed to. When we got to Mrs. Parrish's, we were the first ones there, even before Rev. Rutledge. But Mrs. Parrish didn't act at all surprised to see us, and invited us in and had us sit down in her parlor and gave Pa coffee while she drank a cup of tea.

For the first time I can remember, the two grown-ups I

cared most about in the whole world were acting friendly toward each other. After a while Pa got to feeling at ease and told her some things about him and Uncle Nick. Mrs. Parrish laughed and laughed, and I found myself wishing there wouldn't be a school meeting at all.

But it had to come to an end by and by. Pretty soon a knock came on the door, and when Mrs. Parrish rose to answer it, into the house walked Rev. Rutledge. He seemed a bit taken off guard to find us there, because he started to say something quiet to Mrs. Parrish after she closed the door behind him, but stopped when she walked back into the parlor. When he glanced up and saw Pa, a look of surprise passed over his face, but it was quickly replaced by a smile as he walked forward and shook Pa's hand.

Pa stood and greeted him cordially. They were on fine terms with each other by this time. But on Pa's face, too, I saw a brief look as he rose—his face did not show surprise, but rather disappointment. I glanced over at Mrs. Parrish as she watched the two men shake hands from the entryway. Her eyes were fixed on Pa instead of the minister.

Maybe Pa's growing friendship with Mrs. Parrish was why his letter from Katie Morgan took me so by surprise. I figured I was getting old enough to have him think of me as a grown-up, and I did most of the mothering for the young'uns already. As for the rest, why couldn't he hire someone to do other stuff, or ask Mrs. Parrish to look in on us every once in a while?

But I knew what he'd say to those notions—that I would soon be grown and married, and he'd still have the young'uns to take care of, that Mrs. Parrish had her own business and the affairs of the church to tend to, and that she was likely gonna be the minister's wife before long, and didn't have time to worry about us. And then he'd say that getting a new wife was the only decent solution.

Maybe he was right, but it would take some gettin' used to on my part.

In the meantime, during the first week of October Pa came home from town one day with the news that Mrs. Parrish'd gotten a reply back from one of the letters they'd sent out to a lady about being the new Miracle Springs schoolteacher.

Her name was Harriet Stansberry, and she'd been wanting to come to California from Denver with her brother. She said if the town wanted her, she'd like to accept the new teaching position.

Pa seemed real pleased with the news, and I was so happy to see him taking such an interest in the town's growth. Three weeks later, Pa asked me to come to the next school committee meeting with him.

After everyone had sat down, I was feeling strange, because both Mrs. Shaw and Mrs. Dewater were looking at me smiling. Before I had a chance to wonder too long, Mrs. Parrish said, "Your father's told you about our correspondence with Miss Stansberry, hasn't he, Corrie?"

"Yes, ma'am," I answered.

"After receiving her letter, we decided to offer her the job, which she has graciously accepted. She had one condition, however," Mrs. Parrish went on. "Here," she said, taking a white sheet of paper from the top of her oak secretary which stood next to where she sat, "I'll read you what she said."

She cleared her throat, then read: " 'I must tell you, however, that I am crippled in my left leg. It was broken by a carriage wheel when I was a child, and though I can walk on it, it is not without a considerable limp and some pain. Therefore, I make use of a cane most of the time. I am a good teacher, but some people would not be altogether comfortable having someone like myself teaching their children. So I want you to know that I will understand perfectly if you feel you must withdraw your offer.

"If you do want me, notwithstanding this liability, I shall be most happy to accept the position of schoolteacher at Miracle Springs, and my brother and I will plan to arrive in your community by stagecoach, weather permitting, before the worst of the winter snows set in—hopefully before the first of December. We realize the danger in the mountain passes, but we have been ready to leave Denver for some time and are anxious to come to California.

"There is but one stipulation I would like to make regarding the position. Because of my injury, I will need an assistant. This should preferably be an older young person in your town who would like to not only be in my classroom, but would also be willing to help me as the need arises. A boy or girl of fourteen would be fine, although I have had assistants in the past as old as eighteen.' "

Mrs. Parrish put down the paper and stopped reading.

"Well, Corrie," she said, "will you do it?"

"Me? Be her assistant?"

"Yes, of course. We all agreed you are the perfect choice! You'll be seventeen in a few months."

I glanced around at Pa. He was smiling proudly.

"Don't look at me to tell you what to do, Corrie," he said. "This is your decision! Though what the lady says is true enough—everyone here thought of you first off."

"Oh, why—yes! Of course, I'd love to, but—" I glanced over in Pa's direction again. "But what about the young'uns, Pa, and everything I gotta do at home?"

"The young'uns will be in school with you, so you can all go together and you can take just as good care of 'em there as at the cabin. And as for the rest, I'm fixin' to get you some help with all that."

This was before he'd read us the letter from Katie Morgan. In hindsight I know he was talking about her. But I didn't know it then, and I hardly paid much attention to his words at the time because of everything else about the school I was thinking.

"We thought you'd want to do it," Mrs. Parrish said, "as much as we wanted you to. We've been hoping you would be involved with the school as more than just one more of the students, and we've been glad your Pa's been bringing you to some of our meetings here. That's why we've already written Miss Stansberry, and we hope she'll be on her way to California within a week or two."

"I . . . I don't know what to say," I said.

"Just say you'll be her assistant, Corrie," said Mrs. Shaw.

"If it's all right with Pa," I said.

Pa nodded.

"Then it's all decided!" said Mrs. Parrish. She rose and walked over to me and shook my hand solemnly. All the others did the same.

Pa stood back, watching, proud of what was happening, although my face was all flushed, being the center of attention in the middle of all those grown-ups.

Then we all sat down again, and there followed a lot of talk and planning about the school. They had to go to Sacramento to get some more books and other stuff. The desks and blackboards were already in the church building, but now that they'd hired a teacher who was actually on the way, suddenly they realized they had to get everything else ready as quick as they could. And there was talk, too, about the rest of the money they'd need for the books and for Miss Stansberry's salary.

But I couldn't pay much attention to all the rest of what went on that evening. I was thinking too much about what I was going to get to do, and I couldn't have been happier!

# CHAPTER 16

# THE FIRST DAY

The first day of school was set for December 10, 1853.

Miss Stansberry had arrived two weeks earlier. She and her brother had gotten settled in a two-room cabin at the Dewater place on the other side of town. Then she came and paid a call on us and asked me if I'd want to help her, since I was going to be her assistant at the school. She needed help sending some notices around to the folks telling about the starting up of the school.

That first week of December we wrote out lots of letters and invitations. I got my brothers and sisters to help. They were as excited about the school as I was—all except for Zack. But he did his share too.

Miss Stansberry and I rode around to visit all the families with kids and told them about the school getting ready to start up. Even with her leg being crippled, Miss Stansberry was handy with horses and handled Mr. Dewater's carriage just fine. During that time Mrs. Parrish made a trip with Rev. Rutledge down to Sacramento with one of her wagons to pick up the last of the school supplies. By the time December 10 came, everything was about as ready as a new school could be.

In connection with the school opening, I finally got to write an article for the *Gazette*—my first actual "article" in a newspaper! I don't suppose it was much, but I was proud of it and Mr. Singleton put my name at the end of it. Maybe he still felt bad about not doing the article about the mine after he'd said he would. But I didn't care about the reasons! I got to do it and that was all that mattered, and I hoped now maybe he'd let me write about other stuff too.

When the paper came out on December 8, Pa went to the General Store and bought seven copies—one for each of us, and for the first time I can remember he praised me right in front of Uncle Nick and all the rest of the kids.

"You done good, Corrie," he said. "I'm right proud o' ya!"

What a feeling that gave me! There's nothing in the world like hearing words like that from your own pa, though most folks don't hear them too often. Mrs. Parrish says we have to get from our Father in heaven what our earthly fathers don't know how to give. But for me right then, I was full to the brim with the smile Pa gave me after reading the article.

Here's what I wrote:

On December 10, the Wednesday following this edi-tion, the doors will be open at the new Miracle Springs School. All children and young people between the ages of five and eighteen are invited to attend. Donations for attendance will be accepted but are not required at this time. The school committee—comprised of members of the community including the Rev. Avery Rutledge, businesswoman Almeda Parrish, miner Drummond Hollister—

As Pa read his own name out loud, he paused and glanced around the room with a smile. It was likely the first time he'd seen his own name in print, except on a wanted poster. And Uncle Nick gave him a little gesture of con-gratulation, like he was now a local celebrity.

—Mrs. Jake Shaw, and farmer Harold Dewater and his

wife—have raised sufficient funds throughout the community to finance the school's operation through the Spring of 1854. Hired by the committee as the first teacher of the Miracle Springs School is Miss Harriet Stansberry, who has recently arrived in the area from Denver, Colorado with her brother Hermon. She has had teaching experience, and her classroom will prove an enriching experience for all youngsters in attendance. Miss Stansberry will be assisted by Miss Cornelia Hollister, daughter of committee member Hollister.

Pa couldn't help smiling again, and he looked briefly around at all of us before continuing.

The school building was newly built earlier this year and is also used on Sundays and special occasions for church services officiated by the Rev. Rutledge. Anyone desiring further information concerning the Miracle Springs School should contact Mrs. Almeda Parrish at the Parrish Mining and Freight Company in Miracle Springs.

—By Corrie Belle Hollister

Of course Mr. Singleton helped me with it and made it better. Words like *comprised* and *officiated* and *sufficient funds* and *finance the school's operation* were not things I would have thought of all by myself. And anybody could tell that he wrote "will prove an enriching experience for all youngsters in attendance." But he put my name on it, and just told me that's what an editor's supposed to do—make your writing better than you can make it yourself. For now I accepted Mr. Singleton's words and was happy that something I'd written (most of it, anyhow!) was being read by a hundred people in all the communities where his paper went. That was almost as exciting as the opening of the school!

The first day of school was a day to remember! There'd been some rain the night before, but the sun came out when

Wednesday morning came. We were all up early, hardly able to sleep. Even Zack was excited. Pa had taken us to the General Store and bought Zack and Tad new shirts and me and Emily and Becky new dresses for the occasion.

By now Pa wasn't embarrassed at all to show that he was eager for the school too. Being on that committee had made him feel that he was part of making a good thing come to Miracle. Maybe it made him feel that he was being a good pa to us in this one way, when he felt like he was failing us because of all the problems with men like Hatch and Krebbs making life unsafe for us.

Anyhow, that morning he was up early with the rest of us and said he wasn't going to do any work that day. He cleaned up and put on a new shirt. I felt so proud when we rode into town on the wagon—all six of us, clean and spar-kling in our new shirts and dresses, Pa sitting tall in front and me beside him. All the young'uns were talking a mile a minute, and though neither Pa or I said much, we were both thinking that this was an important day and that maybe we had a part in bringing it about.

Pa led the horses right up by the school and church building, set the brake, then hopped down, and we all fol-lowed. Miss Stansberry was on the porch greeting some other children, although we were there almost before anyone else. The minister and Mrs. Parrish were there too, standing at the foot of the steps. Pa went up to them and they all shook hands.

The few other families arrived soon after us, though most of the parents just went back to their work after dropping their children off. About ten minutes later, Miss Stansberry and I went inside to get the last few details ready before she rang the bell to announce the start of class.

Just as I walked in the door, I glanced back. All around the building children were running and yelling—the younger ones, that is. The few older ones were standing around awkwardly waiting.

The last thing I saw was Pa walking off toward the main part of town with Rev. Rutledge and Mrs. Parrish. I could only see their backs, and of course I couldn't hear what they were talking about. But it was just seeing them walking along together that struck me. A year or two ago Pa might have been walking with a couple of gamblers toward the Gold Nugget saloon for a drink. Now here he was walking in the other direction—probably to one of their houses for tea and talk about the school or the church and what they had been able to do as a school committee—with the minister and an upstanding Christian lady who would never set foot in a saloon except to rescue five orphaned kids. I couldn't help thinking that maybe our coming to Miracle Springs had been good for Pa too!

The desks in the schoolroom were arranged in rows facing Miss Stansberry's. She sat in front, and behind her was a big chalkboard across the front wall. Most of the desks were double, and some seated three in a row, but there was one single one that she'd put off to one side for me, sideways and between hers and the rest, facing the middle. She wanted me to be able to participate with the rest of the class most of the time, but to be ready to get up and help her easily too. She said I would be her legs when she had things to pass around or needed to erase the chalkboard. I was easily the oldest person in the class. Zack, at fourteen, was the next oldest.

In trooped the small swarm of kids, mostly under ten, talking and buzzing like bees. Many were dressed up and scrubbed for the occasion. They scrambled around for seats, and Miss Stansberry quietly waited for the hubbub to subside before she stood up and greeted everyone.

"Good morning," she said in a cheerful voice. "Welcome to our new Miracle Springs School. I am so glad you've come! My name is Miss Stansberry, and I will be your teacher. Most of you know Corrie Hollister—"

Here she glanced in my direction and I could feel my face getting red.

"Corrie is going to be my assistant," she went on, "because, you see, I am crippled in one leg."

She walked out from around her desk, limping noticeably and not using her cane.

"So Corrie is going to help me when I need a faster pair of legs than my own. I would like you to call her Miss Hollister."

As she said this, some tittering broke out and I glanced over to see Tad saying something to Becky. But Becky wasn't listening because she was leaning in Emily's direction and had been, I think, the cause of the laughter.

"I realize this will be difficult for *some* of you," Miss Stansberry added with a smile, looking toward my brothers and sisters, "and so Corrie and I will forgive you if you forget."

The boys and girls were instantly at ease with this woman who had come from Colorado to be their teacher. I already liked her very much, and I knew they would too.

"Now, we're going to spend most of today just getting to know one another. I'll need to find out about you, and I'll tell you about me. One of the first things I need to know is who is here and what all your names are."

A chorus of high-pitched voices all started talking at once, but was immediately silenced by Miss Stansberry's hand slamming down on her desk.

"Perhaps the *first* thing we need to do is get something straight about talking out of turn!" she said sternly. "There will be no more outbursts like *that*!"

I had just begun to wonder if the older ones like Zack and I would be able to get any learning done in the midst of ten to fifteen five-to-twelve-year-olds. The sudden complete quiet that descended over the entire room was encouraging.

Miss Stansberry didn't have the chance to go on with finding out people's names, because all at once I realized all the kids' heads had turned around toward the back of the room. I followed their gazes and looked toward the school-room door, where I found myself gasping in amazement.

There stood a young man of sixteen or seventeen, tall and slender, with muscular, wiry limbs. His face was brown and clear, his eyes looked almost black from where I sat, and his hair was pure black and straight. If I had seen only the face, I might not have recognized him at first because since I had seen him last he had taken on many of the characteristics of manhood. But the tan buckskin shirt tunic he wore, laced up with strips of rawhide, and the braid of his hair, let me know in an instant who this unexpected visitor to our school was.

"Little Wolf!" I exclaimed, jumping up from my seat and running over to where he stood. "Are you . . . are you here for—"

"I have come to go to school," he said in a voice strangely deep since I last had heard him.

He did not smile. At first his face did not even reveal that he knew me. Coming here must have been extremely difficult for him. Seeing the disbelief lingering in my expression, he went on, relaxing somewhat as he did. "It is important that I learn what I can, for California no longer belongs only to the Indian and the Mexican."

"But your father?" I said.

"My father has agreed. Though he still resists the white man, he knows I must be educated if I am to have a chance of succeeding in this new world that is rapidly coming."

As we spoke, the others in the room watched in dumbfounded silence. I then took him to the front of the class and introduced him to Miss Stansberry. She suggested that he take a seat next to Zack.

Before the first week was out, not only my desk but a

small cluster including two other double desks sat off to one side of the room for the oldest among Miss Stansberry's students, including Zack and I, Little Wolf, and Artie Syfer, who came three days later and was fifteen. The only other older girl, seventeen-year-old Elizabeth Darien, didn't start in the school until February.

Eventually we had two classes in one, and the five of us older ones took care of ourselves a lot of the time, with Miss Stansberry giving us instruction during times when she'd assigned quiet desk work to the younger class. All us older ones helped her a lot. All three of the boys, even Little Wolf, really got to like her and were almost too eager to help.

But even though we were all just about the same age— Elizabeth was even older than I was, and Little Wolf might have been too—I kept being the unspoken "teacher" of the older ones when Miss Stansberry was busy. I was still her assistant, and none of the other three older ones could read, so they'd often ask me and Zack for help.

It didn't take long for Little Wolf to feel comfortable, and pretty soon he and Zack and Artie and I got to be good friends. I was so happy for Zack to have some boys his own age to be with. He brightened up a lot and started really looking forward to going to school every day. When the three of them would go off together, I didn't mind, because Miss Stansberry always treated me like her friend. She and I always had school things to talk about during free time and at lunch.

Tad and Becky and Emily had the time of their lives, although it wasn't altogether pleasant having the assistant's ten-year-old sister being the class cut-up. But there was no changing Becky! Emily, who was twelve, made up for Becky's rambunctiousness by studying hard. And Tad did what all the other eight-year-old boys in the class did— worked as much as he had to, but spent most of his energy on recess.

Maybe nobody is what you expect them to be like. Miss Stansberry certainly wasn't like I figured her to be. Knowing that she was crippled, and finding out she needed an assistant, made me expect her to be helpless or weak, and maybe not too interesting a person. But once she was in Miracle Springs, once I knew her personally, I realized I had figured on a dull, uninteresting, feeble lady with a soft, boring voice.

I couldn't have been more wrong!

I'm not good at fixing people's ages. One minute I'd almost think Miss Stansberry and I were friends and practically the same age. Then something would happen to make me realize she had taught in two or three other schools before coming to Miracle and was closer to Pa's age than mine. When we knew each other better I finally asked her age. She said she was twenty-nine.

At first glance there was nothing unusual about Miss Stansberry. Her hair was blond and pulled straight back from her face in a bun. She was thin, which made her look taller than she was, although I don't think she was more than 5'5" or 5'6". When I stood facing her she was an inch or two taller than I was. Her skin wasn't pale like an invalid's—it had a good creamy flesh tone. But when she got riled it could change to all shades of pink and red. When she was sitting quietly at her desk, her mouth seemed small, but then when she smiled it widened out, showing her teeth.

At first I didn't even notice the color of her eyes. I think they were blue. Rather than the color of them, I noticed their activity—they were always roving about the classroom, wide awake, taking in more than her mouth or any other part of her features would have told you. By the second day of school, I could tell that nothing would get past this lady! Her voice wasn't loud, but it was a bit on the deep side for a woman, a pleasant voice to hear. That voice made her even more in control when she spoke, and soon everyone in the class learned to shut their own mouths and listen when Miss

Stansberry opened hers.

The first day she was nice, smiling and laughing with us, making the school enjoyable. Early in the afternoon, Jeffrey Hobbes forgot to leave some of his brawling outside after he came in from lunch. He was cutting up and being wild. Miss Stansberry let him interrupt only once. The second time, he turned around to tease little Mary Johnston, who didn't need any help disrupting things despite the innocent look on her face! When Jeffrey turned back toward Mary, Miss Stansberry kept right on talking calmly, while she slowly limped in their direction.

All of a sudden—wham! Down on the middle of Jeffrey's desk came Miss Stansberry's cane with a loud crash! Jeffrey nearly jumped out of his skin!

I watched it all from my desk. The class was totally silent. Mary sat there with her face pale white and her eyes huge.

Miss Stansberry slowly made her way back to the front of the room, then turned around to face the class. She hesitated a minute while every one of the children stared at her.

Then she smiled broadly, showing no sign of anger, and said in a very quiet voice, "When I was young, I was taught that the moment a grown-up opens his or her mouth to speak, all children should immediately close theirs, even if the grown-up is not talking to them. This is especially true with teachers. I do not know if that is how your parents have taught you, but in *this* classroom that is the rule. I hope I do not have to remind you of it again."

Right then I think all of us knew that our new teacher was a lady with gumption and that her being crippled wasn't a handicap at all.

But you'd hardly know any of this about her just by seeing her walking down the street. If you did look a second time, it would likely be on account of her cane, and maybe you'd feel sorry for her. But if you were close enough and looked a second time, her face would draw you back for a third glance. She wasn't so pretty all by herself, but that face needed a closer look.

When Pa was nice enough to invite her out to our place for dinner one Sunday afternoon, I saw Uncle Nick do all that I just described. He looked at her once, kind of glanced down in the direction of her cane, then looked back again, but this time his eyes were drawn to her face. She had brushed her hair down that day and it fell to her shoulders, so she looked different, and in that moment she'd taken her glasses off to scratch one of her eyes. So she looked a little more attractive than normal. But when he thought no one was noticing—and I suppose I was the only one who did— I saw Uncle Nick glance in her direction a third time, and this time he looked straight at her eyes.

After school one day she and I walked over to the General Store together. We happened to meet Rev. Rutledge on our way inside, just as he was coming out the door, and I saw him do the same thing. He already knew her pretty well, but after he first greeted us, he glanced back at her face twice. It was just two quick little looks, but I couldn't help noticing. It seemed everyone found more in her face to wonder about every time they saw it, and they just couldn't keep from going back.

I liked Miss Stansberry, and I think most of the other people around town did, too. Before a month was out, folks forgot all about her being crippled.

# CHAPTER 17

## OUR SECOND CHRISTMAS

When Christmas came, we had a big dinner at *our* place!

It was Pa's idea. He and Uncle Nick had steadily been working on the cabin all year. Now that they could afford to buy what they needed, and had a growing family of seven in all, the place had kept getting smaller and smaller. Pa added our room right after we came, and by now he'd had also put in another bedroom off on the other side of the cabin for himself and Uncle Nick. He was even talking about a third room, so the two boys could share one room and we three girls another!

In the meantime, though, in the process of putting on his and Uncle Nick's room, he'd redone the main room. It was now a little bigger with more of a separate kitchen-place to work when I was cooking and fixing meals. It wasn't just a *cabin* anymore but a good-sized house. I think Pa was proud of the place and wanted to show it off a little.

Or maybe he just wanted to be hospitable. Ma always said hospitality was what turned a house into a *home*, and Pa had mentioned that a time or two.

Whatever his reasons, one day about the middle of December he said to me, "Corrie, what would you think if we was to have some folks out here for Christmas afternoon?"

"I'd like that, Pa," I answered him.

"I mean a great big fancy dinner. We'll have it right here, and we'll let folks see that we're a family and this is our home."

"Yes, Pa!" I replied, excited already. "You mean folks like Mrs. Parrish—"

"Sure," he answered back quickly, "her and her minister-friend—"

"He's our friend too, isn't he, Pa?"

"Yes, of course—the Parrish woman, Rutledge, maybe your new teacher and her brother—wouldn't want them to have no place to go right after comin' to town—an' Alkali."

"Oh, Pa, I can't wait! Do you want me to tell Miss Stansberry and Mrs. Parrish when I'm in town for school tomorrow?"

"No, Corrie, I'm the man of the house. I'll do the invitin'."

I'd noticed him mention being the man of the house or the head of the family several times lately. I think it was still heavy on his mind, like he'd explained when he'd read us the letter from Miss Morgan that he had a responsibility to provide for us and protect us and all. How Christmas dinner fit into that, I wasn't quite sure, except that I think Pa had been looking for ways to do what I already thought he did better than any man I knew of—being what you'd call a "family man."

He did invite them too, the very next day. He wouldn't even let me go along. Wanted to do it himself, he said. He even took a bath and put on a fresh shirt for the occasion, as if going to Mrs. Parrish's just to invite her to dinner was an event in itself. It looked to me like at last the two of them were starting to get along real well. I found myself secretly wishing something would go wrong with Miss Katie Morgan's plans to come out West.

There was a change in Mrs. Parrish too. I noticed it for the first time when she arrived out at our place that Christmas morning. She'd always been so nice to me and I knew we were friends. Although she and Pa'd had their differences, she was civil to him and they'd been getting along fine for a long time.

But when she came out that Christmas morning, it wasn't just that she was *nice* to me and the kids, she suddenly seemed a part of our lives—all of us, Pa and Uncle Nick too. She wasn't like a stranger helping us out. She looked like she really belonged, like she wanted to belong to *all* of our lives—not just the part of us that came to town and visited her in *her* house.

Of course she came with Rev. Rutledge as usual. But as soon as they got there they went their separate ways, and the minister didn't really seem to know what to do with himself. He tried to talk to Pa and Uncle Nick; they were polite and answered his questions about the mine and what they were doing around the place. But there was a kind of awkwardness too. It was clear he was trying to fit in where he didn't really belong.

I don't fault him for that, because that's what a minister's got to do sometimes—he's got to be interested in what people are doing. And Pa was as polite to him as he could be. Pa had come to respect the minister's willingness to dirty his hands and get blisters building the church and pitching in and helping folks when he could.

Even on that day, I saw them once standing by the creek together talking. The minister was kneeling down scooping up a handful of the gravelly dirt and Pa was pointing to something—probably a flake of gold—and explaining something to the minister. And I knew that the part of Rev. Rutledge that didn't act like a fuddy-duddy about man's work, Pa thought a good deal of. Yet there was still a difference between them—ministers, it seemed to me at least, just couldn't ever *really* be like other men. Or maybe it was just that other men could never completely forget that a man was a minister, and therefore couldn't help treating him just a little different. I won't say Pa put on his good behavior around Rev. Rutledge. Pa wasn't that sort of man. But he didn't talk to him like he would to Alkali Jones either.

The minute Mrs. Parrish set foot out of the minister's buggy that day, it was like *she* was one of our family, and Rev. Rutledge was the only guest. Always before, when we'd visit at her place in town, it was the two of them—Mrs. Parrish and the minister—with us kind of set apart. But this day it was different!

She marched right into the house, greeting everyone warmly, shaking Pa's hand and smiling at him and thanking him for inviting her to be part of our family's Christmas. She carried a big basket in her hand full of rolls she had made and cranberries and several pies. All the kids were clamoring around her as she went in, Pa following too; and when she set the basket down on the table and started pulling out the pies, Pa laughed and said he'd asked for them. It was such a nice friendly atmosphere, just the way Christmas ought to be!

And then as the men looked on, she pulled off her coat, took off her bonnet, handed them to Pa, then looked at me and Emily and said, "Well, girls, what's to be done? Let's get this Christmas feast underway!"

She strode into the kitchen like it was her own with Emily and Becky and me following behind her, proceeding to lift lids and sniff and poke around to assess what I'd already done. Within five minutes we were all working away on different parts of the meal. Mrs. Parrish sure brightened up the place!

When the men started to walk outside, I saw a look of hesitation on Zack's face. Ordinarily he would have gone off with the men in a second, but I think even he could feel the warmth inside the house just from having Mrs. Parrish there. When she asked him if he'd like to help by setting out the plates and silverware on the table, he almost looked relieved to have a reason to stay inside with Mrs. Parrish and the rest of us.

Alkali Jones was the next to show up and not long after him Miss Stansberry and her brother Hermon rode up in their buggy. Miss Stansberry came inside to help us while all the men took a walk up the creek to the mine. It was an hour later before everything was ready. It took the meat a good while to cook—Mr. Jones had brought a salted ham and Pa'd killed four fat chickens for the meal—and we had to cut up a lot of potatoes for that many mouths.

At last we were ready, and how small that house seemed with twelve people sitting around the table, even with the extra planks Pa brought in! Everybody had such fresh and happy looks on their faces—Mrs. Parrish and Miss Stansberry had rosy glowing cheeks from being inside and working over boiling kettles and the hot stove. And all the men had that crisp look of walking into a warm room from the cold outside. But it was the smiles most of all that said to me this was what Christmas was supposed to be like.

When Pa pulled out Ma's Bible, I thought I was going to start crying for joy. I thought he'd forgotten all about it earlier in the morning when we'd given each other our gifts. But he hadn't at all! He'd just been saving it for now, like he really was trying to let all these other folks be part of our family.

"Before we get this eatin' shindig underway," Pa said, "I think I oughta read the Christmas passage. It's somethin' me and Aggie started after Corrie was born. I don't mean to be intrudin' on your territory, Reverend, but I reckon if me and these kids're gonna have to get along without her—"

Pa stopped, but only for a second. I could tell this wasn't easy for him to do, but was something he felt he had to do.

"If we're gonna get along without her, then I reckon there's some things in the way of religious instruction maybe

I'm gonna have to start attendin' to."

He stopped again, opened the Bible, and started reading the familiar words from Luke: *"And it came to pass in those days that there went out a decree from Caesar Augustus, that all the world should be taxed. . . ."*

As he read, there was not just a silence in the room but a deep sense of something else too, something like contentment or peace. Even Uncle Nick and Mr. Jones had looks of respect on their faces. A year earlier they might have kidded Pa for being too "religious." But now I think they realized he was becoming even a stronger man than before, that the family side of him was taking a firmer hold on things. Pa didn't seem embarrassed about doing what he was doing in front of the minister. I was so proud of him!

Mrs. Parrish saw it too, because when Pa finished and sat down and closed the Bible, she was looking deeply into his face with a glistening around her eyes.

There was just a moment's hesitation, then she said, "Thank you so much, Mr. Hollister, for sharing that part of your family's tradition with the rest of us! It makes us feel very much included in your family on this holy day."

Rev. Rutledge added an "Amen," and there were a few other comments and thank yous. Then Mrs. Parrish said— and in thinking it over afterward, I'm sure she did it to save Pa being put on the spot—"It looks to me like the food's about ready to eat. Rev. Rutledge, would you be so kind as to offer thanks to the Lord for us?"

I could see that Pa was relieved, for reading from the Bible is a different matter from praying out loud in front of a lot of people. By the time Rev. Rutledge finally got around to his "Amen," Pa probably wished he had done the praying, because it was time to start thinking about how to warm the food up again!

# CHAPTER 18

## PA'S ANNOUNCEMENT

It was sure a different Christmas dinner than last year!

Everything had been so tense then, with angry words exchanged between Pa and Rev. Rutledge, ending with Pa's leaving the house. Who'd have ever thought that a year later we'd be sitting around a table together again, laughing and talking like everyone'd been friends for years? And by the end of the meal even Mr. and Miss Stansberry seemed like part of our Miracle Springs family.

"So tell me, Mr. Jones," Miss Stansberry was saying, since she happened to be sitting next to the old prospector, "you say you were the first to discover gold in this area?"

"That's right, ma'am. It was all on account—"

"Come on, Alkali," interrupted Pa with a laugh, "we've all heard that story a dozen times, and you don't want to bore the schoolteacher with somethin' she'll see right through!"

"On the contrary, I would like to hear it."

"It ain't nothin' but a parcel of make-believe, Miss Stansberry," put in Uncle Nick.

"Nevertheless," she replied, turning to Uncle Nick, "I think I ought to be allowed to judge that for myself. But before Mr. Jones continues, I must ask you to please call me Harriet."

"My pleasure, ma'am," said Uncle Nick, giving her a nod of the head. "Now please, Mr. Jones, in spite of what your friends say, I want to hear your account."

Pa and Uncle Nick leaned back in their chairs as if expecting a good laugh, and Alkali Jones lit into his story of finding gold in the Miracle Springs Creek. All the others listened in rapt attention, while Pa and Uncle Nick, with Zack joining in their fun, chuckled and winked through it all.

When he was through, the minister said, "Well, I must say that is quite a tale, Mr. Jones."

"Don't you believe a word of it, Reverend," laughed Pa.

"Aren't you being a little hard on your friend, Drummond?"

"Alkali's used to it by now, ain't ya, Alkali?"

"Aw, Drum," shot back Mr. Jones in his high-pitched voice, "you durned newcomers thinks you know everythin', but if it hadna been for us old timers in these parts, there wouldna been no gold for the likes o' you!" Then, so that no one would take him too seriously and think he was really arguing with Pa, he let out with his high cackle, "Hee, hee, hee!"

"An whose claim's keepin' you in beans an' new boots?" put in Uncle Nick, not wanting to miss out on the sport of giving Alkali Jones a good ribbing.

"Hee, hee, hee! I found it, an' the two o' you's makin' me work your claim for my own measly little share! Hee, hee!"

"Is there actually more gold to be found?" asked Hermon Stansberry, to no one in particular.

"That depends on who you talk to," said Pa.

"The hills are full o' it, if ye ask me," said Mr. Jones. "Why, jist the other day I was up on Baseline ridge, an' I seen—"

"Oh, not another strike, Alkali!" said Uncle Nick, shooting Pa a quick wink.

"Jist hold on to your hat, Nick," Alkali shot back. "I seen ol' man Strong, you know the ol' varmint that lives up there in the hills trappin' coons and shootin' bear. He ain't never had no interest in gold. He says you can't eat gold an' it won't keep you warm at night, so he sees no good in the stuff. Well, he told me even *he's* spotted gold in his stream, an' he ain't even lookin' fer it!"

His words silenced even Pa and Uncle Nick for a minute.

"What is your opinion, Mrs. Parrish?" asked Mr. Stansberry. "I understand your business supplies the miners with much of their equipment and supplies."

"Yes, I do," replied Mrs. Parrish, then smiled with fun in her eyes. "But most of the men in these parts do not share their views with me—even their views on the future of the gold rush."

She glanced over in Pa's direction. "Would you say that's a fair assessment, Mr. Hollister?" Still the humor was on her face. "Aren't most miners—men like yourself, for instance—reluctant to make a woman their confidante?"

"Them's your words, ma'am, not mine," answered Pa.

Mrs. Parrish laughed. "Cryptic to the end! Very well, I see I'm going to have to answer Mr. Stansberry's question myself." Then she turned more serious and looked back at Miss Stansberry's brother. "I would say, yes, there *is* a great deal of gold still in California to be found," she went on. "But that is merely a guess on my part. Opinions vary widely, as you can imagine. There are those who thought it was played out in 1850, yet new strikes continue to be made. Our own town here boomed at first, then slowed down. People left their claims, only to suddenly spring back with new strikes throughout the area as a result of what happened right here on Mr. Hollister's land. My own feeling is that gold still exists in abundant supply, but that in coming years it will be increasingly difficult, first to locate, and then to extract."

"The lady's exactly on the target," added Pa. "Harder to find, harder to get at."

"And it's takin' bigger, more expensive equipment, too," said Uncle Nick. "Big outfits is comin' in from all over the place."

"Squeezin' the little guys like us clean outta the gold fields, that's what they's doin'!" said Alkali Jones.

This time his words weren't followed by a laugh. "Pannin' fer gold in a stream ain't findin' much these days, less ye gets lucky like ol' man Strong! Naw, fer fellers like us it's mostly gone."

"That must be good for you, at least, Mrs. Parrish," said Miss Stansberry. "Selling the new gold companies their machinery?"

"Unfortunately," replied Mrs. Parrish, "the way of the small business is probably doomed to go the way of the little one-man claim. My business has always been with local operations, transporting things for them—supplies, small equipment. But the big outfits that are coming in bring their own machinery. They see someone like me, and a woman to boot, as little more than a General Store for miners— strictly small time."

"But you provide a valuable service for all the miners for miles, Almeda," said Rev. Rutledge. He hadn't said a word during the whole discussion about gold mining. "You mustn't be too pessimistic. I'm certain all the men in Miracle Springs will continue to need the goods and services you offer for many years to come."

"The Reverend's right, ma'am," said Uncle Nick, and for some reason I was surprised by his kind words. "None of us coulda got by like we have if it hadn't been for your company an' the ways you help the men."

Both Pa and Alkali Jones nodded their heads and mumbled words of agreement. Mrs. Parrish seemed genuinely touched.

"There, you see what I mean, Almeda," Rev. Rutledge added. "These men hereabouts aren't about to desert you after all you've done, notwithstanding what the larger companies may be doing."

"Well, I must say, that is kind of you, Avery," Mrs. Parrish sighed, "kind of you all! But, I don't know—I do wonder about the future sometimes. A woman, alone like I am, running a business that perhaps there won't be a need for one day. Sometimes I think I ought to find a rich miner or rancher to marry, and think about being a wife instead of a businesswoman!"

My head shot up at the words. I didn't know if she was being serious, like her voice had sounded just a moment before when talking about the future of her store, or if she was joking again.

Her words caught everyone off guard. As I looked across the table, I saw the minister, who'd been looking right into her face, glance away and start fiddling with something on his plate. His neck showed just a touch of red in it and he didn't say anything more.

As he looked away, there were a couple of "Ahem—ahem's" around the table, people clearing their throats. But when I saw Mrs. Parrish's face, I could tell in a second that she'd been funning, because she threw me a quick little smile.

Now Alkali Jones's quick wit saved the conversation. "Well, ma'am," he said, and you could almost hear his high cackle ahead of time, "I don't know no ranchers here 'bouts needin' no settlin', but I knows where ye might find yourself a rich miner! Hee, hee, hee!"

Uncle Nick and Mrs. Parrish seemed to appreciate his humor, but neither Pa nor Rev. Rutledge did much laughing.

One thing I was learning from watching Mrs. Parrish around other people was how she was always watching them, always trying to put them at ease, always trying to say or do something that would keep them from being on the spot or from feeling small. She didn't want the conversation to get awkward for anyone—or for herself—and so her next words steered the talk another direction.

"Well, I must admit," she said cheerily, "this is certainly a more cordial Christmas gathering than I was able to provide last year!" She laughed, and gradually most of the others joined in.

Miss Stansberry looked at her with a question on her face, so Mrs. Parrish continued. "The children and Mr. Hollister had not been together long, and Avery had only been in Miracle Springs a month. I had not been altogether gracious in some of the things I had said and done toward Mr. Hollister, and no doubt—" and here she turned an apologetic smile in Uncle Nick's direction—"toward Mr. Belle as well. Anyway, we had what you might call an uncomfortable Christmas gathering at my home, for which I have always felt bad. I am just grateful that Mr. Hollister and Mr. Belle—and the children, of course!—" She looked around at each one of us quickly, then resumed, "I'm glad they have all opened their home to us so graciously!"

"Amen—amen!" added the minister.

But her bringing up last year's Christmas only seemed to deepen Pa's silence and he didn't say anything. Afraid, maybe, that it was going to turn out like last year after all, Mrs. Parrish struck up again, though now I thought I heard some nervousness in her breezy tone.

"And now that I think of it, Mr. Hollister," she said, "haven't we had something like this discussion about the future of the gold fields before?"

But it wasn't Pa who answered, but Uncle Nick.

"That's right! I recollect the day! It was with that lowdown Royce back when folks was sellin' off their claims!''

"The weasel!" added Mr. Jones. "Why, if it hadna been fer Tad an' Zack here, the durned varmint woulda had the whole blamed town an' valley by now!"

"What's this? Have two of my students done something I should know about?" asked Miss Stansberry, glancing first at Tad, beaming with pleasure, and then at Zack, who looked more embarrassed than proud.

"Heroes, that's what those two are!" put in Rev. Rutledge.

"I want to hear all about it!" Miss Stansberry said. "It sounds exciting!"

"Exciting's hardly the word for it," added Mrs. Parrish. "These two lads did nothing short, I venture to say, of changing the very course of Miracle Springs' history! And certainly Corrie's part can't be overlooked either. She overheard Royce's plan and then ran into town to—"

All this time since Mrs. Parrish's comment about getting married, Pa had kept quiet. Though the talk around the table had picked back up, he'd just been staring down at the table like he was thinking about something else. Now all of a sudden he looked up, took in a deep breath, and interrupted Mrs. Parrish's story.

"I got somethin' to tell you all," he blurted out. "I'm sorry to break into your story, ma'am, and it's not like I ain't proud of my kids for what they done. But one of the reasons I wanted to have some of you here today—though Nick and the kids, we already talked about this, but you, ma'am, an' the minister, an' Alkali—well, I got somethin' I gotta say and I figured this'd be just about the easiest way to get you all in one place like this, and just say it."

When he stopped to take a breath, it was so quiet around that table you could have heard a sparrow chirp clear up at the mine. Nobody so much as lifted a fork to eat another bite.

"I know I'm kinda spoilin' your nice conversation, but your sayin' what you done, Alkali, put me in mind of what I want to say, so I reckon I just gotta rustle up my gumption and say it."

Again he paused, sucked in a breath of air, and forged ahead.

"Well," he said, "I been thinkin' real hard about the kids here, and about what I'm needin' to do for them, to be the sort of father I want to be to 'em, and what's for their best, an' all. So I talked to some folks and I put an advertisement in some papers out East, an' I got a letter back from a nice-soundin' young lady from Virginia who's willin' to come. So I wrote her, and I'm fixin' to send her some money to pay to get her here, and she's gonna come an' be a wife to me and help me raise my kids like they oughta be raised. There! That's what I gotta say!"

He sighed real big and kind of relaxed back in his chair.

"Whew, Drum!" whistled Alkali Jones. "When you say somethin', blamed if you don't say a mouthful! Ya mean to say you's gonna git yerself married again?"

"That's what I just said, Alkali," answered Pa, sounding almost irritated at having to repeat it.

"Well, if that don't beat all! Hee, hee, hee!"

"Well, well! Ahem—congratulations, Mr. Hollister," said Rev. Rutledge, half rising out of his chair and offering Pa his right hand.

Pa shook it, but his heart didn't really seem in it. He didn't look the minister directly in the eye as he did so.

"Yes, Mr. Hollister," added Miss Stansberry warmly. "Congratulations! That is wonderful news!"

Somehow, though, it didn't feel as wonderful as it ought to. As I glanced around the table, none of my brothers and sisters had smiles on their faces. I suppose we'd get used to the notion of Pa having a new wife, but I couldn't help thinking about Ma.

Mrs. Parrish just looked down at her plate and got real quiet.

# CHAPTER 19

# A TALK AFTERWARD

It's a good thing dinner was mostly over when Pa told everyone about Katie Morgan, because after that it was quiet with the sounds mostly of forks scratching around on plates and chewing and passing plates around. Pa squirmed in his seat a little. His sudden announcement threw a bucket of cold water on what had been a pretty lively and fun talk around the table.

Miss Stansberry and Rev. Rutledge kept on talking, but mostly about her coming and what she thought California was like and how the school was getting along. She asked him about the church, and they laughed over things having to do with sharing the building for their two "ministries," as they called them.

Alkali Jones tried to get Pa talking about mining again, but without any success. Then he turned to Uncle Nick and was talking away to him, but I got the feeling Uncle Nick was trying to listen across Mr. Jones to what Miss Stansberry was saying, so he was involved in both conversations at once. Neither Pa or Mrs. Parrish said much of anything, so the rest of the meal was a little strange.

I was sitting next to Pa. Finally I asked him, quietly— because I just wanted to know for myself—when Miss Morgan was coming. I guess everyone heard me, because they all turned to listen to Pa's answer.

"April, Corrie, or May," he said, "or whenever she can get passage on a ship. Folks are pouring west now, and I reckon sometimes they're filled up."

That loosened Pa up some, just getting his tongue working again, and gradually the talk started to flow better as we got up from the table. The men went over by the fire and lit up their pipes, the women—including Becky and Emily and me—started clearing off the things from the table. But no one asked Pa the question I wanted so badly to ask: When was he planning to marry Miss Morgan?

"We'll clear up some of these things," Mrs. Parrish announced, "and give your stomachs a chance to rest, and then put out the pies!"

"Now you're talkin'! Hee, hee!" laughed Alkali Jones, and other enthusiastic comments followed.

I looked around at the men standing by the fire filling their pipes and talking, and at us kids and Miss Stansberry and Mrs. Parrish in the kitchen putting the food away and stacking the plates to take outside to wash. Listening to all the sounds and voices, I thought to myself that it had turned out to be a right fine Christmas after all. I was worried there at the table for a few minutes when it got quiet, and I couldn't help thinking about all the trouble a year earlier. But now everyone's good spirits were back.

A few minutes later, while I was taking the leftover chicken off the bones so we'd be able to divide it up for everyone to take home, I realized Mrs. Parrish wasn't in the cabin. At first I figured maybe she'd gone out to the outhouse or to take some dishes to the pump-sink outside, but when she was still gone ten minutes later I thought I'd go see.

By then Miss Stansberry had Becky and Emily organized into a cleaning troop between the table and the stove, and the three of them were chattering away. Mr. Stansberry was showing Tad his whittling knife. Zack was with Pa and Uncle

Nick and the minister and Alkali Jones. So I figured nobod-y'd miss me for a few minutes. I cleaned the grease off my fingers, wiped them off with a towel, and went outside.

It was a sunshiny day, but cold. I could see my breath in the air. I glanced around. Mrs. Parrish wasn't at the pump, and I was already getting chilly. So I went back inside, got on my coat, and came back into the fresh, clean air that felt so good against my face—especially with a full stomach!

I looked up and down the creek as I started walking. At first I didn't know where to go, but then I saw Mrs. Parrish. She was about halfway up toward the mine, leaning against one of the big man-size rocks the creek worked its way around. I walked toward her, not really knowing what I was going to say. Then it suddenly dawned on me that she must have come out here to be alone.

Embarrassed, I started to back away, but it was too late. She'd heard me and turned her head around.

"Corrie," she said, smiling. "You found me!"

"I didn't mean to bother you, ma'am, I just didn't see you and got to wondering if—"

"Oh, think nothing of it, Corrie," she said. "I've had plenty of time alone with my thoughts. I'm sure the Lord knew some pleasant company was just what I needed."

I didn't say anything.

"It's been a wonderful Christmas, hasn't it, Corrie?" she said brightly.

"Yes, ma'am."

"Just the kind of day to remind us of the Lord's coming to earth." She paused a second, then added, "How are you finding this Christmas for *you*, Corrie—after a year here, a year with your father, a year thinking more personally about God's life with us?"

No one would ever accuse Mrs. Parrish of beating around the bush when she had something to say! But my thoughts were still of Christmas and pies, and I wasn't very quick about an answer.

"I don't know, ma'am, I guess I hadn't been thinking just now about it."

"I'm sorry," she laughed. "I suppose I always get more pensive on Christmas day than most people. But I always try to slip away by myself at least twice on days like this, especially Christmas, just to keep myself from being so caught up in the hubbub and the conversation and the food and the merrymaking going on around me, to remind myself of what it's *really* about—that Jesus came to live among us, and to help us be like Him."

"I thought of all that this morning," I said. "I got up early and prayed some—and, of course, when Pa read the Christmas story. I guess I had forgotten about it for most of the day."

"There's nothing wrong with the merrymaking," she said. "Christmas is a festive time, a time to be happy with family and friends. But as I said, I like to remind myself about its true meaning as often as I'm able. Your Pa's voice had a real nice sound to it when he read," she added, bringing Pa up without even a pause. "It must make you happy to have him working to be a good father and family man."

"Yes, ma'am, I reckon," I said. She must have heard the hesitation in my voice.

"You sound a little doubtful, Corrie," she said, looking at me steadily. I didn't say anything right off, and she gave me time to think out my answer.

"I'm pleased enough about Pa," I said finally. "You know that, ma'am. You know I think he's a fine man, and I'm just proud as I can be. Him inviting all you folks here today was such a wonderful thing for him to do! But, I don't know, ma'am, it's just that him getting married again—well, that's a turn of events that's kinda hard to take hold of."

"Ah, yes . . . I know what you mean," she replied with

a kind of half smile that seemed to hold back more than it said. "I must admit it took me by surprise, too."

"Do *you* think he ought to marry again, ma'am?" I asked.

"Oh, Corrie!" she answered with a laugh that sounded a little jittery. "That is hardly a question that it seems I have any right to consider. What your father does is his business, after all."

"You're like part of our family, Mrs. Parrish," I said.

"That's kind of you to say, Corrie." She put her hand on mine and smiled.

"It's true, ma'am, and so I think that gives you the right to say what you think."

"Of course, I have tried to do my best for you children—"

"And you have, ma'am!" I said. "You've been just—just like—you've been better for all of us than we deserved!"

Before the words were out of my mouth, I was crying, though I didn't know why. Her hand, still on mine, gave me a squeeze.

"And it just doesn't seem right somehow," I went on, but now the words were getting all jumbled in my thoughts, "for Pa to bring somebody here we don't even know to take care of us. We don't need anybody else! We're doing just fine the way it is, with all of us and Pa and—and you, ma'am, and I just don't see why—"

I couldn't finish, because I was sobbing pretty hard by now.

For a long time Mrs. Parrish just let me cry, stroking my head with one hand while the other held mine.

When she finally did speak again, her voice was so tender, it reminded me of Ma comforting me when I was little.

"There's an old saying, Corrie," she said softly, "that wives have to learn and have been repeating to themselves for years. And until they learn it, life can be downright miserable for them if they're going to try to understand everything their man does."

She paused and looked away. I hadn't seen that far-off gaze in her face for a long time. The few times I had seen it, it always reminded me of someone thinking about something that happened a long time ago. I didn't know if Mrs. Parrish was thinking about her husband or about something else, but her words seemed to be coming out of something that had happened to show her what an important lesson it was to learn.

"And this is how folks put it, Corrie," she finally said, turning back toward me. "Sometimes men have just got to do what their hearts are telling them to do. Half the time to the women in their life—whether it's a wife, a sweetheart, a friend, or, like you, a daughter—it doesn't seem to make sense, but once a man feels that he's got to do something, he *has* to do it or he'll never be able to live with himself afterward."

"But what if it's something he doesn't need to do?" I insisted. "Like with this Miss Morgan coming? We don't need any help! Pa's a good pa and we're getting old enough to take care of ourselves."

"I think I understand a little how you feel, Corrie. But once a man's set on something, whether it makes sense or not, or even whether it's right or not, he's got to go ahead with it for his own sake. If he's wrong, well, that's something he has to find out for himself, and no amount of female persuasion is usually going to make any difference.

"And, Corrie, who's to say your father *is* wrong? I've never been a father—I've never even been a parent. And though I love you and the others like you were my own, the fact is that I can't really *know* what it's like for your pa inside, feeling the responsibility of caring for a family without a wife, with all the troubles he's had following him around. It must be a terrible burden for him sometimes. And I do know this, that he wouldn't be doing this if he didn't feel it was the right thing to do for all of you."

"Well, if he's gotta find a new wife—" I began, my tears starting up again.

I was arguing with myself, though I didn't really realize that till I thought about it later. Ever since Pa'd read us Miss Morgan's letter I'd been all mixed up inside about it, and now all at once everything I'd been thinking was coming out at Mrs. Parrish. "If he's gotta find a new wife, then what's wrong with somebody around here we know? Why couldn't he get someone like the widow Jackson that lives over by Fern lake? She's nice and comes to church and is always nice to us kids. Or why couldn't he—why couldn't he marry somebody—somebody like you!"

I started sobbing again as the words I hadn't planned burst out.

Mrs. Parrish looked sharply away. Through my own tears I saw her turn her head. My first thought was that I'd hurt her by what I said, and anytime you can get your mind thinking of somebody else, even if just for a second, you forget your own troubles.

"I'm—I'm sorry, Mrs. Parrish," I said. "I didn't mean to say something to upset you. I didn't even know what I was saying!"

She turned back toward me with the tenderest smile I'd ever seen on her face. Her cheeks were a little red and her eyes were blinking a little harder than usual. Right at that moment she looked prettier than I'd ever seen her before.

"Oh, Corrie—Corrie!" she said in barely more than a whisper. "You dear, dear girl!"

She drew in a deep sigh. "You haven't hurt me, Corrie," she said softly. "That was one of the nicest things you could ever have said! But sometimes a woman's emotions can't be trusted. You'll understand that better when you get a little older. Then you'll know what it's like to suddenly find your eyes misting over when you don't know why. But—what am I saying?—I guess you know about that already!" she added, laughing.

"I reckon I do."

"I forget you're already a woman in many ways! I apologize."

"Now it's my turn to say I didn't take offense."

She smiled. "I suppose both of us will have many new things to get used to, many adjustments to make," said Mrs. Parrish.

"You too, ma'am?"

"Well, your father's marrying is bound to change—change . . . the way—well, you and he won't be coming over to my house for tea before school meetings anymore!" This last part she added hurriedly, as if she only just thought of it.

"We'll still be friends, won't we, Mrs. Parrish? You'll still come and visit and talk to me about—you know, about everything?"

"Of course, Corrie! Nothing will ever change our special friendship. But Miss Morgan—I suppose I'll have to get used to calling her the new Mrs. Hollister!—she'll be your friend too, I'm certain of it. And she'll want you to confide in her also."

"But I don't want to confide in her!" I half-shouted back, my anger and frustration coming out again. "I don't need any one but Pa and you!"

Mrs. Parrish smiled. But she didn't speak immediately. She seemed to be thinking. Then finally she said, "Have I told you about everything working out for good, Corrie?"

"I don't remember exactly," I answered. "I suppose I've heard you talk about it before."

"There's a verse in Romans, Corrie, that says everything will work out for our good in the end *if* we love God and are called according to His purpose. And I think perhaps we need to remember that right now with your pa marrying again."

"But I don't see how *everything* can be good?"

"It doesn't say that everything is good. It says that *in* everything God is able to work out good, to make good come out of it."

"For everybody?"

"No. For those that love God—that is, for Christians who are called according to His purpose—in other words, those whose lives are ordered by God's ways, not their own. It means that if a Christian is trying to live by obeying God's ways and doing what God wants, rather than living for himself, God will be able to make all things work out for good in the end. Even if something bad happens, if you are trying to live by God's principles, not selfishly, then good will come out of it for you in the end."

"What you're saying, then, is that if Pa's going to marry Miss Morgan, good will come out of it."

"Yes, I guess that's what I'm saying. I can't say whether he was right or wrong to write her and ask her to come to California. I only know that for you and me—*if* we are faithful to live as Christians by God's principles—it will work out for good in the end. We don't need to worry about your Pa, except to pray for him. All we need remember is to obey God, and then we can trust good to be the ultimate result."

Both of us were quiet for a spell.

"I guess you're right," I finally sighed. "But it's hard to trust God when things look like they're going in a way you don't want them to go."

"Remember the fog in front of San Francisco, Corrie? Many times we can't see what God sees. He may be doing things we have no idea of. He can see a lot further ahead than we can."

I smiled up at her. "I know you're right. But it's hard to grab hold of the kinds of things you say sometimes."

"It takes time to get some of these lessons deep enough into your heart that you can start living them. And hurts and pains are a required part of the learning too. Nothing much worth learning comes without pain. Maybe now God's giving you a chance to feel some anxious thoughts so you can grow a little closer to Him by trusting Him to work out what's best."

"I hope that's it," I said.

"But don't you think we've been away long enough? They're going to think we skipped out to leave all the cleaning up for them!"

Mrs. Parrish took a step or two away from the rock, then reached her arms high above her head and took in a deep breath of the cold Christmas air.

"Oh, Corrie!" she said, "It's so wonderful here! This is the day of all days to remember that we needn't fear for what lies ahead. You have a home, a family, this beautiful place, and a loving Father in heaven watching over your every need!"

She turned back toward me and embraced me warmly. We held each other tight for a moment, then stepped back. Tears sprang to our eyes again, but neither of us said anything.

Then she took my hand and we began walking back down the slope toward the cabin. I glanced in that direction just in time to see Pa, who'd been standing on the porch, turn and go back inside. I wondered if he had been watching us. But I don't think Mrs. Parrish saw him.

"I think it's time we spread out those pies!" she said. "Knowing how men are, your pa will probably already be hungry again!"

# CHAPTER 20

# THE REST OF CHRISTMAS DAY

When we got back to the cabin, the spirits inside were high again.

In one corner Alkali Jones was telling one of his tall tales. The laughter of the kids and the gleam in his eye told me he was spinning a good one, probably no more true than his occasional claim that he told Sutter where to build his mill.

Miss Stansberry still held a dishtowel in her hand, but instead of using it on anything she was talking to the minister with Uncle Nick standing to her right, listening to every word. I don't think I'd ever seen Rev. Rutledge and Uncle Nick say two words to each other without Pa or Mrs. Parrish around. Now there they both were with Miss Stansberry.

Pa and Hermon Stansberry were at the fire, and it looked like Pa was explaining something to him about one of his guns. Pa was looking toward the door, and the minute we came in he burst out, as if he hadn't seen us just a moment before, "Where you ladies been? We was about figurin' on diggin' into them pies without the two of you!"

Mrs. Parrish laughed and threw it right back at him, "Don't you dare, Mr. Hollister! When I bring pies to such a festive gathering as this, I reserve the right to cut them myself!"

She came into the room as if it were her own house and marched right over to the basket of pies and started pulling them out. The minute she was back, the younger kids deserted poor Mr. Jones. His best story couldn't hold a candle to being with Mrs. Parrish!

"Now, children, what would everyone like, do you suppose?" she said, testing a knife with the edge of her thumb.

"Apple . . . pumpkin . . . mince!" came the shouts all at once.

"Please, please!" she replied with a pretend scowl and a wag of her finger. "Who do we serve first?"

"The ladies," said Emily.

"No, the company," insisted Tad.

"Well, since I am both a lady *and* company," returned Mrs. Parrish, "as well as the one who made the pies, my answer is that we serve the head of the family first." She turned toward Pa with a little nod and smile. "Mr. Hollister," she asked, "what is your pleasure?"

"Well, ma'am—thank you," said Pa, taken a little by surprise, but pleased at the honor. "I reckon I'll have a slice of your apple."

"Very well. Zack, hand me that pie there, will you?"

"To *begin* with, that is!" added Pa.

Mrs. Parrish laughed. "Yes, of course, Mr. Hollister. I wouldn't want you to go away hungry! That's why I made plenty—I know how fond you are of pies!"

"And how would you know a thing like that, ma'am?" Pa's voice had a tone in it I don't think I'd ever heard before, at least toward Mrs. Parrish. He was always so serious around her and now it sounded like he was teasing her.

"There are ways to learn these things, Mr. Hollister," replied Mrs. Parrish as she handed Pa his pie, then began cutting the others.

"I want to know how," he insisted.

"Let's just say I have my own set of spies."

"My own kids tellin' on their pa!"

"Oh, Pa, I just told her you liked pies!" I said. "There can't be much harm in that."

Pa kind of grunted, but threw me a wink as he did, just to make sure I knew he wasn't serious about being upset, then drove his fork into Mrs. Parrish's pie.

"And right tasty pie it is, too!" he said through his first large bite. "Worth waitin' for, and worth bein' spied on to get a hold of!"

Mrs. Parrish and I both laughed, and by now everyone else was gathered around. While Mrs. Parrish cut, I took orders and handed out the plates of pie. She'd made two apples, so even though there were almost a dozen of us, everybody had enough seconds to stuff themselves all over again, with pie left over in the end.

The rest of the day, both Pa and Mrs. Parrish were real cheerful and more friendly to each other than I'd ever seen them. I couldn't for the life of me figure what it could have had to do with Pa's announcement at dinner. Maybe it had something to do with Mrs. Parrish's going out to be alone, and the talk she and I had. But whatever it was all about, I liked it real well.

With the warm fire, the food, and all the different people with us, it felt so good that I didn't ever want the day to end. And if Pa's marrying again was what it took to make him and Mrs. Parrish as close to each other as I was to both of them, maybe it was a good idea, after all.

I guess Mrs. Parrish must've thought so too, because she was buoyant the rest of the day. I'd never seen her like that. Maybe when she'd been outside alone thinking, she'd come to the conclusion that Pa's decision to get married was a good one and she was happy about how much better it would be for all of us.

Darkness had already fallen, and before things started quieting down in the cabin, the men had wandered back to

the table two or three times to pick and nibble at the left-
overs. I was surprised at how long everybody stayed. But
there was enough of a moon that evening to light the ride
back to Miracle, and everyone was enjoying the day too
much to leave.

When it fell quiet for a moment, Mrs. Parrish rose, silently left the house, and returned from her buggy a minute
or two later holding a large bag.

"I brought each of you some presents," she said, glancing around at the five of us Hollister kids. "My apologies to
the rest of you," she added, looking at the Stansberrys, Uncle Nick, and Mr. Jones with a smile and shrug. "But you
know what they say, Christmas is for children!"

"We'll enjoy your giving to them just as much," put in
Miss Stansberry.

Then Mrs. Parrish reached into her bag and began pulling out little gifts, each wrapped in bright paper—dolls for
the girls, a colorful wooden top for Tad, a pocketknife for
Zack, and a new book called *Moby Dick* for me. When all
our exclamations and thank-yous had died down some, she
pulled one more little package out of her bag.

"I must confess, I have one for you, too, Mr. Hollister,"
she said, handing it to Pa. "Apologies again to the rest of
you!" she added looking quickly around the room. "I saw
this the last time I was in Sacramento, and I immediately
thought, 'This looks like something Drummond Hollister
would enjoy.' So I bought it, and here it is."

"That's right kind of you, ma'am." I could tell Pa was
embarrassed by all the fuss, but he didn't show it as his
fingers tore off the paper and he took the nice carved pipe
in his hands.

"It's a *fine* looking pipe. You really pulled a surprise on
me—Mrs.—Mrs. Parrish," said Pa. "I can't figure what to
say, except thank you, ma'am."

Mrs. Parrish nodded but didn't reply.

"What's that white stuff there?" asked Pa.

"That's ivory, Mr. Hollister," she said softly. "They carve it from the tusks of elephants in Africa."

Pa gave a low whistle, indicating that he knew the pipe must have been expensive, while he kept turning it over and around in his hand.

Meanwhile Alkali Jones walked over to the corner, picked up his fiddle, and plucked softly at the strings.

"I say, Mr. Jones, do you know any Christmas tunes?" asked Rev. Rutledge. "Perhaps we might sing a chorus or two."

That was all the invitation Mr. Jones needed to begin demonstrating that indeed he did. And if he didn't know a song that Rev. Rutledge wanted, then "if the Rev'ren'd be good enough t' hum a bit o' it," he'd be sure to pick up the tune in no time!

What a perfect way to end a wonderful Christmas day—singing and clapping and smiling, while Mr. Jones fiddled and Rev. Rutledge led us in singing "Joy to the World," "Hark the Herald Angels Sing," and "The First Noel." He even taught us a couple I'd never heard.

But we hardly needed Mr. Jones. We'd sung in the church services plenty of times, but I'd never realized how beautiful a singer Mrs. Parrish was! Her voice was an instrument all by itself! And, of course, Rev. Rutledge could sing and so could Miss Stansberry. It was a lively and pretty-sounding music that came from our place that evening!

After the more rousing songs, a quiet came over us all the moment we started singing "Silent Night." After the first verse, Mrs. Parrish interrupted to tell us all the story of Franz Gruber and of the snowy mountain night when the words of the song first came to him. When she was through, we started singing again, with Rev. Rutledge helping us with the words, all the way to the last verse:

"Silent night, holy night,
Wondrous star, lend thy light;
With the angels let us sing,
Alleluia to our King;
Christ the Savior is born,
Christ the Savior is born."

Everything was silent for a long time. No one in the cabin said a word. Then finally Rev. Rutledge looked over at Pa and said, "Mr. Hollister, it just somehow seems fitting for us—would you mind if I offered a Christmas prayer?"

Without a moment's hesitation, Pa answered, "Not at all, Reverend. I think that'd be a mighty fine thing to do."

We all bowed our heads and closed our eyes, then Rev. Rutledge began to pray. For the first time his words didn't sound far off to me. It didn't seem that he was trying to make sure God heard him up in heaven someplace, but like he was talking to Him right in the room with us.

"Our Father," he said, "we are all so thankful to You right now for this day—this Christmas day! We are thankful because of what this day means—that on this day Your Son, God's own Son, became a little baby and was born on the earth. God, we thank You that there is such a day as Christmas, and that there was a baby Jesus, who lived among us and grew up to be a man who would die for us. We know that He came to us on Christmas day in order to teach us how to live, how to behave, how to think, and how to obey You. So God, we pray that You would help us in our daily lives to do those things—not just remembering Jesus on Christmas day, but remembering *every* day that He walks beside us to help us be Your sons and daughters. Help us, our God, our Father, to make *every* day Christmas day in our hearts, a day when the life of Jesus is born ever new to us! Amen."

# CHAPTER 21

## NEW YEAR, NEW CHALLENGES

The year 1854 opened with a gigantic snowstorm the day after New Year's. It was four days before Pa finally rode Jester into Miracle. When he came back he said that no one else had been able to get to town either, and that Miss Stansberry had cancelled school until the roads were melted off.

The old timers of the area said they never remembered so much snow that low down out of the mountains. Alkali Jones, of course, had stories to top everyone's, and he claimed that long before gold was discovered, *he* had seen snow six feet deep where Sacramento was now. Nobody believed him. But they listened, every now and then throwing winks from one to another to show they weren't swallowing a word of it.

When we finally did get back to school, a lot of things started changing. There are times we look back on as being turning points, and after those times nothing is the same again—like when Ma died, or that first day when we rode into Miracle Springs with Captain Dixon.

This was one of those times. It wasn't sudden, not one particular moment, but a spread-out time of change. I suppose it started with Pa's letter from Miss Morgan. Nothing could be the same after that. And the idea of a second Mrs.

Drummond Hollister took a lot of getting used to. I wasn't altogether seeing things from Pa's standpoint. I should have been happy for him, and down inside I knew he was doing it for us kids as much as for himself. But the selfish part of me was afraid of what Miss Morgan's coming might mean.

Christmas day at our house had been a day to stick in the mind for a long time. There had been so many difficulties from the first when we came to California, getting all the people and feelings and relationships figured out—first we found our Pa, but Pa and Mrs. Parrish didn't get along too well. Then Uncle Nick got into trouble. When the minister came, he and Pa did a lot of arguing. Then Pa changed from being so gruff, and his life became different than his rough past. Finally Miss Stansberry came, and the school started up.

There had been so many changes! Yet there we all were in our cabin—together, talking, having fun, laughing, singing—Uncle Nick, the minister, Alkali Jones, Pa, and Mrs. Parrish! It felt like a high point, the perfect end to all the problems we had all had that year.

But it seemed almost fated to end just as it was beginning. The minute Pa told everyone about Miss Morgan and about him marrying again, I could feel that things were going to change again, that we might never again have a day where everything was as good as that Christmas day.

Maybe it was selfish of me, but I didn't know if I relished the thought that a year from then there'd be a new woman taking care of things in the Hollister kitchen instead of me. Mrs. Parrish might not ever spend Christmas with us again. She might not even be Mrs. Parrish the next year, but Mrs. Rutledge instead.

Not all the changes were things I worried about. After that Christmas day, once we got back to school, I started feeling a special friendship with Miss Stansberry. After that day she felt a part of our family, and I noticed her always smiling warmly and taking a moment or two with Tad and Becky and Emily. She knew just how to treat Zack, helping him with his learning, but in a way that made him feel like he was one of the older and grown-up pupils. She had such a knack for making Zack feel like she really needed him in the school that he started perking up, working hard on his papers and reading, doing schoolwork at home, and trying all the time to please her.

Pa'd say things like, "What's got into you, boy?" half joking at Zack working on some assignment, and Zack'd just shrug.

But I could tell Pa was happy about it—though not half as proud as Zack was when Miss Stansberry praised him in front of the class for his hard work and improvement. It wasn't long before she had him helping with the younger boys. Even Little Wolf went to Zack for assistance a lot, and Zack was proud of that, since he was several years younger than Little Wolf.

Miss Stansberry was kind to me too. She gradually quit treating me as one of her students and began treating me like another teacher. Whatever she'd said about *needing* an assistant, all of us knew by that time that she could handle most anything that would come up. No one thought of her as crippled anymore—I don't even think we remembered it half the time. I think she wanted me as her assistant as much for my sake as her own.

In March I turned seventeen, and that had plenty to do with some of my worries. I didn't think of it at the time, because when I'm *in* a situation I don't really know why I think certain things.

But looking back on it now, deep inside I realized that seventeen was nearly grown up. I wasn't a little girl any more. And maybe that's why Miss Stansberry treated me differently as time went on. Late in the spring she even asked me if I'd like to call her Harriet.

Before Miss Morgan's letter I didn't need to think much about what would become of me. There was nothing much to think about except helping Pa with the young'uns, cooking, and keeping the house. I never really thought much about the future. I hoped I'd get to write some more for Mr. Singleton, but I never thought about having to leave Pa and the cabin.

But with Miss Morgan coming, it seemed that Pa might not need me much any more. Being seventeen, I'd be grown pretty soon, and it gets cumbersome with too many grown-ups in a little house. She'd take care of the kids and the cooking, so there wouldn't be much for me to do. And I was getting too old for school. I couldn't keep being Miss Stansberry's helper for ever!

I had never thought much about my future—just a little about being a teacher or writing some newspaper articles. But now I realized that people would start to figure I ought to get married.

And if I tried to do some kind of work like teaching or working for a paper, they'd start to call me an old maid! I didn't figure I was the marrying kind, and wasn't interested in being one. Yet if I tried to do some kind of work of my own, it might mean leaving Pa and the kids.

I knew Pa was trying to help, but Miss Morgan's coming didn't do much for me except make me afraid of what might happen to me next.

So that spring of 1854 was a hard time for me. I went for lots of walks by myself and wrote lots of thoughts in my journal. I was moody and quiet sometimes, and I wasn't altogether pleasant to the others.

I tried to pray whenever I'd get to worrying, but I couldn't tell if God was paying much attention or not. I knew I ought to talk to Mrs. Parrish about it, but sometimes I was embarrassed to tell her what I was thinking and feeling because it seemed selfish, and she was always so thoughtful of other folks.

But on Easter Sunday afternoon, just a couple of weeks after my seventeenth birthday, I had a talk with her that I'll never forget. And of all the things that made the first part of 1854 so memorable, that was the biggest day of all. It was a turning point that made all the others seem small.

Mrs. Parrish took me for a ride out into the country and told me, "I think the time has finally come, Corrie, for me to tell you something I've been wanting to share with you for a long time."

Pa had gotten a letter from Miss Morgan the day before. It wasn't the first letter we received, and it didn't say anything different from the others. But maybe because of my birthday, because I was thinking about getting older and wondering what was to become of me, that particular letter unnerved me.

Or maybe it was the way Pa seemed to be gradually getting excited about her coming, because from the letters she sounded like a fun lady. And he was talking more regularly about how things would be after she got here, and I was feeling a little hurt that he didn't seem to care much about me and what I was feeling.

The letter said:

I don't know exactly what day I will arrive, since so much of the passage time, I am told, depends on the weather. I will stop over several days at a hotel in San Francisco, and from there I will notify you of my arrival. I will then take the steamer up the river to Sacramento, where I hope you will be able to meet me. If there are other details, I will write again. I will tell you now, so that whenever and however I manage to get there, how you may recognize me. I do not favor hats, but on this occasion I shall be wearing a floppy white hat with a red flower. It is the only hat I own. I am looking forward to meeting all of you—children, brother-in-law, yourself . . . your whole clan. You have warned me to be prepared for a humble mountain cabin. But it will be a pleasure for me to have a stove and kitchen to call my own after so many years with my aunt. Tell Corrie and Becky and Emily that I am so happy to have such big girls for my stepdaughters— that is, if you decide to keep me, Mr. Hollister!

That was not all she wrote, but it was enough to bring a lump to my throat, and as soon as Pa was finished reading it I went outside to be alone.

I didn't want to be anybody's stepdaughter! And I didn't want to be called a "big girl," as if I were ten years old! And I didn't want to share *my* kitchen with someone I didn't even know!

I couldn't tell any of what I was thinking to Pa. He'd either get mad at me or else feel bad himself, and I didn't want to cause him any more misery.

I'd already overheard him telling Uncle Nick once that he was having second thoughts about what he'd done. And now that he was planning to go through with it, I didn't want to upset him any more.

Worst of all, I felt so selfish! Why couldn't I be happy for Pa, happy for Miss Morgan, like everybody else? If this was for the best for all the rest of the family, how could I be so mean as to worry about no one but myself? I wanted to be good and I tried to ask God to help me think better thoughts, but down inside I felt miserable.

The next day, Easter Sunday, we went to church. I sat there the whole time trying hard to keep from crying. I didn't hear a word Rev. Rutledge said. I don't even remember what he spoke about. I just sat there glum and staring forward, with my mind tumbling about on all the things I was wrestling with inside, and knowing I wasn't behaving like God would want. It was Easter Sunday, when folks were dressed nice and happy and smiling to one another, and that just made it all the worse!

Some folks have a way of being able to look at you and know just what you're thinking. Mrs. Parrish was always that way with me. She walked over to me after the service, pulled me a few steps away from the others, and said, "How about if I drive out this afternoon and you and I go for a ride together?"

# CHAPTER 22

## EASTER SUNDAY— NEW BIRTH

By the time we'd driven out to a little meadow a couple miles out of town, Mrs. Parrish had gotten out of me all the worries that were on my mind, and a few more even *I* didn't know were there!

One or two questions was all it took and I gushed out with it all.

By the time I was done, I was crying and feeling like a baby, and feeling all the more foolish for thinking my anxieties had to do with growing up. Right then I'd never felt *less* like a woman and more like a little girl!

"And you feel both mixed up about all the changes that are coming, *and* a little guilty because you think you're being selfish, is that it?" asked Mrs. Parrish.

"That's about the size of it," I answered. "Just when it seemed my world was getting smoothed out, now all of a sudden I feel like I did after Ma died, not knowing what's to become of me."

"Well, perhaps I can help," she smiled. "Perhaps *the Lord* can help, I should say," she added. "Come, let's go walk. This meadow is one of my favorite places. I often come here when I want to get away and think or pray."

She tied her horse to a tree, then led the way across the

grass, greening and now growing briskly in the spring warmth.

"Let's sit over there on those two large rocks, Corrie," she pointed.

When we were comfortable, she took a deep breath, then began.

"I've been wanting to tell you some things for a long while, Corrie," she said. "But the time has to be just right, or else it's impossible to understand them. I could have said all this to you much sooner, and part of me wanted to. Yet I knew it would mean more to you if I waited until the time came in your life when you were hungry to know these things."

She paused and thought a moment. "Corrie, do you remember the conversation we had our first Christmas together—when I took you and Emily and Becky to the dressmaker's?"

"Oh yes, Mrs. Parrish!" I answered. "You told me a lot about what sin means, and how we all need Jesus in our lives to take away the sin. I wrote it all down in my journal."

Mrs. Parrish smiled, then very seriously asked, "You do know that Jesus is still alive, don't you, Corrie?"

"Yes, ma'am. That's what today's about—Easter. Everybody knows that, don't they?"

"Maybe they know it in their heads, but do they fully realize what it *means*—in the daily moments of their lives?"

"What does it mean?" I asked.

"Just this, Corrie—and this is the most wonderful truth in all the world. Since Jesus is alive, He is with us—right now, this very moment!"

"I guess I've heard that, but it's kind of hard to catch hold of—I mean, you can never *see* Him."

"That's because He's not present in His body, but in His Spirit." Her eyes were glowing with excitement. "And there's a very special place God created for the spirit of Jesus to live after He came back to life—to live forever! Do you know where I mean?"

I thought I knew what she was getting at. "Inside us?"

"Exactly, Corrie! In our *hearts*!" she replied enthusiastically. "In my heart—" she laid her hand on her bosom, "—and in yours, Corrie. That's Jesus' home, in the hearts of men and women!"

"Really?" Her excitement was catching. "In everybody's?"

She gave a sigh, and a cloud passed quickly over her face.

"No, Corrie, not everybody's," she said.

"Are there too many people?" I asked, "and not enough of Him to go around?"

"Oh no, that's not it at all! God is so big that He could fill up every heart on ten thousand worlds and still have only begun. No, the problem is that not every heart *lets* His Spirit live there, even though that was the reason it was made."

"You mean God doesn't automatically live in our hearts?"

"Oh no, Corrie. God is such a gentleman that He will never come into a place unless He's invited. So He only lives in the hearts of the men and women who open the door to that little place down inside them. It's like—"

She stopped and thought for a second.

"Well, think back to Christmas day and that wonderful dinner we all had together. What do you suppose Rev. Rutledge and I would have done if we'd driven up, gone to the house, and found the door locked? Then up drove Harriet and Hermon and they came and joined us. They asked why we didn't go in, and we told them the door was locked tight.

"We knew your father was inside. What should we have done—gone out to your pa's tool shed to find a sledgehammer to break down the door?

"No, we wouldn't even have wanted to go in unless he himself, the head of the house, invited us in and opened the door to us. As it was, we went in and enjoyed a day of hospitality, good food, and wonderful fellowship, because your father invited us to come and opened his home to us."

She paused a moment to let it all sink in.

"That's how God is, Corrie. He wants to come in and make His home with us. But He waits patiently and never beats down doors. You see, there's only one key to the door of every heart, and we're the only ones who possess it. God may be all powerful, but on the other hand, that's one thing God *can't* do—force open our doors."

She paused, and the most peculiar smile came over her face. I could tell that the words had sparked some memory in her own life. She said nothing for another moment, and I sat silently, feeling like I was watching her relive some time in her past—a happy moment, but one that carried with it a certain pain as well.

"So to answer your question," she finally went on, "God *wants* to live in everybody's heart, and I hope someday He will, I don't know. But for now He only lives where the doors have been opened from the inside."

Again she stopped and the same odd smile returned to her expression. "Opening the door can sometimes be very painful. I can tell you that from personal experience. I did not always see things as I do now, Corrie. God had to put me through some heartbreaking disappointments, and I resisted for a long while. Perhaps one day I shall be able to tell you about it," she added rather wistfully.

"I would like that, ma'am," I replied.

"But not today . . . to start on *that* story would take all afternoon!"

She laughed. It was good to see the joy return to her face. It seemed she had put her memories back into the closet of the past once again.

"Again, from my own personal experience, I can tell you that after God *has* come inside, everything changes. He helps

our inner selves to become more like Him. God's desire—
in my heart, yours, your father's, your uncle's, Rev. Rutledge's, or anybody's—is to make us become like Jesus—
not just in outer actions, but inside. With His Spirit living
inside us, gradually we do become more gracious and forgiving and loving and unselfish and considerate *on the inside*."

Even before she was finished I was crying again.

"And that's what you want, isn't it, Corrie?" she said
gently.

I nodded.

"You want to be more like God wants you to be, but
with everything making your life confusing right now, you
realize you're not at all like you think you should be, like
you want to be? Is that something of what you're feeling?"

I nodded again.

"I know that feeling, Corrie," she said. "I know what
it's like to feel like you're bad, to feel like you've failed, to
feel like you've disappointed the people you love the most.
And you see, that's why Jesus wants to live in our hearts.
He can help us!

"He can not only help you face your uncertain future,
He can help you become the person you long to be deep
inside. None of us is what we'd like to be. The Bible says
we're sinners. But God can help us. That's why He wants
us to unlock the doors of our hearts and let Him come in
and live with us there."

"That sounds too good to be true."

"It's just so good it *must* be true! Oh, Corrie, God is so
good to us! He loves us more than we can realize and has
such a wonderful life to give us! Yes, I'm a sinner, just like
the worst man in Miracle Springs. But inside my heart the
Spirit of God lives. And He is slowly remaking me, and
teaching me to live and think and behave differently than I
would if He were not helping me."

"Oh, I *do* want to be good, Mrs. Parrish!" I exclaimed. "I want God to live in my heart, too, and to help me like He is you! Do you think He is there?"

"I don't know, Corrie. He may already be there, drawing you toward Him. One never knows when that little invisible door opens and He slips in. I truly believe that the door of some people's hearts' open before they are ever aware of it, and God's Spirit finds an easy and natural entrance, perhaps in the early years of childhood. Some hearts seem open to God right from birth.

"Others are born with great resistance, and it may take years and years of God's patient knocking before they finally hear Him. For some persons there is an exact moment when they consciously open their heart. For others it is a gradual process. In your case, Corrie, I suspect that God has long been with you without your even knowing it. I sense that your heart is open toward Him, and that you want to be His daughter."

Even as she spoke, I could feel my eyes filling with tears once more.

"I do, Mrs. Parrish!" I said. "I do want to be His daughter and to live in a way that pleases Him—down inside, like you said, not just on the outside!"

She tried to say something, but hesitated. I could see a tear falling down her cheek. At first I didn't understand why, but I did later.

"You . . . you can't know what joy it gives me to hear those precious words, Corrie," she said at last, and her voice was husky with emotion. "And they please God far more than either of us can possibly realize. I sensed when I saw you in church this morning that the day had finally come when you would want to know these things and were really ready to begin living in a deeper way as a Christian."

She paused, then looked into my eyes with the most wonderful smile on her face.

"Corrie," she said, "I love you, and I know you are dear to God's heart . . ."

She stopped, then reached across and took both my hands in hers. Then she closed her eyes and started to pray.

"Oh, loving Father! How I thank You for this dear friend you have brought to me! Show her, Lord, more and more of Yourself every day. Nurture her dawning faith, and let her reflect the image of Your Son. Strengthen her heart's desire—"

She stopped. I opened my eyes to glance at her. She was softly weeping.

I closed my eyes again. I couldn't help being a little nervous.

"God," I prayed out loud, "I really do want to be good like You want me to be. And I want to be kind and loving like Mrs. Parrish talks about, on the inside. I want to be Your daughter, and I don't know if that door to my heart's open or not, or if maybe You're already there. But if You're not, I'd like you to be, and—"

Suddenly I couldn't say anything more. I felt a rush inside me, like the breaking of a dam on a stream, like something was being pulled out from the very depths of me. My voice cracked and my eyes were full, but I struggled to get out the words—

"Help me, Lord. Help me to live like you want me to. Help me not to resent Miss Morgan's coming. Help me to know what I'm supposed to do."

That was all I could say for a minute. It was already more than I figured I could pray out loud in front of anybody.

But then almost without thinking, I added, "And I pray for Pa too, Lord, that you'd help him to do the right thing. Amen."

Mrs. Parrish added a quiet *Amen* after mine.

I opened my eyes. Mrs. Parrish was looking at me with a radiant smile. Her cheeks were wet with tears.

# CHAPTER 23

# THE RIDE HOME

I felt better after that.

It wasn't so much that now all of a sudden I figured all my worries would go away. But riding back to Miracle, Mrs. Parrish explained that once I had really given myself to God and asked Him to help me be a person who was more like He wanted me to be, then my whole outlook could change.

"You see, Corrie," she said, "when a person desperately *wants* to walk closer to God the Christian life begins to be so much more thrilling. Most people are content with their lives as they are. They don't think about growth, change, about developing new habits and attitudes. They just take every day as it comes and aren't really trying to be any different from one day to the next. Growth and development toward more godly behavior isn't what they base their lives on. But then from out of nowhere comes some trouble that they don't know how to handle. And then they finally begin to realize that they need some help. They see that they need to open the door and invite someone else into their house, someone who can help them become the kind of person they now see that they want to be. But until that time, they feel self-sufficient and satisfied and content with the way they are, and feel no need for growth and change. It is very difficult for people to be close to God if they are perfectly content to remain locked inside their houses all alone."

"And that's why you waited until today to tell me about opening the door of my heart to let Jesus live there?" I asked.

"Don't misunderstand me, Corrie," replied Mrs. Parrish. "I truly believe you have loved God for a long time. You and I have had many good talks together about being Christians. I would not have you think that I consider all that meaningless. It's just that *now*—now that some of these hurts and frustrations and confusions inside you have awakened a hunger to grow and be better—now you can really begin sharing your life with God more deeply every day. It's not that what came before wasn't good and valuable, but now that you realize your need, you can begin depending on God more, and trusting Him for more and more things in your life."

"Trusting Him—how?"

"Trusting that He will take care of you, trusting Him to work good for everyone out of Miss Morgan's coming, trusting Him for your pa, trusting Him for your future—for everything, Corrie! If you've given yourself to Him as His daughter, then you can trust Him to be a wise and loving heavenly Father, and to take perfect care of you!"

"So I shouldn't worry about my future, or whether Pa will think I'm in the way in the kitchen? Sometimes I just can't help worrying."

"It's all right to be concerned and to think about things. But remember what I told you a while back, about how God can turn everything and make it into good? Corrie, your whole attitude toward life slowly begins to change when you realize that God is with you every moment, helping you grow, strengthening you, helping you know what to do. Pretty soon all those worries don't look so big, because you realize He knows all about them too and has the solution all figured out ahead of time."

"But what if I can't?" I asked.

"Can't what, Corrie?"

"Can't do all those things—trust God better and be nicer and not worry so much. What if God being with me doesn't change my attitude and make me strong like you said?"

"Oh, but it will, Corrie! There is no *what if* to it. When God lives in a heart, things *do* change. He makes sure of that—He helps!"

She stopped, and her enthusiastic look suddenly turned thoughtful. I could tell she was reconsidering what she'd just said.

"Well," she finally said, still with the serious look on her face, "there is one *if* to it, now that I think about it. Not all people do grow and change and get to be strong Christians."

"Why is that?"

"Well, Corrie, I told you that God doesn't force His way into our lives. And He doesn't force us to do His will either. We have a *choice* to accept Him and submit to the changes He wants to work in us. God comes into our lives, saying, 'I'll come into your heart, and I'll give you joy and I'll make you strong, and I'll help you become more like Jesus, and I'll gradually turn you into the person I created you to be.' That's His gift to us, His part. But we have to cooperate. We need to respond to His love with obedience. Our part is this: we have to do what He says. God *will* change us and make us better, but He won't work against our will. He can only work the changes if we are holding up our side and doing what Jesus told us to do. We need to say 'yes' to Jesus—not just to His desire to live in us, but to His desire to rule our lives as well. Our obedience to Him makes it possible for Him to do the changes He wants to do."

"Well," I said slowly, trying to take in all she was saying, "I reckon that's fair."

"Completely fair! Everything God does is fair, though sometimes the fairness is hard for folks to see. And this argeement—God doing His part, us doing our part—explains why some people never change and others do, and why there are nasty, selfish people in the church who think they are good Christians. Being a Christian is more than knowing in your head who Jesus is—it's surrendering your heart to His ways. The changes in our lives depend on whether we are obeying God, not on our religious talk or how much about the Bible we know or whether we go to church all the time."

"So going to church and reading the Bible and praying and all that doesn't matter?" I asked.

"Oh no, Corrie, I didn't mean that! Those things are very important. But they're only important if they help you learn to do more of what Jesus said. Otherwise, I'm afraid they are meaningless. Do you understand?"

"I think so," I answered slowly. "If I open the door of my heart to let Jesus live there—and I think I have, haven't I, Mrs. Parrish?"

"You have, Corrie! Yes, His Spirit *is* inside you."

". . . if I've done that, then He will make me better and will help me have better thoughts and trust Him more . . . *if* I try to do what I'm supposed to—if I obey what Jesus said to do."

"Yes, that's it exactly! And that's why it *is* important to read the Bible—especially the four gospels—so you can find out what Jesus said, and the kind of people He wants us to be."

"I see."

"And then there's one last catch, Corrie."

"Another one?"

Mrs. Parrish laughed. "I'm afraid so! But this is the last one, I promise. After this, I think you'll have plenty to think about for a good long time!"

"All right," I said, returning her smile. "But I've already got more than I think I'll be able to remember."

"Well, this last thing may be most important of all. Do you want me to tell you now or save it for another time?"

"Oh no. Tell me now. I want to hear it! But when I write all this down in my journal, I'm going to have to come and ask you lots of questions to help me remember everything you've said."

"Agreed. Now, Corrie, we must remember that God's work in our hearts takes a lifetime. The changes we're talking about, learning to trust Him, obeying more like Jesus did, being more loving to people—none of that happens to us all at once. We're still the same people. We still have the same bad habits. And though God wants to remake us—and does!—it's a very slow process."

"Because we don't do our part very well?"

"Partly. But even when we are good and *do* what we're supposed to do, it still takes a long time for us to get to be very much like Jesus. So try not to get discouraged if you get to feeling like you're not the kind of person you want to be. It takes years and years of practice—of *trying* to trust God more, of *trying* to have better attitudes toward people, of *trying* to be unselfish—before you begin to feel you're getting anywhere."

"That does sound discouraging."

"Perhaps I'm not explaining it very well." She paused, thought for a moment, and then said, "If we are cooperating, then God *is* bringing about the changes. But they're happening so deep inside us that *we* can't see them for a long time. You *are* His daughter, a daughter of His grace and love. And He *is* gradually making you more and more like Jesus, but way down deep where His Spirit lives—in your heart—and the changes aren't always visible on the surface. Do you see what I mean?"

"I think so. Kinda like when Pa and Uncle Nick are working in the mine, you can't see them when they're way down inside it. They may be digging out all kinds of gold, but if you're standing looking at the outside, you can't see it."

"That's it exactly, Corrie! God is mining for gold inside

our hearts, but we can't see how much He's getting, and maybe won't see it for years and years."

"And is it kinda like—from what you said before about it being something both God and us have to be working on—is it kinda like we're doing the gold mining with Him, but can't see it?"

"The great thing, Corrie, is that *we* decide how full of gold our own mine is!"

"How's that?"

"Remember what I said about the years of practice in *doing* the things we're supposed to do?"

I nodded.

"Well, every time you or I do some little act of kindness, even though afterward we might not *feel* any different, a tiny little change happens deep inside us. We've added a tiny piece of gold to the mine! Every time I deal fairly with someone in business that I could have taken advantage of, every act of kindness you do to one of your brothers or sisters, every gentle word, every forgiveness, every unselfishness, every time you or I lay aside what *we* want for the happiness of someone else, every prayer we utter on behalf of another, every generous act—they're all little nuggets of gold, Corrie. Some Christians are filling their mines with rich veins, while other are letting opportunities pass every day, and their mines are filling up instead with nothing but dirt and worthless rock."

"But when do we find out?"

"I suppose most people won't know until they die. But once you've been walking through life for five or ten or fifteen years, every once in a while you begin to get glimpses of gold coming to the surface.

"You see, Corrie, the Lord is working away in the mine of our hearts all the time, from now until the day we die—all night, all day, every moment. And all those little specks of gold we fill our mines with, today, tomorrow, next week, next year, *every* little kindness and unselfishness for all the rest of our lives—they all add up together.

"In the end, our hearts are either rich with the gold we have put there for God to develop into a Christlike character, or else they are still empty, even though God has been picking away all our lives to find some gold to put to use. We don't see this work going on, but every moment we are either putting gold in the mine of our heart or we are putting dirt and rock there.

"That's why, at the end of life, some people are radiant with the love of God and others are miserable old grouches. It all depends on the millions of tiny choices we make all day long, every day—golden choices of unselfishness or dirty choices that turn out to be worthless in the end."

I looked up just as she finished speaking, and we were driving up the road to our house. I guess the conversation was finished for now, because already I could hear the yells of Emily and Becky and Tad running out to meet us.

It was probably just as well we were home. I had plenty to think about for now!

# CHAPTER 24

## THE DAY FINALLY COMES

It was May when Miss Morgan got here.

Pa said he'd told her all about his past in New York—actually his words were, "everything she needs to know"—and she still wanted to come. He said, "I reckon she more or less knows what she's gettin' herself into." As much as Pa didn't want the wrong folks to know about New York, he seemed to be trying hard to be honest about himself whenever he could.

There'd been considerable anticipation around town. After all, Pa was well known. With us kids and the gold mine and all, there'd been quite a bit for folks to talk about concerning Pa already. And once word started spreading around about him sending for a mail-order bride, Pa was on everybody's lips. It was the first time around here that anything like that had happened.

Pa hated it, of course. Occasionally, one of the men would come out of a store or one of the saloons with some comment or a laugh and a wink, like, "Hey, Drum, when's yore pretty little catalog bride comin'?" or "I'll tell ya what, Hollister, if she ain't to yore likin', send her my way." Whenever he heard shouts coming his direction, he'd walk on or turn the other way, ignoring them altogether.

Something told me that Pa almost wanted to forget the

whole thing. After all, nobody had heard any more of that man Hatch from south of here. Uncle Nick had been behaving himself. And all my worries after going to San Francisco with Mrs. Parrish turned out to be nothing at all. In fact, I was embarrassed to have gotten in such a tizzy about it, thinking Buck Krebbs was going to follow me here just because he happened to see me all alone. After all, he had known where Pa was all the time. Why was seeing me in San Francisco going to make any difference to him?

At the time I was scared that he'd tried to get me when I was by myself, that seeing me might put the idea into his head to try it again. But now I felt foolish for making all the fuss—especially since that was what started Pa out thinking he needed to get a new wife.

But Mrs. Parrish told me there weren't any accidents that happened to God's people. And since I was one of them, then all that was part of "God's story for my life," as she called it, including the new chapter that was about to begin, the coming of Miss Kathryn Morgan.

I couldn't help wondering if Pa wished he'd never written those letters. But he'd already sent the money back East, and maybe he didn't want the men around town to think he was backing down. Before long it was too late, anyway. Miss Morgan was probably already on her way.

We knew about when she'd be coming, but then came the letter saying she'd be coming into Sacramento on the steamer arriving from San Francisco on May 11th, at 2:45 in the afternoon.

Maybe only Pa and I were secretly harboring our reservations about the whole notion of a new woman about the place. Everyone else seemed excited.

It was such an "event" that three or four hours after the letter arrived, the whole town knew Pa'd be heading down to Sacramento the next day to fetch his new bride-to-be. The more hoopla there was about it, the more reserved Pa got.

He seemed mighty anxious inside. Maybe he was thinking more about Ma than Miss Morgan. Sometimes he'd sit up late at night, just sitting beside the fire, holding the one picture of Ma we had, or holding her Bible, although I don't think I ever saw him reading in it. He'd get up or sigh, almost as if he was saying to himself, *Well, sometimes a man's just gotta do somethin' just 'cause he thinks it's the right thing to do, even if he ain't too keen about it.*

At the same time, even though he wasn't saying much these days, part of Pa couldn't help being just a little bit excited too. I think he was hoping that maybe he'd like Miss Morgan a lot.

The whole town would likely have gone to Sacramento with Pa if he'd let them! Pa had become kind of a local hero, and everybody was watching his every move and wanting to be part of it. Alkali Jones, Uncle Nick, others of Pa's friends—they all would have gone.

But Pa said no—it was just gonna be him and the kids.

Zack and Little Wolf had been getting to be good friends, mostly riding horses together a lot up in the hills around Miracle.

Little Wolf's father was raising horses now, and he didn't seem to mind his son being around a white boy. They'd go up in the hills, high up toward the Sierras, and they'd race and even help break some of the horses. So when we found out about the trip to Sacramento, Zack begged Pa to let Little Wolf come along. Pa said he could. The two boys would ride their horses.

Pa was planning to take our wagon, even though it was just an old buckboard, and clunking along the bumpy roads wasn't any too comfortable. But the afternoon before we were to leave, we heard the hoofs and rattling and clatter of someone coming up the road.

Pa was the first one to the door. All I heard him say was, "What in tarnation. . . ?" The end of his sentence finished up with his mouth hanging open.

Outside sat a new-looking, all-black brougham carriage, covered on top, with a nice little door and a window into the inside compartment. Two of the Parrish Mine and Freight Company's finest looking horses snorted and danced in place in front of it. Mrs. Parrish was just that moment jumping down onto the ground.

Pa walked out with a bewildered expression on his face, followed by the rest of us.

"I hope you won't take offense, Mr. Hollister," Mrs. Parrish said with a smile, shaking Pa's hand. "I well remember when you told me some time ago that I should not interfere with your family's affairs."

While she spoke her face was smiling, like she knew Pa wasn't going to fuss like he used to, and showing that she wasn't afraid to kid him just a little.

". . . but I must say, that old rickety wagon of yours is not the proper coach for a man of your, shall we say, your standing in the community, to pick up his future bride in. No, no, Mr. Hollister, I said to myself that you simply must have something finer on this occasion."

She paused, to give more emphasis to her next words.

"So, as you can see—I have solved that little problem for you."

She held out the reins in one gloved hand.

"But, I—I don't reckon I understand what—"

"Don't worry," she laughed. "It won't cost you a dime. Nor me, either! I have a friend up in French Corral, a wealthy banker who has done a good deal of business with me. I knew he had this brougham and rarely used it. So I rode up yesterday and borrowed it for you. I've taken full responsibility. You don't have to worry about a thing."

"You caught me unsuspecting, Mrs. Parrish," said Pa at last, forcing a smile. "But there just ain't no way I can—"

"Just take the reins and don't say a word, Mr. Hollister."

Now her voice was more serious. She was still smiling, but not at all making light of the situation. At that moment I saw how much Mrs. Parrish had come to care about Pa. At first it had been just for us kids that she'd done things and been nice. But this—I could tell as she handed him the reins and looked steadily at him—she'd done just for Pa.

Pa seemed really touched. "Ma'am," he said, "I am obliged to you! That's just a mighty thoughtful thing to have done."

"Not another word about it," replied Mrs. Parrish. "Just bring your Miss Morgan back here safe and sound. Now," she went on, turning back to the carriage, "it's made to seat four inside. With the children, you might squeeze in five. But if not, someone can sit next to you up on the driver's seat. And there's a rack on top for her luggage. Take some rope with you to tie it down."

Pa walked all the way around it, taking in every line and curve, examining the wheels, while Mrs. Parrish undid her horse from the harnesses.

"So I'll just be back off to town," she said, throwing the saddle she'd brought over the horse's back and cinching up the straps. "And I'll see all you back here in four or five days!"

She went around to each of us with a hug and a personal word. She held me an extra second or two, then just looked deeply into my eyes without saying anything. I knew what that look was meant to say.

Early the next morning, Pa climbed into the driver's seat, and Emily and Becky and Tad and I clambered up into the fancy black carriage. With Zack and Little Wolf excitedly leading the way on their two horses, we were off on our two-day trip to Sacramento.

# CHAPTER 25

# THE ARRIVAL OF MISS
# KATHRYN MORGAN

On the afternoon of May 11, we stood alongside the Sacramento River at the same landing I already felt I knew, watching the big white steamer glide slowly up to the wooden dock.

We scanned the deck and the people on it as the boat slid up, looking in vain for a white hat. But none was to be seen.

When the boat finally came to a stop, two men jumped down and tied the huge ropes to two pylons. A third man hauled out a short wooden ramp, banged it down onto the dock while keeping one end hooked to the boat, and the passengers started filing down the incline and off the boat.

I don't reckon anyone would have had much trouble picking *us* out! There we stood, five kids and an Indian, crowded around a big, rugged-looking man, with his hat in his hand, and a look of apprehension on his face.

"Will she be nice, Pa?" asked Tad's innocent voice.

" 'Course she'll be nice. Now just be quiet and help me look," came back Pa's answer—a little too gruff, but I guess both Pa and Tad were nervous.

It didn't take much more looking. The second she came into view we all spotted her. It was the only floppy white hat and red flower in the whole place! She was shorter than most of the other women, which was why we hadn't seen her on deck.

I don't know quite what I expected to happen. There we were, and there she was, all of us frozen in time looking at each other. I suppose it wasn't any longer than a second, but those kinds of moments have a way of stretching out. You can get inside them and think about all kinds of different things, and then come back again, and still only a tiny fraction of time has gone by. This was one of those times. Everything stood still on the outside, while my mind was racing on the inside. And then when I woke up to the real-life present, we were still just standing there staring as she marched toward us, smiling, with her hand stretched out.

"Mr. Hollister!" she said bright and cheerily, "I'm Kathryn Morgan!"

"Er—howdy, ma'am," Pa stammered as he shook her hand, "Drummond Hollister, at your service, ma'am. These here's the kids."

"Let me try to guess," said Miss Morgan before Pa could get around to introducing us. "You're Corrie," she said turning and smiling at me.

I nodded.

"It's easy to see you're the oldest," she said. "And something else your Pa told me is easy to tell too—you're nearly a grown-up young woman—and a very pretty one."

"Thank you," I said, blushing. "Welcome to California."

"Oh, thank you!" She looked around and took in a deep breath. "So this is the land of fortunes," she said. "Funny, I don't smell the gold in the air. To hear folks back East talk, you'd think the gold was just lying around on the ground. Is there *really* gold here, Mr. Hollister?"

"Oh yes, ma'am," said Pa. "You'll see it soon enough, I reckon."

"Oh, I almost forgot. I brought you a little present, Corrie," she said, looking down into her handbag and reaching around with her hand. "I brought you all something—they're not much. I didn't have extra room, but I thought it might be nice to bring you all a little piece of Virginia. So, Corrie, I brought you a seashell from the Atlantic Ocean."

She handed me a beautiful little reddish-white shell that had a twisted circular pattern on it. Once a sea animal, probably something like a snail, had lived inside it, she said. "If you hold the open end to your ear on a quiet day," she said, "they say you can still hear the sea where the shell came from."

She stooped down next to me and greeted Tad. "Do you know how I know that you're Tad?" she said.

" 'Cause I'm the littlest?" asked Tad, staring with his big eyes into Miss Morgan's smiling face.

"That's right! And do you know what we say back in Virginia about little things?"

Tad shook his head.

"We say that the best things come in the smallest packages! Here, Tad, look what I have for you." Again she reached into her bag, this time pulling out a shiny green rock. "This is a Virginia rock, Tad, like your sister's shell. Every time you look at it, you can remember how big this country of ours is."

She turned to Becky, standing next to Emily. "Let me see, you two girls—" She glanced back and forth between Becky and Emily. "You are not that far apart in age, but I would say you—" She looked at Becky again. "You look to be about eleven, am I right?"

"In three months," answered Becky.

"So you are Becky!"

"Yes, Miss Morgan, and I drew you a picture!" From behind her back Becky pulled out a folded white piece of paper. "It's a picture of Pa working in his mine," said Becky.

"And you drew it for me?" exclaimed Miss Morgan. "Why, Becky, thank you! That makes me feel very special." Her smile brightened.

"That means that you are Emily," she said, turning to Emily, who only smiled shyly. "I'm so glad to meet you at last, Emily!"

Before she had a chance to say anything more, she felt a tug on her coat. She turned back toward Becky.

"What about my present?" said Becky.

Miss Morgan laughed. "I hadn't forgotten you," she said. Digging into her handbag again she pulled out two little wads that looked like rags. "Inside these wet rags are a little tuft of grass and a start of some Virginia moss, both packed in good black Virginia soil. I've tried to keep the roots damp in these rags, and I'm quite sure they will both grow. Here girls," she said handing them to Emily and Becky. "I want you to plant a little garden, with these and maybe some other things. We'll water them, and before you know it, you'll have a little patch of green Virginia right in your own back yard."

She stood up and looked around to the other side of Pa, noticing for the first time that there was an extra person. Zack saw the quick look of confusion on her face, and said, "This here's my friend from the school, Little Wolf."

"Which means you must be Zack," said Miss Morgan. She shook his hand. "Why, you're gonna be as big a man as your pa one of these days," she said, "and a strong one, too! You've got a powerful grip for a—let's see, you're how old, Zack?"

"Fourteen and a half, ma'am," he answered.

"Yes, of course. Well, like I said, you seem awfully strong for fourteen."

She was sure doing her best to make friends with everyone right off!

"Little Wolf?" she said, turning to Zack's friend. "Is that a nickname?"

"That is my name," replied Little Wolf. "I am of the *Maidu* tribe."

The smile left Miss Morgan's face. "I see," she said blankly. Then turning again to Zack, she handed him a small, thin piece of light-colored bark. It had some color and markings on it I couldn't make out at first.

"It's a piece of painted bark," she said, "with an Indian proverb written on it in Cherokee. Before they were driven back to Oklahoma, they used to be one of Virginia and North Carolina's *civilized* tribes, not like the Sac and the Fox, who massacred my parents."

I thought her eyes gave a quick glance in Little Wolf's direction, but just as quickly she was looking at Zack again. "The Cherokee's great chief Sequoia developed his alphabet in 1821, the first Indian tribe to have a full written language of their own. So let this always remind you, Zack, of the difference between peaceful and violent ways."

A brief silence followed. Pa'd been standing watching everything without saying a word, and still Miss Morgan kept the conversation going.

"And for you, Mr. Hollister," she said, "I have the best gift of all, a symbol of beginnings, of new life. She reached inside her bag one last time, and pulled out something small and brown that fit easily in the palm of her hand.

"A pine cone, ma'am?" said Pa, taking it from her and looking at it, seeming to wonder what she found so special in an object so common.

"Not just any pine cone, Mr. Hollister. A Virginia pine cone! Oh, I know you have pines in California. But this cone, with the seeds still inside it, has come three thousand miles. And when we plant these seeds and watch the little seedlings grow, they will remind us that it is possible for a tree—and perhaps for men and women as well—to grow in new soils and strange surroundings."

I think Pa knew what she meant and took the pine cone and put it into one of his coat pockets with a nod of thanks.

"Now along that line, just one more thing," she said. "I also brought you all some apple seeds for the very same purpose. You've heard of Johnny Appleseed, haven't you? Well, we'll help him in his work in Miracle Springs! But I've got them packed away someplace safe, so we'll worry about them later."

"Speaking of your bags, Miss Morgan, ma'am—"

"Please, Mr. Hollister," she interrupted, "if we are going to be married, don't you think we ought to get over the formalities? No more calling me *ma'am*, if you please. Call me by my name—my *given* name."

"You want me to call you Kathryn, ma'am?"

"No, I want you to call me *Katie*, without the *ma'am*. That's what everybody at home calls me—Katie. And I see no reason to change it now. You children may call me Katie, or Kathryn, or Miss Morgan—whatever your father would like."

"You kids call her Miss Morgan, you hear," said Pa.

"And you, Mr. Hollister?" she asked. "How would you have me address you?"

"Well I reckon you can call me Drummond, 'cause that's my name, though most of the boys call me Drum. You can use that, too, if you like."

"I like Drummond. It's a good, strong name."

"Well, Kathryn, ma'am," said Pa, not even realizing he'd ignored both Miss Morgan's requests in one breath, "like I was fixin' to say, you'll be wanting to get your bags. I reckon they got them unloaded by this time."

"Yes, I asked the steward to take care of them for me."

She turned, glanced around for a moment, spotted the

steward, and was instantly off in his direction. The rest of us followed.

She was sure lively. She had told us her aunt said she wasn't timid, and I guess her aunt was right.

# CHAPTER 26

## KATIE

We took two days getting back to Miracle, stopping that first night in Folsom and the second in Colfax at some boarding houses Pa'd made arrangements with on the way down. It sure was an interesting drive.

There was so much to get used to!

Inside the coach the talk was lively, Miss Morgan asking Emily and Becky and me and Tad all kinds of questions. Emily was reserved at first, although Becky and Tad made up for it, chattering away as if Miss Morgan was their best friend they hadn't seen in a year. Being the youngest, their memories of Ma might have started to get vague sooner than for the rest of us. Or maybe the pain of memories was dimmer, and so that made it easier for them to accept her right away.

It was a little crowded inside, and at first I put Tad up on my lap. But it wasn't long before Miss Morgan hoisted him up onto hers, and there Tad was content to stay. His big brown eyes were glued to her face. And Becky would sit no place but right beside her, talking away, sometimes all three of them at once.

Emily and I sat across from them, listening and looking out the windows. I was thinking a lot, too. But Miss Morgan didn't let us go for too long without joining in the talk.

There were long periods of quiet when everyone's energy would get used up for a while. Even Tad and Becky needed to rest their mouths and minds sometimes. At such times I'd try to watch Miss Morgan out of the corner of my eye. I didn't want her to think I was staring at her, but I couldn't help wondering what she was thinking about us all when she drew in a deep breath and looked outside at the countryside passing by.

And I wondered what was going through Pa's mind, too, outside up on the box guiding the horses, as he listened to the sounds of laughter from inside. What might a man be thinking, to hear the voice of a woman he hardly knew, a woman he'd brought west to be his wife, laughing and talking with the children of his first wife?

We made lots of stops. It seemed like somebody needed to go to the outhouse every ten minutes or so. But since there wasn't one, we had to make use of the woods instead. And Pa was trying to be considerate of Miss Morgan too, I could tell.

After some of the stops we'd rearrange and shift places. I sat up with Pa some of the time, and so did the others. Miss Morgan sat with him a time or two as well, but I couldn't hear what they talked about.

Halfway through the second day we were bouncing along during one of those quiet times. Becky was up front with Pa, so the commotion inside was less. Tad was asleep next to me, leaning against my shoulder. Miss Morgan and Emily across from me were each looking out their windows.

She'd been trying to get me at least to call her Katie, but I wasn't quite used to it. I was old enough to be an adult, she said, and if Pa wanted the younger ones to keep calling her Miss Morgan out of respect, that was okay with her. But she hoped to be more like a sister than a stepmother to me, she said, and she'd like me to call her Katie. I smiled and said I'd try.

When we were all being quiet for a spell, I had a chance to look at Miss Morgan a little more carefully than I could while she was moving about and conversing away with us.

The first thing I couldn't help noticing about Katie was her mouth. I've noticed that most people have a particular part that draws my eyes first. When I meet someone new, I find myself staring at one place on them—usually some part of their face. Often it's the mouth or the eyes, of course. But every once in a while I come across someone with an unusual nose or a high hairline or a hat I can't take my eyes off. And sometimes I even find myself staring at somebody's ears!

For as long as I can remember I've noticed people's faces and tried to imagine which part of them was opening into the *real* them, that part of them that thought and felt, their "soul" I guess you'd say. With some people I find myself looking into their eyes and knowing that I'm seeing a little bit "inside" them. Mrs. Parrish's eyes are like that. When they're looking into my face, or filling with liquid because she's feeling something deep, or when they're sparkling with love, I just can't look at anything but her eyes. And when I'm talking to Mrs. Parrish, I talk to her eyes, because that's the part of her that makes her who she is.

With other people I find myself talking to their mouth, and with others I kind of work back and forth between the eyes and mouth. I remember one little boy back in Bridge-ville—he couldn't talk at all, so he had to make folks understand him without words. His whole face was moving every second, and I never had any trouble telling whether he was happy or sad or whatever. His eyes and mouth and nose and eyebrows and ears and forehead all moved about, and I knew what was inside his mind. After I knew him a while, I almost forgot he couldn't talk.

Katie Morgan's mouth was what drew my attention first. And always after that when we were looking at each other, I talked to her mouth and watched what it did. Her mouth, like Mrs. Parrish's eyes, was that little window in her face that looked down inside the real her.

It was a wide mouth, that spread out into her cheeks when she smiled. Her teeth weren't big, but she showed them every time she spoke, nice, even white teeth. It was a mouth that always had something to say, even when she was just quietly thinking. Even then the lips would be subtly moving, shaping themselves with thought, moving this way and that, up and down, sideways. And when she talked— which was a lot of the time—then the mouth was more active than ever. The teeth, the lips, the laughter—everything about her mouth was used when she was communicating.

The voice that came out of the mouth, too, was part of all that. It was a high voice, though not too high, a pleasant voice to listen to, that sounded like it would be able to sing. While Pa's voice sometimes reminded me of a high, rugged mountain, and Mrs. Parrish's made me picture a summer sunset, Katie's brought to mind a cheerful stream, full of clear snow water, rushing down a hillside in spring.

Actually, Katie's whole face was wide, wide enough so it had room for her big smile. Her nose was ordinary and her forehead wide. She had medium brown hair, combed down the middle and falling off to the right and left to just above her shoulders.

Katie's eyes were green, and they opened real big when she was trying to be astonished, so that white spread all around the black and green parts in the middle. At times like that I'd look at her eyes instead of her mouth, because they could flash and show expression too. Her whole face was like that—active and expressive. It wasn't a face I could ignore if she was looking at me. She made sure you looked back.

What she'd said in her letter was true. I don't reckon Pa figured she was beautiful the first time he set eyes on her as she got off the boat. But then when you caught her eyes and mouth in just the right expression, she was pretty enough. I don't suppose Ma was beautiful either, and Pa sure loved her. And prettiness doesn't count for much if it's hiding ugliness down inside. Katie Morgan was average-looking— just like most women, I reckon.

She'd said she was a little stocky, and I suppose that's a good enough word. I noticed her height right off. I was likely two or three inches taller than her, and she was a little on the thick side, though not plump. It was a hardworking sort of build, sturdy and strong. When she shook my hand, her grasp had been firm and her hand large and rough. I didn't see anything dainty about the rest of her. You could just tell by the way she walked and moved, and by the look of her hands and face and arms, that she was a woman who would be able to do what she needed to get by, and that she'd probably get along in the West just fine.

She was dressed in a nice-enough looking dress, blue and a creamy color, sort of between yellow and white. It was probably her best dress. If I were coming to meet a new husband, I'd wear my Sunday clothes for sure. But as we sat in the carriage and I had the chance to take in a little more about Katie's appearance than I had noticed on the dock, I could see that spots of the blue were faded here and there, and underneath the elbows the cloth was wearing a mite thin. It was not a new dress, and not at all fancy.

Funny how you notice little details about people more and more that you didn't see at first—like the dress Katie was wearing. And after two days of being absorbed with her mouth, watching it, listening to it, having conversation back and forth, getting to know her as she talked—as we rode along that second day when it was quiet and Tad was sleeping, I found myself looking at her eyes almost for the first time. She was gazing out the window. Her mouth and whole face was still and calm.

And what I saw—or thought I saw—was a look in the

eyes of question and wonder. Looking out over the California gold country for the first time, maybe she was thinking about Virginia, thinking about how far she'd come, thinking about that man up there in front shouting at the two horses. I don't suppose she could help wondering if she'd done the right thing, wondering what was going to become of her in this strange new land, wondering if she—like the seed from the pine cone—was going to be able to grow in this new California soil. I thought I saw a hint of loneliness too, just for a second, like she was already homesick. I'd been worried so much about myself and how hard her coming was going to be on me.

Suddenly I found myself feeling sorry for her.

# CHAPTER 27

# NEVER THE SAME AGAIN

Eight or ten miles from Miracle, Zack and Little Wolf galloped on ahead.

By the time we reached town, word of our coming had spread and a dozen or so people were hanging around doors and windows, hoping for a sight of the new Mrs. Hollister-to-be.

But Pa wanted none of their gawking faces. At the first sight of them, he could tell what they were up to. He lashed the reins and shouted to the horses, and we flew down Miracle's main street like a black blur. I hardly had time to show Katie two or three buildings, and we were already out the other end, crossing the creek, heading round the bend and starting the long circular climb toward our place.

He slowed down after that, but it was still a bumpy, clattering ride up the hill, across the creek two or three more times, to the claim. We were glad to be home when we heard Pa's "Whoa!" and felt the horses come to a stop.

"Well, here we are!" said Pa, climbing down from the front and opening the door for us.

Katie stepped out, glanced around, and drew in a deep breath with a look of satisfaction. Just then Uncle Nick walked up.

"Nick, this here's Miss Kathryn Morgan," Pa said, as

he tied up the two horses to the hitching rail.

Uncle Nick looked Katie over, with not a frown exactly, but a serious expression, and certainly not a friendly one.

"I'm happy to meet you, Mr. Belle," said Katie. "I hope we can be friends. The children have been telling me all about you!"

Uncle Nick didn't say anything.

"And they've been telling me about your sister," Katie added. "They're very fond of her, you know. And I hope you don't think I will ever presume to take her place."

Uncle Nick's face seemed to brighten just a little. "She was a fine lady, Aggie was," he said, speaking to her for the first time. "She made Drum here a fine wife."

"I am so sorry she didn't make it here with the children," Katie replied. "I only hope I can be half as good a wife as she was. I just want to be a help to you all here." She sure knew how to make herself pleasing!

Uncle Nick gave her another look, a little longer one this time, then threw his glance in Pa's direction. "She might do after all, Drum! She ain't no Agatha Belle, but you mighta done okay for yourself!"

Before Pa could answer, Katie said, "I thank you kindly for your approval, Mr. Belle. I will take that as a compliment!"

"Corrie, take Miss Kathryn inside and show her the place while we get the bags down," Pa said. "Zack, get up on top there and untie that rope."

Katie and I went inside, followed by the three younger ones. Zack helped Pa. Little Wolf had galloped off over the hill to his place just outside Miracle. I don't know where Uncle Nick went. We didn't see him again till suppertime.

It was about four-thirty in the afternoon when we got home. The sun was just thinking about settling down over the hills downstream. So the first thing we did was to start making supper. It reminded me of Christmas day with all three of us girls and Katie in the kitchen at the same time. Pa stuck his head in the door to say, "I'm taking the carriage back to the Freight Company. I'll be back inside forty minutes." I thought it was funny that he'd leave again so soon after getting home. And it was curious, too, that he didn't mention Mrs. Parrish's name about the carriage. But I hardly had a chance to think about it more, and before I knew it he was back and we were ready for supper.

Pa had halfway fixed up his and Uncle Nick's room for Katie to stay in after she got there. He didn't really do much except take their stuff out. He and Uncle Nick were planning to stay in the barn until the wedding, which didn't please Uncle Nick too much. He'd said that he didn't see why Pa didn't just put her up in a boardinghouse in town someplace instead of turning them out of their own home. But Pa said they couldn't tell what kind of woman she was if they were always having to ride into town to fetch her every day. If anyone needed to stay in town, Pa'd said, then Uncle Nick could. Uncle Nick went off in a huff, but he didn't go to Mrs. Gianini's, and that first night he was out sleeping in the barn with Pa. It was a good thing summer was coming and most of the cold weather was past.

Well things were sure different around here after that. And I realized they'd never be the same again.

There wasn't much actual talk about the wedding—not at first, anyway. It was more or less taken for granted, and we just went about living our lives every day, knowing it was out there and the day was steadily approaching. I knew Pa'd been planning on having the ceremony sometime in June, after Katie had been here about a month. He told Uncle Nick once that he figured "a month was long enough to find out if she's gonna take to the kids or not."

In Pa's mind, the marriage was still just mostly for us. But I knew he wanted to make the best of it for himself too, as long as it was something he felt had to be. I didn't know what day Pa was thinking of, but I figured it would be in the middle of June, probably on a Sunday after the church service was over.

He'd went into town a week after Katie got to Miracle to see Rev. Rutledge. I figured it was about the wedding plans.

# CHAPTER 28

## MAY 1854

Those five weeks between May 13 and the wedding on June 24 were weeks of getting accustomed to new ways.

Every one of us around that place had plenty of change and adjusting to do, getting familiar with having Katie around. It was like when we'd come and had had to get used to Pa. Now that we were used to him, everything was changing again. Now that I think of it, I suppose it was hardest of all for Katie. But she hardly ever showed it.

I wrote a lot in my journal that month. With Katie there, I had more time because I wasn't having to do as much work myself. So I had a chance to write and read more than usual, and take some long walks.

Actually, it wasn't as hard for me after Katie got there as I'd thought it would be. Katie must have known that there'd be things I'd be struggling to get used to. She seemed to go out of her way to be nice—and not just to me. She was nice and cheerful to everyone.

We'd get up in the morning and she'd send us off to school with lunches and a wave. I still helped to get the younger ones ready to go, but it was nice having help with the breakfast and lunches. When we got home, she'd always say something like, "Well, Corrie, what do you think we should do about supper tonight?" still halfway treating me like I was the woman in charge of the house. I wasn't, of course, but she was considerate and that made me feel a mite silly for all the worrying I'd done earlier.

All in all, the first week or two wasn't so bad. It was like having a maid around the place—which was a peculiar enough thing for folks like us!

We were gone at school most of the day, till mid-afternoon, so I can't say what things were like then. Pa and Uncle Nick kept working away up at the mine pretty much as usual. Alkali Jones was here probably half the days. Katie kept busy in the house and I could see things she'd done—cleaning and arranging—when I got home. It had looked all right to me before, but she seemed to find ways to make it look better. After a while the cabin started to take on a more homey look. She started working on curtains for the windows and would ask Pa for this and that—some shelves here, some new linen or bedclothes there—and Pa would oblige with whatever she wanted.

Miss Stansberry sometimes talked about wishing she could be "a fly on the wall" listening to somebody else's conversation. I laughed when I first heard her say it, but I wished the same myself when we were at school—to be a fly on the wall of the cabin!

Did Katie and Pa ever have lunch alone? What did they talk about? Or did they ever go on walks or rides in the wagon alone together, as if they were courting? Those were the kinds of questions I couldn't help wondering about.

But I didn't know any of the answers. I never saw them alone together, except by accident. From looking, you'd never have known they were planning to be married the next month. It still seemed like a "business" kind of deal, like she was going to work for Pa instead of be his wife—tend the cabin and kids and keep the place clean.

Pa was as nice to Katie as he'd be to anyone. He'd show her consideration and compliment her on a nice meal. And lots of times he'd say, "Thank you," to her for different things. He seemed like he was trying to act like a good husband ought to.

I think Pa wanted to be nice to her, maybe even for Ma's sake, to do some things better now that he hadn't done with her. But he didn't touch Katie or put his arm around her—and as long ago as it was, I can still remember him putting his arm around Ma almost every day. And they didn't laugh or have fun together or go outside alone or anything. She called him Drummond. He still called her Miss Kathryn. After a while she kept pestering him about it. I thought of her as *Katie* in my mind, but to her face I still called her Miss Morgan like the other kids.

Tad and Emily and Becky all loved her, of course—she saw to that. If Pa'd brought her all the way from Virginia mostly to be like a nanny to his children, then she was up to the task. At first little Tad had followed Uncle Nick around like a puppy dog. But now that there was a new person around, the luster was gone from Uncle Nick's shadow. Tad and Becky were Miss Morgan's constant companions, and she didn't seem to mind. The three of them were always talking. Emily kept to herself a little. I think she would take longer to accept a new stepmother, just like Zack and me.

I wish us three older ones could have talked about the feelings we were having, and how Ma and Pa fit into them. But there's a big difference between seventeen and fourteen and thirteen. Brothers and sisters aren't always accustomed to talking to one another about important things, anyway. So probably even though we were sharing lots of the same feelings, we didn't really talk about them to each other.

I wasn't the only one who was growing. Zack would be fifteen in the summer. He was shooting up, getting tall and lanky and his voice was getting deep. It wouldn't be long before there'd be three grown men up there working the mine.

Emily, too, was getting shapely like a young lady. I wish Ma had lived to see quiet little Emily gradually blossom into a woman. Right now she was sort of in between. The little girl would laugh out in the merriest way, but suddenly without warning that part of her would hide and out of her rich, blue-green eyes would come a glance that made her look for an instant to be twenty years old.

I was amazed when I saw it. Emily had always been my kid sister, and now all at once I began to realize that we'd both be women before we knew it. On her face I could almost see the two parts of her—the woman-child and the childlike-lady—going back and forth, neither quite knowing which was supposed to be in control.

I wish Emily had someone to help her through the growing-up struggle, like I'd had Ma and now had Mrs. Parrish. Maybe one day I could be a little like that for her. Or perhaps she and Katie would hit it off like I had with Mrs. Parrish—though I couldn't tell if Katie would understand things in the same way Mrs. Parrish always seemed to.

Uncle Nick seemed to get accustomed to Katie pretty quickly. He didn't complain about the barn much after the first day or two, and he acted more friendly toward Katie, even on the second day. It wasn't long, in fact, before he and Katie seemed to be pretty good friends and would laugh and talk together. They were a little closer in age than either was to Pa, and Uncle Nick was pretty rambunctious himself, like Katie seemed to be, so I expected they would get along fine.

Once Uncle Nick realized that Katie was going to be a help around the place and that he didn't need to be jealous of Ma's memory on account of her, I think he decided to accept her as part of the family.

He started making an effort, just like Pa, to be a mite

more gracious, with a woman around the place now. He and
Pa'd make a point of washing their hands before supper or
of cleaning the mud off their boots before coming in the
cabin. They even started taking regular baths in the creek,
and with Katie washing their clothes, it smelled more pleasant when everyone was inside.

The townsfolk and the people in the shops liked Katie
right off. Nobody in Miracle Springs knew Ma, so they were
all just happy for Pa and they all said Katie seemed like she'd
do just fine in California. There was talk about several other
men writing for mail-order brides too, now that they saw
how well Pa had done!

It was a Tuesday when we got home from Sacramento.
The following Saturday evening Pa was talking after supper
about going to church the next day and seeing folks for the
first time with Katie with us.

"It's only fair that I warn you, Drummond," said Katie
after she realized what Pa was talking about, "that I'm not
a religious person. I don't intend to be going off to some
church service every Sunday."

Her statement took Pa by surprise. We all waited to see
what he'd say, but he let her go on.

"Oh, I don't mind going with you once in a while. And
I'll do my duty to you and the kids. I won't stand in the way
of them getting their proper share of religious training, if
that's what you want for them. It's just that for me, church
is not something I have much use for."

"Mind telling me why?" said Pa.

"My aunt was a devout lady. She went to mass every
week, and had the priest come over to the house after she
was sick. But I never saw any good it did her—just a bunch
of rituals that wasted half her life. And a long time ago I
decided I was going to make better use of my time than
that."

"There's a lot of decent folks think church holds folks

together and makes a community work better," said Pa.

"I don't doubt the church has a function," Katie answered. "But all the priests and preachers and half the church people I ever met were just as hypocritical as the crooked shopkeepers and land swindlers, so I never saw much use of getting involved."

I was just about to say something but Pa spoke up again, and his words surprised me.

"Well, here in Miracle Springs we got a decent man for our preacher, and I don't think anyone for miles would say he's a hypocrite. There's as much difference between Rev. Rutledge and Royce as day and night."

*Good for Pa!* I thought, *sticking up for the minister.*

"Royce?"

"The banker. He's our local version of what you call land swindlers."

Uncle Nick laughed from over by the fire. "Don't you know, Drum, he's just trying to make an honest profit like any businessman!"

"Who've you been talking to, Nick?"

"Royce has changed," laughed Uncle Nick. "No more shady land deals. Now he swindles folks the honest way! If you wanna know my opinion, Katie, I can abide preachers a lot sooner than I can bankers! Them's the ones I don't trust!"

Now Pa laughed. "You're right there. Royce woulda had this whole claim of ours if Corrie and Tad and Zack hadn't foiled him. Low-down clean through. But talking about that minister again, I helped him build that church of his and he proved himself a worthwhile man in my book. And he's got some other good folks in that church too."

"You may be entirely right. I'll go with you tomorrow and you can depend on me to do my duty as your wife and for your children. Just don't expect me to become one of this man Rutledge's followers.''

Nothing more was said. Pa settled back in his chair and was even more quiet than usual for a spell.

# CHAPTER 29

# AN AFTERNOON IN MIRACLE SPRINGS

We all piled into the wagon the next morning to go into town for church. Uncle Nick didn't usually go with us, but he did that day, and it was nice, feeling like a whole family.

It's funny I would say that with Katie there, but that was how I felt. And naturally everybody was all eyes as we rode up.

Katie must've known everyone was curious about her, but she just walked into the church like there was nothing out of the ordinary and she did this same thing every Sunday. Pa led the way in and didn't stop to make any introductions, just nodding to his friends here and there.

We took up a whole row of chairs, the eight of us—a Belle, six Hollisters, and a Morgan-soon-to-be-a-Hollister. I don't suppose he could have helped noticing it, but Rev. Rutledge didn't say or do anything out of the ordinary, and the service went on pretty much like always.

The minister did say one thing that stuck with me. He was talking about how it was when we expect things to go a certain way and then all of a sudden our plans are upset. Or when we think we're supposed to do one thing and find out we can't.

He said that God never blocks one path unless He's got

another one for us to take. He said it was like walking through a forest and all of a sudden finding a huge tree fallen across the way. Sometimes God puts those trees there to make us move in another direction we might never have discovered otherwise.

What he said reminded me of Mrs. Parrish talking about everything always working out for the best if we're doing our best to obey God. Katie's coming was like a tree across the path of *my* life. It might not have been how I wanted it to be, but if God really was the one who was behind everything that happened to me, then it was bound to turn out good in the end.

Right then I realized I ought to try to think of Katie not like something that had come across my path that was intended to hurt my life, but as a tree God had sent to move me in a new way—maybe toward something that wouldn't have been able to be otherwise, something that was even *better* than the first path through the woods.

Anyway, I think that's what Mrs. Parrish would have told me. She was forever looking for the good side of things that happened. She said it was more than just being optimistic. She said that's what God *wanted* us to do—to always trust Him to work everything out in the best of all possible ways.

I sneaked a peek around to where Mrs. Parrish was sitting listening to Rev. Rutledge. She smiled at me as if she knew what I was thinking. *It must make her proud,* I thought as I turned back and faced the front again, *seeing this church and all the people in it, knowing that she was the one who got it going, and who first wrote to Rev. Rutledge.*

I never heard anyone say it, but I guess she was the most influential person in Miracle Springs. I couldn't think of anyone whose life hadn't been changed in some way on account of her—her business, the money she helped folks with, the church, the school. I wondered if *she* even knew all she'd done! I found myself wondering, too, if there were any trees in her path.

My thoughts drifted to Katie again, then back to the tree and what Rev. Rudledge was saying.

*Lord,* I prayed silently as I sat there, *I do ask You to make Katie's coming be a good thing for all of us, especially for Pa. I want him to be happy and to do what he thinks is best. I pray that You'd make everything happen just like You want it to, and help me to be loving and to help Katie if I can, even though I didn't like the idea of her coming at first. And help me to do like Mrs. Parrish says and trust You for everything, and to know You'll make it for the best.*

After the service was over, we went slowly out, shaking the minister's hand. He was all smiles to Katie, welcoming her to Miracle and telling her that Pa was a fine man and had a wonderful family. She smiled back and was pleasant, but recalling to mind what she'd said about ministers the night before, I wondered if the smile on her face was real, or just put there until church was over.

I'd always heard folks say things to Rev. Rutledge as they shook his hand and went outside, "Fine sermon this morning, Reverend," or maybe, "Your words blessed my soul, Reverend." Mostly it was the older women who sometimes came who said things like that. But this morning as Rev. Rutledge took my hand and smiled at me, I suddenly found myself saying almost that very thing. "I want to thank you for what you said about the trees falling across our path, Rev. Rutledge," I said. "I think that is going to help me with—with—"

Suddenly my words dried up. I was embarrassed and hoped Uncle Nick behind me hadn't heard.

But Rev. Rutledge smiled broadly at me. "Are you saying there's been a tree across your path, Corrie?" he asked.

"Yes, sir, I reckon that's it."

"Well, just let the Lord help you get around it, and you

can count on Him to set your feet down on an even better path than the first one."

"Thank you, sir," I said. "I'll remember that!"

When I got outside and down the steps, Pa and Katie were already with Mrs. Parrish and the two women were shaking hands for the first time.

"I am so happy to meet you at last," said Mrs. Parrish warmly. "This is quite a man you've come to California to wed, Miss Morgan! One of this community's leading citizens!"

Pa mumbled something, but I didn't hear it. Mrs. Parrish threw back her head and laughed.

"Leading citizen, you say?" said Katie inquisitively.

"Oh yes!" answered Mrs. Parrish, loving every second of putting Pa on the spot. "Why, the stories I could tell you!"

"You don't know nothing to tell about me!" exclaimed Pa. I couldn't tell at first if he was riled, but then I realized he was just joining in the fun.

"I *would* like to hear it all!" said Katie.

"I had hoped to talk you all into coming over to my house this afternoon," Mrs. Parrish went on, "so I could get to know Katie a little better. What do you say, Mr. Hollister?"

"*Mr.* Hollister?" said Katie. "You know him as well as you say and you still address him so formally?"

"He's not given me leave to do otherwise," responded Mrs. Parrish.

"Surely, Drummond, if you allow me to call you by your given name after only one week, this lady who has been your friend so long deserves no less."

"You can call me whatever you like," said Pa, not exactly getting upset now, but not liking it too much having two women talking about him.

"Then, Drummond," said Mrs. Parrish, "would you do me the honor of a visit this afternoon? Perhaps you could stop over now and we could have tea and coffee and some biscuits."

She drew his name out slowly, like she enjoyed saying it. "I'd like to have you for dinner one Sunday after church," she went on, "but I'm sure you already have plans today."

"I have a lamb leg on the fire," said Katie.

"Well then, you'll just have time for a nice visit and then you can go home to it."

Without any further discussion, in five or ten minutes, after Pa was through seeing and shaking hands with the other folks wanting to meet his mail-order bride, we were back in the wagon on our way to Mrs. Parrish's.

She must've been planning on us coming. She had several trays of crackers and little biscuits out, and she made coffee and tea and was very hospitable.

Mrs. Parrish was our best friend in town. And now it seemed Mrs. Parrish wanted to make herself a friend to the newest member of the family, Katie Morgan.

They chatted freely. "Every time a new woman joins the community," said Mrs. Parrish, "I am so thrilled. When I first came, it sometimes seemed I went for weeks on end without seeing another one of our kind! Now at least the men don't outnumber us more than twenty or thirty to one. And our numbers are growing fast!"

After a while Mrs. Parrish got up. "Corrie," she said to me, "I have something for you. Would you come into my room with me? We'll just be a minute," she said to the others. "You all go ahead and have something more to eat."

I got up and followed her.

When we were in her room with the door closed, she turned and said with an expectant look, "Well?"

"Well, what?" I returned.

"What do you think? How are things with Miss Morgan?"

"Oh, fine, I reckon. She's nice enough."

"She seems very nice, Corrie. I think you should be pleased."

"I'm trying to be, Mrs. Parrish. I prayed for her during church a while ago. But it still takes some getting used to."

"I know, dear. And it probably will for quite a while. But give the Lord time. Remember what I've always said, He not only brings good, He gives nothing but the best."

"You keep reminding me, and I'll keep trying to believe it more."

She smiled. "That is a fair deal. I agree. But—here!" she reached toward a little package on her dresser, "this is what I brought you in to give you." She handed it to me. It felt like a book.

"It's brand new—just published. I had it sent to me from a bookstore in San Francisco."

I unwrapped it. It was a book, bound in cloth, with the simple title *Walden* in gold across the cover, with the words underneath, and smaller, "Life in the Woods."

"I think you'll like it," she said. "It's by a man named Henry David Thoreau. I've been following his writings for some years. When other men were fighting the Mexicans and discovering gold and making fortunes here in California, do you know what he did?"

I shook my head.

"Thoreau went out into the woods all by himself, taking virtually nothing, and lived alone by a lake near Concord, Massachusetts, called Walden Pond. Like you, he kept a journal, and this is the result."

She pointed toward the book. "Something tells me you and Thoreau have a lot in common, Corrie Belle Hollister. He loved nature, as you do. He found nature speaking to him. He discovered much about himself and about God's world and his fellow man, all from his unique ability to find quiet and calmness within himself.

"He was then able to hear voices speaking to him—God,

nature, and his own inner being. And he possessed the God-given talent to make his thoughts and observations known. He reminds me of you, Corrie. I do not doubt that the world is going to know your name one day, and that you will be telling the world many things. Who knows—someday people may even be reading a book with *your* name on it!"

"That *would* be something!" I said.

"You can never tell what God might do, Corrie. Sometimes those trees across our path, like Avery was talking about today, are thrown there by God because He has some wonderful *new* thing to do in our lives that we'd never see with our eyes fixed straight ahead. I have no doubt at all that He will take you on *many* interesting and unexpected paths, and as long as you are obeying Him and trusting Him, they will be wonderful ones! But I suppose we had better not leave my other guests alone any longer!"

"Thank you for the book, Mrs. Parrish. I'll treasure it!"

"I just pray it encourages you to be faithful to your journal and your other writing. I feel God is going to use your writing, Corrie. And perhaps making a friend of Thoreau will help."

# CHAPTER 30

## A DETERMINED LADY

Katie's talkativeness and cheerfulness came into our house like a summer wind.

She was the kind of person I couldn't help liking. And I think Pa liked her, too. But after a couple of weeks, I found myself starting to wonder what it was going to be like having her there forever. Gradually she stopped being just a visitor. Our home began to seem more like it was *her* home, where *she* was in charge.

Maybe she figured that was how Pa wanted it. That was why he brought her here, wasn't it, to manage the household? That's how wives did it.

And maybe that's how Pa *did* want it, how was I to know? But to my eyes it began to look like she was getting pretty determined about how things were to be done, when it wasn't even her own place yet. But then again, in less than a month it *was* going to be half her place, so maybe everything was just as it ought to be.

One afternoon Uncle Nick and Pa were later than usual coming down from the mine. Uncle Nick was the first to come inside, and he no more than stepped foot inside the door when Katie half-hollered over her shoulder to him, "Come on, Nick, get washed up. Supper's ready and I don't want it getting cold. You too, Drum," she added to Pa as he walked in. "Come on, kids, everyone around the table!" Nobody thought to say anything, we all just did as she said. Pa and Uncle Nick turned right around to go back out to wash their hands. I guess it was a little thing, but I noticed.

From the very beginning she was always cleaning up around the place. At first it was nice. I thought I'd been doing pretty good filling in for Ma, but once Katie arrived, with her sweeping and dusting and scrubbing, I realized how little I really had done.

What Pa noticed, I think, wasn't the cleaning so much as the straightening and rearranging. Often I'd see him stop and look around for something that wasn't where he kept it. She'd see the puzzled look on his face, ask him what he was looking for, and then go get whatever it was for him.

One night he and Nick were sitting in front of the fire smoking their pipes, their feet up on a low table in front of them. They still had their boots on, and they weren't any more clean than boots generally are. As Katie approached I saw Uncle Nick give Pa a quick wink, then scrape his boots together so that some of the dirt fell off onto the table.

Sure enough, Katie saw it and marched right over. "I just cleaned that table today, and I'll thank you to keep your boots off it and your dirt outside!"

"Aw, for crying out loud, woman," said Uncle Nick, "this is our cabin, not no fancy hotel!" He was joking with her, but she didn't realize it. Her next words were heated.

"Now you look here, Nick Belle. Your brother-in-law brought me here to keep a nice and tidy house for him. If you don't like the way I do it, then I suggest you find another."

Uncle Nick was so shocked at what she said he didn't say anything more for a minute. The smile stuck on his face for a moment, then slowly faded.

"Now hold on there, Miss Kathryn," said Pa. "Nick didn't mean no harm. But he's right about what he said.

This is our place, and we ain't used to trying to keep every speck of dirt out of it. I reckon you'll just have to get used to a little dirt here and there."

Katie looked at Pa, seeming surprised for a moment, but with no intention of backing down.

"I see," she said slowly. "Well, if that's the way you want it, I'll comply somehow. But that's no way to run a house, Drummond Hollister, I can tell you that."

She turned and walked away, leaving Pa and Uncle Nick exchanging looks that said more than they'd have wanted Katie to see. Nick was smiling and winking again. Pa was serious.

And despite what she said about complying, when Pa and Uncle Nick finally got up, I saw her go over, pick up the two pipes lying there, empty the tobacco from them into the fire, and then put them up on a mantle shelf. Later, before he went out to the barn, I saw him walk over that direction looking for it.

"Where's my pipe?" he finally said, half-muttering, to no one in particular.

"Up on the mantle," said Katie.

Pa located it, then headed for the door.

"You're not going to smoke out in the barn, are you?" Katie asked.

Pa half shrugged that he was.

"Oh no, Drummond. Not with all that straw out there, and the children and me sleeping so close by. It's not at all safe. No—you do your smoking in here."

I thought Pa was going to say something, but then he apparently thought better of it. He turned around, strode quickly back to the fireplace, tossed his pipe back on the mantle, and left the house without another word, not even a good night to the rest of us.

Five minutes later, from out in the barn I heard a loud laugh from Uncle Nick and I knew Pa'd told him what had just then happened over the pipe. Uncle Nick got a kick out of Katie's ways. I think sometimes he even goaded her on just to rile her. But it seemed it was starting to annoy Pa.

Even though Katie may have been a mite bossy, we sat down to nice meals together like a family ought to, and everybody's manners improved, especially Zack's and Uncle Nick's. Pa was pretty mannerly anyway. But Uncle Nick was noticeably cleaner, and he started shaving more regularly. He hardly ever went into town in the evenings after Katie got there. He just seemed to like being around the place.

After a week or two, he and Katie were getting along real friendly, although he teased her something awful—like with the boots on the table—causing little scuffles between her and Pa. But that was always Uncle Nick's way—teasing, kidding, laughing, causing trouble, having fun—and I could tell he enjoyed having somebody new to do it all with, especially a woman only a few years younger than him. When he realized Katie was strong-headed enough to throw it all right back at him, I wondered if he'd finally met his match. Katie would come right back with a remark to one of his wisecracks, sometimes with a quick glance or smile in my direction to say, "See, men aren't so tough. You just have to know how to handle them."

Well, she might have had it figured out how to handle Uncle Nick, but I wasn't sure her way was going to work with Pa. Maybe on account of Pa knowing she was going to be his wife, everything was more serious. Marriage must do that to folks.

The third Sunday after Katie got there, Pa was moving around getting himself and the wagon ready to go into town. Then as we were getting set for breakfast, he said, "You kids get dressed in your Sunday duds soon as you're done eating, so we can get into church on time."

"I didn't know we had plans to go into town today,

Drummond," said Katie, pausing and looking up at him as she stirred the eggs scrambling on the stove.

"Well, it's Sunday, ain't it? I just figured that we'd—"

"I told you before, Drummond," Katie interrupted, "I do not intend to make a regular ritual of listening to that man's religious pronouncements about trees and paths and God and forests and whatever else it was he so enlightened us about two weeks ago. And last week wasn't much better, though I put up with it. But I told you I wasn't going to make it an every-week thing."

"You tell him, Katie!" kidded Uncle Nick, giving her a little jab in the ribs. Uncle Nick was always trying to protect folks from getting too serious.

Katie's eyes flashed and she glanced at Uncle Nick. At first I thought she was going to lash out at him, but it wasn't anger gleaming out of her eyes.

"You shut up and stay out of this, Nick," said Pa. "This is between me and Miss Kathryn and the kids. I'm telling you all that I'm taking *my* family to church this morning. Be ready, all of you, after breakfast!"

He turned and left the house, and we didn't see him for half an hour. It was a pretty quiet meal. We'd all heard every word and I think the argument frightened us. Uncle Nick did his best to cheer us up around the table by saying it was all going to work out fine.

We went to church, just Pa and us five kids. Afterward, we played for another half an hour while Pa and Rev. Rutledge talked about the wedding. When Pa came outside and climbed back up in the wagon, he said, "Well, it's all set— the fifteenth, after the service."

"That's in just two weeks, Pa," I said.

"Might as well get the thing done, Corrie. She's doing all the things a wife's supposed to do. Might as well make it official and get on with it. Where's Becky?" said Pa, suddenly looking around and realizing he was one youngster short. I hadn't even realized she'd slipped away.

"She's over in them woods, Pa," said Zack, pointing out behind the church building. "There's a little grove of firs and she goes there all the time during school."

"Run and fetch her, will you, Zack?"

"Sure, Pa." Zack was off the wagon and out of sight in a few seconds. He'd not only grown taller, but he was faster as well.

In a couple of minutes he and Becky reappeared, and we set off for home.

Uncle Nick was right. Everything was fine after we got home. The incident before breakfast blew over and no one mentioned it again. I reckon making plans with the minister must have settled things in Pa's mind, because he didn't seem to be annoyed at things Katie did after that. He told her that he and the minister had set the date, and she nodded her approval.

"There are many things we will have to discuss, Drummond," she said.

"I reckon," said Pa. "We got two weeks."

"Which isn't long," persisted Katie.

Pa nodded. There were no more fusses after that.

Two nights later, I found myself lying in bed awake. Gradually, Pa and Katie's voices reached my ears from the other room. Nick was already out in the barn. Everyone but me was asleep, and I guess they thought I was too. I figured they were talking about some of those things Katie said they needed to "discuss." I just lay there, not paying much attention, just hearing the low sound of their voices.

But suddenly I realized they were talking about me! I immediately strained to listen.

" . . . going to be eighteen next year . . . time a young woman gives thought . . . future comes sooner than . . ."

It was Katie's voice talking, but I could only hear pieces

of what she said. When Pa spoke I could make out his deeper voice clearly.

"There's plenty of time for all that later."

"I can tell you from my own experience, Drummond," Katie answered back, but again I only heard some of her words, ". . . goes by quickly . . . those years with my aunt and uncle . . . now here I am over thirty . . . lost opportunities . . . just now getting married . . . time we thought about . . . she's marrying age, Drummond."

What! Katie talking to Pa about marrying me off already! I quickly forgot my resolve to be nice to her and the prayers I'd been praying for her, and tried to listen more intently.

"I ain't gonna have Corrie getting married any time soon," said Pa, and I breathed a sigh of relief. "Besides, she ain't of a mind to be marrying just now anyway. She's got writing to do and maybe teaching. She asked me about college a while back."

" . . . good thing to have dreams . . . realistic too . . . life in the West . . . need a husband . . . chasing foolish fancies . . ."

"It ain't so foolish. She's written for that paper of Singleton's, and she's helping the Stansberry lady with teaching. Corrie's no ordinary young lady, I tell you. She had to grow up in a hurry when her ma died, and I figure she can do just about anything she sets her mind to."

Oh, Pa! I was so proud to hear him say those words!

"Yes, well . . . discuss it again . . . don't have to settle Corrie's whole future right . . . still think it wouldn't do any harm to look . . ."

"I'll tell you again, Miss Kathryn. I may be making you my wife for the young'uns sake. But what becomes of Corrie is for her to decide."

Pa's voice had a finality to it, and I could feel that he believed in me! Just hearing those words made me so happy!

"Yes, well, that's fine . . . we'll see what comes . . . did want to talk to you also . . . the other children . . . school clothes . . . won't do for them to be chasing around . . . rags don't befit the children . . . was it that lady called you—a leading citizen?"

"I ain't no leading citizen and my kids ain't dressed in rags."

" . . . only thinking that . . . do have the money, Drummond, to present a better face . . . your family and you . . . people think of you more highly if . . ."

"I ain't out to impress no one, or my kids neither."

"About Zack . . . he's—"

"He's nearly grown, too, just like Corrie. I ain't gonna be putting no harneses on him, neither. He's a good boy, and—"

I didn't hear the last of Pa's sentence. How I wished Zack could have been listening right then!

" . . . agree . . . wonderful young man . . . only feel I would like . . . suitable . . . with that young Indian—"

"Little Wolf?" exclaimed Pa. "He's a good kid, too, and harmless."

"He *is* an Indian, and I don't want him around here . . . don't know what might . . ."

"His father trains horses up over the hill! Got a good stable. Them two boys is like brothers. They're talking about riding together some day, racing horses even. And I ain't gonna be telling Zack he can't do something like that. He's got his heart set on it, and that's a good enough thing."

Pa's voice had an irritated sound to it again. I guess Katie knew it, because she didn't say anything more about either me or Zack or getting the young'uns better school clothes. They kept talking for a long time, but settled back into less disagreeable topics. I finally went to sleep with plenty of thoughts still floating around inside.

Like I said before, things would never be the same again. In less than two weeks that lady sitting out there would be Pa's wife!

# CHAPTER 31

## A TALK WITH PA

The very next day, when we got home after school, I could tell Pa was being quieter than usual. There'd been lots of things running through my mind all day, from listening to Pa and Katie the night before. I couldn't help it. I was worrying again.

I'd been writing, of course, but I wanted to talk to someone about it too. Because of other things I was thinking about, I knew I couldn't talk to Mrs. Parrish.

Maybe part of me knew that there were things on Pa's mind. I suppose that's what drew me out to the barn that afternoon. I knew he was there and I knew he was alone, and I hoped maybe we'd be able to talk a little. We hadn't for a long time.

When I walked in, I expected to see him shoveling out the stalls, or raking up straw, or fixing or building something. Pa was always busy with his hands. But instead he was just standing there, leaning against a saddle slung over a rail, a piece of straw in his mouth, staring out the window toward the woods across the creek. Just standing there still, not doing anything, not moving.

"Hi, Pa," I said.

He didn't seem startled. It was almost as if he expected me. He turned around slowly. I'll never forget that look on his face—not a smile, but neither was it serious. It was almost a look of relief. I had the feeling he was glad it was me instead of Katie.

"Hi-ya, little girl," he said. He hadn't called me that since before he had left New York. I'd forgotten all about it. For a second I was six or seven again! But the present jumped right back at me a moment later.

He didn't say another word right then, but when I was close enough, he stretched out one of his great long arms, put it around me and drew me into a close hug for several seconds. When he released me and I stepped back, our eyes met, and I could tell we each knew what was on the other's mind.

It was a special moment with Pa. Right then, despite what he'd just called me, I knew he was looking into my eyes as a grown-up, as someone he cared about, and as someone he needed. Even men, I knew, needed someone to understand, needed someone to feel things with, and at that moment I knew I was that someone for Pa.

"Won't be long now, huh Pa?" I said with a smile.

"Yeah," he sighed, letting out a long breath. "Week from Sunday, I reckon."

Again it was quiet.

"Quite a gal, Miss Kathryn, wouldn't you say?" he said. He was making conversation, not asking my opinion.

"You're right there, Pa," I said. "She's got what folks call spunk."

Pa laughed. "Yep, that's a good word for it—spunk! But you can't help kinda liking her though."

"Yeah," I agreed. "I reckon most anybody'd like Katie Morgan once they met her."

"What about you, Corrie?" Pa said. "What do you think? Do *you* like her?" Now he *was* asking my opinion.

"Of course, Pa," I said. "I like her okay."

"You figure she'll be a good step-ma to the young'uns?"

"I reckon. They all seem to like her a lot. She's friendly and nice to everybody."

Pa thought for a moment.

"And what about you? You think you'll be happy with her being *your* step-ma?"

"I don't know, Pa," I answered. "It has been kinda hard for me to get used to, I suppose. But I want you to be happy and do what you think's best. And anyhow, like Katie said, I'm getting older and I won't be around that much longer."

"What makes you say that?"

Suddenly I realized I'd said too much. I felt my face redden, but I couldn't take back the words.

"I heard you and Katie talking last night, after I was in bed. I'm sorry for listening, Pa. I couldn't help it."

"What'd you hear?"

"Oh, about her thinking I oughta get married pretty soon, before I got too old and turned into a spinster, I suppose."

Pa shifted his weight uneasily. I could tell he was embarrassed that I'd eavesdropped.

"She had no call to be saying those kinds of things, and I straightened her out too, I want you to know."

"I do know, Pa," I said. "I want to thank you for those nice things you said. I felt so proud that you thought that about me. I didn't know you knew me so well—you know, about the writing and teaching and things I want to do."

"I ain't such a dense ol' goat as I look, Corrie Belle!" Pa laughed. "And I've had a talk or two about you with that Parrish woman too. She thinks mighty highly of you."

I nodded. Pa bringing up Mrs. Parrish just complicated everything in my mind.

We were both quiet for a minute. Pa left the saddle he'd been leaning against, and walked over toward a bale of straw. He looked like he was going to sit down, but then he just gave it a kick and shuffled along farther.

"I don't know, Corrie," he finally said. "There's just something wrong."

He let out a big breath I could hear clear over where I was halfway across the barn. Then he turned and walked slowly back, kicking at the loose straw with his boot on the wood floor. "You know what I mean, Corrie? You can just feel when things ain't quite right. She's a nice enough young woman, and I doubt a fella'd do better writin' off blind like I done. But I can't help thinkin' of Aggie. And Miss Kathryn just ain't ever gonna be like a 'mother' to my kids. She's more like Nick—like a younger sister or something. I just don't know that I can ever get so I love her the same as your ma."

I knew now wasn't the time for me to say anything. Pa wasn't a talkative man as a rule, but when stuff started coming out of him, like I'd only seen it do a time or two before, it came out like a river instead of a trickle! I was glad Pa felt he could be that downright honest with me.

"I know a marriage can be a good one without all that being in love sort of thing. It ain't that I'm expecting anybody to be my wife like your ma was. But when I look in Miss Kathryn's eyes, there just ain't nothing there that pulls me and says 'This here's the woman I want to be like a new ma to my kids.' Nick and she do okay together, though they can squabble too . . ."

Pa paced to the window of the barn and looked out.

"There they are now, walking down to the creek, Nick helping her with that second pail of water."

He turned back toward me.

"You see what I mean, Corrie. It's different with me. Sometimes I think Nick oughta get himself a woman like that. He's always needed someone to hog-tie him and keep him outta trouble. But I want a woman who knows what she's about and keeps her distance a mite more'n Miss Kathryn seems to be able to."

He stopped, then looked up at me, almost as if he was wondering if I was still there or if he'd just imagined me and had been talking to himself all this time.

I smiled. "Couldn't you—couldn't you maybe talk to her again, Pa? Or do you think maybe it's . . ." I fumbled for words. I didn't know what I was trying to say. I didn't know what Pa wanted me to say. My words just kind of ended in the middle of nothing.

But Pa just kept on going. "That's it, don't you see? There just ain't much I can do. I'm a man of my word. Besides that, I figure I'm probably blamed lucky to find a woman like Miss Kathryn who's willing and able to throw in with an ol' gold miner with nothing but a big cabin already full of kids and kin. What else is a man my age gonna do, anyway?" He stopped suddenly and gazed out the window again.

"Well, you remember what Rev. Rutledge said about trees crossing our path," I said.

"Yeah, I remember, Corrie," he said slowly after a long thoughtful pause. "Matter of fact, the Reverend was making a lot of sense to me that day. Half the time I can't make heads or tails of what he's talking about. But I did understand what he said about the trees."

"Me too," I said. "I guess we both got trees falling in our way."

"Maybe it's the same tree," said Pa with a sly smile.

I laughed. Quickly his face sobered up again.

"The one thing the minister didn't say, though," he added, "is what you're supposed to do when the tree falls and you can't go no farther. Sometimes after the tree has blocked one path, it takes a while tramping around in the brush to find the new one! You understand what I'm driving at?"

I smiled again. "I think I do, Pa."

He looked into my eyes like he had when I'd first come

into the barn, then he looked me over from head to toe.

"I meant what you heard me say last night. You ain't an ordinary young woman by a long stretch!"

"Thank you, Pa." I knew my eyes were getting wet, but if you can't cry at a time like that, what's the use of tears, anyhow?

"No, sir. And I love you, Corrie, love you a lot."

I put my arms around his waist and hugged him. It felt so good to have his arms reach around and hug me back.

# CHAPTER 32

## ALONE WITH THOREAU

Pa'd been having me take one of the small wagons into town with Snowball every morning to get us all to school, so he wouldn't have to take us in and come back. We left Snowball and the wagon with Marcus Weber for the day, then he'd have her all hitched and ready for us when school was out.

The day after my talk with Pa, about halfway up the hill toward home, a rider on horseback flew past us. Then just as we were driving up to the cabin, back he came toward town.

"Who was that, Pa?" Zack asked as we got down, glancing back along the dust just settling back down onto the road.

"Friend of your uncle's," said Pa.

"What'd he want that he didn't want to hang around for?"

"Oh, nothing. He just thought he seen one of them polecats Nick fleeced in that poker game back in the fall."

"That fella Hatch?" said Zack.

"No, no, it weren't Hatch," said Pa. "Who was it Hammond thought he seen in town?"

"Barton," said Uncle Nick, sauntering toward us.

I looked at Zack and shivered. I remembered *that* name!

"But even if it was Barton," Uncle Nick went on, "I

didn't wind up with any of his money. He ain't got no call to have a grudge against me."

"Yeah, but them kind o' lowlifes stick together," said Pa. "I think Hammond's right. You oughta lay outta sight for a few days. Them kind never forget."

"Naw, what could Barton have against me?"

"Hatch mighta sent him."

"Hatch ain't got the brains to think o' something that clever!" said Uncle Nick, glancing at Zack with a smile and a wink, enjoying his own wit.

"And I ain't sure *you* got the brains to keep outta trouble when it comes looking for ya!" shot back Pa. "Where'd Hammond say he saw him?"

"East of town, out by the church building, kinda hanging around that new livery of Markham's."

Pa thought for a moment. "Well, I don't like it. You lay low and keep away from town. We'll keep a good eye out for ol' Hatch for a few days. Like I say, you get varmints like that together and you can never tell what kinda mischief they'll pull."

When we went inside, we were kinda quiet—all except for Uncle Nick, who kept joking and making light of the whole affair. Pretty soon Pa and Nick headed back up to the mine. Katie was working at cutting up some potatoes.

I wanted to be alone, so I fetched my book and went back outside and wandered along the stream. After Mr. Hammond's visit I wasn't exactly of a mind to go for a long walk in the woods, but I did want to get out and away from everybody, even just a *little* away.

So I went up past the mine, waved to Pa, walked across the board Pa'd put down across the creek, and went just a little farther up, not quite out of sight of where Pa was working. I felt safe there, but alone at the same time.

I'd brought my journal and pen with me. I don't reckon I'll ever think of my journal writing again without thinking of Mr. Thoreau. His *Walden* was just about the finest piece of journal writing I could imagine. He's a fine writer, and what he thought of to write about! He must have had some active imagination. I hadn't read much of it at all yet, but I found myself opening it to different parts, and wherever my eyes fell, on any page, whatever he was talking about was so interesting to read!

To write like that—what a dream that would be! I wanted to start right then making everything I put down in my journal better and better.

But it's not just the writing, it's how Mr. Thoreau taught himself to watch and listen and observe all the stuff going on around him. Most folks are too busy, and their lives are too noisy, ever to see the little tiny things. But Thoreau watched bugs, listened to grass growing, heard the sounds of the sky, and paid attention to every little thing. Yet from those little things he seemed to know so much more about life's *big* things too—as if the little things held secrets to big things!

When I read in *Walden* a quietness and an aloneness came over me. More than the fact that Mr. Thoreau *was* alone when he wrote it, I felt quieter and still just from reading it.

Most folks seem to like lots of noise all the time—they want to be talking and laughing and doing things. But sometimes I wanted to be still, to be quiet, to think, to be alone. I wanted to see the world more like Thoreau saw it. Most of the time I figured other people didn't understand that. They thought I was in a sad mood or didn't like talking to them. Every once in a while, when we were having a recess or before or after school when there was some time, I liked to wander off to that little fir woods where Becky had been the other day. I liked all the other kids, but there were some moods that I couldn't share with other folks, and I just had to think and walk and listen to the woods and the water and

242

the sky and the animals to make it all come out right. Reading Mr. Thoreau's book satisfied that part of me that needed aloneness every once in a while.

In one place he talked about a tree he'd planted:

The sumac grew luxuriantly about the house, pushing up through the embankment which I had made, and growing five or six feet the first season. Its broad pinnate tropical leaf was pleasant though strange to look on. The large buds, suddenly pushing out late in the spring from dry sticks which had seemed to be dead, developed themselves as by magic into graceful green and tender boughs, an inch in diameter. . . .

I didn't even know what the word *pinnate* meant, but I liked how he described watching that tree grow. I really sensed from his telling about it that the tree was *alive*.

We'd planted some of the seeds Katie had brought us already, south of the house where Pa said we could start a little fruit orchard. So after I read this, I determined to pay attention to every detail as those trees grew from seeds to seedlings to trees, watching them bud and flower and bear fruit in the springtime, then go dormant in the fall.

In another chapter of his book, a chapter Mr. Thoreau called "Solitude," he said:

I have never felt lonesome, or in the least oppressed by a sense of solitude . . . I find it wholesome to be alone the greater part of the time. To be in company, even with the best, is soon wearisome . . . I love to be alone. I never found the companion that was so companionable as solitude. We are for the most part more lonely when we go among men than when we stay in our rooms. A man thinking or working is always alone, let him be where he will. Solitude is not measured by the miles of space that intervene between a man and his fellows. . . . Society is commonly too cheap. We meet at very short intervals, not having had time to acquire any new value for each other. We meet at meals three times a day, and give each other a new taste of that old musty cheese that we are. We have had to agree on a certain set of rules, called etiquette and politeness, to make this frequent meeting tolerable. . . . We live thick and are in each other's way, and stumble over one another, and I think that we thus lose some respect for one another. Certainly less frequency would suffice for all important and hearty communications. . . . The value of a man is not in his skin, that we should touch him.

I guess I don't understand all of what Mr. Thoreau says, and I don't agree with all that about being alone, because I like people and I like to talk and be with them. I certainly don't fancy the idea of going off to live alone for two years! But still I like what he says, and I don't want to forget it. The danger seems to me being altogether one way or the other, so you can't be learning in different directions in your life.

Maybe that's another reason I liked his book, because I wanted to grow in *lots* of ways—not just as a teacher or a writer or a woman or a Christian, but in *all* those things, and lots of other ways besides.

Thoreau wrote more in *Walden* about being alone, but also about how much he loved nature and the world:

I am no more lonely than a single mullein or dandelion in a pasture, or a bean leaf, or sorrel, or a horse-fly, or a bumblebee. I am no more lonely than the Mill Brook, or a weathercock, or the north star, or the south wind, or an April shower, or a January thaw, or the first spider in a new house. . . . The indescribable innocence and beneficence of Nature—of sun and wind and rain, of summer and winter—such health, such cheer, they afford forever! And such sympathy have they ever with our race.

But the favorite passage I discovered those first days of reading in *Walden* was about ice forming on Walden Lake. Maybe I was drawn by the intricate detail of the things he noticed. Once we get slowed down, and get our minds so they're paying attention, a whole new world is suddenly there to discover that most folks never see. But God made that little world as part of the world of men and women. And I can't help wondering if we can't understand all God wants us to if we only see the big things.

When I read this passage, I couldn't help thinking of Mr. Thoreau himself. I could hardly believe a grown-up man being so still, so quiet, having so much time just to watch and listen, to see how thick the ice is, to lie down flat on the ice—it must have been cold!—and just stare through the water. Just thinking of him doing it made me laugh, but I'm glad he did, because his writing about it showed me a little of how I ought to look at the world.

I tried to imagine knowing the world like Thoreau knew that pond, or knowing another person that well. Or myself! What would it be like to be able to look inside my *own* thoughts and feelings like he did that frozen lake?

That's how I want to know God someday too—the little things about Him as well as the fact that He holds all the power in the universe. The same God that designed water to skim over with something hard and shiny called ice when it gets to just the right coldness, is the God who makes a thousand thunderstorms. The same God who made the little bug and the sand he scoots on, is the God who made me. And I don't want only to know the thunderstorm God, I also want to know the God who cared enough to make bugs.

Here's what Mr. Thoreau wrote about the ice:

The pond had in the meanwhile skimmed over in the shadiest and shallowest coves, some days or even weeks before the general freezing. The first ice is especially interesting and perfect, being hard, dark, and transparent, and affords the best opportunity that ever offers for examining the bottom where it is shallow; for you can lie at your length on ice only an inch thick, like a skater insect on the surface of the water, and study the bottom at your leisure, only two or three inches distant, like a picture behind a glass, and the water is necessarily always smooth then. There are many furrows in the sand where some creature has travelled about and doubled on its tracks. . . . But the ice itself is the object of most interest, though you must improve the earliest opportunity to study it. If you examine it closely the morning after it freezes, you find that the greater part of the bubbles, which at first appeared to be within it, are against its under surface, and that more are continually rising from the bottom; while the ice is as yet comparatively solid and dark, that is, you see the water through it. These bubbles are from an eightieth to an eighth of an inch in diameter, very clear and beautiful, and you see your face reflected in them through the ice. There may be thirty or forty of them to the square inch. There are also already within the ice narrow oblong perpendicular bubbles about half an inch long, sharp cones with the apex upward; or oftener, if the ice is quite fresh, minute spherical bubbles one directly above another, like a string of beads. But those within the ice are not so numerous nor obvious as those beneath.

I like Thoreau's way of observing and describing. He went on to tell what happened when the ice got thicker and harder to see through, and how he'd break it to see what would happen, and what happened to all the different kinds of bubbles when the ice got thicker. The first thing that comes to my mind now when I think of him or of *Walden* is a picture of Mr. Thoreau stretched out on that freezing cold ice!

On that particular afternoon when I'd been reading in

his book and writing down some of these favorite passages in my own journal, thinking about how I could be more observant and a better writer, I finally got tired of reading and writing and put the books down. I stood up and stretched my arms and legs, sucked in a deep breath, and looked around me.

There wasn't any ice, and there wasn't likely to be any for a long spell. But I thought to myself maybe I could still do what Mr. Thoreau did and see some other tiny things that God had put around me.

I was standing on the edge of the woods, about twenty yards away from the stream that wound down to the mine where Pa and Uncle Nick were still working. I looked up. Overhead the pine trees were tall and mostly filled up the blue of the sky. Then I looked down at my feet. Pine needles. Dead, fallen pine needles by the thousands—maybe the millions—were scattered all through the woods.

I thought about looking at them closer, like Mr. Thoreau did with the ice. So I lay down on the ground, flat, with my elbows in the grass and dirt and my head propped on my hands about six inches from the ground. And I just stared at the earth.

Then I picked up several of the pine needles and examined them. They were in little clumps of three, held together by the most curious stuff at one end that easily ground away to a tan powder when you rubbed it between your fingers.

*Why did God make it so that three needles were hooked together?* I wondered.

What a great notion, to have the needles die every year and fall from the tree when new ones come. And what a nice carpet they made for the forest floor! I scooped through the grass and pine needle carpet with one of my hands. The pine needle mass was two or three inches thick! To have gotten that thick, they must have been falling right in that spot for years and years—maybe hundreds, or even thousands of years. And yet probably no person, no human being had looked right *there* at *those* pine needles ever since God made the world. That little spot of ground might have been sitting there for thousands of years, just waiting for me to come along on this day and lie down and play with the ground with my fingers, and wonder about the things that came to my mind because of it!

I got up and brushed my hands off on my dress, then went back to the rock where I'd been sitting and wrote about the pine needles in my journal.

*I don't suppose I'll ever be a Thoreau,* I thought to myself as I read over what I wrote a few minutes later, *but I reckon I have to start somewhere.* More than likely Mr. Thoreau never figured a girl from California would be reading his words when he first wrote them in his journal either. That's just how I felt when reading over *my* journal nine years later to make a book out of things I wrote. I never dreamed anyone else would ever see them. And I knew what Mr. MacPherson would say the minute he saw this chapter about ice and pine needles and my thoughts about Mr. Thoreau's *Walden.* He'd say, "Get rid of that kind of stuff, Corrie! People want to hear what you *did* and what *happened*, not always what you're thinking about. You're too pensive for your own good!"

I had to ask him what "pensive" meant, and he said it meant a person who was always losing himself in thinking and pondering things. So I told him that's why I kept a journal, because I liked to think to myself on paper. He just humphed and shrugged, muttering something about young women and their "unhealthy cogitations"—whatever that was. But he didn't need to worry, because plenty was going to "happen" before long.

In the meantime, my afternoon with Thoreau and *Walden* and my journal was over and I walked back across the creek. I'd completely forgotten about the apprehension I'd felt a couple of hours before.

As I approached the house, I saw Katie with Becky and Emily off toward a clump of oaks that bordered the clearing where the cabin stood.

"What are you doing?" I asked, walking up.

"Watering my grass," said Becky.

"And my moss," added Emily.

"It's starting to green up real nice," said Katie. "I think it survived the trip."

I said to myself that I'd have to make a point to come back here alone. It would be interesting to study the two little growths up close, like Mr. Thoreau would, and see if there *was* any difference between the green, growing things of Virginia and California.

# CHAPTER 33

# THE NOTE

The next day at school I was more "pensive" as Mr. MacPherson would say. I was thinking about Pa and Katie and the wedding coming up just nine days away, and I suppose I was seeing lots of things through different eyes too, because my mind was full of *Walden*. So I wasn't paying heed to things like I should have been.

After school I couldn't find Becky. Pa had gone to town that morning, so when I didn't see her around after school, I vaguely remembered Pa saying something at breakfast about "if any of you wanna ride home with me . . ."

My thoughts were occupied with other things. So when none of us could find Becky anywhere, I figured Pa had fetched her without any of us seeing him, and I loaded the other kids up in the wagon and headed home.

We rode up and there was Pa. But he'd been home for two hours and hadn't seen anything of Becky. Then we started realizing we had something to worry about.

Pa immediately started to saddle Jester.

"I'll go back in, Pa," I said. "It's my fault for leaving her."

"Naw, it's okay, Corrie."

"We could both go," I suggested. "It'll make it easier. We'll have to check all around town and one of us'll have to

249

ride out to Miss Stansberry's. Becky could be anyplace."

Pa thought for a moment. "I reckon you're right. We'll ride in on Snowball and Jester, then we'll split up if she's not still around the school someplace. You go to the Stansberrys' and I'll go see Mrs. Parrish. One of them's sure to know where the little tyke is."

Five minutes later Pa and I were galloping toward town.

Four hours later we returned, just the two of us. No one in town had seen Becky. She had disappeared.

We were silent all the way home. We'd talked to everybody we could think of. I don't know what Pa was thinking, but I know he was worried. I was praying.

A couple of times he muttered something about what a fool he had been to think bringing Katie here would change things, and mumbling about troubles following him for the rest of his life. I suppose we were both blaming ourselves for what happened.

It was pretty silent that evening. Inside the house it might as well have been a tomb.

Katie tried to cheer everybody up, and a couple of times I thought Pa was going to yell at her to shut up and let us all be sad in peace. But finally she realized she wasn't helping and quieted down on her own. Pa just sat there, his feet up on the table, and she didn't even say anything about the dirt.

Just as it was getting dark, we heard a horse galloping up outside.

Pa jumped to his feet and ran out the door, leaving it wide open. Every one of us followed him.

It was Sheriff Rafferty.

"You find her?" shouted Pa as the sheriff reined in his horse.

There was no reply. Rafferty slowed to a stop, then dismounted, threw the rein over the rail, and walked toward Pa. It was clear from his face he didn't have good news. He was holding a piece of paper.

"Sorry, Drum," he said. "All I got's this." He handed Pa the paper. "Weber found it nailed to a post outside his livery in this envelope with your name on it. No one saw how it got there. He brought it to me."

Pa grabbed it, fumbled hurriedly with the envelope, and unfolded the paper. As he read, a sickening look of dread spread over his face.

You'll get yer daughter back, Hollister, when you fork over $50,000. The loot's mine, I'm jist gittin' what's comin' to me! An' jist in case yer not lyin' about not knowin' where it is, I figure yer mine's worth plenty. So you jist git the money, or fifty thousand in gold, or the deed to yer place. It don't matter to me. Try to find the little girl, and I'll kill you and her both! If there ain't no money by next week, we're leavin' yer brat to the wolves. They'll find her in less than two hours! And then I'll grab another o' yer kids and we'll go through this all again. So pay up, Hollister, fer yer own good! I'll git word to you where to take it.

"Krebbs!"

Pa's voice held sounds of wrath and despondency and self-blame and hatred. He walked a few steps away, one hand on his head, the other at his side with fist clenched.

"We gotta do some serious talking, Drum," said Sheriff Rafferty.

Pa turned back around to face him.

"There was also this," the sheriff went on, pulling another envelope from his pocket. "This one had *my* name on it. I guess they figured if they couldn't get you one way, they'd put me on your trail."

Again Pa slowly opened the envelope and took out a folded paper. It was an old, half-torn, yellowed and ragged warrant for Pa's arrest.

"Well, I reckon it's all caught up with me at last," said Pa with a sigh. "You better come on in, Simon."

Pa led the sheriff inside. The rest of us followed and closed the door behind us.

# CHAPTER 34

# THE REFUSAL

The minute we were inside, Pa ordered all us kids into our rooms, but he didn't pay much attention, and we left the doors open. We were all ears, hanging on every word that followed.

"What's this all about, Drum?" asked the sheriff. "I know your kid's in trouble and we'll do what we can. But I'm a sworn lawman and I got a duty too. So I'm asking you, is this warrant on the level?"

"It's a pack of the darndest lies that—!" I heard Uncle Nick exclaim. But Pa's voice cut him off.

"No it ain't, Nick, and you know it."

Then he turned to the sheriff. "I suppose you could say it's on the level, Simon. But there's always two sides to these things."

"Well, I'm listening, Drum. You're my friend, and I figure I owe you the benefit of the doubt. But if this warrant's in effect and they're still looking for you, then—well, then I don't know what! It's my job, you know, and friend or not, I gotta—"

"I understand what you're up against, Simon," said Pa calmly. "How about if I tell you what happened. Then if you figure you gotta take me in, I'll go with you peaceably— as long as we get Becky back first. After that, well maybe it's time I faced the music and quit hiding from my past. That's what I got me a wife for, 'cause I always knew something like this might happen."

"Sounds like a straight deal to me," replied Sheriff Rafferty.

"And you gotta let me and Miss Kathryn get done with the wedding first too," added Pa. "That way, I'll know the kids are gonna be safe."

"When is it?"

"Week from Sunday."

"Agreed, Drum. Now get on with it."

Pa heaved a deep sigh. The room was completely silent for a minute or so, then he started.

"Well, you know how when I first came here I didn't let on my name was Hollister. I went by Drum plain and simple, and let folks think that was my last name."

As Pa spoke I tiptoed to the open door so I could peek out just an inch. I saw Mr. Rafferty nodding his head.

"And Nick, too," Pa added. "Most folks around here still call him Matthews."

"You in this too, Nick?" said the sheriff, glancing up at Uncle Nick.

"Never mind him," said Pa. "If you take me in, you gotta be satisfied with that. You ain't got no warrant on Nick, and I want to know he's around to keep the mine going, for the kids' sake."

The sheriff seemed to chew on his words a while, then looked over both Pa and Uncle Nick.

"For a man sitting trying to explain to a lawman why there's a warrant out on him, you seem to be putting lots of conditions on what I can and can't do."

I thought at first that he was being serious, then I wondered if he was joking with Pa. But nobody laughed, and I never did know.

Pa just shrugged. "I don't figure you got much choice,"

he said. "You ain't gonna get my story otherwise. And you and I both know that if I decide to fight, you'd never take me in. I got too many friends in these parts. So I don't see that you got much choice."

"Just go on with your story."

"Well, that's the reason when we came west, why we—why *I* didn't use my real name. That's an old warrant, before we got caught. We were part of a jailbreak, and after that the law mostly figured we were dead, which was why we thought we'd be safe. But I reckon technically, seeing as how we escaped, that warrant would still be valid."

"What were you in for?"

"You're not gonna like hearing it."

"It was a bum charge—a frame-up!" said Uncle Nick.

"What was it, Drum?" said the sheriff again.

"The worst, Simon—bank robbery and murder."

The sheriff let out a low whistle. "That's bad," he finally said.

"Nick's right, though," added Pa. "We'd been riding with the gang, that much is true. So I reckon you could say we were accomplices on the robbin' part. But we weren't nowhere near any killin'."

"And you were part of a break?"

"Yeah, we busted out, along with a bunch of others. We didn't cotton to the notion of dangling from the end of a rope for something we didn't do, so when we had the chance we lit out and came out here."

"And so who's this fella Krebbs who's been bull-doggin' you these last couple of years? He got something to do with all this?"

"He's part of the original gang that pulled the job. He and several of the others got away clean. Krebbs always figured we had the loot. So when he heard we'd busted out, he got a whiff of our trail, and he's been tracking us ever since."

"You got the money, Drum? If you do, turning it back in would go a long way toward proving to the law your intention of living straight from now on."

"Come on, Simon!" said Pa in disbelief that he would even ask. "Look around! Look at my hands. Look at how hard me and Nick work up there in that mine every day. You think we'd have been bustin' our backs all these years if we had that fifty thousand stashed someplace?"

Rafferty gave a half-shrug and nodded thoughtfully. "Probably not. But I had to ask."

Pa settled back in his chair, waiting for what the sheriff would say next. I glanced over at Katie. She hadn't said a word the whole time. I wondered what she was thinking— probably that she'd gotten herself mixed up with more than she'd bargained for!

"Well, Drum, your story makes sense. I've always fig- ured you for a man of your word. So I'm inclined to believe you. But I think you better tell me the whole story. It's dark now, and those varmints obviously have your young'un someplace we won't find tonight. We got time, so I want you to start at the beginning."

Pa let out a heavy sigh, and launched into the tale that none of the other kids but me had heard. I'd tried to explain things to them, but I was glad they were hearing it from Pa's own lips. I wanted them to know how it had really been between Ma and Pa, and why he'd had to leave us without any word.

Twenty or twenty-five minutes later he was done. He didn't shed tears this time, like when he'd first told me the story. But I knew it had been hard for Pa nevertheless. There were still hurts he felt from what he'd done.

There was a long quiet in the room.

Sheriff Rafferty was the first to break it. The next sound we all heard was the ripping of the warrant in half.

"I believe you, Drum," he said. "Like I said, I figure

you for a man of your word, so I'm gonna pretend I never saw this."

I could almost feel the relief that spread over Pa's face.

"Now we gotta get your little girl back," said the sheriff. "What do you want me to do, Drum? You got fifty thousand?"

Pa laughed, a bitter laugh that didn't have any joy in it.

"Are you kidding?" he said. "Fifty thousand? It might as well be a million! Me and Nick's got maybe $3,000 in the bank. Here we figured that was real good for a year's work, more'n most men see in their lives. Now it looks like nothin'!"

"You want me to round up some of the boys and get together a posse?"

"And do what?" said Pa. "We ain't got a notion where they are."

"With enough men and enough time, we could find them."

"We ain't got time! And like he said, Krebbs'd just kill Becky, then snatch one of the others. I know him. He's a mean one. He won't stop till he's got the money. The way I figure it, I gotta pay him or we'll be runnin' from him forever."

"How we gonna raise fifty thousand, Drum?" said Uncle Nick. "There ain't nobody in this town who's got that kind of cash."

"There's one, Nick."

"You don't mean that lowdown—"

"That's right—Royce."

"Royce'd never give you that much money!"

"Not *give* . . . loan. That's what bankers do, they loan money."

"How would you pay him back?" asked the sheriff.

"If Nick and me put away $3,000 in a year, all we need to do is work a little harder. Zack's getting to be a man. He can help. We can make five, maybe ten thousand a year outta that mine. We could have Royce paid back in five years!"

"Work harder!" groaned Uncle Nick.

"For Becky, we'll put in fourteen hours a day up in that pit!" said Pa. "And you'll be with me! Besides," he added after a little pause, "I don't see what choice we have. We don't know where they are. Krebbs'll kill Becky if we don't give him the loot. You know him, Nick—you know he'll do it sure as the sun shines. And the only way to get that kind of money is from Royce. It's all we *can* do."

"There's the claim," suggested Katie. "What about that?" For the first time since she'd come, her voice sounded timid.

Pa shook his head. "We can't do that, Miss Kathryn. The mine and this claim's all we got. Leastways, if we pay him, after five years the mine and the cabin and the land's still ours. No, we'll pay him."

Pa's voice had a decisive sound to it. No one said anything else for a little bit. Then Sheriff Rafferty got up out of his chair.

"Well, I reckon you'll be coming to town in the morning to see Royce," he said. "Come and see me when your business is settled. We still want to do our best to nab this bushwhacker."

He shook Pa's hand, then left.

The next morning bright and early we all rode to town.

Everyone wanted to go, and with Buck Krebbs on the loose, Pa was in no mood to argue. He told Katie to keep Tad and Emily with her near the wagon. I guess he figured Zack and I were big enough to take care of ourselves. Uncle Nick stayed with Katie, I went to Mrs. Parrish's office to see if she'd heard anything, and Pa went to the bank to see Mr. Royce.

The whole town was abuzz with talk of Becky's kidnapping. Mrs. Parrish knew everything, and the minute I walked in she ran toward me and embraced me. I told her what Pa was doing.

A few minutes later I saw Pa through the window walking out of the bank and back toward the wagon. I rushed outside, not even thinking to close the door.

Pa was walking toward the wagon. Katie was still sitting in it with Tad and Emily. Uncle Nick was on the ground leaning against one of the wagon wheels. Zack was behind the wagon kicking a rock in the dirt. I ran up just as Pa got there.

He just looked at Uncle Nick and shook his head.

"What?" exclaimed Uncle Nick.

"He turned us down," said Pa. "He laughed in my face. I said, 'Have you heard about my daughter?' and he said, 'I heard something to that effect, and I'm sorry, Hollister, I truly am, but fifty thousand is a huge sum of money.' I told him we were good for it, and that's when he laughed."

Pa couldn't help sounding angry. But there was more desperation in his voice than bitterness or hatred.

"The oily scoundrel's probably in on the whole thing!" cried Uncle Nick angrily.

"I thought of that," said Pa.

"He's nothing but a double-dealing snake!"

"A snake who's the only one around here with money."

"You told him we'd work it off?" asked Uncle Nick, calming a little.

"Yeah. I even said we'd sign over the mine as collateral for the money. That's when he laughed again. 'A hunk of ground for fifty thousand?' he said. 'And when the mine plays out a year from now, where does that leave me? No thanks, Hollister. Far too risky an exchange! Look, I'm sorry about your kid. But this is business. And this would be a bad loan, pure and simple. Any banker in the country would turn you down flat.' That's when I walked out. I couldn't listen to another word. But I could feel his gloating eyes on my back. I knew the rascal was smiling inside, getting his revenge on us for spoiling his little scheme last year."

Pa was silent. He and Uncle Nick both stared at the ground, trying to decide what to do. I hadn't noticed at first, but now I saw that Mrs. Parrish had followed me out of her office. She was halfway across the street and coming toward us.

Pa didn't see her. All at once he lifted his head and said to Uncle Nick, "Nick, you go over to Rafferty's. Bring him to the title office. You and me's gonna sign over a quitclaim on the mine to Krebbs. It's the only way we'll ever see Becky again."

Without another word, he walked off down the street in the direction of the Miracle Springs Land Office.

# CHAPTER 35

## THE OFFER

The moment Pa headed off, Mrs. Parrish changed her bearing across the street so that she would intercept him. They were only about twenty feet from the wagon when she stopped him.

"May I have a few words with you, Mr. Hollister?" she said.

"I've gotta get down to the title office, ma'am," replied Pa, still walking.

"If you would just spare me a moment or two," she persisted. "What I have to say may affect your plans."

"You know about Becky?" said Pa, stopping and looking directly at Mrs. Parrish.

"Yes. I know everything. As I came out of my office a moment ago I could not help hearing of your conversation with Mr. Royce."

"A skunk!" said Pa.

"I would not want to disagree with you, Mr. Hollister." Mrs. Parrish paused a moment. When she continued, her voice was different than I had ever heard it sound before. It almost had a quiver to it. "Perhaps you would allow *me* to help you."

"You, ma'am?"

"Yes. Please—I want to help. I can't bear the thought of

262

you giving up the mine."

Pa stared at her intently. "Just what is it you aim to do, ma'am?" he asked. "I want you to know I appreciate that you're fond of my kids, but right now, just how do you figure you can help?"

"Let me give you the fifty thousand dollars."

Pa's face clearly showed the shock he felt from her words.

"You . . . you . . . would *do* that, ma'am?" Pa half-stammered.

"If only you'll let me." Mrs. Parrish was now looking Pa deeply in the eye. "Please, say you'll let me help, won't you, Drummond?"

Pa didn't know what to say. He looked down at the ground, scuffling in the street with his boot. I knew he was thinking real hard. I couldn't help remembering what he'd said once when Mrs. Parrish had offered to help one time before: "I ain't takin' no handouts from a woman!"

"I know it would not be an easy thing for you to do," Mrs. Parrish said. "And there would be no way to keep it quiet. But to save your daughter, and the mine . . ."

She let Pa finish the thought for himself.

Finally he looked up, but still said nothing.

"And for the future of your upcoming marriage!" added Mrs. Parrish. "I'll not only be doing it for you and your children, but also for your bride." She glanced toward Katie and the rest of us. "Think of it as my wedding present, just a little early."

At last Pa spoke. As he looked at her, his face showed that he'd been conquered.

"You've got that kind of money, ma'am?" he asked quietly.

"I can get it."

"No handout—it'd be a loan?"

"Of course."

"I'll pay you back every cent—with interest!"

"You just name your terms, Drummond," she said with a slight smile, "and I'll satisfy your every request."

Pa shook his head and sighed.

"Then I'll go along, I reckon," he said.

"Fine! You do whatever else you need to and meet me in my office in an hour." Mrs. Parrish turned and started to walk away.

Pa stopped her. "Ma'am," he said, "I really am much obliged to you."

She smiled, then crossed the street back to her office, while Pa turned in the direction of Sheriff Rafferty's office.

In a few minutes Mrs. Parrish came back out of her office carrying a small parcel of papers. She did not even look across the street where I still stood by the buckboard with Katie and Zack and Tad and Emily. She walked straight to the bank and inside.

Pa and Uncle Nick didn't come back for quite a while. Fifteen minutes later Mrs. Parrish walked out of the bank. I had wandered up the walk in that direction, but when she came out she headed straight back to her office without saying a word to anyone.

After she'd closed the door of the bank behind her, I saw Mr. Royce come to one of the windows, then spread the curtain aside with his hand and watch her as she walked away. He had a gleam in his eye and a horrible look of triumph. Mrs. Parrish wasn't carrying any papers.

An hour later Pa came back. He went over to Mrs. Parrish's—alone.

After a minute he and Mrs. Parrish came out together. They walked to the bank and inside. Ten minutes later they came out again, Pa carrying a large leather bag.

Mrs. Parrish went back to her office, and Pa went down to the sheriff's. When he came out his hands were empty. He came straight to the wagon, called to us, then he jumped up onto the seat. We all piled in. He yelled to the horses and we were off toward home.

"What do we do now, Pa?" asked Zack.

"We wait," said Pa.

# CHAPTER 36

# THE PLAN

We didn't have to wait long.

Sheriff Rafferty came riding up in a cloud of dust just about an hour after noon. "This is it, Drum!" he shouted, dismounting as his own dust overtook him, and running toward Pa with a letter in his hand.

Immediately everyone swarmed around. Mr. Jones was there now too, both to share the anxious waiting with his friend and to help if he could.

"A kid rode into town a few minutes ago and delivered this to me," the sheriff said. "I didn't know him. Told me he lived down by You Bet. Said a stranger gave him five bucks to ride to Miracle and give this letter to the sheriff. The kid said he said sure, the man gave him five dollars and the letter, then rode off. That's all the kid knew."

Pa took the letter and read it out loud.

Give this letter to Drum Hollister. It's fer him.

Hollister, I hope fer yer kid's sake you got the loot. Put it in a coupla saddlebags an ride out the trail to Deadman's Flat over the Chalk Bluff Ridge. Go a quarter mile past Steephollow Creek. There's a road off left with a sign—To Negro Jacks—stuck to a tree. Behind the tree's a dead stump, half-hollered out. You

265

throw the saddlebags in there! Don't try findin' us cuz we ain't there. We ain't nowhere near there, but we'll get the loot an when we does we'll let the girl go. If you ain't got the cash, you sign over yer deed on yer claim to Buchanan J. Krebbs an' put that in the saddlebags instead. Do what I says, Hollister! Remember the wolves!

"Well, let's go!" said Pa. "Where's the money, Simon?"

"Hold on just a minute, Drum! Let's talk this out a spell. There's still a chance we can figure out where these guys are. We don't want to give them the money if we don't have to."

"I thought we had all this settled!" snapped Pa. "There ain't no other way but to do as Krebbs says."

"Well, I ain't so sure," said the sheriff. "I been thinking while I rode out here—if we could just figure out who's in it with him—"

"Somebody's in it with him for sure," interrupted Uncle Nick. "Krebbs can't read or write his own name! He's the dumbest—"

"That's right!" said Pa. "I plumb forgot. He couldn't have written these two notes."

"Barton!" said the sheriff. "He's had schooling. I've run into him a couple of times. Saw him reading a newspaper once. He could have done it. And Hammond saw him the other day, probably watching the school from across the way by Markham's place."

"He must've seen Becky going off toward the woods," I suggested.

"Barton's from Dutch Flat," Mr. Rafferty went on, hardly noticing my idea. "And I know ol' Negro Jack. His place ain't four miles from there!"

"I bet that polecat Hatch is in on it with 'em!" said Uncle Nick.

"Krebbs always had a way of smelling out the lowlifes around a place," said Pa. "I don't doubt but what you're right, Nick. I'd wager plenty that Dutch Flat's where they're holed up."

"Okay, now we can't go riding in there with twenty men," said Mr. Rafferty. "They'll kill the girl."

"They'll be hiding her someplace safe," said Uncle Nick.

"What'd he mean about wolves?" asked Mr. Jones, speaking for the first time.

"Oh, nothin', Alkali," said Pa. "It was just some threat they made in their first note."

"What threat? What'd they say?"

"They said if we tried anything they'd high-tail it outta there and leave Becky where the wolves'd find her."

"And they's down by Dutch Flat, ya say?"

"That's how we got it figured," answered the sheriff.

"Well, there's a pack o' wolves that's seen sometimes down jist south o' there. Ya heard o' 'em—on Frost Hill."

"So if they were hiding her away someplace—" began Mr. Rafferty, but Uncle Nick's voice cut him off.

"The cave!" he cried. "They've got her in ol' Hatch's cave! That's it, I tell ya, Drum! When that ol' cuss had me there, I could hear the wail of wolves and he kept tellin' me he was gonna leave me there to get eaten by 'em."

Everyone was quiet, thinking hard.

Sheriff Rafferty turned and walked away, slowly, looking first at the ground, then up at the sky. It only took him about two or three minutes.

Suddenly, he spun around and strode back to where the rest of us were standing.

"I think I've got it," he said. "I think we just might be able to save Becky *and* keep our hands on the money. Now look here, Drum—just in case they've got somebody watching us, you'll ride out like he says, alone, with the saddlebags and the money. But we'll follow, about five or ten minutes behind you. You dump the bags, but we'll keep half our men there. If any of them come to get it, we'll ambush them.

Meanwhile, the rest of us will circle back up across Chalk Bluff Ridge and down on the other side of Dutch Flat. Isn't that where Frost Hill is, Jones?"

"Yep. Ya come down off the ridge, across Bear River."

"And where's the cave?"

"Right there, Squires Canyon."

"Okay, we'll split up, half guarding the money, half circling back behind the cave."

"I'm riding to the cave," said Pa. "She's my girl."

"Fine by me. But you'll need help," said the sheriff. "They'll have a guard, but probably only one or two men. If you and two or three of the boys get the drop on them, you should get her fine. One of you ride back to Miracle with the girl, the others ride back up the ridge to where we're waiting at Deadman's Flat. Once the girl's safe, we'll send the money back to town, then all the rest of us'll ride on to Dutch Flat and see if we can smoke out this fella Krebbs."

"What if they come for the money and see you there before I've got Becky out?" asked Pa.

"They couldn't get anyone to the cave before you got there. You'd have a lead on them. And they'll never figure us to know where they're hiding her."

"That may be," said Pa seriously. "But if anything goes sour, you give them the dough, you hear?"

"Fair enough," said Sheriff Rafferty.

There was a pause. The men looked around at each other, anxiety and determination on all their faces, as if to say, "Let's get this done!"

Finally the sheriff drew in a deep breath and said. "Well, if we're agreed, I'll ride into town. Several of the men have already volunteered to help. Nick, Drum, Alkali, you men round up whoever you can on this side of town—Shaw, Hammond, whoever might be willing, I'll get the money from the safe in my office and be back here with the men in, say, an hour."

Pa nodded.

Just as the sheriff was in the saddle and wheeling his horse back down the road, Pa glanced around.

"Where's Zack?" he said.

"He rode off," said Emily.

"Tarnation!" exclaimed Pa. "Which way? Did you see him, Emily?"

"Over the hill by the mine, I think, Pa."

Just then the door opened and Katie walked out.

"Zack said to wait till you were through to tell you this," she said. "He said to tell you he went to get Little Wolf, and not to worry about Becky."

# CHAPTER 37

## THE RIDE

Pa ran to the barn.

"Blue Flame's gone!" he yelled.

He ran back. "Nick, Alkali," he said, "you round up whoever you can, like Rafferty said. I'm gonna ride after the sheriff and see if I can catch him and tell him to be back sooner'n an hour if he can. Otherwise, I'll try to cut Zack off across the ridge if those two ride that direction and through Miracle on their way to wherever they're going. I think I know where!"

Pa was already mounted and on his way as he was yelling out his instructions. "Fool kids!" he said to himself as he galloped after the sheriff. "Liable to get themselves killed, along with all the rest of us!"

Within two minutes everyone was gone, and it was just Katie and me and the two younger ones. Suddenly I realized we were alone, and I remembered the sheriff's words about wondering if they had someone watching us. Buck Krebbs was sure familiar enough with our place!

I went inside to show Katie where Pa kept his rifle and I asked her if she knew how to use one. She said she did. Knowing Katie, I wasn't surprised.

Mr. Jones got back first. He had Patrick Shaw and his eighteen-year-old son Caleb with him. Uncle Nick was next with two other nearby miners. All the men had rifles.

Pa and the sheriff came about twenty minutes later. Altogether they brought another six or seven men. Zack wasn't with them.

I begged Pa to let me go. I promised to stay behind and out of the way.

"Not even if *you* had fifty thousand dollars, Corrie! I got two kids out there already, and that's two too many."

"About the money, Pa," I said. "I think Mrs. Parrish might have done something awful to get it."

He looked down at me from where he sat on his horse, wanting to ask me what I meant but knowing there was no time. Sheriff Rafferty was already explaining the plan to the men.

"Don't worry, Corrie. I aim to do my best to get it back."

He reined his horse around, joined the others, and after a few last-minute words, Pa took the saddlebags with the money and sped off over the hill to join the trail running east. The sheriff and the men waited about five minutes, then followed.

The rest of us went inside.

Everything was still and quiet for three hours. We heard nothing more until we heard a horse outside. It was Little Wolf, alone. The first thing I noticed was the blood on his arm.

Frantically I ran to him, shouting out questions. And between Little Wolf's story and the information we got later that night, I found out all that had happened.

————

Pa rode east, then south across Washington Ridge, by Fowler Spring and Sailor Flat, over Buckeye Ridge, across Chalk Bluff Ridge and down into Deadman's Flat. The whole time he was watching out, but never saw a soul. That was about an eight- or nine-mile ride.

He got there all right, found the Negro Jack sign, and tossed the saddlebags in the hollow stump. He said he didn't think Krebbs had anybody there yet; they probably didn't figure Pa'd be so quick getting the money. So Pa sat off to the side and waited, but he didn't think anybody'd been watching or trailing him either. In ten minutes Sheriff Rafferty came with Uncle Nick and the rest of the men.

They split up. Pa took Mr. Shaw, Miss Stansberry's brother Hermon, and Marcus Weber with him. Everyone else hid in the woods nearby waiting to see if Krebbs or anybody'd come for the saddlebags. Pa and his three men took off west, up on top of Chalk Bluff Ridge, then followed the ridge trail southwest so as to come around and down on the far side of Squires Canyon where the cave was.

Before they were even halfway along the ridge, right by Red Hill spring, they saw a rider coming toward them. Quickly they got off their horses and led them off the trail, drew their guns, and got ready for a fight. But when the rider got closer they put their guns away. It was Zack.

———

In the meantime, when we'd all been back at home, the minute Zack heard what Pa and the sheriff planned to do— and he had a big grin when he was telling about it!—he sneaked around the back of the cabin, gave Katie his message, and got Blue Flame out of the barn as quietly as he could. He said he knew Pa would say no if he asked, so he just didn't ask. Little Wolf knew the woods better than any five men in Miracle put together, and he figured the two of them would have the best chance of rescuing Becky if she was in the cave. He saw Pa heading for town looking for him, but by that time he was way up on the side of Buck Mountain.

By the time Pa and the sheriff and the rest of the men were gathering at our place, he and Little Wolf were already crossing Scotts Flat halfway to Gold Run. When they got to Gold Run, they skirted the edge of town, rode up toward Dutch Flat, and turned off the road before they got to Blue Devil Diggings, so as not to be seen by anyone riding south out of Dutch Flat. They tied their horses, then walked slowly up to where Zack and I and Pa'd been before. Zack remembered the area pretty well and he knew from there they'd be able to get a good look down into the canyon and at the cave.

Sure enough, there were two men standing outside the mouth of it.

They slipped up closer, quietly, until they were within earshot.

The two men were Hatch and Krebbs.

"I'll be back this evening," Krebbs was saying. "If they ain't brung the loot yet, I'll bring ya some grub."

Hatch said something, but Zack didn't hear what it was.

"That ain't none o' yer concern, ya old buzzard!" Krebbs said. "You jist do what I says, an' you'll get yer cut. You stay put right where you are, and if anybody 'ceptin' me comes around here, you blow their heads off. Ya got me, Hatch?"

Again Hatch said something.

"I know there ain't nobody gonna come. There ain't no way they gonna find where we got the kid if they had a year. But I want somebody here anyway, an' that's what I'm payin' you fer."

With that, Krebbs turned and rode off up the far end of the canyon.

Nick and Little Wolf spied out the area a bit more. They figured the horses were best where they were, not far from where we'd tied them when we rescued Uncle Nick. Then they set about a plan to lure Grizzly Hatch away from the cave.

For Little Wolf, that wasn't so difficult, though it took them twenty or thirty minutes to get into place—Zack behind a boulder above the cave, Little Wolf down in the canyon, about fifty feet in front of it. When Zack signalled that he was ready, Little Wolf began making sounds to get Hatch confused—throwing his voice, making animal sounds, then a call like a wolf.

But Hatch wasn't as easy to fool as Buck Krebbs had been. His beady eyes spotted Little Wolf almost as soon as the first bird-call was out of his mouth.

The first sign that he'd been seen was the explosion of Hatch's shotgun. If Little Wolf hadn't been mostly behind a tree, it might have been worse. As it was, some pieces of buckshot found his leg and wrist.

"I see ya, ya redskin varmint!" cried Hatch. "Let that learn ya not to come around here!"

Little Wolf started down the canyon, then looked back. When he saw Hatch wasn't going to follow him, he knew he had to try something else. He pulled an arrow out of his quiver and let one sail toward Hatch, thunking into a pine tree about five feet away, exactly where he'd aimed.

That made Hatch mad, which was just what Little Wolf wanted.

"Why, you no good animal!" screamed Hatch in a rage. "You won't take a warning! We'll see if a belly full o' buckshot is more to your liking!"

He tore down the hill after Little Wolf.

Little Wolf started to run, and for the first time he felt the pain in his leg. He tripped and fell just as Hatch released the load from the second barrel. It flew over Little Wolf's head, ripping a six-inch piece of bark off a Ponderosa pine.

If he hadn't fallen just then, Little Wolf would have been dead.

He jumped to his feet and flew down the canyon limping, hearing Hatch cursing behind him and fumbling to reload his gun. Within seconds Hatch was after him once more.

In the meantime, Zack scrambled down the hillside,

went inside the cave, and found Becky. She was dirty, hungry, and afraid, but her spirit wasn't broken. Zack said her first words to him were, "Hi, Zack. I was just getting ready to escape."

He signalled her to be quiet, untied the ropes around her hands and feet, then picked her up in his arms. Cautiously they left the cave. Zack looked all about, heard Hatch yelling a hundred yards away, then made a dash with Becky down the hill into the canyon, then up the other side just like I'd done with Uncle Nick. Halfway up the opposite side, he heard the sharp report from Hatch's gun again. He jumped in terror, nearly throwing Becky to the ground, knowing the danger his friend was in. But he continued on up the hill, finally put Becky down, and hand in hand they ran the rest of the way to the horses, where they fell onto the ground in exhaustion.

Twice more Zack heard Hatch fire. Every time he wondered if he'd ever see Little Wolf again.

Then came a long silence lasting five minutes or more. From far down the canyon came another shot. Almost the same instant, there was a rustle in the brush behind him. Zack turned. There stood Little Wolf, his face pale, sweat and dirt on his forehead, but smiling broadly.

"I finally managed to get the old goat chasing his own tail," he said out of breath, "but he was not so easy a prey. He is a man of cunning, despite his look of a crazy old fool."

"You're hurt!" said Zack.

"Yes, I am hurt, but not badly. He is not so bad a shot either," Little Wolf added with a tired smile, "for a man on the run. But, little one," he said, kneeling down beside Becky, "you are safe and well?"

"Yes, Little Wolf," said Becky. "Thank you for saving me."

"Your brother is the one with courage. He came to me and told me we must save you."

"We have to get out of here," said Zack. "Come on, Becky. You and Little Wolf have to get home."

"Where are you going, Zack?" asked Becky.

"I gotta get to Pa."

"Let me ride the Chalk Bluff Ridge," said Little Wolf. "I know it like my own hand."

"No," insisted Zack. "You must get home and out of danger. Your father must tend your wounds. But first, take Becky to Mrs. Parrish in Miracle. She will know what to do. Might be nobody's at our place. Then you go to your father."

Little Wolf looked into Zack's face, so much younger than his own. "I will do as you say," he said. "I am too weary to argue, and perhaps you are right."

Little Wolf mounted his pony, and Zack handed Becky up in front of him. "Be careful until you are past Gold Run," warned Zack.

Little Wolf rode off. Then Zack mounted Blue Flame, worked his way north, past Blue Devil Diggings, back across the Bear, and up Chalk Bluff until he regained the trail on the ridge. Then he swung Blue Flame northeast and made for Deadman's Flat.

# CHAPTER 38

# THE FIGHT AT NEGRO JACK'S

When Pa and Zack met on the trail, there wasn't time for Zack to do much explaining. Pa'd have to wait to hear the whole story along with me and everyone else.

All Zack said was, "Becky's safe! She's on her way back to Miracle with Little Wolf."

The next moment, Pa, Zack, Hermon, Stansberry, Marcus Weber, and Pat Shaw were riding like the wind back to rejoin the sheriff and the rest of the men.

Even before they'd started down off the ridge toward Steephollow Creek, they could hear the gunfire.

They rode in from the north, the way they'd come from Miracle earlier. Pa could tell as they approached that Rafferty and Uncle Nick were pinned down. But they still had the entrance to Negro Jack's covered, so Pa figured the money was still there. Otherwise Krebbs and his men wouldn't be hanging around fighting.

Krebbs had a man watching after all, Pa discovered later, who had taken off for Dutch Flat the minute the sheriff and his men rode in. By the time Little Wolf had outsmarted Grizzly Hatch back at the cave, Buck Krebbs and his men were riding north out of Dutch Flat for a showdown.

Pa and the others came down slowly off the ridge, hoping to keep from being seen. When they got in a position to outflank Krebbs and his men and get a good bead on them, they opened fire.

The surprise of the attack must have helped because the rocks and trees they'd been hiding behind were no longer any good. Now they had to move to protect themselves from their exposed positions, and while they were scrambling back in retreat, the men with the sheriff were able to get higher up on the hill and gain a better vantagepoint.

The exchange of gunfire went on for ten or fifteen minutes, but neither side was any closer to being able to send someone in to snatch the saddlebags without being seen and getting shot.

I guess Zack was feeling heroic, because for the second time that day he slipped away without Pa's seeing him.

Suddenly, the next thing Pa knew, there was Zack, behind a small boulder, not fifteen yards from the *To Negro Jacks* sign. Immediately Pa knew what he was trying to do. At almost the same instant, Pa saw Buck Krebbs about the same distance away from the stump on the other side, behind a thick fir, hidden from Zack's sight.

"Zack, no!" yelled Pa, standing and shouting through his cupped hands.

But it was too late. A sharp crack from a Winchester exploded through the air. The slug ripped through the calf of Pa's right leg and he fell to the ground. The same instant Zack made his dash for the stump. He laid his hand on the leather saddlebags, when an evil voice froze him in his tracks before he could make good his escape.

"Don't do it, boy!" said the voice. "Let go o' the bag."

Zack looked up.

There was Buck Krebbs ten feet away, a sneer revealing black and yellow teeth. In his hand was a revolver aimed directly at Zack's head.

For two or three seconds both stood dead still, staring each into the other's eyes, weighing the odds, asking himself what the other might do.

Lying on his belly seventy-five feet above them, blood oozing from his leg into the grass and dirt, Pa had slowly pulled his pistol from its holster and was now drawing it into position. Wincing in pain, he grasped the gun in both hands and stretched out his arms in front of him, squinting as he gazed down the black steel gunbarrel.

Suddenly, Zack clutched the saddlebags and darted toward the nearest tree.

The split second it took for Buck Krebbs to refocus his aim was too long. As his finger began to squeeze the trigger to liberate the bullet that would end Zack's life, Pa's .45 sounded from above.

The gleam went out of Buck Krebbs' eye. He crumpled to the ground where he had stood, shot dead through the heart.

With the money gone and their leader dead, Barton and the rest scattered to the hills. It was over.

Sheriff Rafferty and Uncle Nick jumped out of their hiding places and ran down the hill, congratulating Zack, then tending to Pa's wound. The slug hadn't hit either a bone or an artery, but it was a nasty gash and the slug was still in his leg. They had to get him home and to the doctor's without delay.

# CHAPTER 39

# THAT NIGHT

That afternoon Doc had to come out to our place to tend *two* patients.

After leaving Becky with Mrs. Parrish in town, Little Wolf had ridden to our place instead of home, like Zack had said. He wanted to see if we were there, to tell us Becky was safe and where she was. But by the time he arrived, he was so weak and faint that he couldn't go another step.

I ran toward him yelling, "Where's Becky? What happened? Are Pa and Zack safe?"

Little Wolf told me later he didn't hear a word I'd said. The moment I reached him he half-fainted and collapsed off the side of his pony into my arms. It was all I could do to keep from toppling over with his weight!

All he was able to whisper was, "Becky . . . safe . . . with Mrs. Parrish . . ."

Katie saw through the window and rushed out to help me. We carried him inside, found his wounds, and dressed them as best we could.

He must have been hit more than just that first time. It looked to me that he had a dozen little pieces of shot scattered in his leg and arm, and his clothes were covered with blood. It was no wonder he was faint!

When we got him laid down, I reminded Katie about the

gun, told Emily to lock the door behind me, and said I was riding into town to get the doctor and see how Becky was.

I got back in about half an hour. Doc's buggy was about fifteen minutes behind me, and by the time he had most of the shot out of Little Wolf's leg and ointment and bandages on the wounds, Uncle Nick and the sheriff were riding in. So he started right in on Pa.

By evening Pa was on the mend too. Doc gave Pa two or three glasses of whiskey, and after it had taken effect and Pa was half-asleep, he dug the slug out of his leg. I could hardly stand it. I thought I would throw up a couple of times. There was more bleeding, and Pa yelled out. But when it was over, Doc said the wound was clean. He dressed it, and told Pa to stay off it for a couple of weeks.

"Stay off it, Doc?" Pa exclaimed, wide awake now after the painful surgery. "I can't lay around for two weeks!"

"Then all I can say, Drum," replied the Doc, "is keep your weight off it if you can. Use a cane or a crutch or something. The more you use it, the longer it'll take to heal."

Little Wolf wanted to go home, but he was even weaker than Pa. He had not only lost blood, the exertion from the long ride had worn him out and he remained pale all day. Doc said we should keep him at our place at least overnight.

"Keep him in bed, warm, and get as much of that soup down him as you can. I think I got all the shot out. He'll be much stronger tomorrow."

Zack rode over to his place to tell his pa what had happened.

Not long after the Doc left I suddenly remembered about the money.

"Pa," I said, "what about the money and Mrs. Parrish?"

"You're right, little girl," said Pa, rolling over in the bed and facing me. "I plumb forgot."

"I'm scared of that man Royce, Pa."

"What's he got to do with it?"

"Mrs. Parrish got the money from him, Pa."

"From his bank. Outta her account, like anyone else. I went with her to get it."

"Pa, I think there's more to it than that." It was the first chance I'd had to tell him about seeing her go to the bank with those papers, and the look on Royce's face afterward.

Pa was already half out of his bed by the time I finished. "Why, that woman!" he said, "I hope she ain't gone and done nothing foolish! Here, Corrie, help me with this leg!"

He was already struggling to stand.

"Pa, the doctor said you had to—"

"Never mind the Doc! I gotta get that money back to town."

"Lay back down, Drum," said Uncle Nick, who had wandered over to see what the commotion was all about. "I'll take it to her."

"No, this is something I gotta do myself. What's gotta be said's something nobody but me can say."

"I'll take in the money with a letter from you," suggested Uncle Nick.

"Don't you understand? That woman saved our hides, and this place of ours too! You don't thank somebody for that with a letter. Besides, she may have just—"

He stopped, fumbling to get his arm through his coat sleeve "Well, never mind that—we'll just hope it's not too late."

He grabbed the single crutch the Doc had left him, grabbed his hat, and made for the door. "Somebody come and help me up the horse. Nick, where's them saddlebags?"

Uncle Nick brought him the money and boosted him on top of Blue Flame, who was still saddled from Zack's ride to Little Wolf's father's. Pain filled Pa's face from his swollen leg, but there was no talking him out of what he knew he had to do.

"Can I go with you, Pa?" I asked.

Pa looked down at me, thought for a moment, then shrugged and said, "I don't reckon there'd be anything wrong with that. Sure, come on."

I flew into the barn and saddled Snowball as fast as I could. I didn't want Pa to think of some reason for changing his mind.

It was well into evening when we rode into Miracle Springs, but the June sun still had another hour of life left. The town was quiet. A few people who saw Pa ran over to greet him with smiles and shouts and congratulations, but Pa just kept walking Blue Flame straight down the dirt street, hardly so much as acknowledging the well-wishers who came out to greet him. He had a determined look in his eye and he rode straight for Mrs. Parrish's.

When we got there, he dismounted without any help, although when his legs hit the ground his face twitched from the pain. He slung the saddlebags over his shoulder, stuck the crutch under his armpit, then said to me, "Corrie, I know you like to be around all that's goin' on so you can write everything in that journal of yours. But this here's somethin' I gotta do alone. So you just wait here."

He went inside and I waited.

Fifteen minutes later he came back out, without the saddlebags. His face was wearing a look I wish I could describe, but I could write for two pages and not get it right. I'll have to be satisfied to remember it in my mind.

He didn't say a word. As he was getting on the horse, I saw Mrs. Parrish come to one of the windows and pull aside the curtain and look out, just like the banker had done.

I smiled and gave a little wave. But she didn't seem to notice. I guess she wanted to make sure Pa got on his horse okay. When I glanced over again a moment later, she was no longer there.

As we rode back through town again, word must've spread around that Pa was there because now all sorts of folks were out on the streets. Riding there beside him, I felt like we were in the kind of parade I've read about in New York City! Everyone was shouting and calling out things to Pa as if he was some kind of town hero. And this time he was laughing and returning the greetings and waving back. I guess whatever had been on his mind before was taken care of now.

I couldn't help but think it seemed a mite strange. Here all these folks came out to see Pa, treating him like he'd saved the town from destruction. And back home where we were headed a houseful of folks were celebrating Becky's rescue, and there was food and good smells and lively talk, and everybody was feeling happy. And yet back in town Mrs. Parrish was all alone, and nobody even seemed to know that *she'd* been the real hero of the day. It didn't seem just fair that she wasn't part of the celebrating.

Just then we saw the minister walking down the sidewalk. He waved, and we waved back. But Pa had stopped to talk to the sheriff for a minute, so Rev. Rutledge kept going without pausing for a chat. He was walking in the direction of Mrs. Parrish's. I was glad. Maybe she wouldn't have to spend the evening alone after all.

As we continued on our way a couple of minutes later, I glanced back for one last look at Mrs. Parrish's house before we turned up the street that led out of town. She was on the porch with Rev. Rutledge. It looked like she was explaining that she was just leaving, because he turned around and walked away.

Mrs. Parrish went out toward the little stable beside her house where Marcus Weber was standing waiting for her, holding the reins of a saddled horse. She was carrying the saddlebags Pa had brought her.

Mr. Weber helped her up, then she dug in her heels and went flying away out of town to the south. I turned back, and Pa and I rode north past the last of the buildings, and up the hill toward our place.

The rest of that night was spent in celebrating, waiting on the two invalids in the cabin, and hearing all the stories there were to tell—starting with Becky's version of events, then Zack's and Little Wolf's, then Pa's.

"But I'll tell you something," said Pa as he finished his account of the gunfight at Deadman's Flat, "when I crawled to my feet and stumbled down the hill to see if Zack was safe, and I saw Buck Krebbs lying in the dirt, there wasn't any joy in my heart."

It was a somber way to end a day that had turned out better than we might have hoped the night before.

"No sir, a dead face is an awful thing to see, especially when I knew it was my hand that took his life. God forgive me, I had to do it, else he'd have killed Zack for sure. But don't any of you kids ever think killin's a right thing. It's a dreadful thing, I'm tellin' you! Buck was our enemy, but I'll never forget that look on his dead face, and I pray God can do somethin' better with him now than he was able to down here. He was a bad man, but that don't make killin' him a pleasant thing."

We all went to bed late that night with plenty to be thankful for, and also a lot to think about.

I didn't know if it was a right thing to do or not, but I couldn't help praying for Buck Krebbs one last time. I remembered the Bible verse that said we were to pray for our enemies.

Maybe it was too late, but I figured I ought to do what the Book said. So I did.

# CHAPTER 40

## PREPARATIONS

The next day was Sunday.

Little Wolf felt much better and went home. I figured we'd all stay home, but Pa insisted on going to church. His leg was still swollen, and there wasn't any way he was going to do much walking, crutch or no crutch. Four of us together carried him to the wagon, where he lay down in the back on some blankets. Uncle Nick drove the wagon, and the rest of us gathered in back around Pa. Even Katie went with us, sitting up front beside Uncle Nick.

It was a fun ride to town, although Pa didn't say much. Buck Krebbs was still on his mind, I could tell. Maybe he felt he needed to make peace with God and himself over the killing, and he figured church was the best place to do it.

But the service hardly fit Pa's mood. Everybody cheered when they saw us pulling into the meadow in our wagon, and they all ran toward us, hugging and shaking hands and showing their happiness that everybody was safe. During the service Rev. Rutledge thanked the Lord for his protecting hand over Becky and Zack and Pa and everyone else that had been involved.

When church was over, after the last song and prayer, Rev. Rutledge stood up in front and said, "I have one final announcement. I realize it is probably unnecessary, but in case there are any persons present who do *not* already know—next Sunday, one week from today, after the morning service, at one o'clock in the afternoon, you are all invited to attend the wedding of our own Drummond Hollister to Miss Kathryn Morgan, newly arrived from Virginia."

Several of the men whooped and turned around to give Pa a wink or a few words. Katie smiled pleasantly at the women who glanced at her. But if anything, the minister's announcement seemed to dampen Pa's mood all the more.

Pa stayed in bed the rest of Sunday and all the next day. Doc came out again on Tuesday and pronounced the swelling reduced.

Pa hobbled around a little Tuesday afternoon, then went back to bed. His spirits were depressed, I could tell—probably from not being able to get up and be about and working. He never was one for sitting still doing nothing.

On Wednesday Mrs. Parrish rode out in her buggy to fetch Katie and me. From the very first word of the wedding several weeks ago, Mrs. Parrish had taken it upon herself to see that Katie had a new wedding dress for the occasion. Now it was time for the final fitting and last minute alterations, and she asked me to come along to Mrs. Gianini's. "Women get together, and men get together," she told me, "before weddings. And this is *our* chance!"

Mrs. Gianini was all business, fussing with pins and her tape, and muttering this and that about the hem and sleeves and lace and veil and ribbon. The dress was of light blue, with a high neck, and wide, loose shoulders and upper arms. The bodice was close-fitting, and below the waist the dress filled out with several petticoats underneath. The buttons and lace were of pale yellow, as was the cummerbund around the waist and the bow tied in back.

"It's beautiful, Mrs. Gianini," said Katie after she had put on the dress for the final time and stood in front of the mirror. "So beautiful! I never expected anything like this out here. I don't know how you did it, but this style you and Almeda chose doesn't make me look so round."

"We wouldn't have our Drummond Hollister's bride with anything less," said Mrs. Parrish, smiling at Katie, a smile that seemed to have a hint of sadness in it, though her voice never betrayed it. "He's a 'leading citizen,' remember."

As she gazed over the bride-to-be, the look on Mrs. Parrish's face reminded me of how she looked at me sometimes. Her eyes were so full of love, almost motherly, but not without that look of pain that I never quite understood either. She had done so much for me—and for Pa. And now she was having this dress made, probably at her own expense, for Pa's new wife whom she barely knew. I couldn't help thinking what a selfless woman she was.

"You look lovely, my dear," Mrs. Parrish added, standing back and regarding Katie as Mrs. Gianini took in a last tuck about the waist, then pinned it in place. "I know Corrie's father will be proud when he sees you coming down the aisle on Sunday."

"Won't he already have seen her in the dress after we get ready and drive in?" I asked innocently.

All three of the women laughed together.

"Oh no, Corrie!" said Mrs. Parrish. "Don't you know, a bride and groom must never see one another on their wedding day until the moment when she starts down the aisle." They laughed again.

"My ma always told me I wasn't the marrying kind," I said. "I reckon she was right. But how will Katie and Pa not see each other?"

"Oh, Katie will spend Saturday night with me, of course," replied Mrs. Parrish. "We'll get her all ready right here. You and Becky and Emily shall help me! And we'll have to get you three all dressed up too. Your pa will be so proud to see all his women looking so beautiful!"

As always, Mrs. Parrish's enthusiasm was catching. Pretty soon all four of us were laughing like little girls. I was so happy that Katie and Mrs. Parrish looked like they were going to be friends! I couldn't have stood it if Mrs. Parrish couldn't be at least a little bit like part of our family!

When Mrs. Parrish and I happened to be alone in another room for a few minutes, I asked her about the papers and Mr. Royce and the money. She opened her mouth as if she was about to reply, then thought better of it and stopped herself. A strange look came into her eye.

Then she said, "Corrie, what happened with the money is between your father and me. I know you and I haven't kept secrets from one another. But this time I'm going to have to do just that. It is not that I don't want you to know. But if the story's to be told, I want your father to be the one to tell you. You see, it's his secret now, not mine. So that means it's his to share or his to hold on to, as he sees fit."

By Thursday Pa was a lot better, although he was still acting quiet. His leg still hurt a lot, but he was able to hobble around pretty well.

Friday morning came, and Uncle Nick didn't show up for breakfast.

"Zack, run up to the mine and fetch him, will you?" said Pa.

But Zack came back alone a couple of minutes later. "He ain't up there, Pa."

"Anybody seen Nick today?" Pa asked the rest of us.

No one had.

Still nobody had seen him by the time afternoon came. By evening Pa was getting fidgety, and starting to mutter. Uncle Nick didn't come home that night.

Saturday Pa was furious.

Here it was the day before the wedding, and Katie and I had lots of things to do. Mrs. Parrish was out twice to our place, and Katie and I went into town with her for an hour in the afternoon. Through it all Pa was ranting about Uncle Nick's disappearance.

"The hare-brained idiot's gone off again!" he kept saying. "Probably drunk someplace, losin' away every dime he's got to some gambling shyster!"

Saturday night came. Still no sign of Uncle Nick.

"That numskull!" Pa said over and over. "His sense o' timing's about as lame as his smarts with cards!"

"What are we gonna do, Pa?" I asked.

"What do you mean what are we gonna do? There ain't nothin' we *can* do! We don't know where he is. The loco fool is gonna miss the wedding!"

Mrs. Parrish rode out one last time, this time to get Katie and take her to town for the night.

"You all sleep well tonight!" Mrs. Parrish said as they got ready to leave. "Tomorrow's going to be an exciting day!"

Then she turned to Pa and said in a more serious tone. "Mr. Hollister, do you need anything? Any help with, you know, with your brother-in-law—"

"I appreciate your thoughtfulness, ma'am," Pa replied. "But I'll be fine." It was the gentlest I'd heard Pa talk in two days. "Alkali's comin' out in the mornin'. He'll help me get dressed and all."

"And don't you worry a thing about the younger children, Mr. Hollister," she said. "You just get everybody to town, and I'll make sure everybody knows what to do. You'll be very proud of your family, Mr. Hollister."

"Thank you, ma'am," said Pa.

They each gave a little wave, then Mrs. Parrish and Katie were off toward Miracle.

The rest of us went back inside and got ready for bed, everyone listening, I think, for the sounds of Uncle Nick's horse riding up.

But we all fell asleep without hearing it.

# CHAPTER 41

## THE BIG DAY

Most of the town showed up for the wedding.

Just the fact that Pa'd written for a mail-order bride was curious enough, so lots of folks were interested. And I don't suppose it's all that usual for a man to get married with five of his own children sitting in the front row watching!

But most of all, Pa was a highly respected man around Miracle Springs. It wasn't just that he had friends. It was more than that. I suppose Pa represented what a lot of folks wished for themselves. Here was a man who'd come to town running from the law, using an alias, with nothing to his name. Now Miracle Springs was celebrating its first wedding with him! At least with Sheriff Rafferty he'd been cleared. He had a family, a good claim, and a chance to settle down.

Maybe they were proud of Pa. Maybe some envied him a little. But whatever their reasons, almost everyone piled into that little church that Sunday afternoon. They'd brought in extra chairs from the Gold Nugget, but some of the men still had to stand up in back.

Even with all the people, there was one less than there should have been. My mind kept turning over the question, just like Pa had said as he glanced around at the cabin and up toward the barn and mine one last time: "Where in tarnation's Nick?" And now we were sitting silently in the

291

church, thinking the same thing.

At last Pa and Rev. Rutledge stood up in front. Pa looked so handsome in his black suit. The music started to play— it was Miss Stansberry at the piano in the back of the church.

I turned around to look.

There stood Katie in the gorgeous dress. Slowly, an inch at a time, she began to walk up the aisle between the chairs.

Softly the music played, the only other sound the faint rustle of Katie's dress as it moved along the floor.

My eyes scanned so many faces in that second. Half the town's saloon girls were here, dabbing their eyes with pink and white handkerchiefs, as if "ol' Drum gettin' hitched" spelled the end of all the wild nightlife of Miracle Springs.

Katie was about a third of the way down the aisle now. I suppose she looked pretty. People say that brides always do. I didn't really notice her face.

I turned back to the front. Rev. Rutledge stood tall, with a nice minister-looking smile on his face. Pa beside him was just staring, not smiling at all.

Miss Stansberry started through the processional song again.

You could hear the sounds now of people starting to turn around and watch as Katie approached Pa. She was almost beside me now, still walking slowly. More handkerchiefs came out of hiding. Right behind me I saw that Mrs. Parrish was holding one too. I caught her eye and she tried to smile, but I saw a look of sadness in her face.

All heads turned with Katie, back toward the front of the church, where she had just about reached Pa's outstretched hand. But amid the noise of turning and looking and the piano's tones there now came another sound—faint at first, then steadily louder.

It was a horse galloping up. Louder it came, until it was right next to the church building.

But instead of gradually fading away in the other direction, the skidding hoofbeats and whinnying of the horse caught us all by surprise. Glances began to scatter about the church at the sound of a rider dismounting and the loud booted clomping of footsteps coming up the church stairs two at a time.

The music stopped. Katie turned around.

Suddenly the door flew open and crashed against the back wall.

There in the open doorway stood Uncle Nick!

His face wore three days' growth of whiskers. His clothes were filthy, he still had on his hat, and the dust from his hasty approach seemed to billow into the room on his heels.

He stood there a split second, taking in the scene. Then he ran forward halfway up the aisle, and shouted: "Drum, you blamed fool . . . you're marryin' the wrong woman!"

Instantly the church was in an uproar.

Katie's mouth was hanging open. Rev. Rutledge stood stock-still in consternation, not knowing what to do. Pa stared at Uncle Nick for just a second, his face growing red with fury.

Then he strode forward toward him as fast as his bad leg would let him hobble. He looked as if he was fixing to knock Uncle Nick's block off!

"Just a dadburn minute!" cried Uncle Nick. "Hear me out, Drum. After what I got to say, well, then you can do what you like! Don't you know by now, you ol' goat . . ." and as he said it, he ran the rest of the way up the aisle and stopped just beside where Mrs. Parrish was sitting, ". . . this here's the woman you oughta be marryin'!" He grabbed her hand and held it in Pa's direction before the shocked Mrs. Parrish could think to withdraw it.

"She's the woman who loves you, you idiot! You're so blind you can't see the nose on the front of your face!"

Uncle Nick dropped Mrs. Parrish's hand, went the rest of the way down the aisle, took Katie's hand, and added—

as if to end the discussion—"Don't you know Katie's the woman *I* got *my* eye on?"

Now the commotion *really* erupted!

Everyone was half out of their chairs and balking and stirring about. Pa was still standing there where Uncle Nick had left him, speechless. I glanced behind me quickly. Mrs. Parrish was staring down into her lap and quietly weeping. She was still holding her handkerchief and not even bothering to use it.

Realizing what a stir he'd caused, and maybe embarrassed at his outburst, Uncle Nick by this time had run back outside. Katie went after him. Rev. Rutledge was scurrying about trying to restore some semblance of order, but he wasn't succeeding too well.

I think everyone knew the wedding was over—for right now, at least. Some folks walked outside, others still sat looking around bewildered. Some of the ladies were uttering comments along the lines of, "Well, I never—" and "Gracious sakes, in all my days . . . ."

"Wait! Wait, people—please!" Rev. Rutledge shouted, trying to be heard above the chaos and confusion. "Take your seats until we get this all sorted out! . . . Mr. Hollister!"

But Pa was moving slowly away from Rev. Rutledge now, limping toward where I was sitting. He didn't hear the minister calling his name. I don't think he was aware of the church quieting, and the turning of every eye upon him to see what he was going to do. He was coming toward the row where all of us kids were sitting, but he wasn't looking at us. His eyes were fixed on someone else.

By the time he got to Mrs. Parrish, the church was quiet again.

Pa stopped.

I reckon she could sense he was there. After a moment, Mrs. Parrish slowly looked up. Her eyes were all wet. Pa stood gazing down on her with the nicest, most sheepish, half-embarrassed smile I could ever have imagined on his face.

She half-laughed, but it was sort of a half-cry, too. Her handkerchief quickly went to her eyes, and she glanced away. But only for a second. She looked right back at Pa, and her eyes found his.

"Mrs. Parrish, ma'am," said Pa sort of timidly, "I reckon there's a thing or two you an' me oughta be talking about."

"Yes, Mr. Hollister," she said, nodding, dropping her gaze and smiling softly. "I think you are right."

Pa reached out his hand. She took it, rose to her feet, and joined him in the aisle while everyone sat and watched them.

As they started toward the door, Mrs. Parrish said, "But don't you think, *Drummond*—" She said his name slowly, and though I'd heard her use his given name a time or two before, now it suddenly meant so much more as she said it. "Don't you think that it's finally time you started calling me Almeda?"

Even from where I was sitting in the front pew, I could see the back of Pa's neck getting red.

"I reckon you're right, ma'am," he replied.

Mrs. Parrish looked up into Pa's face with a most radiant smile. I could tell that she loved him. I think she probably had for quite a while.

They walked through the open door, outside, and down the stairs. I could hear Pa's uneven footfall as he struggled down the steps. Inside the church it was dead silent.

Suddenly I was on my feet. I ran back to the door and looked out.

Pa was limping across the meadow next to the church with Mrs. Parrish beside him. I could tell they were talking, but their voices were much too soft and far away to hear.

Mrs. Parrish slipped her hand through Pa's arm and looked up at his face every so often.

Nobody else was around, so nobody ever heard what they said to each other. I asked them both, more than once, to tell me what they'd said.

But Pa would only reply, "That is one conversation, Corrie Belle, that ain't never gonna find its way into your journal!" It was a good while before he said any more. But seeing the two of them like that was a sight I will never forget.

Behind me, the noise of commotion was rising again. Now it grew even louder than before. The wives didn't know whether to be scandalized at the proceedings or happy. The men were all telling their versions of "I knew ol' Drum would . . .", or "Did I tell you the time when Drum . . ." Some of the saloon girls were still crying. Others were laughing and making jokes and already heading for the door to leave. I suppose Alkali Jones said it best. His only comment was, "Well, if that don't beat all!"

I don't know where Katie and Uncle Nick had gone, but now Uncle Nick came back into the church, more calmly this time. Katie was right behind him. He put up his hands and tried to get everyone's attention.

"Hey, you all—quiet down!" he called out, motioning with his arms. "I got somethin' to say!"

Pretty soon most of the folks' eyes were on him.

"Well, I reckon I done it, huh?" he said, "I made a plumb nincompoop outta myself!"

Everyone laughed.

"But the way me an' Katie's got it figured is that Drum looks to be a mite too occupied right at the moment—"

More laughter and some shouts from a few of Uncle Nick's rowdier friends. "And it seems a shame, with Katie comin' so far an' all, an' all you good folks comin' here today—well, it seems a shame to put such a colorful pretty wedding dress an' a church full of guests to waste. So we figure we oughta go on ahead with this here wedding. An' since Drum's busy, I'll take his place! Katie says none of you'd object . . . and *she* don't object, neither!"

Now the place really erupted with shouts and cheers, and finally a round of applause.

Rev. Rutledge had a look of astonishment all over his face. But everyone else seemed to agree that the idea made all the sense in the world.

" 'Course Katie'd like me to get cleaned up just a tad," said Uncle Nick when he could be heard again. "So if you folks don't mind waitin', I'm gonna hightail it home an' shave off some o' these whiskers an' throw on some clean duds, an' I'll be back inside an hour. That oughta give you time to round up Drum and tell him about the change in plans!"

A wave of laughter swept the room. Uncle Nick turned and ran out the door. Several seconds later we heard the galloping hoofbeats like those that had started the uproar. They quickly died in the distance.

Everyone started milling around in little groups, and slowly filed outside. Katie marched through the crowd to where Rev. Rutledge was standing and spent about five minutes with him, making whatever arrangements she had to, I reckon. Then she came over to me and the other kids. Even if she wasn't going to marry Pa after all, she was still going to be kin, so I guess she felt it was her duty to see to us. She knelt down and explained to Tad and Becky and Emily what had happened, and told them she was going to be their Aunt Katie.

And an hour and a half later, as we all left the church for the last time that day, that's exactly what she was.

# CHAPTER 42

# WONDERING ABOUT
# THE FUTURE

Uncle Nick and Aunt Katie went to San Francisco for a honeymoon.

If I thought the town was buzzing before, now there wasn't *anything* more the subject of conversation—from the school to the Gold Nugget to the General Store to the groups of men standing around the streets—than what Uncle Nick had done at what was supposed to have been Pa's wedding! Those folks who hadn't attended were kicking themselves for weeks!

I suppose the one person who wasn't thrilled with the sudden way everything had gone topsy-turvy was Rev. Rutledge. He went through the wedding ceremony with Katie and Uncle Nick with a smile on his face. And I think down inside even he could see how much better it was for Pa to walk down the aisle—still in that handsome black suit, with Katie on his arm—to give her away to Uncle Nick, than it would have been to marry the two of them.

Still, the change was bound to affect his fortunes probably as much as anyone's, and nobody saw him much for several days.

All us kids were positively *dying* to know what was going to happen next. That night we pestered Pa with question

298

after question. But he wouldn't say much. There was a kind of crafty smile on his face, but he just kept saying, "We'll see, kids . . . we'll see."

He did make more than his usual number of trips into town during the next few days, and he hardly went up to the mine at all. Mr. Ashton and Marcus Weber ran the Mine and Freight Company mostly by themselves for the next week.

I knew Pa and Mrs. Parrish were trying to figure a lot of things out. They'd had their differences. They had both had another wife and husband whose memories they still loved. And they both had homes and businesses they didn't want to give up. But neither one of them would let on a word about what they intended to do about all those things.

And when they finally did say—well, that was another whole story!

# MY FATHER'S WORLD

# MY FATHER'S WORLD

MICHAEL PHILLIPS
JUDITH PELLA

BETHANY HOUSE PUBLISHERS
MINNEAPOLIS, MINNESOTA 55438

Cover illustration by Dan Thornberg,
Bethany House Publishers staff artist.

Copyright © 1990
Michael Phillips/Judith Pella

Published by Bethany House Publishers
A Ministry of Bethany Fellowship, Inc.
6820 Auto Club Road, Minneapolis, Minnesota 55438

Printed in the United States of America

---

**Library of Congress Cataloging-in-Publication Data**

Phillips, Michael R., 1946–
  My father's world / Michael Phillips, Judith Pella.
    p. cm. — (The Journals of Corrie Belle : v. 1)


  1. Overland journeys to the Pacific—Fiction.
I. Pella, Judith.  II. Title.
III. Series: Phillips, Michael R., 1946–    Journals of Corrie Bell : v. 1.
PS3566.H492M9    1990
813'.54—dc20                                                    89–78391
ISBN 1–55661–104–8                                             CIP

To

Patrick Jeremy Phillips

# Books by the Phillips/Pella Writing Team

## The Journals of Corrie Belle Hollister

*My Father's World*
*Daughter of Grace*
*On the Trail of the Truth*
*A Place in the Sun*

## The Stonewycke Trilogy

*The Heather Hills of Stonewycke*
*Flight from Stonewycke*
*Lady of Stonewycke*

## The Stonewycke Legacy

*Stranger at Stonewycke*
*Shadows over Stonewycke*
*Treasure of Stonewycke*

## The Highland Collection

*Jamie MacLeod: Highland Lass*
*Robbie Taggart: Highland Sailor*

## The Russians

*The Crown and the Crucible*

# The Authors

The PHILLIPS/PELLA writing team had its beginning in the longstanding friendship of Michael and Judy Phillips with Judith Pella. Michael Phillips, with a number of nonfiction books to his credit, had been writing for several years. During a Bible study at Pella's home he chanced upon a half-completed sheet of paper sticking out of a type-writer. His author's instincts aroused, he inspected it more closely, and asked their friend, "Do you write?" A discussion followed, common interests were explored, and it was not long before the Phillips invited Pella to their home for dinner to discuss collaboration on a proposed series of novels. Thus, the best-selling "Stonewycke" books were born, which led in turn to "The Highland Collection."

Judith Pella holds a nursing degree and B.A. in Social Sciences. Her background as a writer stems from her avid reading and researching in historical, adventure, and geographical venues. Pella, with her two sons, resides in Eureka, California. Michael Phillips, who holds a degree from Humboldt State University and continues his post-graduate studies in history, owns and operates Christian bookstores on the West Coast. He is the editor of the best-selling George MacDonald Classic Reprint Series and is also MacDonald's biographer. The Phillips also live in Eureka with their three sons.

# CONTENTS

9

# PROLOGUE

A few months back, Uncle Nick said to me, "You oughta make that diary of yours into a book."

"Who would read it?" I said. "No one cares what a little girl wrote when she first came West."

"You ain't a little girl now, Corrie Belle Hollister," he answered, looking me over from head to foot. "No, siree. You done a mite lot of fillin' out since you came to California ten years ago. Why, I remember that day I walked into ol' Drum's place and saw you standin' there—"

He paused for a minute with a smile on his face.

"Besides," he went on, "I think a whole lot of folks back East would read anything you wrote, now that you're a famous reporter from one of the Union's newest states."

"Aw shucks, Uncle Nick," I said. "I'm not famous, and you know it!"

"That ain't what Drum says."

"He doesn't count," I said back. "He's prejudiced!"

"Your name's in all the big papers in Chicago and St. Louis and New York. If that don't make a body famous, then I reckon there's no gold in them hills, neither."

"There really is about none left, Uncle Nick," I said.

"Well, the gold may be gone, but they're still readin' what you're tellin' 'em, and that's a fact, Corrie."

"Nobody cares about a reporter's name," I told him. "They only read the story, that's all."

11

"Your ma taught you not to lie, Cornelia." His voice was stern, but that little twinkle in his eye said he was just teasing me. "Lord knows our pa taught us both better'n that, though your ma kept to it a mite straighter than I did. But, Cornelia," he said again, "You know people are interested in *you*, not just what you write. A young lady reporter, sendin' stories all 'round the country from the rough and wild gold fields and minin' towns of California's mother lode—why to them city folks, somebody like you makes the wild West a romantic and interesting place. I reckon you're just about one of California's most famous young women."

"It ain't so," I argued, and I tried to make my voice stern, but he saw right through my act. He always does. He's still kid enough himself to understand me, even though he's seventeen or eighteen years older than me. He's just like my ma. She was always a step ahead of me, and Uncle Nick's got that same Belle blood and quick eye.

I wouldn't talk any more about it to him right then. But he kept badgering me about the idea, and pretty soon I found myself getting used to it. I still couldn't see why anybody would want to read my diary. But seeing a book with my name on it was a thought I couldn't get rid of.

I asked my editor at the *Alta* about the notion of a book.

"That's the most fool idea I've ever heard," Mr. Kemble said. "You're a reporter, Corrie . . . a hack. You're no book author."

"And you reported in 1848 that there was no gold in California," I said quietly.

"What's that got to do with it?" he shouted, not liking to be reminded of his infamous story in the *California Star*.

"Maybe your prediction about me'll be the same way," I said timidly.

"Come on, Corrie, we've got real news to cover! Here the country's in the middle of a war with itself. People pouring into California by the thousands. Folks back East are interested in what kind of place this is out here. They don't want to read the reminiscences of some runny-nosed kid."

I guess Kemble's words riled me some. Pretty soon I found myself taking Uncle Nick's side on the idea of a book.

By that time, though, I suppose I should have known my editor better than I did. He may have put up a blustery front, but he wasn't one to turn his nose up at an idea that might be good. The day after our talk he fired off a letter to a friend of his who worked for a publisher in Chicago.

Then two months ago the friend wrote back and said that his company wanted to make a book based on my diary. Mr. Kemble brought up the subject again, and told me what he'd done.

"The narrative portion of the story will be edited, of course," said his friend in the letter that came addressed to both of us. "But we want you to retain the colorful phrasing and homespun flavor of the language in the dialogue. We feel it will add realism and authenticity to what you say."

I was so happy I threw my arms around Mr. Kemble and hugged him.

We got right to work on it. I was only fifteen when I came to Miracle Springs, and my writing was pretty rough. But we worked on the sentences, trying to correct the grammar without losing any of the "homespun flavor," as Mr. Kemble's friend Mr. MacPherson put it. He did say, after all, that he didn't want me to try to make every single word into high-sounding book English.

But until then, here's what happened, every so often in just the words I used in my diary, with a few things added here and there so you can make some sense out of it.

Uncle Nick says you will like reading it. Mr. Kemble still says he think's the whole notion's foolhardy, though down inside I think he's just as excited about it as I am.

I don't quite know which one to believe. I reckon you'll have to make up your own mind.

Corrie Belle Hollister
Miracle Springs, California
1862

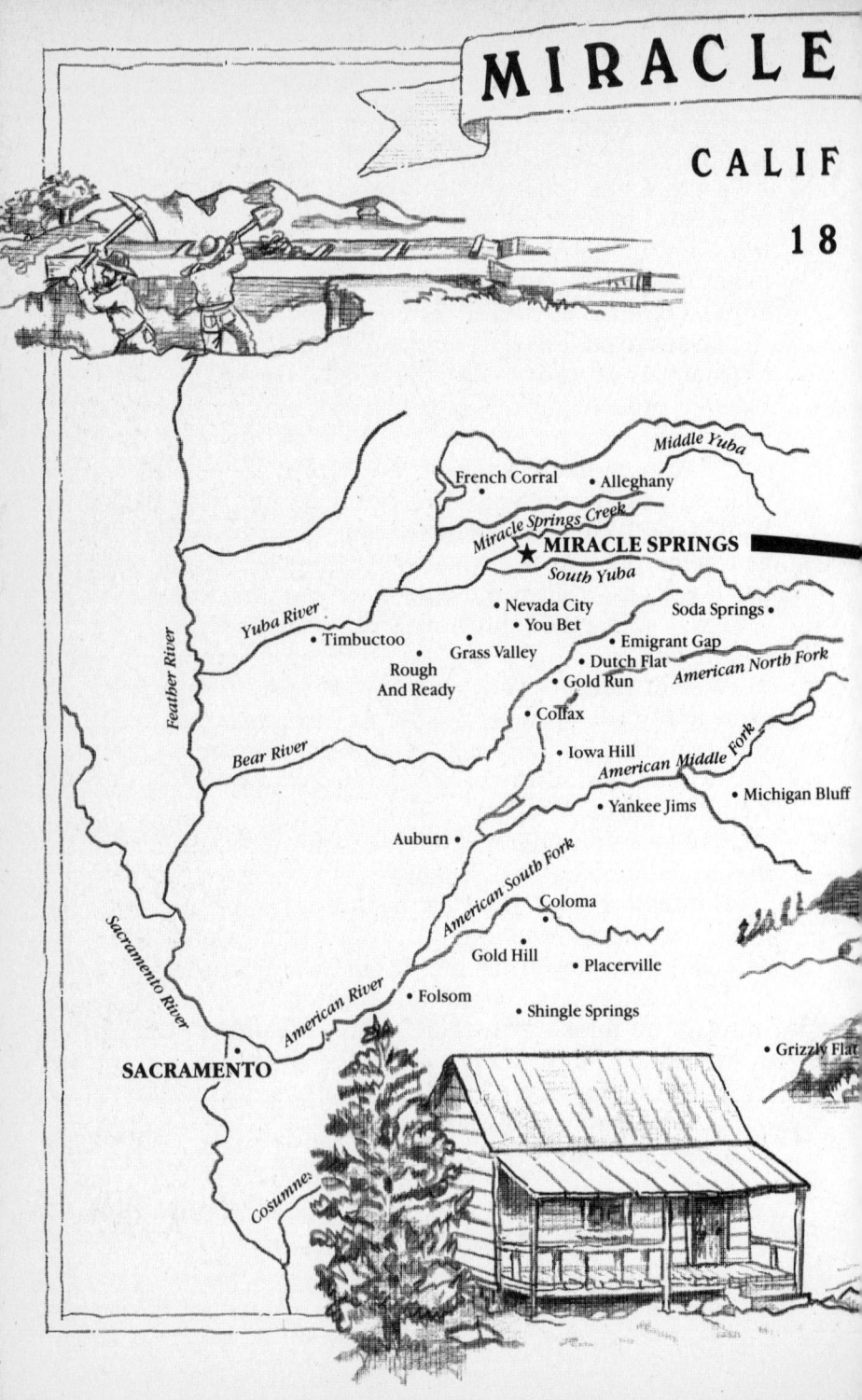

MIRACLE

CALIF

18

French Corral • Alleghany

*Middle Yuba*

*Miracle Springs Creek*

★ **MIRACLE SPRINGS**

*South Yuba*

• Nevada City

• You Bet

Soda Springs •

• Timbuctoo

Grass Valley

• Emigrant Gap

*Yuba River*

Rough
And Ready

• Dutch Flat

*American North Fork*

• Gold Run

• Colfax

*Feather River*

*Bear River*

• Iowa Hill

*American Middle Fork*

• Yankee Jims

• Michigan Bluff

Auburn •

*American South Fork*

Coloma

*Sacramento River*

Gold Hill

• Placerville

*American River*

• Folsom

• Shingle Springs

• Grizzly Flat

**SACRAMENTO**

*Cosumnes*

# CHAPTER 1

## GETTING TO CALIFORNIA
## IN 1852

Ma always told me I should keep a diary.

"Corrie," she'd say, "when a young woman's not of the marryin' sort, she needs to think of somethin' besides a man to get her through life."

I think she was making a roundabout comment about my looks, though she never came right out and said I wasn't comely enough to snag a husband. I guess she figured a diary would be a good idea, too, since I had my nose in a book all the time, and I ought to get some practical use from all that reading.

"It sure ain't gonna get you no feller though," she'd say, "any more'n that nose full of freckles!"

"What's keepin' a diary got to do with marryin'?" I asked her.

"No man wants a wife that's smarter'n him—" She paused, then added with a sly wink, "Leastways, not so's it's obvious!"

Then she took my chin in her rough, work-worn hand, and smiled down on me with that loving look that was almost as good as a hug, and said—as if to make up for saying I wasn't a marrying kind of girl—"I reckon you'll do okay though, Corrie."

I was just a kid then, probably not more than ten, though

I can't exactly remember. I didn't know what all the fuss was about. The last thing I wanted back then was to marry some ornery, dirty-faced boy. So what she said didn't bother me. I was perfectly content with my books.

"You could be a teacher, Corrie," Ma said more than once. Then she'd go on to speculate, "Teachin's a right respectable way for a spinster to get by in this world."

She talked a lot about women getting on in the world alone, probably on account of Pa's leaving like he did. It was hard on Ma, being left with the farm to tend, and four kids and another on the way. I suspect more than once she wished she'd been a spinster herself!

Back then, when I remember her first talking to me about what I ought to do, I didn't have the faintest notion what a spinster was, and I was hardly of a mind to start preparing for my future. But whatever spinster meant, I did know what a teacher was, because I liked our Miss Boyd. As for teaching myself, I'd have to wait and see.

"If you're going to know book learnin' and all that, Corrie," Ma said, "you gotta do more'n just read. You gotta learn how to write good, too. And I figure there ain't much better a way than to keep a diary."

Well, maybe Ma was right. Though I never did much about her advice after that.

Until I got to be fifteen, that is. By then I knew what a spinster was, and I knew about plain-looking girls. And I knew why the two always went together. So I began to see what it might be like to be alone in the world, and to figure maybe Ma's idea about me teachin' was a good one, though I was still a mite young to be going to a teacher's school or college to learn how. Besides, Miracle Springs doesn't even have a school for kids, much less a college.

Once Ma was gone, I knew I had to get thinkin' mighty fast about something. She was right about that. The kids were looking to me for tending, right out there in the middle of nowhere. And it sure wasn't likely to be any different

once we got to where we were going. Even if we found Uncle
Nick, they were still going to be looking to me to be a kind
of ma to them—and a teacher, too. Even if it was only little
Tad, and Becky, Emily, and Zack, I was bound to be teaching them a thing or two since Ma couldn't.

So I figured it was time I started that diary.

Of course I didn't know how. I knew how to write, and
that was about it. So I just started to put down what happened, though it didn't seem there was much exciting in it.

I sure did miss Ma. She'd have told me what a diary was
supposed to be like. I wish I'd started back when she first
told me to do it. Or even last spring when we left our little
patch of ground in upstate New York to come out West.
Then I would have written about the wagon crossing after
leaving St. Louis, about the plains of Kansas, the grand
herds of buffalo, the scare with the Sioux near Ft. Laramie,
the day Emily and I almost got left behind picking berries,
and the snow that was still on the mountains in Utah in July.
Most of all, I wish Ma could have been there to show me
how to do it right.

But even if I had started back then, I probably wouldn't
have written about the desert and what happened to Ma. I
never want to remember that, though I'll never forget it.

So by the time I got started writing things down, we
were in California, and the long trip was mostly behind us,
just like Ma wanted. But she'd never get to see it.

"We gotta get over them mountains before the snows
come," she kept saying, telling the wagon-master every day
to hurry us along.

He always just smiled and said, "Not to worry, Mrs.
Hollister. We'll be past them Sierras by the first weeks of
October. You'll be relaxin' in front of your brother's warm
stove long before the snow ever comes."

Ma couldn't help worrying. She had some terrible foreboding about the winter. It didn't help that folks were still
talking about the Donners, who had so much trouble cross-

ing the mountains seven years before. All through the summer, hot as it was, she kept thinking about the snows getting ready, someplace up by the North Pole, I reckon, to sweep down and kill us all at the California border. I wish we'd had a few handfuls of that snow when Ma took her fever. Captain Dixon called that awful stretch of desert the Humboldt Sink. I thought the ground was hot till I laid my hand on Ma's flaming cheek. I wanted to cry, but Ma was always so strong, and I decided it would help her to think that maybe I was learning to be strong, too.

So I didn't cry. I didn't pray either, though I tried once or twice. But no words would come. It felt like trying to coax water from that horrible dry sand. I wish I'd tried a mite harder. Sometimes I wonder if God would have let her live if I just could've gotten those words out.

We finally did get to California. Captain Dixon was right. He got us over the Sierras before the snows. But the mountains were getting cold, and I was glad when we reached the Feather River and Captain Dixon said it would only be a few more days before we'd be able to see the Sacramento Valley. He said when we got there, it would feel like summer by comparison.

Not long after that, we neared Sacramento City. Several of the wagons took off on their own, but Captain Dixon stuck with those few of us that were still together, because he said he was paid to go all the way to Sacramento and there he would go. I don't know how we'd have made it without him and some of the other men helping us drive the wagon and tend the team. I figured he was just about as fine a man as there could be.

As good as it felt to get to California, I don't mind confessing I was beginning to feel a little scared, too. The wagon train had become kind of a family, especially after Ma died. Everyone was so kind to us. Suddenly I realized that in just a few days Captain Dixon would leave, and my brothers and sisters and I would be all alone.

I knew we'd be with our uncle on his ranch, but seeing him for the first time was going to be a fearful moment. I was hardly more than a baby when he struck out on his own, and his visits were rare enough after that. All I knew about him is what Ma had told us.

I supposed we'd know soon enough. When we left Independence, the Captain said it would be the middle of October when we arrived, and he wasn't far off. Back then we thought Ma would be there to find Uncle Nick. But now we were on our own.

"Don't you worry none, Corrie," the Captain told me. "If we don't find your uncle right off, I'll take care of you and the young'uns. There's a nice boarding house, and there'll be room for all of you, and a place for your wagon and horses, until I locate your uncle and tell him how things are."

That Mr. Dixon was a nice man.

# CHAPTER 2

## WHY WE CAME WEST

The hills were the color of autumn as we descended from the mountains—pretty enough, but not quite so bright with orange and red as back home.

As I looked around, I thought that even if they hadn't discovered gold here four years ago, I would have liked to come. Of course, it never was the gold that made Ma start talking about the West. After Pa left, she struggled to make a go of the tiny farm. It wasn't much good before that, but Pa must have had a way of keeping it going when most men would've given up. Ma never talked much about Pa.

For a few years pure stubbornness kept Ma going. She said she wasn't going to give anyone a chance to say, "I told you so." I think she mostly meant her own pa. But more than that, she was determined to keep the farm going for Pa's return. Then word came to us that Pa was dead, and it seemed to take the vigor right out of her tired body.

After that, she couldn't keep it up so well, what with the five of us kids to tend besides. Her pa, my Grandpa Belle, offered to help, but she would have none of it. They weren't on the best of terms. But when he died last year she took it hard—we all did, because we loved him and he was a good man even though he could be mighty stern sometimes.

Not long after Grandpa died, Ma had a visit from a neighbor who had just returned from California. He had gone to try his hand at gold mining, but apparently it didn't work out because he didn't stay long. He must have seen Uncle Nick, Ma's brother, because she started talking about going out West to see him. She had no family in New York, unless you counted a couple of cousins she hardly knew. She said it was family that mattered and she didn't care what Uncle Nick had done—I didn't know at the time what she meant. But he was family, she said, and they ought to be together.

Uncle Nick left home a year before Pa did. Though he came back two or three times, he was almost a stranger to me. I could hardly remember what my own pa looked like. I'd never be able to recognize Uncle Nick.

Ma said he used to bounce me on his knees. "He'd croak out a lullaby too, now and then, Corrie," Ma said, "when he figured no one was lookin'. You know what plumb fools men are about lettin' a body see their feelin's. He always tried to be the tough one, but I knowed him better."

After Pa left, we never saw hide nor hair of Uncle Nick, either—not until that fellow come to see us after Grandpa Belle died. I don't know all he said to Ma, but he did say he'd seen her brother and heard that he owned a ranch near a place called Miracle Springs, California. Ma figured he must have struck gold in the mines because there couldn't have been any other way for our uncle to afford a spread of land.

When Grandpa Belle's "estate," as Ma called it, was settled, she came into a little sum of money. It was only a few hundred dollars, but more than we'd ever see again in once place, Ma said. Most folks told her to put it into the land, but by then she had no heart left for it. She said it was time for us to pull up stakes and strike out for something new. She always said she was more like her brother Nick than was good for her.

All the folks at home thought she'd taken leave of her senses. "Why, what are you thinking, Agatha Hollister?" I overheard one lady tell her. "It's a fool's errand if you ask me, a woman traveling west alone, and with five young'uns to boot!"

But Ma was a determined woman, and she said no one ever accused her of being faint-hearted. Besides, my thirteen-year-old brother Zachary was old enough to handle a wagon and team right well.

She said she reckoned I could take a fair load on my shoulders too. "You're the oldest, Corrie. And I figure you're just about as grown-up as a girl of fifteen ought to be—with gumption to match."

I still start to cry when I hear Ma's voice coming back to my mind like that. But sometimes her words make me proud.

It probably *was* crazy. Ma said so herself ten times a day those first months on the trail—especially since she had no way to notify our uncle that we were coming. But when Ma set her mind to something, that was that!

"Too much of that Belle blood, I tell you, Corrie!" she said. "It'll be the death of me yet! You just make sure when you get older you keep your own Belle blood in check."

*Oh, Ma! It makes me so sad when I think that you're not here to tell me things anymore!*

But I know what she'd say. "Come on, Corrie. This is a time to pull in your chin, wipe away them tears, and be strong. Don't betray that Belle blood in your veins, Corrie."

The farther west we got, the more I could tell Ma wanted to lay eyes on that "land of promise" they called California. She would have made it, too, if she hadn't slipped and broken her ankle and then gotten that infection. The Humboldt Sink is practically in California. She was so close.

Even now, when I close my eyes and let my mind wander back to that day Ma died, I can see it all as clear as if I was going through it all again. I was in the wagon sponging down her burning skin with the precious few spoonfuls of water Captain Dixon thought could be spared. It hardly made any difference, because the cloth in my hand turned hot in seconds. But at least I felt I was doing something useful.

"Corrie," Ma had said to me, her voice weak and as brittle as the parched earth outside, "fetch me something from that trunk. It's a book wrapped in a lace handkerchief. You'll see it right on top."

I found it easily enough. I remember her packing it when we left home, but I had never really looked at it before. I held it out to her but she was too weak to take it.

"You go ahead and look at it, Corrie," she said.

It was a small Bible, just a little bigger than my hand. It had a pure white leather cover and gold edges on the pages. I had never seen anything so fine and beautiful.

"Your pa gave that to me on our wedding day, Corrie." The corners of her lips strained at a smile. "It was his way of tellin' me he was ready to settle down and be a family man. I'll admit that before we was married, he was kind of a wild one. But I reckon he had good reason. He was orphaned young, left to be raised by his no-account older brother, who was killed before your pa was old enough to take care of himself. His brother's crowd was a bad influence, and he just never had a chance to learn decent ways. But I saw his heart, Corrie. I knew it was good, and I loved him for that." She sighed and had to stop talking for a minute to rest.

I gave her a sip of water. Maybe I shouldn't have let her go on, but Ma was determined, and I probably couldn't have stopped her, anyway.

"Your Grandpa Belle opposed our marriage," she went on. "By then, my brother and your pa had started runnin' together, and I guess my own pa thought Nick had been led astray. I knew better—Nick had his own wild streak. He was just a kid, and by then your pa wanted to change his ways, Corrie. And he did, too, after we was married. He worked hard on that farm and he was a good husband and father—I couldn't have asked for better.

"Everything that happened afterward . . . well, it just

happened. I don't blame him none. And I don't want you to either, Corrie. Sometimes a man can't shake his past no matter how hard he tries. I'm gonna be seein' your pa mighty soon, and I'll finally have the chance to say all these things to him."

"Ma, don't—"

Even if she hadn't stopped me, I couldn't have finished anyway. My throat was getting choked up listening to her.

"Corrie, I have to tell you all this! You're a big girl. You gotta face the fact that I'm gonna die soon. I only wish I hadn't dragged you all out here in the middle of nowhere. But you gotta be brave, honey. Won't help none to do nothin' else."

"Ma," I said through my tears, "you oughta rest." It was a stupid thing to say, I reckon, but I think I just didn't want to hear anymore about her dying.

"I got all the years of eternity to rest, Corrie dear. And I gotta tell you about your Uncle Nick, too," she went on, ignoring my plea. "I never said nothing before, 'cause I didn't want to put no one in a bad light. But now I have to tell you that your uncle was in some bad trouble. That's why he came out West. I thought he died with your pa, but when I heard he was still alive and was out here, I knew I had to come find him.

"Nick's all you got now. I figured when we got to that camp where his ranch is, I'd be able to find him easily enough. Now you're gonna have to do it alone. Captain Dixon said he'd help, but he's got his own responsibilities too, so you gotta look out for yourself. Just remember what I always told you—a woman's gotta be strong, she's got to be able to make her way alone if she has to. Ain't no weak-kneed woman gonna make it out here, Corrie. You hear me? You gotta be as tough and strong as a man—maybe tougher, 'cause they won't make it easy for you."

I nodded that I understood, though my mind was racing with the thoughts that Ma was about to die. I tried to be brave, but I just couldn't stand it!

Then she reached up from where she lay and took my chin feebly in her fingers like she used to do. They were so hot, I was afraid they would burn right into my chin.

She smiled. "What I said a long time ago, Corrie," she whispered, gazing at my face with a peaceful, contented smile, "about you not being of a marryin' sort. Well, I was wrong, Corrie. You've turned out to be a right decent lookin' girl. You're gonna get along just fine without me, Corrie. I know you'll make me and your pa proud!"

"Oh, Ma!" I cried, burying my face in the folds of her dress.

"Come now, we'll have none of that!" she said, though her voice was too soft to carry much of a threat. But I wiped my eyes and pulled myself up and tried to look cheery.

"Now there's more I need to tell you about your uncle," she said. "He's usin' a different name—not Belle. The fellow that told me he was there said he's going by Nick Matthews. Don't ask me why, but that's who you got to be lookin' for. Don't even mention the name Belle, just in case he's in trouble. Can you do that, Corrie? I know it's an awful load to put on a young girl, but there ain't nothin' else for it."

"I'll try, Ma." I took her hot limp hand in mine.

"That's a good girl, honey. And you keep that Bible. It's yours now, to remember me by. And to remember your pa, too. He was a good man."

Then she added—the last words she ever spoke—"It's by the mercy of God we got this close. Find your uncle, Corrie. You'll need him now more'n ever."

# CHAPTER 3

## SACRAMENTO

Sacramento was bigger than I'd imagined.

It hardly seemed possible that such a bustling place could be just three or four years old. But that's what Mr. Dixon said. When you took a closer look, you could see its newness in the dirt streets and the clean look of the timber in the simple, single-level buildings, and the freshly-painted store signs.

There was activity everywhere—people on foot or horseback, wagons of every shape, size and kind rumbling up and down the streets, people calling to one another. Here and there in the din I heard shouts of "gold" and "new strike." As we rode by a saloon I heard one man saying to another, "Did you hear 'bout them varmints what jumped ol' man Ward's claim over yonder by Grass Valley?" But we were out of earshot before I heard what the other man said in reply.

I was glad Uncle Nick didn't live in this town. I'd never lived in a big city before, and I didn't have a hankering to start now.

I was sitting up front next to Zack, who was driving the wagon. I could tell he was trying hard to act like a man. Some of the other kids in the train had jumped from their wagons and were whooping and running about excitedly. But Zack sat still and straight, reins slack in his hands, eyes steady on the team, a serious look on his face.

Poor Zack. He had to grow up awful fast, especially since we left the East. Along with that resolute look in his eyes, I could see the pain, too—a different kind of pain than just from the hard work his calloused hands showed he'd done the many months on the trail. But he held the team steady, gripping the leather straps, eyeing the new town, with just a hint left of my little brother. I could see it in the way his lips were parted a crack in wonder. He was almost a man, but still a boy at the same time.

I suppose Ma might have said something similar about me. I turned around and poked my head inside the wagon.

"Hey, kids," I called. "Come on up here with me and Zack. The three of you gotta see all this!"

Eleven-year-old Emily's curly blonde head peeked out first. She was the pretty one in the family, all delicate like a China doll I once saw in a store window. She sure wouldn't have to worry about being a spinster or a teacher. I gave her my hand and she wiggled onto the seat next to Zack. After her, with a little help, scrambled seven-year-old Tad. He was small for his age, and as the baby of the family, had been petted and pampered. Now he plopped into my lap.

"Is this Sacramento?" he asked.

"Yes," I answered him.

"Can I drive?" he asked, reaching for the reins.

"You're too little," responded Zack in his most grown-up voice.

After Tad, nine-year-old Becky bounded out of the wagon and up to the front, squeezing her chubby little body in between me and Emily. Becky always made me think of one of those bubbly springs we saw on the trail. Ma used to say she was plumb "full of vim and vinegar!" If she had her druthers I suspect she'd have jumped right down onto the street with the other kids and been off out of sight like a shot. She wasn't afraid of anything, nor did she have the good sense that goes along with a healthy dose of fear. I put

my arm around her shoulder to steady her a bit. I wanted
us all to make a good impression on Uncle Nick.

Gradually, after the first awe of seeing the long-anticipated town wore off, I found myself concentrating on the
faces I saw. I began to examine every one we passed, wondering if one of these folks might turn out to be Uncle Nick.
How would I know, anyway? I didn't know what he looked
like. Somehow I guess I thought I'd see some resemblance
to Ma.

"Shucks, Corrie," I could hear Ma say as we bounced
along, "there ain't no way you can tell a man from some
female kin o' his."

Still, I couldn't help thinking about all her talk of the
Belle blood, and I thought that maybe I'd be able to tell.

There were all kinds of folks in Sacramento. I suppose
it wasn't much different than I imagined it would be after
listening to Captain Dixon talk to all the grown-ups around
the campfire at night. There were lots of rough-looking,
grizzled prospectors. They looked just like some pictures
Ma had shown us. One or two were leading mules all loaded
down with gear. But there were men dressed in nice city
clothes too—probably the ones who had found lots of gold.
And there were plenty who looked like the men in the Midwest too, with their high, leather boots, buckskin coats, and
wide-brimmed hats. All around, horses and wagons moved
in every direction.

There weren't too many women. Ma said there wouldn't
be. She figured she might even find us a new pa once we got
here. The few women I did see were all dressed up in fancy
silk or calico. I didn't suppose they did much prospecting,
judging from their get-ups.

Captain Dixon rode up on horseback next to our wagon.
"Well, you young Hollisters," he called out cheerfully,
"here we are! What do you all think?"

A raucous chorus of shouts flew back at him from around
me. He laughed, unable to distinguish between the high-
pitched voices.

"I'll take you kids on down to Miz Baxter's boarding house. Then I'll see what I can find out about your uncle."

He paused and rubbed the whiskers on his chin thoughtfully. "Someone with the name of Nick Hollister oughtn't be too hard to locate," he added.

"His name ain't Hollister," I said quickly.

"That's right. I do recall your Ma sayin' he was *her* brother. Never thought about the man's last name. What is it then? You don't want me chasin' round for the wrong man."

"Matthews," I said, "Nick Matthews." I felt my cheeks flame, 'cause I know better than to tell lies. But this was different—it was Ma's wish. And she did say it was the name he went by. Zack threw me a surprised look, and I was just glad he didn't say anything.

Captain Dixon must not have noticed it; he just nodded and rode off on his palomino with us following in the wagon.

Miss Baxter's Boarding House was located in a quieter part of town, down a side street from the main road. It was a frame house painted white and was the most civilized building in town—at least it was the most civilized one we had yet seen. There was a white board fence around the front yard, and a row of geraniums planted along the front of the house were still in bloom, though it was the middle of October. Inside, the house was furnished plainly. Miss Baxter said she was waiting for a shipment to arrive from the East. But what was there was nice; I hadn't seen a parlor or a kitchen or even a real floor in months.

Two hours after Captain Dixon deposited us with Miss Baxter, and she'd fixed us a fine supper of chicken and dumplings, the captain walked into the front room where we were sitting by the fire waiting. I thought he looked more sober than usual.

"Seems your uncle ain't nowhere in town," he said. "He's most likely up in Miracle."

"What'll we do now?" asked Zack, sounding more than

ever like the little boy he was struggling not to be.

Captain Dixon scratched his head thoughtfully.

No one said anything for a long time. I suppose we were all too shy to ask what was really on our minds. But someone had to ask, and since I was the oldest, it was my job to do it.

"Captain," I said, my voice sounding small in my ears. After all, Captain Dixon only signed on to take the wagon train to Sacramento, not to traipse all over tarnation with a passel of kids. "Do you think maybe we could go up there after him?"

Captain Dixon didn't say anything for a while, then he kind of mumbled, "Well, lemme see. Yep, that's an idea all right—" As his words trailed away half-finished, he went off to the other room and talked with Miss Baxter. They kept their voices low so I couldn't tell what they were saying. In a minute or two he returned.

"Miz Baxter says you can all stay here tonight. We'll git an early start come daybreak. It's a three-day ride to Miracle."

# CHAPTER 4

## MIRACLE SPRINGS

I can hardly remember anything about the next three days except their being long.

When Captain Dixon said he'd take us to Miracle, we were five happy kids. The thought of waiting around in that unfamiliar city, not sure if Uncle Nick would ever turn up, was none too appealing a thought. Especially if we had been left alone, having to scour through the crowded, rough streets searching for our uncle on our own. So we all joyfully hugged Captain Dixon—all except Zack, that is. He just shook his hand like a grown-up man.

But the long drive took some of the fire out of our enthusiasm. There's nothing worse than thinking you're all done with something, only to have to start all over again. After all those months on the trail, another three days should have been nothing. But they were the longest of all.

Anyway, we finally got there about mid-afternoon of the third day. Miracle was nothing like Sacramento, except that it was new. But I suppose everything around California was practically new, because of the gold rush.

Captain Dixon told us that the people who started this town all came two years ago, after a rich strike was discovered on a little tributary of the Yuba River that came to be called Miracle Springs. The town just naturally got named after the springs. There weren't more than two streets and a few buildings in the whole town, and five of the buildings were saloons. Most of the population was housed in a ramshackle conglomeration of tents of all different sizes and shapes.

Captain Dixon said that the people of Miracle hadn't decided if their town was a mining camp, a for-real town that was going to grow like Sacramento, or if it was already becoming a ghost town. The two-year old strike was gradually playing out, and only the serious miners were still scratching a few dollars out of the mines and streams. But quite a few families, and here and there a farmer or two, had come to the area hanging onto their hopes for the future.

"Ranchers like Uncle Nick?" I said.

"I suppose so," replied the Captain vaguely.

For such a little town, a lot of people were milling around the streets. It was Saturday, the Captain reminded me—the day everyone comes to town. As we pulled the wagon up to a stop in front of one of the biggest of the buildings, the town's only General Store, Captain Dixon told us to stay close to him.

We trailed inside behind him like a brood of little ducklings following their mama. For the first time in months, I felt at home. The store was filled almost to bursting with everything imaginable, and reminded me of the Mercantile in Bridgeville, the little town near our farm in New York. The smells of leather, licorice, pickles, feed, peppermint, and burlap all mingled together in a wonderful, homey way. But I wish I hadn't picked up a bar of lemon verbena soap. The strong aroma immediately brought tears to my eyes; Ma used to use it all the time, and it reminded me so much of her. I had to fight back tears the rest of the day because the smell lingered on my hands.

It was easy to guess the proprietor by his appearance, dressed in a white shirt and string tie, with a leather visor stuck on his forehead over dark, brilliantined hair. I suppose the proprietors of stores like these all looked the same. At least he was dressed just like kind old Mr. Johnson back in Bridgeville. This gentleman stood behind a coarse wooden counter, absorbed in sorting through a stack of important-looking papers. He stopped when the door closed behind Becky, looked up, and his thick eyebrows raised right up to his visor as he watched us approach. He had the biggest, bushiest eyebrows I'd ever seen. He said nothing, but his eyes shone with both question and surprise as Captain Dixon walked up to the counter with his little batch of silent ducklings in tow. Maybe folks weren't used to children here in Miracle. I didn't know what to expect. But when he opened his mouth, his voice was friendly.

"Afternoon. Can I help you folks?"

"We're looking for someone," said Captain Dixon.

"I see—" His voice trailed off as his eye followed Tad, who had wiggled his hand from mine and was going for a bright red ball he'd spied.

"Perhaps your children would like a sweet treat?" the storekeeper continued, stopping Tad, as I supposed he intended, in his tracks.

"Uh—they ain't my kids," replied Captain Dixon. "I'm just looking after them until I can get them to their kin."

"And might that be who you're looking for?" asked the storekeeper as he began passing around a glass jar of hard candy.

I was kept busy trying to listen with one ear and contain the squeals of delight from the others at the same time.

"That's right," said the captain. "I'm Jim Dixon, and I'm looking for a Nick Matthews."

The man stopped suddenly, the jar just out of Tad's reach. All at once he seemed oblivious to us kids, and didn't even notice Tad's heroic attempts to wrap his dirty little fingers around a piece of candy. Finally I took out a piece and gave it to Tad. But the storekeeper continued to stare at Captain Dixon.

"That so?" he finally said in a questioning voice. "The young'uns' father?"

"Their uncle."

"You certain of that?"

"Sure as I can be, never havin' met the man. But I knew their ma."

"Hmmm—"

"You know him then, Mister?"

"In a manner of speaking."

"Know where we can find him?"

"Not exactly," replied the storekeeper. "Though he's got a claim hereabouts, but I never—"

"I know who Nick is!" chimed in a voice from the back of the store where a display of saddles was piled.

We all glanced around eagerly in the direction of the new voice. A man came toward us slowly, older and more weathered than anyone I'd ever seen, even more 'n my old Grandpa Belle. His face was covered with a matted gray beard which continued up the sides of his cheeks, around his ears, and up over the top of his head—one big clump of hair, with only his two eyes and a red nose peeking out from it. Toward the back of his head he wore a battered old slouch hat, but his hair seemed too unruly to be contained and spread out in all directions from underneath it. His clothes Ma would have long since tossed out as rags, and around his neck was tied what looked to be a blue bandanna, though it was so covered with grime you could hardly tell the blue from the brownish-gray of his beard. As he approached, two half-sets of teeth made their appearance out of the mass which covered his face—neither the most complete nor the whitest teeth I had ever laid eyes on, but at least the smile surrounding them seemed friendly.

"What's that you say, Alkali?" said the storekeeper.

"Ya heard me well enough," answered the old prospector, his grin widening.

"This here's Alkali Jones," said the storekeeper by way of introduction. "Knows everything and everyone in Miracle, and been here longer than all of us put together, I don't doubt."

"Hee, hee! I reckon yer right 'bout that," said Jones.

"Pleased to make your acquaintance," said Captain Dixon. The two men shook hands. Mr. Jones' hands were as brown and tough as an Indian's.

"What can you tell me about Matthews?" asked the captain.

"Mayhap the young'uns oughta step outside," said Alkali Jones. I thought I detected a slight wink in the Captain's direction as he spoke, but I could tell it wasn't meant for me. "These all be Nick's kin?" he squeaked. "Hee, hee!" His high-pitched voice sounded like gravel scraping over glass.

"That's right, they're his kin. So I figure what you've got to say you can say to us all."

We moved a few steps away, but were too curious to take the old miner's suggestion and go outside.

"Have it yer way, stranger. Don't say I didn't warn ya." He paused, and then, still half-trying to keep his words from us, said in a low voice, "He's done skipped."

"Skipped? What do you mean?" asked Captain Dixon.

"Skipped town, that's what! What else could I mean? Hee, hee!"

"Why?"

"The sheriff's after him, that's why! Ya must be a tinhorn, stranger—why else would a man like Nick pull up and leave his claim?"

"How long ago?"

"I dunno. Last week some time, weren't it, Bosely?" The storekeeper half nodded, half shrugged.

"What did he do?"

"Some say he shot a man, Mister," said the storekeeper seriously. "Others say he was framed."

"Whichever it be, he ain't been seen in Miracle since," added Mr. Jones.

"Well, isn't there anybody in town who can tell me anything about it, or where he might possibly be?" asked the captain.

"The sheriff sure doesn't know," said the storekeeper. "I heard he's been clear down to Placerville looking for him."

"Them that knows ain't sayin', I can tell ya that! Hee, hee!"

"And who might that be, Mr. Jones?"

"Friends o' his."

"Where might I find these friends?"

"Likely over t' the Gold Nugget. Ya passed it on the way in t' town."

"I see," said the captain thoughtfully. "Well then, I'll just leave the kids here while I go have a talk with these gentlemen."

"I wouldn't be doin' that!" said Mr. Jones, wiping his grimy shirtsleeve across his nose. "Ya don't want t' be disturbin' them now . . . no, siree!"

"These kids here have been on the trail for months," exclaimed Captain Dixon. "Their poor ma took sick and died when we were almost here, and now they're orphans except for this Matthews fellow. So whatever's going on ain't more important than this!"

I wanted to cheer for the captain, standing up for us like he did, but I just stood there and kept quiet.

"That's up t' you, of course," said Mr. Jones. "All's I knows is there's been a mighty se-erious game o' poker since last night. An' 'bout two hours ago Nick's partner put their claim on the table, an' then lost it square."

"Don't matter. I'm gonna see him," insisted Captain Dixon.

"Have it yer own way, stranger. I'm jist tellin' ya he said he'd shoot anyone who interrupted the game afore he'd had a fair chance o' winnin' back the land."

"Drum's no hothead," put in the shopkeeper. "I don't think he would—" but he was cut off in mid-sentence.

"Ya know as well as I do, Bosely, that this fracas with Nick's got him a mite riled."

"How much longer do you suppose the game'll last?" asked Captain Dixon.

"No tellin'."

Captain Dixon sighed, thought for a minute, then bustled us kids outside. He went back into the store, I guessed to ask directions, then took us to a boarding house. This one was run by an old Italian woman named Mrs. Gianni. She took us to her kitchen and set about fixing us something to eat. The Captain told us to wait there while he went to see what he could find out.

# CHAPTER 5

# IN FRONT OF THE GOLD NUGGET

We sat in Mrs. Gianini's boarding house around a rough table covered with a red-checkered cloth. Slabs of apple pie were on the table in front of us. It was nearly the best pie I ever tasted—almost as good as Ma's. But I couldn't eat much. Zack ate his and finally began to work on mine.

We'd been waiting so long that a little bit more oughtn't have mattered much. But after an hour I could hardly stand it any more. I began to wonder if that nice Captain Dixon hadn't just given up and gone back to Sacramento.

Then I remembered that old miner's words. Could someone have shot the captain? Surely Ma's brother couldn't have friends like that. I told myself those were just wild tales like the ones we heard about Kit Carson and Davy Crockett.

Finally the waiting became too much to bear. The other kids had finished their pie, Tad was getting cranky, and Becky was wiggling around. I didn't want to wait another minute.

"Look here," I said, trying to sound firm like Ma, "I'm going to find out what's going on."

"But Captain Dixon said to stay put," said Emily in her dainty way.

"Well, supposing something's happened to him?"

Zack's head shot up with a worried look as he caught the meaning in my words.

"I'm goin'," I said firmly, rising up off the chair.

"Well if you go, we all go," put in Zack. "We gotta all stick together."

I didn't argue. I didn't feel quite so brave as my words sounded, and I was glad for the company, even if it was just a passel of young'uns.

Mrs. Gianini told us to stay where we were, but we all bounded out of her place, leaving her with her hands in the air. The little ones held each others' hands and followed on mine and Zack's heels as if we were the ma and pa of the bunch. But inside my stomach was a knot. I was worried and scared, and I missed Ma terribly.

The sun was setting as we marched down the street, and the shadows made the town look all the more threatening. I noticed the brawling noise now, too. Laughter and shouts and catcalls poured out from the saloons. I could hear several gruff men's voices trying their best at "Oh, Susanna," but they sounded off-key, even to my tin ear. They were probably drunk. An even more off-key piano was being played along with them. It might have been comical if I hadn't been so anxious inside.

We found the Gold Nugget Saloon. It was noisy, with lots of men hanging around outside. I didn't relish the thought of walking up to the place, much less going inside, but I didn't know what else to do.

There was a place like the Gold Nugget in Bridgeville, but Ma didn't let us go near it. "Decent folk don't go into drinkin' houses," Ma had said. What little I knew about California told me that a drinking house way out here must be even worse than the ones in the East. I told myself that we had a mighty good reason to be there, but it didn't make it any easier to step up onto the wooden steps and go inside. I looked at my brothers and sisters, but they just looked back at me with big, wide eyes. They were looking to me to decide what we ought to do. My stomach was still all knotted up. Surely one of those rough-looking men standing around the place was going to start making fun of us. But finally I took in a breath, turned around, and started toward the swinging doors.

All of a sudden a female voice spoke up behind us. "Do you children need some help?"

I stopped dead in my tracks and turned around. I was more than a little relieved to be stopped from going inside that place, even if just for a minute.

There stood a woman, about Ma's age, or maybe a few years younger. She was tall and trim, but sturdily built. Even dressed as she was in a blue calico and matching bonnet, I could tell she wasn't afraid of work. She was pretty, but in a rough, earthy sort of way, and her tanned skin looked as if she spent a lot of time out in the sun.

"My name is Almeda Parrish," she went on to say to our blank faces. "I run the Parrish Mine and Freight Company. My office is across the way and I happened to notice you children. Do your mother and father know where you are?"

"Our ma and pa are dead, ma'am," I answered, trying to sound respectful.

"Oh, I'm terribly sorry." And I truly thought she was. "But this is hardly the kind of place for children. Do you want someone inside?"

"Well, Ma'am," I answered, "we just came from New York, and Captain Dixon, that's our wagon boss, he went to find out about our Uncle Nick. But he left over an hour ago, and we got kind of worried waiting on him. We've been—"

Without warning, tears welled up in my eyes, and I bit my lip to keep them back. I felt like such a baby.

"And this—Captain Dixon? You say he's your wagon boss?"

"He brung us all the way from the East, Ma'am," put in Zack, coming to my rescue.

Mrs. Parrish didn't seem to mind a girl crying. She stepped right up to me and put her arm around me. Then she said, "There, there, child. Don't you worry, we'll get all this straightened around."

When I had gotten all my tears out, she went on to say in a thoughtful tone, "Nick. . . ? Nick who?"

"Nick Matthews," spoke up Zack again.

She pursed her lips and nodded slightly, but said nothing. I didn't like the look that came over everyone's faces around here when Uncle Nick's name came up.

At that moment, a man walked out of the saloon doors.

"Sir," said Mrs. Parrish with authority in her voice. The man stopped and paid attention. "There is a man by the name of Dixon, a Captain Dixon, in this establishment," she said. "Would you go back inside and tell him to come out immediately? There are some children here very anxious to see him."

"That might not be sich a good idee right at the moment, Ma'am," he returned. "Ya see, the game's downright tense, an' any disturbance—"

"Well!" exclaimed Mrs. Parrish, "Of all the nerve! To think a game of poker is more important than this. I'll just have to go in after him myself!"

She hitched up her calico dress with both hands, and marched right inside as if she were Daniel walking into the lion's den. I peered over the top of the two swinging doors and could tell that the men inside were just as surprised as me at seeing a fine, well-bred lady suddenly intrude upon their private world. There were other women inside, but they were dressed a whole lot differently than Mrs. Parrish.

"Why, Mrs. Parrish, this is indeed an honor—" the man standing behind the bar began to say. But she paid no attention and marched right on past him.

She disappeared into another room at the back of the saloon. I could hear voices from inside through the open door, but I couldn't make out what anyone was saying. From the loud female voice it was plain that Mrs. Parrish was giving the men gathered there a piece of her mind.

In about two minutes Mrs. Parrish came out again, followed almost immediately by Captain Dixon. Several others straggled along behind them. Some of the men looked pretty mean and all wore guns on their hips.

"I'm sorry, kids," said Captain Dixon walking right up to us. "I'm afraid I wasn't too successful at finding out much about your uncle. None of the men were too talkative while their game was going on. About all I know for sure is what we heard before—that he's not here."

Just then, another man walked through the swinging doors, and the eyes of several of the onlookers swung around and glared at him. Unconsciously, I backed up several steps along the wooden sidewalk, and the younger kids clung close to me. Mrs. Parrish eyed the man intently, while all the other men who had wandered out of the saloon crowded around by the doors, some with grins on their faces, chuckling among themselves, looking ready for a good show.

The fellow was awfully tall. He had dark circles under his red eyes, and wore a full beard. A big hat was pulled down clear to his ears. I'd have guessed him to be thirty-eight or forty years old, but it was hard to tell. He'd probably been at the card table all night, like the man at the store said. His shoulders were broad; he could have hoisted both Becky and Tad up on them and hardly felt it. He wasn't unpleasant looking, but kind of fearsome all the same. He was dressed shabbily, his dusty old trousers held up with faded suspenders over a patched flannel shirt.

"Well, Mr. Drum," said Mrs. Parrish in a stern voice, "as you can see, the situation is as serious as I tried to tell you inside. Now, are you going to tell us where we can find Mr. Matthews, or not?"

"You ain't told me nothin' yet." He glanced at us kids with deep creases forming between his thick brown eyebrows. "What's this all about?"

"As I tried to tell you, these children are looking for your partner."

"Who are they?" asked Mr. Drum.

"It seems they more or less belong to Nick Matthews," said Mrs. Parrish.

Mr. Drum rubbed a coarse hand over his mouth. "Well, I've known Nick a long time and I know for certain he ain't got no young'uns."

"These are his nieces and nephews—he's their uncle!"

The lines on Mr. Drum's forehead and around his eyes got deeper. A look of real shock passed over his face, and he didn't say anything for a long time. When he finally did speak, his voice sounded as if he had just had the wind knocked out of him.

"Nick's nowhere to be found," he said.

"Are you expecting me to believe he'd just pull up and leave, without telling his partner—"

She was interrupted by the laughter of the men standing around.

"Ya must not know Nick Matthews too well!" shouted one of the men. "Why, he's a lightin' off fer somewhere new ev'ry month!"

"And he don't tell me his every move," added the big man called Drum. As he spoke, he kept throwing quick glances in our direction. "This sure ain't no place fer a bunch of kids. Where's their ma, anyway? Why'd she send 'em all by themselves after Nick?"

"I thought you understood, Mr. Drum," said Mrs. Parrish, her firm tone softening. "Their mother died en route to California."

Mr. Drum fell silent once more, his face like a stone wall.

"Hee, hee, hee!" came the rasp of Alkali Jones from among the onlookers. "I guess since Nick's gone, them's yore young'uns now, Drum! Hee, hee, hee!"

He spun around and glared at the old miner, then turned back and looked each of us over one at a time, his ruddy California color getting paler as he took in each of our faces.

When he came to me, I detected something that took away the fear I was feeling. His face still wore a scowl, but his eyes seemed to say that in spite of the bluster he might put on in front of all the tough-looking men in the saloon, down inside he was the kind that could feel sorry for a brood of homeless orphans. But the next moment, I began to think I'd read his eyes all wrong.

The exchange of looks and thoughts took only a few seconds. Then Mrs. Parrish spoke again.

"Well, Mr. Drum, what do you have to say for yourself?"

He shot her a glaring look that seemed to say, *Mind your own business, you busybody female!* But what came out of his mouth was, "I got nothin' to say for myself, 'cept that this is . . . some surprise. And I don't rightly see why you think it's got something to do with me."

"You are Matthews' partner."

"And Nick's gone!" he shot back. "How many times I gotta tell you that, lady?" He seemed more nervous than angry.

"You're closer to their kin than any of us," persisted Mrs. Parrish. "Mr. Dixon here has to be getting back to Sacramento—"

Captain Dixon nodded as she spoke.

"—And I only met these children ten minutes ago," she went on. "So I think it's high time you either told us where to find Mr. Matthews, or got on your horse and went to find him yourself."

"Even if I knew where he was—" he persisted, "which I don't—I wouldn't just ride off so the sheriff could follow me and haul Nick in for somethin' he didn't do!"

I figured by now it was my turn to speak.

"We're real glad to make your acquaintance, Mr. Drum," I said, trying to smile cheerfully. "My name's Corrie. I'm the oldest."

I curtsied like Ma taught me.

The man looked at me again. A strange expression came over his face, but it only lasted for a moment. Then he glanced around at the others.

He wiped his hands across his eyes as if he hoped that might make us all disappear. But we were still there. I told him the kids' names. A pitiful looking lot we were, having spent months on the trail with nary a bath in a month of Sundays.

"There sure are a heap of you," he said softly, scratching his whiskers. "And all such big, grown-up kids, too."

"There's a heap of you, too!" said Tad in a soft voice with wide-eyed awe.

That got a laugh from everyone, especially the men in the saloon, and a few others who had wandered up from the street to see what this strange little gathering was all about. But the fellow in front of us didn't laugh. He still seemed a little apprehensive about the sight of us all.

"Hey, Drum," called out one of the men, "seems to me you're cut out right well for nurse-maidin'!"

He pretended not to hear, but I know he did.

"So, Mr. Drum, what might your intentions be now?" asked Mrs. Parrish, still sounding very stern.

"Well, Mrs. Parrish," he answered after a moment's thought, "I'm meanin' no disrespect, but I reckon it ain't none of your dad-blamed business."

Then he turned back toward the gawking faces at the saloon door. "And it ain't none of yours, neither!" he snapped. "So git!"

No one waited to be told twice. They scattered like birds at a turkey shoot. Apparently his was a voice people listened to in Miracle Springs.

Mrs. Parrish wasn't as easily spooked. Even Captain Dixon took a step back, but Mrs. Parrish settled her hands on her hips and didn't budge.

"As one of the few voices of *decent* civilized society in this town," she said, "I think it *is* my business. Anyway, I am making it mine. These children came here looking for a home, and now it seems you are the only link there is to that home."

"A home!" From the expression on his face I don't think the thought had yet occurred to him. "You can't expect—! Even *you* can see, Mrs. Parrish, that Nick and I ain't fit to be taking care of no kids." He glanced a look at me as if to say, *I'm sorry*.

"We'd be able to help out on Uncle Nick's ranch," I offered, not wanting to sound too eager, but hardly able to keep quiet any longer. "I'm a fair cook, and Zack's a good hand with a plow and animals. As for the young'uns, they can learn. We won't get in your way. Then you can go find Uncle Nick and tell him we're here."

"Ranch? What ranch?" Mr. Drum said.

"The ranch a fellow from California told us Uncle Nick had."

"Since when do you and Nick Matthews own a ranch, Mr. Drum?" said Mrs. Parrish. I couldn't tell if her voice sounded angry or smug.

A reddish color started to come into Drum's face. I don't think he liked being questioned by a woman in front of all his friends from the saloon, several of whom had wandered back toward the door.

"Now, look here!" he said suddenly, a sharp, cross look coming over his face. "Not that it's any of your business, but Nick and I did have a ranch once—won it in a poker game and lost it the next night. How was we to know some-one'd go spreading it around that we was ranchers, or that Nick's . . . sister . . . would take it in her blame fool head to come out West after . . . him."

"Listen here, Drum," spoke up Captain Dixon. "Don't you go speakin' so of the dead, 'specially in front of her own children. Mrs. Hollister was a fine, brave woman."

Mr. Drum looked ready to knock us all down and bolt. He opened his mouth as if he were going to say something, but nothing came out.

"Indeed, Mr. Drum," added Mrs. Parrish, and now her voice *was* angry, "you ought to be ashamed of yourself to speak so!"

Mr. Drum looked as if he was about to suffocate.

"And as far as the question of your and Mr. Matthews' reputations go," Mrs. Parrish went on as if she didn't see what distress he was in, "I must agree to some extent. Yet it appears *you* are all these children have. Technically, if Mr. Matthews doesn't return, then I would think these children would inherit his half of your property. You might as well face it, Mr. Drum—these youngsters may be your new partners."

"Look here, Mrs. Parrish, who knows when Nick'll be back? Why, I ain't even got a decent place for them to bunk down." He was looking more and more like a trapped polecat with all the eyes of the town on him. "What about you?"

"I'm not their kin," she answered matter-of-factly. "I have no connection to their uncle, or to any property to which they might have a legitimate claim. You do. And practically speaking, my business takes me too frequently away from home." She glanced at me apologetically.

"So does mine!" exclaimed Drum. "And I ain't got no intention of havin' no woman tell me my responsibility to-ward—my—my partner's kids!"

He was looking at Mrs. Parrish, but I thought I saw him throw just a momentary glance at me as he spoke. Something in his eyes seemed to want to say, *I'm sorry . . . I'd take you in if I could. But not now, not like this . . . not with the whole town staring at me!*

He spun around and bounded down the steps, striding across the dirt street to where his horse, a pretty bay mare, was tied at a hitching rail. Somehow all the fears I had over the past several weeks never included standing in the middle of a strange town with everyone turning us away.

But there went our only hope of locating our uncle, galloping off down the road, leaving only a cloud of dust and five pairs of disappointed, staring eyes behind him.

# CHAPTER 6

# THE TOWN BUSINESS WOMAN

Even though Mrs. Parrish was a kind lady, the menfolk in town seemed almost afraid of her. As we walked away from the saloon, I wondered about her being the only real lady in a town full of rough, gold-mining men. But they depended on her business for their livelihood, and so maybe they had to watch their step around her.

She almost reminded me of a stern schoolteacher who one just couldn't help liking, even for all her sober looks and strict words. I liked her anyway. Ma would have liked her, too. Now, *she* was a woman who could get on in the world by herself. She sure didn't look like she needed a man around!

She took us right to her house. Captain Dixon had to be on his way, but he took our wagon to Mrs. Parrish's and unhitched the team. She ran one of the town's livery stables there as part of her business, so they made arrangements with the man there for our two horses. I heard her tell him that she'd see to our care " . . . until that Drum comes to his senses, or until Nick Matthews gets back in town."

We all gave the captain big hugs. How we hated to see him go! He'd been about the only familiar face we'd known for quite a while now, and was just about the closest we'd gotten to having a father. Mrs. Parrish was nice, but we'd only just met her, and seeing Captain Dixon go off down the street brought a fearsome loneliness into me all over again.

He promised that he'd come to see us before he left for the East to guide another wagon train to California. I wondered if we might be going back with him. But with both Ma and Grandpa gone, we had no one to go home to back in New York. That little wagon was the only home we had left. We wouldn't be any better off in the East than we were here in Miracle. And I'd rather be orphaned and alone in California, than to face that trip across the country again with a batch of young'uns to watch after. I was practically just a kid myself!

It was late by the time the captain left and we all got settled in. Mrs. Parrish had a nice frame house—there were only two or three other houses in town, but hers was the nicest. I suppose most of the men lived in one of the two boarding houses, in the collection of tents at the end of town, or out on their claims in the hills someplace. It sure was nice being in such a pretty place. It was all done up fancy-like with beautiful carved furniture, chairs with needlepoint seats, chintz curtains, and fine china in the prettiest cherrywood hutch I ever saw. Mrs. Parrish said her husband had it all brought from the East, from their home in Boston. It came around Cape Horn, she said, in 1849, when she and her husband came to California.

She was a widow now. She didn't talk much about her husband except for that, and I didn't want to be impolite and ask too many questions.

She had two extra beds with feather mattresses. I could hardly believe how soft they felt after all those months sleeping in our wagon. Tad and Zack were asleep in seconds. Emily and Becky squirmed and giggled until I could get them settled down. But I couldn't sleep. With all the change, and everything that had happened, my mind was just too full.

Finally I got up and went to a little desk where Mrs.

Parrish had left a small lamp burning for us. I got out the old school notebook I was keeping my diary in, and wrote about the day—how we had come to Miracle Springs and about meeting Mr. Drum at the saloon. I tried to draw a picture of the front of the saloon. Lots of times I'd make drawings along with what I wrote, to help me remember. I couldn't help shedding a few tears. After all this time of anticipation, Uncle Nick was gone. And Mr. Drum left us here without even wanting to help us find him. I remembered that peculiar look in his eyes, as if he might have wanted to help if everyone wasn't watching. I felt so alone. I don't think I ever felt so lonely—even right after Ma died—as that moment standing there on the dusty street of Miracle Springs, watching that bay mare fade away from sight, and knowing nobody wanted us.

It helped to write it down that night. I was glad Ma got me thinking about keeping a diary, because it made the next few weeks easier to bear. I needed to be able to talk to somebody, even if it was only to myself. Most of what I wrote nobody'd ever lay eyes on. But just saying it made me feel better, like having a silent friend I could tell things to. And if I hadn't been keeping a journal, I wouldn't be able to remember a lot of what it was like when we first came to Miracle Springs.

I wrote late into the night by the dim light of Mrs. Parrish's lamp. It must have been past midnight when I finally crawled back into bed between Emily and Becky. But as tired as I was, I kept waking up all night, thinking that at any minute Uncle Nick would come to the door and take us to his ranch.

# CHAPTER 7

## MRS. PARRISH TALKS TO US

I woke up the following morning to a steady rainfall.

Emily and Becky were still sleeping soundly, and Becky had an arm wrapped around my neck. I gently loosened her arm and slipped out of bed. The sun was barely up, but the clouds made it even darker outside. The black sky reminded me that it was almost the end of October. Even in California, winter must be coming soon.

Mrs. Parrish fixed us all a fine breakfast of pancakes and sausages. The men in the mining camps called them flapjacks, she said, and prided themselves on tossing them way up in the air to flip them over. Then she had to leave for her office down the street.

Before she left, she showed us her bathtub in a little room all its own, showed us where to get the water, and told us to help ourselves to baths and anything else we needed. That was her polite way of saying we looked, and probably smelled, like a bunch of mountaineers. She told us where to find the pantry if we got hungry, and then invited us to come by the office later. She didn't say a word about Uncle Nick. I wasn't sure if that was good or bad, but I didn't want to ask.

After she left, I got the young'uns into the bath. All three of them could fit in that big tub of hers at the same time! I figured it'd be okay for me and Zack, since we were older, to have our own separate baths. While the kids were splashing around, I went to the kitchen to wash up the breakfast dishes; I'd asked Mrs. Parrish to leave them for me to do.

After a while Zack came in with that grown-up look on his face. "Corrie," he said, "I been doing some thinking."

He sat down in a chair by the table and took a leftover pancake from a plate. No matter how much might have been on Zack's mind, he could always eat.

"What about?" I asked, scrubbing away at the grease on the skillet.

"You know all them stories we heard about kids not that much older'n us who came out West by theirselves?"

I nodded. Half of them I never believed. "We ain't heard *that* many stories," I said.

"Well," Zack went on, paying my comment no heed, "there ain't no reason we couldn't do the same."

"I don't think I heard any stories about kids as young as us doing it," I added.

"Aw, come on, Corrie! We don't need Uncle Nick or nobody else. Pa left us and we all made out fine. Now Ma's gone, but we're older, too. We could get by."

"I ain't so sure," I said.

I didn't like the tone of Zack's voice. He sounded angry. It never occurred to me to be angry with Uncle Nick. It wasn't as if he had known we were coming and just skipped out on us, like Pa had done.

"I could get a job. Maybe even do some mining."

"Zack, you're only thirteen."

"That's old enough!" he shot back at me. "I might even strike it rich."

He bit into a piece of hotcake as if he was taking his frustration out on it. I decided I'd better not say anything more.

"Anyway," he went on in a minute, "I bet I could make us a living, just like Pa did, while you take care of the kids. Then when Emily gets big enough, she could take care of

Becky and Tad and you could get work, maybe taking in laundry or such like. Lots of women do that kind of thing."

"But that's just it, Zack," I replied, "I'm not a woman. I don't know enough about things—you know, about life, and all that—to take care of all of us. Especially way out here where there's hardly any civilization. And what about school? Ma always wanted us to have a good education. Seems to me we ought to go back to New York."

"And do what?"

"We got friends who'd likely help us."

"Ma would never want us to live off charity."

I was silent. Zack had me there. Ma was a proud woman all right. It was one thing to ask family for help, but quite another to go to complete strangers. Mrs. Parrish was nice, but we couldn't stay with her forever.

Maybe Zack was right. If we were young like Tad and Becky or even Emily, it would be different. Maybe then folks would feel as if they ought to take care of us. But Zack and I were old enough—at least, almost old enough—to take care of ourselves. But I didn't feel that way most of the time. Since Ma'd died, it hadn't been very comfortable being the one everybody looked to for decision-making. And I couldn't help thinking about what Ma had said about Pa when he was young, how hard it had been on him being all alone. I sure didn't want that to happen to any of us.

I was more than a little confused. I just didn't know what we ought to do.

Later in the day, all spruced up and fresh, we left the house and walked over to the Parrish Mine and Freight Company. On the way, I kept craning my head this way and that, looking for somebody that might be Uncle Nick, or some sign of Mr. Drum's bay mare. But neither was anywhere in sight.

The Mine and Freight Company was a hodgepodge of activities. Our eyes were wide open with curiosity when we walked in. Mrs. Parrish gave us a friendly greeting, and then took us on a little tour and told us about the company. They still operated a gold mine in the foothills several miles from town, and did some assaying of what the mines brought in. They even ran a bank, she told us, until Miracle got a real bank a year ago. Mostly the company was a freight outfit. They ran wagons—and pack mules, when necessary—between San Francisco and the Sierras.

"My husband," she said, her voice proud, "believed that the money to be made in the gold rush was not in the mines at all, but rather in supplies."

He was most likely right too, cause Mrs. Parrish lived better than any prospector I had yet seen.

The office itself was an orderly room with several file cabinets, and a big, thick oak counter across the front. Behind it sat two nice, oak desks, and next to them cabinets full of cubbyholes which had papers and files sticking out of them. One of the desks had Mrs. Parrish's name on it. At the other one sat a man she introduced as Mr. Ashton, her clerk.

Mr. Ashton looked like a city fellow. He didn't fit my image of Miracle Springs. He was dressed better than any man I'd seen in town, but he was balding and scrawny. He was nervous, too, and seemed to try hard to ignore us. When Mrs. Parrish presented us to him, his lips twitched up into what I guess was supposed to be a smile, then he went right back to work.

Behind the office was the huge livery stable where the company's stock and wagons were cared for between deliveries. Marcus Weber, a burly, free Negro, presided here as blacksmith, Mrs. Parrish said. He was more friendly than the clerk, and even helped Tad and Becky climb up on a couple of mules. His teeth were pure white, and he put them to good use when he smiled.

Our horses, Snowball and Jinx, looked very contented munching on hay and swishing flies away with their tails. I thanked Mr. Weber for taking such good care of them.

"Miz Parrish, she dun tol' me t' treat 'em like they was my own," said Mr. Weber, grinning.

"Not that he doesn't treat everyone's animals that way," Mrs. Parrish added with a laugh.

I thanked her, and tried to offer her money, but she wouldn't hear of it. I couldn't help wondering where all of this was going to lead. The youngsters were real taken with the office and the livery, but I couldn't keep from thinking, *What is to become of us? What should we do? And where will we live if we stay here and do what Zack suggested, trying to make it on our own?* I wasn't so sure I liked the idea of trying to be a ma to four children when I was barely more than a girl myself.

Mrs. Parrish must have been thinking of this, too, because as soon as we'd seen all around her place, she sent Mr. Ashton home for his lunch, and told us kids to sit down in some spare chairs around her desk.

"Children, I have been giving your situation much thought and prayer," she said, folding her hands together in a very ladylike way on the top of her desk and giving us a sweet look. "The younger children will not be able to understand all that is happening, but you, Corrie and Zachary, are old enough. And I think it is important for you to clearly grasp all the aspects of the situation facing you so that you will see why I must do what I have decided to do."

She stopped and cleared her throat daintily. "Do you have any questions?"

We all shook our heads.

"It is not my intent to speak ill of anyone," she went on, "but I think you should know, if you have not already guessed, just what kind of man your uncle is."

She stopped again and looked intently at Zack's face, then mine, for a long spell. Then, seeming satisfied, went on.

"This land here in the West is very wild and uncivilized. In many places, law is non-existent. Men have had to make their own law and have often resorted to methods that, in the East, would be found unthinkable. Survival has become the most important pursuit—along with getting rich—and the weak do not survive. At least that is how many of these westerners feel. I do not hold that opinion entirely myself, although I do see how it can come to be such in a frontier like this. Surely the weak do perish in the West, but survival should never take precedence over morality."

She paused again, took a deep breath, looked us over and probably saw the dumfounded looks on our faces, which told her we didn't understand what she was talking about. But she plunged ahead anyway, and what she said next, I think we understood well enough.

"Now, your uncle came here when the land was raw and wild. You can hardly imagine the difference five years can make. The population has multiplied many, many times over, just since 1847. And that first year or two after the first strike was a wild and reckless time. Some say it's not much better now, but at least it's begun to settle down some. I have never known your uncle well, and I'll not presume to make excuses for him. But the fact is, your uncle has lived a rather wild life here in the West. I am afraid this is not the first instance of his crossing paths with the sheriff, and as often as not I believe the trouble starts around a poker table. He is not, I believe, a lawless sort. I have heard that he and Mr. Drum have even helped the law out in some cases. But his is not a settled life, perhaps not even a safe one. Do you understand what I am saying?"

By now I had the gist of what she was trying to tell us.

"Mr. Drum doesn't seem like an outlaw," I said.

"And neither is your uncle," replied Mrs. Parrish. "Actually, Mr. Drum has seemed to be a steadying influence on Mr. Matthews. They've worked a claim together since before my husband and I were here, and some say they have done pretty well by it. Mr. Drum's always kept mostly to himself, only now and then pulling your uncle out of a scrape. Your uncle's a talkative sort of man, but no one knows much about his partner. In any case, with your uncle now gone and in fresh trouble, I'm just not so sure how advisable it is—"

"Are you meaning," I asked, even before she'd finished the sentence, "that it wouldn't be good for us to live with Uncle Nick? Or that maybe it's just as well he left town?"

I stopped, looking over at Mrs. Parrish to see if I could tell what she was thinking.

"Because, if you are," I continued, "—well I don't mean to disagree, Ma'am, especially since you probably know what you're talking about. But he's still our uncle, and—"

I took a deep breath. It was hard to speak out like that. Ma always taught us kids to be quiet around adults. But this was such a confusing situation, and I hardly knew whether I was supposed to think like a child or a grown-up. I was sure Mrs. Parrish had every right to box my ears, but I kept going.

"—And, well . . . after what you just said, maybe he even needs us a little, just like we do him."

She didn't box my ears. In fact, Mrs. Parrish just sat there and smiled at me. "You're a very perceptive girl, Corrie," she finally said. "You have put into words exactly what I have been thinking and praying about. I think perhaps this is God's further confirmation of my decision. I realize you hardly know me, and perhaps in normal circumstances it would not be my place to make decisions about—"

"Mrs. Parrish," I interrupted, feeling uncomfortable doing it, but knowing I had to speak, "my brothers and sisters and I are just kids. And we're real confused about what to do."

"You're hardly a child anymore, Corrie," she said, smiling sweetly at me. "Why, you're practically a lady."

"Thank you, Ma'am," I replied, feeling my cheeks getting hot. "But I'm still confused. I don't know much about God, but it seems maybe bringing you across our path might just be something like He'd do. Anyway, we're right obliged for the interest you're taking in us, because you and Captain

Dixon are the only adults we got left, at least maybe the only ones left with half-sensible heads. And now that the Captain is gone . . . well, we'd be right glad to hear whatever you want to say to us."

"Thank you for your confidence, Corrie. I hope I shall prove worthy of it."

She spread her hands out on her desk and looked down at them, and I even thought I saw a bit of flush creep up in her cheeks. But she went on in a brisk businesslike manner. "Now," she said, "here are my thoughts. I believe you should be with your uncle if at all possible. Not only because he is family, but because perhaps you can be good for him. As you said, Corrie, maybe you do need each other. Of course this is ultimately a decision the five of you have to make together, and certainly much depends on whether he is located and what is the outcome of this present fracas."

"Mr. Drum said he didn't do anything wrong," I put in optimistically.

Mrs. Parrish smiled. "Another thing you must understand about the West is that no one *ever* thinks he's done anything wrong, as long as he had a reason. And partners *always* stick up for each other. But time will tell, and we'll hope your uncle is cleared."

"What should we do now?" I asked.

"My counsel is that you do not try to go back where you came from immediately, but stay here in Miracle Springs and try to make a life for yourselves—at least through the winter. I will help you adjust, as I know others will also. And we'll pray really hard that your uncle will either be found or will return soon, and that this whole thing will get cleared up. Though you do have to realize that your Uncle Nick is not . . . well, let's just say he's not accustomed to family life. Even if this trouble with the sheriff blows over, the adjustment will no doubt be very difficult for him."

"What if he never shows up at all?" asked Zack, still sulking.

"Hmmm . . . yes, that is a problem." She folded her hands together and tapped her finger against her pursed lips. "But we must just hope that will work out somehow. And we certainly need to pray about it."

"Ma'am," I said shyly, "I believe in prayer, and Ma put a lot of stock in it. But I don't think I've quite got the hang of it, because it doesn't seem to work too well for me lately."

"Let's pray right now," she said.

"Here?" I always thought the most important praying had to be done in church. I didn't know what to make of the notion of praying right in some business office. What if someone came in and saw us?

"Here and now. Let's all join hands."

I didn't say anything more, and we all obeyed her.

"All right," Mrs. Parrish continued. "I'll do the talking, if you'd like. You can listen and learn. It only takes a bit of practice, and some faith too."

So she bowed her head, right there in that Mine and Freight Company office, and we did the same, and she prayed. Her words were simple, not much like the preacher's in Bridgeville, which were flowery and hard to follow. Mostly she prayed for Uncle Nick, that God would be with him right now no matter where he was, and work to soften his heart. I found myself wondering if God'd be with him even if he was in the Gold Nugget Saloon, but I didn't say it. She also prayed for us, using our names as if God knew and cared about each one of us.

It was an interesting prayer to listen to, and I thought it was the nicest I'd ever heard. I felt good after she was done, thinking that the minute we lifted our heads Uncle Nick would walk right through that door and take us home.

But he didn't.

# CHAPTER 8

# PICNIC IN THE WILDERNESS

The next day Mrs. Parrish took us on a picnic. It was a day I wasn't likely to forget.

I awoke early in the morning. The rain, which had been coming on and off, had stopped. The first thing I noticed, however, was that Emily was not in bed beside me.

I glanced around, and she was gone from the room. Thinking she'd gotten up and wandered to some other part of the house, I got out of bed as quietly as I could, dressed, and went to look for her. But she was nowhere in the house at all.

Finally, I went outside. I found her standing still, looking at the closed stable door.

"Emily," I said, walking to her, "is something the matter? You're up so early."

She turned and looked at me with a smile. "Oh, I'm just going to feed Snowball," she said.

"I'll go with you," I said. "It might still be a little dark inside the stable."

"No, thank you, Corrie," said Emily a little shyly. "But I'd rather go alone."

Still thinking she might be afraid in the stable by herself in the semi-dark, I started to object. But then I stopped. I could understand how she might want to be alone with her horse, even in a dark, strange stable. Snowball was the special friend Emily talked to when she was sad. We each had our own ways of trying to cope with missing Ma, and I knew Snowball helped Emily. So finally I reasoned that I just better leave the two of them alone for a spell.

I smiled, then helped her open the big stable door. Then I walked back toward the house. But at the last minute, I stopped and turned back to watch Emily disappear inside.

I couldn't help myself. Instead of going into the house, I softly crept toward the stable, then stopped and peeked through a crack in the door. I could see Emily with her horse.

In her hand Emily held the apple Mrs. Parrish had given her the night before at supper. She had saved it for her friend. She held it up to Snowball, whose big, white fleshy lips opened and took it from her, eating it in a single, quick bite.

"You know," I could hear Emily saying softly, "you look just like a big white snowball that came down from heaven one day in a cold snowstorm. I don't think Ma could have given you a more perfectly fittin' name, 'cause it's just like you."

She paused for a moment, then added, "I miss Ma, Snowball."

Her voice was sad, and thinking of Ma made her start to cry. But with only Snowball to see, she didn't seem to care about a few tears falling to the ground.

Snowball put her white chin on Emily's shoulder, as if she could sense the tender girl's feelings. Emily patted the wet nose lovingly.

"But you understand how I feel, don't you, Snowball?"

Snowball seemed to sway gently, as if she were saying, "Yes, I understand." I moved quickly away from the crack in the door. Suddenly it didn't seem right to intrude upon this special time between Emily and Snowball. Besides, if I watched any longer, I would start crying myself!

The sun came out gloriously a little while later. The sky was clear and blue, reminding me of an Indian summer back home.

At breakfast, Mrs. Parrish said the day was so fine she thought we ought to go on a picnic. She got no argument from us!

She had to go to her office for a while but I volunteered to fix lunch. By eleven o'clock, after the sun had a good chance to warm up everything, we all climbed into her wagon, a buckboard drawn by two of the finest-looking mules I'd ever seen.

"Could we take Snowball?" asked Emily as she got in. "She could pull your wagon real fine."

Mrs. Parrish laughed.

"I'm not so sure your Snowball would get along with either of my mules."

"We could take both Snowball and Jinx," persisted Emily.

"We'll do that next time, I promise," smiled Mrs. Parrish. "I wouldn't want to try out a new team I wasn't used to, and that wasn't used to me, especially with five children in the buckboard with me. Accidents do happen, you know."

Emily's disappointment was visible all over her face. "You really love your Snowball, don't you, dear?" said Mrs. Parrish.

"She eats apples right out of my hand, Ma'am," answered Emily, brightening.

"That's lovely. Maybe you could show me when we get back. There are some nice apples in the pantry."

Satisfied, Emily's spirits rose. Mrs. Parrish snapped the reins crisply and clicked her tongue in her cheek, and we were off.

We took a different road than the one into Miracle from Sacramento City. The terrain got more rugged and hilly, but Mrs. Parrish handled the team well. I could see that her mules were a better choice than our horses would have been.

We drove for about an hour. The country was so beautiful it made me tingle inside. We'd seen many grand sights in the last few months, but there was something about this land of California that made all the rest pale in my memory. Everything seemed bigger and richer and more alive. I could just imagine what it must be like in spring and summer.

Finally, Mrs. Parrish pulled the rig off the trail we'd been following. There was nothing that could rightly be called a *road* up there. In another minute we stopped, and we all bounded excitedly from the wagon, scattering in different directions trying to find the perfect place to settle. There was a small grove of old oak trees, a sparkling stream, and a clearing of soft grass where the afternoon warmth of the sun made me forget it had just rained the day before. We lugged a blanket or two and Mrs. Parrish's big basket over to the clearing. I helped Mrs. Parrish spread out the biggest blanket, though Becky kept bouncing all over it so we had to keep rearranging it.

"Becky," said Mrs. Parrish, smiling at her antics, "why don't you take this bucket and fetch us some water from the stream?"

Becky grabbed the bucket and flew down the little rise to the water. The rest of us then spread out the lunch.

We wanted to explore right away, especially the two boys and Becky. But we were hungry, too, so Mrs. Parrish suggested we eat a little first and then go exploring around the area, and then maybe finish our lunch afterward. So as soon as Becky got back with the bucket, which was only about half full, we sat down on the blanket. Mrs. Parrish said a blessing and then took to serving us out of the basket.

Something about eating outdoors made everything taste wonderful. It wasn't like eating on the dusty trail like we had hundreds of times in the last months. This was an official picnic, with a blanket and everything. I wish Ma could have been with us. She would have liked Mrs. Parrish.

By the time I'd finished my apple, the urge to wander and run about had disappeared. The warm sun felt so good on my face, and the fragrant earth, still moist and warming up from the sun, was sending out so many delicious, grassy smells that I thought this must be what heaven was like. Maybe Ma was up there right now, having a picnic of her own and watching us with a smile on her face.

Ma was on my mind a lot. Sometimes I'd come to myself and realize I'd been thinking a long while about something she'd said or something we'd done together. That happened on this day as we sat there and I was looking around at the woods and grass and trees and blue sky and clouds. Ma wasn't really one to talk about God all that much, not like Mrs. Parrish did. But every once in a while something would kinda burst right out of her, and now that she was gone, every once in a while I'd remember something like that she said.

It was so quiet and peaceful sitting there, I recalled a time Ma and I were out walking alone together back home. It was a day just like this one—warm, with nice smells, the grass springy under our feet. It was just the two of us, and Ma had her arm around me, and we weren't really saying much.

Then all at once Ma exclaimed, "It's a beautiful place, airn't it, Corrie—this world God made!"

"It sure is, Ma," I said.

"An' don't you ever forget, Corrie, that God's your father too. And you don't need to worry none about not havin' an earthly pa. 'Cause God'll watch over you all the better for that."

"Yes, Ma," I said, though it's only now, with her gone, that I'm starting to realize what she meant.

"This great big beautiful place, it's your Father's world, Corrie, and you're *His* daughter too, not just mine. And this world's your home wherever you go in it. Always remember that, Corrie, 'cause you won't always have me."

Her words hardly stuck in my mind then, but they turned out to happen sooner than she figured. And now as we sat there with Mrs. Parrish it all came back clear as if it'd happened yesterday. And I looked around again and thought about what Ma'd said, *"It's your Father's world, Corrie, and you're His daughter . . ."* And the memory made me feel a little more at home in this strange place, just like Ma said I should.

I suppose the others were thinking thoughts of their own too, 'cause we all just kept lying there relaxed and cozy in the sun, listening to Mrs. Parrish tell us so many interesting things. She told us what it had been like right after the gold rush broke out, and we were full of questions. It's a wonder she didn't get sick of us! After a while, I saw even Zack starting to warm up to her and smile a time or two. She and Captain Dixon were like a ma and pa to us for a spell, at a time when we really needed them. I'll never forget what they did for us. People can be mean and selfish, I don't doubt. But then people can be nice sometimes, too, and when they are, it sure makes the world a better place. I just hope when I grow up, I can be that way to somebody who needs it— kind and understanding like Mrs. Parrish was to us.

She must have answered a thousand questions, then gradually we began asking about her. She and her husband got here early in 1849, almost with the first group of im- migrants from the East. She said her husband had been having itchy feet for a new adventure for some time, and that the minute news of the gold strike broke in the East he was talking about the opportunities to be had.

"Why, I was practically packing up our things the next week!" she said with a laugh. "I knew from the very start that he'd have to go. It was in his blood from the first in- stant," she added, and a faraway look came into her eyes, as if she was having to fight away some tears that the memory brought. I knew the feeling, because I had it almost every night when I was alone and awake after the young'uns were asleep. I'd think of Ma, and it would come over me again that she was really gone and wasn't ever coming back. I knew the kind of pain Mrs. Parrish felt and so I asked no more questions about her husband.

"Men are that way, you know," she said after a little pause, looking at Zack and Tad with a different kind of smile. "Sometimes there are things they just have to do, and there's no use trying to stop them. Conquering something new . . . bold . . . adventurous—it's part of the way God made men."

She took a deep breath, and glanced away, probably trying to push back the memory, and then looked back with a fresh smile on her face, just as Tad asked:

"Did you and your pa come on a wagon too, Miz Parrish?"

She laughed. "No, honey, we came in a ship around Cape Horn. But I came with my husband, not my pa. Do you know where Cape Horn is?"

Tad shook his head. I didn't know exactly where it was either, but Ma always said it was a way only the rich could afford.

"Cape Horn is at the very bottom of South America," Mrs. Parrish went on. "We got on a ship in New York and sailed all the way down the coast of the United States, through the Caribbean, down past Brazil and Argentina and the rest of South America, around the Cape, and then up the other side, past Peru and Panama, then Mexico, and finally here to California and San Francisco."

"Wow!" exclaimed Tad. "That musta taken years!"

She laughed pleasantly again. "No, Tad, but several months."

Mrs. Parrish never said much about her life in Boston, but she must have been rich. The only thing she said was that she was one of only a handful of women in California in 1849, and that she had to forget her genteel Boston ways mighty quickly.

"Mining was hard work back then," she said. "It still is, of course, but methods were so primitive at first. That's why we wanted to bring in newer and better equipment for the men to use."

"Did you mine for gold, Mrs. Parrish?" asked Emily.

"I didn't much myself," she answered, "though I tried my hand at the pan a few times and helped my husband with the sluice box. We were mostly here to set up the business, but Mr. Parrish couldn't keep from trying his hand at anything that struck his fancy. We made a pretty good strike, too, that first spring after we were here. But then he came down with tuberculosis the next winter and couldn't keep up with the work. That's when we decided to get into the freight business to go along with selling supplies. 'If we can't get it out of the ground, Almeda,' I remember him saying to me, 'then we'll haul it over the ground for those that do. We'll sell them the equipment to mine with, let them do all the hard work, then transport it once they're done. It's an ingenious scheme!' And it was, too. I've made a good living these three years. I'm only sorry my husband couldn't have lived to see his scheme, as he called it, materialize.''

Again that faraway look came over her face, and she looked away.

After a few more questions we started talking about the town. She told us that two years ago Miracle had a population of over two thousand.

"It was mostly men, and almost every one of them a miner with a dream of getting rich in a month or two. Most of them didn't live right in town, of course, but on their claims in the surrounding foothills, in shacks and cabins and whatever they could throw together. They weren't concerned with their living quarters, only their search for gold. But after a winter or two, with most of the men working eighteen- and twenty-hour days, and not finding the riches they dreamed of, a good many left. There's probably only a thousand or so left around Miracle now. There's still gold here, and the town's still one of the active ones in the foothills, but only a few really find much.''

We'd been so absorbed in everything Mrs. Parrish was saying that we didn't even notice when Becky wandered away. Mrs. Parrish had been telling of a fellow who had come from the East with a box of "California Gold Grease," expecting to rub it all over his body and roll down a golden hill while a fortune stuck to his skin. Zack laughed and was about to tell Becky, who was always getting into a pile of dirt, that that kind of gold mining would suit her, when we suddenly realized she wasn't there.

We looked around nearby, but she was nowhere in sight and none of us had any idea when she'd slipped away. Usually Becky's presence was plainly noticed by everyone. But I recalled Ma saying more than once that when Becky got quiet, trouble was brewing. We called and yelled, but all our shrieks brought no response.

Mrs. Parrish told me to stay with Tad and Emily while she and Zack went to go search in the woods. The little clearing, surrounded by trees and that wonderful stream, had seemed so inviting an hour earlier. Now all of a sudden it appeared dim and dangerous. This country was not like the little wood at the edge of our farm near Bridgeville. This was the frontier, the wild West, vast and unexplored.

Then my mind started thinking about Indians. The Indians around here were supposed to be friendly, but my imagination immediately conjured up images of the Sioux, Comanche and Apache we'd heard so many awful stories about coming across the plains.

But I wasn't as worried about Indians as I was about cliffs and gulleys and rock slides and deep pools in the streams. Becky might get herself into any kind of danger, even as tough and brave as she was, in this rough, foothills country.

In the distance, the calls of my brother and Mrs. Parrish floated through the air unanswered. Growing afraid, sensitive Emily wrapped her arms tight around me and Tad snuggled close.

About half an hour passed, and Zack and Mrs. Parrish's beckoning voices grew dimmer and dimmer as they went farther from the clearing. I wanted to get up and go help them, but I knew I had to stay with the youngsters. Just when I thought I could stand the uncertainty no longer, off in the distance I saw a man on a horse approaching.

I hardly had time to know whether to be glad or afraid, because when the rider got a little closer, I saw that it was none other than Uncle Nick's partner, Mr. Drum.

He rode into the clearing, sitting proud in the saddle, so sure of himself.

"What's going on here?" he asked in a gruff tone that made me tremble a little inside.

"We came for a picnic with Mrs. Parrish," I answered timidly, just staring up at him. He looked about ten feet tall from where the three of us still sat on the ground. "But Becky's gone and got lost."

"A picnic . . . in these parts?" he half-exclaimed, shaking his head grimly. "Blasted woman! Where are they lookin'?"

I pointed to where I had last seen Zack and Mrs. Parrish. Without another word, he wheeled his bay mare off in the opposite direction. I couldn't tell from the look of annoyance on his face if he was going to join the search or was fed up with the lot of us and had taken off again—this time for good.

More time passed. Pretty soon, as the quiet around us seemed to get deeper and more eerie, I started to think maybe Zack and Mrs. Parrish had gotten lost, too. I had no such worry about Mr. Drum. Finally Zack came trudging out of the brush all covered with dirt, followed in another minute or two by Mrs. Parrish, who looked especially dismal. She knew better than any of us what getting lost in this country could mean.

I told them Mr. Drum had come, but neither of them seemed too excited. Maybe they had no hope he would take up the search. But I tried to keep faith. And when I saw the bay mare nose its way through the bushes, I couldn't help grinning real big. There was Becky perched up on the saddle in front of Mr. Drum, his strong arm around her chubby frame.

"This who you're lookin' for?" he said, reining in his

horse. He then lifted Becky out of the saddle as if she weighed no more than a feather and set her down. He was looking very stern, his mood made all the worse by the delighted look on Becky's face. She didn't seem the least remorseful for all the stir she had caused.

"We were at our wits' end, Mr. Drum," said Mrs. Parrish in a more helpless tone than I had yet heard from her. "It is providential that you came by when you did."

"Providential's what you call it, is it?" he replied in a tone full of meaning that went far beyond my years.

Mrs. Parrish just looked at him and wrinkled her brow, as if she didn't have any notion of what he was talking about. "What do you mean?"

"You're sayin' it's just pure coincidence that you came up this way?"

"I assure you, we were just out for a picnic."

"And you didn't know me and Nick's claim was up here?"

"I have no idea where your claim is."

"Is that so, Mrs. Parrish?" he said suspiciously. "Why, I'm real surprised that a woman of your moral and religious reputation would stoop to lies, especially in front of children."

He might have been riled, but I also thought maybe he enjoyed putting Mrs. Parrish on the spot. The two of them didn't seem to like each other much.

She looked down at the ground, pink flushing her cheeks. I couldn't tell at first if she was angry, and about to shout something back at Mr. Drum about his nerve at making such an accusation, or if maybe she was embarrassed at what he'd said. I guess I would never really know. At least she didn't yell at him.

"Well," she said after a moment, "I don't know *exactly* where your claim is."

He continued to nod skeptically.

"And even if perhaps I did hope to encounter you or that missing partner of yours," she added, the heat rising in her voice, "it was a precious small hope that I would discover any help for these poor children from that quarter!"

Mr. Drum opened his mouth to reply—a response which was bound not to be too nice, because what she said made him mad. But before he could, their conversation was interrupted by Tad's voice.

"Did Uncle Nick come home yet?" he asked, "Are you here to take us to his house?" It was an awfully bold question from such a high-pitched voice. I wish I could have taken it back for him.

"Now look, I ain't—" Mr. Drum began. Then he stopped and got down off his horse. Slowly he walked toward Tad, then knelt down beside him on one knee. Tad's eyes were huge as he watched the man approach.

"Look, boy," he said softly. "I'm doing everything I can to find your uncle. I rode clean out to Soda Springs yesterday, but he wasn't there. Tomorrow, I'm going to get up before sunrise and ride down to Gold Run, Yankee Jim's, Coloma, Shingle Springs, and Placerville. And if I still ain't found him, I may go out to Grizzly Flats. Them's all places he sometimes gets a hankering to see. But until I can find him, there just ain't much more—"

Mrs. Parrish's voice interrupted him before he could go any further. "I have to leave morning after next myself," she said, first to him and then with an apologetic glance at me. "I was trying to find the right time to tell you."

She paused, then looked back at Mr. Drum. "These children need a guardian, Mr. Drum. Today's near mishap is further evidence of that."

He rose and walked back toward his horse.

"Wouldn't have happened at all if you hadn't got the fool idea of bringing them out into this wilderness!" he retorted.

"Be that as it may, the fact remains that in another place, in New York where they came from, they might possibly have been able to fend for themselves. But such cannot be expected of them in this land. And I'm afraid their claim to an interest in the stake you and your partner, their uncle,

74

share, binds their fate inextricably to yours—whether you find Mr. Matthews or not."

"You just don't understand, Mrs. Parrish." He was not arguing now. In fact his voice sounded almost contrite, pleading. The large, tough-looking man seemed to be struggling with some feeling inside which he wanted to keep from showing anyone.

"I do not know you well, Mr. Drum," said Mrs. Parrish. "You have been an enigma in these parts ever since you and Matthews came, so folks tell me. But one fact has always come through as part of what people say about you—your reputation, as I believe men call it. And that fact is that you are a man of honor. I simply cannot believe that you would be so derelict in your duty as not to step in if their uncle cannot be found. These children must not be left unprotected."

"It won't do them no good to have a man—especially one like me—carin' for them."

"I disagree," said Mrs. Parrish firmly. "In this country, I might even go so far as to say they need the care of a man *more* than a woman."

"I'm sorry, Ma'am, I just don't see it your way. They need a ma right now, and since they ain't got one—" His voice seemed to quiver momentarily. "Then I figure they need a woman, and you seem to be *it*. If you ask me, Ma'am, it's you who's hidin' from your duty to the kids. And besides, like I said before, you don't understand nothin' about me, and I'll thank you to keep your nose outta tryin'."

He turned and swiftly mounted his horse, and that was the end of their talk. I almost felt like the man was hiding something, and that if he kept talking one minute more he might . . . but that's plumb silly! Grown-ups, tough men like him, don't cry.

He glanced around at each one of us kids, with a look that said he hoped we might understand, even if she didn't, then dug his heels into the bay's flanks and was off.

# CHAPTER 9

## A SURPRISE FOR US ALL

Two days after the picnic, we got more than one surprise. The first came when Mrs. Parrish called us for breakfast.

I honestly couldn't tell if she was the same lady—except for her feminine figure, I might have even thought she was a man. She had on well-worn buckskin breeches, and a tan leather jacket with long fringe on the bottom and sleeves. On her feet she wore a pair of high leather boots. And when breakfast was over, she grabbed a dusty, wide-brimmed hat, a pair of heavy gloves, and led us outside.

We walked with her down to the freight office, and waited while she brought one of the empty wagons around. She had already gone over everything with us at her house, what we were to do while she was gone. Now we just waited to say goodbye.

When she came around the corner of the building, driving that team of mules with the reins in her hands, something inside me swelled up—pleasure, maybe, at something so rugged and western. Maybe it was just that she was a woman, like I might be someday. I don't know. But it made me feel proud to see her perched up there on the seat of that wagon, calling out orders to them mules and swinging them into line, looking just as natural as she did behind one of her fine Chippendale tables or at her desk in the freight office. She was a fine-looking, strong woman, who seemed able to do most anything.

She jumped down off the wagon and gathered us children around her. "You know," she said gently and apologetically, "I wouldn't go today if I didn't have to. But this is the last big supply run before winter sets in, and I must take all three wagons." She was back to talking in her soft Boston voice, and coming from a buckskin-dressed woman, looking fit for riding on the range, it did seem a mite unusual.

"I will be gone at least two weeks, maybe more. But as I said, I want you to make yourselves at home in my house. Mrs. Gianini will look in on you from time to time. I wish I didn't have to leave you, but—"

Before she could finish her sentence, the sound of approaching hoofbeats made us all abruptly turn our heads. Mr. Drum, on his bay mare, half-skidded to a stop right there in front of the freight office, followed by a big cloud of dust from the street.

He jumped off his horse and strode up to us. He looked around quickly, then stared right at me for a second. His eyes seemed to be swimming in tears. As I returned his gaze, suddenly something inside my brain seemed to dawn, and all at once I realized I *knew* those eyes staring at mine! In an instant, all the funny little questions that had been nagging me the last couple of days started to fit together. At the same time, I told myself it couldn't possibly be!

There wasn't time to reflect on it, however. Just as quickly, he looked away from me, placed his hands on his hips, and spoke in a voice that was resolved, even if he had difficulty saying what he intended.

"I've come for the kids," he said.

"Did you find Uncle Nick?" asked Tad excitedly, having no idea what was happening.

"No, boy, I didn't find your uncle," he replied. "But I don't figure that matters none now."

"What do you mean, Mr. Drum?" asked Mrs. Parrish, surprised as any of us.

"Just that, Ma'am," he said. "You see . . . my name ain't Drum—well, not exactly, that is."

"I'm afraid I don't understand," she answered. "Nor do I see what this has to do with the children."

"Perhaps if I could just have a word in private with you, Ma'am," he said.

She nodded, saying nothing, and he followed her into the office. The four younger children watched with bewildered eyes. But I knew what he was telling her. I should have known from the first. My heart was beating wildly now!

When they came back a minute or two later, Mrs. Parrish had a handkerchief in her hand, which she used to dab at her eyes every so often. She was the first one to speak.

"I have some very wonderful news to tell you all," she began. Her voice was soft and husky. Then she turned to Drum and said, "But I think you should be the one to tell them your real name."

The man stepped forward, cleared his throat awkwardly, then stumbling over the words, began, "You see, kids, when I came here, I was in a heap of trouble, like your uncle is now. So I didn't want folks to know who I really was. I changed my name a little, and let the rumor get out that I was dead, so the men looking for me would stop trying to hunt me down. But like I told Mrs. Parrish, Drum's not my name—well, not my last name, anyway. More like a nick-name, you might say, which I let folks *think* was my last name. Really it's my first name—Drummond. . . ."

Even before the word was out of his mouth I found myself moving toward him, tears blurring my eyes. I reached his side and slowly put my arm around his great big waist, hardly hearing the rest of what he said to the other kids.

"Drummond, that's my name . . . Drummond Hollister. You see, kids, I'm your pa, and I ain't dead at all."

# CHAPTER 10

## ANOTHER WAGON RIDE

The ride out to the claim was almost eerily quiet. Nobody said a word till we were over halfway there, and Pa seemed content to let it be that way, looking straight ahead and holding the reins in his hands.

He and Marcus Weber had hitched up Snowball and Jinx to our wagon, and before we knew it we were sitting there again, as we had for most of the last six months, riding out of Miracle Springs with none other than our own pa sitting on the bench driving, his bay mare following along behind. It was sure some sudden change.

I knew Becky, Emily, and Tad were probably more bewildered than anything. They'd all been too young even to remember Pa. After all, he left even before Tad was born. But I figured Zack remembered him. He'd have been around four or five, and I knew his silence wasn't just from the bewilderment of the sudden turn of events. Even though Ma had never bad-mouthed Pa, the harshness of her life—all our lives—after he left spoke for itself. Zack and I were old enough to feel hurt and even angry sometimes.

It didn't help that Grandpa Belle never had a good word to say about Pa, and even at times seemed to go out of his way to speak ill of Pa in our hearing. Zack thought a lot of Grandpa—a boy needs a man around, and Grandpa was all Zack had. So I had a feeling some of Grandpa's words were going around in Zack's mind. I could tell he was struggling with just how he was supposed to feel about this man who was his pa, but who had left him when he needed him most, like Grandpa used to tell him. Maybe some of the same things were going through Pa's mind too.

As for me, now that we were all there in the wagon together and I had a chance to think, I could hardly believe I didn't recognize Pa right away. The beard changed his looks considerably, of course, and the hat. But you'd have thought I'd have known the eyes and voice right off.

Funny, though, how the mind plays tricks on you. Maybe some part of me, way deep down inside someplace, *did* remember the voice. And I noticed his eyes the first time he walked out of that saloon. But another part of the mind can block out the memory altogether. The feeling of pain comes back, the hurt of the loss, and wipes out the memory. "It's God's mercy you kids is young," Ma used to say, "You'll forget your pa soon enough, and his being gone will be easier on you."

But Ma never could forget Pa, and I don't doubt her pain was awful. She hardly ever said anything against Pa and even tried to hush Grandpa when he'd get started. There were times when she did flare up about Pa though, like when Tad was a baby—colicky and crying, and chores needed to be done, and us older kids were bickering or whining over some little thing. Or when some snooty neighbor would make some careless remark about us being abandoned. Then she'd come close to blaming him for everything, but I think it was just her way of hiding the shame and hurt she felt at being left alone. With all that, I know she never stopped loving him. Her words on the day she died seemed to prove that, though I guess I never heard her say it too often.

We all sat there quietly, bouncing along the dirt road, Pa encouraging the horses along every now and then with a slap of the reins. Zack and I sat on each side of him, staring straight ahead, and the three little ones dozed in the bed of the wagon. Here we were—orphaned less than two months ago, left alone on the streets of Miracle Springs with no one wanting to take us in, handed around from one place and one person to the next—from Captain Dixon to Miss Baxter, to Mrs. Gianini, to Mrs. Parrish, and now all of a sudden here we were sitting in our *own* wagon again with our very own pa! You'd have thought we'd have all been shouting and laughing with joy. But we all sat silent and somber. I guess it didn't feel so much different than if he had been a stranger sitting there. There would probably have been more talking if it *had* been Captain Dixon. We certainly knew him better than this strange man called Drummond Hollister. All we knew about him was what Ma had told us—which was very little—and what Grandpa Belle had said, which was more than we wanted to hear.

"I'm real sorry about your ma," Pa said, breaking the silence abruptly.

An awkward moment or two followed. No one said anything.

"How'd it happen?" he asked, still staring out over the horses' heads.

"Fever," I said, "out in the desert."

"She broke her ankle, Mr. Drum," piped up Becky from behind.

He started to answer her, thought better of it, and kept it in. I didn't know whether to correct her or not, but I kept quiet too. Zack was stone-faced. He didn't seem to like Pa at all.

We rode on for another ten minutes or so. Then all at once, without even planning it, I heard my own voice: "Why didn't you tell us who you were right off, sir?" I blurted out. "Why'd you say you didn't want us?"

The words sounded bold in my own ears. Probably the way they really came out was soft and sheepish. And even though Pa just kept staring straight ahead, I could tell he'd heard me and was thinking hard.

"Well . . . Cornelia," he hesitated at my name. I think it was uncomfortable for him to say it for the first time, but I liked hearing him say it.

" . . . is that still what they call you?" he asked after a pause.

"Folks started calling me Corrie, sir," I answered. "I guess it was after you . . . left."

I thought I saw Pa wince, but with the beard it was hard to tell.

"Well . . . Corrie," he said, "when Dixon came into the Gold Nugget sayin' something about a bunch of kids looking for a fellow named Matthews, I didn't pay much heed. For all I knew, he mighta been one of the sheriff's men tryin' to get an angle on Nick. An the game was mighty hot, so the boys shut him up real quick. But then that Parrish woman barged in like she did, upsettin' everything, and insistin' I come out and do something about them—you kids, that is, . . . well, it kinda caught me off guard."

He stopped and a questioning look came over his face.

"How'd your ma ever find out about Nick?" he asked.

"A fellow from Bridgeville came back from California and told her he'd seen Uncle Nick and that he was using a different name."

Pa shook his head. "Nick never said nothin' to me—the blamed fool! He's determined to get the both of us strung up yet!"

"But," I said—maybe I was being forward, but I still had my questions—"after you came out and saw it was us, why didn't you say anything right then?"

" 'Cause it was a shock to see you standin' there," he said matter-of-factly. "And besides, hearin' about your ma's dying, just then—well, it sort of—"

He stopped again.

"You must know what I mean," he half-blurted out after a moment. "She was my wife, you know . . . mother to my kids. It weren't none too pleasant to hear out of the blue that she was dead."

I couldn't help wondering why it took him all this time to start having feelings of affection for Ma and the rest of us. It didn't seem to me that he'd have cared one way or the other about her dying. Maybe I was being too hard on him. But maybe I had more hurt in me than I realized, too. I couldn't see how Ma could have been so forgiving of him. It just didn't make much sense to me what he was saying.

"You still could have told us who you were," I said.

"It just ain't that simple," he said. "I had lots of things on my mind."

"Things more important than us?"

"Things kids can't understand. I had to have some time to think."

"But we had no place to go, and you said you wouldn't take us!" I was afraid I was going to start crying any minute. I should have stopped, and I knew he had every right to box me if I went on, but I just couldn't stop the words from pouring out. As I remembered all he'd said outside the saloon just three days ago, I felt more and more hurt by what he'd done.

"I know . . . and I'm sorry about that," he said, his voice *sounding* earnest enough. "But I had to try to find Nick and see what he knew about all this; I had to look out for him— the blasted idiot! Don't you see? I had to talk to him before I could say anythin' out in public."

I guess I *didn't* see, but I kept my mouth shut. Even though part of me was wanting to break out and give Pa a bunch of hugs and kisses, another part of me—maybe the part of Grandpa in me—was riled and hurt. And I just couldn't get the two parts to agree on what to do.

"The men were all listenin' . . . and they all think I'm Drum. And I gotta keep it that way! For your good as well as my own . . . and Nick's."

"Did you find Uncle Nick?" I asked softly, after another minute.

Pa sighed. "No, he ain't nowhere anybody's seen him,"

he said. "On top of everything, now he's gone and got himself in trouble with the sheriff *here*, as if we didn't have trouble enough already! And now with the five of you showin' up outta nowhere, and with someone back East who can identify him . . . I don't know what we're gonna do. He may have brung us a pack of trouble!"

He gave the reins a little flick of his wrist and coaxed the horses over a patch of bumpy ground.

I decided it was best for me to keep my thoughts to myself for a while. For the life of me I couldn't figure why any of what he said made it right for him to ignore us, and not let on he was our pa. I didn't see how it made it right for him to leave Ma and us alone all those years either, or to let us think he was dead.

The clicking of his tongue, the groaning sounds of leather and wood, and the jostling wagon wheels filled in the silence. We certainly weren't off to the joyful kind of start you'd expect from such a family reunion. Ma had been our family, and with her gone we really didn't have one anymore. Pa had never really been part of our family. When he left, he cut himself off from us. Whatever that meant to us kids, it hurt Ma real bad. And I didn't see how we were going to be able to forget it that easily. He may have been our pa, but that still didn't make him part of our family.

I guess Zack must have been thinking some similar sorts of things, 'cause all at once he blurted out, and didn't even try to hide the resentment in his voice: "You still ain't told us why you deserted us and left me with no pa!"

I could see Pa's eyes wince at Zack's blunt question—I couldn't tell whether from exasperation or real pain. He drew in a deep breath, resignation building on his face, and then, without turning his head, replied, "You don't understand how it was at all, boy," he said. "There just ain't no way you can understand!"

He picked up the whip and flipped it. The leather thong at the end of the line gave a sharp crack as it slapped against Snowball's rump. The horse jumped into a trot.

# CHAPTER 11

# OUR NEW HOME

Pa and Uncle Nick had a cabin on their claim, less than a mile from the clearing where Becky had gotten herself lost. Once we got there, I could see why Pa had gotten so vexed with Mrs. Parrish. I wondered if it *was* an accident we'd had our picnic right there.

The cabin was small and dirty. If Ma had seen it, not knowing it was Pa's, she'd have either called it rustic or just a shack—depending on what kind of mood she was in. I didn't want to say anything negative right away, but after spending two days at Mrs. Parrish's, I suppose our faces showed our disappointment once we were all crowded inside.

"It ain't much, I admit," said Pa. "But Nick and I didn't build it with five kids in mind. I'll add a room on in the mornin'," he said matter-of-factly, like it was nothing.

At least it sounded hopeful. In fact, he decided that since it was still early in the day, he'd go right out and start cutting some timber. He told me to bring our stuff inside and take care of the young'uns, and then turned to Zack. "Let's go . . . Zachary."

Zack glanced toward me, and I nodded for him to go along.

"You got a nickname like your sister, boy? What do folks in a hurry call you?"

"Just Zack, sir."

"That's always what I figured to call you when you got bigger. Well, Zack, you're pretty big now, I reckon, so you grab that axe there and come with me."

Zack had been completely quiet since his outburst on the wagon. I'm not sure if Pa was trying to be nice by taking him. But at his age, there was nothing Zack wanted more than to be treated like a man. So even though I could still see the silent anger on his face, I knew he was pleased.

"You keep them young'uns outta the creek and away from the mine," he sternly admonished me, and then he tramped off into the woods, with Zack hurrying to keep up.

Emily and I, with a little help from Becky and none at all from Tad, spent the day cleaning and trying to make a place where the five of us could sleep. We had our sleeping gear out in the wagon, but finding a place to bed down, especially as disorderly as everything was, became a chore. I'd never seen a place so in need of cleaning as that one-room cabin!

By sundown we had the house as close to shining as a bare-wood cabin can get, with a pot of beans bubbling over the open fire in a big black pot. I even got a tablecloth from Ma's things to put on the coarse board table set in the middle of the floor. Becky completed the look of civilization with a bowl of wild flowers. I'd been so busy I didn't see her slip away. I didn't ask how far she'd gone or where she'd gotten them. But at least she hadn't gotten lost this time. I gave her a big hug and smiled at her. I could tell the flowers were her way of trying to make Pa glad we were there. All of us were a little scared I think, still not knowing if Pa was going to be mean or nice to us. All we really knew of him was what Ma had said, but we couldn't help wanting to make him like us.

When Pa walked through the door, I tried to read the reaction on his face. I had already begun to figure out that he wasn't likely to say what he felt in so many words.

He glanced at the flowers, turned toward the fireplace to smell the beans, then set his gaze on me.

"What have you gone and done with my place?" he said, his voice sounding gruff. Then I caught the faint spark of fun in his eyes. When I didn't respond, a smile broke on his lips—just a tiny one. "Why, I'd grown right attached to all the dirt and clutter around here!"

"I hoped it would be all right if we cleaned up some," I answered finally, swelling with pride inside. Somehow I could tell he was pleased.

"Guess I'll have to learn to live with it," he answered, the smile gone now.

Zack followed him in, then Pa set his rifle in a corner and unbuckled his gun belt. It was the first time I'd noticed that he wore a gun. He slung the holster on a hook by the door, then strode over toward the fire, took a closer look at the beans, and nodded in approval.

"Looks like your ma made a right good cook outta you, too," he said. " 'Course I guess you been doing the mothering yourself since . . . Aggie died."

I nodded. I'd never heard anyone call Ma that before.

"Let's see, Corrie you'd be what—hmmm . . . fourteen? No, fifteen?"

"Fifteen," I said.

"I ain't likely to forget that winter of '37. Coldest dang January I can ever remember, and your ma swellin' up real big carryin' you. I cut up more logs that month to feed that fire and keep her warm. . . . No, I ain't likely to forget that!"

We all stood there kind of aimless and awkward, wondering what to do.

"Well," said Pa finally, breaking the silence, "what about supper?"

He helped us get everything on the table. We had to go out to the wagon for some bowls and utensils, because I hadn't gotten everything unloaded. Then we all sat down to eat. Pa didn't say a prayer, he just started eating. So we all did the same. No one said much. We just ate quietly, staring into our bowls of beans and munching at my attempt at cornbread. It wasn't too good. I'd have to get used to cooking over Pa and Uncle Nick's fireplace.

We were about halfway through our meal, when all of a sudden Pa noticed the tablecloth. He put down his spoon deliberately, and took the edge of the white linen between his fingers, rubbing it gently. Then he spoke—his voice sounded soft and faraway—"The minister's wife back in Bridgeville gave this to your ma the day we was married. It was always real special to her 'cause it was nicer than anything we could ever afford."

We just listened in silence. It was hard to know what to say at times like that. One minute Pa would seem real friendly, then the next he'd get that gruff look again that seemed to say, "Get outta my way!" It was going to be a while before I knew how to respond to either of his two sides.

When we were done with the meal, I took the two girls with me outside to wash up the dishes. There was no water pump, only a crude table with a couple of buckets on top of it, filled with water from the creek.

When we went back inside, Pa was sitting on a stool oiling and cleaning his gun. There weren't any chairs, only two stools and the bench we kids had sat on while we ate. Tad was sitting in a corner silently watching Pa. Zack busied himself poking at the fire, and then finally laid on another log. We three girls just sat on the bench and folded our hands in our laps.

We were all tired, and would have liked to have gone to bed, but I didn't want to say anything. We were all going to have to sleep in that one room together.

Tad finally got up, walked over to Pa, and as bold as you please said, "I have to go to the outhouse."

Pa looked up with a blank expression, then glanced from me to Zack.

"We have an outhouse back home," said Zack.

"Guess I'll have to build that tomorrow too," Pa muttered. "Well, Zack, take your brother out to the woods."

"I'm big enough to go by myself," Tad insisted. But when he opened the door and stared out into the night, he hesitated.

"You afraid of the dark, boy?" asked Pa, a bit roughly.

"No . . . sir," stammered Tad. "I ain't afraid of nothin'."

"Well boy, you'd better learn a thing or two about California," said Pa. "Why there's wolves out there, and bears, and . . ." He winked in my direction, but Tad didn't catch the humor.

"Really?" Tad whispered seriously.

"Yep. Didn't your ma tell you? We Californians gotta be tough."

Tad cleared his throat nervously, "Could *you* take me out?" he asked.

Pa's expression changed. This was not what he expected. No doubt he would have preferred taking his rifle and going outside to face one of his imaginary bears. But with resolve, at last he laid down the gun he had been cleaning, got to his feet, and, glancing around kind of helplessly, headed for the door.

When they returned about five minutes later, Pa's only words were, "It's time to be bedding down."

I think he'd had enough of his kids for one day.

# CHAPTER 12

# THE FIRST FEW DAYS
# TOGETHER

After that first awkward day, we were kept too busy to worry much about how strange we felt about everything. We tried to get the place livable, and Pa kept talking about winter coming on and all we had to do.

Some men came from town on the third day, and helped with the building of the extra room. It wasn't very big, but it fit us kids fine. There were five beds—two bunks, one for the girls, one for the boys, and a single bed for me. We each had our own place to sleep, and we hadn't even had that back home.

Pa built a bigger supper table, too, with sturdy benches on both sides. After being cooped up in a covered wagon for so long, all these changes were heaven to us. Pa kept muttering little comments about "making do till winter's past" and that he'd "have to see about things when Nick gets back." As much as I didn't want to think so, it almost sounded like he was planning on our being there only temporarily, until he could find some reasonable way to send us back home. But then it did seem that he was going to an awful lot of trouble just to put up with us for a few months. I had to try to be happy for the present and not think too much about the disappointments that might come later.

On the fourth day, Pa took the canvas canopy off our

wagon, and took it into town for supplies.

"Bye, Snowball," Emily called out after him as he disappeared down the road; then she and I turned back toward the cabin to join the others. It was a strange moment, but pleasant in a homey way, walking up to a cabin we'd laid eyes on only a few days before, all alone now, with our Pa trusting us to stay by ourselves.

Late that same afternoon he returned with that big wagon loaded down. We ran out to meet him rumbling up the road, and when he stopped, Zack and Becky clambered up into the wagon. There were straw mattresses for all the beds, and lots of extra blankets. We had been sleeping on the rough, cold boards with our ragged, moth-eaten blankets from the trip west.

But that wasn't all! Besides the bedding, he had dishes and some pots and pans. The equipment I had been using from the wagon was old, charred, and broken. To my delight, there was also a small pot-bellied stove and two new chairs! It was just like Christmas unloading all the new things! All the while Pa kept a gruff look on his face, and kept saying things like, "Now you be careful with that!"

But even with those new chairs and benches, new beds and dishes and all that stuff, it seemed to me that there was something missing. When I closed my eyes, I could still see us as a family back home. But Ma was in the picture in my mind, instead of Pa. Maybe she was sitting by the fire sewing, or reading a book to us, or maybe we were all singing hymns together. Sometimes we didn't even say much, just sitting there listening to Ma's rocker creak back and forth, or lying in bed hearing her humming softly to herself until we fell asleep.

But when I opened my eyes, everything was strange and new. Ma wasn't there, and Pa sat fixing a harness, sharpening a tool, or cutting a piece of leather for something. Everything was quiet. There was no singing, no humming. Just quiet. I was pleased with what Pa had done, but there's something about a ma that can't be replaced by any man, even your own pa. And it seemed as we sat around in the cabin that we just weren't a real family, even with all the homey new things Pa had brought back from town.

Besides all the stuff that was in the wagon, Pa brought with him the old prospector we'd met at the General Store, Alkali Jones. He helped Pa and Zack and me unload. For such an old man he was strong enough, but I guessed from the look of him that he was tough. Tough like an old buzzard. And his voice did nothing to make the similarity in my mind go away.

He was a peculiar fellow. An ornery old cuss, folks called him. After a while I got kind of used to the creak of his voice and that cackling laugh. I had plenty of practice. Everything seemed to amuse him.

After the wagon was unloaded, the girls and I busied ourselves getting dinner. In the several days we'd been there, Pa'd never given us many chores or jobs. Every once in a while he'd tell Zack to bring in some firewood, and the night before he said, "Best be getting some dinner started for the young'uns, Cornelia." I guess he was so used to living alone that he figured we'd all know what to do. He never seemed to realize that except for me and Zack, the kids were young and needed a lot of tending. I guess he figured I'd do all that, too. I had done it, after all, since Ma died.

Tad traipsed along with Zack to cut up some firewood. Pa and Mr. Jones went into our bedroom to finish up the beds, so we could use them that night. I went to fetch some of the new pans that were sitting in a box over on the side of the cabin where they were working, and I overheard Pa and Mr. Jones talking. I knew eavesdropping wasn't proper, but I couldn't help myself. Besides, their voices were so loud that I likely would have heard anyway.

"You make a new strike or somethin', Drum?" asked Mr. Jones.

Pa told us not to call him *Pa* when Mr. Jones or anyone

else was around. When Becky asked why, he just said he'd have to talk to Uncle Nick first to see what they ought to do. I didn't know what Uncle Nick had to do with it, but Pa seemed to have some pretty strong reasons for still wanting folks in town to think he was Mr. Drum. But whatever they were, he wasn't telling us.

"Why you askin'?" said Pa.

"You practically bought out the General Store. Hee, hee! Where'd you get money like that?"

"I got the stuff on credit."

"Why, you'd think them kids was yourn! Hee, hee!"

"What'd you expect?" said Pa, a little too defensively, but Mr. Jones didn't seem to pay any heed. "They're my partner's kin, after all. Couldn't just leave 'em out in the street."

"Well, I figured you ain't got no cash. That game the other night cleaned you out."

"The mine still produces a few ounces a week, if I work it."

Alkali Jones let out with that cackle of his again. "That's the rub, now ain't it? Kids'll take a heap o' *ounces* to bring up, I 'spect."

"Where do you leave off knowin' so blamed much about kids?"

"Don't know nothin', thank the good Lord! But five extra mouths to feed is five extra mouths. An' even that pie-eyed Bosley at the store will be expectin' his money by and by. Hee, hee!"

"I got it all figured out," said Pa confidently. I couldn't tell from his voice whether what came next was part of his Mr. Drum act, pretending to be indifferent toward us, or whether he was confiding his real feelings on the matter to Mr. Jones. "Come spring," Pa went on, "them kids'll be gone. You know Nick, Alkali. Even if he gets himself cleared with the sheriff over this mess with Judd, you don't think he's about to take up as no pa to a passel of kids his sister sent him, do you? Nah, come April, we'll be free men again. But I had to take 'em in 'til then or that Parrish woman might have made things too hot for me. I'll hang on to all this stuff I bought 'til late summer when the new wagon trains arrive, and then I'll sell—at a nice profit, to boot. I'll pay off Bosely and have a little extra for myself!"

Quietly, I grabbed the pans I needed and forced myself away from the door. At that moment, I knew why eavesdropping was wrong—if nothing else, it makes the listener miserable! The part about leaving in the spring didn't bother me as much as all the talk of money, and thinking about Pa having to go into debt because of us. I'd almost forgotten that he wasn't a rich rancher like we'd expected Uncle Nick to be. He must not have had any money at all, and it didn't seem like he had much of a regular income from the mine. And to make it all worse, it sounded as if he was pretty familiar with poker games and gambling tables. I'd been thinking so much about all the changes in my own life that I hadn't stopped to consider what our coming meant for Pa and Uncle Nick.

Right then and there I whispered a little prayer. It might be wrong to listen to someone else's conversation, but maybe it was good I heard this one, because I needed to know these things so I could *do* something about it. I didn't quite know exactly *what* I would do. But I asked God to show me, and I finally got an idea after we were done eating that evening.

We were sitting around the blazing fire listening to Mr. Jones tell story after story about his life in the West. He sure livened up the evenings! I'll never know how much truth there was to his tales, but they were interesting.

"Danged I wish I had my fiddle with me!" he said, turning toward me with a big grin, "But since I don't, let me tell you about a time, Miz Corrie, when I hugged a bear to death."

We were all listening with huge, open eyes.

"Me an' my companions was all sittin' about our campfire eatin' our vittles, when we heard a growl so deep we practically jumped clean outta our boots. We didn't know what that dad-blamed noise was, but I told the other green-horn prospectors, 'Leave it to ol' Alkali here, an' he'll take care of it.'

"So I got up and walked a little deeper into that there box canyon we was camped on the edge of. I was lookin' all 'round and didn't see nuthin', when all of a sudden I turned around and there was a great big brown bear standin' face to face with me."

"Were you scared?" asked little Becky innocently.

"No, Missy! If you think starin' down a bear's hard, why you jest wait 'til I tell you 'bout the time I jumped clean across the lake to get away from the pack o' wolves that was after me! Hee, hee!

"Well, I tell ya, I jest stood there for a minute eyein' that mean ol' cuss of a bear. An' then the story 'bout ol' Davy Crockett came to my mind, so I grinned real big at him, made a leap toward the varmint, an' grabbed him and hugged him hard 'til he couldn't stand it any longer, and he jest dropped to the ground." I saw Pa look at Zack and wink.

Another one of Alkali's stories took place in '48 just after gold had been discovered.

"Me an' a handful o' others was gettin' mighty 'xasper-ated by the pickin's down t' Coloma way," said the old miner when he had us all listening again. "By then, Californians an' Mexicans was pourin' into the mine fields an' things was gettin' mighty close. Hee, hee! If we'd only knowed what was a comin' in the next year! Well anyways, we moved upriver a spell, an' puttered around fer a few days but didn't hit no payload. An' then ol' Charlie Pelham up and got hisself bit by a rattler an' just plumb died. Jest like that! Well, Charlie, he was a good friend so we gave him a right fine funeral. We even had an ex-preacher in our gang, so's it was as official a layin' to rest as you ever wanna see. Now we was all standin' round that open grave, an' preacher

Jones, he was a prayin' his heart out fer the departed soul o' ol' Charlie. But he went on and on with them sentimental notions an' my mind began to wander some. I guess I was starin' down at my boots an' was a diggin' my toe absent-mindedly in the dirt, without even payin' no attention to what I was doin', when suddenly I seen somethin' sparklin'! Prayer or no prayer, I fell down on my knees an' grabbed at the little pebble like thing, an' before I realized what I was sayin' I yelled out, '*Gold!*' Hee, hee!

"Well, I can tell you this, that was the end of that there funeral. I mean, it was plumb over! The preacher, he left off his prayin' pronto, an' we all commenced diggin' quicker than a polecat's spit can hit the ground. Without no disrespect to poor ol' Charlie who missed all the fun, he didn't get right proper covered up fer two days! Hee, hee! Why, I drew two hundred dollars worth o' dust an' nuggets that first day alone, and the others was close on my heels! Turned out to be one of the richest strikes on the American River. We drank to Charlie Pelham that night an' thanked him fer the right nice inheritance he done left us!"

# CHAPTER 13

# MY IDEA

Mr. Jones was a fine spinner of tales, and I right enjoyed them. But on this particular night I could hardly wait till he was finished, 'cause I wanted to get Pa alone and tell him my idea. But even after Alkali finished up and ambled out to the tool shed for the night, I still had to get the young'uns ready for bed.

That seemed to take forever, especially with the excitement over the new beds and all. When everyone had finally settled down, I peeked out the door of our room to see if Pa was still awake.

"What're you doing?" asked Zack.

I closed the door. "I had a mind to say good night to Pa, that's all," I whispered back to him.

"Why? He don't say good night to us."

" 'Cause I want to, that's why. Now quiet, Zack, and go to sleep."

I opened the door again and crept out.

The kerosene lamp was turned down low, but the fire still burned bright and sent out odd-shaped shadows against the walls. Pa was on his knees, bent over the hearth laying on another oak log, and his shadow looked like a giant's.

I cleared my throat shyly, because I still felt a little timid around him. He turned at the sound I made. Maybe it was from the warm reflection of the fire on his face, but all of a sudden he didn't seem quite so terrifying.

"Could I—" I began, then hesitated.

"Somethin' the matter?"

"No, sir. But if it ain't too disturbin', I wanted to talk to you."

He finished with the fire, wiped his hands off on his shirt, and pulled over one of the new chairs.

"You ain't disturbin' me," he said finally. "Come and set yerself down."

I did that, and he sat on the stool just opposite me.

"What's on your mind, girl?" he asked. He sounded like he really wanted to know.

I took a deep breath.

"I done something today that I knew was wrong, and I'm real sorry. But I don't think I'm altogether sorry, 'cause maybe it was something I needed to know—"

"Hold on, child!" he said. "I ain't quite following you. Slow down a mite and tell me what happened."

"Well, sir, I heard you and Mr. Jones talkin' before supper about money. I know it wasn't right of me to listen, but—"

"Don't you think nothing of it."

"Well, to tell you the truth, I never gave it a single thought before then, but we'll be costin' you plenty to take care of."

"I'm sorry you heard that," he replied earnestly. "but it's nothin' for you to worry about."

"But we barged in on you uninvited."

"Don't pay that no mind, Cornelia," he said, a hint of his old brusqueness coming back into his voice. "What's done is done."

"But I want to give you some money. It's only fair we pay our own way."

"Ridiculous!" he said with a wave of his hand. "I'm your pa, and it's my duty to take care of you. Besides, you got less than I do."

"That ain't true," I answered as respectfully as I could. "You see, Ma had some money. She left that to me. And it seems only right that—"

"Don't tell me what's right! Besides, I ain't about to take no money from the kids I ran out on nine years ago."

It was the first mention he'd made of his leaving us. I don't think he meant to say it either, because just hearing himself say it seemed to sober him, and he sat staring into the fire for a long time. Neither of us said a word. We just listened to the fire.

Finally, I ventured to say something more. "In a way, maybe it's really your money after all," I said, "or else Uncle Nick's."

He cocked a bushy eyebrow toward me. "How'd you figure that?" he asked.

"The money came from Grandpa Belle's estate," I answered. "That's how we had money to come here. Ma herself said it was real odd Grandpa never left nothin' to Uncle Nick, and she said that as soon as we got to California she was going to give him his due. I forgot all about it until now, but there's near two hundred dollars put away. And if it ain't your's as Ma's husband, then what about Uncle Nick? I'd feel real pleased if you could find a way to put it to use, for us to pay our way."

The mention of the sum seemed to sober him further, but only for a moment. Then he replied firmly. "And it'll stay put away, too. Nick'd gamble away that money in one night and then it'd be gone. And I ain't none so sure I want it in my hands neither."

"You could pay off your bill at the store," I suggested.

He looked at me, half amused, I think, and half perturbed. "Cornelia," he finally said, "you ain't struck me as an impertinent child 'til now. Don't you know better than to argue with grown-ups? Now, I want you to listen to me good. Your grandpa willed that money to your ma. So it was *hers*. And unless she left something in writin', it's now *yours*, not Nick's. That's the law. He wanted your ma to have it, not Nick, and with good reason, too. And it's God's truth your ma wouldn't have wanted me to have my hands on it! Maybe with just as good a reason."

"But why would Grandpa—or Ma, for that matter—not want their son or brother to have his share?"

"There's plenty neither of them knew about Nick," he answered. "And about as much your Ma *thought* she knew about me, but didn't."

He fell silent for several moments, gazing steadily into the fire. I began to think the conversation was over, when he looked back at me and spoke again.

"You know, I was here in California in '48. Most of the men that were here then are wealthy men today, 'cept them that was still doing nothing but fightin' the Mexicans, or doing what I was doing. I heard someone say once that you had to be either a fool or an idiot not to make a killin' back then. Well, Sutter and Jim Marshall are fools, and I suppose that's why they ain't made a dime off the gold rush. I don't know which I am—probably a fool, too, for getting mixed up in the kind of deals I did, 'cause I don't have nothin' to show for it neither."

He stopped and took a deep breath. I hardly dared make a sound. It was so strange for him to talk like that. As if he'd forgotten I was there. He gave the log in the fire a kick with his boot and then started talking again.

"I remember one week back in '49 when I had ten thousand dollars in dust and nuggets in my saddlebags. It lasted me one trip to San Francisco."

He paused and sighed. "You ever hear the saying, 'Throwin' good money after bad,' Corrie?"

I nodded, but now that I think about it, I'm not so sure I had heard it before. I just nodded without knowing why.

"Well, your Grandpa Belle knew what he was about. He knew me and Nick well enough to know what was the right thing to do with his money. So I don't want to hear no more about it. You keep that money. Put it someplace safe—one day you'll be needin' it. Now get you to bed. It's late."

I stood right up and walked back to our new room. At the door, I paused and took another look at Pa. He was staring right at me with the most peculiar look on his face. But when he saw me looking, he quickly jerked his head away and stared back into the fire.

I crawled into bed still thinking about that look—a sad, faraway expression, as if he was feeling some ache in his heart that had nothing to do with me or our talk.

Seeing his eyes for that brief moment, I felt as if I was eavesdropping again, seeing a little part of Pa that he had wanted to remain a secret.

# CHAPTER 14

## THE INDIANS

Before winter set in for good, my brothers and sisters and I wanted to get to know our new home and all its surroundings as best we could. Pa was always admonishing us about getting lost or running into a den of foxes or a mother bear or a bee's nest. But he didn't keep us from wandering out and doing some exploring, so we took advantage of it.

"This ain't no New York farmland," he said, every time we were about to go for a walk up the hill, through the woods or along the creek.

That, it certainly wasn't. In fact, just a few short years ago, no one but Indians had roamed this part of the country—except for a few Mexicans that may have wandered this far north. My mind was full of the possibility that there were still a whole lot of paths and sections of forest that had never been explored. There could even be new gold to discover somewhere! It gave me goosebumps to think that perhaps I might be the first person to lay eyes on a meadow or a particular formation of boulders, or to climb to the top of some hill and be the first to look out on the valley beyond. It was such a new and exciting land, with so much to learn, so many possibilities for adventure, I didn't want to miss a thing. Yet the growing chill in the air told me that time was running out, and that soon I'd be forced indoors.

On one of those crisp, chilly fall days we went hiking

along the creek just east of Pa and Uncle Nick's claim. The creek had been one of our unspoken boundaries. We had more or less grown accustomed to our particular side of it, and knew how to find our way up and down its length and back to the cabin. But on this day, I found myself looking across to the woods and fields on the eastern bank, thinking how lovely it all looked and wondering what lay out beyond. I had no doubt that there, just past the rise which cut off my view, I would discover true virgin territory. And right then I determined that if I were still here next spring, I would make it my project to strike out and explore over there, maybe even spend a night alone under the stars. I would be sixteen by then, and surely capable of spreading my wings, as Ma would say, farther afield.

But on this day, especially since I had the young'uns with me, I had to content myself with the western side. The others had run off to survey up and down the creek. I had been standing there for quite a while, gazing into the distance, alone on the little bank with only the sound of the water gurgling along in its stream bed at my feet. I was thinking about one of Alkali Jones' tales about the strike that had given the creek and the town its name.

"I was standin' right aside him, hee, hee!" he cackled, "right when he fished out that big nugget!"

According to Mr. Jones, nothing in the whole of California had managed to happen without his help.

"Big as a man's fist, I tell ya!" His eyes shone, just telling the story. "Pure gold, it was! Biggest nugget I ever seen! 'It's a miracle.' I yelled, an' all the others came runnin'. A downright miracle it was, too, an' afore long all the folks for miles around began callin' the stream Miracle Springs, an' the town grew up right on top of it."

So there I stood on the bank of Miracle Creek, just a couple of miles downstream from the spring where Mr. Jones and his friend had supposedly found that first big nugget, and maybe four or five miles upstream from the town. I didn't see any gold sparkling in the water that day, though I had no doubt there were still fortunes to be had from this stream, and I hoped maybe someday I might have a share in one. I bent down and took a scoop of the clear, cold, sweet water in my hands, still thinking about gold, and noticing nothing but the water rippling along beneath me.

But when I glanced up, not a stone's throw away stood two Indian braves. My heart nearly stopped! In my surprise I almost toppled head first into the water.

Somehow I managed to keep control of myself, and held back a strong urge to jump up and flee. Yet the sight was so fascinating I didn't really want to run away, either. I was overcome by such a feeling of wonder at actually seeing two Indians so close, face to face, looking like . . . well, just like two ordinary people. Not savages, like the ones that attacked our wagon train in Wyoming, nor like the ones we'd seen back East in books, all made up with paint and fake head-dresses, but like other people . . . only Indians.

Ma always said my curiosity was going to get me killed like the cat some day. I only hoped today wasn't going to be that day!

I suppose the two Indians were father and son. The younger one was about my age. He was tall and brown, like the older man, and both were dressed only in buckskin loin-cloths reaching almost to their knees. Their long, black hair shone—glistening in the sunlight, but was otherwise plain. I think coming upon a white girl out in the middle of the woods, kneeling all by herself at the edge of the stream, had surprised them as much as they had surprised me.

I especially noticed shock in the boy's face, but the man's was as solemn and unmoved as a rock. They had bows and quivers of arrows strapped to their backs, but I didn't notice that at first. Even if I had, I don't think it would have wor-ried me. Though I was taken aback by their sudden ap-pearance, for some strange reason, after the first instant I wasn't afraid. They looked kind of wild, but not mean. The boy was staring straight at me with a look—curiosity, interest, possibly a hint of unspoken friendship, but certainly no menace. Maybe he'd never seen a white girl his own age up so close either.

All those thoughts went speeding through my brain in only a few seconds; then I could feel my legs going numb beneath me. So I slowly rose to my feet, smiling so they wouldn't get the wrong idea. The man's face did not even flicker in response, but the boy's started to soften into what I hoped might be a smile too.

"Good morning," I said, not even knowing if they would understand me. But before they could respond, all at once there was a rustling in the brush behind me, followed by the laughs and calls of my four brothers and sisters.

As they broke into the clearing where I stood, the two Indians leaped back, then turned and ran away like two frightened deer. If they'd only waited another second to see that the cause of all the noise was nothing but four little kids!

I was perturbed at the rude interruption, and gave Zack and Emily a long scowl, though later I realized they couldn't have had any idea what they had done.

My anger with them dissolved as we walked home, but I was still quiet, and the disappointment lingered with me. I wondered if the two Indians might have talked to me if given the chance, and what they might have said. All I could think about was finding another chance to go back to that same place in hopes of finding them again—this time alone!

We took a different way back, and I got a little confused about where we were. We strayed past the southern boundary of the claim, and there we had our second interesting encounter of the day.

There were three men on horseback riding toward us.

They were coarsely-dressed white men, maybe miners, but definitely not farmers or city fellows. They looked rough and wore guns at their sides.

The appearance of these men didn't startle me like the

Indians did. In one way they were friendlier, smiling as they paused before us and tipped their hats. But I was immediately afraid. Their eyes didn't smile with their lips, and their voices seemed filled with mockery. I clutched Tad to me.

"How do, young folks," said one of the men.

"Hello," I replied, giving a tight smile.

"Ain't too common to find kids in these parts." He looked us over with just a slight squint. "You must be Nick Matthews' kin that ol' Drum's taken in?"

I nodded, wondering how he knew. Though I suppose in an isolated place like this, when five kids show up on a man's doorstep, word gets around.

"Well, you kids better skedaddle on home. We seen signs of Indians a way's back an' it ain't safe to be out."

"We can take care of ourselves," said Zack.

I could have kicked him for his insolent tone. The last thing I wanted was to rile these men.

But the man who had been speaking just laughed and turned to wink at his companions. I didn't altogether like the look of that wink either. As he turned, I noticed an ugly scar on his cheek, making him look all the nastier.

"Thank you, sir," I said, then nudged my brothers and sisters on. The instant the men were out of sight we took off as fast as we could go.

We found Pa up to his knees in the creek, shoveling gravel from the trenches into the sluice box at his mine. We were all red-faced and sweaty from running so hard, and even his untrained eye could tell we'd seen something to throw a scare into us.

"What's wrong?" he said in the gruff tone I was learning was his way of covering up a real concern. "You run into a bear or something?"

"Corrie seen Indians!" burst out Becky excitedly.

"And *then* we seen three mean-looking men on horses!" put in Emily.

"What's this?" he said, setting down his shovel and looking at me.

I told him about the Indians. "They looked friendly," I said, as I finished.

"It was plumb foolish of you not to run," he said. "There might have been more of them."

"I didn't want to upset them," I said lamely.

"You're just lucky they didn't try nothin'."

"I'm sure they wouldn't have harmed me."

Pa rubbed his hand through his beard thoughtfully. "I don't know, you may be right. California Indians are generally the most friendly of the lot. Why, back in the old days they worked right beside us in the mines, even though most of the miners cheated them bad. But that's changed in the last couple of years—most white men just couldn't abide having Indians as friends, much less equals. They drove the Indians away and made them downright hostile. It's best to steer clear of them now."

"I wanted to talk to them so bad."

"Well, you get a fool notion like that out of your head pronto! If we leave them alone, they'll leave us alone. Now, what about those other fellas you was talking about?"

"Aw, they just wanted to warn us about the Indians," said Zack.

"They looked mean," Becky added.

Again Pa looked at me. "They *do* anything?"

"No, sir," I answered. I couldn't help feeling a little proud that he seemed to respect my judgement, though it was probably just because I was the oldest. "But they were pretty stern-looking and carried guns."

"Everyone in these parts carries a gun. They give their names?"

"No, sir, but one of them seemed to know we belonged to you."

"One of them had a big wide scar on his face," piped up Becky.

"On his cheek?"

"Yes, sir," I said.

Pa frowned and rubbed his beard again.

"Well, you stay clear of them, too, you hear?" he added with a finality that indicated the discussion was over. Then he hoisted up the shovel and went on with his work.

It wasn't too many days before I'd nearly forgotten about the scar-faced man and his companions. But I could not get the two Indians out of my mind.

I felt sorry for them after what Pa had said about the gold miners' treatment of them, and I wanted a chance to prove that all whites weren't like that. I thought the Indian boy and I might even be friends, and it would be especially nice for Zack to have another boy near his own age.

Of all of us, I think everything that had happened was hardest on Zack. I had my writing in my journal to occupy me, Becky and Emily had each other for companions, and Tad was young enough to adjust without too many problems. But Zack really had nothing much to keep him busy. For some reason I didn't understand, Pa wouldn't let him help at the mine.

But having an Indian brave for a friend probably wouldn't have solved the problem anyway.

# CHAPTER 15

## AN EVENTFUL DAY IN TOWN

The next day it rained, and the day after that, and the day after that. It hardly stopped long enough for us to go outside for ten minutes without it starting up all over again.

We all got pretty bored and restless.

I especially noticed it in Pa. He couldn't go out and mine or work much outside, and I suppose he'd about had it with the company of a cabin full of kids. Every once in a while he'd question me again about the three riders we saw, and always afterwards he'd get real quiet and thoughtful, almost sulky.

As the hours of the dreary days passed, he grew more and more sullen and short-tempered. By afternoon on the third day of rain, he was hardly saying a word—not that he ever said much, but now he was downright glum. The rain finally stopped, but it was still dark and gloomy with heavy clouds overhead. I was starting supper when all of a sudden Pa, who had been sitting hunched up in front of the fire, suddenly hitched himself to his feet and half muttered something like, "Well, I'm a fool, but I gotta know if he's hanging around . . . and my fingers are itching for some action, anyway. . . ."

He strode to the door, taking a minute to put on his gun belt and pull his coat over his shoulders. In the doorway, he spoke almost as if it were an afterthought. "I'm going to town," he said matter-of-factly.

I just stood there, not knowing how to respond, as usual.

"For how long?" I finally asked.

"No telling."

"What about us?" I said.

"Do what you like," he answered. "You're welcome to come along if you want."

"We're needing some things," I suggested.

"Suit yourself," he replied, still not looking up.

I watched him another minute, but realized he'd said all he was about to say. So I turned and called inside to the kids. "Come on, you all!" I yelled. "On with them coats. We're going to town!"

"Ya-hoo!" shrieked Zack and Tad.

While the kids were getting themselves ready, I grabbed some bread and apples for us to eat on the way. I didn't want to keep Pa waiting. But when I ran outside to tell him we'd all be going with him, he'd gone up the creek to check something at the mine, so I figured we weren't in such an all-fire hurry after all. Besides, the wagon and team still needed hitching up.

About half an hour later, we all piled in the back of our wagon. Zack sat up front and handled our two horses, while Pa rode along on his bay. We made a jolly crew, laughing and talking, and I could almost imagine that everything was going to work out fine for us in our new home. But Pa didn't enter much into our jovial spirits. He just sat there silently on his horse and plodded along behind us.

It was getting well on toward evening when we finally arrived in Miracle Springs. Pa took us to Mrs. Gianini's, with a stern reminder that we weren't to call him anything but Mr. Drum, and he ordered us some supper. He didn't eat with us. He said he'd be back later and left. I thought about going to see if Mrs. Parrish was back from her trip, but it was pretty late by the time we finished eating. In fact it was too late to do much of anything. I wondered why I had wanted all of us to go along in the first place.

Sitting around in Mrs. Gianini's boarding house, we played a few games of checkers and she showed us some travel books. But pretty soon Tad started to nod off. I kept glancing toward the door wondering when Pa was going to come back. When Becky and Emily started to doze, Mrs. Gianini clicked her tongue disapprovingly, and shot a glance first at her clock and then at the door. Finally, she rose and told us to come upstairs where she had made up some beds for us.

Next morning we were all up at first light. I helped the kids get dressed, and brushed Emily and Becky's hair, and then we went downstairs. There was still no sign of Pa. We found Mrs. Gianini singing to herself in the kitchen.

"Ah, did the bambinos sleep well?" she asked when we walked in, giving Becky's pudgy little cheek a soft pinch.

"Yes, Miz Geeneene," said Becky. The plump woman laughed heartily.

"Where's our—where's Mr. Drum?" I asked, glancing around the room, still seeing no evidence of his return.

Mrs. Gianini clicked her tongue in the same way she had last night. Her thick jowls shook in a comical way.

"Your-a uncle's partner . . . he no come-a back," she said in her heavy accent.

"Did he—leave word about what w-we were to do?" I stammered.

"*Santa cielo!*" she exclaimed. I didn't understand any Italian, but from the expression on the lady's face, her answer didn't seem too hopeful. "You poor little bambinos. When I get-a my hands on that Drum, or that Nicolas Matthews for getting himself into trouble, with you coming—!" Rather than finish her sentence, she just waved her arms above her head in frustration.

Breakfast didn't taste nearly so good as last night's supper, though that was not the fault of Mrs. Gianini's cooking. We kids started at every sound outside, looking up expecting to see Pa. It was like that first day we came to Miracle, only now it was even worse, because things had started to look promising. We cleaned our plates, then went outside.

"Where's Pa?" asked Tad.

"I don't know, Taddy," I answered.

"You know as well as I do he's down at that drinkin' house," said Zack. And he was all for marching right down there and walking in on him. But I couldn't quite bring myself to agree to it. Even if I was a little angry that he had gone off and left us without so much as a word, I didn't want to hound him so much that he'd start to hate us. Besides that, it still didn't seem quite proper.

I was anxious to see Mrs. Parrish. When I suggested we go to her place, everyone cheered—everyone except Zack. He just followed behind sullenly.

Emily, Becky, and Tad ran right for the livery where Pa had left the rig. They were anxious to see Jinx and Snowball. Zack said hello to Mrs. Parrish, then ambled off aimlessly down the street. I hoped he didn't plan on looking for Pa.

"Well, Corrie!" said Mrs. Parrish with a friendly smile. "How are you?" She took my hands and looked me over. "You seem a bit pale. Are you eating well? Is your father—"

"Oh, our Pa's taking real good care of us, Ma'am," I answered quickly. But Mrs Parrish could tell I wasn't saying everything there was to tell.

"Come and sit down," she said in her gentle voice.

She led me into the Freight Office and sat in a big leather-covered chair by her oak desk. "I've got some water boiling," she said. "I'll fix us some tea."

She went about getting cups and saucers, sugar, cream, and a little plate of cookies, while she continued to talk. "How have you all been adjusting—if you don't mind my asking. It must be quite a change. I've thought about you and prayed for you often, and wanted to visit—"

"Oh, I know you're an awful busy lady, Mrs. Parrish."

"It wasn't that at all. I've been back in town several days

now, but I thought it was best to leave you all to yourselves for a while. I didn't want to appear the meddler."

"We would never have thought that, Ma'am."

"You might not have, but such a thought might well have come into your father's mind. It's nice that you all came into town together."

I looked down at my lap. I didn't think I was going to cry, but I wasn't going to take any chances. I felt about for my handkerchief just in case.

"What's wrong, Corrie?"

I didn't say anything for a moment or two. "I just don't understand," I finally blurted out, even though I hadn't wanted to say anything. "Things were going so well, it seemed. I really thought he didn't mind too much our being there."

"What happened?"

"I don't know, maybe nothin'. I just don't know where Pa is, that's all."

"Doesn't sound to me as if that's quite all."

"Well," I fumbled, playing with my handkerchief and hoping I didn't have to use it, "I don't want to speak ill of Pa. He's trying real hard. But this does take a lot of gettin' used to, I reckon. It's just that I thought when we all came to town we'd be together. I didn't figure on him runnin' out on us. But now it seems he's gone just like before. I don't know what to think."

"When did he go?"

"He got us supper at Mrs. Gianini's last night, then left. He didn't even have any supper himself."

"And he left no word?"

I shook my head.

"Why that—!" Her voice rose and her eyes flared, but then she seemed to think better of herself and went on in a milder tone. "I'm sure there must be an innocent explanation. Some business probably has detained him."

I nodded. That's what I had thought first, too. At least

that's what I'd hoped. But somehow I think we both knew we were "buildin' castles in the sky," as Ma used to say.

"But I almost forgot! I have some exciting news," said Mrs. Parrish in a light tone. I could tell she was trying to cheer me up, but I didn't mind. "Two days ago I received a letter from back East in response to an inquiry I had made. I wrote to the pastor of the church I had attended in Boston, asking if he knew any ministers who might feel the call to come west. Miracle is still a pretty wild and woolly place, but I don't think it need always be that way. When the mining plays itself out, this could well become a respectable town—with a school and a church, and lots of nice people putting down their roots. More and more families are coming to California. We need to grow, and our towns and western ways need to mature to accommodate civilization."

I could tell from her voice that she was excited, that this all meant a lot to her.

"That sounds real nice, Mrs. Parrish," I said.

"And now it looks like we are well on our way toward that goal! A preacher is coming to Miracle. According to this letter, he ought to arrive in a few weeks."

"But how's he going to cross the Sierras so late in the season?"

"He's coming by the Panama route. I'll meet his ship in San Francisco. Isn't it wonderful, Corrie? We will have our very own church!"

"Is the town going to build a church?" I asked.

"We don't need a *building* to have a church. The early Christians often met in one another's homes."

"Don't seem like even your house would be big enough."

Mrs. Parrish smiled, then gave a little chuckle.

"Oh, to have the faith of children!" she said. "Or, young ladies, I should say! But perhaps you are right, Corrie. We may just have a big turnout, if only for curiosity's sake. I will have to give all of this more thought."

"Does seem that a town with five saloons ought to have at least one church," I said.

"Truly spoken, Corrie," she replied. "And I believe in time it will. But until then . . . you have given me an idea."

She tapped her finger thoughtfully against her lips. "I wonder what the new preacher would think. . . ."

If Mrs. Parrish's intention had been to make me forget my troubles with Pa, it almost worked. I found myself caught up in her enthusiasm. It was so nice the way she treated me, as if I were a lady just like her. I wasn't even close to being a lady, but I couldn't hide my pleasure at how nice she was to me. I never had anybody talk to me quite like that.

But our nice conversation ended suddenly.

The office door burst open, and Becky, her face red from running hard, burst in jabbering excitedly.

"They're gone! They're gone! A man took 'em, and Emily's cryin', and nobody can stop her!"

# CHAPTER 16

## THE HORSES

It took a minute to get Becky calmed down, and even at that we still couldn't understand what she was trying to say. Finally Mrs. Parrish led her outside by the hand. By that time Becky began tugging at her arm, leading us to the livery stable behind the office.

There we found Emily perched on a bale of hay with Marcus Weber seated beside her. His big, black muscular arm was wrapped around her sobbing frame. He looked up, both helpless and relieved at our arrival.

"What happened, Marcus?" asked Mrs. Parrish.

"I 'spose I shoulda come fo' you, Miz Parrish," said the gentle Negro, "but you's allas sayin' fo me to take charge o' the stable, an' . . . well, it all seemed legal-like, an' that there feller was wearin' a gun, an'—"

"What man, Marcus?" interrupted Mrs. Parrish, patiently but firmly. "Tell me exactly what happened."

"He took Snowball!" shrieked Emily beside him, and then burst into a new fit of crying.

"The hosses, Ma'am. The feller done took the chil'en's hosses."

"What man, Marcus?"

"I don' know, Ma'am. This here feller, he done had a bill o' sale signed real official like—signed by Mr. Drum hisself. So the man, he jest took off with the hosses an' now

115

this here young'un's jest about to break her po li'l heart! I guess it's all my fault."

I hurried over to sit on the other side of Emily to try to calm her, while Mrs. Parrish did her best to comfort the miserable blacksmith.

"It is not your fault, Marcus," said Mrs. Parrish. "This man, did he say Mr. . . . er—Mr. Drum *sold* him the horses?"

"Yes'm."

Mrs. Parrish was about to say something. But all at once she stopped, her mouth hanging half open, staring straight ahead.

I turned my head around and followed her gaze. There in the doorway of the livery stood Pa, with Tad and Zack behind him.

I had almost forgotten about Tad. I guess when the commotion started he must have run off after Zack, and somehow the two of them met up with Pa. Anyway, there he was.

All of a sudden, I guess something inside me just kind of popped, because I jumped up off that hay bale and ran over to him.

"How could you?" I cried.

He looked back at me with genuine shock at my reaction. "They was just horses," he said.

"Just horses!" I said. "They were our . . . our pets . . . they'd come all the way with us! Snowball was Emily's special friend!"

My voice was shaking, all the frustration I'd been feeling coming out all at once. I'd never before in my life spoken to an adult like that. "You had no right!" I yelled.

"I was up against a wall," he replied, still bewildered at all the stir he'd caused. "I needed some quick capital."

Mrs. Parrish turned to Marcus Weber. "Marcus, will you please excuse us?" He quietly left the stable. When he was gone, Mrs. Parrish turned her glare right on Pa.

"Did you gamble those horses away, Mr. . . . ah . . .

Mr. Drum?" she asked angrily.

"Things just got out of hand."

"You could have had Ma's money!" I cried. Tears of anger and anguish were streaming down my face. I had tried so hard since the beginning to see things Pa's way and to stick up for him. But now I felt he had betrayed us. "I was going to give you that money!" I said again. "But why the horses?"

"I don't take money from kids!" he shot back, his voice rising. I couldn't tell if he was angry or just frustrated.

"But you would sell their horses, Mr. Drum? Not only their pets and friends, but the only link they still possess to a past that has been torn away from them—a past full of a great deal of pain at your hand!" she added, glaring at him as she spoke.

"Oh, for criminy sakes! You're makin' me out to be some kind of thief!" retorted Pa. " 'Sides, it ain't none of your affair, Miz Parrish. We're kin, an' kinfolk stick together, ain't that right, kids?"

None of us said anything. I don't guess we were feeling too much kinship right then.

"Someone has to look after the interests of these children!"

Still she scowled at him, but he just glared right back. For an instant I thought he might strike her, he looked so mad. But finally he just let out a sharp breath.

"What's done is done," he said finally, in a tight, strained voice.

A stifled sob from Emily made us all painfully aware that Pa was right—the horses were gone. It *was* done, and it wasn't going to be so easily resolved. All our eyes turned momentarily toward her.

"Ain't a one of you thinkin' about me and the tight spot I was in," said Pa. "Listen here—if I hadn't come up with them horses, I might've taken a couple of slugs. I had no choice."

"That doesn't make it right," I said, sinking helplessly back on the bale next to Emily.

Pa looked around at all of us. "Since when is a man answerable to a bunch of kids and a busybody woman that's got nothin' to do with his affairs? If you don't like the way I do things, just remember it wasn't me that asked you to hitch up with me. I told you from the beginnin' it wouldn't work!" He spun around and strode out of the stable.

Mrs. Parrish ran right out after him. I had never seen a bolder woman, nor a braver one. I figured my pa'd been pushed just about as far as any man was likely to go.

By the time she caught up with him he had rounded a corner and I couldn't see them. But their voices came through the wide-open stable doors as clear as gunfire through cold, night air.

"You are not leaving those children again!" said Mrs. Parrish, and it wasn't a question but an order.

"Since when is it your business to tell me what to do?" shot back Pa angrily.

"You have a responsibility."

"So do you, lady, and it ain't pokin' your nose into my life!"

"Now look here, Mr.—"

"Now *you* listen, Mrs. Parrish," interrupted Pa, and his voice was cool, almost calm—but not like the calm of a spring day, more like the dead quiet before a thunderstorm. "You may run half this town," he said, "*but you don't run me*! I'll do as suits me best, and I'll thank you to mind your own affairs!"

"And what about the children?" Mrs. Parrish was just about as cool. I knew if I could have seen her as she spoke she wouldn't be flinching a muscle.

"It seems apparent to me that they've had it up to their eyeballs with me, just as much as I've had it with them!"

I heard the sound of horses hooves and a jingling harness.

"And so you intend—" Mrs. Parrish began, but whatever she meant to say was lost in the sound of clopping hooves.

In a moment she returned alone. Pa was gone on his horse. Mrs. Parrish looked sad for our sakes, but inside I could tell she was boiling mad at the same time. She seemed used to having her way with how things went.

I felt awful. And it didn't help when Zack lit into me.

"Now look what you've done!" he said. "Yellin' at him and driving him away like that."

"Don't blame your sister," said Mrs. Parrish. "Whatever blame there is to be dished out belongs to your father and no one else." She was infuriated with him. "Well . . ." she added, "and some to me, I suppose. I should have guarded my words more carefully."

Tears ran down my cheeks. Deep down I couldn't help but think Zack was right, that it was my fault Pa had run off. Mad as I had just been with him, part of me still wanted to believe in him. Part of me kept thinking that if only I had kept still like a proper, obedient child, things would have been okay. We would survive somehow without the horses. But we needed our Pa and I hoped he needed us a little too. Having to grow up so fast was awfully confusing at times!

"Come now," said Mrs. Parrish after a moment. "You children can stay with me."

The stable was silent a minute, with only the soft shuffling of the horses in their stalls. Then all of a sudden I found myself speaking up boldly again.

"Thank you kindly, Mrs. Parrish," I said, "but we best be gettin' home."

"I doubt your father will return there tonight."

"I know, Ma'am, but that's where we belong now. It's our home. We'll manage. I can take care of the young'uns, and Zack can handle a rifle if need be."

She let out an exasperated, yet not unfriendly sigh. "It seems determination runs in your family."

I couldn't help smiling a little. More than once I heard Ma observe that the stubborn streak was most strong on my *father's* side.

"I'm afraid that's probably true, Ma'am."

"But you don't even have horses to get you there now," she added.

Now it was my turn to sigh. I had completely forgotten the cause of this hubbub in the first place. Jinx and Snowball were *gone*. Mrs. Parrish walked quickly outside to find Mr. Weber. When they returned she was talking to him. "Marcus," she said, "will you hitch up a couple of our horses to the children's rig and drive them home?"

"Yes'm! Be most glad to!" He jumped up, obviously eager to make amends for his part in the misunderstanding.

Mrs. Parrish went over and conferred quietly with him while we stood glumly about. In about ten minutes the wagon was ready and we were off, saying good-bye to Mrs. Parrish, who promised to come up to see us the next day.

# CHAPTER 17

## ALONE AT THE CABIN

We'd never been alone in the cabin at night.

In fact, I can't remember us five kids being alone at night anywhere before. I recalled my conversation with Zack when we first got to California about fending for ourselves. It seemed pretty silly. I felt like a little girl, not a woman.

I could hardly sleep. Every little sound jerked me wide awake.

Luckily, the little ones slept. But I heard Zack tossing and turning in his bunk over Tad's.

I thought I should just get up and go into the other room and light a lamp so I could read or write in my journal or something. I'd been wanting to make a drawing of the cabin. But then I was afraid the light might attract attention. And when I thought of that, I began to think of Indians, and pretty soon I was imagining that all the sounds outside were the padded noises of moccasin-clad feet!

Then I started to think about what it would be like to be massacred. If something like that happened, Pa would sure feel awful then. But that thought didn't make me feel any better. I wasn't angry at him anymore, especially now that I realized more than ever how much we needed him here with us.

But now he was gone.

Would he ever come back? Especially after my outburst

made him think we didn't want him?

No, he had to come back. He was our pa, after all, and I could never stop trying to believe in him.

Suddenly a sharp explosive sound shook the quiet night. *Crack! Crack!*

Twice it came, and I knew it was gunfire!

It echoed deafeningly through the night, then all was still once more. The silence seemed even deeper than before, though it lasted only a second or two, for we were all wide awake now.

"What was that?" said Zack in a tremulous whisper.

"Gunshots," I whispered back.

"Ma . . . Ma. . . !" came three smaller voices.

Shaking all over, I folded back the blanket and crept out of bed. I tiptoed over to a window. Zack was at my shoulder a second later.

"What do you see?" he said.

Peering out, I could see nothing but darkness. I found myself wishing for those small night sounds I had been listening to before; it was dead still outside now.

All at once I heard a sound at the front door. My blood froze. I glanced at Zack, hoping it had been my imagination. But the look of terror on his pale face told me the sound had been real enough.

Clasping one another by the hand, we crept into the other room. As quietly as I could I took down Pa's rifle that hung over the hearth and handed it to Zack. He would have been happy to know that at that moment he looked more a man than I had ever seen him before. Though he was only thirteen, I was sure glad to have him beside me! But I was too distracted to say anything just then.

Now someone was pounding on the door! My heart was in my throat.

"Who's there?" I said finally, in a voice barely more than a squeak. Behind me Zack cocked the rifle and held it steady.

"It's me . . . you chil'ens all right?"

The voice sounded familiar, but wasn't the one I expected. It was Marcus Weber.

"W-we're safe, Mr. Weber," I said in a voice of tremendous relief. "Let me unbolt the door."

The big Negro blacksmith was indeed a welcome sight when I swung open the big wooden door. But his usual congenial look was replaced with serious concern. He came in quickly, shut the door, and told me to bolt it right away, which I lost no time doing. Then I lit the lantern.

"What's going on out there?" asked Zack, lowering the rifle, relieved he hadn't had to use it.

"There was prowlers about," said Mr. Weber.

"Indians?" exclaimed Becky and Tad together. Emily was still too frightened to speak.

The black man's brow creased into deep furrows. "No, siree . . . them weren't no Indian tracks I seen out dere— an' if they's one thing I knows, it's tracks. Someone else be prowlin' 'roun' yo uncle's mine."

But who could have been out there, nosing around so close to the cabin?

"Was it them that fired the shots?" I asked.

"No, that was me, Missy," answered Mr. Weber, patting the pistol now tucked securely in the holster at his side. "I seen 'em creepin' roun' suspicious like, an' so I fired in de air to scare 'em off. I was afeared they might be Indians too, but a close look at their tracks showed it had to be white men. But thank the good Lawd, they didn't put up no fight."

"But what brought you here, Mr. Weber?"

Now the worried look on his face turned into a sheepish grin. "Well . . ." He hesitated a moment before plunging ahead, "Miz Parrish, she done asked me to stick aroun' after I brung you kids home. She didn't want to say nuthin' 'cause . . . well, she figured yo might not take to the idee too well."

I *had* been acting a bit contrary this afternoon. I don't know what got into me. Ma would have said I was being too ornery for my own good, and she would have been right. If

Mrs. Parrish hadn't been so wise, I don't know what would have become of us tonight. So now it was my turn to look sheepish as I spoke.

"I sure am glad you turned up, Mr. Weber. And I thank you kindly for putting yourself out like that to protect us."

"Aw, it's my pleasure, Missy, an' that's a fact!" The blacksmith's worried creases softened into one of his warm smiles.

"You're welcome to stay in here the rest of the night," I said.

"Please stay, Mr. Weber," added Becky in a sleepy, innocent voice. He laughed, and it helped clear away the last of the fear to hear his merry voice echo through the cabin.

He knelt down on one knee, took Becky's tiny, soft white hand in his huge, rough black one, and said, "I'm much obliged fo' yo' kindness, Missy. But iffen it's all the same to you, I think I'll jest bunk down in that tool shed out dere by the mine. That way, I'll hear any unusualness right off."

"Okay, but come in for breakfast in the morning," I said.

"That I'll do right gladly, Missy!" he said to me, rising.

So we all got settled down into our beds again. I tucked the little ones in and tried to pray a prayer with each of them like Ma might have done. Then I crawled back under my own blanket.

I slept a lot easier after that, knowing I wasn't the oldest person around anymore, and feeling the safety of Marcus Weber keeping watch over us.

As I snuggled down into my bed, with the words of the prayer I had just prayed with Tad still in my mind, I realized that Someone greater than the blacksmith was looking over us kids too, just like Ma'd told me. I guess I'd been forgetting that lately. Sure, things had been confusing, and weren't going so smoothly. But it could have been much worse! We had food and a place to sleep. And we'd already met people who were kind to us. I decided to start counting my blessings, starting with Marcus Weber's presence out in the tool shed—even including our pa, because down inside, I still had the feeling he might turn out to be a blessing in the end.

# CHAPTER 18

## BREAKFAST WITH MARCUS WEBER

The events of the next morning muddled my notions all over again about Pa being a blessing.

We were all eating breakfast and having a good time. Marcus Weber was there with us. I fixed a special meal in appreciation for what he had done last night—fluffy buttermilk biscuits, heaps of scrambled eggs and sausages that Mrs. Parrish had sent back with us, and gravy from the drippings sprinkled over everything. Mr. Weber said that biscuits and gravy were his favorite southern meal and he missed them. I probably didn't make them just like he remembered, but I did my best, and he seemed real appreciative. He made his own coffee on the stove, and the fragrance from the fresh-brewed pot, mixed with the sizzling sausages in the skillet, filled the cabin and made it seem cheerful and homey. We were laughing and talking together, and Mr. Weber was doing his best to entertain the younger kids with stories. I suppose we looked a pretty contented lot for the first time since we got to Miracle.

"Why, Miz Corrie," said Mr. Weber, "you is one fine cook! You's gwine t' make some feller a right fine missus one day."

I blushed and giggled. "Not me, Mr. Weber. I figure I'll just be a schoolteacher."

"Ma says Corrie's too interested in books to get a husband," chimed in Becky impudently.

"Stuff an' nonsense!" exclaimed the blacksmith. "Meanin' no disrespec' to the dead, that is. Why look at Miz Parrish! She's one of de smartest people I knows, an' she got hersel' a right fine husban'—I knowed him person'ly. An' they is plenty o' fellers like him, eben in dese parts—jist you wait an' see."

"Are you going to get married, Corrie?" asked Tad.

"No, Tad, don't be ridiculous," I said, but the others had a good laugh over his question. It felt so good to see everyone laughing that I didn't mind that it was at my expense.

Then without warning the door opened and in walked Pa.

His clothes were all dusty as if he'd been riding a great distance. His beard was scruffy and his hat had dirt caked on it. He strode in as though he'd only been gone an hour, took off his coat, unstrapped his gun belt and hung it up on its peg, then came over and sat down in the chair at the head of the table where he usually sat.

"I'm starved," he said just as normally as you please, "what's for breakfast?"

I got him a plate and he helped himself freely to several biscuits. There were still plenty left.

"Well, Marcus," he said after taking several large bites, "what brings you out our way?"

"Miz Parrish, she sent me up t' keep an eye out fer the kids while . . . while yo was gone, Mr. Drum."

"Oh, she did?"

His eyes narrowed some, but then he seemed to change his mind about what he wanted to say. "Well, that was right neighborly of her," he said. "I'll have to thank her next time I see her. And thank you, too, Marcus."

"Much obliged, sir." Marcus looked down at his plate as if he wasn't sure about something. Then he lifted his head and looked straight at Pa, "I scared off some prowlers here las' night," he said.

"Oh?" For a moment, the easy-going nonchalance Pa had been demonstrating seemed to slip, revealing a flicker of real concern. "You kids okay?"

"Yes, sir," I answered simply.

There was so much I wanted to say to my pa. But I could find no words. Yet when were there *ever* words to say what I was feeling? When was it ever easy to say things straight from the heart? Maybe never. Seems we were all trying so hard to protect ourselves from facing any more hurt, that we just couldn't let ourselves be honest with each other. I wanted so much for Pa to like us and accept us. And maybe he was suffering hurts I didn't know about. More than anything, I wanted us to be able to get to know one another. That's the way families were. Yet that was the one thing we didn't seem to be doing—getting to know each other. It was a reminder all over again that we weren't really a family.

Pa finished his breakfast, then he and Marcus Weber went out to take a look at the footprints and horse tracks from last night.

Nothing was ever said about what happened at Mrs. Parrish's; not about what I had said to him, not about the horses, not about Pa's leaving. Maybe it was better that way. What good would a lot of talk have done anyway?

Pa didn't act angry toward any of us. He was just the same as always. Things just went on as if nothing had happened.

Emily kept mostly to herself for a few days. I could tell she was heartbroken over Snowball. I tried to interest her in other diversions, and a time or two I thought I caught Pa making a special effort to talk to her. But she was pretty silent. What he'd done had really hurt her and it wasn't going to be easy for him to win back her friendship.

# CHAPTER 19

# AN UNEXPECTED VISITOR

The next few days went by uneventfully.

Pa didn't say much, kind of stayed out of our way, and spent most of his time up by the mine. Although I think he was embarrassed by what he'd done, he never brought it up, and neither did we. Zack was real sullen.

About three days later, when we were sitting around in the evening, the next big change came in our lives. It was pretty quiet, I had just finished putting Tad to bed and was coming back out into the main room of the cabin, when all of a sudden the door burst open and in walked a man we'd never seen before.

It didn't take longer than a second or two before we knew who it was.

"Nick!" Pa exclaimed, jumping up from his chair. "Where in tarnation you been?"

"Down t' Yankee Jim's," replied our uncle, flipping his hat onto the vacant peg by the door, and walking over toward the stove to see what he smelled in the pot.

"I went down there looking for you after you left," Pa said. "I scoured the countryside from Auburn to Shingle Springs, but no one had seen hide nor hair of you."

"I hid out down at Grizzly Flats for a spell. I didn't get to Jim's 'til after you was gone, but—"

He stopped and glanced around at the open mouths and wide eyes all staring at him.

"Hey, Drum," he finally said after he'd eyed us all, "who're all these kids?"

"Let me just ask you one thing first," said Pa, eyeing him intently. "Did you see a feller from back home some time last year?"

"Last year? How am I supposed to remember that?"

"You don't remember?" Pa returned sharply. "After all we done to hide who we are, you don't recall if you seen someone who can identify us? I always knew you was dim-witted, but this takes the cake. You just can't keep from gettin' us into a peck of trouble!"

"Come on, Drum, I don't see what—"

"Well, I don't suppose there's an easy way to tell you other than just saying it."

"Telling me what?"

"Aggie didn't make it," said Pa slowly. "Your sister's dead, Nick."

The men just looked at each other a second or two. The cabin was silent.

"These are your nieces and nephews, Nick," said Pa finally. "Me and Aggie's kids. They was all on their way out here when Aggie took a fever. But the kids made it—got here two, three weeks back. Kids," he said, turning to us, "say hello to your Uncle Nick."

I stood up and curtsied. Zack went over and silently shook Nick's hand. The younger ones just stared. Tad had gotten out of bed and stood watching in the doorway.

Uncle Nick just glanced around, first at one of us, then the other, all around, and finally back at Pa, without saying a word. Finally he slumped down into one of the two rocking chairs in the room and let out a long deep breath.

As I watched, I wondered what he was thinking. His face, beneath the scraggly several-day's growth of brownish whiskers, showed no apparent emotion. He stared vacantly ahead. Were his thoughts ones of sorrow about Ma? Or annoyance that we kids where there in his place? Or was he thinking about his own trouble with the sheriff and what he should do?

He was a handsome man, several years younger than Pa. Pa must've been thirty-nine or forty. Ma said he was twenty-two when they were married, and Ma a year younger. So I'd guess Uncle Nick to be thirty-three or thirty-four.

His hair was kind of a curly golden-brown, falling down into bushy sideburns around his ears. I saw Ma's family right off in the eyes, and in the prominent nose, too—a straight nose, not too big, but what they call the Roman look, I think. He had a strong resemblance to Zack. Even though he was kind of gazing off into the distance, his face had a lively appearance. Just from looking, I figured him to be more talkative than Pa. He may have been in trouble, but he didn't look anxious or upset about it. In fact, in spite of whatever his difficulties were, he looked like the kind of fellow who enjoyed life and didn't let too many things get him down.

All of a sudden I realized I was staring. I looked away hastily, then went over to the stove. The least I could do was be hospitable, I thought. After all we were in *his* home.

"Would you like some stew and bread, Uncle Nick?" I said, getting a plate.

He jolted himself out of his reverie. "Why, that sounds mighty nice," he said. "What's your name, girl?"

"Cornelia," I answered.

"Yeah, o' course! How could I forget little Cornelia! You musta been two or three when I left New York."

"I last saw her when she was seven," put in Pa, "and you only left a year ahead of me."

"I guess you're right," laughed Uncle Nick. "You lose track o' time out here, you know."

"Speaking of names, Nick," said Pa, "the young'uns here know all about the *Matthews* dodge."

Uncle Nick nodded thoughtfully.

I set the plate down on the table. He sat down at the

bench and tore into it like he hadn't eaten in a week.

"Corrie," Pa said, "why don't you get the young'uns bedded down? Me and your uncle's got some things to talk about."

I motioned to Becky and Emily to come with me. Zack just kept sitting, and Pa didn't say nothing more. I took the girls into the bedroom and got Tad back into his bunk. When I came back out about ten minutes later, Zack was still sitting there listening, and no one paid much attention to me. Pa's voice sounded serious.

" . . . but don't you know what a blame fool thing it was to do?"

"I didn't think," Uncle Nick replied lamely. "Anyway, that fella recognized me first."

"You should've ignored him, denied who you was—anything."

"I didn't think there'd be no harm. It was Pete Wilkins. I grew up with him. It was awful good seein' someone from home, from the old days."

"You're telling *me* about home, about the *old days*!" Pa burst out. "At least you didn't have to leave a wife and kids!"

"Maybe you're right. But I'll never get to see Aggie again, either."

"I guess we made a mess of our lives," said Pa more sympathetically.

"You mean *I* made a mess, Drum."

Pa didn't answer, and I couldn't tell if he was agreeing or just didn't have anything to say.

Finally Uncle Nick went on, "What's done's done, anyway. What's the use of gettin' all riled at me now?"

" 'Cause maybe it ain't done with yet," answered Pa. "Didn't you hear what I just told you about them men the kids seen? Then that Parrish woman's Negro, he scared someone off the other night prowlin' around here. I tell you, Nick, Aggie ain't the only one who found out from that fella where we was."

"Pete wouldn't of said nothin'."

"They could've been watchin' the house, and Aggie."

"But everyone thought we was dead."

"Maybe the law did, though I'm not even sure about that, anymore. But the Catskill bunch . . . they wouldn't give up so easily. More'n likely they got wind of Aggie's leaving and tailed her."

"Followed her all the way out here? Come on, Drum. You don't really believe they coulda done that without someone seein' 'em?"

"Aggie didn't know them. They coulda been part of the wagon train and no one would have been the wiser. All they had to do was see where she lit, and they'd have us."

"Na, I can't buy it! You said yourself you didn't see 'em in town."

"Well, somehow they got to us after all this time. You heard what I told you the kids saw. With a scar like that, who could it be but Krebbs?"

"Plenty of fellas has scars."

"Prowling around here at night . . . askin' questions about us. We never had no trouble all this time, till the kids showed up."

Uncle Nick said nothing in reply. He just sat thinking over Pa's words. "I jest can't believe they coulda trailed the kids so far."

"Men'll do anything for that kind of loot, and as long as they still think we got it, they'll never give up."

He stopped for a minute, then shook his head and muttered in exasperation, "Blast it! I thought we'd finally shaken that bunch of scum! Now the kids're gonna be in just as much danger as ever."

He thought a minute more, then something new seemed to occur to him. He looked up at Uncle Nick with renewed anger. "Which reminds me," he said, "it sure don't help none for you to keep gettin' yourself into fresh trouble. What were you thinking pulling your gun on Judd like that? Sometimes, Nick, I think you're still that fool trigger-happy teen-aged kid I pulled outta that free-for-all back in Schenec-tady."

"Just 'cause you saved my hide once doesn't mean you gotta treat me like a kid the rest of my days. I can take care of myself."

"You can take care of yourself like the hothead you are! I'll treat you like a man, Nick, when you stop needing me to nursemaid you! Now on top of the kids, and being found out by the Catskill Gulch Gang, I suppose I'm gonna have to get you outta this latest scrap and somehow make things right with the sheriff."

"Judd was itching for it. I told you that—it was his doing!"

"Just 'cause a man wants to start something, doesn't mean you gotta pull your gun and oblige him, right in front of the whole blamed town!"

"He called me a cheat."

"Judd's a bigger fool than you are and everyone knows it. So what if he called you a cheat. Besides, he was more than half drunk. Nobody was payin' heed to a word he said."

"I don't like a man spreadin' lies about me."

"So you pulled your gun on him, and then an hour later Judd is found dead in the alley next to the saloon, and every-body's wonderin' where you are! What good did it do you to protect your honor? If you'd a just kept your mouth shut and your gun in your holster, you wouldn't be in this fix."

Uncle Nick just sat where he was, sulking. Finally he burst out again, getting in one last argument in his defense. Funny, it almost reminded me of Zack whining back at Ma when he didn't want to do something.

"I didn't do it, I tell you!"

"I believe you," said Pa, with a sigh of frustration.

"It was that half-brother of his, Kile."

"Proving that and clearing you's not gonna be easy."

"There's bad blood in that family," said Uncle Nick.

"Everybody knows it, including the sheriff. And he knows Kile's been layin' for him, too."

"I know it, and you know it. But until the sheriff gets proof, you better just lay low here, and me and the kids'll not let on we seen hide nor hair of you. It'll do you good to keep out of the saloon and your hands off a deck of cards!"

# CHAPTER 20

# THE SHERIFF PAYS A VISIT

When we woke up the following morning Pa was gone. I didn't find out until later that he'd ridden off before daybreak north across the middle fork of the Yuba to some place called French Corral. Uncle Nick told us later that he'd gone looking for some old mountain man called Brennan, who was supposed to be distant kin to the fellow they'd been talking about named Kile.

At the time, however, all we saw was that Pa was gone, "on business," as Uncle Nick put it.

As a result we kids got to see more of Uncle Nick than we might have otherwise.

As I guessed, he was more talkative. Pa was still a little threatening to us all, but Uncle Nick was so friendly and good-natured he almost seemed like one of us. Before the day was out, he had Becky and Emily laughing and chasing him around the cabin with Tad up on his shoulders hanging on for dear life. Zack still hung back, but Nick even managed to coax a smile or two out of him, wrestling around with him on the floor of the cabin before dinner. He was just so lively we couldn't help having a good time around him.

After dinner, Pa'd always just sit down and everything'd get real quiet for a spell. But Uncle Nick didn't seem the sitting-around type. He always had to be doing something.

" 'You ever shot a Colt, boy?" he said as he got up from the table.

"Who, me?" said Zack.

"Who you think I'm talking to, your kid brother? What about it, have you ever?"

"Uh, no sir," Zack answered.

"How about we give it a try?"

Still bewildered, Zack wasn't sure what to think. Uncle Nick pulled his pistol out of its holster on the wall and, with an inquiring look on his face, waved it butt first toward Zack. Gradually it began to dawn on Zack what he meant.

"Yes, sir!" he said, jumping up and following Uncle Nick outside.

They walked up toward the mine together. I couldn't hear what they were saying, but I could tell by the excitement in Zack's voice that he was feeling good about the interest Uncle Nick was showing in him.

For the next half hour or so we could hear shots firing from up the creek, followed every so often by an excited yell from Zack.

Later that night, before bed, Uncle Nick sat with all of us and told us stories about himself and things he'd done. He never mentioned the trouble we knew he was in, but we still enjoyed it. We went to bed that night happier than any night since we'd got there, and all of us were really glad Uncle Nick had come back.

Pa got back about ten the following morning. He didn't say much, just got Uncle Nick aside and the two of them talked seriously for a while. Uncle Nick seemed to protest what Pa was telling him, but in the end they seemed to reach some agreement. Then Pa got back on his bay and galloped off again.

This time he was gone about two hours. Uncle Nick was quiet the whole time, fidgeting around nervously. After a while, he went out and saddled up his horse, then came back into the cabin and packed up some things in his saddlebags, as if he was planning to go someplace. Finally, he got his gun belt down from the peg by the door and strapped it around his waist. He had a determined look on his face, completely different than the carefree expression of the day before, when he'd been playing and laughing with us and showing us things all around the claim. He looked like I imagined a gunfighter would look, and I couldn't help wondering if he was an outlaw after all.

When Pa's horse came into view down the road, he had another rider with him. Uncle Nick told us to get inside the cabin. We obeyed, but as we were going I saw him loosen his horse's rein where it was tied on the hitching rail, as if in readiness for flight. But still he just stood there in front of the cabin as the two riders approached.

We went inside and closed the door. Zack and I were too curious not to know what was going on. So we went into the bedroom and watched from the window.

Pa rode up and got off his horse. He was the first of the three men to speak.

"Nick, I told the sheriff here that you'd give yourself up, long as he talked to old man Brennan first."

"That right, Matthews?" the other man said, still sitting in his saddle and looking down at Uncle Nick.

Uncle Nick nodded without much enthusiasm.

"You're in a barrel of trouble, Matthews," said the sheriff. "I've a good mind to run you in and slap you in jail right now. But this partner of yours seems to think he can clear you."

"I didn't shoot Judd," said Uncle Nick.

"Well, we'll see. That's not what the folks that heard you and him arguing in the saloon think."

"We may have argued. That don't mean I killed him. I never killed a man, and that's God's truth."

"Maybe you did and maybe you didn't. But I got to go on evidence, and the evidence all points toward you. In the meantime, is what Drum tells me true? Are you willing to place yourself in his custody and promise to stay put 'til I talk to Brennan, and give yourself up and face trial if it comes to that?"

"I ain't about to go to jail," said Uncle Nick pointedly.

"Be reasonable, Nick," put in Pa. "If you run again, they'll have to put a price on your head. Then you'll take a slug in the back."

"Listen to the man, Matthews," said the sheriff. "Running away just says to everyone that you're guilty. If you give yourself up willingly, I can try to make things easier for you, and it'll say to a jury that you know you're innocent. I'm inclined to believe your story, but you got to do your part."

"It's the only way, Nick. I talked to Brennan yesterday, and he'll tell the sheriff that Kile slept out at his shack for two nights after the incident. He'll tell what Kile told him, too."

"Okay, I'll stay put," replied Uncle Nick at length. "But old Brennan better not double-cross us."

"Good," said the sheriff, looking relieved. "Now you two stay where you are. I'll ride up to French Corral tomorrow and see if I can't get Brennan to corroborate your story."

He spun around on his sorrel, then galloped back the way he had come.

Pa and Uncle Nick tied up their horses and walked slowly inside, hanging up their guns by the door.

"It's the only way you're gonna get out from under this," Pa was saying.

"I still don't like it," said Uncle Nick. "Though it's not that I don't appreciate what you done for me."

"Yeah. Maybe next time I'll just let you dangle from your own rope."

Uncle Nick didn't answer, just plopped down in a chair like he'd had a tongue-lashing from his own pa, and stared straight ahead. Nothing more was said about the incident the rest of the day.

# CHAPTER 21

## MIRACLE SPRING'S BIG DAY

Three days later the sheriff returned. Zack heard the conversation that Pa and Uncle Nick had with him outside.

"That man Brennan told the sheriff that Kile had been around and confessed to killing Judd!" Zack said. "As soon as the sheriff said that, Uncle Nick let out a big sigh of relief. The sheriff was upset though," Zack went on. "Because when he asked Brennan where Kile was, the old man just replied, 'I ain't about t' turn one o' my own kin int' the law. I told ya what he said, but I ain't gonna tell ya where the varmint is!' "

"Then what happened?" I asked.

"The sheriff just told Uncle Nick to watch out and not to get himself involved in any more trouble. He said he wouldn't go so easy on him next time."

"And what'd Uncle Nick say?"

"Oh, he sorta thanked the sheriff for being so understanding," said Zack. "But he didn't like saying the words. I think Pa made him do it," he added.

The next few days passed peacefully enough. Now that the cloud over Uncle Nick was gone, at least for a while, he seemed even more fun-loving than before.

In those days of quiet, I did a lot of thinking. We had been in Miracle Springs for a month. The reflection of the setting sun each day on the gold, red and yellow leaves said that fall was truly in the air. Already many of those colorful leaves had fallen to the ground and were decaying underfoot.

So much had happened since the previous spring, when those same leaves were growing from tiny buds. Then, I was three thousand miles away from this place. Now, here I was in California, with my brothers and sisters, our ma gone, and a whole new life before us.

On the outside I was still the same fifteen-year-old girl who left New York. But inside I felt like I'd aged twenty years. I could hardly imagine more adventures—good and bad—happening to one person in a single lifetime, although books I've read about people like Robinson Crusoe and Leather-Stocking in *The Last of the Mohicans* make what's happened to me seem a bit tame.

But, I suppose that especially here in the West, lots of things are bound to happen to everyone—some happy and exciting things, and some tragic things, like losing our ma. I guess she would say that's what life's all about.

One of these fall mornings began with a surprise when Pa woke us all bright and early. That in itself was unusual, for he'd never gotten us up a single day since we'd been there. Usually I'd rise at first light to find him out of the cabin and already at work somewhere about the place. But on this morning he called us out of bed while it was still dim and gray outside. Bacon was frying in the skillet on the stove and coffee was already brewing when I came out.

"Thought you young'uns might like to go into Miracle today," he said in a voice more chipper than usual. Uncle Nick's return and the temporary clearing of the trouble with the sheriff seemed to have raised his spirits.

"Oh, we'd love it!" I replied as I began to stir up some buckwheat batter.

"Big doin's in town today," he went on. "Why, history's likely gonna be made. You kids won't want to miss that."

Just then Uncle Nick walked in from outside. "You going to town today, Nick?" asked Pa.

"You think it's safe?"

"Judd's kin ain't gonna bother you none. They know you didn't do it as well as I do. And if you keep yourself outta trouble, the sheriff ain't gonna do nothin'."

"I wasn't thinking of that," said Uncle Nick. "I was thinking of the other trouble that you think mighta followed us here."

"Oh, yeah," said Pa. He lowered his voice as he continued. "But if it is Krebbs that's nosing around, our staying out of town's not gonna stop him. If that was him the kids seen, he already knows our place. And if we can spot him in the crowd in town, then it might even be to our advantage. At least we'd know for sure he was here."

"Yeah, but he ain't actually laid eyes on either of us yet. It could just be a coincidence."

"If it's Krebbs, it's no coincidence. He's out for our blood, I tell you. That is, if he can't find the hundred grand. And we sure ain't got it!"

Uncle Nick sighed. Neither of them were paying much attention to me, but I was straining every nerve to hear what they were saying.

"I shoulda listened to you in the first place," Uncle Nick said. "Them was a bad bunch to get mixed up with. But all I could think of was how easy that bank was gonna be and how much money there was inside."

"Well, like you said the other day, we done what we done and we can't undo it. So we just gotta watch ourselves now."

When there was a lull in their talk, I asked, "What's going on in town?"

"Newspaper's coming to the area, that's what," answered Uncle Nick as if he had struck El Dorado. "You especially oughta be interested in that, Corrie."

"Me?" I said, and stopped stirring to glance over at him.

"Sure. I seen you night after night scrawling in that there journal of yours. What're you raising here, Drum?" he said to Pa as he flashed a wink in my direction, "Some female Bill Shakespeare?"

I blushed. "I'm just writing down my experiences, that's all—Ma said I should."

"And your ma was right," put in Pa to my defense. He thought Uncle Nick was giving me a bad time, and he hadn't seen the twinkle in his brother-in-law's eye.

"Well, around these parts," Uncle Nick went on, "just being able to write proper puts you up there with them author fellers."

I still didn't see what he was getting at.

"What does a newspaper coming to town have to do with me?" I asked.

"Well, even a no-account ignoramus like me knows that them newspaper fellers write. Seems like with all your writing in that there journal, you'd have something in common with them. Or at least that you'd be interested in them coming to Miracle."

"Yes—yes, I am, Uncle Nick," I said. "I guess I never thought of it in that way before."

"I expect your ma'd want to see you get some kind of education," added Pa, "even in this uncivilized country, where there ain't so much as a school for you." He mumbled the words almost as an apology, as if he was embarrassed at saying something thoughtful. "The newspaper'd be a good thing for you to know about and get involved in."

I smiled. It was nearly the first time he'd shown any real interest in any of us. So newspaper or not, I knew this was indeed a special day!

After breakfast we all loaded up in Pa's old buckboard, hitched to his own bay mare. It was not as comfortable as our old wagon. Emily still missed Snowball, and the bay showed in no uncertain terms that she did not appreciate being put to this kind of labor. But none of us said a word. We all silently realized it was a subject best left alone.

When we got to town there was almost a carnival atmosphere in the air.

Uncle Nick said he hadn't seen it this lively since the actor Edwin Booth had performed in town. "It ain't just the paper, you see," he explained. "As hard as these fellers work around here, anytime they can turn somethin' into a celebration, they'll do it. The paper's just an excuse to whoop it up for a day or two."

A raised platform had been built in front of the largest saloon in town where the two main streets intersected. It was draped in red, white, and blue banners just like election day back home. There was no one on the platform yet, but Uncle Nick said there'd be plenty of speeches before the day was done.

We stopped and piled out of the wagon while Pa tied the horse to a hitching post. Some of he and Uncle Nick's friends came up, and there was a flurry of back-slappin' and guffaws. When Pa turned to us and said they had some business to attend to, his friends all winked and chuckled. Then he told us to have a look around. They walked off down the street toward the Gold Nugget, and we were left gaping at the sights and wondering what to do.

Down near the livery stable there was a sharpshooting contest going on in a big corral. Not far from where we stood, down one of the other streets, several Indians in war paint were doing some dances to the steady beat of the tom-toms. Then down the same street in the opposite direction was a fellow holding a "medicine show."

The boys wanted to see the sharpshooters. They didn't even wait to ask but just dashed off excitedly, Tad running to keep up with Zack.

I was curious about the Indians, wondering if one of them might be the Indian brave I'd seen out by the stream. But Emily was afraid, and I can't say I blame her, for they did have a rather alarming appearance at first. So finally we decided on the medicine show.

I'd never seen anything like it before. A big box-like wagon stood in the middle of the street, painted all over with pictures and banners, and the words "Dr. Aloyisius P. Jack's Famous Miracle Rejuvenator" printed in fancy, colorful letters on the side. A man I figured was the famous Dr. Jack stood on a little platform at the back of the wagon. He was dressed in a bright yellow frock coat that hung to his knees over tan pinstriped trousers and a red vest. If he meant for this outfit to attract customers, it worked, for there were twenty or thirty men, mostly miners, gathered around. He wasn't a big man, but standing up on that platform in those bright clothes and his black stovepipe hat, he looked mighty impressive. His eyes glinted and shone when he talked, and his long, brown beard wagged to give just the right emphasis to his words.

"I can see the town of Miracle Springs is not short of intelligent men . . ." he was saying. "Men of vision! Men of wisdom! Men of. . . ."

He seemed to falter as he scanned the crowd. Then to my horror I realized he was looking right at me!

" . . . and young ladies, too!" he went on in a merry tone. "Ah, yes, I can see this is a town of no mean populace!"

The audience chuckled and applauded, and all at once Emily, Becky, and I found ourselves being jostled nearer to the front.

"Welcome one and all!" Dr. Jack went on. "Ladies—" he winked at us as he said the word, "and gentlemen! With great pleasure I present to you the most stupendous medical discovery of this century! My very own 'Miracle Rejuvenator'! And is it not appropriate that it should be named as your fine town?"

"What's it do, Doc?" yelled someone from the crowd.

"A most intelligent question!" shot back the doctor. "Most intelligent, indeed. The secrets of my Rejuvenator are vast, to be sure. It contains herbs and potions that I, myself, procured at great peril and personal danger from the great Cherokee Indian Chief Oouchalatah. Tell me, my friends of Miracle Springs, have you ever seen an Indian with gout or ague? The prevention of these two maladies are but two of the marvelous feats of Dr. Jack's Rejuvenator. Stomach ailments too will be a thing of the past. Regular use of my elixir improves vision and strengthens the blood— and you all know what that can mean on those cold nights at the diggin's!''

I didn't know what it meant. But lots of others seemed to, for several started waving money and yelling.

"Gimme a bottle of that!"

"One dollar, folks," Dr. Jack was saying again. "One slim dollar to possess the benefits of youth again!"

He glanced down at me. "And, young lady, surely there is someone you know who can benefit from this wonderful tonic?"

"I haven't got a dollar," I said.

"I got ten cents," piped up Becky. I felt like stuffing a sock in her mouth.

"Do you now?" mused the doctor. "Well, little lady, I just happen to be running a special for ladies such as your-self—ten cents a bottle!"

But before Becky could get her fingers around her money, one of the onlookers who had already made his pur-chase yelled out, "Ooo-wee! This here's one-hundred-proof whiskey!"

Dr. Jack cleared his throat deprecatingly. "I must admit that one of the ingredients does happen to be a small amount of alcohol—to enhance the flavor only!"

I waited no longer, yanking Becky and Emily away from the so-called "medicine" show. As we broke through the crowd we nearly ran headlong into Mrs. Parrish.

"Hello, girls," she said cheerfully. "I just saw your brothers, and was hoping to run into you. I'm so glad your father brought you."

"Uncle Nick's here, too," chimed in Becky proudly.

"Ah, so your uncle's back?" she asked, looking at me with a worried frown.

"Yes, Ma'am," I said. "Pa brought the sheriff out to the cabin and got Uncle Nick's problem all straightened out."

"That's wonderful," she replied. "I just hope it stays straightened out."

"Pa said this was an important day for Miracle," I said.

"Indeed it is. Every influence that brings civilization more and more to the wilds is to be enthusiastically welcomed." She paused thoughtfully. "I am a bit surprised he saw it in that light, however. Surprised, but still pleased."

"Why do you say that, Ma'am?"

"I just thought that men such as your father and uncle, you know, from their *background*—"

But she let her words trail away unfinished. I guess she didn't want to speak ill of Pa or Uncle Nick in front of us, though her look didn't suggest she was going to say anything bad. Actually, she looked pleasantly surprised, just like she'd said.

Anyway, she started up again on a different subject almost in the same breath. "Well, girls, the formal festivities are about to begin—mostly long-winded speeches—but historical, nonetheless."

She cast down her eyes almost timidly—a very uncharacteristic gesture for her, then added, "I myself will be delivering a few short remarks as well."

"How wonderful, Mrs. Parrish!" I said. "We wouldn't miss it."

"It won't be much. Many of the town fathers, so to speak, thoroughly resent having a woman up on the platform with them. But since I operate the second largest enterprise in town, they had no choice—especially when I insisted. I have an ulterior motive, however. I want to advertise for another historic event which will be coming up shortly."

"Ma'am?"

"Don't you remember? The preacher will be here in less than two weeks—almost any day now."

"Oh, yes."

"Come along," she said, taking Becky's hand. "I'll walk you over. But I'm afraid after that you'll have to be on your own."

The throngs of people scattered around town were beginning to migrate toward the raised, banner-covered platform. Mrs. Parrish found us a place near the front. Seated at the back of the platform, a band was playing "Oh, Susanna." Four men were seated on chairs in front of the band, all looking very important in their brown and black frock coats and matching trousers, silk ties and waistcoats, wearing stovepipe and derby hats.

One of the men I recognized as the sheriff who had come out to the cabin about Uncle Nick. Mrs. Parrish said his name was Simon Rafferty. He was a big, barrel-chested man, and his general size, solid build, and huge cigar, made him look more like a locomotive than a speech maker. I guess since Miracle had no other officials, he was the most important dignitary we had.

Next to the him sat a tall, younger man whom Mrs. Parrish told me about as we approached the platform. His name was Franklin Royce, and he looked very important. But whereas the constable seemed to be *trying* to look important, Mr. Royce just did. You would never mistake him for anything but an important man. There were two other men with them—the General Store owner, Mr. Bosely, and another man I didn't know. I thought he must be the newspaper man, for surely he would have to be on the stand. I liked the look of him immediately. He had kind eyes behind his spectacles, though his thin, taut lips seemed unaccustomed to nonsense. Maybe he was just a little frightened about the speech he was going to have to make. He must have been about forty, though his thinning hair was more blonde than gray. His skin was pale and looked soft to the touch—a sure sign of someone who hadn't been long in the West.

Mrs. Parrish joined the men, who all stood and tipped

their hats to her as she took the fifth and last chair on the platform.

I must say, Mrs. Parrish looked just as important as the men as she sat up there. In fact, she was almost regal in her gray silk dress and the matching hat with its pink feather tilted just so on her brown hair, all pinned up on her head in soft ringlets. I wondered if I'd ever look *half* as lovely as she did.

The band was striking up "Old Dan Tucker" when Uncle Nick came up beside me. I was beginning to wonder if we'd see him again before it was time to go home. But here he was seeking us out! I smelled a faint whiff of whiskey on his breath as he spoke.

"You kids having a good time?" he asked.

"Oh, yes, wonderful, Uncle Nick!" I answered.

"Now comes the boring part," he said.

"Where's Pa?" I asked.

"Shhh!" he replied with a finger to his lips. "You remember what he told you on the way in—he's still just Mr. Drum! Can't nobody find out who he is 'til we take care of this little problem we have with the fellers from back home."

I don't know if Pa'd have wanted him saying all that to me. Always before when they talked, they were very secretive. But I'd heard enough to figure they were in some kind of trouble from home, too, and that men were looking for them—dangerous men, by the sound of it.

"But Mrs. Parrish knows," I whispered.

"Yeah, and your pa said he was a fool to tell her. But he told her to keep quiet."

"She won't tell," I said. "She's a real fine lady. Look, there she is up on the stand getting ready to make a speech. Doesn't she look grand?"

Uncle Nick gave a more interested look, then rubbed his stubbly chin. "Well, by Jove, you're right, a handsome woman at that!" he finally said.

"So, where's Pa—er . . . Mr. Drum?" I asked again.

"Over with some of the boys. He'll be here pretty soon."

The speeches started, and mostly what followed *was* boring, as Uncle Nick had predicted. About halfway through the first speech, Pa wandered over to where we were all standing.

The speakers all talked about "this fair town" and the "flowering of civilization" and the "wealth not only in mineral, but in human resources, also."

I never heard a town get so many compliments, and wondered if they were really talking about ramshackle Miracle Springs with its sprawling, ragged conglomeration of tents and claims and cabins, its five saloons and rough inhabitants. But maybe they were speaking in terms of what they hoped Miracle would one day be like.

When Mrs. Parrish got up, she finished off her speech by reminding everyone that Miracle would "truly come of age when we receive our first man of God." She told everyone to set aside Sunday, November 27, for that very auspicious occasion when the first services would be held. There was scattered applause as she sat down, but I had the clear impression there would not be nearly so good a turnout on that day as this.

"What's that woman thinkin'?" grumbled Pa. "Sunday's our day of rest from work, not a day to fill up with meetin's!"

Somehow, though, I had the feeling Mrs. Parrish would see to it that there was a decent showing for the preacher's first Sunday!

After the speeches were over, and the crowd gave several cheers for the newspaper's editor, Mr. Culver Singleton, everyone began to disperse back toward the various sideshows or the saloons. Mrs. Parrish stepped down off the platform and walked toward us. With her were Mr. Royce and Mr. Singleton. Introductions were made, and I couldn't help feeling quite honored at the nice things Mrs. Parrish said when she told Mr. Singleton about us. The man named

Royce already seemed to know Pa and Uncle Nick. They tipped hats and shook hands, but no smiles were exchanged. What a world of difference there was between my rough-looking, quiet Pa and the two city-bred men in their fancy suits! But it didn't make Pa any less in my eyes.

"Well, Drum," said Mr. Royce, "how's that little mine of yours doing?" His voice sounded almost condescending.

"Fair to middling," answered Pa.

"Have you reconsidered my offer to sell?"

Hearing the words, Uncle Nick, who'd been on the edge of the conversation not paying much attention, now angled his way to the forefront and answered the question directed at Pa.

"We told you last month, Royce, our claim ain't on the market."

"Even though I'm offering you more than what it's worth?"

"Not more'n what it's worth to us."

"What do you say, Drum?" said Mr. Royce, looking at Pa. "Does your partner speak for you?"

"He does. The claim ain't for sale." He didn't seem to like the other man's tone, and his eyes narrowed and seemed even harder than usual.

"I heard you lost it in a card game not long ago," persisted the banker.

"Got it back."

"I simply don't understand your attachment to the place. Some of the other men to whom I've made offers have been more reasonable."

Mr. Royce spoke casually, but I could tell he was driving at something.

"I've had geologists all over that area, you know, and the scientific conclusion is that the gold for several square miles is played out."

"Then why are you so all-fired intent on gettin' your hands on it?" said Uncle Nick heatedly. The whiskey must've begun reaching his brain.

Royce chuckled—a little nervously, I thought—but quickly regained his composure.

"I'm a banker, Mr. Matthews. I'm pledging my future to this area. I'm interested in acquiring good land, land with water and timber, for the future settlers who will come to Miracle Springs to make their homes here. Of course a banker must keep abreast of mineral developments in an area such as this, but I assure you, gold is of secondary concern to me."

"And that's why you're buying up whatever claims you can, for the streams and the trees?" asked Pa, hardly hiding the sarcasm in his voice.

"Well, that's putting it a bit simply perhaps, but I suppose that catches the gist of it, Mr. Drum."

"You say the gold is played out for several miles, Mr. Royce. Just how far exactly?" asked Mrs. Parrish.

"Not to worry, Mrs. Parrish," the banker replied. "The Parrish mine is well out of that range and should have a few more profitable years left."

"This is a simply fascinating conversation," said Mr. Singleton enthusiastically. Until then he had, though silent, been keenly observing the speakers. "*The California Gazette* will want a feature article on this subject."

"I should be glad to supply you with an interview," said Mr. Royce.

"Thank you kindly, sir," replied the newsman. "But a woman's perspective might be a novel approach. In fact, I can see *two* articles, one featuring the big mining operation like yours, Mrs. Parrish, contrasted with a small two-man partnership. Might you consent to an interview, Mr. Matthews?"

"What?" said Uncle Nick, rubbing his face like he had just awakened from a deep sleep. "You mean you want to put what I got to say in that newspaper of yours?"

"I believe you are representative of a large percentage of

my readership, and thus your perspective would lend greater appeal. You must give it some thought, and you too, Mrs. Parrish."

Then the newspaper man smiled weakly at Mr. Royce who seemed suddenly to have been edged out of the proceedings. "And in the future," he said to him, "I'm sure I shall also want to run an article on the banker's view in all this."

Then some folks came and led Mr. Singleton away.

Mr. Royce used the opportunity to return to the subject of Pa and Uncle Nick's claim. He turned to Uncle Nick, who had begun sauntering away.

"I understand, Matthews," he said, "that the population around your little cabin has grown considerably of late." As he spoke he nodded in our direction. "In light of that, I can understand your reluctance to part with the only roof over your head. Because of these new developments, I am prepared to double my previous offer for your land. It would give you the opportunity to move into town and start a new life for yourself and the young folks here—your long-lost kinfolk, as I understand it."

"We told you before, Royce," said Pa, not even giving Uncle Nick a chance to reply, "our mine ain't for sale. We'll do just fine where we are—all of us."

"I only thought for the children's sake—"

"The children will be here only through the winter anyway."

My heart sank as Pa said the words, but I tried not to show my disappointment.

"Oh, I see. I understood they had no other family but your . . . uh, your partner here, and that—"

"Well, you understood wrong! You may be able to smooth-talk Pickins and MacDougall outta their claims, and I ain't heard what Larsen's decided to do about your offer. But Nick and I ain't selling!"

Mr. Royce said nothing further, merely tipped his hat and ambled slowly away.

"There's something about that man I don't like," Pa muttered. "I don't think I altogether trust him."

"I hope you don't take Mr. Royce's words completely to heart, Mr. Drum," said Mrs. Parrish. "Geology reports can be misleading at times."

"Oh, I don't," Pa replied.

"You and the children's uncle have put a great deal of labor into your claim. I would hate to see you give up on it."

"Royce can keep his geologists," said Pa.

Then followed an awkward silence. It was Uncle Nick who broke it. "Mighty fine speech you gave up there, Ma'am."

"Thank you. I hope it inspired you to attend our first church services here in Miracle Springs." She said the words addressing my uncle, but I could see her glancing over toward Pa as she spoke.

"Well . . . uh, let me see—when was that again?"

"The children need to have their spiritual education enhanced, you know, Mr. Matthews . . . Mr. Drum." Now she looked over at Pa.

His mood changed abruptly. I don't know if he didn't like Mrs. Parrish meddling with us kids, or if he just wanted to be left alone to do his own thinking about religious matters. But he clearly didn't much like her giving him counsel about us.

"The kids'll get along just fine," he said, "without no one telling me what kind of education I oughta be giving 'em. Now if you'll pardon me, Ma'am," he added stiffly, touching the brim of his hat, "I gotta git along."

He spun around and strode off down the wooden sidewalk. Uncle Nick just stood there a moment longer, then walked off in the other direction toward the Gold Nugget. We stayed with Mrs. Parrish and she never mentioned our pa again.

# CHAPTER 22

# DINNER WITH ALKALI JONES

Over the next several days, mining and the status of gold in the streams and rivers and hills about Miracle became a major subject of conversation. Pa never discussed the mine with us kids. But when he was talking to Uncle Nick, or to anyone else whenever we'd go into town, that's mostly what they talked about. And I could tell he was more concerned about it than usual. He seemed to spend every spare minute either at the mine or at the stream.

I wanted to learn all I could about gold digging. It was such an important part of everyone's life around here. Pa was short on details, but Uncle Nick would answer my questions whenever I'd ask him.

I did learn a little about the two basic kinds of mining—placer and quartz. Most of the small claims around Miracle were placer operations in the rivers and streams. They used sluice boxes of many types, and lots of water. Pa and Uncle Nick had several sluice boxes situated on the stream at places where the water would run swiftly through them and sift out the gold as they dredged up dirt and gravel with a shovel and threw it into the top of the box. Watching them shovel and sift the dirt, and then pick through the bottom sections of the wooden chute looking for the specks of gold left behind, I could tell it was a lot of work for what little they found. I tried to draw a sketch of them working to put in my journal.

A person could find a lot more gold with quartz mining, but only rich men and mining companies could afford to do it profitably. Instead of above ground digging in streams, quartz miners dug and blasted their way into the side of a hill where they figured gold might exist, hollowing out a cavern that went inside the mountain. They searched about, hoping to run across a whole vein of the ore.

Pa and Uncle Nick began placer mining in the stream, but they dug out a cave up there at the mine, too, so I guess they had been trying their hand at both methods. They were digging it out by hand with a pick rather than dynamite, and Uncle Nick said it was slow going because it was just the two of them. But he said that's where the real gold is— inside the mountains, not in the streams. Pa warned us several times to keep away from the mine, especially the younger children.

"You gotta stay clear of the cave," he'd tell Tad and Becky every day. "You never can tell when one of them roof timbers'll give way." Then turning to me and Zack, he'd add, "You keep 'em outta there, you hear?"

One day, Alkali Jones came out to the cabin and stayed for supper. I learned more from the talkative old miner in that one day than I might have in weeks from our tight-lipped pa and carefree uncle.

"I tell you, Drum," said Mr. Jones, "that's jest stuff an' nonsense about the gold bein' all dried up."

"Franklin Royce's geologists come all the way from Harvard College in Massachusetts," said Pa. "Leastways, that's what he claims, though I don't believe them neither."

"Aw, what do they know about minin' way back there?"

"If they was workin' for anyone but Royce, I might have to pay 'em some heed. But like the Indians say, Royce tends to speak with a forked tongue."

"He's a snake, is that what yer meanin'?"

"Maybe that's a mite harsh, Alkali. I don't like him much neither, but he is a banker."

"One an' the same, iffen ya ask me."

"I gotta agree with Alkali," put in Uncle Nick. "I think the varmint's up to no good around here. I wouldn't put nothing past him."

The talk lulled as I brought a plate of fresh biscuits to the table. Pa lifted two from the dish, buttered them, ate one in two huge bites, and then spoke as the other two men did likewise.

"Well," said Pa, "our placer operation on the stream is slowing down, and there's no denying it. What do we get, Nick, an ounce, maybe two a week, if we're lucky and work at it? That is if I can keep you here working at all!"

Uncle Nick grinned half-sheepishly and looked over at Mr. Jones.

"Weren't it the underground potential you was lookin' for in this claim when ya got it in the first place?" asked Jones.

"Wasn't really looking for nothing," Pa answered. "Not long after we got here, Nick won it in a Monte game from old Phil Potter."

"Phil was always talking about a bonanza vein and such like," said Uncle Nick. "But I think all that was just so we'd let the claim cover the pot on the table, which was worth more'n we ever took from this stream. Probably nothing but talk."

"I don't know," mused Pa. "He was from the coal mines over in Cornwall, England, and all his friends hereabouts said he knew his stuff." A slow smile spread over his face as he recalled the incident. "That was some game," he said. "You had them cold, and they never knew it."

Uncle Nick laughed. "And now they got their revenge—sticking us with a dead mine!"

"Potter'd be bound to know more'n any blamed Harvard geologist!" said Mr. Jones.

"Too bad Phil ain't around no more," said Pa. He popped the second biscuit into his mouth in one piece. The talk slowed while he chewed and the other two men concentrated on their plates.

When the meal was finished, Pa leaned back in his chair and lit up a cigar. Mr. Jones put his feet up on a log and filled up his pipe, and then lit it with deliberate satisfaction. Uncle Nick threw a quick tickle toward Tad and Becky, then shadow-boxed a couple punches in Zack's direction. The resulting giggles from all three contrasted with the serious talk always coming out of Pa's mouth. I think Uncle Nick might've liked to be more involved with us kids, but was just a little afraid of what Pa might say. Even though he was a man to us, every once in a while I'd catch a look in his eye that made me think he almost looked on Pa as a pa too, more than just a big brother—or brother-in-law. But the talk soon settled back again around the topic of the future of the mine.

As the smoke curled silently up in the air from the cigar and pipe, the girls and I started to clear the supper things off the table. But I moved quietly, hushing the little ones up every so often so I wouldn't lose the thread of the conversation.

"So what're ya aimin' t' do, Drum?" Mr. Jones finally asked, punctuating his words with a wisp of smoke. He talked mostly to Pa, more or less acknowledging him as the head of the partnership, even though it seemed to be common knowledge that the claim was in Uncle Nick's name. Folks in town called it the Matthews claim. To all but their best friends, Pa tried to pretend he was just in the background. I still didn't know why.

"That's one of the reasons I wanted to see you, Alkali," replied Pa. "I know you're bound for Marysville—and you'd find better pickings over yonder on the Feather. But we were thinking—and me and Nick's talked this over and are in complete agreement. If you wanted to stay in Miracle, you could work here with us and help us get the mine deeper into the mountain. Three men could do a lot of things two men just can't."

"There's lots of fellers who'd jump at the chance o' teamin' up with the two o' ya, Drum—younger an' stronger than me. Hee, hee!"

"Yeah, but none we'd trust like you. Nick and me, we've got . . . well, let's just say there's some of those fellers you mentioned who would be a mite too inquisitive to suit us, and we got some things we just can't let get out."

"Nobody can stop that mouth of yours," laughed Uncle Nick from where he stood by the fire, "but you know when to keep it shut, too."

"Thank ya kindly—that is, if yer meanin's what I think it is!"

"Don't worry," added Pa, chuckling himself. "Nick was paying you a compliment."

Mr. Jones might have blushed his pleasure at my pa's words, but it was impossible to tell for certain since so little of his skin showed through the hair and grime. His beard was at least four inches longer and two inches thicker than Pa's.

"It might turn out Royce's eastern fellers are right," Pa went on. "I'm guaranteeing nothing. All our efforts could be for nothing—"

"Pshaw!" exclaimed Alkali Jones with a wave of his hand in the air. "That's the least of my worries. I been workin' all my life fer nuthin', anyhow! Hee, hee! No reason to stop now!"

"I'm going on nothing more than Phil Potter's word and my own gut instinct."

Mr. Jones winked coyly. "Ya may like t' keep it quiet, Drum—an' I know ya got yer secrets houndin' ya from wherever ya come from—"

Pa shot him a keen glance. But a moment's look apparently satisfied him that Mr. Jones knew nothing more than he was saying, and meant no harm by the statement.

"—but I know you! You know yer own share o' that geology stuff."

"I may know a thing or two," consented Pa, "and I'm trusting to that."

"That strike o' yers, when ya went over t' Rough an' Ready by yerself back in '49—that was more'n pure luck."

"Maybe. Though it didn't do me much good, and here I am still scratching the soil for nothing more than dirt."

"The gold's here," said Uncle Nick. "I can *feel* it!"

"There's no cash in feeling it in a lame-brained head," said Pa with a wink in Mr. Jones' direction. "You gotta feel it in your hand!"

Mr. Jones took the opportunity to let loose a high-pitched cackle.

"And we still gotta account for Royce's statement," Pa went on, serious again. "What reason would the man have to spread false rumors?"

"To scare folks off and buy claims up cheap!" said Uncle Nick.

"He could never get away with it," Pa replied. "If there really was much gold left, he'd never pull a swindle like that off. This ain't '49 or '50. We're not just a batch of greenhorns anymore."

"Don't ya believe it, Drum!" said Alkali Jones. "You and I and Nick may be too smart fer that. But there's still enough of the other kind around."

There was a long pause while the two men smoked in silence, rocking back and forth on the legs of their two chairs. Uncle Nick still stood with his back to the fire. I guess Zack had been listening to the conversation, too. Now he looked over to where Pa and Mr. Jones were seated.

"Mr. . . .uh . . . Mr. *Drum*," he said hesitantly, his high-pitched voice both cracking and lowering as he spoke. "I could work at your mine."

Pa stared up at him as if it was the first time he had even noticed my brother. But before he could say anything in reply, Mr. Jones spoke up.

"Hee, hee, Drum! Looks like you don't need me after all! Hee, hee!"

I could see a cloud come over Zack's face. Right then there was nothing he hated more than being treated like a child.

"I'm a real good worker," he said defensively.

"The mine ain't no place for kids," said Pa, exactly as he had a hundred times before.

"Hey, Drum, hold up a minute," said Uncle Nick, with a hint of fun in his voice. He saw an opportunity to speak up for us kids when Pa couldn't say too much to contradict him. "Watch how you're talking about my sister's boy! He's no runt—even a mite big for his age."

"If I'm t' be one o' the princeeples in this here operation," chimed in Alkali Jones, "well, I figure we need jest about all the help we can git."

"He's just a boy, Alkali," said Pa. "Blastin' and pickin' our way into that hillside is man's work."

"Why, jest look at them muscles shapin' up in his arms," Mr. Jones went on. "Drivin' a rig across them plains got him in fine shape fer gold minin'. 'Sides, he's yer partner's kin. So ya can trust him better'n ya can trust even the likes o' an ol' coot like me! Hee, hee!"

Pa saw he was out voted. He took a long, agonizingly slow puff on his cigar, all the while looking Zack over from head to foot as if pondering his friend's words. Finally he spoke again.

"You know how to do what you're told, boy?" he asked sternly.

Zack nodded.

"Well then, maybe we'll give you a try one day. But mind you, there ain't going to be no larkin' on this here job!"

I found that last statement a strange one considering what a hard time Pa was always giving Uncle Nick for getting into scraps that took him away from the work. Yet working the mine seemed to have suddenly become more important to everyone. I wondered if it had anything to do with us being there, or if something inside Pa just wanted to prove Mr. Royce wrong.

Whatever the reason, activity at the mine began to pick up. The buckboard, drawn by Alkali Jones' mule, made several trips into town bringing back loads of mining supplies and cases of dynamite. Meanwhile, Tad insisted that he was almost as big as his brother and should be allowed to work, too. And Becky's natural recklessness and curiosity kept her constantly in the way. It was all I could do to keep Tad and Becky out from under the mens' feet.

But winter was coming on too, and days of rain kept halting the work altogether. Uncle Nick said that in the spring they'd really be able to get going.

I couldn't help thinking that if Pa had his way, by springtime we Hollister children might be on our way back East.

# CHAPTER 23

## SOME TIME ALONE

One of my favorite diversions during those chilly days of late fall was to sneak away from the cabin for a walk in the woods.

Taking care of the young'uns, and trying my best to put a decent meal on the table for Pa and Uncle Nick, and sometimes Mr. Jones, every night, tired me out from morning till bedtime. I wasn't a ma yet, but being those kids' oldest sister made me wonder sometimes why anybody'd *want* to be one. I didn't understand it back then, but now I know why Ma used to collapse in a chair and let out an exhausted sigh.

So I didn't get a chance to get away by myself too often. But sometimes I'd leave Zack or Emily in charge, or convince Tad and Becky that it was time for a nap or "quiet time," and then slip away for thirty or forty minutes—or even an hour, if I thought I could get away with it.

One morning, Pa said he had to go into town for some things, and Uncle Nick soon had everybody else loaded in the back of the wagon to go along. Pa didn't seem to mind, and finally looked around at me where I still stood by the cabin. "Ain't you coming, Corrie?"

I hesitated a moment. "I thought maybe I'd just stay home this time."

He looked at me kinda funny, then turned back and

snapped the reins and took off, while Uncle Nick and Tad ya-hoo'd in the back.

Five minutes later, there I was—*all alone* at the cabin! There was nothing but silence inside, and the sounds of the wilderness outside, to keep me company for several hours.

I could hardly contain my delight! But what should I do with this precious time?

Almost before I'd stopped to think about it, I tucked a copy of Sir Walter Scott's *Ivanhoe* under my arm and wandered out toward the creek. A month before the woods had been pretty with all their bright colors. Yet now, even with most of the leaves brown and dead and fallen to the ground, it was still lovely.

The air was crisp and chilly, and I pulled my winter coat tight around me. The chill stung at my cheeks even as my feet crunched over the dead leaves all over the ground. *This is just what I need*, I thought to myself. *Some time alone*. I didn't worry about myself all that much, but every once in a while I found myself thinking about grown-up things—or maybe I should call them growing-up things. I was starting to become a young woman, and there wasn't anybody to talk to and share with, no one who truly understood the new and sometimes frightening feelings that were coming and going inside me. I suppose Zack was feeling the hurts and uncertainties of trying to grow up, too, but he was only thirteen. And then, of course, he was a boy, and boys just don't feel things the way a girl does.

I didn't mind the cold as I walked along. In fact, it seemed to suit my mood just fine.

Pa was very much on my mind; he always was these days. It had been hard enough getting used to Ma's dying. But then all of a sudden to have Pa back in her place—that was some change to reckon with!

At first, with the horrible uncertainty and aloneness, I'd been so happy to find out about Pa. I remembered that first day, when he told us who he was, and I walked over and put my arms around him. I couldn't believe it was really him, and I wanted so much to love him! I began to feel a little hurt, though, when I thought about his not wanting to claim us. What that might have to do with him keeping his name secret, I still wasn't sure. But I still thought we might somehow make the best of it, even though he was quiet and sometimes gruff and didn't seem to want us around much.

When he gambled away our horses, and caused all that hurt to Emily, it made me downright mad. He had no cause to do such a thing, and it made me start thinking about everything Grandpa'd said about him—how he'd brought trouble and hardship to his family thinking only about himself, what a poor example of a husband and father he was, leaving Ma to fend for herself. Ever since the incident with the horses, I'd wondered if maybe Grandpa had been right in everything he said. Pa wasn't treating us much better than he had Ma, and now he was even talking about sending us back East somewhere.

I was angry at him—even bitter, I guess—on account of Ma. I tried to keep it inside. And having Uncle Nick around the place had helped, because if he hadn't been there, I'm afraid I might have said some things I shouldn't have to Pa. He treated Zack so badly. I wouldn't have blamed Zack if he hated him. He didn't act like a pa at all to him.

As I walked along in the woods, Ma came to my mind. In the daily effort just to do what had to be done, and in trying to figure out how I was supposed to feel about Pa, I'd more or less forgotten how much I missed her. But now, with the anger rising in me against Pa, I realized that maybe Ma'd still be alive if it hadn't been for Pa's deserting her.

*Oh, Ma,* I found myself thinking, *I wish you were still alive, and it was you we were with—not Pa!*

Tears began to sting my cheeks, and all of a sudden the urge to run came over me. I took off and raced over the uneven terrain. It felt good, almost as if I could run the pain out of my heart by making it pump faster and faster. The ground was uphill; I was running up the creek, and after about a quarter of a mile, I finally collapsed in a breathless heap against the trunk of a huge old oak. I half-giggled, half-cried, struggling to catch my breath, still not sure which of my mixed-up emotions was going to get the upper hand.

The sudden sound of my own voice surprised me and made me feel all the more alone. Crying can be done alone, but laughing isn't much good unless you've got someone to share it with. And laughing and crying together doesn't feel quite right any time. I leaned my back up against the tree and sat, still breathing heavily from my run. I was too keyed up to read, so I laid my book aside for a while.

I could hear the gurgling of the creek only a short stone's throw away. I peered over at the opposite bank, still and deserted. It brought to my mind that day several weeks ago when the kids and I had been out here and had seen the Indians. I'd just about given up seeing them again, when all of a sudden, I heard a sound!

It hadn't come from across the creek where I might have expected, but from *behind* me—so close it rang in my ears!

I started to my feet. Terrified, the first thing that came to my mind was Alkali Jones' story about the bear!

If it was some wild animal, trying to flee would do me no good. I froze, still pressed against the oak. All I could think of was how awful it would be to get eaten by a bear. Hastily, I brushed a sleeve across my wet eyes.

Then the sound came again. It was a snapping twig. But only one twig, not anything like what you'd expect from a charging bear. Gathering up all my courage, I turned my head and twisted my body as quietly as I could, and then leaned to the side and peered around the tree trunk.

It was *him*!

The Indian boy had come back! I was so relieved not to see a bear that I forgot to be afraid. I stood up, though my knees were still a bit wobbly, came out from behind the tree, and smiled at him.

"Hi," I said. "Do you remember me?"

He stared at me. I thought maybe he couldn't understand English, but then he gave a little nod.

"I remember," he finally answered. Just the sound of his voice was music in my ears!

"My name's Corrie," I said. "What's yours?"

"I am Little Wolf."

"How did you learn English?" I asked, wanting to inch closer to get a better look at him.

"I must go," he said, and started to leave, almost as if he sensed my intent.

"Please!" I called out quickly, "don't go yet."

He paused.

"I'm—I'm new here," I said again. "Would you . . . would you be my friend?"

He half turned back toward me, with the most peculiar expression on his tanned face.

"I am of the Nisenan tribe—Indian," he said, as if that was the only answer necessary.

"What does that matter?" I replied.

He studied me for what seemed a long time. His dark eyes were filled with intelligence and thoughtfulness, as if the notion of such a thing had never occurred to him. I couldn't tell whether his hesitation was the result of my being a girl and he a boy, or because we were from different races.

"You are strange for a white girl," he said finally.

"How do you mean?"

"You do not show fear. You do not run away or scream."

"I'm not afraid. Why should I be?"

"I have been taught that white men fear us."

"From the first time I saw you with your father I knew you would not hurt me."

"But there is trouble between my people and yours."

"Not between you and me."

"My father says there will always be strife between us."

"I don't hold with any of that," I replied. "My pa doesn't either. He says white folks have been unfair to the Indians."

"White man is our enemy."

"But *I* am not your enemy. It doesn't seem right that you hold against me what others have done."

He didn't say anything for a minute. It was clear this kind of talk wasn't going to get us anywhere, and I didn't want him to run off. So I decided to change the subject.

"How did you learn English?" I asked again.

Still he did not speak for a moment. I couldn't quite make out the look on his face. It seemed that he might want to be friends, but that he felt he ought not to be. Finally he answered.

"My father learned it in the mission school. He said it is good to know the white man's tongue to keep from being cheated by him."

"Does your father hate the white man, Little Wolf?"

"They have been my father's friends. They have also cheated him and stolen from him. White men killed my father's brothers."

"I am sorry."

Our eyes met as I said the words. We looked at one another, maybe even into each other's eyes, for a long time. I felt as if I had finally made him believe that I was sincere.

But he never said another word. As quickly as he came, he turned and ran off, disappearing into the woods. Maybe nothing more needed to be said, right then. The look in his eyes told me that if he had the chance, he would be my friend. I hoped my eyes had told him that I would try to be worthy of his trust.

I'd had enough of a walk. Taking up my unopened book, I slowly headed down the creek the way I had come.

When I got back to the claim, I went to the big rock that sat about fifty yards from the cabin, scrambled up, and sat down. I'd gone there several times—it was my thinking place. Today as I climbed up and perched atop it, my mind was full of Little Wolf, Ma, and Pa. The thought of the one brought happiness, the other sadness, and the third anger. If I wasn't careful, I'd start crying again!

I decided not to say anything about Little Wolf when the others got home. Maybe something inside wanted to hold onto my own personal secret, but I was partly afraid it'd rile Pa if he knew.

I'd tell them sometime. But for now I would just keep quiet about my walk up the stream.

# CHAPTER 24

# A TALK WITH UNCLE NICK

All the rest of that day I was moody and glum. I guess I was feeling homesick, realizing all over again how terribly far from home we were and how much life had changed for us. I missed home, I missed the way it used to be, and I missed Ma.

I was so afraid I'd start crying and not be able to stop, that I kept to myself after the others got back from town.

A little while after supper, I looked around and realized I hadn't seen Tad for a while. I put down the skillet I was scrubbing, and went into the bedroom. He was lying face down, alone on his bunk. I walked over and sat down beside him. "What's the matter, Tad?" I asked, laying my hand on his head.

"I miss Ma!" he sobbed. He was only seven, and trying hard to be like his older brother, but he sat up and threw his arms around me. As much as I wanted to be brave and grown-up, I felt the tears trickling down my own face.

I didn't know how to comfort him. All afternoon I'd been thinking about Ma, too—and all the familiar things I'd never see again: the swimming hole down on Elway Creek where we spent so much time in the summer, the woods, and the delightful hours spent with my sisters picking berries. And the sweet-smelling hay in the barn and my special hiding place in the loft where I'd while away the hours playing make-believe games. And, oh, the smell of Ma's bread filling the whole house on baking day!

"I know," I said, my voice choking. "I miss Ma, too." I couldn't think of anything else to say.

Then I heard the door creak on its new hinges. I looked up and was surprised to see Uncle Nick standing there framed in the light of the sunset coming through the window from the other room.

"What's wrong?" he asked quietly. His voice was full of sympathy.

"Tad's missing Ma," I answered.

Slowly he walked into the room and sat down on the edge of the bed next to me. Tad was still sniffling.

" 'Course you'll miss your ma, boy," he said, with sincere compassion. "We all do. I miss her myself sorely. It's just that us grown-ups have learned how to keep our sadness from showing. And I reckon the missing'll last a spell, for both you and me. But I knew your ma real well, and I think she'd be wanting you to be a big boy—to be tough about it, even though you're still sad."

"H-how do you know?" choked Tad, sucking in tentative gulps of air.

"I just do."

Uncle Nick rubbed his chin and glanced off in the distance, as if he was thinking. By now Becky, Emily, and Zack had wandered into the room, too. And then Uncle Nick started to reminisce, something he didn't do too often.

"When we was kids—your ma and me—there was this swimming hole, down t' Elway Creek—"

I wanted to burst in right then and say I knew the place. I'd never thought that if Ma had grown up not far from our farm, then Uncle Nick must have too, and would know many of the same spots. It changed everything to think of Ma as a little girl and Uncle Nick as a little boy!

But I kept my mouth closed. I didn't want to interrupt Uncle Nick's story.

"We was swimmin' and divin' and havin' a grand ol' time," he was saying, "until I went and slipped in the mud puddle we'd made with our games. I was probably jist a mite older than you are now, Tad. Well, down I went with a crash and a snap. I didn't know how a busted arm could pain so! I was screamin' and blubberin' my eyes out, but your ma, she put her arms around me and held me 'til I calmed down. Then she says, 'We gotta get home.' I started up my bawlin' again. 'Now, Nicky,' she says, 'you gotta be tough and strong. This is one of those times you gotta act like a man.' And she kept sayin' it 'til we finally got home. And that's how I think I know what your ma might say to you right now, too. She'd want you to be strong. Cryin' won't bring your ma back, but maybe thinkin' of the good memories will help."

"You really think so?" Tad took a long resolved sniff.

"Sure do, son."

By now the other kids had sat down and all five of us were listening intently.

"You knew Ma when she was young?" asked Emily shyly from where she sat nearly concealed behind Becky.

" 'Course I did!" laughed Uncle Nick. "She was my sister—my *big* sister. You don't think a man could grow up like me without being a little runt of a lad once, do you?"

"Oh-h-h," said Emily with awe. I snickered a little at what he'd said, but I think it awed all of us—both to think of Uncle Nick as a little boy, and to think of Ma in a way that made her seem alive again.

"Tell us another story!" said Becky bravely. I knew that's what we all wanted, but only she had the nerve to ask.

Uncle Nick was quiet for a while, and I thought this brief special time together was over. I wished it could be like this always.

But then to my surprise, Uncle Nick spoke up again.

"Well," he said, "you kids all know how big sisters can be." The four younger ones—everyone but me—all nodded.

Uncle Nick winked at me, and I smiled.

"Well, your ma was no different," he went on. "It was always, 'You climb the tree first to get the apples, then I'll take a turn.' But of course her turn never would come. Or, 'You take down the first batch of laundry from the lines, and I'll get the next,' when she knew all along there was only going to be *one* batch. She always managed to sucker me into doing things for her somehow! A right cagey young lady your ma was, I can tell you that!

"Well, one day I figured out how to get her back! We was playing hide 'n' seek and your ma was *it*. I pretended to go off and hide, but instead I went home. The thought of her lookin' and lookin' for me and gettin' worried, 'cause she usually found me right off—why it was enough to make me laugh to myself all the way home. Our ma was baking bread, and so I sat back as comfortable as you please eating a big hunk of bread, grinning from ear to ear, expecting her to come bursting through the door all in a sweat. After a while I got another piece of bread, and soon a half an hour, and then an hour went by. By the time I started on my third slice, *I* was the one getting worried. I could hardly swallow that bread, good as it was. And I sure couldn't tell my ma about my worry, since I'd be sure to catch it then. So finally I got up and ran all in a fever back to the old oak tree in the clearing that was our *free* spot. And there was my sister, sitting under the tree reading a book, as if she hadn't never missed me at all! She was just waiting for me to come back, and was determined to outlast me!"

We all laughed.

"Weren't you mad, Uncle Nick?" Zack asked.

"Maybe for a minute or two," he answered. "But I admired your ma too much to stay mad for long. She was smart. I respected that. She made life interesting for me. She wasn't no prissy china doll, afraid to get messed up. Anyway, even if she could be ornery to me, she was always there when I needed her, too, sticking up for me. I sure could get into a heap a trouble for a scrappy young kid! But your ma never let me down."

He paused and smiled. "I'll never forget the Bible Memory Verse contest in church. Like I said, your ma was smart, and she won the dad-blamed thing most every month. She knew more verses than Saint Peter! Our Sunday school teacher gave a ticket for each verse memorized, and at the end of the month the winner traded in the tickets for a prize—the more tickets, the better the prize. Well, all year I had been admiring one prize in particular—a fine-carved wooden horse. But since the only verse I had ever been able to memorize was, 'Jesus wept,' my chances of ever gettin' it were mighty slim. I didn't tell no one, but I guess somehow your ma found out, because all that month she kept finding ways to give me her tickets, mostly in trade for doing chores. She figured I'd be too proud to take her tickets if she just gave them to me, or if she won the horse and gave that to me. The way she had it figured was for me to feel like I *earned* the tickets, even if it was sort of by what you might call illegal means."

Uncle Nick chuckled at the memory, then continued. "The big problem came during the church service when the winner was asked to come forward before the whole congregation. When I stood up, our Sunday school teacher, Mr. Alexander, couldn't believe it. But all the folks was applauding so hard and praising him so for his amazing progress with a mischievous kid like me that he didn't have the heart to tell them the truth. I won that carved horse, and, even if it was ill-got, so to speak, I always prized it special-like because of what your ma—"

Uncle Nick's voice seemed to catch over the words and he stopped a moment.

"Well, your ma was a fine sister," he finally said.

"Why'd you ever leave Ma and come to California?" asked Tad. By now his tears had dried and he was fascinated with this rare and unexpected side his uncle was revealing.

But Tad's question was as ill-timed as the horse had been ill-gotten, because Uncle Nick's talkativeness suddenly stopped. He drew in a deep breath, then let it out slowly. When he finally spoke again, his voice sounded heavy and far away. All of the lightness and fun was gone.

"Well, son," he said, "that is a hard question. And one I can't answer for you."

He sighed deeply again.

A spell had stolen over us that night, and I felt sad that it had to end. But the tone of Uncle Nick's voice told me that Tad's question had intruded upon painful ground.

"That's something, son," Uncle Nick added, "that you'll have to find out from your pa . . . if he ever decides to tell—"

He stopped short and looked up.

Pa was standing in the doorway glaring at him.

# CHAPTER 25

# THE ARGUMENT

From the expression on Pa's face, we all knew the instant we saw him that he was furious.

"Nick!" he barked out, "what do you mean fillin' my kids heads with notions of their ma?"

"Nothing, Drum," replied Uncle Nick, bewildered at the outburst and half rising off Tad's bunk. "I only thought it'd make 'em feel better to—"

"Well, I don't want you thinkin' about what's right for my kids! They're *my* kids, you hear, and I'm their pa, not you!"

"I didn't think—uh, there'd be no harm," stammered Uncle Nick. "They was just missin' Aggie, that's all."

"No harm! What do you know about missin' Aggie? It wasn't you that had to leave a wife and kids! And then tellin' me I oughta explain to 'em why we left! That's what caused the trouble in the first place, not being able to say *why*! And you want me to tell 'em now, after it's too late, after all these years—after I've lost my Aggie? You want—"

Pa's voice broke off momentarily. Sitting there listening, I had no idea of the feelings that were flooding through Pa as he stood in the doorway yelling at Uncle Nick. I was only aware of my own anger at hearing him fault our uncle for just trying to be nice to us.

"Curse you, Nick!" Pa yelled again, recovering himself.

175

"You and that foul breed you ran with. You were nothin' but a fool kid and I shoulda never tried to help you! You cost me my wife . . . and now my own kids can't stand the sight of me. Well, I won't be having you play pa to 'em, you hear me! Get out, I tell you . . . just get out!"

Pa turned and walked into the other room.

Without another word, Uncle Nick followed him, his head hanging low. Seconds later, I heard the outside door shut tightly. The five of us sat still as mice, terrified over the outburst, though we had no idea what all the words meant. The only sound in the whole cabin was our breathing.

All the hurt and bitterness I'd felt earlier in the day was slowly rising to the surface again. When it suddenly boiled over, I found myself on my feet running into the other room, where Pa stood with his back turned.

"Uncle Nick was just being nice to us!" I shouted. "You had no call to yell at him like that!"

Pa stood still as a statue and said nothing.

"He's the only one around here who has been nice to us!" I continued. "You never say a thing! You treat us like you wish we'd never come, and like you can't wait to get rid of us! But Uncle Nick's our friend!"

Slowly Pa turned around to face me. He was full of grief and anguish, but my eyes were too full of tears to realize it. I only saw the same face of stone.

"Corrie, I . . . I—" he tried to say, but I lashed out at him again without giving him the chance to finish.

"Grandpa was right! And now you're treating Uncle Nick and us just like you did Ma."

"Oh, Corrie . . . you just don't understand how it was. If only I could make you see—"

"I understand what I heard!" I shot back angrily. "You're nothing but a mean man! Uncle Nick oughta leave here like you left Ma! And maybe we'll all just leave too!" I was crying hard and didn't know half of what I was saying.

"Please . . . don't talk like that," he said, his voice sad. He reached out a hand, and I think he wanted to touch me. But I hit at him and forced his arm away.

"If it weren't for you, Ma'd still be alive!" I shouted bitterly. "You ran out on her! You deserted all of us. And now she's dead—all on account of you! I hate you for what you did to Ma!"

I turned away from him and ran for the door, threw it open and ran outside. Night had fallen by now, but there was a moon up. I ran and ran, sobbing wildly as I went. I had no idea where I was going, I just wanted to get away. Finally, exhausted from my outburst and the exertion of running, I came to a big tree near my thinking rock, and threw myself down at its trunk and wept bitterly.

I must have cried for five or ten minutes. I was in such turmoil over what had happened, angry and sobbing and hurting inside, that I lost all track of time. Love and hate were battling within me and I couldn't even tell the difference.

Eventually I began to breathe easier and stopped crying. But I still lay there, unaware of the night cold, my emotions spent, my heart aching.

I'm not sure what I expected next, but I never could have anticipated what *did* happen. When Little Wolf came upon me earlier in the day, the sound had startled me. Now I remained still, though I knew someone was approaching. I felt no inclination to jump up or run away. I just waited . . . waited until the footsteps stopped and I could feel someone standing behind me.

I knew it was Pa.

He drew nearer and knelt behind me. Then I felt his hand lightly touch my shoulder. It was the first time he had touched me since our arrival in Miracle.

"Corrie . . ." he said quietly, "will you let me talk to you?"

I nodded. But I still couldn't turn around to face him.

"There's a lot of things kids can't understand," he went on, "especially when they're young."

"I ain't so young now," I said, finally finding my voice, "and I still don't understand why you left Ma and us like you did."

"You're right there, Corrie," said Pa. "You ain't young. You're a mighty fine young lady. But you were young then, and I know you were hurt, and your ma was hurt. You were all hurt, I know that . . . and it's my fault. But there was just so much about it you *couldn't* possibly understand."

"So why won't you tell me, so maybe I can understand now?" I said impatiently, looking the other way.

Pa withdrew his hand and sat down with a sigh. It was several minutes before he spoke again. When he did, his voice was different somehow—quiet, filled with sadness and regret. Just the sound of it softened my anger. "Your ma and your Grandpa Belle never knew what was going on with Nick. We all knew he was runnin' with a bad crowd. Your Uncle Nick was a mighty rambunctious lad back in them days. And he finally got himself in so deep over his head that I knew if I didn't try to bail him out, he'd likely either get himself killed or spend the rest of his days behind bars. Either way it would have broken his old pa's heart.

"I ain't tryin' to lay the whole blame on Nick. It was easy, too easy, for me to slip back into my old ways, my ways before I married your ma. An' I shoulda known better than to try to help Nick by goin' into the pit with him. It was stupid, but I got myself mixed up with the gang he was ridin' with. Fool that I was, I thought I'd be able to get him out of the fix he'd gotten himself into, and that we'd be able to just ride away clean and pick up our lives from there.

"And that's where I made my big mistake, Corrie. The thing went sour on us. Real bad! Before I knew what had gone wrong, two men were dead and me and Nick were arrested for bank robbery and murder. So *both* of us were going to have to spend our lives in prison. On top of that, the Catskill Gang got it in their heads that Nick and I had the money from the bank. We weren't even there that night—I swear it, Corrie! I nearly had to sit on Nick, but I managed to keep us both away. Jenkins, one of the gang who was shot that night, found us just before he died, and I reckon the others figured he told us where the money was. The others all made a clean getaway, but Nick and I didn't even know what had happened, leastways not enough to get our hides away before the law found us.

"Your uncle and me was sent to prison, Corrie." He said the words as if he could hardly stand to hear them. "You can imagine how ashamed I was. My own shame was likely enough to make me do what I did, but even then I woulda at least tried to see your ma if ever I got the chance. She was too far away to come to the trial or the jail, thank God for that, at least! I had only one visitor in jail—your Grandpa Belle. He laid the blame for the whole thing on me and I didn't argue with him—I guess I still don't. He said I led Nick astray right from the start and maybe that was right, too. When we was kids, Nick always looked up to me, and I could be a rough one before I met your ma. Grandpa Belle said Aggie couldn't hold her head up no more in the community because of me, and it'd be better if I was dead. All he said made sense at the time, 'cause I hated myself and what I'd done enough to believe it—to believe Aggie'd even think such things. But even if I thought she'd have me back—if I ever did get out of prison, though they'd have probably hung us eventually—I figured I was too rotten for her, anyway. And I thought about what it would be like for you kids to go through your lives having a jailbird for a pa. It didn't matter that I was innocent. No one believed me. It was all the same as if I'd done all I was accused of."

"Ma never said anything about all that," I said.

"I reckon your ma didn't want you to think poorly of me," he replied in a voice full of despair. "She couldn't say nothin' good about me, so she just didn't say anything. I'm surprised your Grandpa Belle didn't say nothin', but she musta made him keep quiet—'bout that, at least. The fracas took place far enough away that I reckon no one else around town knew much about it."

"But then we heard you was dead—what about that?" I asked. I wasn't very angry anymore.

"There was a big riot in prison only a few weeks after we got there," he answered, still with that trapped tone to his voice. "Upwards of twenty-five prisoners escaped. Nick and I were lucky, I guess, 'cause we just got carried along in the thing and ended up outside. We got to the woods surroundin' the prison and found some of the prisoners who had been killed. We exchanged clothes with them. When the bodies were found, the guards thought it was me and Nick who died. We were pretty desperate, Corrie. But now I can see we was just gettin' deeper an' deeper into a life of lies."

"You let Ma—and us—think you were dead?"

"It seemed best, Corrie. I still believed all your grandpa said. I was a jailbird—an *escaped* jailbird, now. I could only bring more shame and misery to your ma. I'll never stop regrettin' what I did . . . I just kept going . . . Nick and I . . . we left everything—"

His voice broke, but he struggled to continue.

"Do you realize what I did? I left my wife, my four kids . . . my God! Becky was just a baby . . . Aggie was still carrying Tad. I didn't even know my youngest son's name before you got here!"

Again he stopped. Slowly, I turned to look at him. Tears were streaming down his cheeks. I could see them glisten in the moonlight. I'd never seen a man cry before, and now here was my own pa, the rough, quiet man I'd just blown up at, the man Ma had forgiven on her deathbed . . . here he was, sitting not two feet from me, sobbing like a child.

Something in my heart gave way. Suddenly I felt full of compassion for him.

"But . . . but Ma would have understood," I said. "She would have come West with you. You could have told her, Pa."

"I couldn't face her, Corrie." He shook his head dismally. "I've fought Indians without flinchin'. I faced down a stalking mountain lion and shot it. You woulda thought I had enough courage—but I didn't. I kept thinkin' 'bout what her pa said 'bout being better off if I was dead. I kept thinkin' of the shame I'd caused her. And I'd never be safe again either. Not even now, I ain't safe, between the law and the Catskill boys that want me."

"But don't they think you're . . . dead, Pa?"

"I don't know no more," he replied. "After Nick let your ma know he was still alive and here in Miracle Springs, anybody could find us. An' I ain't so worried about the Catskill crowd as I am about the law. If they ever find me, it'd be back to prison, and . . . I don't know what'd become of you kids. And now that I got you back, I—"

His voice faded into a strangled sob, and he couldn't say anything more.

I found myself rising to my feet slowly. I put my arms around his big, broad shoulders.

"Oh, Pa!" I said, crying hard. "I'm so sorry . . . I didn't mean what I said back there at the cabin . . . you were right—I didn't understand. I'm sorry . . . I didn't mean to hurt you more."

Pa reached up and clasped one of my hands, then rose to one knee. I took a step back, and for a moment I just stood there looking into his tear-stained face, and he into mine.

Then he released my hand and opened his arms wide. In an instant my head was on his chest. I felt his strong arms close around me and we held each other tight.

"Corrie, Corrie," he said, "I've thought of you every day for the last eight years, prayin' somehow the Almighty would let me see you again."

He paused and managed to take in a deep breath. I was sobbing on his chest, still holding him tightly. "Your ma and you kids had every right to hate me for what I done . . . but . . . but, Corrie, can you forgive me . . . for leaving . . . for not being a pa to you all these years?"

Again the tears streamed down his face, and the agony of regret in his voice was more than my heart could stand.

"Oh, Pa . . . Pa," I cried, "of course I forgive you! Ma never hated you. When she died, she told me she forgave you. I don't hate you either, and I'm so sorry for what I said!"

"It's over now, Corrie," he said, reaching up and gently stroking my hair. "I'll never think of what you said again. If we can just find a way in our hearts to get over what's past, then . . . then maybe we can start over again . . . as pa and daughter."

I stood back a little, and attempted a smile. "I think we can, Pa," I said. "I really think we can!"

He smiled back at me, and I embraced him again, this time not just as a man I called Pa, but as a father I was learning to love.

# CHAPTER 26

## A NEW BEGINNING

When Pa and I finally walked back toward the cabin about twenty minutes later, he left me at the door.

"There's one more apology I gotta make before I go in," he said, then turned off and headed up toward the mine in the moonlight.

I wasn't quite ready myself to go in and face the rest of the kids. I knew they'd pester me with a million questions, and after what had just happened I needed some time to be quiet. My feelings were still running pretty deep, and I didn't know if I could face their looks without bursting into tears all over again.

So I sat down on the wooden porch and waited.

About fifteen minutes later, I heard Pa and Uncle Nick approaching. I couldn't make out their words, but every once in a while I'd hear Uncle Nick laugh, so I figured it'd been patched up between them. When they came into view, Pa had one arm slung around Uncle Nick's shoulder and was looking earnestly at him. All I heard was Uncle Nick's response.

" . . . think nothing more of it, I tell you. I deserved it."

"You're wrong there—I was out of line."

"Don't matter. It's over. You're always telling me that the stream needs a good storm now and then to flush the gold outta where it's hiding. I reckon people are like that, too."

"Well, however we got here, you've been a good partner to me," said Pa, still serious, "and I want you to know it. And we gotta stick together to get through the rest of it . . . oh, Corrie," he said, looking up suddenly and seeing me sitting there. "Ain't you been in yet?"

"I wasn't quite ready," I answered. "I needed a little more time to settle myself."

"I guess we all did," laughed Uncle Nick, trying to lighten the mood. "After we all blowed up at one another, eh? Nothing like a good rainfall to clear up the air, I always say!"

Pa glanced at me and winked, then I stood up and the three of us went inside where the four younger kids were still silently waiting in the bedroom.

From the looks on their faces, I think their worst fears were that someone was going to wind up getting killed. But after they saw Uncle Nick, whose face had recovered its joviality, and they heard a laugh from me, they began to relax. I think they could see the change in Pa too and that eased the tension more than anything.

I can't honestly say that after that day everything immediately got better between Pa and me. There were still lots of questions, and some hurts remained. Pa didn't completely change overnight, but neither did I. He still had his quiet times when I couldn't tell what he was thinking, but he smiled a little more. And I noticed him taking time with the younger kids more than he used to, calling them by name, and hoisting Emily or Becky or Tad up in his arms.

Kids are quick to forgive, and they returned whatever he gave them in love many times over. It was more difficult for Zack. The more effort Pa made to be friendly, the more he hardened himself against Pa, as if he was determined not to let go of the bitterness he had been holding so long. And Pa didn't know how to win him over. He'd been carrying his own grief and guilt so long, it was all he could do to try to overcome that.

I tried to talk to Zack.

"He's trying to be a real pa to us, Zack," I said once.

"Then why'd he keep it a secret who he was when we first came to town?" he snapped back.

"I don't know," I answered. "But he must have had his reasons."

"Yeah, like when he left Ma and us in New York!"

"I already explained that, Zack," I reminded him. "He'd been through an awful lot."

"It still don't seem fair."

"Think how you'd feel, Zack, if it had been you. Being in prison, thinking you'd brought shame on your whole family."

"There musta been some other way!"

"Maybe so, but everybody does things different." I was getting frustrated with him. "I ain't got all the answers, Zack. Why don't you ask him? Wouldn't hurt if you'd talk to him once in a while, you know, instead of just sulking around."

"I ain't sulking!"

"Well, you sure coulda fooled me."

I didn't know what to tell Zack. I still had a lot of the same questions myself. But I thought Pa at least deserved a second chance. After all, he'd asked me to forgive him, and I figured I owed him that much. He seemed sincere, and I believed him.

I did ask Pa again about that first day, when he came to town and pretended not to know us. I knew Zack'd never get around to asking him, so I brought it up again when Zack was within hearing.

Pa said so much had come at him all at once, it was like being hit with a face full of buckshot. All of a sudden, he said, he was standing in front of kids he'd never expected to see again, not even recognizing any of them but me, hearing that his wife was dead, and wondering down inside if it all was some new trick by the New York gang to get him and Uncle Nick.

"I was battling with grief, Corrie," he said. "If it was all true . . . well, just imagine—I'd just been told my wife was dead . . . the wife that I'd never stopped loving, and it just brought it all back over me like a flood. As I stood looking at you all, a powerful bunch of feelings were going through me all at once! Yet, if I let on you were my kids, and what my real name was, the whole town would know in a second. And I was still having to think about protectin' myself and Nick. And all the while, there was that dad-blamed Parrish woman shoutin' at me about what I oughta do, and then Nick in trouble over Judd's killin'—and off somewhere. And even if what that Dixon feller was sayin' was all true— if I let on I was Hollister, not Drum, and *that* got around . . . well, you'd all be in danger again.

"Can't you see the terrible fix I was in? Why I didn't know what I oughta do . . . and all the time I couldn't help thinkin' of Aggie, knowin' I'd never get a chance to see her again and explain . . . and set things right?"

He turned away and quit talking. I never saw him cry again after that first night. But there were a few times I think he was close, especially whenever we'd talk about Ma. More and more I began to see how much he really did love her and how it had pained him to do what he did.

"So, maybe it wasn't right of me to pretend," he told me later. "But without having the chance to think everything through . . . well, I done it, and I guess it's too late to go back and do different. 'Sides," he muttered, "I ain't at all sure we got that Catskill bunch off our backs, yet. So you just make sure whenever you're in town or there's other folks around . . . you keep them kids from calling me Pa! It may be hard for you to understand all my reasons. I know your brother is carryin' a heap of anger, and maybe one day I'll have the chance to make it all right with him. But . . . well,

I *am* your pa, after all, so maybe you just gotta trust me when I tell you it's for the best."

He was right. I didn't understand everything. And I couldn't very well make Zack think any better of him. But even if Zack was bent on carrying a grudge, I felt like giving Pa the benefit of the doubt, and trusting him as much as I could.

We were trying to make a new beginning of it. Pa was still Pa, and we were still uncertain about a lot of things, so it was bound to take some time before we could all trust one another like we should. But knowing how Pa felt inside sure made it easier.

# CHAPTER 27

# A TALK OVER BREAKFAST

The 26th of November came quickly.

Alkali Jones was still working with Pa and Uncle Nick at the mine—not every day, but often. Every once in a while, either when a big day of work was planned, or when they'd work till dark, Mr. Jones would stay the night at the cabin. And the Friday night before Saturday the 26th was one of those.

At breakfast that morning, the topic of the next day's events came up at the table.

"Well, I hear that new preacher lit into town right on schedule," said Alkali Jones around a mouthful of scrambled eggs.

"Yep," acknowledged Pa.

"Looks like the town's about to git itself tamed fer sure," Jones went on in a regretful tone.

"Don't be so sure," said Pa. "No greenhorn preacher from the East's gonna be able to keep some of these men from raising a little Cain now and then."

None of us kids made any comment. But I couldn't help thinking how excited Mrs. Parrish was about the preacher's arrival. I hoped I'd be able to see him.

"Can't seem to git away from it, can we, Drum?" said Mr. Jones.

"What's that, Al?"

"From dad-blamed civilization, o' course! Why, I left Arkansas in 1830 'cause it were gittin' too full o' settlers. Wandered on down Texas-way an' got there jest in time fer all that fracas with Santa Anna. Luckily, I got my hide outta there before Bowie an' Houston an' Crockett got made heroes in '36! Texas wasn't a bad place then—a man could breathe. But then they went an' turned the blasted outfit into a state, an' I says to myself, 'Can civilization be far behind?' "

"You was sure ahead of us," said Pa.

"When did you leave the East, Drum?"

"Well, let's see . . . what was it, Nick, when we lit out from New York? Forty-four, I think. But we didn't get here 'til a few years later."

"Well," went on Mr. Jones, enjoying telling his tales as much as ever, "I figured California was jest about as west as a man could go. So I joined up with ol' John Fremont. I was thinkin' there could hardly be a more remote an' worthless piece o' land than this, an' nobody here but a few Mexicans. Seemed like no one'd trouble us here. Then blamed ol' Jim Marshall had to up an' discover gold! Why, civilization's jest intent on houndin' me t' my grave! Where are fellers like us goin' to go from here, Drum?"

"There's places, I reckon."

" 'Course, you got yerself all strapped down with responsibilities now, Nick, ain't ya?" He eyed my uncle with a mischievous grin. "The wilds ain't fer you no more, no, siree!"

Uncle Nick only nodded in response, and gave a noncommittal grunt.

"But I suppose ya gotta hand it to this new preacher feller," Mr. Jones went on, as unaffected as usual by everyone else's silence. "What's his name?"

"I don't know—Rutman . . . Rodman . . . something like that."

"Well, I suppose ya gotta give him credit. He musta got a bellyful of guts to come to a place like this an' try to bring religion to a pack o' wild sinners like us! Hee, hee! Don't ya think, Nick?" laughed Mr. Jones, turning to my uncle.

"Ah, them fellers is just fanatics," said Uncle Nick, joining in the spirit of Mr. Jones' laughter. "It don't take no guts when a man's plumb loco."

"I dunno," Mr. Jones persisted, but not poking fun this time, and sounding almost serious, "I heared he come the Panama route."

"What's that got to do with it?" said Uncle Nick.

"Why, *that* takes some gumption, 'specially fer some greenhorn city feller. I'd rather fight redskins or Santa Anna than that cursed yellow fever *any* day!"

"He probably just prayed them mosquitoes away," said Uncle Nick sarcastically.

"Hee, hee!" chuckled Mr. Jones. "I can't rightly remember the last time I was in a real church. Not that I ain't a God-fearin' man! But where's a feller goin' to find a church on the trail? Right, Drum?"

Alkali couldn't seem to interest Pa in the discussion, so he turned back to Uncle Nick.

"How 'bout you, Nick? You ever find many churches along the trail?" Both men laughed.

Their talk about the preacher's coming got me to thinking. Ma always made sure our family was a God-fearing one. We went to church almost every Sunday, except when the weather was too bad. She taught us out of the Bible about what was good and what was bad. And I guess I hardly knew anyone who didn't go to church at least some times.

Grandpa Belle didn't go much the last two years, because his rheumatism got too bad. But he still respected God. He would no more poke fun at a man of God than spit in God's own eye! But, now, here were Uncle Nick and Alkali Jones talking about the preacher as if they thought he was some no-account dunce, and the whole town apparently never thought about church at all. I wondered if all the unbelievers had come to California!

I could still remember our minister in Bridgeville

preaching all about how sinners and heathens would face God's wrath and hellfire. I never was quite sure what a heathen was, though I had an idea they were folks in jungles someplace. But plain sinners were another matter, because he used to talk about them as if they were the people in big cities who went into saloons and who shot people.

And now suddenly I found myself wondering about Uncle Nick. He wore a gun and gambled and drank whiskey. And I couldn't help wondering if he was a sinner too and would wind up in hell someday. I figured he wasn't the best man in the world, but I was getting to like him, and I sure hoped he wasn't a sinner. Pa crossed my mind too. He hadn't really gotten into their discussion, but then he wore a gun and had been in trouble along with Uncle Nick, so I just couldn't be sure what to think.

The subject of the new minister and church came up again later in the day. I guess my worry must have showed on my face.

"What's ailin' you, Corrie?" Pa asked.

"Nothing," I said casually, trying to shake the mood away.

"I 'spect you kids'll be wantin' to hear that new preacher tomorrow," he went on without much enthusiasm.

"Yes, sir, I would," I answered. "If you're planning to go," I added, thinking to myself that somehow I *had* to get him to that service.

"Aw," put in Zack, "the one nice thing about living here was that we didn't have to go to church."

"Zack! What a thing to say!" I must have sounded a lot like Ma, because Zack looked surprised at my outburst.

"I like church," said Emily.

"I'd rather go on a picnic," said Becky.

"So, Corrie," said Pa, turning back to me and looking serious, "you want to go?"

I swallowed hard. "Yes, sir," I replied. "I really do."

"Do the rest of us have to go, just because Corrie wants to?" Zack asked with a sulk.

There was silence then. Even Alkali Jones said nothing. All eyes turned toward Pa. He was facing the first big decision about us kids since he decided to take us in, just because Zack had tossed out that question.

He looked around at all of us, from one face to another. He even looked over at Mr. Jones, who didn't seem about to offer any help at all. Then he took a deep breath and said,

"I reckon if one goes, we all go." His tone made it sound more like he was passing some kind of sentence on us than talking about going to church. " 'Sides," he added, summoning a little more enthusiasm, "it's kinda an historical occasion, like the newspaper comin'. So we oughta be there just for that reason, if nothin' else!"

"Should be a mite interestin' to see the Gold Nugget decked out fer a church!" piped up Alkali Jones. "Hee, hee! I wonder what that ol' bartender Jasper'll do? Hee, hee!"

"Howd'ya suppose that Parrish woman managed that?" said Uncle Nick. "I never knowed Jasper t' put no store in religious things."

"That's a mighty feisty woman," said Mr. Jones. "She gener'ly gits what she's after. They say she's got the preacher out here. 'Sides, maybe Jasper owes her money. Hee, hee!"

"A tough one, all right," said Uncle Nick. "I owed her a little money a while back, and she durned near took it outta my hide!"

I smiled to myself.

Leave it to Mrs. Parrish to turn a saloon into a place of worship! The last time we'd talked, she said she had an idea about the service. That must have been it! She probably feels the same way about a church service as she does about praying—you can do it anywhere.

It made sense, too. If there was one place where there ought to be preaching going on, it was in a saloon. But the folks back in Bridgeville sure would be scandalized by such goings on!

It made me realize again how different California was from the rest of the country.

# CHAPTER 28

## THE GOLD NUGGET CHURCH

The next morning, when I awoke, it was still almost black out, but after a while I began to see the first streak of dawn through the window. I got up quietly, tiptoed over and leaned my elbows on the sill, looking out just as the shapes of the hills and trees began to become visible.

Just then, I saw two deer nibbling the last of the green grass on the little knoll by the stream. I hardly noticed them at first, because their colors blended with the gray of the early mist. But as I continued to watch, their forms became more distinct. Slowly tiny bits of pink began to show in the east. Two rabbits scurried by and then disappeared into their burrow. Red and orange followed the pink across the sky. The deer scampered off into the woods, and all was perfectly still again. For several minutes more, I gazed on the peaceful scene.

After a while, I crept back into my bed and watched as the light grew more and more dazzling through the window, until at last came the moment when the sun burst out into the new day.

What a wonderful sunrise! Something about it seemed to speak to me, as if God himself had made it just for me to enjoy that morning, saying in His own way that I was His child.

Finally, I pulled myself out of bed. I couldn't just lie

there looking at the sunrise—today was Sunday, and we were going to church!

The night before, I pulled all our best clothes from the big trunk that had carried most of our possessions from home. I ironed out the wrinkles as best I could, then gave the young'uns their baths. Now I just had to get everyone up and dressed.

There were groans and complaints from Zack and Tad, mostly protesting their stiff collars. Zack's pants were about two inches too short, reminding us all how quickly he was growing, and how much time had passed since the last time we'd gone to church in Bridgeville, just before we came west. In fact, all our Sunday clothes were on the snug side. But we had to make do, and I thought we looked pretty fine in spite of everything.

Even Pa put on a clean white shirt for the occasion, tucked into a pair of clean, but worn, trousers. The neck of his grimy longjohns stuck up above his shirt collar, tarnishing the effect a little.

When Uncle Nick got up, he just put on his work clothes, seeming to ignore the fact that it was Sunday. He went outside and was heading off for the mine, when Pa stopped him. Uncle Nick muttered something about having some things to tend to.

"You get in there and change them clothes, Nick Belle," Pa said. "You're going into town with us."

Uncle Nick moped back into the cabin and did as Pa said, revealing again that no matter whose name was on the claim, Pa was still boss around here.

The whole town didn't exactly turn out to hear the preacher. There were no banners or sharpshooters or medicine shows. But still there was a fair showing of folks— maybe just the curious, or those who didn't have anything better to do. When we drove into town, a good number of people were already heading toward the Gold Nugget Saloon, and I discovered that more ladies than I had ever imagined lived in these parts.

Along the streets and sidewalks, men were loitering about, watching the proceedings, obviously without any intention of joining them.

"Hey, where ya goin', Drum?" called out one in a sneering tone. But Pa kept the wagon moving steadily forward.

"Matthews," shouted another, "come join us down at the Silver Saddle after ye've dropped off your brood!"

I thought I detected a forlorn look pass over Uncle Nick's face.

"Don't tempt him, Jim," said another. "He's a family man now."

This brought a rousing laugh from the small group.

We finally reached the door of the Gold Nugget, pulled up, and all piled out. There were a few men standing around there, too, and Uncle Nick sauntered over and began talking to them.

After a few moments, I heard, "Let Drum take 'em. He's a religious sort of feller. Come on with us."

Pa walked over, far from cowed by their remarks, and turned a dark glance toward the men. He didn't say a word, but they seemed to understand and shrank back quickly. He took firm hold of Uncle Nick's arm, whispered something in his ear, and without further conversation Uncle Nick turned away and walked with us up the wooden steps. The other children bounded in. But I couldn't help hesitating. Pa started in too, then he turned back toward me.

"Something wrong?" he asked.

"No, sir," I answered. "It's just that I ain't never been in a saloon before."

A faint smile flickered across his face. Then he quickly turned serious. "I'm sorry there ain't no real church for you, Corrie," he said. I could tell he meant it.

"Do you suppose having church in a saloon is all right with God?"

"How in blazes am I supposed to know, girl?" he said, then put his hand on my shoulder and nudged me inside.

Twenty or thirty people were seated in chairs that had been placed in rows in front of the bar—mostly men, but probably six or seven ladies. There weren't any other children.

I saw Mr. Ashton and Mr. Weber from the freight company, and Mr. Bosely from the General Store. Mr. Rafferty the constable, was also there, and Mr. Singleton the newspaper man, and even Mr. Royce. The rest of the crowd were miners and a few farmers. Mrs. Gianini sat with one of the farmer's wives. Mrs. Parrish played the piano, and it would have been fine playing too if it hadn't been for the tinny-sounding, old saloon instrument.

The biggest surprise of all was to see Alkali Jones there. I guess I hadn't really expected to see him at all. But there he was—standing just inside the swinging doors, leaning against the saloon's back wall, waiting for Pa.

"Hey, Drum," he called out in a loud whisper, "I thought ya'd never get here, an' leave me standin' here playin' the fool. Hee, hee."

I don't know if I'd have even recognized him if it weren't for his laugh!

He wore a brown broadcloth suit that looked as out of place on him as his brilliantined hair and beard. Slicked down, the old miner looked like a wet cat whose fur had suddenly been soaked, leaving nothing but skin and bones.

"Quiet, ya old coot!" whispered Pa right back as we walked toward the back row. But Mr. Jones paid him no heed.

"Why, I ain't worn a stitch o' these duds since. . . ." He rubbed his slick beard. "Lemme see . . . since my brother Ezekiel's weddin' back in Arkansas."

"Didn't you wear it last time you went to church?" asked Tad innocently, not realizing he was supposed to whisper.

Several heads turned toward us, and I could feel poor Pa's embarrassment at being caught in such a situation, helped none by Alkali Jones' high-pitched chuckling over Tad's question.

Finally we sat down, much to Pa's and Uncle Nick's relief.

Mr. Rafferty introduced everyone to the Rev. Avery Rutledge. He was not an old man, like I imagined most preachers were supposed to be. He was probably Pa's age, or a year or two younger.

He was handsome in a rather stiff and severe way, a bit on the pale side, tall and slim with shoulders that slumped slightly forward. He surely wasn't robust and muscular like Uncle Nick, but his dark brown eyes beneath the wire-rimmed spectacles were keen and forceful. When he spoke, his voice showed just a hint of nervousness. But he made up for that by speaking a little louder than I thought he needed to, and the preacher-tone of his voice gave it a commanding sound. I doubted he'd be much good in a fist fight, but one word in that voice would probably be enough to discourage most foes. As he stood in front of us, however, his eyes flitted about from face to face, and that detracted a mite from his otherwise forceful appearance.

Mr. Rutledge handed out papers with hymns written on them. We got off to a good start with his leading, and Mrs. Parrish playing "O, for a Thousand Tongues." The piano was louder than all the voices put together, but the voices you could hear were mostly of the women. Even the few gravelly sounds from the motley-looking group of miners—some in monotone, some wandering about in search of the right key, and others like Uncle Nick, who just tried not to be conspicuous—were something priceless to hear and see. I found myself almost forgetting we were sitting in a drinking house!

During the third verse, just as we got to the words " 'tis music in the sinner's ears," all at once there came a commotion at the saloon door behind us, and three or four men came clamoring in.

"Hey, what's going on here?" one of them said.

"What's become o' this here town?" railed another.

"Can't a feller git a decent drink no more?"

"The bar's closed," someone called out. I think it was Mr. Bosely.

"Well, we want a bottle o' whiskey! Where's Jasper?"

"I'm here," called out a man standing against the far wall. I hadn't noticed him before. "But the man's right," he added, though he didn't sound too happy about it. "The bar's closed for an hour."

Mrs. Parrish gave up trying to keep playing the hymn. Finally, Mr. Rutledge spoke up, leveling his gaze toward the intruders.

"Despite the fact that this is a saloon," he said, "we are conducting a worship service, and there will be no whiskey served. But you are welcome to join us."

"So you're the preacher man who thinks he can take our saloon away!"

"Hey, Joe, this I gotta see. Maybe we should stay."

"Yeah. If Matthews can sit through the man's rantin', I suppose our whiskey'll wait an hour."

I could feel Uncle Nick squirm under the words. He fidgeted in his seat and half turned around toward them. I think he was getting set to shout some wise-crack back at them, when Pa gave him a sudden poke in the ribs with his elbow to shut him up.

The men took several of the empty seats, their hard-soled boots echoing on the oak floor of the Gold Nugget, while Mrs. Parrish resumed the hymn, playing as loudly as she dared in order to drown out the ongoing ruckus coming from the back row.

By the time we'd sung two more verses, things had settled down again. Mrs. Parrish played right into "What a Friend We Have in Jesus," and Mr. Rutledge led us in all the verses of that hymn, too. By the time it was done, he'd got his composure back enough from the interruption to start his preaching.

He just started right in, without a word of introduction,

and carried on with one of the loudest most hair-raising sermons I ever heard. He sounded very sure of everything he said, but I couldn't shake the feeling that he'd already preached the same sermon several times before. Every word sounded like he was reading it. But I knew he wasn't, because he had no papers in front of him. I guess he'd memorized it, like the readings we had learned in the school back in Bridgeville.

"And so, my friends," he said as he neared what I hoped was the end of his sermon, "I admonish you again to turn aside from any evil which encumbers you, and to run with godliness the race of life. Only by laying down the evil of our sinful past will we escape the wrath of God, which is as sure as our own corrupt nature, which was born in iniquity. Repent, I say, and enter into the glory of—"

All at once, without warning, a voice spoke out from the congregation:

"Now, I been sittin' here listenin', Preacher," the man said, "an' what I'd like t' know is what ya think men like us oughta do in a place like this?"

Noticeably flustered, a look passed over Rev. Rutledge's face I hadn't seen the whole morning. It was a look, well . . . almost of fear. But it passed from his eyes in an instant, and he quickly struggled to get his sermon back on track.

"I . . . er . . . as I was saying," he went on, clearing his throat nervously, "I would have all men, myself included, turn aside from any and all evils. The wrath of God will come like a thief in the night, and we must—"

"Are you sayin' we're a lot o' evil sinners?" called out another.

Not to be thrown off again, Mr. Rutledge took this interruption more in stride, and proceeded to shake the very rafters of the saloon with his voice. "Yes, my friends," he answered loudly. "A lot of sinners we all are and you are all included in that! Yes, there is sin in every man's heart, and in the saloons of Miracle Springs! But God will not be mocked! He will—"

"Come on, Reverend! Ye're not gonna tell us we gotta give up our poker an' our whiskey?"

"The Lord will exact godliness—" began the preacher in reply, but the men who were now set to disrupt him didn't let him finish.

"Ah, them religious words may be all right for folks back East where you come from, Reverend. But out here things is different. We ain't got nuthin' to do but have a little fun now an' then. Ain't that right, boys?"

Murmurings and a few calls and whistles erupted from around the room.

In vain Mr. Rutledge tried to speak again, but by now no one would let him.

Mrs. Parrish stood. "Please . . . please . . . you must—"

But her voice was drowned out in boos and catcalls, mostly from the back of the room where the fellow called Joe still sat with his friends. We all sat for a few more awkward moments, wondering what was going to happen. All at once I felt movement in the seat next to me, and before I realized it, Pa was on his feet.

"Let the man finish!" he thundered, and in an instant the room was still. "This man came a long way to preach to us," he continued. "Now I say we heed what the lady was tryin' to say, and let him do it!"

He took his seat; I think more surprised than anyone else at what he had done.

Rev. Rutledge mumbled some words of thanks, and quickly finished his sermon, but without ever quite regaining the emotion and fervor of before. I think he was glad to have the service over with, and he didn't stay around much afterwards to chat.

Pa didn't say anything as we filed outside, only led us back to the wagon with a sour expression on his face. I wanted to see Mrs. Parrish, but we were off and on our way back to the cabin before I even had a chance to look for her.

On the way home I thanked Pa for taking us. But he only grunted in reply.

# CHAPTER 29

## A SURPRISE

As December settled in, the days moved quickly, and I realized once more what a different spot we were in than back home. We hadn't had snow yet, though it got real cold and frosty at times. But when I strained my eyes toward the high Sierras I could catch glimpses of the expanse of white on their peaks. Back in New York we may have had more snow, but we sure didn't have mountains like that.

I wondered what Christmas would be like without Ma.

One thing for sure, it wouldn't be easy. Holidays were family times, and now, even with things gradually getting better with Pa, it was still pretty mixed up. A holiday like Christmas needs a ma to make it special. It would probably be the most difficult for Zack and me, because we would remember how it used to be back home. I didn't want to start crying in front of Pa. I didn't want to make him think I was sad. He didn't need anything else to worry about, and he was trying hard to do the best he could.

All month I wondered what he would do about the holiday, although I didn't want to say anything. But on the 17th we got an invitation from Mrs. Parrish to join her for Christmas dinner. She rode all the way out from town in her rig to deliver it to us personally. She included all seven of our Hollister-Belle clan, and said she hoped we'd all be able to come.

I got my crying done in bed when I was falling asleep on Christmas Eve, so on Christmas Day I tried my best to make it a special day for the kids. Uncle Nick and Pa got up and went out to the mine, just like any other day. The girls and I fixed breakfast, and they came in as usual about an hour later to eat.

I had made some small presents for everyone—dresses for Emily and Becky's dolls out of an old dress that didn't fit Becky anymore, and neck scarves for Tad, Zack, Uncle Nick, and Pa. After we were finished eating I gave them out, feeling a little awkward when I handed Pa his. It seemed so small.

"Merry Christmas, Pa," I said.

He looked surprised as he took it from me. "What?" he said in confusion, "Is this Christmas?"

"Yes, Pa," piped up Becky. "You didn't forget, did you?"

"Well tan my hide, girl!" he said scooping Becky off the ground, "now that you mention it, there is something mighty familiar-sounding about this date."

He set her down, then sat on a stool and began deliberately scratching his head with one finger. "Hmmm. . . ." he muttered. The three younger kids were watching him with wide eyes, incredulous that he had forgotten Christmas. But I thought I detected a hint of mischief in his eye, and it wasn't long before I knew I was right.

"Nick," he said, looking over to Uncle Nick, "did you hear what these kids are telling me . . . that this is Christmas?"

"I heard it, but I don't believe it," he replied.

"Yes, it is, Uncle Nick," said Tad excitedly. "It is—I promise!"

"He promises, Nick," said Pa real seriously. "Could you and me have lost track somehow?"

"Ain't likely," said Uncle Nick.

Pa scratched his head again. "Well," he said at last,

"there's only one way to find out for sure."

"What's that, Pa?" said Tad, taking the bait.

"Well—I reckon we'll have to find out if ol' St. Nick's been here."

"And he don't mean me!" said Uncle Nick.

"But you know," added Pa, "that a heap of things is different in California." He looked at Tad with a very serious expression. "By the time Santa Claus gets to California, he's plumb tuckered out and anxious to get home. So he don't fool with chimneys and stockings and tiptoein' around trying to stay outta people's way."

"He doesn't?" said Tad, amazed.

By this time, Uncle Nick was having a hard time not breaking into a laugh. But he kept his reaction to a smile.

"What does he do?" asked Emily, who had been listening intently, not quite sure what to believe, but letting her curiosity finally get the best of her.

"Well, blamed if he don't just drop off his packages any ol' place he can, usually off someplace where folks ain't likely to hear him. Hmmm," he said, stroking his beard, "I wonder if there's any place like that around here?"

"How about the mine cave?" suggested Uncle Nick.

"Nah—I don't think he'd use a place that ain't safe for kids. Probably someplace a mite closer to the cabin."

"The tool shed!" shouted Becky.

"Yeah!" yelled Tad. They both looked at Pa.

He returned an innocently questioning look, as if to say, *Who knows? It just might be.* Then he said, "I suppose it's worth a look."

Like a shot, Tad and Becky were out the door, followed by Emily. Zack and I were a little excited by now too and we sort of half-ran out after them. Uncle Nick and Pa came along too, but they walked.

By the time we got to the shed, which wasn't more than twenty yards from the cabin, already shouts and calls were coming from inside. Tad burst out as we approached.

"Santa's been here Pa!" he shouted. "There's presents and everything!"

"Well if that don't beat all!" said Pa, glancing around at Uncle Nick. "Ya hear that, Nick? These kids is right—it *is* Christmas!"

Tad reached up and grabbed Pa's hand, and excitedly led him inside the shed. Emily and Becky were already distributing the brightly-colored wrapped packages.

"There's only five, Pa," said Emily apologetically.

"Oh . . . well . . . that's another thing about California," he said, stooping down to her. "Out West, Santa's only got enough presents left for kids."

Satisfied, Emily turned back to the flurry of activity in the small shed. They were big packages too, but not heavy. The younger ones weren't waiting to be told what to do. They were already eagerly ripping into the pretty paper. I looked over at Pa kind of sheepishly.

"Well go to it, girl," he said. "It's got your name on it, don't it?"

Finally, I let my little-girl enthusiasm go. I sat down on a log and lit into my package. In a few seconds, I was taking the lid off the box, and reaching inside to lift out the prettiest hat I had ever seen. It had a wide straw brim, and was decorated with pink and blue ribbons which tied in the back and hung down several inches. It was so beautiful! I'd never had such a lovely bonnet in my life.

I looked up to see the others trying on hats of their own. Becky's and Emily's were beautiful too, with lace and tiny flowers. Of us all, I think Zack was proudest of his, though he was careful not to show his true pleasure. Very deliberately, he placed the tan leather hat on his head, its brim curled up just slightly—exactly like Pa's and Uncle Nick's. And even little Tad wore a smaller version of the same western hat.

Then all of a sudden, as if the thought had occurred to each at the same instant, the four younger ones tore out of the shed for the house in search of a mirror. I was the last to rise.

Uncle Nick had run off after the kids, but Pa was still standing there waiting for me. I looked up at him, and there was a look in his eyes I'll never forget—a look of pride, like he was feeling genuine pleasure at our happiness. I couldn't help it—even though I had resolved not to, I felt my eyes filling with tears.

"Thank you, Pa," I said quietly, looking deeply into his eyes.

"Don't mention it, girl," he replied. "That's what Christmas—and fathers—are all about."

He placed an arm around my shoulder and gave me a squeeze, then we began walking slowly toward the cabin together.

"You look mighty pretty in that bonnet," he said. "I think your ma'd be pleased!"

I couldn't help wondering and hoping that Ma was somewhere watching all this, our first Christmas without her. And I did hope she'd be pleased—not only with me, but with Pa too.

When we got back inside, Pa gathered us together and told us all to sit down, then said, "There's one other thing we gotta do, this being Christmas and all. Your ma and me started doing this the first Christmas after Corrie here was born, and we did it every year after that, 'til . . . well, you know—'til I had to leave."

He reached up to the mantle above the fireplace and took down Ma's little White Bible, opened it to Luke's Gospel, and began to read. I don't think I'd ever realized what a nice voice Pa had. But now as he read, a deep recollection of *his* voice stirred in my memory—not just Ma's—reading this very scripture. I had heard Pa read this before! Knowing that somehow made this reading all the more special.

"*And it came to pass in those days,*" he read, "*that there went out a decree from Caesar Augustus, that all the world—*"

"Ma always read us this," interrupted Becky.

Pa kept his eyes on the page, but I knew what he was thinking. Usually he was quiet for a spell after someone mentioned Ma.

"Yeah . . . I reckon she did," he said at length, then continued: "*that all the world should be taxed. And this taxing was first made when Cyrenius was governor of Syria. And all went to be taxed, every one into his own city. And Joseph also went up from Galilee, out of the city of Nazareth, into Judaea, unto the city of David, which is called Bethlehem. . . .*"

No one said another word. We all sat quietly, even Uncle Nick, listening to Pa read. When he was finished, he closed the Bible, and stood to place it back on the mantle. I think we all felt, even without Ma, that it was really Christmas. I didn't say much for the rest of the morning. The other kids were running around excitedly, all wearing their new hats, and Emily and Becky dressing up their dolls.

But it was a quiet morning for me. I felt a little like Mary, with a lot of things to ponder in my heart.

# CHAPTER 30

## CHRISTMAS DINNER

A little before noon we all dressed in our Sunday clothes and headed into town to Mrs. Parrish's.

I was already happy about the way Christmas had turned out, but when we walked into Mrs. Parrish's house, it was like tasting it for the first time all over again. She had a lovely decorated tree in the parlor, strung with fine lace and beads, and covered with delicate glass ornaments. Tiny candles clipped to its branches gave it a special glow. I could have stood there for an hour gazing at it.

Around the rest of the house were garlands of holly and evergreen branches, and the fragrance of cloves and cinnamon filled the air. With these pungent scents mingled the delicious smell of roast goose, fresh-baked bread and pumpkin pie.

It was all too wonderful! I just couldn't help thinking of Ma, and how she would have enjoyed being here with us!

Mrs. Parrish praised the neck scarves I'd made. I blushed, but for once was glad for the color in my cheeks to hide that I was feeling overwhelmed by the day. Then she kindly complimented our new hats and bonnets.

"Santa left them in the shed," said Becky.

"You don't say!"

"Uncle Nick and Pa even forgot it was Christmas," said Tad, still incredulous of the fact.

"My, that *is* serious," she said, glancing up at the two men in mock disbelief.

Mrs. Parrish warmly welcomed Pa and Uncle Nick with handshakes, and they exchanged a few pleasantries. "I hope you won't mind," she said, "but I have taken the opportunity to invite someone else—"

Before she finished another knock came at the door.

"—who would have otherwise been alone today," she added, "and it seems that he is here now."

She excused herself and went to open the door. When she returned, the preacher was with her.

"Rev. Rutledge," she said, "I don't believe you've had the opportunity of being formally introduced to my friends here."

"This is Nick Matthews," she said, turning to Uncle Nick.

The two men shook hands.

"And Mr.—uh, Mr. Drum. Mr. Drum, may I present Avery Rutledge."

"Pleased to meet you," Pa said.

"You're one of the men from our first church service," said the preacher.

"We were all there," replied Pa nonchalantly.

"Oh, but you were more than just *there*, Mr. Drum. Why, you saved my hide! I've been hoping to meet up with you ever since to thank you."

Pa shrugged. "I just thought you deserved a fair shake, that's all. Weren't nothing special."

"On the contrary, Mr. Drum," broke in Mrs. Parrish. "You saved the service. I too have wanted to thank you."

"A regular hero!" said Uncle Nick with a grin.

"Look, it was nothing!" said Pa, a little testily. I could tell this was getting under his skin. If there was one thing he didn't want to be, it was a hero in a church service. I was fairly certain he regretted speaking out like he did.

"Well, nevertheless, we're very appreciative," said Rev. Rutledge. "I'd hoped to find one or two strong men in the community who would ally themselves with me in my cause to bring Christ to the lost lambs in the mining camps."

Pa said nothing more.

"Let me also introduce Nick's nieces and nephews," Mrs. Parrish said lightly, changing the embarrassing subject for Pa. One by one she said our names, and we all curtsied and bowed appropriately to the Reverend.

"I'm very pleased to meet all of you children," he said, smiling.

"Well," said Mrs. Parrish, "as soon as Marcus gets here, we'll be able to—oh, there he is now," she said, just as we heard another knock at the door.

As she went to let in the blacksmith, I saw Uncle Nick sidle up to Pa, give him a jab in the ribs with his elbow, and whisper, "So, you're the preacher's new ally to bring religion to us lost lambs, eh, Drum?"

"You keep your nose outta it, Nick, ya hear?"

"Now, if you'll all gather around the table, we can begin our meal," Mrs. Parrish said.

When we were seated, she served everyone a cup of hot cider. "Corrie, would you like to help me bring out the food?"

"Yes, Ma'am," I answered, happy to be able to help on this festive occasion. Then while the others sipped at their cider, we brought out platters of food from the kitchen, all piled high and steaming.

Rev. Rutledge sat there politely waiting, and if it hadn't been for him, Uncle Nick and the kids would probably have just dug into all that food in front of them. But with the preacher's patient example, everyone else waited too. At last Mrs. Parrish and I sat down.

"Reverend, would you give thanks for us?" Mrs. Parrish asked.

"I'd be honored, Ma'am," he answered.

He bowed his head, and all the rest of us did the same. As he prayed, I wanted so badly to open my eyes and see what Pa was doing, not to mention Uncle Nick. But I didn't dare.

"Almighty God our Father," he began in his solemn preacher's voice, "we thank thee for this most holy of days, when thine only Son Jesus Christ became incarnate, entering the world as a little child. Make us ever mindful, O Lord, of thy wondrous gift to us, on this day and on all days, and let us live lives acceptable in thy sight, always striving to do thy will in all things. We thank thee for this provision out of thy bounty, and we pray thy special blessing on the loving hands that have prepared it for us. Through Christ our Lord we pray . . ." Then after some hesitation he added, ". . . Amen."

Within seconds the table was a commotion of passing plates and reaching hands, the grown-ups doing their best to help the children who were seated next to them. When our plates were heaped with more food than we kids had seen in a long time, we set about to eating. We kept quiet while the grown-ups talked, enjoying every bite of Mrs. Parrish's fine cooking.

"It's too bad about Mr. Larsen's cabin," said Mrs. Parrish as she passed the plate of steaming goose again.

"Was he plumb burned out?" asked Uncle Nick. "I ain't seen him since the fire."

"To the ground, Mr. Matthews," answered Mrs. Parrish. "From what I understand he lost everything."

"I shall have to make a call on him," said Rev. Rutledge. "Perhaps later you might tell me where I can locate him, Mrs. Parrish."

"You're probably too late for that," said Pa.

"It is never too late for a Christian word of comfort and sympathy, Mr. Drum," said the minister.

"I was just meaning that Tom Larsen might already have pulled out."

"Just like that?" asked Mrs. Parrish.

"Royce made him an offer on the place a few days before the fire," answered Pa. "He turned him down then, and from what I hear it was none too friendly a meetin'. Though word is now that he's gonna take Royce's money while he can and get outta town."

"That's a shame. Tom Larsen is the sort of man we need around here."

"Not too bad for Royce. He's gettin' the place for a song."

There was a lull for a few minutes while we all concentrated on the meal Mrs. Parrish had prepared.

"It is so wonderful to have children present for Christmas dinner," said Mrs. Parrish at length.

"It sho' is!" remarked Mr. Weber. "Why, Christmas back home was nuthin' iffen it wasn't a day fer de chillens all scurryin' roun' de place! An' this goose, Miz. Parrish, it puts me in sech a mind o' Christmas when I was a little chile'!"

"I'm happy you are enjoying it, Marcus," said Mrs. Parrish. "And we are all honored that you could join us too, Reverend," she added, turning to the preacher.

"The honor is all mine, Almeda," he returned. "I must say, after the first few weeks I'd begun to think I'd made a mistake coming here. But a festive day like this helps restore my faith again."

"Surely you're not serious, Avery?" said Mrs. Parrish with concern.

I couldn't help noticing that they used each other's given names.

"I'm afraid I am serious, Almeda," he replied thoughtfully.

She continued to look at the minister questioningly.

He acknowledged her concern with a brief smile, but then went on, "I have to admit," he said, in a down-to-earth voice, "that I was quite shaken by what that fellow said the first Sunday—that is before Mr. Drum came to my aid. Do you remember his comment that religion may be all right for the folks back East, but that out West it was different?"

Mrs. Parrish nodded her head.

"Well, what if he's right, and I'm *not* cut out for preaching in this setting? What if the religion I bring isn't going to mean anything to these men?"

This was an altogether different Rev. Rutledge than the man I'd heard preaching that Sunday. Different, too, from the man who'd just prayed before the meal a few minutes ago. His preacher-voice was gone, and he sounded like— well, just like a regular person, not someone who planned everything he was going to say ahead of time. I'd never thought about a preacher having feelings before now.

"Nonsense, Avery!" said Mrs. Parrish. "God's truth must be carried to all men and women everywhere, and it's the same Gospel here and in the East and everywhere."

"I'm sure you're right," he mused, "But I've been doing more thinking this last month than I ever have before in my life. Whatever else comes of it, I realize I'll have to modify my methods some to ever reach men like the wild bunch who have inhabited this place."

I saw Uncle Nick glance quickly at Pa. I guess Rev. Rutledge saw it, too. "The kind of men who were trying to disrupt the service," he quickly added, "nothing like the fine examples of Christian manhood we're blessed with in our midst today."

It was his preacher voice again, and it was Mrs. Parrish's turn to look down at her plate without replying. A brief awkward silence followed.

"Well, Reverend," said Uncle Nick, breaking the quiet, "I hear you came West across Panama way. There's been some discussion as to which be worse—the mosquitoes in them jungles, or the savage Apaches on the plains. I dealt with my share of Indians, and I reckon at least once in a while a body can reason with them, if push comes to shove. But I suppose them 'skeeters bite first and ask questions later, eh?"

Everyone chuckled. Pa broke into a grin at Uncle Nick's humor, and glanced in my direction with a quick wink.

But the minister, who dabbed his mouth carefully with his napkin, seemed suddenly offended after so cordial a beginning to the conversation, and focused his eyes solemnly on Uncle Nick.

"Crossing the jungle was a harrowing experience for many in my party," he said sternly. It looked like his preacher voice was back for a while. "Several of my traveling companions succumbed to yellow fever, Mr. Matthews, so please excuse me if I find little amusement in your comment."

Our laughter stopped at the sharp rebuke, and I could tell Pa was irritated. He pursed his lips and cocked his eyebrow disapprovingly.

"You should have tried your luck with the Apaches then, Reverend," he said dryly.

"I do not believe in *luck*, Mr. Drum," rejoined the minister. "The Lord's divine providence is my stay and my salvation."

Pa opened his mouth to shoot back a reply, and by the look in his eye I didn't think it would be any too pleasant. But Mrs. Parrish broke in.

"Avery, I'm sure everyone would be so very interested to hear of some of your plans for Miracle Springs."

All talk of his doubts had vanished now, and he spoke with that commanding voice we'd first heard at the Gold Nugget church. "This is truly a field ripe unto harvest," said the Reverend. "A man of God should find no end of avenues for ministry. My first project, of course, shall be the construction of a proper place of worship. Meaning no offense to you, Almeda—I know you meant well, and perhaps it *was* the only place available, but it is nothing less than a travesty to be forced to gather for worship in such a vile place as that saloon. It makes me quake within to think of God's displeasure."

"Perhaps," said Mrs. Parrish, with a touch of hurt at his comment, "but you will find that out West we must sometimes make do with what we have."

"But we must never degrade ourselves to the level of the ungodly. The Word of God says, 'Be not yoked with unbelievers.' "

"It does indeed," replied Mrs. Parrish. "But I think the scripture you're referring to says not to be *unequally* yoked, Avery. It seems to me that makes a world of difference. As you quote it, Paul would have been saying not to associate with sinners, and that is something our Lord would never condone."

"I was only trying to make the point—" rejoined the minister, but before he could finish Pa cut him off.

"The lady's right, Reverend," said Pa with just enough edge in his voice to make me feel uneasy at what was coming next. "I ain't no Bible scholar, but it seems to me that Jesus spent a lot of his time out meetin' people where they were. I expect if he was livin' in Miracle, you might find him in the saloons as much as any other place. That's where you're gonna find most of your sinners, Reverend."

"It is one thing to go out on the highways and byways of life to win sinners," returned Rev. Rutledge, his face reddening a bit, "but quite another to expect them to find spiritual succor in the very den of iniquity wherein they first fell."

"I think it was in a church, not a saloon, where *I* first fell from grace," muttered Uncle Nick.

"You are baiting me, are you not, Mr. Matthews?"

"Well, I'll tell you like it is, I seen just as many hypocrites in church as I ever did in the Gold Nugget. At least in the saloon they wasn't pretendin' to be what they wasn't." I was surprised by Uncle Nick's boldness.

"So you consider all churchgoers hypocrites?"

"That wasn't what I said," replied Uncle Nick.

"Would anyone like another helping of anything?" asked Mrs. Parrish, trying her best to redeem the uncomfortable situation.

"This is the best goose I ever et, Ma'am," put in Marcus Weber.

"Indeed it is, Almeda," added the minister. "A mighty fine meal . . . mighty fine indeed! I know we're all very appreciative."

"Yessir," went on Mr. Weber. "The Rev'rend here, he sure be right, Ma'am."

"Thank you, kindly. I'm glad you could all come. And I do believe the pumpkin pies are ready. Avery, would you mind helping me take them from the oven?"

The two rose and left the room, Mrs. Parrish seeming to breathe a sigh of relief that the conversation had gone no further.

But the break proved only temporary. I could feel the tension building as we ate our pie a few minutes later. I didn't follow the gist of everything that was said, but it was clear neither my uncle nor my pa thought too much of all the Reverend's smooth-sounding words.

"I have been quite pleased with the turnout at the services," said Rev. Rutledge as he sipped his coffee. "What with the contributions I brought from the faithful in Boston and the generosity of local offerings, I believe it will not be long at all before we can begin construction on a church building right here in Miracle Springs."

"That's wonderful, Avery!" exclaimed Mrs. Parrish. "And I don't think we will have any difficulty finding a site."

"I've spoken with Mr. Royce at the bank, and he assures me he will be able to help us secure property at a good price, and possibly assist with the financing as well."

"That be land he's stolen from hard workin' sinners, if you don't mind me saying it, Reverend," said Uncle Nick. "If Royce builds your church, you ain't likely to get much of a flock."

"He strikes me as one concerned for the welfare of the community, and as ready as anyone to extend the hand of brotherly kindness. A fine Christian man, I would say."

"A snake is more like it!" shot back Uncle Nick. "If you're wanting to find sinners, Reverend, I'd take that Gospel of yours and preach it in his bank!"

"I'm sure no man is without his faults," said Mrs. Parrish quickly, before Rev. Rutledge had the chance to respond. "Now, who would care for another piece of pie?"

"Iffen you's got plenty there, Miz Parrish," said Marcus Weber sheepishly. "It's de bes' I ever dun ate. And tha's de truth!"

The minister didn't seem sensitive to the fact he was scratching away at a live hornet's nest, because the moment there was a pause in the conversation, he started in again about building a new church.

"Once we do find a location, and come to terms with the financing, I see nothing to stop us. I'm certain if the Lord's blessing is with us, we will see a completed church by next summer. I believe there are plenty of able-bodied men who would be willing to lend their talents to the project, fine men who are not ashamed to stand and be counted for the cause of Christ. Men much like yourself, Mr. Drum—"

As he spoke, he turned in Pa's direction, and it was clear he was attempting to smooth over the recent bumpiness of the conversation with what he felt was a compliment.

"Men of courage, saying to their community, as you did when you stood up and spoke out on my behalf, that they are part of the church's ministry to the lost. Fine Christian men who—"

"Look, Reverend!" Pa suddenly burst out in a loud voice. "When are you gonna get it through that head of yours that I ain't of the same mind as you? I gave up all that righteous stuff . . . well, years ago—when I figured I wasn't fit for it, an' it wasn't fit for the likes of me. Your brain's so filled with old-fashioned talk and Bible verses no ordinary man like me can understand, that you don't have sense to see what's right in front of your nose. I'm one of them sinners you're always talkin' about, Reverend! I may go to some of your meetings, and I may help you build your blamed church, and I'll read my—I'll read the kids here the Christmas story 'cause I believe in givin' the Lord his due. But stop makin' me into somethin' I ain't! I don't rightly know why I stood up to make the boys shut up that day. I half-regretted it ever since, and I sure ain't gonna do it again!"

He stopped and took a deep breath, then turned to Mrs. Parrish. Everyone was absolutely still.

"I thank you kindly for the meal, Ma'am," he said in a softer tone. "But I'd best take my leave—I got business in town."

He stood, then looked in my direction with what appeared a fleeting, unspoken apology in his eyes, then added, "I'll be back for you kids in an hour or so."

Then he turned and made for the door, saying as he went, "You coming, Nick?"

Uncle Nick hesitated a moment, then rose, tipped his hat toward Marcus Weber and the minister, then to Mrs. Parrish, "Ma'am, I thank you too, for makin' this day special for us all." Then he too was gone.

An awkward few minutes followed. At length, Rev. Rutledge sighed, and shook his head with a look of great pity.

"Sometimes, I do not understand the ways of God," he said. "To my limited vision, it seems a deplorable turn of fate that men like that should be given charge of these precious little ones."

"Only a few moments ago you were calling at least one of them a fine Christian, Avery," said Mrs. Parrish softly.

"Ah, but that was before I knew the true state of his heart toward God. He is clearly in rebellion against his Maker."

"Be that as it may, I truly feel they are doing the best they can for the children," persisted Mrs. Parrish. Her defense of Pa and Uncle Nick came as a surprise. She didn't have the best to say for them in times past, and I wondered who was doing the changing—they, or her.

"Yo' betta b'lieve they is," put in Mr. Weber, who had been silent for most of the meal. "Well," he added, pausing for a moment's reflection, " 'ceptin' fer them hosses, that is."

"I fear their best may not be enough," continued Rev. Rutledge.

"There's little other choice, regardless," said Mrs. Parrish.

"Surely there must be some decent family willing to take them in."

"He's our kin!" I suddenly heard myself saying. "Nothing's going to make us leave him—that is, unless he says so." The words were no sooner out of my mouth, and I wanted to sink under the table, for I could feel all eyes turned toward me.

"Yes, child," said the minister, and his voice was gentle and full of compassion. It was his normal voice, not the stern, preachy one full of memorized words. "I truly hope it will work out for you—and for your uncle. I can see that you care a great deal for him, and I'm sure he does for each one of you, too. I will be committing this situation with your uncle and his partner, as well as the souls of the two men, to much prayer."

It sure didn't help matters when, an hour later, Uncle Nick came to the door again with the smell of whiskey on his breath. Pa was sitting on the buckboard waiting, and didn't even get down. Uncle Nick and the preacher exchanged not a word.

Both Pa and Uncle Nick were quite talkative on the way home. Maybe it was the whiskey, maybe it was just their way of letting off steam.

"Some high and mighty cuss, wasn't he!" exclaimed Uncle Nick.

"We ain't exactly saints, Nick, now are we!" laughed Pa, seeming proud of the fact.

"Well, you always said you'd rather be an honest sinner than a dishonest hypocrite. You shoulda told him that, Drum!"

"And I'd still rather be!"

"I'm with you, pard!" laughed Uncle Nick. "I'm with you!"

# CHAPTER 31

## NEW DRESSES

A week after Christmas, Mrs. Parrish came to call. It seemed every other day was full of surprises.

She asked Pa if she could take us girls into Miracle Springs with her until suppertime.

"A ladies' day on the town," she said with a mysterious grin.

"They're old enough that I don't have to watch 'em every minute," he replied. "If they want to go, it's all right by me." He wasn't exactly friendly. We hadn't seen Mrs. Parrish since Christmas Day and I think her presence reminded him of what happened.

But the girls and I could hardly contain ourselves!

Once Ma took me into Bridgeville. "Just for fun," she'd said. I'll never forget that day, because I felt so much a special part of Ma's life, as if we were friends.

I felt the same way on this day in town with Mrs. Parrish. I hadn't known her very long, but the few times spent with her had been important ones. I suppose in a way she made up a little for the loss of Ma. I don't know what Ma would think if she knew I thought such a thing. But knowing Ma, she would be glad I had someone to rely on. As much as I wanted things with Pa to work out, there are times when a girl needs a woman to talk to.

When we got to Miracle Springs, the first place we went

was the General Store. I would have been content to just *look* at all the fine things, but Mrs. Parrish had other plans.

"Good morning, Mr. Bosely," she greeted the store-keeper.

"Morning, Ma'am. Fine day, isn't it?"

"It certainly is. May I see your new shipment of calicos?"

"Parrish Freight brought them in, Ma'am. I would have thought you'd already looked them over."

"I did, briefly. But now I have three young ladies who will want to look them over."

Mr. Bosely grinned. "I see! I'll be right back."

He went to a back room out of sight. Mrs. Parrish turned to the three of us, knelt down so that she could talk on Becky's level, and then said, "Girls, I hope you won't think me presumptuous, but I want to give you Christmas presents. I thought you might each like a new dress."

I gasped in surprise, and couldn't say anything. But as usual, Becky was not at a loss for words.

"Oh, goody! Just for us?"

"Just for you," laughed Mrs. Parrish.

"What about Tad and Zack?" she said, as if she had discovered a terrible flaw in Mrs. Parrish's idea. "They can't wear dresses."

Mrs. Parrish laughed again. "Don't worry, Becky. I've thought of that, too. I thought they might each like a shirt and vest."

She stood, and now spoke to me. "But before I went any further, I needed to have you come into town for fittings."

Finally I found my voice. "That's so kind of you, Mrs. Parrish. But it's too much. You don't have to—"

"*Have* to, child?" said Mrs. Parrish smiling. "Don't you understand? You are my *friends*! Please, Corrie, allow me to do this, won't you? It's as much a pleasure for me as for you."

"Are you sure, Ma'am?" I asked. I suppose I didn't really understand, at least not quite like she meant it.

"I've always wanted children, Corrie. Especially little girls to do things for. Seeing these dresses on you will give me great happiness."

"Well, if you put it that way. . . ." I began. Then Mr. Bosely returned, and all else was forgotten.

He was carrying five different patterns of calicos. Mrs. Parrish must have ordered them with us in mind, because the minute we saw them, each of us knew immediately which cloth we wanted for our new dresses. Becky's hands went right for the red. Emily took more time with her choice, though I think she knew from the beginning, but was just too shy to announce that she wanted the pink. I chose sky blue.

While Mr. Bosely cut off the needed lengths, Mrs. Parrish explained that Mrs. Gianini was an excellent seamstress and would make the dresses, and that she was expecting us that very morning to measure and fit us. It was all more than I could comprehend. Ma had always made our clothes in the past. But to have a fancy new dress, with the lace Mrs. Parrish was asking Mr. Bosely about even as we looked at the fabric, made by a seamstress—it was all too exciting to imagine! We hadn't had anything new since we'd left New York.

The pleasant Italian lady welcomed us as warmly as ever, and after some time complimenting our choice of fabrics and discussing styles with Mrs. Parrish, she said it was time to get started. She took the younger girls first, and told Mrs. Parrish that tea was brewing in the kitchen, and we could relax and visit. Her dark eyes were twinkling and her pink cheeks glowing as she took charge of Emily and Becky. It wasn't hard for me to see that she felt the same way as Mrs. Parrish about the opportunity to do something for the little "bambinas," as she called Emily and Becky. I watched her plump frame shuffle into the sitting room, an arm around each of my sisters, thankful that they had more mothers than me to help look after them.

# CHAPTER 32

# A TALK WITH MRS. PARRISH

While the younger girls were occupied, Mrs. Parrish and I remained in the kitchen. She poured us each some tea, and then offered me a cookie from a delicate China plate. Mrs. Gianini called them *biscottes*, and they were something like a sweet biscuit with a faint licorice flavor.

"Well, Corrie," she said, sitting down at the table opposite me and taking a sip from her hot tea, "you are practically a full-fledged Californian now. What do you think of this land?"

"It sure is pretty, I'll say that much," I answered.

Then I paused. Mrs. Parrish could tell I was thinking, and waited for me to continue.

"Back home Zack trapped a baby raccoon once," I went on. "It was so cute and furry. Ma kept saying, 'You kids be careful. That little coon'll grow up one day and'll turn wild just like that.' 'Course we didn't believe her. We figured he'd stay cute and cuddly forever. But Ma was right. One day all of a sudden, he turned savage and bit Zack in the arm. Real bad too. Ma said Zack was lucky he didn't have rabies. And so we had to let our pet raccoon go back to the forest."

I stopped again, and once more Mrs. Parrish just waited for me to think out what I was trying to say.

"I suppose I feel about our new life in California a little

like we was watching a baby raccoon grow up. You just can't tell yet how it's going to turn out. It might turn out good, it might not. Maybe that's not such a good . . . what do you call it?"

"Analogy?"

"Yes'm, that's it. Maybe it's not such a good analogy, comparing California with a baby raccoon. But it's something like how I feel inside. I can't tell yet what's going to come of it all—good, bad . . . or maybe some of both."

"I don't know if it's a good analogy or not either, Corrie. But it is certainly very perceptive. Do you think like that often?"

"Well, I guess I'm always thinking, Ma'am. Trying to make sense of things."

"You ought to write your ideas down."

I felt my cheeks suddenly get warm. "I have been writing down a lot of things lately, Ma'am," I told her.

"Are you writing letters—keeping a journal . . . what?"

"I don't have anybody to write a letter to. And it's nothing very fancy, just a diary, putting down in writing what happens and whatever else comes to my mind. Ma suggested I do it before she died."

"That's wonderful! I would love to read it."

"Oh, I'd be too embarrassed, Ma'am," I replied. "I'm probably a terrible writer."

"I doubt that, Corrie. Besides, practice makes perfect."

"I am trying to write it better all the time. But it sure doesn't sound like the books I read. It's just the way I talk, Ma'am. Nobody'd want to read that!"

"I think you may be wrong about that, Corrie. I'm certain it would be fascinating for a good many people to read about a young girl's life and reaction to the new land of California."

"Well, maybe, but I do know how much I appreciate all you have done for me and my brothers and sisters since we came," I said.

"As I said, this is as much fun for me as for you," replied Mrs. Parrish. She took a cookie. "Mrs Gianini really is a superb cook!"

"I was meaning more than the dresses, Mrs. Parrish," I said. "You've done so much since we came to California. You've . . . well, you know—with Ma gone and all . . . sometimes I don't know what I would have done without your kindness."

She reached over and laid her hand, still soft and smooth in spite of her work, on top of mine. Her eyes looked into mine, and were full of tears. I could tell she knew what I was feeling.

"Dear Corrie," she said softly, "you've made my life richer, too. Each one of you, really, but especially you. You are more than just an acquaintance, Corrie. You are my friend. I want you to know that I will be here for you whenever you need someone. I would never presume to take your mother's place, but there are times when a girl needs the companionship or the listening ears of a woman."

"Thank you, Mrs. Parrish," I said. I guess I was crying by now too. "I think Ma would be thankful you came along in our lives when you did."

"If ever you need to talk about anything, I hope you will feel free to do so."

I looked down at my tea. I think she knew I was thinking hard about something serious, because when she spoke again she was really earnest.

"What is it, Corrie? What's troubling you?"

"I guess I've been confused about both Pa and Uncle Nick," I said, "especially since the preacher came."

"Confused . . . in what way?"

"Well, neither of them makes a secret of their reluctance about church. Since Christmas, Pa's said some—I don't know—negative things, especially about the minister. And then the way he and Rev. Rutledge argued at your house . . . and of course there's Uncle Nick's drinking and gambling. And Pa's too, I suppose. I know Uncle Nick and Ma went to church when they was kids. And Pa read to us from the Bible once. Inside I want to believe Pa's a God-fearing man, Mrs. Parrish. But sometimes I get real scared, and I wonder if he cares for God at all. He's told me he and Uncle Nick were involved in real bad things and that's why they had to leave the east. I don't want to think ill of him, Mrs. Parrish, but Mr. Rutledge, I'm sure he'd count my Pa as a sinner and an evil man and on his way to hell!"

I started to break down, but did my best to hold back the tears.

Mrs. Parrish gave my hand a squeeze, and tried to comfort me.

"There, there, child . . . you just cry all you need to, and then we'll talk some more."

I was quiet for another minute. Mrs. Parrish handed me her handkerchief and I wiped my eyes. She looked over at me with a deep smile on her face. I tried to smile back, but what came out was a half laugh and half cry that made me feel kind of stupid all over again.

Mrs. Parrish laughed with me.

"You love your father, don't you, Corrie?" she said.

"Oh, of course," I replied, sniffing. "I'm trying to, but he's just a puzzling sort of man."

"I know he is, Corrie. But I do think you love him. Otherwise, you wouldn't feel this hurt over him."

She paused, seeming to think over what to say next while I blew my nose and took a deep breath.

"Corrie," she said, "is your concern that you think your Pa might be a heathen . . . a bad man?"

"Yes, Ma'am. I suppose that's it."

"And because he's not a churchman, and spoke rudely about Reverend Rutledge, you're afraid he is a sinner?"

"I guess so. Along with the gamblin', and what they did in New York."

"Ah, yes. Those are rather serous issues, aren't they."

"Do *you* think those are sins, Ma'am?"

"No doubt they are, Corrie. I'm sure you're right there."

"So do *you* think my Pa's a sinner?"

"Tell me first of all what you think a sinner is, Corrie."

"Doing bad things, I suppose, and not going to church and not caring about God."

"But what about a person who *didn't* do bad things, and who went to church *every* Sunday, and who was always saying religious things . . . would that kind of person be a sinner?"

"Oh no, Ma'am."

"What if that same person, acting very good and religious on the outside, had bad attitudes and resentments and unkindness down inside his heart where no one could see it, what then?"

I didn't have a quick answer to give her.

"In other words, what if one man on the outside seemed to be a sinner, but was kind inside, and did things to help people whenever he had the chance; and another man was very religious and never drank or gambled or did anything that looked wrong, but inside he was mean and vengeful?"

"I think I see what you mean, Mrs. Parrish. But it does make it awfully confusing."

"Yes, it is complicated. But you see, when Jesus spoke of sin, he didn't talk so much about the outward things a person did—like the drinking and gambling—but more about the inside, what a person thought in his heart."

I nodded. She was certainly good at explaining things.

"There's one particular place in the Bible where Jesus is talking about sin, and he says that it's not the outward things that a man *does* that make him a sinner, but the things that are *inside* his heart—things like pride and anger and unkindness toward others, and selfishness. You see, Corrie, we're all sinners in that way."

"Everybody?"

"Yes. I am, and Rev. Rutledge . . . and even you, Corrie, and your brothers and sisters. We all have those kinds of attitudes deep inside us. And Jesus says they are just as bad as things your uncle or Pa or any miner in Miracle Springs might do. It's a terrible thing to kill a man, or to steal. But Jesus says it might be just as much a sin to think horrible thoughts about someone, and to want to kill him in your heart."

"That seems mighty hard to believe, Mrs. Parrish."

"To our small minds, yes it does. It's easier to point the finger at someone *else's* sin than try to discover our own. But sin is on the inside, not so much in what we *do* but in what we *are*. We are all sinners—all of us. So yes, your father is a sinner. But so are the rest of us. I need the Lord Jesus just as much as he does."

"I've never heard anything like that, Mrs. Parrish."

She laughed. "There are many who don't seem to have realized these truths, Corrie, even many church people."

"Why don't they talk about that in church instead of all that loud repentance stuff?" I asked.

"Ah, Corrie," sighed Mrs. Parrish, "that is indeed a good question. Too often we are so busy talking *about* the truths of God, that we forget to get around to *doing* them. God wants us to be good, to be the kind of person that Jesus was—not on the outside, but inside. But it's much easier, for instance, to talk about repentance, than to actually go to another person and ask his forgiveness for something you did against him. Being a godly person inside, that can be difficult."

"Rev. Rutledge didn't sound like he was saying the kinds of things you are, Ma'am. Meaning no disrespect, he sounded just like every other preacher I've ever heard, like he was pointing his finger at all the sinners in town."

"I know, Corrie. But I think he's been a little nervous, not really knowing how to preach to the kind of men there are around here. Preachers are growing and learning and even struggling, just like everyone else. He's a good man,

Corrie, and he loves God. He just needs time to grow, as we all do."

"This is all so new to me, Mrs. Parrish," I said.

"I've given you a great deal to think about," she replied smiling. "Enough for one day, I think. But there are other things about living the way God wants us to. I hope I get the chance to tell you about them someday, too."

"Oh, I'd like that," I answered.

"We'll be sure to talk again—real soon."

Just then I heard the happy sounds of young voices, followed by running footsteps heading toward the kitchen. Becky and Emily had been in the other room just long enough. I didn't know whether the Lord or Mrs. Gianini had had the strongest hand in keeping them there, but I was glad Mrs. Parrish and I got to have our talk.

# CHAPTER 33

## TROUBLE AT THE MINE

I found myself thinking about a lot of new things after my talk with Mrs. Parrish, although I didn't have the chance to write in my journal for days. Pa and Uncle Nick were working constantly at the mine, with Mr. Jones coming out almost every day. So I was extra busy keeping vigil on the children, because the men were setting charges. They let Zack help quite a bit, too, except when the dynamite was set to blow—then they'd make him get way back down the hill. The noise of the explosions was deafening, and many times sent Tad and Emily nearly into tears. If Becky shed any, it was only because I wouldn't let her go near all the excitement.

But just because I didn't write for a while doesn't mean I wasn't busy pondering all Mrs. Parrish had told me.

It's funny how I had started out concerned about Pa. Afterward I found my thoughts turning my own direction. Mrs. Parrish was teaching me a lot about life and how I wanted to live. She said she's had to learn what she knows painfully. But she has a quiet peacefulness now, even with her husband gone. Maybe I won't ever be as genteel as she is. But if I could grow up with some of that same contentment on my face, I'd be satisfied. I wanted to ask her sometime how she got that peace, and whether it was something I might hope to have when I was finally a grown woman, too.

229

When I did find time to start writing about my conversation with her, and what she said about attitudes and kindness and sin and church and all, I found myself really wanting to say things right. I felt that all she said was important, and that I might want to read it again sometime. But so much of it I didn't completely understand. Finally I made the decision to show Mrs. Parrish part of my diary. It was kind of embarrassing at first, because a journal is a personal thing. But I wanted her to help me remember as much of that conversation as I could. So we talked about it again, two or three times, and she helped me fill in what I forgot from the first time I'd tried to write it all down. I think she was a little shy about seeing me write down her words too. But she knew she was doing it as a favor to me, and knew it would likely help me to remember what she had said.

I was still trying to to find time to write about my talk with Mrs. Parrish when Uncle Nick and Pa took the wagon into town to get some more lumber to shore up the roof in the mine shaft. I thought for sure I'd have some spare time then, as soon as I finished baking bread. But so much happened that before I knew it, I had two major incidents in my life to tell about.

Right in the middle of my batch of bread, Tad knocked over the bucket of water. My dough was spoiled, and not only did I have to start all over again, I had to go back out to the creek for water.

I picked up the bucket and started out for the creek up by the mine. About halfway there I heard a strange sound, like chopping, or the sound of a pick against rock, followed by the whinny of a horse. I looked down the road, wondering if Pa and Uncle Nick had forgotten something and were coming back. It was an hour or two too soon for them to be returning with the lumber. But the road was deserted.

The whinny came again—clear, and not far from the mine.

I continued on in that direction.

When I reached the mine, instead of going right down to the creek for water, I made my way slowly toward the mine opening. I saw nothing out of the ordinary. But as I circled around it, on the hillside above, where the top of the shaft sloped down, I saw the horse—a chestnut, tied to the branch of a tree.

The animal looked vaguely familiar, but I couldn't quite place it. Then suddenly I heard a heavy footstep behind me.

I turned sharply. The scar-faced rider we had seen two months ago was walking toward me right from the mine. Only a moment before, I had passed right by the spot. Where had he come from?

"Howdy, Miss," he said in a gratingly false tone. His face was all sweaty and his hands were dirty, as if he'd been working. "Out for another little stroll, are ya?"

"No . . . I was just going for water." He should have been doing the explaining, but I was too scared to ask any questions

"All alone?" he said, an evil gleam in his eye.

"My Uncle Nick's back at the cabin," I stammered, looking toward the ground, "and he asked me to—"

"Now, Miss, you oughta know better'n to tell lies. Fact is, your Uncle Nick's way off in Miracle Springs, and ye're all alone here with them little kids. I watched from up on the hill, an' I seen him go."

"Well, if you wanted to see my uncle," I said, "why did you wait till he was gone?"

He laughed, but it wasn't a pleasant sound at all. Apparently the laugh was the only answer I was going to get to my question. Then he returned to the subject of my errand.

"You ought t' wait for yer menfolk t' get back home. A pretty little miss like yourself shouldn't be fetchin' such a heavy load."

"I can manage," I said.

"Well, I'll help ya. Lemme take that there bucket and I'll go fill it for ya." He stepped toward me.

I shrank back. "I can do it myself."

"Shy, are you, Missy?" His coarse, ugly face broke into a leering grin. "Ole Buck's jest tryin' to be friendly."

He moved quickly toward me and laid his rough hand on my shoulder.

I squirmed out of his grip and tried to run, but before I could get away his other hand shot up and grabbed me. My heart was pounding wildly now. I was really scared.

"You're a supple little thing—an' ole Buck likes 'em young an' willowy. C'mon, I can show you a real good time."

"P-please," I said, "let me go . . . I have to get back." He had me pinned against the rock at the edge of the mine now and I could hardly move. But I was afraid to struggle because he would only grip me tighter with those awful hands.

"Well, I sure can't have you runnin' back an' tellin' your uncle I was here, now can I?"

"He wouldn't care," I answered quickly.

"Ha, ha," he laughed. "There you go lyin' to ole Buck again! You know better'n that, now don't ya? I think maybe I better jist take you along with me!"

"No, please!" I yelled. "The children—they'll miss me and know something's wrong!"

"Maybe I should take the whole brood o' ya," he answered, then laughed again. "That way, I'd be sure no one'd tell!"

"Please—I won't say anything, if that's what you want."

"That's what I want, Missy, but I want more, too." He thrust his face so near to mine that his whiskers scratched me. He tried to kiss me, but I twisted my face away and his awful mouth only brushed my cheek.

I felt sick and faint.

His breath was repulsive. Somehow I managed to keep my legs from giving out beneath me. Yet even if I didn't pass out, I could not fight off this burly, strong man much longer.

He pressed closer and shoved the back of my head against the rock.

"Let me alone—please!" I begged, tears now streaming down my cheeks. "I won't tell no one."

"Don't be scared o' Buck, Missy."

"Help—!" I tried to scream, but his hand quickly shot up and clamped over my mouth.

"Now, Missy, that won't do a' tall—"

But the man's voice cut off sharply when the sound of footsteps could be heard nearby, followed by the light rustling of leaves and pebbles sliding down the embankment above us.

"What in tarnation?" he muttered, but then stopped speaking, realizing his danger. Slowly he loosened his hold on my shoulder, but kept one hand firmly over my mouth to keep me from calling out, while he listened intently.

All was quiet for a moment, then came the clicking sound of a rifle or pistol cocking.

"How in blazes could they have gotten back—" he began, then stopped short.

Again he thrust his face into mine, but all hint of vulgar playfulness was gone, and in its place was pure evil.

"You listen to me, Missy," he whispered in a sinister threat. "One sound outta you, and I'll kill your uncle and that fool partner o' his. I ain't so sure Drum ain't more kin to you all than your uncle. Then I'll come back an' kill you an' the kids too. You hear what Buck's sayin'?"

I nodded in terror.

His hand came off my mouth and went straight to the gun at his side. He let go of me completely, then turned, and with gun drawn and eyes scanning the woods about us, began stealthily moving off in the direction of the noise.

There was another sound, this time from further off. It was like a rock hitting a tree, but I couldn't be sure.

Buck twitched at the sound, uncertain fear replacing the grisly confidence on his face, then he moved off toward it, gun drawn in readiness.

I watched immobile, too petrified to move.

All at once, I felt another hand clamp over my mouth from behind. As I was watching Buck, from around the opposite side of the cave mouth, someone had silently crept up to my side.

My heart beating frantically, I jerked my head around.

It was Little Wolf!

As he stood there in his fawn-colored buckskin, one finger was pressed against his lips indicating silence. Slowly he removed his hand.

"Run back to the cabin," he whispered.

"But—but—who is out there?" I whispered back, nodding in Buck's direction with my head.

"No one," he answered. "The wicked man chases sounds, that is all."

"But the gun? We heard—"

"A trick sound my father taught me with the tongue," Little Wolf whispered with a smile.

"But the sounds came from over there—" I pointed, still puzzled.

"No more questions. The Indian has had to learn many things the white man still does not understand to live from the land. But to make noises and then sneak away is not such a feat. It is something we must do every day when tracking the deer or the bear. Now—you must go!"

"But what about you?"

A smile broke across Little Wolf's face.

"The bad man is not such a clever foe. I will keep him chasing his tail until your uncle returns. I have watched him before and I know his ways. No harm will come to you."

I looked into his eyes, trying to speak a word of thanks.

But before I could say a word, Little Wolf had moved to the other side of the mine opening to glance around the embankment at Buck's retreating figure.

I turned and ran back down the hill to the cabin.

Before going inside, I stopped and looked back. I was frightened for Little Wolf despite what he had said. He was now circling back the way he had come, up the embankment on the opposite side of the mine from where Buck was looking for him. I saw him work his way from tree to tree until he was almost within Buck's line of vision again. Then he stopped, withdrew an arrow from his quiver, laid it into his bow, and sent it toward Buck.

*Thwack!* The arrow sunk deep into the trunk of a medium-sized pine tree about five yards from the prowling white man.

He turned suddenly. I couldn't see his face, but I can just imagine how fearful he was.

Little Wolf stood still, in broad view, waiting for Buck to see him. I couldn't understand why he didn't hide!

"Why, you dirty savage!" roared Buck the moment he eyes focused on his adversary. In the next instant, the air was filled with gunfire as Buck let off a barrage in Little Wolf's direction. But by now the Indian was invisible once more, and the next moment I heard Buck cursing loudly, and lumbering deeper into the woods after his elusive enemy.

I saw neither of them again, though I heard several more rounds of gunfire, always followed by frustrated swearing and angry threats. But each time I heard Buck's voice, it was farther and farther away.

I had been so frightened for Little Wolf, that I didn't realize until then that he was purposely drawing Buck after him, farther and farther from the mine and the cabin.

Finally, I stepped inside and locked the door.

The bucket I'd taken to the mine was still there, but I wasn't about to go after it. I could wait for my water.

# CHAPTER 34

# LATER THAT SAME NIGHT

There were no more sounds from the woods for several hours.

In fact, the next sound I did hear was our wagon coming up the road. Pa was alone with the load of lumber. Uncle Nick had stayed in town for a while. As soon as Pa was in the door, I told him what had happened.

I'd never seen him look the way he did when I finished my story. I don't know if it was only because of the threats to me, or if it was anger roused because someone had trespassed on his claim. But his eyes were flashing, and without a word or a moment's hesitation, he grabbed his rifle from the corner and headed for the door, with a stern admonition to keep it locked.

I have no idea what he actually did or where he went. I'll probably never know, because he didn't talk about it when he returned at dusk. Uncle Nick had gotten back shortly after Pa left, and we'd all had supper.

The awful face of the man who called himself Buck was hard to erase from my mind, but almost worse was the look on Pa's face when he'd stalked out of the cabin in the early afternoon. There was such a look of vengeful violence in his eyes! It had me worried the whole time he was out.

After he finished his supper, he went outside again to tend his horse. I felt I had to talk to him, so I followed him out. I found him leaning against the fence staring straight ahead. I was almost afraid to approach him, but he heard me and looked up before the second thoughts I was having allowed me to retreat.

"Kinda cold to be out, ain't it, girl?" he said. His forehead was creased, the muscles in his neck taut.

"I was . . . nervous, Pa," I began.

"Don't worry. That slimy snake ain't gonna git near you again!" His voice was full of hatred.

"I was nervous about *you*, Pa," I said. "You seem—so—"

"I'll be all right," he muttered.

"You didn't find him, did you? I mean, the man's not—"

"Nah," he answered, sounding regretful that Buck was still out there. "I couldn't find him nowhere. But when I do, I'll kill him."

"But that won't help anything, Pa," I said. "It'll only get you into trouble."

It was probably impudent of me to say such a thing, but I could remember Ma saying the exact words to Zack when he wanted to get back at a bully in school. And her admonition had kept Zack from a needless fight, because it made him stop and realize that it would do more harm than good. Though they didn't seem to have the same effect on Pa coming from my mouth as they did when Ma said the words to Zack.

"The trouble I'm in," he mused, almost talking to himself, "I got in long ago. I thought I'd managed to run away from it, turning my back on my family in the process. But now it looks like the trouble's found me out in the end."

I didn't know what to say.

"But don't you worry none, Corrie," he said. "I won't do nothin' foolhardy. Just remember, this is the *West*, and what a man does for himself around here is sometimes the only justice to be had."

"Then maybe *I* should be the one to go after Buck," I

said. It was a stupid thing to say, and I don't know why I blurted it out.

"Don't talk foolishness, girl."

"But it was me he attacked, not you."

"Doing justice is a man's job. And since I'm your pa, it's my responsibility."

"I'd rather you just let it go."

"Well, you don't know the whole story," he added, without offering to tell it.

"Tell me about it, Pa," I pleaded.

"I can't now. Maybe the time will come . . . I don't know."

"I don't want anything to happen to you, Pa."

"Don't worry. Nothin's going to happen to me."

But just hearing him say the words made me more and more worried.

"Now get yourself inside. It's gettin' late. Time for the little ones to be in bed."

I went back inside, a little reassured, but anxious about Pa.

Later that night, I lay awake in bed unable to sleep. The events of the day still churned in my mind. I hadn't said much at all to Uncle Nick about the incident. But as I lay there, I could hear his and Pa's voices in the other room. I couldn't make out what they were saying, but at the mention of Buck's name, my ears perked up, and I sat up straining to listen.

" . . . I still can't believe it could be Buck Krebbs," Uncle Nick was saying.

"Believe it," replied Pa. "You heard what the kids said before—the scar on his face, now this thing with Corrie."

"But if it *was* Buck, and he was prowling around our place, why would he tell her his name? He'd have to know she'd tell us, and then we'd be onto him."

"None of that Gulch bunch was overloaded with brains,

Nick," said Pa. "And Buck was the biggest dimwit of them all."

"You think he's looking for the loot?"

"What else?"

"So, did you get any lead on him?"

"Nah. Everybody's tight-lipped."

"Some of the boys say Royce has brought in some out-of-town low-lifes."

"What for?"

"No one knows."

"I never did trust that shyster," muttered Pa.

"You think the others are here too?"

"Aw, who can tell?"

Just the sound of Pa's boot kicking at the fire told me that he was standing in front of the hearth, no doubt with his hand resting on a hook in the large wooden beam just over his head. That's where he always stood when he was thinking, staring down into the fire's red-hot embers.

"Even if he did follow Aggie and the kids, I can't imagine Buck making it all the way out here alone."

"Yeah, but don't you think that if ol' Buck saw a chance to grab the money on his own and high-tail it to Mexico or someplace, he'd as soon doublecross the others as put a slug in either of us?"

"Yeah, you got a point there," said Pa.

The two were silent again, and before I heard another word, I was sound asleep.

# CHAPTER 35

## OVERHEARD CONVERSATION

Late in January, we finally got some snow. It was nothing like what we had in New York, but on the distant hills it was heavy, with scattered patches in the valley. Actually, it made a lovely picture—the pure white mounds broken by the rich red earth, evergreens standing tall and fresh all around our claim, the stream winding its way down the hill, and a slate of blue sky overhead.

The weather wasn't bothering the mining too much. The shaft was pretty big now and they were concentrating their blasting in a drift which would be an offshoot from the main tunnel. They were working hard, but hadn't hit any paydirt yet.

Quartz mining with only two or three men wasn't done too often. Hauling up the big chunks of rock was back-breaking for one man, and usually only the bigger operations could afford carts to go in and out of the mine, and a stamp mill to smash and crush the rock to get the gold out. But Pa and Uncle Nick were determined. They tried all sorts of things to separate the ore more efficiently, but so far they hadn't found much.

Then yesterday the three of them spent a lot of time talking about trying to put together what they called a chili mill. Mr. Jones said he knew some Mexicans who could help them get one going and who knew all about the operation.

So this morning Pa and Uncle Nick headed into Miracle Springs again, this time for more lumber, rope, and cable. Pa was saying something about the millstones, but I couldn't tell if he was going to get them or if Mr. Jones was going to go down to Grass Valley for them.

Pa looked worn and haggard when they left. I remember thinking that I hoped something would happen soon, for his sake. After all they'd been through, and with the added burden of us kids, I was afraid if they didn't find some gold before long, he might quit, or take to gambling again.

After the sounds of the wagon died away, and the breakfast dishes had been cleaned up, I decided to go for a walk. I told Zack to keep a close eye on the kids.

"Aw, Corrie, you know I don't like to stay in the cabin playin' ma."

"I won't be gone that long," I insisted. "You don't have to stay *in* the cabin. Just keep an eye out for them, that's all."

"But I was gonna go up and work at the mine."

"Did Pa give you permission?"

"Well, not exactly."

"I didn't think so. You stay away from that mine," I said firmly. "And you keep Tad in sight. He's been dying to get up there, and you know what Pa said. Keep him close by the cabin."

Zack just shrugged his shoulders, then asked, "What if that man comes back?"

"He won't," I answered. "We haven't seen any strangers for a month, and Pa says that fellow's long gone by now. But if you hear somebody you don't know, just bolt yourselves inside. I won't be that long."

As I left the cabin, I thought that if I found a good drift of snow I would go back and get the kids so they could play in it. But I didn't want to say anything, otherwise I'd never get my walk alone. As I walked, I couldn't get Zack's words out of my mind. Maybe Pa had only said what he had about Buck to keep us from worrying. I knew that man had to be still on his mind, because this was the first time all month he had left us alone, even for a minute.

The day was so lovely that it was easy to push my nagging doubts aside. I was determined to enjoy myself. The air was clean and crisp, and I didn't mind that the cold penetrated even my warmest New York coat. The snow was starting to melt in places, but there was still plenty everywhere. I walked north at first, then east toward some snow-covered hills. I warmed up quickly under the hazy winter sun.

After about half a mile, I reached a steep ridge. It probably wasn't the smartest thing to climb it with all the snow, but I'd been there before, and I knew that from the top was a spectacular view of the lowlands.

Slipping and sliding, I finally made it to the crest, and the sight today was even more beautiful than usual. I felt like a fairy princess surveying the realm of her winter wonderland. Ma was always so practical. She would probably scold me good-naturedly for my fanciful notions, and tell me not to let my imagination run loose. But I figured that as long as I could be practical when I had to be, it was okay to daydream sometimes. I expect even Ma would have allowed me that much.

I could have stayed there for hours taking in the view, but my practical side started to awaken and tell me I should be getting back. Just before beginning my descent I noticed something I hadn't seen before.

Way down below I could see the road into town. I'd never realized it came so close to this ridge, winding in a great half-circle around the hill. I think the whiteness of the snow made the dark dirt road more visible.

This would surely be a short-cut, I thought, to the claim. Or—and I shivered with the thought—a way to sneak up around to the back of the mine like that dreadful man must have done, without anyone detecting him on the road that passed our cabin.

Even as I stood staring at the road, in the distance a

horse-drawn wagon came into faint view. At first I thought it must be Pa on his way home.

I scrambled down from my perch to descend the hill on that side, thinking to meet Pa on the road, forgetting for a minute that he could not possibly be returning so soon.

By the time I'd made three-fourths of the descent, I could see that the wagon was too small and too fancy to be Pa's. But I hardly had time to think further, for all at once a rider on horseback came into view. I hadn't seen his approach. There was an exchange between him and the buggy driver, who then snapped his reins and drove off the road under the cover of some trees. They were heading right toward me.

My heart nearly stopped! The man on horseback followed, and it was none other than Buck Krebbs! All I could think of was getting away as fast as I could. But they surely would have seen me! So I crouched down in the brush, praying they wouldn't see me and would go on by. But they stopped where they were, and I was stuck.

I held my breath, not moving a muscle. Even with my heart pounding in my ears, I found myself straining to hear what they were saying. In the still, crisp air, I recognized the buggy driver's voice, but couldn't place it. His back was turned to me.

"Well, Krebbs," he said, "I hope you don't botch the job this time."

"Now look here!" he snapped back, "I couldn't help it if that blame fool girl showed up afore I could git it done."

"If a little girl's going to keep you from—"

"She wouldn've kept me from nuthin'! I coulda handled her just fine! But then that crazed Injun attacked me!"

"There are men I could hire who wouldn't be afraid of a lone Indian—a mere boy, I understand."

"It was his arrows that coulda killed me as dead as the next guy! You ever seen one a them sharpshooters?"

"No—no, can't say that I have, Krebbs, but—"

"You couldn't hire a local who'd keep as quiet about

244

your dirty work better'n ole Buck, an' you know it! 'Sides, I took care o' Larsen's place, didn't I?"

"Well, I just hope you can do as well with Matthews'."

My mind was reeling as I listened, trying to remember where I'd heard the name Larsen before, but the instant I recalled, the man's next words made everything become clearer.

". . . I want their place burned to the ground come sunup tomorrow. You got that, Krebbs?"

"Got it."

"Luckily, my scheme may not hinge entirely on your part."

"Whaddya mean by that? I risked my neck to come back here in broad daylight!"

"I'm paying you well enough."

"No more'n the job's worth. Don't forget, I rode with Matthews back in '43. 'Course that weren't his name then! I seen him in action. That's why when his six-gun comes out, I intend t' be behind him, not in front o' him!"

"I don't care about your personal vendetta against the man, Mr. Krebbs, just so long as you do what I'm paying you for. Whatever else you hope to get out of it, that's your own business."

"I got my reasons," muttered Buck, "I'll get the job done."

"In any case, you won't have Matthews to worry about for long, or that partner of his either for that matter." The icy voice made me shiver, but I just couldn't place it. Suddenly I was colder than ever, and it wasn't from the snow.

"Now, just you wait a minute! If you're plannin' to kill 'em, you just hold onto your hat. They ain't no good to me dead!"

"Relax. I'll let you have the honor. All I want is them outta the way. After that, they're all yours. And when I show Matthews what I got, with his cabin nothin' but ashes and his mine caved in, he'll clear out faster'n them kids can hang onto his coattails. Even that stone-faced partner of his, Drum, won't be able to talk his way out of this one!"

"Whatcha got?"

"None of your business!" came the curt reply. There was a brief pause, then apparently thinking Buck deserved to know at least a portion of his plot, he went on, "Let's just call it a little insurance policy I discovered very recently." And shaking his head, "To think that I've had it all along."

As he spoke, he pulled out a piece of paper and waved it in the air.

"What's a little piece o' paper gonna do to men like Matthews and Drum?"

"Even a man like Nick Matthews has to abide by the law, Mr. Krebbs. And this little piece of paper, as you call it, gives me immediate legal right to his entire property unless he can come up with $150 in cash."

"So why do ya want me to burn him out?"

"Call it double insurance. Matthews is so hot-headed, he would probably try to shoot his way out of this. But if I know that Drum fellow, he'll no doubt think there is some way around this IOU, and I would rather not have to fight him in some Sacramento court. There's something about that man I just don't like. He's too cool for me. I think he's hiding something."

"He's hidin' plenty! I can tell you that! Ya know them kids—"

"I don't care about the kids, Krebbs!" the driver interrupted. "I don't care what name they used to go by. I don't care what your devious scheme may be regarding them. All I want to make sure of is that your little act of sabotage convinces both of them of the folly of trying to resist."

"Just so long as you know I ain't settin' a torch to the place 'til I've gone over every inch o' it."

"Just do the job, Krebbs."

"And I'm warnin' you now, don't git no crazy thoughts o' tryin' to git out o' payin' me for *your* dirty work!"

"You'll get your money. I paid you for the other jobs."

Then like a flash, Buck drew his gun and waved it in the driver's face.

"You'll bring the money to that deserted shack on the ol' Smith claim in one hour," he said in a threatening tone, "or you'll be spending the rest of a very short life lookin' over your shoulder. And you can ask the fellow who *calls* himself Drum how long I stay on a man's trail who double-crosses me! Why, he ain't no more a Drum than Nick is a Matthews! You understand me? You cross me and I'll track you down no matter where you go or how many times you change your name!"

"This is what comes of doing business with low-lifes," the driver said with disgust in his voice.

"One hour! Or I'll be after you!"

With that, Mr. Krebbs swung into his saddle and was gone. The other man remained a moment longer, still shaking his head. Then he walked back to his buggy, got in, and went back the way he had come.

I let out a huge sigh of relief, and waited till both men were well out of sight. My first thought was to warn Uncle Nick and Pa. If I followed the men into town from here, I might be able to get there in less than the hour it would take them to do whatever they were going to do at the Smith place.

But what if the man confronted Uncle Nick *before* going to pay Krebbs his money? What if he forced Uncle Nick to surrender the claim like he said he could?

I just had to get to either Pa or Uncle Nick before he did. I started toward the road, while I thought through a plan.

Then all of a sudden, I stopped short in my tracks. Another idea suddenly occurred to me. I spun around and hurried back the way I'd come down the hill. I *had* to go to the cabin first, even if it delayed everything!

Ten minutes later, I burst through the door, breathless and sweaty. I headed for the bedroom without a word.

"Where you been so long, Corrie," Zack moaned, "You

said you'd only be gone a short time!"

"Zack," I said when I came back to the front room, "I'm sorry, but I can't even stay. I've got to go to town!"

"Why?" he asked.

"There's no time to explain. Now listen, if you see or hear anyone hanging around outside, take one of Pa's guns and get you and the kids out into the woods, but not too far from the cabin, so you can keep a watch on it."

"I thought you said to keep them inside."

"Never mind that. I've just overheard two men talking about burning down the cabin!"

Zack's face was clouded with fear. The younger ones were too bewildered make a peep.

"Corrie, please don't leave us here—alone," he begged.

"I have to, Zack! There's no choice. I don't think they plan to do it 'til tonight, and by then Pa'll be back. But I had to tell you, just in case, so you watch careful, and keep that gun at the ready."

I paused to looked deep into his eyes. I still saw the fear. But he knew I was trusting him with a man's job, and in spite of being afraid, I think he was proud. In that instant, with the lives of our younger brothers and sisters depending on us, I think both Zack and I took several big steps toward growing up.

I hugged him impulsively. "I love you, Zack. You pray for me, and I'll pray for you. The Lord will be with us."

Then I turned and ran out the door before I lost my courage.

"Corrie. . . !" Zack called out after me.

I stopped and looked back.

He was standing in the doorway. I could see tears in his eyes, but he stood tall like a man with a job to do.

"I love you, too," he said, dabbing at the tears with his sleeve.

I smiled and took off with all my strength down the road toward town.

# CHAPTER 36

## A REVELATION OF FAMILY TIES

I left the cabin at a dead run, but that pace sure didn't last for long. The snow that had been so beautiful before was now a curse, what with the mud and slush slowing my pace at every turn. I slipped and stumbled, mud sloshing up over my boots and stockings and caking all over the bottom of my dress.

I wondered if I'd ever make it. My breath came in frosty gasps, and my lungs hurt dreadfully. Still I kept running, keeping my fingers clutched tightly on the small parcel I had gotten from the cabin.

It must have been the longest I'd ever run in my life. By the time I reached the outskirts of town, I had slowed to barely better than a walk, hobbling and limping on my numb feet. All I could think of was whether I'd be on time!

Then I heard the sound of a wagon coming toward me! I couldn't believe my ears or my eyes. It was Mrs. Parrish!

"Corrie—what is it?" she called anxiously, stopping the wagon.

I ran to her as she climbed down to the road, and nearly collapsed in her outstretched arms. It was at least a full minute before I could speak.

"I've got to find Pa!" I finally gasped, "Before it's too late . . . what'll we do if he loses the claim. . . ?"

She could make nothing of my ramblings.

"Climb up here in the wagon, Corrie," she said. "You need to rest a minute, then you can explain everything to me."

"There's no time!" I panted, climbing up after her. My legs and feet ached. "We've got to find Pa or Uncle Nick!"

Without waiting for further explanation, Mrs. Parrish wheeled her horses around, snapped the reins, and sent them charging back the way she had come. My heart gradually slowed its pounding, my chest stopped aching, and I managed to tell her the story briefly. Whether she caught everything I yelled above the din of the charging horses and the clatter of the wagon, I don't know. But she certainly realized the urgency of my mission once it dawned on her that I'd run all the way into town from the cabin in the snow and mud.

About halfway through town we spotted Pa's bay mare tied up outside a place called Lil's Saloon. My heart sank in despair when I saw the buggy drawn up next to it—the one that had brought the man out to talk to Buck Krebbs.

Mrs. Parrish helped me out of the wagon. My feet were still numb and unsteady, but the moment I hit the ground I took off running again straight toward the saloon's swinging doors.

I ran right inside, Mrs. Parrish behind me. We stopped short in the dim light to take in the scene. All the men were so intent on their conversation they didn't even notice us at first. We heard what was apparently the end of a very heated argument.

The place wasn't very crowded this time of day. A knot of men stood around a table against the far wall. My uncle was seated, his arms folded across his chest, his face hard and drawn. My first thought was to recall what had happened with Uncle Nick and the man called Judd over a poker game. I hoped he had been able to control his temper this time!

Pa was seated with Nick; a bottle of whiskey and two half-empty glasses sat between them on the table. Alkali Jones stood behind them, and three or four men I didn't know were gathered nearby, along with the sheriff. And directly in front of Uncle Nick was the driver of the buggy outside. Suddenly I remembered his voice—it was Mr. Royce, the banker!

"I hate to see it come to this, Matthews—or—whatever your name really is," Mr. Royce was saying.

"Do you?" my uncle replied, his lips so tight they hardly seemed to move.

"I'm a businessman, and this note is due and payable on demand." Mr. Royce turned to the sheriff. "It's all perfectly legal, isn't it, Simon?"

Mr. Rafferty was obviously reluctant to take the banker's side. "I've examined it, Nick," he said, "and it's legitimate. Potter borrowed money and put up the claim for collateral."

"Unfortunately," Royce went on with affected sympathy, "when you won his claim, the outstanding obligation fell to you. And I'm afraid unless you can come up with the $150 on demand, as the note specifies, the claim reverts to the bank."

"I ain't givin' up the claim for no piece of paper that I ain't had nothing to do with!" snapped Uncle Nick.

"The law—" Mr. Royce began to emphasize again.

With that, my frozen feet sprang to action and I stepped forward.

"Pa—Uncle Nick!" I cried. "They're gonna burn up the cabin!"

The group of men parted spontaneously as I ran up to the table. In the confusion, no one seemed to notice that I'd forgotten to call him Mr. Drum.

"Corrie . . . what in blazes!" Pa exclaimed, looking up. "What in tarnation are you doing here?"

"I came to warn you!"

"But how'd you get here?"

"I ran—all the way. You've got to stop them, Pa! The kids are up there alone, and these men are gonna do what they did to Larsen's place!"

"Who, Corrie?" asked my uncle from across the table. I turned to him, but before I could answer, Pa noticed Mrs. Parrish standing behind me, and leveled his gaze upon her.

"Your—I should say, Mr. Matthew's niece has gone to considerable trouble to speak with you, Mr. . . . Mr.— Drum!"

"We can take care of our own business, if you don't mind, Ma'am," said Pa, annoyed at her comment.

"I have no intention of interfering. I just happened to meet Corrie as she came into town a few minutes ago. I think you ought to hear her out."

Pa sighed and pursed his lips together. It was hard to tell if he was mad or worried. But now he turned to me again. Without comment, his eyes told me to speak and get it over with.

"It's him!" I cried, pointing toward Mr. Royce. "I saw him and Buck Krebbs talking—"

"So Krebbs *is* in town!" exploded Uncle Nick, half rising out of his chair.

"I don't know where he is now," I answered. "But I came upon the two of them no more than a mile from our cabin. I was out for a walk, and overheard them talking just off the road—"

"Really, this is—" Mr. Royce started to speak. But Pa shot him a look that stopped his words cold.

"You shut up, Royce!" he ordered. "Go on, Corrie what did you hear?"

"They were talking about a job Mr. Krebbs was supposed to have taken care of the day he attacked me up by the mine. Mr. Krebbs wanted his money, but Mr. Royce insisted he do a successful job first. They talked about Mr. Larsen, but I didn't catch enough of it to make sense of it, until they started talking about burning the place to the ground. And that's when I knew I had to warn you! I don't know where Mr. Krebbs is, but the kids are still at home by themselves, and these men said they were going to do it tonight!"

"Come now," said the banker, "you certainly are not going to believe the fanciful rantings of a half-exhausted child!"

Pa jumped out of his chair, sending it to the floor behind him with a crash. He looked a foot taller than Mr. Royce at that moment, and I could almost see smoke coming from his nostrils.

"Are you calling my daughter a liar?" he thundered. If I had been Mr. Royce, I would have been shaking from head to foot.

At the word "daughter" a general murmuring began to filter through the saloon.

A peculiar smile spread slowly over Royce's lips, as if the revelation of this secret gave him further fuel to use against Pa.

"Your *daughter*, you say? I thought this brood belonged to Matthews—ah, but then that's not his real name, is it?" The part about Uncle Nick's name he muttered almost to himself.

"You heard right!" interrupted Uncle Nick, now rising himself and coming to Pa's rescue. "They *are my* kin—my sister's kids!"

"It's all right, Nick," said Pa softly, "there ain't no sense keeping it quiet any longer. Yeah, that's right, Royce," he said, again to the banker. "This here's my daughter, and she ain't been brought up to tell no lies!"

Still wearing that smug smile, the banker said, "I was merely attempting to point out that sometimes children have vivid imaginations."

My natural shyness was gone and I felt indignant at being called both a liar and a child. I was so proud of Pa for standing up for me that I figured I could stand up as well.

"I did not imagine a word of what I heard you saying!" I said, in the strongest voice I could muster.

"Well," said Royce in a slightly altered tone, a thin line of sweat forming on his forehead. "It may well be that she saw Krebbs and me together. The thieving man accosted me on the trail and we did have words. In fact, he tried to rob me. But I assured him I was carrying no cash, and that I would have him arrested if he so much as touched me. He frightened off pretty easily. But if you want to go after him, I say take the law with you and grab him. Men like him are a threat to our community."

"Me gunnin' down Krebbs would be mighty convenient to you, wouldn't it Royce?" said Uncle Nick in a low growl. "That would eliminate the only verification to Corrie's story."

"It's neither here nor there to me." Mr. Royce sounded smug, despite his moist forehead. "Regarding the girl's allegations, whether Krebbs is dead or alive seems to me to hardly change the fact that you have no more proof than my word against hers. And the word of an upstanding town father against that of a flighty child of—shall we say, of dubious parentage—"

Before he could finish, Pa's fist crashed down on the table. He took two strides toward the banker and it looked like he was about to knock him onto the floor.

Uncle Nick and Mr. Jones jumped out from behind the table to restrain him. "The vermin ain't worth it, Drum," said Uncle Nick, suddenly playing the unaccustomed role of peacemaker.

Restrained but hardly pacified, Pa stood glaring at the banker.

"—whose father's real name we apparently don't even know," went on the courageous Mr. Royce. "My word against hers hardly seems a fair contest. What possible evidence could the child bring? And after all I've done for this town, who would believe it?"

"We'll see, Royce," growled Pa between clenched teeth.

"And all this is beside the point, anyway. The problem of the IOU still must be addressed," said Mr. Royce, attempting to again assume the tone of businessman, ignoring Pa for the moment and turning his focus again toward Uncle Nick. "Even if I were everything this foolish girl says, your claim still legally belongs to the bank. Now, I'm going to tell you one final time, *Matthews*—" He spat out the word with contempt. "I am calling your note due. You must make good on that $150 debt, or I will take possession of the mine. There is no court in this country that would tell you differently."

"Well, I ain't got no $150. And I ain't giving you our claim. You can do your best to come and try to take it from us!"

"The sheriff has the authority to arrest you if you persist in your refusal and cause any trouble over this."

Now Alkali Jones' squeaky voice broke into the conversation for the first time. "Hee, hee! I'd like to see him try! Hee, hee!"

"I want to avoid any violence," said Mr. Royce, his smugness slipping once more, "but the law is the law."

"There's another kind of law in these parts, Royce," said my uncle, "and it stands for a dang sight more'n your babble."

"Come now, Matthews," said Mr. Royce with a smile, "you and the so-called Mr. Drum here—you're family men now. Surely even you, despite your reputation, would not resort to gunplay—"

All at once I woke up and came to my senses. Why was I listening to all this? I held the solution to everything right in my hand!

"Pa—Uncle Nick!" I blurted out. "It's right here! I went back to the cabin for it, and I plumb forgot! I heard Mr. Royce telling Mr. Krebbs about the IOU, too. So I ran back for it."

I slapped the velvet pouch I had been carrying down on the table. "There's your money, Mr. Royce!" I cried. "It's my Ma's inheritance. You can take your $150 from it!"

I flashed a look of triumph at Mrs. Parrish, then smiled at Pa.

He and Uncle Nick just stood staring at the pouch, but made no move for it. Neither did Mr. Royce.

"It's yours, Pa," I said, "just like I told you before."

"What about it, Matthews?" asked Sheriff Rafferty.

Uncle Nick glanced at Pa dumfounded. He had known nothing about the money. All eyes were on Pa, waiting for him to speak. But the real expression to watch was that of Mr. Royce. He couldn't hide his chagrin, and it seemed he didn't know what to do next.

Pa remained quiet, stroking his beard, gazing without expression at the pouch. Finally, he looked up at me, and it seemed a mask fell off his face. It was as if he were letting go of a personality that wasn't really his, part of him he'd been trying to hang onto in order to keep back the secrets of his past. Suddenly, he was no longer a stranger who happened to share my family name . . . but my *father*—the man who had loved his wife and children, and who had suffered terrible guilt over being forced to flee and leave us behind.

"Why're you doing this, Corrie?" he said softly, and it was like we were the only two people in that saloon. Everyone else was silent. "Why—after all I done, after my leaving your ma, after the way I treated you. . . ?"

"All that's past, Pa," I answered. "Anyway, we're kin, and I guess that's reason enough. Please take it. That's what Ma would want, if she knew how things were now. I know it, Pa—I know she would! And—it's what *I* want, too."

He took the pouch slowly in his hand, and dumped out the wad of bills. Methodically, he counted out one hundred and fifty dollars, put the rest back into the pouch, and handed it back to me. Then he gave Uncle Nick the money.

"Here's your payment, Royce," said Uncle Nick. As the

banker took it, he looked as crestfallen as ever I've seen a man. "Take it, Royce, and give me that IOU!"

Royce reluctantly handed him the piece of paper.

Now it was Pa's turn to speak again. He looked him coolly in the eye. "Now I'm telling you, Royce, if you or any of your hired hooligans ever comes near my family again, you'll live to regret it! Now . . . get outta here!"

Clutching the money in his fist, the banker spun around red-faced and slipped out a back way. A belated cheer rose from the men in the saloon, above which could be heard the high-pitched cackle of Alkali Jones. As the cheer subsided, there was a barrage of questions thrown in Pa's direction about his newly-revealed family ties.

But before he could answer, even as the doors were still swinging from Royce's exit, they crashed open once more. My brother Zack came racing into the room!

# CHAPTER 37

## THE CAVE

Zack stormed in, all out of breath and muddy, just like I was.

"Pa . . . Corrie!" he cried. "It caved in! He only got away from me for just a minute, but—"

"Slow down, boy," said Pa, trying to stay calm and laying a steadying hand on Zack's shoulder.

"Oh, Pa, I'm real sorry. I didn't mean to let him go near it—"

"Who—go near what? Tell me what happened!"

"I couldn't get him out—Tad's trapped inside the cave!"

"The mine?" Pa cried, his worst fears suddenly realized.

"He slipped away; I didn't know where he went at first, but I shoulda guessed. You know how he's always wanted to go down there and work with us. Well, first I heard him call to me. I went runnin' after him, but then I heard a rumblin' sound . . . and fallin' rocks . . . and dirt and dust was billowin' out of the mouth of the cave . . . and Tad's coat was laying in front of the opening! After that I shouted and shouted, but Tad never answered back!"

"What then?" asked Uncle Nick.

"As soon as the rocks stopped falling, I ran inside and tried to dig my way through the pile—there was a huge pile of rocks and dirt . . . it looked like a whole section of the roof just gave way—and one of the big timbers was lying

257

there half covered by the rocks, like it'd just broken in two from the weight . . ."

"I wonder if it had a little help," mused Uncle Nick.

Pa flashed a look at him. I knew they were both thinking of Buck Krebbs.

"I was calling out *Tad, Tad,* but I couldn't hear anything, and I knew I'd never dig through it myself . . . so I locked the girls in the cabin and ran off down the road. About a mile out, this man came along and gave me a ride into town on his horse."

For the first time, we all noticed that a man had followed Zack into the saloon. I didn't know him, but Pa seemed to.

Even as Pa said, "I'm much obliged to you, Shaw," the saloon became a flurry of activity. Pa and Mr. Jones and Uncle Nick talked hurriedly together, then broke up and headed for the door. Several other men were grabbing their coats and running outside.

Pa was the first one out the door, and I heard his horse galloping away before the rest of us reached the sidewalk. Other riders weren't far behind him.

Uncle Nick called out to whoever would listen, "Anybody have a cable to move them rocks? We'll need some extra picks and shovels too."

I heard someone reply, "I'll bring rope!" By that time, Mr. Jones had the wagon and team ready, and without even waiting for him to stop, Uncle Nick jumped aboard, took the reins from Mr. Jones, and sent the horses flying down the street, his hat tipped back on his head, and his light hair flying in the wind.

Before I could feel left behind, Zack and I were in Mrs. Parrish's wagon, and she was whipping her two horses into a full gallop. We were bounced along as she shouted to the horses for greater speed. "Hee-yeaah! Hee-yeaah!" she cried, half standing, flipping the reins with her wrists. But I think the horses were already running as fast as they could. Several more men on horseback passed us on the way, but it was certainly the fastest trip I'd ever made between town and the cabin!

The moment we got there, Zack and I ran up to the mine, while Mrs. Parrish went straight to the cabin to make sure Becky and Emily were all right.

The mine shaft was jammed with men—scrambling, shouting, all trying to help at once. Pa and Uncle Nick were right in the middle of them all, frantically heaving away rocks bigger than a man's head as if they were pebbles. Sweat was pouring down Pa's face and his eyes were intense with anxiety. But it was more than fear for a child's life that I saw written there. *Any* child in danger would stir the heart of a decent man to do heroic things. But the look on Pa's face at that moment was the fear of a man for the life of his *own* son!

Some of the rocks were huge, bigger than Tad himself, and took two men exerting themselves to the full, to push them out of the hole. The cave-in left piles of debris and white rock unlike any that I had ever noticed before.

Ten minutes passed in no time . . . then twenty . . . then half an hour. The men were beginning to tire from working so hard and so fast, but they still didn't seem to be getting through. No one said much. The only sounds were the groans and puffing of the men, the crashing of rocks on the pile outside, and every so often a call from Pa: "Tad . . . Tad. . . ! Can you hear us, boy?"

Mrs. Parrish came up the hill now, and stood forty or fifty feet back, her arms around Becky and Emily. From the look on her face, I knew she was praying hard. So was I.

All at once a cry came from Uncle Nick. His voice was muffled from deep inside the cave, "We broke through!" he yelled.

I hurried to the shaft opening, but it was so dark inside all I could see was dust and vague figures of the men moving about.

Apparently Pa was trying to crawl through the small hole that had been made.

"Ye'll never make it, Drum!" I heard Alkali Jones' voice. "It's too blamed small!" There was no high-pitched laugh this time. His voice was more serious than I had ever heard it. "Let Nick try."

A moment of silence followed.

"Tad . . . Tad. . . !" came the muted voice of Uncle Nick through the hole. But still there was no response.

Just as my eyes began adjusting to the dark, I saw the form of Uncle Nick pulling his head back out of the hole. He wiped the grime from his eyes and said, "Still too small . . . I can't make it either."

"We'll have to get more of this outta here!" shouted Pa, who began to tear away at the rocks again.

He was interrupted by the sound of Zack's voice. "I think I can fit in, Pa," he said.

Pa stopped and turned around, gazing at his eldest son for a moment.

"I don't know what's in there, boy," he said. "Could be dangerous. Once there's a cave-in and you've lost your timbers, you never know—"

"I want to try," said Zack. "This is all my fault, and I've got to at least try to get him out!" There was no pleading in his voice, only determination.

"It ain't your fault," answered Pa. "And I'm afraid of the wall comin' down more."

"Then I better move fast," said Zack, edging toward the hole.

Pa stopped him. His eyes, filled with pride, met Zack's. "That's right brave of you, Zack," he said, then paused, still looking Zack over as if seeing him for the first time. "Okay," he said a second later, "get in there . . . and you be careful!"

"Yes, sir!" replied Zack, and a moment later he was wiggling and squirming through the small opening.

First his legs, then his feet disappeared. There was silence for a moment. Then, "It's pitch black in here!" he called back, sounding very far away.

Then we heard him calling Tad's name.

Everyone waited, holding their breath, but we didn't hear anything more. After a minute or so, Pa yelled through the hole after Zack. There was no reply. All remained deathly still while we waited.

My hands were in such tight fists, my knuckles were white. All sorts of terrible thoughts were racing through my brain. What if Tad was badly hurt . . . or dead? It would be my fault, not Zack's! I was the one to blame, the one who had let Ma down. Tad was her baby!

The next minutes seemed like ages. It could not have been more than five minutes, but then I thought I heard something—Zack's voice, more muffled than before. I couldn't tell what he was saying.

Then came the dreaded sound of more rock and debris falling.

I glanced at Pa. His face was white as a sheet.

"C'mon!" he yelled. "Let's clear away more of this rock!"

His hands were already bleeding, but he started to tear away at the pile more frantically than ever. Before anyone could move to help him, Zack's voice came again, clearer this time.

"I got him!"

The next moment, Tad's head thrust through the hole, his face covered with grime and blood from a gash on his forehead. Then his little body wriggled through, and he was free.

A great cheer went up from the men, who immediately fell back to make room. I grabbed Tad in my arms and hurried him outside, where he blinked and squinted from the bright sunlight.

Zack was out of the hole next, and he and Pa emerged from the mine side by side. Before he came to us, Pa turned to Zack and extended his hand. "That was quite a thing you

done in there, son," he said. "No man coulda done better
. . . I'm right proud of you."

Then Pa reached for Tad, scooping him up in his strong
arms like he was a feather.

"You okay, lad?" he asked, his voice shaking a little.

"Yes, Pa."

"You gave us quite a scare, Tad."

"I'm sorry. I made it fall down—but I wanted to help
with the mining. Was it my fault?"

Pa gave a big laugh. "You couldn't have caused that
cave-in, son," he said. "I think it had a little help from the
outside. I'm just glad you're safe."

I'm sure Pa intended to say more, but the words
wouldn't come. He quickly looked away, and when he
turned again, I could see the grime on his face was splotched
with moisture.

"Blasted dust!" he muttered, brushing a hand across his
face. "Can't keep it outta my eyes!"

"Hey, this is some family you got, Drum!" shouted Patrick Shaw, the man who'd given Zack the ride into town.
He had just talked to Mrs. Parrish, and seen the young girls
for the first time.

His statement took Pa by surprise. He looked at him as
if he was thinking over all the implications of Shaw's innocent comment.

"Yeah," he replied slowly. "I guess you're right, Pat. It
sure is."

He paused briefly, then added. "But there's only one
thing you're mistaken about." He looked toward the men
milling around the mine. "Hey!" he called out, "Mr. Shaw's
just brought up a topic that seemed of considerable interest
to all of you back at Lil's. I figure this'd be just about as
good a time as any to make a clean breast of it, once and for
all."

The men gathered 'round with growing interest.

"My name ain't Drum," Pa went on, glancing momentarily in the direction of the sheriff, perhaps having second thoughts about what he was about to say. But he didn't stop.

"Well, that is, it ain't my family name, though it's served me well as a given name all my life. The man you're all gawkin' at is a Hollister by birth—Drummond Hollister, to be exact."

"But why, Drum?" spoke up Alkali Jones, perhaps the most dumfounded of anyone; besides Uncle Nick, he had been Pa's closest friend for several years. "You in trouble with the law or somethin'?"

Pa shot him a quick glance, but then only said, "I had my reasons. What's past is past."

"What about 'ol Nick?" Jones pressed.

"I married Nick's sister. Anything else, he'll have to tell you himself—if he wants to."

Before Mr. Jones had a chance to say anything more, the sheriff walked up to Pa, looking straight at him. I was a little scared, but Pa didn't flinch. He just looked right back at him straight in the eye.

"I gotta tell you," the sheriff finally said, "there've been some folks hereabouts curious about you suddenly turning up with a family out of the past with a different name."

"You got a problem with that, Rafferty?" asked Pa.

The sheriff only had to think for a second or two before he answered. "Nah," he said. "I been in the diggin's long enough to know that half the men here are using assumed names." Then a smile broke out on his face. "Shoot, half of them are lawmen now!"

Several of the men standing within hearing of their conversation chuckled.

"So my havin' a past I'd rather keep quiet about don't bother you none?"

"Far as I can see, you ain't done nothin' to arouse no suspicions, Drum—or whatever I'm supposed to call you! Like I said, half the men who came here looking for gold's got their name on a sheriff's office wall someplace. My job's to keep the law here in Miracle, not go borrowin' trouble by asking too many questions about everyone's past."

He stopped, then flashed a sharp glance at Uncle Nick. "But that brother-in-law of yours is another matter. I'll be lenient for your sake, Drum, but only so far."

"Don't worry about Nick, Rafferty," said Pa. "He'll keep to the straight and narrow—if I got to hog-tie him!" He also shot a glance at poor Uncle Nick.

My uncle squirmed a little, but his sincere smile let us all know he intended to try.

"So the two o' you *is* kin!" exclaimed Alkali Jones, who could keep quiet no longer. "And the young'uns?"

"They belong to my sister and Drum," Uncle Nick said enthusiastically. I think he wanted to tell more, but thought better of it in public. Still no mention had been made of his using the name Matthews, and I figured he wanted to keep it that way.

"Well, blamed if that don't beat all! Hee, hee, hee!" croaked Mr. Jones.

A general murmur of contentment, mingled with nods and smiles and comments like "*I knew there was something. . . .*" spread through the small crowd. There was a good deal of back-slapping and hand-shaking.

Suddenly something jolted my memory. With all the commotion over Tad, its full impact hadn't registered till just this moment. A smile broke out across my face.

"Pa!" I said excitedly, "What was it exactly that you said to Mr. Royce?"

"I don't rightly know, girl," he replied with a puzzled look. "I just told him to keep his scoundrels away from us, that's all."

"No—no—that's not it! What did you say *exactly*?"

"I don't know," he insisted.

"You said that if any of his hooligans ever came near . . ." I paused, trying to get him to remember his exact words.

"Oh, yeah. I told him if his hooligans ever came near my family again, I'd—"

All at once he stopped. The word *family* had brought him up short, and suddenly he got what I'd been driving at.

Gently he knelt down, keeping Tad on his knee. Zack and I were standing beside him. As if understanding what was coming, Mrs. Parrish, with tears brimming in her eyes, nudged Becky and Emily toward us. They stood right in front of Pa. He reached out with his rough, grime and blood-smeared hands and took first Becky's and then Emily's small, white palms in his. Then he glanced around at Zack, then me. He seemed to hold my eyes a moment longer than the rest, then looked back at the little ones.

"This sure has been some day," he said finally. "I don't reckon I've had one quite like it in a coon's age!"

"I guess we been a heap of trouble for you, Pa," blurted Zack.

"Yeah, I suppose you have," he said. Then a slow smile spread across his face. "But I don't guess I been much better."

Timidly, I rested my hand on Pa's shoulder.

"Did you . . ." I began shyly, "—did you really mean what you said to Mr. Royce?" I asked.

"About keepin' his good-for-nothin' rascals away from you all? 'Course I did!"

"No," I said quietly. "I mean—did you mean—you know, what you called us?"

He thought again for a few seconds. "I guess we ain't been much of a family up 'til now, have we?" he finally admitted.

None of us said anything, but by now the younger girls' initial intimidation was gone and they were crowding closer to Pa, and Tad's arm was wrapped around his neck.

"Well," he went on, "maybe we can have a clean beginning—starting today! What do you all think?"

I had never told the kids what went on the night Pa and

I had our talk outside. I did tell them some of the reasons why Pa left us, but I had never told them about his crying and asking to be forgiven. Somehow, it seemed it was meant to be our own private moment. Pa had been a lot different since then, really making an effort to make up to us the lost time.

But right then, with all of us gathered around him, for the very first time I felt all our hearts were open to one another. He and I had gotten a little head start in trying to understand each other. But now I felt it was going to happen with all the kids and Pa—even Zack.

I looked straight into his eyes and smiled. He smiled back, and I think he was remembering our earlier talk.

"We'd all like a clean beginning, Pa," I answered for all of us.

Then Tad stirred in Pa's lap. I guess he'd been still long enough. As he started to stand, I noticed his hand was clutching something. Pa noticed it at the same time.

"What you got there, son?" he asked.

"A pretty rock from the mine," replied Tad innocently. He opened up his hand to show us.

The crowd of men who had been watching silently, slowly gathered around us. Pa was still kneeling next to Tad, the rest of us leaning against Pa. Uncle Nick stood beside me.

The incredulous silence lasted only a moment, finally broken by Alkali Jones' shrill voice.

"Well, blamed if little Tad hasn't discovered ol' Potter's vein after all! Hee, hee!"

"He's right, Nick!" called out another, who was examining the heap of quartz chunks piled outside the mine opening. "That cave-in loosened the lode. This here quartz is full of gold!"

In an instant, all the men were shouting and running back to take a look for themselves. Uncle Nick, not one to be sentimental, was off with the others like a shot. But Pa slowly rose to his feet, not as exuberant as might have been expected. Then a slow, easy smile crept across his face.

Of course, the claim was in Uncle Nick's name—*Matthews* that is. But maybe Pa's composed reaction to the discovery had another cause. Maybe he felt a little like I did— that in reality, we had made an even greater discovery just moments before little Tad had showed us his rock.

We had found each other at last. Perhaps we were ready now to be the family God had wanted us to be from the very first day—when we unexpectedly met our father in Miracle Springs.

# CHAPTER 38

## THE NEWSPAPER MAN

The town was abuzz for a week.

In the boarding houses, in the mining camps along the streams and rivers, and in every saloon, all folks were talking about was the new vein, and Pa's "new family", and how he and Uncle Nick were kin, and wondering about how we came to be separated. At least that's what Mrs. Parrish and Alkali Jones told us—and who should know better than those two? It wasn't long before the newspaper man, Mr. Singleton, paid us a visit, wanting the whole story.

"I can tell you, Mr. Singleton," Pa said to him, "it ain't that I don't want folks to know that I found my kids after all these years. But there's no way I'm gonna tell more'n that."

"I'll pay you for it, Mr. Hollister—pay you real good."

"But you see, money ain't so much our worry no more," he said with a smile.

"How good?" piped up Uncle Nick. He was still not above turning an easy profit if he could find one to be made.

"Oh, as high as thirty or forty dollars, if you give me exclusive rights to three stories," the newspaperman replied.

"Nick!" said Pa sternly. "What're you thinkin'? Have you forgotten already that there's certain folks we still best stay clear of? We ain't puttin' no news about us in no paper!"

"What about the children?" asked Mr. Singleton. "We

could change their names, tell about their coming west, the wagon train, the hardship of the journey, their Ma dying on the trail, adjusting to this new life. It's a wonderful human interest drama—just the sort women love to read. I have no doubt it would be reprinted in papers all the way back to the East Coast."

"Would we be famous, Pa?" asked Becky.

We all laughed.

Pa shrugged. "I still don't think it's a good idea," he said. "There'd be those who'd put two and two together—"

"Those boys from the gang can't even read!" piped up Uncle Nick.

"That don't mean I'm ready to start bellowing our whereabouts to the whole world! One of the reasons I left home and came out here in the first place was to keep the kids out of danger, and I sure ain't of a mind to start up our troubles all over again."

"What about the gold?" asked Mr. Singleton. "That's a story you could hardly object to."

Pa shrugged again. "Nothing much I could do to stop you even if I wanted to, on that score," he said.

"Why, it's as much as started a second gold rush," went on the editor. "I've never seen such a fever of activity and excitement as in the last week. This'll put Miracle Springs on the map!"

"I'd like to see 'ol Royce get his hands on a single piece of property *now*!" chuckled Uncle Nick.

"My only trouble," said Mr. Singleton, "is that I'm too busy to get the story written in time. I'm still just working to get the paper on its feet, what with advertising and setting up the presses and all. And I've got a big area to try to cover—all the way from Sacramento north. This story about the new gold is already spreading fast. If we don't run it soon, it'll pass us by. Are either of you gentlemen interested in helping me? It was your strike. You could tell it from the 'inside,' as we say."

Pa and Uncle Nick looked at each other, but neither said anything.

I didn't speak either, but the wheels of my mind were turning just the same. Later that same evening, as we sat down to supper, I resolved to say something to Pa about my idea.

We took our seats around the wooden table, then Pa reached out both his hands. Tad on his left took one, Emily on his right took the other, and the rest of us around the table joined hands in turn, including Uncle Nick where he sat between me and Zack. Since the day of the cave-in, Pa had tried once or twice to pray before a meal. I could tell it made everyone happy when he did it. No one would ever replace Ma. But holding hands and praying together like that, even if it wasn't too often, sure did make us feel like we really were a family.

"God, thank you for the good day you've given us," Pa prayed. "And for health and blessings . . . and we ask you to provide what we need—and we thank you for this food— for the hands of the girls that worked to get it ready for us. Watch over us . . . protect us from harm at the hands of evil men . . . uh, amen."

Pa didn't pray fancy. But I could tell he meant every word, and inside my heart I always prayed a little silent prayer of thanksgiving that he was making such an effort to be a good pa to us.

About halfway through the fried potatoes, beans, and cornbread, I got up my courage. "Pa," I said, "what would you think if I talked to Mr. Singleton about writing about the gold in our mine for his paper?"

Everyone was silent, looking first at me, then to Pa.

A thoughtful look came over Pa's face as he sat motionless, his fork halfway to his mouth. Slowly, he turned in my direction.

"*My* daughter, writing a newspaper story?" he said at last.

"I'd like to try."

"What makes you think you could do it?"

"I don't know," I answered. "Maybe I couldn't. But I've been writing a lot in my journal, and working hard to make it sound better."

"Well," he shrugged, finally taking a bite of cornbread and chewing it thoughtfully. "It's okay by me, so long as you don't write nothin' about us. 'Course, it ain't me you gotta convince, it's that newsman Singleton."

"Oh, thank you, Pa!" I exclaimed. "I'll talk to him on our next trip to town!"

# CHAPTER 39

## A FAMILY TALK

It felt good for all of us to be together after such a memorable day at the mine. But there were still questions and uncertainties to be dealt with.

The next night, when we were all sitting around the fire, the subject came up again. Uncle Nick was tooling a piece of leather; Pa was sharpening an awl. The rest of us were just watching them with nothing much else to do.

Becky finally broke the silence. "Is that bad man, Mr. Krebbs, gonna come back and try to get you, Pa?" she asked.

He glanced over at her, surprised that she even knew the man's name. But we'd all been more curious and paid closer attention to conversations we'd overheard than Pa realized.

"Krebbs, you say?"

"Ain't he the man that's after you?"

"Well, he's one of them, that's for sure," sighed Pa.

"How many more are there?" asked Zack.

"Oh, I don't know how many's left after all this time. How many were there back then, Nick? Six or eight?"

"That'd be about it," Uncle Nick nodded.

"And them's the Catskill Gulch Gang?" Zack inquired, edging his chair closer to Pa.

"How'd you know about them?"

"I heard you and Uncle Nick talking, and Corrie told me some things."

"I thought Zack should know, Pa, so I told him some of what you told me." I hoped Pa wouldn't be riled that I'd done so.

But he just nodded his head thoughtfully. I forgot how much he was changing.

"You done right, Corrie," he said. Then his voice took on a gruff tone. Two months ago, I might have thought he was upset, but now I realized it was just his way of teasing us.

"You know, Nick, I reckon these here young'uns are sharper than I thought. We better watch what we say!"

Uncle Nick got serious. "And ya know, Drum, we ain't out of the woods yet. I reckon these young'uns might just be big enough to know what's happened and what could be coming."

Pa looked at each one of us as if he was sizing us up against Uncle Nick's words.

"Pa," I said slowly, still a little unsure of myself, "if there's still some kind of trouble following you, even with Krebbs gone, well . . . we're all part of the family now. Seems like maybe . . . we could help somehow."

Pa sat back on his stool, let out a long sigh, and was quiet. I could tell he was thinking real hard. For eight years he had been a nameless recluse, a drifter with no ties, no home, living in a wild and reckless land—that had to have rubbed off on him some. Now, all of a sudden, he had a family—five children, at least three of them still very dependent. And all five were counting on him, depending on him to care for their needs, to protect them, to love them. It must have been very difficult for him at times.

At last he spoke, and when he did it was in a tired-sounding voice, with a tinge of resignation, as if he knew that re-living the past eight years and facing the troubles that might lie ahead, even for the sake of his own children, wasn't gonna be easy.

"I ain't proud of anything that happened," he began.

"I'd like nothing better than to never have to tell you kids what kind of man your Pa is—"

"If the kids are to be told," interrupted Uncle Nick sternly, "then at least they deserve to be told the way it really was." Without further delay, he began to tell us the story.

"You kids listen to me, and I'll tell you the *whole* truth about it. It was *me* that rode with the gang, not your pa," he insisted, pointing to himself. "I was just a kid, though that ain't no excuse for what I done. I was hot-headed, and pretty stupid to boot! I knew that gang had a bad reputation, but I just closed my eyes to all the upbringin' your Grandpa Belle gave me. I was a young *fool*, there just ain't no other way o' puttin' it.

"Now your pa, he was as good a family man as you'll ever want to meet, devoted to your ma, and lovin' every one of you kids as you came along—'course you was just babies then, and don't remember. But I seen your pa holdin' you all in his arms—all except for you, Tad, 'cause you weren't born yet. A gentler man with a baby you're never gonna meet, I can vouch for that!

"Well, your pa saw that I was headed into deep trouble, and so he tried to talk some sense into my thick head. I wouldn't listen to him o' 'course, and then next thing I knew he up and joined the gang. I thought it meant he'd started to see things my way, but he done it so's he could keep me in sight and be able to haul me out of trouble when it came! He never intended to become a real part of the gang, but just to stick around long enough to give me a chance to see the light. I finally did, that is, after I seen what kind of evil they was capable of. But by then it was too late. See, they had planned this big bank robbery. Up 'til then, it was just petty stuff—bullyin', raisin' Cain. But then this robbery came up, and afore I knew it I was in on the plans. Your pa wasn't as trusted a member of the gang, so he and a few others didn't find out about it until the night before. I didn't say nothin' 'cause I was afraid of what they'd do to me if I opened my mouth.

"The night before the robbery, they told the rest of the gang the plans. We was all supposed to meet the next day, an hour before the bank closed. Your pa acted like he was going along, but after everyone else went off, he took me aside alone and gave me the biggest tongue-lashing I guess a grown man's ever had. I was nearly ready to listen then—I sure didn't want to end up in prison. But I also knew if I backed out with the knowledge of what they was up to, my life wouldn't be worth buffalo's spit. Fool that I was, I was still thinkin' to go through with it, figurin' to save my neck. But your pa could see it all clearer than me—that I was tryin' to save my neck by stickin' it into a noose!

"The time got closer and closer. I was really scared. Your pa was scared, too—scared I'd really go through with it. Finally, just an hour or so before we all was to meet, your pa laid right into me—slugged me so hard my head spun. You remember that, Drum?"

"How could I forget? It was the only time you and I ever fought," said Pa shaking his head.

"We tussled there in that—livery stable, wasn't it?—'til we could barely stand up on our own feet. But I saw then how much your pa cared for my crazy, foolish hide. I saw that maybe I'd be hurtin' more people than myself if I went through with that robbery."

"I shoulda knocked your block off sooner, Nick," smiled Pa. "In fact, I know just what to do next time you get out of line."

Uncle Nick laughed, rubbing his chin as if remembering the old pain. Then he was serious again. "Your pa saved me from that robbery, but I'd already made too many mistakes to get off so easily, I guess. The gang got off with the loot—leastways I figure they must have, or Krebbs wouldn't still be on our tail. But the law was hot on 'em all, and they scattered all over the place. A couple gang members that I know of were shot, and one lawman was killed. One of the wounded was Jenkins. He'd kinda taken a likin' to me and he knew where I was staying, so he came there to hide out. But he wasn't too careful, 'cause he led the law to my place. I think he mighta told them we weren't involved, but he died before they could get another word outta him.

"So there we were, known members of the gang, caught with one of 'em who'd been shot in the robbery. We'd gone from the deserted livery stable back to my place to get cleaned up, so we had no alibi, no way to prove we was innocent. That's what comes of mixin' with the wrong people.

"My sister never knew half of what happened. You just told her you was going to help me, didn't you, Drum?"

"I figured she'd try to stop me," said Pa, "and I couldn't think of no other way to do it."

"And he didn't want your ma, or my pa, Grandpa Belle, to know what a no-account I'd become," added Uncle Nick. "So we wound up in prison, your pa and I. You tell the kids about the escape, Corrie?"

I nodded, and Uncle Nick went on, "So that's how it was, kids, that's how it really happened."

Zack looked at Pa. I could tell he was trying real hard to understand it all, but it was only natural he'd have questions. "Ma woulda understood, don't you think, Pa?"

"She might have, Zack. She was a good wife," said Pa, "But I guess I was too filled with my own shame to think of that. Before we got married, Aggie told me she couldn't live not knowin' from one day to the next if I'd end up in jail or with a bullet in me. She said she had to believe I'd never go back to that kind of life. Back before I met your ma, I ran with fellers near as bad as that Catskill bunch. Well, I loved your ma and wanted to change, and I promised her I would. She trusted her life and future to my word. And all I could think of was that I'd failed her—and all of you, too. Even if I hadn't been too ashamed to face her, I woulda never have put her through a life of running with me."

He paused and his eyes clouded for a minute as all the

painful memories returned to him. "You see, son, when a man's been in prison, it don't take long for him to start *feelin'* like a criminal, even if he's innocent. You get to feelin' dirty just from what you gotta do to survive. Well, all that together with everythin' else made it so I couldn't make myself go back, no matter how much I wanted to, no matter how much I loved Aggie and you kids. I guess in a way I didn't go back *because* I loved all of you so much. It's the kind of grown-up logic—cockeyed and confused—that's a mite hard for young'uns to understand, I expect."

There was a long silence, just the sound of the crackling fire filling the room. The little ones probably didn't understand all this, but I know they sensed Pa's sincerity, and that would surely make up for whatever confusion there was over the facts.

Before long, a question from Zack brought us back to what had started the conversation in the first place.

"What's gonna happen now, Pa?"

"Well," Pa answered, seeming relieved not to say anymore about the past. "Nick and I suspected all along that the fellers who escaped the law after the robbery musta figured Jenkins told us where the loot was stashed. He musta been carryin' it when they scattered. The rumor we heard before we left New York was that none of them had the money, and they reasoned Jenkins told us where it was. We hoped playin' dead would throw 'em off a mite. Maybe it did; maybe they never bought the story—but it was too much money to give up so easily. So Krebbs and whoever he's got with him just kept followin' us."

"I guess Krebbs has perseverance, if nothin' else!" chuckled Uncle Nick. "I only wish I coulda got a hold of him long enough to tell him he's barking up the wrong tree."

"Probably wouldn't have believed you anyway," said Pa. "I don't know why he didn't make an outright attack in the first place, unless he figured he could make some money out of Royce first, and make us suffer later. We'll have to be careful, I reckon, but now that Krebbs knows we know about him, I think he'll lay low for a while. Like a snake in the grass, he'd sooner attack us when our back is turned." He scratched his whiskers thoughtfully.

"You ain't going to have to go back to jail, are you, Pa?" asked Tad, his voice anxious.

"No, Tad. A few folks know my real name now, and that might be a problem," said Pa, doing his best to sound unconcerned. "But folks here in California don't seem to care much about a man's past. Too many have come here to get away from pasts they'd rather forget. They wanna start clean, and California's far enough away from civilization that it's possible for them to do it. The law back East thinks Uncle Nick and I are dead. Someone'd have to go to a heap of trouble to prove it otherwise to them. New York's a *long* ways from California."

"Maybe we could move away from here," said Zack eagerly. "Go someplace where they ain't heard of you—just in case."

"No, son. That'd be doin' just what I done to you and your ma before. I ain't runnin'. What comes, comes. I suppose that's one reason when I first saw you, I considered not tellin' you who I was. But now that you know—now that I have my family again—I ain't givin' you up, and I ain't gonna hurt you again—not if I can help it."

"Pa," I asked pensively, "couldn't we find a way to clear your name with the law, to prove you didn't have anything to do with that robbery?"

"We might just stir up dust that's best left settled, Corrie. I reckon if trouble ain't lookin' for you, you best not go lookin' for it."

I knew Pa was right, and I was ready to accept him as he was and not worry about what *might* come. Yet I couldn't help thinking that Pa was a mighty fine man, and that it wasn't right that folks should think of him as a robber or any such thing. And I couldn't shake the feeling that Pa would feel better about himself if his name could be cleared. But I didn't say any more right then, though the feelings didn't leave me.

The talk had been so serious, both Uncle Nick and Pa looked almost worn out by it all—especially Uncle Nick, who I'd never seen so serious for so long a spell. But I think as painful as it was for them to talk about it all, it was also a relief for them to get it out. How well I remember, when we kids would have a fight, Ma would always make us "clear the air," as she called it, by apologizing and talking about it. That's what this talk reminded me of. It felt so good to have it all out in the open, and it helped to make us all closer too.

Pa must have sensed this, because after a few moments of quiet, he said, "Kids, I'll never know if I did the right thing, but I'm glad you know everythin' now, even if you may not understand it all. I hope you'll be able to forgive me for the hurt I caused you. I guess all we can do now is forgive and start fresh."

I stood up, put my arms around his broad shoulders, and gave him a hug. It didn't take long for the others to join me, eager to gather around and express their affection to their pa.

Pa looked intently at each one of us, taking time to gaze into our eyes. When he got to Tad, he gave his thick mop of sandy hair a tousle, and Tad smiled broadly.

But it was quiet, softspoken Emily, usually wrapped in her own thoughts, who spoke for us all. As Pa held her eyes for what seemed a long time, she said simply, "I love you, Pa."

He looked at her as though he'd heard something he thought he'd never hear again. Then he took her in his arms and held her tight. After he released her, he stretched his arms wider to embrace all of us.

"It's me who loves you," he said. "Every one of you. You're the best kids any father could hope to have."

# CHAPTER 40

## SPRING IN THE CALIFORNIA FOOTHILLS

The months passed quickly, and we got on pretty well as a family, considering all we'd been through.

After the full burst of spring in Miracle, along about April, the last group of wagons heading East passed nearby our claim. Needless to say, we Hollisters weren't among the travelers. We rode out to watch the caravan go by. I guess it was sort of a way to symbolize to us that we were here to stay. We watched until the last wagon was clean out of sight—Pa and all us kids; then we headed back to the cabin. There was no doubt after that day that California was our home for good.

I can't say things were perfect after the day of the cave-in at the mine. But they were a heap better than when we'd come here last fall. There was a happy spirit about the claim, and I don't think it was just because of the gold Pa and Uncle Nick and Alkali Jones were pulling out of the mine. I know it had just as much to do with what had happened between us all.

No one saw a trace of Buck Krebbs after that. Pa, Uncle Nick, the sheriff and several other men stayed up all that night after the cave-in waiting for him to show up. But he never did. They figured he somehow got word of what happened and lit out over the hills. Uncle Nick did say a couple of months later that he heard a report of him down near Stockton.

Pa and Uncle Nick got to talking about him every once in a while. They never did find out if he tracked them west alone or if others of the gang were out here, too. And they never knew exactly how he and the banker Mr. Royce got hooked up. Most important, they never knew whether Buck Krebbs ever found out that they didn't have the money. They couldn't help worrying about it some, for our safety more than anything.

But at least I can say that no one out of Pa or Uncle Nick's past bothered us for a long time. I can't say we forgot all about it, but we did quit worrying about it. And by the time we finally ran into Buck Krebbs again, it was . . . but that's part of another story.

Alkali Jones kept coming out most days to help Uncle Nick and Pa at the mine. I don't think he cared a hoot about the money he'd make. He just liked working a claim with some gold in it for a change! They told the story of Mr. Royce's fake geologists every other day, and then they laughed and laughed. Mr. Royce kept trying to buy up land in the area, but folks got wise pretty quick, both about Mr. Royce and about the mining potential of the land. The few purchases he was able to make later on were more fairly priced. And the fires completely stopped after Buck Krebbs' disappearance.

Reverend Rutledge didn't go back to Boston, as he had threatened he might. By the beginning of summer—that was in 1853, he had raised about half the money he needed for his church, and *none* of it came from the bank. On that point at least, he seemed willing to take Uncle Nick's advice to heart. I gradually began to understand more of his sermons. I'm not sure if it was actually because of better understanding on my part, or rather because he stopped making them so complicated and high-sounding—probably a little of both. He still spoke in that preacher voice sometimes, but I think he sincerely tried to be more down-to-earth.

The church quit meeting in the Gold Nugget when the numbers dwindled down to ten or fifteen people, and started gathering in various people's homes, usually at Mrs. Parrish's. Reverend Rutledge and Mrs. Parrish were seen around town together quite a bit, and they both seemed excited about the church's prospects for the future. Pa and Reverend Rutledge were on speaking terms again, but they didn't seem to have a lot to say to each other.

Pa really became a family sort of man. He never drank anymore at all, and always stayed home or took the young ones with him when he went into town. As far as I know, he never played cards again. Uncle Nick was about the same as ever. He was bound to head for town occasionally for an evening, returning home with the smell of whiskey on his breath. But I think he was trying hard, too, to be as good an example to us as he could. Pa got the title on the property changed over to both of their names so Nick couldn't gamble it away like he had once done himself.

I still had fifty dollars of Ma's money. Pa didn't need it, and told me to save it till something came up. The strike Tad discovered turned out to be pretty rich. We didn't become millionaires, but with hard work it brought in twenty or thirty dollars a day. Pa was bound and determined to put the money to good use, "Not squander it like before," he said. But he didn't trust Royce's bank, so he had Mrs. Parrish take it to a bank in Sacramento for him when she went in for supplies.

There were some mighty wonderful changes taking place. Zack grew two inches before summer and was helping at the mine just like the men. In fact, Pa started treating him so much like one of them that Zack quickly shed his sullenness and brightened up. He and pa were together more now, working and talking about what they could do with the mine and the sluices. Pa seemed to like having Zack at his side. And I believe he and Zack gradually became friends.

Emily didn't stop glowing after the day in April when Pa went into town for some lumber. When he came back, there were four horses to his team instead of the usual two. While he was still a hundred yards from the cabin, he called out, "Emily! Come outside and see my new team!"

She went to the door and stood watching for a minute as he came up the road. Then suddenly she recognized the two lead horses.

"It's Snowball . . . and Jinx!" she cried, running out to meet the wagon. Her friends were back, and at least Snowball seemed to remember her.

Pa never mentioned anything about how he'd gotten them back. But I found out from Patrick Shaw that Pa had to pay twice what the horses were worth to get them from the fellow who'd won them in the card game.

Seven-year-old Tad became Uncle Nick's constant shadow, but Nick didn't seem bothered by it. Several times a day I'd see him stoop down to Tad's level and put an arm around his shoulder to explain something they were working on. Tad was also frequently seen perched on Uncle Nick's shoulders, bouncing along on a walk somewhere.

Becky didn't change so noticeably—she remained as ornery and full of energy as ever.

Once in a while, Uncle Nick would read a bedtime story to the children, with Tad or Becky sitting on his lap, and the others snuggled up under his brawny arms. What a sight that was! Of course, he only did that when he could talk Pa out of it. Most nights Pa would read, and all five of us gathered around. Even Zack and I wouldn't miss such a moment with Pa.

Whenever I could, I went into town to visit Mrs. Parrish. She and I had more good talks about living the Christian life. Pa didn't have much to say when I mentioned her, but I think he was interested in what I was learning about the Bible and spiritual things—more than he let on. I kept hoping that maybe someday he and I would be able to talk about such things together.

When my birthday rolled around, my mouth nearly dropped open when Pa walked in the cabin about mid-morning. He was clean-shaven and scrubbed like I'd never seen him before.

"What're you starin' at?" he asked with a grin.

"Pa!" I exclaimed. "I hardly recognized you! Why'd you shave off your beard?"

"Well, I'll tell you," he said. "Your sixteenth birthday seemed like a fittin' occasion to say 'off with the old!' "

"What do you mean?" I asked. "I kinda liked it."

He thought a minute, then said seriously, "I'll tell you, Corrie, the beard was always part of my mask, part of my hidin' who I really was, just like the name and all the rest of it. Well, I don't want to hide no more. I am who I am. My name's Hollister, this here's my home—" he gestured widely with his arms, taking in the claim, "—this is my land, this is my family . . . and this is my face! I'm through with hidin'. Oh, I ain't gonna write to the law back in New York and tell them where to find me, but I sure ain't goin' to go skulkin' around no more, either. We're safe, and I think we can start fresh. This is just my way of showin' it."

He placed his strong hands on my shoulders and looked at me full in the face, and smiled. "So that's my birthday gift to you, Corrie Belle Hollister—just *me*! With my proper name, and the face the good Lord gave me, and a hearty 'Best wishes to you on your birthday!' "

I couldn't help smiling. I put my arms around his waist and leaned my head against his chest. His arms closed gently across my back. It was a wonderful feeling. I don't suppose anyone could understand that feeling better than a daughter who, after a lot of years of doubting, finally knows that her father really loves her.

"That's the best birthday present a girl could ever have, Pa," I said honestly. "I'll never forget it."

Well, I've said how all the others were growing and changing but when I try to reflect on how I changed, it's hard to say. If you are changing yourself, you can't always see it, 'cause its goin' on right *inside*.

It was March when I had my memorable sixteenth birthday, and though Pa said I'd grown, I still felt like a kid, even though I was more content than any time since Ma had died.

I remember how I stumbled at prayer when Ma was sick, and how little I understood how much God could have to do with people's lives, and how much He was really interested in our lives. Now, thanks to Mrs. Parrish, I was beginning to see God as more than just some distant, unapproachable Being. I began to believe that He could really go through life with a person, like Mrs. Parrish said He did with her—helping her, giving her strength as she needed it, making her into a better person—the person He wanted her to be. I hoped someday He'd be that close to me, like He was her.

Oh, and about Mr. Singleton. I did finally have that talk with him. At first he thought I was joking. He looked at me strangely, as if he was thinking, *But you're just a young girl! What could you possibly know about writing an article?*

But when I told him about my journal, he agreed to look at it. And once he'd read some of it, he realized how serious I was. His expression changed considerably, and soon he was saying things like, "Well, young lady—if you can submit a piece that is satisfactory to us, we will see what can be done with it."

Just his calling me a young *lady* instead of a *girl* was a step in the right direction. And he'd consented to let me at least *try* to write something for the paper—and that was all I was asking!

I went home that day very excited, determined to do my best with this chance. I didn't get an article written for his paper immediately. It took a lot of help from him, and some from Mrs. Parrish, before I—

But there I go again, starting to tell the next story before

I'm done with this one! Buck Krebbs, my first article in the *California Gazette*, the building of the church, what happened to Alkali Jones and the trouble Uncle Nick got mixed up in down at Dutch Flat—all that will have to wait.

Now I reckon I've told the story like it was, the best I can remember it as it happened.

I often wonder what Ma would think of all this. I can't help being sad that she couldn't be here to share it all with me. Pa still doesn't talk freely about religious things, but he does say he's sure as anything Ma is up there in heaven looking down on all our goings on, and is pleased.

I think he's right.

## IN REMEMBRANCE OF MY MA

*Ma, it breaks my heart to think that you're not here*
    *Though sometimes I feel you with me, and hear your voice so clear.*
*I know you're happy that we have found, the best*
    *home we could have imagined when we headed west.*
*When you left us out there, it was fearsome. My heart felt black*
    *Without you with us, all I could think was we oughta turn back.*
*But I knew what you'd say, the wisdom you'd impart.*
    *You'd want us to be brave, have courage: Take heart!*
*So when we got over the mountains and were finally here,*
    *I did my best to stand tall and hide my fear.*
*And whenever my heart sank and my hope started slowing,*
    *I'd recall the words of yours that would keep me going:*
*You said God takes care of the children that are His own,*
    *Even when they're afraid and completely alone.*
*So I thank you, Ma, for preparing me,*
    *And I thank you, God, for taking care of me.*
*And for bringing me safely, though fears in my heart swirled,*
    *To this land where I discovered my Father's world.*

*—by Corrie Belle Hollister*